1636

COMMANDER CANTRELL IN THE WEST INDIES

1636

COMMANDER CANTRELL IN THE WEST INDIES

ERIC FLINT
CHARLES E. GANNON

1636: COMMANDER CANTRELL IN THE WEST INDIES

Copyright © 2014 by Eric Flint & Charles E. Gannon

A Baen Books Original

Baen Publishing Enterprises
P.O. Box 1403
Riverdale, NY 10471
www.baen.com

ISBN: 978-1-4767-3678-5

Cover art by Tom Kidd
Maps by Gorg Huff

First Baen printing, June 2014

Distributed by Simon & Schuster
1230 Avenue of the Americas
New York, NY 10020

Library of Congress Cataloging-in-Publication Data

Flint, Eric.
    1636 : Commander Cantrell in the West Indies / Eric Flint and Charles E. Gannon.
        pages cm. — (The ring of fire ; 14)
Summary: "Eddie Cantrell is married to the king of Denmark's daughter and is sent by Admiral Simpson to the Carribbean to secure access to the most valuable commodity on that continent—the oil which the up-time machines and industry need. Making his way to the New World, Eddie must face often hostile natives, rambunctious Dutch ship captains, allied colonies on the brink of starvation and the hostile Spanish presence" — Provided by publisher.
    ISBN 978-1-4767-3678-5 (hardback)
1. Time travel—Fiction. 2. Alternative histories (Fiction) I. Gannon, Charles E. II. Title. III. Title: Sixteen thirty-six. IV. Title: Commander Cantrell in the West Indies.
    PS3556.L548A618667 2014
    813'.54—dc23
                                                                2014009924

10   9   8   7   6   5   4   3   2   1

Pages by Joy Freeman (www.pagesbyjoy.com)
Printed in the United States of America

With profound gratitude, I dedicate this book to the entirety of the Ring of Fire community, who were enthusiastic in their welcome, and have proven to be a singularly helpful and dedicated group of pros and fans. Their tireless work as researchers, fact-checkers, and proof-readers enriched and improved every page of this manuscript, as well as the other ones I have had the honor of contributing to this series.

—Charles E. Gannon

What he said.

—Eric Flint

Contents

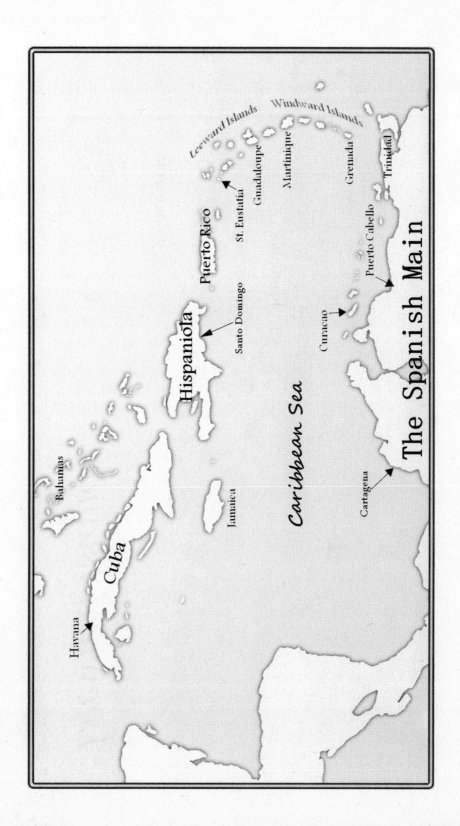

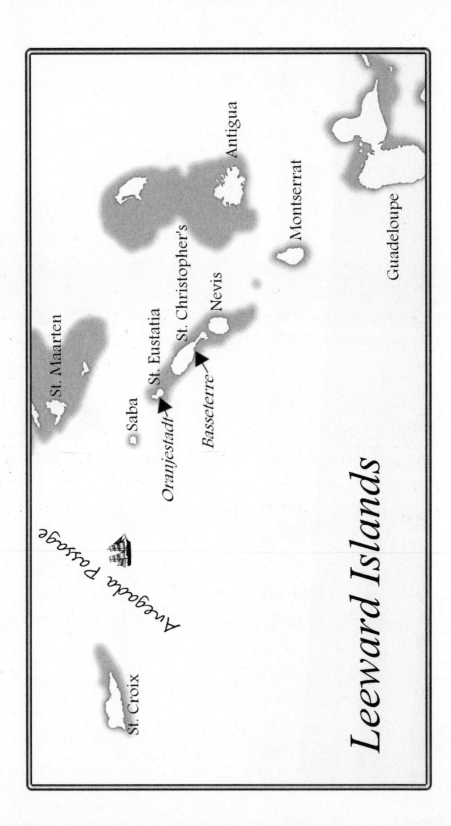

Leeward Islands

Grenada

Grenada Passage

The Dragon's Mouths

Port of Spain

Gulf of Paria

Trinidad

Pitch Lake

Spanish Main

Part One

April 1635

The heavens themselves, the planets, and this centre

Chapter 1

Grantville, State of Thuringia-Franconia

Lieutenant Commander Eddie Cantrell looked down at the stump six inches below his left knee as an orderly removed his almost ornate peg leg. Physician Assistant Jessica Porter—formerly Nurse Porter—approached with his new fiberglass prosthetic. The jaundiced-gray color of the object was not appealing. "Wow, that's uglier than I thought it would be," Eddie confessed as the orderly left.

Jessica shrugged. "It may look like hell, but it works like a charm. We've special-cast more than a hundred of these, now." She fitted it tentatively onto the stump, and looked up at Eddie.

He concentrated on how it felt: a little odd—smooth and cool—compared to the wood and leather lashings that had just been removed. He supposed anything else might feel strange now, having spent a year and a half getting used to the cranky, creaky peg leg that had been specially fashioned for him by King Christian IV of Denmark's medical artisans. But now that Eddie paid closer attention to the new sensations of this prosthetic—"Actually, that feels much better. No rubbing."

Jessica snorted in response. "Yeah, it ought to feel better. It's custom-made. That's why we made you stop by when you brought your princess bride with you last fall, to get a wax mold of your—" Jessica missed a beat, floundered. "Of your—your—"

3

"My stump," Eddie supplied for her. "That's okay; might as well call it what it is." Which, he reflected, Jessica must do dozens of times a week with other amputees. But it was probably different with him. He was a fellow up-timer, a person she had known before the Ring of Fire had whisked their whole town back through time to Germany of 1631. And so, right in the middle of the Thirty Years' War, into which meat-grinder Eddie himself had been thrown.

He looked down at the stump that had gotten caught in those pitiless gears of a new history-in-the-making. "So, that wax mold you took of my stump—?"

Jessica nodded as she secured the new leg. "We filled that mold with a mix of fiberglass and pine resin and presto: your new prosthetic."

Eddie moved the new false limb tentatively. The weight was negligible. "It's hard to believe that's local—uh, down-time—manufacture."

"Every bit of it," nodded Jessica as she stood and stepped back to take a look. "They got the process from us, of course. We made the first few here at the Leahy Medical Center. But after that, there was no stopping all the down-time medical folks, particularly in the new university programs, from dominating the business. Good thing, too: we couldn't have kept up with the demand, here."

"I thought fiberglass would be too hard for the local industries to make."

Jessica shook her head. "That's because you're thinking of the stuff we made speedboats out of, back up-time in the twentieth century. That's ultra-high strength fiberglass. The individual strands were very thin, and very uniform. I doubt any of us will still be alive when that technology makes its debut in this world. But this,"—she tapped the prosthesis; it made a much duller sound than the wood—"this is made of much cruder fibers. Down-timers can make them with a number of different drip-and-spin processes. Then they just pack it into the mold as tight as they can, pour in the pine resin, and, after a little more processing, out comes the prosthesis.

"That's not the end of the process, of course. It needs smoothing and careful finishing where it fits onto the stump. But we didn't stop there," she said, her smile finally returning. "We added something special for you."

"Oh?" Eddie wondered if maybe it had secret compartments. That would be kind of cool.

"Yep. Try stepping on it, then stepping off."

Eddie shrugged: no secret compartments, then. He took hold of his cane, pushed off the examining table, stood tentatively on both legs, then stepped forward with the prosthesis. Well, that felt just fine. And step two—

—almost dropped him to the ground. As his real foot came down and he shifted his primary weight onto it, the heel of the prosthetic seemed to start rising up a little, as if it was eager to take its own next step. It wasn't a particularly strong push, but he hadn't been expecting it, and he flailed for balance.

"Wha—what was that?" he asked, not minding one bit that Jessica had jumped over to steady him.

"That was the spring-loaded heel wedge. Cool, huh? When the sole of the prosthesis is fully compressed, and then you start to shift your weight off it to take the next step, it gives you a little boost. Like your own foot does."

Eddie frowned. "Well, yeah, I guess. But I wasn't ready for it."

Jessica shook her head. "Sorry. Should have thought of that. We don't experience that with the other amputees."

"Why?"

"Well, they're either recent amputees, so they never adjusted to a regular peg leg. Or they come here because someone has told them that up-timers at Leahy Medical Center make the *best* prosthetics, ones with springs in them. So naturally, the first thing we have to do is sit them down and explain every detail, including the phases they're going to go through in getting accustomed to using the new limb. Sorry; I should have observed the same protocol with you, should have warned you."

Eddie grinned and shrugged off her apology, then took a few more steps. Now that he knew to expect that little boost from the prosthetic's heel, it wasn't so bad. In fact, Jessica was right: this was more like real walking, not the flat footed limp-and-waddle he managed with the peg leg and a cane. With this, he could feel the potential for walking like a whole person again, like his old self. He could even imagine how he might be able to work in a little swagger, something to show off to Anne Cathrine...

"Eddie, I'm guessing that smug smile means that the prosthetic is a success?"

"Uh, yeah. Thank you, Jessica."

"Not at all. But tell me something, Eddie."

"Sure." He considered sitting, found he was still comfortable standing, something that rarely happened when he had been wearing the peg. "What do you want to know?"

"Well . . . why did you stay in Denmark once you were no longer being held as Christian IV's own, personal prisoner of war last year? I mean, I know there was the wedding with his daughter, but—"

Eddie nodded. And reflected that in the past, he might have grinned while he explained. But in the past year, life itself had acquired a new gravity that made him less ready to grin and shrug his way through the living or recounting of it. His high school days, not quite four years behind him, now seemed a lifetime away, a collection of memories that rightly belonged to someone else. "Mostly, I stayed up in Denmark because of love, Jessica."

"You mean the princess didn't want to come down here?"

"Oh, no, she was extremely eager to see Grantville." Like pretty much every other down-timer who had the means to do so, the number one locale on Anne Cathrine's list of "places to visit" was the town of miracles that had fallen out of the future into Germany.

"So why not bring the princess back home, Eddie? You get tired of us?"

"Jessica, first of all, Anne Cathrine is not a 'princess.' She's a 'king's daughter.'"

"And the difference is—?"

"The difference is huge. Her mom—her dad's second wife— was nobility, but not high enough for anyone to consider her kids potential inheritors of the throne. It's called a morganatic marriage."

"Thank you, I still read trashy historical romances, so I'm familiar with the term."

"Oh. Sorry. But princess or not, she's one of the brightest apples of her father's eye. He loves all his kids—he's a really good guy, that way—but he's especially fond of Anne Cathrine and her younger sister, Leonora."

"Another blond, buxom beauty, I'm assuming?"

Eddie decided not to point out that Anne Cathrine's hair was decidedly red-blond. "Uh, no, not at all. Leonora is a brunette.

And . . . well, she'll probably be a pretty attractive woman. But she's already sharp as a tack. Not pushy, but has a real sense of her self, of what's right. And doesn't like having her dad determine her future."

One of Jessica's eyebrows elevated slightly. "She sounds like a handful for King Daddy. Good for her. And good for the Princess Anne Cathrine that she chose you."

Eddie shrugged. No reason to add the somewhat embarrassing footnote that Anne Cathrine and he had been surreptitiously "pushed together" by King Daddy, who despite some of his lunatic schemes, understood full well just how advantageous it was to have his daughter married to one of the up-time wizards who had been instrumental in shattering his naval attack on Wismar last year. Happily, Anne Cathrine's heart had already been moving precipitously in Eddie's direction, so King Daddy's stratagems had been, practically speaking, more of an emphatic imprimatur than an imperial order.

Jessica leaned back, arms crossed. "So if she wanted to stay in Grantville for a few weeks or months, instead of three days last fall, why shouldn't you and she have done so?"

"Because of how it would have looked, Jessica. I was the king's hostage after Luebeck, and his convalescent patient." He gestured down toward his leg. "But instead of ending up as a diplomatic football, I became part of the whole war's diplomatic solution."

"How's that?"

"Well, you know the old story: how 'young lovers' from two sides of a conflict become the basis of peace between enemies. Funny how a little intangible 'feel good' stuff like that can go a long way to easing tensions, making things a little smoother at the truce, and then the treaty tables. Which rolled right on into the deals that led to Denmark's entry into a restored Union of Kalmar with Sweden."

"Okay, but all that was finished even before you got married. So why not come back sooner?"

"Well, that whole 'young love' angle could also have lost a lot of its fairy-tale glow unless we got married pretty quickly, since, er . . . since—"

"Since there was no way of knowing how long it would be before the young wife might become a young mother. And how it might embarrass King Daddy if there were fewer than eight months between bridal bed and birthing bed."

"Uh . . . yeah. Pretty much." Eddie hated that he still—*still*—blushed so easily. "And once I was officially part of the family, I needed to get introduced all around Denmark. And any noble that did not get to host us for a short stay or a party or some other damned meet-and-greet event was sure to get their nose out of joint. And of course, the order in which we went to all these dinners and dances was how King Christian demonstrated this year's pecking order amongst his aristocracy."

"And he got to show off his own prize-stud, up-timer wizard, bought fair and square at the territorial negotiation table last summer."

"Yup." Although, truth be told, Eddie had found the whole circus of his semi-celebrity more than a bit of an ego-boost. Who would have ever guessed that his marginal nerdiness would one day make him a star? Back up-time, in the twentieth century, his identity as gamer, military-history nut, and educated layman on all the related technologies had made him one of the boys that the hot-looking high school girls had looked straight through—unless they needed help with their homework. But here in the seventeenth century, those same qualities, along with his service and wounding in the recent Baltic War, had made him the veritable crown prince of geek chic.

Of course, the down-timers didn't see the geekiness at all. To them, he was simply a young Renaissance Man, a creature all at once unique, and brave, and furnished with powerful reservoirs of knowledge that were surprisingly deep and unthinkably wide. And Anne Cathrine was his first and most ardently smitten admirer. Which suited him just fine since, reciprocally, he was her biggest fan, as well.

"And so as soon as King Christian was done with you, your prior master, Admiral Simpson, snatched you back to Luebeck?"

"Well, Admiral Simpson never stopped being my C.O., even when I was a prisoner of war. Afterward, too. So when you get right down to it, all the gallivanting I did in Denmark was really an 'extended leave to complete diplomatic initiatives.'" Eddie swayed into motion, put his right hand out, used the cane in his left to steady himself. "Jessica, thanks so much. The prosthesis—the leg—feels so natural. It's going to make a huge difference in my life."

Jessica smiled. "Well, that was the objective. And you've got a lot going on in that life. Seems, in some ways, that the Ring of Fire has been a good change for you." She glanced down; her smile dimmed. "I mean, I'm not saying that it was worth losing a leg over, but—"

"I know what you mean, Jessica. Without the Ring of Fire, I'd probably have been working a nowhere job, trying to figure out a way to pay for college as the weeks and months mounted up, and I had less and less in the bank to show for them. Sure, I'd have both legs—"

"But you wouldn't be so alive, wouldn't have so much to look forward to?"

"Yeah, I think that's it. Up-time, I just might be surviving day after dull day in my parents' basement, but here, I'm living life. For real. And so is she."

Jessica frowned, not understanding. "'She'? Who? The princess?"

Eddie nodded, released Jessica's hand, and started moving—with surprising ease and surety—for the door. "Yup."

Jessica held him with her wondering voice. "How did the Ring of Fire make her—well, more alive?"

Eddie turned. "It didn't *make* her more alive, Jessica. It *kept* her alive. In the old history, Anne Cathrine died on August 20, 1633. But for some reason, when we arrived here in 1631, our actions sent out waves of change that radiated into her life as well. Who knows? Maybe a ship carrying plague didn't make it to Copenhagen, or she missed a dance where she was exposed to typhus, or any one of another million possible rendezvous with death that she was prevented from making. All I know is that she's here now, and very alive. But back up-time, where she was part of what we called 'history,' she was dead ten days after her fifteenth birthday."

Jessica's mouth was slightly open. She seemed to be searching for something to say. And was failing.

Eddie nodded. "Thanks again, Jessica," he said. "Say hello to your folks for me." He swung around the door jamb, tugging the door closed behind him.

Chapter 2

Grantville, State of Thuringia-Franconia

Colonel Hugh Albert O'Donnell, the expatriate Earl of Tyrconnell, slugged back the contents of the small, clear shot glass. The liquid he gulped down burned from the top of his gullet to the bottom of his gut and filled his head with fumes that, he still suspected, might be poisonous. But at least this time he wasn't going to—

The burn flared at the back of his throat and he coughed. And choked and sputtered. He looked up at his hosts—Grantville's two Mike McCarthys, one Senior and one Junior—who looked on sympathetically. The older man also seemed to be suppressing either a grimace or a grin. Hugh put the shot glass aside politely.

"Can't stomach moonshine, eh?" There was a little friendly chiding in Don McCarthy the Elder's tone.

"Alas, and it pains an Irishman to say it, I cannot. It is not as similar to *poteen* as you conjectured. And it has not 'grown on me' as you Americans say—not the least bit, these past six nights. My apologies."

"Ah, that's all right," said Mike the Younger, who disappeared into the kitchen and promptly returned with a perfectly cast squat bottle, half-filled with liquid of a very promising amber color. "Want to try some bourbon?"

10

Hugh struggled to understand. "Is it a drink of that line, of that family?"

"'Of that line—?' Oh, you mean the Bourbons of France? No, no: this is American whiskey—*uisce beatha*—made in some of the Southern States. Interested?"

At the words "whiskey" and its Gaelic root-word, *uisce beatha*, Hugh felt his interest and even his spirits brighten. He sat a little straighter. "I am very interested, Michael."

Smiles and new drinks all around. But the small glasses were poured out very carefully this time, as though the "bourbon" was precious nectar—and then Hugh realized that indeed it must be. The label, the bottle, the screw-on cap: all bore the stamp of machine-manufactured precision. This was a whiskey from almost four hundred years in the future. It would be a long wait indeed before any more was available. Hugh resolved to savor every drop. He raised his glass. "*Slainte*."

"*Slainte*," replied Michael McCarthy, Sr. with a quick, wide smile.

Michael the Younger mumbled something that sounded more like "shlondy." He obviously saw the grin that Hugh tried to suppress. "Maybe you can teach me how to say it later?" Mike Jr. wondered sheepishly.

Marveling at the taste of the bourbon, Hugh nodded. "If my payment is more bourbon, you may consider yourself furnished with a permanent tutor in the finer points of Gaelic." Hugh felt his smile slip a little. "Well, as permanent as a tutor may be when he must leave on the morrow."

"Hugh," began Mike Jr., "I'll say it again: Dad and I would be happy—very happy—if you'd reconsider and stay a few more days."

O'Donnell waved his hand. "Forgive me for having struck a melancholy note. Let us not ruin this fine drink with dark thoughts. Besides,"—he hoped his light tone would change the mood—"the name of this whiskey reminds me that I need to practice my French pronunciation. Which, up until now, has usually been employed in the exchange of pleasantries over the tops of contested revetments and abatis."

The answering smiles were polite, not amused. Michael Sr. rolled the small glass of bourbon slowly between his palms. "Why are you brushing up on your French?"

Hugh sighed. "A man must eat, Don McCarthy."

"I'd have thought that would hardly be a worry for you."

Hugh shrugged. "While I was in the employ of the king of Spain, you would have been quite right. But I am no longer the colonel of a regiment, nor a knight-captain of the Order of Alcantara, nor may I even remain a servant of my own godmother, Infanta Isabella of the Lowlands, since she remains a vassal of Philip IV of Spain. I am, as you would say, 'unemployed.'"

Don McCarthy leaned back. "So—France. You are becoming a true soldier-of-fortune now."

"You may say the dirty word: yes, I am now a 'mercenary.' I have little choice. So too for all us Irish 'Wild Geese' in Spanish service. Our employer's 'alliance' with England runs counter to any hope that Philip will make good his promise to liberate Ireland. It is a failure that is anticipated in your own histories—although there, the reasons were somewhat different. Besides, I do not wish to find myself fighting you."

"Fighting *us*? How?"

"How not? Spain's enmity toward your United States of Europe is unlikely to abate soon. So, if I am not willing to become the physical instrument of that hatred, I must take service elsewhere. And that decision reflects not just my loyalty as your friend, but the practicality of a seasoned officer: becoming a military adversary of the USE seems best suited to those who are in an intemperate rush to meet their maker."

Michael Sr. smiled a bit. Michael Jr. frowned a bit.

Hugh leaned toward the latter. "What is it, Michael?"

"Nothing. Just thinking, is all."

"Thinking of what?"

Michael Jr. seemed to weigh his words very carefully before he spoke. "Well, Hugh, we might be working for the same boss, soon."

"You, Michael—working for the French? How could that be? Just last year, they attacked the USE."

"Well, yes...but that was last year. We have a treaty now."

"Michael, just a few days ago, did your own father not quip that the honor of nations is, in fact, an oxymoron?"

"Dad did, but I'm not counting on French honor." He snorted the last two words. "I'm thinking practically. My guess is that the French are going to be lying low for a while, at least with regards to the USE. So it should be safe for me to do a short stint of work for the French, just to make some extra money. To handle some extra expenses."

Hugh frowned, perplexed. Then, through the kitchen doorway, he saw Mike Sr.'s German nurse bustling busily at a shelf lined with his many special ointments, potions, and pills.

Michael Sr. spoke up. "Yep, I'm the 'extra expense.'"

"Perhaps I remember incorrectly, but isn't your wife—?"

"A nurse. Yes, but she's needed elsewhere, and there's not a whole lot she can do for me that any reasonably competent person can't."

"And the USE does not provide you with adequate care in exchange for both your wife's service, and your son's?"

"Oh, they provide, but it's pretty costly, taking care of a crusty old coot like me."

Hugh smiled, not really understanding what a "coot" was or how it might acquire a crust, but he got the gist by context.

Michael leaned towards his father, subtly protective. "So I found a way to make a lot of money pretty quickly, I think. But it involves going over the border."

"To France."

"More specifically, to Amiens."

Hugh started. "You mean to work for Turenne?"

Michael nodded, looked away.

Hugh did his best to mask his surprise. "Really? Turenne? And his technical, eh, 'laboratories?'"

Michael nodded again. "I negotiated the leave of absence a while ago. My bags are pretty much packed. Literally."

"And Stearns, and Gustav, will allow you to provide technical assistance to Turenne?"

Michael shrugged, still looking away. "This down-time version of America is still a free country. We brought that with us and kept it. Mostly. Besides, I'll only be showing the French how to achieve something that I'm sure they've already studied in our books."

Hugh nodded, wondered what this "something" might be, and also if there might be some way for Michael and he to combine their westward journeys. He leaned back, feeling a surge of relief at even this nebulous prospect of having a comrade as he began to seek his fortune in France. It was a relief to think one might not start out on a new career completely alone, almost as comforting as the fire which threw flickering shadows around the walls and even painted a few on the back of the front door.

✧　　✧　　✧

Six days ago, Hugh had knocked on that front door—unannounced—to begin his second visit to Grantville. This was a considerable departure from the formality of his first visit, made about three months earlier.

That initial visit had been something of a low-level affair of state. Technically still the earl of Tyrconnell (in everyone's opinion but the English), Hugh Albert O'Donnell's name was known to some up-timers not only in reports from this present, but also from the tales of their own past. And it had been that past, and the future that had followed from it, that Hugh had come to explore.

Grantville's official libraries had been helpful in the matter of general history, but had little mention of Hugh or his illustrious forbears. Rather, it was his first passage through the front door of the McCarthy house that changed his world forever. Although it was Michael Jr. who had invited Hugh to use their home library, it was the father—an elderly ex-miner suffering from black lung—who was the more ardent (or at least outspoken) Fenian, possessing an impressive collection of both historical and contemporary texts on the subject. Like some enfeebled but passionate bard, Michael Sr. could recall twice the number of tales that were in the books, and was singularly well-versed in the lore of Ireland's many troubles—troubles which had continued on, Hugh was devastated to learn, for almost another four centuries.

On the last day of his first visit, Don McCarthy had waggled a gnarled finger at him. "Sir O'Donnell—"

"Don McCarthy, this will not do. I insist that you address me simply as 'Hugh.'"

"Then stop calling me 'Don McCarthy'—'Hugh.'"

Hugh could not stop the smile. "You are the eldest of your family and have the wisdom of many years. I would be a boor not to title you 'Don.'"

"Don" McCarthy made a gruff, guttural sound. He had learned that, although the thirty-year-old earl was always gentle with his hosts, he had a winning way of getting what he wanted. "I have a book," the elder McCarthy grumbled at last.

"You have many."

"Yeah—well, this one talks about you."

"I am mentioned in many of the—"

"No, Hugh. This one has a special chapter about you. About your family, your life—your death."

Hugh felt the hair on the back of his neck rise up straight and stay that way. The old McCarthy patriarch reached up a slender journal. Hugh remembered taking it with the same mix of avidity and dread that he would have felt if given the chance to handle one of the legendary serpents that possessed both the power to kill and confer immortality.

And the chapter, written in 1941 by Brendan Jennings, OFM, had proven to have both such powers. In his first hurried read of *The Career of Hugh, Son of Rory O'Donnell, Earl of Tyrconnell, in the Low Countries*, Hugh discovered that he and the last of his men were to die in 1642, only seven years hence, in the service of Spain, fighting the French at sea off the coast of Barcelona. And thus was sparked his resolve to leave direct Spanish service and encourage his men to consider carefully any offer that might draw them away from their benefactress—and his aunt—Archduchess Isabella of the Spanish Lowlands. It was a decision that might simply lead him to an even earlier death, Hugh reasoned, but that was only one possibility. And so, he hoped that he, and many of his men, had been granted a new lease on life.

But within a few minutes, Hugh discovered the darker curse lurking in the pages of the book. It indicated that his wife had died in 1634. And so she had. Eighteen-year-old Anna Margaritte de Hennin had often visited the court of the infanta Isabella, who had been instrumental in brokering Hugh's marriage to her. What had started as an act of prudent policy had blossomed (as Isabella had wryly predicted) into a passionate romance, but one which had ended in bitter tragedy. Anna Margaritte lost both their first child and her life in the week before Christmas, torrents of post-partum blood pouring out of her as if some demon within could not kill her quickly or thoroughly enough.

Hugh stared at the book. The warning had been here. It had been here since the American town had materialized in the middle of Germany in 1631. It had been here before he had married Anna Margaritte. Before they had spoken of children. The warning of Anna Margaritte's death in childbirth had been here, waiting. And he had not come, had not read it.

And so they had conceived a child in blissful ignorance and she had died in horrible agony.

Hugh did not remember leaving the McCarthys' house. He remembered putting the book down carefully, remembered gathering most of his belongings and notes, and the next thing he knew, he was riding west, into the deepening night. His two guards caught up with him, frenzied with worry, three hours later.

After returning to his regiment, Hugh spent days recovering from the shock of what he had read, and then weeks thinking about what course of action he should take, and when.

At last, just before spring, he began writing the most difficult and delicate letter of his long career as a correspondent with kings and cardinals, princes and pontiffs. When he completed the letter in early April, he leaned back and tried to see anew this document that had even plagued his dreams. And so, skipping the long prefatory parade of titles and overblown felicities, he read the beginning of its second paragraph with, he hoped, fresh eyes:

> *"So as not to besmirch the names and honor of my kind patrons—who ensured I kept my own titles when my sires died—I regretfully announce my resolve to take leave of their service, that I may better serve my native country and kinsmen. This decision in no way signifies any deficiency or decrease in the love and esteem in which I hold my many benefactors. I have naught but gratitude for their innumerable kindnesses, and I depart their service heavy with the sorrow that I shall surely never know the like of their love again."*

And, given the many contexts (and pretexts) that had gone into the making of Hugh's current situation, he reflected that his words were true enough on all counts. The persons who had truly been his surrogate family—Archduchess Infanta Isabella; Sister Catherine, prioress of the *Dames Blanches*; Father Florence Conry of St. Anthony's—had been generous, compassionate, even loving. And of his more distant benefactors—the careful Philip, his recidivistic court, and its hopelessly blinkered courtiers—he could only say that their "love" had indeed been unique. No group of "benefactors" had ever stood in such a strange and often awkward relationship to its dependents as had the Spanish crown to the relatives of the exiled Irish earls O'Donnell and O'Neill.

Three days later, Hugh was finally able to bring himself to fold the letter and press his seal down deep into the pool of red wax that bled across the edge of the top sheet.

The following morning he posted the letter to his patrons and lieges, sought permission for a leave of several weeks, received it, dashed off a missive to the McCarthys that might or might not arrive before he did, and set off for his second visit to Grantville, alone.

He had arrived at their fateful yet welcoming front door six days ago. He had ventured back out beyond it a few times, but had spent most of the days—and nights—reading. Reading reading reading. And when he was not reading, he was making notes, comparing accounts, examining how the dominoes of polities and personalities had fallen during what the up-timer histories called the Thirty Years' War. Judging from how current events had already veered dramatically away from those chronicled in the up-timer books, Hugh quickly concluded that although the current wars might or might not last as long as Thirty Years, they would have an even more profound and lasting effect upon the map—and life—of Europe. And, no doubt, the world beyond.

But ever and again, he would find something that reminded him of how his late arrival to Grantville and its histories had allowed him to follow the fateful track of that other future just a few months too long. Too long for his wife, his son, and at least a hundred of his regiment who had been lost fighting for the interests of a Spanish king who, it was now clear, would never fight for their interests.

And on this, the sixth night of his stay, while sitting in the worn living room of Don McCarthy, these specters of regret had been gathering within Hugh once again as Michael McCarthy, Jr., had emerged from the kitchen with the dreaded "white lightning" that the up-timers seemed to consider divine nectar. He had found himself recalling all the faces that had come to swear allegiance under his banners, and which were now buried in the loam of foreign fields.

He broke out of his silent reverie without preamble. "I could no longer command a unit that bore my name like a lure, so as to attract the *cultchies*—the simple country boys—like bees to pollen."

The McCarthys did not comment as the first round of moonshine was poured out, but he felt their eyes.

"It was hard watching them die in foreign service, far from home, dismally used. But I could make myself do it, so long as I was able to believe we were purchasing the good opinion of our Spanish allies, that we were securing their permanent regard for our honor and character, as well as skill on the battlefield. And that, therefore, Philip would finally be moved to act—if only to keep faith with the promises he had made to men of such quality and integrity." He took a look a small sip of the white lightning. "What a fool I was."

Michael Sr. responded in a low, steady voice. "Hugh, you were brought up by good people to be a good man, and true. But nations—even those ruled by kings who claim to prize honor and loyalty—cannot keep faith with those same virtues. It's in the nature of nations to make promises they don't keep. Unfortunately, no man can know beforehand which of the promises made to him will turn out to be the worthless ones."

Hugh heard the attempt to take the onus off him. He shrugged it off. "I was gullible—in this and other matters. I was not merely a child but a simpleton to believe the initial priestly rubbish about Americans as the spawn of Satan himself. If I hadn't put such faith in Philip's court clerics, I might have thought for myself and come here earlier. I might have read my own future—and in it, seen and avoided Anna's death in childbirth."

"You could not have known." Don Michael's tone was soft yet strangely certain.

"I could have. I could have found better care for her."

"She was Flemish aristocracy. She had the finest doctors of Europe."

"The finest doctors of Europe, even of the Lowlands, are not *your* doctors. My reading has not been confined to the future plight of Ireland, Don McCarthy. I have spent many hours in your libraries. I have learned of obstetrical bleeding, of *placenta previa*. And so I learned that what killed my wife was ignorance: my ignorance, our ignorance."

"Son,"—and McCarthy sounded sincere in affixing that label— "son; you couldn't have read that in time to save her."

"With respect, Don McCarthy, you were here almost three years before her *accouchement*. At any time, I could have—"

"No, Hugh. I'm not saying that the books were not here to be read. I mean that you weren't ready to read—and *believe*—them."

He looked to his own son, whose often unreadable gray eyes were crinkled in what appeared to be pain.

And suddenly Hugh understood that these strikingly plain-mannered beings had been trying to lead him to the realization that now snapped on in his mind like one of their impossible "light bulbs":

—it was Anna's *death* that had jarred him enough so that, shaken from his old perspectives, he could see the world through the new lenses brought by the up-timers. Before she had died, he would not have traveled to read, nor have believed or trusted the content of, the books in Grantville that might have saved her. But when their unborn child had killed her by tearing out the very root of the umbilicus that had already choked him, Hugh's happy complacency ended. Their two deaths had midwifed the birth of his new consciousness.

The change had not been instantaneous. His former habits of thought had not died suddenly, as if decapitated by the single blow of a headsman's axe. No, it had been like a fall from a great height, starting when the midwives and doctors left him alone with Anna's haggard corpse and the tiny, blue-black body of he who was to have had his father's name, and titles, and boundless love. Sitting there with that tiny form in his hands, Hugh had started falling into a hole at the center of himself: falling falling falling—

And when he finally awakened from that long fall, weeks later, he opened his eyes upon a different world. It was a world that was unguided by Divine Providence, and in which his kinsmen had languished and died hoping hopeless hopes. And then had come the strange letter from Grantville.

It had been a strange letter indeed. It conveyed, first and fore-most, condolences—of which there had been many others, most far more grandiloquent in their invocation of tragedy and the mysterious will of God. In contrast, this letter—from an up-timer named Mr. Michael McCarthy, Sr.—while clearly heartfelt, had been singularly straightforward and plainspoken. Yet, it landed like a thunderbolt before Hugh's eyes. In part, this was because he had never thought to receive any such expression of solicitude from an up-timer. But even more arresting was McCarthy's lament that the death of Hugh's wife and heir were also "terrible blows to all O'Donnells—and to the many generations of patriotic Irish who came after you."

This added a strange, almost surreal dimension to his loss. Posterity had, somewhere, already been lastingly impacted by the death of his child and his wife. And the more Hugh reflected on that, the more he felt it grow like a tapeworm in that part of his mind that digested new facts. He and his line were known in the future. And that future could be discovered by going to Grantville.

And so he had. And now he sat in Don Michael McCarthy's living room, sharing this magical bourbon with him and his son. He sighed, sipped again, wondered if life was really any less capricious than the unpredictable dance of flames in this hearth built from eerily identical up-time bricks. He watched the fire send flickering shadow-demons capering along the walls. But less energetically now; it was burning low.

Michael Jr. noticed the fading flames and got up; he gestured for Hugh to remain in his seat. "I'll get another few pieces of wood. Stay put." He looked for his coat. "Damn. That's right; it's in the wash."

Hugh tried to hide his smile. Michael had attempted to ride Hugh's war-trained charger earlier in the day. The high-spirited stallion had been tolerant enough when the up-timer was in the saddle, but was impatient with his awkward attempt at dismounting. One sharp, tight turn had flung coat-wearing Michael down into the mud and manure.

Hugh rose. "Michael, I will—"

"You will not. You're my guest."

Hugh took his distinctively embroidered cape from the knob on the coat-closet door, revealing his scabbarded sword. "Then at least stay warm in this."

Michael seemed ready to decline, then nodded his thanks and took the cape. Hugh sat back down, contemplated the firelight sparkling through the bourbon, wondered what foreign fire he'd be staring into a year from now.

Presuming that he was still alive to do so.

Chapter 3

Grantville, State of Thuringia-Franconia

Eddie emerged onto the rapidly dimming streets of Grantville and pushed up his collar against the faint chill. *You'd think after spending almost a year and a half on the Baltic I'd have a little better resistance to cold, but no.* Having recovered from borderline hypothermia while recuperating from the amputation had left him weakened for quite a long time. In particular, he had been susceptible to chest colds that, up-time, would have been annoyances cleared up by any halfway decent decongestant. Down-time, they were potential death sentences in his then-weakened state. And ever since, cold weather cut through him like a knife.

He strolled west, deciding to take a look at the three trailer homes that had served as his first down-time abode. He smiled to think of the early days when he and Jeff Higgins and Larry Wild and Jimmy Andersen had played D & D there, the game having acquired a strange significance given their displacement in time. It wasn't because of the "historical value" of the game—because there wasn't any; role-playing games were about excitement, not accuracy—but because it was somehow a symbol that not everything had changed with their arrival in war-torn Germany. Not every waking minute was toil for food, scrambling to preserve or rebirth technology, find allies, and repel utterly murderous foes.

A quick session of D & D, where imaginary warriors and wizards strove to slay evil trolls and troglodytes, was also a reassurance that life had not boiled down only to a mere continuation of existence. There was still time for fanciful adventures, for larking about a fictional world with his very real friends.

But then Jeff had married a down-time firebrand named Gretchen Richter, and her entire loosely-associated clan had moved in. Overnight, fancy had given way to kid-powered frenzy. And that, too, had been reassuring and endearing in its own way. It was as though the house was constantly alive with rambunctious sounds of hope, thanks to all the healthy, lively children that were forever charging around and through its small rooms and tight hallways. Yes, in all its permutations, Eddie reflected, it had been a good house.

He almost walked past the tripartite structure, so changed was it. Gone were the bright, albeit fading, colors of the siding. The local tenants (who paid a pretty penny for the privilege of living in an up-time domicile) had given it a second layer of wood shingles, dug a number of discreet latrines in the back to relieve the burden on the indoor plumbing, tidied up the yard, and replaced two of the doors (and their frames) with solid local manufactures. They had also erected what looked like a huge, wooden carport over the entire structure, evidently in an attempt to preserve the metal and vinyl conglomeration from the elements. However, it created the impression that this was not so much a home as it was an oversized shrine commemorating trailer parks everywhere.

Through the windows, oil lamps glowed to greet the dusk, and then shadows moved with slow purpose toward the largest of the kitchens. A brief pause and then a sharp white-yellow light seemed to blot out all the other fire-orange glows about the house. Clearly, someone had turned on an electric light. Immediately, silhouettes of all sizes began gathering around it, some bearing what looked like outlines of cooking implements, others arriving with already-open books.

It looked ritualistic, Eddie admitted, but he knew damned well it was not some strange species of cargo-cultism, a trait Larry Wild had often ascribed to the down-time Germans before he was killed off the coast of Luebeck almost two years ago. This was the prudence of practically-minded folk, amplified by the parsimony of war survivors. Germans who had lived through the now-truncated Thirty Years' War were generally not spend-thrifts. Every resource they had was kept as long as possible, its life extended by using it only when absolutely necessary. And when that intermittent and gentle use nonetheless wore it out, the object was repurposed—right down to its last component. Objects with limited service lives became especially revered objects: not because of their wondrousness, but because of the mix of singular utility and utter irreplaceability that character-ized them. It would be a long time before the up-time boosted labs and workshops of even the best down-timer engineers and inventors were producing freon filled cooling compressors or a wide selection of vaccines or antibiotics.

But the down-timers were also coming up with new compen-satory technologies, one of which now intruded upon Eddie's reverie. Just down the street from where he stood staring at the house that had been his first haven in this often frightening new version of the Old World, he heard a distant toot. Like a child's train whistle, but louder. He turned and, already moving far faster than he ever had with his peg leg, Eddie Cantrell hobble-ran in an attempt to catch the new monorail trolley that was approach-ing the stop on East Main Street, just a block behind him.

The strange vehicle chugged slowly into view: a simple wooden front car that resembled a rough-hewn and vastly shrunken ver-sion of a San Francisco cable car. Except there were no cables, and there was only one track, comprised of split logs, their flat-cut centers lying flush upon the ground, their sun-bleached hemicircular trunks facing up. The operator reached down, dis-engaged the drive-gear, applied brakes. The train slowed and the passengers in the front car swayed, as did the crates and boxes in the high-sided freight car behind it.

Eddie timed his hobble so as to wave his cane and shout when he came down on his good leg. "Hey, wait up!"

If the operator heard him, he gave no sign of it. Instead, he stepped down to help an elderly passenger up into the lead car.

Which, on closer inspection, was a radical departure from any form of up-time rail transportation Eddie had ever seen. In addition to the two, flanged, steel track-wheels—salvaged from small automobiles, and now leather-strapped on their contact surface with the rail—there was, for lack of a better term, a larger wagon wheel attached to the side of the car as an outrigger. It kept the car upright, and ran along the smooth up-time roadbed. The front car's very small steam engine, puffing faintly, was of entirely down-time manufacture. Not terribly efficient, and both heavy and crude, but none of that mattered: it provided reliable power to the up-time car wheels that pulled the car along the wooden track at a comfortable six miles an hour or so.

"Hey!" shouted Eddie again, and this time, missed the timing with his cane. But his new foot's spring-compressed heel popped him into his next step, and what should have been a nasty fall turned into an arm-flailing stumble.

Which apparently attracted the attention of the operator. "I wait!" the man assured him loudly, squinting at Eddie's gait. "We always wait for our soldiers."

Eddie waved his thanks, noted the driver's extremely thick accent. Swabian, from the sound of him, likely rendered homeless by the border wars between the up-timers' first allies—the Swedes of Gustav Adolf—and the upstart dukedom of Bernhard, originally one of the dukes of Saxe-Weimar. As had so many other refugees from all the neighboring provinces of Germany, this driver had probably come to Grantville to find his fortune—and no doubt, from his perspective, had accomplished just that. There was a palpable eagerness as he turned from seating the elderly passenger and came forward to offer a hand to Eddie. The prompt, energetic gesture radiated that special pride particular to those down-timers who operated the new machines that their own artisans had crafted from up-time ideas and inspirations. It was as though they were simultaneously saying, "See? We are helping build this new world with you!" and "Do not discount us: we are just as smart as you are." In truth, given how little of the up-time science and engineering they understood when Grantville first fell out of the future, and how much of its technology they were now mastering and adapting, it was arguably true that, on the average, the Germans were smarter than the up-timers. Markedly so, in a number of cases.

Eddie smiled his thanks at the driver and accepted the hand up into the passenger car. With only room for twenty, who were currently packed in like sardines, there was no seat left for him. Seeing the unnatural stiffness of Eddie's left leg, one of the comparatively younger men stood quickly, gestured towards his spot on a transverse bench. Eddie smiled, shook his head with a "Thanks, anyhow," and held on to the rail as the car lurched forward to resume its journey with a sigh of steam.

The other passengers were mostly mothers with children, older folks, and two other amputees. One of the passengers seemed to be a workman, hand truck tucked tight between his legs. *Probably delivering the cargo in the back*, Eddie surmised.

They had hardly gone a block when the driver stifled a curse and backed off the steam, letting the little train begin to coast. Seeing Eddie's interest, he pointed forward. "Another train. I must pull off."

Eddie saw the oncoming train, almost a twin to the one he was on, approaching from about two blocks away. But there was only one rail. "Um...how do we—?"

The driver seemed gratified, rather than annoyed, by the question. "See ahead, the curve into the smaller cross-street we approach?"

"Yeah, you mean Rose Street?"

"Yes. We take that curve and wait."

"Like a train being diverted into a siding."

"Yes. But it is only one track, so we slow down to wait in the little street."

And applying the brakes gently, they slid around the relatively tight curve with only a slight bump. But the operator frowned at the brief jolt.

"Problem?" asked Eddie.

"Not with the train; with the track," he answered. "It is wood. It wears out quickly at the joints."

"Then why use wood?"

He smiled. "Because wood is also very cheap. So is the cost of putting new track into place. Much cheaper than iron. Or steel. Maybe you forget that, since there was so much of that metal in the future?"

Eddie smiled back. "Yeah, there was—but no, I didn't forget. I deal with that problem every day."

The driver's slightly graying left eyebrow rose. "Yes, and so?"

"I work with Admiral Simpson. Building the new navy."

"Ah. Of course you would know about iron shortages, then." He paused, looked at Eddie more closely. "So you are...are Commander Cantrell, yes? The hero?"

Eddie felt a rapid flush. "I was just—just doing my job."

As the other engine huffed past, the man's eyes strayed to Eddie's left leg. "I think you did a little more than just your job, maybe." He looked up. "I am honored to have you on my train." His English became slightly more precise. "Where may I take you, Herr Commander Cantrell?" There was also a hint of a straighter spine and the faintest bow. Not enough to imply a new, distant formality, but enough to show acknowledgement and respect.

"Oh, just up the street to—"

"The Government House? We shall be there very soon."

"The Government House?" Eddie echoed. "What's that?"

The man smiled. "It is officially called the 'Administrative Annex'—the old presidential office building. It is where all the decisions were made before the capital was moved to Bamberg. But as you must know, there are still many decisions being made there. And I suspect it will continue to be so."

"But then why relocate the capital to Bamberg?"

The driver smiled sagely. "Oh, Bamberg will certainly be the center of attention, and home to most of the bureaucracy. All the fine lords and burgermeisters will journey there and make speeches and drink too much and diddle the barmaids—if their wives have not made the journey with them."

"And here at the Government House?"

"Here is where the business of putting certain decisions into practice will remain. Certain sensitive decisions. It is interesting to see which offices remain here—renamed, but still here. Offices which must make important decisions very quickly. And how else should it be? Here, all the leaders, all the decisions, are still only a phone call away. But here, also, there are many up-time radios and the people who know best how to use them. Here is running water, and electricity for computers, and heat and light for winter hours that reach far into the night." He shifted a gear, opened the throttle, looked behind, and began to reverse back out onto the main line of the track that ran along East Main. "Bamberg is certainly the capital, the center for important talk. But Grantville, Commander Cantrell, remains the center for important action." And with that, he shifted the train's gear back into its original position, tugged the whistle cord, and, as if to give emphasis to that hoarse toot, opened the throttle to resume their journey to Government House.

Chapter 4

Grantville, State of Thuringia-Franconia

Hugh sighed and sipped his bourbon again. Michael McCarthy, Jr., having shrugged into O'Donnell's heavy, distinctively embroidered cloak, thumped through the front room and out the front door.

Hugh let his head lean back on the sofa and closed his eyes, savoring the smooth aftertaste of the bourbon and letting the faces and voices of the past fade away. In their place, he let the utterly mundane sounds of the guttering fire and Michael Jr.'s progress fill his mind. Over the hissing crack of logs rapidly breaking down into embers, he heard Michael trot down off the porch and around to the garage-become-stable. A moment later, Hugh's charger greeted the up-timer with a congenial nicker.

And then, Hugh heard a fast, sliding patter of stealthy human feet: the almost liquid sound of an assassin closing on his target.

Hugh bounded out of the McCarthys' sagging sofa. He landed next to the coat-closet, hip-pinned his sword's scabbard against that door, and drew the saber in one, clean sweep, still moving as he did. He was already sprinting through the abbreviated foyer when a crossbow quarrel—almost certainly a blunt, from the sound of it—smashed loudly through the garage-side window closest to the front door. Someone had seen him moving, had taken a shot.

But why a blunt *quarrel?* wondered Hugh. That fleeting puzzlement didn't slow him any more than the front stairs. He leaped down all five, already running as he landed. As he approached the corner of the house, he heard a dull thud, a grunt, and the muffled bump of someone bouncing off the pliable up-timer wall-shingling that they called "vinyl siding."

Hugh went low as he snaked around the side of the house, saw Michael Jr. face down on the ground, a cloaked figure over him, club ready, reaching toward him—

But not trying for a quick kill—a split-second observation which, again, did not delay Hugh. Trusting that the unseen crossbowman had not had time to both reload and aim his weapon, he leaped forward, saber whirring back and then forward with the speed that only a trained wrist can deliver.

The cloaked assailant looked up, quickly raised his club: a reflex more than a purposeful parry. Hugh's Toledo blade clipped the wooden truncheon at an angle. The wood stripped back and then splintered.

Michael's attacker was thrown back by the blow, alive only because his club had absorbed a cut that would have gone through his collar-bone. But, rebounding from his own collision with the house's vinyl siding, the thug turned his momentum into a sideways barrel-roll that brought him back up to his feet in a moment. He sped into the darkness—

And I'm out of time, Hugh thought—and dropped prone just a second before a crossbow bolt sliced through the air where he had been standing. The quarrel impaled the vinyl upon the wood behind it with an almost musical *throoonk.* Hugh did not need to look up to know that this bolt had not been the kind used to stun small game. He jumped to his feet, sprinted along the reverse trajectory indicated by the quivering tail of the quarrel. He found the weapon that had fired it abandoned on the ground twenty yards away, in the lee of the neighboring house's shed. The dark night was quiet all around.

Staying low—as a lifetime of habit and training had taught him—Hugh frog-trotted back to Mike Jr., who was already raising himself up on his elbows. The displaced earl of Tyrconnell put an arm on his friend's not-inconsiderable bicep. "Here. Let me help you, Don Michael."

For a moment, Hugh thought that his middle-aged host was

going to refuse. Then he felt the arm sag a bit as Michael grunted his gratitude and allowed Hugh to roll him into a sitting position, back against the house. But he was evidently not too stunned to speak. "So now I'm 'Don Michael,' too? What does that make me—royalty?"

"Aristocracy," Hugh corrected gently, wondering how the up-timers could command such wonderful knowledge of machinery and the physical sciences, and yet make social errors that would mark even a five-year-old down-timer as slow, perhaps simple. "I should have used the title before now."

"Before now, you were using it only on my da. I figured that was because he's almost eighty. So am I really 'aristocracy'—or just another old coot who can't defend himself any longer?"

The answer came from the corner of the house. "Speak for yourself, sonny boy." Michael McCarthy, Sr., was there, on his feet and unaided, but with one hand firmly clutching the corner-board for support. The gnarled fingers of his other hand were wrapped around the grip of a .45 automatic.

Michael Jr. goggled. "Da—you shouldn't be walking on your own. And is that your pop's old service pistol? I didn't know you kept—"

"Plenty you still don't know about me, Junior," interrupted Michael McCarthy, Sr. He tried to suppress a wry grin, almost did, but then his efforts were undermined by a bout of violent, phlegmy coughing.

Hugh was over to the ailing father in a moment. Michael Jr. following only a second behind, remonstrated, "Dad, you shouldn't be up—"

"Someone was shooting at my son and my guest—and damn if he didn't bust a window, too. So yes, you're God-damned right I got up, and brought a little bit of persuasion with me." He shook the .45 for emphasis—just as his wheezing phrases became a spasmodic coughing fit that was painful for Hugh to hear. He'd heard similar sounds often enough. War-time camp conditions in the Lowlands had killed almost as many of his men as blades and bullets. Now, lessons learned from up-timer books had begun to change that. Dramatically. But for a chronic condition such as Michael Sr.'s, there was little to do but delay the inevitable.

As they helped Michael Sr. back around the corner of the house, the door banged open and spat out the old man's German nurse,

Lenna. Her fierce glance conclusively damned the two younger men for all the martial (and therefore male) idiocy that plagued the world. She almost shoved them aside in her outraged urgency to help Michael Sr. up the stairs, but at the top, he stopped, turned, snapped the .45's safety into place, and tossed the weapon down to Michael Jr.

Who stared at it, and then him.

"You're going to need it," the old man said, almost apologetically, and then disappeared into the darkness of the unlit doorway.

Michael Jr. stared after him and then back down at the gun.

Hugh put a hand on his shoulder. "Michael, are you hurt?"

Michael waved the concerns away with his free hand. "Nah. Hell, I've caught worse when a wrench slipped off the hood of a car I was working on. But what about you? Are you okay?"

Hugh paused, as he often did when Americans used that strange word, "o-kay." It had too many meanings, and each had its own maddeningly distinct contextual rules. "I was not injured—this time."

"'This time?' What do you mean?"

"I mean that I must assume that there will soon be another attempt on my life."

"Whoa—an attempt on *your* life?" Mike rubbed his head. "If this growing bump and my short-term memory don't lie, it was *me* they were trying to kill."

Hugh smiled, reached up, put a gentle index finger on the cloak Michael was wearing. It was the ornately distinctive one he had borrowed from Hugh just minutes before. "You took a blow that was meant for me, Michael."

He stared for a moment before asserting, "Well, then let's get over to the police station right away and—"

"It is not necessary that we involve your nation's public militia, Michael."

"The hell it isn't, Hugh. Look, you are a foreign dignitary, and someone just tried to assassinate you on our turf. And worse yet, they obviously had you under observation in *my* home."

"Michael, I am no longer a foreign dignitary. I have resigned my rank and titles in Spanish service, and my earldom is attainted. I am, as some of your novels would put it, 'just a regular guy,' now."

"Bullshit. Regular guys don't attract assassins. I'm taking you to the Army—"

"Michael, your kindness is a great honor, but I must refuse. I am not here in any official capacity. I am but a man visiting my friends."

"Then—as your friend—I insist that you come back into the house until we can figure out—" Michael ceased speaking as soon as Hugh began to shake his head.

"Michael, would you have me repay your kindness and friendship by bringing death over your doorstep? These two blackguards showed unexpected—indeed, inexplicable—restraint in their first attempt on my life. They are unlikely to do so next time. So, no, my friend, I will not further endanger you and your good father by accepting the hospitality of your hearth again. I must leave. Now."

Mike stared up at Hugh for three full seconds. Then he looked at the .45 in his own hand and nodded. "Okay. Then I'm coming with you."

Before Hugh could utter a negation through the surprise and secret gratitude that washed over him, Mike had pounded back up the stairs, across the porch, and through the front door that had changed Hugh's life. And if the fates were as kind as they were strange, perhaps he and the younger McCarthy would not merely share the road to Amiens, but share professional fortunes as well. After all, any business with Turenne would ultimately be concerned with military matters—and Hugh had a long and varied acquaintance with those. Of course, it was too early to broach the topic of any kind of joint enterprise with Michael just yet, but the journey ahead would afford ample opportunities to casually learn more about the American's business in France, and if there was any way a displaced Irish earl might help with it...

Mike wasn't gone long—five minutes at most—before he reemerged, backpack in one hand, his other tucking the .45 under his belt. "I'm just about ready to go."

"But—doesn't your family have only one horse?"

"Yeah, but she's *my* horse. Besides, my stepmother is doing her nursing in another city and Dad ain't riding again any time soon."

"Are you sure this is a good idea?"

"You mean, because you're someone's target?"

"Yes."

"Well, I've been thinking about that. Actually, if I come along, it still might put you in danger. I *could* be the guy those assassins were trying to kill."

"Michael, admittedly you are a most important person. As a senior instructor at the technical college, I'm sure any number of foreign powers have a pointed interest in you. But you *were* wearing my cloak when you were attacked. And if anyone wished to assassinate you, they could have chosen a hundred other moments that would be both less complicated and more subtle. I am forced to conclude that I was the intended target."

"Okay—but then wouldn't there also have been a better time to get *you*?"

"In my case, this timing might actually *help* to explain why they made their attempt here and now."

"How so?"

"If an English agent got hold of my letter of resignation during its progress to Philip, then they will have learned that I no longer enjoy the relative protection of my official positions and my own regiment. They might very well send assassins—or maybe kidnappers—to intercept me before I can secure the protection of a new patron. After all, John O'Neill and I are still declarable as princes of Ireland. As offspring of royal blood, we remain worrisome to the English occupiers."

"Yeah, but England seems to have toned down a little bit on the 'Irish Question' right now."

"Officially, yes. And largely thanks to you Americans. But that might be why these assassins tried to use nonlethal methods, at first. King Charles—or factions in his court—might find it less complicated to simply imprison me in the Tower of London."

Michael nodded. "Okay, so maybe you *are* the bullet-magnet. But there's something else you should know, Hugh."

"Yes?"

"It's also possible there's been some loose talk about the technology that I'm bringing to Turenne."

"Others know about it?"

"A few. One is going to have to come with us."

Hugh did not try to stop his eyebrows from rising.

Mike hurried on. "Yeah, I know: another fellow-traveler is probably not what you were bargaining for. But this guy is part of the package. Turenne is going to need him. At least for the first few months. And if this guy, or any of his friends, talked, and rival powers heard the whispers, then—"

"—then they would want to make sure that Turenne will not enjoy the advantage of this new technology," Hugh finished for him. "So first they would try to take you hostage and secure the advantage for themselves, but failing that, they might resort to a more 'permanent' solution—"

"Right, which would make *me* the bullet magnet. Again."

Hugh smiled. "Evidently, we cannot know with certainty who is endangering whom. So we will share the peril equally. Now, you mentioned that we must pick someone up on the way. Who is this person?"

Mike started walking toward his nag. "He's a toymaker."

"A toymaker? What kind of toys does he make?"

"Secret toys."

"Truly? Tell me, Michael, what kind of toy would need to be kept a secret?"

"I'll tell you as we ride."

Chapter 5

Grantville, State of Thuringia-Franconia

Ed Piazza, President of the State of Thuringia-Franconia rubbed his eyes. "Are those the latest production reports, Anton?"

Anton Roedel, former clerk for the city council of Rudolstadt and now Executive Secretary to the President, nodded. "Yes, Mr. President. The production numbers from the new coal mines should not be considered a basis for long-term projection, though. Their operating managers indicate that—"

"Yes, Anton," Piazza smiled, "I was listening when you read their letters to us."

Farther down the conference table—a battered brown institutional slab that had started life in the teacher's lounge of Grantville's elementary school—Vince Marcantonio, Piazza's chief of staff, stretched and groaned. "Please tell me that's the last of the reports, Anton."

"Yes sir, I thought it prudent to conclude with—"

There was a knock on the door.

Warner Barnes of the State Department sighed. "Now what?"

Francisco Nasi, Mike Stearns' spymaster, shrugged. "That would be the arrival of 'unofficial' official business."

"Huh?"

Piazza grinned. "C'mon, Warner, you've worked in the State Department long enough to recognize euphemistic 'code' when you hear it."

"Oh no," Barnes sighed, "not covert crap. Not now. That shit takes forever, and I want to get home."

"Before the evening gets cold?"

"Before my *dinner* gets cold and my wife blows her stack. This happens every time you and Francisco come back from Bamberg with a 'special agenda' for us to go through. This time, I don't think I've even seen her in the past seventy-two hours. She's out the door before I'm out of bed. I get back after she stops waiting up. You're a damned home wrecker, Mr. President."

Piazza nodded. "My apologies, but let's not keep our 'unexpected' guest waiting." Raising his voice, he called, "Come in!"

"Watch," growled Secretary of the Interior George Chehab from his sulky slouch at the very end of the table, "I'll bet this becomes the longest, drawn out business of the whole damned evening. Mark my words—"

But then his jaw shut with a snap, followed by a guilty gulp: Eddie Cantrell stuck his head into the room. He looked a little puzzled as he scanned all the faces.

"Uh...hello, Mr. President, gentlemen. I'm sorry if I'm interrupting. I was told you'd be concluded by this ti—"

Piazza smiled and waved him in. "There's always more work to do than there are hours in which to do it, Eddie. No worries."

The recording secretary looked at Eddie, then Piazza, then turned a new page, and started scribbling.

Eddie glanced uncertainly at Anton and back again to Piazza.

Piazza nodded faintly, so faintly that he was pretty sure that the only two people who saw it were Eddie, who was looking straight at him, and Nasi, who saw everything, anyway. "No need to itemize the report from Admiral Simpson, Eddie. Just leave it with us. We'll probably go over it after Mr. Roedel departs."

Anton seemed to start slightly, then resumed his scribbling.

Eddie nodded. "I understand, sir. Perfectly."

And he and Piazza shared a smile, just as they shared a complete understanding of why a review of the report was being deferred. By waiting until Anton was gone, there would be no official record of Admiral Simpson's strident, not to say fulminative, arguments about the materials, money, specialists, priorities, and other assets he wanted—no: needed!—in order to have a snowball's chance in hell of getting a blue water navy ready by the promised date.

"Those folders under your arm," Piazza said, nodding at the

leather-bound attachés that passed for "folders" in Early Modern Germany, "I take it they also contain brand new requests from Admiral Simpson?"

Eddie's smile was rueful. "Yes, Mr. President. They most certainly do."

"And what would the esteemed admiral want now?"

"Well, pretty much everything he wrote you about last month. Except lots more of it."

Piazza put out his hand for the folders. Eddie moved to walk them over. Piazza saw the limp, remembered the missing leg, jumped to his feet to get the folders, mentally cursing his forgetfulness and excusing it at the same time. *Damn it! Eddie was just a kid—just a smart, awkward kid—only four years ago, staring at cheerleaders, dealing with acne, and coping with the low ceiling of his possibilities in a small West Virginia mining town. And now he's a handicapped veteran. But I still see that kid, when I look at him.*

And that was when Piazza saw the look on Eddie's face: that "kid" wanted to walk the folders over himself. And the way he held himself as he limped closer—straighter, in a military posture—shamed the image of Eddie Cantrell, Nice Kid, forever out of Piazza's mind. He was sad to see that old image go, but felt an almost tearful pride at the image that had now permanently replaced it: Lieutenant Commander Edward Cantrell, veteran and hero at the tender age of twenty-three.

Piazza extended his hand for the folders that Eddie could now reach out to him and he said, quietly, and as seriously as he had ever said anything in his life, "Thank you for bringing these to us, Commander Cantrell."

"My pleasure, sir."

"*—And my duty,*" Piazza heard as the unspoken subtext behind those words. He nodded. "Before you go, Commander, we have something that you need to take with you."

"A return communiqué, Mr. President?"

Piazza smiled. "No, Commander." He turned. Francisco Nasi held out a large, varnished wood box, with a strangely intense look in his dark eyes, as if he was hoping they would convey something that he could not, or dare not, frame as spoken words.

"Sir?" said Eddie, puzzled, as Piazza turned and proffered the box to him.

"Open it."

Eddie did and seemed to redden for the briefest moment. "Is this—?"

"That's the finished medal, Commander. Allow me."

Piazza took the box back, lifted out the first Navy Cross that the United States of Europe had awarded to a living recipient, and put it around Eddie's neck. Who straightened and saluted.

Piazza straightened, "For your actions in and around Wismar, 1633, as per the citations read at the official ceremony," and saluted back. Then he relaxed a bit. "I know you did this last year in Magdeburg, with all the pomp and circumstance, but since the artisans and politicos were still arguing over the final design of the medal, and hadn't gotten around to—"

"Thank you, sir." Eddie looked Piazza in the eyes and then around the table. "It means more than I can say that you—that all of you—did this." All present had risen and come to attention as the real medal was conferred. Then Eddie frowned and glanced back in the box. "Uh—"

"Yes, Commander?"

"Kind of a big box for a medal, sir. And damned heavy."

Piazza smiled again. "I thought a congratulatory gift was in order. To commemorate the occasion and to help you in your future endeavors."

Eddie lifted out the wooden panel upon which the medal had rested. He stared, and then looked up at Piazza. "How did you know?"

Francisco Nasi may have smiled briefly. "I was sitting just down the table from you at your state dinner in Magdeburg last year. Perhaps you remember having a friendly dispute with the admiral over preferred side arms?"

Eddie lifted out the gift with almost reverent hands. An almost slender automatic pistol caught the light and sent gleams skittering off a blued hammer. "An HP-35. Manufactured just after the World War II, if I read the markings correctly."

Piazza grinned. "You do. Although you may be the only person in this world who would call it an HP-35. 'Browning Hi-Power' was the preferred term in the States, Commander."

Eddie, completely oblivious to Piazza's correction, turned the weapon over to confirm that no magazine was inserted. "How—where did you find this?"

Piazza looked down, shrugged, and was slightly annoyed when

Nasi almost drawled, "Actually, it wasn't hard to find at all. It seems a person we know very well had it in his possession. Had an opinion of the gun similar to your own, Commander, and chose it over many others. Even though it was distinctly nonregulation in your up-time US Army. This person has often claimed that it never failed him, and that he preferred the larger magazine size to the stopping power of the larger . . . er, 'forty-fives'?" Nasi sent a glance at Piazza, checking his terminology.

Eddie followed Nasi's gaze. "You, Mr. President? This is *your* gun?"

"*Was* my gun, Commander. It is yours, now. Use it with pride and honor. As I know you will."

"Sir, I can't take it. I couldn't—"

"Rubbish, Commander. You've already taken it. And it's the right gift for a young man who has no choice but to go in harm's way with only one leg. By comparison, I am an increasingly paunchy man whose fate is to sit at a big desk although I have two perfectly good legs. Seriously, now, who has more use for that gun? Who needs every bit of advantage they can get?"

Eddie's eyes raised from the weapon and fixed on Piazza's face, assessing. "Mr. President, you're about fifty-five, now, right?"

"Not a day over fifty-four. Don't put me in the grave any earlier than I have to go, Commander!"

"So during your tour in the Army, you were in—?"

"Yes, I was there, Commander. And since the Browning worked in the jungles on one side of this planet, I'm pretty sure it'll work just as well in the jungles on the other side. I hope you don't have to use it at all, of course, but if you do, you may find it's nice to have a thirteen-round magazine when you can't usually see what you're shooting at very well—if at all." He left unspoken the fact that there were plenty of Glocks and M-9s to be had, which boasted even larger magazine sizes. But the Hi-Power was renowned for its reliability and kindness to small-handed or easily unbalanced shooters—as Eddie Cantrell now might be.

Eddie looked down and held the gun firmly with both hands, almost as if it were a holy relic. For a second, Piazza saw the eager, earnest kid again.

Eddie looked up. "I don't know what to say, Mr. President."

Piazza laughed. "I think 'thanks,' will be sufficient. Otherwise, I can tell you're going to get maudlin on me. Well, more maudlin. Now look here, Commander, I do have one bone to pick with you."

"Sir?"

"How dare you come down to Grantville and not bring your bride?"

"Sir, I didn't think that protocol—"

Always Earnest Eddie. "Protocol be damned, Commander, we just wanted to see her again."

"'See her,' sir?"

Really? You still don't get the ribbing? "See her, Commander. Perceive her form. Appreciate her beauty. Feast upon her feminine pulchritude with our own, envious eyes. You get the picture?" And he grinned.

Before Eddie could get the surprised look off his face, George Chehab rasped, "How could you not know what we meant, son? She's a class-A knockout, that Danish Ann Margaret of yours."

"Uh, Mr. Chehab, her name is actually Anne Cathrine."

"Trust me son, she is a young Ann Margret. But more curvaceous."

"Now George," warned Vince Marcantonio, "let's not get too blatant in our admiration of the young lady."

Chehab smiled and shrugged. "Okay, but damn, I confess to disappointment that she didn't come down with you, Commander: severe, genuine, personal disappointment. She's as charming as she is beautiful, and we'd have liked to show her more of Grantville last year."

Eddie nodded. "Yes, sir. A return visit tops our list of things to do. When time permits."

And the room became quiet again, the jocularity chased out by the shadow of things to come. Serious things. *Time to get back to and conclude the matters at hand,* Piazza admitted. "Well, Commander, we are very glad to have seen you and presented you with your long overdue medal—and gift. I take it you will be returning to your duties immediately?"

"Yes, sir."

"Not even time to sneak a quick visit to Copenhagen?"

Eddie shook his head. "No, sir. Much as I'd like to. What with being a new husband and all."

"Amen to that," breathed Warner Barnes sympathetically, who knew because Piazza had briefed them months ago, that Anne Cathrine was "inexplicably" not with her husband in Luebeck. Of course, there was a simple, if unpleasant explanation for her absence: she had been purposely kept away from Luebeck at the behest of a group of Swedish officers. Anne Cathrine, they correctly asserted, was inquisitive, clever, enthusiastic, and probably could have deduced military secrets from fragments of conversations overheard in Eddie's quarters. Of course, the great majority of the command staff also held that she'd have been even more likely to die rather than give up those secrets. But there had been concerns among some ultranationalist Swedes that a new bride—and a Danish one, at that—should not be in close proximity to secret projects and documents. Nonsense of course, and driven by their distrust of Copenhagen's loyalty to Stockholm in the forcibly reforged Union of Kalmar. But those officers wielded enough political power that some concessions had to be made, and this one was consented to because it imposed politically-inconsequential costs upon only two persons: a love-lorn and sex-starved new husband named Eddie Cantrell and his pining bride.

"That's hard, lonely duty you've pulled up north, Commander," nodded Piazza.

Eddie either misunderstood or was trying to change the topic. "Well, I do like learning how to sail and command a ship, but much of the Baltic is iced over and all of it is cold and stormy as hell in February and March. Every time a training tour is up, I'm grateful to be back in HQ for another few weeks. Suddenly, sorting through an endless stack of papers doesn't seem so bad, when you're doing it in a nice, warm office."

"Well, I'm sure a lot more papers have accumulated in your absence. You certainly have done quite a job of depositing a hefty new pile here with us." Piazza gestured to the leather folios on the table.

Eddie glanced at the "folders" and nodded, taking the president's hand. "It's been a pleasure to see you again, sir."

"And you, Commander. Safe travels. And I almost forgot to ask: how are construction schedules holding up in the shipyards?"

"They're passable, Mr. President," an answer which Eddie punctuated by one moment of extended eye contact, a moment that was, again, probably lost on everyone except Nasi. Sagging a little, Eddie leaned on the table for support. "But everything will come together eventually." And with that, his finger grazed across the exposed corner of the bottom-most folio.

Which was all code for: *construction is on schedule and the new technologies have reached production phase, details of which are in this folder I just touched.* And the delivery of that message, and the coded details scattered as harmless phrases throughout the papers in that folio, were the only reasons that the young commander had actually been sent down to Grantville.

The new prosthetic had been a great cover-story—flawless, actually—but the coded reports on Simpson's classified projects, and his actual completion and readiness dates, could not be entrusted to airwaves or routine couriers. Even secure couriers were problematic because there was always the chance that their role was already known and that they would be waylaid at a most inopportune moment.

No, the best means of sending secret data—for which the codes were the second, not the first line of defense—was to send them in plain sight, so to speak. And that meant using a routine contact, such as Admiral Simpson's staff expert on technology initiatives and fellow up-timer, to convey a single secure communiqué as part of a perfectly plausible trip that had been planned upon months ahead of time. And it meant that there were only three people who had known the identity of the courier in advance: Simpson, Piazza, and the courier himself—Eddie Cantrell.

Who had now reached the door. He turned, saluted, received their returns, and with one boyish smile—like a parting endearment from his rapidly disappearing former self—he was gone.

Anton Roedel finished his scribbling. "Mr. President, shall I read back the—?"

There was a knock at the door. Anton speared it with a glance sharp enough to gut a fish. "Sir, are we expecting another—?"

Nasi interrupted smoothly, with a friendly smile. "That will be all, Mr. Roedel. Please drop off the evening's secure communiqués at the encryption office, will you?"

Roedel's eyes went back to the door briefly. "Yes, but—"

"We need those messages to go out as soon as possible, Mr. Roedel. So please, waste no time delivering them to the encryptionist on duty."

Roedel glanced at Piazza who nodded faintly at the secretary and added a placating smile. "On your way, now, Anton."

Who evidently was still miffed at being sent out when, clearly, there was yet another unexpected visitor waiting beyond the door. Chin slightly higher than usual, Anton Roedel gathered his papers and notes, squared them off, put them carefully in his own leather folio, and exited like a spurned ex-girlfriend.

It was Nasi who, three seconds after the door closed behind Roedel, called out "Come in."

The person who entered through the door Eddie had exited was small, slightly stooped, and dressed indifferently, a hint of seediness in the worn seams of his coat and his britches. He looked around the room's lower periphery, not raising his eyes to meet any of those looking at him. Pressed to categorize him, Piazza would have guessed him to be a vagrant who had some-how, impossibly, strayed off the street, past the guards, and into the highest offices of the State of Thuringia-Franconia.

Nasi nodded at the man, who exited far more swiftly and eagerly than he had entered.

Warner frowned, looked at Nasi and then around the table. "What, no message? Was the guy—lost?"

Nasi shook his head. "No, he was not lost. He was the message."

"What?"

Chehab leaned forward. "The messenger coming through that door could have been one of three persons. Each one meant some-thing different, so their face was their message, you might say."

"And this one means—what?"

Nasi looked at Piazza. "It means that a pair of mechanics who were reported in town four days ago have just now departed."

Warner blinked. "Mechanics?"

Chehab shrugged, looked away. "Fixers. Freelance wiseguys."

Warner blinked harder. "What? You mean hit men, assassins?"

Nasi smoothed the front of his shirt. "Not necessarily."

"And what does *that* mean?"

"It means it depends who hired them and what for." Piazza looked over at Warner with what he hoped was a small, reas-suring smile. Warner Barnes was a relatively new and infrequent member of the group and wasn't familiar with how, or what kind of, things were done in this "sleepy subcommittee"—which also functioned, unadvertised, as the State of Thuringia-Franconia's intelligence directorate.

Warner still hadn't read between the lines. "And we just stood by while these two murderers were walking our streets?"

Piazza shrugged. "What would you have had me do? We don't have any outstanding warrants on them."

Nasi added, "They do not even stand accused of any crime."

Warner sputtered. "Then how do we know they're assassins, mechanics, or whatever?"

"Via the good offices of our preeminent international banker, Balthazar Abrabanel. His discreet connections with the Jewish 'gray market' frequently provide him with information about persons like these. They are often called upon to aid in, er, 'collections.'"

Piazza leaned in. "And we have confirming reports of their identities and reputations from the Committees of Correspondence. These two aren't political activists, but are well-known to the, um, action arms of the Committees."

"And Abrabanel and the Committees—they actually hire thugs like these?"

"Not often. And never these two in particular."

"Why not these two?"

Nasi shrugged. "Well, as has already been implied, this pair has a reputation for preferring to resolve matters...too kinetically."

Warner goggled. "So they're rougher than the average brute and we let them walk around our town, unwatched? All because some of our shadier contacts know who they are? Listen, Ed—"

Piazza shook his head. "Warner, they're not a concern of ours."

Warner gaped, tried another approach. "Okay, if you say so. But maybe we should put a tail on them while we make a quick inquiry into their whereabouts while they were here, make sure they didn't use their visit to harm any of our—"

Piazza looked at Nasi, who in turn looked at Warner, and interrupted him sharply. "Mr. Barnes. Allow me to be quite clear about this: those two men are gone. And being gone, they are to be left alone. Entirely alone. That is this committee's official policy on the matter. Is that understood?"

Warner blinked in surprise, probably more at the tone than the instructions, Piazza suspected. "Okay, yes, Don Francisco. Although I just wish I understood why—"

Piazza stood, making sure that his chair made a loud scraping noise as he did, which momentarily silenced Barnes. The president rubbed tired eyes and then stared straight at Warner before he could resume his objections. "It's been a long day, everyone. Let's go home."

Part Two

May–June 1635

The ladder to all high design

Chapter 6

Amiens, France

"Lord Turenne, we have finished searching their gear. Nothing suspicious, sir."

Turenne nodded and dismissed his orderly with a wave. He had watched from a narrow casement window when, hours ago, the strange trio had first approached the portcullis of his "testing facility." They had surrendered their arms as though they expected to do no less, submitted to the further indignity of a close personal search, and were then led into the courtyard to await a more thorough check of their rucksacks and gear.

While waiting on that process, Turenne had compared their self-written letters of introduction with the fragmentary dossiers he already possessed on two of the three men. The French intelligence was patchy at best, but confirmed that such persons did exist, that the individuals in the courtyard answered to their general descriptions, and that the positions and abilities they claimed in their letters certainly conformed to those attributed to them by the analysts in Paris. But neither source provided any clue as to why the group's two persons of note might be traveling together or why they desired an audience with Turenne himself. However, they had both been clear and politely specific regarding that latter point: they were not interested in speaking with the senior military authorities in Paris, nor Turenne's chief of staff Robert du Barry. They required an audience with Turenne. Otherwise, they explained—again politely—they would take their leave, and take their proposal elsewhere. Given his busy schedule, Turenne would normally have dictated a brief note, wishing them *bon chance* and pleasant travels to whoever was the next influential person on their list.

But one of the two credentialed strangers was an American technical expert. The other was the storied son of an exiled Irish earl, and had played a pivotal role in repulsing Frederik Hendrik's drive on Bruges just four years ago. If Turenne had ever encountered a more peculiar pair of traveling companions, he could not recall it.

There was the anticipated knock on the door. Turenne elected to stand. "Enter."

Du Barry, along with two guards armed with Cardinal breech-loading carbines, brought the unlikely duo into Turenne's office. Du Barry looked to Turenne, who waved a desultory hand at him. "I am safe here, Robert. You may go."

With a backward bow, du Barry and the two guards departed—and headed to join two other guards secreted in small rooms adjacent to this one, the entrances concealed behind bookcases and mirrors. The code "I am safe here" had sent them to these secret stations to oversee their viscount's protection.

However, as the door closed behind Turenne's security entourage, the land-displaced Irish earl and the time-displaced American looked at the walls, and then exchanged glances. Then they looked at Turenne. And smiled faintly.

So much for preserving the impression of trust and a private meeting. Turenne surprised himself by returning their smiles. "Please understand, gentlemen, in my position, to be contemptuous of possible risk is to be contemptuous of one's own life."

The taller and younger of the two spoke. "We understand completely, Lord de la Tour d'Auverge."

He waved away that title like cobwebs. "My dear Comte, er, *Earl* of Tyrconnell, let us dispense with these titles. They are so cumbersome, particularly mine. I am simply Turenne."

"And by that usage, I am simply O'Donnell."

"And your companion?"

The American stepped forward, hand half-extended, but then he glanced at the room's bookcases and mirrors. *Mon Dieu, is it so obvious?* Turenne came around his desk. As he extended his hand in the American fashion, he imagined a nervous du Barry whelping kittens in his sally port. "I welcome your hand, *Monsieur*—?"

"McCarthy, Michael McCarthy. Junior. A pleasure, Lord Turenne."

Plain manners and plain spoken, but forthright, honest, and unbowed. Turenne had heard this about most of the Americans. To many of his aristocratic peers, it made the up-timers intolerable abominations, like ogres who had learned enough of the ancient virtues of Athens and Pericles to become both supremely ridiculous and dangerous at the same time. But Turenne found the effect refreshing. He could already anticipate how, with a man of this demeanor, one could get to ideas, could get to agreements, and could get down to work, very quickly. And without the interminable folderol of titles, and protocols, and curtsies. "I welcome both of you to my, well, you might call them 'experimental laboratories.'" And with that greeting, Turenne resumed his seat. And waited.

O'Donnell heard the unasked question in the silence. "We apologize for taking the liberty of seeking you at your place of work, and with no proper application for an audience. But our circumstances and the import of our proposal are both such that this direct approach seemed best, if regrettably brusque."

"I see. Which explains much, Lord O'Donnell, since you could certainly have asked one of your correspondents for a thoroughly adequate introduction." *Or could have used them to bypass me altogether,* Turenne observed silently. "Unless I am misinformed, your seal is well-known to the pope and Philip of Spain."

Hugh nodded. "It is."

"Yet here you are, on my doorstep, without any of the letters of introduction which would have assured you of immediate audience, and spared you the distasteful experience of being searched and examined like a common highwayman."

The American answered. "Had Lord O'Donnell secured those letters, he would also have alerted those same persons to our meeting with you."

Turenne nodded and looked at the displaced earl. "Lord O'Donnell, if I am not mistaken, you have been in the court, and then direct service, of Archduchess Infanta Isabella of the Spanish Lowlands, since you were two years of age. Have you now chosen to seek service elsewhere?"

The Irishman's face took on a melancholy expression. "I had little enough 'choice' in the matter, given what the histories of Grantville have shown me."

"I can sympathize, sir. My own career was changed as a result of those documents. Cardinal Richelieu advanced me on the strength of deeds I had not yet performed, and now, never can, for that history has been irreversibly changed. Is it the same with you?"

"According to their books, I am a dead man in seven years."

Turenne felt his stomach contract, suddenly cold. "*Mon Dieu*—Lord O'Donnell, my apologies. I had no idea, or I would not have spoken with such insouciance."

O'Donnell waved aside the apology. "We all have different fates. And that was mine if I remained in Spanish service. And probably the fate of many hundreds of my countrymen, as well. And all for naught."

Turenne had read a précis of the European histories that had arrived with Grantville. "Sir, again you have my sympathies, but I must also be frank. I see no promise that the new history we are now embarked upon will make France any more ardent a supporter of Irish interests. Given the recent combination of our fleet and England's to defeat the Dutch, I must sadly project that there might even be less reason for hope."

"I do not place my hope in France, Lord Turenne. I place it in you."

The surprise of those words left Turenne both baffled and a bit wary. "Me? Why me?"

But it was McCarthy who answered. "Because, Lord Turenne, your nationality isn't what's important in this case. What's important is that you obviously understand, *really* understand, the kind of changes my town has brought to your world."

"Your opinion flatters me, Monsieur McCarthy. But then why is the earl of Tyrconnell not joining his banner to that of your USE, and Grantville in particular? It is the very embodiment of those changes."

"Which is probably why that's not the wisest choice for Lord O'Donnell. His former liege King Philip isn't exactly a fan of ours, and vice versa. Besides there's the matter of his men's Roman Catholicism."

Turenne nodded. Of course. Many of O'Donnell's "Wild Geese" were extremely devout Roman Catholics, and most had been driven from their lands to make room for resettled Protestants. Their religious fervor and grudges would be a poor fit for the USE, which, despite its lopsided polyglot of different faiths, was founded upon the strong military spine and current leadership of the Swedish Lutheran Gustav Adolf. "So then, Mr. McCarthy, I suppose it is *your* presence which is the greater mystery. As I understand it, you still retain your post as a Senior Instructor at Grantville's Technical College. If I also understand correctly, I would be a fool not to detain you on the spot and make your future freedom contingent upon your helping us with any number of mechanical challenges that my researchers currently find insurmountable."

McCarthy smiled. "But you won't do that."

Turenne kept himself from bristling at the American's self-assured tone. "Oh? And why not?"

"Well, first, it's not the kind of man you are."

"Indeed? And just how would you know what kind of man I am?"

"I know about the letter you wrote to Mike Stearns last year, expressing regret that your men killed Quentin Underwood during their raid on the oil field at Wietze."

Turenne suppressed any physical reaction to McCarthy's observation, even as he thought: *Interesting: that epistolary gesture has borne some diplomatic fruit, after all.*

McCarthy continued. "Detaining me would also ruin any hope of accord with Lord O'Donnell, thereby permanently and personally inflaming the Irish regiments in the Low Lands against you and France. But most important, forcing me to work for you wouldn't accomplish anything, since you obviously know that men who work against their will neither give you their best work, nor can they be trusted."

Turenne nodded. "All true. But I find it odd that you do not include your status as an American as a further restraint upon me. After all, keeping you against your will could be inflamed into an international incident."

McCarthy shifted. "If I were here as a representative of the USE, that would be true. But I'm not here in that capacity."

Turenne studied McCarthy carefully. "No?"

"No, Lord Turenne. Right now, I'm a free agent."

"You have renounced your citizenship in the USE?"

"No. But I've never taken a day off from my work at the college. It took me a few months to persuade my bosses, but I arranged to take all those days at once, added to a leave of absence. They didn't like that much, but they don't really have any one else with my skills." He shrugged. "I can do as I please with that time."

"And it pleases you to come here for—a visit?"

If McCarthy found the bathos amusing, he gave no sign of it. "I came here to make money, Lord Turenne."

Who, being unaccustomed to such a frank admission of monetary need, neither expected nor knew how to respond to McCarthy's statement. And it seemed that McCarthy himself had not been entirely comfortable uttering it. Unsure how to navigate this delicate impasse, Turenne leaned back—

—just as O'Donnell leaned forward: "Lord Turenne, Mr. McCarthy is a proud man. His father, Don McCarthy, is severely ill and requires constant and increasing care. More care than Michael can readily afford."

Turenne experienced a moment of utter social disorientation. "But does not the American government—?"

"With your indulgence," interrupted the Irish earl smoothly, "neither the USE nor Grantville itself provide for the private needs of even its most important personages. Within reason, they are expected to see to their own expenses."

Turenne looked at Michael and found two subtly defiant but pride-bruised eyes looking back at him. If this was an act, it was an extraordinarily good one. "I see," said Turenne, who remembered something else connecting pride and the name "McCarthy" in the intelligence he'd read on Grantville. Specifically, the McCarthy family was noted as holding an extensive book collection, and ardent political sympathies, that were both radically pro-Irish. And here sat an up-timer named McCarthy with a displaced Irish earl. The pieces were coming together. "So now I know why you are here. But I still have no idea what it is you wish to propose."

McCarthy's posture did not change, but his eyes became more expressive, less defensive. "We propose to help you with some of your current 'logistical initiatives,' Lord Turenne."

Turenne was not sure whether he should be amused or aghast at the blithe certainty underlying such an offer. "And just what initiatives are those, Mr. McCarthy?"

"Well, to start with, I think we have a way to help you achieve some of your long-term objectives in the Caribbean."

Turenne frowned. "Mr. McCarthy, I am rather busy, but out of deference to your background, I made time for this meeting However, I hardly think that France needs to consult with you— or, respectfully, the earl of Tyrconnell—on its strategic posture in the Caribbean."

McCarthy shrugged. "I don't propose to advise you on general regional strategy, Lord Turenne. I have a very specific objective in mind."

"Oh? And that would be?"

"Trinidad."

Turenne leaned back a little and narrowed his eyes. With every passing second, the conversation was becoming more interesting and also more dangerous. Michael McCarthy, Jr., and perhaps higher-ranking Americans, had been doing their homework, evidently. And now began the delicate dance—for which Turenne had little taste—of learning how much the Americans knew and conjectured, even as McCarthy might now be trying to determine the same thing about him and France's own speculations. Turenne studied the expressionless up-timer and thought: *he is a mechanic, a man who works with wheels. And he himself may be filled by wheels within wheels. A spy? Perhaps. But perhaps an emissary, as well. And both roles would require extreme discretion at this point.*

"Trinidad," echoed Turenne eventually. "An interesting location to focus upon. Why there?"

"The petroleum deposits at Pitch Lake. They're right on the surface."

"True. But why would I want to travel across the Atlantic for oil?"

"For the same reason you took all the engineering plans from the oilfield at Wietze before you disabled the facility. You wouldn't have been interested in those plans if you didn't realize that France needs its own aircraft, vehicles and other systems dependent upon internal combustion engines. And that, in turn, means France *must* have oil. And getting oil quickly necessitates owning surface deposits that you can access with only minimal improvement to your current drilling capabilities."

Turenne acknowledged the truth of the deductions with a wave of his hand. Denying something so obvious would only make him seem childish. "So, even if we accept your conjecture, I am still no closer to getting oil, even if I am willing to cross the Atlantic. Pitch Lake is held by the Spanish."

"It is on a Spanish island. That's not quite the same thing."

So they also had access to tactical intelligence on Trinidad. That was interesting. "You seem unusually familiar with, and sure about, the disposition of Spanish forces on Trinidad," he said.

McCarthy nodded. "A young American visited the island not too long ago, on board a Dutch ship. They landed near Pitch Lake and there were no Spanish to be seen, just a few of their native allies. So as regards Pitch Lake, either the Spanish don't know what they're sitting on, don't know what to do with it, or don't care about it."

A concise and accurate summary of all the possibilities. But the dance of dueling intelligence portfolios was not yet over. "Even if it is true that the Spanish have no town or garrison at Pitch Lake, it does not follow that the Spanish are inherently uninterested in it. It is a relatively short sail to Cumana and even Puerto Cabello, where they have a considerable depth of power. In order to hold out against a response from those bases, one would need a small flotilla, at least, to hold Pitch Lake."

"That presumes the Spanish are even aware you have taken possession of it." And McCarthy almost smiled.

So here at last was the first hint of something mysterious, unprecedented: a sure sign that the conversation would soon turn toward an unforeseen up-timer capability, upon which this pair was obviously basing their proposal. "And you have a way to ensure that the Spanish would remain unaware if Pitch Lake were to be seized?"

"Not permanently, but long enough that you wouldn't need to commit large forces to landing and initial defense. Sizable forces would only be needed once Pitch Lake was securely invested and held, to further fortify and secure it against Spanish attempts at reconquest."

"You speak of summoning 'sizable forces' as if I was the French military commander of the Caribbean, Mr. McCarthy. I assure you, I have no such authority. Nor does our senior factor on St. Christopher."

"I am aware of that, Lord Turenne. That is why our proposal for seizing Pitch Lake calls for only one ship."

"One ship?"

"Yes, Lord Turenne. A prize hull, currently at moorings in Dunkirk. The *Fleur Sable.*"

Turenne frowned. The *Fleur Sable* was a severely damaged Dutch cromster, recently taken by the "privateers" operating out of Dunkirk. She had earned mention in his intelligence dispatches when two confidential agents in her crew—one English, one French—both attempted to negotiate with the victorious pirates in the name of their respective governments. Heads (theirs) had rolled in the confusion and the ship, a potential item of international embarrassment, remained unsold and unrepaired. As Turenne remembered her, the oversized *Fleur Sable* was square-rigged at both the fore- and mainmasts and lateen-rigged at the mizzenmast, meaning that she was not only capable of making an Atlantic crossing in good shape, but also had reasonable maneuverability in capricious winds.

Turenne looked at his two visitors with newfound regard. They had selected this hull carefully and well. And they obviously knew that, given his contacts and authority in the region, Turenne could acquire a single battered (and therefore underpriced) hull for "experimental purposes" easily enough. But that did not dispose him toward ready agreement. "And how do you expect me to crew this Dutch sieve?"

O'Donnell answered. "Among the ranks of the Dunkirk privateers, there are currently French sailors, and even a few officers, who were unjustly dismissed from Louis XIII's service in disgrace. As I hear it, almost all of them wish to return to his service, and success on a mission such as this might dispose him to hear their appeals with greater favor."

Turenne was careful to make no motion, change not one line in his face. *Merde! The audacity—and elegance—of the plan!* And it just might work, if this odd pair did indeed have some way of seizing Pitch Lake without being intercepted first or detected shortly afterward. "His Majesty might indeed see fit to restore such men to his favor and service, but I am of course powerless to make such a promise."

O'Donnell smiled. "I fully understand, Lord Turenne."

Turenne wondered whether Richelieu would want to send him a medal or send him to the headsman when this operation was finally revealed. But France needed oil, easy oil that could be reached by her neophyte drillers, and Trinidad's accommodating seeps and shallow deposits were a matter of record, well-detailed in the books at Grantville. But there were still problems with the plan. "Of course, you have not yet discussed who will land on Trinidad itself and take control of Pitch Lake."

The big-shouldered Irish earl nodded. "Well, let us begin by acknowledging that this force cannot be made up of French soldiers, lest you officially embroil your sovereign in an attack upon Spain."

"Exactly. So who would serve as the landing party and foot soldiers?"

O'Donnell cleared his throat. "My men. Five dozen, hand-picked."

I should have seen that coming. "And they will serve France because...?"

"Because you will provide sustenance for the rest of my *tercio* while they are on this mission."

"And so let us presume you have reached and invested Pitch Lake with your forces. In whose name do you intend to claim it, for what country? Ireland?"

"A tempting idea, but rather futile, wouldn't you agree? No, I will take it as a private possession, for sale to the highest—or preferred—bidder. So you see, my part of this operation is to be a purely corporate venture."

Turenne's head was dizzy with the possibilities and pitfalls. Corporations seizing national holdings? Was the word "corporation" just a legitimizing euphemism for "free company?" Would private ownership by dint of military conquest be recognized by any other sovereign state? On the other hand, what would national recognition matter if the "corporate" forces held it firmly? And the Dutch East India company had already made several forceful rebuttals to the common monarchical contention that all the lands of the Earth rightly belonged to sovereigns, who then bestowed their use upon a descending pyramid of vassals.

However, despite the foreseeable legal wrangling, Turenne saw one other certainty clearly enough: by proposing that he take Pitch Lake as a private entity, O'Donnell was allowing France to remain blameless of overt conquest. Of course, once O'Donnell's seizure of Pitch Lake was *fait accompli*, it was almost certain that Richelieu would move quickly to purchase the site. And then France would have its oil, and Turenne would be able to fuel the machines needed for the nation's defense. But still, the most nagging problem of all was that—"Logic and precedent dictates that the operation cannot be carried out by one ship. Unless, as you claim, your single ship can arrive at Pitch Lake completely unseen and land its small force intact, having suffered no losses in chance encounters. And so I must ask: can you do this?" He looked at McCarthy, certain from O'Donnell's expression that the answer did not lie with the Irish earl. "Can your American technology turn a small ship invisible?"

"No, but if you can see far enough ahead, you can detect and dodge opposing ships. Before they detect you."

"And do you have some means of seeing farther ahead than the lookout in a crow's nest?"

"I don't," said McCarthy. "But a friend of mine does."

"Oh? What friend? The German fellow you came with, the one downstairs?"

"Yes, sir."

"And what does he do? Build very tall masts?"

"No, sir. He builds hot air balloons."

Turenne, despite his well-practiced self-control, couldn't keep himself from snapping forward in his chair. "He builds *what*?"

"Hot air balloons, Lord Turenne. Right now, Siegfried's got a model that carries about twelve pounds aloft." McCarthy shrugged. "I think with a little guidance, some material support, and access to the inventories of your silk merchants—"

Turenne was on his feet, calling to the door and then the walls. "Orderlies. Please bring in the other visitor." After nodding briefly at O'Donnell, he turned back to the up-timer. "Mr. McCarthy, did you have plans for this evening?"

"Well, yes. I—"

"Your plans have just changed." Turenne finally smiled at the American. "And if all your hypotheses are correct, you will need to clear your itinerary for the next six months."

Chapter 7

Off Luebeck, Baltic Sea

Eddie watched the slide and tilt of the inclinometer diminish, peripherally saw that his ship's hull was nearing the center of a long, smooth trough between the modest Baltic swells, and shouted, "Fire!"

The second gunner pulled the lanyard; the percussion lock atop the breech of the eight-inch naval rifle snapped down.

Flame jumped out of the weapon's muzzle. The blast shook the deck, rattled all the ship's fixtures, and buffeted Eddie's clothes and those of the gun crew as if, for a moment, they had been standing sideways to a hurricane. The gun leaped backward in its carriage, slamming furiously against its hydraulic recoil compensators as smoke gushed out of it in a long, lateral plume.

A moment later, water geysered up approximately half a mile off the starboard beam.

Beside Eddie, Admiral Simpson adjusted his binoculars slightly. "Thirty yards long of the target, Commander Cantrell, but you were dead-on the line. Your azimuth needs no adjustment."

"I just wish I could adjust the waves," Eddie muttered.

Simpson's wooden features seemed ready to warp. Eddie knew to read that as a small, but well-suppressed smile. "Sounds like a request for the twentieth-century luxury of electric ignition systems, slaved to adequate inclinometers."

Eddie tapped the deck fitfully with his false foot. "I guess so, sir." Chagrined that he hadn't hit the target once in ten attempts, he was reluctant to stop this part of the gun's first sea trial, but the protocols were set. "Swap out the ignition system," he ordered the gun crew.

Simpson raised an eyebrow. "You look annoyed, Commander." His tone turned ironic. "Well, don't fret over getting a proper inclinometer. I'm sure the arbiters of our destiny, the Department of Economic Resources back in Grantville, will put it on the top of their 'to fund' list when they get these test results. Even though they ignored my seven-page brief which predicted this outcome."

Eddie was glad that Simpson hadn't phrased his facetious assessment of the navy's budgetary overseers as a request for his subordinate's opinion of them. Because, truth be told, Eddie could see both sides of the funding argument. Grantville's resources were pinched more tightly than ever. Despite being part of the populous and productive State of Thuringia-Franconia, the town-become-a-city had less, rather than more, wiggle room when it came to supporting cutting-edge technologies.

It hadn't started out that way, of course. When Grantville had materialized, no one understood what it represented in terms of knowledge and advanced materials. Hell, there had been a lot of people who simply refused to believe in its existence. But then, with its decisive intervention in the Thirty Years' War in support of Gustav's Swedes, Grantville became an object of intense scrutiny. And as it integrated into the economic and fiscal life of the United States of Europe that it had largely midwifed into existence, and the broader domain of world events, its singular features came under singular pressure. Every monarch, great and small, wanted devices from the future, yes, but that wasn't the greatest drain. It was all the extraordinary down-time innovators who realized the potentials of steel, of rubber, of electric motors, of plastic, and then designed genius-level devices or processes based on them. All they needed was just a modest amount of x, y, and/or z, and they could usher in a bold new era of—well, whatever bold new era their invention was sure to usher in.

The crowning irony of it was that, after you filtered out the crackpots (which was usually not very difficult; they tended to be self-eliminating), the great majority of these extraordinary innovations would probably have done exactly what their inventors claimed: they would have revolutionized some aspect of life as it was in the 1630s.

But there were thousands of such innovators, and only one Grantville. Only one source for all that up-time-quality steel, and rubber, and plastic, and everything else that was both handmaiden and midwife to these new inventions. And while Mike Stearns had led Grantville in the direction of sharing out its unique wealth rather than hoarding it, there were practical limits as to how far that could go. By now, the daily influx of inventors, treasure seekers, and curio hunters into the precincts of Grantville had emerged as both a singular fiscal opportunity (inns, hotels, eateries, short-term rental properties had sprung up like weeds) and a singular civic headache (congested streets, overburdened utilities, inflation, and a far more complicated and multi-lingual law enforcement environment). And straddling it all was the State of Thuringia-Franconia's beleaguered Department of Economic Resources, which had to set policy on how the town's unique resources should be meted out.

John Simpson understood their job, may have even had a spe-cies of theoretical sympathy for it, but he was a man who had been given an official mandate that had also become his personal mission: to build a navy which, with its small number of hulls, could defeat any conventional force in the world. And the pri-mary factor in achieving that extraordinary potency was up-time technology, either in terms of design, or in terms of actual up-time machinery. Unfortunately, it was that latter desideratum over which the admiral and the Department of Economic Resources, or DER, eternally wrestled, since there could be no increase in the amount of advanced technological systems. Grantville was almost four hundred years away from the riches of the American military-industrial complex, or even Walmart. There were never going to be any more motors, tires, televisions, or computers than there were right now. Not for a century or two, at the very least. And almost everything that Admiral Simpson wanted for his Navy, a hundred other people wanted for some other project.

The electronic inclinometer and fire-control system was, Eddie had to admit, one of those resource wrestling matches about which he felt the most profound ambivalence. On the one hand, that system was not technically *essential* to the operation of the new ship's guns. And there was no accomplishing it "on the cheap."

Down-time materials and technology were simply not up to the task of fabricating one that was sufficiently sensitive and reliable.

But if he had had a system that could the measure the attitudinal effects of wave action on his hull, and then send an electric pulse to fire the gun the moment that the ship was level, he would have been able to hit today's target—a forty-foot by twenty-foot wood framework mounted on a barge—on the fourth, or maybe even the third, try. Instead, after the first three shots—which had been required to make the gun's basic azimuth and elevation adjustments—he still kept missing the target by thirty or forty yards. But not because his targeting was off, or his crew was sloppy, or the ammunition was of irregular quality. No, it was because of these comparatively tiny three- and four-foot swells.

The roll in the deck beneath his feet was almost imperceptible. From moment to moment it rarely varied by more than one degree. But since that motion was not predictable, and since a fraction of a degree was all it took for him to drop a round short or long, it represented an irrefragable limit upon his accuracy. It was a random variable over which he had almost no control.

What little control he did have was through the combined sensory apparatuses of a down-time inclinometer and his own eyes. But the inclinometer, although the best that could be fashioned by exacting down-time experts, was simply a very well-built three-axis carpenter's level: it was not sensitive or responsive enough. And of course, the human eye was an invariably unreliable instrument—although when combined with trained human judgment, it could furnish by prediction much of what the inclinometer could not provide quickly enough.

That precision provided by electronic firing controls was simply not important to naval weapons and tactics of this era. The contemporary down-time guns were fairly primitive smoothbore cannons that evinced all the individual idiosyncrasies of their unique, by-hand production. And so, lacking the range and uniform performance of up-time weapons, it was inevitable that they were most effective when fired at very close ranges, and in volleys. That way, some balls were sure to hit.

Obviously, such weapons would have derived much less benefit from an inclinometer-controlled firing system. As Eddie had explained to Anne Cathrine, putting an up-time inclinometer on a down-time cannon was a lot like putting four-wheel disc brakes and airbags on an ox-cart. She had simply stared at that reference, so he had tried another one: it was like putting lip-paint on a pig. She got that right away.

But with the new eight-inch, breech loading, wire-wrapped naval rifles that Admiral Simpson had designed for these steamships, the want for truly accurate and speedy inclinometers was making itself felt. Profoundly. The extraordinary range and accuracy of these weapons made them, ironically, far more vulnerable to the inherent instability of a sea-going ship. This had not been so important a consideration during the Baltic War, where engagement ranges had been short, the waters relatively calm, and the hulls had been comparatively bargelike and stable. But now, highly responsive fire control was a paramount concern. The hulls that were the prototypes for Simpson's blue water navy—a large one similar to a bulked-up version of the Civil War era USS *Hartford;* the other, a slightly shrunken equivalent of the USS *Kearsarge*— were ocean-going, and if they stood high, rolling seas well, it was in part because the shape of their hulls helped them stay afloat by moving as the water did. Ironically, they were far less stable firing platforms, but fitted with guns that required, and would richly reward, superior stability. Or fire control correction.

Simpson had won the fight to get the guns he needed, and their recoil carriages, but not the electronic inclinometer and fire-control system. Eddie could see the value in both sides of that latter argument, which had essentially boiled down to, "there are finite resources and the navy can't have first pick of all of them," versus, "why go to the expense of creating the most powerful and lethal guns ever seen on the planet only to give them the same sights you would find on a zip gun?"

As time had worn on, Eddie's sympathies had moved increasingly toward Simpson's own—probably, he conceded, because he would soon have to ship out in one of these new hulls and wanted to be able to reliably smack the bad guys at distances of half a mile. By way of comparison, the down-time cannons were notoriously ineffective beyond one or two hundred yards, and were laughable at four hundred. And so if that made engagements with such ships a very one-sided proposition—well, Eddie had learned personally that in war, mercilessly exploiting an advantage wasn't "unsporting." It was sound tactics. Indeed, anything else was the sheerest insanity.

"Commander Cantrell?"

Eddie swam up out of his thoughts, saw blue waves and then Simpson's blue eyes. "Uh... Yes, sir?"

"The gun crew has swapped in the new ignition system. You may commence firing at your leisure." Simpson put the binoculars back up to his eyes.

Eddie stared unhappily at the fast-fuse that was now inserted into the aperture that had, minutes ago, been fitted with a percussion cap nipple. The hammer for that system was now secured in a cleared position.

The gun chief, a Swede, saluted. "Ready to begin firing, Commander."

Eddie sighed. "Reacquire the target, Chief."

"Aye, sir." He stared through his glass, then nodded. "Reacquired, sir. Range and bearing unchanged."

"Very well," answered Eddie, "stand by for the order to fire." Eddie felt for the wind, watched the pattern of the swells, looked for another long, flat trough between them—and saw one. He glanced at the inclinometer. The yaw and pitch were too small to register and the roll was subsiding, the bead floating gradually toward the balance point. Eddie saw it move into the middle band, approach dead center—

"Fire!"

The second gunner touched the glowing match at the end of the handlelike linstock to the fuse. It flashed down in a lazy eyeblink: quick, but far slower than the near-instant response of the percussion-cap ignition system. The gun discharged, sending out its sharp blast of sound and air pressure.

But that lazy eye blink had been a sliver of a second too long. The ship had rolled a fraction past the perfect level point of the inclinometer. Water jetted up almost one hundred yards beyond the target, and very slightly to the left.

"And that shot," observed Simpson, "had the advantage of being fired at an already ranged and acquired target."

"I may have timed the swell incorrectly, Admiral."

"Nonsense. Your timing was as good, or better, than during the trials with the percussion lock. You know the reason for the greater inaccuracy as well as I do, Commander."

Eddie nodded. "The fuse delay. There's just no way to compensate for that extra interval."

"Precisely. The comparative difference in the burn-time of powder fuses reduces the accuracy of the weapon so greatly that it's barely worth the cost of building it. Percussion caps not only ignite much faster, but with far greater uniformity. But let's not leave any room for argument. Since the bean counters in Grantville want concrete justification to release funding for a uniform provision of the percussion system, we shall give it to them." He watched the second loader turn the breech handle and pull sharply; the half-threaded breech block swung open and fumes rolled out, along with a powerful sulfur smell. "Give every shot your best estimate, Commander. I don't want any more trouble with the DER than is absolutely necessary."

Eddie squinted, stuck a finger at the horizon two points off the port bow. "Looks like we may have some other trouble before that, Admiral."

Simpson frowned, looked, spied the almost invisible gray-sailed skiff that Eddie had just noticed, bobbing five miles to the southeast. Grumbling, the admiral jammed the binoculars back over his eyes, then was silent. Eddie saw his jaw work and a moment later, Simpson uttered a profanity which was, for him, so rare as to be shocking.

"What is it, sir? Pirates?"

"Worse, Commander," Simpson muttered through clenched teeth. "Unless I am much mistaken, that is the press."

Chapter 8

Luebeck, United States of Europe

At a nod from Simpson, the two Marine guards stood at ease, but remained flanking the man who had hired the skiff. The fellow did not look particularly anxious. Then again, he did not appear particularly comfortable, either.

Simpson took his seat; he glanced at the chair beside him, which Eddie quickly occupied, grateful to be off his one real leg.

Simpson scanned the few scant reports he had on the man and his activities. Scanned them long enough to have read them five times over, Eddie realized.

The man from the skiff cleared his throat. "Admiral, I wonder if I might—"

"Herr Kirstenfels—if that is your real name—I have not finished studying the information we have on you and your actions today. I will speak with you when I have concluded."

"But Admiral, I only—"

It was quite clear what he wanted: a chair. But Simpson, who had kept this slightly pudgy man from sitting since he was taken into custody, simply waved him to silence.

Herr Kirstenfels shifted his feet but did not resume his request.

After another minute, Simpson put down the papers and folded his hands on the desk in front of him. "Herr Kirstenfels,

65

I presume you are aware that you not only put your own life at risk, but also the owner of the skiff?"

"Yes, Herr Admiral, I know this now. May I please have a seat?"

Simpson frowned. "Herr Kirstenfels, you are hardly in a position to request anything, but I will allow you to be seated." The admiral pointed out a chair to one of the Marine guards, who promptly fetched it and put it behind the detainee. Who sat on it and winced: it was as small, hard, and ugly a chair as humans could craft. Which, as Eddie knew from prior witness, Simpson kept on hand for exactly this purpose. "Now, I wonder if you know how much trouble you are in."

"Perhaps I do not."

Eddie suppressed a frown. Kirstenfels' admission sounded humble enough, but it also sounded faintly coy. Not what one would associate with an appropriately cowed, even intimidated, civilian. The undertone in his voice did not suggest fear, but watchful maneuvering. *Hmmm . . . did we catch this guy, or did he want to get caught?*

What Simpson had heard, if anything, was not suggested in his response. "I shall provide a brief outline of the situation in which you find yourself, Herr Kirstenfels. You entered a test range during official operations. You did so with the admitted intent to observe our weapons trials. Since we did not announce the trials publicly, I must conclude that you bribed or extorted that information out of a representative of the USE's armed forces or government. And that alone constitutes grounds for a full investigation by my staff."

If Simpson had meant to frighten Kirstenfels, it apparently had not worked. The smallish man merely nodded, listening carefully to each of the specifications read against him. When the admiral had concluded, he reflected momentarily, and then asked, "But have I broken any laws?"

Simpson's color changed slightly. "That remains to be seen."

"Pardon me, Herr Admiral, I should have been more precise. Were any of the actions you cited just now legal violations?"

"Your presence on the test range certainly was. Your possession of information regarding the trials may be."

"Well, Admiral Simpson, as to the latter, I did not suborn or solicit information illegally."

Eddie noticed, and so did Simpson, judging from the slight stiffening of his neck, the carefully official language.

Kirstenfels expanded upon his claim. "I simply overheard the conversation between some of the land-based test crew talking about the gun with the sailors who were preparing to go out with it on today's trial."

—*A convenient and utterly incontestable alibi,* Eddie conceded silently.

"And as far as being on the range during the test is concerned, I do not know how that could be illegal, Admiral."

"What do you mean?"

"I mean, if the trial was supposed to be a secret, how could anyone know it was illegal? Since your men were speaking about the weapon tests in a public place, I rather assumed it was not secret. And I never did hear anything about that stretch of the Baltic being off-limits to the public."

"That is because 'the public' does not often venture into those particular waters, and because we had distributed navigational restrictions to all the ship operators and owners currently in port."

"Ah. But that is still not a declaration of illegality, Herr Admiral. Rather, it is an official attempt to make the area temporarily unreachable to the public. Those are two very different things. Wouldn't you agree?"

John Simpson was motionless, but Eddie could read that as one of the clear signs of growing fury. Simpson had a particular sore spot when it came to the press. In his view of up-time events, they had been uncharitable to his country and his comrades in the way they depicted the Vietnam War, in which he had lost his own foot. The press had once again been opportunistic and accusatory when he was a captain of industry afterwards. And Eddie could see that Simpson would soon leave a crater where this hapless reporter was now sitting, if he gave voice to even a small measure of his rage. Which was not in the interests of the Navy—

But Simpson surprised Eddie by exhaling at a slow, controlled rate and then smiling, albeit without the faintest hint of genuine amity. "Well, Mr. Kirstenfels, it seems you wanted to get access to me for an exclusive interview. And now you have it, don't you?"

Kirstenfels stammered for a moment, obviously surprised at being sniffed out so quickly. "Er . . . well, yes, I suppose that may have been part of my—"

"Come now, Mr. Kirstenfels, what else would be sufficient

motivation to sail near a live-fire range? Certainly nothing having to do with our guns."

"Well, in point of fact, your guns are a matter of keen interest to me."

"So it seems. I have reports that, during the land-based proving trials, some of our perimeter guards escorted you back beyond the no-trespassing line." Simpson's restored smile was anything but genial. "You are an artillery enthusiast, perhaps?"

But Kirstenfels, despite his unprepossessing appearance, turned out to have more than his share of sand. "Perhaps, but not in the way you mean, Admiral Simpson."

"Then why don't you explicate?"

"Thank you, Herr Admiral, I will."

And Eddie could tell from Simpson's suddenly rigid jaw, that he had just given the reporter what he wanted: not merely an opening, but an invitation.

The reporter had produced a pad and one of the new, if crude, pencils that were starting to show up in a variety of forms. "You see, Admiral Simpson, I have been duly impressed by the tremendous range and accuracy of your new guns."

"They are not really new," Simpson corrected.

Kirstenfels nodded. "No, of course not. They are modeled on the ten-inch naval rifles you used in the Baltic War, except these are breechloaders rather than muzzle-loaders. But I was surprised to see the mounts for them being readied on the frigate-style ships you are building at your secure facility in Luebeck."

"Oh, and why is that?"

"Well, for the very reason you demonstrated on the water earlier today. Guns such as those require a very stable ship in order to be accurate. The monitors you first put them on have exactly that kind of stability in the mostly calm waters where you employed them, but not the sea-going frigate-style hulls you are currently fitting with steam engines."

Well, Eddie reflected, the steam-engine "secret" was going to come out at last. Which was just as well: it had always been pretty laughable as a "classified" project. After all, it was simply a logical progression to move from steam-powered monitors to steam-powered blue-water ships. In fact, all their projections had presumed that some external observers would have surmised, and then confirmed, that development long ago. Eddie and Simpson privately conceded that Richelieu had probably received definitive intelligence reports on that aspect of the ships' construction no later than March.

But "investigative reporting" was a new phenomenon, and frequently, even the best down-time newspapermen missed telltale clues of what might be transpiring simply because they did not have nuanced enough knowledge of up-time technology to understand how small details were often indicative of whole stories. It was the old problem of the expert tracker who is tasked to find an animal he has never seen or heard of.

But in this case, Kirstenfels was a reporter who obviously understood the greater significance of the (literally) "smoking gun" he was investigating. "My reading in Grantville last month suggests that those long guns would be almost useless while riding up and down the swells of the Atlantic. But there are other bodies of water—strategically significant bodies of water—for which they might be far more suited."

Eddie saw no hint of reaction in Simpson's perfect poker face, but reasoned that his CO's observations must be similar to his own. Kirstenfels evidently knew a lot about his topic, but probably did not understand the ignition variable: that with calmer seas and a percussion cap instead of a fuse, the rifles would be fairly accurate out to their medium ranges. But he certainly did understand the broader strategic implications of putting guns like those on ships that could travel on the ocean. Even if these ships were not being built for high seas battles, they might be intended to sail and steam into engagements on calmer, bounded bodies of water.

"I am speaking, of course, of their potential usefulness in the Mediterranean," finished Kirstenfels.

Which was both a correct and an incorrect guess, Eddie allowed. Eventually, that was where the new class of ships would probably be needed and hopefully, be decisive. But before then—

Simpson raised an eyebrow. "Mr. Kirstenfels, that is, to put it lightly, a most improbable surmise. What could possibly possess the USE to become embroiled in a Mediterranean conflict?"

Kirstenfels actually hazarded a small smile. "I could think of several possibilities. Ottoman expansion. Any serious threat to Venice, where the USE—and Grantville in particular—is heavily invested. An increase in the Spanish adventurism on or near the Italian peninsula, possibly including an attempt to eliminate Savoy's small but troublesome fleet."

He settled back in the chair that had been built—unsuccessfully, evidently—to prevent such relaxed postures. "However, the specific nature of the conflict is hardly the key datum in my surmise, Herr Admiral. I have been studying the ships you are building. They are high weather designs. That is more than you need if you were just going to punt around the Baltic."

Simpson's chin came out defensively. "Perhaps you've overlooked how rough the weather gets up here. In all seasons."

Kirstenfels nodded politely, but didn't look away. "Yes, but by that reasoning, then your choice of smaller craft becomes even more puzzling. The smaller hulls you've been procuring for portage on the larger ones are invariably very shallow-draft. They are lateen or yawl-rigged, have low bows, are narrow in the waist. Not for the Baltic." Kirstenfels glanced out the lead-mullioned windows at the choppy gray swells beyond the bay. "Five months out of the year, these waters would swamp such boats on a regular basis. They are, however, perfectly suited for the Mediterranean: river and inlet scouting, touching on shallow coastlines, and regular ship-to-ship and ship-to-shore exchanges."

A slow, ironic smile had been growing on Simpson's face as the reporter laid out his case. Kirstenfels' answering frown deepened as the admiral's grin widened. "This amuses you, Admiral?"

Simpson seemed to stifle a chuckle. "Oh, no, no. Please continue. I like stories. Particularly fanciful ones."

For a moment, Eddie glimpsed Kirstenfels without his mask of bourgeois suavity and well-groomed calmness. Intent and beady eyes stared and calculated, unaware that he had just been taken in by his own gambit, that the ships' ultimate goal was the Mediterranean—just not yet. But all hungry newsman Kirstenfels knew was that his finger had slipped off whatever sensitive spot had first irked Simpson, that the story which he had been building was about to slip away from him. He was annoyed, anxious, resentful at the easy unvoiced mockery with which his hard-gained evidence was being dismissed, and his conjectures along with them.

Kirstenfels' eyes lost that brief feral glaze. He tried a new tack. "Well, since you enjoy fanciful tales, let's try this one. That the fleet you're building is not bound for the Mediterranean at all, but for waters with somewhat similar characteristics and sailing requirements. Specifically, the Caribbean."

Simpson seemed to allow himself to smile. "Ah, now there's a new one. Tell me more."

Kirstenfels didn't get rattled this time. "I'd be happy to, Herr Admiral. Beyond the indisputable fact that the flotilla you are currently building would be supremely well-suited for operations in those waters, some of you Americans are likely to be relatively familiar with those waters. And you have a special interest in projecting your power into the New World, since the Caribbean has something the Mediterranean doesn't."

"Oh? Like what?" Simpson seemed to be trying to hide a smile once again.

"Like Trinidad. Like Pitch Lake. Like easily reached oil."

Simpson allowed the smile to resurface but it was faintly brittle, and Eddie knew what that meant: *that surprised him. And now Kirstenfels has hit the nail right on its head. If I don't do something, he's going to see and figure out the meaning of the look on Simpson's face and then the cat will truly be out of the bag—*

Eddie grinned, covered his mouth hastily.

Kirstenfels looked over at him sharply. "I have said something amusing, Commander?"

Eddie put on a straight face, shook his head earnestly. "No, Mr. Kirstenfels. I'm just, well, surprised that you figured out our secret."

"Your secret?"

"Yes, sir. About taking the flotilla to the Caribbean. It's no good for us to deny it any longer, now that you've put all the facts together."

Kirstenfels' frown returned. And Eddie could see the wheels of presupposition turning behind his gray, uncharitable eyes: *I know they will not tell me the truth, so my guess about the Caribbean must be incorrect. But they want me to believe it in order to throw me off the real scent. Of course, I should check to see if this, too, is just a ruse—*

Kirstenfels looked at Simpson whose face was once again wooden. "So, Admiral, since we are free to talk about the Caribbean, then—"

With a sharp look at Eddie, he cut off the reporter, "I cannot comment on any operations we might, or might not, have planned for the Caribbean." The faintest hint of the histrionic had crept into his voice, at which Eddie nearly smiled: *very well played, Admiral.*

And Kirstenfels had obviously taken the bait. The instant he heard that slightly theatrical tone in Simpson's prohibition on further conversation about the Caribbean, a tiny smile crinkled his lips. Eddie could almost see the thought bubble over the newsman's head: *So, the admiral play-acts at upset and worry. The two of them hope to mislead me into thinking my guess about the Caribbean was accurate. All in order to divert me from my first, best hypothesis: that they really* are *preparing for action in the Mediterranean.* A smug expression flitted across Kirstenfels' features and was gone all in the same instant, but Eddie knew the look of vindication and triumphant certainty when he saw it.

Simpson had folded his arms. "Is there anything else, Mr. Kirstenfels?"

The newsman rose, cap in his hands. "No, thank you, Admiral Simpson. Am I free to go?"

Simpson looked as though he had swallowed a gill of spoiled vinegar. "Unfortunately, you are, Mr. Kirstenfels. But any subsequent incidents will have consequences. You have been directly and personally warned not to pursue any further investigation into the ships we are building here or their potential uses. If you disregard that warning, I will hand you over to a judge to determine just how profound your disloyalty is in the eyes of the government of the USE. The Marines will see you out."

"And I presume I am not allowed to ask any questions of your men that might be construed to be an inquiry into their ultimate destination in the Mediterranean?"

"Or the Caribbean," Simpson added peevishly. If Eddie hadn't known better, he would have truly believed that the admiral was now irritated at having to play-act at such lame and obvious conceits as prohibiting Caribbean inquiries.

"Or the Caribbean," Kirstenfels agreed, almost facetiously from the doorway. "Good day, gentlemen."

Simpson stared at the door for five silent seconds before turning toward Eddie and matching his smile. "Thanks for the quick thinking, Commander. He had me on the ropes for that first second, when he hit on the Caribbean."

"My pleasure, Admiral. You're quite the poker player. Masterful last bluff, by the way."

The older man's smile became slightly predatory. "Do *you* play poker, Commander?"

"Not with you, sir."

"Ah. Well, in this case, that caution might indeed be more helpful than a gamesman's daring. At any rate, I'm sure we'll be hearing about our Mediterranean flotilla any day now."

"Yes, but Kirstenfels' report will be so premature that it will actually be meaningless."

"'Premature,' Commander?"

"Yes, sir. As you pointed out honestly enough, we have no reason to go down there. But you left out an important qualifying word: '*Yet*.'"

Simpson's rare light-hearted mood extinguished as sharply as a candle in a cold breeze. "Situations can change very dramatically and very quickly, Commander. We could find ourselves wishing for a Mediterranean fleet much sooner than our own timelines of 'international eventualities' suggest. But enough: we've lost a lot of time misdirecting that ambulance chaser. What's the latest status update on the New World mission, Commander?"

Chapter 9

Convent of the Dames Blanches, Louvain, The Low Countries

"Your Highne—I mean, Sister Isabella?"

The urgency in the novitiate's tone caused the infanta Isabella to start—that, and a brief pulse of religious guilt. Once again, Isabella's thoughts had drifted away from her devotions and novenas and veered into memories of her long-dead husband Albert and poignant fantasies of a family that might have been. "What is it, my child?"

"There is a...a penitent here to see you."

"A penitent?" Isabella sat a bit straighter. Sister Marie was neither a very mature nor a very wise novitiate, but she certainly knew that only priests could hear confessions and that they generally did not situate themselves at convents to do so. So this "penitent" was clearly someone traveling incognito, a subtlety which had obviously eluded, and therefore baffled, the country-bred novitiate.

Isabella smoothed her habit, touched her neck as if to assure herself that it was still there, and nodded. "Show the 'penitent' in."

If the young nun was surprised that the sister who was also the archduchess of the Spanish Lowlands was willing to receive a "penitent" in the unusually well-furnished room that had been set aside for her biweekly retreats, she gave no sign of it.

But when Sister Marie returned, she was decidedly flustered.

"Sister Isabella...this penitent...I am not sure. That is, I think...I fear I have—"

"Yes, he is a man. Do not be alarmed, child. None of the men I know bite. At least, they don't bite nuns. Usually."

Sister Marie first flushed very red, then blanched very white. She made a sound not unlike a whimpering squeak, then nodded herself out and the visitor in.

Isabella smiled as she turned. So which one of her many renegade charges had been resourceful enough to find her here—?

She stopped: a large figure draped in a cloak of gray worsted had already entered and sealed the room. The cloak was ragged at the edges, loosely cowled over the wearer's face. Whatever else Isabella had expected, this rough apparel and stealthy approach was not merely discomfiting but downright—

Then the hood went back and she breathed out through tears that, at her age, came too readily and too quickly for her to stop. "Hugh." And suddenly, in place of what the wool had revealed—a square chin, strong straight nose, and dark auburn hair—she saw:

—the cherubic face of her newest page, sparkling blue eyes taking in the wonders of her formal, or "high," court for the first time. Sunbeams from the towering windows marked his approach with a path of luminous shafts, which, as he walked through each one, glanced back off his reddish-brown hair as flashes of harvest gold. When summoned, his final approach to the throne was composed, yet there was mischief hiding behind the tutored solemnity of his gaze.

Isabella had affected a scowling gravity with some difficulty. "Are you sure you are prepared to be a page in this court, young Conde O'Donnell?"

"Your Grace, I'm sure I'm not!" His voice was high, but strong for his age. "But I will grow into this honor, just as I grow into the clothes you and the good archduke always send me." And then Albert had laughed, and so had she, and the little boy smiled, showing a wonderful row of—

His white teeth were still as bright now as then, she realized as she reached out and put two, veined, wrinkled hands on either side of Hugh's face. "My dear boy. You have returned."

"Dearest Godmother, I have."

And the pause told her, in the language of people who have long known each others' hearts, that he had not just returned from Grantville, but from the long, dark travail that had started when he had turned away from his young wife's winter grave almost five months ago. There was light in those dark blue eyes once again.

"Tell me of your trip to Grantville."

He did. She listened, nodded several times. "And so you have decided to leave Spanish service."

He blinked. "You have your copy of the letter? Already?"

"Of course. And you most certainly make an eloquent appeal for the home rule of the Netherlands, and link it to your own cause most cleverly."

"So you think well of this?"

"Of the letter? The writing is like music, the idea eminently sound, and sure to save thousands of lives. And, of course, Philip will not countenance it."

"Perhaps not. But I must try. Even though Olivares is obstinate about retaking the United Provinces."

"So now you have ears at Philip's court, too?"

"No, but I see what's happening to his treasury. Yet he remains dedicated to spending countless *reales* to retain lands that have already been, *de facto*, lost to the crown. Once Fernando declared himself 'King in the Low Countries,' no other political outcome was possible. But Olivares has no prudence in the matter of the Lowlands. He spends money like a drunken profligate to prop up the economy while slashing even basic provisioning for its *tercios*. His fine faculties no longer determine how he reacts to events here. He is driven by pride and obstinacy."

She smiled. "I will make a prince of you yet, my dear Earl of Tyrconnell. You have a head for this game."

"That is because I have a peerless tutoress. Whose many wiles still surprise me: how did you get hold of my letter weeks before my man was to deliver it?"

"Dear boy, do you not think that I know what confidential agents you employ, and that I keep them better paid than you can afford?"

She saw surprise in his eyes and remembered how the first sight of them had been a salve to her wounded soul. He had arrived in her privy court as a stumbling toddler, shortly after she had lost her third—and last—child in infancy. In those days, she thought her attention to little Hugh's education and fortunes was merely a clever self-distraction from her own sorrows. But now, being surprised by him like this, and finding her heart leaping up with a simple joy, she realized, perhaps for the first time, that he had been a surrogate for her losses, her childlessness. And he—fatherless a year after he arrived, and his mother a shadow figure trapped in the English court—had been, for all intents and purposes, an orphan, as beautiful and bright a child as might have stepped out of Eden. But there had been ambitious serpents all around, serpents sly and protected by titles, so she had often been compelled to protect him by employing methods as subtle and devious as theirs.

And she would still need to protect him now. "I must say that the timing of your decision to leave Philip's employ is... dismaying, my dear."

"Not as dismaying as finding that my godmother's intelligence network includes my own servitors."

"Hush, Hugh. How else could I know if one of them had finally been suborned by enough English pounds to betray you? But this time, it simply alerted me to your impending departure."

Hugh's eyes dropped. "What I found in Grantville left me no choice *but* to depart. Even if I was willing to go on to the fate those histories foretold, I cannot also lead my countrymen into pointless deaths. But I know well enough that Philip will not deem those sufficient grounds for my resignations, not even if he were to suddenly give full credence to the revelations of Grantville. All that he will see is that I have become a base ingrate."

Isabella smiled. "Perhaps. But here is what *I* see." She laid one hand back on his cheek, hating the palsied quiver in it that she could not still. "I see a man who blamed himself, and maybe the Spanish clergy's initial nonsense about the 'satanic' Americans, for his wife's death. And I see a nobleman who had to discover and act upon what the future held in store for his land and his people. And so you went to Grantville. And you have acted as you must. Now, tell me: having visited twice, what did you think of the Americans?"

"They are... very different from us." Hugh looked up. "But I had suspected that, particularly after they sent me both condolences for Anna and an invitation to visit them all in one letter."

"Yes, their manners are often—curious. Sometimes even crude. But on the other hand, so many of our courtesies have lost the gracious intentions that engendered them. The American manners are—well, they may be simple, but they are not empty. But enough of this. If you come to me disguised in this rude garb, I presume we cannot have much time, so—to business."

"Yes, Godmother. In part, I had come to tell you to expect the copy of my letter to Philip within the week. Which you have had for over a month, I gather. But I also came to tell you something else."

"Yes?" Such hesitancy was most unlike Hugh, and she felt her fingers become active and tense.

"My men will not all stay in your employ."

She closed her eyes, made sure her voice remained neutral. It would not do to impart the faintest hint to Hugh that she knew more about his most recent activities and the condition of his *tercio* than he did. "I presumed some of your men might wish to leave, since Philip has not sent sufficient pay in many months. A reasonable number are free to go at once. I will see to their release from service. But I cannot afford to have an entire *tercio* disband overnight. It will take some months to achieve a full release. And we will have to weather a torrent of displeasure from Madrid."

"And my many thanks for bearing the brunt of Philip's imperial temper, but that is still not what I came to tell you."

Isabella became nervous again. Her intelligence on Hugh's movements and meetings was uncommonly good and multisourced. But surprises were still possible, and at this point, the smallest surprise could derail the delicate plans she had set in motion.

"Godmother, it may yet transpire that Philip will think worse of me than merely being an ingrate. Though Spain may have made some temporary alliances of convenience, her interests are still ranged against almost every other nation of Europe. And so, if my employ is not with Philip, I might find myself confronting his banners, rather than beneath them."

Despite anticipating this, Isabella still felt a stab at her heart, wondered if it was emotion or the frailty of age. "Dear boy, this is dire news."

"How can it be otherwise, dearest Godmother? But before I depart to—to distant places, I want you to *know* this:"—and he stopped and reached out a hand to touch her cheek, down which tears promptly sped in response—"I will never suffer my sword, or those of my men, to be lifted against yours."

"I remain a vassal of Philip, so how can you make such a promise?"

Hugh looked at her steadily. "I make my oath and I pledge my life upon it." And then he studied her more closely, a hint of a smile at the corner of his mouth. "But I foresee that my promise may not be so difficult an oath to keep as you suggest. I see other changes afoot, Godmother. Don Fernando proclaims himself the king in the Low Countries, but not the king *of* the Netherlands? What careful distinctions. They almost seem like mincing steps and mincing words, if I didn't know him—and you—better."

As his smile widened knowingly, she felt another stab of panic: *does he suspect our plans? He must not! Not yet, anyway—for his own sake.* And his next words did indeed quicken her fear that Hugh might have stumbled upon the subtle machinations she had activated for his eventual benefit and of which he had to remain unaware, for now.

"And Fernando's careful steps towards greater autonomy also lead me to wonder: which Americans have had your ear in the privy chambers? And how has Philip reacted to your receiving their counsel, and to Fernando's unusual declaration? No, do not tell me. If I do not know Philip's will on this matter, or your plans—and you do not know mine—then Philip can never accuse you of being a traitor to his throne, no matter what might occur."

Isabella managed not to release her breath in one, great sigh of relief. No, he had no specific information. He discerned the looming crisis—the inevitable conflicts with Madrid—but nothing more specific. Thankfully, he had not learned of their plans or his envisioned role in them.

Hugh was now completing and expanding the oath with which he had begun. "So finally, know this too, Godmother. Once I have returned from my travels, if you call for my sword, it is yours. And, if Don Fernando finds himself estranged from his brother's good opinion, and still in your favor, he may call for my sword as well."

Until that moment, Isabella had always cherished a view of Hugh as the wonderful, smiling boy that had made her childless life a little more bearable. Now, he was suddenly, and completely, and only, a man and a captain, and, possibly, an important ally in the turbulent times to come. The ache of her personal desolation vied with the almost parental pride she felt for the boy who had become this man. The contending emotions washed through her in a chaotic rush and came out as another quick flurry of tears. Through which she murmured, "*Via con Dios*, dear Hugh. Wherever you may go."

He smiled, took his hand from her cheek, and put his lips to her forehead, where he placed a long and tender kiss. She sighed and closed her eyes.

When she opened them, he was gone.

Amiens, France

As du Barry entered, Turenne looked up. "What news?"

"We have word concerning the earl of Tyrconnell's clandestine northward journey, sir. He slipped over the border into the Lowlands without incident four nights ago. Soon after, he apparently began the process of bringing the first group of troops down to us, the ones that will go with him to Trinidad."

"Excellent. And how do you know this?"

"Reports from our watchers near his *tercio*'s bivouac report a smallish contingent making ready for travel. Several hundred more seem to be making more gradual preparations for departure."

"I see. Did Lord O'Donnell ask for their release from service at court in Brussels?"

"No, sir."

"Then how did he manage it?"

Du Barry reddened. "I regret to say we do not know, Lord Turenne. Once he crossed the border, our agents were not able to keep track of him. He is far more versed in the subtleties of those lands and those roads. For a while, we even feared him dead."

Turenne started. "What? Why?"

"The very last reports inexplicably placed him in Colonel Preston's camp just outside of Brussels during a surprise attack upon a council of the other captains of the Wild Geese *tercios*. Our observer necessarily had to hang well back, so as not to be picked up in the sweeps afterward. By the time he returned, he could find no trace of O'Donnell, nor pick up his trail."

Turenne thought. "Is there any chance the earl himself staged that attack? As a decoy to distract our observers, and to escape in the confusion of its aftermath?"

Du Barry shrugged. "Not unless Lord O'Donnell was also willing to sacrifice a number of his own men to achieve those ends, sir. And his reputation runs quite to the contrary of such a ruthless scheme. His concern for his men is legendary, and a matter of record. The only friction he ever had with his godmother the archduchess, other than some puppyish clamorings to be sent to war too early in his youth, were his complaints over the recent welfare of, and payrolls for, the common soldiers of his *tercio*."

"Complaints for which he had good grounds, as I hear it."

"Indeed so, Lord Turenne. Although his godmother herself has had no hand in causing the *tercios'* pay to be in arrears. That is determined by the court at Madrid." Du Barry shifted slightly "While on the subject of the earl of Tyrconnell's Wild Geese, sir: is it your intent to really allow hundreds of them to cross over the border into France in one group? I suspect there might be some, er, pointed inquiries, if you were to add so many mercenaries to your payroll, and all at once."

Turenne stared at his chief councilor and expediter. "What are you driving at, du Barry?"

"Sir, with the recent increased tensions at court between Cardinal Richelieu's faction, and that of Monsieur Gaston, a sudden hiring of hundreds, and eventually perhaps thousands, of new foreign mercenaries could appear to be motivated by domestic rather than foreign worries."

"Ah," sighed Turenne with a nod. "True enough, du Barry. And if it reassures you, I do not intend to allow the earl of Tyrconnell's larger force to cross into France until we have full satisfaction in the matter of the tasks which lie before him in the Caribbean. However, in the meantime, we will provide for them as promised by sending the necessary livres over the border to the sutlers for their camps. We cannot hire them outright as long as they remain in service to Fernando and, I presume, Philip. So any money sent to them directly would be rightly construed as a sign that we had engaged their services while their oaths were still with their original employers. They, and we, would be rightly accused of base treachery.

"But mere provisioning cannot be so construed, for they are simply the designated beneficiaries of largesse which their countryman Tyrconnell has purchased for them. And so, even before they come to our colors, we will have bought their loyalty with 'gifts' of food for their hungry families. And by letting them clamor ever louder for permission to march south, we acquire something that I suspect Lord O'Donnell has not foreseen."

"And what is that, sir?"

"Leverage over the earl himself."

Du Barry frowned. "Now it is I who do not understand what you are driving at, Lord Turenne."

Turenne smiled. "Let us presume that the Wild Geese in Brussels' employ are becoming ever-more desirous of being allowed into France. Now let us also presume that the earl of Tyrconnell succeeds in his bid to wrest Trinidad from the Spanish. We may still need leverage over him in order to ensure that we remain the recipients of what he has seized.

"I hope, and believe, that Richelieu's factors in the New World will offer the earl a fair price, and promptly. The ship dispatched by the *Compagnie des Îles de l'Amérique* to discreetly observe O'Donnell's progress carries not only the cardinal's personal agent, but also a great deal of silver.

"But if the negotiation with O'Donnell does not come off as planned—well, we must retain an incentive to compel him to turn the oil over to us. And if we still have the power to deny his increasingly desperate men entry to France at that time, he will have an additional incentive to look with particular favor on any terms our representatives offer him."

Du Barry nodded, then asked in a careful voice, "Would he not have an even greater incentive to comply if we already had his men in our camps, unarmed and vulnerable to our...displeasure?"

Turenne frowned. "I will go only so far, du Barry. Leverage should not become synonymous with extortion, or kidnapping. I refuse to offer physical shelter to men that I actually intend to use as hostages. Let others play at such games: I shall not. I will keep my honor, my good name, and my soul, thank you. Besides, our agents in Brussels report that whispers about the Wild Geese's possible departure en masse have fueled official concerns regarding their loyalty. Those concerns may be manifesting as even further constraints upon their provisioning. Furthermore, the commanders of the Spanish *tercios* are finding their Irish comrades increasingly worrisome and are pleading with Philip to remove them entirely."

Turenne stood and poured a glass of wine as he outlined the logical endgame of the evolving political situation in the Spanish Lowlands. "Consequently, as the poverty of the Wild Geese increases, so will their desperation. Given another half year, they will all be clamoring to come to Amiens, where we shall be happy to accept them at rates favorable to us. And the earl of Tyrconnell, being a true, albeit young, father to his men, will not deny them that livelihood."

Du Barry edged closer. Turenne took the hint and poured out a second glass with an apologetic smile. "Do not worry, du Barry. Matters are in hand."

Du Barry took the glass; he raised it slightly in Turenne's direction. "I toast the assured success of your plans, my lord, for they are so well-crafted as to need no invocation of luck."

Turenne halted his glass's progress to his lips. "Plans always need invocations of luck, du Barry. For we can only be sure of one thing in this world: that we may be sure of nothing in this world. A thousand foreseeable or unforeseeable things could go wrong. But this much we know, for we have seen it with our own eyes: France has a workable observation balloon, now. But the rest, this quest for New World oil?" Now Turenne sipped. "I avoid overconfidence at all times, my dear du Barry, for I am not one to snub fate. Lest it should decide to snub me in return."

Chapter 10

Major Larry Quinn of the State of Thuringia-Franconia's National Guard led the way down the last switchback of the game trail, which spilled out into a grassy sward. That bright green carpet of spring growth sloped gently down to where the river wound its way between the ridge they had been on and the rocky outcropping that formed the opposite bank.

Quinn looked behind, as the other two people in the group were navigating the declination. One, a young man, did so easily. The other, a middle-aged woman, was proceeding more cautiously.

Larry smiled. Ms. Aossey had never been particularly fleet of foot, even when she had been his home room and science teacher in eighth grade. And she was more careful now. Which, Larry conceded, only made good sense: a broken leg in the seventeenth century was nothing to take lightly, not even with Grantville's medical services available.

The young man with Ms. Aossey looked back to check her progress, putting out a helping hand. She accepted it with a brief, sunny smile. He returned a smaller one, complete with a nod that threatened to become a bow.

Larry's own smile was inward only. The understated politesse he had just witnessed was typical of twenty-year-old Karl Willibald

Klemm. Larry had spotted the telltale signs of intentionally suppressed "good breeding" the moment the young fellow arrived in his office, having been referred there by Colonel Donovan of the Hibernian Mercenary Battalion.

Although admitting that he was originally from Ingolstadt, Klemm had not divulged the other details of his background so willingly. And Larry understood why as soon as the young Bavarian's story started leaking out. At fourteen years of age, Klemm had been recruited to play for the opposing—and losing—team in the Thirty Years' War. As a Catholic, Klemm explained that he'd been impressed into Tilly's forces in 1632, but not as a mercenary. He had been made a staff adjutant for a recently-promoted general of artillery. That general had not survived the battle against Gustav Adolf at Breitenfeld. At which point Klemm decided that his next destination would be any place that was as far away from the war as he could get to on foot.

Larry Quinn had been unable to repress a smile at the young man's careful retelling of the events surrounding his induction. Young Klemm had been "impressed" by Tilly's own sergeants at the age of fourteen, and then just happened to be assigned to a general of the artillery. Larry had wryly observed that this was not typical of the largely random acts of impressment whereby youths had been made to serve under the colors of both sides, usually as unglorified cannon-fodder.

Klemm had the admirable habit of staring his questioner straight in the eye when addressing a ticklish topic. No, Klemm admitted, he had not been randomly recruited. He had been plucked out of school by members of Tilly's own general staff.

And at what school had that occurred?

Again, Klemm had not batted an eye, but his jaw line became more pronounced when he revealed that he had been in classes at the University of Ingolstadt.

The rest of Larry's questions met with similarly direct, if terse answers. Yes, Klemm had been in his second year of studies at the tender age of fourteen. Yes, he had been in mathematics, but also the sciences and humanities. Yes, he supposed the work did come easily to him, since he was usually done before the most advanced students in each of his classes. Except in the humanities. But he somberly observed that this "failing" was because he often lacked the adult sensibilities to adequately unpack the layered meanings in most art. He had still been "just a boy" at school. Then, he had gone to war.

Tilly's "recruiters" had apparently been well-briefed by young Karl Klemm's predominantly Jesuit tutors. The youth not only had an extraordinarily sharp and flexible mind, but possessed what later researchers would call an "eidetic" memory. Larry doubted the existence of such savantlike powers, but was suitably impressed when Klemm scanned a paragraph, then a list of numbers, then a set of completely disparate facts, and was able to recall them perfectly afterwards.

Given the data-intensive nature of the artillery branch, it had been perhaps inevitable that Klemm had been assigned there. It had been the intent of his recruiters for him to function as a human calculator during sieges and other extended shelling scenarios. There, the ruthless laws of physics dictated results more profoundly than upon the fluid battlefields where human unpredictability, and even caprice, played a greater role in determining outcomes.

But that rear-echelon role hadn't kept Karl Klemm from seeing the full scope of horrors on display in the Thirty Years' War. Nor had it insulated him from the vicious attitudes of an increasing number of the Catholic troops. Not only were Tilly's men weary with war, they had been forced to forage from (then pillage, and ultimately sack) towns, both enemy and allied, for supplies. Predictably, with its ranks swollen by amoral and brutish mercenaries whom Klemm could hardly distinguish from highwaymen, the rank-and-file of Tilly's army was not receptive to a clever young fellow who was clearly the darling of the army's highest, aristocratic officers. The resentment and hate that the soldiers could not express toward those officers themselves was redirected toward this younger, more vulnerable object of their approbation. And so young Karl Klemm had learned to keep his head down and his gifts hidden.

He had approached the Hibernian Mercenary Battalion without referring to his background with the enemy's army or his unusual skills. Rather, he had heard they were looking for persons who might be handy at refurbishing broken up-time firearms. He had applied to become a mere technician. But one of the battalion's two proprietors, Liam Donovan, had the shrewd eye of a professional recruiter and saw much more than that in young Klemm. And so had sent him on to Larry's office.

That had been when Karl was thin, jobless, and shivering in a coat much too old to ward off the frigid fangs of the middle weeks of February. Now, three months later, in a riverside meadow, releasing Lolly Aossey's hand as if handing off a partner in a gavotte, he seemed a different person.

"Karl," Larry called.

"Yes, Major Quinn?"

"Has Ms. Aossey finished boring you today?"

Lolly rounded on Quinn, who was smiling mischief at her. "So I was a boring teacher, Larry?"

"Not usually, Miz Aossey, but let's face it: a fifty-minute lesson on earth science is now a reasonable replacement for the sleeping aids we left back up-time."

"Hmpf. Do you agree with Major Quinn, Karl?"

Klemm knelt to study the soil. "I cannot speak for anyone else, but I find geology rather fascinating."

That's Karl, ever the diplomat. Larry looked back at Lolly. "So why did you want to come down here from the hills?"

Lolly walked over to where Karl was strolling, now running his hands along the sheer skirts of the ridge as he studied the strata of its rocky ribs. "So that Karl could look at what surveyors and drillers would designate extremely soft 'unconsolidated formations.'"

"And what are those?"

Lolly turned to look at Klemm with one slightly raised eyebrow. Karl, seeing that as his cue, supplied the answer promptly. "An unconsolidated rock formation takes the form of loose particles, such as sand or clay."

"You mean, it's not really rock."

"No, Larry," scolded Lolly. "That's not what it means at all. Sand, for instance, starts out as solid rock."

"Like gravel."

Ms. Aossey nodded. "Exactly."

"So how is coming here better than going to a sand pit?"

"Because, Larry, a sand pit such as you mean is not a natural occurrence. And that's what Karl needs to see, to experience: the formations that arise naturally around such earths, and vice versa."

Karl brushed off his hands, put them on his narrow hips, looked at the rock thoughtfully, then at the ground. "And unless I am much mistaken, Ms. Aossey wishes me to become especially familiar with the compositions particular to alluvial or coastal deposits. The other two times we have gone on a field survey, we visited similar environments."

Lolly stared at Klemm. She said, "Very good, Karl," and clearly meant it, but there was also a surprised, even worried tone in her voice.

Quinn kept himself from smiling. The problem with training clever people for even highly compartmentalized confidential missions was that their quick wits could often defeat the information firewalls erected by the planners. From a few key pieces, they could begin to discern the shape, or at least the key objectives, of the operation.

Karl Klemm demonstrated that propensity in his next leading comment. "In fact, I find it puzzling that we are spending so much time in areas with these formations."

Lolly, who was inspecting some small outcroppings of marl that disturbed the smooth expanse beneath their feet, distractedly asked, "Why, Karl? They are good challenges for you: not always the easiest areas to read, geologically. They can be quite tricky unless you know what to look for."

"So you have taught me. And very well, Ms. Aossey. But that still begs the question of why we are studying them at all."

Lolly stopped, a bit perplexed. Quinn now had to hide a small smile. He was no geologist, but he had learned to read people pretty well, and he could see where Karl Klemm was headed. Lolly didn't, apparently. "We study them because they are some of the formations you might encounter when you travel with Major Quinn to the New World."

"Yes, I might. But it seems odd to focus so heavily on these formations, since I will not be expected to survey them closely, let alone exclusively." Karl poked at an upthrust tooth of marlstone. "Or will I?"

Lolly shot a surprised and alarmed glance at Quinn, a glance which said: *Oh. My. God. Could he have guessed where exactly you're taking him? And why? And if that cat is out of the bag, does he have to be sequestered until you leave?*

Quinn simply shrugged.

Lolly Aossey crossed her arms tightly. "Well, Karl, you never know where people might want to dig. Or for what."

"That is true, although one immediately thinks of the New

World's coastal oil deposits. However, it does not stand to reason that the USE would be interested in those, or any, oil deposits known to reside in unconsolidated rock formations."

"And why is that?"

"Because we cannot tap such deposits, not with our current drilling technology. A cable rig will not work. The constant pounding collapses the walls of the hole. To drill in soils such as these, which in the New World predominate around the Gulf coast oil deposits, you would need a rotary drill. A technology which we do not yet possess." He looked up from the marlstone. "I am correct in my conclusions, yes?" He did not blink.

Quinn watched and heard Lolly swallow. Looking like an adolescent who'd been caught telling a lie to her parents, she spread her hands in gesture that marked her next utterance as both an explanation and appeal. "Well, Karl, now about that rotary drill—"

Chapter 11

Undisclosed location near Wietze, USE

Ann Koudsi finished her morning cup of broth—it had been unseasonably chilly overnight—and nosed back into her books and progress charts again. As the second in charge of the rotary drill test rig, and ultimately, the superintendent who would be responsible for the new machine and its crew in the field, it was her job to be The Final Authority on all things pertaining to its operation. That, in turn, meant minor or full mastery of a wide range of topics, including practical geology, mechanical engineering, the physics of pressurized fluids and gases, and even organizational management. To name but a few.

So it was not merely frustrating but alarming and infuriating when, once again, concentration on the words, and charts, and formulae did not come easily. Indeed, she discovered that she had been reading the same line about assessing imminent well-head failures because, instead of seeing it, she was seeing something else in her mind's eye:

Ulrich Rohrbach, down-time crew chief for the rig.

Which was not just foolishness, but utter, stupid, and danger-ous foolishness. As she had kept telling herself over the last nine months. It was foolishness to allow him to court her at all. Fool-ish that they had started taking all their meals together. Foolish that they had spent Christmas visiting what was left of his war-torn family: a widowed sister and her two perilously adorable kids. More foolish still when they had started holding hands just before Valentine's Day, a mostly up-time tradition which he had somehow learned of (Ann secretly suspected their mutual boss, Dave Willcocks, of playing matchmaker). And most foolish of all had been their first kiss as they were laughing beneath the Maypole just weeks ago.

And there were so many reasons *why* it was all extraordinarily foolish. First, Ulrich was a down-timer, albeit a perfect gentleman and more patient than any up-time American would have been in regard to the glacial progress of their relationship. It was foolish because Ulrich barely had a fourth grade education, although, truth be told, his reading had become much faster and broader in the past half year and revealed that his mind was not slow, merely starved. And it was foolish because he just didn't look the way she had imagined the man of her dreams would look: he was not tall, dark, or particularly handsome. But on the other hand, he had kind eyes, thick sandy hair, dimples, a wonderful bass laugh, and a surprisingly muscular build, which, compacted into his sturdy 5'8" frame, would have put any number of up-time body-builders to shame.

And what had been especially foolish about their first kiss was her own response: not merely eager, but starved. She had absolutely embarrassed herself. And why? Because, as she learned when she started flipping backward through the months on her mental calendar, it had been at least—well, it had been a long, long, *long* time since she had had sex.

So all right, maybe her physical reaction—her *over*reaction, she firmly reminded herself—to the kiss had been understandable. But Ulrich wasn't likely to understand it. Or, more problematically, he was all too likely to understand it the wrong way: that her sudden avid response had been to *him*, personally, rather than to his, er, generic maleness. And so how would she explain that to him so that he wouldn't get more attached or more hopeful?

Are you sure that's really what you want to do? said a voice at the back of her mind, the one that had been growing steadily louder and more ironic for the past three weeks.

Her response was indignant and maybe a little bit terrified. Of course she wanted to let Ulrich know that she wasn't interested in him, *per se*. She had work, *important* work, to do. And after all, where could a relationship with him wind up?

Well, let's see, said the voice, *it could start in bed, then move to a house, which would quickly acquire some small, additional inhabitants—*

Ann Koudsi stood up quickly, her stomach suddenly very compact and hard. She did not want to get married to a down-timer. No matter how nice, or how good-natured, or how gentlemanly—or how damnedly sexy—he was. It wouldn't end well.

Right, agreed the grinning voice, *because it wouldn't end at all. Just like it hasn't ended for the hundreds of other up-time-down-time marriages that have occurred over the past few years.*

She paced to the bookshelf to get a book she didn't need, opened it, furiously thumbing through the index for she had no idea what.

Unless, said the voice, *what it's really about is home.*

Ann stopped thumbing the pages, forgot she was holding the book.

Yes, that's it, isn't it? If you marry a down-timer, it's the final act of acceptance that you're here in the past for good. That so much of your family, so many of your friends and almost everything else you ever knew and loved, is gone like that awful song said: dust in the wind. You won't embrace anyone in this world because you won't let go of the people in the other *world.*

Ann discovered she had clutched the book close to her chest, could feel her heart beating with a crisp, painful precision.

But here's the problem, girl: you can't hold on to what isn't there, what no longer exists. And if you wait too long, if you push Ulrich away too hard, you just might lose the best thing—the best man—you've ever laid eyes on in this world or the—

A distinctive metallic cough broke the stillness of the remote, steep-sided glen in which they had set up their test rig. Ann looked up, disoriented and startled. That was the drilling rig's engine, starting to run at full speed. But today's test run had been cancelled—

Then she detected an almost subaudible hum: the rig's turntable was spinning at operating RPMs.

Ann dropped the book and was out the door, sprinting for the drill site, which was located in a dead-end defile a quarter mile away. There was no fire-bell or even dinner-gong to ring to get them to stop, because other than the three cabins for the workers and the one for the senior site engineer—her—there was no one else nearby. And nothing with which to make alarm-level noise. "No reason to attract undue attention," Professor Doctor Wecke of the Mines and Drilling Program of the University of Helmstedt had explained coyly to her when she had accepted the position. She had wondered at the isolation of the site and then wondered if Wecke's caution about gongs and the like wasn't a bit ridiculous. Why worry about noisemaking bells when you spent most of the day running a loud, crude, experimental rotary drilling rig?

As she ran, Ann saw the expected plume of steam from the rig's engine obscuring the black cloud of its wood-fired boiler, and glimpsed a small figure well ahead of her, also running toward the drill site. That figure was moving very quickly and angling in from the main access road that led off to the rig's supply and service sheds. Then she saw its gray-dyed down-time coveralls. Distinct from the typical brown ones of the rank and file workers, that could only be Ulrich. He must have heard the engine start, too. Had probably been in the materials depot, checking the quality of the new casing before it went in the hole to shore up the soft, unconsolidated walls that would be left behind by the next day's digging.

The next *day's digging:* that deferral to tomorrow had not been merely advisable, but essential. Today's run *had* to be called off because too many of the main crew, the veterans, were down with the flu. It was one of those brief but vicious late spring bugs that spreads like wildfire, burns through a body by setting both brow and guts on fire (albeit in different ways), and then burns out just as quickly. Even old tough-as-leather Dave Willcocks, head of the rotary drill development team and liaison to the academics and financiers back at the University of Helmstedt, had fallen victim to the virus. Which was a source of some extra concern at the site and beyond: this was the first sign that Willcocks was anything other than indestructible, and at seventy years of age, there was no knowing if this was just an aberration in his otherwise unexceptioned robust health, or the first sign of impending decline. Ann had seen, all too often and too arrestingly, that people aged more quickly in the seventeenth century, and the transition from good health to decrepitude could, on occasion, be startlingly swift.

Ulrich had reached the rig, seemed to dart around looking for something. Or someone, Ann corrected. He was clearly trying to find who was in charge, who had overridden today's suspension of operations.

From far behind her private cabin, Ann heard another engine kick into life with a roar. That was an up-time sound, the engine on Dave Willcock's pick-up truck. Good, so that meant he was on his way. Ann didn't like that he was up and about, but right now, her strongest sensation was relief. No one back-talked Willcocks. His word was law on site, and that was what was needed to shut down the rig without a moment's delay. Without Dave or Ulrich or her there to oversee the commencement of operations, there was no telling what errors might be made.

Ulrich had reached the platform upon which the derrick was built. Now only a hundred yards off—but with a wind-stitch suddenly clutching at her left side—Ann could see him engaged in a shouting match with someone up there. Someone very tall and very lean and very blond, almost white blond—

Oh shit, Ann thought, *he's arguing with Otto Bauernfeld.* Bauernfeld was the senior overseer for Gerhard Graves, who was the nosiest and most intrusive of all the investors. Imperious and contemptuous both, the Graves family had tried double-crossing David Willcocks and his associates when they undertook their first joint drilling project, a simple cable rig. So this time, Willcocks, his team, and now the university, had unanimously wanted to reject Graves' money—but they simply couldn't afford to. The project would not have been possible without Gerhard Graves carrying twenty percent of the upfront costs. And Otto Bauernfeld, as Graves' visiting factotum, had adopted an attitude to match his master's: presumptuous, dictatorial, and arrogantly dismissive of the rank-and-file workers. "Shit," Ann repeated. Aloud, this time.

She sprinted the last thirty yards to the gravel-ringed drill site, earning stares as she went. Pebbles churned underfoot, slowing her down, but she was able to catch the shouted exchange between Ulrich and Otto Bauernfeld as she traversed the last few yards of loose stone.

"You must shut the rig down, Herr Bauernfeld. Mr. Willcocks has ordered us not to drill today, not even to—"

Bauernfeld looked far down his very long nose at the medium-sized but very powerful Ulrich. "Who are you, and why should I care?"

"I am Ulrich Rohrbach, the site foreman and design consultant. I must ask you to—"

"I do not take orders from you, workman. Now, do not obstruct me any further."

"Herr Bauernfeld, I must insist: on whose authority do you ignore and violate Project Director David Willcocks' strict prohibition against drilling today?"

"I ignore it based on the only authority that truly matters on this site: that stemming from my patron's heavy investment in this project. Which you should understand. I am here for one day—one day, and no more—and must see the progress you have made in developing this drill. My superior expects an impartial report, and he shall have it."

"Herr Bauernfeld, with a little warning, I could have—"

"You are a worker. And an employee of Herr Willcocks. Who will be pleased to tell me whatever he thinks will please my employer. But Herr Graves wants the truth and I know how to get it for him." Bauernfeld stuck this thumbs into his belt and leaned back, quite pleased with himself. "It was simply a matter of getting the crew to run the drill without your interference. Which they did readily enough, when I told them who my superior was, and the personal consequences they would face if they displeased him. So, now I shall see the operation as it truly is, and with my own eyes."

"You are not seeing the operation," Ann panted.

Bauernfeld halted as she gasped for breath, and then doubled over to ease the cramp in her gut. Still looking up, she could see the uncertainty in his eyes, the waver in his demeanor as he tried to decide where she fit into his complex constellation of class and professional relationships. A woman of no particular birth, but an up-timer: a person who actually worked alongside laborers, but also a person of considerable achievement and education. There were no ready social equations that defined her place in his social scheme of things.

But then his eyes strayed to her clothes: grimy, practical coveralls, gray like Ulrich's. Something like a satisfied smile settled about Bauernfeld's eyes. "Frau Koudsi, the rig's motors are running and the drill-string has been lowered. And now—see? It is turning: the drilling has begun. So I am most certainly seeing the operations of your drill."

"Proper operations involve more than turning on the machines." Ulrich's voice was so guttural that he sounded more animal than human.

Bauernfeld speared him with eyes that suggested he would have preferred to respond with the back of his hand instead of his tongue. "Your workers know the steps well enough, I perceive."

"You perceive wrong, then, you ass." Ann felt herself rising on her toes to make her rebuttal emphatic. "These aren't our first crew. Almost all of them are second crew. Replacements who usually carry gear, clean the facility. They're like apprentices at this stage."

Bauernfeld became a bit pale. "And the—the journeymen, or 'first crew,' as you say?"

Ulrich waved an arm angrily back at the workers' sheds. "Back there. In bed. Sick with the same flu that has Herr Willcocks in bed, and why we shut down operations today."

Bauernfeld was now truly pale. "But...all seems to be in order. These men know their tasks."

"Do they?" shrieked Ann over the motor and the drill, wondering how long they had to convince Bauernfeld to tell the class-cowed workers shut the rig down—or how long it would take for Dave Willcocks to drive down here, if he wouldn't listen to reason. "Did you flush the mud hose? Did you check its flexibility? Did you check where it connects to the kelly for signs of wear or fraying? Did you turn the drill in the hole long enough to warm the mud already there *before* putting weight on the bit? And did you warm the new mud in the tanks before pumping it in?"

Bauernfeld scowled at the last. "And how could the temperature of mud possibly matter?"

Ann pointed behind her at the mud-tank. "*That* mud is being pumped down in that hole, Herr Bauernfeld. At extremely high pressure. Among other things, it scoops up the shavings—the debris made by the drilling—and dumps it there, in the shaker tray, where the debris is removed and the mud is returned to the system."

With uncertain eyes, Bauernfeld followed the progress of her pointing: from mud pit, to mud tube, to where it connected to the swivel atop the drill string, to where the return tube dumped the fouled mud into the shaker tray. "And to do this," he said slowly, "the mud must be warm?"

Ulrich leaned in, face red, voice loud with both urgency and anger. "No, but it cannot be *cold*."

"But why?"

Ann rolled her eyes. *Can Bauernfeld really be so stupid? Well, he might be.* "Look, you sit down to breakfast and get thin, hot porridge. How easy can you pour it into your bowl?"

Bauernfeld shrugged. "Easily enough."

"Right. Now let it get cold. Try pouring it."

Bauernfeld's eyebrows lowered, but then rose quickly. "It is thicker. It will be harder to—"

"Exactly, and that's why the mud can't be too cold. But last night we had a hard frost, and the men running the drill haven't dealt with this. They don't know how the resistance builds, particularly with the shavings collecting because the thicker mud can't clear them quickly enough. They have no idea what that could do to—"

Ann heard a faint groan in the mud-carrying standpipe where it ascended the nearest leg of the derrick. "Uh oh," she breathed and looked up at the swivel.

Ulrich was already staring at it but with a surprised expression. "Looks like the swivel coupling is holding," he breathed. Carefully.

Ann nodded, was aware of Bauernfeld's confused gape. He followed their eyes, but did not know what to look at. Which in this case was the swivel atop the spinning drill string. That had been the most problematic piece of machinery to make reliable and robust. Not the swivel itself—that was a fairly straightforward fabrication job—but where the flexible mud hose connected to it.

While the hose did not fully "spin" with the swivel, there was a lot of random and varying motion imparted to it as the drill string sped up, slowed down, encountered resistance, spun free. In short, the linkage between hose and swivel had to be both strong and flexible.

And that was a difficult requirement for seventeenth-century materials. There was no rubber available, yet. That would involve tapping New World trees en masse or growing them elsewhere. And synthetics were a pipe dream, an up-time reality that was now a distant fantasy. So they made do with leather. Layered with canvas. Stitched carefully. Reinforced by brass rivets and clamps, where feasible. And at the connecting collar, where the changes in pressure and torque were most intense, precious (which was to say "retooled up-time") steel rings added extra reinforcement.

And so far, despite the rapid spin-up and overly thick mud,

the epicenter of their engineering headaches and operational worries was holding up. Ann felt a smile try to rise to her lips. *Heh, progress at last—*

But that impulse did not last longer than the eyeblink which refocused her on the very real dangers of continuing operations. So the mud hose's linkage to the swivel was good: so what? The mud was too cold, meaning there were about a dozen other failure points that could be potentially—

The groan in the standpipe returned as a loud surging wail and the whole tube began shuddering, the oscillations racing up its gantry-ascending length.

Ann turned to the engine operator, prepared to talk him through the spin-down instructions—

But Bauernfeld had gone completely pale, discerning in the combination of her desperate motions and the quaking of the standpipe, that he was standing right next to an impending disaster. "Shut it off!" he screamed at the engine operator, "Turn the engine off! Stop the drill string!"

"*NO!*" Ann and Ulrich howled together. But it was too late. The disaster was already unleashing itself when Bauernfeld shouted his crude, and therefore counterproductive, orders. The standpipe, shaking mightily, now put pressure on a connection which had never been a major point of design concern: that point where it joined to the mud-hose, which hung free between the gantry leg and the swivel atop the drill string. However, since that hose was more rigidly affixed to its point of connection with the standpipe, the excessive pressure in the system now made it shudder violently. At the very fringe of where it met the pipe's connecting collar, a brass rivet popped, a seam opened—

"Run!" Ann shouted. "Clear the rig!" And then she felt a blow on her back. The air was driven out of her, and she was flying—but being carried, too. The momentary disorientation became realization: Ulrich had tackled her off the platform. And a powerful emotion rose up to meet that realization. *I love him. I do! I know that now. But this is going to hurt. And we could still die. Very easily.* And yet, her eyes never left the rig.

With a screaming pop of suddenly released pressure, the mud hose stripped itself off the top of the standpipe, flinging the attachment collar high into the air. Freed, the hose's sudden wild writhings resembled the overdose-death throes of a mud-vomiting anaconda. One worker, among the youngest, staring openmouthed at the sudden spectacle before him, did not move in time. The hose spasmed through a vicious twist and cut him open from chest to navel, viscera flying in all directions. Almost bisected, he was dead before he hit the ground.

The wild whipping and slashing caught two more persons. Bauernfeld himself managed to dodge the hose, but his left hip and groin were caught in the spray pattern of the mud. Although quickly losing pressure, that viscous jet was still spewing with a force well above one hundred PSI. Bauernfeld went down with a warbling shriek of pain and surprise, white bone showing through a wash of blood and shattered intestines—less than two seconds after he had shouted his final orders.

Those orders now went into full, monstrous effect. The partially trained rig operator not only cut the engine, but, hearing Bauernfeld's "stop" order, had thrown the long lever that engaged a large, counterweighted arresting gear.

The effect on the drill-string was dramatic. With many tons of pipe already spinning in the three hundred foot hole, there was simply no way to, as Ann's mother used to say, "stand on the brakes." Instead, the arrestor groaned, its cable snapped, and the counterweights were launched sideways, one smashing down a nearby utility shed, the other tracing a ballistic arc into the side of the ravine.

But, even though it was brief, that sudden, strong resistance at the head of the drill pipe forced a rapid drop in rotational speed of its uppermost lengths. However, the much weightier part of the entire drill string assembly was still turning in the hole, its massive inertia being what had quickly shattered the braking mechanism, which had only been designed to gradually slow, not immediately stop, the string.

Now, the differences in inertia and resistance at the two ends of the drill string simply tore it apart. The threaded ends which joined the top pipe in the hole with length that was still free-spinning above it screeched and gave way in a shower of sparks. The lower length of pipe, grinding shrilly against the sides of the borehole, slowed quickly, but its single sweep smashed everything in its path. The upper length, no longer anchored on the bottom, swung wide and fast, ripping free of the kelly and swivel. It spun away like a side-slung baton, clipping the northernmost leg of the derrick, and swatting three workers aside like so many inconsequential—and now quite shattered—flies. The combined kelly-and-swivel assembly swung around like a misshapen bolo, cracked through two gantry struts and spent the rest of its energy by slamming full on into yet another of the derrick's legs.

Showered by the mud spewing up from the shattered standpipe, Ann swung to her feet, blinking—when Ulrich retightened his arm around her waist and started running away—

—Away from the groaning, tilting, unraveling derrick that pushed slowly down through the curtain of mud as it toppled toward them.

Ann got her own feet under her somehow and, with Ulrich now pulling her by the hand, they sprinted away. This time, Ann did not look back.

She heard the smash, felt the ground shiver a moment before the slight concussive wave of the impact buffeted her back. Splinters, whining like darts, bit into her right thigh and buttock. She only ran harder.

Which was just as well. More debris, ejected upward, came down in a lethal torrent where she had been running just two seconds before.

A pulley, rolling on its edge, wheeled past her briskly, lagged when it reached the gravel perimeter of the site, wobbled lazily and fell over. As if that was a signal to Ann and Ulrich that the danger was indeed past, they turned, still holding hands.

The rig was gone. Except for four feet of the drill pipe that had sheared off while partially in the bore hole and two feet of savaged standpipe that had not gone over with the derrick, nothing was left standing upright on the platform. The steam engine had been ruined by debris, its boiler knocked over and the firebox already flaring dangerously. Mud oozed outward and downward in all directions. Smoke—black, brown, and gray—fanned upward into the sky. The workers who had cleared the rig in time were already being joined by members of the sickly "first crew," who, wan and haggard, spread out through the wreckage with them, searching for survivors.

Behind them, brakes screeched, gravel spattered, and a car door opened. A moment later, Dave Willcocks, looking haggard and pale, was standing alongside them, staring at the ruin that had been their grand experiment. "Jesus Christ," he swore. But he didn't stare at the wreckage for more than a few seconds before heading toward the disaster to assist in the rescue work, just a few steps behind Ann and Ulrich.

The time that followed was without a doubt the most gruesome experience in Ann's life. The scale of the blunt force trauma inflicted on fragile human bodies by the disintegrating oil rig was genuinely incredible. It was as if the gods of the earth, awakened and risen in fury, had just torn people apart.

She couldn't even find any flicker of vengeful satisfaction in Bauernfeld's fate, although he'd been directly responsible for the disaster. The wound that had killed him was...horrible, a perfect illustration of the old saw *I wouldn't wish that on my worst enemy.*

Eventually—thankfully—the immediate rescue work was over. Those who'd survived had been stabilized and had been taken away to receive real medical care. Repairing the property damage would take a lot longer, but there was no immediate urgency involved. So, tired and blood-spackled themselves, Ann and Ulrich and Dave Willcocks came back together to discuss the situation.

"I heard about Bauernfeld coming here," said Willcocks. "Got the message from your runner, Ulrich, the same moment I heard the rig start. His doing, I take it?"

Ann looked out of the corner of her eye. Ulrich frowned at David Willcocks' question, looked away, clearly trying to fabricate a face-saving story for a man who was now dead. An incompetent, arrogant man whom Ulrich would probably now risk his own good reputation to protect.

Ann turned and looked Willcocks in the eye. "Yes, this was Bauernfeld's doing. All so he could make a report to Gerhard Graves without any input or 'interference' from us." She turned her eyes back to the smoking ruins. "I'd say his methods were ill-considered."

Another car door opened and closed behind them. Footsteps rasped on the gravel, and then Dennis Grady, head of contractors for the State of Thuringia-Franconia's Department of Economic Resources, their project's other fiscal godfather, came to stand beside Ulrich.

Ann started. "Mr. Grady, what are you doing up here?"

He looked away from the devastation with a baleful expression. "Why, to check on your progress."

Ann—broken-hearted but also quite suddenly aware that not

only was she in love with Ulrich, but had been for almost three months now—felt conflicting emotions of joy and loss roil and bash into each other. They came out of her as a burst of laughter. "Our progress! Wow, did you pick the wrong day for a visit, or what?"

Grady shrugged. "Machines can be rebuilt, if they're worth rebuilding."

Grady's serious, level tone was like a bucket of cold water in Ann's face. *So this isn't the end of all our work, maybe?* "And what determines if they're worth rebuilding?"

"Well, how was the rig doing before this happened?"

"That is the irony of this disaster, Herr Grady," Ulrich sighed. "Tomorrow, we were scheduled to get to four hundred feet. And the equipment had been working quite well. We had to be careful not to push the system too much. The mud flow cannot keep up with our top operating speeds."

"Why?"

Ann thought Dave Willcocks might explain, but instead he nodded at her to continue, smiling like a proud uncle. She shrugged, answered, "The rate that we get fresh mud in the hole determines how much we can cool the system. It bathes the hot drill bit, removes extra friction by carrying away the cuttings. But the mud hose is the bottleneck. We can't push the pressure in the hose over two hundred fifty psi without risking a rupture. That reduces how much we can cool the system, and how fast we can clear cuttings out of the hole. And that determines our upper operating limit."

"But if you stay beneath that limit—?"

"We were making good progress, and this design was holding up pretty well."

"We still have challenges," Willcocks put in. "We've got to have better threading between the separate sections of drill pipe. And I'm not sure that we've got enough horsepower from the current steam engine to really do the job when we get under six hundred feet."

"But in principle, this design is functional?"

"Functional, yes. Ready to drill, no."

Grady shook his head. "But I didn't ask you about readiness."

David frowned. "Two months ago you did."

Grady shrugged. "That was two months ago. Things change."

"Like what?"

"Like never you mind. Look, it was always a long-shot that you'd have a rotary drill ready for the New World survey expedition, anyhow. And as things are developing, we won't need it until next year, probably. By which time, I expect it will be ready." Grady glanced at the smoldering ruin, through which rescuers were picking their careful ways. "Well, *this* one won't be ready, but you get what I mean."

Ann almost smiled, but it felt wrong, somehow. "Thanks, Dennis. I wish I could be happier. But we've lost so much: so many people, so much hard work, and a chance to set foot in North America again."

"Oh, now hold on," said Grady. "Just because you won't have a rotary drill, doesn't mean you're not still going along for the ride to the New World. We need your scientific and technical skills on site, and there *are* drills besides your rotary wonder, you know."

Ann shrugged. "I ought to know. We were working cable rigs at Wietze for the better part of two years."

"And you'll be working them again, half a world away."

Ulrich looked flustered, possibly heart-broken. "So then, if Ms. Koudsi is—is gone, who shall resume building the rotary drill?"

David kicked at the gravel. "I guess that would be me and the technical assistants that have been helping you out here. And I could bring up Glen Sterling from Grantville. And actually, we did learn something important about the drill design today: that the weak point is no longer at the juncture of the swivel and the mud hose, but at the juncture of the mud-hose and the standpipe."

"So how much time do I have to help David with the improved model before I leave?" Ann asked Dennis, while looking at Ulrich.

"None, I'm afraid," answered Grady. "We've got to get you up north for special training and equipment familiarization. Besides, there's not going to be much breakthrough engineering going on for a few months. I figure it will take that long just to get all the drill pipe and casing out of the ground." He looked at David for confirmation.

Willcocks nodded. "Gonna be a bitch of a job. But it will be our golden opportunity to own the next rig outright, without worrying about financiers."

Grady frowned. "Oh? How's that?"

"Herr Graves' representative caused this failure. Every surviving witness will testify to that. And from what Herr Bauernfeld told me on the way down here, he had papers in his bags indicating that he has a 'clear mandate from his employer' to ensure that he saw the rig in operation without me or any of my supervisors around to meddle with it. I told him that wasn't permissible. Sent a letter to his boss on the topic, too.

"But he disregarded multiple direct orders from the lawful site operators and majority owners, and went ahead with his 'private test.' So he and his employer are directly culpable for all this—the loss of life, the loss of the rig, and the expense of recovering all that pipe and casing, since it's too rare and costly to leave sitting in the ground." David's grin was one of savage revenge, not mirth. "It's going to cost that bastard Graves his stake in this whole operation to be able to walk away from this disaster without getting roasted alive by the courts."

Grady nodded. "Yep. Sounds about right." He turned to Ann. "Now, are you ready to pack your bags and head north to the Baltic?"

"I am," answered Ann, "But on one condition."

Grady raised an eyebrow. "And what's that?"

"That I get to choose my crew chief." She turned to Ulrich and smiled. "That would be Ulrich Rohrbach. If he doesn't go, it's no deal."

Ulrich stared at Ann, smiling back, his mouth open a little, jaw working futilely to find words—but not very hard. He was too busy looking at her, Ann was delighted to see, like an infatuated puppy.

Grady cleared his throat. "Well, Mr. Rohrbach, how about it? Are you also willing to go to the New World and drill for oil without a rotary rig?"

Ulrich did not look away from Ann or even blink. "Where do I sign up?" he said.

Chapter 12

Luebeck, United States of Europe

Nodding to the after-hours Marine guard, Eddie entered the ante-chamber outside John Simpson's office. As he did, his stomach growled so loudly that he expected a Marine to enter behind him, sidearm drawn, scanning for whatever feral beast was making a noise akin to being simultaneously tortured and strangled.

And if being two hours overdue for supper wasn't enough, he'd just received yet another letter from Anne Cathrine. It was alternately sweet, steamy, and sullen at having to spend her nights watching her father pickle his royal brain with excesses of wine. She made it emphatically—indeed, graphically clear—just how much, and in what ways, she'd rather be spending those nights with Eddie, indulging in excesses of—

Nope, don't go there, Eddie. You have a job to do, which doesn't include learning to walk with a stiff prosthetic leg and an equally stiff—

The door opened. "Commander, there you are," said Simpson.

Yes, here I very much am. A bit too much of me, in fact. Eddie cheated the folders he was carrying a few inches lower, shielding his groin from ready view. However, nothing slackened his line quite so quickly or profoundly as hearing the CO's voice, so he was safe by the time he had entered the room and saluted.

As soon as Simpson had returned the salute and invited him to sit, Eddie produced one of the folders—rough, ragged cardboard stock of the down-time "economy" variety—with a black square on the upper right-hand front flap. "News from the rotary drill project."

"Not good?"

"Disastrous, sir. The rig literally blew apart. But it wasn't a technical failure. One of the owners' inexperienced factors decided to show up for a surprise inspection and start the morning by playing platform chief."

"And how did that turn out?"

"Five dead, six wounded. The rig is a write-off. They're still trying to fish all the drill pipe out of the hole."

Simpson may have winced. "Well, so much for the overly ambitious hope that they'd have that drill working by the time we left, and be boring holes by fall."

"Yes, sir. But the Department of Economic Resources still wants to send the mainland prospecting team with our task force."

Simpson shrugged. "Well, that only makes sense, assuming the test rig was reasonably promising. That way, by the time they get a working rig ready, they'll know where to start drilling well holes."

"That's the ER Department's thinking on the matter, sir. They've shifted all the actual drilling crew and operators over to the Trinidad cable rig team."

"Which is just as well. That oil will be a lot easier to find."

"Yes sir, although there's a whole lot less of it."

Simpson looked up from the paperwork. "Commander, let's not go round on this again. First, Trinidad's oil will come to hand comparatively easily and it is sweet and light. Just what we need. And we're not equipped to ship more oil than they can produce, won't be for at least eighteen months. Second, and arguably more important, Trinidad has an additional strategic benefit of pulling our rivals' attentions away from our other operations."

Eddie knew it was time to offer his dutiful "Yes, sir"—which he did—and to move on. "All the regionally relevant maps, charts, graphs, and books that will comprise the mission's reference assets have been copied and are en route from Grantville. We still have two researchers combing through unindexed material for other useful information on the Caribbean, but it's been ten days since they found anything. And that was just some data on a species of flower."

"Hmmph. I suspect the focus in the Leeward Islands will be on agriculture, not horticulture."

"Yes, sir." Which was typical Simpson: he was the one who had insisted on extracting every iota of up-time information available on the West Indies, Spanish Main, and environs. And now he was turning his nose up at the tid-bits he had insisted on pursuing. *I suspect he's going to be a very cranky old man. Well, crankier.*

"Did you find any more data on native dialects in the Gulf region?"

Eddie shook his head. "No, sir." All they had turned up were a few snippets of a local dialect alternately referred to as Atakapa or Ishak. And those snippets were so uncertain, they would be better described as "second-hand linguistic rumors" than "data."

"Provisioning and materiel almost ready?"

"Getting there, sir. Without the rotary drill equipment and pipe, we'll have a lot more room than we thought. But we're still taking on plenty of well casing for Trinidad. Each section is about the length, weight, and even girth of pine logs. So we got a lumber ship from the Danes to haul it."

Simpson frowned. "'Lumber ship?'"

"Yes, sir. Their sterns are modified. In place of the great cabin, they have an aft-access cargo bay, so the logs can be loaded straight in through the transom. Sort of like stacking rolls of carpet in the back of your van."

"Military stores?"

"Almost all are on site now, sir. We're still waiting on the molds and casts for the dual-use eight-inch shells. Which are working well in both the carronades and the long guns. All our radios are tested and in place, as is the land-station equipment. And the special-order spyglasses came in two days ago and passed the QC inspection."

"And the local binoculars?"

"There's an update on that in this morning's files, sir. The Dutch lens makers have demonstrated an acceptable working model to our acquisitions officer, but they haven't worked out a production method inexpensive enough for us to afford multiple purchases for each ship. My guess is that they'll have the bottlenecks licked by this time next year."

Simpson made a noise that sounded startlingly similar to a guard-dog's irritated growl. "Another key technology for which appropriations were not approved. Like the mitrailleuses."

Eddie sat up straight, genuinely alarmed. "Sir? They're not—not going to approve any mitrailleuses for the steamships? Why, that's—"

"Insane? Well, as it turns out, the Department of Economic Resources is not completely insane. Only half insane. Which is, in some ways, worse."

Eddie shook his head. "Sir, I don't understand: *half* insane?"

"Speaking in strictly quantitative terms, yes: half insane. Instead of approving one mitrailleuse for each quarter of the ship, they've approved exactly half that amount."

Eddie goggled. "A . . . a *half* a mitrailleuse for each quarter of the ship?" He tugged at his ginger-red forelock, doing the math and coming up with a mental diagram. "So only two? One on the forward port bow, the other on the starboard aft quarter?"

Simpson nodded. "That's about the shape of what the wiser heads in Grantville have envisioned." His voice was level and unemotional, but Eddie saw the sympathy in his eyes.

"But sir, how do you defend a ship against an all-point close assault with only two automatic weapons? If they come all around you in small boats—"

"Which they probably won't. As the holders of the purse strings were pleased to point out, yours is only a reconnaissance mission. So to speak. And you have no business going in harm's way, particularly at such close quarters. But if fate proves to take the unprecedented step of deciding to ignore all our reasonable expectations and plans"—Simpson's bitter, ironic grin made Eddie's stomach sink—"well, I just cut an order to Hockenjoss and Klott for a special antiboarding weapon. Two per ship, to take the place of the two missing mitrailleuses."

"Well, sir, I suppose that's better than nothing," Eddie allowed. And silently added, *but not by much, I bet.*

Simpson shrugged. "Certainly nothing very fancy or very complicated. Essentially I've asked them to build a pintle-mounted two-inch shotgun. Black powder breechloader. It's already picked up a nickname: the Big Shot. It should help against boarders." He must have read the dismay in Eddie's face. "I know what you're thinking, Commander. That such a weapon will be useless against the small boats themselves. That was my first reaction, which the committee has now heard repeatedly and, on a few occasions, profanely. I'll keep fighting for the full mitrailleuse appropriation, but I think I'm going to have to spend all my clout just getting percussion locks standardized for the main guns."

Eddie nodded. "Yes, sir. Which is of course where your clout belongs. Those tubes are carrying the primary weight of our mission."

"Well said, Commander. And if you find yourself in a tight spot—well, to borrow a phrase from another service, improvise and overcome."

Eddie tried to be jocular, but could hear how hollow it sounded when he replied, "Oo-rah, sir."

Eddie's failed attempt at gallows humor seemed to summon a spasm of guilt to the admiral's face. It reminded Eddie of one of his father's post-binge reflux episodes. "It's bad enough that we're not getting all the resources we were promised, but having delayed your departure to wait for them was a bad decision. My bad decision. I should have insisted on keeping the mission lighter and going sooner. That would have given you more time in the Caribbean before hurricane season, less of a squadron to oversee—and fewer hangers-on, I might add."

Eddie shrugged. "Sir, your gamble to wait and get us more goodies may not have panned out, but that's in the nature of gambling, wouldn't you agree? If you had been right, we'd be leaving here with more combat power, and a mission which would have represented a much more complete test of the ships and systems you're planning to shift into standard production. And if the rotary drill had been ready, the cash back on the venture—and the need to rapidly expand our maritime capacity to capitalize on it—would have given you all the clout you needed for what you want. All the clout and more, I should say."

Simpson looked at Eddie squarely. The younger man wondered if that calm gaze was what the admiral's version of gratitude looked like. "You have a generous and forgiving spirit, Commander. I'm not sure I'd be so magnanimous, in your place. After all, it's not just you who now has less combat power, less time before the heavy weather sets in, and more official requirements added on while your departure was delayed. Your wife is now subject to the same vulnerabilities, too."

Eddie nodded. "And don't I know it, sir."

Simpson actually released a small smile. "You sound less than overjoyed to have your wife along for the ride, Commander. Not SOP for a newlywed."

"Sir, with all due respect, none of this is SOP for a newlywed. Am I glad that I won't spend a whole half year away from my beautiful wife? You bet. Does it make me crazy anxious that she, and her quasi-entourage, are heading into danger along with me? You bet. The latter kind of diminishes the, uh...hormonal happiness caused by the former."

Simpson chuckled. "You are developing a true gift for words, Commander. If I could spare you from the field, I'd make you our chief diplomatic liaison."

"Sir! It's unbecoming a senior officer to threaten his subordinates. I'll take cannon fire over cocktail parties any day!"

Simpson glanced down toward Eddie's false foot. "And this from a man who should know better."

"Sir, I do know better. I've experienced both, and I'll take the cannons."

"Why?"

"Permission to speak freely?"

"Granted."

"Because, sir, battles are short and all business, and cocktail parties are long and all bullshit."

Simpson seemed as surprised by his answering guffaw as Eddie was. "I take it, Commander, that you are not enamored of the, er, 'social consequences' of being accompanied by your wife?"

"Sir, I would be more enamored of taking a bath with a barracuda. Even though Anne Cathrine isn't a genuine princess, Daddy is sure acting like she is. I now have my very own traveling rump court. Well, it's not *my* court. I'm just a part of it. An increasingly lowly part of it."

Simpson frowned. "Yes, and from what I understand, Christian IV has saddled you with another senior naval officer, which bumps you yet another place down the chain of command."

"Oh, that's not even the worst part." Eddie tried not to succumb to the urge to whine, which was attempting to overwhelm the none-too-high walls of his Manly Reserve.

"Oh?" Simpson now seemed more amused that sympathetic.

"Admiral, you haven't heard the latest roster of my fellow-travelers. Essentially, Anne Cathrine, not being a genuine princess, doesn't warrant genuine ladies in waiting. So we get a collection of other problematic persons from, or associated with, the Danish court, plus naval wives who have been given land grants in the New World."

One of Simpson's eyebrows elevated slightly. "But Christian IV doesn't have any New World land to grant."

"Not yet."

Simpson frowned. "I see. So I'm guessing that, along with the not-quite royal contingent, we have a just barely official entourage of courtesans, councilors, and huscarles? Some of whom enjoy special appointments by, and are probably assigned to carry out undisclosed missions for, His Royal Danish Majesty?"

"Yep, pretty much, sir."

Simpson nodded. "Yes, leave it to him to sneak in something like this in exchange for the ships he's committing to the expedition. Given the condition in which we received those hulls, I'm not so sure he isn't getting the better end of the deal." Simpson fixed Eddie with a suddenly intent stare. "Has he either intimated or overtly instructed you to take any orders directly from him?"

"No, sir. Why?"

Simpson rubbed his chin. "Well, because technically he could try to work that angle."

"I'm not sure I follow, sir."

Simpson steepled his fingers. "In recognition of your marriage and service, Gustav made you Imperial Count of Wismar. That made you imperial nobility of the USE. Technically. And that made it easy—well, easier—for Christian to get the nobles of his *Riksradet* to accept your creation as a Danish noble, too."

Eddie blinked. "Sir, I'm not a Danish noble. Not really."

"No? If I'm not mistaken, one of Christian's wedding gifts to you was land, wasn't it?"

"Yes, sir. Some miserable little island in the Faroes. I think it has a whopping population of ten. That includes the goats."

Simpson did not smile. "And since your received the land as part of a royal patent, you were made a *herremand,* weren't you?"

"Uh—yes, sir. Something like that. I didn't pay too much attention."

"Well, you should have, Commander. You became Danish nobility when you accepted that land. And therefore, a direct vassal of King Christian IV. Who, unless I'm much mistaken, has bigger things in mind for you. In the meantime, we'd better inform the task force's captains that, in place of all that pipe they were going to be hauling, they're going to be billeting more troops. A lot more troops."

Eddie was relieved. The mission was no longer purely reconnaissance, although that was not common knowledge. Not even among all the members of the ER Department. "How many more sir, and where from?"

"Just under four hundred, Commander. And all from the Lowlands."

"So they're Dutch."

Simpson shook his head. "No. They're from the Brabant."

Eddie stared. "From the *Spanish* Lowlands?"

Simpson simply nodded.

"Sir—we're taking Spanish soldiers to fight for us in the Spanish-held New World?"

"Commander, here's what I know currently. The troops are being provided by the archduchess infanta Isabella. As I understand it, these troops will have sworn loyalty to her nephew Fernando the king in the Low Countries, but not her older nephew, Philip the king of Spain."

"But Fernando is Philip's younger brother, his vassal—"

"Precisely. And that's why we're going to stop our speculations right there, Commander. The story behind Fernando sending troops with us to assist Dutch colonial interests in the New World is one that is well above your pay grade at this early point in the process. I know that because it's above *my* pay grade. I am not yet on the political 'need to know' list. And I suspect the mystery will remain right up until the infanta's troops are being berthed aboard your flotilla. Which probably won't happen until the very last possible day."

Eddie shook his head. "Every day, this 'little reconnaissance mission' not only gets bigger and more complicated, it gets increasingly surreal." Eddie glanced at the map of the Caribbean that Simpson had produced from his own folders. "Hell, we can't even be sure that there are any remaining Dutch colonies for us to help. And vice versa."

Simpson spread his hands on his desk. "Well, we know that once the Dutch West India Company got their hands on the histories in Grantville, they got a two-year head start on their colonization of St. Eustatia in the Leeward Islands. By their own report, they redirected some of their best administrators there last year. Notably, Jan van Walbeeck, whom history tells us was very effective in improving the situation down in Recife."

Eddie shrugged. "And who returned to the Provinces from there just a week before Admiral Tromp arrived in Recife with the remains of the fleet that was shattered at the Battle of Dunkirk. Pity Tromp and Walbeeck couldn't have overlapped even a few days in Recife. If they had, we'd know a lot more about how the situation in the New World may be changing."

"Quite true. But at least we know that Tromp arrived in Recife, and was making plans to relocate, since the colonies in that part of South America were untenable after the destruction of the Dutch fleet at Dunkirk."

"Yes, sir, but relocate to *where*? The two or three friendly ships that have come from the New World since the middle of last year can't tell us. Even the *jacht* that Tromp himself sent last March only confirmed that he expected to commence relocating in April, but not where."

Simpson scoffed. "And can you blame him for not being specific? Imagine if the Spanish had stumbled across that ship, seized it, interrogated the captain. Then they'd know where to find him. From an operational perspective, every day that Tromp can work without Spanish detection is a found treasure. He will have to ferry a sizable population—well, 'contingent'—from Recife to whatever new site he's selected, house those people, find a reliable source of indigenous supplies, establish a patrol perimeter, fortifications. All without any help from back home. He has his work cut out for him, Commander."

"Agreed, sir. But the flip side is that while we're coming with the help he almost surely needs, we don't know where to deliver it to him."

"No, but we know the best places to look. Right now, there are three noteworthy Dutch colonies in the Caribbean and the northern littoral of South America. We know they've sent people and supplies to St. Eustatia. We know there's a small settlement on Tobago, just northeast of Trinidad. And we know that they sent an expedition under Marten Thijssen last year to take Curaçao."

"And that assumes Thijssen's mission was a success."

"Yes, it does. It also assumes that Tromp's stated intent to abandon Recife was not disinformation. But that seems very unlikely.

Deceiving the Spanish on that point wouldn't buy him any durable advantage. In a few months' time, the Spanish would learn that he hadn't left, would blockade Recife, and grind him down. With the Dutch fleet in tatters, there's no relief force to be sent."

"So let's consider the three reasonable options. Curaçao is perilously close to the Spanish Main, just north of the path of the inbound treasure fleet. A great location from which to hunt the Spanish, but not a great location in which to hide from them. And the colony on Tobago is small. Too small: one hundred and fifty persons, at most."

Eddie nodded. "So, St. Eustatia."

Simpson nodded. "Exactly. St. Eustatia is in the middle of the Leeward Islands. So it's out of the way and not much visited by the Spanish. Yet history shows that, in time, 'Statia's central location could make it a powerful trading hub, once the traffic in the Caribbean picks up in intensity. It's also small enough to be defensible, but not so small as to be a rock from which there is no escape."

Eddie nodded. "Yes, Admiral, it all makes sense, but I'm still worried that even our last word of the Caribbean—from the Dutch fluyt *Koninck David*—still didn't include any mention of Tromp. Or much about St. Eustatia at all."

Simpson shrugged. "As I remember the report, the *Koninck David* left the Straits of Florida for its return to Europe in August. They wouldn't have been anywhere near 'Statia for half a year before that, in all likelihood. And although they didn't have any reassuring news for us, the American with them, young Phil Jenkins, also reported that the Spanish presence in the area was still pretty sparse. Which is historically consistent: until the Spanish were significantly challenged, they remained pretty close to their fortified ports and key colonies. With the abandoning of Recife, all the Dutch colonies are, practically speaking, off the beaten path. And St. Eustatia more than the other two."

"I agree that's where Admiral Tromp is likely to be, Admiral—if he's anywhere at all."

"What are you implying, Commander?"

Eddie produced one of the many history books he'd been poring over for the last several weeks. "I'm implying that in this period, the Spanish are realizing the need to establish the Armada de Barlovento, the squadron that enforces their territorial claim over the entirety of the Caribbean. If the ships that survived Dunkirk left Recife with even half of the ships that were already there, that's still a major force in the Caribbean. Too major for the Spanish to ignore, if they detect it."

"*If* they detect it—a very big *if*, Commander. But your point is well-taken. Even though our history books show that the Armada de Barlovento is fairly anemic right now, events since our arrival may have already led the Spanish to resharpen its teeth in this timeline. If so—well, then heed the Department of Economic Resource's exhortations, commander: remember that this is a recon mission only, and not to get embroiled in close range gun duels with the Spanish."

"Or pirates."

Simpson smiled. "Or them either." He stood. "Commander, I think that concludes the day's business. And unless I'm much mistaken, you have a lot of paperwork and correspondence ahead of you yet." He raised a salute.

Eddie jumped up and snapped a crisp response. "Yes, sir. Looks like I'll be burning the midnight oil. Again." And with that, he pivoted about on his false foot and made for the door, deciding that tonight he'd definitely need to use his remaining coffee ration. Definitely.

Simpson's eyes remained on the door as it closed behind Eddie Cantrell and then strayed to the folder on his desk marked "Reconnaissance Flotilla X-Ray (Cantrell)." He resisted the urge to open it yet again and inspect its ever-changing roster of ships. Each new diplomatic, military, or resource wrinkle in the USE seemed to make themselves felt as revisions to the complement of hulls. And with every week that Flotilla X-Ray's departure had been delayed, its size and composition shifted.

Its original composition had been sufficient for its originally simple mission. And likewise, Eddie had been the only possible candidate for the flotilla's senior up-time officer. Indeed, he had as much naval combat experience as any other up-timer (with the exception of Simpson himself). However, that experience was paltry by comparison to the great majority of the flotilla's down-time captains and commanders, who had spent most of their lives at sea. Many began as common sailors working "before the mast," and during some parts of their careers just about all of them had traded broadsides with their sovereigns' foes. Although the down-time naval officers who had been training for the mission clearly respected Eddie for his combat experience and storied daring, they also were very much aware that he was a relative newcomer to their profession, and was almost completely unfamiliar with the nuances of the sailing vessels upon which they themselves had grown to manhood and in which they were infinitely more at home than any place ashore.

What Eddie had in lieu of their profound nautical skill—as much from his up-time reading and gaming as from recent training—was an innate sense of the tempo and requirements of a flotilla operating under steam power. He was the only officer in Flotilla X-Ray who had that almost instinctual insight. Even those down-time crewmen who had been intensely trained in the technical branches, and who had long ago outstripped him in the expertise specific to any given subsystem of Simpson's new navy, still lacked his totalized sense of how all those complex parts fit and flowed together, producing both incredible synergies of military power, but also incredible vulnerabilities to breakdowns in either machinery or logistics.

Simpson kept staring at the folder, kept resisting the impulse to open it and reassure himself that Eddie was being given an adequate force to complete his mission and to be able to over-master or outrun any foes that might present themselves. After all, the admiral told himself, feeling sheepish as he echoed the Department of Economic Resources, it was a simple recon mission. There was nothing to worry about. So what if Reconnaissance Flotilla X-Ray was bound for the New World, beyond the limits of the USE's power to help, or even readily communicate with it? The flotilla was still fundamentally a shake-down cruise for the first production models of Simpson's first generation of steam-powered warships. They, usually with Eddie on-board, had been put through extensive sea-trials, and, except for a few quirks, had performed admirably—even superbly, if Simpson were to say so himself. They were good ships, and Eddie was a good, if young, officer.

Simpson studied the flaps of the folder, edges dirty with the wear of his worried fingers, of his impatient thumbs prying back the dull covers. Commander Cantrell and the rest of the flotilla would simply conduct the preparatory operations in the Gulf and the Caribbean and then, when the time was right, Admiral John

Chandler Simpson would bring over his new navy of mature, second generation ships, as shiny and lethal a weapon as this world had yet seen.

The consequent "pacification" of rivals in the New World would ready his blue water fleet for the more serious and definitive battles that it would almost certainly have to fight against one or more of the armadas of the Old World. It was impossible to foresee which nation, or collection thereof, would ultimately find the rise of the USE so intolerable a phenomenon that it would feel compelled to correct that trend in the most decisive manner possible: a no-holds-barred confrontation of navies. But in the dynamics of the rise and fall of nations, the uncertainties regarding such conflicts had never been *if* they would occur, but rather with whom, and when, and where.

That thought, however, made Simpson's eyes wander to the thinner folder lying alongside the one for Flotilla X-Ray. This one was marked with a white triangle: an intel synopsis, containing a review of pending threats that might require naval intervention, sooner or later. France, Spain, even the Ottomans, could conceivably stir up enough trouble to keep Simpson's larger, finished fleet from a timely deployment to the New World. However, none of those powers appeared to be disposed or deployed to do so.

But then again, John Chandler Simpson knew that appearances could be deceiving and that the only thing certain about the future was that there was never, ever, anything certain about it.

He pushed the folders away, rested his chin on his hand, stared at the door through which Eddie Cantrell had exited, and succumbed to his now-habitual array of worries—half of which were common to all commanders of young men regardless of the time or place of the conflict, and half of which were the dark legacy of every father who had ever sent a son to fight a war in a distant land.

Chapter 13

Brussels, The Spanish Low Countries

"So the Spanish tried to kill the pope? And *did* kill John O'Neill in Rome?"

Thomas Preston, oldest officer among the Irish Wild Geese who served in the Lowlands, and Maestro-de-campo of the eponymous Preston Tercio, stared back at the group that had summoned him and delivered this shocking news. Seated at the center was Fernando, king in the Low Countries and brother of Philip IV of Spain. To his right was Maria Anna of the House of Hapsburg, Fernando's wife and sister of Emperor Ferdinand of Austria. And sitting to one side, but in the largest, most magnificent chair of all of them, was the grand dame of European politics herself, the archduchess infanta Isabella, still an authority in the Lowlands and aunt of both Fernando and Philip. And therefore, Preston's employer for the last twenty years. Oh, and then there was Rubens, the artist and intelligencer, sitting far to one side of the power-holding troika that ruled here in Brussels.

Maria Anna leaned forward slightly. "Colonel Preston, I assure you, my husband would not tell you such things unless they were true."

"Your Highness, I apologize. I did not intend that response

118

as a sign of doubt, but of disbelief. It is shocking news, to say the least."

Fernando nodded. "To us, also, Colonel. And that is why we asked you to meet us alone. It may cause, er, unrest in the Irish *tercios*, if it comes to them as rumor. Coming from you, however, we might hope for a different reception."

Thomas Preston shifted in his suddenly-uncomfortable seat. "Your Highness, the reception might be *some*what different—but not as different as if it came from one of the Old Irish colonels."

Maria Anna's eyebrows raised in curiosity. "'Old' Irish?"

"Yes, Your Highness. My family name, as you are probably aware, is not an Irish name at all, but English. That makes us Prestons 'New' Irish, associated with the old, pre-Reformation landlords who eventually married into the Irish families. We are often wealthier than our Old Irish neighbors—which makes us suspect to begin with, I fear—but no amount of money will ever equate to having ancient Gaelic roots, to being one of the families whose names are routinely associated with the High Kingship's tanists—"

"The tanists?" Maria Anna echoed.

It was Isabella herself who answered. "The royal families of Ireland designate one of their number as chief among them. And it is usually from among these that, in elder times, the current king's successor—the tanist—was chosen."

"Ah," breathed Rubens, "so this is why Hugh O'Neill the Elder was known as 'The O'Neill.' He was the chieftain of that dynasty and all those subordinate to it."

"That is my understanding, but I suspect that Colonel Preston would add details I have missed or misunderstood. Most pertinent to our concerns, though, is that there are—or were—only two scions of the royal houses remaining free, outside Ireland, who had clear entitlement to becoming tanists of the vacant throne: the recently deceased John O'Neill, the earl of Tyrone, and Hugh O'Donnell, the earl of Tyrconnell."

"*Attainted* Earls, My Grace," added Rubens.

"Yes, yes," she replied testily, "so the English have it. The same English who just happened to steal Ireland from its own people, and whose attainting of its few remaining nobles is merely the conclusive legalistic coda to their campaign of usurpation and rapine. It is not as if any legitimate monarch on the Continent,

Catholic or Protestant, cares a whit for the juridical rationalizations of England's theft of a whole nation. But let us return to Colonel Preston's point. The Old Irish will, unfortunately, not hear this news as well from him as they would from one of the survivors of their royal families. But there is nothing to be done about that. The last O'Neill, who is not directly in the line of titular inheritance, is Owen Roe, and he now commands the pope's new bodyguard. The last O'Donnell is my godson, Hugh Albert, and he is..." She paused, either catching her breath or mastering a quaver in her voice: Preston could not determine which. "...is engaged in other matters and unable to return at present."

Preston sat straighter. Whereas John O'Neill had been insufferable and Owen Roe tolerable, Hugh O'Donnell had been a good fellow: clever, a shrewd soldier, well-educated, well-spoken, and without regal airs. So why the hell wasn't he here? He'd disappeared in April, and now, when he was needed most—

"Colonel Preston," Fernando articulated carefully, as if aware that he would have to reacquire the mercenary's attention before continuing.

"Yes, Your Highness?"

"I should add that news of the earl of Tyrone's death, and the attempt on the pope's life, are only precursors to the primary reason I asked you to join us today."

"Precursors, Your Highness?"

"Yes. First, I welcome you to share your opinion on how your men will receive the news. This is material to the next matter we must discuss."

"Well, Your Majesty, I am not one to make predictions, especially not in regard to my own somewhat mercurial countrymen. But I feel sure of this: ever since news came that Urban had been forcibly removed—rather, 'chased out'—of the Holy See, and was being actively pursued by Borja's own cardinal-killing Spaniards, every one of my senior officers has expressed their support for Urban. When they learn that Borja and his Spanish army tried to murder the pope and killed John O'Neill while he was trying to rescue an up-timer and his pregnant wife... Well, let's say my biggest concern will be to make sure that they don't start picking fights with our 'comrades' in your own Spanish *tercios*."

Fernando raised a finger. "You happen to have used an interesting turn of phrase, Colonel Preston. In fact, those Spanish *tercios* are *not* mine, they are my brother's. They are on Spanish payroll, direct from Madrid."

Preston heard Fernando's tone shift, heard it move from the full-voiced, natural cadences of a frank conversation into one laced with slower, quieter insinuations. *Careful, now, Thomas. When a well-manicured Spanish gentleman starts addressing his topics on the slant, you can be sure there's a snake in the grass somewhere nearby.* "Yes, Your Highness," Preston agreed carefully, "the Spanish are paid directly from Spanish coffers. Unlike us."

Fernando smiled. "Precisely. Unlike you." And then he looked down the table at Rubens.

Which told Thomas Preston that now he was going to hear the real dirt, the snaky facts of real politick that Fernando could not afford to utter with his own lips. That way, if later asked to admit or deny having mentioned those facts, he could offer a technically truthful denial. Kings: even the best of them had a bit of viper's blood running in their veins. Thomas supposed they'd be dead, if they didn't.

Ruben moved his considerable bulk closer to the broad, gleaming table at which they all sat. "Colonel Preston, given recent events, we are concerned that this year, when the time comes for our hired troops to renew their oaths to Spain, that there may be, er, resistance in your ranks, particularly."

Preston waved a dismissive hand. "Then let's skip the renewal of the oath. After all, it has no explicit term limit. The renewal is symbolic."

"Yes, and it is a most important symbol. So, in order to preserve that symbol and yet also preserve the genuine loyalty of the four *tercios* of Wild Geese that are the ever-stalwart backbone and defenders of this realm, we have come up with a reasonable expedient: to simply change the oath."

"Change the oath?"

"Yes."

"In what way?"

"This year, when you take the oath, it will omit the reference to Archduchess Isabella as being Philip's vassal. You will take your oath to her as you have for twenty years, but without mentioning King Philip of Spain." Rubens paused, his eyes sought Preston's directly. "I presume you see the political practicality of this adjustment?"

Oh, I see it, painter. I see everything you hope I'll see without your having to say it. On the surface, the change of oath was just to minimize any possibility of disaffection or departure arising from any mention of direct fealty to the increasingly unpopular King of Spain. But, there was an underlying subtlety which, Preston was quite sure, was the real intent of the change of oath. *We'll only be swearing fealty to Isabella. And, unless I'm much mistaken, to her nephew.*

Rubens' next words confirmed his suspicions. "However, as a precaution, we will not point out the fact—which could be easily misconstrued, of course—that, in agreeing to renew your oaths to Her Grace the Infanta, that your service is most likely to be commanded by her nephew, whom she has been pleased to confirm as the senior power in her lands. So, although you now also serve the king in the Low Countries, that additional, extrapolative detail will remain unadvertised. For the moment."

Yes, for the moment. But Preston had been a pawn on the chessboard where kings played their games for many decades and could see where this political compass was pointing. With the oaths of the Wild Geese transferred directly to Fernando, their obedience and their fates were locked to him, not to Spain. Yes, technically Fernando was still a vassal of Spain, but how long that would continue was debatable. And so, when and if the Lowlands became fully and officially separate from the throne in Madrid, the Irish *tercios* would follow suit. And they would indeed comprise the loyal core of its army, since Philip's *tercios* in the Lowlands would most assuredly not follow the same path. But, problematically, they would still be in the same country. Preston flinched at the thought of his *tercio* squaring off against their former Spanish counterparts. That would be a bloody, internecine business indeed—

"Is this change in the oath acceptable to you and your men, Colonel Preston?" Rubens asked. His small eyes did not blink.

"I will have to put it to them. However, given recent events, I think it will not only be acceptable but preferable. However, they will ask a question I cannot answer: how will they be paid? Already, the *reales* from Spain are few and far between. If it wasn't for the deal Hugh O'Donnell struck with the Frenchman Turenne, earlier this year, I don't know what we would have done for food these past three months. But that supply is almost over—and truth be told, I was never comfortable with the arrangement."

"And why is that?" Maria Anna asked.

"Because, your Highness, until France and Madrid cooperated at the Battle of Dunkirk, the French had been the enemies of this realm, ever threatening the southern borders of the Brabant. I should know; I spent many months in garrison there, over the years. And then suddenly we are at peace—but it's a peace which is already fraying. So in taking bread from Turenne, we took bread from a past, and very possibly future, adversary of this court. I was not comfortable condoning it, but I was less comfortable seeing my men's families starve. So when O'Donnell arranged it by serving Turenne along with sixty of the men of his *tercio*, I had little choice but to accept it. And, I must speak frankly, it brought trouble along with it."

"Oh?" asked Rubens. "What kind of trouble?"

"French trouble, Your Grace. Their agents have been lurking around our camps, letting it be known that the king of France is hiring mercenaries, and can pay them in hard coin, not cabbages and watered beer."

Rubens looked at the ruling troika. They just kept watching Preston. None of them blinked, but Maria Anna might have suppressed a small smile.

Rubens rotated one thumb around the other. "And have any of your men left our service for theirs?"

"No, but I worry that they may. I've heard rumors—rumors from this court—that some nobles here speak ill of us Wild Geese, say that we should be grateful for the scraps we're given, and that some of us are already taking service with the French."

"Yes," said Ruben, twirling his moustache, "we have heard the same thing. Largely, because we spread those rumors ourselves."

Preston gaped. "You what?"

Maria Anna leaned forward; Preston tried to ignore the way it compressed her bosom. "Colonel, the privations of your people have never been intentional, but in the last two months, we discovered that they lent credence to the belief in Paris that our grasp upon your continued loyalty was weak, and that certain members of the Wild Geese were indeed finding it necessary to seek employment elsewhere. To be more specific, to seek employment with the French themselves."

Preston felt heat rise in his face. "Your Highness, one of us did. The very best of us, some might say. Hugh Albert O'Donnell may have fed us, but he did it by agreeing to serve Turenne. Turenne! He's Richelieu's hand-picked military favorite. If the earl of Tyrconnell will take service with the French, then why shouldn't they think more of us will follow? And sixty of us did, the ones who went with O'Donnell."

"And whose service there fed you," Isabella observed from behind gnarled knuckles folded before her on the table.

"Yes, Your Grace, but at what cost? Where was Hugh when the pope was threatened? Where does he tarry, now that he is the last earl of Ireland, the last hope of his people? Where has he been since late in April?"

"Evidently working for his employer," Rubens observed smoothly.

"Yes, evidently. Abandoning us to work for the French. Which makes him, for all intents and purposes, a traitor!"

Isabella was on her feet in a single motion, cane brandished in one hand, the other pointing in quavering fury at Preston—or maybe at the word "traitor," which seemed to hover invisible in the air. "You call Hugh Albert O'Donnell a traitor?" she cried.

Preston stood his ground. "Your Grace, if he serves your traditional enemy, that makes him—"

With a swiftness that belied her age, her infirmity, her arthritis and the gray habit of her order, she dashed her cane down upon the table: the heavy oak rod splintered with a crash. "A *traitor*?!" she shrieked, livid. "How dare you say—how dare you *think*—such a thing!"

The room was not merely silent, but frozen, all eyes on the trembling, imperial, terrible old woman who had risen up like a wrathful god from an elder age to silence them all with her fury and undiminished, magnificent passion.

Preston swallowed, but did not avert his eyes. "Your Grace, I mean no disrespect, but how are Lord O'Donnell's actions *not* those of a traitor? Before Philip set Borja upon Rome, before the pope was threatened and John O'Neill was slain, he turned back all his honors and Spanish titles and went to work for France. For France, Your Grace. Your enemy, Spain's enemy—and now, his employer. How is that *not* traitorous?"

"Colonel Preston, do you truly not see any other way to interpret Lord O'Donnell's actions?" When Preston shook his head, Isabella continued. "Hugh was the only one of you Wild Geese except Lord O'Neill who was made a naturalized Spanish citizen by the Crown, who became a knight, and a fellow of the court at Madrid. But then, when he saw that the same Crown never intended to make good its promises and debts to you and your countrymen, I understand that he came to your camp incognito, and explained his dilemma. Specifically, what response could he make if Philip had asked him, as an intimate of the court and loyal gentleman of Spain, to function as Madrid's special factotum and commander here? Which, given the current situation, could mean leading either his, or Spanish, *tercios* against those loyal to me, if Philip's displeasure with the Lowlands were to become so great. Was Lord O'Donnell to obey orders to attack me, or to attack you and his fellow countrymen, if that is how the loyalties of such a moment played out?"

Preston felt as though the chair he was seated in had been turned upside down. Or the world had. Or both.

"Think it through, Colonel. Lord O'Donnell had to step down from his post. And in doing so, it was incumbent upon him to return the beneficences he had received, and remove himself from Spanish territory. But not before he visited his men and yours, and enjoined you to think carefully to whom your allegiance would lie if faced with the eventualities that now seem to be hastening upon us. Philip is already attempting to compromise our non-Spanish *tercios*."

"Your Grace, all this I see plainly. But—France? Why not some other power? Why our old foe?"

Isabella reseated herself slowly. It was an almost leonine action, despite her age. "Because, it is through our old foe that he will orchestrate a solution to both your problem and our problem: money. Enough money for the Lowlands to survive without recourse to Madrid's coffers. Enough money for your families to eat, and your men to have ample coin in their pockets."

Preston knew the room wasn't spinning, but at the moment, it felt as though it was. "And how will Hugh's service to France make possible this solution? And why has he not communicated this to us, as well as to you? My Grace, I mean no offense, but we are his countrymen: why has he not reassured us with the particulars of his plan?"

Isabella closed her eyes. "Because it is not *his* plan. It is ours. And I,"—she opened eyes suddenly bright and liquid, but from which she refused to let tears run down—"and I could not tell him of it."

"But why? If he doesn't know how serving the French will more profoundly serve us, then by what inducement has he left us to—?"

Maria Anna silenced him with a small, sly smile. "My good Colonel Preston, I counsel you not to let these unexplained—and apparently inexplicable—events perturb you. You will note they do not perturb us. Indeed, our plans are well set. But it is often necessary that a cog spinning in one part of a complex machine has no knowledge of how its peers are turning elsewhere in the same device."

Preston frowned at her words, heard two of Isabella's sentences once again in his head: *It is not his plan, it is ours. And I dare not tell him of it.* Implying that the truly ignorant cog in Maria Anna's machination was not Preston, but O'Donnell himself.

And he felt the oblique implication strike him so hard and so suddenly that the room seemed to tilt momentarily. Had O'Donnell's apparent defection been *planned*? Had he been maneuvered into it so that he was then a properly situated, yet unknowing, piece of some larger stratagem?

He looked quickly at Isabella, who was looking intently at him. He did not see canniness; he saw—

Love. Maternal love. Intense, irrational, desperate. But why would she do such a thing to O'Donnell, unless it was—?

To save him. Of course. Now it made sense. And suddenly Preston saw how, since the arrival of the up-timers and their library's revelation of the duplicity of the Spanish in regard to their Irish servitors, the grand dame of European statecraft had realized that in order for her cherished god-child to survive—and thrive—she would have to shift the game board so that he could weather the change in fortunes.

Yes, there was no doubt about it. It was clear enough that, in the days before the up-timers, she had, every step of the way, protected him, groomed him, got him a knighthood. Of course, then Father Florence Conry had almost ruined it all with his hare-brained proposal to invade Ireland. But whereas the priest had envisioned a force jointly led by the Earls O'Donnell and O'Neill and the predictable co-dominium that would arise in its wake, Madrid had embraced a different solution. Philip was no fool, and he had the benefit of the count-duke of Olivares' advice, to boot. So Philip had summoned young O'Donnell, knighted him in an order more prestigious than O'Neill's (which had been Isabella's intent), but then chose him to lead the Irish expedition alone. It was a politically prudent choice, one which Isabella had not expected, probably due to O'Donnell's youth and his clan's less storied name. But the Spanish king and his counselor had seen the qualities, and restraint, in the younger man that would make him both a more capable general of armies and a more capable revolutionary orator than his mercurial peer, O'Neill.

But, since the invasion never came off (largely derailed by Isabella herself, as Preston recalled), the only lasting effect of all this maneuvering was that it ensured that the already difficult relationship between O'Donnell and O'Neill became as bad and bitter as it could be. It hadn't helped that, in addition to simply choosing the younger over the older, Philip and Olivares had made their assessment of Hugh's superior qualities well known at court, and thereby, throughout Europe.

So Isabella had saved her godson from the disastrous invasion, just as she had taken pains to ensure that he was college-educated, naturalized, knighted, and furnished with a tremendously advantageous marriage. All done to both ensure his success, and ensure his survival. A target of English assassins since birth, the higher Hugh O'Donnell's station became, the more pause it gave to those who sent murderers across the Channel: were they plotting the death of a renegade member of the Irish royalty, or an immigrated Spanish gentleman? The former was an affair of no account, but the latter could easily become an international incident, and was therefore best avoided.

And having thus protected and provided for her charge, Isabella of the up-time history had died in 1633, presumably satisfied that she had seen him safely married with a title and land. But within the year, those plans had come undone, here as there. His wife having died without producing surviving issue, he lost more than his love; he lost the land and titles that had been her dowry. In that world, with his godmother dead, he had had little choice but to do what he might as the colonel of his own *tercio*. That he had recruited and commanded well there no less than here, that much was clear. But there, Fernando had evidently inherited Philip's utilitarian attitudes toward the Irish, and had spent them like water. Which was sadly prudent, Preston had to admit. After all, as the opportunity to reclaim Ireland became an ever-thinner tissue of lies, the Spanish masters of the Wild Geese feared that they would be increasingly susceptible to subornation by other, rival powers. And so the last of them were sent to Spain, and then to their destruction in putting down the Catalan revolt that began in 1640.

But what about in this altered world, where Hugh had no future with Spain and none in the Lowlands either, unless it officially broke with Madrid? What place for O'Donnell? Indeed, Preston realized with a sudden chill up his back, what place for the Wild Geese, for Ireland? And evidently, the old girl Isabella had hatched a scheme to correct some, maybe all, of these problems. But it was a scheme so deep, and probably so devious, that it had to be kept from one of its primary executors: Hugh Albert O'Donnell.

Isabella had obviously seen the understanding in Preston's eyes. "So you see, now."

The Irish colonel swallowed, nodded. "I believe I do, Your Grace. Just one question. Is there something my people, my Wild Geese, can do to help?"

"You already have."

Preston started. "I have?"

"Specifically, four hundred of the men of Lord O'Donnell's *tercio* have. They were not sent to garrison in Antwerp as you, and they, were originally told. They were sent there to board ships and have now joined a task force in order to fulfill their part in our plan."

Preston was too stunned to feel stunned. "And if they succeed?"

Fernando leaned forward. "If they succeed, our futures are secure. Both yours and ours. For many, many years to come."

"And if they fail?"

Isabella sat erect. "Colonel Preston, I am surprised at that question. Tell me, as the most senior officer of my Irish Wild Geese, how often have they ever failed me?"

"Only a very few times, Your Grace. But their determination in your service has a dark price, too."

"Which is?"

"That, rather than retreat, they die trying."

Isabella sat back heavily, looking every year of her age. She responded to Preston—"I know, Colonel, I know"—but her eyes were far away and seamed with worry.

Part Three

July 1635

What raging of the sea

Chapter 14

St. Kilda archipelago, North Atlantic

"Commander Cantrell, propellers are all-stop. Awaiting orders."

Eddie Cantrell looked to his left. The ship's nominal captain, Ove Gjedde, nodded faintly. It was his customary sign that his executive officer, Commander Cantrell, was free to give his orders autonomously. Eddie returned the nod, then aimed his voice back over his shoulder. "Secure propellers and prepare to lower the vent cover."

"Securing propellers, aye. Ready to lower prop vent cover, aye."

"And Mr. Svantner, send the word to cut steam. Let's save that coal."

"Aye, aye, sir. Cutting steam. Let free the reef bands, sir?"

Eddie looked at Gjedde again, who, by unspoken arrangement, reserved rigging and sail orders for himself. The sails had been reefed for the engine trials and with the engine no longer propelling the ship, it would soon begin to drift off course.

The weather-bitten Norwegian nodded once. Svantner saluted and went off briskly, shouting orders that were soon drowned out by the thundering rustle of the sails being freed and unfurled into the stiff wind blowing near the remote island of St. Kilda.

Well, technically speaking, they were just off the sheer and rocky north coast of the island of Hirta, largest and most populous islet of the St. Kilda archipelago. If you could call any landmass with fewer than two hundred people "populous." But even that small settlement was pretty impressive, given how far off St. Kilda was from—well, from everything. Over fifty miles from the northwest-ernmost island of the already-desolate Outer Hebrides, and almost 175 miles north of Ireland, Hirta and the rest of the islands of the group were, for all intents and purposes, as isolated as if they had been on the surface of another planet. And, since it was rumored that most of the inhabitants were still as influenced by druidic beliefs as by Christianity, it was not an exaggeration to say that, even though the natives of St. Kilda *did* dwell on the same planet, they certainly did inhabit a different world.

"Commander Cantrell, there you are! I'm sorry I'm late. I was detained below decks. Paying my respects to your lovely wife and her ladies."

Eddie swiveled around on his false heel. Time at sea had taught him, even with his excellent prosthetic leg, not to lose contact with the deck. "And you are"—he tried to recall the face of the man, couldn't, guessed from context—"Lieutenant Bjelke, I presume?"

The man approaching—tall, lithe, with a long nose and long hair that was several shades redder than Eddie's own—offered a military bow, and tottered a bit as the ship rolled through a higher swell. "That is correct, sir. I tried to present myself to you immediately upon coming aboard, but I found myself embarrass-ingly, er, indisposed."

Eddie smiled, noticed that Bjelke's pallor was not just the result of pale Nordic skin, but a manful, ongoing struggle against sea-sickness. "Is that why you did not attempt transfer to this ship until today, Mr. Bjelke? Waiting for good weather?"

Bjelke, although only twenty, returned the smile with a court-ier's polish. Which was only logical: his father, Jens, had been the Norwegian chancellor for more than twenty years and was certainly one of the nation's wealthiest nobles. If one measured his stature in terms of influence rather than silver, he was argu-ably its most powerful lord, having been given the Hanseatic city of Bergen as his personal fief just last year. Henrik Bjelke had, therefore, grown up surrounded by wealth, influence, and ministers of etiquette.

Fortunately, his father was also a fair and industrious man, hav-ing studied widely abroad and now compiling the first dictionary of the Norwegian language. And Henrik, his second son, had apparently inherited his sire's talents and tastes for scholarship. Originally bound for the university in Padova, the arrival of Grantville had caught both Henrik's interest and imagination. Like many other adventurous sons (and no small number of daughters) of European noble houses, he had gone there to read in the up-time library, augmenting that education with classes and seminars at the nearby University of Jena. It was perhaps predictable that he was assigned as Eddie's adjutant and staff officer, as much because of Christian's keen interest in the young Norwegian as Bjelke's own unfulfilled desires to pursue a military career. He had ultimately done so quite successfully in the up-time world of Eddie's birth, rising to become the head of the Danish Admiralty.

However, Bjelke's familiarity with things nautical had been a later-life acquisition. For the moment, it was clearly a mighty struggle for him just to maintain the at-sea posture that was the down-time equivalent of "at ease" in the presence of a superior officer with whom one had familiarity (and with whom the difference in rank was not too profound). Eddie discovered he was inordinately cheered by Rik's unsteadiness. *At last! someone with even* less *shipboard experience than me!* He gestured to the rail.

Bjelke gratefully accompanied the young up-timer to the rail, but stared at it for a moment before putting his hand upon it. The "rail" was actually comprised of two distinct parts, one of iron, one of wood. The iron part consisted of two chains that ran where the bulkhead should be, each given greater rigidity by passing tautly through separate eyelets in vertical iron stanchions. Those stanchion were form-cut to fit neatly into brass-cupped holes along the bulwark line, and thus could be removed at will.

However, mounted atop those stanchions, and stabilizing themselves by a single descending picket that snugged into a low wooden brace affixed to the deck, was a light wooden rail. Each section of the rail was affixed to its fore and aft neighbors by a sleeve that surrounded a tongue-in-groove mating of the two separate pieces, held tight by a brass pin that passed through them both at that juncture. Henrik tentatively leaned his weight upon it. It was quite firm. "Ingenious," he murmured admiring the modular wooden rail sections and ignoring the chain-and-stanchion railing. "Your work, Commander?"

Eddie shrugged. "I had a hand in it."

Bjelke smiled slowly. "Modesty is rare in young commanders, my elders tell me, but is a most promising sign. I am fortunate to have you as a mentor, Commander Cantrell."

Eddie kept from raising an eyebrow. Well, Henrik Bjelke had certainly revealed more than a little about himself, and his role vis-a-vis Eddie, in those "innocent" comments. First, the young Norwegian obviously knew the ship upon which this vessel had been heavily based—the USS *Hartford* of the American Civil War—since he was not surprised by the presence of what would otherwise have been the wholly novel chain-and-stanchion railing arrangement, which reduced dangers from gunwale splinters and, in the case of close targets, could be quickly removed to extend the lower range of the deck guns' maximum arc of elevation. However, Bjelke had pointedly *not* been expecting the modular wooden rail inserts that Eddie had designed for greater deck safety when operating on the high seas. That bespoke a surprisingly detailed knowledge of the ship's design origins, even for a clever young man who'd spent more than a year in the library at Grantville.

Secondly, Bjelke confidently identified the innovation as Eddie's, which suggested that he'd been well-briefed about the technological gifts of the young American. Which went along with the implication that his elders considered Cantrell a most promising officer.

And that likely explained the third interesting bit of information: that Henrik Bjelke had not been encouraged to look at this assignment as merely a military posting, but as an apprenticeship of sorts.

And all those nuances, having a common emphasis on familiarization with up-timers and their knowledge, seemed to point in one direction: straight at His Royal Danish Majesty Christian IV.

Eddie had to hand it to his half-souse, half-genius regal father-in-law: USE emperor and Swedish sovereign Gustav Adolf might be running around physically conquering various tracts of Central Europe, but Christian had launched his own, highly successful campaign of collecting and captivating the hearts and minds of persons who were poised to become high-powered movers and shakers of the rising generation. His son Ulrik was betrothed to Gustav's young daughter. His daughter Anne Cathrine was married to the most high-profile war-hero-technowizard from now-legendary Grantville. And now, he had added sharp-witted Henrik Bjelke to the mix.

And that addition brought distinct value-added synergies to many of King Christian's prior social machinations. Bjelke's appointment no doubt bought the gratitude of various influential Norwegians, who had, so far, been the "forgotten poor cousin" of the reconstituted Union of Kalmar between Sweden and Denmark. Bjelke's appointment also provided Eddie with a gifted aide who was unusually familiar with up-time manners and technology, and who no doubt understood that this mentorship was an extraordinary opportunity to put himself on a political and military fast track.

Of course, thus indebted to Christian, it was also to be expected that Henrik Bjelke, willing or not, would also serve as the Danish king's—well, not *spy*, exactly, but certainly his dedicated observer. And last, the bold Bjelke might just be valiant enough to help save Eddie's life at some point during the coming mission, thereby ensuring that Christian's daughter did not become a widow and that the familial connection to the up-timers remained intact. Alternatively, Bjelke, learning up-time ways and now having first-hand access to up-time technology, might also make a reasonable replacement husband for a widowed Anne Cathrine. Yup, the old Danish souse-genius had sure gamed out all the angles on this appointment.

About which Eddie reasoned he had best learn everything he could. "So what do they call you at home, Lieutenant Bjelke?"

"At—at home, Commander?"

"Yes. You know, the place you live." Although, Eddie realized a moment later, that the son of Jens Bjelke wouldn't have just one home. More like one home for every month of the year...

But that didn't impede the young Norwegian's understanding of Eddie's intent. "Ah, my familiar name! I'm Rik, sir. An amputated version of my proper name, so that I might not be confused with all the other Henriks in our family and social circles. Not very dignified, I'm afraid."

Eddie smiled. "Well, I'm not very dignified myself, so that suits me just fine, Rik. You got attached to the flotilla pretty much at the last second, I seem to recall."

Bjelke's gaze wavered. "Yes, sir. There were impediments to overcome."

"Impediments? Political?"

"Familial, I'm afraid. My father does not share in my enthusiasm for a military career."

Hm. Given the scanty biographical sources from up-time, that might actually be the truth, rather than a clever way of explaining away what might have been a maneuver by Christian IV to get Bjelke added to the flotilla without Simpson or Eddie having enough time to conduct research on his possible ties to the Danish court. What Christian had either not planned upon, or simply couldn't outflank, was the possibility that Simpson and Eddie had compiled dossiers on all possibly mission-relevant personnel without waiting for assignment rosters.

Which they had done. It had been time-consuming, but worth it. Although Eddie lacked any detailed information on many of the flotilla's senior officers and leaders, he had a thumbnail sketch for most of them. In fact, Ove Gjedde was the only notable exception.

Eddie nodded understanding at Bjelke's professed plight. "But your father finally listened to your appeals?"

Rik blushed profoundly, and Eddie could have hugged him: *and he blushes faster and redder than I do, too! Damn, even if he is a spy, it's almost worthwhile having him around so that another officer looks and acts even more like the boy next door than I do!* But Eddie kept his expression somber as Bjelke explained. "My father remained deaf to my appeals for military experience—but not to King Christian's."

Eddie was surprised and reassured by the frankness of that admission. He doubted Christian would have been happy with Bjelke drawing such a straight line between his own presence and the Danish king's desires. And while it was possible that this was disinformation meant to impart an aura of trustworthiness to Rik, a look at the younger man's face and genuine blush-response told Eddie otherwise. Bjelke was simply a polished, well-educated young man who was likely to prove courageous and capable in the years to come, but right now, was a youngling out on his first great adventure. If there was any duplicity in him at all, it would be minor, and contrary to his nature. Eddie could live with that. Easily.

"Well, Rik, however you got here, you're here. So, welcome aboard the *Intrepid*. First order of business is to make you at home."

"Thank you, sir. My man Nils has seen to my berthing and I must say it is a welcome change from the *Serendipity*. Those accommodations were most... uncomfortable."

"Well, I'm glad you like your stateroom"—*more like a long closet*, reflected Eddie—"but when I suggested we make you at home, I meant familiarization with the ship. Do you have any questions about the *Intrepid* that your briefers didn't answer for you?"

Rik brightened immediately; if he'd been a puppy, his ears would probably have snapped straight up. "A great many questions, Commander. Although not for want of my asking. Frankly, my briefers, as you call them, knew fewer particulars about your new ships than I did. I had studied the classes of American vessels that were the foundations of your designs, which they had not. And they could answer only a few questions about how they differed, other than the guns and the steam plants. Seeing them, it is clear that you have made other significant modifications."

Eddie nodded. "Yep, we had to. This class—the Quality I class—needs to be an even more stable firing platform than the original *Hartford* was."

"Because of the increased range and capability of her eight-inch pivot guns?"

Eddie shrugged. "That's a large part of it. But it gets more complicated. First, the *Hartford* had its broad side armament on the weather deck. We put ours below."

"Better performance in bad weather?"

"Well, that too, but it was actually the result of some complex design trade-offs. First, we wanted maximum clear traverse for the pivot guns. So that meant 'clearing the gun deck,' as much as we could. There was already a lot that *had* to go on up there. We needed our antipersonnel weapons on the weather deck so they could bear freely upon all quarters. And although we have a steam engine, that's for tactical use only. Strategically speaking, we're just a very fast sailed ship. Meaning we've got a full complement of rigging and sail-handlers on the weather deck as well. So, the only way we could clear the deck was to put the guns underneath.

"What we got out of that was a more commanding elevation for our naval rifles. But it also allowed us to bring a lot of the weight that was high up in the *Hartford* down in our design, thereby lowering the center of gravity."

"So, putting the broadside weapons on a lower deck also made the ship more stable."

"Exactly. But then, we didn't want to put our crew down in the bowels of the ship. So we had to put the crew quarters inboard on the gun deck. The only reason we were even able to consider doing that was because our broadside weapons are carronades. They're a lot shorter than cannons, and their carriages are wheeled so as to run back up inclined planes when they recoil."

"But that still wasn't enough, was it, sir?" Rik looked over the side at the noticeable slope that ran out from the rail down into the water. "So to get the rest of the room you needed for inboard crew berthing, you pushed your battery farther outboard by widening the beam of the gun deck."

Eddie nodded his approval. "Bravo Zulu, Mr. Bjelke."

"'Bravo Zulu?'"

Eddie smiled. "An up-time naval term. 'Well done.' Learned it from my mentor."

"Ah. That would be Admiral Simpson."

"The same. And so, yes, we widened the gun deck, which meant another change from the original *Hartford*. She had pretty much sheer sides, which is just what you'd want for a fast sloop. But when we designed the Quality I class, we realized that not only would adding that outward slope of the sides—or 'tumble home'—be a good thing to add in terms of deck width, but for stability in higher seas, thanks to how increased beam reduces roll."

Bjelke leaned out over the rail. His eyes followed the waterline from stem to stern. "Yes, these are the structural differences I saw, and at which I wondered. Thank you for explaining them, Commander." He pointed at the somewhat smaller steamship pulling past them at a distance of four hundred yards, her funnel smokeless, her sails wide and white in the wind. "I see the same design changes in the smaller ship—the Speed I class, I think?—but less pronounced."

Eddie nodded. "Yeah, we decided to keep her closer to the original lines of the sloop. So we put only one pivot gun on her, kept the tumble home shallower, and freeboard lower and the weather deck closer to the waterline. She sails sharper, faster, more responsively, and has three feet less draught."

"So better for sailing in shallows, up rivers, near reefs."

"Yes, and strategically speaking, our fastest ship. In a good breeze, she'll make eight knots, and she's rigged for a generous broad reach. Unless she's fully becalmed, she can make reasonable forward progress with wind from almost three-quarters of the compass, assuming she has the room to tack sharply."

"And yet you do not label her a steam-sloop, as was the ship that inspired her."

"You mean the *Kearsarge* from the Civil War?" Eddie shrugged. "Well, as I understand the Civil War nomenclature, if a ship had a fully covered gun deck, she wasn't a sloop. Even if she had a sloop's lines, she'd still be called frigate-built. Although frigate-built doesn't necessary imply a military ship."

Rik smiled ruefully. "I grew up on farms. Even though many of them were close to the water, I confess I do not have a mariner's vocabulary yet. I find these distinctions confusing. Because, if the reports I hear are true, you are not calling the other ship—the *Courser*, I believe?—a frigate, either."

"No, we're calling her class a 'destroyer' and the *Intrepid*'s class a 'cruiser.' As class names, they're not great solutions. But at least they're up-time terms that haven't been used to describe ships, yet, so they'll be distinctive and somewhat descriptive in terms of role. If you're familiar with the up-time history of those classes of ships, that is. But anything else we tried to come up with ran afoul of the labeling confusion that already results from the current lack of international naming conventions.

"In fact, 'frigate' would have been the most confusing label we could have settled on. Ever since down-time naval architects started doing research in the Grantville library, most of the shipyards of Europe have started building new designs, the straight-sterned frigate chief among them. So if we called our new steam-ships frigates, they'd routinely get confused with the new sailed vessels currently under construction throughout Europe."

Bjelke nodded attentively, but Eddie saw that his focus was now split between their conversation and something located aft of their current place at the rail. As soon as Eddie noticed Rik's apparent distraction, the young Norwegian moved his eyes, ever so slightly, upward over his superior's shoulder and toward the new item of interest.

Eddie turned and saw, back by the entrance to the companionway leading down to the officer's quarters, that his wife—and her "ladies," as Bjelke styled them—had emerged to stand on the deck in a tight cluster. They were not an uncommon sight topside, but they usually reserved their appearances for fine weather, not overcast skies. However, despite the mild wind freshening from out of the southeast, they were all dressed for cold weather, apparently. Or were they? Eddie squinted, saw no coats or shawls, which made him only more confused. *So why the hell do they have kerchiefs covering their heads? And all three of them, no less. Damn, I've never seen a lady of the aristocracy allow herself to look that, well, dowdy. And now they've all adopted the same frumpy look? What the heck is that abou—?*

"Commander, given the arrival of the ladies, perhaps it would be convenient for you if I were to take my leave?"

Eddie nodded. "Probably so. Tell my wife that she can"—and then a voice inside his head, the one that was partially schooled in the etiquette of this age, muttered, *No, Eddie, that won't do. Think how it will look, how it will seem.*

Damn, ship protocol was tricky, and yet was still kind of free-form in this era when navies weren't really navies just yet, and had protocols for some things, but not for others. For instance, take the simple desire to have his wife join him alone at the rail. He couldn't very well wave her over. That would be an obvious blow to her stature, and mark him as an indecorous boor, which would work against his accrual of respect as well. But if he sent Bjelke over to summon her, that would be like making the young Norwegian nobleman his valet and also be entirely too formal, to say nothing of downright stupid-looking. Yet, if Eddie left the rail to go over to Anne Cathrine, then it could be difficult to extricate themselves from the presence of their respective attendants—Bjelke and the ladies—if they didn't *all* know how to take a hint—

Eddie discovered that, for the first time since he had stepped on a deep water ship, he had a headache and an incipient sense of seasickness. Which he allowed, probably had nothing to do with the sea at all.

But Bjelke offered a slight bow to Eddie, and inquired, "Might I—with your compliments—inform the ladies and your wife that you are currently without any pressing duties? And that I would be happy to escort any and all of them wherever they might wish to go?"

And for the third time—*wasn't that some kind of spiritual sign, or something?*—Eddie felt a quick outrush of gratitude toward the young Norwegian. Bjelke's simple solution allowed the junior officer to decorously depart from his commander, greet the ladies, and inform them of the status of the ship's captain. Then Anne Cathrine could approach or not—with Bjelke and her ladies in tow or not—and this idiotic etiquette dance would be over and Eddie would have thus achieved the hardest nautical task of his day thus far: finding a way to converse with his wife, on deck and in private, for a scant few minutes.

Eddie nodded gratefully—hopefully not desperately—at Bjelke, who smiled and with a more pronounced bow, left to carry out his plan.

Which worked like a charm. He arrived at the ladies' group and presented himself. Cordial nods all around, a brief exchange, then he walked with Anne Cathrine halfway across the deck, and by some miracle of subtle body language, managed to successfully communicate to Eddie that he should meet them about halfway. Which done, effected a serene and stately rendezvous between man and wife as the crew watched through carefully averted eyes.

Bjelke nodded to both spouses and retraced his steps to the two remaining ladies. Eddie smiled at Anne Cathrine and as they walked back to the rail, the young American breathed a sign of relief. Another terrifying gauntlet had been run.

Chapter 15

St. Kilda archipelago, North Atlantic

Once they arrived at the rail, Anne Cathrine looked up at Eddie, face serious, but her eyes seemed to twinkle. "Hi," she said, not bothering to suppress the dimple that this use of Amideutsch quirked into being.

Commander Eddie Cantrell felt the protocol-induced queasiness in his stomach become a midair dance of happy butterflies. "Hi," he said. Or maybe he gushed: he wasn't really sure. He was never exactly sure of what came out of his mouth when he was around the singularly beautiful and stammer-worthy sex goddess that was his almost-seventeen-year-old wife.

But instead of indulging in any more of the small signs of endearment that they had evolved over the past year to communicate in a playful (or, better yet, racy!) secret banter when in somber and dignified social settings, Anne Cathrine bit her lower lip slightly. She looked out to sea, tugging fitfully at her head scarf. *What the hell is it with the head coverings, anyhow? It's nice weather, not really too windy, and—*

Anne Cathrine looked up at him again, smiling through a slight frown. "So, how did your find your first conversation with Henrik Bjelke?"

Eddie almost started at her tone: measured, serious, possibly concerned. "Um . . . fine."

"I am glad, Eddie. Very glad."

"You sound as if you were worried."

"About Bjelke? No, not particularly. I very much doubt you have to worry about him. He is still an outsider at the Danish court, and too young to threaten you. Much."

"'Much?'" Eddie echoed. He hoped it hadn't come out as a surprised squeak.

Anne Cathrine turned very serious now, her very blue eyes upon him. "Dear Eddie, although this is a USE mission, conceived by the leaders of Grantville and given royal imprimatur by Gustav of Sweden, the majority of your commanders are Danish." She smiled. "Or hadn't you noticed?"

He grinned back. "Nope. Completely slipped past me. Past Admiral Simpson, too."

She lifted an eyebrow, curled a lip in a slow smile that Eddie associated with other places, other exchanges—*down, Eddie! down, boy!* Then she was looking out to sea, again. "Joking aside, Eddie, there are ambitious men in this flotilla, men whose personal interests may not be well-served if you are *too* successful."

"Me—successful? Wait a minute, it's not like I'm in charge of the flotilla. Heck, I'm something like the third rung down on the command ladder. Maybe less. It's hard to know how rank would play against nobility in this kind of situation. So it's not as if the success or failure of this mission is *mine*."

"Now it is you who must 'wait a minute,' Eddie. You may not have the highest rank, but everyone in every ship—and back home—knows this mission to the New World was your idea. Yours. Admiral Simpson was intent on going to the New World, yes. Such plans were already afoot, yes. But it was you put forward the idea of making it a reconnaissance and a ruse all bound into one mission. If this stratagem works, you will receive credit as its architect. At the very least."

Eddie scratched the back of his head, remembered that gesture probably didn't radiate a dignified command presence, and snatched his hand back down to his side. "Yeah. Well. Okay. So who are all these Danish guys with hidden agendas?"

"First, my love, they might *not* have hidden agendas. That is the problem with hidden agendas: that they might or might not be there at all. Wouldn't you agree?"

"Well, sure."

"Excellent. So now, who first? Well, the commander of the task force, for one."

"Admiral Mund? He seems, um, barely communicative."

"And so he is, but that does not mean he is without ambition. He is a minor noble, although he does not flaunt his title. Which is probably just as well."

"Why?"

"Because he was granted a tract on Iceland." Anne Cathrine shivered. "It is not a very nice place to be a landholding noble."

"You mean, sort of like the Faroes?"

"Hush, Eddie! You must know that Father did not give you that land for any reason other than to furnish you with the highest title he might within the nobility of Denmark. And, I suspect, as an entrée to greater things."

"So I've suspected, also." He crossed his fingers, offered silent thanks to John Chandler Simpson.

She looked at him. "Then you are indeed learning the ways of these times, Eddie. Which is necessary, I am afraid. Now, the person you must be most careful of is Hannibal Sehested."

"You mean the guy who displaced the captain from his cabin on the *Patentia*? I met him at court, just this spring. Seems like a nice enough guy. Shrewd, though."

"He always has been a nice enough fellow in his behavior toward me, too, Eddie. But he is also, as you observe, shrewd, and history showed that he was shrewd enough to advance his fortunes in your up-time history's Danish government. Even though he made himself an enemy of the man who was to become its most influential member, Corfitz Ulfeldt."

"The guy who was a traitor, up-time?"

"Yes, the man who was to betray my father. And who would have married my sister Leonora in just over a year." Again, she looked over her shoulder at the shorter of her two "ladies," but this time the glance was both protective and melancholy. "Corfitz was already betrothed to her, you know. Had been since 1630."

"But...but she was only nine years old!"

Anne Cathrine nodded gravely. "Eight, actually. And here you see the fate of the daughters of kings who are not also full princesses. We are objects of exchange, no less than we are objects of Father's genuine love. He arranges marriages that ensure the nation of secure bonds between the king and his nobles, since familial ties to the throne are craved above all things by men of that class. And if, thanks to those ties between crown and *Riksradet*, we all live in a time of domestic harmony, prosperity, and peace, then would we king's daughters not be ungrateful if we failed to consider ourselves 'happy'?"

Eddie mulled that over. "That's what I call taking one for the team. And doing so for the rest of your life."

"If by that you mean it is a sacrifice, well—I think so, too. Although many thought me ungrateful for feeling that way."

"Well, they can go straight to—okay, I know that look: I'll calm down." *Hmmm: calming down—that reminds me.* Eddie turned so his back was to Ove Gjedde. "So, while we're dragging out the dirt on the Danish upper crust, tell me: what do you know about Captain Gjedde? He's the one guy that the admiral and I couldn't find anything useful about. Seems he led the expedition to set up your trade with India, but after that, not much."

Anne Cathrine frowned. "I am sad to say that I do not know much more of him than that. I do know that Father respects him, but—well, Captain Gjedde is not an exciting man. As you have remarked to me several times on our journey thus far. And he is still recovering from wounds he suffered in the Baltic War. From fighting against your Admiral Simpson's timberclads, if I recall correctly."

Oh. Well. He must really be a big fan of up-timers, then. Particularly the ones who had a direct hand in blasting his ship to matchsticks...

Evidently, Anne Cathrine could read the expression on his face or was displaying an increasing talent for honest-to-God telepathy. "No, I do not think his reticence is caused by your being an American. He is more mature than that, and has seen his share of war. Like many older military men, he does not confuse the actions of following a king's order with the will of the men who must carry it out."

"Yeah, he looks old enough to have achieved that kind of perspective. What is he? Sixty, sixty-five years old?"

Anne Cathrine looked somber. "Forty-one."

"What?"

"He was always a somber, old-looking man, but his wounds from the Baltic—they drained him. He has not been at court since he suffered them, last year. But then again, he was never much at court.

He doesn't enjoy it. And while Father respects his abilities, Captain Gjedde is not the kind of man that he takes a personal interest in. The captain excels at navigation and can predict the weather like a wizard from the old sagas. But he does it all quietly, calmly. Not the type of man to capture Father's often mercurial imagination."

"Not like young Lord Bjelke."

"No, indeed. And of course, Father's interest in Bjelke is also self-protective."

"How do you mean?"

"I mean that Henrik Bjelke was, historically, not always a supporter of my father or his policies. He could yet prove quite dangerous, I suppose."

"Really? Jeez, Rik seems like a pretty good guy, actually."

"Yes, Father thinks that as well. He just wants to make sure that history does not repeat itself. And so he has involved Lord Bjelke in his plans for the New World." She looked over her shapely, and surprisingly broad, shoulder to where Henrik was escorting the ladies on what promised to be a quick looping promenade to the taffrail and back to the companionway. "In fact, I think Father put him aboard for a very special purpose."

"You mean, to watch me."

Anne Cathrine's eyes went back up to Eddie's and he felt wonder, appreciation, and perhaps the tiniest bit of sadness in them. "Ah, you are becoming adept at our down-timer machinations, Eddie—or at least, at perceiving them. Which, as I said, is a positive thing. But still, even so, I hope you will always be—I mean, I hope it won't make you—"

"Jaded? Subtle? Snakelike in my new and sinister cunning?"

Anne Cathrine tried to keep a straight face but couldn't. She laughed softly and swayed against his arm for the briefest of contacts. "You—how do you say it?—you 'keep it real,' Eddie. For which I am grateful. And which is one of the many reasons I love you so. But let us be serious for one moment more. Young Lord Bjelke's history and eventual friendship with Corfitz Ulfeldt, in your world, caught my father's attention. So I believe he wants Henrik indebted to him, and yes, hopes to gain a loyal observer in the fleet, as well. But I think Papa has another purpose, as well."

"Which is?"

"Marriage."

"Marriage? Of Bjelke? To whom?"

Anne Cathrine looked over her shoulder again. "To Sophie Rantzau. Or maybe my sister." She frowned as she watched the two ladies in question finish their circuit of the stern. "I cannot tell."

"Huh," Eddie observed eloquently. "Huh. A military mission to the New World as a means of kindling a strategically shrewd shipboard romance? Your dad sure sees some odd opportunities in some odd places. Why not just play matchmaker at court, where he can meddle with the young lovers personally? Which, let's be honest, is one of his favorite pastimes."

Anne Cathrine smiled and swatted him lightly. "For which you should be very grateful, husband. Otherwise, where would we be today, had he not played the part of Cupid?"

"Where would we be? Well, let's see. I'd still be rotting in the dungeon with a crappy peg leg on my stump, and you'd be married to Lord Dinesen, or some other wealthy noble."

"Yes, who would no doubt be three times my weight and four times my age. So, I'm not sure which of our two fates would be more grim."

"Yeah, well, when you put it that way—"

"Trust me, dear husband, that would literally have been my fate. The marriage you helped me avoid when you were my father's prisoner wasn't simply a staged engagement. My wedding to Dinesen was a very real possibility."

"No. Your father would never have made you marry that—"

"Eddie, you keep mistaking what loving parents of your time consider wise actions, and what loving parents of my time consider wise actions. I am a king's daughter, and so almost a princess in stature within my own country. But much less so elsewhere, because in marrying me, a foreign throne will not have gained any formal influence—or potential of inheritance—in the lands of my family.

"And so I was not to be married off to a crown prince of one of the other courts of Europe, but wedded to a Danish nobleman. And who among those men had enough wealth and influence to be a *de facto* dowry for my hand?" Her face hardened. "Old, ambitious men, most of whom spent their whole lives counting their money, counting their estates, counting the ways in which they might move one step higher in the nasty little games of social climbing that are their favorite sport." Eddie thought she was going to spit over the side in disgust.

But instead she rounded on him, her eyes bright and unwavering.

"So you see, my darling Eddie, it is you who saved me, not the other way around." Her eyes searched his and he could almost feel heat coming out of them, and off of her. Her face and body were rigid with the intensity of passion that he loved to see, to feel, in her. When she got this way, she was just one moment away from grabbing and holding him fiercely, and what usually happened next—oh, what usually happened next!—

Didn't happen this time. Anne Cathrine seemed to remember her surroundings, looked away, readjusted her kerchief—*that damned kerchief! what the hell?*—and stared out to sea. She pointed at the *Courser*, now nearly two miles ahead of the *Intrepid* and widening the gap rapidly. "That is the smaller of your steamships, yes?"

Huh? She knows perfectly well that it is. But all he said was, "Yes, Anne Cathrine. That's our destroyer."

"A fierce name," she said with a tight, approving nod. "And that one gun in the middle of its deck, sitting in its own little castle, is the most dangerous of them all?"

He smiled. "That little castle is what we call a 'tub mount.' The round, rib-high wall protects the gun crew from enemy fire, shrapnel, fragments. As does the sloped gun shield. The rifle can bear through two hundred seventy degrees and fire several different kinds of shells to very great ranges."

"It is the same as these guns on your ship?" She pointed to the two naval rifles on the centerline of the *Intrepid*'s weather deck.

"Yes, but, umm...this isn't *my* ship, sweetheart. It's—"

"Yes, I know. It's Gjeddes'. But he has let you run it, with the exception of the sail-handling, since we left the dock."

Eddie shrugged. There was no arguing with the truth.

Anne Cathrine was pointing over the bow. "And that sail up ahead, that is the Dutch-built yacht?"

"Yes, the *Crown of Waves*. A good ship. She's out ahead of us as a picket."

"I thought you have provided us with balloons to look far ahead, so that pickets were no longer needed?"

He smiled. "Pickets are always needed, Anne Cathrine. Besides, we don't want to use the balloons if we don't need them, and if the winds get any stronger, an observer could get pretty roughed up, to say nothing of damage to the balloon itself."

"I see. And the other ship like your *Intrepid*—the *Resolve*—that's her, falling to the rear?"

"Yes."

She was silent for a long time. "Your ships are so big compared to ours. Even compared to the *Patentia*, the *Resolve* is easily half again as long and half again as high, except at the very rear. And still—"

"Yes?"

"Eddie, should your warships have so few guns? I know up-time-designed weapons are terribly powerful, but if they should fail to operate, or the enemy gets lucky shots into the gun deck—" She stopped, seeing his small smile.

"Trust me, Anne Cathrine, we have enough guns. More than enough. It's more important that our magazine is big enough to carry plenty of excellent ammunition to keep our excellent guns well supplied. Which is the case."

She nodded and turned her eyes to the ship lumbering along beside the *Patentia*. "Not a very handsome ship, the *Serendipity*."

Eddie let a little laugh slip out. "No, she's not much to look at." The *Serendipity* was a pot-bellied bulk hauler, with the lines of a bloated pink or fluyt. "But she's steady in a storm, and seven hundred fifty tons burthen. And we need that cargo capacity. So ugly or not, we're lucky to have her."

"Not as lucky as to have the *Tropic Surveyor*," countered Anne Cathrine with an appreciative smile and a chin raised in the direction of the last ship of the flotilla.

And Eddie had to admit that *Tropic Surveyor* was a handsome ship, her square-rigged fore- and mainmasts running with their sheets full. The large, three-masted bark had a fore-and-aft rigged mizzen and twelve almost uniform guns in each broadside battery. Her lines were unusually clean, reflecting the first influence of frigate-built designs upon traditional barks. Her master, a Swede by the name of Stiernsköld, was known to be a highly capable captain who, if he had any failing, tended toward quiet but determined boldness.

Anne Cathrine's attention had drifted back to the *Patentia*, however. "What are all those men doing on deck, and who are they?"

Eddie glanced over; he saw a growing number of men at the portside gunwales of the *Patentia*, many pointing at the island peaks to the south, some nodding, some shaking their heads. Eddie smiled. "Those are the Irish soldiers who came up from the Infanta Isabella of the Lowlands."

Anne Cathrine frowned. "I still do not understand how mercenaries who have been in Spanish service for generations—"

Eddie shook his head. "I don't understand it either. Not entirely." *And what little I* do *understand I can't share, honey. Sorry.*

"Do you at least know why they are on deck there—and look, more of them are gathering at the rail of the *Serendipity*! What are they *looking* at?"

The voice that answered was gravel-filtered and deep. "They think they are seeing their homeland."

Eddie and Anne Cathrine turned. Ove Gjedde was behind them, his eyes invisible in the squinting-folds of his weathered face. Neither had heard him approach.

"Their homeland?" Anne Cathrine repeated.

"Yes, my lady. Because the last week's wind has been fair, there has been some loose talk that we might sight the north Irish coast late today." He sucked at yellowed teeth. "That will not happen until tomorrow, sometime. But I am told that the Irish got word of these rumors. And as you may know, most of them have never seen Ireland, but were born in the Lowlands. Their eagerness is understandable." Gjedde made to move off once again.

Eddie offered a smart salute. "Thank you, Captain."

Gjedde returned a slight nod that was the down-time equivalent of a salute between officers of comparable rank, made a slightly deeper nod in Anne Cathrine's direction, and began slowly pacing forward along the starboard railing, hands behind his back.

Anne Cathrine stared after him. "He did not return the new naval salute, as per your admiral's regulations."

"But he does follow the rest of the regs. To the letter."

Anne Cathrine watched the spare man move away. "Captain Gjedde seems to grow more somber every time I meet him."

Eddie shifted his eyes sideways to his wife. "While we're on the topic of 'more somber'..."

Anne Cathrine glanced at him quickly, fiddled with her kerchief and tucked a stray strand of gold-red hair back under it. "I do not know what you mean."

"Sure you don't." If they had been alone, he would have put an arm around her waist and pulled her closer. "C'mon, Anne Cathrine, what gives? You're acting... oddly."

"I am not." At that particular moment she did not sound like her usual sixteen going on thirty-six. She just sounded like she was six.

Eddie smiled. "Uh, yes, you are. And what's with the head covering?"

Her hands flew up to her kerchief and she stepped away from him quickly. "Why? Has it come undone?" Satisfied that it was still firmly in place, she raised her chin and looked away. "There is nothing wrong. Nothing."

Huh. So there *was* a connection between his wife's hinky behavior and the kerchief. "Anne Cathrine, honey, don't worry. Tell me what's going on. Let me help."

She looked at him, her eyes suddenly glassy and bright, then glanced away quickly.

What? Has she lost most of her hair? Fallen victim to some strange depilatory disease particular to the high seas of the northern latitudes? "Anne Cathrine, whatever it is, it's going to be all right. Just tell me and—"

"Oh, Eddie—" She turned back to him and, oblivious to onlookers, cast herself into his arms. "I'm sorry—so sorry."

"Sorry? About what?" He tried to ignore the fact that even through his deck coat and her garments, he could still feel his wife's very voluptuous and strong body along the length of his own. And in accordance with the orders given by the supreme authority of his ancient mammalian hindbrain, certain parts of him were taking notice and coming to general quarters. Well, more like standing at attention...

"Oh, Eddie, my hair! I should have seen to my packing, my preparations, myself. But in the rush to get everything aboard, and with all the last-minute changes—"

"What? Have you lost your hair? That's okay; we can—"

She pulled away from him. "Lost my hair?" She pulled herself erect. She might not have the title of a full princess, but she could sure put on a convincing show of being one. "Certainly not. But I—I neglected to oversee my servant's preparations. And now I, I..." She looked down at the deck, then reached up and tugged her kerchief sharply.

Eddie was prepared for anything: baldness, scrofulous patches, running sores, dandruff the size of postage stamps, medusan snakes—anything. Except for what was revealed.

Anne Cathrine's red hair came uncoiling from the bulky kerchief in a long, silk-shining wave that came down to the middle of her back. Eddie couldn't help himself: he gasped.

Seeing his expression, Anne Cathrine pouted. Her lower lip even quivered slightly. "I knew it."

"Knew what?" Eddie heard himself say. He was still busy staring at his wife's hair and trying to tell his lower jaw to raise and lock in place.

"Knew that you would be aghast to see my hair like this, without the curls. Oh, I tried, Eddie, I did. My servant forgot to pack the heating combs, and neither I nor Leonora—nor Sophie—know how to do our hair any other way. Commoners can make curls with wet rags, I'm told, so we tried that, but none of us did our own hair often." *Or at all*, Eddie added silently, now quite familiar with coiffuring dependencies of noble ladies. "I have been trying since we left to keep some curl in it, or at least a wave, but this morning, we all agreed there was nothing left to try."

"It's beautiful," Eddie croaked.

Her smile looked broken. "You are a wonderful husband, to say that. But you can barely speak the words. I know the expectations of fashion, Eddie. And here you see the truth at last: I have straight, plain hair. No tumbling curls, not even a tiny ripple of a wave. Plain, straight hair."

He reached out and touched it. "Hair like fire and gold spun into silk," he breathed. "And in my time, that kind of hair was very much in fashion. Hell, I didn't think hair like this was ever *out* of fashion."

She blinked. "So—you like it? You like my hair this way?"

Eddie gulped. "Oh, yes. I like it. Very much. Very, very much." He roused himself out of his pre-carnal stupor. "But know this, Anne Cathrine, the hair is not important to me. What's *under* it is." He touched her cheek. "As important as the wide world."

Anne Cathrine's smile—shockingly white teeth—was sudden and wide. She caught his hand on her cheek and held it there. "Truly," she said, "I am the luckiest woman in the world."

"And a princess, to boot," Eddie added with a grin.

"A king's daughter," she corrected, and moved toward him again—

"Sail, sail on the port bow! Rounding the rocks, sirs. She's running before the wind!"

Chapter 16

St. Kilda archipelago, North Atlantic

Eddie transferred Anne Cathrine's hands from him to the rail—"Hold on, Anne Cathrine, and be ready to take the ladies below"—and made for the stairs to the observation deck atop the pilot house. "Orderly?"

"Yes, sir?"

"Glasses topside, please. And call Mr. Bjelke back on deck. Smartly."

"Yes, sir!" The response was already dwindling aft.

As Eddie made his way up the stairs—*damnit, can't this leg go any faster?*—he heard Gjedde's voice behind him. "No point in breaking your neck, Commander. Things do not happen quite so quickly in this century."

As Eddie thumped his prosthetic down upon the observation deck—another change from the *Hartford*—he turned to offer a smile to the older captain, whose mouth looked a little less rigid than usual. It might have even had a faint upward curl at one side. If he hadn't spent so much time with Simpson, he might have completely missed that hint of a smile. *So, Gjedde doesn't* hate *me. Either that, or he's hoping I'll get offed in the next hour or so . . .*

Eddie went straight to the speaking tubes, popped back the covers, and toggled the telegraphic command circuit. "Circuit test," he shouted.

"Tests clear," came the muffled shout from under his feet where the intraship telegrapher was stationed.

The orderly bounded up the stairs, passing a new-pattern spyglass to Gjedde, and holding a case out toward Eddie, who snapped it open and lifted out the precious up-time binoculars. The signalman hustled past with a hastily muttered *"Verlot!"* and was immediately ready, pad to his right, left index finger poised on the telegrapher's key. "Comms manned, Captain Gjedde."

Gjedde shook his head. "You will make your reports to, and take your orders from, Commander Cantrell. He will direct this ship through her first combat."

Eddie turned, stunned, "What?"

Gjedde bowed. "Your command, Mr. Cantrell. Compliments of your father-in-law, Christian IV."

Why that old son of a— "Then Captain Gjedde, I say three times: I have the bridge. What's the word from the foretop crow's nest? What manner of ship, flying what colors?"

After a pause, the report came back. "A carrack sir. Old design. Spanish colors."

Spanish colors? Up here? What the hell were they—?

Apparently, telepathy was a strong trait in the Danish; now it was Gjedde who seemed to read his mind. "Not so unusual. They supply the Irish with guns and powder, from time to time. Sometimes the Scots, too. There is no shortage of rebels against English occupiers up here, and Spain is only too happy to provide them with assistance."

Eddie nodded. "I understand, but why ever they happen to be here, it seems that they've seen us. They ran between *Crown of Waves* and *Courser* like they were waiting for that opening. I suspect they saw our smoke, peeked around the northwestern point of Hirta—at Gob a Ghaill—saw our flotilla, measured the breeze, and realized their only way to avoid us was to run before the wind after our advance picket had passed them, but before our main van drew too close."

Gjedde nodded, the visible slivers of his eyes sharp. *"Ja,* that is how I see it, also."

"Very well. Signalman, relay this to intership telegrapher for immediate send. 'To Admiral Mund aboard *Resolve.* Message starts: Have spotted—"

"Sir," said the radioman, "incoming message from Admiral Mund."

Well, speak of the devil—"Read it as you get it, Rating."

"Admiral Mund commanding *Resolve* to Commander Cantrell, presumed to be in temporary command of *Intrepid*. Message begins: By joint order of Emperor Gustav Adolf and His Royal Highness Christian IV, I relinquish operational command of Reconnaissance Flotilla X-Ray to you for duration of first engagement. Stop. Awaiting instructions. Stop."

Oh, so all *the heads of state are seeing if I have the goods when the shit starts flying. Well, no reason not to give them a good show*—"Radioman, send the following under my command line. To Admiral Mund, on *Resolve*: message received and acknowledged. Stop. To all ships: general quarters. Stop." He turned to see Bjelke pound up the stairs to the observation deck. Eddie gave him an order and a welcoming nod in the same instant: "Sound general quarters, Mr. Bjelke. Orderly, make sure our passengers understand that 'general quarters' means 'battle stations.' Only duty personnel on deck."

"And if they don't understand that, sir?"

"Then correct their misunderstanding. With main force, if necessary. No exceptions. Including my wife. Especially my wife. Is that clear, mister?"

"Very clear, *ja*, sir!" And again the young orderly was off, with a rising tide of coronets and drums carrying him on his way.

Bjelke returned to his side. Gjedde watched from the rear rail of the observation deck. Eddie thought for a moment, then turned to the signalman, "Forward mount, get me range, bearing, and speed of the Spaniard. Then send to *Crown of Waves* and *Courser*: I need their precise heading and speed."

"What are you thinking, Commander?" asked Bjelke.

"That whatever the Spanish do or do not understand from having seen us, we can't let them escape and report. Just knowing that a flotilla of USE ships is on a course that would suggest a New World destination is bad enough. Anything else could be disastrous. They might have seen the smoke and presumed that one of our ships was on fire, or that we have whalers with us who were putting blubber through some of the new shipboard try-works. But someone with better information on the USE's activities is likely to figure that this carrack spotted our steam warships. Word of this encounter can not—*not*—reach people with that kind of knowledge."

The radioman called out. "All messages acknowledged, except *Crown of Waves*. I think something is wrong with her radio-set, sir. Lots of lost characters. And they seem to be losing some of ours, too."

Well, now *it's a real military engagement: we've got commo snafus.* So without the radio—"Send to *Courser*: Radio on *Crown of Waves* inoperable. Stop. Your position gives best line of sight and shortest range. Stop. Relay command signals to *Crown of Waves* via semaphore and aldriss lamp. Stop. End of Message. New message to *Resolve* starts. Drop to rear of formation. Stop. Remain at one mile distance. Stop. Deploy balloon ASAP. Stop. Maintain close rear watch. Stop. Message ends."

Bjelke's left eyebrow raised. "Rear watch, sir? A trap? Up here?"

"Traps are most effective where they're least expected, wouldn't you agree, Lieutenant Bjelke?"

"Aye, sir."

"So we eliminate that admittedly slim possibility first, then take the next steps."

Gjedde folded his arms. "And what steps are those?"

"To box the Spaniard in. Radioman?"

"Just received acknowledgment from *Courser* now. Captain Haraldsen passes along word that Major Lawrence Quinn sends his compliments and will oversee technical coordination on that hull."

Eddie felt his heart rate diminish slightly. It was good to know the other—the only other—military up-timer in the flotilla was out there, lending a hand. The down-timers were competent, eager, and obedient, but sometimes, they just didn't get how all the parts of a steam-and-sail navy worked together. In all probability, the most important test during this shakedown cruise would not be of Simpson's new ships, but of the crews of his new navy. "Send Major Quinn my greetings and thanks. And have him relay this to the *Crown of Waves*: set course north by northwest, paralleling the Spaniard. Course for the *Courser*, the same."

"Speed, sir?"

"What God and sail-handlers will allow, radioman. We are not raising steam."

Bjelke made a sound of surprise. Eddie turned to look at him. "You can speak freely, Rik."

"Sir, I thought combat was exactly the time when you *would* order steam. Is that not one of the main purposes of this cruise, to see how the steam ships fare in actual combat, under power?"

"Normally, yes, but this time, I'm worried about detection. If this ship is not alone then, trap or no trap, raising steam means sending a message to any and all of the rest of an enemy formation about where and *what* we are."

The radioman cleared his throat politely. "Message from *Resolve*, Commander."

"What does Admiral Mund have to say?"

"Sir, he points out that in order to deploy the balloon, he will have to clear his stern of canvas. And if he does so, if he slacks the sails on the mizzen and swings wide the yard to clear the deck for air operations, he will slow down and fall further behind."

"Send that this is not an operational concern. He'll still have better speed than either *Patentia* and *Serendipity*, whom he must remain behind and protect. More importantly, please remind him that decreasing his ship's speed makes it a better platform for the balloon. When you're done sending that, send to the *Serendipity* and *Patentia* that they are to crowd sail. I don't want them lagging behind too far, and stretching out our formation. And have the *Tropic Surveyor* close on us as she is able, crossing our wake when we clear Gob a Ghiall."

"Aye, sir. Sending now."

Bjelke frowned. "You want the bark to the south of us, closer to the island?"

"Absolutely, Lieutenant. Because if the enemy has more ships behind that headland, I want to give them something to deal with while we bring round our rifles and teach them just how long our reach is."

Gjedde may have nodded. "And so, what will *Intrepid* be doing?"

Eddie smiled and, by way of answer, waved Svantner over. "Lieutenant, do we have solutions for range, bearing, and speed of the Spaniard?"

"Yes, sir. Mount One has rechecked first findings and confirms the following with highest confidence: the Spaniard is now just under a mile off, making two and a half knots and heading north by northwest true."

"*Crown of Waves* and *Courser*?"

"Now on parallel courses with the Spaniard, sir. *Crown* is making three knots and a bit, *Courser* is almost at six."

Eddie made a mental map plot. The Spanish carrack was in a tight spot. If she turned to either port or starboard, she'd be turning into the paths of faster, better-armed ships, and losing the wind in doing so. And since the ships boxing her in—*Crown of Waves* to the south, *Courser* to the north—could sail closer hauled and faster, their speed and maneuverability would be even less affected if they made a matching course change. He had the Spaniard straitjacketed. Now to shorten the chase—

"And our speed, Mr. Svantner?

"Five knots, sir. We can make a bit more if we steer a half point to port, and put the wind just abaft the starboard beam."

"Do so, but keep me out of a direct stern chase. I don't want to shrink the target profile."

"Sir?"

"I don't want to have to shoot straight up that Spaniard's narrow ass; I want a little more of his side to aim at."

"Aye, aye, sir!"

"Mr. Bjelke, send the word to Mount One: stand ready."

"At once, Commander!"

Gjedde unfolded his arms as Bjelke hurried down the stairs. "About fifteen minutes then."

Eddie turned. "I beg your pardon, Captain?"

"Fifteen minutes before you start firing. The range will have dropped to under half a mile, by then."

Eddie smiled. "Less."

Gjedde narrowed his eyes. "How?"

Eddie felt his smile widen. "I would be delighted to demonstrate, sir."

Gjedde crossed his arms again and frowned. "Please do."

Eddie gave a partial salute and turned to his First Mate. "Mr. Svantner, has the Spaniard reacted to our course change yet?"

"A bit, sir. She shifted course slightly to the north, keeping us at distance."

"But closing on the *Courser*, yes?"

"A bit sir, yes."

"Then send to *Courser*: change heading one point to port. Full sheets on the spencer masts. Give that Spaniard a reason to run the other way."

"Aye, sir."

Eddie turned—and caught Gjedde smiling. His face became

stony in an instant. "So. You'll scare him into tacking. Each turn of which costs him time and momentum."

Eddie shrugged. "It's what you taught me, second day on ship. Seems like the right plan, here."

Gjedde nodded. "Seems so."

The radioman uttered a confused grunt, checked an incoming message a second time. "Sir, signal from the *Courser*. But it doesn't make sense."

"Read it, radioman."

"From Major Quinn, technical advisor aboard *Courser*, to Commander Cantrell on *Intrepid*. Stop. Regarding course change. Stop. Aye, aye, Commander...Hornblower?" The radioman's voice had raised to an almost adolescent squeak. "Stop. Message ends. Sir, is Commander 'Hornblower' code, sir?"

Eddie smiled. "In a manner of speaking, rating. In a manner of speaking. Svantner?"

"Yes sir?"

"Tell me when that Spaniard starts to come around to port. As soon as he does, we'll crowd him from the south with the *Crown*."

Eddie checked his watch. *And in about ten minutes, we'll end the chase. For good.*

Nine minutes later, Commander Eddie Cantrell called for the range.

After a moment's delay, the intraship communications officer piped up, "Seven hundred yards, sir."

"Mount One, acquire the target."

The intraship piped up so quickly that Eddie suspected he was in constant conversation with the mount's commanding officer. "Acquiring, sir!"

"Send word to load with solid shot."

"Aye, sir." A pause. "Gunnery officer requests confirmation on that last order: *solid* shot?"

"Solid shot. Tell him we're not going to waste an explosive shell until we have a proven targeting solution."

"Solid shot, aye, sir. And Mount One reports a firing solution. Range now six-hundred-fifty yards."

Perfect. "Fire one round and continue tracking. Svantner, reef sails."

The wire-wound eight-inch naval rifle roared and flew back in its recoil carriage, smoke gouting out its barrel as a long, sustained plume. A moment later, a geyser of water shot up about thirty yards off the Spaniard's port quarter.

Eddie raised his glasses. He could see arms waving frantically on the deck of the carrack. While the Spanish had no idea exactly what kind of gun was shooting at them, it was a certainty that they knew it was like no gun they'd ever encountered before. And that it was also far more deadly.

"Reload," Eddie ordered as he felt the *Intrepid*'s forward progress diminish, its sails retracting upward, "and adjust. Watch the inclinometer."

From where he stood, Eddie could observe the gun's crew go into its routine like one well-oiled machine in service of another. The handle on the back of the gun was given a hard half turn and the interrupted-screw breech swung open, vapors coiling out and around the crew. The cry of "swab out!" brought forward a man holding what looked like, at this range, a gargantuan Q-tip. He ran it into and around the interior, ensuring no embers or sparks remained to predetonate the next charge. Meanwhile, a half-hoist brought up the next shell—akin to a short, somewhat pointed bullet eight inches at the base and sixteen inches long—and the loaders swung it out of the cradle and into the breech, where another man promptly pushed it in until it was snug. Powder bags were loaded in next and then the breech was sealed while the second gunner inserted a primer in the weapon's percussion lock.

"Loaded!"

"Primed! Hammer cocked and locked."

"New firing solution," called out the chief gunner. "Right two, up one!"

The second gunner hunkered down; he made a slight adjustment to a small vertical wheel on the side of the mount, and another to a small horizontal wheel. "Acquired!"

The intraship pipe at Eddie's elbow announced, "Mount One reports ready, Commander."

"At the discretion of the gunnery officer,"—*watch the inclinometer more closely!*—"fire."

There was a pause while the gunnery officer studied the levels that indicated roll, pitch, and yaw, and then he shouted, "Fire!"

The second gunner pulled the lanyard, and the long black tube roared again.

Eddie saw the shot go into the water only ten yards in front of the carrack's bow. And he also realized why the gunnery officer was always a fraction off on measuring the roll: because from his position on the deck, he could not watch the sea close to the *Intrepid*. Standing only seven feet higher, Eddie had a much better view. He could keep an eye on the inclinometer even as he read the proximal swells and troughs.

One of which was coming. The *Intrepid* came off the crest of a two-foot riser, slid down into a long trough—and Eddie knew the inclinometer was going to be perfectly level the moment before it was.

"Fire!" he yelled forward over the weather deck at the same moment that the inclinometer showed level.

The eight-inch rifle spoke a third time as Eddie jerked the binoculars back up to his eyes—

—Just in time to see the shell tear into the carrack, just aft of its bow on the starboard side. Planks and dusty smoke flew up and outward—and, puzzlingly, from the portside bow as well. Which, Eddie realized an instant later, had been caused by the round exiting the hull on the other side.

The Spanish ship reeled, first to port, then tottered back to starboard, the bow digging into the swells heavily. She wasn't taking water, but it was possible that her stem—the extension of the keel up into the curve of the prow—had been damaged and her forecastle was starting to collapse, riven by the tremendous force of the shell. As the smoke began to clear and the human damage was revealed—bodies scattered around the impact point, others hobbling away, several bobbing motionless in the cold northern waters—Eddie barked out his next order through a tightening throat. "Load explosive shell. Maintain tracking."

He waited through the thirty seconds of reloading. The *Intrepid* was now moving slowly, so her position was barely changing. And the carrack, which had already lost a great deal of her headway by being forced to tack back and forth in response to the harrying ships to either side, had been moving at barely one and a half knots before she was hit. And now, with her bow damaged and her crew panicking—

"Mount One reports ready."

Eddie kept his eyes just far enough from the binoculars to watch the inclinometer. "Fire," he ordered calmly.

Perhaps he had become so used to the sound and buffeting of

the big guns that he didn't notice it. Or perhaps he was simply too fixated on the fate of the ship that he was about to kill. Either way, he could not afterwards remember hearing the report of his own gun. Instead, burned into his memory, in slow motion, was the impact of the shell upon the carrack.

There was a split-second precursor: a light puff of what looked like dust. That was the shell, slicing through the starboard corner of the stern so swiftly that it was inside the vessel's poop before the shock waves sent rail, transom, and deck planks flying in a wide, wild sphere of destruction.

But in the next blink of an eye, that was all wiped away by the titanic explosion that blasted out from the guts of the ship itself. The poop deck literally went up in a single piece, discorporating as it rose, bodies shooting toward the heaven that Eddie hoped was there to receive them. The mainmast, the rearmost on the two-masted carrack, went crashing forward, tearing the rigging down with her and stripping the yard clean off the foremast. Black smoke and flames spun up out of the jagged hole that had been the ship's stern, and the men on her decks were a moving arabesque of confused action. Some were trying to fight the fires, others were making for the rail, others were trying to give orders, several were trying to get her dinghy over to the port side. None of them were achieving their objective.

"Check fire," Eddie croaked. "Crowd sails and move to assist."

Ove Gjedde, as still and silent as a forgotten statue, now reanimated. Suddenly at Eddie's elbow, he asked, "Commander, you are planning to assist?"

Eddie stared at the men who were now in the water. Their cries were audible even at this distance. He nodded. "We have to."

Gjedde made a strangely constricted noise deep in his throat. "Commander, I do not wish to intrude upon your prerogatives—"

The radioman looked up. "Commander, message from *Resolve*. Coded urgent, sir."

"Read it, please."

"Aye, sir. Message begins. Admiral Mund of *Resolve* to Commander Cantrell of *Intrepid*. Stop. Balloon at three hundred feet has spotted three, possibly four ships fifteen miles south of Gob a Ghaill headland. Stop. Heading is due north. Stop. Currently making slightly less than three knots. Stop. Awaiting instructions. Stop. Message ends.'"

Eddie could sense Gjedde standing uncommonly close to him. *He wants me to break off, but that isn't right. We can save those men.* "Send this reply, my command line. Message starts: to Admiral Mund, *Resolve*. Stop. Lead flotilla north by northwest on heading parallel to *Crown of Waves* and *Courser*. Stop. *Intrepid* will effect rescue operations and follow all haste. Stop. Secure balloon immediately to minimize possibility of enemy sighting it. Stop. Message ends."

Gjedde was frowning. For some reason, Eddie imagined himself as Bilbo Baggins at one of those moments when he had pissed off Gandalf mightily. Avuncular Gjedde continued to stare at him, seemed to be weighing his next choice of words very carefully.

Finally he began, "Commander, this is not wise. I must point out—"

"Commander Cantrell," the radioman muttered, "another message from *Resolve*. Again, coded urgent."

Eddie held up a hand to pause Gjedde, nodded at the radioman. "Go ahead."

"Message starts. CO *Resolve* to acting CO *Intrepid*. Stop. First action is concluded. Stop. Command changes are now terminated. Stop. Secure from general quarters. Stop. Captain Gjedde resumes direct command immediately. Stop. Rescue operations hereby countermanded. Stop. Flotilla X-Ray immediately heads north by northwest true, at best speed of slowest ship. Stop. Compliments to Commander Cantrell for successful first engagement. Stop. Message ends."

Eddie was still watching the men struggling in the chill gray waters, saw that some of them seemed to be weakening already. Those who had been clustered around the dinghy got it into the water, where it promptly foundered. Probably some splinter or shrapnel had punched a hole in it and they had not noticed that damage in their frenzied attempt to escape their ship. Which was a prudent course of action: the carrack, her stern savaged as if some kraken of the deep had taken a vicious bite out of it, was settling back upon her rudder, and listing slightly to starboard. At the rate she was going down, her decks would be awash within the hour. And her crew—

Gjedde put a hand on Eddie's arm, drew it and the binoculars it held down slowly. "There is nothing to be done, Commander. If we stayed to rescue those men, the Spanish would see us before we could get away again. We must break off now, at best speed, to remain undetected. You must know this."

Eddie didn't want to know it, but he did. "Perhaps they'll be picked up by the Spanish then."

Gjedde didn't blink. "You know better than that, too, Commander. They may see the smoke or they may not. If they do not, it is unlikely they would come close enough to see wreckage or hear cries for help. And even if they do, it will be fifteen hours from now. There will be no one for them to rescue and few enough bodies to see, should they chance to come so close to the site of our engagement."

Eddie looked over the bow. Only three hundred yards away, now, the Spanish were struggling in the water, and the first were already losing the battle to stay above the cold gray swells of the North Sea. He nodded. "Aye, aye, sir. You're the captain."

Gjedde's eyes fell from Eddie's. Suddenly, he looked even older. Then he turned on his heel and began giving orders. "Mr. Bjelke, secure from general quarters and give orders to unload battery and personal weapons. I want no unnecessary or accidental discharges as we run from the Spanish. Pilot, set us north by northwest true. Mr. Svantner, pass it along to crowd all sail. There will be no rescue operations."

As the crew of the *Intrepid* scrambled to set about their duties, Eddie noticed that the *Tropic Surveyor,* which had been traveling under full sail the whole time, was drawing abreast of them. Lining the starboard gunwales were more of the Irish mercenaries, who peered ahead at the wreckage and the ruined carrack.

The Spanish, seeing the ships approach, called out for quarter, for aid, for mercy for the love of god.

As the *Intrepid* passed them at two hundred yards off the portside, their cries were half swallowed by the sound of the wavelets against the ship's hull.

But the *Tropic Surveyor* passed them at a distance of only one hundred yards to her starboard side. The Spanish cried out to the men lining her rail, perhaps seeing the facial features and even the tartans and equipage they associated with their traditional Irish allies.

But the Irish made no sound, and watched, without expression or, apparently, any pity, as more of the Spanish began to sink down deeper into the low rolling swells of the North Sea.

Chapter 17

East of St. Christopher, Caribbean

Through the salt spray and dusty rose of early dawn, Hugh Albert O'Donnell compared Michael McCarthy, Jr.'s pinched, weather-seamed eyes with Aodh O'Rourke's pale-lipped scowl. The latter, staring at the balloon as it swelled up and off the poop deck, muttered, "You'd not get me to swing 'neath that bag o' gas." Then Hugh's lieutenant of eight years nodded to the up-timer beside him. "No offense to your handiwork, Don Michael."

"Don" Michael—whom Hugh had convinced, at no small expense of effort, to accept the honorific—simply shrugged. "No offense taken. I'm not riding in it myself. That's for young Mulryan, here."

Mulryan, an apple-faced lad with an unruly shock of red hair, nodded. "An' it's not so bad, O'Rourke. After the fourth or fifth time, yeh forget the height. Seems natural, 't does."

"To you, maybe," O'Rourke grumbled, and then moved aside as feet thumped up the stairs from the weather deck behind him.

Hugh swayed up from his easy seat on the taffrail as Captain Paul Morraine rose into view. He was followed by a taller, thinner man whose arrival resulted in an almost uniform hardening of expressions and veiling of eyes: Morraine's immediate subordinate, First Mate George St. Georges, was not a favorite with the Irish, nor with his own crew. Only Michael's expression remained unaltered. The two senior officers of the *Fleur Sable* joined the group just as McGillicuddy, chief of the balloon's ground crew, set his legs firm and wide to help his men tug on the guidelines. Straining together, they drew more of the swelling envelope up toward them and away from the mizzenmast, the yard having been dropped to accommodate this process.

Morraine nodded at Hugh. "Lord O'Donnell."

Hugh nodded back. "You wish to have your mizzen back as soon as possible, Captain?"

The left corner of Morraine's mouth quirked. For him, this was the equivalent of a broad grin. "It is so obvious?"

Hugh smiled. "Well, yes. And sensible as well. But at a height of six hundred feet, we will see what lies before us and enter the channel between St. Christopher and St. Eustatia as fast and unseen as the wind that's rising behind us."

"Which I do not wish to miss, sir. Monsieur McCarthy tells me this is a swift procedure, yes?"

McCarthy shrugged, inspecting the billowing envelope. "It'll be aloft in fifteen minutes, up for ten, down in ten, deflated enough for you to remount your mizzenmast in another ten. So, forty-five minutes, barring mishaps."

Morraine nodded, nose into the wind. "Just in time, I would say. I want to be see the lights of Basseterre behind us by midnight."

St. Georges sniffed distastefully at the pitch-soaked combustibles already smoking in the hand burner that Tearlach Mulryan was readying. "I, for one, am worried that your observer will not see all the ships before us."

Mulryan raised a mildly contentious index finger. "Ah, but I will, sir. Six hundred feet altitude and this improved spyglass"—he tapped the brass tube in his rude "web gear"—"will show us the horizon out to thirty-three miles or so, and we'll see the top of most any masts at least ten miles farther out."

"So you have said." St. Georges sniffed again, this time at Mulryan's claim.

"And so we have seen in the trials we've conducted since leaving France," Morraine followed with a calm, if impatient glance at his XO. "However, we will want to keep your men below decks much of the time, now, Lord O'Donnell. In the event our reconnaissance is incomplete, or Fate forces an encounter upon us, it would not do to have a passing ship see our complement to be markedly greater than the expected crew of this vessel."

"Agreed, Captain. Point well taken. Besides, my men will be busy at their own tasks."

"Which shall be?"

"Sharpening their swords and cleaning their pieces."

Morraine's left eyebrow arched. "Indeed. I took the liberty of inspecting the armorer's locker after your men came aboard. All snaphaunces, even a few flintlocks. Expensive equipment, if I may say so."

"Say away, for it's true enough. But Lord Turenne agreed that it makes little sense to go to all the expense of mounting our expedition, and then arm the shore party with inferior firearms."

"It is as you say. But almost half were pistols and the new-style musketoons. Most uncommon."

"As uncommon as our task, Captain." Hugh leaned back against the taffrail. "We'll not spend much of our time at ranges greater than fifty yards, if my guess is right. So while we'll want the ability to pour in a few volleys, I expect we'll have little time or reason for serried ranks and maneuver. As I hear it, Pitch Lake itself is the only 'open field' we'll encounter. But there's plenty of bush to worm through. So I suspect most of the fighting will be quick and close."

Morraine nodded. "Reasonable. Let us hope you do not have much fighting to do, though. Sixty men is not many for such an enterprise, even on the sparsely populated islands of the New World."

O'Donnell nodded. "I agree." He smiled. "Perhaps you could convince Lord Turenne to send along a few more."

Morraine's lip almost quirked again. "Indeed. I shall mention it to him upon my return, perhaps over our first glass of wine."

Hugh nodded, let his grin become rueful. It was out of the realm of possibility that Morraine would actually ever meet Turenne, much less have the position or opportunity to suggest anything to the French general about operations here in the Caribbean. In addition to Turenne's being a phenomenally busy man, Morraine's appointment as the commander of the *Fleur Sable* had been a somewhat delicate business, handled by faceless bureaucrats at the unspoken but clear promptings of Turenne's immediate subordinates. To have gone about it more openly would have been seen as undermining the naval court which had been well-paid to dismiss Morraine as a scapegoat for a young and thoroughly

incompetent executive officer who just happened to be the son
of an unscrupulous duke. Consequently, it was necessary that
Turenne should never have direct contact with Morraine, lest
both of them come under the scrutiny of that same duke, who,
like most powerful men guilty of suborning a court, would spare
no effort to ensure that the lies he had paid to be called "the
truth" would not be revealed or revisited.

Morraine's point about a scant sixty-man force was true enough.
It left Hugh O'Donnell no margin for error, no extra resources
with which to cope with surprises, reversals, or just plain bad
luck. But the other Wild Geese who had been scheduled to follow
him down from the Lowlands had never arrived. According to
Turenne's last message, Fernando of the Lowlands had personally forbidden their departure, pending a reconsideration of their
contracts and oaths to Spain. It all sounded a little suspicious to
Hugh, but that was several months, and several thousand miles,
behind him now. He would have to make do with the men and
resources he had, and hope for the others to come along in due
course.

Morraine's version of a smile had faded. He looked at the
expanding balloon, then at the seas over the bow. "Well, Lord
O'Donnell, I shall leave you and your, er, 'ground crew' to your
business. The sooner you are done here, the sooner we can be
under way and finish this dirty business."

Hugh kept even the faintest hint of resentment out of his voice.
"Dirty business?"

Morraine paused. "Lord O'Donnell, I mean no offense. As you,
I am estranged from my country. And so I will not be happy
until I may stand proud beneath French colors. I am no pirate."

"Indeed, and so you are not flying one of their dread flags."

"Nor am I flying the flag of France, Lord O'Donnell. And until
I do, my loyalties and intentions must be considered suspect by
all whom we encounter. So I leave you to your work, that we
may both return to service beneath our nation's banners with all
possible haste." He nodded a farewell.

As Hugh nodded in return, he considered Morraine's tight,
craggy, and mostly immobile features. The Breton had a good
record operating in the open waters off Penzance and Wight,
and was patriotically eager to end his estrangement from the
pleasure of Louis XIII. He was also clearly thrilled to have a

cromster's deck under his feet. During her trials off Dunkirk, he had made eager use of her mizzen's lateen-rig, getting a feel for the *Fleur Sable*'s maneuverability. He had demonstrated a keen appreciation of her comparatively shallow draft, and enhanced (albeit not extreme) ability to tack against the wind—operational flexibilities he had not had much opportunity to enjoy while serving in His Majesty's lumbering battlewagons. Hugh just hoped that, like countless commanders before him, Morraine did not overindulge his new enthusiasms during combat. War was a messy business, best approached by leaving wide margins for error and the unexpected.

Morraine's swift descent from the poop deck prompted St. Georges into a hurried attempt to follow, which was suddenly blocked by the balloon's uncoiling guidelines. As he sought clear passage, further obstacles obtruded themselves. Spools of downtimer telegraph cable and McGillicuddy's thick, powerful legs threatened to tumble him. Aggrieved, the third son of a wealthy merchant glared archly at the Irish earl. "I must pass, Monsieur O'Donnell."

Hugh found the make-believe-officer too ridiculous to be a source of offense. St. Georges' class paranoia was as thick about him as the smell of his abysmal teeth. Every time he addressed O'Donnell as "Monsieur" instead of "Lord," he seemed poised to gloat over the slight. "I must pass," St. Georges repeated.

Hugh smiled wider. "And you have my leave to do so."

St. Georges stared down at the tangle of cables, grabbing ground-crew hands, and McGillicuddy's tree-trunk legs. Pointing at the latter, St. Georges raised his chin. "I know nothing of your Irish military *customs,* but in our service, this man must make way for me when I approach. You:"—he addressed the word sharply to McGillicuddy—"move! At once!"

Hugh had just decided that St. Georges was able to annoy him after all, when the aeronaut of the hour—lean and lively Tearlach Mulryan—jumped between them. He made his appeal with a lopsided grin. "Lieutenant St. Georges, the chief of our ground crew, McGillicuddy, regrets being unable to move aside, but he is hard at his duties. The equipment for the balloon is rather cumbersome and hard to control during deployment."

"Then he can at least show proper deference to his betters, and excuse himself."

"Sir, he does not understand French, and his English is imperfect. He is from a remote area of Ireland, and speaks little but Gaelic."

"Then use that tongue to acquaint him with my displeasure!"

Mulryan did so. McGillicuddy listened to young Tearlach's fluent stream of Gaelic gravely. Toward the end, the big crew chief brightened, looked up at St. Georges and smiled. *"Pog ma thoin,"* he offered sincerely.

"What did he say?"

"'A thousand pardons.'"

"That's better." St. Georges marched briskly off.

Hugh turned carefully astern, looked into the brightening east, and did not allow his expression to change.

Someone came to stand beside him: McCarthy. "Okay, what's the joke?"

"Joke?"

"Don't give me that. You're wearing your best poker-face and the ground crew is about to split a gut. What gives?"

"Mulryan translated *'pog ma thoin'* incorrectly."

"So it's not 'a thousand pardons?'"

"No. It's 'kiss my ass.' And by the way, McGillicuddy speaks perfect English."

Hugh glanced at Mike and saw the hint of a smile that matched his own. Then McCarthy shook his head and looked up at the dull blue-gray canvas swelling over their heads. "C'mon," he said, "let's go fly a balloon."

Hugh watched McCarthy snug Tearlach into the heavy flight harness. It was fundamentally just an extension of the gondola, which was itself little more than a tall apple basket. McCarthy, Mulryan, and the ground crew went through all the "preflight checks" that Hugh himself had memorized, having now watched the process a dozen times. But just as he expected to see the final, confirmatory thumbs-up, Michael tugged an old back-pack out of the port quarter tackle locker. From that bag, he produced a heavily modified and retrofitted metal contraption that might have started out as some species of up-timer lantern or field stove, now capped by a home-built nozzle-and-cone fixture. The only identifying mark was no help in discerning the purpose of the device. Near the base of the dark green metal tube, a legend was stamped in bold white block letters: "Coleman."

O'Rourke drew alongside Hugh and jutted his chin at the odd machine. "First time I've seen that tinker's nightmare."

"Me, too."

"And I've been on hand for almost all the development of the balloon, y' know."

"I know."

"And I don't think McCarthy shared this little toy with the French, m'lord."

"I think you're right," Hugh said slowly, watching as McCarthy tutored Mulryan in the simple operation of this new "toy," which, from McCarthy's overheard explanation, seemed to be an up-time auxiliary burner which could be used to extend flight time or gain further altitude.

McCarthy backed away from Mulryan and gave his customary benediction, which was, he had explained, a tradition among balloonists from his century: "Soft winds and gentle landings." And then he continued in a surprisingly fatherly tone. "Now don't be in too much of a rush. First, make a full three-hundred-sixty degree observation just to detect ships and other objects of interest. Then, conduct a close inspection of each before you signal its bearing, approximate range, and heading if she's under way. Then on to the next."

Tearlach was smiling indulgently at McCarthy's unaccustomed loquacity. "Yes, Don Michael, just the way you've told me. Twenty times, now."

"You ready, then?"

Hugh had the impression that Mulryan might have done anything to get away from stoic Michael McCarthy's unforeseen and unprecedented transmogrification into a nervous biddy. The former Louvain student nodded and smiled wider. The ground crew held tight the guidelines and then released their mooring locks with a sharp clack. Tearlach Mulryan started up gently, and then, with a whoop, surged aloft as the crew played out the lines.

Hugh stepped closer, craned his neck, and watched. "Well, Michael, in your parlance, the balloon is no longer in trials, but 'fully operational.' According to your history books, this is a historic first flight, is it not?"

Michael nodded. "First flight for an expressly military balloon, to my knowledge. Up-time or down-time." Then he looked almost sternly at Hugh. "And while we're on the topic of historic events, here's another: this journey to Trinidad will be your last 'flight' as an exile—the last flight that any Irish earl will ever have to undertake."

Hugh smiled at the optimistic resolve, but was a bit perplexed at the borderline ferocity with which Michael had uttered it. "From your lips to God's ear, my friend."

But Michael was looking at the balloon again. "First flight. And last flight. My word on it." He must have felt Hugh's curious stare, but he did not look over.

Hugh stood, arms folded, intentionally radiating avuncular pleasure and approval, as Tearlach Mulryan finished delivering his ground report. The details conformed to what he had relayed from his floating perch using the dit-dah-dit agglomeration of dots and dashes that the up-timers called Morse Code. The channel between St. Eustatia and St. Christopher was all but empty. One vessel, probably a Dutch fluyt, was in the straits but while Mulryan watched, she had weighed anchor and was now hugging the coast westward. She would soon have sailed around, and tucked safely behind, the leeward headland, probably on her way to the relatively new Dutch settlement of Oranjestad. This meant Morraine could begin his approach, and with a strong wind over the starboard quarter, make the windward mouth of the channel before sundown. If the breeze held, Morraine declared he'd stay close to the north side of the channel, running dark along the craggy southern headland of St. Eustatia in order to make an unseen night passage. Barring unforeseen encounters or tricks of the wind, he surmised that, by the middle watch, he'd be raising a glass of cognac to toast the dwindling lights of Basseterre as he looked out his stern-facing cabin windows. Pleased with the prospect of so undetected a passage and such an enjoyable celebration of it, Morraine nodded appreciatively to McCarthy, and disappeared down the companionway into the bowels of the quarterdeck, calling for the navigator and pilot to join him at the chart-table in the wardroom.

Mulryan watched the captain and his all-French entourage depart, and then sidled over toward Hugh and Michael. "My lords," he said with a quick look over his shoulder, "I may have broken our hosts' trust."

Hugh carefully kept his posture unchanged, casual. "In what way, Mulryan?"

"M'lord, I, um, edited my report."

"Did you, now?"

"Yes, m'lord. There's one ship I did not mention. She's directly astern, maybe forty miles, due east. Not much smaller than us, judging from what little I could make of her masts."

"Saw them against the brightening sky?"

"Aye, but not well. I checked her again when the sun came up." He looked at the overcast skies. "So to speak."

"And tell me, Tearlach, why did you choose to 'forget' this piece of information that I'm sure would have been of considerable interest to Captain Morraine?"

"Because sir, unless I am very much mistaken, she was putting up a balloon, too. A white one. Like ours used to be."

Hugh kept himself from starting. "Was it the same design as ours?"

Mulryan grimaced. "M'lord, that new spyglass is a wonder, and my eyes are as good as any in County Mayo, but forty miles is a long way by any measure."

Hugh smiled. "True enough, Tearlach."

"But—another ship with a balloon? What do you think it is, Lord O'Donnell?"

Hugh was considering how best to tactfully phrase his speculations when Michael shared his own—bluntly. "That, young Mulryan, is our master's eye."

"Lord Turenne? He sent a ship after us?"

"He, or Richelieu, almost certainly," Hugh confirmed.

"It only makes sense that he'd want to keep an eye on what we do," Michael conceded. Then, with a smile, "If he can, that is."

Tearlach cocked his head. "What do you mean?"

"I mean that ship can't have seen us today. She was easy for us to spot, silhouetted against the dawn while putting up a white balloon. But, from her perspective, we were against the western predawn darkness, putting up a blue-gray balloon. She didn't see us."

Hugh rubbed his chin. "So that's why you had our balloon painted only after we left Dunkirk. You didn't want Turenne to know you'd camouflaged it."

"Right, and that's why we were four days out before I started running test ascents over three hundred feet. As far as Turenne knows, one hundred yards is as high as we're rated to go. He'll have tried pushing that limit a bit himself, but not as aggressively as we have."

"And he won't have that little toy you gave Tearlach right before he went up."

McCarthy nodded. "Yeah, the boost from the natural gas burner doesn't last long, but it does give you a little extra height. Or time. Which are the edges we need. And by tonight, we'll be so far off, that he won't have any chance to catch sight of us again. Now, 'scuse me. I'm gonna show Mulryan here how to take care of my 'toy.'" And he took the natural gas burner from Tearlach's hands and led the young aeronaut back to the poop deck.

As they left, O'Rourke sauntered over from the rail.

"Heard all that?" asked Hugh.

O'Rourke nodded. "Every word."

"And what do you think?"

"I think McCarthy is shrewd. Maybe too shrewd."

"What do you mean?"

"I know that look, Hugh O'Donnell. You've misgivings of your own."

"But I'll hear yours first, O'Rourke."

"As you wish. So, the ship on our tail couldn't see us today. Bravo. But hardly luck, eh?"

"What do you mean?"

"I mean that McCarthy has had every step of this game sussed out from the start. From before we left France, it seems."

"And that's bad?"

"Not in itself, no. But why didn't he bring us into his confidence on all this earlier? Because rest assured, he's been playing this game of chess five moves ahead of the opposition, he has."

"What do you mean?"

"I mean that he obviously foresaw that Turenne would send a ship after us. And so he saves some special tricks for our balloon, to make it more than a match for the one Turenne has. But in order to have those tricks at hand, he must have anticipated needing them much earlier. So, from the time he started working in Amiens, he must have been expecting that Turenne would be crafting a secret duplicate balloon off-site, even as he and Haas were constructing the original model."

"Strange, O'Rourke: having an ally with that kind of foresight sounds like a great advantage to me, not a source of worry."

"Aye, but that ally is an advantage only if he shares what

he's seen from the peak of his lofty foresight, m'lord. And Don Michael, whatever his reasons might be, did not do so."

"So what are you saying? That he's not to be trusted?"

O'Rourke rubbed his thick nose with a flat, meaty thumb. "I wouldn't be saying so black a thing as that, m'lord. But if Don McCarthy is clever enough to keep important secrets from someone like General Turenne, then isn't it a possibility that he could be keeping important secrets from us, too?"

Hugh nodded and turned his gaze slowly to where Michael McCarthy was tutoring Mulryan, back at the taffrail. "Yes, O'Rourke, there is that possibility. There is definitely that possibility."

Chapter 18

San Juan, Puerto Rico

Barto—the only name he ever gave out because it was the only one he had ever had—ate the third slice of papaya greedily and washed it down with a mix of rum and soursop. The musky taste of the latter mixed well with the local spirit's strong cane flavor. Speaking around the mixture in his mouth, he addressed his host. "So you've business with me, eh? Can't remember when a man in silk trousers had business with me. Now, silk-trousered ladies, on the other hand—" Had Barto's senior "officers" been present, they would have no doubt laughed on cue.

But tonight, Barto had no audience. He was alone with his host, Don Eugenio de Covilla, who now seemed to be attempting to suppress a disgusted sneer, as he had throughout much of the meal. But Barto suspected that his host's duty to Spain and Philip came before indulging in displays of repugnance. "Señor Barto, I most certainly do have business to conduct with a man of your—experience."

Barto leaned back, belched, studied the Spaniard. A minor functionary recently dispatched from Santo Domingo. A dandy who had probably been in fewer fights than Barto had warts (well, a lot fewer fights, by that count). But the Spaniard reeked of oils and silver, and while Barto had no need of the former, he had both a powerful need and lust for the latter.

Ironically, Barto's increased need of silver was a direct consequence of his corresponding increase in good fortune. His "free company" had grown prodigiously in just the past month. Three weeks ago, while drawing near shore at Neckere Island to take on water and any fruits they could find (scurvy having made yet another general appearance), Barto had come upon a sloop-rigged English packet in the throes of repressing a mutiny. Drawn by gunfire as a shark is drawn by blood, Barto quieted his men and commenced to run close against the far side of the headland at which the packet was moored. After putting his best boarders into his smaller boat—a shallow-hulled pinnace—he swept around the headland, the wind full at his back. He was on them in three minutes; the fight lasted less than half that time. He put the lawful owner, stalwart captain, and loyal crew to the sword—the whole lot weren't worth twenty *reales* in ransom—and put the mutineers to work cleaning the deck and transferring stores and cargoes between this new hull and Barto's two others. With the mutineers added to his ranks, he finally had enough men to consider plundering a larger town, maybe one of the small English settlements just recently established in the Bahamas, or the Dutch enclave that was rumored to have returned to Saba. Such a raid would only swell his coffers slightly, but would at least quiet his crews. They were already restless and would soon make their displeasure known to him—in a most pointed fashion, if need be. So, since a full-scale raid would take more time to plan, a smaller intermediary action was required to tide them over and sate their appetites for both rum and blood. A nuisance, reflected Barto, but it was all part of a freebooter's life.

He belched again. "You invited me to dinner that we might talk. So now I've eaten your dinner. What have we to talk about?"

De Covilla smoothed his moustache. "The matter is somewhat delicate, Señor Barto. Do I have your word . . . hmmm, allow me to rephrase: is it understood between us that sharing this information would attract the special disfavor of His Imperial Majesty Philip of Spain?"

Barto smiled. He had thought that, having seized four of Philip's ships, he had already attracted quite as much of that imperial displeasure as anyone could hope for. But apparently he had been mistaken. "I understand. And I hope that His Majesty's representatives will realize that any past, er, indiscretions on my part regarding his shipping were matters of mistaken identity. Night actions, you see."

"Of course." De Covilla's smug smile indicated that he knew Barto never attacked ships after sundown. "Indeed, the representatives of my liege are not only willing to pay handsomely in silver, but to provide you with something else you might find of even more durable value."

"Which is?"

"Which is a letter of marque."

Despite his attempt at bored nonchalance, this so took Barto by surprise that he sat up. "A letter of marque, signed by—?"

"No less a personage than the captain-general of Santo Domingo, Don Bitrian de Viamonte."

Barto sneered. "Viamonte the Invalid? Really? He spent his years as governor of Cuba limping through the underbrush, building towers and forts to fend off, er, 'fortune-seekers' like myself. And now he is interested in hiring the very same free-spirited adventurers whom he meant to kill?" Barto snorted as he laughed into the dregs of his drink. "Perhaps de Viamonte's disabilities are not merely physical, hey?"

He had meant that insult to test de Covilla's mettle, to see if the young Spaniard had enough temper in him to burst through his almost effete courtly exterior. Barto was not disappointed. The well-groomed *hidalgo* rose slowly, hand on his rapier. "You will mind your tongue, Señor. The captain-general may suffer from infirmities that the Lord Himself saw fit to inflict upon his body, but perhaps that was to better stimulate the growth of his keen mind and indomitable will. He determined to reduce Cuba's vulnerability to pirates. He achieved that, and evidently you are not so bold as to have personally tested the walls and militias he raised for that purpose. Now he is set upon hiring men for a special mission. He directed me to seek appropriate persons among the self-styled 'brethren of the coast.' I started with you. However, I am under no compulsion to confer the contract upon you, specifically, and so, if you continue your insolence, I will take my *reales* elsewhere. And depending upon the severity of your further slurs, I may ask for the satisfaction of honor that must be demanded in response to your impugning the character and person of the captain-general. Am I clear?"

Barto smiled and lifted his cup. "Bravo. And I actually think you'd be foolish enough to play at swords with me, which you must know to be unwise. So you've a ready heart under that fine silken vest, I'll give you that. And so, to business."

Whatever de Covilla had been expecting, it hadn't been that. "Do you—do you *mock* me, Señor?" His hand turned slowly on the pommel of his rapier.

Barto made his best sour face. "Mock you? I am simply speaking to you plainly and man-to-man, not like some lace-loaded grandee at court. Let me make my words plainer. You'd be a fool to fight me, but you know it, and are still quite ready to cross swords on a matter of honor. You've got *cojones*, and that's what counts. Experience and age will furnish all the other necessary skills in good time. If you live that long. But that's not what we're here to talk about. So, I say again, to business."

De Covilla frowned, fiddled with his sword's hilt uncertainly, and then sat. "Very well, to business. I have offered silver and a letter of marque. Co-signed by the new governor of Cuba, no less: the field-marshal Don Francisco Riaño y Gamboa de Burgos. Whose name and martial reputation is known to you, I imagine."

In fact, Riaño y Gamboa's name was barely known to Barto, who had no idea what military glories might lurk hidden behind it. But de Covilla uttered it with the utterly reliable conviction of youthful loyalty, and so there might be enough truth in it to warrant credence.

But it wasn't the reputation of the governor or the money or the marque that commanded Barto's attention. Rather, it was the attractiveness of the offer. Or rather, the *excessive* attractiveness of the offer, and the fact that the particulars were not presented up front.

Accordingly, the primary instinct of all successful pirates—wariness—arose in Barto, who frowned his mightiest frown. "Well, this is certainly a most intriguing offer. So far. But I have yet to learn what it is I must do for this handsome—eh, 'reward.'"

De Covilla sipped daintily at his glass of rioja. "It has come to our attention that a ship just recently arrived in the Caribbean will soon make landfall at Trinidad with the intent of taking, and holding, the land around Pitch Lake."

"What the hell for?"

"Does it matter? This banditry is an affront to Philip of Spain's exclusive dominion over the New World as per the Church's own *inter caetera*, and so, it must be prevented."

Barto rubbed his chin. "Very well, but if you know where this ship is bound, and you have Philip's express orders to destroy it, then why not deal with it yourself?"

De Covilla pushed at his goat stew with his fork. "I did not say the orders came from Philip himself, nor that the intelligence came from Europe. Not directly."

Barto leaned his large, hirsute forearms on the table. "Let us speak frankly. I stay alive in this business because I avoid jobs that stink like old fish, and this is starting to smell that way. Make clear the job, the information, and the sources, or I must decline."

De Covilla seemed surprised, but also pleased. "Very well. Last year, a Dutch captain who has apparently started a colony in Suriname—Jakob Schooneman, by name—brought a young American to conduct a brief reconnaissance of the area around Trinidad's Pitch Lake. After a variety of further trespassings and pillagings in His Imperial Majesty Philip's colonies, they both returned to Europe. Some time ago, that same ship, the *Koninck David*, returned and touched on the coast nearby San Juan, probably smuggling. That didn't stop some of her crew from wandering into town for a brief carouse, of course.

"When the *Koninck David*'s assistant purser was in his cups, he told one of our informants that he had overhead this same young American being closely interviewed in Bremen last winter by a good number of his countrymen and unprincipled adventurers. Whereupon a number of this group determined to send a warship to Trinidad to usurp the region around Pitch Lake in order to sell its petroleum riches to the USE. We learned roughly when the ship was due and also that it would not head directly to Trinidad, in order to avoid the heavily trafficked transatlantic route that leads directly into the Grenada Passage, just off Trinidad itself. But more than this we could not learn."

Barto leaned back, folded his arms. So, he was already entering into an ongoing plot rife with treachery, secrets, and informers. However, those were supposed to be his area of special expertise. Accordingly, it made him nervous when the Spanish—or anyone—displayed equal facility with them. Largely because it meant that he might be the one surprised, rather than the one springing the surprise. But balanced against those risks were the incredible benefits to be derived from taking this job, and succeeding. He pushed down his misgivings, and breathed out slowly as he made his response. "So have any of your informers told you how this expedition intends to take, and *hold*, a position on Trinidad? A single ship, even the largest, could not carry enough soldiers and supplies for a quick and lasting conquest."

"We have wondered this, also. But inasmuch as our forces are spread too thin to respond in a timely fashion, this may be precisely what these bandits are counting upon. They hope to have the time to fortify, consolidate, perhaps rally others to their banner while we collect the necessary forces, and authority, from Venezuela, Isla de Margarita and even our more distant colonial *audiencias*."

Barto rubbed his chin. "I have sailed near Trinidad in the past, but not recently. What are the conditions there?"

"They are most unfortunate, since our investiture of that island is indifferent at best. The governor is Cristoval de Aranda, who has held that post without any noteworthy distinction for four years. Indeed, his tenure is somewhat of an embarrassment to the Crown. He has been unable to substantively increase the size of his small colony, which is primarily engaged in the growing of tobacco. Which, it is reported, he then sells illegally to English and Dutch ships, rather than reserving it for the merchants of Spain."

Barto did not point out that it was well known throughout the Caribbean that Spanish ships almost never went to this all-but-forsaken possession of their empire, and that if Aranda didn't sell the tobacco to someone, he would soon be the governor of a ghost-town. Or maybe a graveyard, given the testy native populations on the island. Most of whom preferred any other European settlers over the Spanish. But Barto only nodded sympathetically.

"I suppose Aranda should not be made to bear all the blame himself," de Covilla temporized. "His fortifications are small, guns are few, and the size of his militia laughable. It may not total twenty men, all mustered. Indeed, when he was finally compelled to evict a pack of British interlopers from Punta de Galera on the northeast point of the island a few years ago, he had to appeal to the colony on Margarita Island to raise a sufficient force for the job. Pitiable. However,"—and here the young *hidalgo* fixed a surprisingly direct and forceful gaze upon his dinner guest—"I am told that you, Señor Barto, have a significant force at your disposal, that you are immediately available, and that you specialize in swift, direct, and—above all—final, action."

"That I do, Don de Covilla, that I do."

"Excellent, because that is precisely what will thwart the plans of this new group of interlopers. So, to the details: how many men can you bring with you to Trinidad?"

"It depends."

"'It depends?' Upon what?"

Barto leaned far back in his chair. "It depends upon how many *reales* you have to spend."

"I see. Well, how much would it cost to hire all of your men?"

Barto smiled. "All of your *reales*."

Chapter 19

St. Eustatia, Caribbean

With the dawn silhouetting the culverins that jutted out aggressively over the ramparts of Fort Orange behind them, Maarten Tromp turned to look into St. Eustatia's wide leeward anchorage. Almost thirty-five hulls lay invisible there, except for the spars that stuck upward from them. *Like crosses in a water-covered graveyard,* he thought gloomily, *Which is what this harbor will become, if we—if I—fail to dance every one of the next steps correctly.*

Soft movement behind him meant the only other man in the skiff, besides the combination steersman and sail-handler, had approached. "Should we take you straight to the *Amelia*, Admiral?" asked Jakob Schooneman, captain of the Dutch fluyt *Koninck David*. A merchant, an adventurer, and now, quite obviously, a confidential agent for the United Provinces and possibly for the USE as well, Jakob Schooneman had been absent from the Caribbees for many months. He had made a northern passage back to the New World, touching at several places along the Atlantic coastline, searching for other Dutch ships that could be spared for Tromp's fleet: the last in this hemisphere flying Dutch colors after the disastrous Battle of Dunkirk, not quite two years earlier. Jakob Schooneman's success had been modest, at best.

Tromp nodded, not turning to face Jakob Schooneman, determined not to look him in the eyes until he could be sure of what the captain would see in his own. Tromp looked up at the sides of the hull now looming out of the charcoal-blue mists: the *Amelia*, his fifty-four-gun flagship, and one of the few to survive the withdrawal from Dunkirk. He could still see her as she was during that perilous October flight across the Atlantic to Recife: her hull scarred and holed by cannonballs, most of her spars and rigging incongruously new because almost all of what they had sailed into battle with had been shot away or so badly savaged that they had to replace it as soon as they knew they were free of Spanish pursuit. Only the stout mainmast remained of the original spars, black with both age and grim resolve. Or so Tromp liked to think.

When he could discern the faint outlines of her closed gunports, he turned to the master of the *Koninck David*. "Thank you for coming to see me directly, Captain Schooneman. Your visit was most informative."

"Glad to have been of service, Admiral."

"Which we are happy to return. The lighters will be out with your provisions by noon. You are sure that none of your men wish shore liberty?"

Jakob Schooneman smiled crookedly. "'Wish it?' They most certainly do. I wish it myself. But circumstances dictate otherwise, wouldn't you agree, Admiral Tromp?"

Tromp suppressed a sigh as he looked into the purple-gray western horizon. "Yes, they do." Now close abeam his flagship, Tromp called up to the anchor watch. The ship above him was silent for the moment it took for the watch officer to stick his head over the gunwale, squint down and determine that yes, it truly was the admiral arriving before the full rose of dawn was in the sky. Then the *Amelia*'s weather deck exploded into a cacophony of coronets and drums which rapidly propagated into the lower decks as well.

"Nothing like an unannounced inspection to set the men on their toes, eh, Admiral?"

"Indeed. And it is a serviceable pretext, today." An accommodation ladder was dropped down along the tumbledown of *Amelia*'s portside hull. In response, the skiff's tiller-man lashed his handle fast and grabbed up a pole to bump against the fifty-four-gunner's planking, keeping them off. Tromp put out his hand. "Fair weather and good fortune to you, Captain. You have need of both, it seems."

Jakob Schooneman's lopsided smile returned. "I shall not deny it. And you, Admiral, the same to you."

Tromp nodded, prepared to ascend, thought *Yes, I need fair weather and good fortune, too. For all our sakes.*

Tromp was surprised to see lanky Willem van der Zaan waiting for him at the forward companionway. It was Tromp's wont—indeed, most officers'—to first head aftwards for their berths. But here was Willi, waiting at the forecastle, his cuffs rolled up neatly and pinned, even.

Tromp managed not to smile at the fresh-faced youngster's quick nod and winning smile. "You are up early, Mr. van der Zaan. And more mysterious still, you knew to wait for me here, at the other end of the ship from my quarters. Have you been consorting with sorcerers?"

"No, Admiral. Just watchful."

"You saw me coming?"

"No, sir . . . but I was standing the last leg of the middle watch and saw the fluyt that came in slow and quiet from the north. At night. Passing other ships at anchorage without a hail."

Tromp stared at Willem. "Little Willi"—what a misnomer, now!—had not just grown in mind and body, but subtlety. A year ago, he might not have come to such a quick and certain surmise that the incoming ship's quiet approach signified an ally wishing to make a brief, surreptitious visit. Instead, he would have reflexively sounded an alarm signifying that pirates were upon them under cover of night. "You are very observant, Willi."

"I am the admiral's eager pupil, sir. If I'm not mistaken, that was the *Koninck David*, sir, wasn't it?"

"Mmm. And how did you know?"

"Captain Schooneman's rigging, sir. He's always ready to run as near to the wind as he can."

Because he's often working in dangerous waters, gathering, or carrying, confidential information. Tromp felt his smile slacken even as his pride in van der Zaan grew. *All of which you know, don't you, Willi? Knowledge is what brings childhood's end, and you are indeed Little Willi no longer. Which means that now, you will face the same duties—and dangers—as the rest of us. May*

God watch over you, dear boy, for from here on, my ability to do so will be greatly reduced.

They passed the galley. Urgent sounds of hurry that bordered on chaos spilled out.

"Early to be serving breakfast," observed Tromp.

"Turning out for the admiral," was the respectful correction offered by van der Zaan, as they passed. "I suspect the cook will be putting an extra few rashers of bacon on, today. Do you not wish to inspect?"

Tromp nodded. "Yes, but they are doing well to be about their business so smartly. I shall give them time to make good their special preparations." He turned to his young assistant. "Letting men succeed, particularly in a special task which they have taken up on their own initiative, builds their pride. Which builds their morale."

"Yes, Admiral," said Willi with a smile which also said, *As you have well and often taught me, and as I have well and fully learned.* After a moment, he added, almost cautiously, "You seem distracted, sir."

If you only knew. "Not at all, Mr. van der Zaan. I am simply quiet when I am most attentive."

"Ah. Yes, sir. Of course, sir."

Is that a way of saying, "Of course I will agree to your obvious lie, sir"? Well, no matter.

Willi followed Tromp to the next ladder down. "Where are we headed, sir?"

Tromp stopped, hands on either side of the almost vertical between-deck stairs that seamen called "ladders." He looked at the young man gravely; he knew that the moment he uttered their first inspection site, Willi would know what was in store, what kind of news had come in from the *Koninck David* in the small hours of the morning. "The bilges, young Willem. We are going to the bilges."

Willem van der Zaan's eyes widened. Because he had not forgotten—*how could he?*—Maarten Tromp's weekly litany about preparing for battle: "You check the ship from keel to foretop. You do it yourself. Meaning you start in the bilges."

"The bilges?" van der Zaan almost whispered, looking very much like Little Willi again.

Tromp just nodded and headed below.

✧　　✧　　✧

Tromp was still trying to wipe the stink of the bilge water off his hands when he returned to the galley. The ship was in readiness—he had expected no less—and despite the long wait for action, she was well-caulked and her gear made fast with tight lashings and adequate dunnage. But the inescapable fact was that there was simply less gear than there should have been. Dry goods were low, as was cordage and canvas. They had managed to procure some through the intercession of Sir Thomas Warner, the English—*well, now state-less*—governor of nearby St. Christopher. But sails came at quite a price, since Warner got the canvas via the occasional traffic from Bermuda. Wherever possible, Tromp and his fleet of almost forty ships had adopted local expedients in place of Old World manufactures, but good, reliable chandlery—to say nothing of nails, tools, and metal fixtures of all kinds—was not being produced in the Caribbees, or anywhere in the New World, outside the greatest of the Spanish ports.

Even rags, Tromp reflected, continuing the futile task of cleaning his hands with a towel already inundated with bilge water, even rags were rare enough commodities, here. What weaving the locals did was crude, and not suitable to all purposes.

"Shall I fetch you another towel, sir?" Willi asked as he peered into the evidently expectant mess.

"No use, Willi. Let's not keep the cook waiting."

The watch officers had taken advantage of the admiral's inspection of *Amelia*'s orlop deck and stores to rouse the first watch out of hammocks and make for the galley, where the cook (one of the few that had all his limbs) had set about building his fires and preparing the food, all the while debating provisions with the purser, as usual. However, the moment the admiral entered, the men, regardless of rank or age, looked up expectantly, with the suppressed smiles of boys who've done their chores early and without being told to.

Tromp suppressed a smile himself, nodded to the cook. "Up early today, are we, Ewoud?"

Ewoud effected dour annoyance. "It is as the admiral says. These louts couldn't wait to fill their bellies today. Can't think why. Sir."

"No, me either," agreed Tromp, going along with the act. The men grinned. As had sailors from the dawn of time, they had a natural affinity for a quiet, firm commander who could enjoy and acknowledge a joke without becoming part of it himself. "What feast have you set on today?"

There was a quick exchange of glances—none too friendly—between the purser and the cook before the latter waved at the simmering pots with a hand that invited inspection. "Well sir, this morning I thought we'd depart from local fare, and—"

Tromp shook his head. "A nice gesture, Ewoud—and Mr. Brout," he added with a glance at the purser who had no doubt pushed Ewoud to use the Old World supplies, "but there are to be no exceptions while we are in port. Local foodstuffs only."

"But sir," Brout explained, hands opening into an appeal, "soon, even the peas will spoil if we do not—"

"Mr. Brout," Tromp let his voice go lower, less animated, and then turned to face the suddenly quiet purser, "I assure you, I have the spoilage dates of all our dry goods well in mind. And they do not worry me." *Particularly since, after today, we'll be finishing them up quickly enough.* "Do I make myself clear?"

Brout looked as though he might have soiled himself. "Yes, Admiral. Perfectly clear."

Ewoud was trying hard not to smile, and, satisfied, sent his young assistant—barely thirteen, from the look of him—scurrying to swap around the bags and casks of waiting food. "Tapioca and mango, then. Smoked boar for a little flavor." The mess-chiefs who'd come down from each group of mess-mates sighed. Tapioca and cassava crackers were the new staple of the Dutch navy. Such as it was.

Tromp looked over Ewoud's broad, sweat-glistening shoulders deeper into the galley and saw familiar bags and barrels with Dutch markings. *The last of the foodstuffs we sailed with, of the meals that we thought we'd eat until the day the sea swallowed us up instead.* Whether on the Dutch ships that had sailed into disaster at Dunkirk or on those moored in safety at Recife, there was little variation in the bill of fare that had been loaded into their holds before leaving the United Provinces of the Netherlands.

Each day had begun with bread and groat-porridge, and lunch had been less of the same, but usually with strips of dried meat and also a sizeable part of the daily portion of cheese. Sunday dinner meant half a pound of ham or a pound of spiced lamb or salted meat with beans. On Monday, Tuesday and Wednesday fish with peas or beans was on the menu. On Thursday it was a pound of beef or three ounces of pork and on Friday and Saturday it was fish again. But long before the food ran out, the beer was gone. Since it spoiled comparatively quickly, it was an early-journey drink.

Even before the disaster at Dunkirk, the admiralties of the United Provinces had also taken a page from the books of the up-timers, and citrus or other fruits had been part of the provisions on the way out, and then, were a high priority item to acquire as soon as landfall was made in the New World. Happily, that was easily accomplished. And if the transition from gin to rum had been strange, it was not unpleasant, and Tromp had to admit that it mixed with a wider variety of the local juices. Indeed, it turned a cup of soursop from a rather musky, acquired taste, into a delightful and reputedly healthful drink.

But what started as a few expedient replacements for Old World comestibles had now become a wholesale substitution of them, since the familiar foods of home had no way to reach them. It had been a month since Tromp had enjoyed bread made from anything other than cassava, and longer since he had any meat other than goat. But at least he had two full meals a day, which was more than could be said for the almost three thousand people who were his charges on St. Eustatia. And now, he would have to dip deeply into already-scant stockpiles of durable food—

"Mr. Brout, you are to be given the first helping of breakfast."

"Why—yes, Admiral. Thank you."

"Do not thank me. It is so you may go ashore as soon as possible. You are to requisition as much salt fish, smoked goat, dried fruit, and hard-baked cassava loaves as you can find. Tapioca for porridge, and beans, too."

"I am to 'requisition' it, sir?"

"Yes. We will settle accounts later." *If we're alive to do it.* "You are to return by noon. The supplies are to be loaded by nightfall."

"Admiral, that leaves me little time to negotiate for a fair—"

"Mr. Brout, you do not have time to negotiate. You will see that the holds of our ships are provided with three months' rations, at a minimum. You are to begin by calling upon Governor Corselles. He will have my message by now, and will accompany you to ensure the compliance of your suppliers." *And to watch out for your own profiteering proclivities, Brout.*

Whose eyes were wide. "Yes, Admiral. If I may ask, are we soon to weigh anchor—?"

But Tromp was already out the door and into the narrow

passageway. He was halfway up the ladder to the gun deck before the raucous buzz of hushed gossip surged out of the galley below him.

Willi, at Tromp's heels, laughed softly.

"Something amusing, Mr. van der Zaan?"

"Yes, sir. Very much, sir."

"And what is it?"

"How an admiral of so few and such quiet words can work up so many men so very quickly."

Tromp shrugged and turned that motion into an arm-boost that propelled him up onto the gun deck with satisfying suddenness. Men who were hunched in whispering clusters came to their feet quickly. Over his shoulder, he muttered, "A man who yells does so because he is unsure that he is in command. Remember that, Willi."

"I will, sir."

Tromp, walking with his hands behind his back, nodded acknowledgments to the respectful greetings he received from each knot of befuddled seamen. However, his primary attention was on the guns. The last of the culverins were gone, as he had ordered. In their place were cannon, although one of those was only a twenty-two-pounder, or "demi-cannon." But each deck's broadsides would be a great deal more uniform now: another up-timer optimization that tarrying at their Oranjestad anchorage had enabled. Gone was the mix of culverin and cannon of various throw-weights and the occasional saker, and with them, the variances of range and effectiveness that made naval gunnery even more of a gamble than it already was.

He popped a tompion out of a cannon's muzzle and felt around within the mouth of the barrel. He found it sufficiently dry, and with a paucity of pitting that testified to the routine nature of its care. Salt water was a hard and corrosive taskmaster.

Admirably anticipating his next point of inspection, a gunner came forward at a nod from his battery chief and made to open a ready powder bag. Tromp nodded approval and turned to young van der Zaan. "Fetch Lieutenant Evertsen to find me here. He'll need to complete the inspection. Then make for the accommodation ladder."

"Why, sir? Are you expecting—?"

A single coronet announced a noteworthy arrival on the weather deck.

"Yes," Tromp answered, "I am expecting visitors. Now go."

✧   ✧   ✧

Tromp looked up when, without warning, the door to his great cabin opened and Jan van Walbeeck entered. "You're late," the admiral muttered.

"I am more informed than I would have been had I hurried to be on time," retorted van Walbeeck with his trademark impish grin. He pulled up a chair and sat, heavy hands folded and cherubic smile sending creases across his expansive cheeks. Full-faced for a man of thirty-five, his jowls were apparently not subject to privations in the same way the rest of his now-lean body was. He, along with the other three thousand refugees from Recife, had narrowly avoided the specter of starvation over the past year. But somehow, van Walbeeck still had his large, florid jowls.

Tromp waited and then sighed. "Very well, I will ask: and what additional information did your tardiness vouchsafe?"

"I tarried on deck to exchange a few pleasantries with your first mate, Kees Evertsen. While there, a Bermuda sloop made port. Down from Bahamas, freighting our neighbors' sugar for relay to Bermuda. And as chance would have it, one of our most notable neighbors was on board."

Tromp frowned. By "neighbors," van Walbeeck meant the English on St. Christopher's island, which was already visible as a dawn-lit land mass out the admiral's south-facing stern windows. A "notable visitor," meant the person was not of the very first order of importance, so it was not the governor, Sir Thomas Warner himself. Indeed, the "Sir" part of Warner's title was somewhat in doubt. Technically, shortly before the League of Ostend arose, Charles Stuart of England had ceded all his New World possessions to Richelieu. Or so the French maintained. And it was probably close to, or the very, fact. The English crown's protest over that interpretation was, to put it lightly, muted. However, the popular English outcry over losing its New World possessions had grown intense enough to propel the already paranoid Charles into a dubious course of instituting loyalty oaths and a standing, special court for the investigation and hearing of purported cases of sedition.

So was Thomas Warner's patent of nobility still effective, his governorship still legal? Not under the aegis of English law, but until someone took the island from him, the dispute was pointless. And given how these uncertain times required his full attention and involvement in the well-being of his now isolated colony, Tromp would have been surprised had he been the visitor to

St. Eustatia. But there was another likely candidate. "Lieutenant Governor Jeafferson?"

"Bravo, Maarten! Your powers of deduction are undiminished. It was Jeafferson himself on the sloop, which must have left St. Christopher's in the dark of the night to be here so early. And you know what that means—"

Tromp sighed. Jan van Walbeeck was arguably the single smartest, most capable man he had ever met, and he had met plenty of them. But his irrepressible ebullience—even at this hour of the morning—was sometimes a bit wearing for, well, normal people like himself. "Yes, Jan, I think I do. He's here to finalize and sign our five-year lease of the lands south of Sandy Point."

"Exactly. And thereby kill two birds with one stone: we get the arable land we need, and Thomas Warner gets the guards he wants. And frankly, we need to reduce the number of soldiers we have here on St. Eustatia."

Tromp laid aside his protractor and looked up from his charts. "And you feel certain this will not bring us into conflict with the French colony on the island?"

Van Walbeeck blew out his cheeks. "Who is certain of anything, Maarten? Indeed, who can say who will hold power over us, or these islands, when the lease is up in five years? But this much is true. The French had only one ship arrive last year, and that was before we arrived. As best we can tell, Warner's colony has grown to almost nine thousand, maybe more. The French have barely a tenth of that. So I think that it is unlikely there will be any trouble."

Tromp frowned. "So then, if that is true, I ask—as I have before—why is Warner so concerned with having our guards? What are we not seeing—and he not saying?"

Van Walbeeck nodded. "I think I have a little more perspective on that, now that our farmers and his farmers are talking with each other on a regular basis. Firstly, Warner has all his people gainfully employed, and most in food production of one sort or another. Would that we could say the same. So the same people who man his militia are also the only ones available to oversee the workers and the plantations."

"You mean, guard and drive his slaves."

"Maarten, I know how you feel about slavery, and I share those feelings, but these are the conditions as we found them, and the best we can do is work to change them. And it won't be easy, given the tales our planters are telling his."

Tromp stared at his charts, at the outline of St. Christopher's. "I can only imagine. Our decision to prohibit slaveholding has not made me a popular man."

"You? *You?*" Jan leaned forward. "Maarten, you are not the president of the *Politieke Raad*. You don't have our planters screaming for your blood. Well, not so loudly as for mine, at any rate."

"And Corselles is still no help?"

"How can he be? I frankly feel sorry for the poor fellow. He arrived here with maybe two hundred and fifty souls, all of whom were assured that they will grow rich like the English planters. Which meant, in short hand, that they will own plantations and the slaves that allow the land to be worked at such a fabulous profit.

"And then, just a year after they arrive, we separately descend upon them like a horde of locusts, almost three thousand strong, ninety percent young or young-ish males, short on rations, and with our military leadership determined to eliminate slavery. Which was what pushed almost half of our farmers into league with their farmers."

Tromp nodded. "And this connects to Warner's want for our guards—how?"

Jan sighed. "Let us presume that he does indeed see that our survival may be the key to his, and vice versa. We are both without support from our homelands, albeit for very different reasons. But if we hang on to St. Eustatia long enough, we'll start seeing flags from our home ports. At that point, the advantage is ours. For Warner is a man without a country. So, while he still enjoys the advantage of being our breadbasket, he will naturally wish to enter into accords with us which will stand him in good stead when that balance of power shifts. And his power is in the food he makes, so he is not eager to have his overseers as his full-time militiamen. Food production will drop and with it, his fortunes."

Tromp looked up from the map. "That seems to track true, yes."

"Ah, but there's more, Maarten. He doesn't just want guards; he wants *our* guards. Dutch guards."

"Why? Are we Dutch especially good at guarding things? Even things that do not belong to us?"

"No, but our guards operate under the aegis of our flag. So if the French try cases with them—"

"Yes, of course. Then there is an international incident. And since Warner is no longer in charge of an 'English' colony, he has no such protection of his own."

"Precisely. The only thing that gives the French pause about running Warner off the island is the question of whether or not they can physically achieve it. But if his colony's guards are our men, with the flag of Orange flying above, the French risk a war. And if there is anything we have an overabundance of in this area, it is soldiers."

"Yes, but Warner seems to be acquiring their services far earlier than he needs to. He has little to worry about from such a small French colony."

Van Walbeeck shook his head. "Except that the French colonists are not the direct threat. It is the dissent they have been successful at breeding among the English slaves, and some of the indentured workers from Ireland. And there is rumor that the French commander d'Esnambuc has been parleying with the natives as well. The Kalinago still want St. Christopher's back, you know."

Tromp stood. "Very well. So Warner wants our guards. When will the lease go into effect?"

"It will still be a few months, at least. Our people are eager to put the tracts around Sandy Point under cultivation, but it will take time to get them ready, to gather the equipment, to settle affairs here. And the same goes for determining which troops shall go."

Tromp shook his head. "Since we are so close—a morning's sail—there is no reason to make our forces on St. Christopher a fixed garrison. We shall rotate troops through the station, as we shall their commanders. I want our people to both know that island and to get a break from this one."

Van Walbeeck nodded enthusiastically. "Most prudent. And speaking of guards, I'm wondering if we shouldn't set up some special detachments of them here, too."

Tromp folded his arms. "You mean, here in Oranjestad? We already have greatly oversized guard complements on all our warehouses, on the batteries, the outposts, the—"

"We need them on the women, Maarten. Particularly the visiting English ladies."

"The ladies—?" And then Tromp understood. "Oh."

"Yes. 'Oh.' Maarten, there are fewer than four hundred women on St. Eustatia, out of almost three thousand persons, more if you count our shipboard crews. Most of the four hundred women are already married. And you have seen the effects, surely."

Tromp surely had. Brawls, drunken or otherwise, had been steadily increasing for six months. And however the causes and particulars varied, there was usually a common thread: it had started over a woman. It may have been that the woman in question had never spoken to, perhaps never even looked at, any of the combatants, but that hardly mattered. Like a bunch of young bucks in rutting season, any incident that could in any way be construed as a dispute over mating dominance resulted in locked horns. "What do you suggest?" he asked van Walbeeck.

"Cuthbert Pudsey."

"The English mercenary who's been in our ranks from Recife onward? A one man guard-detachment?"

"Maarten, do not be willfully obtuse. Of course not. Pudsey is to be the leader of, let us call it a 'flying squad' of escorts who will accompany any English ladies who come to call at Oranjestad. And given that it will be a merit-earned duty—"

"Yes. Perfect comportment and recommendations will be the prerequisite for being posted to that duty. With any brawling resulting in a six month disqualification from subsequent consideration. But really, Jan, you do not think our men would actually go so far as—?"

"Maarten, I will not balance the safety of the English ladies who visit—or perhaps, in the future, seek shelter with—us on my projections or hopes. We will assume the worst. And in the bargain, some lucky guards will come near enough to recall that ladies do, indeed, sweat—excuse me, *perspire*—in this weather. That they are not such perfect creatures, after all." Van Walbeeck squinted as the light rose sharply on the table before them. The sun had finally peeked around the steep slope of the volcanic cone that was known simply as The Quill, St. Eustatia's most prominent feature.

"Hmm. It is still the scent of a woman, Jan. And in circumstances such as ours, that will only quicken their starved ardor."

"No doubt, and no helping it. But charged with protecting the English ladies, I feel fairly certain that our guards would more willingly die defending them than protecting me."

"Far more willing," drawled Tromp,

"While you are around," smiled Walbeeck, "I shall never lose my soul to the sin of Pride. You are my guardian angel."

Tromp grunted as he felt the sunlight grow quick and warm on the side of his face. "A more improbable guardian angel there has never been."

"And yet here you sit, wearing a halo!" Walbeeck grinned, gesturing to the sun behind Tromp. "Now, have you decided to stop serving coffee on this sorry hull of yours?"

"Not yet," said Tromp, who almost smiled.

Two hours later, the coronet pealed again. Tromp frowned at Walbeeck's sudden and serious glance at the rum.

"Just one swallow. For perseverance in the face of immovable objects and irremediable ignorance."

"Jan, don't reinforce our enemies' characterization of us."

"Whatever do you mean?"

"You know perfectly well what I mean. Our resolve in battle is too often linked to our bolting shots of gin just before. 'Dutch courage,' they call it."

"Well, I could use a little of that courage right about now..."

The dreaded knock on the door was gentle enough but felt like a death knell to Tromp. "Enter," he said, trying to keep the sigh out of his voice. He flattered himself to imagine that he had succeeded.

The group that entered was not quite as ominously monolithic as he had feared. There were friendly faces among those crowding into the *Amelia*'s suddenly claustrophobic great cabin. Servatius Carpentiere and "Phipps" Serooskereken had been part of the *Politieke Raad* at Recife, and early converts to the exigency-driven agricultural changes that they had brought to St. Eustatia. But Jehan de Bruyne, also a member of that body, had been diametrically opposed from the start, and remained so, now drawing support from original Oranjestad settlers Jan Haet and Hans Musen, whose expectations of quick wealth had been dashed by the arrival of Tromp's ships and slavery injunctions.

Respectful nods notwithstanding, Musen was quick to confirm both the purpose and tenor of this visit by the determinative civil bodies of the St. Eustatia colony. "Admiral Tromp, we are sorry to disturb you on this busy day—"

—not half as sorry as I am—

"—but we have just learned that you will be setting sail soon. Today, it is rumored."

Tromp shrugged. "There are always rumors. Please continue."

Musen looked annoyed. "Very well. Since no one seems to know, or is willing to say, when you might return, we must make an appeal now, relevant to upcoming matters of commercial importance."

Tromp had had cannon aimed at him with less certainty of fell purpose. "Yes?"

"Admiral, you have forbidden the acquisition of new slaves with which to work the plantations here on St. Eustatia—"

"—which we still protest!" Jan Haet put in archly.

"—but we presume that this would not apply to any farms established on land that is not Dutch-owned."

Tromp resisted the urge to grind his molars. *And damn me for a fool that I did not see this coming.* "Mr. Musen, allow me to prevent you from spending time here profitlessly. The rules that apply on St. Eustatia apply equally to any plantations you may put in place on St. Christopher's."

"But that is English land!" shouted Jan Haet.

"But under our dominion while we lease it!" retorted Phipps Serooskereken.

"Immaterial," countered Musen coolly. "The terms of use permitted on the tracts around Sandy Point were made quite explicitly by Lord Warner: use of slaves is expressly permitted."

Jan van Walbeeck smiled broadly, and perhaps a bit wickedly. "Then perhaps you are preparing to swear loyalty to Thomas Warner?"

The various combatants started at him.

"Because, logically, that is what you must intend."

Jan Haet, as ardent a Dutch nationalist as he was a slaveholder, rose up to his full height of 5'5". "I intend no such thing, and you know it, Jan van Walbeeck!"

"Do I? Here is what I know. Fact: Lord Warner may no longer be a lord at all. England has renounced claim to the land he holds and upon which his title is based. Fact: your actions are not constrained by what he permits, but by what this regional authority allows you to do, as a Dutchman, in this place and time. And you have been forbidden from acquiring more slaves.

So unless you wish to renounce your citizenship in the United Provinces, what Thomas Warner permits you to do is secondary to what your government permits. And fact: swearing allegiance to Warner makes you men without a country and therefore invalidates you from working the leased land at Sandy Point, since that agreement exists solely between the representatives of the United Provinces and Thomas Warner." Jan Walbeeck smiled. "But of course, you can always become citizens of Thomas Warner's nation. If he ever declares one, that is."

Jehan de Bruyne had been frowning slightly at the deck throughout the exchange. "I will ask you to reconsider your ruling on slavery one last time, Maarten. I am not sure you understand the degree of dissatisfaction it is causing among our people."

Oh, I understand Jehan. I even understand the veiled threat in your calm tone. Tromp folded his hands. "Mijn heer de Bruyne, your own council, the *Politieke Raad*, voted in support of this measure. And I remain unclear how you can conclude that a slave population poses no credible threat to our security here. You have only to look at Thomas Warner's experience. In the last seven years, he has had to struggle to maintain control over his colony. And why? Not threat from the Caribs: they no longer appear willing to try cases with him. No, his problems arise from resentment and rebelliousness among his slave population."

Musen sniffed. "That is because the French keep stirring the pot."

"That may even be true, Hans, but would we be immune to such trouble? The French see the English as interlopers; why should they see us any differently? Indeed, given the presence of our forces on the island, will they not consider us an even greater problem? Because once we arrive and provide both plantation and border security for Thomas Warner, they will have even less chance to displace him—and us. Unless, that is, we bring our own slaves, whom they would no doubt attempt to suborn as well."

Tromp leaned back and shook his head. "No. People who have no freedom have little to lose. When slaves are being worked to death, they understand quickly enough that soon they will also lose the last thing they value: their lives, and those of their families. At that point, it is only logical for them to risk the probable suicide of unarmed rebellion rather than continue toward the certain suicide of eventually dying of malnourished exhaustion in the fields."

Haet leaned in aggressively. "And then why are the Spanish so successful using slaves, Tromp? They seem to do well enough and get rich while doing it."

Tromp studied Haet calmly but very directly. "Because, mijn heer Haet, the Spanish are not hanging on by their fingernails, as we are. They are routinely resupplied, routinely reinforced, and routinely involved in ruthlessly squashing any hint of resistance in their subject populations."

"And the Dutch East India Company does no less. And thrives!" countered Haet.

Jan van Walbeeck spoke quietly and without any trace of his customary animation. "I have been to those colonies, Haet, have been among their slaves. Have seen, have *felt*, the hatred for us in their eyes, in their gestures, in their quiet, patient watching. Are those Pacific colonies profitable? Yes, most certainly. Are they safe? Only so long as you have guns trained on the slaves, Haet. And one day—and it will only take *one* day—we will be weak, or forgetful, and we will stumble. And they will slaughter us and drive us back into the seas which brought us like a curse to their shores."

Haet snorted. "So you prefer the natives to your own kind, van Walbeeck?"

"Haet, I don't have to prefer them in order to understand that their feelings about us enslaving them on their own land are identical to our feelings about the Spanish doing the same to us in the Netherlands. And you remember what we did to the Spanish when we finally got the chance."

Haet was going to speak, but swallowed whatever words he might have spoken.

Tromp exchanged glances with van Walbeeck. Good: the conversation had remained on a practical footing. The ethical discussions over slavery had long ago proven themselves to be emotional morasses which achieved nothing but the expenditure of countless, profitless, hours. And they invariably led to the slaveholding faction accusing their opponents of succumbing to up-time influence (often true) and, by extrapolation, being Grantville's lackeys (not at all true). Indeed, since adolescence, Tromp had been disquieted by the circuitous rationalizations his countrymen and others employed when resolving their Christian piety with their grasp upon the slaveholder's whip. But, as an admiral, his life had not had much direct involvement with such matters, or the resolution of such issues.

But here in a New World where the Dutch colonies were hanging on by a thread that only remained uncut because the Spanish had not yet discovered it, the domain of the military and the commercial had begun to overlap. With no help or even news coming from the United Provinces, all choices, all decisions made locally had a bearing upon all other local decisions. And so Tromp had been compelled to weigh both the practical and ethical burdens and benefits of slavery.

Van Walbeeck, having arrived in Oranjestad ahead of him, had been an invaluable interlocutor on the matter, and the smattering of copied up-time texts in his library had been the catalyst for their discussions and grist for much deep thought. Leaving Recife, Tromp had been leaning against slavery for practical reasons, which happily aligned with his largely unstudied ethical misgivings. But the past year at St. Eustatia had confirmed him in the belief that, just as he had felt it his duty to become a church deacon if he was to live a Christian life and not merely profess one, so too he could not truly call himself a Christian without also working to undo the institution of slavery.

Van Walbeeck turned mild eyes upon the gathered contingent of councilors. "Any other observations on the matter?"

The quiet, careful Servatius Carpentiere, shrugged. "There will be much unrest among the colonists, particularly since the *Politieke Raad* approved your recommendation to prohibit raising tobacco." His voice was apologetic. One of Tromp's most stalwart supporters, Carpentiere was raising an issue that clearly had been pressed upon him by the colonists, but would certainly play into the hands of the admiral's detractors.

Musen lost no time wielding it as a rhetorical weapon. "You see, Admiral? Your own hand-picked advisers from Recife foresee problems with your decisions. First you prohibit the further acquisition of slaves. Then you urge the growing of cane sugar, which involves immense amounts of labor, in place of tobacco, which is much easier to grow and harvest. And which was why most of us came to Oranjestad in the first place."

Tromp nodded. "Yes. That is true. And when you came, tell me: what did you plan to do with the tobacco?"

Haet, not seeing the trap, blurted out, "Why, sell it, of course!"

"Where?"

"Back in—" and he stopped.

Tromp just nodded again. "Exactly. 'Back in the Provinces.' Or 'Europe.' It hardly matters where, specifically. The problem is that those markets are an ocean away from us here, and our own ports are unreachable, due to the Spanish. What few ships remain sheltered in smaller harbor towns are merely jachts which have no reason to brave the swells of the Atlantic. And even if they knew we still existed here, ready to trade, what of it? Yes, jachts are fast, nimble ships. But useless for freighting smoke or anything else in bulk. So tell me, mijn heer Haet, given the changes since you arrived here, where, now, would you sell your tobacco?"

Musen smoothly changed the footing of his side's argument to a less disastrous posture. "Even if that were to be true, Admiral— cane sugar? The most labor-intensive crop in the New World?"

"And the only one for which we have any local use," replied van Walbeeck. "What else would you grow for high profit? Cotton? The labor is almost as bad as cane but, again, there's the same problem: where would you sell that cotton? The fact that drives all our choices is this, mijn heer Musen: we no longer have access to markets. Our ships cannot come here safely, and we cannot spare any to undertake the equally perilous voyage from here to Europe. And what's more, any regular commerce between us and our homeports would only tell the Spanish—or others—where to find us, where to hunt us down and exterminate us.

"So we grow sugar. We may eat it ourselves, and we may make rum—which has local value even to the natives, in these parts. And which we may further refine into disinfectants and a flammable fluid. And if we cannot grow so much because we have no slaves? Well, first, we have no shortage of able-bodies without tasks to occupy them. And so we will learn that you do not need slaves to grow cane, and thereby set the pattern for creating a durable local economy which is not based upon slavery."

Haet looked as though he might spit. "I did not come here to work like a dog in the fields. I came here to get rich."

Tromp nodded. "Yes. But apparently fate had other plans."

Jehan de Bruyne rubbed his chin. "Or perhaps it is Maarten Tromp that has had other plans."

Tromp kept his head and voice very still. "I assure you, mijn heer, that being defeated by treachery at Dunkirk, and seeing the Dutch fleet reduced to three dozen hulls, was not any plan of mine. And it is that outcome—that and no other—which forces these changes upon us. You wished to be rich? Fair enough. I wanted to return home, to my wife and children. As do many of us who fled to Recife." He stood. "What men want is of little matter to the will of God and the hand of fate. I suggest we focus on a new want that we should all share: the desire to stay alive long enough for our own countrymen to find and succor us. Because that outcome is by no means certain." *By no means, indeed.* "Now, mijn heeren, if we are quite done, I have arrangements to make for the fleet. About which you shall be informed shortly. Good day."

The envoys from both the *Politieke Raad* and the original colonists' Council nodded their way toward the door they had entered through. Van Walbeeck rose to go as well, but Tromp motioned him to stay in his seat with a down-waved palm.

When the rest had left, Jan cocked his head like a quizzical spaniel.

Tromp sighed. "Stay and hear what I tell the captains. Someone will need to report it to the *Raad* and Council. And the rest of the colonists, too."

Chapter 20

St. Eustatia, Caribbean

Maarten had expected the various captains he had summoned to arrive in bunches, being familiar with how the vagaries of currents and oarsmen made it nearly impossible to maintain perfect punctuality when calling a council aboard a single ship in the midst of a wide anchorage.

Nonetheless, just after the first bell of the afternoon watch, the coronet blew only two blasts, the second no more than a minute after the first. Five minutes later, the entire collection of summoned officers were asking Willem for admittance. As soon as the young officer put his head in the door, Tromp made a waving-in motion and spread out the charts he had prepared, the top one being a general map of the Caribbees and the Spanish Main. The precision of its outlines and scale marked it immediately and distinctively as a high quality copy of a map from Grantville.

Cornelis Jol—who was known to all his peers simply as Houtebeen, or Peg Leg—came stumping in first. Immediately after came the big Dane, Hjalmar van Holst, with a broad smile on his face. Although two more dissimilar men would be hard to find, he and Tromp had taken an immediate liking to each other in the years before the disaster at Dunkirk. And that relationship had evolved into personal and political support of the admiral on more than one occasion over the year just past.

After that came his nominal superior, Dirck Simonszoon Uitgeest, who was considerably older and was as taciturn and spare as van Holst was gregarious and expansive. He, and one other attendee, young Pieter Floriszoon, had been in Recife when Tromp arrived. All the others—Klaus Oversteegen, Johan van Galen, and Hans Gerritsz—had escaped from the disaster at Dunkirk. Willem nodded the gentlemen in, then bowed to the admiral, halfway back out the door as he did so.

Tromp shook his head. "Willem. You are to join us and take notes. But fetch Kees, first. If something should happen to me, he must know the role the *Amelia* is to play in the action to come."

Willem looked like he had swallowed a pickled frog. "At once, Admiral," he croaked and rushed off to get Kees Evertsen.

There weren't quite enough chairs for everyone, but it didn't matter. Van Holst planted his feet, crossed his arms and looked ridiculously Norse and good-natured. Simonszoon had already slunk into a bench beneath the transom-spanning stern windows. There were seats enough for the others, but the room began to grow uncomfortably hot. That it was midday in the currently cloudless tropics did not help matters.

Tromp tugged his collar a bit wider and pointed at the map. "You've all seen one of these now, yes?"

Floriszoon leaned forward, admiring it. "No, Admiral. Not I. The precision is extraordinary."

"Yes. And quickly becoming universal. I would be surprised if the Spanish have not acquired their own copies. Although they are among the slowest to innovate in such ways. However, we must presume their charts are now as good as ours."

Van Galen looked eager. "So we sail against the Spanish? Finally?"

Tromp looked at Johan van Galen and reflected how the fleet's long period of inactivity made some men less aggressive, but made a few more so. For the latter, it was as if waiting to weigh anchor and sail into battle was some interminable itch that they simply could not scratch. "Some of us have been sailing against the Spanish all along. And their leader will begin by telling us of any changes he has encountered."

Peg Leg Jol thumped forward with a grin that he swept

around at all the gathered captains, and hunched over the map with positively conspiratorial glee. The Spanish considered Jol an out-and-out pirate, and in that moment, Tromp had to work hard to remember that his countryman was, technically, still a "privateer."

"So, news from the Main, fellows. Hunting continues to be good there. Took a barca-longa just before coming up here. Shot it up too much so we had to give her to the sea, but there was a fine haul aboard."

"Gold?" asked van Holst loudly.

"Better than gold. Letters. She was a mail courier. From what we read, the Spanish are still spending the majority of their time arguing over regional responsibilities. The Cuban governor doesn't like footing the whole bill for general naval protection, the Armada de Barlovento, against pirates and privateers throughout the Antilles, whereas the viceroy of New Spain is unwilling to spend on more than his own *garda costas*—half of whom seem to be freelancing as buccaneers as soon as the Silver Fleet finishes touching their respective parts of the Spanish Main every year."

"Anything about us?" asked Simonszoon quietly.

"Only mistakes. Their entire focus seems to be on Thijssen's seizure of Curaçao. There's a lot of speculation that we met him there after abandoning Recife. The governor of Venezuela has been trying to gather ships together to mount a counterattack, but his colleagues in the other coastal *audiencias* of the Viceroyalty of New Spain seem less than enthusiastic in helping him with that project. However, he has been gathering what forces he can in Puerto Cabello."

Klaus Oversteegen frowned. "Did you visit Curaçao yourself, then?"

Houtebeen Jol shook his round head. "No. Too close to the Spanish. But my sailing partner, Moses Cohen Henriques, roves nearer to their ports, since—having no Dutchmen aboard—even if they were captured, it wouldn't point the Spanish in our direction. He went as far as New Providence, where he made contact with Abraham Blauvelt, the famous 'explorer.'" Jol smiled. Blauvelt was not much less of a pirate that Houtebeen, truth be told. "So we got news from him, as well. All the attention of the Spanish Main, and even Havana, seems to be focused on Curaçao."

"That's good for us," observed Gerritsz soberly.

"Yes, but maybe not so good for Marten Thijssen," mused Jan van Walbeeck.

Tromp nodded. "True enough, but right now, we cannot help him—cannot even send word—without tipping our hand and calling attention to ourselves here." *Although we may be doing so soon enough, anyway.*

Simonszoon shifted from a mostly supine to mostly upright position. "Maarten, this is all very interesting, but you didn't bring us here to listen to Houtebeen tell us what he's already jabbered about in my great cabin when he's in his cups."

Jol smiled at Dirck even as he frowned. Simonszoon smiled back.

In that brief moment of silence created by their gruff camaraderie, Tromp discovered, and not for the first time, how grateful he was to have these two snarling sea dogs in his command. Both privateers with more a decade of experience, they had been the ones least panicked by the fleet's relocation from Recife to its tenuous safe haven on St. Eustatia. They had long experience with the vicissitudes of fate that shaped the lives of seamen, and the changing menu of perils it offered as its daily fare. Where Tromp's other captains had wrung their hands anxiously, these two had reached out their hands for another cup of rum and exchanged tales of the earliest days of Dutch colonization (the Spanish rightly called it "invasion") when danger and uncertainty had been *truly* high. These days, they opined with slow, sage sips at their fermented cane juice, were just a bit unpredictable. Nothing to lose sleep over.

"Dirck's right," agreed van Galen. "We all know your purser has been in town from first light this morning, buying provisions for the fleet. And we've all seen a disproportionate amount of those supplies coming to the ships captained by the men in this room. So where do we sail, Admiral? North again? To take back St. Maarten?"

Tromp shook his head. "No. That would be the last place I would sail, right now."

"Why? When the puny Armada de Barlovento came nosing south from there last year, we boxed them in and sank all four ships."

"Yes, thanks to the watch post the admiral set on the high ground of Saba Island," Simonszoon pointed out with a slow drawl that signified that van Galen's simplistic view of that engagement was beginning to annoy him.

Tromp waved away Dirck's compliment. "Simple prudence. Any capable commander would have taken that precaution. But Captain van Galen, have you considered how very *lucky* we were that day?"

"Lucky? Admiral, it was your skill and our naval superiority that won the day. We started with eight ships to their four and, thanks to the advance warning, had the wind gauge on them before they knew we were sailing the same ocean. And by the time they realized their predicament, the other three of our ships appeared on the leeward horizon, closing the trap. Those square-rigged Spanish apple-barges never had a chance."

Tromp had to glance at Simonszoon to keep him from commencing a low-voiced, laconical evisceration of yet one more nautical fool he was not willing to suffer gladly. "Mr. van Galen," Tromp said patiently, "I mean, have you ever thought how lucky we were *after* the battle?"

Van Galen blinked. "*After* the battle? How were we lucky after the battle? We won a clear victory and even—"

"You half-blind pup," whispered Simonszoon. "Have you never considered what must have happened on St. Maarten after those four ships failed to return?"

Van Galen's stunned silence—an expression of insult giving way to worried suspicion that he had missed a key piece of some naval puzzle—confirmed that he indeed had never considered such a thing.

Simonszoon acquainted him with the immensity of that oversight. "Then let me reprise the events on St. Maarten almost three or four weeks later, when, by any reasonable estimate, the Spanish on the island had to consider the under-equipped Armada de Barlovento to be missing. The commander there—Captain Cibrian de Lizarazu, if last word is accurate—no doubt picked up his goose quill pen and started a letter to his superior, one Captain-General Bitrian de Viamonte in Santo Domingo. In this letter, Lizarazu certainly reported the disappearance of the entirety of that puny Armada, and promised his continued vigilance for any sign of its return.

"But as months wore on, he could only report more silence, and ultimately he and Don de Viamonte considered the Armada de Barlovento lost and the matter closed. Except that then, we must assume that Don de Viamonte—whose physical infirmities and less than dazzling personality have never interfered with his ability to perform as one of Spain's most prudent regional administrators—no doubt sent word to Governor Gamboa in Cuba, along with a request to reconstitute the Barlovento. That worthy may or may not have initially agreed, but over time, it is hard to imagine that he would not ultimately concede to such an appeal. After all, how many times have four warships disappeared without a trace, unless they were engaged by a similar or greater force of adversaries? Pirates flee from strong adversaries, particularly a flotilla of them. So the thinking in Hispaniola and Cuba by early this year must have come round to entertaining the possibility that there is a rival power somewhere in the New World: a power that has reason to attack, and apparently seize or sink, four Spanish men-o'-war. And here's the lucky part, van Galen: they still haven't sent a reconstituted Barlovento south, to follow the path of the first. Because if they did, what's the first major island they'd come to after departing St. Maarten?"

Van Galen's eyes cheated sideways slightly to look at the outlines of Oranjestad.

"That's right, they'd come here. St. Eustatia. If the Spanish knew the problem was so close to their own holdings in Hispaniola and Puerto Rico, they'd waste no time exterminating us en masse. We're too close to the Flota's return route to Spain, too close to their silver pipeline. And too close to major ports that we could fall upon with little warning." Simonszoon leaned back, his dark eyes lusterless. "If you haven't given thought to all that, Captain van Galen, it's time you did. And while you do, consider this piece of extreme good luck: that Marten Thijssen's attack upon and investiture of Curaçao occurred, by blind chance, at precisely the right time to give the Spanish a completely plausible source for completely erroneous conjectures. Specifically, that the Barlovento must have run afoul of Thijssen's flotilla and been sunk. Otherwise, they'd have been looking out for another explanation. Meaning, us."

Pieter Floriszoon was still staring at the map. "Frankly, it seems impossible that they still don't know we are here. It has been a year since we arrived, almost three since Oranjestad was established, and they haven't once checked on what they claim to be their possession?"

Van Walbeeck shrugged. "This is not uncommon for the Spanish,

Pieter. The Spanish haven't made landfall in the Leeward Antilles since they shattered the English and French colonies on St. Christopher's in 1629. They never even bothered to return to ensure that the English colonists who fled into the mountains didn't reestablish their settlement. Which they did. With a vengeance."

"Yet they must have word of the rebuilt colony. Its goods travel back to Europe, and its port is not unknown."

"Not unknown, yet almost never visited except by us. And the Spanish will hear less of those goods in Europe now. Charles the First has forsaken England's New World colonies and so has all but lost contact with his subjects—or former subjects—here. An English ship has no business in New World waters, these days. The French are said to be attempting to revivify their *Compagnie de Saint-Christophe* to grow their colony on St. Christopher, but seem to have a hard time attracting the focused attention of their primary patron, Richelieu. So, except for the two buccaneers we intercepted last winter, who visits these waters anymore?"

"And the Spanish are not curious after losing the three ships they sent south from St. Maarten earlier this year?"

"I am sure they are curious, but Thijssen's attack on Curaçao does offer a likely explanation. Far more so than the proposition that the last Dutch fleet in the world lies lurking, almost immobile, in the Leeward Islands. And when it comes to the losses of their individual ships to Houtebeen and our other raiders, common pirates are a far more likely explanation. Or an opportunistic attack by the god- and king-forsaken English who still endure on Bermuda, Barbados, New Providence, St. Christopher's and Antigua."

Simonszoon muttered, "Some are in the Bahamas, now. On Eleuthera, mostly, if the rumors are true."

Tromp nodded. "I am half-ready to believe those reports. Without regular resupply from home, the English on Bermuda have the same problem we do: too many people and too little cultivated land. Only their crisis is ten times greater. They outnumber us here by at least five-to-one, and Bermuda is not particularly arable. Or furnished with larger neighboring islands, as we are. So of course the English there must strike out toward better sources of sustenance."

"Meaning the Bahamas," observed Gerritsz.

"Yes, and Eleuthera is the outermost of the islands, with good bays, but not much frequented by the Spanish."

"Even the bastard buccaneers of Association Island don't sail that far out, usually," commented van Holst.

"No," van Walbeeck agreed. "But do not expect that the English are going to Eleuthera to find food, so much as establish a gathering point for it."

Van Holst frowned. "What do you mean?"

"Eleuthera is more pleasant than Bermuda, but still not a particularly good source of comestibles. The richer islands of the Bahamas are closer in to the continent. My guess is that the English—well, I suppose they are 'Bermudans,' now—plan on using Eleuthera as a staging area. Their ships will fan out into the better islands from there, and return there as well. Then a different set of ships will convey the foodstuffs they've gathered back to Bermuda."

Simonszoon rose into a sitting position. "Very well. So we have been very lucky, and the English have the same problems we do. But that tells me nothing about why there are dry goods getting jammed into every open space on my ship's orlop deck right now."

"No, it doesn't," Tromp admitted, "but it was imperative that we all have the best current knowledge about what we know or suspect conditions to be in the Caribbean."

"Why?"

"Because in the event that any of your ships must scatter away from each other to survive, you must be able to act independently and wisely to save your crews, your hulls, and hopefully, make it back here to St. Eustatia."

The quiet in the cabin became absolute.

Van Holst nodded. "To where are we sailing, Maarten?"

Tromp removed the top chart. Beneath it was another, this one of the Windward Antilles and Trinidad. He pointed at the latter's large, almost squarish mass. "There." He paused. "At first."

"What does that mean, 'at first'?" Simonszoon almost whispered.

"It means I have annoyingly incomplete information."

"Information that came in with Jakob Schooneman of the *Koninck David*, last night?"

"Yes. Here is what I know: a French ship was sighted by the *Koninck David* some thirty miles southeast of this anchorage, heading due south. Cautiously."

"Cautiously? You mean it didn't want to be seen by us?"

"Perhaps. But more pertinently, it did not want to be seen by the ship it was apparently trailing, and so remained at a distance that allowed it to stay beneath the horizon from its prey."

Kees Evertsen frowned. "Admiral, it is rather difficult to shadow a ship once it is no longer visible. Hard to keep track of its course changes, I'm told."

Grins sprung up at Kees' profound understatement.

"That is true, Kees, but not if the following ship is flying an observation balloon."

Again, absolute silence. Several of the captains seemed to be trying to remember what that word even meant.

Simonszoon stood up, sauntered over to the map. "A balloon? How high?"

"Several hundred feet, at least, Dirck. Yet, at even fifteen miles, it would be less than a dot in the sky. You'd need to be looking at just the right spot, with a fine spyglass, to spot it."

Simonszoon nodded. "So even the tops of your masts could be well below the horizon and, with the balloon aloft, you could still keep your eyes on a ship ahead of you."

"Precisely."

"But why?" blurted van Holst loudly, "and how does Schooneman of the *Koninck David* know that both these ships are bound for Trinidad, which I presume must be why we are now going there?"

Tromp felt his teeth lock together. *How indeed does Jakob Schooneman know what he knows? Indeed, his reports are not made up of facts but intimations, as if he either knows he is missing important pieces of the underlying story, or has been forbidden from revealing them.* "Hjalmar, you do know that the *Koninck David* is the first ship from home to find us here, do you not?"

"Yes, which is why I rather expected that you were gathering us: to announce that we would once again have the help and succor of the United Provinces arriving in the coming months."

"I wish that was the news that I have. And I suspect something like that may be forthcoming. But what you do not know is that when last the *Koninck David* was in these waters last year, mostly along the Spanish Main, she had an up-time passenger. One whose reports on the New World have apparently found interested ears back home."

The captains leaned in closer, like hounds on the scent.

"Among other things, Captain Schooneman bore a letter from

Prince Hendrik's own chamberlain, indicating that the prince bade us listen carefully to the recommendations of the master of the *Koninck David*, who had been acquainted with His Highness's interests and ambitions as they related to pending events in the New World."

When it was clear that Tromp had finished, Gerritsz jumped to his feet. "'Pending events?'" he almost shouted. "What kind of oblique nonsense is that?"

Simonszoon cut a sharp glance at his colleague. "The kind of oblique nonsense that *remains* nonsense when heard by the wrong ears, Gerritsz. Ears that must not learn the secret intents and actions of our Provinces." Looking back at the map, Dirck put his hand beneath his chin. "And so, both Hendrik's 'interests' and this mysterious French ship lead Jakob Schooneman of the *Koninck David* to tell us that we must go to Trinidad?"

"Yes."

"But Schooneman won't offer any further explanation or speculation?"

Tromp shrugged. "When I asked him that very question, he simply responded, 'You know I was on Trinidad last year, don't you?' I replied in the affirmative. He explained that he had touched the coast at Pitch Lake to take on some of the tar, and that there had been no Spanish in sight. Not a single Spanish sail was spied in those waters, in fact. And then he mentioned that he had been made aware of an up-time book that indicated that beneath the tar, there were vast quantities of oil."

Simonszoon almost smiled, turned, and collapsed back into the bench, half supine again. The other captains stared around. "Oil?" asked Oversteegen at last.

"Oil," affirmed van Walbeeck. "Which is of interest to the up-timers, and to any nation that hopes to adopt their technology. It is the best source of energy for their engines, if I remember correctly."

"You do," nodded Tromp.

Kees matched the nod. "Well, that explains the French presence then. They clearly have ambitions to adopt up-time technology."

"Yes, it explains the French, but whose ship are they following?" van Holst asked. "Up-timers?"

"That's unknowable at this point," said van Galen with a dismissive wave of his hand. "But we may be sure of one thing: it means that our presence here could be discovered soon. Within weeks, even."

Van Walbeeck perched his chin on his fist. "And how does the presence of the French ship return us to that concern?"

"Is it not obvious?" van Galen asked, either oblivious to or uncaring of the impatient glares his impolitic tone was earning. "This is the first French ship to even approach these waters since we arrived from Recife—or at least, since our arrival was known to the colonists on St. Christopher's."

"So?" asked Gerritsz testily.

"So what other friendly port does this Frenchman have in these waters? The French on Association Island are, from all accounts, lawless buccaneers. The so-called privateers who operate out of the tent-towns in the Bahamas and the Florida Keys are far away and would be more likely to seize the ship than help it." He thumped the table for emphasis. "No. When the French have concluded whatever skulduggery they are about, they will have to make landfall on St. Christopher's before departing the Caribbees. And from that moment, the candle that measures our remaining days of safety will begin burning down."

Simonszoon folded his arms. "Tell me, van Galen: have you received credible word that the French would send a fleet to expel us from St. Eustatia?"

"No," said van Galen, unperturbed by his senior's droll, facetious tone, "but why should the French not tell the Spanish that we are here? Or, better yet, use the threat of doing so to extort our cooperation?"

"Extortion to do what?" Van Walbeeck queried.

"Why, to help them drive Warner and his people from St. Christopher's. Knowing the French, I suspect they'd garnish the deal by offering to share the island with us. But I suspect they would only concede a tiny fraction of the lands they gained from displacing their hereditary English foes."

"Who, on St. Christopher's, no longer represent that hereditary foe."

"That's a mere detail. Hereditary foe or not, the French want St. Christopher's. And if this ship returns to Europe unable to effect that conquest now, they might be followed by a flotilla which can. Which would mean we'd have very large, and very dangerous, neighbors."

"So what do you recommend?" asked van Walbeeck.

"That we should be prepared to 'entertain' an offer to cooperate with the French in the matter of Warner and his people. If the French can take St. Christopher's without need of reinforcements, they might not summon a fleet. Not for a very long time."

Tromp simply kept staring at the map, and thought: *Van Galen is truly piratical. Not on the superficial level of operations like Jol. No, he is too comfortable with what makes a man a genuine sea wolf: a ready embrace of duplicity and stratagems based on guile and deceit. I wish I could leave him back here, but I've got to bring him along. He's just the type who, unwatched, might go looking for trouble, find it, and bring it right back to our doorstep. I just wish he didn't also have a very good point about the French ship.*

"That will be a matter for us to address when the time comes. And if it arises while we are still gone, then mijn heeren van Walbeeck and Jol will be available to make a suitable response."

Houtebeen Jol started. "You're leaving me behind? With the rest of the fleet? Maarten, surely you must—"

"Captain Jol. I am leaving you behind. But not with the fleet. That's not the place for you."

Jol's injured expression began to shift into a blend of shock and rage. "Why, I'm twice the captain of any—"

"Jol," Tromp said calmly, "I can't afford to tie you down to *any* fleet. Not the one I'm sailing with, and not the one I'm leaving here under the command of Joost Banckert. I need you to keep doing exactly what you're doing: being our ears and eyes in the wider Caribbean. Because, if any Spanish should happen to decide to venture in this general direction while we are gone—"

At which words, Peg Leg Jol held up a hand and nodded. "Yes, Maarten. I understand. I don't like it—but I understand."

Tromp hoped that Jol did understand the full import of his responsibility to St. Eustatia now. Yes, he had to keep Jol at his specialty—a rover—and had increased need of his ability to gather intelligence along the Spanish Main. But if Tromp failed, or worse yet, did not return, then the thin but crucial trickle of supplies that Jol's raiding provided would need to be expanded, and quickly. If the Dutch lost the ten fighting hulls that Tromp was taking south, the Dutch would, in the same act, have come to the attention of one or more foes. And sooner or later, that meant that the Spanish would seek the source of the destroyed ships, and attempt to reduce it by bombardment and blockade.

When it came to building up a reserve of munitions and supplies to endure such an eventuality, and yet to acquire them surreptitiously, Jol had no peer. He was a master at finding single ships before they detected him, shadowing them, closing during the night (no mean feat, and he was its master) and then attacking them early and swiftly so that, by midday, he had the prize in hand. If the ship was in good enough shape and a good sailer, he brought her back with a prize crew if he had the men to spare and the distance was not too great. Otherwise, he took what he could, spars included, and scuttled her. No fires: that could draw attention.

Which was always, of course, his most important objective: to leave the Spanish unaware of his depredations. As far as the viceroy of New Spain and the governors of his various *audiencias* were concerned, these were ships that simply disappeared, as did so many others that sailed alone in the treacherous waters of the Caribbean.

The one difficulty with his operations had been prisoners. Not the presence of them—the Dutch only had three dozen under guard at Fort Oranjestad—but their paucity. Jol had taken eight large ships, so far. Almost all had crews that had been greater than twenty, some considerably more. And yet, only thirty-six prisoners. The Spaniards—indeed, everyone but the Dutch—had long considered Houtebeen Jol more of a pirate than a privateer, but even those detractors who labeled him El Pirata nonetheless grudgingly conceded that when it came to enemies and prisoners, Jol was a singularly humane and considerate fellow. And yet, only thirty-six prisoners.

In the past year, Houtebeen Jol's missions had not been for commercial gain; they had been for the survival of St. Eustatia. More than once, in the early days, widespread starvation had been narrowly averted by the timely return of Jol's twenty-two-gun *Otter*, loaded with Spanish foodstuffs but without a single Spanish prisoner aboard. What could explain such ominously suspicious circumstances? Jol, who had always been an almost insufferably merry fellow, had grown quieter over that year, and did not volunteer an explanation.

To his shame, Tromp had not asked for one. Because, after all, what was the point of doing so? Jol had known well enough that the thousands of newly arrived refugees on St. Eustatia could not feed themselves, let alone prisoners. Furthermore, each Spaniard taken prisoner was one more escape risk, one more chance that someone would alert the viceroys that there was a credible challenge to their power in the New World, but that it was fragile and vulnerable and could be eliminated by a single decisive blow.

Simonszoon had risen. "So, no pirates in our fleet," He poked his friend Peg Leg in the ribs to lighten the mood. "And the rest of us? We're the fleet?"

"You and a few other ships."

Van Holst crossed his arms. "Which others?"

"The *Neptunus*, the *Achilles*, and the *Kater*."

Pieter Floriszoon, who commanded the most heavily gunned of all the Dutch jachts, the *Eendracht*, nodded. "So I'm to be helping Captain Gijszoon of the *Kater*, then."

Tromp looked slowly sideways at Floriszoon. "No, he will be helping you."

For a moment, the young captain's face was blank as he worked through the unexpected inversion of syntax. Then his eyes went wide as the implication hit. "But Admiral, Jochim Gijszoon is an old hand with coordinating the actions of jachts. The oldest, in fact."

"Which is precisely why I don't want him leading our scouting efforts. He is too valuable to put at the tip of the spear when we are maneuvering to secure the wind gauge." The gathered men nodded solemnly at this bit of wisdom that was only one half the real explanation, which they all implicitly understood from Tromp's indirect announcement of Floriszoon's promotion over Gijszoon.

Yes, Gijszoon was the oldest hand at leading the jachts, but was arguably slightly *too* old a hand. Years made some men more bold because they became more certain of themselves and their methods. Not so Jochim Gijszoon. Ever since the news of Dunkirk had arrived, he had acted like a man haunted. He had lost many—indeed, almost all—of his old friends that day, and although his seamanship and leadership skills were undiminished, he had become increasingly cautious, to the point where he was unwilling to take necessary, or at least, advisable and advantageous risks. And if that was an unfortunate trait in the captain of a slower, larger ship, it was a disastrous trait in the captain of the smaller, faster jachts, whose job it was to scout ahead, lure targets to the main body, and out-race adversaries to secure the wind gauge for the rest of their fleet when battle was finally to be joined. The light cavalry of the seas, leading the jachts was not a job for the faint of heart or the skittish, and unfortunately, Jochim Gijszoon had become both.

With characteristically unflappable focus on the practicalities of an upcoming mission, van Holst looked up from the map. "So. We do not know what we must do at Trinidad. But surely Schooneman shared some hint of the *means* whereby we may learn of the objectives that our ships are to pursue there?"

Tromp looked van Holst in the eye. "No. I do not have such information." He didn't give his captains time to formulate the questions he himself would already be asking—stridently—in their place. "I know how this sounds. I had the same reaction. But remember and consider the significance of this detail: the French are *not* making best speed to Trinidad, but are *trailing* another ship. Which sounds very much like Richelieu's *modus operandi*. Something is afoot which he wishes his men to observe, perhaps wishes them to take advantage of, but which he does not wish them to initiate themselves."

"Meaning what?"

"Meaning," Simonszoon put in, "that while Richelieu may be interested in Trinidad, Richelieu is not the primary actor. He is positioning himself to observe and react, not attack."

Van Holst threw out wide hands in exasperation. "But then whose flag *is* taking action on Trinidad? The Spanish already own it. The French are observing, not acting. The English aren't in the game anymore. Our forces are too crippled to make such a move. So who's left? Who is moving on Trinidad?"

"Who wants oil the most?" mused van Walbeeck.

The gathered captains exchanged glances as van Holst asserted. "The up-timers, the USE. As I conjectured."

"And you might well be correct. Let us not forget that this news comes to us via Jakob Schooneman, who has coordinated with the up-timers in the past. But all this is still just guesswork."

Gerritsz shook his head. "All this obfuscation worries me."

Tromp nodded. "Me too, Hans. However, we may be sure of this: whoever is taking action on Trinidad either prefers, or needs, our presence there. And unless Schooneman is lying, Prince Hendrik prefers, or needs, us to be there also. So we go." He leaned away from the chart-table. "Not so different from the missions of our forefathers, after all. Sail into the unknown, lay hold of the opportunities that chance puts before us. Except this time, it seems to be a matter of certainty, rather than chance, that such an opportunity exists on Trinidad."

"Yes," agreed van Holst, "but these 'opportunities' are not going to be wrested from feckless, ill-armed natives. We are set to beard the Spanish lion in its den. And that lion is likely to resist effectively and tenaciously."

"That, too, is true," Tromp agreed, and restrained a quick, unbidden impulse to glance at Little Willi. Protective instincts died hard, and right now, they were shouting loudly in Tromp's ear: *leave him behind, here in Oranjestad! Don't take him into battle! Don't bring another innocent with you, only to be gobbled up by death's greedy maw while you escape those fangs yet again!*

But Maarten Tromp knew that trying to shelter him was futile. Here, in the New World, the saying had it that *there is no peace beyond the Line*—the "Line" being the longitudinal divider known as the Tordesillas Line, west of which all territory was claimed by Spain. So there was no safe place for Willem van der Zaan in the Caribbean, and he might as well start learning the bloody trade into which he'd been born so that he had the best chance of surviving long and uncrippled. And at least he wouldn't be forced to do so under the command of a captain too rash, too timid, too uncertain to maximize the lad's chances of coming through that most difficult of all trials: the first battle. There, everything was new, and terrifying, and the novices died in windrows for one reason above all others: the shock that paralyzed them for one, fateful second. For in that second, as they stood gaping and horrified, they were easy targets for the grizzled veterans who knew that killing a neophyte now meant one less seasoned opponent to face later on.

Tromp looked around the room, where his own collection of grizzled veterans were already comparing notes on sailing conditions farther down the Caribbees and tactical contingencies for handling the different numbers and kinds of enemies they might face. They were, Tromp conceded, probably the very best grizzled veterans in the world.

But, even so, were they enough?

Chapter 21

Overlooking Pitch Lake, Trinidad

For the second time that day, Hugh came to the crest of the northern lip of the bowl-like depression that cradled their objective. And again, as he looked down upon it, he wondered: *I left kith and kin for* this?

Pitch Lake was wrinkled, its uneven folds sagging over upon folds in some places. It was as if an immense black peat bog had grown the hide of an elephant. The foliage around the bitumen expanse was low scrub, although on the modest northern overlook, it was mostly grass with a few trees bent sideways by the prevailing winds. The northern coast at their backs chased around to the west and then down south, the shore keeping a constant distance of about one-and-a-half miles from the tarry bowl. In the west, a forest rose up at about the halfway mark, whereas to the direct south and east, low grass and occasional trees crowded the lake more closely, rising into tall bushes and then true jungle canopy after only one hundred yards or so.

Hugh took in the total tactical picture. Good: this vantage point offered clear sightlines in all directions. And since this overlook backed on the north shore—the deepest water and closest coastal approach to Pitch Lake—it confirmed Hugh's first instincts. "We build the stockade here," he announced with a nod.

Morraine came to stand next to him. "Very good," he said. "But then, you hardly need my approval."

Next to him, St. Georges had his mouth open to object—

Morraine held up a hand. "I am in command on the sea; Lord O'Donnell commands on the land. These matters are his affairs. At most, we can offer our opinion and advice."

"Both of which I welcome, Captain."

"For now, I have none." Morraine stepped back with a slight inclination of his head. "I will leave you to your command, Colonel."

"Very well." And as he turned to address the challenges of this venture, Hugh had an image of himself waving one last farewell to Anna's grave-swallowed coffin. There would be little time for dwelling upon the past, now. He turned to the business at hand.

"O'Rourke, establish four watch posts. One near the north coast, overlooking the anchorage. One at treetop to watch the west coast, one to watch the edge of the eastern forest, one at the south compass point of the lake. All in brush, all under cover, all in direct line of sight to this spot."

"Signaling mirrors?"

"Yes, and double muskets for all. Three day-watches. But we'll pull the outposts in at night."

"No night watch in the outposts?"

"O'Rourke, are you familiar with these jungles?"

"No, m'lord."

"Well, neither are the rest of us. But our enemies are quite familiar with the lay of this land, and so any men we leave out during the night will never see their killers coming. And we won't know our lads are gone until they fail to signal at the appointed time, or we're under attack by those who killed them. Now, let's get those outposts set up."

O'Rourke agreed with a frowning nod and swung away, roaring names as he went. "Brown, Garvey, Finan, O'Halloran, Hanley—"

Hugh turned to Michael, who was studying the area intently. "Michael, would you mind supervising my engineer, Doyle, as we lay out the camp?"

Michael shrugged. "Sure. It's always better to have something to do."

Hugh looked beyond Michael. "And Mulryan, you assist. You,

too, have nothing else to do until your balloon comes ashore with the stores."

"Yes, m'lord. What's the layout?"

Hugh smiled at the young fellow's ready, unpretentious confidence. Mulryan had shown the same broad aptitudes at the University of Louvain, under the Franciscans. They had pleaded with the lad to consider a professorial vocation to show his love of Christ, but as soon as he had been old enough, Tearlach had signed on with O'Donnell to show his love of country, instead.

Hugh knelt to draw a rough map in the dirt. "We'll keep the defenses simple: square palisade, one hundred feet per side. If the available wood permits, ten foot high, but no less than seven. Green wood only. Two foot of soil buttressing the base on the inside. Platforms at corners, another at the center of each expanse, two at the gate—one to either side."

Doyle was adding details to Hugh's dusty top-down schematic. "Where do you want the gate, m'lord?"

"Center of the south wall, on a straight line to the lake. We'll be hauling pitch up here, before long. No reason to put curves in the pathway. Get up the walls before you start on the buildings, Doyle. We'll make do with tents until they're up."

Michael looked at the diagram. "Buildings?"

Hugh drew a square in the center of the north wall. "From the main gate, a lane goes straight though the middle of the compound and ends at the back wall. That's where we'll want a small warehouse with double doors."

Hugh's engineer frowned. "A warehouse? Not a shed?"

"No, Doyle. I know it's much work, but we've got to have a few hard points inside the compound. The storehouse will be one of them. Now, to the west, or left, of the storehouse, we put light sheds for storing and servicing the balloon. We keep those as far back from the gate as possible."

Mulryan frowned. "Pity we can't conduct all the balloon operations from inside the walls."

"The interior space needed for laying out the envelope before and after flights is a luxury we can't afford, Tearlach. It would double the perimeter, and therefore, the walls we have to build."

Michael nodded. "Yep, sure would. Go on."

"The blockhouse goes on the other side of the lane from the

balloon sheds. So it's toward the northeast, or right rear, of the compound."

Doyle goggled. "A . . . blockhouse, m'lord? With respect, the time it will take—"

"I know, Doyle, so get to work on it right after the palisade. And double-time it, man. Do the blockhouse's inner walls first, but prepare the ground for a second course of timber four inches out from the first walls—"

"—the space between to be filled with rocks and mud?"

Hugh turned to look at McCarthy. "Have you been studying 'ancient fortification' techniques, Michael?"

"Some. That's going to take a long time to build."

"To completion, yes. For now, I just want the outer walls, a solid roof with a low waist-works, and an observation tower."

Doyle made his voice ridiculously respectful. "Is that *all*, m'lord?"

Hugh smiled. "We can leave the tower until last. We just need a light framework."

"Oh well, if that's all—"

"Doyle—"

"Pardons, m'lord. I'll just be checking now if I've any miracles left mixed in w' me pioneer tools."

"I'm sure you've got at least one in there."

"Without doubt, m'lord."

Hugh looked up as O'Rourke came back, florid, sweating heavily in his face. "Water, O'Rourke: drink lots of it. Starting right now. This isn't the Low Lands."

"With respect, m'lord, I've noticed."

"Then empty your canteen down your gullet. And after you do, get a water detail going."

O'Rourke nodded, then turned to McCarthy. "Don Michael, if I might look at your map, again?"

McCarthy handed him the map-tube, then kneeled to look more closely at the evolving layout of the stockade. "And what are you going to put on the south side of the compound, near the gate?"

"Tents for the men, huts when we get the chance to build them."

McCarthy scratched tentatively at the diagram. "I wonder: can I get a small work detail from the ship's crew? Just for a day or two?"

Hugh leaned closer to Michael, keeping his voice low. "That's problematic. As it is, it's awkward, having to keep St. Georges and his half-dozen men here. The fiction that they are our guests is unconvincing, at best." Then Hugh conceived of a strangely pleasant solution to the dilemma. "Michael, perhaps you can use St. Georges and his men, instead of a separate work detail."

McCarthy's answering smile was not pleasant. "Perhaps I can."

"And now I must ask—what do you need them for?"

Michael shrugged. "I've asked Morraine to demount two of his eight-pound sakers for the fort. I need to wheel them in, emplace them."

Hugh frowned. "To cover the land approaches, or the sea?"

McCarthy smiled. "Neither. Actually, what I had in mi—"

"M'lord," a new voice interrupted.

Hugh looked up. It was Kevin O'Bannon, softest foot in the regiment, and one of its best shots as well. He and a team of four had put ashore in a cat-boat at dawn, two miles east of Pitch Lake. Their mission had been to sniff out the natives who might be in the area and, according to most reports, kept a fairly constant eye out for trespassers. Hugh stood. "Good to see you back, O'Bannon. Your report?"

O'Bannon scratched his ear. "Sir, I—"

"A problem? Fast, man: tell me."

"No, m'lord. Not a problem. Not one damned problem. The opposite, in fact."

Hugh had been ready to hear, and respond to, any contingency—except this. "What do you mean?"

"No sign of natives, m'lord. At least nothing recent. We found one campsite, about a mile to the east. There were the remains of a small fire that had to be at least two weeks old, maybe a month."

Hugh frowned and considered. This was either very good news, or very bad news. If the natives had—due to disease, disinterest, or disputes—abandoned their unofficial coast watch of this area, then their absence was a stroke of extraordinary good luck. But if the absence was intentional, it might indicate that the *Fleur Sable* had been seen approaching. Which, given her nighttime approach and dark running, would be hard to imagine. The other possibility, but even harder to imagine, was that their arrival had been anticipated, and the natives were merely hanging back for now. But either way—

Hugh clapped O'Bannon on the shoulder. "Good news or no,

mystery or no, you've done fine work and we proceed as if you had seen the Arawaks in the flesh. Set watches and patrols as already assigned. If they're waiting for us to relax our vigilance, they'll have a long wait." He turned to Doyle. "Get your timber from the forest on the western shore, but all from the landward side."

"—because by taking trees from the landward side, passing boats won't see any changes to the forest there."

Hugh nodded appreciatively at Mulryan's foresight. "And so you also know when we'll use the balloon?"

Tearlach nodded. "At night only."

Doyle gaped. "And what are you to be seein' at night? Banshees? The moon?"

Hugh shook his head. "Actually, Doyle, we'll never go aloft when the moon is up. We could be spotted, then. But on the nights we do go up, we'll be looking for lights. On the water, lights show us the positions of ships, and on land, lights mark the presence of natives or Spaniards. Either way, there's a good chance we'll have warning the night before we have any daytime visitors."

Hugh looked around the group, waited. "Well? Am I going to have to build it all myself?" With the exception of Michael, the command staff fragmented outward, each fragment heading for a different cluster of waiting soldiers.

Michael watched them go, watched the different groups set about their assigned tasks. "They love you, you know," he said at last. "All of them."

Hugh looked away, to hide the emotion he felt welling up behind his eyes.

Part Four

August 1635

In noble eminence enthroned

Chapter 22

Southeast of Anegada Island, entry to the Caribbean

Eddie Cantrell was about to put down the water jug, then thought the better of his manners and tilted it toward his guest. Larry Quinn nodded, hand out to receive the pitcher as the younger man reached it across the slightly swaying table.

"It doesn't taste half bad," Quinn commented. "Particularly for desalinated water."

"The condensers are doing pretty well," Eddie admitted. "Which is good: the Caribbean is not a great place to run out of feed water."

Larry poured out a half glass of water. "Ironic. At sea, steam engines are just as vulnerable as humans."

"What do you mean?"

Larry leaned back in his chair and screwed his eyes closed as he apparently strove to find a distant memory. Which turned out to be a line of poetry: "'Water, water, everywhere, and not a drop to drink.'"

"Uh...Wordsworth?"

"Right poetic church, wrong poetic pew. Coleridge. 'Rime of the Ancient Mariner.'"

Eddie tried not to look crestfallen. He was supposed to be the book hound, not Quinn. But then again, although Quinn had read less deeply, he had read more broadly. In a bookstore, Quinn had been a wanderer, a browser, whereas Eddie's attention had been largely confined to the fantasy and science fiction shelves, with frequent forays into military history and relevant technology.

Apparently, Eddie's attempt to conceal his disappointment was not successful, although Quinn misread the cause. "Hey, so there's a little metallic taste to the water. I've had worse on camping trips. And lots worse when I went on maneuvers with the Reserves back in West Virginia. Overall, these ships are functioning just great. You should be really proud."

Now Eddie tried not to sulk. "I'll be a lot more proud when we get the bugs ironed out."

"Bugs? Like what?"

"Like the lower compression ratios we're getting out of the engines. That and the handmade brass fittings and pipe joints all mean less speed because we can't push the engines as hard. And those condensers you're raving about, yeah, they work, but they're finicky. And we've got higher-than-anticipated gear wear on every system that uses down-time alloys. I mean, the local fabricators have made huge, huge strides, but—well, let me put it this way: this may look like a nineteenth-century ship, but there's still a lot of semi-improved seventeenth-century technology under the hood."

Larry knocked back the last of the water, which was in marginally better supply upon the *Intrepid* than it was upon the *Courser*, the ship he had been assigned to. "Eddie, my boy," he said with a big-brotherly grin, "you worry too much. Which, truth be told, is probably why you're so good at this job."

"If I'm so good at this job, then why did we almost botch a balloon recon op again? We rehearsed it so many times on the crossing, but as soon as we get close to the Caribbean and the men see a sail—"

Larry put down his cup with a resounding, but not quite startling, clack. "Look, Eddie. There are going to be teething problems with everything on these ships. Everything. That's why they call it a shakedown cruise." He smiled. "It's a shakedown cruise for you, too. And you did just fine today. I watched you handle each new wrinkle like a pro. Not as calmly as an old pro, mind you—" his smile broadened "—but a pro, nonetheless. You saw how the change in the wind was going to produce updrafts that would also push the balloon in the direction of that Spanish ship right about the same time they came around toward our heading."

"And they may have seen us, you know."

"Hmm, really? The only reason *we* knew they were out there was because we had a sky-guy up in your balloon, sending down Morse code updates of what he could see well over the horizon. So the Spanish *couldn't* see our ships, and would have to be wizards to see our blue-gray balloon. And when you had us tack away to get leeward of them, that gave us all the speed we needed to slip off to the south. It also helped that you hauled in the balloon to counter the updraft, and got your pilot to keep his hands off the burner, even when he was sure the bag was going to deflate and plunge into the sea." Larry poured out another two fingers of the mechanically purified water and toasted his companion. "You were a steely-eyed rocket man—well, balloon man—today, Commander Cantrell. We got away and got our balloon under the horizon in plenty of time."

Eddie scratched his ear. "Thanks, but that's not what bothered me, Larry. It was the retrieval. It took twice as long as it should have. Damn it, I can't keep my fantail cleared that long if we're going straight from being a balloon ops platform into a combat platform."

"I think you're still overestimating the speed with which naval combat takes place in this century, Eddie."

"With respect, I don't think I am. Or, to put it another way, if my deck evolutions can't take place faster and more smoothly than today, we are undercutting our great advantage: tactical speed. Yeah, we can run rings around other sailed ships, but I can't start running those rings until my decks are clear for sailing operations and all my yards are free. Every minute I lose bringing them about to catch a breeze because I'm still reeling in and deflating a balloon is me pissing away my greatest advantage and giving my adversary a slightly more level playing field."

"Yup," smiled Larry, "you are absolutely perfect for this job. A born leader and man of action when you're on deck, and a born worrier before and after. Simpson would bust his vest buttons with pride if he could see you now."

Eddie smiled. "Ah, go to hell, Larry."

"Why, that's pretty much exactly where I'm heading this very afternoon. Louisiana in early summer? Southwest bayou country? Oh yes, hell. Which, in this case, is not blessed with a dry heat."

Eddie nodded and felt suddenly very alone. Larry was the only other up-timer in the fleet, unless you counted Ann Koudsi, who he never saw anyway. She had remained in the *Patentia* for the whole Atlantic crossing, along with her drilling equipment and crew.

But Larry had been a pal and a confidante on the way over the Atlantic. They had compared notes on their respective ships—Eddie was always looking for failure patterns in the new machinery common to both hulls—and the incredibly polyglot population of the flotilla. They had joked, as only they could, about how the D-Day invasion must have been a bit like this, where there had been units of various nationalities mixed into the forces of Operation Overlord. Here, Danes vied with Swedes for the most common demographic of crewmen, but there was no shortage of Germans in the ships' troops and technical services, a few Dutch military types who remained closeted on the *Tropic Surveyor*, and last but certainly not least, the almost four hundred Irish mercenaries who still claimed to belong to a *tercio* based in the Spanish Lowlands. Had the mission planners been able to include a few Mongolians, Micronesians, and Kalahari bushmen, it would have started resembling a floating version of the UN.

But beyond the perspectives and routines the two up-time officers had in common—and the shared knowledge of why Quinn was along, and where the *Courser* was ultimately bound—Eddie had found a genuine chum in Larry. Quinn was only a little bit older, and so became something of a big brother as Eddie struggled with the uncertainties and insecurities that come with a first command. Eddie had, prior to departing Luebeck, girded his loins to face these personal demons in silence and alone. That was part of command image, after all. But Larry had been a sympathetic ear, and his tales—many funny, several scandalous— about his time in the Army and Reserves, had reassured Eddie that he was not alone. Not alone as a new commander—Larry had been there before—or as an up-timer. Because, no matter how (often fiendishly) smart and insightful down-timers were, there was just no way for them to understand what it felt like to lead an expedition back to the continent and land that had comprised the country of one's birth some three and a half centuries in the future. He had been glad for the fellowship of another inadvertent time traveler and had not looked forward to the day when he would lose it.

But that day was today, and that time was now. Larry stood up, looked out the fairly humble stern windows of the *Intrepid*.

"Well, it's about time for me to begin my role as master but not commander of the *Courser*. I wonder how the good Captain Haraldsen is going to like that bit of news."

"Since they're sealed orders with Gustav's signature and signet stamp on them, I doubt Olle will debate them much."

"Oh, it's not a debate I'm worried about," Larry said as he made sure all the items on his web-gear were snug and secure. "I'm worried that Olle, who's been a fine fellow up to now, might get his nose out of joint and dig his heels in at some point. I'd hate to have to pull rank formally and in front of the crew. I don't want to put him in that kind of situation, but I need to know he's going to take orders without delay. Being on our own, and far away from any friendlies, means we've got zero margin for error."

Eddie nodded, rose, and managed not to blink when Larry came to attention and snapped a salute, albeit with a shit-eating grin on his face. "Commander, request permission to debark and commence independent operations."

Eddie returned the salute. "Permission granted, and Godspeed, Major. And...I'll miss you, Larry."

Quinn, who had finished the salute and was already halfway to the door, looked back. "Now that's just an out-and-out lie, Eddie. You've got a twenty-four/seven job on your hands here, as well as a drop-dead gorgeous young tigress-wife who's sure to keep you busy the rest of the time."

"Yeah, well, even so, don't be a stranger. You miss a check-in and I will keelhaul your ass when you bring it back."

"Daily squelch-break, and a quick sitrep every third day, for as long as we're in range. My word on it, Commander."

"Do you think the crew has figured out where you're going?"

"Hell, I think the only ones who even know we're about to split off are the ones we told at the start of the voyage: Haraldsen and his XO. And I don't think it's dawned on Haraldsen yet that he can't remain in command of the mission because he doesn't have the right skill set to carry it out."

"It should be an interesting couple of hours when you get back and break the news, Larry."

"That it should. Take care, Eddie."

With a single long stride, Larry Quinn was out the door.

✧   ✧   ✧

From Anne Cathrine's slightly padded chair in her sitting room (merely two lieutenants' cabins with the paneled partition removed), she watched as Larry Quinn swung energetically down the accommodation ladder to the yawl-rigged skerry that had brought him over from the *Courser*. His visit had been relatively short, and she watched him go with mixed feelings.

On the one hand, it was irksome that her husband clearly shared secrets with his fellow up-timer to which she was not privy. Not that this had been a surprise. Shortly after her marriage to Eddie, older ladies of the court had counseled her not to let such inevitable professional confidences bother her. After all, her husband was a military man with ties to three separate polities, now—Denmark, the USE, and the singular institution of Grantville—and was sure to traffic in secrets which he might not share with anyone, even (some said, *particularly*) his wife. But, despite the ostensible wisdom of those words, Anne Cathrine had never been willing to blithely concede the wider world of power and secrets to men—not even her darling Eddie!—and her father's use of daughters as marriage-primed pawns in his political chess games had only confirmed her in that resolve.

In the case of this voyage, the only impediment to her enjoying full access to her husband's professional life was one Lawrence Quinn: a slightly older up-timer whose mild-mannered self-assurance made him a Man Worthy of Notice for her two ladies, and even for the reclusive Edel Mund, the stolid wife of the flotilla's stolid naval commander, Pros Mund. Quinn's allure had no doubt been further spiced by the aura of mystery surrounding his slightly smaller ship, the destroyer *Courser*. It was quite clear to Anne Cathrine, having grown up in the courts of the high and the powerful, that this ship and its crew had either been, or would be, given special orders. There was no other explanation for the strange exclusion of the vessel from the intership contacts that had been commonplace among all the others in better weather. Even the rumored differences in *Courser's* crewing and supplies were not mentioned, let alone detailed, in the routine intership communiqués. That way, no conjectures could be made as to her final destination and purpose. The only thing Anne Cathrine was sure of was that, sooner or later, the crew of the *Courser* would set of upon a task both hazardous and secret.

And so Anne Cathrine had consoled herself that, ultimately,

Lawrence Quinn would depart, and she would have her husband's first and last confidence in all things, and so, be fully satisfied once again. Except, as she watched Larry's skerry whisked away by a beam-reaching breeze back toward the *Courser*, she discovered that now that his moment of departure was imminent, she regretted it.

Partially, this was because she had come to like the American, despite his annoying claim upon an exclusive confidentiality with her Eddie. Quinn was easygoing, affable, courteous without being affected, and seemed genuinely concerned for her beloved Eddie's well-being. She was quite sure that the older up-timer had, on more than one occasion, offered her husband sage council on how to handle some of the junior officers who chafed at being subordinate to him, since they were not only older than he was, but had lived upon the waves since the age of twelve. While not openly insubordinate, those officers had tested the willingness and ease with which he exercised his authority. Larry had steered Eddie through those first encounters, helping him avoid the predictable extremes: resorting to barking orders and standing on rank alone (the mark of an insecure officer) or pretending not to notice the slights, thereby avoiding any corrective action at all (the mark of an even more insecure officer). Anne Cathrine had no doubt that Eddie would have found his footing as an officer and commander soon enough, but with Larry's extra guidance, her husband's missteps had been very few, and those but very slight. The net result was that, by the time the flotilla had crossed the Atlantic, Eddie was both well liked and well respected by not only the crew of the *Intrepid*, but the entirety of the complement of Reconnaissance Flotilla X-Ray.

But there was another reason she now regretted Quinn's departure. She realized, for the first time, that it would probably make her husband feel lonely and perhaps a bit sad, and she chided herself for not having foreseen that before this moment. Up-timers were truly alone in this world, which was, for them (she still suspected) a primitive, ignorant, and often squalid place.

"Sister, you are scowling like Vibeka Kruse herself, just now." The voice, of her younger sister Leonora, was jocular and wrung a smile from Anne Cathrine in spite of the dark thoughts that Larry Quinn's departure had spawned. Vibeka Kruse had been her father's somewhat plain mistress for some years, whose virulent hatred for the children of his prior marriages was a matter of common knowledge, if not public display.

"I would rather you compare me to the Gorgon," Anne Cathrine replied in the same tone. "What is more ugly than a predatory woman whose hunt has been frustrated by the family of her carnal prey?"

But instead of smiling at the rejoinder, Leonora's eyes grew quite large and round and drifted ever so slightly in the direction of the third woman in the room.

She, the tall and stately Sophie Caisdatter Rantzau, did not *seem* to notice the remark. Perhaps she was too engrossed in her up-time collection of Donne's verse. At least, Anne Cathrine hoped so, because she understood Leonora's meaningful semi-glance in an instant. Sophie was, herself, the offspring of one such beautiful yet Gorgonic woman, whose pursuit of male prey had been frustrated by his powerful family. In fact, it was King Christian IV of Denmark who had "rescued" his besotted eldest son from the scheming of Sophie's own mother: Anne Lykke. She had entranced Prince Christian when she appeared in court but a year or so after her first husband's death in 1623. Christian IV had ultimately imprisoned her, which incensed even neutral nobles against him: the king had no legal right to imprison either a nobleman or noblewoman without specific criminal charges. Christian IV responded with an (unfortunately characteristic) outré counterattack. He charged Anne Lykke with sorcery, claiming she had hired a reputed witch by the name of Lamme Heine to strike down the king once he became an obstacle to her amorous designs upon the crown prince. The resulting furor in the *Riksradet* was as vitriolic and bitter as only truly stupid disputes can be, but left Anne Lykke with a reputation of being a "dangerous woman."

However absurd the scandal, though, even Sophie had suffered from it. Hence her presence on this voyage as a person wanting an increase in royal pleasure. Anne Cathrine, who would have liked to have kicked herself for her impolitic remark about Gorgons and unscrupulous women, looked cautiously sideways at Sophie Rantzau.

Sophie sighed and, not looking up from her reading, remarked, "Rest assured, I am not my mother, much less an admirer of her tactics. She is so—" Sophie tossed a long-fingered hand into the air, fingers miming her mental search for the proper word.

"—so strong-willed?" supplied Leonora tactfully.

The fingers stopped. Sophie allowed a slow smile to accompany her response and looked up. "It is said that there is a fine line between being strong-willed and willful. Wherever that line is, you will find my mother well on the other side of it."

Anne Cathrine beamed, both in relief and a sudden rush of appreciation for Sophie, who was the oldest of the three of them at the advanced age of nineteen. They had been cordial and carefully convivial during the crossing, and the sisters had endeavored to make her feel welcome, but the pre-extant gaps between them—of both social station and family feuds—had been an unaddressed and therefore unresolved factor. After all, Christian IV had not only imprisoned Sophie's mother, but threatened her with a capital crime, and then grudgingly released her on the condition of house arrest. It was perhaps a trifle optimistic to assume that she would welcome friendship from that same king's own daughters.

But in this unlooked-for instant, Sophie Caisdatter Rantzau showed herself to be her father's child in temperament, even though she was her mother's daughter in looks. Cai Rantzau—sheriff of Copenhagen and an eminently trustworthy and even-tempered man—had been admired not merely for his abilities, but for his wry sense of humor. And that sense of humor was now evident in the charmingly crooked smile with which Sophie regarded the two sisters.

Anne Cathrine giggled and put her hand out to touch the much taller woman's arm. "I am so glad you are here with us, away from all—that."

"Yes. It is good to be away from all—that." And Sophie closed her eyes, looking simultaneously pained and relieved.

Anne Cathrine looked at ever-politic Leonora, who showed no sign of inquiring into Sophie's reaction. So Anne Cathrine herself plunged onward despite the risks, as was her wont. "Good Sophie, you repeat my words in a most unusual tone and with a most unusual expression. If you are disposed to share the cause of—"

"I shall do so, my lady Anne Cathrine." Sophie opened gray eyes that were calm and grave. "But, if it please you, not this day."

Anne Cathrine swatted Sophie's arm. "Here, now. This is the last time you will call me Lady Anne Cathrine. I am simply Anne Cathrine, she is simply Leonora, and you will tell us of your woes if, when, and as you choose. Agreed?"

The wry smile was back on Sophie's face. "I would not think of disagreeing. Thank you—Anne Cathrine. Being able to have a conversation as frank as this—well, it is among the reasons I am most grateful to be away from all 'that,' from the endless intrigues that swirl in and around your royal father's court."

Anne Cathrine tilted forward with a conspiratorial whisper. "Me, too, Sophie: me, too." But as she leaned back again, Anne Cathrine found herself longing for that court's plush chairs, even though the last time she had sat in one had been emotionally uncomfortable . . .

Four days before boarding the *Patentia* for her pending rendezvous with Eddie and his up-time-crafted ships, Anne Cathrine's royal father had summoned her to see him in the middle of the day. Which meant that although their meeting would be private, it was also motivated by official business. She had sat—indeed, had sunken into—her wonderfully soft chair while her father outlined his plans for her, for the New World, for Denmark's place in the USE, and how this journey to the New World would advance all of them.

"That is all very fine, Father," Anne Cathrine had said after listening to the lengthy and surprisingly coherent presentation. "But I must ask: why are you telling me all this? Full and open disclosure has not been one of your notable traits, to date."

"Ungrateful child! You cut your royal father to the quick!"

"Possibly. Yet I note you did not deny the truth of my observation."

Christian's answering smile was as sly and long as those he usually wore when he was inebriated and thinking himself surpassingly clever. "Daughter, you make me proud. Your wit is barely less than my little sage Leonora's, and you have five times the courage of any of my other offspring."

"You mean, your female offspring."

A dull look seemed to reduce the intense focus of Christian's eyes for a moment. "I said what I said. I see no need to modify it."

To which Anne Cathrine made no response. The conversation would not proceed well if the king began to brood upon his own regretful implication that she had more nerve and brains than his namesake, the crown prince Christian.

Fortunately, her father was not one to let a silence drag on. Indeed, he was not one to allow a silence to take place at all, and this time was no different. "However accurate—or not!—your initial observation may be, my Anne Cathrine, it is necessary that, on this occasion, you are made aware of all my plans in regard to what Admiral Simpson calls Reconnaissance Flotilla X-Ray."

She nodded, but thought: *Not true, Father. You haven't told me who else is charged with overseeing your interests, who might emerge to express your royal ultimatums when we find ourselves in the Caribbees, nor how, nor when. You have only told me what I need to know so that I will not be surprised and so that I cannot unwittingly foil your plans. But you have told me nothing with which I can help Eddie be on guard for your picked men in our little fleet.* But Anne Cathrine only said, "What makes this full disclosure so necessary, Father?"

"Because I know what you want, Anne Cathrine, even though you've not asked for it."

"And what is it you think I want, Father?"

"Why, to be made a duchess. Or, more to the point, to have Eddie made a duke."

Anne Cathrine was again impressed by how shrewd her father remained, despite all the alcohol he consumed. "And this voyage to the New World is necessary to that eventuality...how?"

"Daughter, certainly you must see it for yourself. If I am to pass over some of my own children to award this honor to your husband—"

—and to thus confer upon me enough power so, come what may, I will not be treated merely as a "king's daughter," but akin to an actual princess—

"—then Eddie must prove himself worthy, and mightily so, in my service."

Anne Cathrine smiled. "Is not his present service to the USE also, in part, service to the Union of Kalmar, and hence, service to you?"

"Well, it is...and yet, it is not. I am one of the monarchs of the multinational hodgepodge over which Gustav presides. But to follow the orders of the USE, and to serve its interest...well, it cannot be equated with service to me, to this crown, directly. If Eddie makes 'prudent' choices when the right opportunities arise, then we may construe his service with Flotilla X-Ray as service to us. Perhaps his actions will show he is worthy of being made a duke. And perhaps you can encourage him in this regard. If so—then, we shall see."

Anne Cathrine rose stiffly. "So we shall," She bowed and turned toward the door. She was amazed, for a fleeting moment, that familial extortion so obvious as that now being plied by her father did not actually have a physical stench.

Christian's voice implored her spine. "Daughter!" His tone softened when she halted and turned back to face him. "Now do not become cross with me."

"Then do not demean my husband."

Christian's eyes seemed to grow more shiny. He straightened in his chair and his voice was loud and sharp. "You dare scold me?"

"I do not. But I do dare to defend my husband when he is held to be deficient in deeds of valor and conquest that, quite obviously, he has already performed. And I observe that the standard to which you propose to hold him is already far greater than what you expected of most of the men to whom you have forced my sisters to become betrothed. How very lucky I was that a landless up-timer fell into our hands. Otherwise, I might have wound up a consort—or should I say mattress?—for that hero of whore- and counting-houses, Friherr Dinesen."

Christian grew very pale, then very red, then returned to normal color. "Anne Cathrine . . ."

At that moment, Vibeka Kruse drifted past the open door. Her idle stroll and excessively sunny smile were akin to an open admission that she had been listening from the hall. Christian nodded at her, rolled his eyes once she had passed, and his gaze swept across the single, small portrait of Kristen Munk—Anne Cathrine's mother—that he allowed to remain in the palace. He smiled sourly as his eyes came away from the picture of the woman for whom his desire had led to an ill-considered morganatic marriage. Anne Cathrine raised an eyebrow, staring at him.

Christian's sour smile became wry. "I was preparing to lecture you, once again, on how—for royalty and their offspring—marriage is not reserved for love, but for duty. But I am afraid my own behavior would hardly support my case."

Anne Cathrine allowed herself a smile that was almost a copy of her father's but said nothing.

"So I allow you this: young Commander Cantrell is everything I could hope for in a son-in-law save in one way. His birth."

"He is not of low birth. Such a concept is meaningless to up-timers."

Christian nodded. "True enough. Which is—and I will deny

this if you ever repeat it—a political trait of theirs I admire, in many ways.

"But our exigencies are dynastic, not democratic; our concerns realistic, not idealistic. There are only so many titles I may grant, particularly hereditary ones, before I begin to dilute the significance of those titles by making them too commonplace."

"That is what Eddie calls 'inflation.'"

"Yes. And I do not argue that he is bold and brave and clever and unswervingly loyal to those whom he has sworn allegiance. But beloved daughter, remember this: he demonstrated all those qualities not while in my service, but while in service against me. Against us. Let him match—even faintly—those deeds while in my service, or showing similar regard for Denmark's interests, and then I can make him what you wish. Indeed, I will seem at once magnanimous and just, raising him up as a hero, unprejudiced by the fact that half of his heroism was exercised against me."

Leonora's low-voiced comment brought Anne Cathrine back to the present. "The *Courser* is departing already." Her sister nodded toward the single porthole in the ladies' sitting cabin.

Anne Cathrine blinked, still slightly disoriented by the rapid shift from memories of Denmark eight weeks ago to the rolling currents of the New World. Sure enough, the *Courser* had most of its canvas in the wind, and was already skimming swiftly southwest, angling away from the rest of Flotilla X-Ray's increasingly southeasterly course.

"Where do you think they are going?" asked Leonora, who had effectively memorized several atlases worth of New World maps.

Anne Cathrine was debating how best to reply when Sophie Rantzau said, "Someplace dangerous, Leonora. Of that I feel certain."

"Yes," Anne Cathrine breathed into the silence that followed Sophie's oracular pronouncement. "Someplace very dangerous indeed."

Chapter 23

Pitch Lake, Fort St. Patrick, Trinidad

Tearlach Mulryan stared down past the spyglass that hung at his chest, and saw the tiny outline of their stockade, which McGillicuddy had dubbed "Fort St. Patrick." The glimmer of lights—the low, steady fires of dry branches dipped in pitch—just managed to pick out the corners of the smaller, dark square that was the recently completed blockhouse. The storehouse, although barely more than a large, sturdy shack, was also completed. Every other faint outline was a tent. Mulryan smiled, glad not to be sleeping in one of those canvas shelters, because, floating four hundred feet above the ground, he was kept wonderfully cool by occasional gusts of the less humid night air. Down on the ground, his comrades sweltered and sought refuge from the incessant attention of an infinitude of mosquitoes.

Beyond the rough darkness of the land beneath him was the smooth, inky darkness of the sea. And the only sounds besides the wind were the distant cries of high-flying birds. That and the surf, Mulryan amended, as he heard the distant sigh of waves rubbing their backs against the steeper slope of the north beach, as well as the faint swells that ran whispering in over the tidal flats that scalloped outwards from the west beach—

His reveries came to an abrupt end: the west beach had lights

240

beyond it. A quick check through the spyglass revealed that it was not one, but three separate lights, probably no more than twenty miles away. That put them much closer than the normal maritime traffic, which traveled primarily from east to west, following the prevailing winds and making for destinations farther along the South American coast. But more significantly, these three lights were all on parallel courses, bound directly for the west shore. Their slow but steady progress indicated that they were probably fore-and-aft rigged vessels, tacking tight against the wind.

Mulryan resisted the powerful impulse to signal his ground crew for a fast descent. Instead he followed the special orders—*protocols*, Don Michael called them—that had been established for handling this eventuality.

Tearlach looked down, and carefully noted the arrangement of the time-marking lanterns on the balloon's servicing pad. As he watched, the quarter-keeping lantern was moved from the 1:15 position to the 1:30 position. Time of observation was fixed. He tapped it down to the ground crew, who now knew that something was afoot. He signaled bearing, course, approximate distance, and best guess at speed. And then he lifted the spyglass back up to his eye and commenced the first of several slow sweeps of the horizon, each one of which would be a concentric circle that overlapped the prior one by about twenty-five percent, all spiraling in to a close observation of the immediate environs of Fort St. Patrick. But before he finished even the first full sweep, Mulryan spotted another light, this one solitary and farther off, perhaps thirty miles to the east. Whether or not that ship was underway, and what its heading might be, were impossible to determine at this range. Meaning that it could very well be nothing more than a typical merchant vessel, moving slowly or at anchor for the night.

But somehow, Tearlach Mulryan suspected that this was not an evening for coincidences, and as he clicked the Morse code data string pertaining to this second sighting, he thought, *And what are you doing waiting out there, my lovely? Have we seen you and your balloon before, or are you a new partner in our dance?* Mulryan felt very sure that he'd know the answer by this time tomorrow.

Presuming, of course, that he was still alive.

✧   ✧   ✧

Barto stabbed a finger down at the left edge of the crudely rendered map of Pitch Lake and its environs. "We land our real raiding party here on the western coast, in force and in secret. The rest of our men remain aboard while all ships hug the shore, beating northward, still using the coastal trees for cover."

"The water is very shallow dere," observed Riijs, the most quiet of Barto's company and unquestionably the most dangerous. A multiple murderer who had fled Frisia, he killed with a quiet efficiency and calm that defied the assignation of any suitable *nom de guerre*. He was just called Riijs—and he preferred not being called at all. "Is it safe passage? And will we not be seen, staying so close?"

Barto looked at Berrick, the Englishman, who shook his hoary head. "I sailed wif them whut sailed wif Raleigh, and they told me that the draft is enough for hulls such as ours. And the trees will hide ye fine. One needn't dally in the breakers to stay in their blind spot, 'cause the high land near the lake is none too high. They can't see over the treetops for miles out."

"And if dey have a watch post dere, on de western coast?" Riijs' voice lacked any discernible intonation.

Barto shrugged. "Then you signal us and we move quickly to deeper water, around the headland, and engage their ship near the north beach. You comb and clear the woods along the west beach, and wait for our diversion. But remember: you don't charge the rise"—for it could not reasonably be called a "hill"—"until you hear our guns."

"So, we use de same signal either way: your first cannonade. And either way, you follow de same plan for engaging de enemy ship."

"Aye. But if we can move slowly and unseen, all the better. Best if you can advance to the eastern edge of the west woods undetected. It's more than half a mile to the high ground, so you can't charge it all the way. And the more time they have to see you—"

"*Ja.* I know. De more of us will die. But I am more worried by dis: do you really tink dey will be so stupid as to focus all dere attention on de north shore when our ships show up dere?"

Barto smiled. "I'll make sure of it. The pinnace and the packet will be loaded with almost eighty men, and will seem to make briskly for the beach. Of course, our foe's 'daunting ship and superb seamanship' will scare us off. And so we'll appear to delay the landing of what will certainly look like our main raiding force."

Riijs was the only one who did not smile at the elegance of the ruse. "It is a gut plan. Let us hope our enemy does not also have a gut plan."

Barto smiled at his coolly homicidal lieutenant. "You worry too much, Riijs."

Who nodded. "*Ja.* Dat is true."

Hugh looked up at Mulryan, who was on the blockhouse roof, standing atop a hastily erected ten-foot platform, spyglass aimed at the western woods. O'Donnell shouted up through the brisk morning breeze, "Are their small boats still heading for the west shore?"

"The treetop outpost signals that the raiders are approaching the tidal flats now. A pinnace and packet. They're full to the gunwales."

Hugh nodded to his command staff. "Aye, that's their main attack force, sneaking up on our 'blind side.'" He shouted up to Mulryan. "Is O'Bannon in position yet?"

"Yes, m'lord. Just got the signal this second."

"Good. Signal back that message is received, and our treetop watchers are to withdraw and fall back to join O'Bannon's team at the first ambush site."

St. Georges, who had missed the predawn preparations, stuck his face into the ring of officers around Hugh. "What do you mean, 'first ambush site?'"

"Good of you to join us, Lieutenant. O'Bannon, my best scout, left before dawn with his original landing team plus a few other men. They've taken up positions at the edge of a clearing near the northern tip of the woods."

St. Georges, still bleary-eyed and endued with a faint vinous reek, pulled his uniform collar straighter. "Why there?"

"Because when we finally put our balloon up, that's where our visitors will no doubt send some marksmen—probably their best, with rifled pieces—to snipe at it. Once they've positioned themselves in the clearing and they've begun to fire, O'Bannon will take them by surprise." Again, Hugh shouted up to Mulryan, "Tearlach, has Morraine acknowledged your earlier signals?"

"Yes, Lord O'Donnell."

"Then down you come, and at the double-quick."

St. Georges looked meaningfully back at the balloon sheds

but saw only the beginnings of activity there. "I see you are not yet ready to put Mulryan aloft. Would not his observation be invaluable at this time?"

"Not as valuable as his becoming a decoy a little later on."

"A decoy? How?"

"I'm not going to put Mulryan up in the balloon until our visitors to the west have all landed, and settled themselves into the woods. Or until they start getting too close to O'Bannon. Whichever occurs first."

"Why wait so long?"

"Because I want the attackers to think their attempt to surprise us has worked. The farther they proceed with whatever plans they've made based on that assumption, the more likely we can turn the tables on them later on."

"I see," said St. Georges.

Hugh doubted he did, based on the Frenchman's hesitation and muted voice. "But once they see the balloon, they'll know that we have them under observation, and they will have to begin improvising. Their first step will be to snipe at the balloon. And that's when O'Bannon will give them their first surprise."

"And when they pursue him?"

"He'll run back fifty yards, through a maze of preset snares, turn and wait."

"And ambush the dogs again when they become entangled. Ingenious," conceded St. Georges.

Ignoring the faintly supercilious tone, Hugh finished the tactical overview. "O'Bannon will do this twice, if he can, and then fall back out of the woods and around to the brush just off the north beach. And I'm hoping that a lot of our visitors on the west shore will chase him."

St. Georges nodded. "Because the more of them that are chasing him—"

Hugh nodded back. "—the fewer of them they'll have to attack the stockade. Either way, O'Bannon and his men will take up concealed, prepared positions just a hundred yards northwest of the stockade. If he's not busy defending himself from following forces, he'll wait there as a reserve, or will harry any attempt to land to our north. Although I don't think they're going to try a landing on the north coast."

"Why?"

"First, it's a little too obvious. Second, the water is deeper there and they have to come closer to put men ashore. Third, I believe Captain Morraine and *Fleur Sable* will make it too costly for them."

That brought a genuine, and somewhat fierce, smile to St. Georges' face. "*Oui, vraiment.*"

O'Rourke frowned down at the map that Hugh had hastily sketched in the dirt as he spoke. "So how many do you think they're landing in the west woods?"

"I wish I knew, but I expect no less than one hundred, perhaps as many as one-hundred-twenty. That assumes they need to keep running crews and some boarding parties on all three ships."

O'Rourke emitted a low whistle. "Steep odds. There are only sixty of us—sixty-six, counting Lieutenant St. Georges and his men. It could become a desperate affair, fighting against those numbers—"

Hugh smiled. "Yes, but their advantage in numbers will also be their undoing."

"How so?"

"They will want to use that advantage to make a quick, decisive attack. Which is why they're positioning themselves to approach under cover, and then charge the fort *en masse*."

"That's just what I'm afraid of."

"Ah, but that's just what I want. O'Rourke, you're to take forty men and get into concealed positions at the edge of the eastern forest. All except for your five best marksmen and three of the green lads to work as reloaders. They're to be prone and concealed out in the brush, forward of the forest."

"I'm taking forty of our sixty men? That leaves you—what?—four for running the balloon, six for O'Bannon's team in the west wood, and ten for the fort itself?"

"Yes."

"And then what? Am I to twiddle my thumbs while these dogs swarm around the fortress gates?"

"At first, yes."

"They'll break in!"

"Of course. That's what I want."

"Are ye daft—m'lord?"

"No, old friend, I am not. When the raiders get the gate open, that's when your marksmen go to work. They'll be bunched up,

so whittle them down, drive them inside the stockade for cover—
and then charge for all you're worth. Leave your long pieces
back with your marksmen. The rest of you close and engage
with musketoons, pistols, even swords if it gets that tight. But I
don't think it will."

"No? And why not?"

"Because when they finally open the gate—"

Barto, watching the almost empty pinnace exit the shallows,
glimpsed movement over the trees lining the shore to the west
of Pitch Lake. As he watched, a swollen, inverted teardrop shape
rose up higher than the palms. Berrick pointed to it with an
inarticulate stutter that always afflicted him during combat.

Barto sucked the salt wind through his irregular and incomplete teeth. "I see it, fool. But what is it?"

"I d-d-don't know, b-but th-there's a m-m-man in a b-basket
b-b-b-beneath it."

And so there was. Hanging near the tapering base of the
upward-falling blue-gray teardrop was a single figure. Its hands
and arms raised towards its face, and Barto saw a split-second
glint of sharply reflected sunlight.

"Bastards! They're watching us from that—thing. With a spyglass."

"B-b-but what is it?"

"What does that matter? They can see us from it and, no
doubt, signal their forces on the ground. Damn it, we have to
move now—and fast!" Turning to his mate, he ordered, "Signal
the pinnace to run large and catch up with us. We've got to put
a boarding party on her, but we'll have to do it on the move,
rather than pausing at the northern headland."

Riijs stared up through the trees at the strange, tapering globe,
which rose slowly, like—like what? Where had he seen this kind
of lazy, steady ascent?

And then he knew: it was akin to the way that heavy embers,
or whole leaves, rose up out of a fire. But this distended sack, and
the single man slung beneath it, kept rising and would soon be
high overhead. He looked through the trees and out to sea. The
pinnace was just dropping from sight around the headland to the
north, trying to catch Barto's sloop. Well, the man hanging under

that swollen sphere had doubtless seen those ships, so that part of their attack was no longer a surprise. But had the observer been aloft in time to see Riijs' landing force?

His uncertainty was not resolved by the runner who came bounding through the brush toward him, breathless. "News from the eastern edge of the woods," the man panted.

"Ja. Say."

"As we thought, there is a stockade on the rise to the north. But if they had outposts, they have pulled them in."

"Do you tink dey saw us?"

"No sign of it from the fort. But who knows what they might see from that," and he glanced through the forest canopy, up to the strange, skyward-receding orb.

Riijs thought. The floating sky-ship created another problem: as commander, where should he position himself? At the edge of the forest with the waiting assault forces, or back here to oversee the marksmen who he would instruct to bring down the sky-ship as soon as Barto's guns fired? Or should his marksmen go to work even before Barto's signal? If the airborne observer had already caught a glimpse of Riijs' main attack force, the element of surprise might be slipping through their fingers, even now—

Riijs focused outward once again; the runner, who had been standing there the whole time, seemed to reappear in front of him. "Go back to de edge of de forest wit deese orders: 'wait for my command to charge.' I will move to a position two hundred yards back from de line. Go." He looked round at the marksmen and loaders he had gathered to him. "All of you: go to de clearing we saw. Load wit small balls and use silk. You will need much range. Wait for my order to start shooting. And you:"—he pointed to one of the loaders—"come wit me. When I tell you to go, you will run back to deese men wit orders to fire on de ting in de sky." Riijs waved for his personal guards to form on him, and then followed after the first runner at a brisk walk, and wondered, "When will Barto fire those damned guns?" To which there was only one sure answer: the sooner, the better.

Chapter 24

Pitch Lake, Trinidad

Barto signaled for his packet to move closer to shore as they came around the headland—and found the enemy ship already bearing down upon them.

And it was a cromster, damn it. But an older one: her mizzenmast was lateen- rather than yawl-rigged. And from the look of how that rigging was dressed—

"Boys, I think we have some navy-trained fool captaining that ship."

"Fool or no, he's got twenty-eight guns to our sixteen," offered Dorsey, the chief gunner. "Probably heavier ones, too."

"Which he's been taught to use in set-piece broadsides, I'll wager. Out in deep water." *In deep water, where the great ships lumber like corpulent apple-barges*—and then Barto saw how he was going to win this battle. "Gianetti, hard a-starboard. Berrick, signal the rest to follow us in."

Gianetti, back at the whipstaff, was wide-eyed. "Starboard? You mean—?"

"Take us into the shallows, Gianetti, as close as you can. And Dorsey?"

"Aye?"

"Give him a portside volley as we come over."

"At this range? Even with shot, we'll fall short by—call it two hundred yards."

"Good."

"You want to waste powder *and* make him think we don't know how to shoot?"

Barto turned to smile at his gunnery chief. "Yes, Dorsey, that's *exactly* what I want him to think."

Riijs heard the distant cannonade and turned to the second runner. "Run hard, back to de marksmen. Tell dem to shoot dat sky-ting and de man beneath it. Remember: silk on de musket balls, a half-measure more of powder. Go." Then, Riijs resumed moving toward his front line but did so at a slow walk. He would not be comfortable until he heard his marksmen firing at the observer watching his forces from the sky....

Morraine felt the *Fleur Sable* lose headway as the wind spilled from his square-rigged sails, and then regain a half-measure of it as the breeze began filling out his lateen.

"Captain, he runs before us," called his pilot.

Morraine nodded, watching the pirate sloop and her two smaller sister ships—the latter packed with troops—run in closer against the shore. They were far in and had to be in danger of running aground. He had a deeper draft and could not follow them very far into the shallows, but he didn't need to do so. He only needed to come close enough to bring all his guns to bear. "Two points more to port, pilot. Crowd them in against the land."

"Captain, we have lost much of the wind, and if we go much closer—"

Morraine slapped the rail impatiently. "Obey, blast your eyes. We have not lost all the wind. We have the mizzen"—he jerked his chin at the billowing lateen sail—"and that will allow us to sail clear again. We are not attempting to board, merely coming over to bring our portside battery to bear."

"Yes, Captain." The pilot made his reply through a nervous swallowing noise.

Morraine looked overhead. The breeze was steady into the lateen. So what if it caught a bit less wind than a more modern fore-and-aft rig? It was not so *very* different. He had put *Fleur Sable* through her paces and she was a well-sprung hull, sprightly and responsive compared to the contemptible monsters he had commanded before. With this hull, surely it was possible to get in a little closer and put a solid broadside into the sloop before turning out to deeper water.

Morraine glanced up. The lateen sail's leading edge began to sag and flutter faintly. But surely such a simple maneuver as he intended was still possible.

Behind Riijs, the chaos started, at it usually did, all at once. From back in the clearing where his marksmen were now sniping at the sky-thing, the intermittent sounds of gunfire redoubled and became a fierce exchange. Riijs, now three hundred yards behind his main force, debated: ignore the sudden appearance of enemy troops behind him and start the charge, or set things to right in his rear area first? There were no lieutenants he could trust with either task. The skirmish behind him was unexpected and could be a trap. Charging the enemy stockade, while simpler, was a sprint into the unknown.

Riijs slapped his oldest bodyguard, Hernandez, on the shoulder, said, "Go bring twenty men from de front line." Then he turned and started sprinting to the rear. First things first.

The gunfire started and stopped a few times as he ran. Then it ceased, just as the runner he had sent back originally burst out of the brush in front of him—and almost got a ball through his head.

"Report," said Riijs, who lowered his snaphaunce pistol and resumed moving to the rear at a trot.

"An ambush. They were waiting—"

"I know dat. How many are dere, what are dey doing, how have we responded?"

"Riijs, we do not know how many there are. There could be twenty shooting occasionally. There could be five, reloading quickly and always moving. Our marksmen are dead—"

But of course they are—

"—and the rest of us have taken cover."

Riijs needed no further report. He had arrived at the rear of the defensive line his remaining men had set up on the safe side of the clearing. The senior among them, a mestizo who went by the strange name of Madre, pointed across the sun-flecked stretch of grass and scrub. "They pulled back. We sent four to follow. They're going to—"

Deeper in the trees that fringed the far side of the clearing, there was a sudden crash, a shout that turned into a scream, a single shot. Silence. Then three ragged pirate voices began shouting and cursing.

Riijs nodded. "Traps. Our enemies planned all dis. Dey reasoned we would sneak in from de west coast, which means dey must have seen us coming ashore. And now dey want us to waste more time here. Which we will not do." As Hernandez arrived with the twenty men Riijs had requested, he looked down at Madre. "Use deese men to hold dis position. Do not follow de enemy further into de bush. Secure your flanks. I will start de attack on de stockade as soon as I reach our front line. Do not follow us. You must make sure dat deese enemy snipers do not threaten our rear."

Madre nodded and looked across the clearing again. "And what about the four—eh, three men we sent after them?"

A second scream and a shot. Silence.

Riijs shrugged. "Dey were dead men de moment you sent dem." He turned and began sprinting back to the main force.

Hugh, standing at his signaling position on the roof of the blockhouse, estimated that it had been a full two minutes since he had heard the rattle of musketry in the west forest. From the sound of it, the pirates had taken the bait once, but had not followed on into the second set of snares. Well, so far, things were going much better than capricious fate usually allowed. He put two fingers to his mouth and whistled twice. Out beyond the western wall of the stockade, in the center of the ballooning field, McGillicuddy's thick outline stopped moving, then his head came around. Hugh pointed up, and then made three down-pulling motions. McGillicuddy nodded and turned to his ground crew, who began hauling in the balloon's guide wires at the double-quick. Yes, Hugh reflected, everything seemed to be going almost suspiciously well, both on land and at sea. He turned to check on Morraine's pursuit of the pirates—

—and saw *Fleur Sable* angling landwards, saw the three pirate ships running before her, saw the mottled aqua moiré of shallows that the pirates had obviously navigated before, and into which Morraine had no business venturing. Not that he'd run aground: he had room enough to come over and avoid that, but if the lateen was out of position to tack back across the wind...

✦   ✦   ✦

"Captain Morraine!" The cry of the leadsman, sounding line high in his hand, was shrill and anxious.

"Yes, yes, I see. Harder to port, Pilot."

Who complied, and then looked up. The lateen sail sagged to half her fullness. Morraine felt his heart quicken.

"Captain!" The leadsman, staring down into the water directly beneath the starboard bow, sounded even more panicked.

Morraine bit his lip, looked down amidships toward his gunnery officer. "Camignon?"

The gunnery officer snapped straight. "Yes, Captain?"

"How much of our portside battery bears on the sloop?"

"Nine guns, Captain. But we are losing the angle."

Which matched Morraine's own assessment: the sloop was running out of his field of fire faster than *Fleur Sable* was turning to track him. "Pilot, hard a-port. Camignon, stand ready! Steady, steady..." Morraine watched the firing angle improve, but then, as his lateen sail luffed and lost more wind, the rate of turn diminished, and the angle began widening out again. "Fire!"

But even as Morraine gave the order, the pirate sloop heeled over hard to port herself, swinging her bow sharply away from land and aiming it directly at *Fleur Sable*. This put the sloop head-on to Camignon's guns, and thus shrank her target profile by two-thirds. Of the nine balls that came roaring out from the port side of Morraine's cromster, three went past the sloop on her port side, four overshot her on the starboard. The other two smashed into her, blasting a deck gun overboard, clipping a sail free, and gouging a smoking pit into the middle of her weather deck. But the extraordinarily maneuverable pirate resumed her portside turn, tacking through the wind smartly to come all the way about. Her course now fully reversed, she headed back to cross in front of the almost completely becalmed *Fleur Sable*.

Like little curs following a wolf, the packet, and then the pinnace, turned about also—but they came straight back out toward the *Fleur Sable*. Morraine saw the men rising up on those crowded decks, boarding hooks held at the ready.

Mon Dieu, those brutes are not a second landing force. They are boarding parties. Which meant, Morraine realized, that he had done exactly what the pirate captain had wanted, and expected, him to do. The low-hulled packet would be under Morraine's guns before they could be reloaded and the sloop would have just slipped past on his port bow. Only the pinnace was far enough out that his guns could—

Then the pinnace heeled over, her five small portside demi-culverins tilted up by her movement. As she began to right herself, the guns fired in volley.

A second before Morraine's eyes told him what was inbound, his ears detected the unmistakable, ferocious moaning of chain-shot, headed straight up into his drooping sails.

Riijs, nearing the end of his long sprint, vomited in midstride: his breakfast came out in a side-streaming rush, and then he was among the rearmost men of the attack force. He looked up and down the tree line, estimating rather than counting. He was about a dozen shy of a full company. Not a lot, but it would have to do. "Stand," he shouted. They rose, the assorted firearms of their bloody trade bristling upward and outward like a ragged hedge. "Ready and—at de trot—forward."

Half a step behind Riijs, who loosened his brace of pistols and drew his cutlass an inch from its scabbard, the eighty-seven remaining buccaneers of the Frisian's main attack force began loping northeast toward the stockade.

Barto, eyes never leaving the cromster, shouted back at his sailmaster. "Spill the mainsail, man; bring to as we cross his bows." Then, to Dorsey: "Has the starboard battery been reloaded as I ordered?"

Dorsey nodded with a gap-toothed grin. "The garbage is ready to go, Cap'n."

Gianetti, who was young for a pilot and new to The Life, called forward through the wind. "'Garbage?'"

Barto shouted over his shoulder. "Do you know what we pirates do with broken nails, old fishhooks, rusted grommets?"

Gianetti, confused by the question, blinked. "No," he shouted back.

Barto turned, smiled. "Then just watch this."

Morraine peered through the tangle of his shredded sails, dangling yards, and tilting masts to try to keep track of the sloop's progress. She had slowed just before she went athwart his hawse. Camignon's voice reached him through the ruin and sting of impending defeat. "Half the portside battery is reloaded and bears."

Morraine glanced quickly to his left; the pinnace was trying to bring its bow around to point at the *Fleur Sable*'s waist, but a quirk of the wind had slowed her. "Fire all, Camignon!"

Seven guns of the *Fleur Sable* spoke. Wood and smoke jetted up from the pinnace, which listed precipitously. Her jigger down, she slowed further, but then the wind freshened and she sped away after the sloop, her deck littered with bodies. Morraine felt a quick surge of hope; he looked forward again—just in time to see the sloop's midship gunwales swing into sight over his starboard bow and the pirate gunners lowering matches to fuses.

"*Down!*" Morraine shouted, and rather than flattening himself against the poop deck, he vaulted the rail and dropped into the quarterdeck's companionway. As he landed there, the discharges of eight cannon came roaring up the length of his spar deck. He had expected grape: he was not prepared for sangrenel. The uneven bits of metal screamed like enraged hornets, then growled and hissed and spat as they splintered, ripped, and chewed their way into and through everything that was upright on the main deck of the *Fleur Sable*.

It was over in a fraction of a second. Morraine rose quickly, wondering if maybe, just maybe, some straggler of that swarm of slaughtering scrap-iron might kill him, too. But he had to live to see the aftermath. Gunners who had been on the far side of their cannons had survived, as well as those few sharpshooters still up in the rigging. Behind him he heard feeble movement and a moan on the poop deck. But everywhere else, men were screaming, spurting blood from impossibly irregular gashes, whereas those who had been caught in the very center of the cone of death lay in mangled heaps, moving weakly as their blood poured out of scores of hideous wounds.

Morraine caught it all in a single glimpse. The very next second, the sloop's starboard bow swung about to roughly kiss his own and pirates swarmed onto his low fo'c'sle. A moment later, board- ing hooks snapped down over his portside gunwales, and like a hoard of spiders, the brutes from the packet flowed up and onto his main deck, killing any who had strength enough to stand.

For Morraine, the situation was as easy to read as a book, which, in this case, was clearly a tragedy: his ship was lost. As he drew both his pistols, he watched half of the scant remains of his deck crew blasted aside by blunderbusses and run through by cutlasses. His own two shots, although each dropped one of the boarders, only served to infuriate and attract the attention of the ravening horde that is a pirate crew intent on slaughter. Six, maybe eight of the unwashed, bangled buccaneers came roaring at him, and Morraine realized that he had only one way to still snatch victory from the jaws of this defeat.

A ball splintered the heavy door frame as he turned and sped for the stairs to the gun deck. Yes, victory could still be his.

If he followed the example of Pyrrhus.

Hugh waved St. Georges and his men back from the gates. "No, damn it, get on the platforms. Don't waste time bracing the doors. They won't hold anyway. They're not *meant* to."

"But *monsieur*, these timbers will buy us precious time as we—"

"St. Georges, do as I say or I will shoot you where you stand." Hugh produced his most coveted pistol, a double-barreled flint-lock, to give substance to his threat.

St. Georges nodded to his six French marines. Each team of three dropped the heavy timber they had been preparing to wedge in behind the gates. "I must point out that, in civilized countries, the conventions of siege craft—"

"*Get on the wall*, St. Georges. Let's see if you can shoot as well as you talk."

With a curt nod, St. Georges dispatched his two three-man teams, one to each platform on either side of the gate. They joined the ten Irish soldiers of fortune already working there, each of whom slowly but steadily fired and reloaded a long-barreled rifle, electing not to touch an impressive array of preloaded smooth-bores, all ready to hand. The marines, following the example of the Irish, did not disturb their own racks of preloaded weapons, but used their regular muskets to fire occasional, careful shots at the distant pirates.

Riijs considered his options. His men were tired from the trot, and most had drained their water skins at least an hour before. The sun was climbing higher and the volume of fire from the fort had picked up. At two hundred yards, this had been deemed a safe range at which to rest and reorganize, but some of the marksmen on the walls were evidently quite accomplished. One of his force had been killed, two incapacitated, and many unnerved by balls that came much closer than they should have. *The defenders have plenty of powder and, if I give them enough time, they have enough marksmen to either chase us back or whittle us down. No,* decided Riijs, standing up and earning a near miss for his trouble, *the time has come.* "All stand." He was answered by the rustle and clattering of eighty-four raiders rising to their feet. Many stared at the two hundred yards of open ground and then at Riijs. Mortal uncertainty—and the contemplation of mutiny—glimmered in the eyes of several.

Riijs brought up his pistol and aimed it at the dense jungle to the south. "You plan to hide dere? The Arawaks will kill you by sundown. And if our boats are sunk, you are stuck on dis island. So. You have one safe place to go:"—he swung around and aimed at the stockade—"dat fort. Everyplace else is death."

Those pirates who had wavered swallowed, nodded.

Riijs nodded back, then shouted. "Musketeers, halt at seventy yards and volley to cover our final approach. Every one else, we charge all de way. Axe-men and maul-men, stay near de front: you'll deal with de gate. Ready? Now—"

"They're charging!" Hugh called down to the wall. But the men there had seen it for themselves. They immediately shouldered their current weapons for one last shot at range. Their rifles spoke; a few of the onrushing figures sprawled. Then they set to cocking the hammers on all the waiting pieces.

At seventy yards, Hugh saw the pirates with longer weapons slow and bring their pieces up. "Down!" he shouted. All but one Frenchman responded promptly.

The pirates' loose volley was still impressive. Balls zipped overhead, splintered timbers, and one found its way through the slowest Frenchman's forehead. He pitched back off the platform as limp and lifeless as a sack of stones.

Only one or two of the pirates were hanging back and reloading. Hugh yelled down to his men, "Stand and fire at will."

The defenders needed little encouragement. With a horde of ruthless attackers at fifty yards or less, the Irish and the French quickly found targets, fired, dropped the spent musket, grabbed the next. At about twenty yards, a few of the pirate muskets spoke again, joined increasingly by pistols and blunderbusses as the distance narrowed. The defenders started feeling the firepower of the attackers. Another Frenchman went down. An Irishman, soft-voiced Murphy, toppled off the platform, an arterial wound spraying like a bright red roostertail as he fell. Others were wounded.

St. Georges, wild-eyed, spun to look up at Hugh. "Monsieur, do you lack the courage to defend your own walls?"

Hugh gritted his teeth and ignored the question. "Abandon the platforms, St. Georges. Fall back to the barricades to either side of the lane. As we discussed."

"Abandon the—?"

"Off the walls, damn you!"

"But without us to fire down upon them, the brutes will surely get in."

"Damn it, do as I say."

St. Georges spat conspicuously but complied. Hugh would worry about offended honor later. For now, he was counting how many men he had lost, and let his eye wander back to the storehouse, where McGillicuddy stood waiting in front of the doors.

Axes started thudding into the gates, followed closely by the dull thump of mauls. From Hugh's vantage point it was difficult to tell just how many pirates were clumped together there, or were surprised to discover that the gates were built more lightly than the walls of the stockade, being fashioned of wide-set trunks that were both thin and dry. The light, gapped construction had been an essential part of Don Michael's tactical contribution to Hugh's overall defensive strategy—a tactic which Michael had insisted on withholding from the French. When asked why, he simply answered, "I don't trust 'em to protect us, so why should I trust 'em to follow our plans or keep our secrets?" Hugh had publicly expressed nothing but confidence in the up-timer's daring tactic, but had nursed his own unspoken doubts about it. Which rose up once again: *Michael, if your plan doesn't work, they are going to rush over us like a wave over ants*—

The sound of thumping and hacking doubled. "Get your men back and under cover!" Hugh shouted down toward St. Georges, who made a wan attempt to comply.

Your funeral, thought Hugh, who turned toward McGillicuddy and raised his fist high. McGillicuddy nodded, raised his own fist, signaling he was ready. Hugh dropped his hand.

McGillicuddy heaved at the left-side door of the storehouse. It swung open, revealing the French eight-pounder that Michael had positioned there, muzzle trained directly at the gate. "Fire," shouted McGillicuddy.

The roar of the saker was underscored by a faint rush of what sounded like immense, growling bees. The bow-wave of the double-loaded grapeshot went straight thought the lightly constructed gate, splintering almost half of it and summoning forth a chorus of shrieks and screams that, though inarticulate, conveyed one fact very clearly:

Many of the remaining pirates had just been wounded or killed.

Riijs wiped blood from the side of his face, checked, found that it was not his own but had instead come sheeting over him when the maul-man who had been hammering at the gate's right-side hinge-points had his left lung blown free of his body. Riijs—who had been standing farther to the right and was thus sheltered by the stockade wall—had escaped death by mere inches. Which did not impress him in the slightest.

Instead, he counted his men as he moved toward the gate. He had lost about fifteen dead and wounded reaching the stockade. This blast of grapeshot had cost him almost twenty more, most of whom were incapacitated or killed outright. Grapeshot rarely inflicted flesh-wounds, after all. That left him a force of about fifty, too many of whom were wavering. But judging from the enemy's sudden abandonment of the walls, Riijs had the sneaking suspicion that—

"Dere are less of dem than we thought. Hernandez, you keep five men out here to watch our backs. De rest of you: through de gate and follow me!"

Morraine used the butt of his pistol to club the pirate who had discovered him on the gun deck. The man fell, but with a long moan. The other pirates, who were slipping in through the gun ports, heard, looked, saw, and started back toward the captain.

Morraine finished staving in the top of the powder keg, laid his pistol down upon it sideways, so that its action touched the loose gunpowder just beneath the copper lip of the cask. He cocked the flintlock's hammer—

—just as he felt something cool slide into the center of his back. Before he could blink, a pirate's cutlass-point came out the front of his doublet, coated in his own blood.

But you are too late, Morraine thought. His lip quirked, and he pulled the trigger of his double-primed flintlock.

Barto had just jumped onto the foredeck of the crippled cromster when, beneath the main deck, and just abaft the mainmast, he heard a loud, hoarse explosion, more like a large grenade than a gun, but clearly greater than either.

In the first split second after the sound, Barto realized he had heard it once before, but could not immediately place it.

In the next split second, he remembered how, when pouring a close broadside into the first galleon he had ever attacked, he hit the ship's magazine, which did not, as tales tell, go up all at once. Rather, there was a loud but muted blast that announced the first fateful ignition of a keg of powder—

And in the last split second, Barto connected the present sound with that earlier one—and thus knew that, truly, this was his last split second.

A louder, timber-ripping roar blasted deck planks upward as the full contents of the *Fleur Sable*'s magazine detonated.

Chapter 25

Pitch Lake, Trinidad

Behind Hugh, there was a shuddering blast that sent a tremor even through the timbers of the blockhouse's roof. He turned and saw, half a mile out to sea, tiny specks flying up in the air, smoke and flame billowing after them, chasing them into the sky. Staying low, Hugh scrambled across the roof to the northern waist-works and peeked over—just in time to see the back half of the pirate packet sink like a stone: her bow was entirely gone. As was the *Fleur Sable*. The sloop listed, engulfed in flames, and then, the ready powder for her deck guns started going off. Like explosive hammer blows, the loose charges tore apart her spar deck, section by section, until, after the fifth blast, some ember or burning chunk must have sleeted down into the reserve munitions she kept below. With a final concussive roar that rivaled the *Fleur Sable*'s, the pirate sloop disintegrated outwards in a fury of self-annihilation.

Riijs heard the two titanic blasts as he and a dozen of his men shouldered open the tattered gate, guns in hand, looking for targets—

—and found themselves facing a dandy in the uniform of a French naval officer, four of that nation's marines standing nervously behind him, apparently uncertain whether they should raise their muskets or not.

Riijs raised his gun. This was going to be easier than he thought.

The dandy stepped forward from behind a rude barricade of wooden crates. "Monsieur, my sword."

And, as if he were on some battlefield where such things actually occurred—which Riijs secretly doubted—the Frenchman drew and proffered his sword.

Riijs stared at it, saw, from the corner of his eye, some other soldiers—mercenaries from the look of them—clambering up on a platform set against the stockade's inner, eastern face. They glanced up toward the compound's central building—a fair approximation of a blockhouse—and then, after waiting a moment for some signal that evidently did not come, went over the wall.

Before Hugh could finish recrossing the blockhouse roof back to his signaling position at the south-facing waist-works, he saw that two of his men had scrambled up one of the platforms on the east wall, and now vaulted the top of the stockade. Deserters? From *his* ranks? No. Not unless—

Frowning, dreading the worst, he rushed to see what was happening near the gate—

Riijs stared at the Frenchman's sword, took it. Now what?

The dandy did not keep him waiting. "Naturally, we would have fought on as honor demands, but our commander, he is an Irish incompetent and all but opened our gates to you. Now he is nowhere to be seen. So shall we arrange a ransom?"

"A ransom?"

"But of course. It is the civilized option, no?"

Ransom? To Riijs, this young Frenchman didn't look or act like any prince. "Who's your father?" he asked.

The dandy actually made a little bow. "I am the son of Geoffrey St. Georges of Rheims."

"And is he a duke? A count?"

"No, my father is a wealthy merchant."

"Den his son is a dead man."

Before the dandy could blink, Riijs shot him through the forehead.

✧   ✧   ✧

Hugh saw the shot as he arrived back at the roof's southern waist-work. The French marines, stunned, raised their muskets. One was fast enough to get off a shot before they went down under a hail of pistol fire.

But not as much pistol fire as Hugh had expected. Indeed, he saw very few ready pistols still dangling from the pirates' sweaty neck-lanyards. And with St. Georges gone, there was nothing obstructing the line of sight between the storehouse and the raiders...

O'Rourke crawled forward from the fringe-scrub of the east woods, and tapped Fitzwilliam on the boot. He pointed out the half dozen pirates clustered around the stockade's gate. "Nice and steady now."

Fitzwilliam raised his very long flintlock. A moment passed. Another. Then he fired and immediately reached toward the loader for another of the weapons.

One of the handful of figures by the gate fell to his knees with a yell that came quite clearly over the one-hundred-thirty yards.

The rest of the Irish marksmen began to fire their long, rifled weapons. Another pirate went down. The others crouched and milled uncertainly.

O'Rourke turned back toward his other thirty men, their faces dim within the edge of the forest. Dim except for their bright, eager eyes.

"So lads, here we go. And no wastin' breath shouting 'O'Donnell Abu.' We'll chant it loud once these bastards are dead. So—up now!"

Despite the forty-odd pirates near the gate, Hugh stood up and looked back toward the storehouse.

McGillicuddy reappeared in the doorway.

Hugh raised his hand just as a loud, enraged shout warned of a figure on the roof of the blockhouse.

McGillicuddy raised his hand also.

Down below, a piece fired; a bullet clipped the wooden waist-works five inches to Hugh's left just as he brought his hand down.

McGillicuddy did likewise as he pushed open the storehouse's right-hand door—and revealed Michael's second French saker.

The crew didn't wait for the command: the weapon roared. The carnage around the gate was immediate and horrific.

Hugh gave the "lock up" sign to McGillicuddy. The crews reached out and pulled the two storehouse doors closed. Hugh ducked back down, scurried to the stairs, and descended them three at a time.

Michael was waiting at the base of the stairs, watching the blockhouse's open doorway from across its wide ground-floor room. "What the hell has gone wrong?"

"I went wrong."

"You?"

"Yes. I took a moment to check on Morraine. Who is dead." Hugh began checking and cocking his pistols.

"And let me guess, while you were gone—"

"St. Georges also went wrong, yes." Hugh looked ruefully at the open doorway. Doyle had intended to hang the door this afternoon. Too late now.

"Okay, so St. Georges messed up. No surprise. But where are his men, and yours?" McCarthy matched Hugh's worried glance at the doorway to the compound. "I kept waiting for all of them to fall back in here and—"

"They're not coming. They're dead or gone. It's just us, now."

"Us?"

"No time to talk, Michael. We've got to hold out until O'Rourke gets here. I'll cover the door."

"Well, then I'm coming along to—"

"No. You fetch the musketoon we gave you and go to the roof. Cover the door, but don't shoot too soon. Let them bunch up."

"I'm a newbie, not an idiot," Michael grumbled, and he was gone.

Hugh drew and hefted two pistols. So now it was a race between how fast the pirates could overwhelm them and how fast O'Rourke's men could get inside the compound.

Had Hugh been a betting man, he wouldn't have wasted any money betting on himself.

Riijs picked himself up off the ground, found he was one of the lucky ones who had, again, survived the grapeshot unscathed, and counted the rest. He was down to twenty-five men. But half of them were either glancing or drifting back out the gate: *fools, turning back with safety finally at hand.*

However, it seemed that their flight might be short lived.

Judging from shouts outside the stockade, the group he'd left with Hernandez was evidently under attack and preparing to fall back *inside* the walls. Which probably meant a threat from the east wood—

But there was no time to think about that now. The first order of business was to take the blockhouse. The gate hung in ruins, so the stockade walls would not keep out a new threat. He had to commandeer the one remaining strongpoint. Which meant no time for better tactics, no time to reload. Just—

"Rush de blockhouse! Now!"

Hugh got to the blockhouse's reinforced doorway just as the irregular wave of pirates drew within ten feet of it, cutlasses drawn. Firing and pulling one pistol after another, Hugh dropped the first three while standing his ground but had to retreat back inside the doorway to get the next one—who sagged but did not go down. Hugh pulled his double-barreled flintlock as the rest, clumping together in their rush, came tight around the door. And Hugh thought, *Now, Michael, now!*

As if on cue, there was a thunderous roar, akin to a shotgun, overhead. Two more pirates at the rear of the press went down, cursing.

But the rest surged forward. Hugh fired his flintlock's two barrels in rapid succession, and drew his saber just in time to parry the first blow from a pirate cutlass.

Once forced back from the door, Hugh had no time to plan, no time to feint, no time to trick his foes: they were all around him. He yanked out his main-gauche and was immediately glad for it. His attackers hemmed him in so tightly that he had almost no time to attack, only parry—and be grateful for every second that he remained alive. Most of the pirates were passable swordsmen, but their shorter weapons were at a disadvantage in this relatively open space. However, two of their number—and in particular, a tall, very pale, very blond, and very calm fellow—were quite good, much better than what Hugh usually encountered on European battlefields. Nevertheless, in the first ten seconds, Hugh had managed to wound two and sever another's windpipe with an unexpected backhand cut. In return, he had acquired a deep slice in his right thigh, a flesh-wound in his left arm, and a growing need to know the answer to one key question:

Where the hell *is O'Rourke?*

The blond pirate, evidently the leader, must have seen Hugh's reflexive glance toward the blockhouse door. He launched a back cut that was actually a feint, taking Hugh off balance just as the true strike came in. Hugh got his main-gauche up in time to block the pirate's cutlass, but not solidly: his long-quilloned parrying dagger rang, spun out of his left hand and skittered across the floor. The blond fellow smiled: removing the main-gauche had obviously been his intent. As he came in again, two of the others followed, coordinating their attacks with their leader's—

The report of a gun, unusually loud and piercing, stopped the swordplay as abruptly as if it had stopped time itself. The blond man sagged and crumpled to the floor—revealing Michael at the base of the steps, legs braced, both hands wrapped tightly around the little gun that his father had given him. Which now spoke again and again. Six more times it fired; three more pirates went down. The last four tried bolting out the door, but Hugh was faster. He ran two through from behind, and cut down another that turned to parry. The fourth and last, falling over the bodies piled in the narrow doorway, begged for mercy that Hugh chose not to show.

When he came back into the blockhouse, he discovered that Michael was trimming the straps on his up-time backpack. Hugh leaned against the wall; he wanted to laugh, both with relief and amusement at Michael's rather bizarre choice of post-combat activity. "Going on a trip?"

Michael looked up, no smile on his face. "Uh, yeah. I've got to go. Now."

Hugh laughed, then stopped, seeing Michael's unchanged expression. "You're serious."

"Yep. Listen, you've done a great job, Hugh. Turenne is going to be very pleased, and I suspect his ship will be along soon to help you."

Hugh frowned. "You 'suspect'? You must *know*. How else were you planning to depart?"

"Well—there's another ship."

"Another—?" And then Hugh stopped and felt cold spread outward from his spine. "Another ship. The ship that Mulryan spotted farther to the east, last night."

Michael nodded. "Dutch. The *Koninck David*, under Jakob Schooneman."

"And why do you only tell me this *now...?*" But he saw the reason before Michael could respond. "This expedition has all been an elaborate ploy, hasn't it?"

"No, the deal with Turenne is real. Sort of. He's already got his balloon and he'll get his oil—*if* Richelieu's agents make you the best deal for it. Just as we agreed."

"Then why this skulduggery, Michael? Why not stay and—?"

"Because that's not part of the plan."

Hugh narrowed his eyes. "Whose plan?"

"Mine. And the USE's."

"So you are their agent. And now that this site has been wrested from the Spanish, will I be expected to turn it over to Gustav Adolf, or directly to you Americans?"

"No, absolutely not. It's yours."

"It's Turenne's."

"It is if he decides to make the best offer. And if you decide to sell it to him. You might want to wait a day or two, see if a better offer comes along."

Hugh frowned. "Turenne paid for this mission. All of it."

"Look, Hugh, right now you own this piece of real estate. Or rather, your 'corporation' does. But tell me, what will you do if Turenne's boss Richelieu won't offer a fair price?"

And Hugh once again suddenly found himself hobbled by his personal Achilles' heel: his reflexive tendency to put faith in self-professed allies and their promises. "I do not know what I would do. I suppose I would have to trust in Turenne's influence."

"Turenne's influence is at Richelieu's pleasure. Here's another poser for you: what if Richelieu decides he's not interested at all? What then?"

Hugh had no answer. "Then, I suppose, we are all lost."

"You suppose wrong. There are other people interested in making you an offer if Richelieu's falls through. Remember, Hugh, you own this land. Capturing it was your mission, and you've succeeded."

Hugh scoffed. "Succeeded? Michael, have you been paying attention over the past few weeks? Our 'secret' approach to Pitch Lake was obviously disclosed to our foes. Within two weeks of arriving here, we have been attacked. And although the enemy we fought was only a pirate band, we can rest assured that they learned of us from a greater power. I'm betting on Spain. Which must therefore know of our landing and, as soon as sufficient force has been gathered, will come and obliterate us. Against which we have little defense, since all of Morraine's crew is surely dead, and our only ship is lost. And you call this a success?"

But in staring long at Michael's gray eyes, Hugh saw that his arguments had made no impact. So how would this debacle still be a success for Michael and the USE? And then, he knew. "You want them to come here, don't you? All of them, and in force: the Spanish, the French, and the Dutch. Our attempt to seize Pitch Lake highlights its strategic importance. And you amplified that impression with your great show of stealth. The balloon was the masterstroke. Who would employ so special and secret a device if the stakes were not correspondingly high? And besides, it was a piece of technological bait that Turenne could neither resist nor ignore. But in reality, it was all just theater, staged to make this miserable patch of tar a seemingly irresistible object, and to draw the attention and the forces of the great powers here." He thought, then smiled. "So if you Americans want everyone's attention focused here, it only stands to reason that your real interest was to distract them, so that they will be less likely to notice when you advance on your true objective here in the New World—"

Mike suddenly grew very pale, and his gray eyes jumped sideways. "I've gotta go."

Hugh leaned back again. "You might as well admit that my conjecture is correct. The change in your color has told me as much." He glanced to confirm that Mike had indeed packed away his pistol and then smoothly brought out the boot dagger he kept as a final hold-out. "And now, having discerned your true objective, I have become a danger to its attainment. So logically, you will wish to move against me."

Michael's pallor was dramatically superseded by a bright, angry flush, and his eyes narrowed. "Damn it, Hugh, that's the first stupid thing you've said."

"How so?"

"Because part of what makes you so valuable is how damned smart you are. Which means it was always probable that you would figure this out, anyway. It's a risk that was considered, and was deemed acceptable."

"But now that I know—"

"—'Know' what? What do you really 'know'? That the Americans might be up to something in South America or Mexico or the

Caribbean? If I had a dollar for every one of those rumors, I'd be a rich man. All you 'know' is that we wanted this to happen."

"And probably, in the long run, hope to own Trinidad yourselves."

But Mike was shaking his head. "No. That's not the point of this."

"Then what is?"

Michael looked away for a moment, seemed to listen—probably for O'Rourke's approach—then he met Hugh's eyes again. "Now listen carefully, Hugh. Right here, right now, you're in charge of Pitch Lake. You make the decisions. And as long as you hold this ground, you have leverage. You have something—at last—with which to bargain, something that will actually make nations pay attention to your cause and keep their promises."

Hugh blinked. He had been a captain of soldiers since before he truly needed to shave, so he was well acquainted with faces of men whose passionate determination was not only grim, but vengeful. And that expression was now set deep into the lines of Michael Jr.'s suddenly aged face. To which he addressed the question, "Why?"

"'Why' what?"

"Why do this for me? Without promise of alliance?"

Michael's eyes did not waver. "You've said it yourself: you, your family, and your nation have had a belly full of broken promises. You've been bled white by the people who strung you along on easy assurances of aid and alliance. And as the years went by, they simply turned you—all of you—into their pet war-dogs." Mike suddenly grew very red again. "No more. Not one bit more. Take this place. Bargain with it. Bargain hard. Recruit any Dutch who hate the Spanish: there are plenty. Recruit the English, who have been forsaken by their own king. Recruit the privateers who thought themselves patriots, but found themselves disowned by their own nations. It won't take many desperate men to hold this place. And if you deal fair with the natives, they'll deal fair with you."

"And how do you know that?"

"Because our Dutch friends in Suriname have been in contact with the Nepoia tribes here on Trinidad for half a year. The Nepoia's own displaced tribal king Hyarima has given Jakob Schooneman his word that he will receive your envoys and deal fair with you. With you alone, Hugh O'Donnell. Think it through, man: why do you think the Arawaks were not here when you landed? Because our Dutch partners convinced Hyarima to make war on the Arawaks, and draw them away from peripheral areas like Pitch Lake. Hyarima and the rest of the Nepoia tribes want to throw off the Spanish control of their towns, and take their lands back from the Arawaks. Armed with trade muskets from the *Koninck David*, I suspect they're making some progress, too."

Hugh wished there was a chair to collapse into. "And so I am to simply sell Pitch Lake to the highest bidder?

Mike shrugged. "That's up to you. If Richelieu makes the best offer, it seems like you owe him the right of first refusal. But whatever you do, remember this: sitting on oil means you're sitting on both great peril and great promise. For yourself and your country. And by your country, I don't just mean the Spanish Lowlands. I mean Ireland."

Hugh felt himself suddenly, inexplicably moved. McCarthy's often veiled eyes seemed not only open, but pleading. And he felt his face smile crookedly, despite his resolve not to. "You have some of the bardic tongue of your forebears, Michael McCarthy. I shall heed your words, and watch my step."

Michael nodded, walked to the doorway, stopped, and handed Hugh a heavy cloth bag. "In case some of your enemies require a little extra persuasion," he explained, and was out the door at a trot.

Hugh heard Michael's hastening boots diminuendo toward the north end of the stockade. He heard O'Rourke's loud and worried approach from the south. He looked at the bodies littering the floor of the blockhouse. And then he looked in the leaden bag.

In an ungracious lump at the bottom he saw Michael's holstered .45, four magazines, and several boxes of ammunition. He hoped he would not need them.

But Hugh O'Donnell conceded that, before too many days had passed, he probably would.

Mike McCarthy, Jr., found Hyarima's hand-picked Nepoia scouts waiting for him just outside the stockade when he reached the platform at the center of the north wall. They tossed up a hooked line. Mike snugged the hook between two of the palisade's timbers and went down, hand over hand.

Staying on east-bound game-paths, they made good time, first moving within the tree line that paralleled the north coast, and then directly alongside the shore itself.

After approximately twenty minutes of brisk walking, Mike caught sight of a lugger beached in a small cove up ahead. The crew, two Dutch seamen, saw them coming, and stood up slowly, casually—

—the same way Ed Piazza had stood up when Mike had entered his office in Grantville almost a year ago to present him with The Plan....

Mike and Ed had made small talk for a few minutes on that day, and then got down to discussing Mike's proposal. McCarthy pointed out that, with the situation changing across Europe, Simpson and Stearns must already be thinking in terms of a journey to develop and tap into some of the singular resources of the New World. "But I know that's not happening too soon," qualified Mike, "at least, not until Simpson's done building his expeditionary force."

Ed kept his posture and his face relaxed, but his voice betrayed him. In a tighter, slightly nasal accent, Ed repeated, "Not until Simpson's done *what*?"

Mike leaned back. "When I was up north on the Baltic coast a few months back, I saw the kind of ships he's building. High weather designs. More than you need if you were just going to sail around the Baltic. I also noticed his mast arrangements, as well as the smaller hulls he's been procuring. Handy, shallow-draft, fore-and-aft rigged boats. Again, not for the Baltic."

"Perfect for the Med, however."

"Sure, they'd work in the Med, except we have no reason to go there and any operations would have to start with a very high-profile run through Gibraltar. That's not been the USE's *modus operandi*, to date. But the Caribbean—and the Gulf—is open access, and more importantly, it has something the Med doesn't."

"Oh? Like what?" Ed seemed to be trying to hide a smile now.

"Coastal oil. In a variety of places."

"True enough. And does your crystal ball reveal our hypothetical destinations there?"

"Nope, and I don't want to know. Because then I'd know too much, and you wouldn't let me leave Grantville, much less go on a Caribbean cruise."

"True enough. For now. But how can you help me if you don't even know where we're—hypothetically—going?"

"Well, part of the trouble with any move into the Caribbean and the Gulf is that there's a good bit of traffic there already. And most of it belongs either to potential rivals or outright enemies, both of whom would like nothing better than to get wind of what you're doing, and either give you hell while you're doing it or make it entirely impossible."

"Okay, so how can you fix that?"

In response, Mike made his "Pitch Lake pitch," including the use of the balloon. Ending with, "And that's why Pitch Lake is the perfect stalking horse for your *real* operation."

"A 'stalking horse'?"

"Sure. Look, all your rivals already know that Pitch Lake exists, so you're not giving away any intelligence, right? And because it's a source of easy oil, it's going to be a pretty appealing piece of real estate, once they start thinking about it a little more. There's minimum difficulty accessing the crude, and they can boil and process a lot of what they need right out of the seeps in the lake itself."

"Go on."

"So if any colonial power in the Caribbean makes a grab for it, the others will probably wake up and follow. They all understand the importance of oil. Hell, Turenne chose to raid the field at Wietze not just to put it out of commission, but to acquire technical intelligence on oil production. So the French are thinking about using oil, which means they're thinking about getting it. And the rest can't be too far behind."

Ed tapped his goose quill lightly on the paper in front of him. "Hypothetically speaking, it might be very helpful to create a diversion in Trinidad. But we're spread so thin as it is, that—"

"I didn't say anything about *our* taking Trinidad, did I?"

Ed stopped tapping the pen. "Why, no—no, you didn't." And he smiled. "Turenne?"

"Yep, Turenne. Indirectly, that is. You give him the opportunity to grab Pitch Lake and get a leg-up on hot air ballooning all in one fell swoop, and he'll take the bait. Even if he suspects he's being played. But he won't have the authority to seize a Spanish possession himself, so he'd have to bankroll a 'free company' of independent speculators. From whom France can then buy the property they've 'acquired.'"

Ed frowned. "That's a pretty small legal fig leaf."

"It's a giant palm frond compared to the legal contortions the Dutch and the Brits have undertaken to justify some of their 'rightful conquests.' But that's okay, because the more ambiguous the French claim is, the more contention there will be. Meaning

France will have to send some local forces quickly to protect her ownership. Spain will attempt a swift reconquest, so they'll need to use local forces, too."

Ed's frown had not disappeared. "I'm not sure the news that Pitch Lake is up for grabs will make its way to Havana and Cartagena as quickly as you're hoping, Mike."

"Then we help it along by leaking it selectively. Some of the Dutch traders that young Phil Jenkins traveled with last year could spread a few rumors in the right ports, at the right time. And the resulting clustering effect around Trinidad should reduce the general traffic in the other parts of the Caribbean. Which gives Admiral Simpson, or whoever he sends, a freer hand and more open waters to make a run to—well, to wherever they're going."

"Mike, I won't deny it: your plan has some promise. But there's one hitch."

"What's that?"

"Hugh O'Donnell. His willing cooperation is central to your plan's success."

"Absolutely."

"Well, from what I know of him, this isn't exactly his style. Ethically speaking, that is. What you're contemplating is just half a step shy of outright land-piracy. If that much. What if O'Donnell decides he just doesn't want to play?"

"He'll play. He *has* to, Ed. He's learned some difficult things about his future. So he needs to make a change, a big change."

"Okay, but how do we, um... 'guide' him into believing that leading an overseas land-grab is the right way to go about making this kind of change?"

"By using a carrot and a stick."

"Huh. I can see the carrot: money, power, and influence are all needful things for an estranged earl. But the stick?"

Mike rubbed his nose, looked away. This was the part he loathed. "Once Hugh leaves Spanish employ, we could lead him to believe that he needs a new patron. Really quickly."

"And how do we do that?"

"Hugh grew up knowing that his godmother, Archduchess Isabella, was shielding him from English assassins. One of The O'Neill's young sons, Brian, was strangled in Brussels about eighteen years ago when his keepers got careless one evening."

"Okay, but O'Donnell is no boy. He won't scare easily."

"No, but if he thinks his presence poses a threat to those he cares about, he'll want to put some hefty distance between himself and them. And that, of course, will give him a strong incentive to snap up any reasonable opportunity to pursue his goals overseas. At least for a while."

"Okay, I'll buy that. It fits his character. But how do you propose to convince him that he's got this kind of immediate bull's-eye painted on his back?"

Mike squared his shoulders. "We hire the necessary agents through our contacts in the underworld and stage an abduction attempt."

"We have 'contacts' in the underworld?"

"Ed, as I understand it, the Abrabanels and their partners not only know whose closets contain which skeletons, but also which confidential agents were responsible for making the skeletons in the first place."

"Ahem...okay, I'm still listening."

"So, we go through those 'channels' to recruit a pair of apparent kidnappers."

"And what would their orders be?"

"Simple: to make a 'gentle' attempt to capture the man wearing the earl of Tyrconnell's cloak. Which I'll make sure that *I* have on when they come calling."

"You? Why should you be the shill for your own con game, Mike?"

Michael felt like vomiting. "Because Hugh has adopted Dad and me like we're family. If one or both of us are threatened because of him—"

Ed nodded. "Then he'll feel guilt and be more tractable, easy to guide, particularly overseas where you'd both be out of harm's way. Okay, but how do we keep you and Hugh safe during this sham abduction? What if the kidnappers get a little too, um, enthusiastic when they try to grab you, or resist O'Donnell?"

"We tell our hirelings to use minimal force, and that if they kill or even wound either the mark or his friends, they get no pay."

"Won't that make the kidnappers suspicious?"

Mike shook his head. "Not if we make it clear that the point of the kidnapping is extortion. When the objective is to acquire surreptitious leverage over people, you can't kill the hostage, or their family, or their friends. Any 'professional' will understand that. So we explain that if the abduction is too difficult to manage safely, it's enough that they give the mark a good scare."

Ed smiled, stood. "Y'know, Mike, this plan might work. I'll think it over and send word in a couple of days." He put out his hand—

Now Michael found himself staring at a different hand—that of a Dutch sailor who was offering to help him into the lugger. Michael took the hand and let himself be guided over the side of the boat. He wondered at the sudden weakness in his limbs, wondered at the wetness on his cheeks, wondered how he had been able to betray O'Donnell, and wondered why the rationalizations he had repeated to himself every day since leaving Ed's office just didn't make the self-loathing go away.

But here—surrounded by Nepoias and common Dutch seamen who probably didn't understand one word of English—he could whisper the real, gut-level, impolitic truth of why he had so profoundly and horribly manipulated the life of Hugh Albert O'Donnell:

"He's their only hope," Mike confessed to the shining waters in a murmur that barely got past the thick ache in his throat. "His family, his men, his country: they'll be dying even sooner, now—unless Hugh can get enough leverage to save them."

But if the Nepoias or the Dutchmen had even heard Michael, they gave no sign. Instead, without a word, they swung the lugger's prow around and began a swift run across the bright blue bay toward the waiting *Koninck David*, and ultimately, a rendezvous with the allies Hugh didn't even know he had.

For McCarthy, the presence of the *Koninck David* was a message in itself, the text of which read: *we have found Tromp's fleet and they are coming.* And if the fates were kind, Tromp's ships would already have linked up with Simpson's advance recon flotilla, which was carrying a letter from the infanta Isabella to Hugh. That probably lengthy missive was all at once a plea, an explanation, and an apology from the one person in power that the attainted earl truly trusted. But Michael was uncertain that any of Hugh's trust would survive a reading of that letter's explication of the many half-truths, deceptions, and wiles that had made possible his seizure of Trinidad.

Michael McCarthy felt his throat tighten again. He stared at the sun's reflection upon the scudding wavelets, letting that light burn into his brain, burn away the guilt, help him to think of nothing.

Chapter 26

Off Saba, Lesser Antilles

Of all the officers and ground crew gathered at the *Intrepid*'s mizzen, only Ove Gjedde seemed immune to yawns. Staring up where the balloon tether disappeared into the predawn dark, Eddie Cantrell was not the only one who yearned for the comfort of his bunk, but he may have yearned for it more than most. Of them all, only he had a wife in his bed, a wife who often awakened right about now. It would not have been accurate to say that she then arose, but rather, that she drowsily greeted the day and her husband—amorously—before catching another two or three hours of post-coital slumber.

But instead of that wonderful conjugal greeting, Eddie was waiting to see what came sparking down the telegraph wire that was secured to the balloon's mooring cable. Which, he decided, was a pretty lousy trade. At least some of his command staff, such as Rik Bjelke, were still catching shut-eye. On Eddie's orders, no less.

Mutiny was apparently in the early morning breeze, though: Rik Bjelke appeared in the companionway that led down to the staterooms. "Captain, Commander: any news?"

Eddie tried to frown. "Nothing except a discussion about how long you're going to be thrown in the brig. What are you doing out of your bunk, mister?"

Rik was smiles and apologies as he made his way over to Eddie and Gjedde. "My pardons, sirs, but I could not sleep. Not even with an extra swallow of brandy. Too eager to hear the news, I suppose."

Which, Eddie conceded, was certainly understandable, but wasn't any help. "Mr. Bjelke, I appreciate your interest in the results of our reconnaissance, but as the day wears on, I need someone at the con who was not already awake at the end of the middle watch. That was supposed to be you."

Rik glanced up into the darkness sheepishly. "Yes, sir. My apologies. I could go below, try to drink more brandy." Gjedde's mouth twitched to resist the emergence of a smile.

Eddie sighed. "Well, I'd rather have you tired than drunk, Rik. You might as well stay on deck until we get word."

"Which should be soon," Gjedde said with a look eastward. The rim of the world was no longer satin black, but dark, downy gray.

Rik's glance traveled from the balloon cable to the reefed sails. "Where are we, just now?"

Eddie felt the wind rise to about two knots, then settle again, and he wondered what their observer in the balloon was experiencing. "St. Eustatia is about twenty-eight miles south-by-southeast. Saba is about fifteen miles south-by-southwest. At about five-hundred-fifty feet altitude, our observer reported seeing multiple light sources in what should be Oranjestad. That's probably good news. The number of original settlers wouldn't generate enough light—or the right type—to be visible at 0400 hours."

"That's wonderful!" Bjelke exclaimed. "So Tromp is there!"

Gjedde's voice was much cooler than the breeze. "Or the Spanish. In which case, Oranjestad has been conquered and we must reformulate our plans."

As if to rebuff the gloom of the Norwegian's caveat, the first bright rim of the sun pushed over the wine-dark horizon. Far above them, the gray-blue canopy of the balloon seemed to materialize out of the diffusing darkness, catching the first feeble rays a moment before they also glowed faintly against the spars and gunwales of the *Intrepid*.

Eddie knew there wasn't light enough for the observer to see clearly yet—that would take a little longer—but he still found himself listening for the first chattering of the telegraph that would announce the fateful report from aloft.

Rik's hands were moving nervously. A glance from Gjedde had the young man fold them quickly behind his back. "So," Bjelke said in a tone that suggested he was casting about for a subject, "evidently no encounters with the Spanish when we passed Saint Maarten?"

"None," answered Eddie. "Captain Gjedde timed our pass perfectly." Which, despite sounding like hyperbole, was a simple statement of fact. True to his intent and his word, Ove Gjedde, piloting for the fleet at Mund's insistence, had slowed Reconnaissance Flotilla X-Ray's approach into the Caribbees so that at 9 PM, they were approximately fourteen miles northwest of St. Maarten. Crowding sail once the last light was out of the western sky, the flotilla ran past the Spanish-held island at a distance of ten miles, each darkened vessel running but one small light well beneath the weather deck of its starboard quarter. Traveling in a westward-staggered echelon, the ships of Reconnaissance Flotilla X-Ray thus presented the potential Spanish watch posts to their east with their lightless portside hulls. The piloting task was not difficult for the ships that followed the path blazed by Gjedde. Each one only needed to keep the starboard-quarter light of the ship in front of them one point off their own port bow.

However, that meant that the success of the passage had been wholly dependent upon Gjedde's ability to maneuver southward into lightless seas on a fairly precise and constant heading. Nonetheless, over the course of the six hours it had taken to sail to their current position on a close reach, the grizzled captain had given fewer than ten commands in accomplishing this feat. This did not count the occasional corrective grunt or gesture when the prevailing winds from the east edged northward and threatened them with the prospect of having to run close hauled.

Eddie discovered that, like everyone else, he was staring up the increasingly visible cable toward the balloon overhead, as if the observer might shout something down. Instead, the telegraph finally began to clatter in the below-decks communications center, too fast and muted for Eddie to make out the message.

The clattering did not last long, which was either a very good, or a very bad, sign. The comm officer's young assistant came up the steep stairs that seamen called a "ladder" two steps at a time and handed a slip to Ove Gjedde. Whose slow, expressionless perusal of it was quite maddening.

Eddie resolved to show no more emotion or anticipation than Gjedde and so, when the older captain proffered the slip to him, he shrugged. "I'm sure Mr. Bjelke would enjoy summarizing it for us." Judging from Rik's nervous foot movements and florid face, this was a very safe conjecture.

Gjedde's lips twitched as he handed it off to his young fellow-Norwegian.

Rik's eyes raced across the lines as he breathlessly summarized. "Approximately thirty hulls observed in Oranjestad Bay. Many have outlines discernible as jachts and fluyts. Although it is difficult to see sufficient details, a large encampment is noted surrounding the town. Its layout is not consistent with a military bivouac." He looked up. "Tromp and the refugees from Recife. It has to be—doesn't it?"

Eddie was surprised by Gjedde's sharp nod. "Unquestionably. But not because of the encampment. The whole colony could have surrendered, after all. And they'd still be living in camp conditions, anyhow."

"Then how are you so sure it is Tromp?" Bjelke asked.

By way of answer, Gjedde glanced sideways at Eddie. Who, although new in his mastery of things maritime, had a life-long interest in and aptitude for things military and strategic. "The types of ships reported, Rik, particularly the jachts. They wouldn't be present if the Spanish took Oranjestad."

Gjedde completed the explanation. "Dutch jachts are among the fastest and most maneuverable boats in the world, Mr. Bjelke, and they certainly hold that pride of place here in the Caribbean, along with the smaller sloops patterned after the Bermudan kind. So if the Spanish fought Tromp, or attacked Oranjestad, they could not have captured so many of them. They, at least, would make good their escapes. Yet there they are, present in the bay. And the fluyts are the further assurance of Tromp's presence and continued control. The Dutch who first settled St. Eustatia had, at most, but two or three such vessels at their disposal. And I suspect if the Spanish had taken such ships along with the town, they would have used those same vessels to deport the colonists to Cuba." He scowled. "It is Spanish mercy, you see. Instead of killing colonists who have violated Madrid's popish *inter caetera* right to all lands west of the Tordesillas line, they take those trespassers to Cuba, where they can be more charitably kept in chains and worked to death. That's what happened to the first Dutch colony on Saba, if I recall the reports properly."

"So, what now?" asked Rik.

Again Gjedde turned to Eddie. "At this point, I believe we are to turn to you for special instructions, Commander."

Cantrell shrugged. "Not exactly, but I'll need to be on hand for the initial contact and negotiations when we reach Oranjestad." *Because there are some parts of this operation that remain very much need-to-know, and therefore, are topics for one-on-one conversations with the folks at the very apex of Oranjestad's military food chain.* "Runner,"—he turned to the boy who'd brought the message— "return to the communications center and inform the duty officer to send to the *Crown of Waves* that she is to pick up the waiting diplomatic parties on *Resolve* and *Patentia* and rendezvous with us. She will then precede the *Intrepid* by three miles as both ships press on to Oranjestad at best speed. The rest of the flotilla will follow."

Oranjestad Bay, St. Eustatia

It was just after 9:30 that a skerry launched from a Dutch jacht drew alongside *Crown of Waves*, which was running with the tompions still in her cannon's muzzles. Of the four men in the small boat, two reached up to take hold of the short boarding stairs that had been put over the side. Once on deck, they stared at the group gathered before them—Eddie, Pros Mund, and the personal secretary of Hannibal Sehested—and then up at the ensign-staff just behind the Danish jacht's taffrail, where no less than four flags were flying: those of the United States of Europe, of the Union of Kalmar, Gustav Adolf's house standard of Vasa, and a diplomatic pennant of Prince Frederik Hendrik of Orange.

The older of the two gestured around at the *Crown*'s weather deck. "This is a Dutch ship, but you are not dressed as Dutchmen, nor do I know any of you."

Eddie looked to Pros Mund. Who, in keeping with his taciturn nature, simply nodded and spoke in passable Dutch. "You are correct in all these observations." He switched to Amideutsch. "One of my officers will explain." He folded his arms and then nodded at Eddie.

Well, that was gracious. Eddie simply smiled and put out a hand. "I am Commander Edward Cantrell of the United States of Europe. From Grantville."

Their visitors' eyebrows rose markedly at the word "Grantville." The older of the two extended a hand. "We are pleased to see you, Commander. Very pleased. I am Philip Serooskereken and this is Matieu Rijckewaert. We welcome you to Oranjestad." He smiled. And he waited.

Which was, Eddie reflected, perfectly understandable. Living in the unremitting fear of Spanish discovery, two ships—one of which is the immense and oddly shaped *Intrepid*—arrive out of nowhere, running a bewildering array of flags that had no reason to be on the same ship, and one of which was the ensign of their own Prince of Orange. What, then, were these ships? Harbingers of strange news from home? An elaborate ruse that bordered on the surreal? Or—the most nail-biting alternative of all—the arrival of long-prayed-for succor from home and/or allies? Well, no reason to keep them wondering. "Mr. Serooskereken, I believe that Admiral Tromp is, well, not exactly expecting us, but had reason to hope for our arrival. It is imperative that we meet with him at once to discuss—"

But Serooskereken was shaking his head. "I am sorry, but I must inform you that the admiral is not in port—"

Not in port? Damn it, what's happened?

"—but that Councilor van Walbeeck may be able to answer your questions, and may have also been told to expect you."

So van Walbeeck made it here alive, and it sounds like he's serving as Oranjestad's senior political leader. That's good. But still— "Excellent. We look forward to meeting with Councilor van Walbeeck, but I wonder if you could tell me where the admiral has traveled to, and with how many ships?"

Serooskereken's experience as a political figure was becoming increasingly evident. He redirected Eddie's inquiry with an easy gesture and relaxed smile. "I suspect Councilor van Walbeeck will be eager to discuss these and many other matters with you. In the meantime, let us arrange for the berthing of your two ships at adequate anchorages and then depart for—"

"With respect, Councilor Serooskereken, we'll need to arrange for seven berths, not two. The rest of our flotilla should be here by three o'clock or so."

Serooskereken's eyes widened, as did his smile. "Seven ships? Well, that is very good news indeed, Commander. The mate in the skerry can arrange the anchorages with your chief pilot, I'm sure. In the meantime, allow me to offer you the hospitality of Oranjestad." His smile buckled. "Such as it is."

Eddie glanced over the man's shoulder. Now less than a mile off their port bow, the tent-city that had burgeoned into existence around the skirts of the original colony's few permanent buildings was starkly visible. While it was neither ramshackle nor particularly dirty, it was strikingly crowded and makeshift.

And suddenly, Eddie was seeing the tent-city that had gathered around Grantville mere months after it had fallen into this world. Refugees had heard of the miraculous town from the future, a self-proclaimed safe-haven for victims of the intensifying Thirty Years' War that up-timer intervention ultimately diffused into a much less sweeping and destabilizing set of conflicts. The promise of food and warmth, as well as an absolute guarantee of religious toleration, had attracted the tired, the poor, and the huddling, hungry masses like moths to a single, distant flame of hope. Yes, Eddie was well-acquainted with the realities of tent-cities, even in one that seemed to be nestled in an island paradise: the smells, the near-despair, the staring eyes and hollow cheeks—

"We look forward to sharing some refreshment with you," he assured Serooskereken brightly. "And of course, you won't mind us bringing some gifts from back home. And some supplies we were tasked to carry for you."

The Dutch councilor looked like he might faint from delight. "No. We would not mind. Not at all."

"Then while you work out the berthing for our ships, we'll signal to our larger vessel to meet us ashore with the gifts and some of the supplies. The balance of the shipment is being carried on our other ships. So if you could arrange for a few lighters—"

"They will be waiting at the anchorages," Serooskereken assured Eddie with an eager nod, and then he followed Pros Mund's gesture toward the *Crown of Waves'* pilot. After a bemused glance at Eddie, the nominative admiral of Reconnaissance Flotilla X-Ray stalked toward the bows, hands behind his back.

Sehested's secretary, who was also the coordinating purser for the flotilla, turned a bright smile on Eddie as soon as both Mund and Serooskereken were out of easy earshot. His eyes were panicked, however. "Commander, I am, er, dismayed. I was not aware that we are carrying gifts for Oranjestad. And I would certainly have noticed it on our cargo manifests if the flotilla's collective lading included any general supplies for—"

Eddie turned an equally bright smile on Lord Sehested's secretary and made his eyes very hard. "You are mistaken. We are carrying both gifts and supplies for this colony. The gifts are coming from the officers' messes on this ship, and the *Intrepid*. Collect all their discretionary provisions and deliver them to Councilor van Walbeeck. He has a reputation for being evenhanded and honest. You will do the same with all the comestibles of the officers' messes on the other ships when they arrive at anchorage."

"But—!"

"I'm not done. You will then off-load thirty percent of the reserve rations on board the *Patentia* and the *Serendipity* as general supplies, again delivered to the attention and discretion of van Walbeeck. He'll know where it's needed most."

"Sir, I must protest. I cannot be held accountable for mission provisioning if our own dried and durable foodstuffs are so severely diminished at the outset of our—"

"We already have replacement provisioning waiting for us on Trinidad, acquired from the Nepoia tribes. So we will be fully restocked within a fortnight." *Please, please let me be telling the truth.*

The secretary was momentarily mollified but retained an erect posture of prim disapproval. "Very well, sir, but surely, given the ladies aboard the *Intrepid*, and the noble personages aboard the *Patentia*, you cannot mean that their messes are to be *completely* transferred to—"

"I said clean them out, and that is precisely what I mean. And not another question about it."

"And if your wife protests?"

"She won't." *She's made of sterner stuff than you, evidently.*

"And if any of the nobles, such as Lord Sehested, should complain?"

"Then they can come see me."

The master purser's voice took on a sinuous quality. "Lord Sehested might expect you to be responsive to his desires to exclude his mess from these unexpected depletions."

"Unfortunate. Because if he does complain, the only response he can reasonably expect from me is 'too bad.'" *And maybe "go to hell" and a punch in the nose if he insists too often or too loudly.*

"Sir, my duties bind me to convey your exact words to Lord Sehested. Are you aware of that?"

"Aware of it? I'm counting on it." *I hope I'm not buying a political battle over a few hogsheads of dried beef, but if Sehested turns out to be a self-indulgent grandee who expects life in the field to resemble life at court, then we might as well have it out now. I can't afford to have class-privilege crap popping up if we face some* real *hardships.*

"Commander Cantrell!" called Serooskereken as he returned from the jacht's taffrail. "I have arranged the anchorage and we are ready to depart. When would it be convenient for your party to join us ashore?"

Eddie glanced at the signalman who was sending prearranged messages via semaphore to the *Intrepid*, then smiled at the Dutch councilor. "How about right now?"

Chapter 27

Oranjestad Bay, St. Eustatia

Anne Cathrine looked up at the humble battlements of Fort Oranjestad and saw Eddie's silhouette as he strolled there with the other civil and military commanders. She repressed—barely—a surge of offended pride: *I should be up there, too.*

And if it hadn't been for the Swedes on the mission, she might very well have been. But the suspicions that had kept her from joining Eddie as he worked on the fleet in Luebeck had followed her, albeit indirectly, into the flotilla itself. Although reunited with her husband, there were still meetings from which she was excluded, plans to which she was not made privy. Most of that was due to the hard-line Swedes who had insisted that their nation's long-range plans were no business of the Danish royal family, not until tests and time had demonstrated that Copenhagen's commitment to the forcibly reconstituted Union of Kalmar was genuine and robust. Gustav Adolf could certainly have overridden those exclusionary stipulations, but Anne Cathrine had to concede that it was a wise king who chose his domestic battles with care, and the Swedish monarch had evidently allowed his hard-liners this minor victory. After all, it cost him little and made them feel useful.

But Anne Cathrine could not overlook the lesser source of

her exclusions from Eddie's business: Eddie himself. In fairness to Eddie, she knew that he would have trusted her with the hidden details of their mission. But the captains and kings who had come to control the shape and fate of his stratagems were not similarly minded. As Eddie had apologetically explained to her, knowledge of various elements of their mission to the New World were on a "need-to-know" basis: a peculiar, hyphenated phrase that had the pragmatic, engineered sound typical of so many other up-time political and military expressions. Eddie assured her that even he, himself, was not fully briefed on all elements of the voyage: he was carrying a set of sealed orders and letters about which he knew next to nothing, to be delivered to a person he had never met.

"Step careful, m'lady," prompted a voice at her elbow. Anne Cathrine looked over at the escort that had been assigned to her and her two companions: a group of Dutch soldiers led by an Englishman named Cuthbert Pudsey, who jerked his own eyes downward hastily. It was to his credit that he had been tutored not to steer a noblewoman by the elbow, but at this moment, it might have been helpful if he had been a bit less proficient in etiquette. Anne Cathrine followed his eyes downward—just in time to see her foot descending toward a low pile of goat dung. Unable to stop her momentum, she hitched up her skirts and cleared it in one graceful hop, much to the delight of a boy who stood waiting beside the odiferous muck with a crude wooden shovel.

She nodded thanks to Pudsey. "Happily, it seems no one else shall have to hazard the same obstacle I did." She glanced meaningfully back at the boy who was already scooping up the dung.

Pudsey frowned in momentary confusion. Then his face brightened. "M'lady, it please ye, but cleaning the street is the lesser part of his work." When Anne Cathrine's face registered no more understanding than Leonora's or Sophie's behind her, he explicated. "We're careful using wood, on a small island such as this, ladies, and we've not had new axes for more'n a year. So, when a fire is wanted for something other than cooking—" He let the sentence hang unfinished.

Anne Cathrine nodded. *Well, that explains the smell.* Following Pudsey's guiding gesture, she continued walking toward a small paddock that backed upon the windward wall of the fort. A tent, arrayed pavilion-style, was pitched therein, under which a most ancient fellow sat on an upended cask, hands on his knees. As the ladies approached, he tilted his head back and squinted, as if the ten yards separating him from them were in fact ten miles. As Anne Cathrine neared, he labored to rise.

As one, the three women rushed toward the old man, exhorting him to remain seated. He—a wrinkled, sun-browned raisin—did not heed them, but rose, and spoke in fluent Dutch. "Ladies, I am told you have just come ashore from the ships recently arrived in our bay, and that you are persons attached to the Danish court." He actually bowed. "Greetings and felicitations to you all. I am your servant, Ambrósio Fernandes Brandão, and have been asked by our illustrious senior Councilor, Jan van Walbeeck to answer what questions you might have about this place and our condition here."

Before Anne Cathrine could think how to best reply to this grandiloquent greeting, quiet Leonora stepped forward with unusual eagerness. "You are that Ambrósio Brandão who authored the *Dialogues of the Greatness of Brazil*?"

Anne Cathrine suspected that very little rattled or surprised the wizened, white-locked sage, but this inquiry had precisely that effect. He swayed a bit and smiled, showing that a full two-thirds of his teeth remained in his head. "I am he, but how—how do you know my name?"

Leonora had, over the years, been introduced to many of the crowned heads of Europe and, in her words, an "interminable" number of their direct off-spring. Never had Anne Cathrine heard her one-quarter as excited as she was now. "Dr. Brandão—for you are also a physician, if I recall correctly—your work on the flora and fauna and natural sciences of Brazil is one of the primary reasons I commenced learning Dutch. I wished to read your work myself one day. All who have read it speak most highly of not only its unusual eloquence, but its exacting observations."

Brandão gabbled like a startled turkey for a moment. Anne Cathrine could barely suppress her smile. *Hardly the mien of a dignified sage. And here is my own beloved sister acting like—what is Eddie's term?—a geek. Or maybe her behavior is better defined by the expression "fan-girl"—except, to be categorized as such, she must emit a sound akin to "squee." Which she has not done. Yet.*

Brandão had recovered enough to ask leave to sit. The three young women nearly fell over each other helping him to re-perch upon his empty, up-ended cask. "My dear Princess Leonora—"

"Doctor, please. I am but a king's daughter, and to you, Leonora."

"Then my dear Leonora, I am at a loss for words. So you have read the *Dialogues* in Dutch?"

Leonora's large brown eyes stared at the ground. "I must confess I have not." Her eyes came back up quickly. "But not for lack of interest. I had no opportunity. Father was uncertain whether I would derive sufficient benefit from the book, and so did not instruct his purchasers in Amsterdam to acquire it. And then the war intervened, so—" Leonora held up her hands in a display of futility.

"I see. I wonder that your royal father was so dubious about your interest in the *Dialogues*. They are not so very difficult, and you must be fourteen, now, yes?"

"Well, yes, but my interest in your book is not a new phenomenon."

"No? When did you conceive of a desire to read it?"

"When I was seven," Leonora answered promptly. And in such a matter-of-fact tone that it was quite clear that there was not the faintest bit of pride or ego behind her reply.

"Ah, er, I see," replied Brandão, whose brief glance at Anne Cathrine was filled with incredulity and no small measure of alarm at Leonora's intellectual precocity. All Anne Cathrine could do was smile and shrug. Which seemed to settle the old man into accepting that the young woman before him was exactly what she seemed: one of the most extraordinarily gifted intellects he had ever encountered. "Well, Princes—my dear Leonora, I suspect that the book exists in Councilor van Walbeeck's personal library, and I would be surprised if he would not consent to lend it to you. But there will be much time to see to that. Let me first discharge my duty as your guide to this place." He glanced more inclusively at all three women. "Surely, you must have some questions?"

Anne Cathrine nodded. "More than we may ask in any one sitting, Doctor. But you might start by telling us how you—I mean, *all* of you—came to be here. We heard rumor that Admiral Tromp had reached Recife, but with only a handful of ships. However, now we find you here with a veritable fleet."

Brandão nodded. "A quick telling will do much injury to the tale, but for now, that is all that time permits. It happened thusly: the ship that brought me back to Recife from Europe in 1633 was the same one which, departing but three weeks later, carried Councilor van Walbeeck back to the Dutch Republic to report on conditions in Brazil, along with the governor of Dutch Brazil, Dierick van Waerdenburgh. Their crossing had an unexpectedly eventful conclusion: they ran into the blockade the Spanish imposed after winning the Battle of Dunkirk, ultimately finding safe harbor in some small port town on the Frisian Islands."

Brandão shrugged. "So, ironically, van Walbeeck and Admiral Tromp passed each other on the high seas, the latter arriving in Recife mere weeks after the former departed. The two working together would probably have quelled much of the dispute and debate that arose over leaving Recife."

Anne Cathrine shook her head. "But was the decision to abandon the colony not obvious? How was Recife to survive, after the rest of the Dutch fleet was sunk at the Battle of Dunkirk? It was an isolated enclave on a Portuguese coast."

"Lady Anne Cathrine, your ready wisdom would have been an aid in those councils. Our position was made more dire by the colony's inability to support itself. As had been the case since its founding, almost ninety percent of the non-native population of Recife was military. It was profitable in that it exported sugar, but it could not feed itself, and depended upon the Provinces for all its staples.

"But men who have sacrificed much, including the comfort of their homeland, to pursue the goal of becoming wealthy land-owners in the New World are not easily convinced to abandon that which they have gained at so dear a cost. Admiral Tromp was hard put to build a consensus to forsake Recife, was harder put still to formulate a plan whereby he was able to evacuate the almost 2700 souls that required relocation. I doubt he would have been able to do it without help from two key persons: a local farm owner named Calabar and the pirate Moses Cohen Henriques."

Leonora leaned forward. "A pirate named 'Moses Cohen'? He is a convert—a *converso*—from Judaism?"

Brandão nodded. "As am I: a *murrano*. Specifically, a Portuguese of Sephardic birth. He is actually somewhat renowned."

The voice that amplified the old doctor's assertion was thoroughly unexpected. "Henriques was instrumental in ensuring Piet Hein's victory and seizure of the Spanish treasure fleet at the Battle of Matanzas Bay seven years ago," supplied Sophie

Rantzau. The corner of her mouth curved slightly as all the eyes in the group turned towards her in surprise. "I do take up the occasional pamphlet or book," she explained. "And, Dr. Brandão, I take it that Henriques was an acquaintance of yours?"

The octogenarian nodded. "It is as you conjecture, Lady Sophie. It was through me that his initial participation was coordinated with Admiral Tromp's commanders in Recife. Moses has—well, *had*—an island that he used as a base off the Brazilian coast. This became a staging area for the evacuation, allowing us to make preparations beyond the gaze of the uninformed persons of Recife, as well as the eyes of whatever informers certainly lurked there. Meanwhile, Calabar's knowledge of the region around Recife guided the maneuvers that both misled the Portuguese at their citadel of Bom St. Jesus and the surrounding native tribes as to our ultimate intents."

"Still," put in Pudsey from behind the ladies, "it were a most delicate dance, right before we left. Tromp offered the *creoles*—who would have refused to go, anyway—double wages to build another fort, further up the bay. When they finished it the day before the evacuation began, it became their prison for a few weeks. Got 'em neatly out from underfoot, it did, and no one harmed in the doing of it. But it were a delicately dance, as I say."

Brandão nodded. "Delicate and complex. Because of the size of the population and the materials needed for resettlement, the relocation was too great to effect all at once. So it was conducted in stages. A small number of troops and the majority of the strictly civilian colonists—including my own Sephardic community, which enjoyed freedom of worship in Recife—were taken by a limited number of ships here to St. Eustatia.

"Meanwhile, under the guise of a quarantine, access to Recife from the countryside was restricted for some time. By then, the rest of the population—the soldiers and, in many cases, their families—were evacuated as well. Slightly more than three hundred souls chose to expand the Dutch colony already present on Tobago. That left almost two thousand persons, mostly soldiers, to be carried by approximately thirty-five ships, all the way from Recife to here. It was a journey of some privation. It consumed all but a small measure of our dried foods."

"How did you live, afterward?" Anne Cathrine wondered. "Did many starve?"

"No, not outright, Lady Anne Cathrine. But the first months were not kind to the very young, the very elderly, or the ailing. Nearly a hundred such persons perished in those first weeks. Sadly, since the Dutch have long experience in the vagaries of colonial life, they were prepared for such an outcome, and consequently, that grim cost did not have the additional sting of being a surprise.

"It would have been much worse, had Tromp not had the foresight to send us civilians on ahead, in enough time to get in most of a growing season before the balance of the evacuees arrived. After we early arrivals had acquainted the colony that was already here with the size of the resettlement that was pending,"—Anne Cathrine noted wince-spawned wrinkles shoot across Brandão's forehead as he tactfully skirted how the refugees had effectively usurped control of the original Oranjestad colony—"we both put new land under tillage and made contact with Governor Warner of St. Christopher to secure the necessary sustenance. Even so, food was, and remains, in short supply." The doctor smiled. "You will find few rotund Dutch gentlemen here, I am afraid. But we manage."

Sophie looked solemnly over the tents that radiated outward from the permanent structures of Oranjestad in mostly even rows. "Still, there must be considerable difficulties. Wastes, for one."

Cuthbert Pudsey rubbed his chin. "We are, eh, encouraged to stroll into the surf when nature calls loudest, m'lady. Not all do, but there's a fine for, eh, being repeatedly uncooperative."

Sophie nodded. "And fresh water?"

Brandão shook his head. "It is still rationed, almost as closely as our foodstuffs, Lady Sophie. Thanks to our many strong-backed soldiers, we were able to build cisterns quickly. But after one season spent in tents during the storm season, their labor was shifted to building permanent shelters as soon as our water supplies were even marginally sufficient." His face fell. "Unfortunately, the temperament that leads a man to become a soldier for coin is often quite unsuited for tasks such as building and farming. Tensions—of all sorts—remain high."

Anne Cathrine heard a host of unspoken problems hovering behind the doctor's conclusion, given weight by Pudsey's own grumble at what he clearly considered an immense understatement of the present challenges. Anne Cathrine looked out over the tents, then back at the bay, where Reconnaissance Flotilla X-Ray had arrived, the comparative immensity of *Intrepid* and *Resolve* creating a strange shrinkage in the apparent size of the other vessels. She focused particularly on the *Intrepid*, where her comfortable stateroom and bed (an actual bed aboard ship!) waited for her at the end of the day. Was it wrong to be glad for the clean linens and comfortable pillows of that bed? Was it wrong for her to have been the slightest bit annoyed when the *Intrepid*'s purser arrived, hat in hand, to explain that the choice delicacies in the officers' mess and the ladies' own private larder were being appropriated "to help the colonists"?

She was not sure if those selfish twinges made her a lesser person. For all she knew, Eddie himself had felt something similar when he had ordered the transfer of all those fine foods. But that hadn't stopped him from doing so immediately, reflexively. She looked up at the battlements. Eddie's silhouette had moved farther down the wall of the fort and was distinguishable from the others only because of his slight limp. She frowned; that meant he was deathly tired. But that would not stop her Eddie: it never did, any more than considerations of wealth or class or race or sex or religion did. Which might be, she thought with an almost girlish flutter behind her breastbone, why she adored him so very much.

Chapter 28

Fort Oranjestad, St. Eustatia

Eddie Cantrell nodded farewell to Hannibal Sehested as the group that was leaving to take stock of conditions in Oranjestad began retracing their steps to the stairs down from the ramparts.

The initial gathering had been a large one. Every commander and councilor and aristocrat from both the flotilla and St. Eustatia had met to share schnapps, stories, and get the measure of each other. Now, the councilors and aristocrats were finally departing, led by Phipps Serooskereken. Trailing in his wake, Hannibal Sehested, Rik Bjelke, and the original governor of the colony, Pieter van Corselles, exchanged comments on the relations with the English of St. Christopher's and Nevis. Following behind were three councilors who seemed to be Tromp supporters—Calendrini, Carpentiere, and Van der Haghen—and an equal number who glared balefully whenever the admiral or his policies were mentioned: De Bruyn, Haet, and Musen. However, the six of them had been on good behavior and mostly stayed on neutral conversational ground: the stories of their escape from Recife.

Which, from the sound of it, had been a pretty dicey proposition. Tromp and the rest of the military were in agreement that, in the wake of the disastrous Battle of Dunkirk, there was nothing to prevent a repeat of the earlier attempt to starve Recife

292

into submission, originally carried out by the victor of Dunkirk, Admiral Oquendo, in 1631. Even back then, it had been the sheerest luck that the patrolling jacht *Katte* had spotted the Spanish, who—again, luckily—stopped over at Salvador after being sighted. And even if the Dutch and Recife were that lucky again, could they afford a reprise of the ferocious and costly naval battle which followed? Because even if the Dutch once again repulsed the Spanish, how would they replace lost ships? And how swiftly and well could they repair the damaged ones? It was akin to the final siege of a nation's last uncaptured city: with no hope of relief remaining, the outcome was a foregone conclusion. The only variable was how long and grim the eventual defeat would be.

So, before the Spanish arrived with news of destroying the Dutch fleet at Dunkirk, Tromp—on the advice of the mixed-race *criollo* named Calabar—carried out a sharp, successful assault against the Portuguese stronghold of Bom de Jesus. That apparent bid to expand the Dutch colony prompted discussions of a five year truce as the Portuguese and their native auxiliaries licked their wounds and plotted how best to use the time.

Of course, that Portuguese fixation upon securing and getting a truce was precisely the misdirection Tromp had intended to engender. Long before the local enemy commander, Duarte de Albuquerque, had recovered enough to contemplate breaking the truce, Tromp had abandoned Recife and embarked upon the exodus that ultimately brought most of the colony safe to its new home on St. Eustatias.

Eddie had found the tales and anecdotes of that exodus interesting and informative, and would have listened with reasonable avidity on some other occasion. But right now, he had a mission to move forward, and he had not been able to do so until now. There were details that he could not share with anyone but the two persons currently at the top of the colony's chain of command: Jan van Walbeeck and Vice Admiral Joost van Trappen Banckert. And those were the two locals who had elected not to accompany the general tour, and now stood with Eddie and Pros Mund, surveying the wide anchorage of Oranjestad Bay.

Mund broke the silence. "Must we continue to stand here? I would prefer walking."

Van Walbeeck offered a small smile. "With your indulgence, let us remain a few moments longer. It is good we are seen here together. Once we walk further leeward, where the walls are over the shore, the people have no view of us."

Unlike the Dutch adventurers of the New World, who usually had to combine an aptitude for statecraft with military acumen, Mund's perspective was purely that of a wartime captain. "And how does this help you and your colony, van Walbeeck?"

"In several ways," the genial Dutchman replied. "First, to be seen together in public means that we have no major quarrels that must be kept hidden."

"But we have no such quarrels," Mund interrupted testily.

"Of course not," van Walbeeck soothed. "But there are doomsayers in every crowd, Admiral Mund. And they would seize upon a wholly closeted meeting as a means of concealing our differences. Our appearing publicly here—and the others from your flotilla now touring the town with our councilors—will silence those cynics, or at least show their anxieties to be groundless."

Mund made a noise that was half grunt, half sigh. He had little patience for civilian perceptions or judgments of what he believed were purely military affairs.

"Besides," van Walbeeck continued, "Commander Cantrell wisely asked that we find a private place to discuss more sensitive matters. With the lookout discharged temporarily from this post, I can think of no place simultaneously so proximal and yet so private. Now, your questions?"

Eddie was about to commence his inquiries about Tromp and his squadron, but Mund jumped in first. "What do you know of Thijssen and Curaçao? Is he secure there?"

Van Walbeeck seemed as surprised as Eddie at the query. If Joost Banckert was surprised—by this or anything, ever—he had the poker-playing face to conceal it completely. "Marten Thijssen has indeed driven the Spanish from Curaçao and has set about building a fort overlooking the natural harbor at St. Anna Bay. More than this we do not know. Word of this came to Cornelis Jol by way of the privateer Moses Cohen Henriques."

"Privateer?" Mund scowled. "I have heard the word 'pirate' assigned to him. He has no letter of marque, certainly."

"That may have been true before the evacuation of Recife, but Admiral Tromp thought it wise to provide him with the appropriate papers."

Mund darkened and his jaw worked angrily—but before he

could speak, Banckert added a blunt declaration. "Tromp was right to do so. I fully support his decision. I would have done so myself, had I been in his shoes."

Mund shot a fierce look at Banckert, but did not make whatever comment he had been about to utter. Which would probably have been an untactful comment about the suitability of Henriques for their letter of marque, given how piratical the Dutch were themselves.

Eddie sought, and found, a topic which redirected the discussion just enough to get off this possible point of contention, but not so much that the other men would feel themselves being steered toward safer conversational waters. "You sound concerned about Thijssen, Councilor van Walbeeck. Do you foresee problems?"

"I am concerned that the plan to take Curaçao was, well, ill-advised."

Mund's curiosity swept aside his irritation. "How so?"

Van Walbeeck shrugged. "The notion of seizing Curaçao pre-dated the Battle of Dunkirk. I was in Recife when the discussions began and so only became acquainted with them upon my return home, but the Nineteen Heeren of the West India Company had determined that, given its natural harbor and location, Curaçao would be an excellent advance base from which to harry Spanish shipping along the Main."

"You disagreed?" Mund pressed.

"I wondered if that motivation remained prudent," van Walbeeck amended smoothly. "Remember, the mission to take it was not launched until late spring of last year. The ships were collected from scattered berthings as far as the Baltic, given the Spanish blockade of Amsterdam. How, I asked, were we to resupply Thijssen? Who could provide him support, here in the New World?" Van Walbeeck smiled. "And for having the temerity to ask that latter question, the Nineteen decided I should also become my own answer to it. Without having any certainty that Maarten—Admiral Tromp—would come to St. Eustatia, it was decided that I should come to the colony here at the head of a small group of additional settlers and reinforcements, as the United Provinces' on-site coordinator."

Banckert added, "'Coordinator' is a fancy Company word for the fellow who must make sure that all our New World posses-sions support each other when threatened. Easier said than done."

The long-suffering smile on van Walbeeck's face suggested the veracity of his countryman's observation. "At any rate, my concerns were waved aside. The Nineteen wanted Curaçao, and with the news that we had lost St. Maarten as well, they reasoned that there was even more reason to go ahead with their plans."

Eddie shook his head. "I don't understand how losing St. Maarten makes Curaçao a more urgent target."

"Salt pans," Banckert answered flatly. "That was one of the great values of St. Maarten: flats in which to salt fish or even meats for shipment around the Caribbees. When we lost St. Maarten, the Company turned its eyes toward the only other flats we might take: those at Curaçao."

"But they refused to seriously address the risks of doing so," van Walbeeck resumed. "With our naval forces so crippled and constrained, it seemed likely to me that the Spanish would become more aggressive, here in the New World. With a reduced need to patrol the route of their silver fleet against our raiders, they may now have enough surplus forces to mount an assault against Thijssen. Indeed, my greatest worry was always that his raiding along Tierra Firma would become *too* successful, and I fear that may have occurred. Cornelis Jol brought world that the governors along the Spanish Main have been gathering a small armadilla in Puerto Cabello. It is hard to imagine what they intend for such a force, other than an attack on Curaçao."

Eddie knew that timing made his next speculation unlikely, but it would serve to shift the conversation where it really needed to go. "Perhaps they intend to send it to Trinidad?"

Van Walbeeck glanced sideways at Eddie and his smile became sly. "Ah. Trinidad. An island of which we have had some mention recently. From the fluyt *Koninck David* and her master, Jakob Schooneman. An acquaintance of yours, perhaps?"

Try "an agent of ours." And now, of your own Prince Hendrik, as well. "A shared asset," as Nasi likes to say: he's read too many up-time spy novels. "Captain Schooneman is known to us, yes."

"And so you feel that the Spanish strength building at Puerto Cabello may be intended for Trinidad. Why?" Van Walbeeck's eyes were bright, very alert.

"Oh, I don't know," drawled Eddie. "Maybe Captain Schooneman might have an answer. Where is he, anyway?"

Van Walbeeck laughed and clapped a friendly hand down on

Eddie's shoulder. "Well done, young Commander: you sent the ball right back to me. So, enough dancing, yes? You guess that Tromp is headed to Trinidad in the wake of Jakob Schooneman himself and you are correct. Now you tell me: why? The message that Schooneman brought was, to understate the matter, surpassingly cryptic."

Eddie shrugged. "You've probably already guessed the reason: oil."

Banckert nodded once, sharply. "Yes, we guessed that. It was the obvious answer to 'why' you would go to Trinidad. But how do you plan to take it? And I am not referring to overcoming the Spanish on the island. They are so weak there that it could be years before they were aware of an intrusion. I am interested to learn what you plan to do about the competition?"

Eddie felt his brain screech to a stop, head in a new, unpleasant direction. "What competition?"

"Several weeks ago, we had report of a French ship passing St. Christopher's, trailing what was thought to be a balloon. It was following an earlier ship that Schooneman told us was bound for Trinidad. That first ship would have arrived there weeks ago, presuming the winds were at all favorable."

The ship carrying Mike McCarthy and O'Donnell went through almost a month ago? And was followed by a French ship with its own balloon? Which, given its presence in these particular waters, was probably the ship Richelieu was sure to send. Which would mean that the whole timing of the operation—the leak to the Spanish about an upcoming incursion at Trinidad, McCarthy and O'Donnell's arrival there—was all running ahead of schedule...

"I was unaware the, er, competition would be so—prompt," Eddie gabbled. "Accordingly, we will need you to make all possible haste sending more lighters to our ships. We've got to complete unloading your provisions, as well as some special radio gear which we'll use when we return here. In the meantime, I need you to detail exactly when Admiral Tromp left for Trinidad, with what ships, and the sailing characteristics and armaments of those vessels. And, as soon as we've finished with all that, we've got to set out after Admiral Tromp with our fastest ships. Preferably before sundown." Eddie felt Mund's eyes on him, wondering, frowning. *Because now you can smell that even you, the commander of the flotilla, are not privy to all that will be revealed once we get to Trinidad. And you won't like that one damned bit.*

Van Walbeeck looked as alarmed as Eddie felt. "Commander Cantrell, surely we have the time to complete discussing these matters in a more leisurely mann—?"

"Councilor van Walbeeck, I would very much enjoy an extended conversation, but every hour I delay the flotilla's departure increases the chance that we won't arrive at Trinidad in time."

Banckert blinked. "In time for what? To get your oil?"

"No. To save our men."

Part Five

September 1635

A universal wolf

Chapter 29

Fort St. Patrick, Trinidad

Hugh Albert O'Donnell stared down from the top story of the fort's blockhouse at the French skiff that was approaching the shallows of the north shore. The rowers, six to a side, leaned into their task with a will while, toward the stern, a well-equipped soldier and a man in a shiny silk waist-coat sat calmly riding through the swells. The dandy in the bright clothes, Hugh thought, would be the mouth of Richelieu.

That dandy had taken his time about arranging for his visit. The French ship had arrived three days after Michael McCarthy, Jr., had gone over the wall to rendezvous with the Dutch fluyt *Koninck David*. For several full days, the French sat approximately two miles off-shore, doing nothing but putting up their balloon. Hugh had been tempted to show he and his lads could still do the same, but he let good planning trump pride. *Better they think we lost our balloon on the* Fleur Sable. *No reason to let them know anything about what we do or don't have.*

The regrettably cautious and cynical character of that thought had become an increasingly significant part of O'Donnell's attitude toward his backer's agents. After all, why had the French waited so long to send a boat ashore? What had they been looking for Signs that it was, indeed, O'Donnell and his men in possess of Pitch Lake, rather than the Spanish or their servitors? He'd wanted to believe the French were simply being that cautious, but it made less sense with each passing hour. On the second day, O'Donnell had all but ten of his men march beyond the wall, form up in ranks, and fire a well-timed salute with their pieces, synchronized with discharges from both cannons. Yet the Frenchman had remained motionless in the waters of the Gulf of Paria, waiting and watching—for what?

Hugh and O'Rourke had come to the same conclusion before they voiced it to each other. The French were looking to assess how weak they were, if there were any signs of desperation, of food or water shortage, of medical want. Which meant that the captain of the ship was thinking far more about the Wild Geese's bargaining position than he was about their well-being. Perhaps Michael McCarthy, Jr., was right: perhaps the French would have to be dealt with at arm's length, after all,

In a way, however, the French indolence was a blessing in disguise. Given the ruthless pragmatism that probably motivated their delay, Hugh had used the time to strengthen his own negotiating position. He set his men about further grooming the fort and ordering their logistics. The bodies of those few pirates that had not fled into the forests were located and stripped for gear before being carried down into the waters off Point Galba a few hundred yards to the west. The current's acceleration around that slight promontory carried off the bodies, which there had been insufficient tools or time to bury. Alternately, a mass pyre would have alerted the Arawaks to their ongoing presence near Pitch Lake. Leaving the bodies open to the air would have created an equally compelling signal—a steady, sky-climbing gyre of vultures—while simultaneously inviting disease and vermin into the area.

While the powder for the two French sakers was not sufficient for an extended duel with nearby ships, it did provide an excellent magazine for their small arms. That was expanded handsomely ⁓n the powder horns taken from the pirate corpses were in: the attackers had not had much opportunity to fire at ⁓ Geese. A few volleys during the charge to the fort had for the majority of their powder expenditures. The rest ⁓battlefield harvest produced a plenitude of weapons, ⁓elts, and other useful gear, all in good condition ⁓rary to apocryphal tales of the slovenly nature of pirates, Hugh and his men discovered the more nuanced truth behind those legends. On the one hand, pirates did indeed have little care for objects or tasks that were not directly involved in the furtherance of their livelihood. Regrettably, this included personal hygiene and cleanliness. According to several of the Wild Geese who had spent some time as hog butchers, their porcine stock-in-trade had been far less odiferous and dirty than the pirate bodies they released into the surf. However, when it came to their weapons and equipment, it seemed that freebooters were, if anything, freakishly fastidious. Their weapons were in good to excellent condition, as were their tools, powder horns, sewing kits, and other accoutrements.

As Wild Geese's armory and other stockpiles grew, Hugh saw to it that their fort did, as well. Under Doyle, the Irish mercenaries had improved the walls, finished the blockhouse, built reasonable huts to function as barracks, and sunk one nighttime privy within the walls and two daytime privies without. Torn clothing was mended. Game traps were set and fishing parties established. Ripening fruit trees were found and fresh water supplies were located and surrounded with snares that would ostensibly show if the Arawaks had ventured near them. And daily drill and training kept the men mindful of and ready to perform their first function: soldiering.

So by the time the French sent their first boat ashore, inquiring if the comte Tyrconnell would find it convenient to receive a visit from Cardinal Richelieu's personal representative, Sieur Jean du Plessis d'Ossonville, Fort Patrick and its men had been growing stronger and more fit, rather than weakening. The mild annoyance and dismay on the face of du Plessis' messenger suggested that his master had been hoping for the reverse.

That had been yesterday. And now, sweeping a feathered hat back on to his balding head, du Plessis himself had at last arrived to visit, make an offer for Pitch Lake, and in so doing, very possibly determine the fate of hundreds, even thousands, of expatriate Irish families in the Spanish Lowlands. Hugh could imagine Michael McCarthy's sardonic comment on the upcoming meeting, could almost hear it as if the up-timer had been there himself: "No pressure; no worries." O'Donnell started down to meet du Plessi

They arrived at the gate at more or less the same time, H smiling and walking toward his guest, hand out. Techni du Plessis' knightly title was as minor as they came, but Hugh had little patience for the formalities of rank and class outside of court. Besides, any man or woman who elected to face the dangers of the New World to make their fortune shared a kind of aristocracy of spirit, of courage, so far as he was concerned.

But du Plessis apparently had a different sense of social stratification and a keen sense that while Hugh might have the far greater title, he commanded far fewer resources. The Frenchman stood very straight, put out his hand very far, and announced himself, "I am Sir Jean du Plessis d'Ossonville, senior factor for the *Compagnie des Îles de l'Amérique* in this place, and personally appointed by his Eminence, Cardinal Richelieu. And you are?"

The tone was distant, faintly dismissive, not quite condescending. Not quite. *And besides, am I supposed to believe you don't know who I am, that you weren't given a description of me?* No, Hugh decided, this meeting was probably not going to evolve toward an amicable agreement between partners, not judging from du Plessis almost defiant greeting.

"I am, as I suppose you conjecture, Lord Hugh Albert O'Donnell, Earl of Tyrconnell. Please come in where we may speak more easily."

Du Plessis nodded serenely and entered the blockhouse, but was surprised when O'Rourke started following them up the stairs to the second floor. "And your man—he is to hear our discussion?"

"My 'man' is Aodh O'Rourke, whose counsel and loyalty have ever been among the greatest gifts with which God has elected to grace my life. And your companion—?"

"Shall remain down here," du Plessis concluded, with a glance at the well-armed soldier, who did not meet his superior's eyes but came to a stop at the base of the stairs. Hugh continued leading the way up.

Once seated and refusing refreshment of any kind, du Plessis leaned back in one of the two rude chairs available, one hand ʒ to prop upon his hip. He waited, his chin slightly higher ⁓ really ought to have been. And he waited some more, ꭈut a window instead of at his hosts. He might have ꭓ for a portrait.

ʼd almost feel heat radiating from the silently fum- ꭙehind him. But instead of becoming aggravated ꭟnell simply leaned back, sipped at his water and thought at his guest: *I've no need to start this conversation, my dandy French friend, but you are under orders to do so. We'll see how long it takes you to give up this silly game you're playing.*

It took about half a minute for du Plessis to realize that he could not keep affecting bored toleration as he waited upon an inquiry from, and therefore the implicit supplication of, the other party. Flipping an irritated wrist, he gestured beyond the walls of the blockhouse. "So it seems you have taken Pitch Lake, after all, Monsi—er, Comte Tyrconnell. But with more loss than expected, I observe."

Hugh shook his head. "There was never any discussion about the possible level of casualties, Sir du Plessis. There was no basis for such discussion, since we had no idea what we might find upon our arrival, or afterwards."

"Perhaps I mis-state, your Lordship. I was referring more to the imbalance of casualties. I find no surviving Frenchmen here, but few enough of your own men seem to be missing."

Hugh managed not to bridle at the implication of favoritism, also managed not to point to the blatant incompetence and cowardice of St. Georges, and the probably marginal incompetence of Morraine in maneuvering too close to the shallows. "That is because all but a handful of your men were aboard the *Fleur Sable* when she was destroyed. And I emphasize: destroyed. She was evidently struck in her magazine, or suffered some similar fate. None of which I could change or ameliorate, I'm afraid."

Du Plessis seemed irritated that his first attempt to secure superior footing in the prenegotiation grappling phase had been unsuccessful. "Perhaps that is true, my lord—"

O'Rourke snapped a correction before Hugh could stop him. "You need not wonder if the Earl of Tyrconnell's words are *perhaps* true. He tells no lies."

Du Plessis stopped; he looked simultaneously outraged at O'Rourke for interrupting, but also suddenly alarmed at having been caught up on what could easily become a point of honor. He had little choice but to start over with an apology. "My regrets. I simply meant to say that even if we presume that the Earl of Tyrconnell's overview of the battle and its vagaries are complete, it does not alter the simple fact that, for the French Crown, thi has been an expensive expedition. Much more expensive th anticipated."

Hugh leaned forward over the table. "Many things here were not as anticipated. Such as the attack itself. We were barely here two weeks before we saw their sails approaching. And it was not a matter of chance that they clashed with us here. They came knowing, or speculating, enough about our positions to approach us under the cover of the western wood while they feinted at making their primary landing on the shore just north of here."

"And so? I am sorry that fate was unkind to your adventure, but, to borrow your own words, it was hardly in France's power to change or ameliorate that."

Touché—almost. "Sir du Plessis, I must reemphasize that it seems unlikely that we were the victims of unkind fate. Rather, given how closely the pirate attack followed our arrival, one must also suspect a more logical cause: incaution on the part of those who knew of our mission. Or, more extremely, betrayal."

Du Plessis forgot to keep his hand on his hip. "Lord O'Donnell, do you suggest that Lord Turenne himself would stoop so low as to—?"

Hugh waved a hand. "I suggest nothing of the sort. Lord Turenne is an honorable man, and too intelligent to play at such self-defeating idiocies, besides. No, whoever hired the brigands that came with the intent of driving us off—for surely, the pirates themselves would have conjectured that we lacked any riches worth plundering—was willing to work with a crude and unpredictable implement to smash us out of the way. But many more people in France knew of our destination than people in my employ. Indeed, before boarding the *Fleur Sable,* only three persons knew we were bound for Trinidad."

Du Plessis was mollified but still vexed. "First, Lord O'Donnell, your implication still does great disservice to your backers, implying, as it does, that we are incapable of controlling the actions of our own servitors—"

Of course—because bribery is unknown in La Belle France.
…ite the fact that it's a way of life from Rheims to Marseille.
…rthermore, the information of your anticipated arrival here
…ve trickled down through channels unknown to either of
…sations overheard through doors, or in places thought
…ll too often how foreign agents discover secrets. And
…'d the three members of your own party be above
…is regard?"

Hugh resisted the bitter smile he felt trying to bend his mouth. "Because, Sir du Plessis, all three of those persons were in direct mortal peril as a result of the pirate attack: myself, my aide-de-camp O'Rourke, and Michael McCarthy, Jr., the up-timer."

Du Plessis acted as though Hugh had given him a trump card. "And up-timers are of course known for their ready embrace of, and loyalty to, actions undertaken by the French crown."

Hugh decided not to make an issue of du Plessis' richly sarcastic tone, but also could feel that his patience was becoming perilously thin. "Perhaps not, but Don McCarthy's risk was as great as mine. He and I were trapped in this blockhouse, fighting off more than a dozen of the pirates ourselves, at the end. It was a close thing."

"An altogether *too* close thing," grumbled O'Rourke from behind.

But in that brief moment, Hugh had to ask himself: *and how, really, do I know that Michael, or his superiors, were not in fact the ones who ensured that our enemies knew of our arrival here? Perhaps the risk he took by my side was simply part of his mission, too. But why? Why inform our enemies? It tempted failure and death. And all for what?*

But there was no time to scrutinize that possibility any further. "Sir du Plessis, I do not bring up the apparent betrayal of our mission here to cast aspersions upon France. I do so to demonstrate why considerations of expense or casualties did not enter into my initial discussions with Lord Turenne. We understood this mission was rife with uncertainties. However, despite the unpleasant surprises we have encountered, we have taken this place as agreed. Accordingly, we should be happy to learn the terms you bring from His Eminence, Cardinal Richelieu."

Du Plessis' hand went back to his hip. "With all humility, Lord O'Donnell, the terms you are to be offered for this land were not fixed by His Eminence, but presented to me as a range of options that I was at liberty to adjust, according to the situation I found upon arrival. I have surveyed this fort and its environs from our balloon for several days. My visit here has confirmed what we detected. Consequently, here are the terms that seem just, and even generous, for France to offer in exchange for this plot of ground." He held out a slip of paper in O'Rourke's direction.

From the shift of his aide-de-camp's feet, and then the tone of his voice, Hugh was relatively sure that O'Rourke had adopted a broad, arms-folded stance. "*Your* man is downstairs, Sir du Plessis. We can summon him up here, if you need him to deliver your mail."

Du Plessis became very red, then his chin went back. He rose, hand still on hip, approached the driftwood-table behind which Hugh was sitting and dropped the paper on it before returning to his seat.

Hugh raised an eyebrow, picked up and unfolded the parchment sheet—

Jean du Plessis d'Ossonville resisted the urge to produce a handkerchief to dab the sweat from his brown. Weeks of pursuing careful relations with the Caribs of Guadeloupe had not been half so unnerving as walking into this lion's den of desperate Irishmen. It would have been a great deal easier had he and his fellow-factor for the *Compagnie des Îles de l'Amérique*, Charles Liénard de l'Olive, not needed to shift some of the silver originally intended for the Wild Geese into their own overtaxed coffers. But that would hardly matter to Richelieu if they were able to report success on both islands without incurring any additional expense. And His Eminence certainly wanted to lay hold of both the islands, but presumably for very different reasons. Du Plessis could well imagine what those different reasons might be, but Richelieu was not, to put it lightly, in the habit of informing minor nobles of his long-range plans. However, it was quite clear from the color building in the earl of Tyrconnell's face that he would soon make his feelings and opinions on the offer for Trinidad quite clear indeed.

The Irishman did not disappoint du Plessis' expectations. "Surely this is a joke. And a very bad one."

"Surely, it is not, Lord O'Donnell."

"In that event, it is an insult."

"I regret that you elect to conceive it so, my lord. We consider it a most generous offer: half a year's pay, in advance, for all those men and their families who leave the Spanish Lowlands and come over the border to serve under French colors."

"Sir du Plessis, that would not even be a particularly attractive hiring incentive, particularly not to long-service mercenaries such as the Wild Geese. Yet that is all you are willing to offer for the mercenary contract you offer us *and* for the technical help that built your balloon *and* the successful completion of this mission to Trinidad? I fail to understand how you can make this offer to us intending it to be anything *but* an insult."

"Allow me to share what *I* understand, my good Earl of Tyrconnell. I understand that you have a great many mouths to feed in and around Brussels. I furthermore understand that Cardinal Richelieu, in consideration of the service you have performed here on Trinidad, has elected to both feed them and to pay your men at their present rate. And he is willing to relay your first half-year's payroll to you here and now, in this place, as a sign of his goodwill, and as an indication that you will never need to wait upon the prompt satisfaction of his payrolls. Unlike the case with your *tercio*'s present employer."

Du Plessis saw that this line of debate was angering the semi-civilized Irishman even more—which meant, in all probability, that his remarks were cutting deep because they were landing upon the tender bruises of unpleasant truths. Perhaps, though, he should have increased the amount of the bribe, or "special service commission," that he had explicitly set aside for O'Donnell himself in the written offer. But, being inherently unprincipled, high-ranking sell-swords often became greedier for bigger bribes once their appetites were whetted, so it probably would not have made a difference. Besides, it was too late to adjust that number now. The offer had been made, and due to the presence of the colonel's aide-de-camp, the thinly disguised bribe could not be confidentially renegotiated or even remarked upon. Well, that was the Irishman's loss and the *Compagnie des Îles de l'Amérique*'s gain.

The Irish earl, like a tiresome dog with a well-worn bone, seemed insistent upon returning to the terms of the settlement. "Assuming, for one improbable second, that you and His Eminence are serious in making this offer, it ignores a number of problematic realities. Such as this: what if no more of my men are allowed to leave their employ in the Spanish Lowlands? What then?"

"Then that is most unfortunate for them, but I do not see how you could reasonably hold us accountable for the actions of another sovereign lord." Du Plessis congratulated himself on the smoothness with which he had furnished that rebuttal. He had foreseen this objection, had planned and even scripted the best way to deflect it.

And if his planning continued to prove itself adequate, it seemed likely that he and his partner Charles Liénard de l'Olive would manage to stretch Richelieu's somewhat scant fiscal underwriting to secure two islands for the price of one and thereby specially acquaint His Eminence with their shrewd resourcefulness. Liénard, a French settler on St. Christopher's, had brought du Plessis a fair stratagem for investing Guadeloupe with a French colony last year. His timing had been auspicious: not only were du Plessis' failing family fortunes reaching an alarming nadir, but Richelieu had just sent word to those interested that he was rejuvenating the mostly mismanaged and moribund *Compagnie de Saint-Christophe*. Never having met its mandate to seed other French colonies in the Caribbean, Richelieu had charged one of his councilors, Francois Fouquet, to reinvent the enterprise as the *Compagnie des Îles de l'Amérique*.

Ironically, most of the new investment money had gone to Pierre Bélain d'Esnambuc, who was still tussling with the English for control of St. Christopher's. Most of the remaining silver was earmarked for the purchase of a base on Trinidad from a group of Irish adventurers who had surreptitiously seized it for the Crown of France, or from any non-Spanish who might have ousted them from the place. It mattered little to Richelieu and Fouquet who was paid for that slip of Trinidadian coast.

Indeed, Liénard's and du Plessis' own venture in Guadeloupe was of such decidedly tertiary interest to the cardinal that he had only agreed to their request to retain one of the two ships with which they had journeyed to the New World because they had agreed to go to settle matters at Trinidad, and leave the other ship and most of the professional troops there.

But Richelieu's and Fouquet's eyes and hands were far away from the strings of the purse that they had entrusted to du Plessis. Who realized swiftly enough, that, if the holders of Trinidad—Irish or otherwise—could be made to accept less money, then the livres saved thereby could be used to ensure more reasonable funding for the colonization of Guadeloupe. And surely no one would notice if a few hundred more found their way back to France to defray some of the more onerous debts looming over the good name of the family du Plessis.

However, the attainted, therefore landless, and therefore relatively powerless earl of Tyrconnell was determined to keep quibbling over the terms of the exchange. "Sir du Plessis, in all our discussions with Lord Turenne, we were assured of a fair price for our success here and for helping to make the balloon which you have been using. But what you have offered is not a fair price at all; it does not even include any pay for the time that my men have spent upon this mission. Frankly, no sovereign would dare make such an offer in Europe, lest word begin to spread among mercenaries to avoid service with that crown."

"But we are not in Europe, my lord." Du Plessis was no longer able to resist tugging a handkerchief out of his sleeve and dabbing at his damp brow. "And just as we did not stipulate what number of casualties we considered reasonable, you did not stipulate what sum of silver seemed fair. What I have offered is, I repeat, what we think is both fair and generous." Seeing that the Irishman was becoming more, rather than less, determined in his intransigence, du Plessis deemed it time to reveal the threat he had been hiding. It would have been more convenient if the benighted bog-hopper had inferred its possibility from the conversation, but that was not to be expected with single-minded sword-swingers such as he. "I feel that I must point out, my good Earl of Tyrconnell, that my mere presence alone is a sign of reciprocal good faith. A most profound sign of it, in fact. One that is worthy of your gratitude, I should think."

O'Donnell looked stunned and du Plessis managed not to scowl or sigh. *Really? Can this mercenary truly be so dense? Are they not all schooled in guile and duplicity from the cradle?* "It has perhaps escaped your attention, my lord, that, for half this sum—indeed, much less, I suspect—we could find another pirate band much like the one which nearly overwhelmed you here. And we could offer them a contract akin to the one which you conjecture brought that first group to these shores: seize Pitch Lake. They would be glad for the coin and, were we to recruit among the *boucaniers* of Tortuga or their kin in the Bahamas, we could garnish that offer with letters of marque, and pardons for any offenses committed in France or its possessions." Du Plessis looked out the window at the long, low breakers. "It would delay us for two, maybe three, months, but we would have what we wish and for a much lower price than we are offering you now. So perhaps your gratitude might be improved by considering my offer in the context of that alternative. Which I remain willing to forego."

O'Donnell's sharp reply caused him to start. "No, my gratitude is not improved. Not at all." Thus far, the displaced earl had seemed a bit slow to utter conversational ripostes. But the crisp decisiveness in this counter made du Plessis wonder: *did I mistake "measured responses" for "slow" ones?*

The colonel's next comments made that conjecture seem all too likely. "Sir du Plessis, it was understood that Cardinal Richelieu's agents would have the right to make the first offer for Trinidad, and if it was at all fair, that we were honor-bound to accept it. However, while we might argue long and inconclusively as to whether your offer is in any way 'fair,' here is something that is simply *not* a matter of debate: Lord Turenne never implied that he would wrest this hard-won ground from us by force if we did not take whatever offer was made to us. Indeed, if that were the case, then the entire notion of this 'negotiation' is simply a sad charade. Out of respect for Lord Turenne's intents, I will allow you the opportunity to withdraw your current offer, and present a new one—one which does not include any odious bribery, by the way."

Du Plessis rose. Well, the Irishman was clearly as stubborn as the rest of his recidivistic race, and, in addition to being impervious to reason, was beginning to demonstrate a distressing gift for both logic and eloquence at exactly the wrong moment. Time to let the desperate nature of his circumstances do the arguing that would ultimately bring him round to accepting du Plessis' terms. The Frenchman tucked his handkerchief back inside the margin of his cuff as he said, "Lord O'Donnell, my first offer is my only offer. I will return tomorrow to hear your response to it. I bid you good day."

And, without waiting for leave to do so, du Plessis started down the stairs but a bit more quickly than usual. He was still not entirely certain that the troglodyte named O'Rourke, or even the earl himself, might not throw a knife into his departing back.

However, just as du Plessis arrived on the ground floor and called the guard to his side with a gesture not unlike that he used to summon his hounds, an unusually-dressed man of middle age, and with the flat-footed gait of a rank commoner, entered the blockhouse with several of the Irish mercenaries around him. At first it seemed that he was another visitor, arriving under guard, but then du Plessis noticed the smiles on the faces of the Wild Geese, the gentle banter with which they engaged the newcomer, and he understood: this was the American, the up-timer who had built the balloon for Turenne.

Du Plessis drew up to his full height, which was still two inches less than the American's, and attempted to look down his nose at the workman. "So, monsieur, perhaps you will be able to prevail upon your lord to accept my offer. I suppose you have some measure of influence with him?"

The American stopped, stared at du Plessis and then barked out a laugh. "Some measure, maybe," he chuckled. "But thanks for telling me he's turned you down. Now I know where I stand when I give him *my* offer." The American actually winked as he brushed past du Plessis and started up the stairs two risers at a time. "And you might want to stick around to hear the outcome. It could save you the problem of making another trip here and mussing up your waistcoat."

Michael McCarthy, Jr., knew that, the moment his head rose above the second story's floorboards and he saw Hugh, he'd be able to tell if his friend had decided to disown him or not.

If anything, it didn't even take that moment. Hugh was on his feet, beaming, by the time McCarthy's brow had cleared the planks that hemmed in the stairs. "Michael! Are you well? This is strange timing indeed." Hugh paused as a rueful smile crept across his face. "Or is it?"

Mike stared around the mostly finished second story approvingly. "If you mean, was I watching today's proceedings from some hiding place, no." He turned toward Hugh. "As for how I'm doing, I'm passable. You?"

Hugh nodded, put out his hand. "I am well enough. Better for seeing you, I think."

Damn it, that smile and frankness of his is like a magic spell; no wonder so many Irish mercenaries followed him to their death, up-time. "It's good to be seen," Mike admitted as he shook Hugh's hand, nodded at O'Rourke, who nodded back with a careful, but hopeful, smile. "Look, I don't mean to interrupt, but—"

"Not like you're interrupting anything, Don Michael," grumbled O'Rourke. "The Frenchman bearing Richelieu's terms was pretty much done buggering us, I think."

Mike winced. "That bad?"

"Worse," O'Rourke snarled, "but I'm too much a gentleman to give a full description of the reaming."

Hugh glanced over his shoulder, his attempt to muster an expression of disapproval completely undermined by his amused grin. "Always the way with words, eh, O'Rourke?" He fixed his attention back on McCarthy. "But he has the right of it, Michael. As you may have anticipated."

Mike rubbed his chin. "Yeah, that French guy didn't look too happy, coming down the stairs. I kinda reckoned you hadn't reached a meeting of the minds."

"To say nothing of suitable terms. But that is a different topic, for a different time. I am delighted to see you Michael, but surprised. I had suspected you would be well on the way to—well, wherever you were going."

Carefully now, Mike. "Actually, Hugh, I'm here for the same reason that he is."

Hugh leaned back slightly. "You are here to—to make an offer for Pitch Lake? *You?*"

Mike waved a hand testily. "Yeah—I mean, no, not me personally. I mean, yeah, I'm the guy sitting here in front of you but I'm not—" *Sheesh: this is harder than getting shot at.* "Look, Hugh, I thought I was done here, that somebody else was going to do all the fancy talking. At least, that was the plan. But from what I can tell, the guys making those plans got their schedules fouled up, and now, the ones who were going to present the deal to you are still en route."

Hugh did not blink, did not even nod. "And how do you know all this?"

Mike shrugged. "We have a radio on the *Koninck David.* Starting last night, it started going haywire. Fragments of transmissions, but nothing very clear. Then just before dawn, we got a clear signal."

He pointed northward. "Hugh, right now, there is a fleet sailing this way. One of the ships was designed by up-timers. It's powered by steam and it has a large radio. They'd been trying to reach me on the *Koninck David* for days because they were worried that you'd have to make a decision before they could get their deal in front of you. So when we were finally able to exchange messages early this morning, they asked me to convey the broad outlines of what they are willing to offer for Pitch Lake. And here I am."

"And this offer, it is from the USE and Gustav, after all?"

"In part. But it is equally from Prince Hendrik of the United Provinces and from your former employer, Fernando, King in the Spanish Lowlands."

Even the indomitable O'Rourke goggled openly at this constellation of improbably cooperative political luminaries. Hugh leaned forward after a long moment of silence. "The USE, the

United Provinces, and the Spanish Lowlands—all in agreement, and working together?"

"Yes. Although it shouldn't come as a *complete* surprise, Hugh. C'mon, how many times now has your godmother had up-time visitors? Seems like there are always a few of us in her court, to say nothing of our books. And we did make sure that Fernando got his Austrian bride safe and sound out of Germany, courtesy of one of our aircraft. And we've been working to help the Provinces against Spain itself—not the Lowlands, but Spain—in all sorts of subtle ways. This is no different. Well, except that it's a whole lot less subtle."

"I should say so," agreed Hugh, who still did not blink. "I am not surprised at the cooperation between the USE and the United Provinces. They have many common interests, and share many of the same predilections. For technology, for instance. But the Spanish Lowlands—"

"Maybe you were too close to the changes there to see them clearly," Mike offered. "Or maybe not. Who was it, less than half a year ago, who told the leaders of all the Wild Geese *tercios* that they might soon have to choose between loyalty to Philip of Spain and Fernando of the Lowlands?"

Hugh became a bit pale. "Yes, I said that."

"Well, follow it to its logical conclusion. If Fernando ultimately parts company from Madrid, how will he survive? Who might be his new friends? Certainly no one allied with Spain. Certainly not the French, who'd like to extend their borders north of Brussels. The English are in disarray, Austria is a shadow of its former self."

"And so Fernando and my godmother are willing to ally with Protestants?"

"Why?" asked Mike around a smile that assured Hugh he knew better. "That bother you?"

"Certainly not, Michael. You know I have become quite sympathetic to Grantville's enlightened policy of religious freedom. But my godmother and her nephew—"

"Are not so different from yourself, Hugh," Michael interrupted with a grin. "Unlike the fossils creaking around the court in Madrid, they understand that the times, they are a-changing. And is the USE a 'protestant' union? Hell, if it was, I—and the millions of other Catholics, from rulers to peasants—would be in a pretty tough situation. But we're not. Because what unites the USE is not a common faith, but rational political agreements. And, slowly but surely, shared values. Such as religious toleration."

Mike waved in the approximate direction of Europe. "Fernando sees this clearly, although I'm pretty sure it was your godmother who pointed it out to him. Hell, she can see new trends and changes coming before anyone else in Europe, so far as I can tell. She had been cooking up a scheme like this on her own when some of us from Grantville approached her with an idea about how to kill a bunch of birds with one strategic stone: seizing Trinidad."

Hugh nodded. "So. This has my godmother's blessing, you claim."

"Hugh, you don't have to believe me. There's a sealed letter from her being carried on one of our ships, the *Intrepid*. I'm sure it will explain the underlying tangle of statecraft spider webs better than I could given a year's time."

Hugh rose and came around to sit on the desk directly in front of Mike. "The desirability of the oil is easy to understand. But I do not understand how all the other objectives can be met simply by taking Trinidad."

"You will when you hear the offer."

"Which is?"

Mike drew in a deep breath: *all or nothing, now.* "Trinidad, and its oil production, is to be a shared venture. The split is: fifty percent belongs to the USE. Twenty-four percent belongs to the United Provinces, and twenty-four percent to the Spanish Lowlands."

Hugh frowned. "That's only ninety-eight percent. What happens to the last two percent?"

Mike felt how crooked and desperate his smile was. "Can't you guess?" *Don't you know this is why I pushed and pulled you and the Wild Geese into this crazy scheme—just like your godmother did?*

Mike saw understanding illuminate Hugh's face like the iconic light bulb snapping on. "It is for us. For the Wild Geese."

Mike nodded, explained slowly. "Two percent of all production and proceeds from oil operations on the island of Trinidad will be placed on account for the Irish expatriate community in the Lowlands. That, by extension, puts it at the disposal of the last free and legitimate leadership of Ireland, Hugh."

"We'll have much to discuss with the earl of Ulster, I can see," O'Rourke said sourly from behind the desk.

Mike looked away, having heard the latest grim news regarding John O'Neill. "Maybe not," Mike muttered evasively. "Look, however the details swing, this is a lot of money, Hugh. Do you know how much a gallon of oil—just unrefined oil—sells for right now?"

Hugh shook his head.

"About twenty guilders per unrefined barrel of crude. And the price continues to rise. And will for the foreseeable future. We are sitting less than five miles from where, in my world, some of the earliest, smallest sweet crude gushers produced one hundred barrels a day. Within a few years, there should be a dozen other wells, at least. And many of those will be producing more. Much more."

Hugh's mental math was quite good: the earl's eyes opened wide. "And for how long may we enjoy this entitlement?"

"It is permanent. And can you guess what Fernando has sworn to do when he gets his first proceeds from the speculators, long before the first oil gets back to Europe?"

"Buy an army with which to resist his brother's *tercios*?"

"No, Hugh. He's going to pay all of what's owed the Wild Geese, and fifty percent more, in honor and appreciation of your loyal service. And then he wants *you* to buy that army for him—you and Colonel Preston, working together."

O'Rourke came forward and leaned against the table. "Don McCarthy, this sounds so blasted fine that I know it *can't* be true. As you must fear yourself."

Mike frowned. "What do you mean?"

O'Rourke spread his hands. "So I'll assume that there's a piece of paper somewhere that asserts we are part owners of the oil concession here on Trinidad. And similarly, that the king of the Lowlands has gone on record saying that we are his chosen troops, and that he shall settle all our back pay and then some." O'Rourke shook his head. "But none of it will come to pass, because of the people upon whom it depends: high and mighty lords and ladies that can't even agree whose carriage comes first in a progress, let alone share ownership of something which is, as you yourself said, a strategic piece of real estate. They'll be bickering before the first oil comes out of the ground. And so none of it will ever get to market."

Mike shook his head. "That's a reasonable fear, O'Rourke. But those same lords and ladies foresaw that same problem. And that's why the ownership of the oil is structured as it is."

"Eh?" said O'Rourke.

Hugh saw it, nodded. "That's why the USE owns half of the oil. It can force cooperation among the other partners."

"Or can simply have its own way, I fear," added O'Rourke.

"No, not entirely," said Hugh, suddenly staring at Mike, who realized that the Irishman was starting to realize just how much the up-timer sitting in front of him must have been involved in the formation of this arrangement. "If all the other parties—the Spanish Lowlands, the United Provinces, and we Wild Geese—are all in agreement against the will of the USE, there will be no majority. It will be fifty percent against fifty percent."

"Ah, that's fine, it is," O'Rourke growled. "Deadlocked. Just like clan politics back in Ireland. Everyone with a voice, and so nothing can be agreed upon."

Hugh shook his head. Mike wondered if he had already foreseen the answer to the question he was going to ask: "How is a deadlock prevented, Michael?"

"Majority vote among the four shareholding directors, one from each of the groups. One vote, one director."

O'Rourke persisted in his sour tone. "And so, two votes for each side of any dispute, and again, a deadlock."

"No," corrected Hugh. "Almost certainly not, because it would take the combined shares of all three of the minority shareholding groups to create the first deadlock. Logically, then, their three directors would outvote the USE director three to one, in that circumstance."

Mike nodded. "That's the idea. And stability in the Netherlands is maintained by a similar device. If the United Provinces and the Lowlands resume hostilities with each other, or ally with an enemy of the other, or undertake any one of a list of actions which have been decreed impermissible, then oil proceeds are not distributed to either party but are held in trust until such time as they resolve those differences."

O'Rourke couldn't help smiling. "So each has a pistol to the other's head, both fired by the same trigger. Heh. That might even work. For a while."

Mike smiled. "Nothing is permanent. But if this lasts even five years, the Lowlands and Provinces will have rebuilt themselves and made great progress toward forging a single nation, the USE will have a ready supply of oil flowing, and you, Lord O'Donnell, will have well-paid men, a war-chest, and new allies with which to seek justice for Ireland."

"And Spain will be thirsting for all our blood," finished O'Rourke.

Hugh chuckled. "And just how is that any different from the situation as it stands right now, old friend?" He stood. "No, I think we've just heard the offer we're going to take." He put out his hand to Mike. "And something tells me that the man whose hand I am shaking to seal our commitment was involved in crafting some of its stipulations."

Mike didn't look away, but he couldn't lie. "There were a lot of cooks consulted in the making of this crazy stew," he allowed.

Hugh held his hand, his eyes, a moment longer than necessary. "I'm sure there were, Don Michael McCarthy. And I thank you for being one of them, and for remembering Ireland when the final recipe was decided upon. Now," he said, withdrawing his hand, and striding towards the stairs, "I think we can deliver our final answer to our French guest."

O'Rourke, who'd wandered over to the window, whistled sharply. "I suspect our Gallic friend may have already deduced our response. Come and see."

Hugh and Mike joined O'Rourke at the window. Just below their vantage point, Jean du Plessis was standing on the platform that lined the north wall of Fort St. Patrick, staring out to sea. The three men followed his gaze to the horizon.

Half a dozen ships were emerging out of the heat-misty horizon: two Dutch jachts leading a brace of man-o-wars with forty or more guns. More ghostlike sails seemed to be approaching from farther back in the indistinct distance behind them.

Mike nodded. "Unless I'm much mistaken, that would be Admiral Maarten Tromp of the United Provinces."

Du Plessis must have heard the comment; he turned sharply, eyes as cold as a promise of murder. "So, Lord O'Donnell, this is how you deal in good faith? How convenient for you that your new owners have already arrived."

O'Rourke smiled wolfishly down at du Plessis. "Correction, sir. Those are not the 'owners.' They are the 'co-owners.' Now run along; from what I recall, your fleet betrayed Tromp's at Dunkirk. But if you prefer, you could stay a while and test the limits of the admiral's forgiving nature."

Du Plessis was off the platform and headed for the gate before Mike had finished chuckling.

Chapter 30

Fort St. Patrick, Trinidad

After putting his three announcements before the group, Lieutenant Commander Eddie Cantrell looked for surprise or alarm on the faces of the down-timers and saw little. The news that Cardinal Borja of Spain had driven Urban VIII off the *cathedra* in the Holy See was not news to anyone but Tromp. Hugh O'Donnell and Aodh O'Rourke had heard of the events in Rome before departing Europe. And Tromp didn't seem to care very much. Mike McCarthy, Jr., had heard what Hugh and O'Rourke had, and Ann Koudsi had enjoyed the same access to recent events that Eddie himself had, traveling with the flotilla.

The announcement of John O'Neill's death affected only one person very strongly: O'Rourke. He leaned protectively toward the earl of Tyrconnell and actually glanced around as if checking for inbound assassins from every point of the compass. O'Donnell, now the last legitimate royal heir of Ireland, simply looked saddened. Hugh's reaction was somewhat surprising to Eddie. All reports indicated that there had been no love lost between the two earls. But the same sources had indicated that whereas they were rivals for preeminence in the eyes of the Irish, John also had a number of purely personal grudges against his royal cousin. O'Neill had long nursed a profound jealousy for Hugh, who had completed his degree at Louvain University and had been well liked for his wit and charm. John O'Neill, on the other hand, had inherited his illustrious father's temper and self-seeking instincts, without a corresponding measure of his brilliance and personal magnetism. In some ways, Eddie had to admit, Ed Piazza's analysis—that with the passing of O'Neill, Irish politics became a great deal clearer and less tangled—was probably correct. Tromp's careful face showed no reaction to the news of John O'Neill's death: a prudent reaction from a Dutchman sitting in council with representatives of the Wild Geese and the court in Brussels which they served. The only diplomatically safe reaction was polite and respectful silence, a behavior at which Admiral Maarten Tromp excelled.

However, Tromp's composure was quite undone when Eddie announced the outline of the deal that Mike McCarthy, Jr., had struck with Hugh O'Donnell and his Wild Geese. He started visibly at the news of the accord between the United Provinces and the Spanish Lowlands portions of the newly reunited Netherlands that both made the joint oil-development possible and was in turn made feasible by the common interests thus forged. However, he did not interrupt, and as Eddie continued to detail the agreement's particulars and the various checks and balances built into it, he nodded once or twice.

Well, thought Eddie, *so far so good. Which is better than I was hoping for. Sitting down with major leaders of the contending forces in the Lowlands could have gone sideways at the double-quick. And never mind that one of them is among the most famous admirals in history, and the other is the last heir to the Irish throne and godson of Archduchess Isabella. Which reminds me—* "Lord O'Donnell, I was asked to bring you a sealed letter. From your godmother, the archduchess infanta Isabella." He produced the wax-sealed tube and proffered it to the earl of Tyrconnell.

O'Donnell smiled—*such a bright and guileless smile!*—and took it carefully from Eddie's hands. "I very much appreciate your carrying this letter to me, Commander. Or, if the Wild Geese aboard your ship have told me correctly, should I say Lord Cantrell?"

Eddie felt himself blush, wishing he could wave away the color as easily as he could wave away the title. "I'm just Eddie. That title doesn't mean all that much, I'm afraid."

Hugh cocked an eyebrow. "You own land? You currently enjoy the use of it?"

Eddie nodded. "Yes, to both."

Hugh smiled again. "Then your title is more real than mine—Eddie. My lands are attainted. I am nobility in name only."

O'Rourke's brow had lowered. "There's many as would contest that, m'Lord O'Donnell. With flags waving and swords high."

The attainted earl of Tyrconnell nodded at O'Rourke's somber interjection. "We can safely leave that aside for now. And we can still hope that the swords will not be necessary." His expression transformed into a quizzical grin. "There's one more bit of news—or perhaps 'insight' is the better word—that I'm eager to have, Eddie: just how is it that the pirates seemed to know to come find us here? And so quickly? From the time we entered the Caribbees, we didn't see any other ship except for du Plessis', following us. So it's difficult to imagine how they learned of our presence here. Without some help, that is."

Eddie nodded. He'd been told that the Irish earl was shrewd, so he had half-expected this. "You are right, Hugh. The pirates—or more accurately, the Spanish—had help learning about your mission here. They had to, or they might not have come in time."

O'Rourke leaned forward. "Might not have come *in time*?"

Eddie nodded. "That right, Sergeant O'Rourke. In addition to getting oil from Trinidad, this mission had another purpose: it's a draw play."

"A 'draw play'?" Tromp echoed uncertainly.

"My apologies, Admiral Tromp. An up-time term—a sports term, actually. A draw play is an operation designed to pull an adversary's attention and units to a specific part of the playing field. In this case, that was Trinidad."

Hugh was frowning, rubbing his chin. "Why so?"

Eddie hoped that the two-thirds truth he was telling would be convincing enough on its own. "To draw in any units that the Spanish had in the area so they could be eliminated, either by the *Fleur Sable*, or, if absolutely necessary, by our follow-up force. It was imperative to get them to commit, and lose, any nearby units early on. The strategic logic was that this would leave them unable to even reconnoiter the area before our main forces and drillers arrived, much less make another bid to take it back. That should have taken the Spanish several months, by which time we'd have been well-established here."

Mike was frowning. "I note you said 'should have' taken the

Spanish several months. Which makes me suspect that not every-thing has been going to plan."

Eddie shrugged. "Well, it hasn't."

O'Rourke's brow had beetled down once again. "And why not?"

Eddie put out a hand by way of appeal, wondered how he'd introduce the ticklish answer to that question, but Maarten Tromp saved him the trouble. "I am the answer. I am why things are not going according to plan."

All eyes were on the ever-composed Dutchman. "How could you be responsible for derailing plans of which you were unaware?" asked Ann Koudsi.

"Well, strictly speaking, I did nothing to derail the plans, but my actions and those of Admiral Thijssen have no doubt made the Spanish more easily provoked, and more decisive in response, than they were a year ago.

"Specifically, Admiral Thijssen took Curaçao from the Span-ish in September of last year, although I suspect word of it did not reach any of the *audiencias* on Tierra Firma—excuse me; you call it the Spanish Main—for some months. At almost the same time, I abandoned Recife and relocated to St. Eustatia. From whence, shortly after, we were compelled to intercept the Armada de Barlovento when it ventured south from St. Maarten." He shrugged. "I suspect they had emerged in search of us, never guessing we were just one island further south in the Leewards."

Hugh nodded. "The Spanish conjectured you had reinforced Curaçao, that your actions and Thijssen's were coordinated."

Tromp nodded. "Exactly. Ironic, since we initially had no idea of each other's whereabouts or circumstances. But consequently, the Spanish evidently began considering the necessity of a mis-sion to unseat Thijssen. Which meant that, by the time you and your men arrived here, Colonel O'Donnell, they had coincidentally brought additional forces down closer to Tierra Firma, including detachments from Havana and Santo Domingo. So Commander Cantrell's plan to draw off and destroy the usually paltry forces with which the Spanish patrol this area has fallen afoul of the Spanish decision to build up a greater power here to unseat Thijssen. Consequently, the first Spanish response to your attack on Trinidad"—he nodded at Hugh—"was to recruit a band of cutthroats. Otherwise, they would have had to draw ships from the flotilla they were gathering to oust Thijssen, which would have delayed those plans."

"And when the pirates didn't return with news of success," Mike nodded, "the people who hired them are now getting *really* worried."

Tromp nodded. "Yes. As we sailed here from St. Eustatia, we met one of our privateers, Moses Cohen Henriques, who touches along the Spanish Main both to gather information and raid, intermittently. Evidently, the Spanish are now delaying whatever plans they might have been evolving to attack Curaçao and are coming here instead." Tromp's smile was crooked. "In a way, I suppose you could say that, due to our activities here in the New World, Commander Cantrell's plan to attract Spanish attention has worked all too well."

Hugh nodded. "So, practically, what does this mean to us here? How many Spanish ships, how many troops, and when can we expect them to attack?"

Damn, thought Eddie, *I wish I could be so calm when asking questions like those.*

Tromp nodded. "We do not have anything approaching complete information, but between our own rovers, such at Cornelis Jol, and privateers such as Moses Henriques, here is was we have heard. The Spanish have three separate fleets converging on Trinidad: one from Havana, one from Santo Domingo, one from Cartagena. Their greatest difficulty will be effective rendezvous. That did not particularly matter when they were gathering to strike at Curaçao. They were simply gathering slowly in Puerto Cabello, waiting for their numbers to be complete. Now, because they have no specific intelligence on us, they must be ready to contend with a strong force that might meet them anywhere near Trinidad. And because they must act quickly, they cannot afford the luxury of rendezvousing in a single port anymore. They must attempt to arrive in this area, probably in the lee of Grenada, at approximately the same time and then order themselves for battle. This means they will have pickets out well ahead of their formation, searching for each other. And for us, as well.

"The Cuban fleet will take some time to get here, even though they have been underway for some weeks. Crossing the open water of the Caribbean from the north is a fickle business, as the prevailing winds will be coming abeam whereas the galleons want a following wind to make reasonable speed. The fleet from Santo Domingo is closer, but again, operating with many of the same constraints. However, they may catch a few more favorable winds by moving southward within the fifty miles of the lee-side of Lesser Antilles. The ships from Cartagena will be having the hardest time of it, tacking constantly to keep from being caught in the eye of the east wind."

Seeing the perplexed look on Ann's and Mike's faces, he explained. "'In the eye' means to be sailing straight into the wind. If you do so, you'll find yourself held fast, or 'in irons,' as we say, without any reasonable chance to make headway. This is a constant problem for ships sailing eastward along the Spanish Main, since both the current and prevailing winds are strongly westward, and Cartagena is a long way off. On the other hand, it is quite possible that the ships from Cartagena and other *audiencias* along the Main may have already been gathering closer to Curaçao, and so could be starting their journey from much closer than the fleets from Cuba or Hispaniola."

Tromp stood and gestured toward the map spread out on the table in the captain's combination ward- and chart-room. "It will be some weeks, we believe, before they arrive. And we do not have enough ships to maintain a line of pickets, searching for them. We will need to rely on our three balloons: Admiral Mund's flotilla has two, and Colonel O'Donnell still has his one. Those, along with our excellent glasses, should give us reasonable warning. However, it means keeping most of our ships on station near the Grenada Passage, if we are to intercept them at the time and place of our choosing. So we will presume that we are relatively safe for at least one more week and keep all but two of our ships in close anchorage here in Trinidad to take on supplies and prepare. After that week, we will need to put to sea and seek an anchorage near the Dragon's Mouth, where the Gulf of Paria meets the waters of the Grenada Passage."

Hugh smiled patiently. "And how many ships, guns, and troops do they have? You will forgive me for being so numerically-minded, Admiral Tromp."

Tromp almost smiled in return. "I share your fixation, Colonel, for those numbers will largely determine our fate. Informers who were in Hispaniola three months ago saw nine suitable ships being readied. I think we may assume that these were the captain-general of Hispaniola's contribution to the intended move against Curaçao. I think we may also reasonably assume that most, or all, will have received word to make way against us, instead.

"We have little other than guesswork concerning the other two fleets. However, when Havana has contributed to a larger effort in the Caribbees, it is usually half again as sizable as what emerges from Santo Domingo. Mind you, this is the very crudest of estimates, and may bear little resemblance to what is actually occurring. However, my captains all agree that it would be unusual if, in this particular circumstance, they did not send at least a dozen. They also note, with some alarm, that Havana's ways were more active in the last year than they have been in the preceding five. The new governor of Cuba seems to have received permission from Madrid to recommence his former prodigious rate of ship-building."

"That is not good news," O'Rourke observed softly.

"No, indeed," Tromp agreed. "And as for Cartagena, or more properly, the contributions drawn from along the length of the Spanish Main, we have no basis for estimate. The last time there was a significant problem here, Cartagena was able to muster sixteen ships, not counting lighter *garda costa* hulls, pickets and auxiliaries. However, that was a gathering performed on very short notice. They may have assembled far more, this time."

"So we can expect somewhere between twenty and forty ships, give or take a lot," Mike summarized sardonically.

Tromp did smile this time. "Your numbers are every bit as precise as our own, mijn heer McCarthy. As far as troop totals, this is unknowable. They may hope to rely mostly upon local natives with whom they have alliances, or they may be carrying a thousand seasoned Spanish troops. But I rather doubt the latter."

"Why?" asked Ann.

Hugh looked at Tromp for permission to field the question, who nodded his leave. "Logistics, Lady Ann. These three flotillas have something in common: they must spend a long time at sea to reach us. That means a great deal of food. The more men they bring, the more food, water and other perishables they must carry. Logically, if any of these fleets are furnished with significant numbers of troops, it would be the one from Cartagena. That one can at least touch at various points along the Spanish Main for reprovisioning."

Tromp nodded, seeming to be pleased. Eddie noted that the admiral had a ready and catholic appreciation for competence, wherever he found it. Including, in this case, a commander who, under prior circumstances, would have been his enemy. "The colonel could not be more correct," Tromp averred. "Fortunately, the troops found along the Spanish Main are not the best-trained nor best-equipped of Madrid's New World army. Such as it is." Tromp hastened to provide an explanation for his apparent derogation of Spanish soldiery. "Do not misunderstand me. The Spanish troops we might face are likely to be quite competent, but they will not be trained in drill and field maneuvers as you would encounter in Europe. Here, in a land of jungles, swamps, and grasslands, where most of the opponents are native tribes or perhaps a company of pirates, there are no reasons to keep *tercios* in camps, ready to take the field against organized armies. The New World's wars are skirmishes in remote areas or on the outskirts of towns. Or, occasionally, small cities. There is no maneuvering of serried ranks, no sweeping cavalry attacks against exposed flanks, no clashes of thousands of armored men under the gaze of generals on two opposed ridges. Here, men fight in the bushes, at close range, with little warning of the combat to come, and no expectation of quarter if they lose. The Spanish formations of the New World have adapted to this style of warfare. So while they are not much use in set-piece battles, and are indifferent artillerymen at best, they are as deadly and ruthless a foe as this environment can make them. And you will find, I fear, that this environment is a harsh teacher, indeed."

Eddie distractedly rubbed his palm over the butt of his holstered HP-35's worn grip. *Sounds like it's Vietnam all over again for you, pal.*

"So, other than waiting for them to show up, do we have a plan?" Mike didn't sound annoyed so much as faintly anxious.

"Yes," Tromp said with a decisive nod. "First, we believe that the Spanish have no idea that the up-time designed steamships exist, much less what attributes they might have. Our plan is to allow the Spanish to believe they have a reasonable chance to gain the weather gauge on our fleet. Only then will we use the steam power at our disposal to show them the error of their assessment and to secure the weather gauge for ourselves."

O'Rourke's eyebrows canted skeptically. "You are saying they may be bringing an average of thirty ships to face our—what?—twelve? Admiral Tromp, I know you have seen the full armament of a war galleon up close, but are you sure your memory is furnishing you with an accurate recollection of their firepower, just now?"

Tromp glanced at Eddie, who leaned forward, smiling. "Sergeant O'Rourke, I have a question for you: have you ever seen an eight-inch breech-loading naval rifle in action?"

"Be damned, but I'm not even sure what sort of iron-mongery that might be."

"Well, at some point in the coming weeks, I suspect you'll get a chance to see it in action. I think our naval strategy will start making a lot of sense, then. But in the meantime, we've got some unconventional ground operations in mind, as well."

Hugh had not missed Eddie's leading tone. "For which my Wild Geese might be particularly well suited?"

"They just might be," admitted Eddie, "and as you're probably aware, we brought many more of the men of your *tercio* over with the flotilla."

"Yes, I had the opportunity to chat with a few when we came aboard." And he shot Eddie a most unusual look, a smile that was almost mischievous, as if it concealed a shared secret...

Eddie managed not to start, hoped he hadn't flushed: *damn it, he's halfway to figuring out Quinn's part of our mission! His own troops probably fell over themselves rushing to tell him that we had a third steamship in the flotilla—the* Courser—*which split off from us just before we entered the Caribbean. And Hugh's already guessed what that means: the real reason we're pulling all the attention here to Trinidad is so the* Courser *can fulfill its undisclosed mission with a minimal chance of observation by, or chance encounter with, the Spanish. A mission that no one's talking about, or even alluding to...*

But Hugh was evidently going to let him off that hook. The Irish earl kept on the primary topic of conversation. "So what kind of unconventional action are we talking about, Eddie?"

Eddie leaned in. "Let's call it a special mission, and leave it at that for now. We'll go over the details after we've wrapped up this general meeting, okay?"

"Very well." Hugh's eyes drifted along the map to a point well west of Trinidad. "I must ask: what of Curaçao? Can we not involve the Dutch forces there in our plans, Admiral Tromp?"

"I wish we could," mused Tromp with a frown. "But we have yet to establish contact with whatever colony Thijssen has planted there, and he did not have many ships or men to begin with. Perhaps we will send an envoy, in the months to come, urging him to join with us—"

O'Rourke's smile was small, sad, sympathetic. "But you don't think such a suggestion will set him a-hurrying in our direction."

Tromp shook his head. "No, I don't think it would. And that is unfortunate, for he is too far exposed for his own sake. And for ours."

Ann frowned. "What do you mean?"

Tromp gestured toward the green line of Trinidad's shore, visible out the portside windows. "We are soon to deposit you and your, er, drilling crews, on a very large island, Ms. Koudsi. "We need Thijssen's force here, securing you, the land, and the oil. But I doubt he will quit Curaçao, and I fear that decision may prove his undoing."

Eddie leaned forward, glanced toward Ann. "Speaking of oil, perhaps you'll brief everyone about what you're expecting to be doing for the next half year or so, Ann, and why it could make this a very valuable piece of real estate."

Ann nodded; she leaned her lips against her folded hands, apparently thinking how best to make a simple, cogent explanation out of a very complicated and multifaceted operation. "First," she almost mumbled, "we have several huge advantages drilling for oil here on Trinidad. Probably the greatest of those advantages is how much we know from up-time sources about the early oil industry here. We know, roughly, where the first successful wells were sunk to within two square miles, and we know the sorts of geological formations the prospectors were looking for. So the hardest part of our surveying work is already done."

"Second, the number of wells sunk in relatively close proximity to each other was high, so we don't have to start drilling exactly where the first successful up-time prospectors did. As long as we're in the right area, we should hit oil after a few tries, at most.

"Third, Trinidadian oil is not only sweet and light, but very close to the surface. None of the first wells required more than two hundred and fifty feet of drilling; some required little more than one hundred and fifty. And that's all easily within the depth range of our cable-drilling rigs. We also know that a lot of them were gushers, so we know to go slow and be prepared. That way, we'll suffer less damage and lose less oil. A lot less."

Eddie nodded. "And when do you expect to start drilling?"

Ann grinned crookedly at him. "As soon as your boats finish ferrying my gear to the colonel's fort, and as soon as we get the 'all clear' to start surveying. As I understand it, it's not safe for us to go wandering around inland, yet."

"Not yet," nodded Eddie, "and I suspect the colonel will need to provide you with security contingents, even so."

"Then how will it ever be secure enough to drill in any of the sites we find?"

Eddie nodded. "When you've got a high-confidence find, we'll throw up a security cordon around it. If it's further off, we'll need to patrol an eventual access road as well. Which is why we've asked you to concentrate your initial surveying close to Pitch Lake. It's off the beaten-track of the Arawaks, and with any luck, we won't even need an access road."

Ann shrugged. "I'll do my best. We do know there were some wells sunk in sight of Pitch Lake itself. But that's a lot different from being able to deliver one on the first shot, and by request."

Tromp was shaking his head. "No one expects that, Ms. Koudsi. Nothing of the kind. We understand that you might need many tries and much time before finding oil. Which is why we are trying to formalize an active alliance with the Nepoia tribes. If that can be accomplished, our work here will be much easier."

"And how have those efforts been coming along?" Ann's keen interest vied with her obvious anxiety as she inquired.

"Pretty well," Eddie answered, "but we've had a hard time setting up a meeting with their cacique, Hyarima. He's in the field carrying the fight to the Arawaks right now. But he's interested in meeting his new neighbors." Eddie glanced at Hugh. "Particularly you."

Hugh raised an eyebrow. "I am honored. But I suspect that I, too, will be too busy for that meeting." He smiled. "Speaking of which, when do you need us to start on that special mission?"

Eddie grinned sheepishly, shrugged. "Actually, it would be best if your Wild Geese could leave today, Colonel. Before which, I'll want a few words with you in private."

Hugh smiled knowingly. "Of course, Commander. Well, O'Rourke,

I see we shall be working for our share of the profits along with everyone else. No more lolly-gagging about for us!"

O'Rourke glanced at his earl sourly. "Sure and I'll be missing my life of tropical leisure, m'lord."

Eddie nodded agreeably, but thought: *O'Rourke, you might soon mean those ironic words seriously enough. Particularly given where you and the earl are heading.*

For Hugh O'Donnell, the end of the private meeting with Eddie Cantrell did not mark the end of business. Emerging from the aft companionway, Hugh had found his sergeant pacing the deck of the *Intrepid* like a caged bear. He had immediately summoned all the Wild Geese that were aboard, who swarmed their two senior officers, as eager as puppies to go ashore and mingle with their comrades manning the walls of Fort St. Patrick.

But that was not to be for the half being retained as ship's troops. And of those, forty were hastily transferred to the Dutch yacht *Eendracht*, which was to weigh anchor at dusk and commence carrying Hugh and his men to their distant objective. But before then, Hugh and O'Rourke had much to do in little time: familiarizing the recently arrived officers of the *tercio* with the routines and particularities of Fort St. Patrick; supervising the transfer and placement of a small battery of demi-culverins ashore; and calming Doubting Thomas Doyle who was lamenting the impossibility of completing all the inevitable new construction projects in the time required.

They finished their work ashore just in time to wave farewell to the *Koninck David* and the *Crown of Waves* as those two ships set sail back north. Michael McCarthy was at the taffrail, waving back at them. Word had it that he was bound for 'Statia to perform yet another piece of up-time technological wizardry. Exactly what he was to conjure up remained unknown to all but Tromp and Cantrell, and they were not sharing that information. *More secrets*, thought Hugh. *Nothing but, here in the New World.*

And Hugh was not innocent of secrecy, himself—not until he could share his destination with his men, which for security's sake he could not reveal until they drew close to it. Nonetheless, they would be training for their upcoming operation as they traveled west along the Spanish Main on a course known only to the Dutch captain, his mate, and his pilot. The prerequisite level of mutual trust between the commanders made for a markedly strange situation, reflected Hugh, since he had fought the Dutch since he could hold a sword.

But this first joint enterprise of forces from the newly cooperative Lowlands also presented a wholly unlooked for silver lining in the form of the young and wonderfully alert young captain of the jacht *Eendracht,* Pieter Floriszoon. Good-natured and every bit as weary of religious bigotry as Hugh himself, they quickly worked out their respective command prerogatives—Floriszoon commanded on the water, Hugh on land—and got under way. The prevailing winds were handy, coming from the east abeam the starboard gunwale, and Floriszoon accurately predicted no more than five hours sailing to traverse the Gulf of Paria to the near side of Dragon's Mouth, where they would make anchorage in a protected cove.

Shortly after dark, the *Eendracht* dropped anchor at the appointed place and Hugh went below to take a congenial meal with the almost fifty Wild Geese who were aboard. In addition to the forty troops that had been drawn from the *Intrepid*, ten specialists had been hand-picked from the original group at Fort St. Patrick, all of whom spent the evening telling the new arrivals heavily embellished tales of their time at Pitch Lake.

As the rations of grog were being ladled out, Hugh had noticed O'Rourke getting ready to break away from the below-decks camaraderie. No doubt to button-hole Hugh so that they could finally compare notes on the day's events. There had certainly been plenty of food for thought in the news they had heard, and careful counsel was in order. But, with an unvoiced apology to his old friend, Hugh slipped off alone to examine the day's last potential source of surprises and secrets: the letter from his godmother.

Had Hugh read it before the pirate attack, its contents would have flabbergasted him. She revealed that, for almost half a year, she had foreseen the inevitable effect that Fernando's increasing distance from his brother Philip of Spain would have on her godson, that he would be placed in an impossible position if he remained in Philip's service. Consequently, she had set about her slow campaign to properly position him to be in the right time and right place to take advantage of the changes that were coming.

Her indirect encouragements to meet the up-timers; her back-channel negotiations with that group's President Piazza to maneuver Hugh into a partnership with Michael McCarthy; the up-time brokered agreement between Fernando and Hendrik to share the responsibilities and profits that might arise from tapping oil in Trinidad; the inclusion of the Wild Geese as a smaller but fully entitled partner in that larger deal: what would have shocked him a month ago now seemed like an embarrassingly obvious answer to the apparent coincidences of the past half year. Even so, the amount of invisible negotiation and creation of common points of interest that Isabella had brokered, groomed, and achieved was formidable. It might yet prove to be her finest coup in a career chock-full of diplomatic tours-de-force.

But Hugh could see another level that few, if any, other observers would have detected: that the foundation and driving force behind her grand accomplishment had been her love for Hugh, her largely hidden determination that his legacy, and potential, should be married to resources that might enable him to realize and capitalize upon both. McCarthy's passion for Ireland had been the crucial catalyst she had been seeking, the means of bringing together a strange, wholly unofficial, yet powerful political bond between the interests and persons of the Spanish Lowlands and the interests and persons of the USE.

After reading the letter twice, Hugh spent some minutes just looking at it, cherishing his godmother's familiar, bold hand and the wry wit that lurked behind so many of her comments and observations. For the briefest moment, he seemed to feel her fingers touch his face like a ghost's, reaching all the way from the other side of the ocean.

It took a while to get to sleep. The water was calm, but his mind was filled with surges of other faces and facts: John O'Neill dead, Urban VIII missing, Prince Frederik Hendrik an ally, and a cascade of silver for his Wild Geese and their families. And upon him, the title of the last legitimate earl of Ireland. He wasn't sure whether to feel it as a great weight or a great joke, being such a tremendous reversal from the life he had lived and expected. He was still trying to decide which reaction was more appropriate when the gentle movement of the *Eendracht* finally rocked him to sleep.

❖   ❖   ❖

Ann Koudsi had been rocked to sleep a lot more energetically than Hugh O'Donnell. In a manner of speaking. When she awoke in her cabin in the middle of the night, it took her a moment to reorient herself. First, because it was her own cabin on land—part of the newly built housing for the drilling team on Trinidad—not the even tinier cabin she'd shared with another woman on the *Patentia*. And second, because she hadn't shared a bed with anyone in...

A long, long time. Since the Ring of Fire, in fact—as if the simple act of sexual intercourse would somehow have finalized the disappearance of the world she'd once known and loved.

Now, lifted up on one elbow and gazing down at the recumbent form of Ulrich Rohrbach, she realized just how foolish she'd been. The truth was, no matter how fond she'd been of her up-time existence, it was a pale shadow compared to her new life. She knew she'd never have experienced such adventures, nor had such awesome responsibilities thrust upon her. Never been so challenged—and never shown herself how well she could and would rise to those challenges.

And she'd never have had a lover like Ulrich. A man who admired and respected her as much as he did, without being intimidated by her. Because, despite his lack of formal education and his modest birth, he'd absorbed the up-time belief in self-betterment and applied it with a determination that bordered on ferocity.

There'd been no chance to further their relationship while they'd been on the *Patentia*. There'd been no privacy, for starters. Perhaps more importantly—this was hard to pin down, exactly—Ann herself hadn't felt quite ready. So long as they were in transit from the old world to the new, she'd somehow felt as if her life was still suspended.

No longer. They'd reached their destination—for the moment, at least—and her fate was back in her own hands. This was their first night on Trinidad since the cabin was finally declared ready and they could transfer off the ship. And she'd made the most of it, by God!

For the first time since the Ring of Fire, she was finally able to fully accept and welcome her new life. O brave new world.

Ulrich shifted slightly on the bed. And, then, began to snore.

All right, fine. Some things stayed the same. But it was still a brave new world.

Chapter 31

Entry to Galveston Bay, Texas

Major Larry Quinn glanced over his shoulder at the darkening southern horizon. Even at this range, he could see actinic flashes inside the low line of gray clouds that were beginning to rise up through the hazy air mass above them. He glanced back up the tumblehome of the *Courser*, trying not to sound either anxious or annoyed as he said, "Any time now, Karl."

Karl Klemm swayed down another step of the netting that had been played over the side of the destroyer, then glanced at his feet before starting downward again. This time, however, his foot remained in midair, thrashing about in search of the next foothold, which the gentle sway of the ship had snatched away.

In the boat, two of the elite soldiers of Grantville's increasingly proprietary Hibernian Mercenary Battalion, Volker and Wright, exchanged world-weary glances. Wright looked at Larry. "Major Quinn, should we lend Mr. Klemm a hand in—?"

Larry shook his head and said quietly but firmly, "No. He can handle it." *And hopefully he'll do so before the month is out*, the up-timer added silently. Because with a hurricane coming straight up out of the Gulf of Mexico, and the *Courser* waiting for them to lead it to safe anchorage, every minute counted.

But it was also important that Klemm, the only man on the

Courser who had not started out by embracing a life of risk on either battlefields or the high seas, should learn to master the skills and attitudes necessary to survive beyond the margins of civilization.

Klemm eyed the six feet remaining to the deck of the small, up-time motor boat bouncing against the fenders separating it from *Courser*'s hull. Larry saw the assessing stare, and shook his head. "No jumping, Karl. That's a good way to twist an ankle, and you have to stay mobile."

Karl glanced at Larry, nodded tightly, gritted his teeth and put another foot down, then again, and finally, half-stepped and half tumbled into the cockpit of the bright red 1988 180 Sportsman. He straightened, panting slightly, and looked Larry in the eye. "Apologies, Major. I will work hard to improve my climbing."

Larry nodded for the lines to be cast off and the fenders pulled in, then glanced sideways at the young Bavarian. "You seemed a good enough climber when we were touring various rock formations with Ms. Aossey. Hell, you were as good scrambling up a rock face as I was."

Karl looked about the controls of the motorboat, alert, as if reading the function of each lever and button. "With respect, Major, cliffs do not move as you climb them. So it seems strange to me to try to put my foot where the netting *will* be, rather than where it was when I last looked down."

Quinn smiled. "Fair enough."

"Major," said the middle aged sailor perched on the bow of the motor boat, "we are ready."

Karl looked at Larry. "Shall I help the leadsman with—?"

"No, Karl. You stay here. I want you to learn how to pilot this boat."

Karl's eyes were wide—with apprehension or avidity, Larry wasn't quite sure. "Me?"

"Yes. You have a knack for machines and we'll need at least two people to pilot it when we make our way back up the coast to the Mermentau River. Besides, this boat can be a little finicky."

Klemm stared at the unfamiliar word. "'Finicky?'"

Evidently that colloquialism hadn't made the jump into Amideutsch. At least not yet. "Finicky is, er, sensitive, twitchy. Like a nervous cat."

"Ah. Delicate controls. I shall watch closely."

Quinn eased the throttle forward and turned the wheel to the right. The slow, clockwork mutter of the outboard rose into a ragged purr and the Sportsman sheered away from the hull of the *Courser* at a leisurely pace. Before them, the blue-green waters that marked the narrow entry into Galveston Bay roiled, mildly agitated as they moved over and among that gap's notoriously migratory sandbars. "Leadsman," cried Larry into the wind, "reading."

"Not quite three fathoms, sir."

Damn it, that was close. The *Courser* drew almost two fathoms without her drop-keel down, and because she was heavily loaded for a long mission away from resupply, she was probably drawing a full thirteen feet. That left only four feet between her keel and the muddy sands that she would need to traverse. Larry eased the throttle back. Frequent depth readings were going to be needed in order to make sure they didn't miss a submerged bank or other protrusion that might snag the *Courser* and leave her trapped before the slashing jaws of a rapidly approaching hurricane. "Keep singing out those marks," he shouted toward the bow as he glanced at Volker and Wright.

The two soldiers kept an easy hold on their rifles—down-time copies of the Winchester 1895 chambered for .40-72—one scanning the low, sandy end of the Bolivar Peninsula on the northeastern side of the channel, the other alert for movement on Galveston Island's higher southwestern shore. The glass-smooth water and the lack of birds confirmed what the barometer had started predicting two days ago and what the dark line of clouds on the south now promised: that the approaching storm was certain to be quite ferocious.

"Fourteen feet," called the leadsman grimly. "Silty and thick."

Another one foot rise. Much more, and the *Courser* would have no safe harbor. This was what Admiral Simpson had called the worst-case scenario of the mission: that, arriving along the Gulf coast during hurricane season, the *Courser* could find itself unable to make a run into a good high-weather anchorage. Her ultimate objective, the Mermentau River, was known to be shallow, and the harbors at Port Arthur and the Calcasieu Channel did not exist in this world. Without dredging, they were barely half the depth required. Until one reached the mouth of the Mississippi, the tidal flats were precisely that: very flat, and very shallow. No ports worth the name. And while the *Courser* could lie off the Mermentau easily and safely enough in most weather, she was at severe risk if she stuck to the open water in the teeth of a hurricane.

The only option had been Galveston Bay, a full one hundred miles west of the Mermentau. Fortunately, they had heeded the barometer's warnings and taken no chances, bypassing the Mermentau and making straight for Galveston.

But making straight for Galveston was not synonymous with racing into her bay. Although the channel ranged from one and a half to two miles wide, the shifting silt and sand made the actual pathway something of a slalom course. And in an era without dredging or regularly updated depth charts, the trick to finding safe harbor depended upon trail-blazing the sinuous path of the greater depths.

Consequently, at the start of the first watch, Larry had given orders that the Sportsman 180 should be uncovered, which was achieved by disassembling its disposable warehouse-cocoon on the ship's main deck. Captain Haraldsen, who had finally begun to forgive Larry for taking over the mission when the *Courser* parted from the rest of the flotilla, had been unable to suppress his pointed interest in the up-time boat as, board by board, it was revealed and then made ready for lowering over the stern by a hastily erected pair of davits. Now, Larry just hoped they had put her in the water soon enough. "Give me another reading."

The leadsman shook his head. "Steady at fourteen. Might have risen another inch."

Not good. Quinn looked back at the *Courser.* Haraldsen himself was waiting patiently in the bows, spyglass ready to distinguish any hand signal that might come from the motorboat. Because if the channel continued to rise, the best the *Courser* could do was anchor herself in the mouth of the channel and hope that the path of the storm was such that the headlands broke the worst rush of wind and water, rather than focused it upon her. Still, even that was better than catching the storm out in the Gulf and being pushed up against the land without any control. But being carried out of the center of the channel by a storm surge might be almost as bad, leaving the ship stranded in a position from which they would not be able to get it back into the receded waters. That would mean the end of their mission, and quite possibly, the end of their lives—

"Three fathoms full, again, Major!" cried the leadsman. "And dropping fast. We must have been moving over a silt shelf."

Quinn nodded. "Good, but we're not safe yet. We've got about another mile of channel to go, and we haven't encountered the narrower sand bars." *Assuming there are any narrower sand bars, that is.* Working from a few nineteenth- and twentieth-century accounts that had been located in the Grantville Library didn't exactly provide them with an extensive maritime gazetteer of Galveston Bay. For all anyone knew, the sandbars might have been a later phenomenon or one with a long periodic arc.

But whatever the case, they were well over a mile into the channel, which meant they had reached the point where it had been determined it was worthwhile bringing the *Courser* in for anchorage, even if she could go no farther. "Wright," Quinn called over his shoulder. "Signal to Captain Haraldsen that he should start following along in our wake. Precisely in our wake. Otherwise he is at risk of running aground from bars that we're not detecting farther to the east or west."

"Yes, sir," Wright said, standing and making the appropriate hand signals back to the *Courser*.

"Leadsman," called Quinn. "Reading."

"Three fathoms full and less silt. Feels like we're past the muck."

Larry nodded, pushed the throttle forward. "Okay then, we're picking up the pace. The sooner we blaze a trail to get the *Courser* into the bay, the better the anchorage she might find." The Sportcraft 180's engine sound grew throatier. The prop dug at the water harder, putting a thready vibration through the deck. The leadsman called out largely unchanging reports.

Quinn felt Karl's eyes watching his hands upon the controls. "Catching on?"

Klemm nodded. "Yes. It seems simple in principle. But, like many such things, I suspect it is more difficult than it looks."

"A little," Quinn admitted with a smile. "But once the hurricane has passed us and we're ready to head back to the Mermentau River, you'll get some time behind the wheel. We'll share the piloting when we head back. By the time we're ready to motor into the bayous, you'll be an old hand."

Karl looked skeptical. "If you say so, Major. But the close margins of inland waterways will be a more difficult task, no?"

Quinn frowned. "Different, more than difficult. On open water, you've got to watch the risers and the chop, particularly in a light boat like this one. And you've got to read the skies well, so you can run to an inlet, a bay, or even a beach if heavy weather is on the way. Inland, the worry is that you'll put a hole in her hull, run aground in the shallows, or get snarled in vegetation. Either way, the best rules for a new boater are to look sharp and go slow. That way, you'll last long enough to become an old boater."

The leadsman called more loudly. "Sand bar. Up to fifteen and rising toward port."

Quinn turned the prow slightly starboard, eased the throttle back. "Now?"

"Holding steady. Now dropping. Sixteen."

Quinn held the wheel motionless, maintained speed. "Now?"

"Steady at sixteen."

Quinn called over his shoulder. "Volker, toss back a weighted buoy where we turned."

Karl watched the small float, trailing a bottom-weighted rope, soar through the air, land with a splash well back in their wake. "Let us hope the bar does not rise in this new direction, as well."

Larry nodded. If it did rise up higher, they'd have to backtrack, keep trying different directions until they found one that would get them all the way into the bay. But they didn't have the time for that kind of trial-and-error anymore. He looked back at the southern horizon. The sky was hazy as high up as he could see, and the dark storm bank had risen to show more of itself over the rim of the world. It would be on them in two hours, maybe less.

The leadsman's next shout sounded like a sigh of relief projected through a bullhorn. "Seventeen. No, eighteen. And widening out on all sides. You can cut back to port again, I think."

Which would be a good thing, since their current heading would have fetched them up against the scree and rubble shore of Point Bolivar in another few hundred yards. Quinn swung the motorboat slowly back to port.

"Steady marks, Major. And we're just about out of the channel."

Quinn eased the throttle forward again, discovered that Volker was trying to catch his eye. "Herr Major," he said, just loud enough to be heard over the engine, "who or what are Wright and I watching for?"

"Most likely natives. Possibly Spanish, but our histories say they were pretty hesitant to make landfall along here."

"Because of the sandbars?"

"Possibly. But probably more because of the Atakapas."

Volker smiled. "So the natives don't much like the Spanish?"

"Oh, they do," Wright observed sardonically. "For dinner."

At first, Volker was perplexed. Then his eyes widened. "They are cannibals?"

Quinn was wondering how best to defuse any surge in anxiety over the rumored culinary habits of the natives, but Karl beat him to it. "Actually, Herr Volker, that is a matter of some debate. There was little mention of them in the books in Grantville. However, while most accounts do suggest that they ate their foes ritualistically, it seems that the only Europeans they ever defined as 'foes' were the Spanish."

"Why?" asked Wright.

Quinn shared the last of the scant knowledge that had been gleaned on the Atakapas. "Apparently, the Spanish enslaved and tortured the first groups of Atakapas they came across. And it seems the Atakapas have long memories. At least that's what the history books say."

"The very *few* history books," Wright amended soberly, "based on scant travelers' tales, from the sound of it. Let's hope they're right."

"Well, Mr. Wright, we'll be the first to find out." Quinn watched the last of the headlands that formed the two sides of the channel fall away behind them, Galveston Bay spreading out around them. "Mr. Volker," he called back, "signal to the *Courser* that we've marked their passage, and are now going to scout anchorages." Quinn moved the throttle farther forward and felt the nose of the boat begin to rise as their speed increased.

Larry stole a rearward glance. The hurricane had changed again. Taller, darker, and, given the rate of visual change, moving directly toward them at one hell of a clip. Safe anchorage or not, they'd also need a good measure of luck to come through the storm in one piece.

He turned to survey the wide bay before him and saw little in the way of making their own luck. One of the problems with Galveston Bay was how very flat its sheltering islands were. They were simply sand spits, really, studded with a few rocks here and there. The only feature that rose up to any height was Pelican Island, immediately to their west, which meant it was back across the sand bars they'd just avoided.

Quinn kept a worried frown off his face, as he called forward to the leadsman. "I'm going to take us a little farther east, to see if we can find some deep water in the lee of the Port Bolivar headland."

The leadsman simply stared at the water there, which was entirely too calm and not particularly dark, and then stared back at Quinn.

Who thought: *yeah, I know. Doesn't look promising. Problem is that* nothing *looks promising. Most of all that damned storm.*

Karl was close at Larry's elbow. "Major, without depth charts, how shall we know where best to make a quick search for an anchorage?"

Quinn sent an entirely artificial grin at the young German. "We make our best guess and take our chances." *And right now, our chances aren't looking too good...*

Part Six

October 1635

What plagues and what portents

Chapter 32

Outside Puerto Cabello, Venezuela

Hugh O'Donnell turned, listened, went into a crouch, and motioned the thirty men following him to do the same. Behind them, a faint voice cried out in Spanish, but only to silence a barking dog. Then, all was quiet again in the lightless, mostly abandoned village of Borburata, just five hundred yards behind them.

"Have we been seen, m'lord?" asked one of his senior ensigns, Daniel O'Cahan.

Hugh glanced up at the sky. Stars stared back down, impassive. Too clear for his liking. He'd waited for a near-moonless night, but could only pray for clouds, which had not materialized. "No, Daniel, I think not. The skiffs put us in better than four hundred yards northwest of the furthest huts, which the Dutch say are deserted. And they should know. They've raided here a bit."

The ever-laconic Jimmy Murrow glanced back at the faint outlines of tilted thatched roofs, many half-collapsed. "What's to be had, I wonder?"

"Not much anymore. Less than a hundred souls there. Quiet now. There will be coast watchers ahead."

As if to confirm Hugh's warning, O'Bannon slipped out of the bushes lining the thin strand. "Two coast-watchers, m'lord. About two hundred yards further on."

"About what we thought, then. Where's Purcell? Is he keeping an eye on them?"

O'Bannon's face was unreadable in the dark. "In a manner of speakin'. I should have said there *were* two coast watchers."

O'Donnell nodded. Purcell was as quiet as a cat, handy with a dagger, and disturbingly eager to use both skills. Which he had done tonight. Hugh would rather not have commanded such men as Purcell, but such fine moral scruples were luxuries a colonel could not afford. Having a diverse collection of tactical tools at one's disposal, no matter how devious and dark some of those tools might be, meant more success and fewer lost men. Better a stain on his honor that no one else perceived than a few more trusting *cultchies* buried in a foreign field.

Or in this case, possibly more than a few. It would be nothing short of disastrous if the Spanish had any warning of their approach over the thin arm of land that framed in the northern side of Puerto Cabello's protected anchorage, and was only two hundred fifty yards wide at its narrowest point. If detected, it was quite possible that they'd fail to reach the inner harbor at all, and quite unlikely that they'd capture the ship they had seen sitting almost astride the channel into it. And since the Dutch commander of the up-time-inspired steam pinnace that was set to rendezvous with them had no way of knowing if they were repulsed, or where to retrieve them if they were, it was all too likely that any determined Spanish pursuit would end in the wholesale slaughter of Hugh's detachment.

O'Donnell nodded at O'Bannon, his senior lieutenant in this group. "Any other pickets that you could see?"

O'Bannon shook his head. "No, m'lord. Looks clear all the way down to the inner harbor. Nothing on this arm of land until you reach the guardhouse and the open battery we spotted overlooking the narrows."

Which, for all intents and purposes, meant they could make their way down to the shore of the inner harbor unobserved. The narrows were more than six hundred yards west of their destination, with a small rocky promontory blocking the sight line between them.

O'Cahan didn't sound convinced, though. "Can the Spanish really be that lax? Natives could be just as quiet as and deadly as Purcell, and the jungles are thick wid 'em."

O'Bannon smiled at the cautious new ensign, who was clearly eager to show that he was competent and alert to all dangers. "Not so many natives about as you'd think, Daniel. They stay well back from the bigger towns unless they mean to burn 'em to the ground. And the Spanish aren't worried about their neighbors sneaking in from here on the north beach, because there's naught they can do. So the natives take the northern arm of the inner harbor. Then what? Are they going to swim out into the anchorage and threaten the Spanish ships?"

"No," muttered Jimmy Murrow, "because they're not such bleedin' goms as we are."

"Are you saying you've reservations about our plans, Mr. Murrow?" Hugh asked coolly.

Murrow made a sound as if he was swallowing his shoe. Sideways. "None 't all, m'lord."

"Mm. Didn't think so. You'll be wanting that length of bamboo handy about now, I'd think. And you too, O'Cahan. In a few minutes, it will be time for your midnight swims."

Aodh O'Rourke brought up his pepperbox revolver as the bushes rustled in front of him. "Advance and be recognized."

A swarthy, much-scarred man of medium height and build emerged from between two giant fronds. "It's Calabar," he said quietly. "What are you doing this far forward on the path?"

"Being where I'm not supposed to be," O'Rourke answered, waving to the men behind him to rise and prepare to move.

"And why is that?" asked Calabar, who eased the hammer forward again on his flintlock pistol.

"Because if any of the Spanish bastards had caught you and indulged their taste for torture, I didn't want to be where you'd have told them we were."

Calabar's voice was quiet, distant. "I'd not have told them anything. Not unto death."

"Which is as may be, friend, but I'll not be trusting the lives of twenty mothers' sons to any man's resolve when his captors start playing mumblety-peg with his fingernails. Or his manhood."

Calabar's shadow shrugged. "Very well. The path ahead is overgrown. It is not much used, possibly only by hunters."

"I thought Puerto Cabello was mostly home to fishermen," put in Malachi O'Mara, O'Rourke's second in command, from behind.

Calabar's voice was half-droll, half-annoyed. "As I said, the path is not much used. Are your men ready?"

O'Rourke nodded. "The oil and charges are ready, and the men are arrayed in their pairs."

"You've reapplied mud?"

"We've done as you instructed."

"And look like a horde of Moors, to boot," mumbled Patrick Keenan, from farther back in the column.

"You mind yourself, you blue-eyed Moor," scolded O'Rourke, who kept his focus on Calabar. "Have you seen the warehouses?"

The half-Portuguese *mameluco* from Brazil's Pernambuco coast shrugged. "Their roofs, only. I did not wish to go closer. But they are where Moses Henriques reported them to be."

"And you trust this pirate-friend of yours?"

Again, Calabar paused before speaking. "He is my friend, and I saved his life near Recife, so yes, I trust him. And he is a pirate, but a selective one. He rarely takes a ship lest she be Portuguese or Spanish. Most importantly, no one knows this coast half as well as he does. His men were in Puerto Cabello only two weeks ago and saw war materiel being moved into the warehouses, saw the guards standing watch night and day, saw that most of the crews were being kept aboard their ships, not billeted in town."

O'Rourke nodded. "Meaning the Spanish are presuming they could receive orders to weigh anchor any day. Very well; we'll trust your Hebrew pirate friend." He turned to his men. "Blades, not pistols, until we leave the jungle. If we bump into patrols, we take them quietly. Once at the outskirts of the town, it will be guns and fast feet, lads. We'll not have much time."

Maintaining a tight crouch, Hugh crept down to the water's edge, with Murrow and O'Cahan beside him. O'Bannon had already taken a few men to keep watch over their right flank, just in case a patrol meandered out of the guard post farther to the northwest. He scanned the inner-harbor as the two young men, the best swimmers in his two companies, reblacked their faces and checked their bamboo breathing tubes. In the briefing for the mission, Cantrell had kept calling them snorkels and seemed to presume they were easier to use than past experience had proven them to be.

O'Donnell had used them once, himself, years ago during the

siege at Bruges. It was not unknown to use breathing tubes to cross shallow moats, but it was a risky undertaking. Moats were usually barely a step above open sewers in terms of cleanliness, and using the breathing tubes meant swimming in an awkward position: half on one's back, almost. Which made strong swimmers the users of choice.

That was even more true on this mission, where they would be towing lightly weighted lines out to the *patache* that was almost sitting astride the inner mouth of the channel that communicated between the outer and inner bay. Two days of observation—by a team deposited under cover of a cloudless night on the uninhabited lump of rock and brush named Isla Goaiguaza—had confirmed that the ship was approximately half-crewed, and kept ready to sail at a moment's notice. This was not an uncommon practice among the Spanish, particularly at the smaller ports along the Tierra Firma. More yachtlike in design than any other Spanish ship, the *patache* was capable of sailing close to the wind and was often fitted with oars, as well. Consequently, it would be optimally responsive to any attempt to enter a protected anchorage such as Puerto Cabello's. That she hadn't the weight of shot or of men to fight off a concerted attack was hardly a concern. At the very least, she would buy the greater ships in the harbor time to ready their guns and sails, whether the threat was from a boat full of boarders or a fire ship.

"So, m'lord, do we know whether we're to seize her or sink her?"

O'Donnell nodded as his two swimmers checked the pitch seals on the sewn top-folds of their oilskin bags. "Yes. We seize her. Her sails are reefed but ready and we've got the right wind, coming from the northeast. That's directly abeam, so we should be able to get up the channel at a good speed. Seven knots from the sails alone, if Captain Floriszoon guesses right and his prize crew is up to handling the rigging a-right."

"And when we go past the guns at the mouth of the channel?"

It was a good thing that the observers on Isla Goaiguaza had been furnished with new, up-time-modeled 10x magnification spyglasses. "Our fellows sitting out in the bay got a good look at those guns. Small demi-culverins, at best, so probably ten-pound balls. Not enough to do heavy damage unless they have plenty of time to fire at us. Our real worry is from the guns in the battery across the bay. They have full cannon over there, according to the Dutch and their pirate-friends. But as long as the *patache* is being contested, I'm wagering they won't fire upon their own men. Besides, with any luck, the men of the battery will be more than a little distracted by other events."

"Such as?" prompted Murrow, with a hastily appended, "m'lord."

Hugh smiled. "We'll leave that to O'Rourke. He excels at mischief, you know."

"So he does, Colonel," conceded Murrow. "But once we start the fireworks on board the *patache*, that's likely to draw their attention even so. And so I'm wondering: just how fast can we get up that anchor?"

O'Cahan's rolled eyes caught the faint lights glimmering across the water from Puerto Cabello. "We're not going to raise the anchor, eejit. We're going to cut it."

"And just how are we going to do that?"

"Ships have axes on 'em, y' great gom. For just such occasions."

"And if this ship doesn't have one, or we can't find it?"

"That's why one of our lads is bringing over a small saw."

"Oh." Murrow had stripped down to a loin-clout, with his waterproof pack and the weighted line lashed to the belt that held it up. "And the prize crew? How do we know those damned Dutchmen will get here in time? How do they even know when it's time to come?"

Hugh interrupted with a voice signifying that the discussion was over. "Because, Murrow, we've fireworks and a whistle with us, and the steam pinnace is waiting to detect either, just a mile off the mouth of the channel."

Murrow seemed surprised. "You trust that fire-breathing brass beast? Look how long it took the Dutch to get it to work, Colonel!"

"That's because they were being careful, Murrow, just as they were during all the practice runs we made as we traveled along the Main from Trinidad. Without the steam engine's power, we'd be entirely at the mercy of the wind. This way, even if the wind dies or turns on us, we can still make three knots out of the channel. And if the breeze stays will us, we could do close to ten."

O'Cahan nodded. "It's a well-conceived plan, m'lord—but, well, what if you and the lads don't take the ship?"

Hugh looked squarely at O'Cahan. "You know the answer to that, Daniel. That's why you have the augurs. And the scuttling charges."

"Aye, sir, but we've not had an opportunity to test the charges, lest we waste them. And how do we let you know to go over the side, once they're planted?"

Hugh nodded. "Wish I had those answers, Daniel. It's the best system we could devise. The charges are well-wrapped, and the primers are lit by percussion cap. So as long as you don't dislodge the arming system inside the oilskin, the fuse should light and burn down. The tamping is crude, but should at least buckle a light hull such as the *patache*'s. The two together should breach it. And as for warning us?" Hugh shrugged. "If it goes as badly as all that, I doubt they'll be many of us left to warn. And mind you, no heroics. You stay under the curve of the hull, out of sight. And if you hear the signal, you scuttle the *patache* and leave. And no looking back. That is an order. Do you understand?"

"Yes, m'lord. I expect we'll be putting out the second set of tow-lines for O'Rourke, instead."

"So do I. Now, into the water, lads. Tell me, how quietly can you swim?"

Murrow looked dubious. "As long as I keep my feet from floating up, I thought I'd not make any noise swimming underwater, m'lord."

"Well, I'll let you know afterward. Or I suspect the Spanish on the *patache* might let you know first."

Murrow's eyes were large as he waded into the rippleless water. "I'll mind my feet, Colonel."

"Yes. You do that."

Calabar held up a hand, waving O'Rourke's column down into the ferns at the edge of the jungle. Gesturing for the sergeant to come forward, Calabar pointed toward low, squarish outlines that were located halfway between their position and the sparse lights of Puerto Cabello, only six hundred yards to their northwest. "The warehouses. Simple frame construction. Recent. Almost certainly to house fleet stores."

O'Rourke scanned the bay. Ten large ships pushed their masts toward the stars. Half again as many smaller hulls rode at anchor around them. "That's not the whole fleet from Cartagena, is it?"

Calabar shook his head. "No. They're not all here yet. Those are probably from Maracaibo or Coro. The galleons—any square-rigged ship—has a hard time heading east along Tierra Firma.

The current and winds are both against them, and they can't tack well." Calabar considered. "But the Cartagena fleet can't be too far off. A week or two at the most."

O'Rourke nodded. "Which of the warehouses are our main targets?"

Calabar shrugged. "All are worth destroying. Most only contain food and casks of water and wine, but after all, a fleet without provisions is hardly a fleet. However, if you mean powder and shot . . ." Calabar pointed at a smaller warehouse of superior construction, located at the center of the larger ones. Whereas the patrols moved in a leisurely pattern between the other buildings, the guards around the munitions warehouse circled it endlessly, and in pairs. And they were armored. Of course.

O'Rourke turned to the men behind him. "Listen closely, lads. When we get close to the powder and shot stores, we're going to have to fight genuine Spanish regulars: breastplates and morions all. So don't load lead bullets. Iron's what we need. Double shot for the musketoons and balls for the pepperboxes." He looked across the ground to the warehouses. "Assume they'll hear us coming at about one hundred yards, see us at about seventy or so, if we're running."

"We could crawl to the warehouses," Calabar offered.

"We could, but it's too easy for us to get spread out that way. When we attack, we have to be close enough so that our numbers sweep them aside and give us a direct line to the munitions. So we crawl the first twenty-five yards, then up and crouched approach until we're spotted. Then kneel, fire a round, and charge."

Calabar nodded. "Let us do so, then. Spread your men along the edge of the jungle. I have been here once before, so I shall lead the way."

Chapter 33

Puerto Cabello, Venezuela

Hugh O'Donnell was a fair swimmer but was not enamored of being fully submerged. Particularly on a nearly lightless night. So despite the steady flow of air down the bamboo breathing tube, and the fact that it assured him of remaining within eighteen inches of the surface, he was nonetheless eager to get his head above water as soon as he reached the end of the weighted cord that O'Cahan had secured to the *patache*'s rudder by looping it over the pintle-and-gudgeon joint that was closest to the waterline.

Hugh knew his eagerness to resurface was a danger insofar as he would disturb the water with a sudden breach, so he forced himself to take a final breath through the tube, remove it from his mouth, draw it straight down, and float up slowly.

The stars and faint sounds seemed to rush in at him after towing himself with one hand along one hundred yards of submerged line. The lack of current in the inner harbor had made corrections of balance negligible, particularly since this water was calmer than any of the bays or inlets in which they had practiced during their journey along the Spanish Main. Now out of the silent darkness, he strained his ears and eyes to assess the situation.

Looking back toward the shore, and only because he knew to look for them, he spotted two irregular lines of small bumps protruding above the smooth surface of the inner harbor: the last of his thirty men finishing their submerged approach to the *patache*. He moved forward, keeping a steadying hand on the undercurve of the hull until he could glimpse the waist of the *low-slung ship*. In the water along her side were a cluster of what looked like oversized coconuts—his men's heads—bobbing underneath the shelflike outboard channel that held the chainplates at bottom of each ratline in place. They had approached along the second line, looped over the rigging cleats beneath the channel, and were now concealed from overhead detection as long as they stayed put and hugged the ship's waterline.

A slight disturbance in the water beside him caused Hugh to turn. O'Cahan rose up so slowly that he barely sent out a ripple. He cut his eyes southward, toward the town and the main battery. He tilted his head slowly, quizzically.

Hugh understood O'Cahan's silent question: Should he start across the rest of the channel, running yet another tow-line to the opposite shore for O'Rourke's men? It was a reasonable question. Yes, Hugh's detachment was supposed to wait for the unmistakable sounds of O'Rourke's attack before they took their own next steps, but more time had passed than should have. Still, if anything had gone wrong, there would have been the sound of more distant gunfire. So in all probability, it made sense to have O'Cahan start his swim now, giving him more time. On the other hand, if the attempt to board the *patache* went very badly, very quickly, Hugh would want the young ensign on hand with his augur and scuttling charge in order to—

From well south of the center of Puerto Cabello, there was a sputter of gunfire: sharp, distinctive reports of the new pepperbox revolvers and the brash roars of the double-barreled musketoons of the Wild Geese. The answering fire was irregular and vaguely flatulent in quality. Evidently, some of the Spaniards here were still armed with venerable arquebuses.

Hugh smiled and nodded vigorously at O'Cahan, who drew a deep breath and sank back down into the dark water. O'Donnell started counting heads, listening to the first concerned mutters of the Spanish anchor watch less than six feet overhead, and heard their feet moving toward the opposite, port side of the ship, closer to the sounds of combat. *So far, so good...*

✧　　　✧　　　✧

O'Rourke cocked back the hammer on the third of the five chambers in his pepperbox, drew down on the charging Spanish sergeant, cheated a little low, and kept the cutlass in his left hand ready on his shoulder. At about three paces, he squeezed the trigger.

Aodh O'Rourke was a good shot to begin with, and the excellent Brussels-based workmanship of the pepperboxes made them quite reliable and consistent in their performance. Add to that his long experience in combat and the incredible proximity, and the outcome was hardly surprising. One of the two double-shotted iron balls punched through the bottom rim of the Spaniard's breastplate, the other disappeared through the jerkin that began at the top of his groin.

The man stumbled and almost fell, his blood already running down his legs in black rivulets: the color of nighttime death, when you could see it at all. But Spanish regulars were tough soldiers and even their softest sergeants were still the consistency of cured leather, both inside and out. Teeth shining in a grimace against the pain of raising his rapier and straightening up, the veteran tried finishing his charge.

But O'Rourke knew a dead man walking when he saw one. He gauged the vastly decreased reflexes and flexibility of his armor-sluggish opponent and brought the cutlass off his shoulder in a chop aimed at the head of the stricken Spaniard. Who parried through his grimace—

—But missed the subtle hints that the simple diagonal cut was merely a feint. O'Rourke waited until his opponent had committed to the parry, then shifted the body-crossing trajectory of his blade into more of a downward, outside sweep. The rapier made a light, ringing contact with the cutlass just before a twist of O'Rourke's wrist jinked it over into the side of the Spaniard's right knee.

The veteran fell one way, his rapier the other. With his right leg already half-covered by a glistening tide of blackness, the sergeant spat a defiant curse at O'Rourke. O'Rourke had no time for the foolishness of trading insults on a battlefield, and was equally unwilling to spend a bullet to end either the man's invective or his life. He ran on, shouting for his men to light the fuses and get to the harbor channel. *Besides, it's not as if that old soldier is going to be able to achieve anything while he's busy bleeding to death.*

The munitions warehouse's dedicated patrol had fallen to the pistols and musketoons of the Wild Geese. But in actuality, the attack was the easy part of the mission. It was the escape that worried O'Rourke. Once they were done with the warehouses, they had to run to the inner harbor, skirting the town. They didn't have the time to stop, reload, and conduct a moving gun-duel with randomly appearing Spaniards. But that also meant that those randomly appearing Spaniards would be more likely to kill his men.

As if to underscore the dangerous tendency to expend too many of the charges already loaded in their weapons, one of O'Mara's men, Edmund Butler, used a second round from his pistol to kill the last and badly wounded guard covering the door to the warehouse. "Mind your ready ammunition, Butler," O'Rourke grunted, "There was but one sword-stroke between that man and his Maker. Loftus, Ealam, get those doors open. O'Hagan, you have the charge ready?"

As the doors to the munitions warehouse creaked open, O'Hagan replied, "Ready. De Burgo, get up here with that oil. And—watch out! To yer left!"

De Burgo fumbled the oil, reaching for his pistol. The bag fell, ruptured, and sent a thick petroleum reek up around them.

O'Rourke cursed. "Peter's Holy nut sack, O'Hagan, can't you tell a stray cat from a Spanish soldier? Damn it, a waste of oil and a waste of time, both." He scanned the frenetically running figures of his command, most routing the remaining Spaniards beyond the northern limit of the warehouses. "Sheridan?"

The soldier in question, who had reached the next warehouse, turned round, then ducked as a musket ball clipped the building's corner. "Yes, Sergeant?"

"Get over here with your oil. We need it for this warehouse."

"Yes, sir." He reported as he came. "Ensign O'Mara's having a problem, sir. Both of his sappers' fuses are ruined."

"Ruined?"

"Aye, sir. Probably mud. Soaked through the bags when we were lying in the jungle."

Well isn't that just feckin' perfect. "Right. Butler, make yourself useful for a change. Run to O'Mara, tell him that in place of the fuses, he's to use a trail of oil, touched by a trail of powder."

"But, Sergeant, that could—"

"O'Mara's putting flame to food and wine, not powder. His men will get away in time. Now, no more thinking, Butler: ye're not very good at it. Get on with you."

Butler shrugged, trotted out the door—and went down with a bullet through the gut. Sheridan saw the lagging Spaniard who'd fired the shot, popped a round after the retreating silhouette, missed.

O'Rourke bellowed. "No time for that, Sheridan. Your job is in here. Spread your oil. De Burgo, you take Butler's message to O'Mara. And you'd best do it on the double-quick or you'll be a pin cushion for Spanish rapiers."

O'Hagan sidled up to his sergeant. "What about Butler, though? Do we carry him? 'Cause it's sure he can't walk."

O'Rourke hated what he said—and would have to do—next, more than any other part of soldiering. "It's sure he won't *live*, O'Hagan, not with that wound. Get about planting your charge. I'll see to poor Butler."

Hugh waited for the first of the warehouse explosions before signaling Purcell and then O'Bannon to board the *patache*. Purcell climbed up toward the stern along the aft-anchor line with a steadying hold on the tiller-chains, and O'Bannon slid up over the chainplates and laid hold of the dead-eyes at the amidships ratlines. The rest of the men stayed below the curve of the hull, waiting for their team leaders to affix and toss netting over the side, by which they would ostensibly swarm aboard the deck of the Spanish ship.

A hoarse curse overhead drew O'Donnell's attention to Purcell. The infallible and silent climber was twisting his left hand around vigorously, as if it had been suddenly caught in a trap. Which wasn't far off from what had happened. A slight shift of the rudder had tightened the chain, snagging his left index finger. With another curse, the *tercio*'s best climber toppled and fell into the water with a noisy splash.

O'Bannon's silhouette froze. O'Donnell waved up toward the deck, hoping that the scout's extraordinary eyes could make out the gesture. Evidently they did, because O'Bannon was up and over the gunwale in a blink, snagging the net on one of the cleats as he went.

Rapid footfalls padded on the low quarterdeck overhead—right as Purcell came up gasping. O'Donnell ripped open his oilskin pouch and pulled out Michael McCarthy's .45 just as two muskets fired down into the water and cries of alarm came from the ship's stern. Purcell, hit, grunted, twisted, and rolled to one side.

Hugh tugged himself to the aft end of the rudder with one quick jerk of his left arm; he pinned himself against it as he raised the up-time pistol and snapped off its safey. He brought its sights in line with the stern and the two Spanish guards he saw there, one of whom was reloading, the other of whom had drawn a hanger and was calling for help. Remembering to pause between shots long enough for the barrel to drift down toward his target again, O'Donnell started firing.

Disobeying every rule he'd ever heard or been schooled in regarding such weapons, Hugh did not even bother to count the rounds. He had learned that in a crisis, the initiative lost by striving for perfect execution—even if that only took one second—was often the difference between defeat and victory. In this case, precise shooting and conserving ammunition were simply not priorities. Clearing the stern and terrifying the Spanish with a startling volume of fire were.

And his split-second decision seemed sound. His first two shots missed, but the third punched a red hole straight through the musketeer's sternum. The other Spaniard, who'd been facing the other way, spun around just in time to be missed twice and hit once. He staggered back out of sight. And Hugh realized that he'd been counting his shots, after all. Having started with one round already in the chamber, that left him two more before he was dry.

Letting the weapon hang on its lanyard, he reached down toward the faces clustered around the stern. "Bill Kelly, where's that hand-spike your were carrying? Good. O'Bregan, fetch that coir netting out of the drink and be ready to throw it up to me. The rest of you, weapons in hand."

O'Donnell, driving the hand spike into the pintle-and-gudgeon joint halfway up the rudder, pulled himself halfway to the taff-rail. He clutched at the top of the stern-window shutters for fingertip-purchase while he freed the handspike and swung it over to dig into the edge of the transom, just seven feet over the water-line. From there he'd have to pull himself toward the deck, since jumping wouldn't be much help: one foot was dangling in midair and the other was precariously balanced upon the rudder. If a new bunch of Spanish found him now—

A sudden eruption of gunfire from amidships signaled that the remainder of the *patache*'s anchor watch had discovered O'Bannon's boarding party. But only one pepperbox revolver was speaking in response to what sounded like several Spanish pistols. Cries and readied steel rang along the length of the ship and more shouts were audible beneath the weather deck. The rest of the crew was starting to react and would be coming topside.

Hugh paused, long enough for a half-second of precaution to push through his impulse to act immediately. "Grenades!" he hissed down below. "Who's got 'em out?"

Three men answered tentatively. "But no way to light the fuses, m'lord."

"Pepperboxes?"

Half a dozen replied, even more tentatively. "Can't tell if they're too wet, Colonel," said one. "Looks like the bags leaked."

"Never mind that. Odds are one works. One man fires a gun, the next man holds the fuse of his grenade against the nipple vent. If you get it lit, lob it over the taffrail. Now, damn it!"

Two pepperbox hammers fell before the third one fired, but the grenade's fuse fizzed and died. And now Spanish voices were coming up on deck, and a few were growing louder behind the shuttered stern windows only three feet away from Hugh's midriff.

Another dry snap of a pistol's hammer, then another full discharge, followed immediately by the lively hiss of a lit fuse. The grenade arced past Hugh's head toward the deck, just as he heard the weather braces getting yanked out from behind the shutters of the stern windows. He muttered to the men beneath him in Gaelic, "The two of you with working pistols: aim at the windows. Sweep 'em clean."

The windows opened at the same moment that another grenade sputtered into life, and the one that had been lobbed on the deck went off. The Spanish musketeers who appeared in the stern windows—two black muzzles running out—fell back under a fusillade of fire from not just two, but three of the pepperbox pistols. A moan up on the quarterdeck suggested that the first grenade had at least wounded someone.

Hugh rapped out new orders. "Half of you, in the stern windows and hit them along the lower deck." The second grenade went off. "O'Bregan toss me the netting. Follow with the rest as soon as I've secured it."

Without pausing to consider the possibilities or consequences of failure, O'Donnell simultaneously pushed and pulled himself toward the *patache*'s low-slung quarterdeck, scrabbled madly for a handhold, almost fell, but got three fingers over the taffrail. That gave him enough leverage to get his second hand on it as well. Fear and natural strength helped him heave his whole body up and over it in a single powerful yank. Hitting the quarterdeck at an angle, he rolled toward one of the flag lockers; he saw a ferocious melee amidships and saw heads turning in his direction.

He leaped up, looped the netting twice about the handspike, and snagged its sharp hook around one of the taffrail's balusters. As he tossed the netting out over the transom so it spread down to his waiting men, Hugh caught up the .45 in his other hand, and turned.

Two sword-armed Spaniards were already pounding up the four shallow stairs that separated the main deck from the quarterdeck. But behind them, another one was raising a matchlock pistol.

Hugh drew a careful bead on the pistoleer, let the up-time barrel drop a little, and squeezed the trigger slowly. The .45's sharp roar stopped the two approaching swordsmen for a moment, their eyes wide. The pistoleer grabbed his left thigh with one hand, but fired his matchlock with the other. The resulting stagger spoiled whatever reasonable aim he might have achieved; the ball whined off into the dark, well over Hugh's head.

The two Spanish swordsmen resumed their charge. Hugh gave ground, drawing—and hating—the short cutlass, and hearing the first of his men's hands scrabbling at the taffrail.

Rather than fire immediately, Hugh waited for the two Spaniards to finish closing. He noted the quick exchange of glances that meant they would try to time their blows to be simultaneous, eliminating any reasonable chance for him to parry both. But that wasn't what Hugh had in mind. As they lunged forward, weapons back to strike, Hugh swung the cutlass in his left hand to deflect the blow of the smaller of the two at the same moment that he raised the .45 and fired its last round straight into the chest of the much larger man at a range of three feet. Not because he was more fearful of the larger man—they were often the less nimble, and so, less dangerous, swordsmen—but because he was a considerably bigger target. And Hugh dared not miss, not now.

He didn't. Although the bullet was low and off center to the right, the large man gasped, his overhand slice becoming a wavering and easily dodged swat. The fellow on the left, who was clearly the better swordsman, feinted rather than striking directly. But Hugh's long professional training, even with so cumbersome and inelegant a tool as a cutlass, allowed him to roll his wrist in a tight, defensive *moulinet* and almost trap the real blow between his sword's blade and abbreviated top quillon.

The Spaniard cursed, yanked his weapon back, then started and stared over Hugh's shoulder. A pepperbox roared once alongside O'Donnell's left ear. Three wide red holes, made by .30 caliber lead balls, appeared just below the swordsman's right clavicle. He staggered back and immediately disappeared under a rush of torsos and cutlass-wielding arms: the first wave of Wild Geese had arrived over the taffrail. Hugh drew in a deep breath. *Time to spend a second assessing the situation.*

The fight amidships was a desperate brawl of flashing blades but only occasional gun discharges. Which meant that more of the oilskin bags had leaked, ruining the powder of the pepperbox revolvers that normally gave his men a decisive edge in firepower. Even so, those few that still functioned were doing so decisively. The Wild Geese just arrived from the Lowlands had long trained for this kind of contingency and used the five chambers of each heavy unipiece cylinder sparingly. No fusillades, therefore, but when one of their own number was flanked or threatened by multiple opponents, the triple-charged weapons intervened, eliminating an enemy and thereby allowing the superior swordsmanship of the Irish mercenaries to carry the day. Hugh could see that the Spanish had already become so fearful of the weapons that they held back from assaulting too directly, and thus were not gaining the ground that their superior numbers should have made possible.

But that would not last for long. And judging from the deck-muted discharges and grenade blasts underfoot, the Spanish would soon be pouring up on the weather deck with increasing speed, running from the Wild Geese who'd entered by way of the stern windows. And those growing numbers were already exacting a toll, despite the intercession of the occasional pepperbox. At least half a dozen of the Wild Geese who'd boarded behind O'Bannon were down, and many of those still fighting were doing so with gashed arms, legs, or freshly missing fingers. The Spanish had to be broken, and there was only one sure way to do it.

Hugh gave orders to his boarders as he ejected the spent magazine from the Colt and pulled a fresh one out of the oilskin bag. "Those with working pistols, you've five seconds to load fresh cylinders. The rest: ready grenades with short fuses, to throw at my signal. Or, if you've only a cutlass, charge as soon as we start forward."

Two more of the Wild Geese in the amidships melee staggered and fell, one clutching the Spanish rapier that was still lodged in his chest.

"Ready, men," Hugh cried. "Follow me!"

Hugh sped down the four stairs just as several of the Spaniards on the main deck saw him and made to charge. But they drew up sharply as he shouted. "Now, at the walk—fire!"

Two, and then a third, pepperbox started blasting away, each discharge sending three of the lead balls into the densely packed Spaniards. Several slumped over, others clutched suddenly bleeding limbs. Half a dozen Wild Geese with nothing but cutlasses charged past Hugh and headlong into the flank of the Spanish, who turned to meet them.

But Hugh kept walking forward, .45 raised level with his eye, watching the Spanish, picking out the leaders. At seven paces, and seeing the onslaught against O'Bannon's Wild Geese faltering as the Spanish began shifting to deal with the new threat from the quarterdeck, he brought up his second hand to stabilize the gun. He stopped, chose a tightly grouped cluster of likely targets, and started squeezing off rounds from the up-time weapon with the steadiness and finality of a metronome.

The mass of Spaniards recoiled from the sharp, percussive roars of the .45 and from the falling bodies that were closest to its chosen field of fire. And then three at the back of their ranks broke for the bow at a run.

That was what Hugh had been watching, and waiting, for. "Grenades! Into the crowd at the portside gunwale!"

As Hugh reloaded, and the Spanish roiled in a confusion of men trying to flee, men trying to fight, and men trying to choose between those options, two grenades arced into the largely undecided rear ranks of those lately come sailors who had yet to add their numbers to the fight against O'Bannon's boarders. Several leaped away from the sparking bombs, two diving over the gunwale itself. The first went off at the same moment that Hugh brought up the reloaded .45 and fired through the magazine in one long rush, straight into the milling crowd.

As often happens in battle, the Spanish broke all at once, the way deer do when a hunter approaches too closely. Without any apparent coordination other than an instinctual sense of the disintegrating morale of their fellow creatures, they scattered wildly. Some went over the gunwales, while others ran to the bow and swung down the lines in the water. Two tried escaping below decks along the forward companionway, only to be bowled over by a panicked group streaming upward, who, to a man, joined the rout over the side and into the water.

As the press of the melee broke, it also revealed many of the half-naked Wild Geese who lay dead or writhing on the deck of the *patache*. Hugh forced himself to look beyond them to O'Bannon, and shout, "No time for the wounded, now. We need to get the signal rockets and the whistles. Until those Dutchmen tow us from under the Spanish guns, we're none of us sure of living out the hour."

O'Rourke ducked as a Spaniard swayed around the corner of the harbormaster's ramshackle cottage and fired. The ball bit into the dirt five feet ahead of him. *Thank God that bastard is drunk, and he won't reload in time, so no need to stop and cut him down.*

Half-reminding himself, he shouted to his much-reduced unit, "Sprint for the harbor, lads. Look for the lines just in the water at the foot of the wharf. Bag your guns when you've shot 'em dry. We're running, not fighting, now!"

At that moment, the rolling, intermittent explosions from the warehouses behind them were almost drowned out by a sharp and sustained sputter of gunfire from the middle of the inner harbor. And through the many hoarse discharges of down-time weapons, Aodh O'Rourke heard the distinct, reverberant reports of Hugh's .45 automatic.

He'd been prepared to shout an alert to his men, but they didn't need it. As if it had been a supper-bell rung for hungry hounds, the surviving Wild Geese fixed on the sound of that gunfire and sprinted toward it, their flagging endurance suddenly refreshed, their trajectories homing on the same relative compass point. *Good—*

—or maybe not so good, O'Rourke amended. Passing within ten yards of the eastern end of the low, rude rampart of Puerto Cabello's harbor battery, he could hear urgent shouts in Spanish. And they were loud enough to be easily understandable:

"The *patache* is under attack, too? Is it a diversion?"

"Fool: if it was a diversion, she would have been attacked before the warehouses, not after."

And a third voice: "So they mean to escape on her?"

"Madness. There cannot be enough of them to take her and sail her."

"Not take her? Dolt, those aren't ordinary guns. Hear them? Again?" Hugh's .45 now emitted a slow, sustained pulse of thunder.

"What is it?"

"I don't know. Maybe a new gun made by up-timers or their allies."

"Up-timers? Here? But—"

"Idiot. We must act, not debate. Bring the guns to bear on the *patache*! Quickly!"

"The *patache*? But she is our own—!"

"The *patache* is lost," confirmed an older, calmer voice. As if to prove that assertion, the .45 tore through the other sounds of combat with a fast staccato flurry, counterpointed by the dull crump of black-powder grenades. "Pass the word to the barracks: the raiders are running. Cease hunting them in the streets. Man the battery, instead. Stand to guns one and two. Others will be brought to bear as new crews arrive. Hurry."

"Yes, Lieutenant."

Well, that ties it. Seems I'll be disobeying my own orders to make for the water. But I could do with a little company. O'Rourke scanned the closest silhouettes of his fleeing men. "Hsst! Hsssssst! O'Hagan, De Burgo!"

"Sergeant?"

"Aye?"

"To me. Here, in the shadow of this shed. You've cylinders left for your pistols, yeh?"

A moment of silence. Then nods, and De Burgo's slow bass, "But we're to be running, heading for—"

"Not us three. Not yet. Fresh cylinders, lads. Either of you have grenades?"

Both nodded. "Never had the need or chance to use 'em," appended O'Hagan.

"That's because it was possible we might need them for what we're going to do now."

"Which is?"

"We're going to sow some grapes of wrath in behind that open battery to the west of us. Each of you light a slow match and follow me."

Hugh heard as much as saw the approach of the Dutch pinnace that had been fitted with a down-time steam engine. The demi-culverins at the mouth of the channel spotted her as well. Two spoke, put plumes in the water, almost fifty yards behind her. Either they were very poor gunners, or, more likely, not used to shooting at that fast a target so close to shore. Unburdened except for her operators and the prize-crew for the *patache*, the pinnace was making at least six knots.

Hugh shouted toward O'Bregan in the bows. "Found an axe?"

"No, m'lord. This ship is a pigsty. Nothing's placed proper. We're almost through the anchor line with the saw, though."

"Keep at it. O'Bannon?"

"Sir?"

"Losses?"

"Nine dead. Three more will be by dawn. Half a dozen wounded."

Hugh's stomach sank. That was half of the men who'd boarded. He kept to the tasks at hand. "Set the rest to get the nets into the water over the port quarter. That's where O'Rourke's men will be coming in along the lines that O'Hagan and Murrow swam over to the opposite shore."

"Right away, m'lord."

Hugh nodded, looked around, saw his men at their tasks, wanted to busy himself alongside them, but stayed that impulse. A commander's job was to stay alert, to watch for the next threat or task, not to become embroiled in the ones already being handled. He stared out toward the low ramparts of the inner harbor's battery, the walls of which screened most of Puerto Cabello from view. No sign of O'Rourke's men yet, of their own bamboo breathing tubes bobbing across the hundred and twenty yards of glass-smooth bay water between the *patache* and the guns that could sink her. There were lights, and now drums and coronets, on the Spanish ships deeper in the harbor, but that was of no consequence. They were too far off to see what was happening, and so could not be sure of a course of action. They would learn too late, and still be too far off, to respond.

But the battery: even on a mostly lightless night, they would have seen and heard the savage gunfight on the *patache*. And when it ended without a reassuring flurry of coronets and responses to the fort's many hails, they would know the outcome of that fight as surely as had they been standing on the deck themselves: the *patache* was now an enemy vessel.

Their only hesitation might be to avoid sinking her where she sat astride the inner mouth of the channel. But once they saw, and heard, the approaching steam pinnace above the flash, glare, and roaring of the sabotaged warehouses, it was a certainty they'd respond.

And perhaps they were doing so already. There was a blast near the ramparts. But as the sound died away, and shouting rose up from the dim outline of the battery's covering walls, Hugh realized that it hadn't been the roar of a cannon, or even a range-finding musket shot. It had been a black powder grenade.

Which was to say, it was O'Rourke.

O'Hagan finally reached the ready powder for the middle gun of the battery, grenade fussing fulminatively in his left hand as he cleared a path with the pepperbox in his right. One of the gunners sheltering behind the next cannon popped up and fired a miquelet-lock pistol at him. O'Rourke snapped up his pepperbox, but was too late. The man had already ducked back down.

O'Hagan had stumbled, but, limping, finished his rush up the stairs. He pried the loose cover off a readied powder keg, dumped the grenade in and then prepared to jump down from the battery platform to the ground. And, as O'Rourke had expected, the same gunner at the neighboring gun popped up again, furnished with a fresh pistol. O'Rourke fired twice; the second round hit the man, who disappeared with a yelp. Not dead, but he and any proximal friends were now probably disinclined from trying to fight back anytime soon. And when the seven-second fuse on O'Hagan's grenade had burned down, thoughts of counterattack would almost surely be swept away by a panicked impulse toward self-preservation.

O'Rourke counted through two of the seconds, jerked his head at the gimping O'Hagan, and shouted toward De Burgo, "Help him! Get to the water!" O'Rourke counted another two seconds, then ducked and ran himself, jumping over and around the half-dozen bodies that marked the path by which they'd entered the rear of the battery.

It hadn't been that hard to do, actually. With the noise of the warehouses exploding, the panicked shouting, and the Spanish presumption that the raiders were all in flight, O'Rourke and his two troopers hadn't encountered any guards until they were down in the marshalling area of the battery itself. There'd been powder enough there, too, but most of it was still in tightly sealed barrels that they wouldn't be able to get open in time, not before the gun crews and soldiers would see what they were up to and swarm them. By sheer numbers, if nothing else.

So instead, O'Rourke and his men blended into the chaos as best they could, responding to a few casual inquiries in perfect Spanish as they approached the stairs to the gun platform. There, in the lantern light, their identities became suspect and the shooting had started.

But it had not been random gunplay. Even De Burgo understood, without having to be reminded, that their targets were the soldiers guarding the battery, not the gunners. So when the pepperboxes started snapping quickly, the gun wielding, morion-helmeted Spaniards were the first to go down, not even understanding who was attacking them. The gunners fled behind their pieces. O'Rourke and De Burgo kept their heads down while O'Hagan charged up the stairs to one of the gun's ready powder supply, lighting his long-fused grenade...

...Which went off as O'Rourke cleared the waist-high covering wall at the east end of the battery. "Down!" he shouted, and saw De Burgo carrying O'Hagan to the ground with him.

An eyeblink after the grenade, the powder went off with a roar and a flash. Pieces of wood, mortar, stone, maybe metal struck the other side of the screening wall and went hissing over it. Then another blast, and another—

Panicked screams of women and children and no small number of men began rising up from the town itself. O'Rourke gauged the distance to the water: twenty yards, maybe twenty-five. If any Spanish happened by while they tried to find the lines...

"De Burgo, run down and find the lines. I'll cover you. Signal when you've found 'em. I'll bring O'Hagan and we'll go swimming. Well, towing."

O'Hagan muttered. "Feck, O'Rourke, I'm no cripple. I can—"

"You can be shutting up now, you eejit. You'll get us all killed, hobbling down to the beach on your own like a creaky old gaffer. De Burgo, what are you waiting for? Dawn?"

De Burgo's large dark mass rolled up off the sand flats and loped down toward the water. O'Rourke moved toward O'Hagan at the crouch, turned, kept an eye on the town, and suppressed a sigh. He had one round left in the cylinder. *Better than nothing,* he temporized. *But not by much.*

A Spanish soldier appeared around the far end of the battery, shaken, shouting to locate survivors, ducking when still more powder went off, blowing a sheet of angry white-yellow flame high into the night sky.

Damn it, he'll see me in this light, thought O'Rourke, who doubted he'd make the shot at this range. Another ten paces, though—

"Wait here," he ordered O'Hagan in English, and scrambled up, running toward the soldier, yelling, "Help me! Help me!" in Spanish.

The Spaniard had apparently just noticed O'Rourke peripherally, but approached so openly, and with explosions still roaring behind him and just overhead, the man ducked, his weapon forgotten in his hands. He ran toward the Irishman. "What? What help do you need?" he shouted back.

You just gave it to me by running closer, O'Rourke thought with a twinge of regret. He raised the pepperbox and fired.

The Spaniard stopped as if stunned, then staggered as he saw fire-reflecting blood begin leaking out of the hole in the front of his buff coat. With a groan he sagged down to his knees, eyes pinching tight against a sudden wave of pain.

O'Rourke turned, ran back to O'Hagan, and saw as he did so that De Burgo had found the weighted lines that O'Cahan and Murrow had put here and by which the rest of his raiders were no doubt making their way to the *patache*. O'Hagan hobbled up. The sand covering his right thigh was dark and slick with blood. "Let's get you home, you clumsy oaf," O'Rourke muttered as, shouldering up O'Hagan on the right side, he led them down to the edge of the inner harbor.

De Burgo had already stripped out of his clothes and had his breathing tube out. "Need a hand?" he cried out in English.

O'Rourke shook his head angrily. *A fool for crying out, a double fool for doing it in a foreign tongue—*

O'Rourke never heard the shots: they were drowned out by a

new set of roars from the battery as more ready powder went up. One Spanish ball cut off the lobe of O'Hagan's left ear, two more drilled into the water beside him. Others whined overhead and one struck De Burgo in the shoulder. The big man cursed and staggered before a defiant instinct brought him back upright—and into the path of two more balls that caught him in the midsection.

As the already-dead Irishman sank down into the water, O'Rourke found the line and got O'Hagan's hands on it. As he kicked his shoes off, he felt a sensation like a wide, hot poker go through the large expanse of stocky muscle at the back of his left thigh. *Damn it,* O'Rourke thought, losing hold of his breathing tube as he stumbled. The length of bamboo disappeared into the fire-reflecting water. *Well, it's up and down to breathe for me, or I'm musket-fodder for sure.*

O'Hagan stared at him around his own breathing tube, frowning at the dark stain in the water around O'Rourke's right leg.

"Get going, O'Hagan. You're blocking the line."

O'Hagan shrugged and sank under the water until only two inches of his breathing tube remained, moving slowly but steadily out toward the inner mouth of the channel and the *patache* that sat astride it.

O'Rourke towed himself a yard, drew in a deep breath, dove down sideways and kept pulling himself along the lightly weighted line, hand over hand.

There was a muted bacon-frying sound around him, and something hot bumped off his abdomen: a musket ball, flattened and slowed by the three feet of water under which O'Rourke was sheltered.

Well, lucky me. And all I have to do is stay *lucky all the way to the* patache.

A pity that I've never been a lucky man.

Hugh watched as the Dutch sailors swarmed over the port bow and O'Bregan and Kelly tossed the severed anchor cable to the pinnace's crew. Along with mooring hawsers and lines from the bowsprit, it would serve as a makeshift tow-cable at least until they got out of the channel and away from the Spanish guns. There, a proper towing rig could be improvised on the move. No one was sanguine about stopping to square away the pinnace as a proper tug, not while within reach of possible Spanish pursuers.

O'Cahan, still dripping from helping O'Rourke's wounded raiders out of the water, passed by. Hugh hailed him. "How many made it back?"

"A baker's dozen, m'lord, including that Calabar fellow. Half are wounded."

"O'Rourke?"

O'Cahan shook his head. "No sign of him. Last seen scooting over to make the mischief we saw in the battery. But there's hope yet, sir."

O'Donnell smiled sadly. "There's always hope, with O'Rourke. We might find him rowing out to us on a raft of palm trees in a day or so." He said it more for O'Cahan's benefit than to assert any serious hope of O'Rourke's survival.

But O'Cahan must have detected his commander's suppressed tone of grief. "I'm not just blathering fairy-wishes, m'lord. We've still got weight on one of the lines to the far shore. Probably the weight of one or two men. Hard to tell. But it could be O'Rourke, that stubborn tinker's mule."

Hugh nodded, trying not to get overly hopeful. "It just might be."

O'Cahan sucked breath in meditatively. "My only worry, Colonel, is in waiting for them. We shouldn't spend any longer here than we have to."

"I agree. Get two men and start reeling in the line. If they're not on board by the time the Dutchmen are ready to move"—which, would not be long, judging from their competent progress rigging the tow-lines and raising the *patache*'s fore-and-aft mainsail—"then secure it to the pinnace."

O'Cahan gaped then smiled. "We *tow* them out, Colonel?"

"Why not?" O'Donnell smiled back. "I think we can be certain that they'll be hanging on for dear life. Literally."

"Aye, sir. I'll pass the words and gather the men to start reeling them in. Any other orders?"

Hugh nodded. "One, Mr. O'Cahan. Detail two men to take our dead below deck. The Spanish, too."

O'Cahan seemed startled. "As you say, sir. But, as regards the Spanish, I'm sure the fish are hungry tonight, sir."

O'Donnell stared at O'Cahan. "They always are, Daniel. But they've been fed enough this night." Hugh glanced over the deck littered with the bodies of his men, envisioned the others they'd left behind. "More than enough."

Chapter 34

Oranjestad, St. Eustatia

Anne Cathrine wiped her hands on her apron and stared distractedly as a larger-than-necessary party of Dutch soldiers-become-workmen wheeled half a dozen large boxes out of the fort's landward sally port. They were all stamped in unusually regular block letters and she had to think hard for several seconds in order to decipher the up-time legends: *primary transmitter components; secondary transmitter components; transformers; wiring, non-antenna.* The boxes had been among the first unloaded from the ships of Reconnaissance Flotilla X-Ray, and had been handled with more care than a cargo of silk, fine crystal and irreplaceable gems.

Because, according to Eddie, their contents were every bit as valuable and irreplaceable. A radio, using spokelike lines of transceiving wires elevated on The Quill's volcanic northeast slopes, would be capable of reaching Vlissingen in the United Provinces. The communications would not work routinely, and not enable them to have what Eddie called "voice-grade exchange." But even if a single, two-hundred word message took three days of constant, repetitive signaling or listening to send or compile, it hardly mattered. The fastest other means of exchanging information was by swift ship, and even the swiftest could rarely make an Atlantic crossing in as little as forty-five days. Sixty was more typical. With this powerful new radio, strategic updates could be exchanged promptly, and calls for assistance could reach their allies within the same week, rather than (hopefully) the same season.

Anne Cathrine realized that the soldier-workmen were loitering around their boxes. Unusual behavior, since she had observed that most of the Dutch preferred to finish work quickly and efficiently once they started it. And then she realized that, quite slyly, they were all stealing looks at her.

She felt heat rise up in her face, accompanied by a wild mix of outrage, shame, and, worst of all, flattered vanity. At the same moment, a long hand came down upon her shoulder gently. Sophie Rantzau stood just behind her, staring at the men with unblinking gray eyes. After a moment, they gave up their pretense of lounging about and returned to their chores. The youngest, a fellow whose blond hair was almost white, actually flushed, bowed an apology, and set his shoulder to one of the crates with repentant vigor.

"Well," observed Sophie mildly, "at least one of them has some breeding. Or shame."

Anne Cathrine glanced at the young woman's face—Sophie was just two years her senior—and marveled at the gravity in it, the composure. She wondered if anything of mundane origin could ruffle that smooth brow, those chiseled features. And for the briefest moment, she felt envy. Not the petty, childish envy of a young woman craving the looks or possessions or popularity of another. Rather, her envy was one with her admiration for Sophie's apparently effortless transcendence beyond such trifles. At times, her demeanor reminded Anne Cathrine of the tales she'd heard in childhood of the Norns: tall, mystical fate-maidens who were woven in and out of the pagan mythology of the Scandinavian countries in the way that ligaments connected bones and tissue. They connected past and present, action and outcome, free choice and fate in ways that were both various and mysterious, always transmitting and influencing earthly and heavenly power, but never holding it themselves.

She realized that Sophie was looking at her, one eyebrow raised. "You are lost in thought frequently today, Anne Cathrine. Tell me, does the appearance of the radio equipment mean that you have had word of your husband? That he might be returning?"

Anne Cathrine turned back into the full shade of the tent in which Ambrósio Brandão first received the sick of the colony. "No, quite the opposite. He is remaining in the south. And again, he may not say why, or where." She clenched her apron so hard that her fingers became white.

Leonora, watching Brandão examine a young child with a fever, glanced over, her brow dipped in concern.

Sophie nodded gravely. "It would prey upon any woman's soul, since we know that secrecy and hazardous enterprises go hand in hand. But be calmed: your husband is with good men and loyal guards. His steamships are the finest in the world and may strike their foes with impunity."

Anne Cathrine frowned. "Yes, but it will not always be thus, for the war machines of one nation quickly become the war machines of all others."

"Truly spoken," Sophie agreed. "But leave that worry for the future that shall bring it. For now, the unique power of his ships means that there is *less* cause for worry."

It was a logical argument, and comforting in its way, but Anne Cathrine, much as she hated to admit it, was not a creature of logic first and foremost. She was a creature of passion. She was not concerned with reasons or rationalizations. She just wanted Eddie. She wanted him in her cabin, in her arms, in her bed, and in her, and in that order. And she wanted it—wanted it all—right now. "I think I should return to work," she muttered hoarsely, with a quick smile at Sophie, but without eye contact. She did not want her Norn-friend to look into her eyes and see her shallowness, her illogic, and the primal heat that old-wives' tales warned went along all too often with her red-gold hair.

Drawing alongside Brandão, she heard him finishing his examination of a young child no more than four years old, of mixed Amerind and African parentage. "The low fever and the location of the transient pains are consistent with both yellow fever and the dengue. Malaria or a systemic viral infection—influenza, I think you call it—is not out of the question, but unlikely. The location of her aches is overwhelmingly associated with the first two illnesses, and none of the secondary signs of malaria are present."

Anne Cathrine looked at the child's light brown back, patient and calm under Brandão's expert hands, and felt a terrible, gnawing compulsion to run soothing palms along it, to bring a moment's comfort, if nothing else.

Leonora, eyes alert and incisive, watched Brandão's fingers as they gently mixed calming touches with an almost unnoticeable palpation of the lymph nodes of the neck and armpits. "How long," she asked, "until we know which manner of disease is causing the symptoms?" In her sister's tone, Anne Cathrine could hear the intensity and discipline of a budding physician, but also found it oddly detached and disturbing.

Brandão shrugged. "A day, maybe two. Watch for the growth of a rash"—he let his hands tarry at two points on the girl's back—"here, and here, almost like measles. That is a discriminating symptom of dengue. In the meantime, this child must be kept quiet and resting. If this is a hemorrhagic fever, then we do not wish to tax the body, or cause a rise in what the up-timers call 'blood pressure.' This precaution is not decisively efficacious at reducing the possibilities of internal hemorrhage, but is the best alternative at our disposal. Also, this child is to be given—by which I mean, compelled to drink—a cup of water every hour. At the very least. Dehydration is a prime concern, regardless of which malady is at work, here."

From behind, Sophie's voice calmly pointed out, "One cup every hour is three times the adult ration, Doctor. Will Councilor Corselles allow it?"

"I expect so, but it hardly matters. If Corselles forbids it, I will appeal to van Walbeeck and he will approve it. From his time in the East Indies, and then Recife, he knows what an outbreak of a serious disease can do to a colony's morale. He will not take chances here. He will allow us to retain the child in quarantine and use what resources we need to effect a cure."

"Some of the landowners," said Sophie in a quiet, and almost dangerous tone, "voiced their opinion that the surest means to protect the colony is to place the child in an oubliette until she dies."

"Idiots," Brandão declared in a low mutter. "Unless this is influenza, which I very much doubt, they should be fearful of mosquitoes, not this child. That is how yellow fever, dengue, and malaria are spread. And in caring for the child, we may also watch the development of the symptoms to make a more certain diagnosis and provide care appropriately." He turned around to face Anne Cathrine and Sophie. "This is why I returned to the New World, you know."

Anne Cathrine nodded. "To treat the sick."

"Well, yes, that too," Brandão allowed. "But it is the education, the teaching, that I meant to do. The up-timer information and methods change everything, even without all the wonderful devices that they used in their scientific achievements. Surely, married to a man such as your husband is said to be, you must see this even more regularly than I."

Anne Cathrine found it hard to think about Eddie without getting distracted by sensations that were decidedly not logical or learned in nature. "I am uncertain what you mean, Doctor. Perhaps you would explain further?"

"Well," smiled Brandão, "I suppose it *is* different in your husband's areas of expertise, where his knowledge is made manifest through engineers. In the case of medicine, the phenomenon is subtler, albeit no less profound. Indeed, I hazard to say that it is *more* profound, particularly when it comes to the identification, management, and treatment of epidemics.

"Consider the case of this child, and how the library at Grantville has revolutionized how we may approach her illness. Ten years ago, when faced with such maladies in the Pernambuco, we had Dutch physicians, Portuguese physicians, *murranos* like myself, and persons with lesser medical experience whose journeys took them through Recife. Each one of us spoke Latin, but yet, we had no common compendium of epidemiology. And we simply accepted that state of affairs as inevitable. We did not see that we were milling about our own tower of Babel, each of us having different names for the same disease. And just as often, we were unable to agree on distinctions between diseases. For instance, some persons among us insisted that all tropical hemorrhagic fevers were simply different expressions of the same underlying disease. Most held that diseases such as cholera were spread by miasmas operating at the will of God, while a few of us held with Italian physicians that the means of contagion were natural and not simply spread by airs polluted by rotting matter."

He shook his head. "Then, Lady Anne Cathrine, your husband's town appears. There, not only in learned texts in its library, but in the 'home health' pamphlets possessed by even the least educated families, our theories were shamed, shown to be a mixture of bad guesswork and superstition. And the impact upon us down-time physicians was not restricted to such concepts as germ theory and variable vectors of infection, but also by the sheer uniformity of the observations, of the nomenclatures, of the methodologies. It was no longer necessary to guess what caused a disease. It was an established fact, often illustrated by pictures taken through these extraordinary devices you call microscopes. It was no longer necessary to strive across barriers of different language and experience to determine if, in fact, we were speaking about the same diseases. Now all the diseases had names in Latin arising from a single classification scheme applied to their causal microorganisms, and all of which were described according to a proven range of diagnostic and symptomatic variables. In short, physicians were suddenly able to speak a common tongue, wherever they might be, whatever their experience had shown them."

He rubbed the child's back as might a loving grandfather. "And so I knew I had to come back to the New World, where we have brought so many of our diseases. And which has so many diseases that are completely unknown to us. It was incumbent upon me to share the particular features of the many maladies, and also the standardized means of identifying them, of discerning and conducting treatment, of assessing and thereby preventing further spread."

He leaned back and patted the child gently between her shoulder blades. The four-year-old rolled over; her large brown eyes scanned all of them gravely, possibly apprehensively. *Poor child,* Anna realized, *she's probably never been this close to this many white people this long without being ordered about, or, quite possibly, beaten.* Anne Cathrine had noticed that, despite their wonderfully civilized and learned accomplishments in most other areas, many of the Dutch landowners showed a marked disregard for the welfare of the poor creatures whom they compelled to work their upstart cane plantations. "Doctor Brandão, this child, is she a slave?"

"Yes, she is. One of the few who came with us from Recife."

Leonora's careful eyes rolled round to study Brandão. "But we have been told that there is no slavery permitted on this island."

Brandão smiled. "I have observed that, here on St. Eustatia, different persons give different answers when asked about the existence or absence of manumission. The most precise description is, I believe, that there is no *new* slavery permitted. Mostly."

"That is not a very precise definition, Doctor," Sophie observed dryly.

"No," sighed Brandão, "but it is the only one that fits our current situation."

"I was under the impression," Anne Cathrine remarked impatiently, "that Admiral Tromp and Jan van Walbeeck both disapprove of slavery."

"They do."

"Then this is a very strange way of demonstrating their disapproval."

Brandão shook his head. "Despite all the soldiers here, this is not simply an armed camp. There was a civilian authority in Oranjestad before we arrived, just as we brought one with us from Recife. And the question of who holds the greatest power is, often, less than clear."

"So the Dutch colonists have resisted Admiral Tromp's wishes in this matter?" Leonora asked slowly.

"That would be overstating the case in several particulars," Brandão explained through a sigh. "First, not all the colonists support slaveholding. That sentiment predominates only among the landowners. Second, they are not so much resisting the dictates of Tromp and van Walbeeck as they are finding ways to subvert or avoid them.

"Before leaving from Recife, Maarten Tromp unsuccessfully attempted to leave the slaves in that colony behind. But many feared life under Portuguese taskmasters, and in the case of many *mamelucos*, their actual status was ambiguous. Some were bondsmen, some were slaves, and some fell in between: persons whose bond-price had grown so many times greater over successive generations that there was no hope of ever buying their way out of servitude."

"So slaves in everything but name," Sophie observed. Anne Cathrine started at her tone. Although it conveyed anger, it had gone from cool to cold.

Brandão helped the little girl to sit up. Anne Cathrine crouched down, ladled a cup of water out of the covered drinking pail, and poured it into a cup made of a coconut shell. The Jewish doctor nodded his thanks, passed it to the girl, and sighed as he continued his story. "Upon arriving here, the problem became even more complicated. The local workforce was predominantly African slaves, many brought over immediately after the first settlement, some purchased from the English and French on St. Christopher's. And the cash crop was tobacco. So when Tromp arrived he had many battles to fight. He was arriving with a military and refugee group almost ten times the size of the original colony, was making the island a more noticeable and urgent target for the Spanish, and needed to compel the local landowners to change their crop from the tobacco they no longer had a way to sell to the cane sugar that was at least practical and a reasonable commodity even among the settlements of the New World."

Anne Cathrine saw the problem immediately. "Of course. He had to choose between the changes he wanted to make and the changes he *had* to make."

Brandão nodded. "Precisely. He already was in a position where he was, de facto, usurping political and military control without the colony's consent and dictating policy to people who'd come to the New World seeking the freedom to do and work as they pleased."

"Which included owning slaves who would never have such freedoms," Sophie added darkly.

"Ironically, yes. However, it was painfully obvious to Tromp that, on top of all those impositions, he could not presume to change anything else, lest the original colonists rebel. Which would, of course, have been the end of everything. If the landowners from Oranjestad did not cooperate with those from Recife, and if both did not work together to grow the needed foodstuffs for almost three thousand people, the colony would have been as thoroughly destroyed as had the Spanish bombarded it for a week."

Leonora nodded. "And so this is what you mean by no 'new' slaves are permitted. Only those who were already in the two colonies before Tromp arrived are allowed."

Brandão shrugged, took the empty water cup from the young girl, whom he eased back down toward her sleeping palette with his palms. "If it were only so simple as that, Leonora."

"It *should* be as simple as that," Anne Cathrine snapped. "I am sorry, Doctor," she apologized hastily. "My impatience is not with you, but with your implication that there are still other 'exceptions' to Admiral Tromp's rule against slaveholding."

"And you are as forgiven for your impatience as you are correct in foreseeing such connivance. Shortly after Admiral Tromp arrived and his perspectives on slavery became known, the original landowners sent their ship over to Africa yet again."

"To gather more slaves, in defiance of Admiral Tromp's law?"

Brandão shook a gnarled old finger. "Ah, their disregard for his policy was not so straightforward. You see, among their many other accomplishments, the Dutch are masters of circumlocution and legalistic distinctions so fine that a gnat could not perch upon their edge without falling off."

"How can this matter? When is a slave anything other than a slave?"

The old *murrano* physician smiled ruefully. "When there is a document stating that he is not. Consider: the fluyt sent by the Dutch landowners arrives on the western coast of Africa. Ghana, let us presume. Slaves are brought to her master. He says, 'Actually, I am not interested in buying slaves. I am here to purchase the work contracts of bondsmen. I am here to find indentured servants who must work at whatever their master directs, under whatever conditions, for ten years, at which point they may buy their freedom. That is, if they have been able to save enough to do so.'"

"But that is absurd," Leonora exclaimed. "Given the conditions under which they work, any such person would be lucky merely to be alive after ten years. It is unthinkable that they would have the time or opportunity to set aside valuables equal to the price of their bond."

"Naturally. But by *law*, they are not slaves. And Admiral Tromp and Jan van Walbeeck will be hard put to challenge this casuistry successfully. Oh, it does give them the ability to prevent or at least ameliorate the worst offenses of slavery: murder, rape, seizure or outright prohibition of personal goods. These new workers will enjoy the basic protections of our laws. But being signed over into indentured servitude by their African bondholders dodges the technicality of slavery, even though their lives will be little different."

Anne Cathrine stood. "And Admiral Tromp and van Walbeeck will tolerate this subversion of their clear intent?"

Brandão rose, crooked and bent, alongside her. "In the short term, they have little choice but to turn a blind eye. But if, as seems likely, the appearance of your flotilla is the harbinger of more ships flying friendly flags, and bringing aid against both the threats of hunger and of the Spanish, then I suspect Tromp and van Walbeeck will no longer pay so high a price for the cooperation of the landowners and their farms. And that—" Brandão said with a pat on her firm arm—"would be a very good thing indeed. Now, enough speculating. We have serious work before us. One fellow gave himself quite a gash while shoveling manure and is predictably infected. Then there are two Dutch imbeciles who tried to teach themselves spear fishing yesterday and believed that, since they were in the water the whole time, they were protected from the effects of the sun. After that, we will see how much pure ethanol our apparatus has distilled today and shall check on our stores of—"

As Leonora followed Brandão into an adjoining tent, Anne Cathrine felt a hand on her shoulder delay her from following immediately. She turned and saw Sophie's serious Norn-eyes gazing down at her again. "It is not every king's daughter, princess or otherwise, who conceives of a dislike for slavery. Too many see all but their highest-ranked subjects as nothing more than their thralls. And so, their minds and hearts are more than halfway reconciled to slavery as permissable, even desirable." Her gaze wavered, the first time Anne Cathrine had ever seen it do so. "Whatever unfortunate exchanges there have been between our families, I am proud to call you friend. And happy to think that our king has raised a person of such charity and integrity." Sophie nodded and followed the path Leonora had taken into the adjoining tent.

It took Anne Cathrine a full three seconds to recover from her surprise. She made to exit after the others but then remembered the lambent brown eyes that had looked at her so solemnly minutes before. She turned. The small girl now lay on her side, a light blanket pooled around her waist, her jet-black hair slightly tangled from the sweat of her fever, her thumb half in her mouth as she shivered despite the warmth of the day.

Anne Cathrine kneeled down and drew the blanket up a bit higher. As she placed a hand upon the child's cheek, she felt a tear run down her own. But she did not know why.

Chapter 35

Oranjestad, St. Eustatia

Mike McCarthy, Jr., was puzzled by his escort from Oranjestad's small pier, Reverend Johannes Theodorus Polhemius. A man who seemed to alternate between shy silence and garrulous excesses of expostulation, he'd provided the up-timer with the complete dossiers of the eight workers who had volunteered to "learn about radios from the ground up" over the course of their work for Mike.

Two were sailors by trade; six were soldiers. From Polhemius' anxious yet highly generalized accolades about two of the latter, he suspected that pair were simply in it for the extra money. It was also possible they were motivated by boredom, wanting something better to do than waiting around to get a job they liked (going out as part of a ship's contingent) or a job they hated (farming as a contract laborer down on St. Christopher's). But the other six all seemed to genuinely have the blood of gadget-tinkerers running in their veins. One had been a watchmaker's apprentice before declining family fortunes sent him off to sea. Another had been a sapper in the Provinces before journeying to the New World. A third had most recently finished refurbishing various items of ships' chandlery that some half-piratical character named "Peg Leg Jol" had brought back to Oranjestad after raiding a small Spanish port down along Tierra Firma.

He also heard a good deal about their behavior, and piety or implied lack thereof, sobriety or implied lack thereof, and work ethic, which most of them seemed to have in fair measure or even excess. And he also had to fend off Polhemius' numerous invitations to a late breakfast of cassava bread and fish. Happily, he'd dined aboard the *Koninck David* this morning with Captain Schooneman, enjoying the comparative delicacies of turtle and sweet potatoes served with a side of fried plantains.

As they walked through what was still mostly the tent-city of Oranjestad, families stopped to stare at Mike's clothes. Although he didn't have much left in the way of up-time duds, he had brought a western-style brimmed hat to shield against the tropical sun, as well as a bandana. That, and his lack of facial hair drew enough attention that he asked Polhemius, "Reverend, my clothes aren't *that* strange. Why are all these people staring at me like I'm from another planet?"

Still walking briskly, Polhemius turned to stare at him and almost tripped over his own feet doing so; he was a markedly ungraceful man. "But you *are* from another planet, mijn heer McCarthy. A planet almost four hundred years away from ours, in time. They are staring at you not because your clothes are strange to them, but because they know what they signify: that you are an up-timer. Please remember, they have heard of your people, but have never met one. They commenced their journey here less than six months after your town appeared in Germany." He rubbed his large, sunburned nose. "And they know that the, the *steam*-ships are designed by your people, as well as the radio you will be commencing to build today."

"Well, I'm not really *building* the radio—" Mike started, and then gave up. He was building this radio the way a kid builds a model airplane: assembling parts somebody else fabricated, according to painstaking instructions. Oh, sure, he understood the majority of the physics and mechanical properties of the transceiver, but he was mostly an engine and body-work guy. Drive-trains and differentials: that was his comfort-zone. Sending sparks halfway across the world? Well, he just hoped he didn't have to resort to improvisation...

Polhemius looked concerned. "You're not building the radio? But I thought—"

"Well, yeah, I'm building it in the sense that I'm putting it together. But it's not like I'm its inventor."

"Perhaps not, but that hardly matters. The aim of the entire project, to be able to send signals home instantly, is as other-worldly as you up-timers are. Or so it seems to all of us."

Mike heard the words "all of us," and frowned. "Reverend Polhemius, just how many people know what I'm going to be working on over the next few months?"

"The radio? Oh, a great many, I should say."

Well, damn. That wasn't part of the original game plan. "Reverend, I'm a little confused. I was told that we'd try to keep the radio a bit of a secret, at least for a while."

Polhemius frowned. "Ah. Yes. I see. But, as it turned out, we were faced with a dilemma when trying to find you helpers for the construction phase. As our leased plots on St. Christopher's have now become available for tillage, the demand for farm-workers has gone up. Also, we are sending more troops there to protect those farms, along with the English possessions. So, in order to be sure that you would get the kind of workers you needed for this task, we had to explain enough of what it entailed to pique the interest of those with the correct aptitudes. Otherwise—" The reverend held up his hands in a gesture of futility.

"Yeah. Okay, I get it." *Which doesn't make it any better, though. The sooner the town knows, the sooner informers hear. That's just the way of the world. So our secret international radio advantage isn't going to be secret for very long.*

They had arrived at the eastern edge of the tent city where an intermittent arc of shallow ditches had been scraped out of the sandy soil. Bamboo spikes lined their outer berm like irregular, narrow fangs. "Expecting trouble?" Mike asked Polhemius.

The reverend shrugged. "We are in the Caribbees, mijn heer McCarthy. It is always prudent to expect trouble. I remind you that many of the Caribs whom Warner and the Frenchman d'Esnambuc drove from St. Christopher's less than ten years ago still consider these islands rightfully theirs and would be happy for any opportunity to reassert that claim. In the bloodiest pos-sible fashion. The brutes."

McCarthy managed to stifle his impulse to point out the reverend's rather profound double standard regarding barbarous behavior. In his world-view, it was apparently acceptable for white settlers to dispossess the natives of their own land via massacre, but it was "brutish" for those same natives to consider reversing the situation with identical methods. He also suppressed verbalizing his less arch curiosity regarding how the reverend would feel in the natives' place, about being on the losing end of the stick with which the Europeans had beaten the prime lesson of all colonialism into the Caribs' heads: that might makes right, not uncounted generations of habitation and ownership. Of course, it could also be averred that, in the case of the Caribs, it was simply a matter of what goes around, comes around. According to the history books, the Caribs had been the local colonizers less than half a millennium ago, driving the comparatively peaceful Taino out of the Windward and then Leeward Isles in a slow but inexorable campaign of northward expansion-by-genocide. Not for the first time, Mike wondered if maybe that's all history was: a succession of bullies and thieves, each one dressing up their own conquests in veils of fancy rhetoric and moral speechifying.

Polhemius had signaled to eight young men lounging near the only permanent structure near the eastern skirts of Oranjestad: a shack fashioned from discarded planking and spar fragments. They rose, revealing a collection of stenciled crates behind them. "These are the fellows I was telling you about," he said by way of introduction as the group drew closer.

Mike scanned them and, by posture alone, identified the two who were coming along simply for the money and what they presumed would be light labor. While not so rude as to look obviously bored, they were not attentive, scanning the outskirts of the tent-city for objects of interest. First among which were young women, origins and status notwithstanding. Mike managed not to smile. *Okay, guys, I've had overgrown boys like you walk into my shop, looking for a job. Let's see if you're up for it, because I'd rather have two positions that still need to be filled rather than two positions filled by young punks who won't give me a solid day's work.* "You, and you. Yeah, you. Both of you. Have you worked on ships?"

After overcoming their surprise at being singled out, and gruffly, the two started explaining that they were not sailors, of course. But that they had lent a hand while aboard. Here and there. Not so much as to mean that they knew how to work on ships, but—

"That's enough," Mike interrupted brusquely. "So you've climbed masts, worked out on the ends of yards."

They both started babbling out further qualifying statements—

"I said that's enough. You two are lucky, because you get to start work without having to spend today learning about a bunch of dull radio components and wire-splicing, here in the shade. Instead, your job is to go to the eastern side of The Quill and survey its slopes for tall trees. Specifically, you are to locate and tag every tree that's at least thirty feet tall in the northeast quadrant of the slopes. Double tag any trees that have plump, straight trunks up to fifteen feet. There won't be many too close to the level ground, since the wind off the Atlantic pushes most of them over sideways. But as you get higher up, the jungle itself provides a partial windbreak, so you'll find more of them as you climb higher." Mike tossed a bag of white, ribbonlike rags at them. "There are your tags."

One of the pair simply looked at him, unspeaking. The other held the bag, looking helpless. "Hammer?" he asked. "Nails?"

"No nails," Mike announced with a single shake of his head. "Too scarce to use on something like this. And besides, we don't want to kill the same trees we're going to use to mount our antenna lines. Now, get moving. You've got a good walk ahead of you, and a lot of work when you get there."

"We're not going to learn about radios?" said the one who had been speechless. He sounded as if Father Christmas had put coal in his stocking.

"You are learning about radios," Mike said with a smile. "From the ground up. Literally. Now git." He turned to the other six young men.

Except that there were now seven men, and the seventh wasn't as young as the others. He was leaning in the now-open doorway of the shack. He nodded at Mike, a broad easy smile pasted on his big, blunt peasant features. But his eyes were bright and alert, and Mike immediately recalled similar faces from his thirty-five years working on cars and in other mechanical industries. This was the face of the guy all the bosses underestimated, the guy they pegged as being "slow," but who turned out to be the sharpest knife in the drawer, and the guy who not only got his own work done on the shop floor but managed to drag a small passel of prior slackers along with him into genuine productivity. Mike smiled back. "Hey old-timer," he said to the thirty-something fellow. "Glad you could join us."

The man laughed—a deep, easy rumble—and nodded. "Hah.

Ja, old-timer; that's me. Been a second-mate for almost ten years, now. About time I try something new. Maybe skill with radios will get me that overdue promotion to first mate. Or, if not, maybe I'll work for you, hey? Lots of sailors around, these days, but not many people who know radios."

Mike nodded. "True enough. I'm Mike—"

The man bowed a bit. "Oh, we know who you are, Mr. Michael McCarthy. We've been waiting for you to build this radio."

"'We?'"

The man scratched at his thick, and decidedly unruly, brown hair. "*Ja*. Me and the young fellows, here."

Mike nodded, beginning to understand. "So, you were responsible for choosing who was going to be on this job?" He glanced sideways at Polhemius, who nodded almost nervously.

"Yes," the reverend answered, "that is correct. Mr. Kortenaer expressed interest in your project and was also accustomed to dealing with lively young men, such as were needed."

McCarthy saw Kortenaer's eyes twinkle and he suppressed a new smile. *So, the good Reverend Polhemius isn't comfortable providing leadership to a bunch of young roughnecks. They probably don't pray and clean their fingernails often enough for his comfort. So he pulls an older version of them from before the mast to choose and baby-sit them. Which is just as well. Now I don't have to find a foreman, because I've already got one.* "Well, now that you've been kind enough to finish making all the introductions, Reverend Polhemius, I think I'm ready to get to work." Mike put out his hand. "Thanks so much, and I'm sure I'll see you soon again."

Polhemius, who was possibly aware that he was being politely but swiftly brushed off, shook hands while uttering a few abbreviated pleasantries and then strode back toward the western side of the town and his small wood-framed church. Mike watched him go. He turned to Kortenaer, who'd come to stand beside him. "So, if you're going to be my foreman"—the man's smile was as honest as it was sudden and broad—"I need to know your whole name. So I can know who I'm cussing at, you understand."

The answer rode atop a faint chuckle. "I am Egbert Bartholomeuszoon Kortenaer. 'Bert' for short. Now, how shall we start?"

Mike thought. "First we check the components and the wires, and make sure they all made the trip safely. If we're going to have any technical problems, I need to know right away."

"To send home for new parts?"

"Well, that eventually, but mostly to see if we can jury-rig something until then. We need this radio for local strategic coordination, including finding out what happened to a ship of ours."

"The other steamship?" Bert asked. Then, seeing the surprised look on Mike's face, added, "It cannot surprise you too much that we heard. Your crews drink with our crews, and try to impress the ladies of Oranjestad with their choicest rumors."

Mike shrugged. "Yeah. We should have heard from the other steamship, the *Courser,* on our own ships' radios by now. Even if it was just some chopped up Morse code, we should have heard them trying to make contact."

"But all has been silence?"

"Yeah. For weeks, now. So I need to know if we're going to have any mechanical problems up front. In practical terms, that means I need your guys to open the crates carefully and unpack them carefully. One at a time. I don't want the components to touch the ground, so have them put on a table."

"No table. All our new wood goes into building and ship repair," Bert said with a shake of his head. "But—" He turned to the men and ordered them to uncrate a spool of wire first. "Put the wire on a canvas drop cloth. Then, break its crate apart—carefully. Keep each side intact."

"Why, Heer Kortenaer?" asked the very blond and very young one of the group.

"Because you're going to use those crate-sides to make tabletops. The bases will be wormed casks from the ships. I knew there'd be a reason to keep them, and here it is. Then, unload the contents of the next crate, the one with components, upon that table."

"And make another table out of that next crate?"

"There's a bright lad. Now get about it." He turned back to Mike. "What next, Heer McCarthy?"

"Next, you learn to call me Mike. After that, you tell me the most important thing any job-boss needs to know."

"And what is that, Mike?"

"Well, there's a saying that we don't fail because of what we don't know. We fail because of *things that we don't know* we don't know. Understand?"

Bert smiled. "I don't know. But at least I know that I don't know."

"That's the ticket. Now, what problems are lurking around that a dumb-ass up-timer like me has no clue about?"

Bert's smile faded. "It is not that you have no clue about them, Hee—er, Mike. It is that the clues, the signs, of the problems are being kept from you."

Mike repressed a sigh. He'd hoped that his fishing expedition for unseen troubles would be fruitless, but he'd also been sensible enough to know the odds of that were low. And that's just how it was playing out. "Okay, Bert, what local problems could get in the way of setting up the radio?"

As the six young Dutchmen started lifting spools of precious wire onto old canvas, Bert considered Mike's request with a deepening frown. "Well, you will find out quickly enough, I suspect, that not everyone in Oranjestad considers your arrival an event for celebration."

"Oh? Who have I managed to piss off, already?"

"No, no, I am not referring to your coming, personally, Mike. I mean the arrival of the Reconnaissance Flotilla and what it signifies."

"You mean, that the USE is getting involved in Dutch affairs?"

"Oh, not that so much. We're probably just about the most grateful Dutchmen in the world when it comes to receiving help from unexpected benefactors. No, it is about this agreement that has been reached with the Spanish Lowlands. There are some who just won't have it, no matter how beneficial it might be."

Well, that *cat came out of the bag pretty quickly, too.* "Bert, do you have any idea just how the news of the oil deal and the Lowlands' participation already arrived in Oranjestad?"

Kortenaer shook his head. "No, but word of it was running up and down the tent-lines like a brush fire last night. I suspect someone who'd overheard discussions at Trinidad went on liberty from the *Crown of Waves* or *Koninck David* when you arrived just after sundown and offered to trade tales for grog... Well, you know how these things happen."

Don't I just, though. "And so who in Oranjestad has decided they'd rather stay at war with Fernando than get oil-rich?"

Bert shrugged. "The same settlers who came here wanting to grow tobacco, own slaves, and get away from Catholics. I mean no offense, Mike. These are their sentiments, not mine."

Mike nodded. "Understood. But aren't these settlers very much in the minority, here?"

"It is true they number but a few hundred of all who are here, but they are the ones who own most of the land, who were granted the charter to St. Eustatia. Although the soldiers and sailors and tradesmen are almost ninety percent of the population, they haven't the money, the possessions, or the backing of the Dutch West India company."

"Well, from what I hear, the Nineteen Heeren who call the shots of the Company were pretty enthusiastic about the oil trade when Prince Hendrik shared word of it with them a few months ago. Everyone in the New World is trying to grow tobacco and sugar, but right now, we've got the monopoly on oil, and it's worth far more, pound for pound. And it requires far less labor, cheap or otherwise. So the representatives of the Dutch West India Company were very vocal supporters of the oil co-dominium from the start."

"Well," said Bert thoughtfully, "that is good news, and that is bad news."

"And that is as cryptic a sentence as I've heard you speak, Bert. What's it mean?"

"It means that, in the long run, the Company will get what it wants, which is also what makes most sense. But the bad news is that I know these men on St. Eustatia, and their friends and sons who are now working leased plots on St. Christopher. They are almost all staunch Calvinists of the most orthodox type, men who will not abide Catholics. And they will not want to be made less powerful, less important, by the development of oil on another island." He toed the dirt irritably. "Understand, Mike. These are men who *like* owning slaves, who feel powerful commanding them to work in the fields, and commanding the women to—well, you know."

Mike found that he was grinding his teeth. "Oh, I know, Bert, I know. And I guess they know I'm dead set against letting that kind of shit start here, all over again."

Bert started at Mike's tone more than his words. "I—I do not know if they know your personal feelings about slavery, Mike. But it has been made clear, from what little we have heard about the up-timers, that despite your diverse faiths and beliefs, you all hate slavery. I suspect they will not be surprised to find an enemy in you, Mike."

Mike could feel the better half of his nature ready to drop the tasks and tools of setting up an intercontinental radio. Instead, he discovered that he was already thinking of the ways in which he could take the fight to the bastards who got a thrill out of raping slave women while their two-year-olds hid under the bed, eyes wide at the brutality, terror, and humiliation of the violation taking place only a foot over their heads. But he scooped up that rage, crammed it forcefully into a mental vault and reluctantly sealed it, promising the growing fury within, *you've got to wait a bit. Just a bit. First we build a radio. Then we get lots of ships and guns over here. And then... Oh, and then—*

"Mike, are you quite well?"

"Me? Never better, Bert. I love having something to work toward, and you've just given me another very fine purpose to get this radio up and running as quickly as possible. About which: as soon as we've finished identifying the trees we're going to use, we'll need to get a much bigger work crew together to affix the wires to run down and outward from The Quill's cone in rays spreading toward the northeast. So here's what I want to know: is it any more expensive to, well, lease a slave or bonds-man from one of the landowners than it is to hire one of these soldiers or sailors?"

Bert frowned. "It is not so much a matter of cost. It is that the slaves and bondsmen can be made to do work that none of the colonists will agree to do. Working in cane fields is hard. Very hard."

Mike nodded. "I know. But I've heard rumors that right now, the landowners aren't making as much from their cane crops as they'd like. They don't have any way to ship it back to Europe, yet, and they can only use it as a barter good, here in the Carib-bees. So wouldn't it be profitable for them to lease out slave labor for silver?"

Bert shrugged. "Yes, but why should you do so? We have many soldiers who can help us as part of their military orders, working in shifts."

"True. But we'll get them on short, rotating assignments, I'm told. But if we have a large core of steady workers—such as leased slaves—they'll quickly get a higher level of expertise at the job. And then rotating laborers from the military becomes more effective more rapidly."

Bert's smile crept back on his face. "But that's not the only reason, is it, Mike? You want to speak to the slaves, away from their masters, don't you? Before their masters come to realize how you feel about slavery?"

Mike smiled back. "That obvious, huh? But yeah, that's just what I mean to do. Maybe we can get a few hired over from St. Christopher's, as well."

Bert's smile faded. "I think you mean to do a good thing, Mike, but I'm worried it could hurt the very people you mean to help. I counsel you to consider this: let us say you move the slaves to assert themselves. And so they refuse to work. Whatever else may happen, we will all starve. So perhaps, at first, you could simply work in the same direction as Tromp and van Walbeeck."

"Which means what?"

"They are trying to get the slaves converted into bondsmen. I know, I know: there is still great inequity in being a bondsman. But any more rapid transition will destroy the colony. On the other hand, if this colony becomes a place where outright slavery ceases to exist, then escapees from the Spanish colonies, and those of other nations, will flock here. They will come for the same reason we did: to have a chance, no matter how distant and uncertain, to live a better life than the one we knew at home."

"And how is the life of a bondsman that much better than that of a slave?"

"It is, if it follows the model that Tromp and van Walbeeck are trying to get the councilors to accept. In which the slaves and current bondsmen shall all earn their complete freedom with five years of bonded work."

"And then what, Bert? Without any possessions, without any land of their own, they'll be desperate. They'll have no options, no means of providing for their own needs. Which means they'll massacre us to take what they must, or we'll massacre them to keep it."

"Or," temporized Bert calmly, "like peasants have since the beginning of time, they will continue to work the same land, but now will keep a share of what they grow. And that shall be the beginning of their wealth."

Mike started. Bert was of course not aware of it, but in suggesting serfdom, he was rebirthing the basic principles of sharecropping, and Mike knew full well the abuses to which that grim institution was subject. But, on the other hand, it was a hell of a lot better than slavery, and was probably the most progressive policy that the local freemen would accept. With the great majority of them being tradition-minded political moderates, they would reflexively reject an immediate conferral of full equality. But this was a middle course they could probably get behind. Meaning that this was probably the shape of the near future. The hard-liners wouldn't like it one bit, but wouldn't be able to get enough support from fence-sitters to keep their slaves from becoming bondsmen. At best, they'd be able to haggle about the details of the agreement.

Mike looked at Bert, looked at the second crate of radio components being delicately unloaded, looked up at the slopes of The Quill, and conceded that, in this New World, the challenges were never simple, the solutions never perfect, and the need for flexibility never-ending. "Okay," he muttered. "We'll take the gradualist approach. Now, which landowners are hurting enough financially to rent us some well-spoken and charismatic slaves?"

Chapter 36

Chaguamara Peninsula, Trinidad

Even after the partition separating Eddie's cabin from the *Intrepid*'s wardroom had been removed, the space around the chart-table still felt crowded. Pros Mund was next to the map-table with his executive officer, Haakon. Immediately across from them was Tromp, who had brought his own first mate, a bright young fellow named Evertsen. And of course both Gjedde and Bjelke were there from *Intrepid*. Arrayed back in a second rank along the walls were Simonszoon, von Holst, and van Galen and the pilots of their ships, who'd need at least as good an awareness of the situation and planned maneuver as the captains themselves.

A pewter pitcher of water made its way slowly around the circle of men, several of whom muttered about preferring grog, and one who wondered, aloud, if there was any food to be had. Eddie wondered if he should get an orderly to meet those needs, but found Gjedde glancing at him. The old Norwegian shook his head faintly and returned his attention to the map.

That, Eddie allowed with an imaginary slap to his own face, was a prompt he shouldn't have needed. It had been unnerving, learning that the final commanders' conference was to be on his—well, Gjedde's—ship, but that didn't mean he had to worry about catering the event. It was a working gathering, not a social occasion. The captains should certainly have been able to feed themselves before they traveled to the *Intrepid* in their individual skiffs.

And it wasn't as if meeting on the *Intrepid* was any kind of unusual honor. The decision had been based solely on the consideration that it was the one location that could not offend or call into question the comparative status any of the senior officers. It was a lot of rubbish, Eddie thought, but the same kind of seniority and rank issues had persisted down through to the up-time navy of his own nation, so he really shouldn't have expected any different, or any better, here.

Tromp was, by any reasonable measure, the senior commander, and brought the greatest number of ships to the fleet that was currently raising its anchors from the twelve-fathom depths of northwest Trinidad's Scotland Bay. However, Pros Mund was senior among the USE commanders, and although only two ships of his flotilla were present, the *Intrepid* and the *Resolve,* they were arguably far more powerful than all the Dutch ships combined. This was further complicated by the ticklish fact that the most knowledgeable person about the details of how the new cooperative oil ventures between the Provinces and the USE did or did not influence military cooperation in the protection of those ventures was none other than Eddie himself. Eddie calculated that, in anything like a chain of command, he was probably somewhere about fifth or sixth, with Gjedde, Simonszoon, and the *Tropic Surveyor*'s Stiernsköld coming after the uncertain Tromp-Mund dyad.

In short, notions of seniority were completely scrambled and everyone knew it. But they were also too polite to say anything for fear of starting a disagreement that might result in an inability to pursue a coherent response to the Spanish threat that had finally arrived this morning. And no one had to dance more carefully than Eddie. On the one hand, he had to be careful not to step on any superior-ranking toes; but, on the other, was the only person who really understood the technological opportunities— and also, limitations—of the up-time designed steamships that were the lynchpin of their plans.

Happily, Tromp had proven to be a calm, almost ego-less commander whose quiet graciousness had become familiar to Eddie over the course of several shared dinners on both the *Amelia* and the *Intrepid*. And if Pros Mund was, by comparison, standoffish and cheerless, he was patient and prudent enough to realize that Tromp had to insist upon equal command dignities. The Danish admiral certainly cared more about the quality of their plans and leadership than any folderol about seniority and rank, but it was also true that he had to protect his staff, to ensure that his captains were not made to answer to a commander they had never met, let alone (in most cases) heard of. Consequently, Eddie had led both admirals toward a strategy that made a virtue out of being allies whose relationship was as new and unspecified as their chain of command was undetermined.

Eddie pointed to the map, which illustrated yet another reason why this final council of war had been called aboard the *Intrepid*. Not only was it "neutral ground" in that it was not on either Tromp's or Mund's respective flagships, but it put the best up-time maps, clocks, and drafting equipment at the disposal of the entire command staff. Resting his finger next to a red pin stuck fifteen miles northwest of the island of Grenada, Eddie looked around the room. "So this is where the Spanish were when the first sighting was made by our balloon, land-moored at Prickly Point on Grenada, one hour ago. Since then, twenty-six ships have been spotted, of which five are *pataches*. Their main van was making about two knots."

Simonszoon frowned. "Then they're not taking full advantage of the leeward breeze. I saw the morning weather reports from your radiomen who are with the balloon's ground team: almost fourteen knots south by southwest. Perfect for the Spanish square-riggers, coming just one point off their port quarter. Even their high-hulled scows should be able to make four knots with that God-given breeze."

Eddie nodded. "That's right, but they've got the *pataches* out in front of them, looking for any forces we might have in the region. That means their main body has to slow down, let their fore-and-aft-rigged scouts run ahead and around, come close enough to send signals, then work their way out again."

Tromp nodded. "That is good in that it gives us more time, which we will want since we have to tack to windward to meet them. But it is not good insofar as it suggests that the Spanish are being cautious, rather than rushing in hastily."

Mund shrugged. "So we will need to follow what Commander

Cantrell calls plan Beta. We will need to conceal our true intents longer, which will require more careful coordination as we approach the Spaniards."

Simonszoon rested his finger at the southern tip of Grenada. "It also means we shall need regular reports from your balloon, here. They will be able to keep the Spanish under observation as we maneuver to make contact with them in the place and in the formation we have decided upon. The balloon will need to keep us updated so that we may adjust to any course or formation changes *they* might make."

Eddie smiled. He liked working with Dirck Simonszoon, whose laconic wit was a screen behind which he hid an agile and incisive tactical mind. More than any of the down-timers he'd met thus far, Simonszoon appreciated how the adroit use of balloons and radios made it possible to both deceive an approaching foe and maneuver for advantage. That was why it was his ship, the comparatively fleet-footed forty-four-gun *Achilles*, that was to be towed by the flotilla's one available steam pinnace to keep up with the *Resolve* and *Intrepid*. Once the allied fleet came in sight of the Spanish, these three ships would push forward as a flying wing stretching north from the eastern flank of Tromp's main body of Dutch ships. "That's absolutely correct, Dirck. We need those airborne eyes as we close to contact. Which is why I've already ordered the balloon to land, for now."

Simonszoon frowned, then nodded. "Yes, because of their limited ability to keep heating the air in the envelope."

"That, and because as the Spanish get close to rounding Grenada, which we guess will be happening in about four hours, they'd be far more likely to spot our balloon. If it was still up in the sky, that is. Two hours after they draw past Grenada, we'll send it aloft again. They'll be less likely to spot it astern to the north when all their lookouts are concentrating on finding us to the south, east, and west."

Von Holst sounded concerned. "But during those six hours when the balloon is on the ground, how shall we know if they change course?"

It was Tromp who pointed almost fifty miles northwest of their position in Scotland Bay. "Because Gijszoon is out there, with the yacht *Kater* and his own balloon."

"What?" van Galen almost shouted. "You told us he was—!"

"I said nothing specific about his whereabouts, merely that he was on patrol. Which he was, working from out beyond the north tip of the Paria peninsula. He's been sheltering in the Cove of Palmar behind Punta Mejillores and then patrolling approximately thirty-five miles north. With the balloon we gave him, that allowed him to spot either a Spanish fleet coming from the Greater Antilles directly across the open waters of the Caribbean, or for the Cartagena fleet to the west. And as he had a reaching wind both coming out of and going back to his anchorage, he had great flexibility of movement.

"As for the Spanish who have now appeared, they will not see him at his patrol point unless they change course to the southwest or west. But Gijszoon will see that change first and let us know."

"So if we receive no radio signals from Gijszoon, we know that they are still rounding Grenada and heading in their last known direction," von Holst concluded with a nod.

Van Galen was frowning, though. "Unless they decide to turn around and run home, head back up the Leeward side of the Lesser Antilles."

Mund frowned at van Galen's frown. "Yes, but this would not concern us. If the Spanish turn back, the wind will be in their faces. They'll either be in irons, or sailing very close-hauled. And being close-hauled on those big square-rigged galleons, they would be lucky to make headway faster than one knot. Within ten hours we would know that they had turned about, and we would be upon them in two days, at the most."

"Yes, but only your two steam ships could catch them so quickly," van Galen protested doggedly. "And how do we know your ships are as powerful as he claims—" a head jerked insolently in Eddie's direction—"or that you won't take all the spoils?"

"First," Mund answered with slow, crisp syllables, "Commander Cantrell is not the only one who has seen or been aboard these steamships when they are in action. Consequently, you have my personal assurance that he has not, in the slightest particular, exaggerated their capabilities. Second, it is utterly illogical that we would or could 'take all the spoils,' as you put it, Captain van Galen. If by spoils you mean gold or silver, then you are here fighting the wrong battle, both because treasure is not our objective, and because these are not treasure ships. If, on the other hand, you are calling the ships themselves the 'spoils,' consider the complements of my flotilla. I might be able to crew a captured galleon or two as prize hulls, but not all of them. There would be 'spoils' enough for all, in that event."

Tromp turned a slightly testy eye upon van Galen, and asked quietly, "Does this answer your concerns, Johan?"

The Dutch captain glowered at the map and folded his arms. "Yes. For now."

Tromp turned to Eddie. "So this means we will not have *Kater* and Gijszoon rendezvousing with us?"

Eddie crinkled his mouth apologetically. "It's not likely, Admiral. If our guesses are right, we'll be meeting the Spanish only a few hours before dusk, about eleven hours from now. But it will be six hours until we are certain that the Spanish are doing what we expect: to crowd sail once they enter the Grenada Passage and try to slip into the Gulf of Paria via the Dragon's Mouth just after nightfall. That means *Kater* would have only five hours to sail into the eye of the wind and cover almost thirty miles to reach your van. I know that Joachim Gijszoon is a fine sailor, but—"

"But he will not make six knots an hour if he must constantly be tacking through a wind from the northeast. And finding a steady heading in the Grenada Passage can be tricky, particularly right where the Leeward breeze meets the prevailing westward wind that blows along Tierra Firma." Tromp shook his head. "You are right, Eddie, we may not count on Gijszoon's ship. Which means my van will have no jachts."

"Which leads me to ask," von Holst asked, "where is Pieter Floriszoon, the *Eendracht*, and those Irish Wild Geese?"

Tromp shrugged. "Probably tacking against that same westward wind. They could have been here, at the very earliest, a few days ago. They could easily be another week in reaching us. Either way, the Spanish are here now, so we should move with all haste. Are there any other changes to plan Beta?" His glance started on Pros Mund, bounced to Eddie—and stayed there.

Eddie shook his head. "No, Admiral. Just remember that no matter what the Spanish do when they come at your van, keep your hulls in formation, and be the first to show the world what well-gunned ships can do when engaging the enemy in a line. Just like you did in my world."

"So you tell me. In your up-time world, I introduced this tactic in 1640, yes?"

"Correct, sir. At the Battle of the Downs. Which will now never happen. Here, they'll say that the first use of the naval 'line of battle' doctrine was in 1635 at the Battle of Grenada Passage."

"Yes. Assuming we win it," added Gjedde darkly as he glanced out the portside window into a sudden shaft of bright yellow light. He rose, his slate-on-granite voice already rising into cries to unreef the sails and ready the commanders' skiffs.

With the sun now fully up, the time had come for the fleet to get under way.

Grenada Passage, Caribbean Sea

By two PM, Eddie no longer needed the radio relays from the balloon at Prickly Point to tell him where the Spanish were. He could see them himself.

And evidently, vice versa. The lighter *pataches* had already begun angling off to the flanks of the Spanish van, which had altered course perhaps one point in a more southerly direction, making straight for the seven Dutch sails they first saw there. When, a quarter of an hour later, they evidently saw the other three sails of the second group of ships following perhaps a mile behind the main van, their *pataches* began coming forward more aggressively, no doubt in an attempt to get a better look at what this second formation might be. But the main body made no further course change.

And, Eddie allowed, why would it have? From the initial Spanish perspective, their fleet was facing seven Dutch ships that had fewer guns, but were better sailors. But with twenty-one galleons or smaller galleoncetes, they outnumbered the Dutch three to one in large ships, and had the wind right where they wanted it: running fresh and steady over their port quarter. If anything, the Spanish might wonder why the Dutch were willing to maneuver toward contact under such unfavorable conditions. But they would reasonably conjecture that, given their intrusion near Pitch Lake, the Dutch were desperate to keep the Spanish ships from reaching the Dragon's Mouth, and thereby entering the Gulf of Paria. Because once there, the Spanish were too numerous for the smaller Dutch fleet to contain. While the galleons kept the Dutch ships occupied, a squadron of the smaller galleoncetes could easily break off and disrupt or destroy their incursion upon Trinidadian soil. And so, the defiance of the Spanish *inter caetera* would be at an end.

But now the time had come to change the playing board in a way that the Spanish could not anticipate, and, more importantly, would not strategically understand. Not this first time, anyway, Eddie reminded himself. He turned toward Ove Gjedde, who was already looking at him. "With your permission, sir."

"Commander Cantrell, you have the con. I will mind the sails. As usual."

"Very good, sir. I say three times, I have the con. Now, a question, sir: can you get me six knots by canvas alone in this breeze?"

Gjedde looked at Eddie as if the up-timer had insulted him. "You know very well that I can, Mr. Cantrell."

"Then, as soon as we've got the steam-pinnace fired up, I'll be asking you for those six knots." He turned away, raised his voice. "Mr. Svantner?"

"Sir?"

"Ring down to the engine room. Ready the bitumen-treated wood for the burner. No coal yet, but they are to keep it handy."

"Just warming the boiler, sir?"

"Precisely. Mr. Bjelke?"

From Eddie's left elbow, Rik's voice was tense and slightly higher-pitched than usual. "Sir?"

"Send by semaphore to the pinnace towing *Achilles* that she is to make full steam as soon as possible and fall in behind us. She is to alert us at once if she cannot sustain six knots. Helmsman?"

"Yes, Capt—Commander Cantrell?"

"You'll be following the wind as Captain Gjedde tells you, but bring our heading due north."

"Sir, that will have us angling away from Admiral Tromp's ships."

"It will, Helmsman," Eddie affirmed with a smile. "It will indeed."

Lieutenant Admiral Fadrique Álvarez de Toledo y Mendoza glanced sideways while Captain General of the Armada Jorge de Cárdenas y Manrique de Lara's attention was upon the latest report from the crow's nest. And Fadrique wondered, *how did it ever come to this?*

Honored just last January by Philip IV, he had then been dismissed in near-disgrace mere months later by Olivares for being too popular at court and also too outspoken about the danger to the viceroyalties of the New World. Happily, the need for capable admirals in the field was greater than the power of Olivares' displeasure in court. September brought news that he had been reappointed to a military command, largely thanks to his brother who commanded the galleys of the Mediterranean. Taking leave of his wife and children to oversee the re-expansion of the Armada de Barlovento, he quit his villa just ahead of the diphtheria outbreak that, he learned shortly after, had claimed him in the "up-time" world of the heathen Americans.

However, that good luck did not follow him to the New World. Upon arriving, he discovered that the Armada de Barlovento, shrunken to three or four worm-eaten hulls, had disappeared and evidently no longer existed. Worse yet, in reply to the governor of Cuba's plea for an overall naval commander to coordinate activities in the Caribbean, such as finding and eliminating the resurgent fleet of the blasted Dutchman Tromp, Olivares' advisory council, the *Junta de Guerra de Indias* sent none other than the largely ineffective de Cárdenas y Manrique de Lara to do the job. *It should have been* me *they chose to hunt down the Dutch, damn them.* Me! *I've won more battles against them than Jorge has ever fought.* But of course, Fadrique knew precisely why he had been made merely the commander of the decrepit (and now extinct) Armada de Barlovento and why de Cárdenas y Manrique de Lara had been placed over all naval matters in the New World: favor at court.

Jorge wasn't particularly gifted overseeing naval operations, but he was an inspired navigator of the ebbs and flows of the prevailing tides of popularity in Madrid. And so here he was, four years Fadrique's junior, and not even vaguely his peer in matters military, but still in charge of the largest single offensive reprisal that Spain had mounted in the Caribbean in years. It was possibly the largest since Fadrique's own successes in driving the English and French from their settlements in St. Christopher's and Nevis only six years earlier. But the brazen violators of His Imperial Majesty's exclusive right to settlements west of the Tordesilla line had returned as soon as Fadrique's galleons had disappeared over the horizon. Just as Fadrique had said they would. And just as he had warned Olivares—*the whoreson!*—the same thing had occurred in similarly isolated possessions throughout the Caribbean. Chasing and imprisoning violators was not enough.

Deporting them to mines or fields in Cuba or Tierra Firma was not enough. Nor even was extermination. Only by settling and holding the land itself could the Spanish Crown be sure that godless trespassers would not sneak in to usurp it. And of course Olivares had not wanted such talk bruited about, because that level of commitment, that strategy of certain success, also cost more money. Or it meant giving the viceroys and governors of the New World increased authority to raise their own navies and armies, which meant, once again, pulling some measure of power out of Olivares' grasping hands. And that was simply not going to happen, not until some crisis forced that simpering bootlicker to take action.

"Well, Fadrique," de Cárdenas y Manrique de Lara mused, "the reports are confirmed. Two large ships to the east of the Dutch van are now advancing well north of their line. A third is following them. That one may be afire, since it is putting out some smoke."

It was no less than de Toledo has seen through his own spyglass. "That smoke makes little sense. There was no sound of a prior battle as we approached."

"Perhaps they are still recuperating after an earlier encounter with our fleet from Cartagena. That would explain both the smoke of the one ship, and their diminished numbers. This is certainly far fewer ships than Tromp was said to have at Recife."

Fadrique kept any hint of impatience out of his reply. "Perhaps. But none of our *pataches* have located the *patache*-pickets of the Cartagena fleet, Captain-General, not even those which we sent down here so that they might watch for their arrival and report back. Also, the Dutch numbers may not signify prior losses, but current caution. If Tromp is still in the Caribbean, he has been here for better than a year. If seems certain he must have a base somewhere, possibly Curaçao. If so, he must leave much of his fleet behind to protect that base."

De Cárdenas y Manrique de Lara flipped a dismissing wrist at the objections. "Well, then, the smoke could signify a fire-ship. The Dutch are outnumbered and may hope to scatter us, lest we gather too tightly upon any of their number."

De Toledo nodded, answered, "Perhaps," and thought, *Are you mad, or simply stupid?* Fadrique continued carefully. "However, a fire ship puts out more smoke, and blacker. And it is best used in a bay or channel, where maneuver is limited or difficult." *Besides, you ass-kisser, you can see through your own glass that the smoking ship is fully and handsomely rigged, and therefore, well-crewed. Fireships are manned by skeleton crews so they may be abandoned at the last second, in haste.*

De Cárdenas y Manrique de Lara merely pouted. "You may be right, Don Álvarez, but I shall suspend judgment. In the meantime, why do you think these two great ships—built along *fragata* lines, no less—are coming out in front and to the flank of the main Dutch body?"

Álvarez de Toledo shrugged. "The wind is from the northeast. They are to our east, heading north. They hope to get the weather-gauge on us. And, making better than five knots, they are likely to accomplish that."

"But to what end, Fadrique? They are but three ships, and one is burning. And see, the large ones have few ports for cannon. Not even sixteen on the port side that we can see." He rapped the rail along the port quarter decisively. "They must be large merchants, some new kind of argosy, trying to slip past us rather than try cases against our twenty-six-gun broadsides!"

"'Slip past us'?" echoed Fadrique. "How? If they get the weather gauge, they must sail to the west—*toward us*—unless they wish to find themselves tacking in baffling winds, or even caught in irons."

"And so they may, Fadrique. Really, I am surprised you do not perceive their ploy. They shall try to outsail us, to get north of our van. Meanwhile, the regular Dutch ships will slow down, baiting us to use our following wind to descend upon them. I suspect they will turn their tails and run to the Dragon's Mouth, then. And when we crowd even more sail to catch them, these great argosies shall come about to put the wind over their starboard beams and run westward, hugging close against Grenada and escaping behind us."

Fadrique nodded. "I hadn't thought of that." That was because it was the most absurd collection of inanities he'd ever heard. Whatever these large ships were, they were not "argosies." Their hulls were too long and narrow to be effective cargo ships. Besides, their rigging was different and their lines were—strange. And why would they be taking a burning, but apparently conventional, ship with them? Something was not right here...

"Well, Fadrique, whatever these large ships are, and whatever their intents, we have all the speed, and all the hulls, we need to ruin their strategy."

"Certainly, sir. However, I—"

But before de Toledo could offer his tactical counsel, de Cárdenas y Manrique de Lara was declaiming his own. "So then, you shall give the Dutch what they want. You shall take half our ships and strike south at the Dutch van. I suspect they will not give you battle, but if they do, press close and smash them, Fadrique. Seize any that you may, but I am not overly concerned with prizes. I want these Dutch interlopers swept from the waves, and if that necessitates blasting them into driftwood rather than risking a boarding, so be it.

"Meanwhile, I shall take the other half of our ships due east to cut off the three fleeing ships. I shall send the *pataches* slightly northward, to deny them any chance of working around to the leeward side of Grenada. And the rest of our ships will bring cannon to bear against the argosies, which may well be too large to sink quickly. But that will be acceptable. I have a powerful curiosity to see what special cargoes they must be carrying, to abandon their own fleet in so desperate a fashion."

De Toledo was glad to wait through de Cárdenas y Manrique de Lara's lecture of the day's intended tactics. It gave him a few extra moments to distance himself from the absurdity of his commanding officer's assessments and plans. "Captain-General de Cárdenas y Manrique de Lara, are you certain that splitting our forces is wise? The large ships are unusually fast, and it is entirely possible that they might turn toward us, and—"

"And what, Fadrique? Challenge our twenty-six-gun broadsides with their fourteen-gun impotence? Will they hope to swarm us, board us, being outnumbered better than four to one? They mean to flee, Fadrique, of that much you may be sure. And you may also be sure of this: I shall stop them. Now, return to your ship at once. We are drawing close enough to ready the guns, and you must lead your half of this fleet south against the Dutch." And with that, Captain-General Jorge de Cárdenas y Manrique de Lara turned away from his subordinate, signaling that their conversation was over.

Chapter 37

Grenada Passage, Caribbean Sea

At one-mile range, and with the sun starting down toward the horizon, Eddie turned to Svantner to confirm—one more time—the weather conditions he'd been watching so closely. "Mr. Svantner, wind, currents, and sea?"

Svantner didn't even have to inquire. He'd arranged runners to give him updates every two minutes. "Sir, wind is running in from the east-northeast at a steady twelve knots. That is only one point off the direction of the current. Seas are reasonably calm: one-foot waves, sometimes one and a quarter, sir. Conditions remain steady, wind shifting only a point or so from the prevailing direction."

Eddie nodded. He called down to the intraship comm officer beneath his collapsible "flying bridge." "Range and bearing of the enemy's lead ship?"

"Mount One is calling it 1600 yards to the lead packet—er, *patache*—sir, bearing 285 degrees. About 1900 yards to the first galleon behind her, bearing directly abeam at 270 degrees."

Eddie nodded, as much to himself as to the men around him. "Right." He looked up at the *Intrepid*'s funnel. For the last ten minutes, a thin, whitish smoke had been rising out of it. "Rik, have they warmed up the engines and boilers?"

"Yes, sir. They've used about half the wood."

"Tell them to shift to coal. Captain Gjedde, we'll be moving to steam as soon as our boilers are up to pressure. Tell the men aloft to expect her to get lively."

"They are ready, Commander Cantrell."

They ought to be, given how often we've briefed them. "Radioman, instruct the *Achilles* that she is to signal the pinnace to cut her loose and sheer off." Over the muted "Aye, sir," from below the deck, Eddie asked, "Rik? Do I have steam enough for ten knots?"

"The chief engineer says you do, Commander."

"Then ahead three-quarters." *And let's give those Spaniards something to gawk at.*

While still more than a mile away from the Dutch ships, Fadrique de Toledo was distracted by a cry from the lookout in the mizzen's crow's nest. He turned and saw a single gout of smoke coming up from the center of each of the big ships as they started drawing northward at an almost inconceivable rate—and sailing broad-hauled, at best.

And then he understood what he was seeing, and what the smoke had to signify. He had heard reports of the American armored river ships that had destroyed the Danish fleet last year. And had heard rumors that the up-timers were building ocean-going craft with the same motive power—steam—somewhere on the Baltic. Luebeck, probably. He had discounted those rumors as just more of the fear-mongering that surrounded the up-timers, who, if you were to listen to half the tales, could achieve any technological marvel they chose give a few weeks and a few tons of steel.

But these had to be those ships. Logically, their steam power was the source of both the smoke and their sudden burst of speed, which was even now making paltry nonsense of Jorge de Cárdenas y Manrique de Lara's attempt to cut them off. The up-time ships had already raced well north of his lumbering galleons, and were already starting to turn westward into a broad reach with the wind slightly abaft the beam: the very fastest position for ships with such uncommonly maneuverable and versatile rigging and spars. Although the range was too great for Fadrique to be sure, the ships' great speed actually seemed to make them more stable, cutting through the almost imperceptible swells with the ease and speed of a razor-sharp hand-plane cutting smooth the edge of a slightly frayed plank.

"Sir!" called the first mate of Álvarez's ship, the *Nuestra Señora de los Reyes*, "The chief gunners wish to know how to position their pieces. At what range do you plan to come about to commence firing upon the Dutch ships?"

Staring through his spyglass, de Toledo responded, "I shall know the answer to that question in ten minutes time, Roderigo." *Because what happens next to the north—to our rear—will decide what I do about the enemies in front of me . . .*

"Eight hundred yards to the first Spaniard," cried the intraship comm rating from beneath Eddie's feet.

"Very good." Eddie glanced at *Resolve*, about nine hundred yards off the starboard beam and trailing by perhaps one hundred yards. Which was according to plan. Although Pros Mund was clear about his precedence in the chain of command, he was quite content to let his young up-time commander establish the pace of operations, set an example by acting first, and arguably, become a likely scapegoat if things did not go as planned.

But judging from the way the Spanish were reacting, it seemed that those plans were unfolding as envisioned. They were heading straight at the *Intrepid* and *Resolve* in a kind of elongated pack, the five heaviest galleons clumped relatively close to the rear of their van, three slightly lighter ones arrayed in a more open formation to the front. Tactically, it was a reasonable enough arrangement. Notionally, the three lighter ships were to constrain the maneuver of the two up-time cruisers, and ultimately pin them in place by engaging them. That would give the big galleons enough time to approach and gang up on the two ships in whatever fashion seemed most advantageous, surrounding them and battering them beneath the waves or into submission at murderously close range.

Eddie lowered his binoculars and watched the high-pooped Spanish ships persist in lumbering toward him in a close-reach, even though they had lost the weather gauge. And again, why wouldn't they, given their presumedly decisive superiority in guns and numbers? It was typical of battles in the decades before the advent of line-tactics. Ships more or less headed towards each other in much the same way that opposing rugby teams formed a scrum. They rushed together, usually trying to achieve some initial positional advantage that was quickly forgotten as the battle became the maritime equivalent of a dog-piling brawl. If the speed and responsiveness of the contending ships were more or less equal, it was typical that neither managed to attain the upper hand. What resulted resembled, to Eddie's sensibilities, a demolition derby where the contestants had big cannons and attempted to board, rather than ram, each other. However, the devolution into this boxing-match in a broom closet was not a consequence of choice, so much as it reflected a kind of grim necessity. In addition to the difficulty of maintaining control over widely arrayed fleets, it was also unusual for ships to attempt to fire their broadside armament beyond two hundred yards because of both the poor accuracy and drastic reduction in striking power of balls fired at those ranges. Besides, trained gunnery crews were fortunate to get one shot off every two minutes, in part because the guns were so irregular and cumbersome, and in part because the use of bagged powder was, for reasons both traditional and technical, not much practiced yet. So wise captains of the 1630's tended to hold their fire until the ships were "at pistol shot"—meaning one hundred yards, give or take—before they really began firing in earnest.

And even so, despite what seemed the murderously close range and immense cannons of those exchanges, most combats between ships were ultimately decided by musketry and boarding actions. Comparatively few vessels sank outright during battle, although many were so badly battered that they had to be scuttled. Too unreliable because of the damage to both their hulls and spars, heavily damaged vessels were frequently more impediments than they were prizes. Unable to keep up with the truly functional ships, and likely to capsize in even moderately high seas, many a riddled hull was finally surrendered to the sea bottom by those who had taken her at no small cost in powder and blood.

And here were the Spanish, following all the best practices of their day. Which was not in itself scorn-worthy. Even if their galleons were considerably smaller than the two up-time cruisers, they were far more numerous, sported far more and bigger guns, and could still effect boarding actions, given the great height of their poop decks, which the Spanish still conceived as "war-towers."

The only thing that bemused Eddie was that, despite the sudden and unprecedented burst of speed displayed by the two USE cruisers, the Spanish had not changed their formation. Perhaps they were still trying to decide what to do, or perhaps, given how unfavorable the wind was now, they simply intended to keep making whatever headway they could, with the intent of coming about to deliver a broadside once the big enemy ships got close enough.

But that was not going to happen today. Nor was Eddie going to steam into the middle of the Spanish van to invite the accretion of yet another maritime scrum. He leaned toward the speaking tube that led down to engineering. "More steam, please. Comm rating?"

"Yes, sir?"

"Signal *Resolve* that we are commencing evolution Delta. Report when they reply and comply."

"Yes, sir!"

"Mr. Svantner?"

"Aye, sir?"

"Bring us two points to port, and ahead three-quarters."

The intership radioman called up from below. "Sir? Admiral Mund has received, understood, and is carrying out evolution Delta."

"Excellent. Rik?"

"Sir?"

"Instruct Mount One to bear upon the second Spaniard, the more southerly one. I want a firing solution within the minute."

"The southerly one, sir?"

"Yes. Of the two, she's at longer range and we're turning to cross her at an angle. Mund will be doing the same to the northern, closer Spaniard. I want him to have the easier target."

"You are most considerate, sir."

I am most practical. *Mund has worked his gunnery crews as well as he knows how, but he's just learning himself. Intrepid's accuracy is almost ten percent better, particularly with the deck guns.*

Rik followed up his comment with a report. "Mount One indicates they have a solution." He smiled. "The gunnery chief expresses his hope that the commander does not believe that it takes him a whole minute to acquire a target, sir."

"I'm quite aware of that, Rik. But today I need the solutions to be correct, and triple checked, rather than quick. There's a morale war we're waging here, as well, although the Spanish don't know it yet."

"And what morale war is that, Commander?" asked Gjedde from his left side.

Eddie looked over. "The war to break their spirit by convincing them that they are facing a foe so precise and lethal that it makes no sense to stand against him. I don't want a lot of misses, today. And we've got the right weather for shooting. Pretty calm seas, with both wind and current following, now that we've got the weather gauge on them. So there's minimal chop, and what little there is, we're counteracting with our propulsion: we're cutting through those little waves without a bump. All good news for our gunners. And all bad news for the Spanish. And by the time we've fired three rounds, I want them thinking that retreat or surrender are their only reasonable options."

Rik stepped back into the group at the front of the flying bridge. "Mount One reports a triple-checked firing solution, sir. Range is six-hundred-eighty yards. The Spaniard is trying to turn into us, but she's still close-hauled and sluggish. We'll have a target that's in three-quarter profile."

"Very good. Confirm that Mount One is loaded with solid shot and tell them to stand by. Has Mount Two signaled she can bear on the target, as well?"

"Just a few moments ago, sir. They're getting a solution, now. Range is now just over six hundred yards, sir."

Eddie sighed softly. *Which means it's showtime. This is what we trained for. And this is where we see if all our fine technology will perform, and if Admiral Simpson really knew what he was doing when he put me in charge of all this high-octane machinery and all these brave men.* And, somewhere behind that self-focused anxiety, Eddie remained aware that, today, success for him would ineluctably mean death for dozens, probably hundreds, of Spanish sailors and soldiers.

"Mount One reports ready and tracking, Commander." Rik's voice was a little tense, was clearly the verbal equivalent of a light jog to his elbow.

Eddie exhaled. "Mount One may fire at will. Mount Two?"

"Has a solution, now, Commander."

But Eddie was watching Mount One's chief gunner, now perched on a removable observer's pulpit, attached to the side-gunshield of the eight-inch naval rifle. Watching both the swells and the interferometer from that greater height, he leaned forward, like a hunter about to spring after prey—

His order to fire was immediately drowned out by the roar of the naval rifle. With well-trained speed, the gun crew had the breech open, and were already swabbing it.

Eddie saw this only peripherally. His eyes were on the galleon only five-hundred-fifty yards off his starboard bow, where a tall plume jetted upward about ten yards short and to the left side of the enemy ship.

The gun-chief's fulminations in Swedish and German, at himself and his men, were quite audible all the way back on the bridge. In point of fact, it had been an excellent first shot, and Eddie found himself strangely relaxed as he gave the next order to Rik almost casually over his shoulder. "Mount Two, fire when ready."

Mount One was loading another round when the *Intrepid*'s second eight-inch naval rifle roared from abaft the bridge and sent its solid shell through the foremainsail of the galleon, only three yards above the deck.

"Mount One is to fire when ready. Mount Two is to load explosive shell, adjust, and fire."

"Yes, sir!" Rik almost shouted, as Eddie looked down at his watch. Thirty-one seconds since Mount One had fired. Any moment now, she should be—

Mount One thundered again, smoke geysering out toward the galleon.

The shell went into the Spaniard's hull just two yards under the gunwale amidships, but the extent and nature of the damage was not immediately visible as dust, splinters, and debris vomited outward in a wedge-shaped cloud. By the time it had settled, there was more smoke rising up from the deck of the Spaniard. Clearly, the shell had hit something substantial and easily flammable on that first gun deck. Otherwise, the eight-inch shell would quite possibly have exited the hull on the other side.

With the smoke of the impact clearing, the full scope of the damage was now evident. An immense hole with a saw-toothed periphery had been ripped out of the galleon's side. One gun and its crew were nowhere to be seen. The piece adjoining it was over on its side and figures struggled and flopped fitfully in the distant gloom of that savaged center gun deck.

"Mount One is asking if it should load explosive, Commander," Rik asked.

"Tell them to stand by, and continue tracking. The next shell from Mount Two could end the engagement."

"Aye, sir," acknowledged Rik, just as Mount Two thundered behind them.

Eddie prepared himself for the resulting impact by visualizing the effect of the explosive shell on the carrack he had sunk off St. Hirta island, months ago. He had been careful to recall every detail of that explosion, of the discorporating ship, of the shattered bodies, so that he would be prepared for this moment.

But he wasn't. The shell tore into the ship just where the stairs that led down from the poop deck met the maindeck. Entering at a slight angle, it sent splintered wood and gunnery gear in all directions. A flash of powder—probably a readied fusing-quill—touched off as the shell passed deeper into the ship.

In the next moment, the forward frame of the poop deck seemed to blast outward, flame and smoke vomiting through rents made by the murderous pressure that now shot outward and upward through its riven timbers. Fragments—of chandlery, stored spars, cooking pots—ripped skyward through the pilot's post atop the poop deck. The mizzenmast went over, taking out the port quarter rail and several of the mainsail's stays.

The human costs were hard to make out at five-hundred-fifty yards range, but Eddie hesitated before raising the 10x binoculars to his eyes. He knew he needed to assess the enemy ship's state of readiness, but was not eager to see the carnage at a corrected equivalent of fifty-five yards.

Thankfully, the wounded and dead were all below the screening sides of the gunwale. Most of the fever-pitch activity about the deck was concerned with providing aid to the wounded or dragging the fallen out of the way. A swarm of sail-handlers were streaming aft, some reinforcing the mainsails' remaining stays, others starting aloft to rig new lines. Harder to see, on the port side of the spar deck, hurrying men with axes and buckets were wreathed in a steadily growing plume of smoke from below decks. It was unclear if they, or the fire they were fighting, were going to be the winners in their desperate contest. Along the gun decks, blood-smeared gunners heaved splintered wood, ruined tools, and no small number of bodies out the two gaping holes in her starboard side.

Meaning that, although the ship was stricken, she was still capable of putting herself in order for combat. And the troops aboard her, their morions and pieces bobbing as they crowded toward the starboard side, were clearly still spoiling for a fight. Whatever criticisms you might lay at the foot of Spanish soldiers and sailors, you couldn't fault them for a lack of courage. But unfortunately, that meant that Eddie had to give an order he'd hoped to avoid.

Perhaps Rik was reading his mind again. "Do we take them under fire once more, Commander?"

"Yes, Rik, but not with the deck-guns. I want Mounts One and Two to commence tracking our next target." Eddie pointed to the next ship on the extreme southern side of the Spanish formation, which the *Intrepid* would pass still farther to the south, thereby fulfilling its mission as the lower pincer of evolution Delta.

"So, a broadside from the carronades to sink the Spaniard, then?"

"Well, I'd be happy not to sink her, Rik. Remember, the Dutch have a lot more crew than they have hulls. Any Spaniard we can take as a prize is an addition to our fleet. So, solid shot in the carronades. Tell Svantner to bring us one point to starboard and hold her steady. Get me to within four hundred yards of the Spaniard so the battery has a decent shot."

Rik nodded as he cut hand signals in Svantner's direction. "Very good, sir. But four hundred yards won't score nearly as many hits as if we press in to three hundred."

Eddie smiled. "Yeah, as I taught you, Rik. But we can't spare the time to maneuver closer. And actually, I'm counting on a few extra misses at four hundred yards. Firing at three hundred yards would be overkill."

"Would be what?"

"I'll explain later. Pass the word."

Rik was already sending the orders to the gun deck.

Admiral Pros Mund watched eagerly, greedily, and, he had to admit, with a measure of envy, as *Intrepid* steamed swiftly around the extreme southern flank of the Spanish, quickly found the range of the closest ship, and, after two misses, put two shells into the hull's center of mass. An impressive feat of gunnery, even given the current favorable conditions.

But now it is my turn, to defeat my foes and please my king. Unbidden, he recalled the image of Edel's strong but aloof profile, staring hatefully at the snowy lumps and naked peaks of the Icelandic coast, and thought: *and if Christian is pleased enough, then maybe I can also bring her to a place where she will smile once again.*

Resolve, engines vibrating beneath Pros Mund's feet, had worked her way beyond the north extents of the approaching Spanish van. The only exception were the three *pataches* that had almost comically attempted to deny the steamship the weather gauge. Their captains, either showing that they had better sense or better speed than those aboard the galleons, ultimately scattered like so many cream-winged pigeons as the tremendous speed of the up-time ship left them struggling to react swiftly enough. Stranded between and behind the now fully opened pincers formed by the *Intrepid* running along the southern edge of the Spanish van and the *Resolve* skimming along its northern edge, the Spanish *pataches* were now circling, as if uncertain what to do. With the wind turning so it was more from the north, flight to the northeast along the comparatively treacherous windward side of the Lesser Antilles was becoming increasingly problematic. The wind could, instead, catch them in irons, or buffet them back toward their own fleet, or down upon the *Achilles*. But she was a big ship, outgunning them by at least two to one, and more than that by far in weight of shot per broadside. In the time it took for them to get the weather gauge on her, night would be falling and the steamships might be back. On reflection, Pros admitted, it was easy to understand why the *pataches* were biding their time, waiting for some indication of which course of action might prove most prudent.

Haakon, Mund's first mate, approached and bowed. "Admiral Mund, we are at four hundred yards, as you instructed. Orders?"

Mund nodded. "Do Mounts One And Two have the gauge—er, have firing solutions for the Spaniard?"

"Yes, sir."

"They are loaded with solid shot?"

"Yes, sir."

"Then tell them to fire at once and await reloading orders."

"Yes, sir." Mere moments later, both of his ship's great guns spoke. Two geysers appeared in front of the enemy ship, bracketing it to left and right.

"Load solid shot, adjust, fire when ready," he shouted to the orderly, who relayed the orders into the speaking tubes.

On the Spanish ships, musketeers were beginning to ascend into the rigging, finding comparatively stable spots higher up on the ratlines.

Mount One spoke shortly before Mount Two, and put a shell into the low-slung bow of the Spanish galleon, the bowsprit coming down with a crash, stripping off stays and planking that trailed, foaming, in the water along her port side. The shell from Mount Two fell short rather than long this time, but only by fifteen yards.

"Load with explosive shell," Mund said, and told himself he did not feel a thrill to give that order. "And fire at will."

Mount One spoke first, again, and put her shell into the Spaniard's fo'c'sle. Planks, rails, bodies flew up in a blast of dust and smoke, snapping two bow stays of the foremast as the ship veered sharply to port. A moment later, the second shell sliced into the ship's deck just a few feet to the port side of the mainmast, penetrating both the spar and the layered hardwoods of the shaft in which it was set. The explosion was sharp and fierce. Deckplanks sprayed in all directions as the thunderclap of smoke and woodchips sent the mainmast several yards into the air, stripping free of its stays and shrouds, the main topgallant snapping away from the main spar of the mast, sails flying wildly about as if signaling distress. That cyclone of splintering spars severed another foremast stay and the fore topgallant teetered and shook, a telltale sign that the entire mast was in jeopardy.

"She's all but dead in the water," exulted Haakon as they passed abreast of the crippled galleon. "A broadside to finish her off?"

"No, we move to the next target." Mund gestured to the next Spanish ship, a smaller galleoncete, another five hundred yards farther west. "Our job is to work along both sides of their van, crippling ships so that we and the Dutch may take them as prizes later. This ship has only the use of her mizzen, and has fires to control, beside. She will not escape, and cannot maneuver to return fire. If she tries, the Dutch will cross her bow and sweep her decks with grape." *Although I want to take her, blast them. I want—I need—the honors, the favor, of my king.* "Order more steam, and as soon as we have it, ahead full."

"Sir?" Haakon asked carefully. "We are already at the speed that was set—by you—for this phase of plan Beta."

"Plans change, Haakon." Mund drew his sword and nodded to the ensign of the Wild Geese whom he'd put in charge of his boarding team. "The sun is going down and we can have a more decisive victory if we hurry. And perhaps we can yet board a rich prize for the glory of our king." Mund's small, rare smile caused his subordinate to blink in surprise. "We have only begun to hunt, Haakon."

Chapter 38

Grenada Passage, Caribbean Sea

Fadrique Álvarez de Toledo had seen enough to know that the day was lost, and that the most valuable thing he could do now was to save what was left of His Imperial Majesty's fleet and report the presence of these extraordinarily swift and lethal up-time ships to the governor of Havana. If he was able to pull away in good enough order and his ships were not scattered by fleeing into the approaching night, he would dispatch a *patache* to inform Cartagena, as well. But those lazy Tierra Firma bastards had not even been reliable enough to show up for this fight. Although, seen objectively, it was probably a fortunate thing that they hadn't.

Whatever guns were on those two up-time ships, they were like nothing he'd ever seen or even heard rumors of, with the exception of last year's shelling of Hamburg. There, the up-time ironclads had reduced the heavy walls of that city to pulverized gravel in a matter of hours. And if these guns were not quite as devastating in their effects as rumor had described those long cannons, they were accurate and lethal at ranges that made the ships carrying them almost completely unapproachable. Fadrique had watched as the two long, fast ships split apart, bracketing and running along the northern and southern fringes of Jorge de Cárdenas y Manrique de Lara's van of eight galleons. In minutes, and firing from almost six hundred yards, the two ships had, with less than half a dozen shots each, disabled the two leading galleons. And unless he was much mistaken, several of those shells had carried explosives within them, almost like mortars. Then the southernmost up-time ship had unloaded a broadside into its target from the almost unthinkable range of four hundred yards. More unthinkable still was the accuracy and effects of the enemy carronades. The galleon had literally reeled under the force of the blast; its mainmast fell immediately, and an already thin trail of smoke became thicker and darker. Now, as the shadows were starting to lengthen, that hull, the *San Salvador*, was listing severely to starboard and putting out increasing volumes of smoke.

And as if to prove that these results were the rule rather than the exception when fighting against these up-time ships, they had now completed savaging the next two galleons along their path. Once again, they had used the long guns that were mounted high on their weather decks and that had sharp reports, almost like thunderclaps, when they discharged. On this occasion, it was the northernmost of the up-time ships which then fired a *coup de grace* broadside, apparently of exploding shells.

It was hard to discern the range at which the up-time ship had unleashed that broadside. Álvarez de Toledo hypothesized it might have been as little as two hundred yards since its smaller target, the galleoncete *La Concepcion*, had fired back, probably more in defiance than out of any reasonable hope of scoring a hit. And it was impossible to know exactly how many hits had been scored upon the galleoncete or where. But to Fadrique's trained ear, it did indeed sound as if all the shells of that broadside were tipped with explosives. Because after the thunderous crashing and eruptions of smoke were over, *La Concepcion* was still there, meaning it wasn't her magazine that had been struck, despite the sound. But she was fiercely aflame from stem to stern and settling rapidly into the water, listing to port. If Fadrique had still been a betting man, he'd have predicted she'd burn to the waterline by ten o'clock and would roll and go down at about midnight.

But if he had any say in the matter, neither he nor any of his ships would be here to see either of those moonlit events. He swung his glass around to gauge the range to the Dutch: five hundred yards. If he turned to port and came about one-hundred-eighty degrees, he would put more distance between his ships and theirs before heading due west to catch the following wind and so, escape with all haste. He would use that wind to run overnight and regather his ships come dawn. If there was no sign of pursuit, he could then start working his way across the great central expanse of the Caribbean, tacking to make northern progress toward Santiago, the closest place of Spanish strength.

But that portside turn would take him through the very eye of the wind, and his galleons were finicky when tacking. They lost way so quickly that there was always the chance that, if the breeze died as they began to turn into it, that they might not tack across but struggle through baffling winds or, worse yet, get caught in irons. In which case the Dutch, whose ships could sail closer hauled, would catch them astern.

But the alternative, a hard turn to starboard, had its own risks. Yes, it put the wind behind him almost immediately since he only had to make a ninety degree turn, but he was still sailing obliquely toward the northbound Dutch. And at this range—

—well, at this range, he hadn't the time for indecision. "Roderigo, tell the pilot hard a starboard as tight as she'll take it."

"Admiral!" cried Roderigo, "that could bring us within two hundred yards of the Dutch guns, closer if they read our intent correctly."

"We've no choice. Do as I say, and signal the other ships to do so at once as well."

"Yes, sir. I shall—"

There was a cry from the foretop crow's next. "Smoke! Smoke off the starboard bow! And sails!"

De Toledo cursed, swung up his spyglass, and felt a bitter cold in his belly that threatened to unman him. Sharply outlined against the western horizon was a single, thin, but rapidly advancing plume of smoke and the sails of three sizable fore-and-aft rigged vessels: outsized jachts or *pataches*. Bigger than his *pataches*, at any rate. And that smoke could only mean one thing.

"Sir," Roderigo asked hoarsely, "what is it? What are they?"

"The third side of the trap," Fadrique answered bitterly. "And that smoke is yet another of these blasted up-time steam ships. I cannot tell how big it is—those ships are too far off—but it hardly matters. If we turn due west to catch the wind, they shall cut us off. They can sail closer to the wind and are heading northward, across our line of withdrawal."

"So what do we—?"

"We still come about hard to starboard, but we keep turning. Take us through a one-hundred-thirty-five degree turn, so that our final bearing is north by northwest. That and due north are the only open sides of this box ambush they've sprung upon us. And of the two, the northwest allows us to keep the wind over our starboard quarter. We should be able to outrun them. Maybe. Pass the order."

"Yes, sir." Roderigo tarried a moment, concern in his dark brown eyes. "And the rest of our fleet? What of them?"

De Toledo looked behind to the northeast. The southernmost of the up-timer ships was starting to fire on a third galleon, while the northernmost steamship was leaping ahead even faster, bearing down directly upon its third target, de Cárdenas' own flagship, the *San Miguel*. The up-time ship's angle of approach suggested an intent to board. "Roderigo," Fadrique breathed heavily in answer, "the rest of our fleet is already lost. Now let us go, and hope we can avoid being crippled by the Dutch guns as we make our escape."

"Commander Cantrell, a message from Admiral Tromp!" the voice from below decks was surprised but pleased.

"Read it off, rating."

The rating complied. "Message begins. Tromp commanding *Amelia* to Commanders *Resolve* and *Intrepid*. Stop. Radio signal from Gijszoon. Stop. Has rendezvoused with *Eendracht*, steam pinnace, and prize *patache*. Stop. Currently twelve miles west of my van. Stop. Maneuvering to deny Spanish escape to west. Stop. Spanish ships coming about to flee. Stop. Have taken two under fire, attempting to intercept. Stop. May be delayed reaching your area of engagement to help with crewing of prizes. Stop. Will update on pursuit of Spanish soonest. Stop. Message ends."

"Well, Floriszoon and the earl of Tyrconnell showing up now: that's a pleasant surprise!" exclaimed Rik brightly.

Gjedde nodded. "Yes, but that's not." He pointed almost due north as *Intrepid*'s Mount Two roared and put a final shell into the third galleon's sterncastle, flame and smoke gushing out all her shattering windows as the explosive shell went off deep inside her.

Eddie followed Gjedde's finger past the devastated galleon and suppressed a gasp. Even from this distance, it was clear that *Resolve* had not merely closed to broadside range with one of the largest galleons, but could only mean to board her. "My God, what is Mund doing? We agreed that neither of us would—"

Gjedde shook his head; he looked sad but oddly unsurprised. "Pros Mund is the admiral. He is the one person who may elect not to follow the orders that were agreed upon."

"But then why didn't he radio, let us know—?"

"Commander Cantrell," Gjedde said sadly, slowly. "Let us move to the next ship, and try to signal Admiral Mund. And let us shift two points to starboard as we do so."

"Tuck more tightly to the north? Why? Do you want to start boarding galleons now, as well?"

"No, Commander Cantrell. I want to be closer to *Resolve*. In case something goes wrong."

You mean, "more wrong," thought Eddie, but instead he shouted, "Mr. Svantner! Two points to starboard and give me some more steam. We may be changing our plans."

Pros Mund's heart leaped up as the great galleon's mainmast came down. The long pennant that announced it as the flagship of the fleet's admiral went over the side with the topmain spar and disappeared into the wreckage-strewn waters.

After finding the range, his deck gunners had put three solid and three explosive shells into the galleon, which he had feared might sink her. But the towering Spanish ship with a looming broadside of twenty-six-, forty-two- and thirty-six-pounders proved that sheer mass was a quality unto itself. The heavy timbers of the craft were rent in many places, putting out smoke from several, but it remained seaworthy and upright.

The same could not be claimed for a great many of her crew, however. Her top decks were a writhing mass of sailhandlers attempting to save the fore and mizzen, seamen struggling to douse fires, musketeers trying to find enough calm among the chaos to keep a bead on the approaching up-time ship, and a foot-tangling mass of dead and wounded comrades. Along the gun decks, four of the guns had spoken in response, but at slightly better than one-hundred-fifty yards, only one had scored a hit. It was respectable shooting, actually, but futile. The ball had rebounded from the *Resolve*'s stout reinforced timbers, its only effect having been to leave a significant dent in them.

"One hundred and twenty yards!" cried Haakon from the deck.

"Helm," shouted Mund, "one point to starboard. Haakon, as soon as we're alongside the Spaniard, fire port-side battery. Mitrailleuses,"—Mund had moved both to the same side of the ship for this very reason—"prepare to concentrate fire upon the enemy's quarterdeck."

The *Resolve* straightened from her starboard correction, and the portside carronades, all fourteen of them, roared, sending jets of smoke toward the Spaniard that quickly diffused, forming a single, cloudy smear that veiled the other ship.

But even through those drifts of gunpowder-fog, Mund could see that eight of his fourteen eight-inch carronades had struck the galleon, including one of the three he had loaded with explosive shell. The ruin along the first gun deck was unlike anything he'd seen before. Half the strakes were broken at least two places and the interior explosion ejected a spray of gear, balls, and bodies from deep within the Spaniard. The scene on the deck was more frenzied still, with the new casualties and growing panic undermining the ongoing attempts to put the ship a-right for combat. And now that the smoke was clearing, he could see that the quarterdeck, the logical location of both the admiral and a guard of his best marksmen, was returning to order noticeably faster than the rest of the weather deck. That was almost surely a sign that effective commands were still being issued and followed, there.

Haakon was shouting a warning at the same moment that Pros Mund pointed his drawn sword at the Spaniard's quarterdeck and shouted, "Mitrailleuses, fire on the quarterdeck!"

The .50 caliber multibarreled guns began firing rapidly. The two weapons emitted a rippling roar and their stream of projectiles played in tight arcs back and forth across the galleon's quarterdeck.

Mund discovered that he had stopped exhaling in mid-breath. He had seen carnage aplenty in his years before the mast: waves of musketry sweeping decks; cannon balls blasting through bulkheads, sending forth a wide spray of daggerlike splinters that sliced men to ribbons. But nothing prepared him for this: the methodical and relentless cone of death that walked back and forth upon the Spaniard's high quarterdeck with terrible precision and even more terrible lethality. Probably two-thirds of the rounds fired passed high, splintered rails, or chewed at the hull's side, but the one third that did hit dropped men in windrows and shattered every object they hit. The tiller was riven, the compass stand blasted, lights shattered, flag boxes riddled. The bullets not only went through the breast plates of the crowded soldiers, but out the back as well, still carrying enough force to slay men behind the first. But unlike the broad sprays of blood he associated with wide, slow-moving musket balls, these bullets simply rose a brief, maroon-colored puff, or left no external sign whatsoever—and seemed all the more haunting, for that. It was as if the bullets themselves were too focused on killing to make any sign that they had done so, were too busy finding another life to extinguish or limb to maim.

Mund was still staring at the abattoir that had been the crowded poop of the Spaniard when the questioning cry came from the rear mitrailleuse mount. "Do we reload, Admiral?"

"Yes," barked Mund, rousing from his fixated daze and leaping down the steps of the running bridge to join the boarders sheltering behind the portside gunwales. Most were Irish, who he had always heard were a rather loud and raucous lot. But now, as they waited to join the combat, they were among the most silent and ferociously focused troops he had ever seen. "Three points port," he shouted over his shoulder at the pilot. "Bring us alongside her to board." Mund envisioned Edel smiling again, smiling as they neared a new land grant, this one back home in Denmark, maybe along the coast near Skaelskor...

"Admiral!" shouted Haakon again.

Edel and her elusive smile had been swept away by Haakon's cry. "Damn it, man, what is amiss?" he asked sharply, scanning the Spaniard for signs of trouble.

His eyes gave him the answer the same moment Haakon did. "Swivel guns up along the bow, Admiral. Get down—!"

It hardly seemed fair, Mund reflected, as he saw a half-dozen Spaniards swinging their hastily remounted small guns in the direction of his boarders. *Resolve*'s first hits upon the Spaniard had been in her forecastle, had started a fire there and left bodies draped over her gunwale and caught in her spritsail sheets. But Spanish professionalism was not to be underestimated. Even before they brought the fires under control, some of the troops at her waist had evidently discerned that the sides of the uptime ship were too high to allow them to engage her weather deck from their own. So they had sought a better vantage point by relocating to the greater altitude of the fo'c'sle and poop. So a good number of the midship's swivel guns—a mix of falconets, patereroes, morterettes, and espingoles—had been moved to yokes on the bow. It was not part of a subtle scheme to initiate counterfire from a part of the galleon that its attackers might reasonably conclude was no longer in the fight. Rather, it was a product of dumb luck and the training and dogged resolve of professional soldiers who insisted on finding a way to strike back, even when higher orders were no longer forthcoming.

Mund turned to order his own swivel guns on the starboard side, the two-inch "Big Shots" of down-time manufacture, to fire upon their Spanish equivalents. As he did, the morion-helmeted Spanish leaned over their pieces and discharged them in a ragged volley. Pros Mund saw Haakon diving for cover, thought that he should have done so himself before shouting his most recent order, felt a rapid patter of dull thumps in his chest, saw Edel's disapproving frown—

And then he saw nothing at all.

Eddie Cantrell's foul-mouthed alcoholic father had always been outraged when any of his children emulated his colorful use of language. He had communicated that displeasure with either a tongue- or a belt-lashing. So Eddie had come to adulthood with a reflexive tendency to avoid cursing. However, when the *Resolve* sent a second broadside into the ship she had closed with, he let out an oath between clenched teeth.

Although his eyes were still locked to his binoculars, he could hear Gjedde shift alongside him, imagined the Norwegian staring at him. "Is Mund boarding her?"

"No," Eddie grumbled, "he's destroyed her."

As if on cue, the broadside—evidently all explosive shells—went off within the galleon, which seemed to fly apart. The last two masts went down, the mizzen cartwheeling into the water. The sterncastle and forecastle both seemed to detonate from within, planks, window frames, bodies flying outward in a shower of general destruction—

The magazine went up with a roar like two fast thunderclaps. The flash it made was reminiscent of the nighttime battleship gunnery duels that Eddie had seen on the newsreel footage included in countless documentaries on the History Channel. It wasn't just one great light, but a kind of quick-strobe effect of overlapping explosions. An all-obscuring blanket of white smoke fumed outward furiously, catching the slightly roseate light of the descending sun as it did.

Rik swallowed nervously. "How close was *Resolve* when—?"

Eddie sighed. "One hundred yards, maybe a little more. They're safe, but will be catching some of the debris on their deck. Damn it, I wonder what happened, why Mund decided to—?"

"Commander Cantrell," the intraship comm rating called up. "Mounts One and Two report they continue to track our target and are loaded with explosive. Awaiting your orders."

Eddie suppressed yet another sigh and swung his glasses toward the fourth galleon on his target list. She was coming about and starting to make some headway in her attempt to run to the northwest. Not that it mattered. The best she could do was three knots, if she was lucky. *Intrepid* was already doing ten and Eddie could call for more, if needed. "Range?" Eddie asked lazily. Strange how the combat gunnery that had been a nail-biting novelty forty minutes ago had become a comparatively dull routine.

"Five hundred fifty yards, sir."

"Fire at will. Reload and maintain tracking but check fire."

Although Eddie was eager to see *Resolve* emerge from the now-thinning smoke of the vaporized galleon, he forced himself to watch his guns' effects upon their present target. One shell struck the fo'c'sle, penetrating deeply before exploding. Timbers and smoke roiled outward, a cannon upended and disappeared off the opposite side of the shattered weather deck. The second shell passed into the stern windows of the galleon and went off after a beat. It made a muffled noise, and smoke started trailing out the ruined captain's cabin about the same moment that the ship's rudder seemed to loosen and the breeze in the sails tugged the ship into a more westerly course.

"She's sailing before the wind now, rudderless," commented Gjedde. "The shell probably exploded somewhere near her whip-staff or tiller-chains."

Rik nodded, turned toward Eddie. "Shall we come close enough to let the carronades fire some canister-shot into her sails?"

Eddie shrugged. "Even if we didn't, she can't steer, so she's going nowhere fast. But we might as well slow her down a little, even so." He aimed his next query down at the comm ratings working beneath below deck. "Any word from *Resolve* yet?"

"No, sir."

"Then hail them, ask for an update."

Gjedde nodded at the last ship of the Spanish fleet's eastern van. "What about her? I suspect we'll only have to put a few shells into her at range, and ask her to strike colors."

"Because of what she's seen us do to her sister ships?" asked Rik.

Eddie saw what Gjedde was getting at, shook his head. "No, because she's not *really* a sister ship. Look at her waterline, the slope of her tumblehome, the more widely spaced gun ports. She's not a galleon but a nao, a trading ship that the Spanish sometimes rearm for combat."

"She looks quite similar to the galleons," Rik observed with a dubious frown.

Gjedde nodded. "Because there's little difference when the Spanish lay down a galleon from when they lay down a nao. In an emergency, they can reequip her, as I'm sure they've done now. But she'll have a crew more accustomed to trade and running from enemy ships, rather than fighting and heading toward them. She knows she can't outrun us before dark. And, as you said, she knows what our guns can do." He folded his arms. "Since she's already running, I'd say she's half-ready to surrender. Just give her master a good excuse—two shells from the rifles—and I suspect she will strike her colors."

"Commander Cantrell," the intership radioman called up, "I have a report from the *Resolve*. From First Mate Haakon."

Eddie, Gjedde, and Rik exchanged rueful glances. "Please read the message, rating."

"Message begins. *Resolve* to *Intrepid*: Admiral Mund killed by enemy fire. Stop. First Mate Haakon in temporary command. Stop. Unaffected by explosion of galleon. Stop. Minor casualties among deck personnel from enemy swivel guns. Stop. Awaiting orders. Stop. Message ends."

The news was somewhat worse than it might have been, but it was hardly a surprise. The three officers stood quietly on the flying bridge for several long seconds. Then Eddie turned to Gjedde. "I believe this means you are now in command of our ships, Captain Gjedde. Do we continue with the second half of our plan, to chase the Spaniards' southern van?"

"We can overtake them within the hour," Rik added. He sounded eager.

Gjedde stared at the setting sun for several more seconds. "We could, but we shall not. There will not be enough light left to use our guns for very long, and to chase them will take us far away from Tromp's van. Furthermore, the *Resolve* just lost her captain who is also the only senior officer with extensive training in all the technological innovations on the ship. The section heads are all competent, but Haakon was a late addition to the command staff and did not receive enough training across these various areas of new expertise. So even if we had more light, we may not count upon the *Resolve* to perform as she might under better circumstances."

Eddie leaned back and let Rik lead the charge for action, watching Gjedde's response. "So shall we engage the *pataches*, then? They are slipping away to the south, just a few miles to port."

Again Gjedde shook his head. "They are maneuvering southwest because they are fleeing. I suspect they hope to slip between our steamships and Tromp's van, and thence, escape west into the open waters of the Caribbean, following in the wake of the Spanish southern van. They are smaller and more maneuverable, and so are much harder to hit. And there is nothing to be gained in chasing them into the dark. We have enough work ahead of us just to regroup, take what prizes we may, sink what we may not, and decide upon our next course of action."

"Not back to Trinidad as we planned, then?" Rik sounded perplexed.

Gjedde shook his head. "Not all of us."

Eddie was careful to make his observation oblique enough to avoid sounding like criticism. "With respect, Captain, we have over a hundred Wild Geese, twenty other ship's troops, and an oil-prospecting team on Trinidad. It seems we have some difficult choices to make, weighing adequate defense for them against our obvious need to tow our prizes back to St. Eustatia for refit."

Gjedde stared at Eddie but nodded. "Just so. And that is why we may not take as many prizes as we wish. As you say, we must balance how many of the spoils we may take from this battle against how much it costs us to take them at all. And I assure you, Commander, I will not leave Trinidad poorly defended. But we must make a quick run to St. Eustatia if we are to meet

Trinidad's special needs, just as we must provide for the new requirements of our fleet."

"You mean, we need to bring Ann Koudsi and the drillers the gear they need to start sinking some holes?"

"That, and we need to inaugurate a new class of officers and seamen, Commander."

Eddie nodded. "Of course. There are a lot of extra sailors waiting in St. Eustatia who could be reassigned as crew for the prize vessels we take here."

Gjedde's brow seemed to wrinkle. "Yes, but that was not what I was thinking of, primarily."

"Oh, Captain? Then what new class of officers and seamen are you talking about, sir?"

"The ones you are going to train, Commander. Between these new guns, the cruisers, the steam pinnaces, the balloons, and the radios, we are now fighting a very new kind of war. And you are the person who is going to teach a new cadre of officers how to fight it. Now, Commander Cantrell, I believe we have a nao to frighten into submission before we may set about regrouping and taking our prizes."

Chapter 39

Le Grand Cul-de-Sac Marin, Guadeloupe

Jacques Dyel du Parque glanced over his shoulder out into the bay known as Le Grand Cul-de-Sac Marin, where the Dieppe-built bark *Bretagne* rode at anchor. He wished he was still on it, and bound back to Martinique. Possibly all the way back to France. He hadn't yet decided the limits (if any) of his aversion to the Leeward Islands.

His uncle, however, had no such reluctance or regrets, having made his admittedly inconstant fortunes here in the New World, and, most particularly, on St. Christopher's. Which, Jacques readily admitted, was a pleasant enough place, but seemed doomed to be overrun by the English, their Irish bondsmen, and now the Dutch. It was only a matter of time before the island's French colony would be taken over, either by martial conquest or marital cooption.

So, in an act of prudence that was also an attempt at creating a legacy (his uncle, Pierre Bélain sieur d'Esnambuc, had not married and so Jacques had come to understand that he was to be the beneficiary of his intermittent and inchoate patriarchal impulses), Jacques found himself the lieutenant governor of the two-month old colony on the island of Martinique. Which was neither as friendly to husbandry nor as hospitable as St. Christopher's, and furthermore, was the home of natives whose receptivity was, at

428

best, uncertain. However, Uncle Pierre had met with the rather daunting Caribs on his way to fetching Jacques, and reported that the proposal he had made to them in that meeting had significantly improved the local cacique's opinion of their French neighbors/invaders. Jacques remained unsure which term better represented the native attitude toward the pale-skinned visitors, and suspected the Caribs themselves remained undecided.

After sending a skiff to fetch Jacques from his glorified shack in Fort St. Pierre, d'Esnambuc had set course directly for Guadeloupe, inquiring affectionately after his nephew's health and spirits and then immediately closeting himself with the Carib warrior who had accompanied him from Martinique. From the few words he had exchanged with his uncle since then, this fellow, Youacou, was a person of some diplomatic significance by dint of his relations. While not a cacique himself, he was well-placed for Uncle Pierre's immediate purposes. On the one hand, Youacou's maternal aunt had married a renowned hunter from the Caribs of Guadeloupe. On the other hand, Youacou's second-cousin-once-removed had been killed by Thomas Warner on St. Christopher's in 1626, at the genocidal massacre that had since acquired the eponymous label the Battle of Bloody Point. Jacques had not wanted to embarrass his uncle by inquiring how it was that Youacou had been convinced that Thomas Warner alone had been responsible for the death of his second-cousin-once-removed, since d'Esnambuc had fought alongside the English in that battle and, according to stories told by his uncle's long-standing assistants, the battle had fundamentally been fought at his urging. Warner had, it was whispered, been exceedingly reluctant to interpret deteriorating relations with the Caribs as an inevitable prelude to slaughter.

But Jacques had no opportunity to ask such ticklish questions. It was almost as if his uncle was trying to avoid him, or at least to have any sustained conversation with him while they were aboard the *Bretagne*. But now they were ashore, and Youacou had disappeared into the bushes, just as two of d'Esnambuc's men started down the beach to make contact with the French settlers here, who, having arrived almost four months ago, were still living in tents. Just around the next headland, the smoke from their cooking fires rose lazily up toward the cotton-ball clouds.

"Uncle," Jacques began mildly, "I do not know if this is a better time for us to converse?"

D'Esnambuc turned with a genuine smile. "It is, my boy. I am sorry I have had to hold you at arm's length since I spirited you away from your duties on Martinique, but it was essential that you not know just why you were being brought here."

"That sounds quite mysterious, Uncle."

"Not so much mysterious as delicate, Jacques. You remember that I spoke to you of the two men that Richelieu's agent, Fouquet, sent here to colonize Guadeloupe?"

"Yes. One was a former colonist under you at St. Christopher's: Charles Liénard de l'Olive. A bold man, you said, but not particularly politic."

"Precisely my words, I believe. Well, during his partner's absence, it seems he has further mismanaged his supplies and his relations with the Caribs of this island. I suspect he shall be raiding them for food before the year is out."

Jacques frowned. "But does this not match your expectations and hopes?" D'Esnambuc had not welcomed Fouquet's diversion of finances and assistance to the strange pair who had undertaken the settlement of Guadeloupe, and had refused their first requests for aid two months ago.

"It matches my expectations, but my hopes have changed, Jacques." He glanced at their guards, who were patrolling beyond the thin line of palm trees in whose shadows they waited. He lowered his tone so that it almost blended with the sound of the surf. "With the Dutch arriving in such great numbers on St. Eustatia, and now collaborating so freely and extensively with Warner's colony, my hopes that his settlement would wither for lack of support from England are dashed. Indeed, he now has such multitudes of workers and troops at his disposal that it is sheer inertia that keeps him from pushing us off the island altogether."

Jacques wondered if the principle of honoring one's agreements might not also work as a constraint upon the Englishman, but suspected his adventurer-uncle might not appreciate that perspective. "And our changed fortunes on St. Christopher's change your attitudes toward this Guadeloupe settlement in what way?"

"In every possible way, my boy, considering their most recent letter to me. A little less than a fortnight ago, a packet came to Basseterre in St. Christopher's. Despite much circumlocution, the letter's author, Jean du Plessis d'Ossonville, revealed that he had failed in a mission given to him by Richelieu. He was to have purchased a tract of land on Trinidad that had been seized by a group of 'adventurers' who were known—favorably—to the cardinal's allies in France."

Jacques frowned. "Will the Spanish care for such fine legal distinctions? It will not matter to them whether the land in question passed through independent hands before coming into Richelieu's grasp."

"Just as it shall not matter to the crown of France that Spain is offended. The law here in the New World, my boy, is that there is no peace beyond the Line. And even so, we did not field our flag against Spain's to come by the property. Beyond that, everything is a pesky detail of interest only to ministers-without-portfolio and historians."

Jacques shrugged. There was no arguing that almost certainly correct point. "So du Plessis failed to purchase this land on Trinidad. How does this impact our fortunes on St. Christopher's?"

Muttering, "Ah, my boy, my boy," d'Esnambuc ruffled his twenty-year-old nephew's head. Jacques put up with such inappropriately juvenile displays of affection in small part because the man expressing them had also undertaken to furnish him with a potential for wealth far beyond anything his rather neglectful father had assayed. But more so because he knew his Uncle Pierre loved him genuinely and that was worth more than all the islands and livres in the world to Jacques.

"Ah, my boy," d'Esnambuc repeated. "You have a good soul, bless you. Perhaps your prayers will redeem my sins, when I'm gone. But for now, listen and learn. From reading between the lines in du Plessis' letter, I am quite sure that he got greedy in his negotiations with these adventurers on Trinidad. From what de l'Olive told me of him, the fellow is clever and a shrewd bargainer. But I suspect in this case, he bargained a bit too hard. He forgot that in any negotiations, whether with priests or pirates, the objective is to shear the sheep, not skin them. For if they feel the edge of the shears, even if you have them bound to your will in that moment, they will remember that injury and look to repay it to you four-fold."

Jacques wondered if Uncle Pierre was always so prudent as his advice suggested and wondered how many shear-shaped scars Thomas Warner and the other English leaders of St. Christopher bore and still reflected upon with ill-feeling.

If d'Esnambuc perceived a disjuncture between his advice and practice, he did not evince it. "So, in his most recent letter, du Plessis once again requested aid. But this time, he is not only offering to pay for the food that his intemperate partner de l'Olive has now mismanaged into nonexistence, but is offering twice the highest rate I have seen. In livres, mind you."

"So, he is willing to spend the money that was entrusted to him to purchase this land in Trinidad—embezzle it, essentially—to save his failing colony here."

"Exactly."

"So, do you mean to help them?"

"Yes, but not as they asked or expect. There is a reason I did not try to establish a colony here on Guadeloupe, Jacques, despite the fine waters of its own basse-terre and reasonable promise of husbandry."

"The Caribs."

His uncle nodded. "I have fought them once before and am in no rush to do so again. And here they are far more numerous than on Martinique. I would not have planted you in that place, my boy, unless I felt sure we could make it safe. But this place?" Pierre waved a hand dismissively toward the south. "They are thick in those volcanic valleys, and they will remain so."

Jacques frowned. "So, du Plessis and de l'Olive are worried that they must have a success to show Richelieu that will induce him to pardon their failure at Trinidad, and now, are failing here as well. And the natives are populous upon these islands and unremittingly hostile. And the English have new friends—the Dutch, no less—on St. Eustatia and so our days on St. Christopher may be numbered." He shook his head. "Yet you report all these things as if they are harbingers of some great venture that may be undertaken. I do not see it."

D'Esnambuc smiled. "As I said, you have a good heart. Now, be schooled by your uncle who shall have all his successes in this world, not the next, I am quite sure. With the arrival of the Dutch, the Caribs know that their designs to retake St. Christopher's are all but dashed. And we, being pushed out like them, find ourselves sharing islands with them. And the current representatives of France on Guadeloupe are becoming more unwelcome by the day, for the natives know what the five hundred settlers under du Plessis and de l'Olive will do once their food runs out. They will raid their primitive neighbors and take what they need. And then, as it was on St. Christopher's, it will be war to the knife. So, logically, the natives are considering taking that fateful step first. And quite soon. But the Caribs know all too well what our weapons do, how many dozens of young warriors they will lose for every one of us firing from behind the walls of our forts.

"But in this moment, the interests of both parties, Frenchman and Carib, are strangely aligned. We have a common enemy in Warner, for with the Dutch on his side, he ruins both our designs on St. Christopher's. And since he now holds Nevis and Antigua as well, and the Dutch are crawling upon St. Eustatia like maggots on a dead cat in summer, we must all come to the same conclusion independently: that time is running out. And the only way we can change that is by combining our strength."

Jacques nodded, impressed and slightly horrified by the plan implied by his uncle's analysis. "So. You approached the Caribs of Martinique and offered them an alliance in exchange for—what? The English parts of St. Christopher's?"

D'Esnambuc nodded. "For them, and for the Caribs of Guade-loupe, if they both join us in driving the English and the Dutch out. And nothing if only one aids us."

"Whereby you hope the Caribs of Martinique will press the much larger tribes of Guadeloupe to cooperate."

Uncle Pierre shrugged. "It should not be so difficult. The great cacique slain almost ten years ago on St. Christopher's—Tegreman—has much family on Martinique, including a well-respected cousin. His sister's daughter is married to the young son of the cacique here on Guadeloupe. So through those relations, we shall bring the stick of family pressure to bear upon the Caribs, even while we dangle the carrot of reclaiming two islands under their noses."

"And how do du Plessis and de l'Olive fit into this?"

D'Esnambuc pointed at the headland, from whence their scouts were already returning, waving to signal that a safe approach could now be made. "There are at least four hundred desperate Frenchmen over that rise of land. All are armed. All can teach natives how to use firearms. And all that can be done here, and on Martinique, far away from the watchful eyes of Warner and his Dutch friends."

Jacques tilted his head in uncertainty. "But Uncle, training natives to use weapons: what is the point? Where would we get so many extra weapons, and powder, and shot? And with what funds?"

"The 'where' is handily answered by having high friends in low places. You may recall that we have traded more than once with the *boucaniers* who range this far from Jamaica and Tortuga. I have had occasion to be in contact with them recently. They can provide us with almost one hundred fifty pieces, mostly old Spanish matchlocks, and no small amount of powder and shot. And all they want in return is silver."

Jacques nodded. "Which will come from the unspent purse that Richelieu sent along for the purchase of Trinidad."

"Which du Plessis and de l'Olive may eventually report purchased his Gray Eminence sole European possession of the richest of all the islands, St. Christopher, to say nothing of Nevis and Antigua, and bought goodwill and a cohabiting entente between us and the Caribs of Guadeloupe and Martinique." D'Esnambuc rose, carefully picked up his snaphaunce pistols from the canvas in which he had wrapped them as they sat, and started toward the scouts returning from the headland.

Jacques, following, shook sand from his own piece, and wondered aloud. "But how will we share so many islands with the Caribs? It is not feasible, in the long run, since we must turn their jungles and grasslands into cane and cotton fields. How will we resolve that problem?"

D'Esnambuc turned, smiled crookedly, shrugged and shook the pistols he held in his hands. "With these," he answered. "Now, let's meet these two fools from Dieppe."

Jacques had to admit that his uncle's uncharitable characterization of the two governors of the Guadeloupe settlement was, nonetheless, accurate. De l'Olive was a great fool, as could be determined within two minutes of meeting him. Bombastic, self-important, and with a heightened sensitivity to both real and imagined social slights, he was a man perpetually prepared to do battle with anyone and anything, and not for any particularly good reason. He was a fixture of French provincial farce come to life.

Du Plessis was the more educated and measured of the two, whose one crucial failing made him a lesser fool, but arguably a more dangerous one. Although intelligent and shrewd, be believed himself to be far more intelligent and shrewd than he actually was. Jacques was fairly certain that, if one was able to peruse a dossier of his past blunders, one of which had reportedly landed his family in debt and near-disgrace, they would all reveal a common thread. Namely, that du Plessis was ever and again snatching a baffling defeat from the jaws of almost certain victory. He was that species of man who would fail, time after time, and remain mystified how it could occur to one so mentally gifted and incisive as himself. And so he would ultimately bring ruin upon all unlucky enough to cast their fortunes in along with his.

This was clearly the case unfolding here in Guadeloupe. The squalor, short-tempers, and thin, hungry faces of the sprawling, unclean tent-city that was His Majesty's colony of Grande Terre read like a still-life of imminent disaster. And the look on du Plessis' face as he heard Pierre Bélain d'Esnambuc calmly and patiently unfold his bold plan was that of a man who was so distracted by his "inexplicable" failure at reversing the catastrophe rising around him, that he could neither admit to, nor even fully perceive, the brilliance of the seasoned adventurer who had come to offer him an alternative that reconfigured so many of their enemies and obstructions into assets.

Strangely, it was de l'Olive who embraced d'Esnambuc's strategies first, possibly out of an old instinct for following his former and usually successful leader. Or possibly because the hinge upon which the plan turned was all-out war. His first and last comment on it was as self-defining a statement as Jacques had ever heard come from a human. "I like a plan that allows me to cut through our problems with a sweep of my sword. I'm with you, on this!"

D'Esnambuc nodded, pleased, turned toward du Plessis. "And you, Jean, how about you?"

"Eh? I suppose it is quite prudent, quite well reasoned out. Actually. But I am unsure how Touman, the local cacique, will react to it."

"We'll know soon enough."

Du Plessis frowned. "I do not understand."

Uncle Pierre shrugged. "I sent Youacou, a Carib warrior from Martinique, ahead to invite him to a meeting."

"Here? In my camp?"

"Where else should one leader meet another? And he has my guarantee of safe-conduct, so you'd best tell your guards to be particularly polite when they receive him."

Du Plessis and de l'Olive exchanged looks, then de l'Olive nodded to one of the three lieutenants they had present. That bearded fellow left the rude table made of planking and headed for the sentry post that watched over the approaches from the southern, volcanic lobe of the island.

"Excellent," d'Esnambuc nodded. "He will be here soon, so I must make haste to explain the other reason why we must not delay in carrying out this plan. There is a new threat to our interests here in the New World."

Du Plessis perked up. "You are referring to the up-timers, of course."

For the first time in years, Jacques saw his uncle genuinely start in surprise. "You know?"

"I know one of them had managed to sway the mercenary colonel on Trinidad away from doing business with the agents of France. I know that he seemed to be in league with the Dutch. And I know if I see one such instance of cooperation, there must be others."

"There are indeed other instances of cooperation," d'Esnambuc affirmed with a vigorous nod. "According to the merchants in my own town of Basseterre who trade regularly with the English, two large up-time ships powered by steam made port in Oranjestad some weeks ago, then left. They came with other ships, about half a dozen, that had all been sent under the aegis of the USE or the Union of Kalmar, and they have delivered much needed stores to the Dutch."

Du Plessis seemed to grow pale. "If they manage to reinforce the Dutch position on St. Eustatia—"

D'Esnambuc nodded slowly, his gaze compelling the other Frenchman not to look away. "Then we are done. Beyond all hope. We already see that the Dutch are making common cause with the disowned English of St. Christopher, Barbados, the Bahamas, Bermuda. If the USE has decided to pursue interests along with them in the New World—"

"They have," du Plessis stated flatly. "That was why Richelieu was interested in the land in Trinidad."

Jacques understood du Plessis' reference immediately. Being the most recent arrival in the New World and the youngest of the Frenchmen present, he had had both the opportunity and inclination to immerse himself in matters pertaining to the up-timers and their technology. "Of course. They are after Pitch Lake. It is bitumen, and nearby, there is almost always oil. That is how most of their vehicles run, you see. It is the key to the operation of so many of their machines."

Du Plessis was nodding. Uncle Pierre was simply smiling, delighted and discernibly proud at his nephew's knowledgeable addition to the conversation. "Young Monsieur du Parquet knows whereof he speaks. Trust me, d'Esnambuc: the up-time presence here is not fleeting. They mean to have that oil. And that means they must establish a nearby stronghold in the New World. And where better than here in the middle of the Leeward islands, by expanding upon an already-extant port?"

Uncle Pierre nodded vigorously. "Yes, so we must destroy that port, that facility, before they can develop it. And I think you are very right that they mean to develop it as a military base, as well."

"Why?" asked de l'Olive suspiciously.

D'Esnambuc leaned back and folded his hands. To Jacques, his uncle suddenly looked like an improbably well-armed and vigorous school-master. "There is an up-timer on St. Eustatia now who has commenced a most unusual project. He is stringing what seem to be some kinds of cables high in the trees on the northeastern side of the volcanic mountain called The Quill. Specifically, on the slopes that face back toward Europe. I do not know what it portends, but an unusual amount of manpower, both freeman and slave, has been dedicated to the project. It also seems to involve the construction of a sizable steam engine that spins metal wheels, which resemble the blades of windmills trapped within a broad hub."

Jacques folded his hands and nodded. "They are building a radio, I think. A very powerful one. That steam plant you have heard about is to furnish power for it. A generator, I believe they call it. When the steam blasts through the tubes containing those wheels, their spinning generates electricity. I think. But for a radio to require that much electricity, it must be very powerful. And if those wires on The Quill are some kind of antenna—a metal grid which gathers or spreads radio signals—then this radio is not only meant to receive those signals over great distances, but send them as well."

"How great a distance?" Uncle Pierre asked quietly.

Jacques shrugged. "I do not know. My reading about their technology was more broad than deep. I do not know what the limit of such a radio might be."

"Perhaps not," said d'Esnambuc in a quiet, determined tone that sent a chill down Jacques' spine, "but I can find out. And I'll need to do it soon. This same American is making other problems for us."

"How so?" asked de l'Olive.

"He is apparently talking to the slaves working for him about ways in which they might acquire the means to buy their freedom. Likewise, he is speaking to the Dutch townsfolk about the greater safety and ease of having a colony of freemen and bondsmen, rather than spending every waking hour ensuring that their slaves do not flee or revolt."

"And the Dutch are listening to this nonsense?" de l'Olive snorted.

"Some. Perhaps enough. At any rate, no one is silencing this American. Even though he is not making any public speeches or the like, he is becoming famous for his casual conversations about such matters. Or, in the eyes of some, he is becoming infamous. When the landowners heard about these 'conversations,' most of them stopped leasing him slaves to help with the construction of whatever it is he is building on the windward side of The Quill."

Du Plessis frowned. "That should have put an end to his project, right there."

"It should have, but it did not. Tromp apparently found townsmen willing to add to the daily rate of the slaves' leases. The landowners, between their prior agreement and the lure of all that money, could hardly continue to refuse. And the slaves, of course, repeat the American's seditious ideas and exhortations back among their own people."

De l'Olive grumbled. "That's the end of your long-standing scheme for inciting a slave revolt, Captain d'Esnambuc. I remember how diligent you were in trying to bring one off from the time we returned after the Spanish chased us off in '29."

"Yes," d'Esnambuc agreed sourly. "If the Dutch convert their slaves to bondsmen, and they hold to their word, it is difficult to see how we will stimulate an effective revolt. Indeed, St. Eustatia may become a destination for escaped slaves and *encomienda* laborers from all around the Caribbean. And I suspect that Warner would adopt the same policy quickly enough, if he saw it succeeding. So this may well be our last opportunity to not only protect our colony on St. Christopher's, but arrest a trend that could create problems for the *Compagnie des Îles de l'Amérique* throughout the Lesser Antilles."

"Agreed," announced du Plessis, with a slap at his knee. "I think our plan must take precedence over all other efforts, at this point." Jacques was bemused to note how his uncle's plan had become a collective stratagem, in which du Plessis was now not only invested, but ready to claim a share of the authorship.

His uncle was too pragmatic a man to allow any impatience or resentment show, if he felt it. D'Esnambuc simply nodded and pointed his chin slightly southward. "And here comes our company, gentlemen. I believe that is cacique Touman and his entourage. And although it may irk you, I recommend you stand to receive him. Willing cooperation of the Caribs is, after all, the lynchpin of 'our' plan."

Jacques found himself quickly admiring Touman, who sat among both proven and potential enemies without any sign of fear or anxiety. He expressed no happiness, was indeed, quite grave, but was in no way rude. His inquiries were focused and well-considered. When he occasionally sensed that he was being given half-truths, he bluntly asked for a more complete explanation of the issue or item in question. Jacques wondered if his own countrymen would have been so collected and serious and yet polite if the circumstances were reversed, and he frankly doubted it. He knew that he would not have been.

At the end of half an hour, Touman nodded and surveyed the faces of the Frenchmen. He ended on d'Esnambuc and said, "You are bold, to contact my relatives on Madinina, which you call Martinique. And to come before me here on Karukera."

"And why is that, Cacique Touman?"

"Because you are he who slew Tegreman and took Liamuiga — St. Christopher's—from my people, the Kalinago. Had you not come to Youacou on Madinina first, and with only a small guard, I would not have heard the sounds of your tongue, but given orders that it be ripped from your head."

"Cacique Touman," d'Esnambuc said with a sigh. "You are a warrior so you understand that in war, events transpire that we do not intend. The terrible killing of the Kalinago on the island we call St. Christopher's was one such event. Had it not been for the fear in Warner's breast—that, having started slaying your people we would not be safe unless we left none alive—there would have been far less blood spilt. And among the blood that would not have been spilt was Tegreman's own. He was a leader and a straight-standing man. We did not always agree, and did not always part happy with each other, but men do so without killing each other. It should have been thus with him."

Touman stared with narrowed eyes at d'Esnambuc while the other Frenchmen held their breath as if witnessing a duel between well-matched pistoleers. "So with these words, do you claim that your hand was not the one which slew Tegreman?"

"I do claim that," d'Esnambuc replied quickly, truthfully.

"And you claim that your tongue did not give the command that others should kill him?"

"I claim that as well," Uncle Pierre lied just as quickly and convincingly.

Touman continued to look at d'Esnambuc for the better part of a minute, as if trying to read him the way his people read the clouds and wavelets for favorable signs to cross the great expanses between the islands of the Caribbean. At last, he looked away and spoke. "I shall speak plainly. I do not agree to become a part of these plans gladly. My people, the Kalinago, have had little luck trusting the word of pale men from over the sea, regardless of how they differ from each other in their language and dress and customs.

"But this I know: you speak the truth of the changing times in these islands. Although my people no longer do so openly, we visit our islands, even those you hold most strongly. We know the truth of what you say, that many ships and many Dutch came to Aloi, which you call St. Eustatia. And we have heard reports from our distant cousins of great ships that burn fires on their deck as they move more swiftly than the strongest men may row. I had wondered if these tales were true, but I doubt them no longer."

He met the eyes of each of the four white men once and then spoke again. "If you shall provide us with guns as you say, then the Kalinago people shall make this war with you against the English and Dutch of Liamuiga and Aloi. Afterward, we shall live there with you in peace and mutual protection, staying within the borders we have agreed upon today, which shall not change."

D'Esnambuc nodded. "We shall provide the guns as we have promised. You shall have thirty today and your warriors may have instruction in them before leaving."

"And these guns are ours to take?"

"They are. Within two weeks, we shall have at least one hundred more. We hope to have two hundred more. All these guns shall be yours also. We only ask that you do not use them, nor change them, when away from us. We must conserve the powder and shot to train you, and if any part of the mechanisms are changed, the guns may not function as well, or at all."

"I understand. I wonder if *you* understand."

"I do not know what you mean, Cacique Touman."

"Can you not? Whether or not I have heard lies, sitting in council with you this day, you have given me guns, and the promise of many more. Which means you have given me the power to make men from over the sea keep their promises. It does not matter whether it is you, or the Spanish, or these men you say have come from another world of future spirits. We shall not tolerate lies any more.

"Furthermore, we have seen that you do not know the ways of these islands. Without our help, you would soon starve. We will provide what food we may, and trade with our cousins to the south for more. But now you will know—*all* will know"—he shook the matchlock he'd been given lightly—"that nothing may be taken from us, or gained by threatening us. Those who depend upon our food will eat so long as they keep their promises. This I resolve. And so, I am finished." Touman stood. "My people will return tomorrow with food, and to learn more of how to use the guns you have given us. I hope this day marks the start of better times between our people." He nodded, turned, and left. Youacou remained behind for a moment, nodded, and left also.

When both were well gone, de l'Olive rounded on d'Esnambuc. "But Captain! You always said that we must never furnish the savages with guns. You always said if they—"

D'Esnambuc interrupted with a quiet voice that silenced his old follower more surely than a shout would have. "Yes, I did say that. And those were different times. Times when we did not need savages as allies. Times when the Dutch were not selling trade muskets near the Orinoco. But I am unworried."

Du Plessis frowned. "Why?"

"Did you not notice what Touman failed to ask for?"

Jacques nodded. "Metal for casting musket balls and the casting tools. And assurances of a constant supply of powder. They know what guns do, but do not yet have a full understanding of the other items they must possess and the skills they must master, if they are to continue using them."

"Just so, my nephew," Uncle Pierre said.

"But they will learn of these needs," du Plessis sputtered. "They will figure it out within the first few days and—"

"And we shall never let them want for powder or shot. Not now, not until that day comes when French ships sail untroubled from St. Eustatia to Guadeloupe and these lands are brimming with our colonists."

"And then?" asked Jacques, dreading the terrible answer that was sure to be uttered by the uncle he loved so much.

"And then," d'Esnambuc replied in a tone that sounded like an apology, "a day will come when our ships will ensure that the Caribs cannot leave our islands to trade for powder with anyone else. And so, the powder will go away. And so will they."

Part Seven

November 1635

Office, and custom, in all line of order

Chapter 40

Three miles east by southeast of Pitch Lake, Trinidad

Ann Koudsi took off toward the number three hole at a dead run even before the first deep-toned alarm rang out. Her rig workers called the hoop of brass which made the sound a gong, but she thought it sounded more like a cowbell. However, she'd known a full three seconds beforehand that something must be happening, either good or bad, because the relentless percussive slamming of the cable drill rig stopped suddenly, and long before the scheduled personnel break and maintenance check.

As she emerged from the tree line into the small clearing where they'd first found the oil seeps, she scanned the crazed activity around the well. Ulrich was at the center of it, gesturing wildly, his German crew scattering to perform tasks that seemed to take them in every direction.

"Good news or bad?" Ann shouted as she came to a panting halt a dozen yards away.

"Both! Get back, Ann. Please!"

Instead, she rushed across the rest of the distance. She had decided, some months ago, that while she was not interested in taking stupid risks, she wasn't about to allow Ulrich to take any she wouldn't also. It would be bad enough to go on living without him. To know that she had seen to her own safety instead of being there to help, and maybe save, him would be simply unbearable.

"Ann—!"

"Save it. We'll argue later. What's up with number three?"

But even as she asked it, her nose told her the answer: a faint spoiled eggs smell. "Gas?"

"Yes, but then it stopped. And the last shavings that we took up were these." He pointed backward into a bucket. At a glance, she knew: they were near oil. Very near.

That was when the hole emitted what sounded like a muddy burp. It ended in a stuttering hiss that faded away.

She looked overhead. The cable was mostly out, spooling up onto a drum being cranked by two of the largest roughnecks. Two more waited to swing the drill bit up out of the casing and clear of the hole. "How far down are you?"

"One hundred eighty-seven feet. We were going slowly, just as you recommended. You were right about this one, Ann."

"Yeah," she said, purposely trying to sound as sour as the old eggs smell around her, "we'll see about that." She didn't want to get her hopes up, not when there was so much riding on—

"Pans are in place; catch tubes laid!" one of the workers shouted before backing away at a reverse trot.

"Ann," Ulrich insisted, "we can't do any more here. Let's get back, wait and see if—"

The platform vibrated slightly for a second. Out of the hole came a sound like a whale having a titanic episode of indigestion, punctuated by occasional flatulence.

Ann and Ulrich grabbed each other at the same instant and started running. A moment later, surging up from the ground behind them came a sound like a prolonged, slow burp, ending in a sigh—*okay, so not a gusher*—which chased them off the platform with a light, misty shower of fine gray-and-black goo. The oil smell was unmistakable.

Ulrich, his white teeth incredibly bright in the midst of his smudged face, turned to her in the boyish glee that so endeared him to her. "You've done it, Ann! You've—"

"*We've* done it. We. Us. And keep running. Never trust an oil well until you've capped it, and I'm not getting near that one for at least an hour." But as they ran farther up the trail, back into the comparative safety of the tree line, she could not suppress the surge of elation that arose with the word: *Oil! We've struck oil!*

Santo Domingo, Hispaniola

Fadrique Álvarez de Toledo y Mendoza pushed away the cup of decidedly inferior rioja but schooled himself not to allow the gesture to become so forceful as to signal displeasure. After all, he was a guest in the modest palace of Santo Domingo's captain-general, and the fellow, while lacking the body of a soldier, seemed to have the heart of one, since what he was suggesting was tantamount to political suicide. And given how petty and vicious Olivares was becoming these days, it was not beyond imagining that poor crippled Don Juan Bitrian de Viamonte y Navarra would receive a summons to Spain that would mark the end of his titles and honor and money. And a semi-invalid such as he might not survive very long without the ease and medicines his position made available to him. So, it might reasonably be said that de Viamonte was risking his life as much as any other man who decided to serve Spain's best interests, even if that meant dangerously bending or misconstruing the intent of Olivares' many dicta. And as for inferior rioja? Since Fadrique's duties seemed certain to keep him in the New World for the foreseeable future, he might as well accustom his palate to what was available this far from the vineyards of home.

The other man at the table was a youngish fellow, one Don Eugenio de Covilla, who had introduced himself as the confidential liaison between Captain-General de Viamonte and the redoubtable governor of Cuba, His Excellency Francisco Riaño y Gamboa, a hard-bitten old soldier whose physical and mental toughness were legendary. Gamboa had proven the truth of those legends even before he had fully arrived at his new assignment in Cuba. His ship having capsized off the coast of Mariel, the white-locked septuagenarian swam ashore with nothing but his royal patents and sodden clothes. And in the year that he'd been at his new post, he had made significant changes, as well as significant enemies. A field marshal prior to becoming the governor of arguably the most important Spanish city and island in the New World, he was aggressive in combating corruption and was not willing to look the other way when Spanish merchants conducted their (admittedly far more profitable) trade with the itinerant merchantmen of other nations, or with the so-called Brethren of the Coast. But, popular or not, given the alarming reports now emerging from the Lesser Antilles all the way down to the eastern edge of Tierra Firma, seventy-year-old Gamboa was precisely the sturdy warhorse needed to take on the Dutch and their new allies.

Whether de Covilla would represent Gamboa's wishes as forcefully as the Cuban governor himself was another question entirely. Frankly, Fadrique did not envy the young *hidalgo* his job. Being the mouthpiece for the blunt, and even impolitic, Gamboa meant he would frequently become a most unwelcome messenger in the palaces of men who stood far above him in both rank and access to courtier's ears back in Madrid.

Fadrique stared down the table at Captain-General de Viamonte, who was finishing his wine, probably at the order of doctors. His withered arm was tucked against his far side and largely out of sight, but his patchy hair and labored breathing were unfortunately beyond concealment. It was obvious looking at the man why he had been bounced out of the governorship in Havana to make way for Gamboa, but the doing had not been the old general's, who was said to have a high regard for de Viamonte's quiet competence. Rather, Fadrique's present host had been undermined at court by the Marquis of Cadereyta, Don Lope Díez de Aux de Armendáriz, who, prior to his recent ascension as the new viceroy of New Spain, had been a skilled captain-general and admiral of the flotas that went to and from Seville. He had couched his public disapproval of de Viamonte in terms of the man's conventional and uninspired policies, of not having the dynamism necessary to a position as trying and so wanting bold action as the governorship of Cuba. Privately, he made no secret of loathing the infirmity and inwardness of de Viamonte, and so, was only more resentful of the man's quiet resistance to de Armendáriz's attempts at bullying concessions out of him regarding the equipage and provisioning of his various flotas, and Havana's defenses.

Fadrique shifted in his chair impatiently. "So, then, what news, Don de Viamonte?"

"I will learn it along with you, my good Don de Toledo. De Covilla here is just off the advice *patache* this morning and we have not had the time to talk."

Fadrique turned to the young fellow, who nodded his respect again, as he had upon meeting Fadrique. He glanced back at the captain-general. "Then, sir, with your leave—"

"By all means, Eugenio. Please share the messages from His Excellency Governor Gamboa."

De Covilla smoothed his vest, put aside his wine, and folded his hands. "First, he sends his compliments and greetings to you, Don de Viamonte, and especially commends your speedy and bold decision to send three ships as couriers to Spain as soon as you received news of the battle in the Grenada Passage."

Bold indeed, Fadrique reaffirmed silently. Olivares was renowned for confusing those who alerted him to bad news with being the causes of that news. De Viamonte might have a frail body, but he had courage enough for any five men to send prompt news without flinching or second thoughts. A pity that Spain tended to push aside or pillory those loyal and imprudent enough to do their duty even when it was sure to anger Olivares.

De Covilla had not paused. "He also confers his approval of your initiative to restore the shipyards here in Santo Domingo to full production capacity. He has followed your example and given identical orders to the shipyards on Cuba. He has also exhorted, in the strongest possible language, that the new viceroy of New Spain, Don Lope Díez de Aux de Armendáriz, and the viceroy of Peru, Don Luis Jerónimo Fernández de Cabrera Bobadilla Cerda y Mendoza, follow similar programs of reinstating their shipbuilding industries at their maximum level of production."

Fadrique tried not to look dubious or disgusted. Armendáriz, while capable, was also known to be self-interested, secretive, and, it was rumored, perverse in his affiliations and actions. He might trouble himself to become part of the solution to the growing Protestant threat in the New World, but he was just as likely to allow the regions most directly influenced to bear the brunt of the expenses. The only reason to have strong hopes otherwise was that Armendáriz, a *criollo* from Quito, had made his name in the world by commanding the flotas. He, as well as any man alive, was likely to fully understand just how disastrous any loss in control or security of the sea-lanes would be to the fate of all of Spain's New World possessions. And whereas Peru's Don de Cabrera was a reliable fellow, he was stuck on the other side of South America: a strange place from which to govern the affairs of Cartagena and the majority of Tierra Firma, but that was Spanish governance for you. Getting a timely message to him, and getting his authorizing response, would be the biggest problem, and represented a considerable delay.

"Last, he agrees with you that, as practicable, we should identify all recent wrecks in shallow waters and commence salvage operations at once. He has already contracted two masters of intercoastal trading ships to undertake this activity."

Álvarez de Toledo leaned forward. "What is this? You are sending diving bells down to wrecks, now? For coin to pay for the shipbuilding?"

But Don Juan Bitrian de Viamonte shook his high-domed head. "No, Don Álvarez, for cannons, balls, and if they are still serviceable, the very nails themselves." He continued when Fadrique's expression showed his increasing perplexity. "Don Álvarez, we may lose men to accident and high weather during salvage operations, yes. But, God save me that I must say so, we have no shortage of men. However, what of the ironmongery with which we must build and outfit the ships that we are even now commissioning in our yards? And of the armaments which we must provide for them?" He shook his head sadly. "These objects are our new wealth, my dear Álvarez de Toledo. For we have no capacity to make such objects ourselves, and if Olivares does not send them to us in considerable bulk, all our efforts to build a fleet here shall come to naught. We have no choice but to find and refurbish that which we have already lost once."

Fadrique nodded, realized his eyes had opened wide, and simply did not care that his admiration for the wizened little man was so frank. By God, if one of every ten Spaniards had both his clear mind and gigantic *cojones*, their empire would cover every inch of the globe. "As you say, these are our new wealth, Don de Viamonte."

De Covilla had turned his body as well as his head to face Fadrique. "His Excellency Francisco Riaño y Gamboa is glad to welcome you to the New World and of course wishes it might have been under better circumstances. However, he is extremely glad that you were present to manage the scope of the difficulties that befell our fleet in the Grenada Passage, commends you for your prudence in saving as many ships as you did, and for taking steps to distribute intelligence of our new enemies not only to himself and Don de Viamonte, but to Governor de Murga in Cartagena."

"His Excellency is a kind man, to thank me for losing a battle."

"He does not see it so, Don Álvarez de Toledo. However, he anticipated that you might be just so harsh with yourself. So he bade me communicate to you how he perceived the outcome of the most recent battle. It may be that the unfortunate Admiral de Cárdenas split your fleet in the face of the enemy for the wrong reasons—for how often is such a stratagem a good one?—but the governor observed that it was nonetheless a fortunate choice. Because had all of your fleet engaged the USE steamships, far fewer of our ships would have returned home. Conversely, had you all sailed together against the Dutch, it seems most certain that the outcome would have been worse still. The USE steamships are, by your report, so swift that they would have taken your fleet in the flank, which, constrained by having engaged the Dutch van, would have been destroyed in bunches. It is difficult to see, therefore, any other course than the one you chose once Admiral de Cárdenas had fallen: to salvage what you might, and quickly.

"So, in consideration of that wisdom, and your many past successes, His Excellency wishes you to know most explicitly that you have his full confidence. And furthermore, that you have full authority to do whatever is necessary to rebuild the Armada de Barlovento, which we must now presume is truly and permanently lost, and to fashion a strategy which allows us to defeat our new foes. His Excellency the Governor is keenly interested in any actions you take in these regards, and asks to be informed of them at once, Admiral, so he may mobilize any local support your initiatives might require."

Fadrique hadn't heard the last part of de Covilla's courtly summary of Gamboa's message. "Did you call me 'Admiral?'"

De Covilla smiled and nodded. "The governor has so ordered your promotion to full admiral, to replace the fallen de Cárdenas. He emphasized, several times, that he was most glad to have you close at hand for this important duty." De Covilla paused and met Fadrique's gaze steadily. "Most especially glad."

Ah, so a special nod from the old boy in Havana. Fadrique interpreted the subtext of Gamboa's repeated emphasis on both his gratitude and relief, which translated roughly as: *Thank God we are no longer saddled with a poseur such as de Cárdenas. Now we professional soldiers can get to work.*

De Covilla's next comment also confirmed Fadrique's assessment that Gamboa's natural impulse was to take decisive, practical steps against the new threat. "His Excellency has also taken it upon himself, and his own authority, to directly call upon the other ship-building towns of the New World to contribute their efforts to build a more credible local fleet." *Going over the head of the viceroys to get fast action? Gamboa's sense of urgency is obviously much greater than his reluctance to make powerful new enemies.* "Accordingly, His Excellency has dispatched advice *pataches* and barca-longas to deliver his vigorous encouragements and exhortations *directly* to the mayors and shipyard masters at Salvaleón de Higüy, San Juan, San Germán, Veracruz, Campeche, Jamaica, Cartagena, Maracaibo, and Caracas. He welcomes Admiral Álvarez de Toledo to add to that list, or make specific recommendations, of course."

Fadrique nodded. "In Maracaibo and Campeche, you must restrict the shipbuilding to small hulls with shallow draughts. Maracaibo has shifting sandbars and Campeche's harbor is too shallow for big ships. And I suggest one further proviso. When we are building warships, we must begin to increasingly adopt the frigate designs that the Swedes and Dutch have been producing for almost two years now."

"I beg your pardon, did you say *fragata*?"

"I did not. I do *not* mean our small versions of these craft, but the larger brig- and barquentine-sized hulls that have no perceptible quarterdeck and but a single gun deck. They should be of about one hundred tonneladas and between twenty and thirty guns, total."

De Covilla frowned. "That may not be received well in Seville, Don Álvarez de Toledo. While the smaller *fragatas* are not so large nor a sizable investment, the class of ship you are asking for will be almost as long and expensive to build as a small galleon. And our craftsmen are not familiar with the design. They would need to be taught."

"In Havana, they are familiar enough with similar designs. And in the other yards, they may be taught. Let us be plain about what Olivares and the Royal Council of the Indies are interested in: getting gold and silver from the New World. To do that, they want to ensure that we have enough high-pooped, heavy-hulled galleons to wallow safely up and down the waves of the Atlantic and so bring the treasure to Seville. That has been a reasonable strategy. Until now."

Fadrique leaned forward. "Formerly, it did not matter if our ships were less maneuverable than theirs, were slow as scows if they lacked a following wind, had quarterdecks so high that they are a constant drag upon the hull as it strives forward against the sea and the air. We had the advantage of numbers, of size, of immense steady platforms from which to fire our immense cannons, and of those high fore and aft castles crowded with our infantry. Our galleons were forts upon the sea, and none could assail them with impunity."

De Toledo jabbed his finger down into the tabletop, the sharp *clack!* drawing attention to the moment. "But now, size is no longer decisive. Even without the up-time ships to support them, the Dutch and the Swedes are producing ships—frigates—with sleeker lines, mixed rigging, a long, low profile, and heavier guns. They are not capable of absorbing as much damage as our galleons, but being swift, they are hit far less often. And, again because they are swift, our advantage in numbers is no longer decisive. They can outmaneuver us and herd us into clusters, bringing almost their full force to bear upon each isolated group in turn. And so, through cunning maneuver, they may contrive to outnumber us at every point of contact, even though we may outnumber them, total hulls to total hulls."

"Well," soothed de Covilla, "regardless of how many changes Count-Duke Olivares is willing to approve, I suspect that he will not bridle at their mere suggestion. Don Lope Díez de Aux de Armendáriz, Viceroy of New Spain, who departed shortly after I arrived in Havana, took the opportunity to recount, at length and in detail, the mood in the Council of the Indies earlier this year. I am pleased to say it is most aggressive in regard to the foreign violation of our *inter caetera* rights in general, and to the Dutch seizure of Curaçao in particular."

"Indeed," de Viamonte murmured. "Please do recount the viceroy's words in as great a detail as you might recall." The captain-general's tone suggested he was not looking for information or revelations so much as he was searching for a weakness, a gaffe, a misstep on the part of de Armendáriz.

De Covilla heard the tone as well; he inclined his head to study some notes he had brought with him. "According to Don Lope Díez de Aux de Armendáriz, he was invited to observe the proceedings of a 'granda junta' of the council. It was attended by the councils of State and War, as well, and was presided over by none other than Don Gaspar de Guzmán y Pimentel Ribera y Velasco de Tovar, comte d'Olivares et duc de Sanlucar la Mayor, himself.

"The count-duke initiated the proceedings by explaining, at some length, that the Dutch capture of Curaçao might endanger, or at least delay, the sailing of this year's treasure fleet, if Thijssen proved highly active in raiding along Tierra Firma. That has not materialized, although the new threats we have discovered more than compensate for the dangers and losses with which Thijssen failed to present us. However, regardless of whatever might have transpired this year, Count-Duke Olivares averred that a Dutch presence at Curaçao was inevitably a springboard for further Dutch raiding along Tierra Firma and further island seizures in the Caribbean. He called for many forms of assistance, including Portuguese ships added to our own, but in particular, maintained that the Armada de Barlovento, or Windward fleet, needed dramatic expansion. The four galleons he believed her to possess as that time were to be increased to eighteen within two years' time."

"So perhaps he is already planning to authorize a full renewal of shipbuilding here in the New World?" Fadrique inquired hopefully.

"Frankly, the viceroy made it sound more as though the count-duke saw this increased need for hulls as a windfall for the yards in Vizcaya. However, given the recent losses here in the New World, I suspect that, for now at least, any increase in the size of our fleet will be a welcome development in his eyes, regardless of where the ships are built."

"So you think he will be, er, open-minded, about the special measures we have taken to address the current crisis?"

"He might well be. The count-duke was quite explicit about the finality of the war he wished prosecuted against those who trespass upon His Majesty's lands, or who threaten their safety. He repeatedly referred to the Dutch as faithless rebels and heretics and, because they were, that they should be slaughtered when captured."

De Viamonte's eyes widened slightly. "And both the Council of the Indies and the Council of War permitted that policy?"

De Covilla nodded slightly. "Don Lope Díez de Aux de Armendáriz did mention that there was worry in the chamber that the Dutch would simply retaliate by massacring the crews of Spanish vessels they intercepted in the Caribbean. Olivares was unmoved, and simply reiterated his insistence that Dutch prisoners be killed in any way expedient, at any time it was convenient for Spanish commanders to do so."

Fadrique could not keep himself from blinking in surprise. "This is not well-considered," he murmured. Which was hardly a surprise in and of itself. Olivares had become increasingly injudicious in recent years, and anything remotely touching upon the Dutch and the interminable problems spawned by the wars in, or troubles pertaining to, the Spanish presence in the Lowlands, excited him to excesses of anger and ready vengeance. "But I think it makes it all the more wise that his Excellency Captain-General Gamboa took such extraordinary steps in establishing our own fleet, here in the New World."

"And why is that, Don Álvarez de Toledo?"

"Because," Fadrique said, drawing his wine a bit closer, "if we do not take matters into our own hands, and find answers that we may vouchsafe with own labor and treasure, then Olivares will do what he's best at: increase our taxes to pay for our own defensive fleet. Which he will likely have built in Spain, where it is easier for him to 'manage' the funds." Álvarez de Toledo sneered openly. "The last time he increased taxes in the New World, I think he almost doubled the New Spain *alcabala* sales tariff. It was an unmitigated disaster. The money went to Spain, and in exchange, we received an undersized shipment of new weapons and ships, along with a veritable army of the count-duke's current flatterers and sycophants. And from what I could tell, it was their especial job to oversee the utilization and distribution of the scant and shoddy resources Olivares had sent, along with ensuring that the collection of the additional tariff continued." Fadrique had meant to take a sip of his wine, but now gulped at it angrily and set it down with a loud clack. "We cannot afford the pointless cost of Olivares' infinitude of sinecures in our coming struggle against the Dutch and their new allies. And we must prosecute that war sooner, rather than later."

"Why?" wondered de Viamonte, frowning.

"Because they will waste no time attacking us again. We suffered the losses, not they. We have slower communications, if we may conjecture that they are making some use of radio. And yet we have a much greater area and more far-flung units to coordinate than they do. Our size has often made us powerful, but against these adversaries, I fear it simply makes us ponderous. This is why we must have faster ships."

Don de Viamonte smiled wistfully. "And up-time radios, too, perhaps?"

"You may have meant that as an irony, Captain-General, but I am deadly serious when I say I would give ten galleons for five radios and their operators." Fadrique spread his hands. "Our empire's size is, in many ways, a disadvantage, if we cannot coordinate its far-flung locales and assets properly. Imagine twenty oxen, tied together in no particular fashion by a clutter of ropes. Their immense power is useless because it is not focused. Now imagine only four oxen in paired yokes, all following the same lead-line. They provide much less raw power, yes, but they can get many times more work done, because they are all pulling in the same direction, all answering to one will and voice. This is precisely the difference between us and our foes. With their steam speed and radios, their much smaller numbers will defeat us almost every time."

"Then what is to be done?"

Could he really not see? "Build faster ships. Get radios. Find alternatives to reduce or eliminate our handicaps. Ensure that we have strong, consistent, central leadership. And remain mindful that they hope to strike us severe blows—mortal, if possible—before we can find their primary base. For once we do, we may bring all our force to bear upon what must be a fairly weak port. Their largest colony, Recife, they abandoned. How much could they have built since? A few ramparts, a few dozen houses? They have no Havanas, no Cartagenas, and they know that we are well aware of that. So they will attack us as quickly as they might, to preemptively protect whatever base and settlement they are operating out of."

"And where do you think that might be, Admiral?" de Covilla asked, leaning forward intently. "Curaçao?"

Fadrique shrugged. "That is a logical location, but I am not convinced it is correct. Not at all."

De Viamonte emphasized his single-syllable question by attenuating it. "Why?"

"Because if it is Tromp who engaged us at the Grenada Passage, and I think it was, then Curaçao is exactly where we would expect to find him, after he abandoned Recife. But siting himself so close to so many of our cities along Tierra Firma, it would be almost an invitation to us to attempt to mass against him, to beat him back into that island's well-protected harbor, no matter the cost. And then we would land our troops at all points of its tiny coastline and destroy him and his colony like burning a badger in its hole. Clearly, they cannot have any significant fortifications thrown up yet, nor supplies to resist a siege, so no matter how numerous his soldiers might be, they would ultimately succumb."

De Viamonte mused before answering. "So he would go someplace he is not likely to be found?"

"Quite possibly. Tell me, when was the last time you sent a patrol to see what was going on in the islands we do not visit frequently?"

De Viamonte's voice was reedy. "Alas, before it disappeared last year, that was a significant part of the Armada de Barlovento's mission. So it remains unaccomplished."

"Hmm. I wonder. Perhaps that part of their mission, is, in fact, the one thing that they *did* accomplish."

The captain-general, who had modest reserves of stamina at best, looked more weary by the minute. "I do not understand."

"Let us consider what we last knew about the Armada de Barlovento, and what is unusual about its disappearance." Fadrique folded his hands and leaned forward. "First, is it not strange that *all* four ships of the Armada de Barlovento should disappear? Even in a terrible defeat, usually one or two hulls escape, live to tell the tale. And that is usually what occurs because you typically meet an enemy without warning, in a place neither of you had thought to meet another ship at all."

"So, you suspect an ambush?"

"Of a sort. Let us suppose that, rather than joining Thijssen in Curaçao, Tromp chose instead a safe port where he hoped to hide, a place farther from the regular route of our flotas."

Fadrique saw de Covilla's eyes widen slightly. A smart lad, evidently. "Tromp would keep a watch on the approaches to such a port, with his own ships ready to trap any others that discovered his anchorage so they could not escape to report."

"Precisely. Now there is no guarantee that this is why all four ships are missing. Storms claim whole fleets, on occasion, and we have little news of it if the high weather comes and goes where our flag does not regularly fly."

De Viamonte shook his head. "So how would you propose to determine if our ships were the victims of an ambush, and furthermore, where Tromp's secret anchorage might be? The Caribbean is a wide sea, and, if your earlier comments about an impending Dutch attack are correct, we may not have enough time to send *pataches* to its far corners."

De Covilla cleared his throat. "There may be another way. Though I am loath to suggest it."

Fadrique frowned. "Come now, young fellow, it is the honor of Spain and our king we are trying to save, here."

"It is the honor of Spain and our king that I mean to protect by *not* suggesting what I just conceived, Don Álvarez de Toledo."

Fadrique narrowed his eyes, nodded. "I think I understand what expedient you may be considering, and your repugnance of it. But you are right: it answers our need. And may show the way forward to meet other challenges, as well."

De Viamonte, who was usually a most astute man, sounded very puzzled and slightly annoyed. "I should be most grateful if you two gentlemen would stop speaking in a code known to you alone, apparently. What solution have you conceived that might answer our need for scouting more widely, Eugenio?"

"Don de Viamonte, I am ashamed to say it, but in the time that I coordinated the activities of the raiders commanded by the bandit Barto, I learned that others of his ilk, the so called Free Companions, range far and wide. Which we knew, of course. But it is also true that there are havens, also suspected by us, where they convene. In these places, they trade their ill-gotten goods, ply themselves with drink, satiate their appetite for women, and share their tales, many of which are fanciful fabrications, but many of which are true. Many of which would therefore include recent intelligences on the ships and powers of rivals and nations. Which might very well include word of the Dutch."

De Viamonte leaned back, his nostrils pinching tight as if he were smelling the reek of such a den of debauchery. But he stiffened and nodded. "You are right, of course. In both regards. It is a vile alternative. And it is also the only one which may provide us the necessary information in time. You have my leave to send agents amongst them, and to let it be known that we would deign to speak with them in our ports. Where we will trade hard silver for information. Although, I fear that many will come to tell us lies we cannot disprove and depart with silver we cannot withhold."

"Not if we make it worth their while to tell the truth," mumbled Fadrique.

"And how should we do that, sir?"

"By offering them ten times as much if they sail with us to plunder the Dutch in their ports and take their fine ships."

"We should *recruit* them?" de Viamonte almost gasped.

"From what young Don de Covilla has said, it sounds as though you already have, once. But if we need to act quickly—and we do—and we need to have eyes, ears, and eventually guns in many places at the same time—which we will—then I fail to see how we can exclude this expedient."

"And we are to let them plunder the Dutch settlements?"

"Is that so much worse than following Olivares' orders to exterminate the Dutch wherever we find them? The pirates may choose to show them mercy, or not. We, on the other hand—" Fadrique let the sentence dangle unfinished, felt sure that a noble soul like de Viamonte's would choose an alternative that afforded some hope for civilians to survive over the ineluctable alternative of being their black-hooded executioner.

De Viamonte did not disappoint him. "But we will still need to control these 'free companions,' somehow."

"They were manageable when promised letters of marque," de Covilla pointed out.

"And so we legitimize their barbarism," the captain-general spat.

"As Olivares has legitimized ours," observed Fadrique.

De Viamonte seemed to hug his withered arm close, shivered as though suffering a chill. "This war will come to no good end," he predicted.

"That is most likely," agreed Fadrique Álvarez de Toledo.

Chapter 41

The rude-planked coffin, draped by a Danish pennant, was lifted out of the skiff by six Danes from the crew of the *Serendipity*. With Gjedde in front and Eddie Cantrell following behind, they made their way slowly past the assembled on-lookers, who numbered close to two hundred, and toward Edel Mund. She stood straight and stiff and very alone at the foot of the west-facing walls of Fort Oranjestad. They marched directly toward her and the Dutch soldiers flanking her on either side.

As the casket arrived before her, the procession stopped. The Dutch troopers raised their already-drawn swords, a wave of silver streaks catching the gold of the late morning sun even as they glinted silver. Then the six men carrying the casket marched through a slow pivot of ninety degrees and paused in that profile position, motionless before Pros Mund's pale widow. After a thirty count, and at Gjedde's gesture, they resumed their slow march, Eddie lagging so that dry-eyed Edel Mund could fall in directly behind the coffin as it made its stately way to the town's humble church.

Maarten Tromp had considered offering his services as a deacon to Reverend Polhemius but had ultimately decided against it. There were too many ways such an act could be misinterpreted:

as being intrusive, as a Dutchman taking a place that should logically belong to a Dane with a similar calling, as having the humility of the act perceived as ingenuine. Any and all of which would only call attention away from the man who was rightly the center of reflection, appreciation, and mourning in this, his last hour among the persons he had left behind.

Edel and a few crewmembers made their way into the church, followed by a large number of ladies led by the three who had come from Christian IV's own court: his two daughters and the tall Sophie Rantzau. At the same moment, Tromp noticed Jan van Walbeeck sidling up to him where they stood under a pavilion outside the church, along with the others who had come to pay their respects to a man they had hardly known.

Van Walbeeck looked about surreptitiously. "You've chosen an auspicious spot for the ceremony, Maarten."

"Have I? The shade is no better or worse here than anywhere else."

"True enough. But I mean that we are standing so far to the rear that we may speak—quietly, of course—without being overheard."

Tromp glared at van Walbeeck. "Jan, I know you are not a conventionally devout man, but this is—well, it is disrespectful to the deceased and our Lord, alike."

Jan winced, shrugged. "I suppose that is true. But I also suppose we may have no other time to discuss matters relevant to the meeting later this afternoon."

Maarten sighed, unhappy. Because, as usual, Jan van Walbeeck was right. Having arrived in port in the late hours of the middle watch, the ships that had returned from Trinidad remained steadily busy until well after breakfast. The few wounded were transferred ashore; the Spanish prize hulls were brought to secure anchorages near the beaches at which they might be safely careened. Secure arrangements ashore were worked out for the half dozen Spanish prisoners they had retained for purposes of debriefing. And of course, the burial of Reconnaissance Flotilla X-Ray's slain commander had to be hastily arranged.

And so, when Maarten Tromp exited the ketch that brought the senior officers to shore in the wake of the funeral skiff, that was the first he had seen of Jan van Walbeeck since departing Oranjestad for Trinidad.

As Polhemius' almost quavering voice called the mourners to their first devotions, the two Dutchmen folded their hands solemnly and leaned toward each other. Van Walbeeck started their whispered exchange. "I notice that Houtebeen Jol is not here. Have you done away with him, or has that great heathen foresworn even his face-saving attendance at funerals and weddings?"

"Neither. And I could ask you the same thing about Joost van Banckert's absence, which is stranger still, since he is a reasonably pious man."

"That he is, but we must have someone ready aboard a flagship to lead the fleet if the Spanish should discover us this hour."

Tromp allowed that this was quite true and quite prudent. "Jol is actually doing much the same thing."

"Protecting us from possible attack?"

"No, but readying his new ship and squadron to weigh anchor and make for Trinidad."

"So soon?"

"I wish it could have been sooner. We could only leave three ships there: *Achilles*, *Vereenigte Provintien*, and *Amsterdam*."

"And is Simonszoon in charge down there?"

"I couldn't spare him. I had to leave the Trinidad squadron in the hands of Hjalmar von Holst. A solid man, and clever enough, but not as brilliant and, er, unconventional, as Simonszoon."

"And so now you are sending that old pirate, Jol."

"Yes. He'll take over command from von Holst, who will be an excellent second-in-command. And Houtebeen will be bringing more ships with him to strengthen our Trinidad squadron: *Sampson*, *Overijssel*, *Thetis*, the fluyt *Koninck David*, and the jachts *Leeuwinne* and *Noordsterre*. They are escorting the Danish transport *Patentia*, which is carrying the balance of the oil drilling gear, along with that clean-lined bark of theirs, the *Tropic Surveyor*."

"Quite a formidable fleet."

Tromp forgot himself and grunted diffidently. Two Dutch women turned and stared at him. He smiled apologetically, took another half step back. Van Walbeeck followed, smiling. "So, *not* a formidable fleet, then?"

"Not if de Murga in Cartagena manages to wring any significant cooperation from the other *audiencias* along Tierra Firma. If he does, he could raise a considerable armada, easily twice the size of what we will have in Trinidad."

Tromp could tell from van Walbeeck's long, silent consideration of this information that he was trying to conceal both his surprise and reservations. His voice was measured and tactful when he finally commented, "Hm. Jol is a good man, but I am still puzzled that you haven't sent Dirck, and more ships, to guard the oil."

Tromp nodded as much of an agreement as their presence at a public funeral allowed. "I can see why you might be puzzled. But no one knows that coast like Peg Leg Jol. And he has the trust of a number of vehemently anti-Spanish reivers that prowl those waters. Not that he or I would ever trust them as dedicated allies, but they are free enough with information if they think sharing it will hurt the Spanish. So Jol's relationship with them gives us a means of remaining at least partially apprised of what our enemy is up to. Quite possibly, they might give us advance word of any move against Trinidad or Curaçao." Tromp paused. "But, that's only half the reason I'm sending Houtebeen down there."

"Or perhaps you mean to say, 'keeping Simonszoon up here'?"

Tromp smiled. "There's no fooling you, Jan. Yes. I want, *need*, to keep Simonszoon up here. For the good of the fleet. By which I mean the whole fleet, ours and that of our allies."

"I don't understand," van Walbeeck whispered as, in response to an invocation from Polhemius, the mourners lowered their heads in silent prayer.

Tromp did not explain until the reverend resumed the liturgy. "With Pros Mund dead, and seeing that we need to find a way for our very different forces to work together more effectively, we must rethink both our command structures and tactical doctrines. To make our combined fleet a unified implement of naval warfare, we must carefully assess how to amplify its tremendous advantages and reduce its unusual weaknesses. And at the center of all those efforts is Eddie, er, Commander Cantrell. He understands our down-time principles of naval warfare well enough, but more importantly, he is the only one who understands the up-time technologies and doctrines thoroughly. He must be the liaison, and translator, even, between our two different naval traditions."

Van Walbeeck only looked more confused. "And so? For this he needs Simonszoon alongside him?"

"In fact, yes, he does."

"Again, I do not understand."

Tromp smiled. "That is because, after your years before the mast, you became a governor, not an admiral. It is all well and good to say that Eddie must bring these two doctrines of warfare, and training, together into a functional whole, but it is quite another thing to achieve it. Think of who his students will be: young captains commanding ships or ambitious first mates. All of them will be more senior than he is and are unlikely to be able to get past the galling fact that the twenty-three-year-old teaching them has one tenth their combat experience and one-one-hundredth of their sailing experience. How effective do you expect his 'instruction' will be to such a class as that?"

Van Walbeeck nodded. "Ah. Now I see. So Dirck Simonszoon, the most laconic and facetious of all our captains, shall be present in the class as well, showing Eddie deference and paying serious heed to his instruction. And thereby, setting an example the others will tend to follow. An excellent plan. But I have one question about Dirck: *will* he show Cantrell that deference?"

"Strangely, I am quite certain he will. You know Dirck almost as well as I do, and you've seen what makes him bristle, and what doesn't. He is temperamentally incapable of suffering fools. And the more such a fool tries to justify or defend his foolishness, the more arch and combative Dirck becomes." Tromp shifted his stance, changed his hands so that his left was now folded over his right. The first notes of a hymn wafted out of the church and were taken up irregularly by those gathered outside. "But Dirck took to young Cantrell right away. I suppose Dirck's temperament is like a coin, furnished with two opposite sides. Whereas he is harshly impatient with people he considers slow-witted, he seems charmed and protective of those he considers quite clever. And you have seen for yourself that young Cantrell is quite clever, indeed."

"And refreshingly modest, too," van Walbeeck added. "So, with Dirck sitting as a respectful pupil in young Cantrell's classes, our young officers transfer the respect they feel for the revered and feared Captain Simonszoon to Eddie himself, and so, they will not challenge him. Which we cannot afford them to do."

"Eddie cannot afford it either," Tromp added quickly, "since he will almost certainly now be first among the Danish and USE commanders that remain."

"What of Gjedde?"

Tromp frowned, thinking. "Both by temperament and orders, I suspect that Gjedde is here as both a mentor and a hand on the reins with which the Danish throne means to govern the progress of Cantrell. Gjedde himself has never sought war-time commands, and is quite vocal about preferring exploration. He will, I think, maintain his current position as Eddie's titular superior, but will not exert that authority except where the young commander may be making a misstep."

Van Walbeeck's sigh suggested he was not fully convinced of the workability of such a scheme. "And what of the other USE captains and junior officers in his flotilla? Will they be so willing to serve under so young a commander?"

"That," replied Maarten Tromp with his own sigh as Polhemius called for the concluding hymn, "is something over which I have no control, Jan. Now let us be first in line to offer our condolences to Lady Mund. That will allow us to be first to leave, and so, the first to arrive for the general meeting."

After looking around at the commanders and councilors who had been called to the meeting, Pieter van Corselles, the original governor of the first Oranjestad colony (and who had since been side-shifted into the post of Superintendent for the Dutch West India Company), shook his head in disbelief. "So after a year of hiding, now we are to make ourselves known? By launching an attack against the Spanish? From here?"

"That is correct, Superintendent Corselles." Jan van Walbeeck said with a mild nod.

"But it will bring them here in droves! It will mean our certain destruction!"

"Actually, if we do *not* attack the Spanish, it will mean our certain destruction. If we do not seek them out and cripple their main fleet, then they will eventually find and engage us here. That is not merely tactically unwise, it is strategically unacceptable."

"I do not disagree with your conclusion," Hannibal Sehested commented, "but I would welcome an explication of your reasoning in the matter."

Tromp nodded. "Certainly. Although I should begin by saying that the two senior commanders in each of our fleets—myself and Adrian Banckert for us, and Captain Gjedde and Commander Cantrell for you—are unanimous that we have no reasonable alternative." Tromp stood and put his finger on the up-time map of the Caribbean, planting it firmly upon St. Eustatia. "Note our position. We are near what you might call the pelagic elbow of the Caribbean. From here, the Greater Antilles stretch westward to Cuba, and the Lesser Antilles drop all the way down to Grenada. Until now, our island has been a relatively remote and, to the Spanish, uninteresting location. Prior to the four ships they sent south from St. Maarten's last year, they had not bothered to examine any of the Lesser Antilles islands since Fadrique Álvarez de Toledo led forty ships on a campaign of expulsion and extermination from St. Croix southward in 1629, thereby enforcing Spain's *inter caetera* claim to all lands west of the Tordesillas Line."

Tromp moved his finger to Puerto Rico, then Hispaniola, and finally Cuba. "Perhaps all these nearby places of considerable Spanish power embolden them to think that no one is mighty enough, or,"—he smiled—"idiotic enough to decamp so close to them, here in the northern extents of the Lesser Antilles." His finger drew an arc from Saba, through St. Eustatia and St. Christopher down to Nevis. "And yet, here we all are."

"All us idiots," Simonszoon growled. He almost grinned when his comment elicited a few equally sardonic laughs.

Tromp merely smiled. "Whether it is foolishness or fate that has brought us here is, for the moment, a debate we need not have. Rather, we must ask: after their defeat at the Grenada Passage, what will the Spanish do now?"

Chapter 42

Fort Oranjestad, St. Eustatia

Corselles, who was neither a seaman nor a soldier, gestured to the great blue expanse of the map on the table. "Why, it is obvious what the Spanish will do next. They will look for us all over. Relentlessly. Our only consolation is that finding us could take many months, maybe another year."

Tromp shook his head. "No. It will not."

"But why?"

Eddie leaned forward. "Because the Spanish that got away from the Grenada Passage brought back information that will help their bosses in Havana and Santo Domingo know where, and where not, to look for the ships that beat them up."

"What information would that be?" asked Sehested, studying the map as if seeing it anew.

Eddie shrugged. "Well, for starters, the mere fact that two immense USE steam cruisers were in the fight means a new team has slipped into the Caribbean. And given that our ships would have come out of the Baltic, they've probably got a pretty good guess at our course across the Atlantic. They will correctly guess that we entered the local swimming pool someplace very near that island-elbow Admiral Tromp was pointing out a minute ago.

"Which means that, unless we happened to stumble across Admiral Tromp's ships right before the battle, and by accident, we were already operating in coordination with a Dutch fleet. And I'm pretty sure they'll know the Dutch fleet they tangled with is not Thijssen's fleet from Curaçao, but the one that abandoned Recife."

"And how would they know that?" Corselles wondered in an almost desperate tone.

"First, the number of ships. As I understand it, Thijssen took Curaçao with just four, and that was the last expedition the United Provinces were able to mount. Next, how would Thijssen, sitting at the middle of the Spanish Main, have learned that we were going to be at Trinidad? And what reason would he have to come out and meet up with us? And how did all that happen just in time to catch a southbound Spanish fleet that he had no reason to suspect was headed toward Tierra Firma?" Eddie leaned back and shook his head. "As the guys in Havana start to put together those facts, and consider the other reports they must be receiving, they're going to become increasingly convinced that it couldn't have been Thijssen they met in the Grenada Passage."

"What other reports?" Sehested asked.

"Well, take the report that they'll get regarding the earl of Tyrconnell's raid on Puerto Cabello. The Spanish strategists would have to be pretty stupid not to interpret it as precisely what it was: a preemptive raid. By destroying their warehouses, we took out the provisioning for any fleet coming from Cartagena, thereby preventing it from joining the other fleet that was responding to our attack upon Trinidad. That is proof positive that there was widespread prior coordination between our forces before we engaged the Spanish off Grenada. Which in turn suggests that the attack on Trinidad was not simply a rogue event, but part of a much larger, well-considered operation."

Sehested nodded. "Which would logically mean, to them, that the wheels of this plan had been turning for half a year beforehand. Longer, since they must logically presume that our flotilla left Europe with the intent of arriving here at just the right time."

Eddie returned the nod. "Exactly. And how would Thijssen, whose base on Curacao is almost halfway to Cartagena, be able to get word of, and coordinate with, such a plan that far in advance? So, once they realize it wasn't him, they figure it can only be Admiral Tromp, who's been off their radar for more than a year. And when they start thinking about it, they'll start make some pretty predictable conjectures. Such as: 'Well, if that was Tromp in the Grenada Passage, then those couldn't have been all of his ships. Which means he has a base somewhere. Where he's been hiding out for a whole year. And if he's feeding even half of the people he evacuated from Recife, then he can't be in some uncharted Brazilian cove because they'd have starved to death by now. And he can't be anywhere on the Spanish Main because our garda-costa and trade traffic along there would have encountered him months ago, at the latest.' And so their eyes drift to a part of the map where there are islands with rapid access to European supply, have a history of excellent fertility, where they know there are still some non-Spanish settlements, and where they know the Dutch tried starting some of their own." Eddie dropped his finger so that it touched St. Eustatia and Saba.

"And then they start wondering about the four ships that went missing—and which you sank—just off Saba late last year. And so, they will eventually realize that all the hypothetical smoking guns are, in fact, pointing right about here." He pushed his finger into the map again. "Oh, they won't figure it out that quickly, because the information will come in dribs and drabs, and they will have to exchange emissaries and letters and speculations and share any reconnaissance results they get. But make no mistake, their light ships will come here looking. And when they do, one of two things will happen. They'll either see us before we see them and live to report. Or we'll see them first, catch them, and sink them without a trace. But even so, that still sends a kind of message." He leaned back. "The first rule of reconnaissance is that if your scout doesn't come back to report, the odds are good that he found something. So then you send three scouts in a group to visit the area where the first scout disappeared. And when they don't come back, well—" Eddie ended with his hands upraised, the conclusion so obvious that he didn't need to articulate it. "Which is pretty much what they already saw happen with the four ships they sent south from St. Maarten."

"Very well, so the Spanish will find us," Corselles agreed with a nervous nod. "But how will attacking them now save us? They are located all across that map, with many places of power. Once they know of us, they will drive us into the sea. Effortlessly."

Van Walbeeck folded his hands. "Pieter, the Spanish are not the monolithic force they may often seem. I have made a close study of their structures of government here in the New World, much of it revealed by research available at Grantville, paradoxically. Here is what I may tell you. In addition to great difficulties and loss of time in communicating with each other across such vast distances, the viceroyalties and governorships and *audiencias* are often rivals, striving to advance themselves at the expense of their neighbors. Knowing this, we may reasonably project the following:

"The greatest single power, the Viceroyalty of New Spain, is centered in Mexico. She is not particularly concerned with affairs in the Caribbean except and unless they impact her single overriding concern: the safety and reliability of the flota as her means of shipping gold and silver to Spain, and receiving supplies in return. She is slow to move and often sees Tierra Firma as a nuisance. Conversely, she traditionally perceives Havana as a competitor for preeminence and royal favor, since that city is the great shipbuilder and maritime defender of the region. But let us skip to a consideration of the Spanish power that is more likely to be concerned with maritime incursions: Cartagena, the closest naval power of any size."

"Not Caracas, and the *audiencias* of Venezuela?"

Van Walbeeck interlaced his fingers. "I do not think so, simply because what little strength she has is continually focused upon her contention with mainland natives. However, although Cartagena will be the most concerned when it comes to our invasion of Trinidad, she may well be fickle or undependable in her responses to the implication of our broader presence in the Caribbean."

"Why?" asked Rik Bjelke, who had remained almost motionless beside Sehested until now. "I thought the governor there—er, de Murga?—was a most active man."

"He is, but he answers to the viceroy of Peru."

Rik seemed puzzled. "But Peru is—"

"On the other side of South America, yes. It is a curious arrangement, an artifact of historical flukes and no small amount of sinecure. However that may be, this will work to slow and limit Cartagena's response. And in turn, that means she will concentrate her forces strictly upon that which threatens her interests most directly: Trinidad. This was confirmed by the surviving captains of the vessels we took as prizes there, several of whom were brought here for further questioning."

Corselles' eyes became grim. "And the rest of the prisoners?"

Tromp waved a dismissive hand. "Back at Trinidad. On one of what are called the Five Islands, just a few miles offshore from Port-of-Spain. They are quite secure."

"Because the island is so remote?"

"That, and because the Nepoia natives have decided to watch it quite carefully. They are most determined not to allow any new Spanish to set foot on Trinidad."

"So," Sehested said, returning to the main topic, "you do not expect either New Spain's or Cartagena's fleets to aid any efforts made against us here, in the northern extents of the Lesser Antilles."

"Correct. For both of them, we can only be reached by a very long sail against the prevailing winds or currents. And for now, at least, we represent no threat to their livelihoods. However, in the case of Cuba and the islands that are her immediate satellites"— Tromp ran his finger to Havana and drifted it slowly eastward to touch Jamaica, Hispaniola, and Puerto Rico—"we must expect an aggressive response. We threaten them in a variety of ways, not the least of which is our ability to sail north and attempt to intercept the flota as it returns to Spain with the silver that keeps Madrid's bloated economy afloat."

"So, you are saying we need to mount a campaign against the entirety of the Greater Antilles?" Corselles looked as incredulous and horrified as he sounded.

Tromp moved toward the map again, shaking his head. "Not at all. We know where they will gather their strength for a strike against us. It is also the same port to which most of the fleet we defeated undoubtedly fled." He jabbed down at the south coast of Hispaniola. "Here. Santo Domingo."

Sehested stroked his goatee meditatively. "Why there?"

"Cuba is too far. Puerto Rico is too undeveloped, particularly on her south coast, and her north coast often has unfavorable winds. But Hispaniola is well-developed, has several large towns, and Santo Domingo has shipyards and quite respectable fortifications. Furthermore, although the prevailing winds there are contrary, they are milder than the breezes that come straight off the Atlantic on the northern coast, and her anchorage could easily accommodate a fleet as large as sixty, perhaps seventy hulls."

"And how far between Santo Domingo and St. Eustatia?"

"Approximately four hundred and fifty miles. Let us assume contrary conditions, with a forward progress of one knot. A fleet, sailing steadily, would still reach us in no more than three weeks. Let us say four weeks, if they touched at Puerto Rico and refrained from sailing on moonless nights. Let us say five weeks if they encounter high weather."

"But that is after they find us, and decide to gather a fleet to send against us," Corselles said hopefully.

Simonszoon shrugged. "Yes, but finding us might not take more than two weeks."

"But at one knot—"

"Superintendent Corselles," Simonszoon interrupted sharply, "you have no doubt noticed that our jachts travel much more speedily than our fluyts, particularly when the weather is unfavorable?"

Corselles looked indignant, but too intimidated to speak. He simply nodded.

"Well, the Spanish *pataches* are akin to our jachts. Not so fast, not so agile, but they tack well and would be here in a week's time, easily. They could make it back to Santo Domingo in half that. So although it might take them six weeks to send a fleet here, their scouts could arrive much sooner than that."

"So we are to strike Santo Domingo," Sehested murmured. "To disable them before they may exterminate us."

"That is the gist of it," Tromp said with a nod.

"And how do you propose to protect Oranjestad, while you are off on this mission?" Corselles' eyes were large and bright. Eddie wondered if the man might be verging toward a breakdown. He hadn't been so anxious when the flotilla first arrived, but it almost seemed that, with relief and resupply finally at hand, his spirit was not pliable enough to face new risks and uncertainties. "And if we manage to defeat their fleet, won't the Spanish simply build another? How does this strategy furnish us with a lasting solution?"

Gjedde looked up. His voice sounded rough from disuse. "It is not a lasting solution. Nothing is. That is in the nature of contending nations. This stratagem answers the immediate threat and buys us time. But that time could be decisive. With the agreement forged between your Provinces and Brussels, you will soon have the renewed support of your homeland. The USE and my sovereign have established interests here, as well. You are no longer alone. Be consoled in this. It is a far brighter outlook than you had three months ago." He folded his hands and lowered his chin again.

Sehested nodded at this interjection and turned to Tromp. "However, there is another, more pressing danger in this stratagem. It means dividing our collective forces into three groups, does it not?"

Tromp sighed. "Yes. It is, unfortunately, unavoidable. We may not leave our forces and interests on Trinidad unguarded. Nor may we leave St. Eustatia without defenses. But we must carry the attack to Santo Domingo unless we are content to wait here until they overwhelm us, even with the up-time steamships."

Corselles' eyes had grown even larger. "So even your ships could not destroy all the Spanish hulls that might try attacking us here?"

Eddie shook his head. "No. They can't be every place at once, and we have a lot of strategic vulnerabilities that a knowledgeable enemy could exploit. The Spanish probably wouldn't even come straight at us. They might realize that our greatest vulnerability on this island is actually food, and so go after St. Christopher's instead, where we get our bulk provisioning. And then what do we do? Keep one steamship here, and send one there? And if they get a toehold on St. Christopher's, they can land troops there, and then try to get them across the channel at night. It's only eight miles, shore to shore." Eddie leaned back. "Look, if the Spanish are at all smart, they'll learn from the mistakes they're sure to make, and which—being Spain—they can easily afford. And once they've learned those lessons, then, even if they can't beat our steamships, they'll outflank us and take us on land. It might be a long fight for them, and it would be costly, but in the end, the only thing the Spanish wouldn't have beaten into submission are those two steam cruisers. And if those two ships have burned up their full supply of coal running back and forth, putting out fires—well, the wind can give us trouble just like anyone else. And we can run out of ammo just like anyone else, too."

"So you're saying your ships *aren't* magic?" Simonszoon leaned over to smile at Eddie.

Eddie smiled back. "Damn," he play-acted, "I guess I let that secret slip." He shook his head seriously. "The fact of the matter is that our steamships are fundamentally offensive platforms. They are at their best when they are on the attack, not defense. And that means, among other things, that the attack on Santo Domingo is going to require more than just warships. We're going to need to bring a number of Dutch fluyts along with us. We're going to need to bring a lot of troops and a lot of supplies, because we can't just beat their fleet. We have to hit the city itself so hard that they can't use it any more. If we accomplish that, then their next closest reasonable base is on Cuba. That means that the next time they try to mount an offensive campaign against us here, they would have to project that force almost twice as far. That means a lot more ships, a lot more money, a lot more men to feed for a lot more weeks. And for us, that means a lot more time before they can mount that kind of offensive. And that's what we're playing for here: enough time for our side to send what we need to prevail."

Corselles looked slightly less nervous. "Very well, but do you really need the fluyts? I have seen these immense ships of yours, riding at anchor. Can they not carry proportionately greater numbers of our troops, of the needed supplies?"

Eddie smiled, shook his head. "Oddly, no. For those of you who have not been below decks on one of our steamships, you would probably find it a strange sight. In the place of throngs of men, there is a lot of machinery and even more supplies. We shoot much faster and so use far more ammunition. The steam engines must be fired by coal, or at least wood, which must be kept dry and handy in special fuel bunkers. We have radios, intra-ship speaking tubes, special areas and companionways reserved for the exchange of stores or for access to secondary systems, such as our condensers."

"Your what?"

"Condensers, Superintendent Corselles. We use them to convert sea water to fresh water."

"So you may enjoy a refreshing drink whenever you choose, on your voyages?" Corselles tone hadn't been derisive, but nor had it been entirely jocular. The laughter that rose up was genuine, but slightly strained.

Eddie joined in, chuckling. "Well, that is a side benefit, Super-intendent Corselles. But the real reason we have the condensers is because you can't run steam engines on salt water. You have to have fresh water. But if you can tell me where to find some bubbling island springs in the middle of the Atlantic, maybe we can leave those condensers behind to help you with your water shortages here on St. Eustatia."

A little polite laughter followed Eddie's reply, but most importantly, he could see in the faces at the table, even Corselles', that he had made his two points. First, that fresh water was an operational necessity not an indulgence, and, second, that it was inadvisable to make jokes based on superficial assumptions.

Tromp leaned his fists on the table. "Although we will be meeting often as we move our plans for the attack on Santo Domingo forward, we do have one last matter that must be addressed now. Speaking as the nominal commander of our allied fleet, we must find a new captain for the *Resolve*, and this means selecting a person who will learn the technologies of the ship, and its operation, quickly and well. The late Admiral Mund was schooled in this extensively at Luebeck, and personally witnessed much of *Resolve*'s final construction. We cannot hope to duplicate that level of familiarity here, but we must have a captain. We must also have a larger staff of technical specialists, led by the *Intrepid*'s executive officer Henrik Bjelke, ready to take the ship into battle. So, after polling my command staff, I consulted with the two senior officers of the USE and Danish flotilla, and we are unanimously resolved that the new captain should be Dirck Simonszoon."

Simonszoon groaned. "Oh, by all that's holy, Maarten. How could you do this to me?"

Tromp smiled. "I've seen you eyeing those guns, those engines, Dirck. And your sailing skill will be key, as well, since *Resolve* only uses her steam engines when she's in combat."

Simonszoon shook his head. "First you took me off my yacht, and put me on a great scow of a warship. And now I am to move from commanding a mere giant to a full-blown leviathan? And with a mere Danish pup to tell me how to run the machines?"

Bjelke, who was not yet accustomed to Simonszoon's broad gibes, started.

Tromp only smiled more widely. "Dirck, you know very well that Rik has the necessary skills for both roles, since you've told me so yourself. Multiple times."

Rik looked as suddenly pleased as he had been suddenly dismayed. Simonszoon only looked annoyed at having had his better nature and opinions publicly revealed. "I was lying. And what of the matter of authority?"

"What do you mean?" asked Joost van Banckert.

"I mean that with Gjedde and Cantrell on *Intrepid*, that puts both of the senior USE commanders on one ship, and none on the *Resolve*. How is that wise? And furthermore, by what authority am I to be in charge there? I am not a part of that flotilla. I serve Maarten Harpertszoon Tromp and the United Provinces, and in that order."

Sehested smoothed his mustache. "I fear the command situation is even more complicated than that, Captain Simonszoon. In the command ranks of our flotilla, Captain Gjedde is now the first senior officer. But arguably, Tryggve Stiernsköld, as a Swedish post captain, is next, and *then* Commander Cantrell. By all rights, therefore, it should be Captain Stiernsköld who is the master of the second steam cruiser."

Eddie scanned the faces, ended upon Stiernsköld's; he was fairly sure what he read there, and that he had an accurate measure of that taciturn yet straightforward man. "Captain Stiernsköld, tell me, do you feel comfortable commanding one of the steam cruisers?"

Stiernsköld shook his head. "No," he said flatly.

Sehested started, stared between the two men as if seeking prior collusion and frowned when he saw there was none.

"Captain Stiernsköld," Eddie continued, "do you think you ever *will* be comfortable commanding one?"

The Swede nodded. "Most certainly. Once I have received adequate training. But I have not. I am told I was included in the flotilla for my abilities with fast, mixed rig sailing vessels, such as the *Tropic Surveyor*. As you no doubt know, Commander Cantrell, I was only briefed on the steamships' capabilities so that I knew what they might do and how best to coordinate with them. I received no training in their operation."

Sehested leaned back, nodded. "Very well. You have made your point, Commander Cantrell, and most convincingly. I withdraw my reservations over the proper chain of command in the ships of the flotilla. But I still cannot countenance a foreign captain—even one so skilled and friendly to our cause as Captain Simonszoon—to be the master of *Resolve*."

Eddie rubbed his nose and schooled his voice to be apologetic yet firm. "Unfortunately, Lord Sehested, that objection is a bit beside the point."

"I beg your pardon?"

"Lord Sehested, so we all understand your position with complete clarity, who appointed you to the flotilla?"

Sehested's frown intensified as he spoke, seemed to be veering toward umbrage. "You know very well that it was your own father-in-law, Christian IV, who asked me to accompany this mission."

"Yes, but on what authority did he make that assignment?"

Sehested opened his mouth but shut it again, his eyes narrowing slightly. Clearly, he saw where this was heading. "He was exercising his prerogative as one of the sovereigns of the Union of Kalmar."

"Yes. Which is not a member of the United States of Europe, nor are any of its constituent powers. Now, the steam cruisers: to whom do they belong?"

"The United States of Europe—whose monarch is Gustav Adolf, who is also *primus inter pares* among the monarchs of the Union of Kalmar."

"That is very true. But it is also quite a separate matter. Gustav Adolf may indeed dictate the actions of the USE in his role as its monarch, but not in his role as the king of Sweden or as the first-among-equals from the Union of Kalmar. Consequently, unless my understanding of the prerogatives that attach to these separate roles is in error, none of the Danish, or even Swedish, members of the flotilla may speak for, or presume authority possessed by, the USE. That would fall to individuals who are nationals of the USE, or who have been directly and explicitly named by Gustav Adolf of Sweden to be operating in its service."

"Such as yourself," van Walbeeck concluded, a slight grin hidden behind his hand, "on both counts."

Eddie shrugged. "It does so happen that I am the senior ranking representative of the USE with the flotilla." *A position which Simpson made absolutely sure of, bless his crusty and irascible hide. It was as if he saw this wrestling match coming from the very moment I proposed the mission.* "Consequently, while it was agreed, from the outset, that I could not hold a field rank equivalent to the many senior Danish and Swedish commanders in the flotilla, my equal share of authority regarding the management and strategy of the flotilla was—and remains—undiminished."

He turned to Simonszoon, whose usually veiled eyes were wide in frank admiration. *Didn't think I had the stones for this sort of down-and-dirty politicking, eh, Dirck? Well, guess what: neither did I.* Eddie didn't miss a beat. "Captain Dirck Simonszoon, as a sign of the amity and alliance between our nations here in the New World, might I ask you to accept the temporary command of the USS *Resolve* as a special commission?"

"Commander—Sir! It would be my honor, if my admiral may spare me from the Dutch fleet."

Tromp smiled. "You have my leave and encouragement to accept Commander Cantrell's offer, Captain. Make the Provinces proud."

Simonszoon scoffed. "And when have I done any less?"

Van Walbeeck grinned. "Do you mean on the deck of a ship, or in a grog shop?"

Dirck pointedly did not glance down the table at Jan, but rather, tugged at his collar. "It's getting hot in here. Let's finish this damned meeting."

Chapter 43

Oranjestad, St. Eustatia

The one large wooden building in Oranjestad—an all-purpose *gemeentehuis*, indoor market, and dance hall—was already starting to fill with eager guests. The somber mood of the late morning funeral that had been conducted not twenty yards away had dissipated completely. That was hardly a surprise: Pros Mund had stepped ashore all of one time, and the whispering behind cupped hands opined that his wife was at best a recluse and at worst an emotionless and aloof exemplar of all that was deplorable in aristocrats.

"A welcome occasion, a party," Tromp observed as he remained well to the back of the slightly elevated platform at the rear of the building.

"A novel occasion," van Walbeeck corrected. "This is the first true party we've had."

Tromp, who had spent many weeks on patrol, and the rest of the time too busy to partake, or even become passingly familiar, with the social life of Oranjestad, started. "Can that—can that be?"

"It most certainly can, Maarten. What did you think? That while you were slaving away for the good of the colony, the rest of us were dancing and drinking?"

"No, no, but I—"

Jan laughed someplace down in his belly, and put a hand on his friend's shoulder. "You are always so delightfully earnest, Maarten. I know you were well aware that our colonists have not had a lightsome time, this past year. But I do suspect that you might have imagined that, out here in the town, the rituals of life managed to go on as before, albeit much diminished."

Tromp reflected. "I suppose I did. I suppose I wanted to imagine it that way. Because if there was some semblance of normal existence, it meant that I—we—were providing for the colonists sufficiently."

Jan squeezed his shoulder. "Well, see now? All your hard work is finally rewarded: a party!"

"Yes," Tromp grumbled, "mostly victualed from the larders of Danes."

"Well, how should it be otherwise? It is a presentation of their king's daughters to the society of Oranjestad. Such as it is."

"We have 'society' in a town that has not had a single party in a year?"

"Of course we do."

"And how do you tell the members of society apart from everyone else?"

"Quite simply, Maarten. The members of Oranjestad society still have real shoes."

Tromp stared sidelong at Jan, saw his smile, and could not resist joining him in a brief chuckle. "It is good to have a moment to leave business behind, my friend."

"It would be," Jan admitted in a slightly more somber tone.

Tromp resolved not to frown. "And what is it now?"

"I have had word from Michael McCarthy. He believes the radio will be ready tonight."

"Tonight? So he will not be here?"

Jan shook his head. "No. And I suspect he is secretly relieved at the coincidence. He sent his formal regrets to Lord Sehested, who seemed relieved to receive them, as I understand it."

"Sehested doesn't like McCarthy?"

"Oh, no. Nothing of the sort. But I suspect he may plan to use this social event as an opportunity to do a bit of politicking. And radio messages to and from Europe would only get in the way. Particularly since those communications would involve contact with up-time authorities."

"Ah," Tromp exhaled, seeing where Jan was leading. "So you think Sehested wanted Eddie on his own, tonight, and without recourse to his leaders?"

"The possibility has crossed my mind. However, one thing is certain: before this party begins, you and I must decide who we shall continue to meet with openly as we frame our plans for Santo Domingo, and who we must exclude."

Tromp nodded. "Because we must restrict spreading word about the radio, which will be an integral part of those plans."

"That, and general prudence against setting loose lips flapping here in our own town. Consider Corselles. He has no role in deciding upon how we shall attack Santo Domingo. However, were he to be kept apprised, he would, alas, be quite capable of giving away subtle strategic details without even knowing he was doing so. And there are other avenues by which necessarily secret information might become widely known. For instance, ship's captains often drink to excess just as much as their sailors do."

"Jan, are you referring to—?"

Walbeeck held up a hand. "I am not mentioning individuals because I am not thinking of individuals. I simply note that, the more persons who are involved in the early planning of our attack, the more chances we have of enemies getting wind of its particulars."

Tromp sighed. "It is sad, but prudent. Besides, there is entirely too much dissent among our own landowners. They have regular contact with our captains, our pursers."

Van Walbeeck shook his head. "And what of our tradesmen and workers who go back and forth from St. Christopher's? They seem to do a more lively trade in rumors and gossip than anything else. And the French there, those who mix in with the English, will carry those rumors down into their capital at Basseterre. And we know that both governors, Warner no less than d'Esnambuc, both turn a blind eye toward trade with the pirates of Jamaica and Tortuga."

"So who is our inner council of war, then? Just the two of us?"

"Well, Maarten, truth be told, I'm none too sure about your reliability, either."

"Very funny, Jan. Who else? Eddie, obviously. Banckert."

"Even though you have to leave him behind in Oranjestad, again?"

"Absolutely. Joost must know what we are doing, and when, and why, if he is to be able to react to unforeseen crises or changes."

"Fair enough, Maarten. Anyone else?"

"I do not think we can include Eddie without including Gjedde. It would be too profound a slight to the senior officer of our allies. And besides, Gjedde doesn't speak much, but when he does, it's always worth listening to."

Van Walbeeck nodded vigorously. "Agreed. Simonszoon?"

"I think we must, and he's not much more talkative than Gjedde, usually."

"What about the ground commanders? Once we get to Santo Domingo, they will need to know everything."

"Yes, but at this stage, they do not need to know anything. As we begin studying the maps we have of Santo Domingo, and gathering reports on its walls and troops, then we will bring them in. Although—"

"Yes?"

"I wish we had the earl of Tyrconnell here. He is a clever fellow, quite experienced, and well educated. More importantly, he has spent his life in Spanish service and knows the smallest details of their protocols."

"Having taken a few Spanish ships and towns ourselves, we are hardly ignorant in such matters, Maarten."

"True, but we still remain outsiders to that knowledge. It is not *instinctive* to us. Conversely, the earl of Tyrconnell was a well-placed insider, trained in Spanish service, including artillery. Besides, he is a prudent man who has spent a lifetime learning how to hold his tongue and be cautious. He had little choice, since the English have wanted his head, and do so more than ever, now."

"Ah. Because he is the last earl of Ireland. Tell me, why is he not here?"

Tromp shrugged. "Because he is doing other important work that only he may do."

"And what, and where, is that?"

"O'Donnell and Pieter Floriszoon split off from our fleet when we drew near Montserrat."

"Why there?"

"The population is overwhelmingly comprised of Irish catholic refugees from Nevis. Apparently they fled after a religious disagreement several years back. He is hoping to rally the support of the settlement there, possibly even draw some new recruits to his colors."

"Well, it still sounds as though he had some help with that.

Without Floriszoon's *Eendracht*, he would have had to ask the recruits to swim back here."

"Not entirely true. He is half owner of the *patache* his men took in Puerto Cabello. We own the other half."

"And so is the earl a proficient seaman, among his other wonderful traits?"

"No, although Floriszoon tells me he has the right instincts for it. And whereas our fellows are teaching the Irish how to be sailors, the Wild Geese are imparting some lessons in weapon-handling and even the finer arts of boarding a ship."

"They are teaching *us* how to board ships?"

"Many of them spent time as ship's troops. The Spanish train their lead-rank boarders quite specially it seems. O'Donnell and Floriszoon are sharing that knowledge and between them, they seem to be making a good team."

"Yes," agreed Jan, "it's all needful skills they are exchanging."

Tromp shook his head. "I mean more than that, and more than the greater and improbable combination of our Dutch sea dogs and O'Donnell's Wild Geese. I'm referring to the pairing of O'Donnell with Floriszoon *personally*, the fact that they get along well, that they have worked together. That is a serendipitous first bridge between Amsterdam and Brussels in this new Netherlands in which we now exist."

"In what way?"

Sometimes, Jan van Walbeeck's fine intellectual insights blinded him to more visceral human truths. Not often, but this was one of those moments. "Jan, O'Donnell and Floriszoon are both young men, both educated, both tired of the religious bigotry that fueled the wars that defined their lives and those of their forebears. We are fortunate that both are philosophical enough in their respective faiths to find ample room for toleration of the other." Tromp leaned back. "I would not interrupt the solidification of that friendship even if it cost me a ship and twenty good guns. Because the cooperation—*willing* cooperation—between the Brabant and our United Provinces, of linking our fates and fortunes as a single nation means more in the long run than any single battle. And it will be fortunate and wise to have men of intelligence and experience who may be liaisons between those two dominions at moments of friction. Men such as O'Donnell and Floriszoon. Much may be done if the leaders of our new country are operating in concert.

Much may be lost if they are not. And men such as these two young captains may be just the insurance the Netherlands needs to maintain enough unity of purpose and mutual understanding to survive the first years of genuine integration. Allies are far more difficult to manage than enemies, after all."

"How timely an axiom," murmured van Walbeeck. "Here comes another one of those potentially difficult allies, now."

Hannibal Sehested, attired in understated splendor that flattered the event without quite making him conspicuous, approached with a broad smile. "Gentlemen," he said in passable Dutch, "how do you fare this evening?"

They bowed, Jan replying as he did so. "Quite well, Sir Sehested, and our thanks for your sovereign's generosity, that we might make merry while making the formal acquaintance of his lovely daughters."

He bowed in return. "I wish the evening could do both better honor to the ladies, and to you, our hosts in this far land. And it saddens me that fate had us choose the date that should turn out to be the same as marks our mourning of Admiral Mund."

"Indeed," agreed Tromp solemnly. "I did not know him well, but he seemed prudent and concerned for the safety of his men." Tromp spotted Eddie entering the building from the rear door, scanning faces as he began roving along the edges of the early-comers. "Ah, Commander Cantrell, do join us." *And save me from this eager young Danish diplomat.*

Eddie, looking very distracted, stopped, nodded and wandered over, remembering to bow instead of shaking hands at the very last second. "Nice to see you all, gentlemen. I wonder if you have seen my lovely wife?"

"I am afraid not, Lord Cantrell, although with half an hour left before her entrance, I would not expect to find her here," Sehested replied. "But this is an excellent vantage point to scan for her, if she makes an early appearance. And as you do, you might perhaps share your insights on our fallen hero, Admiral Mund."

Eddie sounded confused, looked suddenly cautious. "Uh— insights? I can't really say I knew him that well."

"No, of course not. Pros Mund was a private man. And so, the causes of his actions were not always fully understood by those who witnessed them. Indeed, I had not foreseen that he would be such an indomitable lion once was combat was joined. But he was bold indeed, taking so many prizes."

Tromp suppressed a sigh. Now Sehested's motivation for this conversation was becoming clear: to further "discuss" the matter of the Spanish prize ships. Which had caused some debate in the wake of the battle.

Of the twenty-six Spanish ships that were present for the Battle of the Grenada Passage, three had been sunk outright. Five more were so badly damaged by the guns of the USE steam cruisers that they had necessarily been scuttled. Three had to be abandoned before guns or other valuable items could be recovered from them. The fires had been too dangerous and widespread to risk coming alongside. Four had been taken as prizes, although only one—a refitted nao that had struck her colors when the *Intrepid* bore down upon her—was fundamentally undamaged. Of the other three, one—a galleoncete that Tromp's own Dutch ships had been raked with fire and disabled before she could flee with the rest of the Spaniards' southern van—was still capable of independent maneuver. The other two, galleons much pummeled by the two USE steam cruisers, had suffered immense damage to their spars, and, in one case, the rudder and tiller mechanism.

An even split of the prizes was deemed fair in the immediate aftermath of the battle, the Dutch claiming a galleon and the galleoncete that they had taken themselves, while the USE and Danish contingent had settled for the nao and a galleon.

However, upon radioing a report of this ahead to Oranjestad when they finally came into range, Hannibal Sehested had initiated a swift, if polite, challenge to that apportionment of spoils. Specifically, the Danish diplomat had argued that the steam cruisers had performed the greatest deeds of the day, and so, had earned more than half of the prizes. When there was some resistance to this by Tromp, Sehested countered by pointing to the bravery and sacrifice of Mund as a further reason that it was the contribution of the Danes (he began omitting references to the USE at this point) which had made the victory possible at all. Accordingly, they should at least be given the two largest warships—the galleons—instead of accepting the ponderous and decidedly mercantile nao as one of their prizes.

It was uncertain how the debate would ultimately have resolved, had not Ove Gjedde finally, and reluctantly, become involved. He pointed out that the galleons were not particularly useful to his own Danish fleet as warships. In the current circumstances, they were too slow and incorrectly rigged for military operations in the Caribbean, and two galleons would have been difficult to crew, when the flotilla already had enough guns and hulls to man. However, in claiming the nao, Gjedde pointed out that Denmark had also received first choice of her intact stores and cargo, and that being a high weather ship, like a galleon, she would be well-suited to convoying those spoils home to Copenhagen. Sehested was at pains to graciously accept this perspective (which matched the original division of prize hulls) and thanked Gjedde for his "subtle wisdom" in making these choices on behalf of Sehested and King Christian IV. Or, as Simonszoon had commented, for having shown that the Danish diplomat had as much knowledge about ships as a boar had about bathtubs.

But here was Sehested mentioning the prize hulls yet again. Tromp hoped that the Dane would not be so crude as to use his role as the magnanimous provider of tonight's food and drink as a means of exerting pressure to yet again revisit the twice-approved division of spoils.

But that did not seem to be the Danish diplomat's intent after all. "I understand that other bold actions were undertaken beforehand to secure our alliance's resounding victory. I refer, of course to the daring raid upon Puerto Cabello. I had hoped to meet that commander, the Irish earl, here at the party but I am informed that he did not return with your fleet. Is that correct?"

"It is, Sir Sehested. He and one of our captains, Pieter Flo-riszoon, diverted to Montserrat. They had refugees to deposit there, and it was also thought best to also acquaint that island's settlers with the earl of Tyrconnell *bona fides.*"

"Ah, yes," Sehested said with a nod. "It is populated by Irish Catholics, is it not?"

"Yes," affirmed van Walbeeck, "and it is our hope that they might proclaim loyalty to the earl. Which, given his service to Brussels, would mean adding another safe haven for the ships of the Netherlands." He nodded at Eddie. "If we were to be able to count upon Montserrat as another island allied to our cause, along with those inhabited by the English, we would be most excellently situated, having control over all the northern Lesser Antilles. With the exception of our old colony on St. Maarten, that is."

"That would be an excellent development," agreed Sehested, "and it is fortuitous that you should mention St. Maarten. That island is of particular interest to his royal Danish Majesty, Christian the Fourth."

"Indeed? Is he interested in its salt-flats? At some point we hope to return there to reestablish our salt-fish production. Would he wish to join us in this?" asked van Walbeeck.

"No," Sehested said calmly. "He wishes to take and claim the island for Denmark, in recognition of his contributions to the defeat of the Spanish throughout the Caribbean and the rescue of your colony here in particular. Of course, his Majesty would be happy to grant the right to reopen the commercial operations you call 'factories' without tariff or other fee to his Dutch friends, and would be particularly gratified to materially aid those who lost their business interests in the place when the Spanish evicted you last year."

Tromp was stunned but, being a fairly quiet man, knew that his stunned silence was not particularly noticeable. Garrulous van Walbeeck's speechlessness, on the other hand, was a marked contrast with his usual demeanor. His cheeks puffing, he reddened slightly and finally sputtered. "This—this is most unexpected, Sir Sehested."

Eddie Cantrell's arch stare suggested that he had not expected it, either. "Excuse me, Sir Sehested."

"Yes, Sir Cantrell?"

"Is this according to the will of the Union of Kalmar? Which is to say, does Gustav know anything about this—request?"

"No, he has not been apprised of this *requirement*. But after all, your royal father-in-law is a sovereign. In all that the term signifies and entails. This falls well outside the peripheries of consultation between the different monarchs who are bound together in the Union of Kalmar."

"Yes. I see. Please excuse me a moment."

"Do you have a pressing matter, Lord Cantrell? You shall figure prominently as we continue this discussion, I assure you."

Eddie smiled—a bit too brightly, Tromp thought. "I'm sure I do, but as the spouse of one of this evening's guests of honor, I have a little of my own coordinating to do before the festivities begin. Excuse me. I won't be long."

Tromp had to consciously stop himself from calling—"No! Don't leave!"—after Eddie as Hannibal Sehested began discussing the optimal timetable for retaking St. Maarten from the Spanish.

Chapter 44

Oranjestad, St. Eustatia

Anne Cathrine rolled her eyes as, yet again, there was a knock on the door. "We are hurrying as quickly as we may, Matilde," she called patiently and, she hoped, sweetly to the young Dutch girl who had been working as messenger and girl Friday for the three young Danish ladies. Who were deeply involved in making their toilet and the dress preparations necessitated by their imminent presentation to Oranjestad society.

The voice that responded was not Matilde's. "Uh, it's me, Eddie."

"What? Eddie? Husband—dear—I am, that is, we are—" Anne Cathrine glanced at shy, half-dressed Leonora and Sophie Rantzau's calm, casual nudity—"we are indisposed. Most decidedly indisposed."

"Oh. Still? Um, honey, are you still indisposed, too?"

"I am dressed, if that is what you are asking." Anne Cathrine had to remind herself not to sound coyly seductive. Which is how she usually responded whenever Eddie had occasion to ask her about her state of dress.

"Yeah, that's exactly what I'm asking. Because—"

"Yes?" Anne Cathrine stood. The tone in Eddie's voice was uncommonly serious. "Is something wrong, Eddie?"

"Well, yeah. Someone's making trouble at your party. Already."

Anne Cathrine, without having any idea who might make trouble at a party that would not yet start for twenty minutes or how they would do so, gathered her considerable skirts and began walking to the door. "Who is making this trouble? Have you told Sehested about this?"

"Oh, he knows. Actually, he's helping the troublemaker."

"What? Who is this troublemaker?"

"Unless I'm very much mistaken, it's your father."

"*What?*"

"Honey, come on out and walk with me. I'll explain on the way to the main conference room in the fort. I've already sent Matilde to get Sehested and the others."

By the time Eddie reached the wide, shuttered room on the second story of the fort's expansive blockhouse, Tromp, Sehested and van Walbeeck were all there. Sehested rose, smiling, "So, we are to have a meeting to settle this matter now? That is quite agreeable to—"

And then he saw Anne Cathrine enter from behind Eddie, who was holding the door for her. She was not smiling. "L-Lady Anne Cathrine," he stuttered. "This is a most awkward surprise."

"Yes," she replied archly. "I rather imagine it must be."

Eddie could hardly keep from beaming as he thought at her, *you go, girl!*

Sehested spread wide, temporizing hands. "Lady Anne Cathrine, I am dismayed that you were summoned away from a party being held in your honor. Of course, it is also for Lady Leonora as well, and it is a privilege to introduce Mistress Rantzau along with you. But you are the oldest king's daughter, and so—"

"And so it is my duty to be present when the king of Denmark's affairs of state are to be discussed. My husband was quite right to summon me, and I will be pleased to have you present this *requirement* that my royal father has evidently instructed you to impose upon our Dutch allies."

Unless Eddie was very much mistaken, Jan van Walbeeck was ready to explode in amusement and enthusiasm for the spirited and capable young Danishwoman who had, uninvited, swept to the seat at the head of the conference table. Tromp himself hastened to hold her chair, which she acknowledged with a smile as radiant as the rising sun.

The men sat, and she nodded at Sehested.

He shifted slightly in his seat and gazed down at the table. "Lady Anne Cathrine, I must point out that, while I am delighted that you take such keen interest in your father's royal desires and political actions, he did not ask you to represent him here in the New World."

"He did not need to. I am his daughter. I do not need to be told that I should pay close heed to my father's interests. And to my husband's as well, since you told him that this conversation would concern him, too."

"And so it does. But that is predominantly a military matter. And as a king's daughter—"

Anne Cathrine's green eyes were bright and wide, as if daring Sehested to take one step further down the inevitable path he intended: to point out that since she was not a princess, she had no material interest in the royal family's possessions or affairs. She was not in line of succession herself, nor was she a full royal sibling to any of Christian's potential successors.

But on the other hand, she was now sitting at the head of the table, her father's very fiery and competent daughter, with her up-time, Danish-titled husband to one side, and the senior Dutch admiral and administrator in the New World seated on the other side. Sehested's eyes rose from the tabletop, scanning their faces, and Eddie knew what he was looking for: the faintest hint of uncertainty or anxiety. *He's playing poker. He's trying to see whether we're bluffing or whether we will see his bid and call.*

Sehested was no fool, and was evidently good enough at poker to see that the other players were not going to fold, but would see this hand all the way to the bitter end. Which meant that, even if he was perfectly within his legal rights to exclude Anne Cathrine from the conversation, and even the room, he would have destroyed his credibility with the three men sitting around her, to say nothing of his relationship with her. And, princess or not, she had her father's ear and she would clearly not be an advocate for Sehested's interests in court. On the contrary, she might become an implacable and quite effective foe. So Sehested shrugged. "As a king's daughter, you are welcome to hear of your father's wishes. They were given to me as a contingency that might require execution, based upon what we might find upon arriving in the New World, and what actions we might be called upon to undertake once here. However, while I would be saddened to displease you in any way, you must of course realize that, as the agent of your father's will, I may not alter my duty to suit your own wishes."

Chin high, Anne Cathrine nodded. "You would be a poor representative of his interests, if you did. Please continue."

"As you wish, Lady Anne Cathrine." Sehested turned his gaze to Tromp and van Walbeeck. "I hope you gentlemen will not think ill of me if I am quite candid."

"We would prefer that," Tromp said quietly.

"Very well. His Majesty King Christian IV is concerned, and somewhat dismayed, that no provision has been made to reward Denmark for her participation in this mission to the New World. She is not party to the joint ownership of the oil drilling ventures in Trinidad, has been promised no land rights on any of the islands there or here in the Lesser Antilles, and most recently was even denied what seemed a just share of the treasure gained in the recent battle of the Grenada Passage even though her ships were responsible for crippling or sinking all but one of the Spanish vessels that were defeated."

Eddie frowned. "Sir Sehested, you are incorrect in one particular. *Intrepid* and *Resolve* are not Danish ships. They are USE warships."

"Yes. And seventy percent of their crews are Danish."

"Provided to the USE through the kind agencies of Gustav Adolf as first sovereign of the Union of Kalmar, not directly by King Christian IV."

"Your father-in-law the king sees the matter differently. However, that is ultimately of no account, here. His requirements are not contingent upon whatever gratitude these Dutch gentlemen might feel for his contributions to this alliance, although he would have preferred that those finer sentiments had been strong enough to induce them to offer voluntarily that upon which I must now insist. Namely, that the island of St. Maarten be taken with all practicable haste in the name of King Christian IV of Denmark."

Tromp shook his head, more in bemused confusion than negation. "And we are supposed to do that *for* you?"

"Several support ships and troops are all we require. As for the act of claiming, that will be done by our senior representative and the leader of the expedition to St. Maarten."

Eddie frowned. "I don't think Captain Gjedde will wish to—"

"Lord Cantrell, it is you who are the senior representative."

"*Me?*"

"Of course. Oh, you are not the ranking military commander, but you are a noble of Denmark. You are the husband of the king's daughter. And, as your king, Christian IV is happy to pass to you the honor and duty of taking and claiming St. Maarten in his name."

Eddie was about to wax prolific and even profane on what he thought of being bushwhacked to be the executor of that honor and duty, when he peripherally detected a stiffening in Anne Cathrine. He paused, not looking at her because that could signal weakness or lack of resolve to Sehested. But what might have caused Anne Cathrine to sit up a little straighter, lose her relaxed, confident posture?

The answer came to him immediately. *Oh. Sure. Because she's now skewered along with me on her Daddy's two-pronged loyalty test. Prong One: is Eddie loyal enough to take up this duty, which would mean that I'm putting my duties as an honorary Danish citizen before any possible objections that might arise from the USE? But if I defy the order and flunk my test, then King Daddy's Prong Two activates: will Anne Cathrine be more loyal to her father, or her husband?*

Eddie frowned. He'd learned, from both life and countless strategy games, that if an adversary confronts you with a choice, your best chance at winning lies in breaking outside that either-or paradigm. In short, you need to come up with a choice of your own. And Eddie saw a way to do that, and save everyone's reputation and honor, if only they were open-minded enough to play along for the first few steps—

He turned away from Sehested and faced Maarten Tromp. "Admiral, I am put in the uncomfortable position of having to request your assistance in taking St. Maarten as a Danish expedition. With apologies in advance, may I humbly ask for your cooperation in this matter? I assure you, it will earn tremendous gratitude from the highest authorities whom I serve."

Tromp frowned. "It seems that your highest authority believes our instincts for gratitude are sorely wanting, so I am not sure how our cooperation will improve your royal-father-in-law's opinion of us."

Eddie shook his head. "Allow me to clarify. King Christian IV of Denmark is not the highest authority I serve." He detected flinches from either elbow, one from Anne Cathrine and one from Sehested. "I am an officer in the service of the USE and its commander-in-chief, Gustav Adolf of Sweden, who is its monarch. While I suspect he would frown upon the requirement being exerted by his royal cousin's proxy-agent, Sir Sehested, I suspect he would be more concerned with ensuring that our fleet continues to be a functional combat force."

Tromp's eyes narrowed. "Yes. I see what you mean."

"Well, I don't!" van Walbeeck exclaimed. "How does this issue affect the operational status of our combined fleet?"

Eddie shrugged. "As Sir Sehested pointed out, almost seventy percent of the flotilla's crews are Danish. They were trained and furnished to the Union of Kalmar and hence to the USE thanks to my father-in-law's keen interest in technology and training his subjects in its uses. But, unlike me, their first authority is King Christian IV, and I suspect they will listen to a known junior councilor of his court,"—Eddie glanced at wide-eyed Sehested—"before they listen to me. At least in matters of national loyalty, and of discerning which banner they must serve and obey first: that of Denmark, the Union of Kalmar, or the USE. But perhaps Sir Sehested will shed some light on the crux of this matter by answering a simple question: if I were to refuse to carry out King Christian IV's directive, would he, in turn, order the Danish members of my crews to stand down from their duties until I complied?" Eddie turned to look at Sehested and felt his wife lean closer to him.

Hannibal Sehested gestured vaguely at the fleet anchored beyond the shuttered blockhouse windows. "I am the agent of my sovereign's will and so, would be compelled to do as you say. If pressed." He looked at Eddie, and then Anne Cathrine, and lastly at Tromp, very intently. "And I assure you, I truly pray you will not press me to do such a thing." His eyes pleaded more desperately than his words.

So, Hannibal wasn't such a bad guy after all. He was just a man doing his job, and not liking it too much, right now. Denmark had ties with all the allies who were literally or figuratively present in the room. As part of the Union of Kalmar, it was de facto allied to the USE. His king's daughter was not merely married to but genuinely and thoroughly smitten with an up-timer and his people's ways. And there had long been amity and exchange between Copenhagen and Amsterdam. Sehested would clearly not enjoy being placed in a position where he was an agent of potential discord among those forces, all allied in their mission against Spanish domination in the New World.

Eddie nodded. "I understand your duty," he said to Hannibal. "However, in order to fulfill my duties to all parties, I must also predict that ordering our Danish crewmen to stand down would potentially jeopardize our alliance with the Netherlands, with which the USE is now involved in a crucial co-ownership of New World oil supplies." Eddie turned to Tromp. "Am I right in assuming that the United Provinces would be disinclined to comply with King Christian IV's requirement if they are not offered at least a token of appreciation for their willingness to overlook the highly irregular and manipulative manner whereby the requirement was issued to them?"

Van Walbeeck was not able to hide his sly smile as he bumped his elbow into Tromp's. The admiral cut his eyes at his friend and murmured, "Apparently, a token of appreciation would ensure our compliance."

"Very well," said Eddie, who at last stole a second to look at his bride—and nearly lost his composure. Anne Cathrine was smiling at him with an admiring, horny ferocity that made it necessary for Eddie to shoo away visions of her ravishing him here on the tabletop right after she peremptorily dismissed the other three men from the room. He swallowed and pulled his eyes away. "So, er, given that King Christian IV has charged me with accomplishing the task of retaking St. Maarten, and insofar as it requires Dutch cooperation to do so, I hereby secure the willing aid of the United Provinces by ensuring them that, in recognition of their cooperation and amity to help Denmark accomplish that which she could not accomplish alone, that her captains and commercial factors shall enjoy full and tariff-free access to St. Maarten, in perpetuity. This includes all harbor facilities, all trade, and free and equal access to the salt pans of the island in the interest of resuming their former salt-fish production there." He turned back to Tromp and van Walbeeck. "Is this acceptable to the representatives of the United Provinces, presuming we do not undertake operations until some time next year?"

Tromp, eyes still narrowed, smiled and nodded slowly as if watching a pupil solve a problem several steps more advanced than he should have been ready to address. "It is most acceptable, Commander Cantrell. It will be my personal pleasure to work with you in securing St. Maarten for the Danish crown in 1636, given its generous assurance that the United Provinces shall have free and equal use of its facilities in perpetuity."

Eddie looked over at Hannibal. "Do you have any questions, concerns, or objections to this arrangement, Sir Sehested?"

And Sehested, knowing full well that if he objected, King Christian could conceivably blame him for the failure to snatch the island, shook his head and smiled. "No, Lord Cantrell, I have nothing to add or object. I think we may consider our business here concluded. Lady Anne Cathrine, I believe it is time for you to meet your sister and make your entrance to the party. And here, providentially, are your two hosts whose duty it is to escort you into the building."

Tromp and van Walbeeck rose, each offering an arm to Anne Cathrine. She rose with their completely unnecessary assistance and led the way to the exit. Tromp did not just smile but grinned at Eddie as he passed. A step behind, van Walbeeck jiggled the up-timer's elbow conspiratorially. "After the party—some schnapps, perhaps?" Eddie nodded diffidently, was too busy watching his wife—

—Who, as she exited the room, turned her head briefly in his direction and sent him a look that sent all thoughts of schnapps out of the up-timer's head. Eddie knew just what he was doing after the party tonight, and it didn't involve sitting around tossing back shots with a genial, middle-aged Dutchman.

When the trio had left, Sehested rose, his hand out. "Lord Cantrell, well done."

Well done? He took and shook Hannibal's hand. "No hard feelings, then?"

Sehested looked slightly perplexed, slightly confused. "If I understand your idiom, no: no 'hard feelings.' In fact, your solution is a great burden lifted from me. I was unsure if the Dutch could be brought around to help us take an island upon which, to some degree, they have best claim. You found a solution that your father-in-law did not foresee." He stopped, considered. "Or perhaps that was his purpose."

"What do you mean?"

"I harbor a suspicion, Lord Cantrell, that King Christian occasionally sets us tasks for which he has no solution in mind, simply to test our determination, our resourcefulness, our ingenuity. If I am right in this conjecture, then I suspect he will be happier with *how* you achieved this than he is with the achievement itself." Hannibal smiled. "And as for me, I am happy to be sharing this strange adventure with a fellow who at once respects royal authority, yet is no fawning slave to its every whim. To attempt one of your stranger up-time idioms, would it be correct to say that I 'like your spunk'?"

Eddie laughed aloud. "I guess it would, although I haven't heard that expression in quite a while."

"It is out-dated then?"

"Given that it's 1635, I don't see how anything from my time could be called 'out-dated.' And hell, if it is, who cares? And by the way, call me Eddie, from now on."

"Very well, Eddie. And you should call me Hannibal. And we must hurry if we are to be on time. I suspect you will not want to miss your wife's grand entrance."

Michael McCarthy, Jr., pushed through the old sail-cloth that was the curtain that screened off the recovery cots from the dispensary. Aodh O'Rourke's alert eyes were already on him as he entered. "Damn it," Mike grumbled, "are you still laying about?"

"It's a vacation I'm having, Don Michael. Don't be spoiling it."

"Huh. Some vacation. Almost lost your leg to that damn infection that set in on the way back here. I'm guessing it took a few gallons of one hundred proof cane spirits to save it."

O'Rourke grumbled, licking his lips at the words "cane spirits." "Hrm. Then t'was a bad waste of good rum."

Michael stared at him. "You'd have rather had the rum than kept your leg?"

O'Rourke frowned.

"Well?" Mike pressed.

"Never rush a man when he's making a difficult choice, Don Michael. I'll cogitate on it a bit and get back to you. Now what brings you here, anyway? I would have expected you'd be making merry at the party I'm hearing."

"Me? At the party? Hell, I'd rather be hung by my thumbs."

"Which I'm sure some of the landowners would be happy to arrange. So you've just dropped by to check in on my sorry self again?"

Mike shrugged. Evidently Dr. Brandão's three noble Danish nurses had updated O'Rourke regarding the visitors he'd had when still lost in a febrile, trackless delirium. "Yeah. Maybe. But I had to come out this way, anyhow."

"Ah, you're making me feel so special, y'are. And what has you coming to the fort in the middle of the night, or near thereto?"

"First message from Europe just came in. Took three days to get it."

"Three days? I saw the radio we had on the *Eendracht*. Those boyos sent messages in a few minutes. At most."

McCarthy nodded. "That's because they were transmitting over short ranges. When we try to get or receive a signal from over the Atlantic, there's a lot of signal loss and unreliability, and there are certain times of the day when you can send more easily than others. We're working through all that now. So we had to tell the folks in Vlissingen to keep repeating the message. And they did. Over and over and over. But finally, we got the last pieces filled in about an hour ago. Then we were able to run it against the code-book. And here I am with the message."

"Well, good on yeh, Don Michael, for getting that beast up and running. And that steam engine you brought to make the power for it: working as well as you hoped?"

"It is now. Took effort and then some to get it to run on either wood or petroleum by-products."

"On what?"

"Er, the less valuable parts of the oil that we'll be getting from Trinidad."

"So they're producing oil? Already?"

"No, but the bitumen of Pitch Lake can be separated into different components. Some of them make a reasonable fuel on their own, some work best when you use them to inundate wood. That radio itself was the real trick to get running. The Alexanderson alternator that makes it possible is pretty big and pretty delicate. Well, delicate enough that it's a little grumpy after having made an Atlantic crossing in a small ship like the *Intrepid*."

O'Rourke raised an eyebrow. "The *Intrepid* is *small*? Then just how big were your up-time ships?"

"We'll talk about that some other time. Like maybe after half of the farm owners are done trying to kill me."

"It's come to blows, then, has it? I've heard a bit about that ruckus you've started."

Mike shrugged. "Well, no, it hasn't come to blows. But I'm pretty sure some of the landowners would be eager to finish me off in a *single* blow. They're not interested in fisticuffs, O'Rourke. Every slaveholder on this island pretty much hates my guts enough to want to wear them for suspenders."

O'Rourke folded his hands meditatively over his broad, flat belly. "We've a saying in Ireland about such situations."

"To listen to my dad, the Irish have a saying for *every* situation."

"So we do. It's the hallmark of wisdom, don't you know. But here's the saying anyway, you ungrateful pretend-Irishman: 'it's a compliment to be both hated and feared by all the scoundrels in one's own town.' So, it was your rabble-rousing rhetoric that's brought things to their current state?"

"Oh, they probably could have lived with it if it was just coming from me. But, having been the first go-between for Eddie, and Hugh, and Tromp, I had access to the admiral's ear. And van Walbeeck's. And we had conversations about how different colonial powers in the up-time history weaned themselves away from slavery. And they started to put those methods into practice here."

"Hrrmmm," O'Rourke subvocalized. "I'm not surprised to hear it. Maarten Tromp's a man of principle, he is."

"You know him?" McCarthy said, surprised. "How?"

"Well, after the wound from Puerto Cabello turned ugly, that heathen Tromp came by to stare at me a bit on my sickbed aboard the *Intrepid*."

"'Heathen?'"

"Well, he's not a Catholic, is he?" Seeing the bemused look on McCarthy's face, O'Rourke scowled. "Ah, that's right. You up-timers are above petty differences such as the path a man must go to see the face of God."

"We're not above it. We just don't kill each other about it."

"Yes. Well. So the heathen Tromp came to see me and inquire after my health on a few occasions—although, I must allow, he's a most civilized and pleasant heathen, and sure it will be a shame that he's to burn in hell."

"Er. Yes. So you were already familiar with his attitudes about slavery?"

"And tyranny in general, for that matter. As I said, a most principled man."

McCarthy nodded. "Yeah. But he knew he wouldn't be able to sell his reforms based on principles. He persuaded most of the council here by walking them through the up-time historical models I showed him. However the models differ, they all show pretty clearly that any economy dependent on slave-labor is extremely vulnerable to all kinds of disruptions. Van Walbeeck pushed them further along by outlining what he had seen himself while in the East Indies, how every slave population *always* becomes a breeding ground for crippling rebellions. So between those arguments, Tromp got the council to support his directive to recategorize all slaves as bondsmen."

"Changing a term doesn't change whether a man is treated like a slave."

"No, but it does change whether he is property, whether he can be bought and sold. And as Tromp intended, that was just the edge of the wedge to make further changes. The council just recently agreed that all bondsmen will earn their freedom five years from now, or, for those who come later, after five years of service. Next, I think he's going to try put in a rule that new laborers who arrive in the colony against their will or wholly indigent can't be swept into the current debt-peonage system, but must be allowed to enter as regular indentured servants."

O'Rourke smiled. "That must make you even *more* popular with the local men of substance, then."

Mike smiled back. "You have no idea. I'm accused of corrupting Tromp and van Walbeeck, possibly using up-time sorcery to inveigle them to rot the colony from within by welcoming natives, Africans, and Jews. And of course, the arch-Calvinists among them are happy to point to my Roman Catholic background as proof that I am a malevolent being."

"Are you a Catholic, then? I couldn't tell."

"Well, *they* are sure I am," Michael replied, ignoring the veiled remonstration, "since I visited you a couple of times when you were still delirious. And brought some extra food to the other Wild Geese who were recuperating from their wounds, here."

"Ah, you consort with low companions, you do, Michael McCarthy. I knew there was a reason I liked you. Now, do you happen to have some of those infection-killing cane spirits about you? I'm asking for purely medicinal reasons, of course."

"Of course." McCarthy unsuccessfully tried to keep the smile off his face as he rose. "I'll see what I can do."

Part Eight

December 1635

Commotion of the winds

Chapter 45

Santo Domingo, Hispaniola

The sound of a military campaign in preparation was loud beyond the large window that overlooked the veranda of Captain-General Juan Bitrian de Viamonte y Navarra's villa. Nestled tight around the precincts of Santo Domingo was an armed camp almost half again as large as the city proper.

Standing at the window, Fadrique Álvarez de Toledo nodded at the activities among the tents of his troops, and the swift skiffs carrying messages between the ships in the bay. "Our preparations here are well in hand. What of our Free Companies, Captain Equiluz?"

Antonio de la Plaza Eguiluz, at last returned to civilization after many weeks of making contact with cut-throats and *boucaniers* from Jamaica to Tortuga, nodded. "I come from meeting with their gathered forces, near Isla Vaca, far to our west."

"Why there?" asked Eugenio de Covilla as he patted the grease of the roast boar medallions off his lips.

Equiluz shrugged. "It was a reasonable midpoint between the two greatest concentrations of raid—er, Free Companies. A large number make their hidden homes along the coasts of Jamaica, while the more numerous ones frequent the northwest coast of Hispaniola in general and Tortuga in particular. They are none

503

too trusting of each other and so wished a neutral midpoint in which to work out any, er, differences that might exist among their officers. Besides, a *boucanier* of some education from England claimed that one of his country's most famous pirates, who may still be born this year, found it an excellent place in which to gather forces prior to a raid, or to which to retire in the wake of one."

"Who is this newborn heathen reiver?" asked Fadrique.

"I think they called him Harry or Henry Morgan. I did not pay particular mind to the reference. At any rate, the ships of the Free Companies are mostly as we expected: sloops, barca-longas, *piraguas*, a few of our own *pataches*, a few Dutch jachts, and a few more of the same craft built to accommodate the English or 'Bermudan' style of rigging."

"Nothing too large, then," de Viamonte summarized.

"That is so, Your Excellency. And that is what I believe we desired, is it not?"

"It most certainly is," Fadrique said, putting his hand on his hip and feeling notably less flesh between his knuckle and hipbone than he had only eight weeks ago. Being in the field again gave him purpose and vitality, which reduced his need for the rich food and strong drink with which he had formerly dulled the aching wounds that Olivares' displeasure had inflicted upon him. "The Free Companies are the weaker half of our trap, true, but their speed and maneuverability are essential. They must be able to reach broadly and turn quickly. If each hull has no more than a dozen guns, it is still of little matter. Their numbers are important, however." He turned a questioning eye upon Equiluz.

"We can count on a dozen who are reliable enough to actually sail along with our main fleet, as we discussed, Admiral. I have offered letters of marque to another forty-three, most of whom are likely to accept."

"Excellent. How have you arranged for them to be paid for these, eh, special services to His Majesty, Philip of Spain?"

"As agreed, Admiral, they were given one part in twenty of the promised *reales* when they signed to our colors. When I meet with those who have agreed to sail with our main fleet four days hence off Isla Beata, one hundred miles to the west, they shall be given a further nine parts of the twenty. The balance shall be paid upon completion of their task."

"And how do we know these dogs will not simply fly upon receiving a full half of their payment at Isla Beata, having incurred no risk?" De Viamonte tossed aside his napkin angrily. He despised pirates and every minute spent discussing their necessary recruitment and management made him increasingly ill-tempered.

Fadrique interceded, knowing the captain-general would not dare to vent his spleen on an equal. "My dear de Viamonte, it is a surety that some of these dogs will do just as you fear. It is in the nature of soldiers of fortune and adventurers everywhere. However, we cannot ask for a perfect solution, merely one that provides us with the forces to defend the interests of our King and Country. Of the one in five or one in ten that desert without providing the contracted service? We shall put a heavy bounty on their heads. And those of their brethren who survive this battle shall be put on their trail like so many hounds on the scent of a fox." He smiled. "They know each others' dens so much better than we do, and the pursuers will be aware that, if they hurry, they will not only get the bounty, but the silver the blackguards stole from us. And so, by the hands of thieves, we will yet see justice served, Captain-General de Viamonte."

De Viamonte, considering this, smiled tightly and toasted the proposal with a lifted glass of rioja. "I suppose one can ask no more of justice than this: that if it must be imperfect, at least it should be poetic. And our main fleet is now complete?"

Fadrique nodded. "It is. The last eight warships arrived from Santiago de Cuba yestereve at dusk. We now have thirty-five men-of-war and fourteen smaller supply ships. Add to that our dozen *pataches*. And add the dozen Free Company ships that Captain Equiluz will be paying, just before he leads the rest of the dogs off on their southeasterly course. All together, we shall number just over seventy ships."

"Let us not forget the nine naos that shall transport the troops," de Viamonte added.

"I've not forgotten them, but I will not load and bring them with us until our battle fleet has met and defeated the foe."

"Which we have at last found, I hear." De Viamonte turned toward de Covilla. "You are sure that last night's reports are accurate, Eugenio?"

"They are, Admiral. The *patache Tres Santi* encountered a Dutch yacht scouting the Anegada Passage just four days ago.

The gin-swillers broke away as soon as they discovered that they had been spotted."

"This is thin evidence upon which to project the presence of a larger 'target,' Don Álvarez de Toledo," observed de Viamonte.

"On its own, yes," Fadrique agreed, "but this sighting was precisely what we were watching for, given what the Free Companies have told us."

Eguiluz nodded. "I took pains to gather intelligence from pirate captains while they were still at remove from each other, and therefore, were unable to coordinate their stories. Yet their reports usually overlapped in all the crucial particulars: that the English colony is back on St. Christopher's and stronger than before. That a French colony is also there, but more anemic in its growth and vitality. That both engage in occasional trade with the Free Companies, particularly those on the north coasts of this very island."

De Viamonte sounded cross. "Here on Hispaniola? Why?"

"It seems, Your Excellency, that when Don Álvarez de Toledo extirpated the colonies on St. Christopher's in 1629, he took many hundreds of prisoners, particularly the English who stayed to fight at their coastal fort after the French abandoned them and fled into the mountains. Those English prisoners were put to work in *haciendas* on this very island, and many subsequently escaped to join the *boucaniers* of Tortuga. In consequence, they still have friends, or at least acquaintances, among the English of St. Christopher, and make use of those prior associations when engaging in trade. It is they who were most recently at the island, trading old muskets to the French, as I understand it. And it is they who report that the Dutch presence on St. Eustatia grew dramatically since last year."

"And that," concluded de Toledo, "is why the single jacht we saw scouting the Anegada Passage tells me we shall soon have the target we want: the Dutch fleet. Probably led by these two up-time steam ships."

"All that derived from spotting a single jacht?" de Viamonte wondered.

Fadrique nodded. "Yes. A jacht that, according to Don Equiluz, was tacking more than she needed to, which meant she was not heading to a destination so much as searching for something."

"But for what?" de Viamonte asked.

"For us, Your Excellency," de Covilla supplied deferentially. "If I understand the admiral correctly, he deduces from the maneuvering of the jacht that it is sweeping the waters, seeking enemy sails in the Anegada Passage. That is the best place to catch a fair wind to move down along the leeward side of the Lesser Antilles, in the general direction of St. Eustatia. In short, our adversaries are trying to learn if our strength is in port, or on the water headed for them."

"Which is more crucial for them to ascertain than it is for us," Fadrique added. "They have but one base. They cannot afford to sally out in search of our fleet, only to sail past and miss us as we are bound for their home port with the power to utterly destroy it."

De Viamonte nodded. "I see. Well, I suppose being charged with defending ports for so long has made me unaccustomed to think along such risky lines. But you make a sound case for perceiving this yacht as a probable confirmation of what the Free Companies have told Don Equiluz. But tell me"—he turned to the young captain—"should we not suspect that the Companions with ties to St. Christopher will in fact impart warnings of our current actions to their associates there?"

Equiluz nodded somberly. "I had the same misgivings, Your Excellency. That is why I did not extend offers of letters of marque to such men, nor did I even mention our plans. I simply paid them for the information they provided. Even so, I suspect that, before too many months elapse, our recruitment of the other pirates will become known to them, as will its purpose, and so, they shall realize why we were asking the questions we did. However, by then, the actions we plan to undertake against this new Dutch threat will have long been completed." He held up a palm. "There was, unfortunately, no way to solicit information from the Free Companions without, indirectly, releasing some to them as well."

De Viamonte nodded indulgently. "This is in the very nature of asking a question, good Don Equiluz. You always inform the one to whom you address a question that the answer is in some way important to you." He set down his glass. "So it seems our plans are coming together as hoped. The enemy's strength is tentatively located on St. Eustatia and seems to be readying itself, or has begun, to head toward us. Which means that you must commence your difficult tasks of coordination, gentlemen. What you propose is fairly ambitious."

"It is," Fadrique admitted, "but we have the resources to carry it out. Our main fleet has all the warships we could ask for. Our Free Companions have swift, maneuverable ships, and have been furnished with mirror-backed heliographs for signaling and maintaining formation during the night, and lensed reflectors for doing so during fair days."

"And if the weather turns foul, you still believe that will be to our advantage?"

Fadrique felt his lips become rigid, straight. "Captain-General de Viamonte, after what I saw those steamship deck guns do at the Grenada Passage, I may absolutely assure you of this: any engagement in which their accuracy is undermined is to our advantage. Our numbers will prevail, but only if we survive long enough so that they may be brought to bear upon our foe."

"Yes, of course," agreed de Viamonte. "But with so much depending upon a fairly complex plan, I could wish that we had had more time to address all relevant the preparations, particularly with the Free Companies."

"More time is always good," Fadrique agreed openly, but thought, *except that now, with their radios, these up-time supplied bastards have an advantage over us. The clock and the calendar are always their friends and never ours. So our one alternative is to press matters wherever we may. Wherever we determine they wish they had more time, that is precisely where we must act with utter swiftness, even if our plans are not well or fully set.* "But fear not, Captain-General de Viamonte, we are in adequate readiness. And our Free Companies are already straining at their leashes to set upon the Dutch. So the time is ripe to set them in motion."

No matter how hateful the doing of it might be.

Chapter 46

Fifteen Miles East of St. Croix, Caribbean

The soft knock on the cabin door was recognizable as Svantner's. "Come in, Arne!" Eddie called out, picking up his next report.

The lanky Swede slipped into the cabin. "You asked to be notified as soon as the *Zuidsterre*'s sighting was confirmed."

"So, the Spanish have come out to play. Do we have a count?"

Svantner nodded. "Sixty sail, sir. Maybe a few more toward the back of their van. Hard to tell, even from the balloon." He sounded admirably calm, given that it meant the Allied fleet was outnumbered, three to one. Even counting the supply fluyts that were to be kept far away from any combat, lest the troops and ammunition and extra coal on them be lost. But, odds notwithstanding, it was a good thing that both Eddie and Tromp had pushed relentlessly for getting their own fleet under way as soon as possible. Had they put it off another five days, they'd have been meeting these Spanish in sight of Oranjestad itself.

Eddie nodded at Svantner's report. "So it's as Tromp expected. The Santo Domingo fleet has been reinforced from Cuba. Heavily."

"Maybe not, sir. A lot of the ships are smaller than we expected. A lot more *patache*s or other fore-and-aft rigged craft, sir."

That made Eddie pause. "Hmm. Less weight of shot, but more maneuverability. And harder for us to hit." Of course, it was entirely possible that the Spanish had simply scraped together whatever hulls they had available to throw at the new Caribbean threat that had announced itself at the Battle of Grenada Passage. But it was also possible that the composition of this Spanish fleet was not a matter of chance, but careful design... "Arne, signal Dirck and Admiral Tromp that we need to keep a close eye on how the Spanish maneuver."

"What, specifically, are you recommending they watch for, Commander?"

Eddie shrugged. "I wish I knew. But typical Spanish doctrine would have them line up a wall of galleons against us. Either they don't have them to spare, or they're trying something different. And since they've changed the balance of their fleet toward lighter, handier hulls and fore-and-aft rigs, I'm thinking that their tactics are going to emphasize maneuver more than usual."

Svantner shrugged. "They might, but I don't see how they could get the weather gauge on us, sir. We're running before the breeze coming steady from east by northeast. And we'll be north of St. Croix before they reach us, so it's not as though they've got enough room to turn our flank unless we let them."

"All true, Arne. But they know all that, too, and they've known we're coming for at least a week now, what with our yachts playing hide-and-seek with their *pataches* and piraguas in the seas between us. So whatever they've got in mind, they've taken all that into account. Which means either I'm missing something, or they are. Or these are the only ships they've got available near Santo Domingo."

"Probably the latter, sir."

Which was both a reasonable and a comforting conjecture. Which was why Eddie refused to accept it, refused to be lulled into a dangerous complacency by hearing what he *wanted* to hear. "You might be right, Arne, but until we know that's the case, we're going to behave as if it isn't. How long until we reach them?"

"If we push on, we'd make contact at night, sir. Some time during the middle watch."

Eddie started. "What? How strong is the wind?"

"Up to thirteen knots sir. Seas are rising toward three-foot swells."

Too fast an approach and increasingly choppy seas: no good. "Send to the admiral that I recommend we half reef the sails and close slowly. I think our best scenario would be to have the Spanish at about five miles come tomorrow morning. We can use the rest of today's light to tighten up our formation so we've got minimal dispersion to correct at dawn. And we won't put the steam pinnaces in the water until we see first light and determine how high the seas are going to be."

"Very good, sir. Anything else?"

"Yes, Svantner. I want you to bodily throw the chief engineer in the brig."

Svantner blinked. "Sir?"

"I'm kidding, of course." *Well,* mostly *kidding.* "But I swear that if Pabst sends one more of his 'black gang' up here with a panicked request to test the new treated wood before we enter combat, I will cook him in his own precious boiler."

Svantner stared at the deck. "Well, sir, to be honest, a lot of the engineering crew aren't entirely sure why we're carrying a fuel that seems to be—well, an added fire risk."

"Okay, Arne. Then I'll explain it to you, if you promise to go down there and explain it to them."

"Aye, aye, sir," Svantner said sheepishly.

"To start with, where can we get more coal?"

"Uh...nowhere. Not without going back to Europe."

"Precisely. There's plenty of it here in the New World. Coming from a coal-mining town originally, I can assure you of that. But no one's tapped into it yet. And it could be quite a while before they do. So we either burn the coal we brought with us, or the wood that comes to hand."

"Yes, sir. Which is why we haven't burned coal since the Battle of Grenada Passage."

"Right. So, now: burning wood. You've seen how fast we go through it, particularly if we're trying to get the boiler up to full pressure."

Svantner nodded. "Yes, sir. It's gone in no time."

"But if we soak the wood in petroleum by-products, the ones we separated from the bitumen we took from Pitch Lake, then we get some of the benefits of oil burning, even though our engine is designed to burn solids."

Svantner nodded. "Yes, sir. I understand all that. I suspect they do down in engineering, too. But it will still burn quickly, and these oil-soaked, one-inch cubes are not only as dirty as sin, but leave a flammable residue on whatever they touch. In short, what's the benefit?"

"Saving coal by getting the engines to operating heat before we start shoveling it in. Svantner, tell me, have you seen the oil-treated cubes burn?"

The Swede nodded. "Yes, sir. Like the fires of hell itself."

"Exactly. Now, let's say we're closing with the enemy and must get our engines up to speed, but we don't know exactly when we'll need to commence tactical maneuvers. That means we have to get the boilers up to a useful temperature quickly, but don't want to burn any of our irreplaceable coal doing so, or holding them in preheated readiness."

The figurative light came on over Svantner's head. "So the oil in the wood cubes gives us that fast, high heat before we start shoveling in the coal." He nodded again. "Thank you, sir. But Pabst is still worried about the wastes, is concerned it might leave a heavier residue that could smother the draught to the burners."

Eddie nodded. "That's a good thought, but we've separated out the impurities from the bitumen pretty well. So the treated wood should burn just as cleanly as regular wood. In addition, we've chosen woods that burn to a finer ash—a powder, really—that should actually make less trouble than coal dust." He smiled. "Do you think that will make Pabst—and you—rest a little more easily?"

Svantner stared quickly at the deck again. "My apologies, sir. I didn't mean to—I wouldn't dream of—"

"Arne, you needed to voice a concern that impacts the safe and effective operation of this ship, for which you are the executive officer. You'd be derelict in your duty if you didn't bring the matter up with me. You've done your job, and done it well and respectfully. Now, if there's nothing else—?"

"Sir, there is one other thing. Do you think the Spanish know that our steamships burn coal, predominantly?"

Eddie frowned. "I'd expect they do. It would be strange if none of their personnel weren't familiar with at least that aspect of our steam technology."

"Then I was wondering: are you using this wood to mislead them, to make them think we're burning more coal than we are? When I saw the treated wood burning, just before we left Oranjestad, I noticed that the color of that smoke was close to what one sees with the coal."

Eddie made sure he didn't grin anywhere near as widely as he wanted to: Svantner was proving to be more shrewd than he originally seemed. "Well done, XO. That is exactly what I hope they'll think. If they're watching the clock, waiting for us to run out of coal or to start getting stingy with it, they'll be working from the mistaken assumption that we started using it much earlier than we actually did. And every time they make that kind of wrong guess, it puts us in the position of be able to hand them another nasty surprise."

Svantner nodded, chimed in with the mantra he'd learned recently. "Because the side that has to guess, and keeps guessing wrong, loses the initiative. They are playing by the rules set by the opposition."

Eddie nodded, pleased. "And we want them playing by our rules, Mr. Svantner. Until they've lost the game and go home. Assuming there are any left to do so."

Seventeen miles south of Cerro Indio, Isla de Vieques

Admiral Fadrique Álvarez de Toledo lowered his spyglass and spoke over his right shoulder. "Time for you to be getting back to your ship, Captain de Covilla. It seems the Dutch and their heathen friends have taken the bait."

"They are steaming towards us already?" De Covilla sounded alarmed.

Fadrique laughed. "Hardly. They seem to be slowing, probably reefing their sails, from what our pickets report." Which meant that, given the many relays it had taken the report to reach them, from the lead scout-*patache* all the way back to their position toward the rear of the van, the change in the allied fleet had probably been observed twenty minutes ago.

"Then how would that indicate they are taking our bait, Admiral?" De Covilla sounded perplexed.

"As I observed off Grenada, they will wish to conserve their fuel, and also to take us at distance with their deck guns. They would achieve neither if they pushed on now." He gestured behind at the sun which would be kissing the horizon in an hour. "Instead, they would reach us in darkness, a time that all but eliminates the superiority of their gunnery and they would have burned much coal to do so. No, they will approach slowly through the night and leap upon us in the morning, using full sail to overtake our fleet before shifting to their steam power to outmaneuver us tactically."

"Except we will not be where they expect," smiled de Covilla.

Fadrique nodded. "Sailing before the wind all night, we will be ten miles farther to the west, compelling them to chase us. Naturally, they will be frustrated, and will find the poorer sailing speed of the Dutch warships, and particularly their supply ships, to be particularly annoying."

"Perhaps they will abandon the slower moving ships, then."

"We could hope for that, but I doubt it. I have not seen that species of rashness in their commanders, to date. But I suspect that, in straining to catch us, they may not maintain the formation they intend. And that will be serviceable enough. Assuming that all our own plans are in order. About which: have we had another signal from Equiluz?"

"Yes, Admiral. He reports the easternmost scout of his privateers have sighted the western mountains of St. Croix."

"Are our privateers in good formation, reasonably tight?"

"That final part of Equiluz's message failed, sir. As the sun sank, his reflector became dim, then unreadable. We will need to wait until nightfall for our far southern pickets to see his heliograph."

If we see it at all, Fadrique grumbled mentally. This had always been the part of the plan about which he had harbored the greatest misgivings: that an armadilla of pirates-made-privateers, maneuvering independently, and with only one Spanish ship to oversee their compliance, would in fact be where they were needed, when the time came. St. Croix had been the visual anchor point for that southern detachment's furthest eastern picket, and had obviously served that purpose well. Navigating to a position in unmarked, open waters would have been an unreasonable expectation. But if the weather turned, or a mist rolled in—"The weather, Captain de Covilla: what do our scouts report from the east?"

"Clear skies of a pink tint, Admiral. We should have good visibility to receive new messages, at least unto the middle watch."

"Excellent. When you return to your ship, remember to send word that the sappers on board the *San Augustin* must finish distributing the pole-petards to the *piraguas* by midnight. It will take time to rig them on their booms and run the fuses through the pitch-sealed tubes."

"I shall do so immediately upon my return, Admiral. However, I must report that the crews of the *piraguas* are still none too confident that the spikes will hold the petards to a hull, no matter how forcefully they are rammed home."

Fadrique shrugged. "In all honesty, de Covilla, I share their uncertainty. But their duty is to Spain and her God-loving king, so we shall hope that divine grace shall vouchsafe either safety for their bodies or salvation for their souls. A commander in war-time may hope for little else when he sends so many men in harm's way." *Although, truth be told, the men in those petard-carrying* piraguas *will be consorting with more bodily harm than I would happily embrace.* "Now, be on your way, de Covilla, unless you have some other question."

"Just one, Admiral. How can we be sure that the enemy does not have a second contingent of ships, one which might be coming around St. Croix from the south? If so, they would find our southern privateer armadilla and quite ruin our stratagem."

"Yes, they would, but you are watching for spectres of your own fears, my dear young captain. Be assured, the Dutch fleet in front of us is all they can spare to hunt us. Indeed, they have sortied more ships than I expected. But if we further assume they sent at least ten or a dozen hulls to protect their new assets on Trinidad, then they can barely have enough ships left to guard their probable base on St. Eustatia. So, to send yet *another* flotilla southward around St. Croix would necessitate reducing their home guard. And I'm sure the Dutch would not do anything to jeopardize the only safe anchorage they have. I'm sure they left it in well-armed and highly-vigilant hands."

Capisterre Bay, St. Christopher's

Pierre d'Esnambuc shook hands with cacique Touman and strolled over to where Jacques Dyel du Parque waited nervously, staring out over the bay into the darkling east. He looked at his nephew's still-wrapped sleeping roll. "You should get some sleep, my boy," the older man murmured.

"I will soon," Jacques lied. "I wish you did not have to go."

D'Esnambuc sat next to his nephew. "I wish that as well. But

I must lead the ships from Dieppe Bay south tomorrow. There is no captain skilled enough that I may delegate the responsibility of overseeing the attack upon the English upon him. And we must not fail in that mission." He put a hand on his nephew's arm. Jacques tried very hard to suppress the shiver there. "And you must not fail either, Nephew. But if anything unexpected should occur, stay close to du Plessis."

"Du Plessis? I thought you said that de l'Olive was more trustworthy, and certainly more loyal to you. And so, more loyal to me."

"That is true. But de l'Olive is also a hothead and will not think to flee until it is too late. Du Plessis has the one virtue of all cowards: they are quick to their heels. And if he must fly, he will want to rescue you as a means of currying favor with, and forgiveness from, me. And he will be right in expecting that I shall be grateful that he looked out for you."

Jacques shivered even more. "I will not disappoint you, Uncle Pierre."

"I know you shall not, dear boy. But do not get carried away and think you must be a captain in this fight. That is not your role. Your role is far more important, for I have many captains, but only one of our number understands enough about up-time machinery to accurately assess it, divine its purposes, and to inflict enough damage upon it to terminate its functions without utterly destroying it."

"Do you really think Richelieu will be so pleased by having a radio here in the New World? Even though he does not have a matching radio of power in France?"

"'Pleased?'" D'Esnambuc laughed aloud. "Jacques, if what the disgruntled, and now well-bribed, landholders of St. Eustatia have communicated to us is true, the Gray Eminence would rather get his hands on such a radio than any two islands. Because if this radio may do all the things you have told me, then he will understand readily enough that with it, he might take those two islands and many more besides. Think of the coordination that would be possible, the swift confirmation of successes or failures, the proper deployment of forces to where they are needed in a timely fashion and in the right numbers." D'Esnambuc shook his well-shaped head. "You have not lived before the mast and on the battlefield, Nephew—may you never have to do either!—but I have, and I may assure you of this: the radio would dramatically shrink the uncertainty, the confusion, and above all, the titanic waste of such adventures. If Richelieu learns that we have such a powerful device in our possession, it means he will send ships and troops to protect it, experts to repair it." D'Esnambuc thumped the ground in both triumph and annoyance. "The neglect of this colony, of all our island colonies, will be over. Our colonies shall be transformed from a dabbling in New World fortunes to a locus of new and essential power. Our fortunes, and your future, will be assured, my boy."

"In the meantime," Jacques wondered aloud, "how will we manage all of them?"

For a moment, d'Esnambuc seemed to stare at the one hundred scruffy Frenchmen who had traveled along with the almost nine hundred Carib warriors to this sparsely settled coastline near St. Christopher's northern tip. Then he followed further along his nephew's gaze to the natives. Uncle Pierre smiled, almost apologetically. "Oh, them. I do not see much trouble in the initial years, Jacques. We shall do just as we have promised the Caribs. And when the Spanish come—and be assured, they will—we shall be glad of the Caribs' friendship. They know these waters better than anyone else, and are excellent scouts. Their small boats may see our tall ships far off, and yet remain unseen themselves. With them, and perhaps with several of these balloons du Plessis has used, we shall see the Spanish coming from afar, and the natives will join us in fighting them off, harrying any troops they land, raiding whatever cachements they establish ashore. And later, when things are secure—well, I suspect that will be beyond my time, Jacques. But more to the point, it is not a matter that needs resolving this day or tomorrow, whereas we already have enough work for those scant hours, wouldn't you agree? Now, remember, if either du Plessis or de l'Olive resists getting under way before midnight, you must support Touman against them. The cacique is not lazy, and he understands best how long it will take to cross the passage and make an unobserved predawn landing on the windward side of St. Eustatia. Our countrymen will not be mindful of such details that the natives shall rightly deem critical. For instance, the Caribs will want to allow an hour to hide their boats on that part of the shore where the trees come down close to the water. You have seen well enough that such cover is sparse on the windward side of these islands, and the few trees that grow there are stunted and bent by the constant breeze. The natives understand the need to conceal their boats, and appreciate the time it will take to achieve that. They must be in charge of the maritime portion of your journey, and its timing. However, once you are ashore, Touman knows he must defer to du Plessis and to you.

"Caribs, or as they style themselves, the Kalinago, will be good in battle. But their real value to you will be as scouts. Give them time to thoroughly assess The Quill and all that is going on upon it. The wait shall be worth your while, I am sure, and you should easily be in your positions by dawn.

"Once the attack begins, you know what to urge, even if du Plessis forgets or believes he has devised—God help us!—a superior plan. The Kalinagos are to skirmish and their bowmen are to work from forest ambush wherever possible. That said, do not depend over-much upon the musketeers, either ours or theirs. Bring them up like artillery when you run into concentrated defense, then let the Kalinago lead the attack once again. And once you reach Oranjestad, you need only get far enough into it to allow the torch to be your final weapon."

As his uncle squeezed his shoulder affectionately and rose to leave, Jacques realized that there was one topic that had never come up in all the discussion of the attack and its details. "What of prisoners, Uncle Pierre? What should we do with them?"

In the growing darkness, d'Esnambuc's face was a black outline. "They would be a great inconvenience," he said slowly. "I recommend you defer to Touman and the Kalinago regarding the disposition of any persons who surrender."

"But Uncle—"

"Defer to the Kalinago. And do not stay to watch."

Chapter 47

Off Bloody Point, St. Christopher's

The late autumn sun was now southerly enough that, at dawn, it did not rise over the high, green spine of St. Christopher's mountains, but over the flat uplands just north of the French town of Basseterre. Pieter Floriszoon screened his eyes with his hands and looked back at Hugh Albert O'Donnell. "Seems rather quiet, don't you think?"

Hugh shrugged, smiled. "Having never been here, I wouldn't know."

"Well, in my time, I've rarely seen so few boats out fishing. Is it some holiday?"

"None that I'm aware of." Hugh felt the strong tugging pressure fade out of the *patache*'s whipstaff and heard and saw the mainsail begin to luff slightly. "Wind is shifting," he commented.

"So it is," grinned Pieter, who folded his arms and smiled.

Hugh rolled his eyes. This was not a tricky wind, but Floriszoon was probably trying to see if navigating so close to land spooked the Irishman. But as the wind from the northeast shifted to north by northeast, and he went from close reaching to close hauled, it was a simple matter of turning one point to port to bring the wind back into the mainsail and return to close reaching.

The flutter of the mainsail's luffing subsided and the *patache* resumed a brisk northwesterly pace, aimed directly at the head-land known as Bloody Point.

Malachi O'Mara approached from where his Dutch tutor in sail-handling had just relieved him. "My lord, you look a bit of a pirate this morning, you do."

"Mind your tongue, O'Mara, or you'll find out what it's really like to be keelhauled."

"Yes sir!" He approached and watched Hugh's work with the whipstaff meditatively, clearly paying not a jot of real attention to it.

O'Donnell knew a purposeful loiter when he saw one. "Out with it then, O'Mara. For whom are you playing the part of an emissary, this morning?"

"Why, my lord, I wouldn't dream of—"

"We never dream of things we do routinely. So out with it, I say."

"As you say, m'lord. There's some concern among the new lads from Montserrat that maybe we should have gone to Nevis first, after all. Showing up on Governor Warner's doorstep might be seen as being a bit bold."

"They feel that, do they?"

"Well, yes, sir. Respectfully, sir."

"I appreciate their respectful concerns. You may convey to them my resolve to proceed as planned. Governor Warner is not so grand and well-established a lord as he once was. He's been cut loose by his king. So I suppose you might say, having both lost our titles, mine was greater and older than his and I've no reason not to pay him a visit and my compliments directly. Besides, it was he who accepted their deportation to the Irish colony on Montserrat. It is he who would have to repeal it, at least enough so that they might trade freely here once again without any prejudice or suspicion of being agents for the French."

"Or for them to recruit for you among the relatives and friends they left behind?" Floriszoon all but winked at Hugh.

"Just so," the attainted earl replied. "You say his plantation is beyond that headland?"

Floriszoon nodded. "Yes, a mile or so north of Bloody Point. And what town he has is there, as well. The English are far more populous, but also more spread out. They have no single settlements as large as Dieppe Bay or Basseterre. Although now that we Dutch have sent over so many soldiers, I wonder if—"

From beyond the headland, thunder rolled. In a clear sky.

"Cannon?" O'Mara wondered aloud.

"And not just one, so not a signal or a hail," Hugh glanced back over his shoulder. Floriszoon's own ship, the well-gunned *Eendracht*, was only one hundred yards off their port quarter. "Pieter," muttered Hugh, "I'm not liking this."

Floriszoon nodded. "None of the usual French ships in Basse-terre Bay, no fishing boats out. But would the French really be bold enough to—?"

"If our fleet has left to take the fight to the Spanish, they might have drawn off quite a few of your Dutch soldiers, most of whom are scattered about the countryside anyhow, aren't they?"

"Yes, but given a little time, they would be able to gather and—"

"There may not be any time, not if French mean to eliminate the leadership of the English colony first. Which they would do by attacking Bloody Point. Jeafferson lives around here as well, doesn't he?"

Pieter Floriszoon nodded. "We should come about into the wind and into irons, wait for the *Eendracht* to lay to so I can transfer and—"

"Pieter, if the French are shelling Warner's estate and the town"—another cannonade confirmed that—"then we don't have the time to stop and put things in order. We must deal with the situation as we find it. Immediately."

"Hugh, we don't know what we'll see when we come around Bloody Point."

"No, but we know one thing: they won't be expecting us. And we have almost one hundred twenty troops between our two ships, and forty-four guns of respectable size."

"And they may have more. Of both."

"Yes, but they don't have the element of surprise. And if they're shelling, they'll be stopped, possibly at anchor." Hugh turned another two points to port. The sails billowed out as the ship came into a broad reach. "And we have speed a-plenty."

"Your man O'Mara is right," Pieter grumbled as he motioned for the pilot to take the whipstaff and gestured for the captain of the deck battery to join him on the shallow poop deck.

"O'Mara is right? About what?"

"You *are* a bit of a pirate, aren't you?"

❖   ❖   ❖

The *patache* that Hugh and Pieter had named the *Orthros*—since, being jointly owned by Dutch Protestants and Irish Catholics, it seemed fitting to name it after a two-headed hell-hound—came round Bloody Point at seven knots. One mile ahead, and motionless in the water, was a French bark of approximately thirty-two guns. Another similar ship was largely obscured behind her, perhaps eight hundred yards farther north. The morning breeze was blowing westward and so was pushing the smoke of their bombardment back in their faces. Since the French were no longer firing concentrated broadsides, but allowing their pieces to speak at will, the noise was ragged but unrelenting.

"Fat, deaf, and looking the wrong way," summarized Floriszoon as *Eendracht* came around the point behind the *Orthros*.

"For now, let's leave them that way," Hugh muttered as he finished giving orders to his boarders: almost all the Wild Geese and new recruits from Montserrat were aboard the *patache*.

"We'll never reach them undetected, you know."

"I know, Pieter. But tell me, when they see us, what will they do?"

Floriszoon considered. "Crowd canvas and turn to port. Try to get around so their unused battery is facing us. Give us a broadside."

"Yes, but how much speed will they have?"

Floriszoon scoffed. "Given what little time they'll have to react, not even half a knot. Probably not a quarter."

"So once they commit to a portside turn—"

Pieter's eyes studied the position of the closest French ship, and then went wide. "You're not a pirate. You're a madman, to even think of risking a last-second shift to—"

"But would it work, given our speed and maneuverability?"

"Damn, it might. But it will be a rough ride. And a hell of a stop."

Hugh smiled. "Then let's not scare ourselves by wondering about it. Make for her stern and get me in position."

The *Orthros* was only four hundred yards astern of the Frenchman when the lookout in the bark's main crow's nest spotted the two fore-and-aft rigged vessels bearing down on them, the first one's decks fairly bristling with troops. Panicked yells ran the length of the Frenchman, and, as expected, her sails unfurled in such haste that one end of her foremain tangled in its reef-points and had to be shaken out. With only its mizzen fore-and-aft rigged, and almost in irons at that, the ship struggled to bring its fresh, unfired batteries around to face south toward the approaching ships.

But at three hundred yards, the faster of the two—the Dutch yacht—turned another point to port, catching the breeze full a-beam. Accelerating, she heeled over, angling off to the northwest, and away from her partner. On that new course, she'd enter the Frenchman's field of fire that much sooner. The Spanish-made *patache* held course, but with barely half as many guns as the jacht, was certainly the lesser of the two evils bearing down upon the Frenchman.

When they were at two hundred yards, the bark had begun to catch the wind. Her mizzen started filling slowly, allowing her rate of turn to accelerate. Gunners began muscling their pieces into position. Below decks and above, the crews from the landside pieces left off their shore bombardment and crewed the half-manned portside guns. By that time, the jacht had straightened out again, soon to pass almost directly parallel to the Frenchman, whereas the *patache* showed an almost dull-witted obstinacy, maintaining a course that now had her prow aimed at the bark's port quarter. Had she had a ram, it might have made some kind of sense.

At one hundred yards, three guns of the Frenchman's port-side battery spoke, seeking the range. Two white geysers erupted behind the flying jacht and one hundred fifty yards beyond it. The bark slowed its turn, preparing to unleash a broadside at the Dutchman when she closed another thirty or forty yards, which would be in less than twenty seconds.

That was the same moment that the *patache* cut dramatically to starboard. That maneuver spilled some wind out of her sails—she came into a close reach—but she had barely lost momentum by the time she crossed behind the bark. As she did so, she swung hard back to port—putting her on a course to sideswipe the French ship.

Shouted warnings about a collision were lost in the roar of the bark's port side broadside, which discharged just as the jacht heeled harder to port once again, catching the breeze full a-beam and speeding directly away from the Frenchman, showing the enemy battery her narrow stern. Bracketed by geysers, one ball crashed into her deck, mauling a gun and its crew.

But on the starboard side of the Frenchman, the *patache*

closed rapidly, only eight yards separating the two craft. One cannon from the Frenchman's shore-aimed battery discharged at the speeding craft but soared over the heads of the cold-eyed boarders waiting beneath its gunwale.

A Dutch-accented voice shouted from the *patache's* stern— "brace yourselves"—just before the ship turned one more point to port and put her bow into the side of the Frenchman's hull.

Wood screamed, flew up as stripped off strakes and splinters. The lighter Spanish-designed ship rebounded slightly, but her angle of impact had been shallow, so she came back easily with her remaining momentum. The second impact was lighter, so light that the men on her decks were able to remain standing and fling grappling hooks over the Frenchman's shattered gunwale.

Not expecting to fight another ship, the bark had no marksmen in her rigging when the other ships were spotted. The first ones to respond were just climbing up, and so were blown down by massed musketry from the *patache's* deck. Similarly, as the French deckhands leapt to swing their swivel guns about, they found the Spanish ship's patereroes already trained upon them and firing. The would-be counterattackers were blasted away from their pieces, trailing spatters of blood.

The boarders swarmed onto the bark's deck, where the hastily organizing resistance met with a terrible surprise: their attackers were armed with pistols that fired repeatedly. A vanguard of ten Wild Geese led the rest of the troops over the Frenchman's gunwale, their pepperbox revolvers killing a few of the defenders, wounding many. More significantly, that sudden wave of fire surprised and quickly broke the morale of most of the survivors. Fleeing to the poop and the fo'c'sle respectively, the French had given up the midship weather deck before any officers had been able to organize a stand. The rest of the Wild Geese poured over, sniping at any defenders who raised a musket in opposition to the more indifferently armed Montserrat recruits who spread like a tide across the deck, wielding everything from daggers to cutlasses to old Spanish matchlocks. A few went down, but each one who fell was hastily replaced by three others, and more Wild Geese came on along with them, carrying musketoons, fresh pistols, and competent orders for the new recruits.

Meanwhile, the jacht had moved well out of range, and made swiftly for the farther French ship. Seeing the fate of her sister, and unsure of how many more enemy hulls might appear, that ship was crowding sail and making for open water. There, she could take advantage of putting the wind behind her square-rigged mainmast even as she put her stern to a following sea.

With most of the first Frenchman's surviving crew trapped on the gun deck and unable to move up the companionways for fear of the revolvers and cutlasses covering the stairs, the remaining officers and sail handlers huddled behind what cover they could find at either end of the ship. And in their silent, collective consternation of wondering how best to fight back, one of the tallest boarders stepped forward, raised a sword toward the captain on the poop deck and shouted:

"I am Hugh O'Donnell, Earl of Tyrconnell, and on my word, I promise you this: I will have your honorable parole or I will have your heads. The choice is yours."

In the profound quiet that was the immediate answer to his ultimatum, a single man stood on the poop deck. "Monsieur, that choice is no choice. You have our parole."

Hugh watched the second French ship fade into the distance and counted the dead being laid out on the deck. Six of the new recruits from Montserrat had already earned the bitter coin of service to their homeland's last earl, along with two of the Wild Geese. A dozen more of his men were wounded, but only one so severely that he was in any immediate danger. "What now?" asked Pieter Floriszoon who was still flushed and seemed eager to find yet another ship to fight. Hugh wondered who, truly, was the pirate at heart. "I go to St. Eustatia. At once."

"What? But they put troops ashore here, and Warner could be—"

"You will take care of that, and protect this place. We cannot be sure the other ship will not return, and we have no way of knowing if others might not be on the way. You will stay here, with this ship as a prize and with yourself on *Eendracht*."

"And you? You're going to St. Eustatia alone?"

Hugh smiled as he looked back over his shoulder at the men on the *Orthros*. The recruits from Montserrat lofted the French muskets and cutlasses with which they had re-armed themselves. "I think I have company enough. But I'll want your second pilot for the helm. We don't want a ham-handed beginner like myself at the whipstaff, or it will be all of us who'll need rescuing."

"Truly spoken," grinned Pieter. "You can leave the wounded here—"

Hugh shook his head. "Your Dutch doctors are best, and you've told me you have a Jewish surgeon in Oranjestad. If we succeed, they'll want to be close to that care. If we don't succeed—" He shrugged. "There won't be much hope for any of us, perhaps."

"Yes, perhaps. Which is the why you should not go alone. If these French officers are telling us the truth, that there is an attack under way on St. Eustatia, it could be twice as large as they're claiming."

Hugh stopped and held Pieter's gaze. "True, but if the French return here and overwhelm the defense we leave behind, then the English are defeated. And that means you'll all starve on St. Eustatia. So, either way, we must have a force in both places. And *this* is where ships are needed most, not at Oranjestad where your defense fleet is at anchor."

Floriszoon chewed his lower lip slightly and looked away. "Well, when you put it that way—"

Hugh put his hand on the Dutchman's shoulder. "Lend me some of your ship's troops, now. You should be able to scrape together some of your Dutch plantation guards once you put a skiff ashore. But I'll have more want of foot soldiers, I suspect."

Floriszoon nodded. "How many do you think you'll need."

"Thirty more?"

"Take fifty. And then get going. If there's anything I can't stand, it's watching a lazy Irishman loiter about."

Chapter 48

Off Vieques, Caribbean Sea

Eddie Cantrell lowered his binoculars and frowned.

Ove Gjedde's soft-voiced observation was annoying, mostly because it was perfectly accurate. "It is unlikely anything will change so dramatically that you need to examine the enemy every two minutes. They continue to run. We continue to chase. It has been thus since dawn. And the range is closing steadily."

"Yes, steadily. But not fast enough."

Gjedde shrugged at the receding Spanish sails that dominated the western horizon. "Like us, they have fair winds and following seas. Nothing could be better for their galleons. With the exception of our steam-ships, none of our hulls are much faster than theirs."

Eddie nodded, turned about and raised his binoculars to better see the allied fleet behind. Led by the steam-tugged *Amelia* and *Gelderland*, eight more Dutch warships had crowded sail to keep up with the USE steamships: *Hollandsche Tuijn, Zeeland, Neptunus, Utrecht, Prins Hendrik, Eenhoorn, Omlandia, Wappen von Rotterdam.* They were among the lighter and swifter Dutch hulls, none carrying more than thirty-eight pieces, but even so, their speed was not much greater than that of the Spanish galleons. Van Galen had loudly protested the decision to send almost all the bigger ships south with Peg Leg Jol to Trinidad, or to be kept as a home guard at Oranjestad, but now, Eddie's foresight was making itself felt as a lived reality. Once the Spanish saw the smoke from the steamships, he'd predicted they might not come straight to grips but do everything they could to maneuver for advantage. However, while the *Intrepid* and *Resolve* would be able to quite literally run rings around the Spanish heavies, it would be unwise to fully break formation to do so, not until the enemy was firmly engaged.

Van Galen had scoffed at this doctrine as overly cautious; he even came close to suggesting it was cowardice, at one point. But Eddie had maintained that the fleet sent to Santo Domingo had more need of speed and maneuverability than weight of shot. The steamships provided overmastering firepower on their own, but that would do little good if they raced far ahead of the rest of the fleet. So with the exception of the *Amelia* and the *Hollandsche Tuijn*, the other warships of this fleet had been selected for their operational flexibility. So had the five jachts that worked as both pickets and escorts for the four troop- and supply-laden fluyts that wallowed along with the *Serendipity* at the rear.

And yet, despite all those precautions, the fleet's van had begun to stretch out as the swift lead elements pressed to engage the rear of the Spanish formation. It would have been easy enough to achieve with the steamships alone, but whereas many of the Dutch presumed that the steamships would be able to destroy anything that came close, Eddie eyed the unprecedented number of enemy fore-and-aft rigged ships with concern. They, too, were swift and highly maneuverable, several looking to be highly streamlined jachts. With the seas rising, he could envision being unable to bring his guns to bear upon enough of those hulls swiftly enough to prevent being swarmed by the survivors. So whereas van Galen wished to charge straight ahead, confident that the Spanish would scatter and their galleons would flare and die as one after the other came under the eight-inch guns of the onrushing USE ships, Eddie was uncertain of such an outcome. And so far, Tromp and Gjedde had heeded his uncertainty. But, judging from the signals being flagged between the following ships, the impatience among the fleet's captains was growing.

Beneath him, down at the inter-ship comms position, Eddie heard the wireless start clattering. There were only four radios in the fleet—on *Intrepid, Resolve, Amelia*, and the yacht *Zuidsterre*—and messages would not be coming from the latter, since she was not in the command loop and placed well back in the formation. Which meant communiqués were coming exclusively from Tromp or Simonszoon. Which meant, in all probability, another debate.

The runner pounded up the stairs. "Signal from the *Amelia*, Commander!"

Eddie nodded the boy to give the message to his XO. "Summarize it if you would, Svantner."

"Yes, sir," said the Swede, taking the sheet out of the runner's hand and gesturing for him to wait for a reply. "Admiral Tromp is asking you to respond to Captain Simonszoon's respectful observation that with the enemy at only three miles range, we could increase steam and engage them within the hour. We still have better than four hours of daylight left. Without going so far as pursuing the Spanish into the dark, we could inflict considerable casualties upon them and yet be safely regrouped by nightfall." Svantner looked up slowly, deferentially. No doubt he'd been thinking the same thing. And wondering why they weren't doing it.

And why weren't they? Because Eddie Cantrell had misgivings. Nothing more specific than that: simply misgivings. *Doesn't exactly constitute a sophisticated tactical reason,* he admitted to himself. *But damn it, sometimes being in command means knowing when to play a hunch. Okay, so I'm the details-and-data guy in this crowd. So I'm the tech-wizard. And so they all think I don't really have the belly for a close-in fight. And who knows? Maybe they're right. But damn it, that's not what's holding me back.*

He glanced forward at the Spanish sails again. There had to be damn near sixty of them, and there were probably more farther on. If they'd been able to run up a balloon, they'd have been able to get a look at the seas for thirty-five miles in every direction, which would have been comforting to Eddie. But with the wind gusting erratically, and given that any ship conducting balloon ops lost the use of her mizzenmast, and thus, lost speed, the fleet had to rely upon their last long-range observations, now almost sixty hours old.

But even if the visible sixty sails represented all the Spanish ships between here and Santo Domingo, Eddie still kept coming back to one distressing fact, which he murmured loud enough for Ove Gjedde to hear. "These Spanish must know what happened at the Battle of Grenada Passage. They must know what our steamships can do. So, whatever else they intend, they are not going to come about and sail straight into our guns and their own certain death."

"No," agreed Gjedde in a slightly puzzled tone. "That is why they are fleeing."

"Are they fleeing, do you think?" Eddie raised his eyes to his binoculars again. "I'm not so sure."

Gjedde was silent for a long moment. "They are making good speed away from us."

"Yes. But tell me, Captain, you've seen adversaries fleeing before. Do these Spanish look to be in as much of a hurry as they should be if their objective is to break contact, to get away?"

Gjedde's next silence was even longer. "No," he admitted. "And it is puzzling. But still, whatever their reasons for such a measured withdrawal before us, what risk do we take by closing briefly, sinking several, and regrouping before dusk? Because you must directly answer that very question for Tromp, and soon."

Eddie nodded, and thought, *yeah, but if I give the answer I want to give—"Hell, no: we stay in formation, damn it!"—then Tromp's either got to support me against all the other commanders, or ignore me and give them their way. So, the smart move is to give advice that will calm his officers a bit, while also reigning in any excessive overconfidence. Which isn't the best military advice, but the reality of command is that sometimes, the human factors can be just as decisive as the strategic ones.*

"Here's my answer, runner," he said. "Insert stops where needed. To Admiral Tromp. I recommend that *Resolve* move ahead to engage enemy ships at range. Recommend one thousand yards as closest approach. *Intrepid* will remain five hundred yards astern of *Resolve's* port quarter to cover her flank against any lighter ships that may maneuver to close with her from that side. I presume that will be where they wish to do so, keeping the open waters of the Caribbean to their southerly backs. Recommend that both ships drop back again at four PM to facilitate dusk rendezvous with the rest of the fleet. Very Respectfully, Commander E. Cantrell. Please read that back."

The runner did. Eddie waved him on his way, felt the frown return to his face.

Gjedde nodded. "That was wise."

Eddie shrugged. *Yeah, wise. But it's also stupid. I can feel in my bones that it's not the right move. Now, if only I knew why . . .*

Tromp agreed with Eddie's plan, with the exception that he authorized *Resolve* to approach the rear of the Spanish van to a range of eight hundred yards. Apparently, though, he had to exert more than a little of his special authority to make his commanders fall in line with the rest of Eddie's recommendations. Van Galen was particularly resistant, and the semaphore exchanges between his ship and Tromp's *Amelia*, visible through Eddie's fine binoculars even as the main van dropped farther behind, were spirited. In the final analysis, Tromp prevailed upon the inevitable math of the strategic situation. Given that the Dutch ships were slightly faster than the Spanish, they were sure to fully overtake their enemies long before reaching Santo Domingo. In reply to van Galen's point that, with a full head of steam, the USE ships could overtake and destroy them today, Tromp serenely replied that, since it was already noon, waiting another eighteen hours to press home the final attack would make no difference.

The wind was such that the Dutch fleet would be within a mile of the Spaniards' sterns by nine o'clock the next morning. And if the enemy should happen to come about in the middle of the night, their square rigged galleons would be putting their bowsprits into the eye of the wind and so, be in irons. Unable to close or maneuver, they would be lucky to blunder within sighting distance, much less shooting range, of a target. Furthermore, if the Spanish hoped to continue making maximum headway as a fleet even after the sun had set, their stern lights would show any course changes they might make. If, instead, they doused those lights, they would be hopelessly scattered by the first rose of dawn. In short, there was no rush. One way or the other, the Dutch fleet would be upon the enemy tomorrow. Which meant that Commander Cantrell's recommendations for a more measured approach did not threaten the surety of a decisive engagement with the fleeing foe, and so had the virtue of prudence against unforeseen events. Van Galen's flags ceased to signal except to acknowledge receipt of the admiral's last message.

By that time, Simonszoon had raced ahead, prompting Eddie to wonder just how much coal the senior Dutch captain had already burned throughout the day. Perhaps infatuated with the new technology at his disposal, Simonszoon's *Resolve* had been putting out more smoke than the *Intrepid* and had been less assiduous about courting the winds. But there was no way to ask Dirck if he'd been careless about his fuel levels without also insulting him and possibly souring what was both a growing friendship and crucial ally among the command ranks. Besides, there was no longer any time to do so.

By one o'clock in the afternoon, the *Resolve* had closed to within eighteen hundred yards of the rearmost galleon in the Spanish formation, The lighter *pataches* and almost piratical-looking yachts scattered away from the big USE cruiser as she bore down upon them. The eight-inch rifle of Mount One spoke, putting a spout in the water at least eighty yards astern of the galleon's port quarter. The second shot was somewhat better, but not by much. The third rolling report was followed by a white plume erupting thirty yards aft and ten yards wide of the target's rudder.

When the fourth round overshot the ship by fifty yards, Eddie closed his eyes, fearing that he knew what was transpiring on board the *Resolve's* bridge at that very moment. Eager to draw first blood, thrilled but also anxious about taking the up-time ship into combat, the typically unflappable Dirck Simonszoon had given in to the temptation to show everyone in the fleet, and perhaps most particularly Eddie, that he was indeed the right commander for *Resolve*. And so, at the longest range yet attempted, he had started firing at the lumbering Spanish galleon. But since there was no ammunition to waste, he'd had only enough actual gunnery practice to familiarize himself with the inclinometer and the exacting nature of the deck-guns. So in his eagerness to prove himself quickly and decisively, he'd missed.

And then missed three more times. And no doubt felt that if he was proving anything to the rest of the fleet, it was that he did not belong in command of *Resolve*. After all, the young up-timer Cantrell rarely missed more than three times. Unfortunately, the subtleties of wave height, speed, target profile, and the differences between effective and practical range were probably not at the front of Simonszoon's awareness where they belonged, but following behind his increasing frustration and realization that he had engaged the enemy too soon. And even further behind that thought was any latent cognizance that Eddie and Pros Mund had made it look so easy because when they fired, they had always enjoyed the advantages of optimal sea conditions, close range, and significant training.

No doubt Rik Bjelke was trying to provide a patient voice of experience, but Simonszoon, for all his many intellectual virtues, was also a proud man who had never, it was said, encountered the situation that he could not handle. As uncomfortable as the fifth and sixth misses were to watch from the deck of the *Intrepid*, Eddie could only imagine the torture of suppressed counsel and soaring frustration that predominated upon the bridge of *Resolve*.

The *Resolve*'s guns stilled after the sixth miss and, soon after, a prodigious increase of smoke started pouring out her stack. The cruiser jumped forward at what must have been full steam, bearing down upon the Spaniards at almost thirteen knots, her prow slicing through the seas so sharply and powerfully that she was less susceptible to the chop. At eleven hundred yards from the Spaniard, her forward mount fired again, missed long by only fifteen yards, and then the rear mount put a solid shell through the galleon's stern windows.

There was no discernible response from the Spaniard other than a slight loss of speed. Within forty seconds, the *Resolve*'s forward eight-inch rifle spoke again, and this time, an explosive shell blasted a raging furrow three-quarters of the way across the galleon's quarter deck. Fires sprang up in several places, and the ship sheered sharply to starboard, losing way.

Showing the tactical aptitudes that made him such an excellent commander in even these unfamiliar circumstances, Simonszoon immediately ignored that crippled ship, understanding she would not be able to keep up with her fleet and was therefore no longer a threat. Closing to nine hundred yards with his next target, Simonszoon began firing again, but this time, more slowly and steadily. This time, he was probably taking more time to gauge swells, make sure he kept his course and speed rock steady while the gunners adjusted their firing solution, and was listening to the advice of Rik Bjelke. The forward mount's second shot fell just short of the next galleon's prow and the third struck her dead amidships in the gun deck closest to the waterline.

At this range, the impact looked simply like a puff of dust. Seen through Eddie's binoculars, it would have been a split-second tornado of shattered strakes, planking, and gunners. A moment later, secondary explosions started erupting from within the ship. One sent out a brief flicker of orange flame, hastily superseded by a vast plume of gray smoke. While her magazine did not go up, fires built rapidly in her lower decks and she, too, lost speed and heading.

As Simonszoon shifted course to bring his cruiser closer to a third target, Svantner muttered, "Commander, two points off the port bow: *patache* breaking back in toward *Resolve.*"

Eddie shifted his glasses and saw the Spaniard in question. She had been one of the half dozen lighter fore-and-aft rigged ships that had scattered like startled doves at the white-waked approach of the *Resolve*. Since then, she had slowly, casually reversed course, and was now angling in toward the lead USE ship. Behind that *patache*, Eddie saw two more sails slowly tilting over in the same direction, the ships beneath them heeling over into a close-reach to double back in a way that the square-rigged galleons of the Spanish fleet could not.

Eddie felt a painful pulse of premonition flare up in the same, chest-center spot that older men complained of heartburn. He dropped the binoculars from his eyes and scanned the horizon and flanks. Ove Gjedde was doing the same thing, squinting and frowning ferociously.

"You see it?" he asked the old Dane.

Gjedde nodded. "Yes. The smaller ships have not been keeping up with their fleet as swiftly as they did at first. They have been dropping back."

"Into a position from which they can pull just that kind of flanking maneuver." Eddie pushed out his chin. "Well, let's make them think the better of it. Helmsman, bring us two points to starboard so that both our rifles will bear on that *patache*. Intraship, message for Mounts One and Two: Get me a firing solution for that *patache*. And be careful to lead her. She's at speed and leaving a bone-white wake."

"Aye, Commander!"

Gjedde was peering around more aggressively. "Commander, I think you were right."

"Right? About what?"

Intraship interrupted. "Commander, Mount Two reports it has a solution."

"Fire when ready and continue tracking. Same order to Mount One when it reports a solution."

"Aye, sir." And the deck shook as Mount Two, only thirty-five feet behind them, roared.

Gjedde shook his head. "This *patache*, and the others, they are not receiving signals. They are pressing the flank of *Resolve* without orders."

Eddie nodded. "Which is to say, they *already* have orders to do so."

"Yes. This is part of the Spanish plan."

Mount One's discharge sent a shudder back under their feet and a long gray-white plume out over the port bow.

Eddie nodded. "Yes, but the plan is not complete."

"What do you mean?" Gjedde asked.

"I mean there's something missing. They must know we're not stupid enough to charge straight into them"—*well, except van Galen*—"and even at this close an approach to their van, they still can't flank us beyond our steamships' abilities to turn around and both flee and shoot our way out of any attempt to trap us."

As if to prove that point, Mount Two's second shot went through the mainsail of the *patache*, which sheered off to port and away from the two USE ships.

Gjedde nodded. "Yes, that is true. Presuming this is part of a larger trap."

Eddie stopped and felt his misgivings suddenly coalesce into a hard, sharp, painful point directly behind his sternum. "Of course. These light ships, these fleeing galleons: they're not the trap. They're just flypaper."

"What do you mean?" asked Gjedde, but it was the maintop lookout who shouted out the answer that Eddie dreaded hearing.

"Enemy sails off the port beam, coming over the southern horizon! Dozens of 'em and closing quickly!"

Eddie turned to Gjedde. "Now, their trap is complete."

Chapter 49

Slopes of The Quill, St. Eustatia

For the fifth time in as many minutes, Michael McCarthy, Jr., wished he had his father's .45 with him. Two Kalinago warriors appeared out of the trees just ahead of him, making for the antenna's ninth array line. But with the phenomenal senses of jungle-trained hunters, one heard a pebble snap out from under the up-timer's boot and turned.

Mike cursed, both at having to kill again and not having the best tool with which to do it. He raised his Hockenjoss & Klott .44 caliber black powder revolver and brought his left hand in for a two-handed grip. He fired.

The first warrior didn't seem to know he'd been hit square in the sternum. He managed to take two leaping steps, war club raised, before his eyes opened wide. He flinched and fell with a strangled cry.

But Michael missed his first shot at the other, who had either more presence of mind, more experience with firearms or both. The hatchet-armed warrior ducked, sidestepped, then charged.

The sidestep fooled Mike, who missed again. But the Kalinago had probably not encountered a weapon capable of so many shots and charged Mike directly, evidently believing himself safe.

At only four feet range, he learned his error. Mike, gritting his teeth to firm his nerve, fired twice. The Kalinago, hit in the shoulder by the first round, lagged and turned slightly in that direction, just before the next round hit him high in the diaphragm. He fell, bleeding heavily, but still trying to sweep his hatchet at Mike's tibia.

Mike stepped back and moved around the warrior, whose attempts to yell for help and more warriors were no more than hoarse wheezes. Mike, panting in the heat and humidity, crossed to the other side of the ninth and last spokelike array line that descended sharply from the summit of The Quill to its rain-forested skirts. He slipped into the trees and continued to run like hell.

Heading down the slope that would ultimately bring him to the western outskirts of Oranjestad's tent city, Mike finally reached what he'd been striving toward since the attack had begun almost half an hour ago: the groomed *ghut* his workers used as both a run-off sluice for their construction camp, and a wide and direct porter's trail when it was dry. It was hardly an ideal arrangement—almost nothing in the seventeenth century Caribbean seemed to be—but it was a less treacherous path when moving heavy, cumbersome, and yet fragile equipment.

But that wasn't the reason Mike had made for it in the middle of what seemed to be a widespread sneak attack. Instead, he had been told by some of his African workers—well, New World-born *cimarrons*, according to them—that the Kalinago would not suspect a *ghut* to be usable as a trail. The Kalinago were the masters of these islands; they were intimately familiar with how to look at a patch of jungle or the side of an overgrown mountain and predict where the streams and run-offs, or *ghuts*, would be, as well as the game trails, the rocky versus loamy slopes, and the rough gradient of them all.

However, the notion of a *ghut* being widened, groomed, and used as a trail would not be a part of their compendium of natural clues. In fact, quite the contrary, since the courses of most *ghuts* were narrow, rocky, and treacherous. Accordingly, Mike had reasoned it was likely to be the safest path down the western side of the mountain. And from the look of it, he'd been right.

He hadn't been the only person who'd reasoned this out, apparently. Approximately fifty yards farther down the *ghut*, he caught sight of two figures making their way swiftly downward, one a broadly built white man, the other a lithe and muscular black man. Not daring to shout, Michael doubled his already headlong pace, and before long, the other two, hearing the noise, turned toward him, weapons ready.

Mike waved a greeting, got a wave in return and the two waited, crouching cautiously. They rose when he approached, and Mike couldn't help but smile. "Good to see you made it out, Bert, Kwesi."

Bert Kortenaer took his left hand off his musket's forestock and shook Mike's hand. "And good to see you, too, Mike. I confess, I feared you might be one of the first killed."

"Huh. Let's get going while I learn why you were in such a rush to see me hustled to my eternal reward."

"Now, Mike—" started Bert.

"He only means, Michael, that we knew you were restringing wires on the fourth array, today." Kwesi frowned, moving swiftly, steadying his progress with his left hand, his wood axe ready in his right. "How did you get here so quickly? I mean no disrespect, Michael, but you are more of a thinker than a runner."

Michael considered his medium build and less than flat stomach. "I don't know how much of a thinker I am, but you're right that I'm no runner. Never was. But today, it wasn't my head or my feet that saved me."

"No?" asked Bert. "Then what was it."

"Luck. In my case, dumb luck. Literally. I was halfway to array four when I realized I'd forgotten my toolkit back at my tent near array seven. I didn't make it back down yesterday, so decided to stay overnight on the slopes. I was just picking up the tools when I heard the first gunshots."

Kwesi seemed to shiver. "What is happening, Michael? We have seen both Kalinago and white men attacking workers. Together. The white men are French, Mr. Kortenaer says. What are they doing here?"

Mike almost twisted his ankle between a stray root-end and a boulder that had been too large to lift out of the *ghut*. "Trying to destroy our radio, from the looks of it. They've been cutting wires as they go, and if they hadn't stopped to do that, they might have overrun us all before we get to town. Which we need to do as quickly as possible."

"To push them off The Quill?"

Mike stared at Bert. "To keep them from rolling Oranjestad into the sea. When I came to the clear ridge-line near array eight, I got a chance to look down the eastern slopes." Remembering the sight made Mike shiver slightly. "I didn't know what I was seeing at first. It looked like the ground between the trees was rippling. Then I realized: all those were men, moving up the slopes from wherever they landed on the windward side of the island. Which is why they must be here to knock out the radio. They came ashore where we couldn't see, where Oranjestad would not have any eyes or ears."

"There are some farmers near the eastern shore," Kwesi said grimly. "It's where I must work when I am not working for you, Michael."

"Yeah, I know, but all the farms are farther north, in the cross-island fertile belt. I'm guessing these attackers, who must number over a thousand, came ashore farther south, right at the foot of the mountain."

"That's nothing but rough surf and rocks, there, Mike," Bert observed.

"Yeah, but the Kalinago were born to them and they were willing to take the chance to get the jump on us. Which they've pretty much done." Mike's recent memories seemed to flit across his present vision like the images of an old-style slide projector skipping along a wall. He saw three of his most reliable and agreeable workers hacked down to the ground by half a dozen Kalinago who seemed to appear like ghosts out of the wood, the blood flying up with every backswing of their axes. He saw David, the silent Dutch sailor who had come to love the radio and every-thing about it, running to alert the camp at array seven, shot in the back by a Frenchman. And when the tow-headed youngster got up, blood smearing the front of his shirt, to try to continue raising the alarm, four Kalinago arrows burrowed into his back with singing whispers. Mike, not thinking clearly, had emptied his revolver at the first attackers who came close, improbably causing a brief lull in the entire attack. But in hindsight, that had been nothing more than the enemy mistaking the revolver's rate of fire for an unexpected number of defenders on site.

"Who else made it out?" Bert asked quietly.

Mike shook his head. "Don't know. All I saw were people run-ning every direction. Some were us, some were them. Most of our technical crew was not on the mountain last night. Just you, David, and Gerben were up there. But our workers—"

Kwesi shook his head. "My people will flee if they can, but will not die without a fight. Particularly not now that they can hope for freedom in a few years."

Mike nodded as they skittered down the last few yards of the *ghut*. *And if we hadn't made sure of that eventual freedom, your people might be joining forces with the Kalinago right now. And hell, who could blame them if they had done so, anyway? Not like we colonizers have a long, proud history of keeping our promises.* "A lot of the workers were going toe-to-toe with the Kalinago, machetes against hatchets. Gave at least as good as they were getting. I shouted at those guys to run, but a lot just smiled and kept swinging."

"They are warriors, most of them," Kwesi explained quietly. "They were sold to your slave-traders because they were taken prisoner by victorious tribes. Given the promise of freedom, there is honor to be reclaimed in defending the ground they worked with you, Michael."

Mike felt suddenly shamed that he had not stayed on the slopes of The Quill and died with them. Even though he had known, from the moment he saw the invaders, that he had to perform an even more important task: alert Oranjestad. "Let's go," he said as the *ghut* leveled off, leading to Oranjestad's outskirts. "I figure we've got about ten minutes to raise a defense."

Jean du Plessis peered down from the western slope of The Quill, watching the handful of survivors scatter away from its base toward Oranjestad. Behind him, almost all the long, coated wires had been hacked down from there they were secured to high, straight, well-pruned trees. "We are done here then? The radio is disabled?"

D'Esnambuc's nephew, Jacques Dyel du Parque, frowned at the swinging wires. "For now."

"Well, that is as we wanted it, yes?"

Jacques nodded. "Yes, Monsieur du Plessis, but I am concerned that it may not be enough."

"What? Why?"

Jacques pointed at the dozen mite-sized figures sprinting toward the outskirts of Oranjestad. "If they succeed in raising a defense, we may not be able to hold this position. Or remain on St. Eustatia at all."

Du Plessis almost sneered. "And what defense could they raise?"

Jacques raised his finger toward the west as de l'Olive approached, half of his French musketeers just behind him. "Monsieur du Plessis, how many ships do you count in the bay?"

Du Plessis scowled, covered his eyes, although fortunately, the sun was not too far advanced. "About twenty. About a third are jachts. At least three are simply fluyts. None have even weighed anchor, yet."

"Quite true, monsieur. But we did not expect to see so many here, according to the landholders who responded to our bribes. They thought that only a handful would be left."

"What's your point, Jacques?" De l'Olive sounded far less impatient that du Plessis felt.

"Only this, my friend: how many ship's troops would be upon them?"

"A few hundred, at least," de l'Olive murmured with a nod.

"So even though we might prevail in Oranjestad, we might not be able to hold it."

"They shall not shell their own town, even with us in it," du Plessis sniffed.

"No, but you mean to burn it, monsieur. And if you do so, there will be no town left for their guns to spare, and so, no reason for them to remain silent. However, the fort will remain. Which, if my spyglass shows me correctly, is still manned. I would say close to a hundred troops, from what I have counted over the past half hour. They will delay us considerably, no?"

Du Plessis wanted to disagree, but thought the better of it. First, the otherwise ruthless and hard-nosed d'Esnambuc doted on his nephew like a pampered puppy. Second, the young fellow was making sense. Unfortunately. "So what are you suggesting, Monsieur Dyel du Parque?"

The nephew shook his head. "I am loath to say it, for it runs counter to my uncle's fondest hopes, but I do not think we can afford to save the radio. I suspect we will not be able to hold Oranjestad, once we take it. And if my reading is correct, a radio so large as this one will be too cumbersome and fragile to move."

Du Plessis glanced at the wires behind him once again. "Are you saying that we will now have to cut up all these—?"

Jacques shook his head. "No. There is neither the time for that, nor will it serve our purpose. The wire is not irreplaceable. But I suspect the radio itself is. So we must attack Oranjestad, burn it, but make sure we find the radio and demolish it. Then, if we must withdraw, we will still have crippled our adversaries. As we must, if we are to take all of St. Christopher's and expand throughout these islands."

Du Plessis was still getting used to the conceptual changes when de l'Olive nodded and smiled. "You are your uncle's boy, all right. He'll approve. I know it. So, how do we find the radio? What will it look like?"

Jacques gestured toward the cluster of wires that ran down the hill along several converging paths. "We follow the wires. Like the heads of a hydra, they can be replaced. But at the root of them all is the heart of their operation. Which will look like a large machine with wires going into it. And hooked up to some kind of electrical power source."

"Electri—what?" De l'Olive stumbled over the words, gave up.

"More wires," Dyel du Parque supplied, "which carry the energy that the radio uses to receive and send signals. Those wires will be hooked up to a steam plant, or a windmill, or something that takes the work of a turning wheel and turns it into the needed energy."

"And once we find it? Hammers?"

Jacques seemed to flinch in regret. "Yes. Hammers will do."

Du Plessis sheathed his sword, checked his pistols. "Well, then, de l'Olive, you have the information you need. Gather our musketeers and the Kalinagos so armed, also. I suspect we'll need them to break through whatever defense these lazy Dutch manage to throw up in the next few minutes."

Cuthbert Pudsey was gasping for breath when Anne Cathrine bid him enter. "My ladies, make haste! Ye've got to get to the hidey-holes we have built into the—"

"Mr. Pudsey, you may see for yourself that we will not be requiring that protection." Anne Cathrine had already made a trip to the secondary arsenal and returned with an armload of new flintlock muskets, percussion cap pistols, and powder flasks.

"But ladies, your safety was placed in my care, and besides, you are—"

"Mr. Pudsey," Anne Cathrine said, straightening up, "we are able-bodied persons who may help defend this largely unpopulated town. Unless I am wrong, there are but ninety-five men in this fort, true?"

"You are correct, but—"

"And presuming my husband tells me the truth, and my own eyes have not been lying these past weeks, we have few more to spare. Twelve hundred embarked to do battle at Santo Domingo. For which three hundred were furloughed from their defense of the English properties on St. Christopher's, which now has only one company scattered among its many plantations. Furthermore, almost half of the Irish Wild Geese are defending their fort on Trinidad, along with one hundred and fifty Dutchmen. And almost three hundred and fifty more are, necessarily, embarked upon our ships in the bay, should they be required to sail to repulse a Spanish attack. Are my numbers accurate?"

Pudsey swallowed. "I-I think so, Lady Anne Cathrine, but the officers aren't in the habit of informing me—"

"And allow me to conjecture that the landowners have not yet begun to gather in defense of the town," added Sophie.

Pudsey blinked. "How did you know—?"

"Mr. Pudsey," Anne Cathrine snapped, "you may or may not have noticed that the largest landowners are also the largest slave owners, and that none of them are fond of Admiral Tromp or the policies he has championed for their slaves' eventual transition to freepersons. Clearly, they did not respond when the alarm bell on The Quill was rung earlier this morning, nor to the musketry we heard there. Nor have they come here to help defend the town, or secure their own safety. Possibly because many of them have no reason to fear the attackers."

The implication of treason hung unspoken in the air for a second. "And so," Sophie finished calmly, "if we cannot expect help from many of the landowners, how will we defend the town? I know Captain Arciszewski has signaled for Admiral Banckert to send some of his troops ashore, but the attackers will be in our streets before those boats are through the surf." She slipped two decidedly nonmilitary fowling pieces over her arm and walked toward the door in which he was standing. "So, with your permission or without it, Mr. Pudsey, the king's daughters and I will take our places among what few defenders we have."

"I'll get Captain Arciszewski to send fifty men from the fort," Pudsey sputtered hastily. "And I'll come along wid' ye to—"

Anne Cathrine shook her head. "And then who shall defend this fort if half its soldiers leave, simply to protect us? The captain, and you, and all the others must man these walls until Admiral Banckert's relief arrives. Because if we do not succeed turning back the invaders at the outskirts of town, this fort will be our last foothold in Oranjestad, and her guns must not be turned on the fleet."

"But . . . but who shall take charge of the defense of the outskirts when—?"

Leonora shrugged. "Unless I am much mistaken, I believe I have heard Mr. McCarthy all the way from the other end of the town, just before the fire bell began ringing there."

"You did? What was he saying?"

Leonora blushed. "As a lady, I may not repeat it. But we are responding to his summons. All of us."

Hugh O'Donnell glanced at the young man—just a boy, really—who was piloting the *Orthros* at least as much as the man at her whipstaff, a Dutchman simply named Aart. "Are you sure of the depth here, Mr. van der Zaan?"

The lanky, tow-headed adolescent smiled a wide, bright smile. "Oh, Lord O'Donnell, you can call me Willem. Or just Willi. That's what Admiral Tromp calls me."

"Very well, then, Willi," Hugh responded with a similar smile. "Now tell me, how close can we come to the shore in that bay?" Hugh pointed to an inlet just south of the wide sweep of the anchorage in front of Oranjestad proper.

Willi tapped the helmsman on the shoulder, indicated he should sheer to port half a point. "I'd say about ten yards from shore, Lord O'Donnell. But your men will be in five feet of water, there."

Aart shook his head. "Though you've dumped all the ballast on the way here, you'll still run her aground if you go that far into Gallows Bay."

"I don't think so," Willi mumbled with a faint frown. "Right now, the tides give us a little more leeway. And if we did get caught, it would be by such a small bit that we can kedge ourselves off the sand. There's a patch of rocky bottom just a few yards away, if we keep ourselves due west of that driftwood cask on the beach."

Hugh nodded at Aart. "We're going to follow Willi's advice." He looked back into the faces of both the veteran and newly recruited Wild Geese, as well as the Dutch soldiers crowded upon the deck. "All armor off. Bag your weapons and your powder, and hold them over your head. It's not far to shore, but some of you will be up to your eyebrows for a moment or two."

"Lord O'Donnell," appealed Aart, "once again, please consider landing on the main strand just to the west of the town. It's smooth sands there, easy for your men, and easier for me to sail in and out."

"I know," Hugh answered, "but you heard what our lookout spied before we reefed sail and starting hiding our approach. The attackers are approaching the east edge of Oranjestad. If we port to the west, we'll be doing no better than the boats we've seen Admiral Banckert lowering into the water. We'll get there too late. And we'll be coming from the direction that they expect. And there's one thing I've learned in my years of soldiering, Aart—never, ever do what your enemy expects. Which means that as soon as you drop us in the briny, you come about and head back south around The Quill and worry them from the windward side of the island. But don't shell their boats. Give 'em room and the ability to run. We don't want them bottled here on this island with us." He turned to the men behind him. "Now, boys, ready along the starboard gunwale. We go in smooth and silent, make for land, regroup and then fast march. And remember, you don't shout or shoot until I tell you to."

Chapter 50

Oranjestad, St. Eustatia

Anne Cathrine nodded to Michael McCarthy, Jr., who had seemed fairly calm until he caught a glimpse of the three Danish ladies entering the makeshift defenses. Their arrival had elicited the same degree of desperate solicitousness that had so afflicted Cuthbert Pudsey only five minutes earlier. Strange. Although up-time men were so ready to confer equality upon women in so many matters, they were no different than their down-time brothers when it came to the matter of combat. In some ways it made up-time male attitudes towards women frustratingly inconsistent and yet, familiar.

But the three Danish ladies had stood their ground against Michael McCarthy's objections. They pointed out that a dozen other Dutch women were in the defense lines, mostly to reload the muskets of the men who were sheltering in the trenches or behind the hasty, flimsy barrel barricades that flanked them. Michael had countered that those women were the exception, not the rule, and that most of the women had complied with his order to stay away from the coming battlefield. Anne Cathrine had listened through to the end of his exhortations, and then promptly turned on her heel, but not to depart the defenses. Rather, she began crying an alarm among the tents, calling specifically upon women to come out and take their places along the barricades

546

or in the ditches. Michael had rolled his eyes but had been too busy, or maybe too sensible, to waste any more time trying to end what he could not even forestall.

Looking out toward the dust cloud being raised by the approaching enemy, Anne Cathrine surveyed their defenses. Two ditches guarded the eastern approaches to the town. Each offered waist-deep cover for fifteen men, at most. Most of the soldiers were there, along with a few of the townsmen who had turned out to help. The barricades were manned by the balance of the soldiers and townsmen, the workers who'd made it off The Quill, and those few landowners who had decided to throw their lot in with their neighbors.

She approached the northern trench, where Sophie was calmly surveying the enemy's approach, a fowling piece in her long, slender hands. Leonora waited just behind her, ramrod, powder and balls at the ready. Anne Cathrine wondered if there was some argument, any argument, that she could use to get Leonora off the line. At least one of them should take care to survive this battle and so, be a consolation to their father. "Leonora," Anne Cathrine murmured, "should you not be in the infirmary, ready to help Dr. Brandão with the wounded?"

Leonora's smile was small as she shook her head. "I think not, Sister. If these attackers break our ranks here, they will be upon the infirmary in three minutes and slay all there. So here is the best place where I may work to ensure that the wounded actually have someplace to be treated. Besides," she said, patting the closest powder horn, "I have made a study of the loading and reloading actions undertaken by the soldiers at the fort, when they are at drill. I think I shall make a useful reloader for Sophie."

Sophie nodded. "She seems quite adept."

Anne Cathrine raised an eyebrow. "And you? You are a soldier, too, Sophie?"

"No, Anne Cathrine, but I grew up on wooded estates with a father who, as sheriff, took pleasure in hunting for much of the meat that graced our table." She smiled. "He took great pains to pass some of those skills on to me, at least when it came to shooting waterfowl. So I suspect I may be of some use, here."

"I'm sure you shall be. I wish *I* was of more use."

Sophie stared at her. "You really do not see how the other women look at you?"

"What?"

"Anne Cathrine, they see you carrying that pistol, walking behind these trenches. They do not think, 'there walks the king's daughter, who knows not how to help.' They think, 'there walks the king's daughter, who gave us the courage to join our men here on these lines, who moves behind us like our better conscience, proof that to be a woman is not to be weak.' If you were not here, and visibly so, there would be far fewer women here now. And our numbers may yet help decide the outcome of this battle."

"I truly hope so, Sophie, I truly—"

With a savage cacophony of war cries, shouts, and taunts that shared not a single syllable in common, the Kalinago warriors began sprinting across the three hundred yards between them and the meager defenses of Oranjestad. Following them a hundred yards farther back at a modest trot were what looked like musketeers, some European, some native.

Michael McCarthy's voice was loud and surprisingly authoritative. "Hold your fire till they clear the stubble of the closest canebrake. That's about one hundred yards. Reloaders, you need to grab the shooters' spent muskets right away and reload them quickly. If you do that, we'll get off three volleys, which might break them. If you don't, we'll get off two and they're likely to overrun us. Now stay down and under cover until you get the order to fire."

Anne Cathrine rushed into the rear of the trench, next to Leonora, and watched the horde of Kalinago warriors approach. They wore little, bore brutal-looking clubs, stopped here and there to fire their bows. They were good marksmen, but only a few shafts found flesh through the gaps in the cover, and only one of those hits was fatal.

Seeing the Kalinago looming like a wave, and the arrows flying towards them, many of the defenders became restless. One of them in the southern ditch raised up on one elbow, sighted his wheel lock rifle, eased the hammer back—

"You there!" shouted Michael. "You can track a target, but if you fire, I swear to God, I'll shoot you myself." The restlessness in the trenches subsided slightly.

The Kalinago came on, the volcanic cone of The Quill rising up behind them like a green pyramid erected by a cockeyed, atavistic island god. It seemed impossible that the near-naked warriors could run so quickly, so far, and it defied belief when, as they cleared the canebrake, the first of the mob redoubled their already considerable speed into a flat-out charge.

Anne Cathrine watched McCarthy, who, tensely watching the approach, waited two more seconds before he cried. "Fire!"

Almost a hundred muskets spoke in a loose sputter along the barricades and trenches. Perhaps a third that number of the natives staggered, cried out, or fell limp. However, the Kalinago had done battle with Europeans before and expected no less. And today, they still had at least seven hundred warriors in the field.

Anne Cathrine raised her pistol, knew not to fire until the third volley, felt her underarms, back, and brow awash with sweat that owed nothing to the heat of the sun. McCarthy's voice grew increasingly stentorian. "Swap muskets! Reloaders, we're depending on you. Shooters: aim...and...fire!"

The second volley was even more ragged, but did more damage, in part because the persons using fowling pieces and musketoons were now at range. Only fifty yards away, almost forty of the Kalinago went down. Many of the survivors drew up short—but not because they intended to flee, but rather to return fire.

Arrows keened among the barricades and clipped into the edges of the ditches. Several found their mark, promising the fate that was now overtaking those who had been hit earlier: poison-inflicted convulsions. The leading edge of the warriors was now ragged where it had been chewed at by the Dutch musketry, and none of those natives still had bows in hand. Instead, their war clubs were held far back, primed for skull-crushing blows.

Anne Cathrine raised her pistol and looked for a warrior who was either larger or more adorned than the others. She found one, cocked the weapon's hammer, then gripped the handle of her gun with both hands, just as Eddie had taught her. She wished—very strongly, and throughout her whole body—that she could have seen and held Eddie just one more time. Then she was aware of nothing except for the Kalinago warrior she could see over the brass bead atop the end of her pistol's muzzle. To either side of her, the reloaders were pushing the first muskets back into the shooter's hands, then drawing their own pistols or swords. She wanted to glance at Michael McCarthy, wondered if he hadn't called for the last volley because perhaps he'd been hit with an arrow, feared that maybe someone else—she herself?—had to take charge now, give the final order to—

"Fire!" shouted McCarthy.

Anne Cathrine was both too relieved and too focused to double-guess her aim. She fired the double-charged pistol, saw the male torso upon which the muzzle was superimposed stagger and fall out of the sight picture. Along the line, the blast of musketry was more uniform, and louder, with the loaders' pistols contributing to it. And from behind, she heard the sound of running feet approaching—but only a few. Had some of the natives gotten behind them, sneaked in through town from the north—?

She hadn't the time to think. Although the Kalinagos had taken horrible losses with this volley, many of the charging warriors were too far ahead of the wave of casualties to be stunned or panicked by that destruction. They sprinted closer, racing toward the trenches and the barricades, suddenly so near that Anne Cathrine could make out the individual teeth in their mouths as they shrieked their war cries and thirst for mortal vengeance—

From behind, a fusillade of pistol fire startled her. Had the rest of the soldiers been sent from the fort? Turning, she discovered the gunfire was coming from fewer than a dozen men: the Wild Geese who'd still been in the infirmary, now wielding their revolvers with deadly, much-practiced precision among the Kalinago who most closely approached the defensive lines. Several made it to the northern barricade, but there, Michael McCarthy's own, larger cap-and-ball revolver sent out a steady stream of thunderclaps.

Its leading lines of skirmishers slain, the main body of the Kalinago broke and ran for the rear, suddenly silent in retreat. But they did not go far. Upon encountering the musketeers behind them, they formed up into a mass once again. Voices that both berated and encouraged them in two foreign languages—Kalinago and French—soon had them turned back around, crouching as they sorted themselves into archers and skirmishers. Soon, arrows were sailing across the two hundred yard gap. The whining shafts did not find any victims—it was well beyond the optimum range of what were essentially self-bows—but they were keeping the defenders pinned down. Hearing the dying gasps and shuddering cries of even those who had been modestly wounded by the arrows, the allied defenders were unwilling to expose themselves, making communication and movement difficult.

Sophie turned around, a long bang of sweaty hair hanging down in front of her face. "I do not think we will survive the next attack," she commented with what Anne Cathrine heard as her surreal Norn-calm.

"Why?" asked Leonora.

"They know where we are, they know what weapons we have, and they will bring up their musketeers, this time. When we rise to fire at them, they will no doubt fire at us." Sophie shrugged. "How many times can we afford such an exchange?"

The Kalinago, now aided by the French, were obviously eager to find the answer to that very question. With the rain of arrows still coming in at a shallow arc, the skirmishers began arranging themselves into rude ranks.

As they did, one of the most plainly dressed loaders rose up from her position further down the trench to dig a pistol out of a bag she had left unattended a few yards away. When her plain workman's hat fell aside briefly, it revealed the smoke-smudged face of Edel Mund.

"Lady Mund!" Anne Cathrine exclaimed. "What are you—?"

"I am doing the same thing you are, Lady Anne Cathrine. I am fighting to defend this town."

"Then get down, Lady Mund! One of the native arrows could easily—"

Edel's mouth was a brittle-lipped line as she muttered. "I do not fear that."

"Granted we might die here, but none of us deserves to—"

Edel Mund wheeled on the younger woman. "You are wrong. Some of us do deserve to die. Particularly those of us who caused the deaths of others."

Leonora gaped. "But what—what are you saying—?"

"Do you really not understand? Do you not see that it was I who killed my own husband?"

Anne Cathrine blinked, then realized she'd half forgotten about the regrouping Kalinagos. "You—?"

"A fief on Iceland. A generous gift, I suppose, your father intended it to be. But—Iceland. As grim and lifeless a place as God or devil ever conceived or created. And then, Pros was given the chance to come here, to lead a fleet to the New World. To please your father, the king. Perhaps we would have been given land somewhere near Skaelskor, or maybe even here in the New World."

"And how," Leonora asked as the native war cries began rising again, "did that hope kill him?"

Edel Mund glared at her. "The hope didn't kill him, because it wasn't important to him." She closed her eyes. "It was my hope, mine alone. And *I* was what was important to him. Me and my happiness. Pros was determined to do anything to please me, to allow me to escape our fief on Iceland forever. And I"—her eyes became fixed and bright—"and I let him. Did I forbid him to take the risks that I knew—*knew*—he planned to take? To seize Spanish ships for his king to purchase my happiness with those war-prizes? No. I allowed him to destroy himself. All because I wanted a little more sun, and a little less ice, I allowed my husband to go to his death. As fine a man, as good a man, as caring a man as ever lived, despite his stoic silences. And my pettiness killed him, just as certainly as had I driven a dagger into his back myself."

"But Lady Mund—" began Leonora.

Whatever Anne Cathrine's sister had intended to say was lost when, with a single shout that sounded a great deal like "Tegreman!" the Kalinago skirmishers started forward. Now in loosely organized ranks, they came on at a slower trot, closely followed by almost two-hundred native and French musketeers. To Anne Cathrine's eyes, the French were armed with quite modern weapons—snaphaunces and even a few percussion-cap rifles, from the look of them—whereas most of the natives were armed with older Spanish pieces. They would not fire so quickly or so accurately as their French allies, but given their numbers, it would hardly matter.

Even now, as the leading Kalinago skirmishers reapproached the stubble of the last canebrake, the reloaders were just finally passing weapons back into the hands of the shooters. The Wild Geese had taken cover among the crates surrounding the radio shack, and both they and McCarthy were busy reloading. Sophie was right. The defenders would not fire so many times, nor so well, this time, and would be facing a hail of musketry while doing so.

Someone tapped her on the arm. It was Leonora, holding up Anne Cathrine's reloaded pistol. Startled, Anne Cathrine looked down at her younger sister. "But I didn't hand you my—?"

"No, I just slipped the weapon out of your fingers. You were inspecting the battlefield. Confirming Sophie's assessment of our chances, I suspect."

Anne Cathrine nodded, then reached down and gave her sister

a fierce hug. She shot a glance at Sophie, meaning to put the same affection into it, but the Danish noblewoman was already facing the Kalinago, fowling piece raised to her shoulder.

"Ready on the line!" shouted a new, authoritative voice: Aodh O'Rourke's.

The lead skirmishers of the Kalinago, now about seventy yards away, were beginning to separate. If the two ends of their lead rank kept splitting farther apart, neither would be funneled by the barricades into the closest approach to the tents of Oranjestad. Rather, they would flank the defenders on either side and bypass the trenches at the center of their line. And if that happened—

O'Rourke and McCarthy perceived that the danger to their flanks would increase with every passing moment. "Fire!" they cried in unison.

The defenders did, and many of the Kalinago sprawled head-long. But the others did not break stride, and now, advancing at a faster trot through the open space vacated by the two halves of the front rank, came the French and native musketeers. As they raised their pieces, McCarthy shouted, "Fresh muskets! Reload the empties! Quick or they'll—"

A well-coordinated volley split the humid air, more coordinated than Anne Cathrine had been expecting, and she fully expected it to be the last sound she ever heard. But instead, she opened her surprise-shut eyes and discovered that the French and native musketeers had not fired, but, in fact, had been mauled by the volley she had heard.

Turning to look south, she saw more than a hundred men emerging from the virgin forest that hemmed in Oranjestad at the south and which extended to a point within eighty yards of attackers. The new defenders—a half company of Wild Geese—was heading for the lead ranks of the enemy musketeers, led by a tall, auburn-haired man whom the others followed with a surety and confidence that was tangible, even at this range.

Anne Cathrine jumped to her feet and shouted for joy, just as O'Rourke's cry rose up, "O'Donnell *abu*! Now one more volley into those musketeers and break 'em!"

But that's not quite the way things worked out. The volley from Oranjestad's defenders, more ragged and ill-timed than before, was less focused than O'Rourke had hoped. At least half of the muskets were fired at the Kalinago who were trying to flank the barrel barricades. The other half did hit the enemy musketeers while the French leaders were trying to turn that mass to face the new threat coming out of the trees to the south. It did not drop many of them, but it sent ripples of irritation and dismay through their ranks. The natives might have been familiar with their muskets, but not with moving in ranks and certainly not withstanding flanking fire while doing so. A large number of Kalinago angrily turned their pieces back toward the town's defenders, discharged them, and hit close to a dozen of that thin line.

But in the meantime, Dutch musketeers emerged from the wood behind the Wild Geese and discharged a flanking volley into the rearmost ranks of the attackers. The front ranks, when finally dressed, turned toward the loose skirmish line of Wild Geese, raised their weapons, and fired. At almost the same moment, the Irish mercenaries dove into the stubble of the canebrake. Nearly a dozen did not dive down in time, but the rest rose up swiftly, and charged until they were only twenty paces from the furiously reloading French and natives. The pepperbox revolvers were in their hands now and, collectively, the sound they made was even faster and more raucous than when the *Intrepid* was test-firing one of her mitrailleuses.

French and Kalinago alike, the musketeers went down in windrows before this point-blank fusillade. Order disintegrated swiftly. Unwilling to keep reloading in the face of such sustained fire, and surrounded by so many casualties, the Kalinago cast aside their cumbersome matchlocks and came at the Wild Geese with their war clubs. That was when they discovered that perhaps one in five of the Irish mercenaries had not been contributing to the general fire, but waiting, kneeling, to break just such counterattacks.

O'Rourke, hoarse and still pale from his slow recovery, vaulted over the ditch in which Anne Cathrine was taking cover, shouting "O'Donnell, *abu*! McCarthy, if you're an Irishman true, now's the time to show it!"

Michael yelled an answering, "O'Donnell *abu*! For Tromp and Oranjestad!" which brought the Dutch soldiers boiling out of the thin defensive line and at the Kalinago.

Strangely, to Anne Cathrine's eyes, that charge by forty or so defenders did more to break the spirit of the natives and the French than anything else. Maybe they reasoned that the defenders would not charge unless they had seen reinforcements approaching from the rear. Maybe it was the audacity of the countercharge. Maybe they thought the defenders of Oranjestad had gone insane with a berserker death-lust. Whatever the reason, the Kalinago and French broke ranks, shooting as they streamed back toward the low humps of The Quill's northern foothills, apparently intending to reach their boats on the windward side of the island by the swiftest possible route.

The Wild Geese took the opportunity to swap new cylinders into their revolvers and renew their charge, the tall, auburn-haired man leading them after the repulsed invaders. Sophie rose slowly, looking at that man, head forward as if her eyes were straining after the sight of him, as if her ears were straining after his voice.

As she and Anne Cathrine watched, several of the French attackers turned, hurled something small and round at their pursuers just as the auburn-haired man stopped to help up a fallen comrade. One of the small black dots thrown by a Frenchman landed next to him. In the next instant, there was a small flash and a vicious puff of smoke, and Anne Cathrine could not tell if the man had leaped, or was blown aside, by the grenade.

Chapter 51

Off Vieques, Caribbean Sea

Maarten Tromp read back across the recent and voluminous wireless exchanges. With his new executive officer peering over his shoulder, he shook his head and muttered, "I can find no flaw in Cantrell's reasoning." Tromp looked up at the skies, looked out over the three-foot seas. "We must split the fleet. And you must stand by the signalman to provide an explanation to our captains."

Whereas Kees Evertsen would have launched into an animated inquiry as to why the fleet must be split in the face of two larger enemy formations, Adriaen Banckert showed that he was indeed his father's son. The taciturn nineteen-year-old executive officer merely frowned. "Why, Admiral? Cannot we stay close to the USE steamships while they defeat the closest group to the west, and then the next one to the south?"

Tromp shook his head. "We cannot put that measure of faith in their guns, not in these seas. Their aim will be less accurate, and so they will not be able to effectively close with and destroy one enemy force without offering the other their stern."

"So the enemy planned this to be able to inflict more damage upon the steamships?"

"Cantrell thinks that is only a secondary concern for the Spanish. And I think he is right."

Adriaen put his hands behind his back. "Admiral, like the captains with whom I must soon communicate, I must wonder: what, then, are the Spanish after?"

Tromp looked up with a bitter smile, looked over his shoulder and the taffrail. Stretching into the far distance, the long line of Dutch warships gave way to an even more extended line of her supply fluyts. "They are after our conventional, sailed ships. But especially our supply ships." Seeing no change on Banckert's face, he sighed and gestured to the last visible sail of their formation. "The Spanish have been more crafty, and have learned more quickly, than we conjectured. They realized after the Battle of Grenada Passage that the steamships cannot be attacked directly. To do so is to commit suicide. So the main fleet before us has only been bait, a lure to get us to keep chasing the galleons of their fleet. But all the while, what they were really after was to pull us out of formation so that they could threaten our slowest ships. The ships that are carrying the thirteen hundred troops with which we mean to raze Santo Domingo and its facilities. The same ships that are carrying all our spare powder and balls, and which are carrying the extra ammunition and coal for the steamships."

Now Adriaen Banckert's beetled brows rose in understanding and alarm. "Of course. But how did they manage to coordinate the appearance of this second fleet?" He gestured to the rapidly growing mass of fore-and-aft rigged ships approaching out of the south.

"That is indeed an excellent question, Adriaen. But given our current position, I think they used the western mountains of St. Croix as a kind of marker, a place that their line of ambushers were to form up against. I suspect that is why they started approaching us along such a broad front. They were signaling, up and down that line, to maintain position and pass the word to begin their attack."

Banckert nodded. "Still, it is a difficult feat."

Tromp nodded. "It is indeed, even were those attackers as disciplined as the ships of a legitimate navy."

Adriaen's left eyebrow rose. "What do you mean, Admiral? How are the approaching ships not a 'legitimate navy'?"

Tromp smiled. "Oh, they are a force to be reckoned with, but those ships are not in the rolls of any nation's fleet. They are pirates. Well, privateers now, I suppose."

Banckert was so surprised that he forgot to address Tromp with an honorific. "What?"

"Adriaen, tell me, do you imagine the Spanish have ready access to so many fore-and-aft rigged vessels as are approaching us from the south? Perhaps if they drew in all the hulls of the *Garda Costa* and all their advice ships, but that would take more than a year to coordinate. No, the Spanish *recruited* the fleet we see coming from the south. And, I begin to suspect Cantrell is right in guessing that many of the smaller craft in the fleet to our west have the same origins."

"But the Spanish detest pirates. They almost never grant them letters of marque—"

"Adriaen, we confronted them with an entirely new threat at the Grenada Passage. And they have formulated an entirely new response. They set aside their old prejudices to find a means to reduce the effectiveness of the steamships' new weapons. Pirate ships are smaller, faster, more maneuverable, all of which makes them harder to hit. It also means they do not require fair breezes from the stern like galleons, but may sail close to the wind, tacking through it at their leisure. No, Cantrell's analysis is correct. And I think he is also correct in speculating that their nature *as* pirates did help us in one way: they lacked sufficient discipline to wait a few more hours."

Banckert looked at the sun, now well past the midday point. "But Admiral, if they had waited a few more hours, they would have been engaging us at dusk."

"Precisely. Enough light to see us, but not enough light for us to maneuver against them, regroup, or unleash broadsides at a distance. Adriaen, the dark is their friend. And they need not sink or disable many of us to win a great victory here. For if we flee these waters, and we must, then any hull that straggles behind will be fodder for these sea-wolves."

Banckert nodded, understanding Tromp's strategic decision at last. "And so, in order to escape, we must sail south by southwest. That will give us a reasonable following wind, give us the wind-gauge over the more nimble ships to the south. And will bring us away from any threat that the main fleet to the west might pose, should it turn about. Although, Admiral, the wind is against them."

"Against the main fleet's galleons, yes. But all her fore-and-aft rigged vessels can tack and make headway against it, could get in among our square-rigged warships, maybe our supply ships."

"Unless the steamships hold these waters long enough for the rest of us to sail southward, out of—what did Cantrell call it, this 'L-ambush'?—and punch our way through the second fleet."

"The lower and weaker jaw of the Spanish trap," Tromp affirmed with a nod. "Now, send the signals, Adriaen. If our captains wish to have the orders explained, do so once, and succinctly. And in such a way that they know that this flagship neither has the time nor the interest in answering further inquiries. And once we are tightening up our formation, we'll need to ready the steam pinnaces for towing both *Amelia* and *Gelderland*. We'll be pulling ahead along with the jachts to serve as a vanguard."

"Yes, sir." He looked over the bow, toward the big USE cruisers. "At least, with their speed and their guns, they should be safe."

The admiral merely motioned Adriaen toward the waiting signalman. Maarten Tromp knew all too well how easily such confidence could turn out to be wrong.

"Commander Cantrell, Captain Simonszoon has sent a reply to your fuel inquiry."

Well, about bloody time, Eddie huffed silently while he maintained an impassive exterior. Simonszoon's delay wasn't a good sign. If he'd been running his ship right, he should have known how much coal he had left in the bunker. He shouldn't have had to send someone below decks to get a count. "What's his reply?"

"*Resolve* has twenty percent fuel remaining."

It was not terribly surprising that the down-time commander had burned through so much coal. Conserving fast-consumables other than powder and shot could be tricky to gauge, since the depletion accrued as a constant trickle rather than in a few dramatic gulps. But it was damned inconvenient, given the kind of maneuvers the cruisers might have to perform in order to keep the main Spanish fleet from turning about and closing in.

Which might not prove to be as easy a tactical objective as it sounded. As soon as the *Amelia* turned her prow south by southwest, and the jachts began hurrying to form a flying wedge at the head of the formation, the western progress of the main Spanish fleet had slowed noticeably. And although he wanted to keep the pressure on them, Eddie did not dare call on Simonszoon to keep her steam up, or even to make reasonable headway with the favorable wind. Because when the time came to turn and flee, that new heading would put the cruisers in a close reach. If the two big ships were going to get meaningful distance from the smaller *pataches* and jachts of the western Spanish fleet, they'd need to have steam left to make it happen. Possibly more steam than *Resolve* could raise.

Which meant that only *Intrepid* could afford to edge forward and keep the Spanish galleons somewhat at bay. "Svantner, half reef the sails."

"Sir?" asked the startled Swede.

"You heard me, Svantner. We can't afford to move too far ahead of *Resolve*. And she can't afford to move ahead at all."

Ove Gjedde's voice was quiet, ominous. "They will turn upon us, then."

Eddie shrugged. "Captain, with all due respect, they're starting to turn on us already. Chasing them isn't what will buy us most of the time we need. It's the range of our deck guns. Look at the enemy formation. Their admiral is smart enough to be approaching on a broad front."

"But none too quickly, even so," Svantner offered. "They won't engage us until an hour before dusk."

"Yes," Eddie agreed, "and that's just what they want. They're scared of our eight-inch rifles, but even if they weren't, they won't want to arrive at their useful ranges much before dark. If they do, our main-battery carronades will tear them to pieces at five to six hundred yards."

"But then how will they fire on us, sir? It will be dark for all of us."

"Yeah, but there are lots of them and only two of us. And luck is on the side with the most hulls in the water."

Gjedde nodded. "And see what they are beginning to do. The fore-and-aft rigged ships are tacking in irregularly."

Eddie nodded. "Tactically, we up-timers call that a 'serpentine' approach. Usually used to describe infantry movement, but it holds here, too."

"It does indeed." Gjedde exhaled slowly. "It will be hard for our gunners to predict their turns and adjust in time."

"It will be damned near impossible. Which is why we're going to ignore them for now and go after the galleons as soon as they come within thirteen hundred yards."

"So far?" Svantner murmured.

"Yes. If they don't feel safe edging closer to us now, they'll be too far away to trouble us when the light is failing. We can hit them occasionally at thirteen hundred yards, which is all we need to do to maintain their fear of our firepower. And yes, Svantner, I think Dirck Simonszoon has learned his marksmanship lessons pretty well today."

Gjedde nodded. "So you are not as interested in sinking them as terrifying them."

"That's the idea. Now, let's get some firing solutions and go hunting."

The Spanish lost a galleon and a galleoncete before they realized that the USE cruisers were pointedly ignoring the more rapidly closing light vessels. But the Spanish admiral—*one hell of a competent and ballsy guy,* Eddie had to admit—did not react as expected. After about a quarter hour of signaling, his larger ships continued to advance, but slowly, maintaining a wide arc that could easily turn into a butterfly net. True, the cruisers would logically be able to tear right through that net, but if they weren't careful, even a small snag might allow more yachts and *pataches* to swarm around them.

Gjedde frowned mightily at the distant, but still approaching galleons. "He gives us big targets at range, to keep us from turning our guns upon the closer and faster ones that will be able to close with us swiftly come darkness. Clearly, he believes the small ships may inflict considerable damage upon us."

Yeah, that, or he simply realizes he's got no choice, that the big ships won't last long enough to get in range. And anyhow, as long as he's stopped us in our tracks, and sees the rest of our fleet trying to break out to the south, he knows he's running us out of the battlespace. And that's probably what's most important to him. But in the meantime—"Well, let's not insult our Spanish host by refusing his *hors' d' oeuvres.* Do we have a firing solution on the next galleon yet?"

Svantner called an inquiry down into the intraship, got a prompt answer. "Yes, and they've been tracking for a minute, sir."

"Very well. Standard nonexplosive rounds from both mounts. They may fire at will, and continue tracking."

A moment later, the two deck guns went off in such rapid succession that the overlapping shockwaves buffeted Eddie's clothes in two directions, whipsawing his trouser legs from one side of the compass to the other. Both shots geysered up the gray-green seawater, but less than twenty yards off-target.

"Load with explosive shell, watch the swells. Correct and fire at will."

"Aye, sir!"

Eddie watched the chief gunner lean over the rim of the pulpit attached to the side of Mount One's gun shield, stare down at the near risers and then bring down his hand sharply. Mount One's naval rifle blasted smoke outward in a long plume, leaping back against its recoil cylinders. Mount Two did the same a moment later—and, for the first time since the *Intrepid* had become operational, both rounds hit the target at the same time. The entire galleon shuddered to port. The first shell blew her bow into a ruin of strakes sticking up like the back of a skinned hedgehog. The second disappeared into her high quarterdeck, which, an eyeblink later, blew outward in all directions. Not much was left there, other than a partial skeleton of its framing timbers, silhouetted by an inferno raging where the officers' cabins used to be.

Resolve's guns spoke a few seconds later, and although both shots hit water not wood, Simonszoon's ability to work with his gunners was clearly improving. The two rounds bracketed the galleon he'd targeted and Eddie would have taken odds that if he didn't score a hit with the next pair, he would with the third.

As he watched his own gunners crank their pieces around to access the next proximal target, he crossed his arms, felt his stump tired and cramping in the prosthesis for the first time in weeks. *Okay, Mr. Spanish Admiral, if you're willing to put your galleons in range, we'll keep smacking them down. Until your faster ships get inside of five hundred yards, that is.*

Maarten Tromp watched smoke jet out of the steam-pinnace's funnel, and a second later, felt a tug in the deck beneath his feet. "Are we matching pace with the jachts, now?"

Adriaen Banckert nodded. "Yes, sir. They've reefed sails enough that we can keep formation with them."

Tromp looked starboard. *Gelderland*, also under tow, was abeam at three hundred yards. The jachts *Fortuin*, *Zuidsterre*, and *Pinas* were approximately three hundred yards ahead in a rough arrowhead pattern: a wedge to drive through the pirate ships now two miles ahead. Or so Tromp hoped.

He looked astern. The rest of the Dutch warships were making good speed, the wind having freshened and come into a friendly compass point. But they would not be able to add their weight to any engagement that the advance guard initiated for at least an hour.

Meanwhile, the enemy ships to the south had closed ranks, but probably not as much as they had wished. Having sprung their trap early, they had begun in a wide, dispersed arc. Now, closing ranks came at the expense of forward progress, and vice versa. Tromp could only hope that, despite their greater numbers, they were spread too far and too thin to resist the lance-point that he hoped his fleet would be.

"Admiral Tromp?" Willem van der Zaan's replacement, a fourteen-year-old former native of Recife improbably named Brod, arrived with a strip of paper: a communiqué from the ship's wireless.

"Who from, Brod?" asked Tromp.

"Commander Cantrell, sir. Answering your message."

Tromp nodded, watching Adriaen descend to the main deck to inspect the arms and armor of the ship's troops. It would be a miracle indeed if the slower Dutch ships managed to pass through their antagonists without repulsing at least one boarding attempt. "Read the message, Brod."

The lad complied. "Cantrell commanding *Intrepid* to Tromp commanding *Amelia*. Message begins. Now shifting fire to small vessels. Stop. Unable to estimate time remaining before disengagement. Stop. Cannot predict ETA at rendezvous point one. Stop. Sail for home and do not look back. Stop. Message ends."

Commander Eddie Cantrell was busy scanning and describing the new hulls for *Intrepid*'s growing target list, his runner scribbling furiously.

"Target seven. Currently bearing 284 on the compass rose. Range: 800 yards. Approximate speed: four knots. Type: thirty-foot *piragua* with single lateen sail. Armament: two swivel guns. Complement of twenty. Unusual feature: prow-mounted pole or boom.

"Target eight. Currently bearing 294 on the compass rose. Range: 950 yards. Approximate speed: five knots, making three knots headway with tacking. Type: Bermuda-style sloop. Armament: eight demi-culverins, four falconets. Complement of thirty-five.

"Target nine. Currently bearing—"

"Commander Cantrell!"

"Yes, Svantner?"

"Targets three and four have sheered off, given us a wide berth."

"Heading back for *Resolve*?"

"That or looking to get behind us, sir."

"Does sub-battery three have them in range?"

"Aye, sir!"

"The gun chief may fire his carronades both with my compliments and expectations of success."

"Yes, sir!"

Gjedde had been giving the sail handlers sharp, fast orders. He now looked up in a lull as the *Intrepid* came back before the wind, steadying so that the main batteries would have a stable platform from which to fire. "They are playing with us, you know."

"Of course they are. But they're paying, too." It was true enough. After sinking four galleons outright and damaging another seven, the two cruisers' guns had turned upon the fore-and-aft rigged vessels and, since doing so, had sunk three and damaged two. Being small—everything from twenty-gun Dutch jachts that had been cut down to follow the sleek lines that pirates preferred, to ten-man *piraguas*—many of the ships were as lightly built as they were nimble. The smaller ones often capsized after a single hit because the shells from the rifles over-penetrated, punching through the strakes on one side, and blasting out a spray of hull chunks as they exited the other.

Gjedde nodded. "Yes. But without our steam, they are more maneuverable, may exploit more points of the wind. We will not be able to keep the water between ourselves and the *Resolve* clear much longer."

"That's why I sent Dirck instructions to come about and start heading after the main van."

"So soon?" Svantner stared nervously at the smaller ships swarming and circling toward their flanks like distant sharks. They stayed just outside the six hundred yard limit, which was where the spread and accuracy of the carronades could begin to reasonably cope with the speed and evasive tacking of the small boats.

"Yeah," Eddie sighed as the portside carronades spoke. "He's got to get going now." Target four—a small *patache*—skipped ahead of four balls that plunged into the sea behind her like a line of foam-spurting exclamation marks. The little ship heeled over and reopened the range to the *Intrepid*. "We've held them here for two hours and by the time Simonszoon gets enough wind in his sails to make a good pace, it'll be the better part of a third. And he doesn't have enough coal to steam away. He may need that later to close with the main van, or help them out if that southern pirate fleet manages to jam them up. Either way, he's got to rely more on the wind than we do, a lot more, which means he's got to get going sooner."

"Which leaves us on our own," Gjedde said quietly.

Eddie didn't respond. He was afraid that instead of calmly acknowledging the threat implicit in that situation, he'd start shouting: *Well, of course we'll be on our own! And why is that? Because some down-timer hot-shot captain got a little too steam happy, that's why!*

But this was no time to publicly vent his feelings. He wasn't really being fair to Simonszoon, anyway. The Dutch captain—born, bred and raised in the seventeenth century—was having to learn lessons under fire that any up-time teenage kid had learned by the time he got a driver's license. *Always keep an eye on the gas gauge, stupe.* You didn't run out of wind the same way you ran out of fuel.

Still, unfair or not, the situation *was* aggravating. Since they had to stay here another hour or so to cover the *Resolve's* withdrawal, could they expect the privateer ships to get bolder? *Unquestionably.* And if they hadn't extricated themselves by dusk, would this fine naval engagement devolve into a confused brawl? *Absolutely.* Would blunders occur right and left? *Assuredly.* Was this all to the advantage of the outgunned and usually outmaneuvered foe? *That's why the enemy is doing it.*

A mechanical flaw or trick of fate only needed to strike them once, only needed to cause them to stagger, to stumble. Because if they did, these little jackals would be on them in a minute with cannons, cutlasses or whatever else might work.

But all Eddie said was, "I share your reservations, Captain Gjedde. But do you see any other reasonable options?"

Gjedde watched the ship's troops—several dozen of which were Wild Geese—mounting the mitrailleuses and immense "Big Shot" scatter guns on the four heavy-weapon mounts, one located at each quarter of the ship. "No," he answered. "But I recommend that we bring the regular ship's troops on deck. And keep the Wild Geese below, as a reserve."

Eddie nodded to Svantner to comply, who had just received a slip of paper from the runner. "I will muster the regular troops at once, Commander. And sir, a reply from Captain Simonszoon."

"Read it."

"From *Resolve* to *Intrepid*. Message starts. D. Simonszoon hereby relinquishes local command to E. Cantrell. Stop. E. Cantrell is, by my command authority, and if acceptable to Captain Gjedde, hereby brevetted to post-captain. Stop. Apologies and bitter regrets that *Resolve* must withdraw before her sister ship. Stop. Shall not rest easy until we see your lights closing on our stern. Stop. Message ends."

Eddie glanced at Gjedde. Whose lips seemed to crack as he smiled faintly. "Well, are you going to reply—Captain?"

Eddie sighed. He'd always thought ascending to that proud rank and title, even as a temporary brevet, would be an event he savored. But right now, he just wanted to get the hell out of the situation that had caused it. "Runner, send this reply. We'll be right behind you. Protect the rest of the fleet. See you in Oranjestad."

Or, added Eddie silently as the runner disappeared down the bridge stairs, *I'll see you in the next life.*

Chapter 52

The steam pinnace that had towed the *Gelderland* into the fray had barely cast off when a barca-longa crewed by pirates-become-privateers heeled over toward her, firing swivel guns. Several of the Dutchman's crew went down as she labored back through what had been, until she turned, following seas.

"Adriaen," Tromp shouted, "do we have grape loaded?"

"In three of the starboard guns."

"Excellent. Fire at that barca-longa. We need to protect our tugs." Tromp started counting down the seconds he had left to make up his mind about *Amelia*'s next course change, which was largely based upon how long it would take for his gun deck to send a load of moaning grapeshot at the privateer. From what he could make of the swirling hulls in front of him, two of his jachts—the *Zuidsterre* and the *Pinas*—had drawn at least six of the enemy ships to them. Too eager to wait to distribute themselves more evenly among the approaching Dutch ships, the raiders had pounced with the blood-eagerness of their kind. In consequence, they had weakened this part of the net they were trying to cast before the Dutch van.

Amelia's three starboard guns spoke, most of the grape falling short, kicking up a fuming lane across the swells. But the end of that lane rode right up over the low-gunwaled side of the barca-longa and mauled men, mast, and canvas alike. The stricken boat swerved away from *Amelia* and the steam pinnace.

But Tromp hardly noticed that. Only three hundred yards ahead, the *Zuidsterre* had managed to slip out between a pair of small *pataches* and was no longer enmeshed with the enemy. But *Pinas* was pinned in the middle of a triangle of their hulls, taking what modest pounding their batteries could deliver.

Tromp saw her crew falling aside among the smoke and splinters and resolved that her sacrifice should prove to be the means of their escape. "Adriaen!"

"Sir?"

"Do you see the gap between the sloop and *patache* hemming in *Pinas*?"

"Yes, sir."

"Crowd sail and make for it, best speed. And double-charge both batteries. We are going to open a wide hole for the rest of our fleet."

"Sir, Captain Gerritsz signals from *Gelderland* that he is making for the western edge of that melee. We might come under his guns, if we follow the course you order."

"Then signal Hans to either hold his fire or be damned careful with it. We've got to break these ships. The wind is failing us, so we can't wait on a careful duel while their fore-and-aft riggers dance around us. This group has been greedy for our blood and has trapped themselves. We must capitalize on that. So, when you're done warning Gerritsz, signal the rest of the warships to converge here. This is where we are going to break through."

Or die trying, Tromp amended.

At eighty yards, the heavily modified ex-Dutch jacht pulled hard over to starboard, bringing her portside battery to bear on *Intrepid.*

"Mount Two has a firing solution," cried Svantner.

"Fire!" yelled Eddie over his shoulder, not bothering with the intraship relays.

The two ships traded shots simultaneously. The eight guns of the privateer made a broad, throaty blast, but the gunners had waited a moment too long as the jacht recovered from her turn, rolling slightly above level. Their balls whizzed overhead, one putting a hole in the foremain sail, the other clipping the mainmast's spencer mast clean off. The spencer's foldable sail tumbled, fluttering, into the dark like a half-spined pterodactyl with one shattered wing.

The eight-inch naval rifle repaid the privateer by driving an explosive shell into her, amidships. The shell didn't go off until it was well inside the light-hulled vessel, blowing out a wide spray of wood, cannons, bodies, and dunnage into the failing light. As the smoke cleared, a strange, guttural growling rose up. It was the water rushing into the savage bite that had been taken out of the jacht's side, and which stretched slightly below the waterline. The ship began to roll in that direction as the risers lapped into her greedily.

"Commander," snapped Gjedde, "*patache* coming up from the port quarter. At sixty yards."

Damn it. The ones who had swept wide around *Intrepid* were now coming out of the near-darkness to her east, easily finding and steering for the big USE ship's silhouette against the increasingly cloudy western horizon. "Anything else closing?"

"Not at the moment." Gjedde's tone put a discernibly dark emphasis on "at the moment."

"Then Captain, if you would be so kind, send the order to fire all, portside battery, when she's abeam."

Gjedde nodded, leaned toward the intraship comms tube.

For the first time in twenty minutes, no one was asking for orders, which allowed Eddie to take in the bigger picture. Up on the starboard bow position, the mitrailleuse was firing athwart the rays of the setting sun, its rounds chasing after a *piragua* that had ventured inside one hundred yards range and was now hurriedly rowing back out. Just behind the mitrailleuse, near the forward companionway, a junior lieutenant of the Wild Geese was hunched down on weather deck, alert-eyed and waiting for orders to bring up the forty or so of his men whom Eddie had put in reserve as an anti-boarding fire-brigade. Their training, experience, and armament—double-barreled musketoons and pepperbox revolvers—were a final insurance against what the pirates-turned-privateers obviously wanted to achieve: a run in under the effective lower arc of *Intrepid*'s guns, and then, to board. Normally unthinkable, the dying light, massed and maneuverable opponents, and isolation had combined to make it a distressingly reasonable possibility.

The majority of the ship's troops—German and Swedish

musketeers—were already on the weather deck, stalking along the gunwales, watching. Most of their attention was directed into the darkness behind the *Intrepid*'s stern, where dusk had already pulled all the light away from the eastern horizon. That was the direction from which small privateers, and a few Spaniards, too, had been trying to surprise them, running dark. Several had almost chased in under the arc of the steamship's guns.

The *patache* that had approached from the port quarter was the boldest of this group of ships that increasingly tested and baited *Intrepid*'s gunners as the sun's rays ceased to glint off the swells of the wide seas. However, at sixty yards range, the Spaniard's sails still caught a good amount of the dying light and the cries of her gun crews told Gjedde that they were preparing to fire. He did not give them the chance. "Portside battery, fire all!" the Norwegian cried.

The volley had a few trailing discharges. Probably the forward guns were a second late, being muscled into rearward angles to fire before the enemy ship drew fully abreast of them. Of the fourteen regular eight-inch projectiles, five struck along the hull of the ship, which quite literally came apart. There was no dramatic explosion or burst of flames. The tremendous overlapping force of those hits—along with several more that ripped through masts, sails, and rigging—simply shattered the frame of the ship. The strakes and deck-planks split even where they had not been hit: the shock waves, traveling through the wood from two opposed directions, met and tore them apart. The ship rolled even as its keel started groaning; she was at beam-ends within twenty seconds.

Gjedde's voice was anything but elated. "Our carronades were at minimum elevation, resting on their bases. Because so many of their ships sit so low upon the water, we will be fortunate to put any shot on the smallest of them if they reach twenty yards."

Eddie nodded. "That is undeniably true, Captain." The mitrailleuse at the starboard bow was once again stuttering into the setting sun. A sloop that had approached to one hundred yards listed, taking water as the high-velocity .50 caliber bullets punched a trail of splinter-edged holes in her hull and deck.

Svantner was standing just over Gjedde's shoulder. "Shall I ask if the chief has raised enough steam, yet?"

Eddie shrugged. "Might as well."

"You do not think that this might be a wise time to withdraw?" Gjedde asked with one silver-white eyebrow raised.

Eddie sighed. "Oh, I think it would be a great time—Mount One! Jacht inbound on port bow! Acquire solution and fire!—but we can't withdraw yet." When Gjedde's other cloudlike eyebrow rose to join the first, Eddie handed him the note that the runner had pushed into his palm just before the modified Dutch jacht had made its starboard approach. Eddie recited it from memory. "*Amelia* to *Intrepid*. Message begins. Winds from east weaker and less favorable. Stop. Neither side possesses wind gauge. Stop. Combat continues. Stop. Uncertain if we will break free before night falls. Stop. *Resolve* will not arrive in time to accelerate outcome. Stop. Need an additional hour to secure escape. Stop. The fleet salutes you and your heroic crew. Stop. Tromp, commanding *Amelia*. Message ends."

Svantner swallowed. His eyes were much larger than they had been before Eddie had started reading the message. Gjedde simply looked off into the approaching dark. "How long ago was that sent?"

Eddie shrugged. "About twenty-five minutes ago. In thirty more, we can show these jackals our tail. But until then, we must hold this patch of water. If they are allowed to start southward any sooner, they could catch the rest of our fleet during the early hours, or sometime tomorrow. Between the two Spanish vans, they could keep our conventional ships tangled up long enough to inflict damage to the supply ships and transports, or even our warships. And then we'd no longer be a force they'd fear."

Gjedde nodded. "Within months, we'd see their sails approaching St. Eustatia."

"Exactly. So we have to keep that from happening." Eddie looked to where the sun was finally setting. "Meaning that we have to pin them in place, have to stay here for another thirty minutes."

Gjedde looked down into the lightless depths. "Let us just hope that duty does not mean that we shall stay here permanently."

The next ten minutes were unusually calm, as though the Spanish and their privateer allies had heard the resolute words and tones of the *Intrepid*'s command crew and had slunk away from any further battle with so determined an adversary.

Eddie conceded that that had been a nice fantasy, but he knew that the Spanish weren't daunted by their adversaries' courage. No, they were simply waiting for the arrival of their most decisive ally:

nightfall. And once the sun had fallen beneath the far western waters, the enemy ships made their own mortal resolve quite clear.

They were not brash about resuming their attack but began circling in closer slowly. Like nocturnal sharks cautiously approaching a wounded killer whale, they could smell the blood, but knew that the immense predator still had teeth which could rip them open if they were incautious. And so, just as Eddie gave orders to douse all lights on *Intrepid*'s decks and in her cabins, the privateer and Spanish boats began probing at the rapidly shrinking edge of visibility. Hulls flashed here and there, but were gone before a gun could be trained upon them. And as the final hazy, gray-and-salmon smudge of sun-lit cloud bottoms also shrank down behind the arc of the wide world, they came closer and closer still.

The sound of sails luffing as the ships tacked to and fro became the typical first warning of their direct approaches. Three piraguas swept in from the north, small lights flickering along their lengths. A moment later those lights were arcing through the air toward *Intrepid*: flaming arrows, most of which sunk into the side of the big ship, guttering. But the oil-soaked rags affixed behind their points quickly flared again.

Svantner almost laughed. "Do they mean to burn us?"

"No," Eddie said, restraining himself from snapping at the lieutenant. "They mean to mark us. As a target that they can all see. Get the ship's troops to douse those damn arrows, and prepare to deal with more. Captain Gjedde, we'd best find the wind and give the Spanish a more lively target to chase until we break off and run."

Gjedde looked aloft. "Admiral Tromp isn't the only one whose breezes have weakened." And it was true enough: *Intrepid*'s canvas was either lank or luffing, no matter how wind-master Gjedde turned her. "The Spanish have lighter ships with more canvas than hull. They'll be slowed, too, but less so than us. And their piraguas move as much by oar as sail."

"Well, get me what speed you can, in any direction but west."

"That risks collision."

Eddie shrugged. "Standing still makes us an easy target. We'll have to take our chances. At least they are small boats."

Svantner leaned over from working with the helmsman as they tried to find a point of wind that would give them some headway. "True, but if we hit a *patache* or jacht, we could be severely damaged, start taking water."

"Which is why we have pumps. Get me a little more speed, no matter how you do it." More arrows came out of the night, this time from off the port beam. Several found their way up into the sails, but the heavy, fluttering canvas knocked them aside. This time. A crackling of German muskets reached back along the fiery paths that the arrows had followed. If the ragged volley hit anything, there was no sight or sound to indicate it.

As men leaned over the side to pour water and vinegar mixtures down upon the arrows still burning against *Intrepid*'s dark hull, muskets flared in the darkness about seventy yards off the port bow. One of the fire-control party flopped to the deck with a cry, a dark stain spreading across his shirt from the vicinity of his breastbone.

The runner next to Eddie turned wondering eyes into the dark as more German rifles fired at where the enemy muskets had so momentarily bloomed. "How did they see to shoot at our men?" he asked.

Eddie leaned against the railing of the bridge, taking the weight off his cramping stump. "Probably saw a shadow in front of or at the edge of the light from the arrows. They fired at the movement. Enough muskets, and a little luck—"

"*Patache*, bearing on our port bow," came a cry for the foretop.

Eddie swung in that direction and saw the enemy ship approaching, her sails luffing as she struggled to maintain headway against the shifting wind. Which bought Eddie the time he needed. "Svantner, is the port battery reloaded?"

"Yes, sir."

"Very well. If that *patache* comes alongside, fire the first half of that battery. Mount One," he directed into the speaking tube, "do you have a shot?"

"Barely, sir," replied a tinny, indistinct voice that would have been drowned out had any of *Intrepid*'s guns been active at that moment, "and only the quarterdeck."

"That's good enough. Lay open sights upon her and fire as soon as you can!"

"Yes, sir!"

The mizzen lookout cried about more boats approaching from the port quarter. "How are they coordinating this?" Svantner yelped.

"They're not. But when they see the silhouettes of one of their own approaching us, others try to join in, to swarm us. We can't shoot in all directions at once." *But we're sure as hell going to try.* "Lookout, what manner of boats on the port quarter?"

"Sloops, sir," came the voice from aloft.

"Very well. Mr. Svantner, warn the port quarter mitrailleuse that it looks like they'll finally get some action, too."

"Aye, sir," Svantner said with a nod, just as Mount One roared. Eddie swung around in time to see the eight-inch shell plunge into the low poop deck of the *patache* and planks fly up, the mizzenmast having been sliced through an instant beforehand. Severed only five feet above the weather deck, the mast was blown aside so forcefully that she ripped clean out of her stays.

But the wounded *patache* kept coming. Boarders, Spanish troops judging from their glinting beetlelike morions, were clustered in her bows. "The Big Shot on the forward swivel: is she ready?" Eddie cried at Svantner.

"Aye, sir. They're drawing a bead now. Fire at ten yards?"

"Five!" Eddie corrected as the rear mitrailleuse began chattering, presumably at the sloops drawing close to the port quarter. And from the sound of it, that gun crew might burn through their current cassette of ammunition before dissuading the enemy ships from closing. "Aft port battery!" Eddie howled into the speaking tube.

The battery chief's reply came after a moment. The background furor almost drowned it out. "Yes, sir?"

"Your two fastest crews: have them swap out their current shells for canister shot."

"Canister shot, sir? That hasn't tested too well."

"I'm aware. We'll give it a try at point-blank range, Chief. The two sloops approaching from astern are your targets. Once they're within forty yards, fire at your discretion."

"Aye, aye, sir!" The battery chief sounded strangely delighted. Perhaps, being below decks, he didn't have a complete appreciation of just how close the Spanish sharks were circling.

The report from the forward swivel sounded like a shotgun amplified by a bull-horn. Most of the first three ranks of morion-helmeted boarders on the approaching *patache* went down or over its bows, cries and splashes lost in the dark and ridden under her keel. The Big Shot's crew struggled to get another charge into their weapon, did so, fired just as some of the waiting boarders did, dropping one of that crew.

Damn it. "Gallagher!" Eddie shouted at the junior lieutenant of the Wild Geese who had remained in his motionless crouch throughout the entirety of the battle thus far. "Give me a squad at the port bow, on the double!"

As German musketeers began clustering to contest the boarders as well, the after-half of the port battery roared, the carronades' fiery tongues briefly illuminating the sloop that received the majority of their fury. Although only one of the shells hit, the canister-shot stripped away the vessel's sails as if they had been snatched up in a tornado. A dozen of her boarders and crew sprawled across the narrow deck with ghastly, blood-spraying wounds from the lime-sized balls. Then, the flaring muzzles of the *Intrepid* dark once again, there was only the ruined outline of the sloop and the moan of her wounded.

Well, that decides it. "Svantner, pass the word to all batteries. When next they reload, all odd-numbered guns are to reload with canister-shot. It is to be reserved for use on targets within fifty yards."

"Aye, aye, Commander." As Svantner passed the word, a sustained spatter of muskets up near the bow was joined by the rippling coughs of the Wild Geese's musketoons. Grenades went between the ships, without many casualties being inflicted on either side. The *patache*, with most of its crew dead and whipstaff in splinters, was adrift when she bumped her bow against *Intrepid* with a final desultory kiss. The Spaniard swung away from the light impact. "Looks like we'll pass the *patache*, sir. She's got no grapples on us."

"Very well, but I want deckhands with hatchets out to cut any they might land over our stanchions. And do we have those burning arrows put out?"

"Yes, sir, but we've taken a few more. Working to douse them, now, sir."

"Work quickly. I'm going to call for steam in a few minutes and I'd like to be dark when we do it, not surrounded by another swarm of these damn small boats. They're getting too close for—"

Eddie could not distinguish all the cries that started up, almost simultaneously. There were two more contacts off the starboard bow: a piragua and a barca-longa, both sizable and loaded with boarders who did not appear to be Spanish, let alone part of any civilized army in or out of Christendom. At the same time, the second sloop that had been approaching the port quarter, and which had presumably withdrawn after seeing what happened to her sister ship, had swerved in close to the still-reloading portside after-battery. And, last, appearing from behind the shadow of the almost derelict *patache*, came a lateen-rigged pinnace, loaded with Spaniards.

Eddie gave the orders he could. *All swivels and mitrailleuses should engage all targets upon which they could bear. Raise steam. Ready the rest of the Wild Geese.* But then events took over and finally, the well-coordinated battle fought by the *Intrepid* devolved into a series of desperate brawls. The sloop fired her sakers and demi-culverins at the after-battery that had savaged her sister ship. Balls bounced off *Intrepid*'s hull timbers, but several smaller ones from the pirate's swivels played across the gun crews. The two carronades that had been reloaded replied, one landing a solid shell amidships. The sloop heeled away from the threat of further fire.

At the port bow, the boarders from the pinnace threw grapples from a distance of five yards, as did a few doggedly courageous survivors aboard the *patache* that was falling behind, still adrift. The ship's troops and Wild Geese aimed their fire down into the ferocious faces lining those decks, who returned the deadly compliment at the defenders some six-feet over their heads.

As that firefight raged and grenades started flying between the bows of the two ships, the starboard bow mitrailleuse yelled a report quickly down the speaking tube. But Eddie, distracted, missed the words which rolled out of the metal horn and which were clotted in a thick Swedish accent. "What?" Eddie asked.

His runner tugged his sleeve. "He said 'petard,' sir. And 'boom.'"

For one sliver of a second, Eddie froze, then ordered his runner forward to call up another squad of Wild Geese, this time to the starboard bow. The boy leaped down to the busy weather deck and began slaloming his way around deckhands and ship's troops to deliver the summons.

"What is the matter?" Gjedde asked.

"Spar torpedo. Like the ones you Danes used against our ironclads last year. We've got to make sure they don't—"

The starboard side mitrailleuse stuttered its way through one of its cassettes, riddling the new torpedo-armed piragua with bullets. Thank God. "Svantner, call for full steam. We're going to get out of here as soon as—"

But as the second ship off the starboard bow, the overpopulated barca-longa, drew closer, the mitrailleuse did not resume speaking. Eddie looked in the direction of the weapon's mount, saw the loader struggling to get the new ammunition cassette into the weapon, then begin struggling to get it out. It was clearly jammed, and the first grapple lines were already coming over the starboard bow.

And a new squad of Wild Geese had not yet risen up to reinforce that weapons mount. Eddie scanned, saw the commander of the Irish mercenaries waiting for just such an order, then sought his runner—and saw the young fellow, writhing in pain, just aft of the bows. Apparently, one of the few Spanish grenades that had cleared the bedroll-lined stanchions had put some fragments into the poor lad, who was leaving a spattering of blood to either side as he rocked to and fro, clutching his left thigh.

Damn it. Eddie spun on his real leg to look for Svantner—who was ringing up the steam and directing the helmsman. He turned quickly toward Gjedde, who was already staring at him. The Dane moved as if to head to the bows himself. "I shall take care—"

"No, Captain. You keep piloting the ship. I'll be back soon."

Gjedde winced, but nodded as Eddie pounded down the bridge stairs and limp-loped toward the starboard bow, shouting as he went. "Gallagher! Lieutenant Gallagher!"

He had closed half the distance before the young, anxious Irishman waiting at the companionway heard. "Sir?"

"Starboard weapons mount! Boarders!"

Gallagher turned, saw the frenzied activity in that direction, ducked his head into the companionway and started yelling orders.

By which time, Eddie was past him. Clumping up the stairs to the low fo'c'sle, he saw the last of the mitrailleuse's crew gunned down by a volley of pirate pistols and blunderbusses. The same fate had befallen most of the German musketeers, who, having fired their last charges, drew swords as Eddie came amongst them.

"Captain, what are you—?"

"Stand aside. Send the Wild Geese up toward me as soon as they arrive." Eddie stepped up into the mount, pushing aside the bodies of the mitrailleuse's slain crew.

Two grapples were already hooked over the gunwale of the reinforced pulpit in which the weapon was situated. Two Jacob's ladders had been hooked alongside them. Boarders were on their way up. But they weren't the immediate worry.

Eddie had read, and had since seen evidence, that the best marksmen in the Caribbean were not the soldiers of any nation, but pirates. Prizing unusually long French rifles, many pirate crews relied mostly on musketry to take ships, being both so accurate and able to mount so withering a hail of fire, that many merchantmen dared not handle sails or man a tiller. So they surrendered their ship, and usually lived or were, at worst, ransomed. Which, by logical deduction, made the most dangerous men in the barca-longa the musketeers who had wrought such death among the mitrailleuse's crew and nearby ship's troops.

Eddie unholstered Ed Piazza's HP-35, leaned over the heavy-timbered pulpit of the weapon position and, both hands on the pistol's grip, began unloading its thirteen-round magazine down among the pirate-crowded thwarts of the barca-longa.

Bodies started falling, men cursing. Not more than half of Eddie's shots were hits, and less than half of those were lethal or even extremely serious. But the sudden and unexpected volume of fire from so strange-sounding a weapon—each report as sharp and spiteful as a cracking whip made of lightning—almost froze the pirates. In the very next second, they were diving for cover as they became aware of the murderous swath the weapon was cutting among their crew.

Eddie fished in his ammo pouch for the next magazine as he pressed the magazine release. The old box slipped out just in time for him to run the next one up and into the handle—and the first pirate face appeared over the gunwale.

Fortunately, it wasn't a face alone that could kill him—*although this one is damned near ugly enough!*—but rather, the weapon-filled hands that were soon to follow it. Eddie thumbed the slide-lock, brought up the pistol as the slide rammed forward and primed it, and fired twice into that ferocious, nearly animalistic face. At a range of two feet.

Eddie did not see the effect of the bullets. The weapon bucked and the face disappeared. He leaned back out over the pulpit-mount to unload the rest of his second magazine down into the barca-longa—and discovered just how combat-hardened and reactive pirate crews were.

Had he not stumbled a bit on his weakening left leg, the

first volley of counter-fire from the pirate musketeers below him would probably have been lethal, or at least debilitating. As it was, one ball came close enough to audibly whisper past his right ear. Tempted to duck down, Eddie forced himself to assess the scene in the boat: no other readied pieces. The rest of the pirates were either reloading or getting on the Jacob's ladders to board.

Eddie steadied the HP-35 with both hands, tracked along the men who were reloading the muskets and two-tapped each one of them. Again, after the first two seconds, pirates were diving in every direction for cover. And just as the HP-35's slide came back and stayed back, two pairs of grimy hands came up over the gunwale, one holding a long-wicked looking life.

Eddie gulped, ejected the second magazine, fished around for the third one. He took a quick step back—

—and ran into buff-coated Lieutenant Gallagher. "We'll take it from here, if't please you, Commander."

Eddie nodded as two other Wild Geese pushed past and slashed at the grimy hands with their sabers. Shrieks of agony plummeted toward the water as the Irish mercenaries drew their pepperboxes and, hugging low to the rim of the weapon-mount, sent their deadly waves of fire down into the barca-longa. Cries rose up in three different languages to back oars and get the hell away from the steamship.

Eddie half stumbled down the stairs to the main deck, where Svantner was running toward him, a hand extended in concern. Eddie waved it off. "That runner—that boy—he needs help. He was—"

"Already attended to, sir. And you? Are you unhurt."

"Yes, damn it. Now stand still for a second and report. Are we at full steam?"

"Yes, sir. We should be able to pull away and—"

Looking over Svantner's right shoulder, scanning to see how his ship was doing, Eddie caught sight of the rear end of a piragua disappearing beneath the arc of the starboard quarter gunwale, heard the Big Shot swivel gun covering that section of the ship fire. Bodies splashed in the water, but not all of them seemed to have been hit by the immense gun. It looked like some of the piragua's crew had jumped in. And Eddie realized: the piraguas were too low to the water to have any chance of putting boarders on *Intrepid*'s decks. Which meant, if they closed in this far, and their crews were jumping out—

"Spar torpedo! Sink that *piragua*! Any gun that can bear! Sink—!"

Eddie, running stiffly in that direction as he shouted the warning, heard a dull *th-tunk*, as if a spear or hook had embedded itself in the hull timbers. The piragua, rowed at speed, had probably lodged a prow-spike into *Intrepid*. "Shoot the torped—the petard!" Eddie changed in mid-sentence, realizing that older word would be more immediately understood. "Or shoot the boom it's on! Just shoot—!"

The Big Shot spoke again, but its discharge was drowned out by a roar that shook the deck out from under Eddie's feet and sent part of the quarterdeck's stanchion-and-bedroll sides flying up among the mizzen sheets. The hazard bell began ringing in engineering and as Eddie picked himself up off the deck, he couldn't be sure if he was staggering or *Intrepid* was listing.

An iron hand grasped his arm, steadied him. Eddie looked round: Gjedde. "Captain. Are we—?"

"I know nothing more than you. Go to the bridge. I will see. You, sailor! Help the captain to his post. Svantner, do we still have steam?"

"No, sir."

"Why?" yelled Eddie, trying not to sound like he was watching his child, his creation, die beneath his feet. Which was exactly what he was in terror of.

"I do not know, sir. No comms from Engineering."

Damn it. The piragua had hit back by the engines. "Svantner, get below. I'll see to guiding the pilot, but we've got to get solid information about our engines. If we can't steam out of here—"

Svantner nodded his understanding of the mortal consequences of that scenario and was then sliding down the handrails of the companionway into the darkness of the lower decks.

Gjedde reappeared from back near the transom, scanning the near waters for the outline of any approaching ships. "Captain Cantrell, it is as you surmised. We were struck by a spar torpedo."

"Damage?" Eddie found he couldn't breathe, watching Gjedde as he chewed his lower lip.

"Less than I expected, frankly," the Norwegian answered. "I cannot tell if it was because of the inferiority of their bomb— it was simply a petard, I think—or the stoutness of *Intrepid*'s timbers. But other than some shattered strakes, the hull held up remarkably well."

"And for that, you may thank the ship's design," added Svantner, who came bounding breathlessly back up to the weather deck. Gjedde frowned.

Eddie smiled explained. "He means the citadel design: the armor housing we put around the engine and boiler."

Svantner, panting and doubled over, nodded weakly. "Aye, sir. Because of the inner armoring, the hull could not compress too much at that point, and that second layer, so to speak, made any spalling or shattering of the internal timbers almost impossible."

"So the engines—?"

"Are fine, Captain Cantrell. The chief engineer shut them down because he wanted to ease the pressure, just in case any damage had been done to the rivets, seams, or tubes. He brought the steam down to diagnostic levels and is pleased to report all normal and that it shall be restored within the minute. As far as the hull damage is concerned, the pumps are keeping well ahead of the leaks coming in through the seams that the explosion sprung." A gout of new smoke erupted from the *Intrepid*'s stack as if to punctuate the engines' readiness with an exclamation mark. "Orders, sir?" Svantner asked with a smile.

"As if you need to ask!" Eddie said. "Bring her to south by southwest and let's get the hell out of here—full steam ahead."

Part Nine

January 1636

The unity and married calm of states

Chapter 53

The coast of eastern Texas

Larry Quinn raised his hand and pointed to a darker skein of water on the left side of the narrow inlet they were approaching. "There's the deeper water. Steer to that."

Karl Klemm nodded. "Will there be a countercurrent, Major Quinn?"

Larry shrugged. "I doubt it. The mouth of the Calcasieu shouldn't be putting a lot of water out into the Gulf."

Kleinbaum, a woodland and jungle scout who had come highly recommended from his time working for the Dutch in the jungles of the Pernambuco, stared backward from the bow. "We're going *into* the mouth of the Calcasieu? You said we were beaching east of it."

Larry didn't like his tone, but was willing to let it slide. Once. "That's *not* what I said, Sebastian. I said we'd look at the inlet and make a final call when we got here. Needed to look at the land, see if it has regular visits from the natives. Sure doesn't look like it."

"Yes? Well, I think it is unwise to move inland at all. We should stay on the coast, where we can move away more quickly if we encounter the cannibals."

Larry sighed but held his ready temper in check. "First, we have no proof that the Atakapas are cannibals or that they are in this area at all. Which I've repeated at least a dozen times in the past three days. And second, you've shared your thoughts on what we should do quite clearly already—three times on the way in. Any more, and I'd be tempted to construe that as disrespect for your commanding officer."

Kleinbaum stared at the approaching sands of the East Texas coast, slightly roseate in the setting sun. "You brought me along to provide you with my best assessment of the lands we are in," he muttered, his voice as stubborn and retracted as the hunched curve of his back.

"Yes," replied Larry. "But we're not on the land or anywhere near its flora, fauna, or inhabitants, yet. Unless you are telling me that your expertise starts from three miles off shore?"

Kleinbaum clearly did not want to respond, but knew he had to: he shook his head. "But going upriver always invites trouble—no matter where you are."

"Does it?" Larry countered quickly. "Kleinbaum, just so you know, I'm going up into the inlet a few dozen meters so that we'll have some depth in which we can anchor and sleep aboard. Yeah, it will be crowded, but we can scoot in a minute. Whereas if we pulled onto the beach on either side of the inlet, we'd have to haul the boat back into the surf before we could get away. Does that sound like a better idea to you?"

From behind, Larry could see Kleinbaum's jaw working angrily. "No, sir," he answered finally.

Quinn leaned back, raising his binoculars again. On either side of the narrow inlet that ultimately led to Calcasieu Lake, low sand-and-scree shores stretched straight and narrow into the vanishing-point distance of either horizon. Beyond them, low scrub brush and occasional stunted trees gave the land the appearance of having a youngster's tousled head of hair. Nothing foreboding. Hell, nothing much at all.

"Major Quinn," Karl said so quietly that he was almost inaudible over the surging growl of the Sportsman's engine, "I think I remember reading that the Atakapas have an extensive coastal range."

Leave it to Karl to read all the supplemental briefing materials. "That's correct."

"Then why did we start toward the Mermentau River before the *Courser* left Galveston Bay, sir? If something should go wrong— well, there aren't many of us to handle any unexpected problems."

"Karl, that was very tactfully put, but I'm not a particularly tactful person, so I'm going to answer your real question. Yes, this boat and its small crew will head up the Mermentau as soon as we reach it. Alone. Because even once the *Courser* joins us, her forces will be too far away to make much of a difference. Not unless we wait for them to paddle the ship's boats upriver with us. Which rather defeats the purpose of having a motorboat: to explore and make contact quickly. And to be able to leave quickly as well, if need be."

Karl swallowed; he glanced back at Wright and Vogel's lever-action rifles. "I understand, sir. But wouldn't the natives be more inclined to, er, diplomacy if they understood, from the start, that we had a strong force at our disposal?"

Quinn smiled ruefully. "You know, Karl, that was pretty much the first-contact philosophy throughout the colonization of the New World. And most of the time, it set exactly the wrong tone. Can we awe them? Sure. But there are two problems with that strategy. First, they are the masters of this country, not us. So if they want to stay unfound and unmet, they'd have no trouble doing so, particularly if we bring a company of troops to blunder around in the bush and the swamps that they grew up in.

"Second, if we do meet them, do we really want to awe them? Awe is the first cousin to fear, which has its roots in threat. If you consider the accounts of first contact in this part of the country, the smaller the contacting group, the more personal the interactions. You bring too large a group, and you look like invaders or a warchief with an escort. But if you come in smaller numbers, you look like explorers and are treated more as individuals, which is how friendships start." Quinn rubbed his close-cropped hair. "My ancestors spent two hundred years trying to intimidate and control the natives in the New World. And yeah, they got their way, but killed whole nations in the process. This time, knowing a little bit about the different tribes in advance, we're going to try a different approach."

Karl nodded. "This sounds most prudent—and ethical. Although even if they are our friends, that does not mean they will be willing to let us drill holes in their land."

No, thought Quinn, *it doesn't. Which could put one hell of a giant wrinkle in all our fine plans.* But all he said was, "Give it a little more throttle, Karl. Take us in."

Chapter 54

Santo Domingo, Hispaniola

Fadrique Álvarez de Toledo, Admiral of the Armada de Barlovento, hearing the sudden increase in gaiety in the villa's great-room beneath them, raised a glass of rioja toward his host, who sat opposite him at the table in the well-appointed study. "Happy New Year, Don de Viamonte. A fine party, worthy of the grandees of Madrid."

Juan Bitrian de Viamonte y Navarra, who was still flushed from the exertions of dancing the evening's first extended *rigaudon*, waved away the compliment. "First, the party is not so fine as you say, and you know it well. Second, if I am to be able to deflect your tiresome courtesies with good nature, we must agree to first names. And last, the party is not a half-worthy celebration of what you accomplished, my dear Admiral."

"What I accomplished?" Fadrique scoffed. "Now you mock me—Juan."

"I do not—Fadrique," responded the half-crippled captain-general with a warm and genuine smile. "Santo Domingo still stands today because of your triumph at the Battle of Vieques."

"The Battle of Vieques, as too many are styling it, was no victory," countered Fadrique. "It was at best, a stalemate. And we paid for it with eight galleons, two galleoncetes, and three *pataches* sunk or irreparable. All this while running away from a fleet we outnumbered, three ships to one, for almost three consecutive days. And you will note I do not include the losses among our 'privateers,' losses which numbered well over twenty hulls, when we include the actions to the south, where the Dutch escaped." He irritably sucked in a full-cheeked swig of the red wine, as he had not done since resolving to regain his fitness and the finer form of his youth. "Another few 'victories' such as the one off Vieques and we shall be done for, in the New World."

Juan shook his head. "You are wrong, Fadrique. Wrong in so many ways, I do not know where to begin enumerating them. Let us return to my first comment. Had your stratagems not repelled these so-called 'Allied forces,' they would have reached this city. And we have all heard what similar up-time naval rifles did to the fortifications at Hamburg last year. They were reduced to rubble in half an afternoon. Had that happened here, how many more ships would we have lost? How many thousands of men? How many slips in which we may build the ships with which we must fight this new menace? And, perhaps more importantly, how would we have fought a war against them in the Lesser Antilles when our next stronghold truly worthy of that label is Havana, far to the west? How could we have hoped to contest their further expansion, and ultimately, contain and suffocate them on the few islands they currently hold? No, my dear Fadrique, you may have lost ships, but you won the battle. Any outcome which did not end in the leveling of Santo Domingo is a strategic victory of the first order. And yours is the mind and will that produced it."

"Well, I—"

"I am not finished, Admiral!" Juan remonstrated histrionically, his color becoming more normal. "Since I have returned to the topic of lost ships, I concede that yes, you did lose many. But you presumed that from the outset, did you not? And many of those lost used to be piratical scourges that are no longer a worry to us, are they not? You need not answer. I know the rightness of my assertions. And what did you accomplish with those losses?" Juan leaned forward and raised his wine-glass toward the man who had become a friend over the past five months. "You drove off those two steamships, and even significantly damaged one. The same ships which sunk and captured so many of our vessels at the Battle of Grenada Passage and routed all the rest.

Your strategy—to bait them onward until the weather, sea, or light were unfavorable to their guns—was decisive. They did not discern it quickly enough to counteract it. They were lucky to escape, as it was."

"Not so lucky, Juan," Fadrique insisted, emphasizing his disagreement with a jabbed index finger. "The objective was not merely to deflect their probable strike against this city, but to inflict losses among the slower hulls in the rear of their formation. Every fluyt we sink of theirs reduces their ability to project power, to sail great distances with the troops and supplies and powder and coal that they require. It was unfortunate that we tangled with their steam behemoths at all, and see what it cost us! They were cautious enough not to give chase as ardently or swiftly as they might have,"—*as I might have!*—"and so we were not able to strike them at their weak point: support ships. Logistics. And now that we have tipped our hand, strategically, we must expect that they shall not give us such an easy opportunity again." He set down the empty glass. What he really wanted to do was shatter it on the table. "The flaw was in relying upon the pirate bastards in the south. They grew too eager, sprang the trap too early. In another hour, they would have regrouped properly and been abaft the beam of the rearmost Dutch fluyt. Our foes' escape would have been far more difficult and costly, then."

Juan frowned, nodded sympathetically. "Do we know what happened, in the south?"

"What else? Their spleen and bloodlust got the better of them. And I was foolish not to put more of our *pataches* in with them. Equiluz had to hold the mountains of St. Croix in his spyglass toward the far eastern end of our ambush line. Only he was reliable enough to accomplish that. Without him there, the whole sorry lot of them would no doubt have drifted apart in a few hours. And our privateers proved indifferent at sending signals clearly and promptly."

Juan shrugged. "You did the best you could with the resources you had. The Dutch lost a few ships, got a good scare that should give them pause, and ran away. Now, we have coast-watchers who may give us more timely warning of any subsequent approach. And soon, we shall bring the war to these pestiferous 'allies.'"

"Yes, and we've some good officers with which to do it. You know, Juan, I shall confess: I had my reservations about de Covilla when you first introduced us. But beneath that refinement, he's a good soldier. Last one off his galleon before it sank. His men admire his cool demeanor under fire, and they came under fire enough, from those steamships."

Juan traced the rim of his wineglass with his finger. "I have meant to ask: why did you put him up at the head of the van, closest to the steamships? Particularly if you had reservations about his, er, puissance?"

Fadrique shrugged. "By that time, I had revised my initial opinion of him. I also needed a person who knew our entire strategy to manage the pace and range of our retreat before the up-time ships. Most commanders would either have run, or turned and fought. And died. I needed a commander who could resist those two extreme impulses, and who was in our confidence regarding the trap we were setting with the southern privateer force." Fadrique snagged the decanter and poured another two fingers of rioja. "Now, de Covilla has seen combat, has had a ship shot out from under him, and did not flinch. And I know I have an excellent officer, in the bargain."

"Who seems to be making excellent progress with the ladies of my city, this evening."

"Well, it always helps to be a dashing, well-dressed war hero with one's arm in a sling, but with all his pieces still attached. As I said, a fine celebration you have hosted, Juan. And I would rather be here, in good, trustworthy company, than among the viperous grandees that will be clotting the king's ballroom in Madrid."

"Yes, and I wonder how welcome either one of us would be there, given what news we would have to report, and what Olivares might think of our resolve to renew our shipbuilding."

Fadrique frowned as he rolled the glass between his palms meditatively. "Since most of the ships we are building shall not qualify as workhorses for La Flota, and since they are coming from our own pockets, I wonder how much he can object. Although it will be the devil's own work getting him to send over the chandlery and cannon we need for them. But I think he will see the merits of spending a few thousand *reales* once in order to secure the delivery of several millions of them every year. Olivares is often foolish, but still, is no fool. He must know that we cannot brook a serious naval rival in the New World and be able to assure the safety of his treasure fleets. Thanks to your first message, and the one just sent, he should have time to add extra galleons to the fleet he is sending in March. That way, the Dutch and their 'allies' will find it painfully difficult to plunder it when it finally departs Havana with its riches, in late summer."

Juan shrugged. "That presumes he has the ships to spare. So long as Olivares is committed to blockading the English Channel as close as we can to the Dutch coast, too many of our ships are tied down to their duties in Europe."

"Yes, but if Olivares lifts the blockade it will go even worse for us." Fadrique leaned forward. "From what I hear, the Dutch continue to build ships in Amsterdam's ways. As it is, more of their ships will begin appearing in these waters. If Oquendo's fleet is called away or significantly reduced to assist with matters elsewhere, the Dutch will come here in still greater numbers."

Juan nodded. "And then our ability to wear this Allied fleet down will be seriously reduced."

"Exactly. Which are just a few of the reasons why we must push Havana's Captain-General Gamboa to bring de Armendáriz and New Spain in line with our resolutions. He must add the weight of his funds and his shipyards to our own. Similarly, we must get the viceroy of Peru, and de Murga in Cartagena to awaken the slumbering *audiencias* of Tierra Firma and make their own contributions." Fadrique lifted his glass. "Coordination and cooperation, my dear Juan. In the months to come, these must be our cardinal virtues. And if we would hope to see another New Year, we must accept that we will live or die by how well we achieve them—or not."

Oranjestad, St. Eustatia

In Oranjestad's newly completed governor's house, Eddie retreated from the dance floor, assisted by Anne Cathrine. His stump, still recovering from the long hours on deck and the constant tension of both actual and impending battle, was not cramping yet, but he could tell that if he didn't give it a rest, his wife would spend the rest of the evening without a regular dance partner.

The great-hall/ballroom/dining room of the governor's house was airy and clean, but sparsely furnished. The foods and drinks were quite predictable, but the plenitude of rum on this evening either dulled the sensibilities of the attendees or simply induced them not to give a damn. It was a party, there was music, and best of all, it was a new year and they were still alive. Just a month ago, that last fact had remained very much in doubt.

The ratio of men to women was actually much better than usual. No more than five to one, this night. But that had been achieved through a variety of careful machinations. First, many of Warner's English ladies had been invited up to St. Eustatia. Which was to say, they had been furnished with a *gratis* yacht ride to-and-fro, and gifts beside. And even some of the island's French women had made the journey as well, most of them having been unceremoniously abandoned when d'Esnambuc was forced to flee on his one remaining ship without returning to Dieppe Town. Many of the ladies were widows, many had been abandoned years ago, many more were mixed race orphans whose situation in the French colony had always been delicate.

The English governor Warner had accepted the invitation as well, and had brought his wife, children, and several influential members of his now-expanded colony. For the first time in years, it was relatively safe for many of the leaders of the English colony to be absent, in large part due to the repulse of the ships and soldiers of its French neighbors. The troops that the captured French bark had already put ashore near Bloody Point had been tracked down swiftly enough in the nearby hills. Most of the other French forces in the colony had been aboard d'Esnambuc's own bark, the *Bretagne*, which had withdrawn. Once free of pursuit, she had swept around the southern end of St. Christopher's to head up along the island's windward side and so get news of the attack upon St. Eustatia. What d'Esnambuc got instead was a view of du Plessis' ship, the *Main Argent*, fleeing southward toward him, flanked by native piraguas. In the distance, several Dutch jachts, along with the *Orthros*, had been in hot pursuit or landing their ship's troops along the French colony's strands. Seeing that, d'Esnambuc and du Plessis had turned their bowsprits southward and vanished into the gathering night.

On the dance floor, almost a third of the men in semi-finery—Tromp's command staff, a few troopers from the Wild Geese, and officers of various ships of the USE flotilla—made regretful bows and were ushered out the door by an honor-guard led by Cuthbert Pudsey. That bandaged worthy then admitted an equal number of men of similar rank, and in similar partial finery. Eddie smiled. This had been the other method of ensuring that the male to female ratio remained beneath the testosterone-alert levels. The men attended in shifts, while the ladies were allowed—indeed, encouraged—to stay for the duration of the evening. Or, now, morning.

Anne Cathrine surveyed the beginning of the next dance with a high-necked and utterly regal expression of immense satisfaction. "It is a fine celebration."

"It sure is." Eddie craned his neck. "But where are your ladies-in-waiting?"

Anne Cathrine swatted his arm lightly. "I am but a king's daughter. I do not have 'ladies-in-waiting,' or are you implying that I am taking on airs?"

"You? Absolutely not, your Royal Exalted Highness of the Universe and Empress of Supreme and Sultry Sexiness."

"Sshhh, Eddie! People will hear!"

"Let 'em. I'm a truth-telling man, by nature," he half-lied. "But seriously, where are Sophie and Sis?"

Anne Cathrine suddenly looked as coy as a debutante and crafty as a cat. "Well, Sophie chose to forego the festivities."

"What? Why?"

"She's in the infirmary."

"Now? Couldn't they get someone else to cover it?"

"Actually, no. And she was quite willing to make the sacrifice." Eddie was impressed. "Well, that's a hell of a noble gesture."

"Oh, yes. Most certainly." She actually hid the lower half of her face behind her fan and tittered. "Quite noble indeed!"

"What—? Oh, wait a minute."

"Ah, has my war-wizard genius-hero from the future figured it out at last?"

"The earl of Tyrconnell is still recovering in the infirmary, isn't he?"

Anne Cathrine nodded. "Yes, although his wounds seem almost fully healed to me. Except where he lost the last joint on his little finger; that still requires some care. Which Sophie takes every opportunity to provide, you understand. And when I say she takes every opportunity, I mean she seizes it violently, if need be. She almost pushed poor Dr. Brandão aside yesterday, in order to get to Lord O'Donnell first."

Eddie almost chortled at the sudden mental image of tall,

fine-featured, almost severe Sophie Rantzau hip-checking wizened little Brandão out of the way to get dibs on her favorite patient. "And is Hugh—er, Lord O'Donnell—showing appropriate appreciation for her nursing skills and dedication?"

"I cannot tell." Anne Cathrine smiled. "But he has apparently started crafting some verses that he will allow no one else to see."

"Because he's a lousy poet, or because they are about her?"

Anne Cathrine's positively feline leer was back. "His men tell me he is actually a fairly gifted writer of odes."

"Huh. A man of many talents, I guess. And where's Leonora?"

"With Rik Bjelke."

"Really?" He scanned the dance floor but did not see them. "Where are they?"

"Oh, they're gone."

"Gone? Why?"

Anne Cathrine shrugged. "Well, you know Leonora. She got bored with the dancing. So she went outside to show Rik the constellations that we can see here, but not in Denmark."

"You're kidding. She took him out to star-gaze?"

"Yes. And he seemed genuinely interested."

"In the stars or in her?"

Anne Cathrine actually giggled. "Both, I think." She scanned the nearby crowd. Her laughter became a genuine, but very public, smile as two men emerged from the festive throng. "Admiral, Governor. How wonderful to see you this evening. And our thanks for this lovely celebration."

The two Dutchmen had emerged from behind a cluster of officers signing their names on a tired but cheery young lady's dance card. They approached and bowed to Anne Cathrine—a little more deeply now, Eddie thought. Van Walbeeck straightened up with a smile almost immediately. "I saw you two dancing earlier. I must say, you are a handsome couple! Well, you would be if Eddie wasn't half of it."

Eddie almost gargled his rum punch. Anne Cathrine smiled. "Oh," she said, slipping a shapely arm through her husband's, "on that point, Governor, I must disagree."

"Ah, well and loyally spoken, my lady. You are having a good time, it seems."

"Wonderful," Anne Cathrine replied. "And you and your men seem quite jovial, Admiral."

Eddie didn't think Tromp looked jovial. Hell, Tromp *never* looked "jovial." But the Dutchman certainly looked pleased and relaxed. "We are glad to be on land, together, and alive to greet the New Year. And to be in the presence of such beauty as you bring to this party, Lady Anne Cathrine."

Van Walbeeck poked Maarten Tromp in the arm. "Here, now, you sly sea-dog! *I'm* the shameless flatterer. Do not presume to usurp my role!"

Anne Cathrine smiled beatifically. "You gentlemen are both so gallant. You are also so thoroughly under the influence of rum that your eyes have grown kind and easily pleased. Now forgive me as I ask my husband if he is ready to dance again?"

Eddie listened to the opening chords or the next dance: a *gigue*. And a pretty lively one. He shook his head sadly. "Honey, if I dance to that, I won't be dancing again for a week. How about the governor, here? Mijn heer van Walbeeck looks like he could bust a few moves."

"Bust a few what?"

"Like he'd be an excellent dancer. Now, go have fun!"

Tromp stared at Eddie, at the new dance partners who were making their way out on to the floor, and shook his head with a smile. He raised a small snifter of schnapps toward the up-timer. "*Proost*, Eddie. And a very Happy New Year."

"You, too, Admiral."

"I am Maarten, please. I am not so formal as all that. Particularly not with my colleagues."

Eddie thought he'd choke on his punch again or laugh. Or maybe shout with a mix of triumph and pride. Maarten Tromp, an admiral out of the legends of history, had labeled him a colleague and suggested they proceed on a first-name basis. How cool was *that*?

"Well, Happy New Year to you, too, Maarten. I'm just sorry we can't be celebrating it in Santo Domingo."

Tromp stared down at his schnapps. "Not me. That would have been a very bloody business. Even if your guns had reduced the city as quickly as you projected, I suspect we would still be there, up to our knees in refugees, and bodies, and debris, and the misery of the people whose city we had destroyed. No, I think it is better to have New Year's here."

"Well, I certainly agree with that, Maarten. But I can only

hope they have the same tender consideration for us when they come after Oranjestad."

Maarten stirred his rum punch. "And they will come, of course."

"Yep. And by deflecting our drive on Santo Domingo, they debuted a new playbook. And whoever's authoring it is one smart cookie."

"You mean by deferring engagement until night, or by going after our Achilles heel: our support ships?"

"Both, and more besides. The Spanish have never given lighter, fore-and-aft rigged ships any serious consideration as combat platforms. They got into the galleons-as-sea-forts mentality about a century ago, and haven't budged. But this guy, whoever he is, threw that out after one nasty surprise off Grenada." Eddie shook his head. "The Spanish admirals are usually not out-of-the-box thinkers. But this guy is, and that makes him dangerous. Hell, he was even willing to recruit pirates to get enough of the right kind of ships and crews for his ambush. And he almost pulled it off."

"Well, at least we know what to look for, in the future," Tromp offered. "Although I suspect that this fellow had alternate tactics in the event of bad weather, since poor visibility favors his ships in other ways."

"Yeah, I'm sure he had a Plan B. And probably a Plan C for really high seas. Either way, until we retrofit our ships with a fire-control system that's electronically triggered by our interferometers, and also come up with some night vision gear, they're going to try to engage us in unfavorable fighting conditions. And as long as they keep a lot of their lighter ships around to run interference, it's going to be pretty hard to pin down their heavies and sink them."

Tromp nodded. "Yes. He made quite an accurate study of both your gunnery, and the conditions that will nullify its superiority. And he deduced he needed lighter ships to 'run interference' as you call it. And I am not sure how we can parry his riposte. Unless we find some pirates of our own to recruit."

Eddie smiled. "Or even better, some disaffected Englishmen. They do run quite a number of sloops and yachts between here, the Bahamas, Bermuda, and even Barbados."

Tromp smiled and raised his schnapps snifter in a toast. "An excellent project and New Year's resolution." He took a sip, grew somber. "It would certainly have been helpful to have even four or five more such ships when we tried to push through them to the south. We sank or disabled enough of them, but our warships were too slow to exploit the gaps we punched in their trap before they filled it with more of their swift ships. As it was, we were still fighting when light fell. Thank God that the *Resolve* showed up when she did and made steam. The lights from her, and her funnel, gave us a gathering point, kept us from scattering further. By following her, we got moving in the right direction even though we couldn't see each other's signals. By the way, I am now a convert to your insistence that every ship has a blinker tube. It would have been an immense help at the end of that combat. And perhaps we might not have had to lose the *Pinas* and the *Zeeland*."

"Why?"

"Because they were not sinking so much as they were damaged, unable to make headway. Had we been able to find them in the dark sooner, we might have been able to assess the damage and effect enough repairs to allow them to keep up with the rest of our ships." Maarten flipped one impatient palm upward. "But instead, by the time we found them, we were already worried about not getting far enough away, by becoming embroiled in a second day of combat. There wasn't the time to fix much, and we couldn't afford to leave the crews behind. So we had to scuttle them. Such a waste. We need every hull we have. And more."

"No argument from me on that point, Maarten. Are your folks finished refitting the Spanish ships we took off Grenada?"

"Not quite, but soon. Frankly, the Spanish ships are so slow that they will not be much use to us when we sail to war. But they will be serviceable enough as part of our defense forces, either here or at Trinidad, I think." He smiled. "They do quite well as floating batteries, at least."

"What about giving them a better fore-and-aft rig on their mizzen? Or spencer masts?"

Tromp shrugged. "One has clean enough lines to warrant such modifications, and we might do so, if time permits. But the others—they are fortress-scows to carry silver back to Seville."

Eddie finished his drink. "I suppose, all things considered, we came out of it well enough. Even if we failed in our main objective."

Tromp seemed to study him closely, for a moment. Then said:

"I think you underestimate what we gained, Captain Cantrell. As a result of the battle off Vieques, we have resolved what may have been the single greatest weakness we had."

"Which was?"

"You. Or more precisely, everyone's assessment of you."

Eddie must have looked startled, because Tromp's face was briefly creased with an outright grin—very unusual for such a reserved man. "Come now, Eddie. Surely you understood the predicament we were all in—you more than anyone, perhaps. On the one hand, we were dependent on your knowledge and skills. On the other..."

Eddie understood. "I had no...the term we up-timers use is 'track record.'" Seeing Tromp's slight frown of puzzlement, Eddie clarified the term. "That means personal—no, more like professional—history. You knew nothing about my...well, courage, I suppose."

"Not exactly that." Tromp's grin half-reappeared. "The Danes are quite fond of you. Not only married to one of their king's daughters but, in an odd sort of way, they seem to have transmuted your somewhat suicidal ramming of one of their ships at Wismar into a Danish feat."

Eddie didn't bother trying to explain that the supposedly "somewhat suicidal ramming" at Wismar had been entirely an accident. He'd fought and lost that battle too many times already. Legends could have the thickest hides in creation.

Tromp shook his head. "But frenzied berserk courage is not the same thing as cool control under fire, maintained for hours. That, more than anything, is what a commander has to have—and that is what you displayed at Vieques. Displayed in full measure. So no one has any questions, any longer, about your fitness for command. Which means"—he issued a slight chuckle—"that the next time you try to caution us that we don't understand some subtlety of the way up-time technology affects naval tactics, everyone will listen respectfully. Even Johan van Galen. That may prove critical in the battles still to come."

A little embarrassed, Eddie didn't know quite how to respond. Luckily, an interruption came. A side door into the ballroom opened and a squarish man entered. He was not dressed for the party. Rather, he looked like a workman, perhaps come to fix one of the storm shutters.

Eddie smiled: Mike McCarthy, Jr. "Hey, Mr. Mike!" Eddie cried out, reverting to the form of address he'd used as a kid, "over here!"

Mike scanned for the source of the voice, spotted Eddie, nodded curtly, and began the laborious job of winding through the dense throngs of men clustered about any woman on or near the dance floor. When he finally extricated himself from the eager, sweating, would-be swains, he looked about in exasperation. "Jeez," he exhaled, "I really am glad I decided not to come."

"And yet, here you are," observed Tromp with a small smile. Then the admiral became quite grave. "Mr. McCarthy, before the moment slips away, I want to say that this colony owes you a singular debt of gratitude, although not all of our citizens are comfortable admitting, and therefore, expressing it. So allow me to say this for every man and woman on St. Eustatia: had our landowners' slaves not been converted into bondsmen with freedom in their future, I am quite certain they would have either joined the Kalinago during the attack, or simply stood aside. And that would have been the end of this colony, given how very many of our troops were in service elsewhere or embarked on the transports heading for Santo Domingo."

Mike did exactly what Eddie expected: he waved it off. "I'm just a guy with a big mouth, Admiral. Sometimes that big mouth is helpful, sometimes it's harmful. No reason to get worked up too much, either way. I'm just here to drop off a few pieces of news: the radio is working again. I've got two messages that came through clearly from Europe. We were trying to trade signals with Vlissingen all afternoon, which was working as a priority relay to the naval radio shack in Luebeck."

"So you were swapping Morse code with headquarters, but not Grantville," Eddie clarified.

"Yep. First item relevant to our mission: on Christmas Eve, the new rotary drill prototype got down to almost seven hundred feet before breaking down. But the crew was able to save the rig, contain the damage, and protect themselves. By this time next year, we'll be digging holes a whole lot faster and deeper in Trinidad."

And, more important, in Louisiana too, if Quinn's expedition is successful, Eddie thought behind the cover of his broad smile and approving nod. "And the other message?"

Mike smiled. "The other message is for you, Eddie. Personally. From Simpson."

"A personal message for me? From the admiral?"

"Yep. Because it summarized a bunch of politicking back home, it kind of rambled, so I only brought the last part on paper. But I can pretty much synopsize the rest. Simpson sends his warm congratulations on all that you and the 'Allies' have achieved. It is his pleasure to promote you to full commander on the basis of meritorious action. Furthermore, due to the death of Admiral Mund, he agrees to extend your brevet rank of post-captain indefinitely." Mike noticed Eddie's broad grin and shook his head. "Y'know, Eddie, you never get a promotion without new headaches."

Eddie found he was no longer smiling.

"Simpson went on to say that 'growing developments' back home in the USE make it 'imprudent' for Simpson's own new fleet to set sail for the New World. First of all, it's not ready yet. He's still overseeing the first production runs of the improved cruiser and destroyer classes that you auditioned here. He also cited 'uncertain international situations' as a reason to keep the strategic power of the new fleet close to home."

"What kind of international situations?"

"He didn't say, and with Simpson, you don't ask. Know what I mean?"

"Do I ever. Go on, Mike."

Mike shook his head, reached into his pocket, pulled out a telegrapher's sheet and handed it to Eddie with a crooked smile. "I figured you might want to read the rest of it yourself."

Eddie, nodding dumbly, took the sheet and read Admiral Simpson's closing remarks:

Collectively, these circumstances require that the core of the USE fleet remains in Luebeck. Logically, this compels a strategic revision of the mission profile of Reconnaissance Flotilla X-Ray. Specifically, it is no longer a mere reconnaissance-in-force. It is, de facto, the USE's Caribbean fleet-in-being, and the only tool available to accomplish this nation's critical objectives in that region. Consequently, so that our command-grade contribution to what is being called the composite Allied fleet enjoys equal standing with the senior staffs of the other participating nations, King Christian IV of Denmark is pleased to confer upon post-Captain Edward Cantrell the acting rank of Commodore in Danish service. He has confirmed that this rank shall be recognized by all the nations signatory to the Union of Kalmar, as well as the armed forces of the U.S.E.

So I wish you good hunting in the New Year—and Godspeed, Commodore Cantrell.

Still staring at the sheet without really seeing it, Eddie murmured. "Hell. I've been promoted. Several times."

"Yeah," commiserated Mike. "Ain't it a bitch?"

Cast of Characters

Álvarez De Toledo y Mendoza, Fadrique	Admiral of the Armada de Barlovento
Anne Cathrine	Oldest daughter of Christian IV by his morganatic marriage to Kirsten Munk; "king's daughter" but not "princess"; married to Eddie Cantrell
Aossey, Lolly	Geologist
Banckert, Adriaen	Dutch naval officer
Banckert, Joost	Vice Admiral of the Dutch Fleet
Barto	Pirate captain and privateer
Bjelke, Henrik	Norwegian nobleman, officer in Reconnaissance Flotilla X-Ray (RF X-Ray)
Brandão, Ambrósio	Sephardic physician
Calabar	Brazilian soldier, freedom-fighter, plantation owner
Cantrell, Eddie	Lieutenant Commander, USE Navy; assigned to RF X-Ray
Christian IV	King of Denmark

Corselles, Pieter	First Governor of Oranjestad, later local director for the Dutch West India Company
De Burgo, John	Soldier, Wild Geese
De Cárdenas y Manrique de Lara, Jorge	Captain-General of the Armada de Barlovento
De Covilla, Eugenio	Captain of Spain
De l'Olive, Charles Liénard	French adventurer, assistant governor of Guadeloupe
D'Esnambuc, Sieur Pierre Bélain	Governor of the French colony on St. Christopher
De Viomante y Navarra, Juan Bitrian	Captain-General of Hispaniola and Santo Domingo
Doyle, Thomas	Lieutenant and field engineer, Wild Geese
Du Parque, Jacques Dyel	Administrator of Martinique; nephew of Pierre d'Esnambuc
Du Plessis d'Ossonville, Jean	French adventurer, governor of Guadeloupe
Fernando	King in the Netherlands, House of Hapsburg, younger brother of King Philip IV of Spain; married to Maria Anna of Austria
Floriszoon, Pieter	Dutch captain
Gerritsz, Hans	Dutch captain
Gjedde, Ove	Captain of *Intrepid*, RF X-Ray
Haakon, Gorm	Officer in RF X-Ray
Isabella	Archduchess of the Spanish Lowlands, House of Habsburg
Jol, Cornelis "Houtebeen/Peg Leg"	Dutch captain
Klemm, Karl	Technical expert and oil prospector, special operations group, RF X-Ray
Kortenaer, Bert	Radio construction foreman
Koudsi, Ann	Oil drilling expert

Leonora	Second "king's daughter" of King Christian IV of Denmark by his morganatic marriage to Kristen Munk; sister of Anne Cathrine
Maria Anna	Wife of Fernando; Queen in the Lowlands; Archduchess of Austria, House of Hapsburg
McCarthy, Jr., Mike	Technical instructor
McCarthy, Mike	Elderly invalid ex-miner and Fenian
Morraine, Paul	Captain, *Fleur Sable*, expatriate French naval officer
Mulryan, Tearlach	Ensign, Wild Geese
Mund, Edel	Wife of Pros Mund
Mund, Pros	Captain of *Resolve*, and Admiral of RF X-Ray
Murrow, James	Soldier, Wild Geese
O'Bannon, Kevin	Captain, Wild Geese
O'Cahan, Daniel	Ensign, Wild Geese
O'Donnell, Hugh Albert	Earl of Tyrconnell, Colonel of the Wild Geese
O'Rourke, Aodh	Aide-de-camp to Hugh O'Donnell and Senior Sergeant of the Wild Geese
Piazza, Ed	President, State of Thuringia-Franconia
Preston, Thomas	Colonel of the Wild Geese
Pudsey, Cuthbert	English mercenary in Dutch service
Quinn, Larry	Major, USE Army, special operations group commander, RF X-Ray
Rantzau, Sophie	Danish noblewoman, companion to Anne Cathrine and Leonora
Riijs	Leader of Barto's landing force
Rohrbach, Ulrich	Oil drilling foreman
Schooneman, Jakob	Captain of the *Koninck David*
Sehested, Hannibal	Danish nobleman travelling with RF X-Ray; agent of King Christian

Serooskereken, Philip	Councilor of Oranjestad
Simonszoon, Dirck	Dutch captain
Simpson, John Chandler	Admiral, USE Navy
St. Georges, George	French expatriate naval officer
Stiernsköld, Tryggve	Captain of the *Tropic Surveyor*, RF X-Ray
Svantner, Arne	Officer in RF X-Ray
Touman	Kalinago cacique from Guadeloupe
Tromp, Maarten	Admiral of the Dutch Fleet
Turenne, Henri de la Tour d'Auvergne	French general
Van der Zaan, Willem	Dutch cabin boy
Van Galen, Johan	Dutch captain
Van Walbeeck, Jan	Governor of St. Eustatia
Von Holst, Hjalmar	Dutch captain

Glossary of Naval Terms

Ship Types

Note: Ship designs and designations were not standardized in the early seventeenth century. The definitions that follow are therefore approximations that are generally accurate but from which any particular ship might deviate to one extent or another.

Barca-longa   A two- (sometimes three-) masted lugger, a vessel using a lugsail, which is a modified version of a square sail. Often used as fishing vessels.

Bark (or Barque)   A small vessel with three or more masts, the foremasts being square-rigged and the aftermast rigged fore-and-aft.

Fluyt   A Dutch cargo vessel, generally two to three hundred tons, at least eighty feet long, and with a distinctive pear shape when viewed fore or aft.

Galleon   A three- or four-masted warship developed from the heavy carrack cargo ships, but with a longer and lower design. Not usually more than six hundred tons. Typically, the mizzenmast was lateen-rigged.

Galleoncete   A smaller galleon, generally of one hundred to two hundred tons. Many were designed to be able to use oars.

Jacht	Agile and fast vessel with very shallow draft, originally developed by the Dutch to hunt pirates in the shallow waters of the Low Countries.
Nao	A galleon adapted for cargo-hauling.
Patache	A light two-masted vessel with a shallow draft, often favored by pirates and privateers.
Piragua	One- or two-masted native boat that was also adopted by Spanish and pirates. It was narrow, often made from the trunk of a tree, and could be sailed or rowed. Commonly for a crew of six to thirty.
Yacht	English version of the *jacht*.

Gun Types

Note: As with ship types, naval ordnance was not yet standardized in the early seventeenth century. It varied widely over time and between nations. The definitions reflect this extreme diversity.

Cannon	In general use, any type of artillery piece. Specifically, a very large gun that typically fired a shot of 32 pounds or more.
Carronade	Short-barreled gun firing shot that ranged from 6 to 68 pounds. Much lighter than cannons firing an equivalent weight of shot, but had much shorter range. Predominantly used as a broadside weapon, it was originally designed specifically for naval combat.
Culverin	More lightly constructed than cannons, guns of this type fired shot from 16 to 22 pounds.
Demi-cannon	Gun firing shot weighing from 22 to 32 pounds.
Demi-culverin	Slightly larger than a saker, this weapon fired shot from 9 to 16 pounds.
Saker	A small carriage-mounted gun, firing shot of eight pounds or less.

Rigging Terms

Fore-and-aft-rigged A sailing rig consisting mainly of sails that are set along the line of the keel rather than perpendicular to it.

Foremast The mast nearest the bow of a ship.

Lateen-rigged A type of fore-and-aft rig in which a triangular sail is suspended on a long yard set at an angle to the mast.

Mainmast The principal mast of a sailing vessel.

Mizzenmast The mast aft or next aft of the mainmast.

Square-rigged A sail and rigging design in which the main sails are carried on horizontal spars that are perpendicular, or square, to the keel of the vessel and to the masts.

Stay A strong rope or wire supporting a mast.

Yards The spars holding up sails.

Yardarms The tips of the yards, beyond the last stay.

Economics of Labor Relations

Economics of Labor Relations

Gordon F. Bloom, Ph.D., LL.B.
Senior Lecturer, Sloan School of Management
Massachusetts Institute of Technology

Herbert R. Northrup, Ph.D.
Professor of Industry and
Chairman, Labor Relations Council
The Wharton School
University of Pennsylvania

1977   Eighth Edition

RICHARD D. IRWIN, INC.   Homewood, Illinois   60430
Irwin-Dorsey Limited   Georgetown, Ontario   L7G 4B3

Eighth Edition

2 3 4 5 6 7 8 9 0 Q 5 4 3 2 1 0 9 8

ISBN 0-256-01910-X
Library of Congress Catalog Card No. 76–49314

Printed in the United States of America

SUMNER H. SLICHTER (1892–1959)

Teacher and Inspiring Friend

Preface

LABOR RELATIONS and economics in the 1970s have been dominated by the interrelated key issues of unemployment, poverty, race relations, inflation, environmental matters, security-costs conflicts, and public employee bargaining. These issues are not only integrated into each chapter of our completely rewritten Eighth Edition, but in addition special chapters are devoted to unemployment, civil rights legislation, the impact of union policies on inflation, the search for security, manpower planning, and collective bargaining in the public sector.

Because a complete revision was undertaken, current labor problems have been given great emphasis: The impact of the Occupational Safety and Health Act, early retirement, union policies in regard to black workers, and the latest developments in wage theory are among the many issues discussed in detail. All materials dealing with labor relations, race relations in industry, inflation and wage controls, labor force matters, and all figures, tables, and suggested readings have been brought up to date. In addition, the writing has been tightened so that there is no increase in book length despite the many new subjects treated. In short, the authors have striven to make the Eighth Edition as new and fresh as possible.

Mathematical appendixes have been included in several chapters of Parts Four and Five. The mathematical rendering of the relevant economic theory is not essential for understanding any aspect of the text, but will be of assistance to some teachers and to more advanced students, or to those desirous of probing deeply into the theory underlying the discussion of labor relations theory and practice. The authors are grateful to Marti G. Subrohmanyam and to Stephen A. Schneider for assistance in the development of the appendixes in Part Four, and to Martin Kosters and Finis Welch and to the editors of the *American Economic Review* for permission to reproduce in Part Five the contributions of these authors.

As in earlier editions, a major objective has been the integration of economic facts and economic analysis so that the student may acquire not only an awareness of labor problems, but also an understanding of conflicting views concerning their causes and possible solutions. Wherever possible, the authors have incorporated in their discussion the latest views and approaches to various labor problems that have appeared in recent articles in professional journals. Considerable effort has been made to spell out clearly economic principles and the techniques of economic analysis.

The authors have not attempted to write a text with a general theme or a particular slant. Our main interest has been in making available to the teacher and student a text which discusses the field of labor problems in a clear, comprehensive, and interesting fashion. The material contained in the text has been organized in a manner which we felt would make the study of labor problems both enjoyable and understandable to the beginning student. Part One, which contains a general introduction to the field of labor problems, is intended to orient the student to the subject matter. Parts Two and Three give a picture of labor history, union structure and government, and collective bargaining techniques and issues. Part Four uses the tools of economic analysis to illuminate a variety of labor problems. Part Five discusses the economics of minimum wages and shorter hours, including the four-day week, and government programs to protect employees against the insecurities of old age, premature death, unemployment, accident, and illness. The collective bargaining impact of the Occupational Safety and Health Act of 1970 is also considered herein.

Part Six deals with the increasingly important role of the government in labor relations. As in previous editions, it contains detailed, up-to-date analyses of all major labor laws, including the Taft-Hartley Act and the Landrum-Griffin Act. In addition, Part Six contains the chapters dealing with federal and state equal opportunity legislation and administration, and the chapter on public employee bargaining and legislation. Part Seven is devoted to concluding remarks of the authors in which questions of future policy of government, unions, and employers are raised.

Many persons have aided in the preparation of this work. Harriet G. Weinstein supplied research assistance and aided in writing Chapters 15 and 22; Rochelle R. Bookspan assisted with the writing of Chapter 17 and provided editorial assistance; other editorial help was provided by Michael J. McGrath and Joanne M. Caruso. James P. Northrup assisted with research for Chapter 23 and Jonathan P. Northrup for Chapter 16. Deborah T. Kelsall assisted with the typing and Margaret E. Doyle with various administrative matters.

Over the years, many professors who have used the book have aided the authors by constructive suggestions. These include Frank T. deVyver,

Duke University; Charles Killingsworth, Michigan State University; Emanuel Stein, New York University; John P. Troxell, Stanford University; John B. Ferguson, University of Hawaii; Russell S. Bauder, University of Missouri; Myles Hoffman, Temple University; Darrell S. Spriggs, University of Arkansas; John Burton, University of Chicago; Walter Galenson and George Hildebrand, Cornell University; Edwin Young, formerly University of Wisconsin; and Jack Ellenbogen, the General Electric Company.

In the preparation of this edition, our work was aided by the comments of Robert W. Harrington, Illinois Wesleyan University; Edward G. Young, Washington State University; Erwin Kelly, California State University, Sacramento; John B. Parrish, University of Illinois, Urbana-Champaign; John Hannaford, Ball State University; Joel Seidman, University of Hawaii; and Harry Dawson, South Dakota State University. Richard L. Rowan, The Wharton School, has made many helpful suggestions over the years. Other Wharton colleagues whose assistance has been appreciated are Bernard E. Anderson, Charles R. Perry, Stephen A. Schneider, Marten S. Estey, and James Jordan.

Special thanks should also go to the national and regional staffs of the U.S. Department of Labor's Bureau of Labor Statistics, Employment Standards Administration, and Office of Labor Management and Pension Welfare Reports; to the National Labor Relations Board; and to The Conference Board. All were most helpful in supplying information.

The authors are grateful to the following organizations, publishers, and journals for permission to quote copyrighted material: The Conference Board, the Chamber of Commerce of the United States, McGraw-Hill Book Co., University of Chicago Press, Brookings Institution, American Enterprise Institute for Public Policy Research, American Economic Association, *Antioch Review, Southern Economic Journal,* Harper and Row, Houghton Mifflin Co., Twentieth Century Fund, W. W. Norton and Company, Inc., *Quarterly Journal of Economics,* The Macmillan Company, *Harvard Business Review,* the Bureau of National Affairs, Inc., *U.S. News and World Report, Industrial and Labor Relations Review, Industrial Relations, Fortune, Time,* and *Nation's Business,* Yale University Press, and many others cited in the text.

This book represents a joint undertaking for which joint responsibility is shared. The authors hope that their combination of academic background and practical experience in the field of labor relations has enabled them to introduce into this text a viewpoint and ideas which will make the field of labor as vital and interesting to the student as it always has been to them.

The opinions expressed herein are the responsibilities solely of the authors and are not to be attributed to any company or organization with which either author is now, or has been in the past, associated.

The first seven editions of this book were dedicated to the late Sumner

H. Slichter, who not only profoundly influenced both authors as well as the whole field of labor economics during our generation, but also gave to the undersigned his wise counsel and friendship. This edition is dedicated to his memory as a person, a teacher, a friend, and as a constructive thinker, whose works continue to provide the highest standard of analysis, objectivity, and integrity.

March 1977   GORDON F. BLOOM
                                                HERBERT R. NORTHRUP

Contents

toward Incentive Wage Methods. Union Control of Incentive Systems. Measured Daywork. Production Standards and Effective Employee Relations. Profit-Sharing Plans: *Gain Sharing, Buy-Out Formulas, and Scanlon Plans.* Formalization of Wage Structure. Supplementary or Fringe Benefits: *The Nature and Extent of Supplementary Benefits.* Key Fringe Issues: *Pensions. The Employee Retirement Income Security Act. Health and Welfare Plans. Supplemental Unemployment Benefits. Employee Stock Plans. Whither Fringe Benefit Costs?* Wage Costs, Fringe Benefits, and Take-Home Pay. Fringe Benefits and Employment.

Markets. Unstructured Labor Markets. Internal and External Labor Markets. Primary and Secondary Labor Markets. Diversity in Wage Rates: *Geographic Diversity: The North–South Differential. Union Policy and Regional Differentials. Geographic Diversity: City Size. Interindustry Differentials. Interfirm Differentials. Personal Differentials: Sex. Personal Differentials: Race.* Differences in Occupational Remuneration: *Equalizing Differences. Nonequalizing Differences. Noncompeting Groups.* Unions and Wage Differentials. Supply and Demand in the Labor Market.

The Changing Incidence of Unemployment. Who Are the Unemployed? *Unskilled Workers. Youth. The Uneducated. Older Workers. Black Workers.* Occupational Characteristics of the Unemployed. The Location of Unemployment: *Unemployment in the Cities. Unemployment Amid Labor Shortages. International Comparison of Unemployment Rates.* Poverty and Unemployment. The Profile of Poverty: *The Location of Poverty. The Families and Racial Composition of the Poor. Poverty and Unemployment. Programs to Eliminate Poverty.* Types of Unemployment: *Unemployment from the Worker's Point of View. Economic Classifications of Unemployment.* Cyclical Unemployment. Secular Trends in Employment. Technological Unemployment: *The Possibility of Permanent Technological Unemployment. Technological Progress and Employment Opportunities.* Seasonal Unemployment. Frictional Unemployment. Demand versus Structural Unemployment. The Challenge of a High-Employment Economy.

part five
Minimum Wages, Maximum Hours, and Government Security Programs

Other Procedural Safeguards. How the Public Was Affected: *Prohibited Strikes. National Emergency Strikes.* Appraisal of the Taft-Hartley Act: *Ways in Which the Act Encouraged Effective Collective Bargaining. Ways in Which the Act Impeded Effective Collective Bargaining. Effect of the Act on the Growth of Union Organization. Criticism of Administration of the Act by the NLRB. Suggestions for Reform.*

capped. The Vietnam Era Veterans Readjustment Act. Discrimination—
Concluding Remarks.

part seven
Concluding Observations

part one

Introduction

1

The Nature of Labor Problems

UNEMPLOYMENT, wage demands, strikes—these are issues of vital concern today. Hard-core unemployment of minority groups in our urban centers poses one of our most explosive current domestic problems. Continuing union wage pressure adds fuel to the mounting forces of inflation in our economy. And strikes—by teachers, municipal employees, and hospital workers, as well as industrial workers—raise perplexing problems of the extent to which a free society should attempt to curtail the individual's right to withdraw his or her labor from essential occupations. Through radio, television, and the daily newspaper, all of us have become increasingly aware of these and other labor problems which confront our economy. Labor problems have become everyone's problems. They affect every man, woman, and child—every consumer, employer, and employee.

WHO IS LABOR?

The term *labor* is used in many different ways. Sometimes, it is used as synonymous with "the civilian labor force." Such a definition lumps together in the same category the banker and the ditchdigger, the independent storekeeper and the president of the United States Steel Corporation. This heterogeneous group has one common characteristic, namely, that its members work for a living. In this respect, they are distinct from other groups in the population, such as housewives, students, pensioners, those too young or too old to work, the incapacitated, and those who, for one reason or another, find it impossible to seek work. On the other hand, the term *labor* is sometimes used to refer to much more limited groups. For example, when we refer to "skilled labor," we normally mean skilled craftsmen who work for hire for others and who are neither white-collar workers nor professional personnel. This definition excludes both the typist in the office and the doctor in the hospital although both may work for hire and have highly developed skills. Similarly, if one reads that "labor" opposes the use of the injunction as a strikebreaking weapon, it is likely that the term is intended to apply to a limited group of men and women, skilled and unskilled, white-collar and non-white-collar, who are either members of unions or are in groups which lend themselves to union organization. The term *labor*, therefore, may have various meanings and scope, depending upon the context in which it is used.

WHO ARE EMPLOYERS?

In order to understand the nature of the labor market in our economy and the factors which contributed to the development of trade unions, one must understand who provides the jobs for our labor force. Today, most people work for someone else, whether it be a large farm operator, a giant industrial corporation, a governmental agency, or the corner drugstore. Self-employment has continually declined as a source of work. Today, only about 1 in 12 Americans is his or her own employer. About one quarter of these workers are in agriculture, still the largest source of individual enterprise. Other industries with significant numbers of self-employed are construction, trade, and various service industries.[1]

Nonfarm Business

There are about 8 million operating nonfarm businesses in the United States, most of them small proprietorships.[2] If employment in the entire economy were evenly distributed among a great many such small firms, our labor market would be quite different from what it actually is, and it is conceivable that workers would never have felt the need for unions to protect their interests. Averages, however, are deceptive. While small business enterprises are abundant in wholesale and retail trade and in various service occupations, a relatively small number of giant companies employ a substantial part of the entire nonfarm labor force. Manufac-

---

[1] Robert N. Roy, "A Report on Self-Employed Americans in 1973," *Monthly Labor Review*, vol. 98 (January 1975), p. 49.

[2] U.S. Department of Commerce, Bureau of the Census, *Statistical Abstract of the United States, 1975*, 96th ed. (Washington, D.C.: Government Printing Office, 1975), table 801, p. 490.

turing, in particular, is characterized by bigness, and generally bigness in corporate form. Approximately three out of every four workers in manufacturing are employed by corporations employing 100 or more persons.[3]

Most employees in nonagricultural business establishments are employed by corporations. This means that they are employed by a legal entity, which, in turn, is owned by stockholders, frequently numbering in the hundreds of thousands. In 1973, the 100 largest manufacturing corporations accounted for about 45% of all corporate assets.[4] Large corporations control the bulk of our wealth and production; they set the tempo for wage adjustments; they establish the general framework of attitudes and policies which condition union-management relations in the country as a whole.

Because of the wide holdings of stock in this country, it might be argued that the ultimate employer of labor in the United States is the stockholding public. It owns the assets which provide employment and, moreover, it normally has the right to elect directors and so influence corporate policies. As a practical matter, however, corporate decisions tend to be made by a class of persons known as management, who are employed by stockholders to manage the day-to-day business of corporations. Management includes such executives as the officers and directors of corporations, as well as personnel directors, department heads, and foremen. To the average worker in a large corporation, this group—and not the remote stockholder-owners—constitutes the employer. We shall discuss at a later point how the separation of the management function from ownership in American industry and the growth in size of corporations have exercised a profound effect upon the nature of collective bargaining.

It is important to recognize, however, that if we look not simply at the business sector of the economy but at the entire sphere of employment of labor—business, nonprofit institutions, and government—the majority of persons in the labor force do not work for business corporations. They work for governmental, unincorporated business, or nonprofit institutions, or they are self-employed. A major trend in the American labor market has been the growing proportion of the labor force which is employed by nonprofit and governmental institutions. Today it is likely that less than half of the total labor force is employed in the corporate sector.[5]

---

[3] Ibid., table 1260, p. 736.

[4] Ibid., table 825, p. 502.

[5] As of 1969 the corporate sector had already fallen to a minority position. See Neil H. Jacoby, "The Myth of the Corporate Economy," *Conference Board Record*, vol. 8 (June 1971), p. 49. The growth of government employment since that date has accentuated this trend.

Government

We are accustomed to thinking of the automobile industry, the steel industry, and other durable goods producers as the major source of employment in our economy. Yet today in the United States more persons are employed by government—federal, state, and local—than by all durable goods manufacturing industries combined. Government employment has almost tripled since the end of World War II, from 5,474,000 in 1947 to 14,771,000 in 1975.[6] Although the federal government is the largest single employer in the nation, with a total of 2,748,000 civilian employees in 1975,[7] most governmental employees are on the payrolls of state and local governments. Between 1947 and 1975, the number employed by state and local governments rose from 3.5 million to 12 million, a 236% increase.[8] During the same period, federal employment increased only 45%, slightly less than the percentage growth in total employment over the postwar period.

If we add to the total governmental employment about 2 million members of the Armed Forces and about 6.7 million persons employed in private industry who supply goods and services purchased by various governmental agencies,[9] we find that roughly one out of every four persons in the total labor force, owes his or her job either directly or indirectly to governmental action. Since we pride ourselves on the achievements of our private enterprise economy, it is sobering to consider the extent to which government expenditures and government decision-making affect the level of employment.

Agriculture

Agriculture is the only major industry in which the majority of workers are self-employed or unpaid members of families. In 1975, only 1.3 million out of a total of 3.4 million persons employed on farms were classified as wage and salary workers.[10] Generally, hired farm wage workers are young (median age 23), white (83%), and male (79%), and reside in nonfarm places (76%). In 1974, they earned an average of $1,447 in annual cash wages, or $16.60 per day for 87 days of farm wage work.[11] Much farm employment is part-time; employment in large

---

[6] U.S. Department of Labor et al., *Employment and Training Report of the President, 1976* (Washington, D.C.: Government Printing Office, 1976), table C–1, p. 293.

[7] Ibid., p. 293.

[8] Ibid.

[9] See U.S. Department of Labor, *Manpower Report of the President, 1972* (Washington, D.C.: Government Printing Office, 1972), p. 215.

[10] U.S. Department of Labor, *Employment and Training Report*, p. 238.

[11] U.S. Department of Agriculture, Economic Research Service, *The Hired Farm Working Force of 1974*, Agricultural Economic Report 297 (Washington, D.C.: Government Printing Office, July 1975), p. 1.

numbers per farm unit seldom occurs except during seasonal harvest periods.

THE LABOR FORCE

Suppose that we want to find out how many people are in the "labor force" of the United States. How would we go about obtaining this information? Obviously we need two things: first, a definition of what we are seeking, and second, the statistics to fill our classifications.

Definitions

The most commonly used classification of the labor force and its components is that adopted by the Bureau of the Census, which compiles data for the Bureau of Labor Statistics. These definitions have been changed from time to time,[12] but at this writing the following criteria are applied in classifying persons on the basis of activity during the survey week studied.

> *Labor Force:* The sum of persons in the Armed Forces plus persons in the civilian labor force, whether employed or unemployed.
>
> *Civilian Labor Force* (limited to noninstitutional population 16 years of age or more).
>
> *Employed persons* include:
> 1. All civilians who during the specified week did any work at all as paid employees or in their own business or profession, or on their own farm, or who worked 15 hours or more as unpaid workers on a farm or in a business operated by a member of the family;
> 2. All those who were not working but who had jobs or businesses from which they were temporarily absent because of illness, bad weather, vacation, or labor-management dispute, or because they were taking time off for personal reasons.
>
> *Unemployed persons* include those civilians who had no employment during the survey week, were available for work, and:
> 1. Had engaged in any specific job-seeking activity within the past four weeks, such as registering with employment offices, checking with friends and relatives, meeting with prospective employers, etc.;
> 2. Were waiting to be called back to a job from which they had been laid off; or
> 3. Were waiting to report to a new wage or salary job scheduled to start within the following 30 days.
>
> *Persons Not in Labor Force:* This category includes all persons not classified as employed, unemployed, or in the Armed Forces who are 16

---

[12] For an up-to-date discussion of problems in the measurement and definition of unemployment, see U.S. Department of Labor, Bureau of Labor Statistics, *Unemployment: Measurement Problems and Recent Trends,* Report 445 (Washington, D.C.: Government Printing Office, 1975).

years of age or over and are not inmates of institutions. These persons are further classified as follows:

1. Engaged in own homework;
2. In school;
3. Unable to work because of long-term physical or mental illness;
4. Other—this category includes persons who are retired, voluntarily idle, too old or temporarily unable to work, seasonal workers in off season who are not looking for work, and persons who did not look for work because they believed that no jobs were available in the area, or that no jobs were available for which they could qualify.

Data with respect to employment, unemployment, and labor force participation, as so defined, are obtained through monthly surveys of the population based upon a scientifically selected sample of households designed to represent the civilian noninstitutional population 16 years and over. The statistics based upon these definitions are widely used and enter into the formulation of major governmental policy decisions affecting the economy in general and the labor market in particular. At this writing, the Department of Labor is reviewing the concepts which have been utilized over many years in measuring employment and unemployment. In Chapter 14 we shall consider in detail some of the alleged shortcomings of the current definitions.

Characteristics of the Labor Force

The civilian labor force is not a fixed group. It grows with the long-term growth of the population; it responds to the influence of economic forces; and it changes with the seasons. In July there are usually 3 or 4 million more job seekers than in January, as students look for summer jobs and housewives seek jobs in seasonal farm industries. December is another peak month, for it is the time when many persons take part-time jobs in department stores and other firms which do a heavy Christmas business.

Because of the movement in and out of the labor force during a given year, many more persons are employed (and unemployed) during the course of a year than is indicated by the annual averages in Table 1–1. For example, about 102 million persons are estimated to have worked at some time during 1974,[13] yet Table 1–1 shows that civilian employment averaged only about 86 million. On the other hand, only 57 million persons actually worked full-time—50–52 weeks.[14] A total of 18.3 million persons experienced some unemployment during the year,[15] contrasting with the figure of 5 million in the table.

[13] U.S. Department of Labor, *Employment and Training Report*, table B–14, p. 287.

[14] Ibid.

[15] U.S. Department of Labor, Bureau of Labor Statistics, *Work Experience of the Population in 1974*, Special Labor Force Report, June 1975, p. 1.

TABLE 1–1

Employment Status of the Noninstitutional Population 16 Years and Over: Annual Averages, 1947–1975 (numbers in thousands)

| | | Total Labor Force, Including Armed Forces | | | Civilian Labor Force | | | | | |
| | | | | | | Employed | | Unemployed | | |
Year	Total Noninstitutional Population	Number	Percent of Noninstitutional Population	Total	Total	Agriculture	Nonagricultural Industries	Number	Percent of Labor Force	Not in Labor Force
1947	..103,418	60,941	58.9	59,350	57,039	7,891	49,148	2,311	3.9	42,477
1948	..104,527	62,080	59.4	60,621	58,344	7,629	50,711	2,276	3.8	42,447
1949	..105,611	62,903	59.6	61,286	57,649	7,656	49,990	3,637	5.9	42,708
1950	..106,645	63,858	59.9	62,208	58,920	7,160	51,752	3,288	5.3	42,787
1951	..107,721	65,117	60.4	62,017	59,962	6,726	53,230	2,055	3.3	42,604
1952	..108,823	65,730	60.4	62,138	60,254	6,501	53,748	1,883	3.0	43,093
1953	..110,601	66,560	60.2	63,015	61,181	6,261	54,915	1,834	2.9	44,041
1954	..111,671	66,993	60.0	63,643	60,110	6,206	53,898	3,532	5.5	44,678
1955	..112,732	68,072	60.4	65,023	62,171	6,449	55,718	2,852	4.4	44,660
1956	..113,811	69,409	61.0	66,552	63,802	6,283	57,506	2,750	4.1	44,402
1957	..115,065	69,729	60.6	66,929	64,071	5,947	58,123	2,859	4.3	45,336
1958	..116,363	70,275	60.4	67,639	63,036	5,586	57,450	4,602	6.8	46,088
1959	..117,881	70,921	60.2	68,369	64,630	5,565	59,065	3,740	5.5	46,960
1960	..119,759	72,142	60.2	69,628	65,778	5,458	60,318	3,852	5.5	47,617
1961	..121,343	73,031	60.2	70,459	65,746	5,200	60,546	4,714	6.7	48,312
1962	..122,981	73,442	59.7	70,614	66,702	4,944	61,759	3,911	5.5	49,539
1963	..125,154	74,571	59.6	71,833	67,762	4,687	63,076	4,070	5.7	50,583
1964	..127,224	75,830	59.6	73,091	69,305	4,523	64,782	3,786	5.2	51,394
1965	..129,236	77,178	59.7	74,455	71,088	4,361	66,726	3,366	4.5	52,058
1966	..131,180	78,893	60.1	75,770	72,895	3,979	68,915	2,875	3.8	52,288
1967	..133,319	80,793	60.6	77,347	74,372	3,844	70,527	2,975	3.8	52,527
1968	..135,562	82,272	60.7	78,737	75,920	3,817	72,103	2,817	3.6	53,291
1969	..137,841	84,239	61.1	80,733	77,902	3,606	74,296	2,831	3.5	53,602
1970	..140,182	85,903	61.3	82,715	78,627	3,462	75,165	4,088	4.9	54,280
1971	..142,596	86,929	61.0	84,113	79,120	3,387	75,732	4,993	5.9	55,666
1972	..145,775	88,991	61.0	86,542	81,702	3,472	78,230	4,840	5.6	56,785
1973	..148,263	91,040	61.4	88,714	84,409	3,452	80,957	4,304	4.9	57,222
1974	..150,827	93,240	61.8	91,011	85,936	3,492	82,443	5,076	5.6	57,587
1975	..153,449	94,793	61.8	92,613	84,783	3,380	81,403	7,830	8.5	58,655

Source: U.S. Department of Labor et al., *Employment and Training Report of the President, 1976* (Washington, D.C.: Government Printing Office, 1976), table A–1, p. 211.

As can be seen from Table 1–1, the overall rate of participation[16] in the civilian labor force appears to have remained remarkably stable since 1947. However, this apparent stability masks some striking changes in

---

[16] The rate of participation is the percentage of persons of working age (16 years and over) in the population actually in the labor force.

the participation rates of various component groups within the labor force. For example, from 1947 to 1975 the participation rate of males dropped from 86.8% to 78.5%, while the participation rate of females rose from 31.8% to 46.4%.[17]

The decline in the male participation rate has been concentrated among the youngest and oldest workers. Participation by young men has been reduced largely as a result of the increased term of education and the increase in school attendance. Participation by males over 65 has fallen precipitously from 47.8% in 1947 to 21.7% in 1975,[18] reflecting the spread of public and private retirement programs, business policy aimed at compulsory retirement at age 65, and the diminishing importance of agriculture, which historically has enabled older men to work, even if part-time, to an older age than industry now permits.

For women, changing social attitudes toward work by women and the increased utilization of laborsaving products in the home have contributed to an amazing increase in participation rates. From 1947 to 1975 the female population of the United States increased 52%, but during the same period the female labor force increased 123%![19] In 1960 the labor force participation rate for women 16 years and over was 37.1%; by 1970 it had risen to 42.8%; and the U.S. Department of Labor projects a 45% rate for 1980.[20] Participation rates have increased for women in all age groups, but the increase has been especially notable among married women and among women with young children. For example, in 1948 only 11% of married women with children under six years of age were in the labor force, in contrast to 36.6% in 1975.[21] By 1975, there were about 37 million women in the labor force, representing almost 40% of all workers.[22] The implications for industry and for public policy of a work force in which four out of ten workers are women have been momentous. It has required employers and unions to adjust practices and provide maternity leave, and resulted in continuing and increasing pressure for enforcement of equal employment opportunities and equal pay.

The relative stability in the ratio of the labor force to population is all the more remarkable when account is taken of the large number of persons of working age who choose to remain outside the labor force at any given time. For example, in 1975 there were about 12.5 million men and 38.7 million women, age 20 and over, who were neither em-

---

[17] U.S. Department of Labor, *Employment and Training Report*, table A–2, p. 214.

[18] Ibid.

[19] *Wall Street Journal*, March 8, 1976, p. 1.

[20] U.S. Department of Labor, *Employment and Training Report*, table E–2, p. 330.

[21] Ibid., p. 143.

[22] Ibid., p. 142.

ployed nor looking for work.[23] The reasons were varied: school attendance, physical or mental disability, family obligations, discouragement with job prospects, and other circumstances. Most of the women were probably housekeepers—but so were millions of other women in past decades who have since moved into the labor market. Thus, a huge potential labor pool overhangs the labor market and makes it difficult to achieve the goal of a job for all work seekers.

The Projected Growth of the Labor Force

The rate of population growth in the United States is slackening; in fact, the birthrate has plunged to levels below those registered in the depths of the Great Depression. Despite this fact, the labor force will continue to grow at a rapid pace during the decade of the 1970s, reflecting the high birthrates of the postwar years. The labor force is expected to grow at an annual rate of 1.7% until 1980, and thereafter the rate will slow somewhat to 1.2% per annum.[24] Based upon these rates, the labor force will reach 100 million in 1980 and about 107 million in 1985. This means that the average annual net increase in the labor force will be 1.5 million persons during the balance of the decade.[25] About 94% of the increase in the labor force will be attributable to a larger population, with the remaining 6% accounted for by an expected increase in the participation rate.[26]

Not only is the labor force growing rapidly during the 70s but its composition is also changing due to the shifting relative importance of different age groups in the working population. The teenage labor force, with all its special problems, is growing much more slowly in the 70s than it did previously.[27] On the other hand, the number of persons in the age group 25 to 34 is increasing at a dramatic rate, growing by about 800,000 a year, compared with an average of 175,000 per year in the previous decade.[28] Another marked change is occurring in the age group 45 to 54, where the rapid growth of the previous decade has disappeared, and the number of workers may, over the course of the decade, actually decline slightly in absolute numbers.[29] The changing significance of various age groups in the labor force is shown in Figure 1–1. Let us turn our attention now to some of the major components of

---

[23] Ibid., table A–7, p. 223.

[24] Sophia C. Travis, "The U.S. Labor Force: Projections to 1985," *Monthly Labor Review*, vol. 93 (May 1970), p. 3.

[25] Ibid.

[26] U.S. Department of Labor, *The U.S. Economy in 1980*, Bulletin 1673 (Washington, D.C., 1970), p. 4.

[27] Travis, "Labor Force," p. 3.

[28] Ibid.

[29] Ibid.

FIGURE 1–1
Labor Force Developments

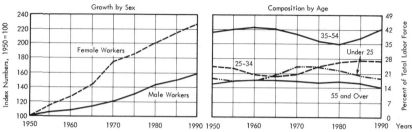

Source: Data, Departments of Commerce; Labor; and Health, Education, and Welfare. Chart, *The U.S. Economy in 1990* (New York: The Conference Board, 1972), p. 9.

the labor force and consider the special problems facing each of them in the years ahead.

Youth

During the 1960s, the number of young people in the labor force increased at a spectacular rate. In 1970, there were 56% more workers under the age of 25 than at the beginning of the decade.[30] These were the wartime babies coming to maturity. However, as has already been mentioned, the growth rate for young workers in the labor force has slackened in the 70s. The number of persons age 16 to 24 years in the labor force will increase by only 19% between 1970 and 1980, and in the following decade will, according to Labor Department projections, actually decrease by 14.6%.[31] The problem of providing jobs for our youth may therefore become more manageable in the decade of the 1980s, but currently unemployment among youth is a serious problem. In mid-1975 nearly one half of all unemployed workers were between 16 and 24 years of age, including about 1.8 million teenagers and 1.9 million persons in their early twenties.[32] In 1975 the unemployment rate for teenagers averaged about 20%, compared to an overall rate for the labor force of 8.5%.[33] Since many young people customarily seek only part-time work, this raises the real question of whether their failure to obtain employment should be given the same weight as that of the laid-off full-time adult worker. We shall address that question in Chapter 14.

A special problem is presented by the rapid increase of nonwhite

[30] U.S. Department of Labor, *Employment and Training Report*, table E–3, p. 331.

[31] Ibid., p. 331.

[32] Ibid., p. 26.

[33] Ibid., table A–19, p. 241.

youth in the labor force. While the number of white youth age 16 to 24 in the labor force will increase by only 16% between 1970 and 1980, the increase among black youth will be almost 40%.[34] In view of the fact that in 1975 about 40% of all black teenagers in the labor force were unemployed (see Figure 1–2) and about 20% of all blacks in their early 20s faced the same dim prospect,[35] the changing racial composition of the youth segment of the labor force poses major problems to the nation in terms of providing adequate job opportunities for unemployed youth.

FIGURE 1–2

Unemployment Rates for Nonwhite Teenagers, 1956–1976

Source: Data, U.S. Department of Labor; chart, reprinted from *U.S. News & World Report,* September 27, 1976, p. 61. Copyright 1976 U.S. News & World Report, Inc.

The increase in the number of young workers has been occurring despite increased school enrollment which normally would postpone entrance into the labor market. A remarkable phenomenon of the past decade has been the increase in the number of young people who work while attending school. Students in the teenage labor force more than doubled in number between 1960 and 1970, whereas young work-

---

[34] Ibid., table E–5, p. 333.

[35] Ibid., p. 26.

ers not in school increased by only 13%.[36] In 1974, 45% of all school or college youth, age 14 to 24, were also participating in the labor market.[37]

Out-of-school youth, including both high school graduates and dropouts, now constitute less than half of the teenagers in the labor force.[38] As might be expected, job-finding difficulties are compounded for those out-of-school youth who failed to complete high school. The unemployment rate for dropouts was about 30% in 1974, almost double that of graduates.[39] In Chapter 15, we shall discuss various programs which seek to improve the school-to-work transition.

The Older Worker

At the other end of the age spectrum is the "older worker." Two categories may be distinguished within this group, each with special problems.

Workers 65 and Over. In 1974, there were about 21.8 million persons age 65 or over in the United States, representing about 10% of the population. At present death rates, this older population is expected to increase 40%, to 31 million, by the year 2000. In 1974, about 3 million persons in this age group were in the labor force—either working or actively seeking work.[40] Among males 65 and over, part-time employment is becoming increasingly common. The proportion of working males over 65 years of age who had part-time employment rose from 40% in 1966 to 45% in 1974.[41] While for many this may represent a conscious choice, for many others it represents an inability to find full-time jobs.

With improving health care and greater longevity, there is increasing evidence that persons age 65 years and over are quite competent to continue working. Nevertheless, current mandatory retirement policies in effect condemn many of these men and women to enforced idleness. In recent years the National Council of Senior Citizens, the American Association of Retired Persons, and even the American Medical Association have attacked the policy of compulsory retirement. It seems quite likely that in the years ahead groups representing older persons will attempt to obtain legislation outlawing this practice. Although until recently there has been little public support for such a move, the growing con-

---

[36] U.S. Department of Labor, *Manpower Report of the President, 1972* (Washington, D.C.: Government Printing Office, 1972), p. 81.

[37] U.S. Department of Labor, *Handbook of Labor Statistics, 1975* (Washington, D.C.: Government Printing Office, 1975), table 11, p. 53.

[38] U.S. Department of Labor, *Manpower Report, 1972,* p. 82.

[39] U.S. Department of Labor, *Handbook of Labor Statistics, 1975,* table 32, p. 93.

[40] U.S. Department of Health, Education, and Welfare, *Facts about Older Americans, 1975* (Washington, D.C.: Government Printing Office, 1975).

[41] Shirley H. Rhine, "The Senior Worker—Employed and Unemployed," *Conference Board Record,* vol. 13 (May 1976), p. 9.

cern about the steady increase in the number of social security beneficiaries and the corresponding decrease in the number of social security
taxpayers could eventually change present legislative attitudes toward
this problem, as will be discussed in Chapter 17.

Workers 45–65. In 1970, there were 28.3 million persons age 45–64
in the labor force. The projected number for 1980 is only 29.2 million.
This small increase of less than 1 million contrasts with the increase of
4 million which occurred during the decade 1960–70.[42] The decline in
the growth of this older worker group is attributable to the changing age
composition of the population and a continued decline in labor participation rates for men in this age category.

Our concern with these workers arises from the difficulty which they
experience in obtaining employment once they lose their current jobs.
The statistics indicate that this age group has a low unemployment rate
—as low as the 35–44 age group—but the statistics may understate the
true rate of unemployment for older workers. These workers are more
likely to become discouraged and drop out of the job market when
they experience difficulty in obtaining reemployment. In any case, it is
clear that unemployment, once it occurs, is definitely longer for the
older worker. In 1975, 25% of the unemployed in the 55–64 age category
and 32% of the unemployed 65 and over—but only 13% of the unemployed
in the 20–24 age bracket—had been jobless for at least 27 weeks.[43]

Women at Work

In mid-1975, nearly 37 million women were in the labor force—about
40% of the nation's labor force and 46% of all women 16 years of age
and over.[44] In recent years, women have been entering the labor force
at a rate more than double that of men. The significance of this trend is
brought out dramatically by the fact that in 1975 adult women accounted for 1.1 million of the 1.5 million increase in the labor force![45]
The extent to which the growth in female participation in the labor
force has outstripped that of males is shown in Figure 1–1.

Marital status is a very important factor in the work experience of
women. Single (never married) women age 25–54 are extremely committed to work—81% of these women worked during 1974; three fourths
worked all year at full-time jobs. Married women are somewhat less
likely to work, but the movement of these women into paid employment
has nevertheless been dramatic. In 1974, among married women age

---

[42] U.S. Department of Labor, *Employment and Training Report*, table E–3,
p. 331.

[43] S. Rhine, "Senior Worker," p. 9.

[44] U.S. Department of Labor, Bureau of Labor Statistics, *Women in the Labor
Force*, November 1975, p. 2.

[45] *Wall Street Journal*, March 8, 1976, p. 1.

25–54 more than half worked; over two fifths worked at full-time year-round jobs.[46]

Despite the progress which women have made in recent years in gainful employment, they are still faced by major handicaps in the labor market. We shall discuss this briefly here and in more detail in subsequent chapters.

First, the range of jobs in which women are found is still limited. Women tend to be concentrated in clerical jobs and in the service sector. Nearly one fourth of all women workers are employed in the service sector, where they make up over one half of all employees. Within the service sector, nearly two thirds of the workers in education and three fourths of those in medical health and personal services are women.[47] On the other hand, women constitute only 10% of all physicians, 7% of lawyers, 24% of accountants, and 14% of chemists.[48]

Second, the large wage differential between male and female workers has persisted over the last two decades despite gains made by women in penetrating various occupational categories. In 1956, the median amount earned by full-time year-round female workers was 63% of the median for male workers. By 1974, the percentage had fallen to 57%.[49] In Chapter 8, we shall examine possible reasons for this continuing differential. It is apparent, however, that the enactment of various anti-discrimination laws by the federal and state governments as well as pressure by feminists has thus far been unsuccessful in equalizing male and female occupational standings.

Third, women characteristically have a higher unemployment rate than do men. In part, this reflects lack of seniority and interrupted work experience. Unemployment among women has become a more serious problem in recent years because of the increasing number of households headed by women. In March 1975, the labor force comprised 3.9 million families headed by a woman, and only 35% of these families had another worker. The 1975 unemployment rate for women who headed families in which there were no other workers was 11.5%.[50]

The disadvantages women experience in the labor market are the result of interrupted job experience, emphasis on traditional occupational choices, limitations on education and training, limited physical strength, and socially accepted stereotypes about "women's jobs" and "men's jobs." These conditions are slow to change, and it is therefore

---

[46] U.S. Department of Labor, *Women in the Labor Force*, p. 12.

[47] U.S. Department of Labor, *Manpower Report of the President, 1975* (Washington, D.C.: Government Printing Office, 1975), p. 60.

[48] *U.S. News & World Report*, December 8, 1975, p. 57.

[49] Ibid., p. 57.

[50] Julius Shiskin and Robert L. Stein, "Problems in Measuring Unemployment," *Monthly Labor Review*, vol. 98 (August 1975), p. 7.

likely to be some time before women actually achieve equality in the labor market.

The Changing Status of the Black Worker

Approximately 11% of the civilian labor force is classified as nonwhite —that is, Negro, Oriental, or American Indian. Over 90% of this group is black. We shall use the terms *black* and *nonwhite* interchangeably to refer to this entire group.

In recent years, there has been a gradual breakdown of some of the age-old barriers between whites and nonwhites in terms of education, occupation, and social status. Nevertheless, important differences remain in the characteristics of the white and nonwhite components of the labor force. Thus, nonwhite persons go to work at an earlier age and remain in the labor force to a greater extent after 65 years of age; nonwhite women have a greater tendency to remain in the labor force after marriage; and because of higher mortality and a heavier toll of disability, nonwhites have a considerably shorter working life than do whites.

A majority of black families still live in the South, but there has been a heavy migration of blacks to the metropolitan areas of the North. In 1974, 58% of all blacks resided in the central cities of metropolitan areas.[51] Blacks constituted over 22% of the population of central cities, up from 16% in 1960.[52] The heavy migration of blacks to the central cities occurred at the same time that many businesses were leaving these cities because of high taxes, congestion, and other ills. Thus, the geographic location of the supply of labor represented by the black population poses problems for the economy in bringing jobs and labor supply into balance. Although blacks continue to be concentrated in the central cities of metropolitan areas, the black population in such cities has experienced a slowdown in its rate of growth since 1970. This slowdown can be attributed to the declines in both the rate of natural increase and of net in-migration.

Blacks have been particularly vulnerable to unemployment, not only because of their geographic location but because of the occupational stratification which has developed for black workers as a result of their lack of skills, on the one hand, and of past discriminatory practices by both employers and unions, on the other. Throughout the postwar period, unemployment has consistently fallen most heavily on the black

---

[51] U.S. Department of Commerce, Bureau of the Census, *The Social and Economic Status of the Black Population in the United States, 1974,* Current Population Reports, Series P–23, No. 54 (Washington, D.C.: Government Printing Office, 1975), fig. 2, p. 9.

[52] Ibid., p. 15.

worker. Since the Korean War period, black unemployment rates have generally been twice those of white workers, except for a slight narrowing of the gap during 1970 and 1971. In other words, relative to the proportion of blacks and whites in the labor force, two black workers have consistently been unemployed for every unemployed white worker.[53] In 1975, the unemployment rate for white workers was 7.8%, whereas for blacks it was 13.9%.[54] Likewise, the 1975 unemployment rate for black teenagers—36.9%—was more than double the 17.9% rate which prevailed for white teenagers.[55] The actual number of unemployed black youths in the trouble spots—namely the central cities—is relatively small. A study made in 1971 indicated that the total number of unemployed black teenagers in the central cities was only 134,000.[56] The problem is exacerbated because of the severe deprivation of those affected and the lack of available unskilled jobs.

Not only do black members of the labor force bear the heaviest burden of unemployment, but when they are employed, their earnings tend to be less than those of their white counterparts. Despite legislative enactments designed to eliminate discrimination against blacks, the earnings gap between blacks and whites has tended to increase during recent years. In 1969, the median income of black families was 61% of that of white families; by 1974, this ratio had fallen to 58%. In that year the median income of black families was $7,808, compared to a median of $13,356 for white families.[57] Although various factors contributed to this result, an important circumstance was that between 1970 and 1974 the proportion of black families with wives in the paid labor force declined from 36% to 33%, whereas the proportion of white families with working wives increased from 34% to 37%.[58] Poverty is an ever-present threat to many black families. In 1974, almost one third of all black families had incomes below the poverty level, more than three times the proportion of 9% for the white population.[59] Earnings of black workers are low because of the kinds of occupations in which they are concentrated, because in any particular occupational grouping they tend to have the jobs at the bottom of the ladder—the most menial and the least skilled—because even on the same jobs blacks may earn less due to lesser seniority.

As can be seen from Table 1–2, although blacks made some progress in occupational status between 1962 and 1974, they are still underrepresented in professional, managerial, sales, and craft jobs. In 1975, while

[53] Ibid., p. 55.

[54] U.S. Department of Labor, *Employment and Training Report,* p. 21.

[55] *Monthly Labor Review,* vol. 99 (June 1976), p. 78.

[56] U.S. Department of Labor, *Manpower Report, 1972,* p. 85.

[57] U.S. Department of Commerce, *Social and Economic Status,* table 9, p. 25.

[58] Ibid., p. 30.

[59] Ibid., p. 41.

TABLE 1–2

Occupational Distribution of Black Persons, 1962 and 1974 (numbers in thousands)

		Employed Blacks			Blacks as a Percent of Total Employed	
				Change 1962–1974		
Occupational Group	1962	1974	Number	Percent	1962	1974
All employed	7,132	9,315	2,183	30.6	10.4	10.8
Professional	382	970	588	153.9	4.7	7.9
Managerial	184	380	196	106.5	2.5	4.2
Sales	115	214	99	86.1	2.6	4.0
Clerical	509	1,414	905	177.8	5.1	9.4
Craft workers	443	874	431	97.3	5.1	7.6
Operatives	1,430	2,041	611	42.7	11.8	14.7
Nonfarm laborers	950	832	−118	−12.4	26.8	19.0
Farmers and farm managers	194	64	−130	−67.0	7.5	3.9
Farm laborers	580	190	−390	−67.2	25.3	13.5
Service workers, except private household	1,284	1,863	579	45.1	19.8	18.4
Private household	1,062	474	−588	−55.4	44.3	38.5

Data for 1962 are not strictly comparable with 1974 data because of definitional changes in occupational categories and because 14- and 15-year-olds are included in 1962 data and excluded from 1974 data.

Source: Stuart H. Garfinkle, "Occupations of Women and Black Workers, 1962–74," *Monthly Labor Review*, vol. 98 (November 1975), p. 27.

only 12.3% of whites were employed as service workers, 25.8% of black workers held such positions. On the other hand, 13.4% of whites were classified as "craft and kindred workers," whereas only 8.8% of black workers fell in this category.[60]

In this connection, special mention should be made of Puerto Rican workers, who in some respects have suffered even more occupational discrimination than have blacks. About one out of every three Puerto Ricans lives on the mainland United States, with a concentration of over 800,000 in New York City. In New York City, only 33% of Puerto Ricans held white-collar jobs, compared to 58% for all residents and 43% for blacks. Puerto Ricans frequently were employed as cooks, cleaners, and health service workers. They accounted for one fifth of the area's male dishwashers and dining room attendants.[61] It is apparent that this is another minority group which has experienced disproportionate occupational difficulties.

Because of the changing structure of the job market, employment in the occupations in which blacks are concentrated will be growing more slowly than employment in other fields. There must be an accelera-

[60] U.S. Department of Labor, *Employment and Training Report*, table A–16, p. 237.

[61] Lois S. Gray, "The Jobs Puerto Ricans Hold in New York City," *Monthly Labor Review*, vol. 98 (October 1975), pp. 12–13.

tion in the rate of transfer of blacks from blue-collar jobs to growth-oriented white-collar occupations if any substantial improvement is to be effected in reducing the already high nonwhite unemployment rate. The need for opening up additional job opportunities for blacks is made even more pressing by the fact that the black work force has been growing at a faster rate during the 1970s than has the white work force. Between 1970 and 1980 the black labor force is expected to grow by 27%, compared to 16% for white workers.[62] The difference in growth rates is primarily a consequence of a more rapid increase in the black population of working age, particularly in the ages under 35. We shall deal with legislation designed to enforce equal employment opportunity in Chapter 23.

Part-Time Workers, Moonlighting, and the Multiworker Family

Although it has been claimed that we live in a leisure society, more people are at work today than ever before in our history. Part-time work grows every year; family members other than the principal breadwinner seek to augment family earnings; and the result has been a higher spendable income for the family unit.

Moonlighting. A significant number of wage earners hold another job in addition to their principal job. This practice, commonly called "moonlighting," involved about 3.9 million workers, or about 4.7% of all employed persons, in May 1975.[63] We shall return to the subject of moonlighting in Chapter 16.

Multiworker Families. Families in which not only the husband works, but also the wife and possibly other members of the family, are a major and growing factor in American economic life. In 1975, nearly half of all husband-wife families had two or more workers in the labor force. The median income of families with a wife in the paid labor force was $16,928 in 1974, compared to $12,082 for families with a nonworking wife.[64]

Part-Time Workers. Part-time employment is generally defined as employment for fewer than 35 hours a week. Part-time employment has been growing at a considerably faster rate than has the total volume of employment. As Figure 1–3 indicates, there are two general categories of part-time employees—those who voluntarily choose to work less than full-time schedules, and those who would like full-time work

---

[62] U.S. Department of Labor, *Employment and Training Report,* table E–5, p. 333.

[63] Kopp Michelotti, "Multiple Jobholding in May 1975," *Monthly Labor Review,* vol. 98 (November 1975), p. 56.

[64] Howard Hayghe, "Families and the Rise of Working Wives—An Overview," *Monthly Labor Review,* vol. 99 (May 1976), pp. 12–15.

FIGURE 1–3

Employees on Part-Time Schedules, Voluntary and Involuntary, 1957–1976

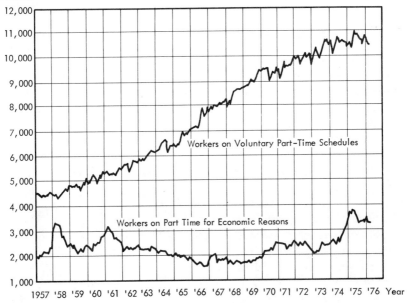

Source: U.S. Department of Labor, *Employment and Earnings*, vol. 22 (May 1976), p. 12.

but are on part-time involuntarily for economic reasons. The former group is by far the more important.

The number of voluntary part-time workers in nonagricultural industries almost doubled between 1960 and 1976—increasing from 5.8 million to close to 11 million. In large part, these workers are white, married females, 25–44 years old. The majority work in sales and clerical jobs.[65]

Involuntary part-time employment represents a failure by the economy to utilize its human resources fully; it is a type of hidden unemployment. As can be seen from Figure 1–3, part-time employment of this kind fluctuates with the business cycle, rising in periods of recession and falling when business conditions improve. In 1975, part-time employment of this type reached a high point, with 3.7 million persons on shortened work schedules.[66]

Part-time employment—both voluntary and involuntary—is particularly common among the very young (under age 18) and those over age 65. Moreover, in almost every age class, women are more likely to be em-

[65] *Conference Board Record*, vol. 12 (October 1975), p. 57.

[66] U.S. Department of Labor, *Employment and Training Report*, table A–31, p. 256.

ployed part-time than are men. Part-time employment is prevalent among nonwhite workers, and as might be expected, involuntary part-time employment falls heavily on this group.

The Quality of the Labor Force

A nation's labor force is the source of its strength and wealth. These attributes cannot be measured in terms of numbers alone. More important are the educational attainments and skills of the people who compose the labor force and the adaptability of these people to the needs of an ever-changing technology.

Measured by a number of criteria, the quality of the U.S. labor force will continue to improve during the decade of the 70s. As the median age of the population rises because of the decline in the birthrate, the average maturity and experience of the work force should increase. Likewise, with the substantially lessened flow of new job entrants, the problems of training unskilled youth should ease somewhat. The upgrading of the educational attainments of the labor force will continue. On the one hand, the proportion of the poorly educated will continue to diminish. In the late 1950s, over one third of the adult civilian labor force—19.3 million workers—had completed eight years or less of formal education. This proportion will fall to one eighth by 1980 and to about one sixteenth by 1990. On the other hand, workers with four years or more of college are projected to increase from 9.6 million in 1970 to 14.3 million in 1980 and to 21.8 million in 1990, at which time they will constitute almost one fourth of the civilian labor force.[67]

The improved quality of the labor force is not, however, an assurance of full employment. There is growing evidence that the rising tide of college-educated job seekers may meet problems in the labor market. Although holders of college degrees are increasing at an average annual rate of 4.0%,[68] there is no indication that jobs requiring such skills are increasing at as rapid a rate. In fact, there is considerable evidence that many college-educated persons are being forced to accept jobs for which they are overqualified. According to one recent report:

> In the last 15 years . . . the number of male college graduates who had to accept positions unrelated to their majors climbed to 20% from 13%, and the corresponding female total rose to 17% from 10%. . . . Over the same period, the proportion of college-educated men who had to settle for nonprofessional nonmanagerial positions increased threefold, and the proportion of women went up fourfold.[69]

---

[67] Denis F. Johnston, "Education of Workers: Projections to 1990," *Monthly Labor Review,* vol. 96 (November 1973), p. 22.

[68] Ibid.

[69] *Wall Street Journal,* January 16, 1976, p. 1.

College graduates who find that the available jobs do not give them the opportunity to utilize and develop their skills, are likely to feel frustrated and alienated from their work. It is an unfortunate fact that many jobs seem dull, boring, and repetitive. There is some evidence that beyond a certain point, increasing educational attainment may be associated with declining, rather than increasing, productivity on the job.[70] The increasing educational attainment of the labor force may cause problems, rather than progress, unless there is a better matching of skills and job needs.

A special problem faces women college graduates, whose numbers are also increasing rapidly. In past years, a large proportion of these graduates were absorbed in primary and secondary education, but with the downturn in school enrollments resulting from the decline in the birthrate, women will move in unprecedented numbers into traditionally male-dominated professional and technical occupations.

It is obvious from the foregoing discussion that despite the rising level of the labor force's educational achievement, training and guidance services will be needed more than ever before. The problem of obsolescent skills, which used to be associated with textile workers in mill towns, is now a pressing concern of engineers in aerospace industries. Indeed, a study of 2,500 design and development engineers suggests that the problem of obsolescence is becoming more severe and that there is a trend toward earlier obsolescence of specialized skills.[71]

OCCUPATION AND SOCIOECONOMIC STATUS IN THE LABOR FORCE

In today's growing and complex society, it is not enough simply to know that there will be 100 million jobs for 100 million workers in 1980. Where will those jobs be? What skills will be required? Which industries and occupations will grow at the most rapid rate? In the following section, we shall examine some of the basic trends which are shaping the nature of our economy and will determine the job needs of the future.

The Decline in Agricultural Employment

As laborsaving machinery has taken over the backbreaking work which used to be required on the farm, the surplus population from our large farm families has gravitated to the cities to work in industry. Thus,

---

[70] Ivar Berg, *Education and Jobs: The Great Training Robbery* (New York: Praeger Publishers, Inc., 1970), pp. 85–94.

[71] Gene W. Dalton and Paul H. Thompson, "Accelerating Obsolescence of Older Engineers," *Harvard Business Review*, vol. 49 (September–October 1971), pp. 57–67.

as industrial employment has risen, agricultural employment has fallen drastically. In 1900, about one out of every three persons gainfully employed was engaged in farming or some other agricultural pursuit. In 1975, by contrast, agriculture accounted for only 3.4 million employees out of a total of 84.8 million persons employed in both agriculture and non-agricultural industries, or about 4% of total employment. (See Table 1–1.) Until about 1970, employment had been declining in agriculture at the rate of about 200,000 workers per year. Since 1970, however, agricultural employment seems to have stabilized at about 3.4 million.

The Shift from Goods-Producing to Service Industries

A surprising aspect of our machine-oriented industrial economy is the decline in the importance of the goods-producing sector as a source of employment opportunities. Table 1–3 shows how employment was

TABLE 1–3
Percent Distribution of Actual and Projected Employment in Nonagricultural Establishments by Industry Division, 1947, 1960, 1970, and 1980

Industry Division	1947	1960	1970	1980*
Total	100.0	100.0	100.0	100.0
Goods-producing industries	42.1	37.6	33.0	31.3
Manufacturing	35.4	31.0	27.4	25.3
Durable goods	19.1	17.4	15.9	15.0
Nondurable goods	16.3	13.5	11.6	10.3
Mining	2.2	1.3	0.9	0.6
Construction	4.5	5.3	4.7	5.3
Service-producing industries	57.9	62.4	67.0	68.7
Transportation and other utilities	9.5	7.4	6.4	5.5
Trade	20.4	21.0	21.1	20.4
Finance, insurance, and real estate	4.0	4.9	5.2	4.9
Services and miscellaneous	11.5	13.7	16.5	18.6
Government	12.5	15.4	17.8	19.4
Federal	4.3	4.2	3.8	3.5
State and local	8.2	11.2	13.9	15.9

* Projected.
Source: U.S. Department of Labor, *Manpower Report of the President, 1972* (Washington, D.C.: Government Printing Office, 1972), table C–1, p. 215; table E–11, p. 259.

divided between the goods-producing and service sectors of the economy in 1947, 1960, and 1970, and also projects the changes expected by 1980. Whereas in 1947 about 42% of the workers in nonagricultural industries were employed in the production of goods, by 1970 the proportion had fallen to 33%. Although the percentage of the labor force employed in goods-producing industries has continued to decline during the decade of the 70s, there has been some small growth in actual employment in this sector. However, the bulk of the new job opportunities will fall in

FIGURE 1–4

Employment* Trends in Goods-Producing and Service-Producing Industries 1947–1968 (actual) and 1968–1980 (projected for a services economy with 3% unemployment)

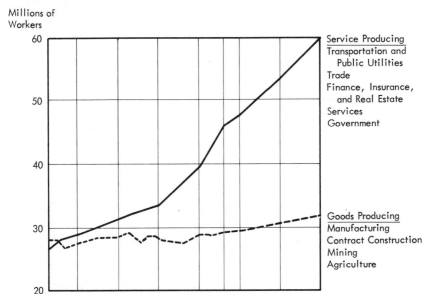

Millions of Workers

* Wage and salary workers only, except in agriculture, which includes self-employed and unpaid family workers.

Source: U.S. Department of Labor, *The U.S. Economy in 1980: A Summary of BLS Projections* (Washington, D.C.: Government Printing Office, 1970), chart 4, p. 18.

the service sector. Figure 1–4 illustrates the diverging employment trends in these two sectors.

By 1980, almost seven out of every ten workers in nonagricultural industries—or 68 million persons—are expected to be employed in the service sector of the economy.[72] The fastest rates of growth will occur in the "government" and "services and miscellaneous" categories. Employment has been growing faster in government than in any other sector of the economy. As already noted, government employment has almost tripled since the end of World War II.[73] One writer has suggested that the shift from goods-producing to service-producing industries would be much less dramatic if government were not included in the service-producing group.[74] During the 70s, employment by the federal government has

---

[72] *Monthly Labor Review*, vol. 96 (December 1973), table 9, p. 39.

[73] U.S. Department of Labor, *Employment and Training Report*, table C–1, p. 293.

[74] Edward F. Denison, "The Shift to Services and the Rate of Productivity Change," *Survey of Current Business*, vol. 53 (October 1973), p. 20.

expanded only slightly, but state and local government employment has continued to grow at a rapid pace. The U.S. Department of Labor projects the employment needs of state and local governments to rise to 16 million by 1985, about 50% higher than the 10.6 million employed in 1972.[75]

Government employment is one area in which the changing composition of the labor force will tend to favor union organization. The militancy demonstrated by unions which have become entrenched among key groups of government employees portends major problems of public policy in the years ahead. We shall explore some of these questions in depth in Chapter 22.

Within the services group, which includes personal, business, health, and educational services, there will be continued rapid expansion in employment. Growth in business services is expected to be particularly rapid, as firms rely increasingly on advertising, accounting, computer, maintenance, and other types of contract services. It is significant to note that while consumer services typically have a high concentration of female employment, these so-called producer services rendered to business firms have a greater percentage of male employment and higher average earnings than are shown for the labor force as a whole.[76]

The fastest growing industries during the period to 1980 will include such glamorous areas as office computing and accounting machines; optical, ophthalmic, and photographic equipment; electronic components and accessories; communications; and plastics and synthetic materials.[77] Although the rate of growth of *output* in these industries will exceed that of industry in general, this does not necessarily imply that these industries will be major sources of job opportunities. Unemployed workers need jobs, not growth rates, and in terms of total numbers of vacancies created, this group is not very significant in the entire economy. One reason is that rapidly growing industries frequently exhibit a high level of productivity improvement, and this tends to limit employment opportunities.[78]

Despite the changing job structure in the decade ahead, manufacturing will account for about the same proportion of overall employment in 1980 as it did in 1950. However, as has already been indicated in Figure 1–3, significant growth in employment opportunities will occur in the service-producing industries listed in the figure. These industries, by and

---

[75] U.S. Department of Labor, *Occupational Outlook Handbook*, 1974–75 ed., Bulletin 1785 (Washington, D.C.: Government Printing Office, 1974), p. 17.

[76] Harry I. Greenfield, *Manpower and the Growth of Producer Services* (New York: Columbia University Press, 1966), p. 1.

[77] U.S. Department of Labor, *Patterns of U.S. Economic Growth*, Bulletin 1672 (Washington, D.C.: Government Printing Office, 1970), p. 33.

[78] U.S. Department of Labor, Bureau of Labor Statistics, *Productivity and the Economy*, Bulletin 1710 (Washington, D.C.: Government Printing Office, 1971), p. 34.

large, represent areas which in the past have been characterized by rather low levels of productivity change. The significance of this shift in the structure of employment will be discussed in Chapter 13.

The Growth in White-Collar Employment

A characteristic trend in the development of American industry has been the shift in employment toward white-collar occupations, such as professional, managerial, clerical, and sales work, and away from the blue-collar occupations of craftsmen, operatives, and laborers. This change in the occupational content of jobs has been associated with the shift from goods-producing to service-producing industries and with the rapid growth of employment in the governmental sector of the economy, which creates jobs primarily for white-collar workers.

This trend toward more white-collar employment has been evident in our economy since the turn of the century and is part of the normal evolution of economic development, which shifts labor resources from agriculture to manufacturing and then to services. The increasing importance of white-collar jobs is not, however, just another manifestation of the shift from goods-producing to service industries; for even within the goods-producing industries themselves—mining, construction, and manufacturing—white-collar employment has grown faster than production employment. (See Table 1–4.)

TABLE 1–4
White-Collar Workers as a Percent of Total Employment in Goods-Producing Industries, 1947 and 1975

	White-Collar Workers as a Percent of Total Employment	
	1947	1975
Mining	9	30
Construction	11	22
Manufacturing	17	31

Source: U.S. Department of Labor et al., *Employment and Training Report of the President, 1976* (Washington, D.C.: Government Printing Office, 1976), p. 150.

By the middle of the 1950s, white-collar workers had begun to outnumber blue-collar workers; by 1980, more workers will be in white-collar jobs than in the blue-collar and service groups combined. However, since 1970 there has been some slackening in the rate of change from blue-collar to white-collar jobs. At the same time, continuing a trend that began in the 60s, the proportion of workers in the economy's hard-to-mechanize menial tasks—garbage collectors, janitors, and hospital orderlies—has increased after generations of decline.[79]

White-collar jobs are not necessarily available only to highly educated workers. Actually, the category encompasses a wide range of educational qualifications. Managerial jobs range from presidents of large corporations to operators of hamburger stands; clerical jobs cover both executive secretaries and file clerks; sales work includes peddlers as well as stockbrokers.

Figure 1–5 indicates projected changes from 1972 to 1985 in major

FIGURE 1–5

Projected Changes in Major Categories of Workers, 1972–1985 (in percent)

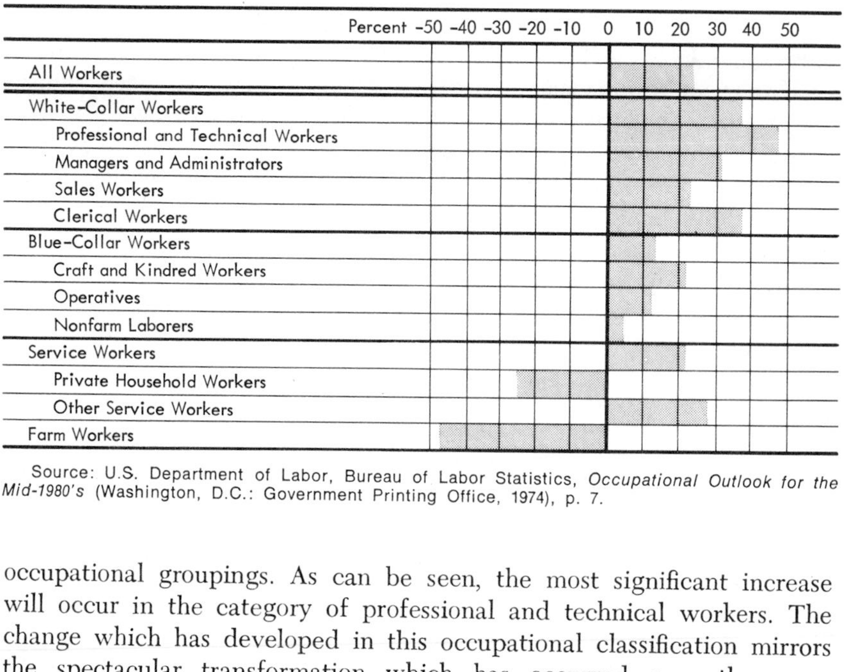

	Percent −50 −40 −30 −20 −10	0 10 20 30 40 50
All Workers		▨
White–Collar Workers		▨
Professional and Technical Workers		▨
Managers and Administrators		▨
Sales Workers		▨
Clerical Workers		▨
Blue–Collar Workers		▨
Craft and Kindred Workers		▨
Operatives		▨
Nonfarm Laborers		▨
Service Workers		▨
Private Household Workers	▨	
Other Service Workers		▨
Farm Workers	▨	

Source: U.S. Department of Labor, Bureau of Labor Statistics, *Occupational Outlook for the Mid-1980's* (Washington, D.C.: Government Printing Office, 1974), p. 7.

occupational groupings. As can be seen, the most significant increase will occur in the category of professional and technical workers. The change which has developed in this occupational classification mirrors the spectacular transformation which has occurred over the years in the labor market. In 1947, the proportion of the labor force in the skilled crafts was double that of professional and technical personnel. By 1975, professional and technical personnel had surpassed skilled craftsmen in numerical representation in the labor force. Whereas in both 1960 and 1970 operatives were the most numerous occupational groups in the labor force, by 1980 they will be surpassed in number by both clerical workers and professional and technical employees.[80]

The foregoing statistics make one point abundantly clear: although technological progress has been changing us into a nation of employees,

[79] Edmund Faltermayer, "Ever Increasing Affluence Is Less of a Sure Thing," *Fortune,* vol. 91 (April 1975), p. 95.

[80] U.S. Department of Labor, *Employment and Training Report,* table A–15, p. 234.

it has not been building a proletariat of production workers bound to the machine. Scientists, supervisors, artists, teachers, professionals, and other white-collar workers have been increasing at a much faster rate than has the working population as a whole. The increasing importance of middle-class occupations has tended to strengthen the forces of conservatism and to some extent has made more difficult the task of union organization. White-collar workers often ally themselves with management groups in their thinking on economic matters; by and large, they have looked upon union organization as a blue-collar movement. Unions have found white-collar workers difficult to organize. Union members are a minority of the 21 million clerical and sales workers. Recent successful organizing drives among teachers and other government employees have made some inroads in the white-collar group, but most white-collar workers still remain outside the union fold. Union leaders, faced by the changing composition of the labor force, must find some way of attracting white-collar workers as members.

Although the trend from blue-collar to white-collar jobs is significant, one should not jump to the conclusion that the American labor force is becoming a conservative group of white-collar employees. The customary definitions of "blue-collar worker" exclude service workers. The latter, however, are a group of growing importance in the economy, with aims and problems similar in many respects to those of blue-collar workers. The number of service workers, other than private household, jumped from 5.5 million in 1958 to 10.5 million in 1975, while their proportion in the labor force rose from 8.8% to 12.4% during the same period.[81] In this category one can find janitors, waiters, elevator operators, guards, watchmen, and hospital employees. Obviously, these are groups which have been prone to union organization. On the other hand, the definition of "white-collar worker" includes such types as postal workers, baggagemen, messengers, dispatchers, newsboys, and others whom many readers would not ordinarily think of as "white-collar workers." A recent controversial book claims that the "working class" is still the majority in America and cautions readers not to be misled by categorical definitions which have been adopted for ease in statistical analysis.[82] Nevertheless, the traditional salaried office worker group does remain largely unorganized.

WHAT IS A LABOR PROBLEM?

We have reviewed briefly the composition, characteristics, and projected growth of the labor force. "Labor problems" typically involve only a certain segment of the civilian labor force. A simple illustration

---

[81] U.S. Department of Labor, *Employment and Training Report,* table A–15, p. 234.

[82] See Andrew Levison, *The Working Class Majority* (New York: Coward, McCann & Geoghegan, Inc.), 1974.

will serve to indicate the criterion which separates the group with which we are concerned from other members of the labor force. Consider the case of John Jones, the independent grocer, who owns his own store and is self-employed. His income depends upon the margin between his sales receipts and the cost of his wares, after covering expenses of operation. Suppose that competition from other grocers compels him to reduce prices so that his income is cut in half. John Jones may now complain that his labor is not being adequately compensated; yet ordinarily, this circumstance would not be considered a labor problem.

Now change the facts slightly. John Jones employs ten clerks in his store. Competition forces him to cut their wages in half. Here, we have a labor problem. What is the essential difference between the two cases? The difference lies in the fact that John Jones is self-employed, whereas his clerks work for wages and are therefore dependent upon their employer for their livelihood. Labor problems grow out of the economic activity of that part of the working population which offers its services for hire to *others* and receives its compensation in the form of wages or salaries. Because they are dependent upon others to offer them employment, wage and salary earners are subject to the risk of unemployment. Because they are dependent upon employers for their daily income, their interests frequently clash with those of the latter group. The result is strikes, lockouts, slowdowns, and other manifestations of labor strife. Finally, because they have this common bond of dependence upon others for their employment and income, a certain feeling of solidarity tends to exist among members of this group, despite the diversity of their occupations. This sense of a common status has led many of them to join together in unions to present a common front to their employers and to the owners of the means of production.

Organized Labor and Labor Problems

Although much of the theoretical discussion in later chapters of this book concerning the labor market, supply and demand, and related considerations is applicable to all persons who work for hire, our major emphasis will be upon organized labor and upon the problems which arise between unions and management in the collective bargaining process. The reason for this emphasis is clear. While less than one out of every four workers is a union member, nevertheless union actions and union policies affect the working of the entire labor market. We have already noted that large corporations control the bulk of our industrial assets and employ the majority of our workers in manufacturing. For the most part, these giants of industry are unionized. As a consequence, agreements reached by management and union representatives in these companies profoundly affect production, income, prices, and employment throughout the economy.

In the manufacturing field, practically all our key industries are strongly unionized. The same is true for the railroads, air transport, and many parts of the trucking, construction, electric light and power, and paper industries. While the growing importance of white-collar employment and the diminishing importance of production workers in our economy may in the long run weaken the position of organized labor, at the present time and for the foreseeable future, organized labor exercises—and will continue to exercise—a major influence on trends in the labor market.

There would undoubtedly be labor problems without unions. For example, we experienced strikes, large wage increases, and a wage-price inflation in 1919 when unions were weak and industry was largely unorganized. But the fact remains that in our economy today the labor problems that make the headlines and require our study are primarily problems in which unions play a key role. We shall, therefore, begin our study of labor problems by reviewing the history and development of organized labor in this country so as to understand better the motivation, objectives, and policies of organized labor.

QUESTIONS FOR DISCUSSION

1. Discuss the various meanings which can be attached to the phrase *labor force*. Consider how the following factors might affect the size of the labor force: war mobilization, massive unemployment, increased social security benefits, the elimination of discrimination in employment.

2. How does the changing occupational structure of employment affect the problem of providing jobs for blacks in our economy?

3. "There is no longer a 'working class' majority in the American economy." Discuss the validity of this statement.

4. Karl Marx predicted that the growth of capitalism would produce an industrial proletariat, squeeze out the small businessman and shopkeeper, and therefore set the stage for communist revolution. To what extent has the development of capitalism in the United States differed from this prediction?

SUGGESTIONS FOR FURTHER READING

Economic Report of the President (annual reports). Washington, D.C.: Government Printing Office.

These annual reports constitute an invaluable source of currrent information on labor, population, business, and other economic trends and statistics.

U.S. Department of Commerce, Bureau of the Census. *The Social and Economic Status of the Black Population in the United States, 1974.* Current Population Reports, Series P–23, No. 24. Washington, D.C.: Government Printing Office, 1975.

A compendium of statistical data relating to Negro population distribution, income, unemployment, housing, education, and other significant economic and social conditions. Such reports are issued at regular intervals.

U.S. Department of Labor, *Employment and Training Report of the President* (annual reports). Washington, D.C.: Government Printing Office.

These annual reports contain concise explanations, supported by up-to-date statistics, of changes which have occurred and are occurring in population, labor force, employment, and other variables in the labor market.

U.S. Department of Labor, *Occupational Outlook for the Mid-1980's*. Washington, D.C.: Government Printing Office, 1974.

An excellent analysis of the factors creating change in the labor market with projections for growth in various occupations.

part two

Union History and Government

2

History of the American
Labor Movement

UNIONS TODAY have a profound effect on the American economic system. The allocation of economic resources, the sharing of the products of industry, political attitudes and alignments, employment and unemployment, legal rights and duties, business stability, technical progress and the rate of innovation in industry, and the policies and attitudes of all levels of government—all are influenced by union policies and programs. Despite the failure of union membership growth to keep pace with the growth in the labor force, union membership today remains high (see Figure 2–1), and union power remains strong. Obviously, economic analysis must concern itself with union policy and practice if such analysis is to present a realistic contemporary picture.

THE CONDITIONS OF ORGANIZATION

Despite differences, all labor movements have certain characteristics in common. Labor movements arise initially out of the separation of the workers from their tools. Someone who becomes an employee instead of a self-employed person loses control over the terms and conditions of his or her employment. With the development of a factory system of labor and a concentration of ownership employing large numbers of workers, the individual's influence over working conditions is steadily lessened. Workers tend to show interest in organizing unions when they feel that their immediate opportunities for advancement in the organizational hierarchy to the employer class are limited. The acceptance of unionism by a worker in a society like ours, with its relatively fluid class lines, does not mean that the worker will reject future opportunities to rise above the working group. It merely means that the worker

FIGURE 2–1

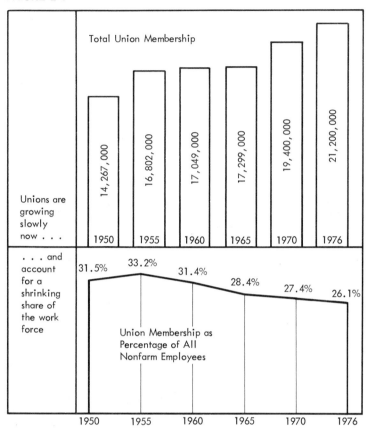

Source: Data, U.S. Department of Labor. Chart copyright © 1972, U.S. News & World Report, Inc. Reproduced from the issue of February 21, 1972, and modified to include 1976.

believes that his or her present economic situation will be best served by union activity.

Workers also join unions to obtain a voice in their wages, hours, and working conditions. Even those satisfied with what they are paid often join unions in order to participate in the determination of the conditions under which they work.

A fundamental condition for the existence of trade unionism everywhere is the existence of freedom of speech, press, and assembly. The so-called unions which operate in dictatorial or totalitarian countries are, in fact, organs of the state, controlled and operated by the state, and lacking in power to act except to transmit state orders. We shall be concerned with unions in the traditional sense: organizations of workers which function primarily as the agents of employees in collective bargaining with employers or management over the terms and conditions of employment. Such unions may engage in a variety of supplementary activities, but their primary interest is in collective bargaining, and, subject to some legal limitations, they are free to act, unrestricted by state control or domination.

Once the initial conditions have been met, labor organizations emerge among employees who have bargaining power which the employer must respect. These are workers possessing a hard-to-replace skill, for example, toolmakers; or workers located at critical spots, for example, teamsters or longshoremen. They may form a union solely of their own, or they may find it necessary or wise to bring in their less strategically located fellow employees. The skilled are the essential core of unionization.

The speed with which a labor movement organizes is a product of economic and political conditions. American labor unions have made their greatest gains in periods of rising prices and labor shortages (1863–72, 1896–1904, 1917–20, 1941–45, and 1965–68), and in periods of political unrest (1827–36, 1881–86, and 1933–37). When prices are rising and labor is in short demand, union growth occurs as employer resistance to large wage increases is tempered by high profits and the difficulties of obtaining sufficient employees. In recent years, the expansion of industries with compulsory union agreements has also spurred union growth.

THE AMERICAN ENVIRONMENT

If, however, the conditions of union organization and growth are similar in various lands, the environment is not. Five fundamental characteristics have contributed to the uniqueness of the American scene, and in turn that of American unions.

Class Fluidity

Penniless immigrants arriving in the United States have seen their sons become business executives, labor leaders, statesmen. In America, one is not born into a status. Since class lines are not hard and fast, workers have been able to advance as individuals. American workers have, therefore, been less interested in trade-union organization than have many of their European counterparts. Indeed, it was not until the Great Depression of the 1930s that large numbers of workers decided that they needed unions at all.

America's loose class lines have not only hindered union development but have shaped unionism as well. In being interested primarily in improving labor's conditions within the capitalist system, American unions reflect their members' basic belief that this is still the land of opportunity.

Resources and Land

The rich resources of America have, of course, aided in preventing the rise of hard class barriers by providing opportunities for advancement. Moreover, the traditional "rugged individualism" of American employers stems from the same sources. In labor relations, employer "individualism" has featured opposition to government or union "interference" in the operation of business and the refusal to recognize unions of employees or collective bargaining until compelled to do so by law.

One of America's great resources has been abundance of land. The westward migrations drained off potential city proletarians. Many workers went West to seek individual fortunes instead of remaining in the East and joining unions to seek group advancement. The movement of industry from urban areas to suburban and rural environments in recent years has further hindered unionization by decentralizing plants and work forces.

Wide Markets

The size of the American market has been an important factor contributing to the growth of American unions. To protect the workers under its jurisdiction, a union cannot raise the price of labor too far beyond that which competitors of the company are paying. A union must organize the length and breadth of the market. Otherwise, nonunion plants, by paying lower wages, may take business away from the union plants and thus imperil the jobs of the union workers. In the 1830s, a union did not have to organize much more than a citywide market. Poor transportation made the city relatively immune from the competition of other areas. Today, however, the market is more likely to cover a far greater area, or even to be national in scope. A union, therefore, must often become a national organization of tremendous size in order to be successful in a national market.

The development of the national market not only stimulated national labor organization but, paradoxically, made that organization more difficult. With a continental market, nonunion competitors can be a thousand miles apart. The resources which American unions require in order to organize an industry are thus very great.

Moreover, the large American market permitted the breakdown of jobs into small specialized units of the mass-production process. Thousands of workers are employed in unskilled or semiskilled jobs, their efforts combining to perform a task done in smaller countries by a single skilled worker. Since the semiskilled and unskilled are easier to replace than the skilled, the bargaining power of labor was correspondingly reduced, and the ability of unions to compel a reluctant management to recognize their existence was considerably lessened.

Heterogeneous Population

Another factor hindering the development of labor organization is the existence of many races and nationalities without a common heritage, with rivalries, suspicions, and often without obvious mutuality of interests. Such heterogeneity presents a labor force which is difficult to weld into a labor movement. The policy of many factories in employing a "judicious mixture" of ethnic groups, or the practice of substituting a new wave of immigrants when an older wave showed signs of becoming restive with the status quo, kept racial and ethnic rivalries alive and made the task of the union organizer all the more difficult. Current animosities among white and black workers attest to continued existence of the racial problem in union organization.

Social and Legal Background

The legal and social system in the United States, itself a result of the environmental factors of the American scene, has strongly conditioned American labor. The strong support of private property among the masses, the high esteem of businessmen in the population as a whole, and the consequent unpopularity among the dominant middle class of trade unionism, which is often pictured as "antibusiness," have all helped to make it difficult to build the American labor movement and to have helped to shape its policies as well. In recent years, however, favorable government laws and judicial rulings have aided unions.

THE BEGINNINGS, 1790–1825[1]

Records of local labor unions and strikes antedate the Revolutionary War, but labor organizations in colonial times were very short-lived. Commencing in the 1790s, however, came the first known unions which survived for a number of years—shoemakers, carpenters, printers, bakers, tailors, longshoremen, and teamsters formed organizations of their crafts and groups. Sometimes organization was defensive against the merchant-capitalist, a new functionary who bought and sold in large quantities over wide areas and therefore broadened the scope of competition. This often either compelled master craftsmen to discontinue independent work and hire out as a journeyman or else forced the master to reduce the wages of his journeymen. On other occasions, organization was spurred

---

[1] Although the authors accept full responsibility for interpretations, they have frankly based the pre-1950 section on secondary sources, including the pioneer works of John R. Commons and his associates, R. F. Hoxie, and Norman J. Ware, but especially on the admirable synthesis of Professor Royal E. Montgomery in H. A. Millis and R. E. Montgomery, *Organized Labor* (New York: McGraw-Hill Book Co., 1945), pp. 1–242. The lack of detailed documentation is for reader convenience and is not intended to understress our great debt to these authors.

by the shortage of skilled labor and by the desire of craftsmen to take advantage of the demand for their services.

These early unions were composed entirely of skilled workers or of strategically located workers, such as teamsters and longshoremen. In fact, throughout history, such workers have always been the first to organize. Those who, by reason of skill or strategic location, can exert pressure or inflict loss by withdrawing their services possess the ability to secure employer recognition long before their less favorably placed fellow workers.

Early unions did not engage in collective bargaining as we know it today. Customarily, the union "posted its prices," that is, announced the wages and working conditions for which its members would work. If the employer refused to agree, a strike would ensue, and perhaps a compromise would be worked out. Only slowly did the custom develop of joint employer-employee conferences at which bargaining occurred prior to direct union action. Even in the later part of the 19th century, when collective bargaining as we know it today was well under way, unilateral union posting of wage schedules was not uncommon.

The Conspiracy Doctrine

The early unions were not received with complacency by employers. The latter found a firm ally in the judiciary, which throughout the 19th century stood firmly with the well-to-do class from which its members were recruited. The ancient doctrine of conspiracy was brought out and applied to "labor combinations in restraint of trade." Although "there was nothing unlawful in combination itself, nothing unlawful in an individual's refusal to work, and nothing unlawful in a workman's desire to obtain better standards of employment,"[2] the early judges found that this all added up to a conspiracy. Thus, in the famous *Philadelphia Cordwainers* case,[3] the learned judge declared: "A combination of workmen to raise their wages may be considered in a two-fold point of view: one is to benefit themselves . . . the other is to injure those who do not join the [combination]. . . . The rule of law condemns both. . . ." Hence the workers were jailed and fined.

The judges were reasoning from their socioeconomic point of view. As time wore on, however, more reasoned justice asserted itself. In 1842, the Massachusetts Supreme Court dealt the criminal conspiracy doctrine a mortal blow by ruling in effect that the legality of a strike depended upon the end sought, and that the mere purpose of requiring all workers to join a union (closed shop) was not per se illegal.[4]

---

[2] Charles O. Gregory, *Labor and the Law*, 2d rev. ed. (New York: W. W. Norton & Co., Inc., 1961), p. 19.

[3] An 1806 case. Cordwainers were shoemakers, originally those who worked on cordovan leather.

[4] *Commonwealth* v. *Hunt,* 4 Metcalf 111 (1842).

CITYWIDE MOVEMENTS AND POLITICS, 1825–1837

Andrew Jackson rode into the presidency on a wave of agrarian and urban revolt against that era's prevailing economic and political inequalities among different classes. Most rankling to the urban wage earner were the length of the workday (sunup to sundown), imprisonment for debt, compulsory militia service from which the rich could buy excuse, the absence of mechanics' lien laws to protect workers in case of employer bankruptcy, property qualifications for voting, and the lack of a free educational system. Workers in New York, Philadelphia, and other seaboard centers attempted to cope with these problems through their unions. The battle was fought both by direct economic action and by political action. The former technique was utilized to improve wages and working conditions, especially by reducing hours to a straight ten per day.

It was in the political field, however, that the unions of this period made their most spectacular efforts. Workingmen's parties were formed and, particularly in New York and Philadelphia, held the balance of power between the Federalists and the Democrats for several years. Anxious to secure the workers' votes, New York's Tammany Hall adopted the basic workers' program—free public education, universal suffrage, and mechanics' lien laws were adopted or strengthened, and compulsory militia service began to disappear. By 1843, the workingmen's parties had folded, but their imprint remained.

The local unions in the cities formed central trades organizations to coordinate their activities, and a National Trades Union was formed in 1834. Although it lasted less than five years, it agitated successfully for the establishment of the ten-hour day in government employment. The workers' problems were primarily local, however, and they were unwilling to cede authority to a national body. The same factor hindered the establishment of national craft unions.

FROM REFORMISM AND COOPERATION TO NATIONAL ORGANIZATION, 1840–1867

The depression which began in 1837 was one of the severest in American history. The ranks of unions thinned out and disappeared in the face of mass unemployment. As new unions were formed, their interests were diverted toward reformist programs which were often more well-meaning than practical. Adherents of cooperation were especially prominent. The thesis that labor's problems can be solved by placing the ownership of the means of production into the hands of the worker and then having the worker share in the profits has always had a great appeal to reformers of every era. Workers, however, soon found that it takes more than manual work to run a business.

The cooperative often could not supply better conditions of employment than the capitalist supplied, and often the cooperative could not even produce goods as cheaply as the capitalist could. It was the practical trade unionist who won out, for he alone could deliver something more substantial than the promised millennium to cope with the problems of wage earners. In the 1840s, the use of anthracite coal stimulated the rise of the steel industry, railroad development began, and increased industrialization and urbanization went forward rapidly. That decade also saw rapid increases in population, wealth and prices, and a consequent increased demarcation between the property holders and the propertyless.

The unionism of this time was confined to the skilled, but it was firmly rooted. During the two decades that followed the founding of the International Typographical Union[5] in 1852, at least a dozen organizations were formed which survive to this day. The Civil War, by separating North from South and dislocating industry and the economy, at first seriously set back the new unions; later, however, by creating a shortage of labor and stimulating industry, it fed union growth. In 1867, an attempt at national federation led to the founding of the National Labor Union.

Knowing nothing of the early struggles of labor, the founders of the National Labor Union permitted political as well as labor organizations to affiliate. Moreover, when the organization's propaganda led to the adoption of the eight-hour day in federal employment, political action was stressed. Other reform objectives, however, failed of attainment. The states did not, as hoped, pass eight-hour laws; producer cooperation and worker ownership of industry failed to materialize; and the "cheap money" program of the Greenback movement did not aid worker aspirations. Slowly, the unions dropped out, and the National Labor Union became defunct in 1872.

THE KNIGHTS OF LABOR

Even before the National Labor Union was engulfed by politics, seven tailors met in Philadelphia, determined to found an organization which would transcend the narrow limits of craft unionism and unite all workers under one banner, regardless of race, sex, nationality, or creed. Thus was created the Noble Order of the Knights of Labor, which as a secret society spread slowly through industrialized Pennsylvania.

Gradually, the secrecy became a liability. Secret organizations were in ill repute in Pennsylvania as a result of the activities of the Molly Maguires, a terrorist group which attempted to achieve social justice by murdering company officials. The Mollies were uncovered by a Pinkerton

---

[5] Unions are called "international" in the United States because they have locals in Canada.

detective, who managed to become a Molly official and thus to achieve fame as the first in a long line of labor spies.

The Knights' secrecy was formally abolished in 1879, when Terence V. Powderly became the "Grand Master Workman." Thereafter, the Knights of Labor attempted to weld together all elements of the working classes. To do so, it permitted craft unions to affiliate directly with its "general assembly" (national organization) and also organized "mixed assemblies," that is, local organizations composed of a variety of workers organized on either an industrial or a heterogeneous basis.[6] The Knights' program stressed political reform, and the organization was closely allied with the agrarian revolt of this period, known as the "Great Upheaval." Powderly was a kindly, friendly Irishman who had a keen sense of social justice, a yearning for a better life, a firm belief in the common virtues and in the American system of private property. Some of his allies, however, were more radical, and they gave the Knights its tone, since the organization's local assemblies were autonomous.

The Knights of Labor reached its apex in 1886 after a strike on the Wabash, Missouri-Kansas-Texas, and Missouri Pacific railroads had forced Jay Gould, the financier who controlled these railroads, to grant recognition. The Knights' membership rose from 100,000 in 1885 to 700,000 in 1886. Members came in so fast it was necessary for the central office to suspend organizing to assure that no lawyers, bankers, gamblers, liquor dealers, or Pinkerton detectives—the only barred groups—would join the Knights.

The decline of the Knights was as rapid as its ascent. Losses in a number of strikes, including defeat in a second Missouri Pacific walkout, and the separation of the skilled men into a rival organization, later known as the American Federation of Labor, turned the tide. In 1888, the Knights claimed only 222,000 members; in 1890, 100,000; and in 1983, but 75,000. From then till the official dissolution 20 years later, its central office was engaged primarily in reform propaganda.

The structure and program of the Knights were ill-suited to the job of running a labor organization. Local organizations, known as "assemblies," often took in all comers, regardless of job or place of employment. The assumption was that all workers had the same interests and needs. The leadership of the Knights spent much of its energy, enthusiasm, and financial resources promoting producer cooperation and various monetary proposals, such as Greenbackism and Bryan's "free silver" program. Meanwhile, the day-to-day needs of wages, working conditions, and especially, organization building, were neglected.

The membership of the Knights was very unstable, composed mainly

---

[6] An industrial union includes all workers in a plant, an industry, or industries, regardless of craft or trade, whereas a craft union includes workers of one craft or trade, regardless of the plant or industry in which they are employed. Heterogeneous unions are those which take membership on any basis.

of unskilled workers who flocked in and out so fast that the Knights was once described as a "procession instead of an organization." These workers, being totally inexperienced in unionism, were great strikers but poor union members, disappearing from the organization as soon as a conflict ended. At first, the skilled craftsmen and their unions were attracted to the Knights, but the ineffectiveness of the Knights in day-to-day, bread-and-butter unionism led the craftsmen to bow out and seek an organization suited to their special needs and ambitions.

THE RISE OF THE AMERICAN FEDERATION OF LABOR

While the Knights of Labor was achieving its great boom, a group of trade-union leaders met in 1881 and formed what was first called the Federation of Organized Trades and Labor Unions and then, after 1886, the American Federation of Labor (AFL). Led by Samuel Gompers and Adolph Strasser of the Cigarmakers' International Union, this group was composed primarily of representatives of the skilled trades who feared that the result of the Knights' activities would be the destruction of trade unionism as they conceived it. They believed that trade unionism could best succeed if it were confined to those able to organize themselves—in other words, to skilled or strategically located groups. They also believed that trade unionism should limit itself to the immediate issues of improving workers' wages and working conditions rather than promote a socialist utopia.

The program of the AFL leaders was thus a pragmatic one, grounded firmly in the principles of American capitalism. They were out to improve the conditions of those whom they represented, and they represented the skilled workers who, because of their strategic location, had bargaining power sufficient to command employer recognition. To the great mass of workers, these leaders said, in effect: "Organizing will help you, but until you are ready for organization, we can best aid you by pulling up our wages and thus indirectly influencing yours to rise also."

Samuel Gompers

Samuel Gompers and his fellow founders of the AFL came to their conclusions concerning the type of labor movement that could prosper in America only after patient study and experience. Early in his working career, Gompers became acquainted with the German Socialists, mainly refugees from the unsuccessful European revolutions of 1848. Through them, he became familiar with the writings of Marx and the other literature of socialism. At the same time, Gompers took an active role in the developing Cigarmakers' Union, and thus he acquired the practical experience of a trade unionist. Although sympathetic with the aims of socialism, Gompers saw clearly that any organization which made a frontal attack on private property would alienate the dominant American middle classes and would find little support even among employees, who were less class-conscious and more interested in getting ahead as individuals than the European socialists thought.

Growth was slow during the first year of the AFL, but as the Knights of Labor declined, the Federation forged ahead. In 1894, the Socialists succeeded in defeating Gompers for the presidency. They were unable, however, to place their man at the helm for more than one year, and Gompers was returned to the office, which he held every year thereafter until he died in 1924. Later the Socialists attempted to form a rival organization known as the Socialist Trade and Labor Alliance. This organization failed, however, to gain a mass following.

In order to insure control of the AFL by national unions, Gompers was careful to reject affiliation offers by political groups. The constitution of the AFL maintained the national unions as autonomous organizations, each with exclusive jurisdictional rights in its territory. An executive committee, composed at various times of 5 to 15 persons, elected from affiliated national unions, plus a full-time president and secretary, governed the Federation between annual conventions. Representation in the AFL conventions was based on dues-paying membership. A combination of a few larger unions could thus control the AFL. The president had little authority. By leadership, force of personality, and an astute sense of politics, Gompers gave the AFL presidency vitality and power until his later and less vigorous years.

The Philosophy of the AFL

The American Federation of Labor, as the true counterpart of American capitalism, traditionally opposed government intervention in industrial relations matters. Samuel Gompers and the business exponents of laissez-faire were one in their belief that the government should confine its role in labor relations to policing and the maintenance of order and should not interfere in industrial relations matters or in the internal affairs of labor or business. Thus, Gompers opposed government intervention in labor disputes even to the extent of opposing government facilities for mediation and voluntary arbitration,[7] foreseeing that such intervention might lead to compulsory arbitration. Moreover, he wanted no part of government assistance in union organization. He did not think that the government should outlaw discrimination against workers because of union membership, believing that such government aid would lead to government control.

---

[7] Mediation or conciliation is the process whereby a third party attempts to secure settlement through persuasion and compromise. Arbitration involves the use of a third party to decide a dispute.

In social welfare matters, Gompers likewise stood for "voluntarism." No less than businessmen, he was against government minimum wages for men, and against government unemployment insurance and other forms of government social security. He believed that such welfare programs would weaken democracy by making citizens too dependent upon the state, that a minimum wage could tend to become a maximum and thus limit union action, and that minimum wages, unemployment insurance, and other social security measures could best be provided by the workers themselves through trade unions. The only exception to this rule was maximum hours and minimum wage legislation for women and children, and for government employees, who he felt were in need of special government protection.

The Injunction and the "Yellow-Dog" Contract

Of all the forms of government intervention, few have been resented by labor as bitterly as the "injunction." It became prominent in labor disputes in the latter half of the 1800s and was a carry-over from the common law, where it was devised to grant continuing relief if damages would not suffice to remedy a continuing harm. For example, if a farmer who depended upon a brook for water observed his neighbor upstream damming that brook, he might, under certain conditions, go to court, petition a judge, and, without prior notice, secure a temporary injunction requiring the neighbor to cease work on the dam, to maintain the status quo, and to appear in court in a given period, usually a week or ten days, to show cause why the injunction should not be made permanent. At the hearing, both parties had the right to plead before the judge as to what his course of action should be. The judge would then render an opinion, either dissolving the injunction or making it permanent. A person's failure to comply with an injunction, whether temporary or permanent, puts him in contempt of court and subjects him to penalties which the judge may impose without trial by jury.

Employers soon saw in the injunction an ideal weapon to curb the activities of labor unions. An employer who felt that a strike was impending could scurry to a judge with a complaint and rather easily secure an injunction requiring the union to stay any action on the ground that grave damages would befall the employer. Then the employer could discharge union members and otherwise undermine the organization so that by the time the hearing was held, the question of whether the injunction was to be made permanent or to be dissolved had become irrelevant.

To supplement the injunction, a legal technique was developed which was soon termed by organized labor, and is now known generally, as the "yellow-dog" contract. This is an agreement between an employer and a worker whereby, as a condition of employment, the worker agrees not to join a union. Unionists maintained that this was not a legal contract, since the worker was coerced into signing it. The courts of New York State upheld this contention by refusing to enforce it, but the federal courts and the courts in most states maintained that the mere fact of unequal bargaining power did not necessarily render a contract unenforceable. Thus, if an employer had signed up his workers to yellow-dog contracts, he might get an injunction requiring a union organizer to cease attempting to induce employees to break their legal contracts!

The climax of government by judiciary came when the Supreme Court ruled that the Sherman Antitrust law, enacted in 1890 to curb cases of business combination, was also applicable to labor combinations and that employees who had instituted a nationwide boycott against a hat manufacturer could be successfully sued for the treble damages provided in the law.

This was the background which led to the 40-year AFL campaign to end "government by judiciary" and to "neutralize" the courts. In 1914, when Congress passed the Clayton Act, which Gompers thought removed unions from the jurisdiction of antitrust laws, he believed that he had won his aim; but the courts interpreted this act differently. Not until 1932, with the passage of the Norris–La Guardia Act, did this AFL legislative drive achieve fruition.

Industrial Relations, 1880–1914

Between 1880 and the beginning of World War I began the first attempts at modern collective bargaining. National agreements negotiated in the stove, glass, and pottery industries; the beginning of regional collective bargaining in the bituminous coal industry; and a large number of agreements in the building and printing trades—all showed promise of a conciliatory tone in industrial relations between labor and management. Under the leadership of John Mitchell, president of the United Mine Workers and onetime Gompers "heir apparent," the anthracite coal industry was organized, and a working agreement was achieved, after two long strikes and federal intervention in the form of a fact-finding commission had forced the "hard-boiled" operators to negotiate.[8]

In the 1890s also, industrialists and bankers under the leadership of Mark Hanna, President William McKinley's campaign manager and later a senator from Ohio, joined with Gompers and other AFL leaders in founding the National Civic Federation. This body sought agreement between labor and industry on broad principles, promoted collective bargaining contracts, and maintained voluntary machinery for the media-

---

[8] Among them was George M. Baer, president of the Philadelphia and Reading Company, who immortalized himself with this statement: "The rights and interests of the laboring man will be protected and cared for not by labor agitators but by Christian men to whom God in his infinite wisdom has given control of the property interests of the country."

tion and arbitration of labor disputes. By promoting collective bargaining, the Civic Federation aided the immediate interests of the AFL. It frowned, however, on aggressive unionism. Since the latter was needed to organize the unorganized, unskilled masses, the Civic Federation's influence was more friendly to established unions than to union growth.

If, however, the AFL had established a beachhead in industry, it found no warm welcome in the new mass-production industries. Andrew Carnegie, the rising genius of the steel industry, had at one time been anxious to deal with the Amalgamated Association of Iron, Steel, and Tin Workers. He reasoned that by encouraging the union, he would encourage price stability; and since he figured that he could outsell his competitors if he held them to equal costs, he promoted unionism to promote sales.

As Carnegie grew in the industry, however, his love for unionism declined. In 1892, he dealt the Amalgamated Association a terrific blow when he ousted it from his Homestead plant (near Pittsburgh, Pennsylvania) in a bloody strike. The course of unionism in steel from then on was downward, and as steel went, so went unionism in mass production. The United States Steel Corporation, which was formed in 1901, principally by Carnegie and Morgan interests under the latter's domination, refused to recognize the steel union, defeated its attempt to force recognition by a strike, and then gradually eliminated it from the plants where it had already been recognized. Mass-production industries which grew up between 1900 and 1933 followed the lead of the steel corporation. Detroit, the automobile capital; Akron, the center of rubber products; the Pittsburgh–Ohio Valley steel center; Chicago, the heart of the meat-packing combines—all kept unionism from their gates except for the briefest of periods during World War I, and other industries followed their lead.

As their spokesman, the antiunion interests found the National Association of Manufacturers an excellent crusader, with its campaign for the "open shop," which, to the NAM, meant the elimination of trade unionism. Between 1900 and 1914, the American Federation of Labor was on the defensive. Although its membership increased to 2 million by 1914, it failed to keep pace with our growing industrial economy. Even in those industries where they had a firm foothold, such as glass, the AFL unions were confined largely to the skilled employees. Coal mining was one of the few union strongholds among semiskilled and unskilled employees.

The antiunion drive of the NAM and its allies served to give most of the new large corporations formed at the turn of the century the opportunity to utilize labor without restraint from unions. Workers who did not like this treatment, or who rebelled, could look elsewhere for a job; that was their only recourse against the power of the giant corporation. Of course, many employers had good cause to reject unionism around 1900. The history of industrial relations provides many examples of unions during 1880–1900 refusing to sign written agreements, calling "quickie" strikes, and placing restrictive rules on expanding industries. Industry did have the opportunity to work out an understanding with the AFL; however, the "fight unionism" program of the National Association of Manufacturers prevailed over the cooperative program of the National Civic Federation.

The IWW

To American radicals at the turn of the century, the success of the antiunion crusade and the support which it elicited from the general public were evidence that the "narrow" dollars-and-cents unionism of the AFL type could not succeed in working out a compromise with the capitalist system. At the same time, the failure of the AFL to interest itself in the needs of the unskilled workers and the workers in such frontier industries as metal mining and logging and lumber drove these groups to seek a solution of their problems outside the AFL's orbit. The metal miners, who for a time had affiliated with the AFL, took their union, the Western Federation of Miners, out of the AFL in 1897. Lack of success in their own fierce labor struggles and an increased radical bent within the organization and among its leaders led the Western Federation of Miners and its allies from the West to make common cause with the Socialist Trade and Labor Alliance and with various dissident AFL locals. In June 1905, these groups launched the Industrial Workers of the World.

The IWW was the champion of the unskilled, but it never built an organization for them. It would not sign agreements, which it regarded as a form of capitalist enslavement. The IWW depended on mass action used directly and without restraint. It hid nothing and apologized to no one for its anticapitalist views. The press built up the "wobblies" as a tremendous organization. Its strength was more carefully appraised by a scholarly observer, who, after witnessing its 1913 convention, termed the IWW a "pathetically weak" organization which "has failed utterly in its efforts to attach to itself permanently a considerable body of men representative of any section of American workers."[9]

WORLD WAR I TO THE GREAT DEPRESSION

As World War I approached, the Wilson administration sought labor support. A threatened strike by the four railroad brotherhoods for an eight-hour day was averted when President Wilson secured the passage of the Adamson Act, guaranteeing the eight-hour day without loss of pay

---

[9] R. F. Hoxie, *Trade Unionism in the United States* (New York: D. Appleton-Century Co., 1924), p. 139.

from the previous ten-hour day to all operating employees of railroads. Tripartite, public-labor-industry labor relations boards were established in critical industries, and the AFL was given official recognition as a representative of labor.

When war broke out, President Wilson called together representatives of labor and industry and won an agreement providing, among other things, for the establishment of a tripartite National War Labor Board, an agreement guaranteeing the right of organization, and a freeze on the closed-shop issue which stated that open shops were to remain open and closed shops closed for the duration. Aided by the shortage of labor, the official recognition by government, and a truce with industry, organized labor's ranks shot up to 5.5 million, which proved to be the highest membership figure prior to 1935.

World War I was followed by serious industrial strife. The nation had a coal strike in 1919 and an industrywide steel strike (whose main demands were for an end to the 12-hour day in blast furnaces and for recognition of the union). The strike failed after being portrayed as a "red menace." Serious stoppages also occurred in other industries, such as meat-packing. Similar to another postwar year, 1946, the year 1919 was one of the costliest in terms of strikes.

The year 1919 was also an inflationary year. Prices subsequently fell sharply as the country experienced a short but serious depression. Labor's gains of the war evaporated as war industries closed and unemployment set in. Industry took the offensive with the "American plan," a version of the open shop dressed up by the first ingredients of personnel administration.

Company Unions

During the war, American industry had realized the high cost of hit-or-miss personnel policies. Industry became concerned for the first time over high labor turnover, foreman training, and scientific salary administration. Moreover, the public was demanding more democracy in industry, and the more forward-looking industrialists saw that they must have something to meet the trade-union challenge besides the famous remark attributed to the chairman of the United States Steel Corporation: "We do not deal with unions as such."

Out of this developed many elaborate schemes of employee representation and company unions. The company unions were deficient in many ways. Certainly, the company union cannot give workers the bargaining power to stand up and fight for an enlargement of their share, since it ultimately owes its strength to company toleration. Nevertheless, during the 1920s, it was the forward-looking employer who sponsored employee representation plans. Company unions also played a role in training future union leaders and in teaching employees to discuss their rights, to learn about business, and eventually to realize the impotence of company unions as bargaining agents.

The AFL Decays

American trade unionism was in a state of decadence during the 1920s, despite the fact that 30 years later the AFL was still led by some of the leaders who were prominent during the 1920s. As technological and mass-production methods created millions of semiskilled jobs, the AFL continued to hold on merely to the craft unions and made no serious attempts to organize the great body of workers. Membership slowly fell from the wartime peak to less than 3 million in 1932. The coal miners' union, which had been the largest in the AFL, not only failed to organize southern West Virginia and Kentucky, but was eliminated from most of the northern mines as well. Even the building-trades unions, which were the bulwark of the AFL, lost their grip on San Francisco and failed to penetrate such new industrial areas as Detroit. Charges of corruption within the AFL's leadership, attacks by liberals and left-wing groups, and the effective antiunionism of employers all took their toll.

To succeed Samuel Gompers, who died in 1924, the Federation elected the United Mine Workers' secretary-treasurer, William Green. A compromise candidate, he remained in office until 1952 but never had the stature or power of Gompers.

Labor under the New Deal

The Roosevelt administration, which came to power in 1933, brought gains to labor which were unprecedented in American history. In the wake of such legislation as the National Recovery Act, the National Labor Relations (Wagner) Act, and the amendments to the Railway Labor Act, trade-union organization increased to an all-time high. With the final impetus of war, continued prosperity, and shortages of labor, union membership quadrupled.

Under the first great New Deal law, the National Industrial Recovery Act, business and agriculture were encouraged to plan scarcity in order to raise prices, and labor was given the right to organize without management interference. Labor's right was not enforceable to any very important extent, but energetic unionism took immediate advantage of it. Gambling the last $75,000 in the miners' union treasury, John L. Lewis sent expert organizers throughout the country's coalfields, and within three months he had enrolled 400,000 coal miners, including those in the previously impregnable antiunion strongholds of Kentucky and southern West Virginia. The International Ladies' Garment Workers' Union resurrected and expanded itself, as did the Amalgamated Clothing Workers in the men's clothing industry. Unionism sprang up in the mass-production industries, unaided, unguided, and confused; but if some organizations sprang into action under the magic of NRA, most of the AFL lay quiet and asleep. Not until after considerable prodding did AFL organizers appear on the scene to help unionization in previously unorganized industries. Then, in industries such as rubber and automobiles, where no AFL affiliate had general jurisdiction, the Federation chartered directly AFL-affiliated, or "federal," locals.

Without a central organization, however, these new locals were often inept in bargaining. Moreover, craft unions of carpenters, electrical workers, machinists, and so on, claimed the right to, and often did, demand that craftsmen in newly organized federal locals be turned over to them. The effect was usually to destroy the federal local and to estrange the transferred craftsmen from the labor movement until organizations suited to their purposes were founded.

In the steel and meat-packing industries, AFL unions did exist. The Amalgamated Association of Iron, Steel, and Tin Workers, however, had had an unbroken record of failures since the Homestead strike in 1892, and its leadership had neither the resources nor the capacity to undertake a large-scale organizing drive. Except for a short World War I interval, the Amalgamated Meat Cutters and Butcher Workmen had never penetrated the major meat-packing centers. Until revitalized in the late 1930s, it appeared content to confine its organization to the small packing establishments and to retail butchers.

The Founding of the CIO

The AFL's failure to organize mass-production industries gave impetus to a movement led by John L. Lewis to issue industrial union charters to organizations in the mass-production industries. Both Lewis and the craft union adherents realized, of course, that if thousands of new recruits came into the AFL, the power balance within labor's ranks would change, and Lewis, as the leader of a revitalized miners' union and the recognized champion of the industrial unionists, would be in a strong position. In 1935, for the third time, the craft unionists refused to permit the issuance of industrial union charters. The arguments of the craft unionists were based upon union structure, but the basic issue was power in the AFL.

Lewis went ahead anyway. The industrial union group, under his leadership and that of David Dubinsky of the Ladies' Garment Workers' Union and Sidney Hillman of the Amalgamated Clothing Workers, and including unions in the oil, textile, and metal mines industries, met and formed the Committee for Industrial Organization for the avowed purpose of organizing unorganized workers. The original unions were soon joined by others, such as the rubber, flat glass, automobile, shipbuilding, and electrical appliance workers' unions, which had pleaded in vain with the AFL for industrial union charters. The CIO immediately offered the AFL $500,000 to organize the steel industry. When the latter's Executive Council turned it down, Lewis succeeded in inducing the leadership of the virtually dormant Amalgamated Association of Iron, Steel, and Tin Workers to put itself in a receivership to a newly organized Steel Workers Organizing Committee headed by Philip Murray, then vice president of the United Mine Workers.

The AFL viewed these developments with alarm. Its Executive Council ordered the CIO to disband. When the latter refused and Lewis resigned as a vice president of the AFL, the AFL Executive Council suspended the CIO affiliates for "promoting dual unionism." The haste with which the Executive Council acted and the probable lack of constitutionality in its suspension were not seriously challenged by the CIO unions, except for the Ladies' Garment Workers' Union.[10] The CIO group had given up the possibility that mass-production industries could be organized within the framework of the AFL. Hence, when the AFL convention met in 1936, the CIO unions were not represented, and the action of the Executive Council was sustained. Two years later the CIO unions were formally expelled.

The CIO Organizes Steel

The CIO challenge to the antiunion policies of the steel industry was met vigorously by the steel companies. Once more, men were spied on and fired for union activity; the rights of assembly and free speech in company-dominated towns were curtailed; and violence, bloodshed, and death erupted on the industrial scene.

The steel companies also used more refined tactics in trying to overcome the new union threat to their traditional methods of controlling labor relations. Large sums were spent on a nationwide advertising campaign condemning unionism as a threat to the country. In addition, considerable effort and money were expended to form and maintain company unions.

This time, however, the steel companies met more than their match. The money, effort, and above all, the activities of union organizers who had already penetrated antiunion citadels made the CIO drive as tough

---

[10] In 1935, the AFL constitution said nothing about Executive Council jurisdiction to suspend an affiliate. Unions could be expelled only by a two-thirds convention vote. If the CIO unions had been represented at the 1936 convention, no two-thirds vote would have been possible. The 1936 convention was reminded by several delegates that the Executive Council had been "in such a hurry" to suspend the CIO that the procedure was questionable. Matthew Woll, a leading exponent of the Executive Council viewpoint, later defended the suspension as follows: "The fact is that if the Council had not acted there would have been possible disintegration within the American Federation of Labor which would have been disastrous. The Council acted not so much to punish those who had formed the CIO, but rather to prevent disintegration from within" (*Hat Worker,* June 15, 1939, p. 11).

and effective as the companies' countercampaigns. The tactics and flair for showmanship demonstrated by Philip Murray and his aides were superior to those of any previous organizing campaign.

For example, the CIO realized that the nationwide advertisements sponsored by the companies gave the organizing campaign widespread publicity which it could not otherwise have obtained. Hence, the union replied softly in its rejoinders to the company publicity, which was often so extreme as to alienate the public. Moreover, the CIO allied itself fully with President Roosevelt's 1936 reelection campaign. His overwhelming reelection was followed by a large influx of steelworkers into the CIO.

Toward company unions, Philip Murray, the leader of the CIO drive, also adopted a new tactic. Instead of regarding them as arch-enemies, he saw company unions as a training ground. The CIO people tried to get control of the company unions and succeeded in large measure. The United States Steel Corporation's money spent for company union agitation frequently served to promote the CIO. By January 1937, it was apparent that the new steel union could close down Carnegie-Illinois, U.S. Steel's biggest subsidiary, if it so chose.

At this point, probably through the friendly offices of President Roosevelt and Senator Joseph Guffey of Pennsylvania, Myron Taylor, chairman of the board of U.S. Steel, and John L. Lewis were brought together. The result was an agreement recognizing the CIO as bargaining agent for its members in all U.S. Steel subsidiaries in the iron and steel industry. The arch-opponent of unionism thus came to an agreement with a new CIO union, a triumph for the latter that insured its existence.

The CIO drive in steel was temporarily slowed down by the defeat of its recognition strikes against several of the major "Little Steel" companies.[11] However, four years later, in 1941 the steel union came back to win bargaining rights in all of these concerns. Today, under the name of the United Steelworkers of America, this union has a membership of over one million and contracts covering nearly all major steel concerns, as well as numerous companies in other industries.

Rubber, Automobiles, and Other CIO Drives

While the steel drive was getting under way, labor erupted in the rubber and automobile industries. These unions were not started from the top down, as in steel, but grew straight from the rank and file. Using a new technique, the "sit-down" strike, workers in the rubber and automobile industries took possession of plants of such giant corporations as Goodyear, Chrysler, and General Motors. This unorthodox and undoubtedly illegal procedure won recognition from these corporations

---

[11] Bethlehem, Republic, Youngstown, and Inland, all giant corporations.

because of general public sympathy with the objective of union recognition. (There never was any attempt by the unionists to seize permanent control of the plants.) The lawlessness involved in the sit-down, however, soon became sufficiently apparent to react against unionism. Shortly abandoned as an approved tactic, sit-downs had virtually disappeared from the American industrial relations scene by early 1938.

In the rubber industry the CIO won bargaining rights at Uniroyal, Firestone, and Goodrich in the 1930s, but the status of the union at Goodyear was not officially recognized until 1941. Today the CIO Rubber Workers' Union is not only dominant in this industry but has spread into the cork, linoleum, floor tile, and other industries.

Although sit-down strikes won the CIO recognition at Chrysler and General Motors, Ford did not yield until 1941, when a strike closed down the great plant at River Rouge. Today the Automobile Workers, after expanding into the aerospace and agricultural implement industries, boast a membership of more than 1 million.

CIO unions also organized packinghouses and stockyards in the large centers, as well as the bulk of the electrical manufacturing industry. The old Western Federation of Miners, now known as the International Union of Mine, Mills, and Smelter Workers, near extinction in 1935, became a CIO charter member and gained over 20,000 workers ten years later, principally in the western silver and copper mines and smelters. A new union, the National Maritime Union, started from remnants of the then decadent International Seamen's Union, AFL, brought unionism to the East Coast seamen for the first time since World War I.

The revolt of the East Coast seamen also did something else. It forced the AFL to reorganize its seamen's union, in effect dissolving the International Seamen's Union and forming in its stead the Seafarers' International Union. To a lesser degree, the CIO had the same general effect on the AFL as the formation of the National Maritime Union had on the AFL seamen's organization. Forced to meet an energetic rival for the first time since it outdistanced the Knights of Labor (the IWW of pre–World War I was no great threat organizationally), the AFL and its constituent unions got out of their easy chairs and really went to work. Although the CIO surpassed the AFL in membership in 1937 and in 1938, when it established a permanent federation, the Congress of Industrial Organizations, it never did after that. For the first time, AFL unions, such as the Machinists and the Teamsters, really made an effort to take in the thousands of workers within their jurisdictions. By 1953, membership in the AFL included almost half of the 16.9 million unionized. By then the CIO, having lost the Ladies' Garment Workers and the United Mine Workers, and having expelled the Communist-led unions, as will be narrated below, could claim but 4.5 million, with the remaining unionized found in nonaffiliated unions.

Once the CIO was firmly established in the mass-production industries, the AFL leaders made no more pretense of opposition to industrial organization. Indeed, if only as a defensive measure, the AFL accepted industrial organization wherever the alternative might be loss of jurisdiction to the CIO. For example, the Machinists were granted exclusive AFL jurisdiction in aircraft manufacturing to counteract the CIO Automobile Workers' drive in the same industry. But although industrial unionism was admittedly eliminated as a basic thorn in the side of labor unity, it was replaced by concurrent jurisdictional claims, as the AFL and the CIO each chartered rival unions in jurisdictions dominated by affiliates of the other and opened its doors to dissident groups of the other. The CIO chartered groups in such AFL-dominated areas as building construction, railway shop crafts, and pulp and paper. The AFL, in turn, welcomed rump groups from the CIO-dominated automobile and rubber industries, and tried mightily to gain a foothold in the CIO industrial union stronghold of steel. Thus each federation built up vested interests in the form of jobholders dependent upon disunity, and each encroached upon the jurisdictional claims of the other.

WORLD WAR II TO THE KOREAN WAR

World War II was a period of expanding union membership. Soon after our entrance into the war, a National War Labor Board was established with union, management, and public representation. The union groups were divided equally between the AFL and the CIO. Despite the strains, the NWLB maintained a high record for peaceful settlement; and apart from numerous "quickie" strikes, labor generally observed its no-strike pledge. The tight labor market and expanding industry aided union membership to grow steadily. But a large number of small stoppages, combined with a few large ones, particularly the miners' strikes under John L. Lewis, caused public opinion to turn against unions.

The end of the war and the lifting of economic controls resulted in a psychological outburst on many fronts. Labor's response was strikes— 1946 was the greatest strike year in American history in terms of mandays lost. Wherever the responsibility may have belonged, the public blamed labor; the result contributed to the congressional election sweep of the Republicans in 1946 and to the passage of the Taft-Hartley Act in the following spring.

The severity of the postwar strike wave came as a surprise to both union and management leaders. During the war, a strike was a signal for a flurry of government and management activity to get the employees back to work. As a result, wartime strikes were of short duration. When the postwar strike wave started, management did not think that the unions could hold out for a long period, and the unions did not think that the strikes would last long. Neither could have been more wrong.

SAMUEL GOMPERS
President, AFL, 1886–94 and
1895–1924

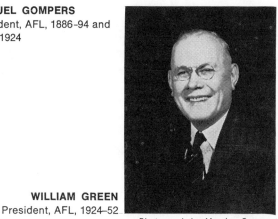

WILLIAM GREEN
President, AFL, 1924–52

Photograph by Rogers Studio,
Seattle

Photograph by Maurice Seymour,
Chicago

JOHN L. LEWIS
President, UMW, 1920–60
Chairman and President, CIO
1935–40

PHILIP MURRAY
President, CIO, 1940–52

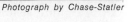

Photograph by Chase-Statler

Photograph by Chase,
Washington, D.C.

WALTER P. REUTHER
President, UAW, 1946–70,
and CIO, 1952–55

GEORGE MEANY
President, AFL, 1952–55,
and AFL–CIO, 1955–

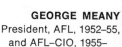

Photograph by Chase,
Washington, D.C.

The General Motors employees were out on strike for nearly three months in the coldest part of the year, from December 1945 to March 1946; Westinghouse employees stayed out almost four months; and strikes in steel, coal, and other industries were also of long duration. Yet the workers did not seem to give serious consideration to returning to work without union approval. Managements, fortified by the knowledge that economic losses resulting from strikes could be partially made up by offsets on previous years' excess profits taxes, were in no hurry to settle until certain that the government would not continue its short-lived attempt to hold the price line after the war as it had done during the war.

Despite the fact that most large postwar strikes resulted in substantial wage increases for the strikers, unions did not gain in favor or significantly in membership during the period between the end of World War II and the beginning of the Korean War. Much-publicized CIO and AFL drives to organize the South were almost completely unsuccessful. Gains in membership which the CIO and the AFL recorded during this period resulted mainly from the expansion of employment in plants already unionized. Press and public often blamed the unions for the price increases which generally followed large wage increases. State legislatures, dominated by rural interests, appeared eager to pass legislation designed to curb unions. And the most popular of these laws echoed the NAM's 50-year-old campaign to maintain the "worker's right to work" by outlawing the union shop or any variation thereof which requires union membership as a condition of employment. Such laws now exist in 20 states, all in the South and the Midwest.

COMMUNIST UNIONISM

Following the Russian Revolution, the American Communist party was organized in 1919, and soon thereafter it set out to capture control of key labor unions, particularly in the apparel industry. Its efforts largely failed, but the party was given a new base of operations by John L. Lewis in the 1930s. Against the advice of David Dubinsky of the Ladies' Garment Workers, which had fought off the Communists earlier, Lewis hired party members to fill important CIO jobs. They organized well, but also used their positions to convert some of the new unions into propaganda transmission agencies for their party.

When the Nazi–Soviet pact of 1939 opened the way for the Nazi attack on Poland, the American Communists opposed the defense program and fomented strikes to interfere with it. Here again, they found common cause with John L. Lewis. He was a confirmed isolationist, with a gradually growing hatred of President Roosevelt, which began in 1937 when the president declined to support the Little Steel strike as strongly as Lewis wished. Lewis thus opposed Roosevelt in 1940 for reasons very different from those of the Communists. He resigned from the presidency of the CIO following the 1940 national elections, and Philip Murray succeeded him.

At first, the Communists obstructed Murray at every turn because he supported the war effort, and agitated for Lewis' return to power. Then, after the German invasion of Russia in 1941, the Communists deserted Lewis and, in Murray's words "lifted [me] to a veritable sainthood,"[12] although Murray's views had not changed. Lewis gradually dropped out of CIO affairs, and then disaffiliated the United Mine Workers from the CIO. The UMW had previously organized "District 50" on a nationwide basis in order to bring into its ranks coke and by-product workers, but it was later expanded to enroll any workers it could. In 1968, District 50 was expelled from the UMW in a dispute over atomic power policy, and in 1972 it merged into the United Steelworkers.

After World War II, the Communist party "line" changed, and Communist union leaders again fought the regular CIO officials on numerous policies, including the reelection of President Harry S Truman, whom the CIO strongly supported. The non-Communist CIO leadership then set out to rid the organization of the Communists. They were voted out of office in the automobile, maritime, shoe, and transport unions, while 11 other unions which Communists dominated either disaffiliated or were expelled from the CIO.[13] Since this 1950 action, only 2 of these 11 have neither disbanded nor been absorbed by other unions: the United Electrical, Radio, and Machine Workers and the International Longshoremen's and Warehousemen's Union. The former has shrunk from 600,000 members to 167,000; the latter, still under the leadership of Harry Bridges, has a membership of 50,000, as compared with a high of 65,000, and it retains its grip on waterfronts of the West Coast and Hawaii, as well as on the plantations of Hawaii.

Today, the Communists are not a significant factor in the American labor movement. They never had a mass following, but their strength was concentrated in a few unions. They lost out when they chose to subvert trade-union objectives to Communist party policy.

RELIGIOUS LEADERSHIP IN UNIONS

In both the 1920s and the 1930s the efforts of the Association of Catholic Trade Unionists and the United Hebrew Trades were important in the defeat of the Communists in many unions. The former gave aid,

---

[12] *Steel Labor,* March 1948.

[13] Mine, Mill, and Smelter Workers; United Office and Professional Workers; United Public Workers; International Fur and Leather Workers; Food, Tobacco, and Allied Workers; Marine Cooks' and Stewards' Association; Fishermen's Union; International Longshoremen's and Warehousemen's Union; American Communications Association; Farm Equipment Workers; and United Electrical, Radio, and Machine Workers.

comfort, and leadership to many antiCommunists in the New York subway system and helped to wrest the Transport Workers' Union from the Left; the latter did much the same thing in the garment industry. Protestants have had no such group, but have had special committees working to bring church and unions together.

When Samuel Gompers assisted in the organization of the United Hebrew Trades in 1888, he had serious qualms about the propriety of organizing a separate Jewish group because he did not believe in organizing workers along religious lines. Gompers, however, supported the United Hebrew Trades on the ground that "to organize Hebrew Trade Unions was the first step in getting these immigrants into the American Labor movement." Gompers was proved right in believing that the UHT would draw Jewish immigrants into AFL unions rather than separate them from such unions. The ACTU has apparently had the same impact.[14]

UNITY AND DISUNITY

In November 1952, Philip Murray, president of the CIO, and William Green, president of the AFL, passed away. Walter Reuther, president of the United Automobile Workers, succeeded Murray; George Meany, secretary-treasurer of the AFL, succeeded Green. Within three years, the new presidents had negotiated a merger agreement, and a new organization—the American Federation of Labor and Congress of Industrial Organizations—was born, with Meany as president.

The merger overcame two pillars of the AFL foundation which heretofore had been too great a stumbling block to unity—the principle of exclusive jurisdiction and the principle of the autonomous national union. The doctrine of exclusive jurisdiction provided that each affiliated national union should have a clear and specified job territory and boundary, which was ordinarily defined in terms of work operations, crafts, trades, occupations, or industrial grouping of jobs, and was occasionally defined in terms of geography. Under this doctrine, no two unions were supposed to have jurisdiction over the same work operations or area. As a corollary, the AFL, by determining union jurisdictions, also determined which union the individual employee should join. Of course, since the passage of the National Labor Relations Act in 1935 (now, as amended, the Taft-Hartley Act), workers have designated by election the union that they desire to represent them. Since workers may not

---

[14] See Philip Taft, "The Association of Catholic Trade Unionists," *Industrial and Labor Relations Review*, vol. 2 (January 1949), pp. 210–18; Will Herberg, "Jewish Labor Movement in America," *Industrial and Labor Relations Review*, vol. 5 (July 1952), pp. 501–23, and October 1952, pp. 44–66; and James Meyers, *Do You Know Labor?* (New York: John Day Co., Inc., 1940), chap. 18, for backgrounds of religious organizations.

follow the dictates of the federation as to union jurisdiction, the principle of exclusive jurisdiction was never fully operative after 1935.

Meany and Reuther did not attempt to merge competing unions when the AFL and the CIO merged. Instead, the merger agreement simply provided that the jurisdiction actually exercised by each affiliate at the time of the merger was to be preserved intact and that established collective bargaining relationships supplanted historical jurisdiction as a basis for unions' territorial or organizing rights. Each union was supposed to organize unorganized groups, or groups outside the merged federation on the basis of its historical jurisdiction, with the federation determining priorities and rights in case of a dispute.

The second significant alteration in the fundamental concept of American unionism as developed originally by the American Federation of Labor has been the modification of the principle of autonomy by the requirement that national unions shall be free of corrupt and totalitarian influences if they are to maintain AFL–CIO affiliation. The AFL–CIO set up codes of ethics and an Ethical Practices Committee, but it could only enforce its codes by expelling an affiliate. This it did, in 1957 disaffiliating three unions, including the country's largest, the Teamsters. Under James R. Hoffa and, later, Frank Fitzsimmons, however, the Teamsters declined to purge its ranks of persons of ill repute and proceeded to compete for the right to represent workers in many jurisdictions. The AFL–CIO has not again shown a disposition to expel recalcitrant affiliates.

Other unions which have remained outside the AFL–CIO fold include the surviving organizations which were expelled from the CIO for Communist domination; the United Mine Workers, whose membership in the coal mines declined with employment from 600,000 to about 200,000; and the Brotherhood of Locomotive Engineers, which has always remained independent. Decimated by declining employment in their industry, the other operating railroad "brotherhoods"—the Locomotive Firemen, the Trainmen, and the Switchmen—merged in 1969 under the name of the United Transportation Union and affiliated with the AFL–CIO.

Although both Meany and Reuther had hoped that membership in the merged federation would spur unions in overlapping jurisdictions to unite, this happened very slowly until recently. Now it has hastened, largely as a result of basic economic considerations—declining memberships and rising costs of operations—plus the aging of leaders who, with impending retirement, are more favorably disposed to mergers. The already noted railroad unions' merger is a case in point, and others have occurred in the paper, printing, meat-packing, textile, and insurance industries, and among government workers and other groups. In addition, strong unions have incorporated weaker ones and thereby expanded their jurisdiction. Thus, the Steelworkers has taken over the Mine, Mill, and Smelter Workers; the Stone and Allied Products Workers; District 50, formerly part of the Mine Workers; and several independents. Despite this heightened merger activity in recent years, competing and overlapping unions are still more common than not.

If labor unity was furthered by mergers, these were, for several years, more than offset by the Meany-Reuther feud which led to the disaffiliation of the Auto Workers from the AFL–CIO. Apparently giving up his dream of heading a merged labor movement, Reuther led the UAW out of the AFL–CIO in 1968.

Obviously hoping to replicate John L. Lewis's success of the 1930s, Reuther joined with the Teamsters, which he had helped to drum out of the AFL–CIO, to form the Alliance for Labor Action, a rival federation. ALA, however, failed to attract a following despite substantial expenditures both in organizing attempts and for civil rights and welfare purposes. Reuther's death in an airplane accident in 1970 cost ALA its driving force. The General Motors strike later that year drained the UAW treasury. In early 1972, the Teamsters and the UAW dissolved the short-lived Alliance for Labor Action. The continued failure both of the Teamsters and the UAW to reaffiliate with the AFL–CIO seems to demonstrate clearly that large unions can exist outside the Federation without difficulty. On the other hand, the ALA experience causes doubt that a rival to the AFL–CIO can be created under foreseeable conditions. Moreover, the UAW has given indications that it might reaffiliate with the AFL–CIO within the next few years.

AMERICAN UNIONS TODAY

Figure 2–1 shows the growth of union membership since 1950 and the percentage of the labor force unionized. The great periods of growth, 1935–39 and 1940–44, preceded these years for the reasons already discussed. Union membership rose slowly for the first 12 years after World War II, but these gains did little more than keep pace with the increase in the labor force. Judging from the fact that the nonunion groups of 1944 were still largely nonunion in 1956, it would appear that union growth in the 1944–56 period stemmed principally from expansion in employment by unionized firms.

Union membership reached a peak of 17.5 million in 1956—one year after the AFL–CIO merger—and then began to decline, not only as a percentage of the labor force but in absolute numbers as well, until 1963. The years between 1956 and 1963 saw the membership rolls of former CIO affiliates especially hard hit, as, first, recession unemployment occurred, and then automation and increased productivity permitted increased production without increased employment.

After 1962, union membership again moved upward, surpassing its former peak in 1966, and surging on to a new high of 21.2 million in

1975. One cause was the sustained prosperity of the 1960s. Industry expanded payrolls in the unionized sector, and union memberships rose accordingly. A second reason for union growth since 1960 has been the tremendous expansion of public employee unions. For example, the American Federation of State, County, and Municipal Employees grew from 210,000 members in 1960 to 700,000 15 years later. Other organizations of government employees made similar gains.

On the basis of these statistics, union growth has failed to keep pace with the growth of the labor force. This is mainly because the increasing numbers of salaried and service workers outside government remain nonunion. Moreover, the traditional areas in which unions have been weak remain unorganized. Thus, despite some highly publicized gains in agriculture, most farm workers are still nonunion, as are southern textile, carpet, and furniture employees. In addition, the construction industry, historically considered a union bastion, has become over 50% nonunion, as builders and users have sought to offset the very high union wages and increasingly restrictive work rules.[15]

The above data on union membership, however, exclude those organizations which have over the last decade converted themselves from various types of associations to bargaining agents. Foremost among these are the 1.5-million-member National Education Association, the powerful Fraternal Order of Policemen, and large civil service groups in New York and California. In a real sense these are unions, and they add nearly 3 million employees to the union membership roles.

Except in periods of great social change, such as the 1930s, union membership has been closely tied to the business cycle, rising in prosperous times with increased employment and declining as production and employment decrease. The expansion in public employment during the 1960s not only increased the expected gains of a prosperous period but also added to union rolls a group relatively insulated from cyclical fluctuations. The increased unionization in public employment, and in such semipublic areas as hospitals, universities, and other nonprofit sectors, adds a new dimension to collective bargaining and public policy which is discussed in Chapter 22.

Meanwhile, unions remain a tremendous force. Despite the decline in the proportion of the labor force which they represent, they are the dominant influence in wage determination and in the determination of the rules and regulations under which people work. The nonunion sector is heavily influenced by union policies and follows closely (or jumps ahead of) what unions obtain for their members. As AFL–CIO President George Meany has noted:

---

[15] Herbert R. Northrup and Howard G. Foster, *Open Shop Construction*, Major Study No. 54 (Philadelphia: Industrial Research Unit, The Wharton School, University of Pennsylvania, 1975).

We [organized labor] have never had a large proportion of the labor force in this country—nothing like Britain, nothing like the Scandinavian countries, nothing like the Germans. . . .

We've done quite well . . . we've delivered more to the American worker than any labor movement that ever existed. . . .

With all our complaints, we have the highest standard of living in the world.

Why should we worry about organizing groups of people who do not appear to want to be organized? If they prefer to have others speak for them and make the decisions which affect their lives, without effective participation on their part, that is their right.[16]

Concentration of Union Membership

In 1976 the six largest unions had approximately 36% of the total union membership. These unions—the Teamsters, the Automobile Workers, the Steelworkers, the International Brotherhood of Electrical Workers, the Machinists, and the Carpenters—all claimed more than 800,000 members, with the first three claiming more than 1 million each and the Teamsters claiming in excess of 2 million.

Table 2–1 shows that the six largest unions have generally accounted for about one third of the total union membership. Although the makeup of the six largest unions has changed from time to time, the Carpenters have always been represented in the group. The decline in the coal industry until recently and mechanization of the industry have reduced the roles of the Mine Workers from 600,000 to about 200,000. On the other hand, the Carpenters' union has been able to remain one of the Big Six not only because it is the largest trade in construction, but also because it has unionized woodworking, furniture, and lumber operations.

Like the Carpenters, the International Brotherhood of Electrical Workers, with a membership of 980,000, and the International Association of Machinists and Aerospace Workers, with 900,000 members, are former craft unions which have branched out and organized factory workers on an industrial basis. For example, the Machinists now include aerospace employees in addition to workers in a great variety of metal-working shops. The Electrical Workers include not only electricians but also employees of all classes in public utilities and electrical and communication products manufacturing. In 1967, they passed the Machinists in membership for the first time in 30 years.

The Automobile Workers and the Steelworkers are the only former CIO unions in the Big Six. Their size is largely the result of the size of the basic industries whose employees they represent, but they have augmented their growth by spreading into related jurisdictions. The automo-

---

[16] From an interview in *U.S. News & World Report,* February 21, 1972, p. 27.

TABLE 2–1
The Six Largest Unions, 1900–1976

Year	Six Largest Unions (in order of membership)	Membership of Six Largest Unions	Total Union Membership	Percentage of Total Union Membership in Six Largest Unions
1900	Miners Carpenters Railroad Trainmen Cigarmakers Locomotive Firemen Locomotive Engineers	335,800	868,500	38.7
1920	Miners Carpenters Machinists Railway Clerks Railroad Trainmen Railway Carmen	1,649,000	5,047,800	32.6
1929	Carpenters Miners Railroad Trainmen Electrical Workers* Clothing Workers Painters	1,028,200	3,442,000	29.8
1953	Automobile Workers Teamsters Steelworkers Machinists Carpenters Miners	5,750,000	16,948,000	34.4
1964	Teamsters Automobile Workers Steelworkers Machinists Electrical Workers* Carpenters	5,850,000	16,800,000	34.2
1972	Teamsters Automobile Workers Steelworkers Electrical Workers* Machinists Carpenters	6,650,000	19,500,000	34.1
1976	Teamsters Automobile Workers Steelworkers Electrical Workers* Machinists Carpenters	7,803,000	21,200,000	36.0

* International Brotherhood of Electrical Workers.
Source: Leo Wolman, *Ebb and Flow in Trade Unionism* (New York: National Bureau of Economic Research, 1936), for data for 1900–1929; U.S. Department of Labor, for 1953, 1964, and 1972; and authors' estimates for 1976. Canadian membership excluded from total membership.

bile union now includes aerospace employees and the bulk of the workers engaged in agricultural implement manufacturing. The Steelworkers have enrolled thousands in metal fabricating, metal mining, and chemicals. Much of the recent membership increase recorded by the Steelworkers results from mergers with other unions, notably the Mine, Mill, and Smelter Workers, and District 50, formerly of the United Mine Workers.

The Teamsters is the country's first 2-million-member union. It has not only taken advantage of the great growth in the distribution and service industries within its traditional jurisdiction, but since its expulsion from the AFL–CIO, it has organized employees in any industry where it could. Moreover, the Teamsters is not only the largest union but also the most powerful. Not only do trucks carry the bulk of goods in our economy, but they also usually complete the delivery of items shipped by rail, air, or water. Hence, if trucks stop, little moves. The strategic position of the Teamsters insures its power.

In the 1970s, one union, the American Federation of State, County, and Municipal Employees, could easily become one of the six largest unions, if not the largest. With nearly 6 million noneducational employees projected for state and local government by 1980, membership in AFSCME could then more than quadruple its current 700,000 membership.

Regional Variations

Union membership in the United States varies tremendously by state and region. Figure 2–2 shows the least and most unionized states. In Michigan, where the United Automobile Workers is dominant, 38.4% of the nonagricultural labor force was unionized in 1974; in fast-industrializing North Carolina, only 6.9% of that work force was represented by unions.

Many factors account for these variations, including the location of industry, historical relationships, and regional worker attitudes. Historically, in the South and Southwest, the bastions of the "open shop," there has been a community feeling that unions are outsiders which represent a negative impact upon local economic and political well-being. All of the states with few union members have passed "right to work" laws which forbid unions and companies to agree to compulsory membership provisions in their contracts. As discussed in Chapter 6, the absence of such clauses weakens unions by permitting the workers whom they represent to refrain from joining unions and paying dues. Paradoxically, the lack of unionism in the southern states makes these states extremely attractive to new industry; but the faster they industrialize, the more likely they are to develop labor forces which are union-oriented. Time, therefore, may erode these regional differences, but they have been pronounced for many decades.

FIGURE 2–2
Regional and State Variation in Union Representation

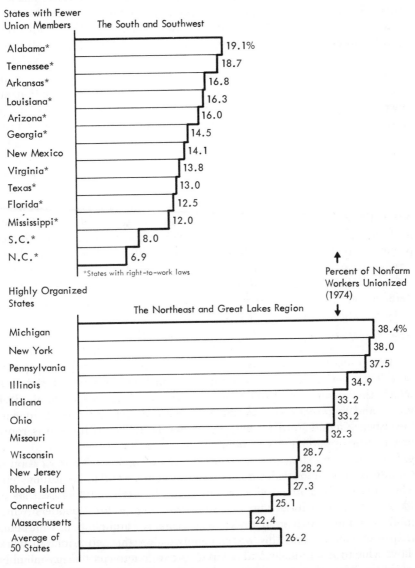

States with Fewer Union Members — The South and Southwest

State	Percent
Alabama*	19.1%
Tennessee*	18.7
Arkansas*	16.8
Louisiana*	16.3
Arizona*	16.0
Georgia*	14.5
New Mexico	14.1
Virginia*	13.8
Texas*	13.0
Florida*	12.5
Mississippi*	12.0
S.C.*	8.0
N.C.*	6.9

*States with right-to-work laws

↑ Percent of Nonfarm Workers Unionized (1974) ↓

Highly Organized States — The Northeast and Great Lakes Region

State	Percent
Michigan	38.4%
New York	38.0
Pennsylvania	37.5
Illinois	34.9
Indiana	33.2
Ohio	33.2
Missouri	32.3
Wisconsin	28.7
New Jersey	28.2
Rhode Island	27.3
Connecticut	25.1
Massachusetts	22.4
Average of 50 States	26.2

Source: Data from U.S. Department of Labor, Bureau of Labor Statistics; reprinted from the May 17, 1976, issue of *Business Week* by special permission. © 1976 by McGraw-Hill, Inc.

Labor in Politics

Gompers' "voluntarist" philosophy advocated the separation of unions and political parties—but not union aloofness from politics. Thus, under Gompers' leadership the AFL avoided involvement with any political party but attempted to support candidates with a prolabor record or platform, and campaign against those considered antilabor, regardless of the party to which the candidates belonged.

Although the AFL–CIO has not altered its official position and still maintains ties to some Republicans, it is heavily committed to, and involved in, the Democratic party. With finances and field-workers, it has provided major support for Democratic party candidates, including presidential candidates, during the last decade and is now a great power in that party. Moreover, by allying itself with various groups, such as those backing civil rights legislation, consumer activities, or old-age benefits, the AFL–CIO has built effective allies which are of immense aid in generating support for candidates and issues.

The AFL–CIO role in politics has continued to expand. Recent election reform laws, which purported to limit campaign spending, actually weakened controls on the use of union funds for politics. The Taft-Hartley Act restricted the use of union dues in political campaigns, but a clause in the 1972 election law overruled court decisions which allowed criminal prosecution of union officials who made political contributions from union treasuries. Thus, unions are freer than at any time since 1947 to spend their members' dues in behalf of political candidates. Since 1972, unions have spent great sums and efforts in political campaigns.

Corporations are now also free to establish political action committees and through them to contribute to candidates. Unions, however, far outstrip corporations in providing assistance to candidates through election workers, computerized election lists, and professional campaign aids. The effectiveness of the union role can be seen by the manner in which the unions mobilized their resources and manpower to register voters and to provide the margin that enabled Jimmy Carter to defeat incumbent Gerald Ford for the presidency in 1976; and by the manner in which union adherents throughout the states have been sent to Congress to such an extent that a majority of its members are almost certain to vote on the union side of any issue crucial to the union leadership. The great success in politics of unions under AFL–CIO leadership is likely not only to induce unions to stress their political role, but also more and more to lead them to seek benefits through political rather than economic action. This will, of course, alter the nature of the labor movement in America, and to a large extent, it appears to have already made the labor movement more politically oriented than ever before.

The Young, the Female, and the Black

The large numbers of young people in the labor market have created internal union clashes, particularly with the predominantly middle-aged union officials. As the late president of a union noted: "The young worker never experienced the Big Depression. He is well educated and has been taught to be independent. He doesn't feel the work ethic that is so important to his parents."[17] Another union official pointed to another problem: "Often when a man gets hired in a plant that has a union shop [compulsory union membership] . . . his introduction to the union is a deduction of $20 or so union affiliate fee on his paycheck. That's not a good introduction."[18]

The generation gap in unions has been rather muted since the recession of the early 1970s taught many young people that there are interruptions to economic progress. Nevertheless, the dissatisfaction of young workers with older union leaders has certainly been a factor in the changing leadership composition of several unions. As noted in Chapter 3, the leadership of American unions is now undergoing change, partly because the World War II generation is retiring; its place is being filled in part by the new labor force recruits of a few years ago. Undoubtedly, these new leaders, like their predecessors, will remain in office long enough to be criticized by young people as being "out of touch."

Women play only a small role in union leadership, though they comprise about 40% of the labor force. A recent report of the U.S. Women's Bureau stated that only about 350 of the top 4,800 union positions are held by women and that even fewer women negotiate contracts. Even those few women who were on international union executive boards were found to have little real authority.[19] No women has ever sat on the AFL–CIO executive council.

Although the AFL–CIO and many unions have supported most civil rights legislation, there is much white-black controversy within unions as in society. One reason is that at the local level, unions and union members, and particularly those very visible ones in the building trades, have more often than not opposed practical equal opportunity for blacks. As a result of this, relations between black groups and unions have often been strained in recent years.

This black-union difference has been exacerbated by the layoffs incidental to the early 1970s recession. This hit blacks in some industries especially hard because they were the last to be hired and therefore, as explained in Chapter 6, the first to be laid off pursuant to seniority clauses. Many civil rights leaders have advocated racial quotas regardless of seniority to correct what they regard as the result of past discrimination, but unions have steadfastly opposed any breaches in the seniority principle.

Within unions, a number of black separatists groups have formed,

---

[17] Comment of Joseph A. Beirne, late president of Communications Workers of America, reported in *U.S. News & World Report,* February 21, 1972, p. 25.

[18] Comment of Leonard Woodcock, president of United Automobile Workers, quoted in *U.S. News & World Report,* February 21, 1972, p. 25.

[19] Reported in *Daily Labor Report,* July 13, 1976, p. A–12.

but these have achieved little success. Thus, in Detroit UAW locals, blacks who have won local officer positions have espoused working within the UAW rather than radical or separatist aims. In the urban transit industry, strong efforts of the predominantly black work force in major cities to win control of locals have been stymied by union policies that permit pensioners to vote. The latter, being predominantly white, have kept incumbent whites in office despite the change in working personnel.[20]

Black union members are still poorly represented in the top union echelons. Slow turnover in union officialdom and the fact that blacks are a minority of most memberships insure this situation, but its continuation is certain to be a focal point of dissent and controversy in the labor movement.

Unions, like companies, thus have problems with different segments of society which desire different relationships. Since union officials must give first consideration to their union leadership role, they will always look at problems differently than will advocates of the role of youth, women, minorities, and other groups. Thus, such problems will always exist. The current solutions are, of course, not necessarily either permanent or superior, as we shall discuss in ensuing chapters.

QUESTIONS FOR DISCUSSION

1. Do you think that union growth will be faster or slower in 1975–80 than it was in 1965–70? Support your answer.

2. Why was the Alliance for Labor Action unable to survive as a rival of the AFL–CIO?

3. If you were the president of the Brotherhood of Locomotive Engineers, an independent union, would you support affiliation with the AFL–CIO? Why, or why not?

4. Has the Teamsters' Union been damaged by its expulsion from the AFL–CIO? If so, in what manner? If not, why not?

SUGGESTIONS FOR FURTHER READING

Bernstein, Irving. *The Lean Years: A History of the American Worker, 1920–1933.* Boston: Houghton Mifflin, 1960.

---

[20] Herbert R. Northrup, "The Negro in the Automobile Industry," in *Negro Employment in Basic Industry,* Studies of Negro Employment, vol. 1, part 2 (Philadelphia: Industrial Research Unit, The Wharton School, University of Pennsylvania, 1970), pp. 99–104; Philip W. Jeffress, "The Negro in the Urban Transit Industry," in Herbert R. Northrup et al., *Negro Employment in Land and Air Transport,* Studies of Negro Employment, vol. 5, part 4 (Philadelphia: Industrial Research Unit, The Wharton School, University of Pennsylvania, 1971), pp. 85–90; and Herbert Hill, "Black Labor, the NLRB, and the Developing Law of Equal Employment Opportunity," *Labor Law Journal,* vol. 28 (April 1975), pp. 207–23.

_____. *The Turbulent Years: A History of the American Worker, 1933–1940*. Boston: Houghton Mifflin, 1970.

Two well-written volumes describing pre–World War II worker problems and unions in a very sympathetic manner.

Caddy, Douglas. *The Hundred Million Dollar Payoff: How Big Labor Buys Its Democrats*. New Rochelle, N.Y.: Arlington House, 1974.

Foster, James C. *The Union Politic: The CIO Political Action Committee*. Columbia: University of Missouri Press, 1975.

Greenstone, J. Donald. *Labor in American Politics*. New York: Alfred A. Knopf, 1969.

Three studies of union political activities, past and present, from very different points of view.

Galenson, Walter F. *The CIO Challenge to the AFL*. Cambridge, Mass.: Harvard University Press, 1960.

An examination of the effects of the rise of the CIO upon the policies and activities of the AFL.

Rowan, Richard L. (ed.) *Readings in Labor Economics and Labor Relations*. 3d ed. Part 2, "Some Aspects of the History of the American Labor Movement," pp. 61–88. Homewood, Ill.: Richard D. Irwin, Inc., 1976.

Various articles by leading authorities on the development, theory, and history of the labor movement.

Terkel, Studs. *Working*. New York: Avon Books, 1975.

Interviews with workers, professionals, and managers who tell in their own words what they think about their jobs.

CASE STUDY READING

Under the guidance of your instructor, read a book or a series of articles about unionism and industrial relations in a particular industry. How does the growth of unionism in the industry you studied compare with the growth of unionism in the country as a whole?

3

Union Structure
and Government

THE GOVERNMENTS of American unions, like those of nations, run the gamut from democracy to dictatorship. The type and structure of a union organization have traditionally depended upon a wide variety of industrial and personal factors, but with the passage of the Labor-Management Reporting and Disclosure Act of 1959 (also known as the Landrum-Griffin Labor Reform Act), federal law became a most important factor shaping union government. Since union government and structure have important repercussions both on union policies and on the economy as a whole, a knowledge of union structure and government is essential background to the economics of labor relations.

ORGANIZATIONAL STRUCTURE AND ITS DETERMINANTS

Union organization usually commences on either a "craft" or an "industrial" basis, but it soon expands beyond these limitations. Today very few craft unions confine their membership to a particular craft, and very few industrial unions have not expanded beyond their original industry. Thus, the International Brotherhood of Electrical Workers takes into membership building-trades electricians, railroad shop electricians, shipyard electricians, and electricians wherever else they are employed; but it has also organized all employees of telephone, electrical machinery, and electronic concerns. Likewise, the original jurisdiction of the United Automobile Workers included all employees in and around automobile plants, whether janitors, electricians, tool and die workers, assembly workers, or any other kind; now, as the United Automobile, Aerospace, and Agricultural Implement Workers, its activities embrace these additional industries also. The Teamsters will accept employees in any occupation or plant. Unions which are outside of the AFL–CIO have no compulsion to respect the jurisdictions of other organizations. The Steel-workers expanded into mining and chemicals by merging unions in these fields.

Sometimes, as in the case of the Teamsters, organizational structure is determined by leadership conflicts. Other factors are often decisive. Early craft unions found that if they did not accept the helpers into their unions, the helpers would take their places in case of strikes. The AFL failed to organize the mass-production industries, partially because it would not accommodate organizational structure to organizational needs. The CIO forced the AFL to adopt a more realistic approach.

Technological factors impact sharply on union structure. Several craft unions—the Brotherhood of Blacksmiths, Drop Forgers, and Helpers, for example—have disappeared from the scene because of technical change.

Government policy alters union structure. The National Labor Relations (Taft-Hartley) Act removes some jurisdictional rules from the hands of union leaders and places them in the hands of the workers themselves and of the NLRB. For example, if a group of textile workers wishes to be represented by the Rubber Workers' Union, and if the leaders of that organization are agreeable, they can petition the National Labor Relations Board for an election. The NLRB then decides who is eligible to participate in the election and holds it. If the workers vote for the Rubber Workers' Union, that union is the legal representative of the workers for collective bargaining, with which the employer must deal, regardless of what union jurisdictional rules provide. The principle of exclusive jurisdiction actually died in 1935 when the Wagner Act was passed; the AFL–CIO recognized its burial in the merger agreement of 1955.

The decisions of the NLRB affect union structure in other ways. For example, if the NLRB declines a union request to separate skilled from unskilled workers, the petitioning union must open its doors to the unskilled as well as the skilled or face the possibility of losing the right, as a result of the adverse votes of the unskilled, of representing either the skilled or the unskilled. This does not mean that craft unions have to take on an industrial character because of NLRB rulings. The NLRB, as we shall point out in Chapter 19, has been careful to maintain the rights and jurisdiction of craft unions.

Union jurisdictional lines often are not clear. In an industry organized along craft union lines, as is the building industry, technological change and the substitutability of one material for another lead to conflicting jurisdictional claims and to jurisdictional strikes—that is, strikes of one craft against another craft doing the work. The outcome of such strikes determines which group of workers will do the work, perhaps which union will grow in strength and size, or the eventual merger of the contesting organizations.

A dispute over which union will represent workers is different from a jurisdictional dispute, since no matter which union wins out, the same workers will continue to work. In representation matters, accidents of location often determine the result and therefore the union structure. If, for example, a metal-fabricating company is located in Detroit, where the United Automobile Workers is strong, it will probably be represented by the UAW; if it were located in Pittsburgh, the United Steelworkers would probably win bargaining rights; in Minneapolis, the Machinists; and so on. In each case, the friends and relatives of the plant workers are likely to be in the dominant union of the area, and so that union is likely to be chosen by the workers in the metal-fabricating plant to represent them.

DETERMINANTS OF UNION GOVERNMENT

As a union grows and takes into membership workers with different interests, not only its structure but also its government is shaped to meet the needs of the members and to take advantage of the experience which develops. For example, the division of the membership along craft, industry, racial, or geographic lines often results in semiautonomous division within unions and in special provisions for the representation of specific groups. Thus, all executive board members in the United Automobile Workers' Union are elected from various geographic areas except two, who are elected "at large" but who, by tacit consent, are a black and a Canadian.

Administrative Determinants

Practical administrative problems also determine union regulations. For example, unions discovered at an early date that strike control would have to be centralized to prevent locals from striking on the slightest provocation, and thus costing the national union thousands of dollars for strike benefits, legal and publicity fees, and even lawsuits by employers if a breach of contract were involved. Many unions do not pay strike benefits unless a strike has been approved by the national executive board; others may refuse to sanction a strike without national approval.

Effects of Rival Unionism

The development of rival unionism on a mass scale in the 1930s materially affected union government. In many cases, the advent of rival unions forced existing unions to open their doors to members previously barred. For example, some unions which once admitted only skilled workers (the Flint Glass Workers and the Molders and Foundry Workers) admitted unskilled workers in order to prevent their organization by the CIO. A number of other unions, such as the Hotel and Restaurant Workers, removed bars to black workers because of the threat of rival unions. On the other hand, the existence of a union with discriminatory racial policies has often caused rival unions to "soft-pedal" their equalitarian policies in order not to alienate the dominant white membership.

Imitative Elements

Many union constitutional provisions result from the fact that the writers of the constitutions merely copy similar provisions from the constitutions of older organizations. The constitution of the first permanent union, the Typographical Union, was copied from that of the Right Worthy Grand Lodge of the Independent Order of Odd Fellows, and then it was gradually amended to suit the needs of the union. Likewise, many railroad unions have constitutions which bear a strong resemblance to the constitution of the oldest railroad union—the Brotherhood of Locomotive Engineers.

Power Elements

A number of union constitutional provisions can be explained only by the desire to increase the power of given individuals or groups. Thus, James Hoffa was able to have the constitution of the Teamsters substantially rewritten to transfer power from subordinate officials to the union presidency. John L. Lewis had great power given to the presidency of the United Mine Workers and reduced the union districts to impotence. In such union constitutions as that of the Carpenters, provisions which give a greater vote to craftsmen than to members of industrial locals are aimed at retaining power for the craftsmen even though they might not make up a majority of the union membership.

Effects of Legislation and Court Decisions

Union government, like union structure, is often shaped by laws or by the decisions of administrative bodies or courts. For example, the adoption of civil rights legislation has forced unions to delete racial bars from their constitutions. Decisions of the NLRB, placing certain groups of workers in bargaining units, have compelled unions to alter their admission policies. Likewise, the courts have ruled that the union leadership did not have authority under certain union constitutions to take specific acts—for example, to expel a member. In a number of instances, the union has thereupon amended its constitution to grant the officers additional authority.

But no act of government has had as great an effect on union government as has the Labor-Management Reporting and Disclosure Act of 1959 (Landrum-Griffin). Under this law, members of labor unions are guaranteed basic rights of free speech, free assembly, and access to financial information, and their officers are required to maintain records and to account for union funds. In addition, unions are required to amend their constitutions, if necessary, to conform to this legislation. The law spells out procedures for the election of union officers, their terms of office, and the frequency of election, and provides rules for the conduct of elections. (See Chapter 20 for a detailed analysis.)

THE NATIONAL OR INTERNATIONAL UNION

The "top" organization of American unions is the national or international union. The officers of the national unions are selected by convention, by referendum, or by a combination of the two, whereby the convention nominates, and the actual contest is determined by a referendum of the entire membership. Unions are required by the Landrum-Griffin Act to have a national convention at least once every five years. Many do so at shorter intervals.

Although union conventions generally provide for the representation of every local, many locals do not send delegates because of the cost. Some internationals have paid the convention expenses of the locals, but the cost of doing so is usually considered too great. As a result, large segments of the membership can be unrepresented at union conventions.

Because the convention is the supreme governing body of most unions, a fair procedure for electing convention delegates is a requisite of democratic union government. Yet most national union constitutions had very little, if anything, to say about how delegates to conventions were to be selected prior to the passage of the Landrum-Griffin Act. Union officials can assure a friendly convention by paying the expenses of delegates from locals beholden to them and by refusing to pay similar expenses for others.

Some conventions are truly deliberative bodies; others are just captive audiences assembled to hear union officers and special guests talk, and to affirm action already decided upon. Even if the convention is truly deliberative, with wide participation by the delegates in formulating, discussing, and adopting or rejecting policies and rules, the real work is done in caucus or committee. In some unions, there is an air of the perfunctory at the convention when actually there have been heated debate and wide participation by delegates in caucuses or committees.

To control the convention committees may be to control the convention. A credentials committee will have a powerful voice in determining which of two contesting groups of delegates can be seated with a vote in the convention. The resolutions committee may be able to bottle up some proposals and report out others, thus controlling the priorities and nature of the floor discussion. The appeals committee hears those who have been disciplined by union locals or officers or who otherwise have a grievance against union judicial machinery. Other committees may perform equally strategic functions. Since either the international president or the executive board almost always appoints the convention committees, the delegates must overturn the convention machinery to change the convention committees.

If, however, the convention delegates elected their committees after arrival, they would probably either have to accept their officers' recommendations because candidates for committee assignments would not be generally known to the delegates, or, as in one convention of the International Association of Machinists, would have to spend nearly a week bickering over committee assignments and transact almost no other union business.

The Referendum

About one fourth of the country's unions elect their officers by direct referendum. The referendum can be a useful tool in promoting union democracy, where the membership has a tradition of participation and a high sense of responsibility, as is the case in the International Typographical Union, or where procedures for getting nominated and insuring fair and honest elections are carefully adhered to. It is, however, no real substitute for a convention. Union members frequently do not take an interest in referenda, so that the decisions made as a result of them have largely been the decisions of active minorities who took the trouble to vote.

National Union Officers

Most national unions are officered by a president, a secretary-treasurer, and one or more vice presidents. The number of vice presidents will be determined by many factors, for example, whether or not regional directors bear that title. In addition, most unions have a national executive board which is theoretically the top governing body between conventions. Members of the executive board are often regional directors or vice presidents.

Although the president, or whoever the chief executive officer of the union may be, is almost always technically subordinate to the executive board, more often than not he is likely to control it. There are, of course, exceptions. In most cases, however, the constitutional power of the union's chief officer is very great; and if he is a forceful personality, he may reduce the executive board to complete subordination, as James R. Hoffa and John L. Lewis did, or simply dominate it, as did Walter Reuther.

The Tenure of National Officers. Most unions have been dominated by one man for long periods of time—in some instances, for 40 or 50 years. In the construction industry, it is also becoming common for son to succeed father—a union leadership dynasty. In any election, the incumbent has a tremendous advantage. He is already well known to the membership, and his every action is news. The challenger must make himself known outside his locality and must have an issue which differentiates him from the incumbent. Patronage, the union journal, and other avenues of communication are controlled by the incumbent. In the fairest of elections, the challenger faces heavy odds. In only a few unions are contests for the top job common.

In recent years, the number of challenges to incumbents, or to the "official" candidate, has increased. This is in part the result of the retirement of leaders who rose to power in the World War II period, but it is also the result of the Landrum-Griffin Act, which makes such opposition less likely to expose challengers to physical or economic harm. This act also reduces the potential for stealing elections to thwart challengers, enabling government action to prevent stolen elections in the cases of the International Union of Electrical, Radio, and Machine Workers in 1964 and of the Mine Workers in 1972.

For the most part, union incumbents do not depend on stolen elections to keep them in power. The Landrum-Griffin Act regulations which provide for honest elections and make provisions for recall and impeachment are not, therefore, likely to reduce materially the length of incumbency of union chiefs. More likely, a new group will retain power for long periods once it, like its predecessors, becomes entrenched.

The long-term incumbency of top union officials is, of course, not unique in American life. Corporation and university officials are frequently in power for long terms, and there are advantages therefrom. In industrial relations, such long terms may promote stability and understanding between labor and management. A union official who is sure of reelection may be in a position to act more realistically with management than one who must constantly bear in mind the effect of collective bargaining on his tenure. That experience is a valuable asset, few would deny. Nevertheless, the advantages of active opposition appear to outweigh the disadvantages. New blood means new ideas, new directions, and often, better representation.

Appointive Officials

In addition to elected officials, most national unions have a sizable staff of paid, appointed personnel. This includes two groups: the specialists or professionals and the international representatives. The former are the lawyers, economists, statisticians, research and educational directors, and the like, whom modern trade-union organizations must employ in order to conduct what has become the highly technical business of running a union and engaging in collective bargaining with management. The latter nearly always come from the ranks of union members.

Professional employees of unions sometimes become key figures in union administration or collective bargaining. Usually, however, the lawyer remains in the background as chief adviser of top officials. And if these officials fail to secure reelection, their lawyers and other professional advisers are usually swept out of office by the new administration. However important the advice of professionals is to labor leadership, that advice can always be purchased from those whose loyalty is above question as well as from those who served the outgoing administration. With extremely few exceptions, professional personnel have discovered that working for a union permits less deviation from the official administration line than does working for government or business.

International representatives have three main functions: first, they are assigned to organize unorganized shops in the union's jurisdiction; second, they assist local unions in negotiations and collective bargaining; and third, they act as political representatives of those responsible for their appointment. Much has been said and written about "interference" by national union officials who prevented local unions from settling controversies except on terms dictated by the national union.

Frequently, however, the national union is a force for peace. Its officers know the costs of strikes, and its staff builds up prestige by successful, peaceful settlements. Local union officers are often too fearful of the consequences of their actions and too inexperienced. The local officers "get out on a limb" from which they cannot rescue themselves. At this point the international representative can step in and use the prestige of the national union to sell the membership on the need for a reasonable solution.

International representatives have little job security, although they may win it for the rank and file through collective bargaining. Theirs is a political appointment (which does not cast aspersions on their abilities), and they must aid the political fortunes of those who appoint them if they are to retain their jobs. In government, the power of patronage is always an important weapon in the hands of the incumbent. So also is the power of patronage in a union. A union official who gave no heed to politics would not last long in office. He must make friends in order to assure his reelection. One of the best ways to do that is to give jobs to people who have contributed to his success and who will continue to work in his interest. The international representative is a political appointee and thus the political emissary of the person responsible for his appointment. For, basically, the union is internally a political organization. It could not be otherwise if it is to be in any way democratic.

Union international representatives, like employees of business, revolt against insecure working conditions. This has led to the formation of unions by union representatives and to demands that such bodies as the AFL–CIO and international unions negotiate with unions of *their* employees. The reaction of labor's top officialdom has been remarkably like that of management 40 years ago—rejecting recognition. The unions of union organizers have repeatedly been forced to go to the NLRB to compel unions to recognize unions of their own employees!

INTERMEDIATE UNION GOVERNMENT

To coordinate the activities of local unions, and to act as an intermediary form of government between the local and the national union, most unions have established what are termed regional offices, district councils, joint boards, and so on. In industrial unions the regional office is the most common. Its jurisdiction varies with the concentration of the industry. For example, the state of Michigan has been divided into numerous regions by the United Automobile Workers, and the rest of the country has proportionately many fewer regions, because the automobile industry is concentrated in and around Detroit. Similarly, the districts of the United Mine Workers are coterminous with the various coalfields; and those of the United Steelworkers are heavily concentrated in the Pittsburgh–Ohio Valley area.

Building-trades unions, which are organized on a craft basis, frequently have all the local unions in an area represented in a coordinating district council. The garment unions call a similar organization a joint board. Railroad unions generally coordinate their locals on a single railroad in what they call a system federation.

Whatever the name, the general purpose of these intermediate forms is the same: coordination of local union activities and joint action of locals in dealing with management. Generally, the regional office is headed by an official who is elected either by the entire union membership or by the membership of the district or region only. In some unions, regional chiefs have the title of vice president; in others, such as the building trades, the head of the district council may be its secretary-treasurer. In any case, the regional office is an important union position which many local union officials covet.

THE LOCAL UNION

The local union is that part of the union structure which the member contacts directly. The conduct of affairs on the local level is thus frequently the means by which the member judges his or her union. Like the government of municipalities, local union government is characterized by much that is heartening to those interested in democratic ways and by much that is unsavory; and the latter, as in municipal affairs, is most often attributable to the failure of the citizenry, or members, to concern themselves with the conduct of their organization. In short, local union government, like municipal government, too often depends on the character of the small minority who bear the burden of operating the organization.

Local Jurisdiction and Size

The jurisdiction and size of local unions do not follow a fixed pattern. Most commonly, the local has jurisdiction over a single plant, and thus the size of its membership depends upon the size of the plant. One of the largest locals is No. 600, United Automobile Workers, which has jurisdiction over the 25,000 workers employed in the River Rouge (near Detroit, Michigan) works of the Ford Motor Company. Other one-plant locals may have as few as 10 to 100 members.

There are, however, many variations from the one-plant local. Craft union locals commonly have jurisdiction over an area. Thus, Bricklayers' Local No. 1 of Louisiana is composed of all union bricklayers in New Orleans. In larger cities, such as New York or Chicago, two or three such locals may divide the jurisdiction.

Industries in which average plant employment is small are frequently characterized by multiplant or "amalgamated" locals. Thus, in the Detroit tool and die jobbing shops, which employ an average of less than 25 employees per shop, one local union of the UAW has jurisdiction.

Amalgamated locals may also develop for other reasons. A number of unions have amalgamated locals which are quite large, apparently to centralize control. Under the amalgamated system, each plant in the large locals is represented on an executive board. Control of the executive board secures control over all plants. By concentrating all its strength in a minority of the plant units, a faction can win control of the local.

Local Union Officers

If a local union is small, it usually cannot afford full-time officials. In such cases, its officers work at their jobs but, by agreement with management, take time off for union business. The union compensates them only for actual expenses, which include time off from their jobs at the job rate. In many instances the international union assigns a full-time representative to aid local unions in the conduct of their affairs.

The larger local unions usually have one or more full-time officials, who are compensated completely from the local treasury. The top-ranking official may be the president, or the latter may be only a figure-head, with the chief power in the hands of a business agent or manager, or a secretary-treasurer. Custom, accident, and the strength of the individuals who occupy these positions are the determining factors.

Only the largest local unions can afford appointed officials to assist elected ones. A few of these do, however, have organizers and other "local representatives" on their payroll. Such appointees help organize new shops, assist in negotiating and administering collective bargaining contracts, and aid the union political fortunes of those elected officials who are responsible for their appointment. They function on a local basis similarly to international representatives on a national basis. Because they are self-sustaining, large locals often operate quite independently of their international union.

The Duration of Local Union Office

Most commonly, local officials are elected for a term of one or two years. In contrast to the situation in the national union, the turnover of local officials is high. This is especially true in the smaller locals, where the leaders and the membership are close, and challenges to local leadership do not involve expensive campaigning. On the average, it is not likely that the tenure of local office exceeds two or four years. Some of the turnover is accounted for by advancement to higher union positions; some, by the fact that local union officials often accept managerial positions—for example, become foremen; but most of the turnover is accounted for by the electorate's desire for a change in administration.

The United Steelworkers elects local officers every three years. In 1973, 34.5% of the top 26,460 elected local officers were new, a clear indication of the extent of turnover in such positions. This union also reports that the turnover for lesser local union offices was even higher.[1]

Local union officials often have few compensations for their jobs. Their salaries as a rule are not particularly high, and often not very much in excess of what they can earn as workers. There are, of course, exceptions, with some local officials inordinately overpaid. In the main, however, status is likely to be more important for the full-time official, for full-time union work is more appealing to many than is a factory job at equal pay. Against that, however, are the long hours, the necessity to work nights when factory employees are free, and the constant reminder that tenure in office is likely to be short.

The Shop Steward

Besides compensated officials, nearly all local unions have shop stewards or committeemen, who are the union representatives in the plant. These officials are usually elected by the group they serve. They work full time at their jobs; but in addition, they collect dues, handle grievances with management foremen, and generally look after union affairs in the shop. They carry the union's message and represent the union in its daily contacts with members. Their relations with foremen often

---

[1] *Steel Labor*, May 1975, p. 10.

determine the type of industrial relations which exist in a plant; for whatever the union-management relationship may be at the top level, stewards and foremen are the persons who must carry it out on the shop level.

Membership Apathy

Despite the evidence that the great majority of local union officials are both undercompensated and honest, a significant number have obviously been neither. Therefore, requirements for fair procedure set forth in the Landrum-Griffin Act specifically apply to local unions as well as to national unions. Local unions must now elect officials by secret ballot at least once every three years. Various guarantees are set forth to insure free elections by secret ballot, reasonable opportunity to nominate candidates, a fair prior notice of elections, no discrimination in the use of membership lists or campaign literature distribution, and safeguards for a fair count of ballots.

If, however, the Landrum-Griffin Act is to achieve its full effect, the average union member will have to attend union meetings much more consistently than he or she ever has before. The outlook for such a turnabout in behavior is not promising.

The business of the local is generally conducted at meetings which are either called by local officials or held at stipulated intervals. Unfortunately, these meetings are not, as a rule, either interesting or well attended. The average union member takes his responsibilities as a member lightly. After a hard day's work, he is much more likely to stay home with his family or to engage in recreational pursuits than to attend a union meeting which may be quite unexciting. In short, his attitude toward his union duty is like that of the average citizen toward his responsibilities as a stockholder, organization member, or citizen.

TRUSTEESHIPS

The constitutions of many international unions authorize the international officers to suspend the normal processes of government of local unions and other subordinate bodies, to supervise their internal activity, and to assume control of their property and funds. These "trusteeships" (or "receiverships" or "supervisorships," as they are sometimes called) are among the most effective devices which responsible international officers have to insure order within their organization. Trusteeships have been widely used to prevent corruption, mismanagement of union funds, violations of collective bargaining agreements, infiltration by Communists —in short, to preserve the integrity and stability of the organization itself.

In some instances, however, trusteeships have been used as a means of consolidating the power of corrupt union officers, of plundering and dissipating the resources of local unions, and of obstructing the development of free speech, free assembly, and free elections within local unions. The fact that most union constitutions are vague about the explicit terms and powers of trusteeships has permitted and abetted misuse of the trustee function.

The reasons why trusteeships may be initiated are typically vague and indefinite, and provide the international president or executive board more often than not with almost blanket authority to take over a local union or even to subvert the will of the local membership. For example, the constitution of the United Mine Workers permitted John L. Lewis and his successors to institute trusteeships and to maintain them for over 40 years.

Title III of the Landrum-Griffin Act sets forth detailed regulations for the conduct of trusteeships, and undoubtedly has curtailed some abuses in their utilization. The U.S. Department of Labor, which administers Title III, has not pushed regulation. For example, although the Department announced in 1964, five years after the passage of the act, that it was suing to eliminate the Mine Workers' trusteeships, not until 1972, after the murder of a union presidential challenger, were the cases pushed and the trusteeships abolished by court orders.

UNION FINANCE

Operating a union in modern American society is an expensive undertaking. Officer and employee salaries, office rent, traveling expenses, postage and other communications costs, publicity, and legal and research activities are some of the daily routine expenses which must be met. In addition, a reserve must be built up; for a long strike, with its increased demands on ordinary services, plus the cost of strike benefits, extra legal and publicity help, and so on, can drain the union treasury of several million dollars. As an extreme example, the United Automobile Workers and its locals spent $142 million on strike benefits in 1970. This included the disbursements during the General Motors strike of that year. The net worth of the UAW, which stood at close to $100 million a few years before, was down to $5 million at the end of 1970; by 1975, higher dues and assessments had brought it up to $162.5 million.[2] As a result of the 1976 Ford strike, however, the amount was again substantially reduced.

Dues and Fees

The funds necessary to operate a union and to service its membership come primarily from the monthly dues paid by the members themselves.

---

[2] See *Solidarity*, August 1971 and September 1975, for UAW financial reports.

In addition, unions derive income from initiation fees and assessments, also paid by members, and from government bonds, property, or other securities in which excess or reserve funds are invested.

In general, the older craft unions have the highest dues and initiation fees. High dues and fees are justified by these unions on the ground that newcomers should compensate the union which has raised wages and standards in the craft, especially since the present high wages permit "Johnny-come-lately" to pay his share so easily. A high initiation fee also serves to discourage applicants and thus give union men a greater part of the available work. The use of the initiation fee as an exclusionist policy is only feasible if entrance to the trade can be controlled by the union. With a few exceptions, only craft unions can exert such control. An industrial union, which depends for its bargaining strength on organizing all employees of the industry or firm, would defeat its purpose by raising its fees high enough to limit membership.

On the basis of the data filed with the U.S. Department of Labor pursuant to the Landrum-Griffin Act, the authors estimate that national unions had receipts well in excess of $1 billion in 1976. In addition, several billion more are now channeled annually into union-controlled or union-management welfare and pension funds. Table 3–1 summarizes financial information for certain unions, including the six largest, several very wealthy ones, and some whose assets are dwindling as their mem-

TABLE 3–1
Union Financial Information, Selected Unions, Ranked in Membership Order, 1975

Union	Dues and/or per Capita Tax	Total Receipts	Net Assets
Teamsters	$49,633,407	$146,130,337	$120,750,458
Automobile Workers	18,000,112	713,148,892	213,129,979
Steelworkers	87,317,736	415,051,675	116,714,779
Electrical Workers (IBEW)	56,201,312	105,215,411	42,176,131
Machinists	39,434,782	45,857,160	46,537,374
Carpenters	30,725,188	76,515,025	32,252,783
Laborers	13,174,603	21,043,717	37,919,523
Hotel and Restaurant Workers	6,075,300	17,919,901	13,020,317
Operating Engineers	10,362,265	23,734,672	38,928,887
Electrical Workers (IUE)	11,473,812	12,614,085	10,492,100
Railway Clerks	9,115,810	12,874,238	7,454,868
Plumbers	14,893,683	38,461,282	34,120,795
Mine Workers	7,304,868	32,674,459	80,726,416
Rubber Workers	8,747,879	14,655,140	9,872,205
Oil, Chemical, Atomic	8,740,561	9,713,694	3,791,524
Chemical Workers	3,711,667	7,101,254	3,239,254
Cement, Lime, and Gypsum Workers	1,631,071	2,172,366	5,015,076
National Maritime Union	3,327,439	5,333,321	9,072,040

For related membership information, see Table 3–2 below.
Source: U.S. Department of Labor, Office of Labor-Management and Welfare Pension Reports.

bership declines—for example, the Chemical Workers. It does not, however, include information on union welfare and pension funds, the assets of which may well be 100 times those of the unions.

Initiation fees tend to vary from double the monthly dues to much more. Many of the older craft unions charge $100 or more for an entrance fee, usually payable in installments. Where initiation fees of $500 or of $1,000 have been asked, for example, in some of the skilled crafts of the motion-picture industry, such fees are as much bars to admission as they are actual charges.

The extent of union assessments varies considerably. Generally, they occur as a result of an emergency expenditure, for an organizing campaign, or for strike benefits. For example, the United Automobile Workers enacted a $25-per-month assessment in 1971 to help defray expenses related to the strikes, particularly the one involving General Motors Corporation.

The Problem of High Fees

Generally, complaints of high union fees refer to initiation fees rather than to dues. Moreover, as has been pointed out, the basic problem is admission policy and not initiation fees. Any legal attack on what are considered antisocial union fees must be directed to the root of the problem—the extent to which unions should be permitted to exclude persons from employment by excluding them from the union.

There is no one criterion for a "too high" initiation fee. Five hundred dollars could be a reasonable fee for the Air Line Pilots Association, whose members may earn more than $50,000 per annum; the same fee is outrageous when charged by the Laborers' Union. A fee is large or small relative to the benefits expected, primarily the prospective earnings.

Most union fees are not excessive by this standard. The main exceptions are found in the building and amusement industry unions. In these industries, union power is great, and union control over jobs extraordinarily complete. Those who are in the unions are thus afforded an unusual opportunity to inflict heavy charges on such applicants as they permit to join.

Section 8(b) of the Taft-Hartley Act makes it an unfair labor practice for a union to charge "excessive or discriminatory" fees. The act further requires the National Labor Relations Board to consider, "among other relevant factors, the practices and customs of labor organizations in the particular industry, and the wages currently paid to the employees affected" in determining whether a fee is excessive or discriminatory. The NLRB has had comparatively few complaints under this section and has ordered fees reduced or discontinued in only a few instances.

The Landrum-Griffin Act attacks the problem of union dues and fees from another direction. It prohibits unions from raising dues or initiation fees or from levying assessments unless a majority of the members of a local union so vote in a referendum or by secret ballot at a special meeting for which due notice has been given; or unless a national union votes by referendum or at a convention, for which appropriate due notice has been given. Failure to follow these provisions has forced a few unions to rescind dues increases or assessments.

Salaries

Unions are, in general, not distinguished as high-salaried organizations. The average union staff member receives less than his counterpart in industry, in terms of salary, benefits, and expense allowances. Actually, union officials are paid on the more modest scale which typifies employees of other nonprofit institutions. Of course, the income of the union representative is usually greater, often substantially, than he would earn in his trade. More often, however, the prestige and interest of the office, rather than the money, are the lures which impel a man to seek union office.

As the data in Table 3–2 show, however, there are a few union officials who receive fairly high salaries and allowances. A salary of from $25,000 to $50,000 does not seem large when compared to the salaries of from $100,000 to $500,000 paid to industrialists. But unions are, after all, nonprofit organizations whose expenses are paid for by workers' monthly dues; and sometimes, those dues come from workers whose income is very small. Thus, the $140,000 in salary and expenses paid to Edward T. Hanley, president of the Hotel and Restaurant Workers union, comes from the dues of low-paid culinary workers. And as the number of seamen and railway clerks declined, the salaries of the presidents of their unions rose. Before he retired in 1973, Joseph Curran of the National Maritime Union received almost $100,000 in salaries and expenses, plus severance pay for a total of $419,663.79. He now receives an annual pension of $53,577.24. His union is down to about 15,000 members and is saddled with pension obligations to retired seamen that it probably cannot meet.

In the Teamsters, a policy of multiple salaries has developed which greatly increases the income of some officials. Thus, one man may receive one salary as a local business agent, another as a regional director, and a third as a vice president. There seems to be little reason for this except personal greed.

We may conclude that union salaries vary with the interest of the union officials in money. Some want more income than do others. And because the salaries of the rest of the union bureaucracy depend upon what the top man receives, there is always interest in more money for the top man if he is willing to countenance having his subordinates push up the scale.

TABLE 3–2

Union Presidents and Their Salaries, Selected Unions, 1975

Union	Membership	President	Salary	Other Compensation
Teamsters	2,100,000	Frank E. Fitzsimmons	$125,000.00**	$ 9,885.86
Automobile Workers .	1,575,000	Leonard Woodcock	46,431.94	20,451.69
Steelworkers	1,300,000	I. W. Abel	75,000.00	12,786.40
Electrical Workers (IBEW)	993,000	Charles H. Pillard	72,687.51	6,384.53
Machinists	945,000	Floyd E. Smith	41,000.00	7,094.52
Carpenters	820,000	William Sidell	62,200.00	9,857.16
Laborers	650,000	Peter Fosco	62,500.00	1,948.88
Hotel and Restaurant Workers	453,000	E. T. Hanley	50,800.00	88,552.00
Operating Engineers.	415,000	Hunter P. Wharton‡	90,000.00	22,396.48
Electrical Workers (IUE)	298,000	Paul Jennings§	35,000.03	13,498.00
Railway Clerks	235,000	C. L. Dennis‖	70,000.04	26,703.25
Plumbers	225,000	Martin J. Ward	56,375.00	29,220.00
Mine Workers	200,000*	Arnold Miller	45,309.42	3,384.79
Rubber Workers	192,000	Peter Bommarito	33,681.88	5,674.11
Oil, Chemical, Atomic	177,000	A. F. Grospiron	32,100.00	16,080.00
Chemical Workers ...	75,000	F. D. Martino	28,750.30	1,379.00
Cement, Lime, and Gypsum Workers ..	37,000	Thomas E. Miechur	29,122.00	2,506.00
National Maritime Union	15,000†	S. S. Well#	53,991.60	11,086.68

* Claimed 270,000 in 1975, but believed overstated.
† Claimed 35,000 in 1975, but believed overstated.
‡ Resigned in 1975 and replaced by J. C. Turner.
§ Resigned in 1976 and replaced by David Fitzmaurice.
‖ Resigned in October 1976 and replaced by Fred Kroll.
In 1973, replaced Joseph Curran, whose salary was $97,000.
** Raised to $150,000 in 1976.
George Meany, president of the AFL–CIO, was voted a salary of $90,000 by the 1971 AFL–CIO convention.
Source: U.S. Department of Labor, Bureau of Labor Statistics, and Office of Labor-Management and Welfare Pension Reports.

Union Financial Methods

A union with a membership of 100,000 and dues of $10 per month would have a monthly dues income of $1 million and expenditures for numerous items, most of which are purchased in bulk. Obviously, it is imperative that unions operate with careful bookkeeping and accounting methods which account for every penny to the membership. Many unions have always done this, but others have not. In addition, local union accounting practice has often been inadequate. Careful practices, such as were adopted by the Steelworkers, the Ladies' Garment Workers, and the Machinists, have not been sufficiently common, especially at the local level. The passage of the Landrum-Griffin Act in 1959, and of pension and welfare control laws in 1958, 1962, and 1975, was designed to safeguard union and welfare funds, now amounting to several billions of dollars.

As a result of these laws, union financial practices have been substantially improved. Although congressional investigators have found that millions of dollars of union and welfare fund assets have been siphoned into the hands of questionable characters,[3] or used, as James R. Hoffa did, for questionable investments in questionable projects run by equally questionable characters,[4] such practices continue because, unless someone complains, the government has limited powers to act, and even then, seems to move reluctantly. Too often, employers must share the guilt of dissipating union welfare funds because they have done nothing to stop this after handing over the moneys. Both Hoffa and employer representatives on a Teamster welfare fund were convicted of conspiring to misuse such funds, and numerous other indictments have been handed down, but the problem remains.

Union Assets

Based on reports to the U.S. Department of Labor, the authors estimate that international unions had approximately $6 billion in assets in 1976. This does not include the tremendous assets of local or intermediate union bodies; nor does it include the assets of wholly or partially union-controlled welfare and pension plans, which, as already noted, are estimated to be many times those of unions. Although union assets are enormous, they do not approximate those of major corporations. A few of the major corporations have more assets than have all unions combined.

Most union funds are invested in low-return government bonds. Union financial managers want their assets liquid for emergencies, and they want to avoid criticism that could come if they invested in the stocks of companies with which they might deal. Attempts to persuade unions to invest in socially desirable projects, such as low-cost housing, or to diversify their investments have been largely unsuccessful.

A conspicuous exception to the usual union investments are those of the Teamsters, whose funds have been invested in a variety of deals, including real estate, gambling casinos, and hotels. Many of these Teamster deals have shown little return and have been the basis for a

---

[3] See, for example, "Diversion of Union Welfare-Pension Funds of Allied Trades Council and Teamsters Local 815," in *Hearings before the Permanent Subcommittee on Investigations of the Committee on Government Operations* (U.S. Senate, 89th Cong., 1st sess., 1965); and "Staff Study of the Severance Pay–Life Insurance Plan of Teamsters Local 295," *Report of the Permanent Subcommittee on Investigations of the Committee on Government Operations* (U.S. Senate, 94th Cong., 2d sess., 1976).

[4] Ralph James and Estelle James, *Hoffa and the Teamsters: A Study of Union Power* (Princeton, N.J.: D. Van Nostrand & Co., 1965), pp. 213–320; and *Teamster Democracy and Financial Responsibility* (Washington, D.C.: PROD, Inc., 1976).

continuing investigation of relations between Teamster officials and the promoters of these ventures.

In most cases, union wealth is a function of the prosperity of an industry. The brisk demand for automobiles in the 1960s made the UAW the country's wealthiest union until it overspent its assets on building projects and the General Motors strike. Declining employment so reduced the income of several railroad unions in the same period that a wave of union mergers occurred. The assets of the Mine Workers remained high despite a decline in the number of coal miners from 500,000 to 100,000, because royalties for its welfare fund were based on tonnage mined, not the number of miners, and because the employer and union trustees of the Miners' welfare fund used its assets to further the UMW policy of protecting its investments rather than for its members. Thus, in the period between 1951 and 1969, 14%-44% of the miners' welfare fund moneys were left in a non-interest-bearing account in the Washington, D.C., bank controlled by the UMW. Other funds were utilized to purchase public utility stocks in order to force these utilities to buy union-mined coal. A court ruled these acts a breach of trust and a conspiracy, ordered the UMW president to resign as a trustee of the welfare fund, ordered that all relations with the UMW-controlled bank cease, and assessed damages against the trustees of the welfare fund.[5]

ADMISSION POLICIES AND THE RACE ISSUE

The great majority of American unions admit any applicant to membership. "If he is good enough to work in the plant, he is good enough to join the union" sums up the prevailing union practice and attitude.

But unions also tend to accept prevailing practice. The union is the servant of its members, not an innovator. If discrimination exists, this is likely to be satisfactory to white union members. That is why black organizations and unions are often at loggerheads, and why much antagonism exists today between many unions and black groups.

Although the AFL preached against discrimination in its early period, many of its constituent unions did practice discrimination. Blacks were antagonistic to organized labor in the pre-1932 period because of this fact. But when the CIO was organized, it made a practice of encouraging black membership. This, in turn, forced the AFL and its unions to adopt a more tolerant attitude. Unions, and especially the CIO, received heavy black support during the next 15 years.

But as black unemployment rose in the late 1950s and the drive of the black for more equal status on all fronts continued, the gulf between the aspirations of blacks and unions widened. Racial equality programs

---

[5] *Blankinship et al.* v. *Boyle et al.*, Civil Action No. 2186–69, U.S. Dis. Ct., D.C., April 28, 1971.

ran counter to the vested interests of white union members—and they control most unions. The attempts of blacks to end this discrimination, and the tendency of unions to institutionalize the status quo, resulted in racial antagonism.

The reasons for racial discrimination by unions lie in the basic economic and technological conditions of a particular industry. The unions which readily admit all applicants—the United Automobile Workers, the United Steelworkers, the International Ladies' Garment Workers' Union—are organized on an industrial basis, the only type of union structure feasible in a mass-production industry. Such unions derive their bargaining power by admitting all the workers in their industries to membership and by bargaining for them without discrimination. If they excluded any racial or ethnic group, they would weaken their bargaining power. Exclusion would invite the excluded group to join another union and to break strikes. Racial exclusion by unions in mass-production industries is not only impractical, but it endangers the unions' very existence.

On the other hand, equal admission practices do not necessarily mean equality of treatment. Union seniority rules often institutionalize existing discrimination in promotion practices, or even add new discriminatory practices. In the steel industry, the United Steelworkers did little to open up rolling mill jobs, traditionally a white man's preserve, to blacks until forced to do so by litigation pursuant to Title VII of the Civil Rights Act. Nor did the United Auto Workers, until very recently, substantially aid the efforts of blacks to expand their opportunities among the skilled craftsmen of the industry.

There are craft unions that have not discriminated, and industrial unions that have. Many other factors are involved; and in each case, they are mixed in different ways. In the railway unions, for example, much can be explained by their character as fraternal societies. The first two railway unions (the Brotherhood of Locomotive Engineers and the Order of Railway Conductors of America) were fraternal and benevolent societies, and discriminatory rules have been traditional in many fraternal groups. As other railway unions came into existence, they copied the bylaws of the older organizations, including the discriminatory rules, as a matter of course, even though by then these organizations may have become more important as bargaining than as fraternal organizations.

Economic factors, however, have been most important in maintaining the discriminatory practices of the railway unions. When employment on the railways declined, the railway unions tried for years to shift the burden of unemployment to black workers, whom they barred from membership. The Brotherhood of Locomotive Firemen and Enginemen and the Brotherhood of Railroad Trainmen succeeded in getting nearly every railroad in the South either to limit the number of blacks hired as brakemen and firemen, or more often, to eliminate blacks from these jobs altogether within a few years. This deprived blacks of jobs which had been open to members of their race since the southern railroads were built.

The AFL–CIO takes a strong position against discrimination in its constitution and in all of its official actions. Nevertheless, it admitted to membership both the Locomotive Firemen and the Railroad Trainmen, now merged as the United Transportation Union, after exacting promises that these unions would delete the offending clauses from their constitutions. This they did, but they continued their restrictive practices for many years until forced to change as a result of the Civil Rights Act.

Many unions expressly protect the rights of workers to join, regardless of race. Such provisions vary from explicit provisions that "no worker otherwise eligible to membership shall be discriminated against or denied membership because of race" (Woodworkers), or that any discrimination because of race will be punishable by a fine of $100 (Bricklayers), to simple provisions that all eligible members, "regardless of race," shall be admitted.

Except in the building trades, racial admission policies are likely to be determined and controlled by the national union. There have been important exceptions. Locals of the United Automobile Workers have discriminated against blacks, despite contrary national union policies; and locals of the Machinists and Boilermakers admitted blacks on an equal basis, despite former national union discriminatory rules. Such local variations have been the exception rather than the rule.

In the building trades, locals have on many occasions discriminated against blacks despite national officer pressure. This industry is still featured by strong local autonomy—and internal racial discrimination. As a result, building-trades local unions have been the targets of numerous civil rights demonstrations and court cases brought by state human relations commissions and by the federal government pursuant to the 1964 Civil Rights Act. Few matters have caused so much bitterness between unions and civil rights groups as the obvious and overt discriminatory practices of some building-trades unions.

Despite the progress in eliminating it, racial discrimination by some unions remains a blot on the labor movement. The fact that the record of the labor movement is about equal to that of most other facets of American life in race relations does not reduce the need to eliminate racial discrimination in unions.

CLOSED UNIONS

Sometimes, unions refuse admission to any newcomers or accept only a favored few, for example, relatives of members. Such unions are found almost exclusively among highly skilled or strategically located groups which are in a position to control entrance to a trade. In addition, closed unions may be found in industries where employment is casual or seasonal (maritime, garments). In a case in Philadelphia, one man tried in vain to gain entrance to the motion-picture projectionists' local for about 50 years—an extreme case involving skilled work in a casual trade.[6]

The closed union is usually a local organization. Generally, national unions are opposed to a policy which limits union membership and may create a sizable group of potential strikebreakers. The local leadership, however, is under pressure to give preference to local members—even at the expense of members from other locals—and closing the union books is one way to achieve this result.

Sometimes, closed unions give limited work permits to nonmembers. This has developed into a racket in many instances, with permit holders charged high fees to work. A number of building-trades union locals have used the permit system to comply with government "goal" or quota requirements on jobs for blacks in federally financed construction. This, of course, serves to avoid admitting the black craftsmen to the union on a permanent basis and thus continues the practice of discrimination in construction in which federal funds are not involved.

The closed union is most common in the building, amusement, and printing trades; the local delivery business; diamond cutting; and mirror manufacturing. In periods of depression, it has extended to the seasonal and casual trades, and even to such industries as mining.

The Reasons for Union Exclusionary Policies

The fact that some trade unions limit their membership should not be regarded as too extraordinary. A great many barriers against economic opportunity are sought by a wide variety of organizational groups —farm, business, and professional organizations as well as labor organizations. Moreover, the policies used by unions to bar admission are like those of other groups. Consider, for example, the historic attempts of the American Medical Association to limit the number of doctors (or to use the AMA's terminology, "prevent overcrowding of the profession"). Constituent groups of the AMA have used licensing laws, race discrimination, discrimination against aliens, denial of licenses to out-of-state doctors, and other equally antisocial means of restricting entry into the medical profession.

Whether a labor organization, a professional society, or a business organization, the reasons for restricting entry are usually the same: work-scarcity consciousness, dictated by fear of unemployment. For example, unions are more likely to close their books in depressions than in

---

[6] *Philadelphia Inquirer,* December 2, 1962, p. 32. Investigation later indicated that he never was admitted.

prosperity. Also, it is true that race prejudice is only one factor in the discrimination against blacks. Undoubtedly, a most important reason for such discrimination is that the color line provides a convenient method of limiting the market.

Public policy generally does and should condemn closed unions. Yet the situation is often not clear-cut. For example, in depressed times, when unemployment among union members in the maritime industry is significant, unions typically "close their books." Because of the hiring hall system, whereby men are selected in rotation to fill the available jobs, admitting new members would result in a further sharing of unemployment in a particular industry where unemployment among those already attached to the industry is severe and where employment even in ordinary tinmes is casual and intermittent. Nevertheless, if the union books are closed to some, but not to others, on the basis of race, creed, or color, or by some other invidious method, then the action is clearly indefensible—and today also illegal.

JUDICIAL PROCEDURES IN UNIONS

In the conduct of their affairs, unions have found it necessary to establish a list of offenses for which penalties may be assessed against the members. Union constitutions give officers considerable authority to impose a wide variety of sentences upon their own initiative, or after a trial has found a member guilty. Many of the offenses are general in character (action unbecoming a union member is such an offense); others are more specific (strikebreaking, for example).

The penalties vary from a modest reprimand to heavy fines or expulsion from the union, which can mean a virtual blacklist for employment. Union judicial processes are thus a serious matter from the point of view of public policy—namely, to what extent should private governments, such as unions, be permitted to levy fines and to deny persons work?

Anyone familiar with the realities of union organization realizes that unions must have some protection against those who would convert the unions into instruments of outside organizations, for example, the Communist party, or those who are agents of the employer, labor spies, or provocateurs. Morever, if unions were unable to enforce any penalties whatsoever against members, workers who violate collective bargaining agreements could not be disciplined by the union.

On the other hand, the vagueness and general character of the offenses found in union constitutions are a grave peril to the civil rights of union members. One of the most abused provisions of union constitutions has been the prohibition against slander. No constitution defines "slander." Yet, the charge has often been invoked to insulate union officialdom against criticism. The same has been true of provisions against "creating dissension" or discussing "union business" in public. Such events contributed to the passage of the Landrum-Griffin Act's "bill-of-rights" sections, guaranteeing members' rights to free speech.

Procedures

Charges against a union member are typically filed by another member. Invariably, they must be in writing and be served on the accused. A trial committee is then usually appointed by the local president or elected by the local. The committee hears testimony and renders a decision, which is usually reported to the local membership for action. A guilty verdict often requires more than a majority vote—two thirds or three fourths—usually by secret ballot. The penalties vary from reprimands and light fines ($5) to expulsions and heavy fines ($100–$5,000).

Virtually all unions provide for appeals through the union hierarchy. A frequent course is for appeal to the regional office, thence to the international president and/or executive board, and finally to the international convention.

In addition to this procedure, a number of unions grant their international president specific authority to initiate and/or hear charges against local members or local unions. Other unions permit the president to order a local to try a member and to take action if the local refuses to comply.

Unfortunately, most union constitutions do not provide for a stay of execution of the penalty pending appeal. Thus, even if a member eventually won a case on appeal, he could be denied union membership (and work) in the interim, which could be as long as four years. The ability of unions to discipline members in this way has been reduced somewhat by the provisions of the Taft-Hartley Act, which do not interfere with the right of a union to expel a member but prevent that expulsion from causing the member's discharge, except for nonpayment of dues; and by the bill-of-rights sections of the Landrum-Griffin Act, which has provided much more ready access to the courts for redress if a member is wronged. Studies of the impact of these laws in terms of actual redress to the individual indicate, however, that restoration of job rights is often not effectively accomplished; or else that the costs of litigation are too formidable for the individual to undertake.[7] Moreover, the protections which Congress attempted to legislate seem to have been undermined by U.S. Supreme Court decisions which permit unions to fine members who refuse to restrict production[8] and which permit unions to sue in court to collect fines from employees.[9]

---

[7] For analysis of this situation and the relevant law, see Thomas J. Keeline, *NLRB and Judicial Control of Union Discipline,* Labor Relations and Public Policy Report No. 13 (Philadelphia: Industrial Research Unit, The Wharton School, University of Pennsylvania, 1976).

[8] *Russell Scofield et al.* v. *NLRB,* 394 U.S. 423 (1969).

[9] *NLRB* v. *Allis-Chalmers Mfg. Co.,* 388 U.S. 175 (1967); and *Florida Power & Light Co.* v. *IBEW, Local 641,* 417 U.S. 790 (1974). For an analysis of these cases, see Keeline, *NLRB and Judicial Control.*

Analysis of Union Judicial Procedures

Justice requires trial before an impartial jury, a full and fair hearing, and speedy determination of cases, including the appeal. Union judicial procedure has not stood up well under these criteria. There have been some significant exceptions to this judgment. The International Typographical Union constitution shows great concern for due process and independent judicial determination for those charged with offenses against the union.

The United Automobile Workers goes even farther. It has set up a public review board composed of seven well-known citizens who have no other relationship with the union. The review board receives copies of all complaints lodged with the UAW international executive board. If a union member is dissatisfied with the decision of the executive board, he may then appeal to the public review board, which has not hesitated to overturn the executive board on a number of occasions. Moreover, the public review board has authority to act directly on a matter "if it concludes that there is substance to the original complaint and that the action of the International Executive Board does not satisfactorily meet the problem." The Upholsterers' International Union is the only other union with a similar public review system.

As a matter of fact, those who bring charges under union constitutional processes more often than not may control the staffing of the trial committee appeal bodies. Thus, local officers, who may bring charges in most unions, usually either serve on the trial committee or appoint it, this being the case in 77 of the 136 unions studied by the Bureau of Labor Statistics. However, 56 of these unions denied a place on the trial committee and appeal body for anyone who was an accuser or a defendant. In addition, the defense is often denied access to information, and witnesses are sometimes intimidated from testifying for the defense, or prompted to testify for the prosecution. The infliction of the penalty prior to the completion of an appeal has also been a severe hardship in many cases. An appeal to a convention which may not meet for five years is often an empty right, especially if the penalty is enforced meanwhile. Moreover, conventions are large legislative bodies, basically unable to give the time and study to appeals from disciplinary actions or other judicial functions. Since convention committees are usually appointed by union officers, such committees usually recommend the denial of appeal from rulings made by these same officers.

Traditionally, the courts have regarded unions as private bodies without a vested public interest. Hence they would not intervene on behalf of a worker disciplined by a union unless the worker were denied the forms of a fair trial, that is, fair according to the union rules, or else fair in general terms if the union rules contravene public law or policy. Moreover, the courts have frequently required union members to exhaust internal remedies before accepting a case—which meant appealing first up the union hierarchy to a convention before bringing the case to the courts. In addition, court litigation is costly and uncertain in outcome because of the numerous technicalities involved.

Congress, therefore, intervened by passing the Landrum-Griffin Act, which requires guarantees of freedom of speech and assembly, freedom to resort to the courts or administrative agencies without reprisal, and safeguards against disciplinary action (except for nonpayment of dues) unless served with written charges, given time to prepare a defense, and afforded a fair hearing, regardless of any contrary provision in a union constitution. Moreover, if the union procedure takes longer than four months, the judicial requirement to exhaust internal remedies is waived, so that court appeal is facilitated. Nevertheless, appeals to the courts continue to be costly and lengthy, although an increasing number of union members are using this avenue of redress.

DEMOCRACY AND BUREAUCRACY

Democratic government is frequently confused with "good" or efficient government. Some of the best-run unions in the country from the point of view of economic returns to the membership, responsibility, financial integrity, and so on, cannot be considered democratic. The Amalgamated Clothing and Textile Workers and the United Steelworkers are cases in point. On the other hand, the excessive delegation of authority, both executive and legislative, to union officials, who in turn employ a large appointive bureaucracy, is not necessarily a structural defect of large political units. It endangers democratic principles but is not proof of a lack of democracy.

Moreover, union constitutions meet fairly well the key structural requirements of democratic government—general suffrage, free election of legislators, and control by the legislators of the expenditure of funds and other executive actions. To be sure, the governments of unions frequently vary widely from the constitutional forms; and in actual fact, most unions are operated by political machines, whose members have a vested interest in perpetuating themselves in office. This is, however, no unique indictment, since virtually all organizations are run by active minorities.

The most valid tests of democracy are found in the extent to which a union—or any other organization—adheres to the principles laid down in the Bill of Rights—the first ten amendments to the U.S. Constitution. For example, are the union's members protected in the rights to free speech, assembly, and press to an extent that enables them, without fear of reprisal, to criticize their leaders and work openly for the defeat of those leaders? Is there a judicial system within the organization which protects individual members in the exercise of these rights and which effectively insures a fair trial for those accused of crimes against the organization?

On the basis of these standards, Congress, in the light of evidence such as that presented in this chapter, found unions so wanting as to require that a legislative bill of rights for union members be imposed by law.

LABOR RACKETEERING

The deficiencies in trade-union government which have been discussed in this chapter do not necessarily involve *racketeering,* as the term is commonly used. What racketeering involves is the conversion of the union to the private benefit of the union official. A union official may engage in all sorts of undemocratic practices and still not convert the union into an instrument utilized primarily for his own benefit. Anthony (Tony Pro) Provenzano, a Teamster national vice president from New Jersey who lives in Florida, is a different case. A onetime truck driver, he rose through the ranks to his present position, allegedly with the aid of violence, underworld connections, and Hoffa support. A young ex-Marine who opposed him was murdered. Other opponents have been beaten up or have disappeared.

Tony Pro was convicted of extortion, and the U.S. Department of Labor sued to have his union offices vacated because of election irregularities. But while he was in jail, his brother ran his local for him. Tony Pro was reelected local union president and national vice president after waiting the required number of years after his release that is specified in the Landrum-Griffin Act. Now he has again been indicted for financial malpractice, and he has been questioned about the disappearance and presumed death of Hoffa, with whom he fell out while both were in jail.

Not all labor racketeers grow up in the labor movement. Some are full-fledged lawbreakers before they become union functionaries. An example is Johnny (Dio) Dioguardi, alleged Mafia member, who was brought into the Teamsters by Hoffa. Dioguardi created a number of "paper" local unions which sold protection to employers, and which also gave Hoffa the votes to control the New York City District Teamsters' Council while the latter was Teamster president.

Causes of Racketeering

Labor racketeering is likely to flourish in those industries in which employment is unstable and strikes are extremely costly. In such instances, notably trucking, the building trades, longshoring, and the amusement industries, the labor force changes so fast that opposition to leadership is difficult. More often than not, there are more men than jobs, so that the power of dispensing jobs is great, and the fear of unemployment inhibits opposition. When opposition arises within the union, a beating or a murder can squelch it. Employers, meanwhile, acquiesce in order to avoid strikes, property damage, or beatings.

Racketeering and Public Policy

Racketeering is thus a cancerous growth on the labor movement. It affects only a small portion of the unions, but a significant enough group to be of public concern. Moreover, union racketeering is often a part of a larger setup featuring crooked business and political deals.

Obviously, such racketeering is more a police matter than a labor relations matter. Too often, local authorities are unable or unwilling to cope with the situation; and sometimes, state officials are in no better position. A bistate authority established by New York and New Jersey is now trying to control crime on the New York City waterfront. Among the laws it must enforce is one barring those recently convicted of felonies from serving as union officials. A similar provision has been incorporated into the Landrum-Griffin Act. It has made it more difficult for racketeers to utilize unions as fronts for rackets, but it has certainly not ended the problem.

THE GOVERNMENT OF THE AFL–CIO

The government of the American Federation of Labor reflected the deliberate desire on the part of the founders of that organization to lodge the principal power in the hands of the national unions. The AFL constitution gave its president no authority to intervene in the affairs of its constituent unions. Consequently, a mild-mannered leader like William Green took refuge in his lack of authority when pressured to act against an affiliate. Stronger personalities, such as AFL founder Samuel Gompers or George Meany, used the prestige of office to assert leadership when an affiliated union misbehaved, without violating the technicality that national unions are autonomous bodies.

Since the CIO was organized by former AFL unions, it is not surprising to find that its constitution was similar to that of the AFL. Thus the CIO constitution gave the president no statutory authority over affiliated unions. Until the death of Philip Murray in November 1952, however, the CIO executives, Murray and John L. Lewis before him, had great influence over affiliated unions. This was true because Lewis and Murray had, each in his own way, strong leadership personalities, and because both were the heads of powerful affiliated unions, besides heading the CIO itself: Lewis, of the Mine Workers, which he later took out of the CIO, the organization he did so much to found; and Murray, of the Steelworkers. It was also true because Lewis and Murray helped to organize many of the unions affiliated with the CIO, and other leaders in the CIO looked up to them and greatly respected their judgment. After Walter Reuther succeeded Murray as CIO president, he had the backing of the United Automobile Workers, of which he remained president, but much less complete support among other CIO unions. This perhaps contributed to his willingness to merge the CIO with the much larger AFL.

Figure 3–1 describes the formal governmental structure of the AFL–CIO. It is much like that of the AFL (and of the CIO, which was modeled on the AFL). Originally, the AFL–CIO had a formal executive committee to act for the council, but the committee was abolished after a few years when it did not prove useful.

The supreme governmental body is the convention, which meets biennially. Between conventions, the federation is ruled by its Executive Council, composed of 33 officials of affiliated unions who are also vice presidents of the federation, plus the AFL–CIO's only two full-time salaried officers, the president and the secretary-treasurer. AFL–CIO vice presidents receive no salaries from the federation.

National union control of the AFL–CIO conventions is insured by the method of representation. Each national union is entitled to send delegates to the convention in accordance with a formula based upon the membership for which monthly per capita tax has been paid to the AFL–CIO.

In contrast, directly affiliated locals—that is, local unions which are affiliated with no national union but are attached directly to the federation—are accorded just one delegate, as are city and state federations and departments.

Most delegates to AFL, CIO, and now AFL–CIO conventions are officials of affiliated unions. The rank and file are more apt to be represented directly at conventions of affiliates. This does not, of course, imply that the AFL–CIO conventions do not represent rank-and-file opinion.

The AFL and the CIO organized local unions for direct affiliation only when no affiliated national union had jurisdiction over the persons involved. After the merger, most of these unions were turned over to a national union. City and state councils are coordinating bodies which were chartered by the AFL and the CIO in cities and states for the purpose of giving direction and leadership to affiliated unions and to represent the AFL or CIO point of view before city and state officials. Often the leaders of these central bodies have considerable influence in their areas. They assist unions with bargaining, represent them before public bodies, and generally aid and coordinate their activities. The merger agreement provided that the state and city AFL and CIO organizations had until December 1957 to merge voluntarily. After that, the AFL–CIO took nearly another decade to accomplish all the mergers.

The Industrial Union Department (IUD) was created to give the CIO unions a coordinating body within the merged federation. Other unions with industrially organized segments have since joined this department,

FIGURE 3-1. Structural Organization of the American Federation of Labor and Congress of Industrial Organizations

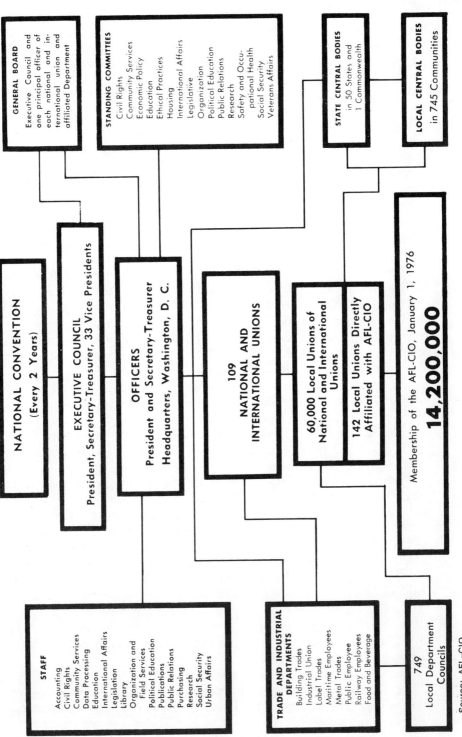

Source: AFL-CIO.

but at first it remained a focal point for the old CIO group, and a platform from which Walter P. Reuther, head of the department, could expound his views, as he had done formerly when president of the CIO, and coordinate organizing, negotiating, and research efforts. Since the mid-1960s, the IUD has attempted to coordinate bargaining among unions which deal with the same company or industry. Such "coalition" bargaining tends to transfer the locus of union power from the various local and national unions to the IUD and to enlarge greatly the scope of bargaining, and therefore the impact of strikes.

The Union Label Trades Department promotes "union-made" goods. The six other departments act as bargaining agents, activity coordinators, and jurisdictional dispute mediators among workers in the railroad shops (Railway Employees Department), shipyard workers (Metal Trades Department), building-trades workers, maritime workers, public workers and food and beverage employees. One international union can be a member of several AFL–CIO departments; the International Brotherhood of Electrical Workers, for example, is affiliated with at least five.

The AFL–CIO services its affiliates with a wide variety of functions, coordinating their activities; mediating disputes among unions; supplying news, publicity, and economic and legal assistance; and leading and coordinating political activity, including lobbying at all governmental levels. The federation receives its funds from a per capita tax of four cents per month which each international union supposedly pays on each of its members. We say "supposedly" because sometimes the larger unions tend to report to the AFL–CIO a membership considerably less than they have in order to keep down their cost of belonging to the federation. As a result, AFL–CIO membership figures which are based upon the per capita taxes received may not be accurate.

The power of the AFL–CIO over its affiliates is greater than that which was held by the old AFL, but it remains limited despite the vigorous leadership of George Meany, president of the AFL since 1952, and of the combined federation since the merger. Article VIII (7) of the AFL–CIO constitution establishes procedures to implement the doctrine, adopted in the new merger constitution, that affiliated unions shall be free of corrupt influences and totalitarian agencies. The Executive Council is empowered to conduct an investigation, to direct an affiliated union to take action on these matters, and on a two thirds vote to suspend an affiliate pending action by the convention. This was the procedure followed in the suspension of the Teamsters' Union and other unions which the convention then expelled.

The AFL–CIO, for a short period, regulated the conduct of its affiliates to a degree not even considered by the AFL of William Green's bygone days. The passage of the Landrum-Griffin Act, however, lessened federation interference in the affairs of its affiliates. For with the enactment of legislation, the government took over the policing of union government and finances, and did so after the AFL–CIO expulsion of the Teamsters had demonstrated the basic lack of ability of the AFL–CIO to curb large affiliates which could "go it alone" after expulsion—the federation's most drastic penalty. Evidences of racketeering in such affiliates as the Painters and Hotel and Restaurant Workers have since elicited no action from the AFL–CIO headquarters.

QUESTIONS FOR DISCUSSION

1. Explain why the tendency toward increasing centralization of unions has occurred.
2. What do you think is the greatest weakness in union government? What remedies would you propose?
3. Why do you think discrimination and racial prejudice exist among unions?
4. Go to a local union meeting. Observe the conduct of affairs. Compare it with the local's constitution, and report to your class who runs the local— and how.

SUGGESTIONS FOR FURTHER READING

Edelstein, J. David, and Warner, Malcolm. *Comparative Union Democracy: Organisation and Opposition in British and American Unions.* A Halsted Press book. New York: John Wiley & Sons, 1976.
    An in-depth study of union government and internal political opposition within British and American unions.

Herling, John. *Right to Challenge: People and Power in the Steelworkers Union.* New York: Harper & Row, 1972.
    A history and analysis of the split in the Steelworkers ruling group which led to the defeat of the incumbent president by the former secretary-treasurer.

Hutchinson, John. *The Imperfect Union: A History of Corruption in American Trade Unions.* New York: E. P. Dutton & Co., Inc., 1970.
    An analysis of the character and extent of union corruption, utilizing especially the McClellan Committee hearings which led to the passage of the Landrum-Griffin Act.

Rowan, Richard L. (ed.) *Readings in Labor Economics and Labor Relations.* 3d ed. Part 3, pp. 143–226. Homewood, Ill.: Richard D. Irwin, Inc., 1976.
    A series of significant articles on union structure, government, and administration.

part three

Collective Bargaining

4

Organizing and Negotiating

How do workers become organized in a union? What happens when collective bargaining begins? What are the wage and nonwage issues which concern labor and management in the collective bargaining process? What about strikes, "industrywide bargaining," "coalition bargaining," and "labor monopoly"? These vital questions will be the subject of our discussion in this and the following three chapters.

ORGANIZING

The unorganized plant may be called to the union's attention in a variety of ways. Often employees contact the union to interest it in establishing a local union for them. At other times the employers with whom the union deals stress the competition of nonunion firms and give the union representatives names and places as well as facts and figures. And frequently, the union itself will map out a drive to bring the nonunion plants within the fold.

The nature of the organizing campaign will depend upon the skill of the union leadership and its objectives. For a small group, the union drive may consist exclusively of personal contact of workers by the union representative. Organizing campaigns involving large companies include radio and newspaper publicity, leaflet handouts, large public meetings, and other methods of arousing enthusiasm in addition to the essential personal contacts.

As soon as possible, the organizers attempt to establish contact with sympathetic workers in the plant. Such workers act as volunteer organizers within the plant and form the nucleus of the budding union organization. As the union following increases, membership meetings are held, and a program for building a local union is developed.

Today the large firms in most industries have been organized. Increases in membership come only from the laborious task of attempting to unionize relatively small firms. Where large companies still remain unorganized, they are "tough nuts to crack." If they have held out this long against union organization drives, the employees involved are not likely to be interested in unionization. The employees of government, federal, state, and municipal, and of nonprofit institutions, such as hospitals, are now the most inviting organization targets. These groups include large numbers of unorganized employees who have recently demonstrated a strong interest in unionization.

Winning Union Recognition

Whereas once the question of whether employees desire union representation could be determined only by force, the Taft-Hartley Act provides that "representatives . . . selected for the purposes of collective bargaining by the majority of the employees in a unit appropriate for such purposes shall be the exclusive representatives of all the employees in such units for the purposes of collective bargaining. . . ." Congress gave to the National Labor Relations Board the power to conduct elections or otherwise to determine what union, if any, shall represent a given group of workers for collective bargaining. Once a union is certified by the NLRB as the bargaining agent, the Taft-Hartley Act provides that an employer must deal with it.[1]

WHEN THE UNION ENTERS

A union organizing campaign, by its very nature, upsets existing relationships and unbalances emotions within a plant. The job of the union organizer is in many respects that of initiating the transfer of the employee's loyalty from the employer to the union. To accomplish this, he is likely to point up existing or imagined grievances, to promise extraordinary and often unattainable benefits, to appeal to the worker to join with his fellows at the peril of being a social outcast, and to aggravate the aggression and hostility which exist dormantly within many individuals.

The purpose of the union, of course, is to win the representation election conducted by the National Labor Relations Board, or otherwise to gain recognition from the employer as the bargaining agent. To accomplish this purpose, the union must sell itself to the workers; and as in political campaigns, almost no holds are barred. Under such circumstances, the employer is under extraordinary temptation to develop a keen emotional animus toward the union and its personnel. Many em-

---

[1] See Chapter 19 for details of Taft-Hartley Act administration.

ployers believe that they must keep the record straight for their employees, that they should advise their employees to vote in representation elections so that decisions will not be made by default, and that they should correct grievances which are called to their attention by the union organizing campaign. Employer communication to employees in such situations is becoming more and more common.

Employers who attempt to convince their employees that they are better off without a union may be charged with violating the Taft-Hartley Act by intimidating workers in the free exercise of their rights to choose their bargaining agent. Union organizers, on the other hand, complain that they are often denied equal opportunity and facilities to air their viewpoint to employees; and when organizers stage mass rallies or picket at the factory gate so as to influence employees leaving or entering the plant, they may find that the employer has obtained an injunction prohibiting such activity. Some of the problems involved in the exercise of free speech by employers and in picketing for organization purposes will be discussed in Chapter 19 in connection with analysis of the Taft-Hartley Act.

Problems of Early Adjustment

If the union wins bargaining rights, the parties sit down at the conference table to negotiate an agreement which will govern their relationship for the next few years. Then there is a real need for clear heads and mutual understanding, not name-calling and emotionally generated heat. But such a change in attitude, although undeniably beneficial to stable labor relations, cannot be achieved overnight. Charges, recriminations, and abusive remarks in the heat of the preceding battle are not quickly forgotten. The union has the job of making good on as many promises to the employees as it can, and of establishing itself firmly not only with those employees who voted against it, but also with those who have been lukewarm. The union representative, therefore, is likely to make extravagant demands and to be unwilling to compromise.

The employer, on the other hand, often retains the view that the employees were better off without the union, and is disinclined to yield any concessions which would strengthen the union position and thus indicate to employees who were either lukewarm in their adherence to the union or who voted against union representation that there are substantial benefits to be gained through retention of the union as bargaining agent.

As a matter of fact, stable bargaining relations are not likely to be achieved until two developments occur: (1) management accepts the idea that the union is in the plant to stay; and (2) union members and leaders understand that their union is not all-powerful but instead that the basic job of running the business is still largely a management function. Until the new union and management learn to understand their new relationship and achieve a *modus operandi* within this relationship, there is likely to be some strain and strife in union-management dealings.

Management has the opportunity to start bargaining relations off on the right foot by dealing with the union honestly and fairly as a permanent institution and by forgetting any unpleasantness that developed during the organizing campaign. Management can also be helped by employing competent advisers who are experienced negotiators and who understand the significance of the first contract in the longtime union-management relationship. Otherwise management may concede issues that seriously interfere with the profitable operation of the business, while fighting the union on other issues which, in the long run, may be less significant. For example, it may be far less costly to grant demands for extra vacation benefits rather than concede to the union a veto over how many persons are required to man certain machines or over the introduction of new and more productive equipment, even though a concession on these latter points does not involve any immediate cash outlay.

Union leaders can also ease the tensions by sending in new personnel to conduct negotiation of the contract—persons who cannot be charged with responsibility for any false accusations or violence which may have occurred in the course of organizing the plant—and by having the courage to explain to extremists among union members that some demands are out of the realm of the possible.

Negotiating the Contract

Negotiation of a contract, whether by a new union or an established union, is heavily a matter of effective preparation before negotiations commence, but also a contest of wits between the representatives of management and the representatives of the union. In many cases, the general pattern of the contract will have been set before the negotiators even sit down at the conference table. This is true not only for the amount of any wage adjustment sought by the union but also for the general content of the contract. Quite often the union will present the employer with a form of contract used by other organized employers in the same industry or by the same union in another industry. Or it may be that the employer will submit a form of contract which contains various clauses taken from other contracts in the industry or area.

Even if neither party presents a proposed contract, the "big bargains" —like those between the United Automobile Workers and General Motors, the United Steelworkers and United States Steel—or the big bargain in the particular industry or area may well have decided the general tenor of the agreement. But even where the general pattern has been set, the course of bargaining between the employer and union representatives will determine the extent to which the general pattern will be modified to suit the needs and peculiarities of the particular firm involved.

Collective bargaining has been facetiously referred to as "collective arguing." Since both parties sit down together with the intention of bargaining, they may try to conceal the ultimate position they are prepared to take and commence bargaining from extreme positions. If the union is prepared to settle for a 75-cent-an-hour increase, it may submit a demand for $2 an hour. Although the union's intention, when it makes such extravagant demands, is usually apparent to a skillful management representative, submission of such demands at the outset of negotiations accomplishes two useful purposes from the point of view of the union. In the first place, there are always extreme elements in the union who vociferously urge that large wage adjustments be obtained. The union negotiators must, therefore, present such a demand and retreat from this extreme position only after they appear to have made a last-ditch stand in the face of overwhelming employer opposition. In the second place, human nature is so constituted that management may be readier to settle at a lesser figure, and management representatives will feel that they have done a better job of bargaining, if the union demand starts higher than if it starts lower. The employer cannot, of course, know precisely what the union minimum demand really is. By starting from a high figure, therefore, the union hopes to improve its chances of picking up a few cents an hour which it might not otherwise have obtained had it started at a figure closer to the true minimum.

This method of bargaining is not always either smart or successful. Experienced management negotiators often refuse to make a genuine offer until the union "gets realistic." Often the only result of fantastic union demands is a delay in negotiations or an increase in bad feeling. In a number of strikes in recent years, union negotiators did not recede from such demands until after a long strike. Apparently these union officials believed that this approach was necessary to convince the rank and file of their militancy; or else they underestimated management's capacity to resist.

Collective bargaining frequently looks like a show. Sometimes the purpose of the oratory and gesticulations is to impress the parties on the other side of the table. Sometimes there may be an actual audience, as is the case when the union business agents bring with them a large negotiating committee representing the membership. Then the business agents are anxious to impress the negotiating committee with their skill as negotiators and the fact that the employer is a tough party to deal with. So they play to the galleries. Occasional walkouts by the union or management representatives from the bargaining table have come to be accepted as part of the byplay of collective negotiations.

The union, of course, does not have a monopoly on "acting ability."

Employers have also become proficient in the art of predicting dire consequences if they are compelled to grant the union demands. When a representative of an employer association, or an outside consultant or lawyer, handles the company negotiations, he may also engage in theatrics to impress management personnel on the negotiating committee. Sooner or later, however, both sides get down to business, and usually a contract is hammered out. (See Figure 4–1 for an index of the subjects covered in a typical agreement.)

Dissatisfaction with the "haggling" approach to collective bargaining has induced some employers to come to the bargaining table with a

FIGURE 4–1
Index to a Typical Collective Labor Agreement, Showing the Range of Subjects Covered

INDEX

Paragraph		*Page No.*
SECTION I SCOPE AND PURPOSE		
1	Purpose of agreement	1
SECTION II RECOGNITION		
2	Bargaining unit definition	1
3	No discrimination or intimidation	1
4	Management clause	2
5	Work performed by supervisors	2
6	No strike—no lockout	2
7	Watching and maintenance service	2
8	Union cooperation	2
9	Equal employment opportunity	2
SECTION III WAGES		
10	Minimum rates of pay	3
11	Rates of pay above minimum	3
12	Rate revisions	3
13	Pay for working on higher class job	4
14	Pay for working on lower class job	4
15	Pay for reporting for work and no work available	5
16	Employee address and telephone record	5
17	Pay for less than four hours' work	5
18	Pay for emergency call-in work	5
19	Night shift differentials	5
20	Paid holidays	6
SECTION IV HOURS OF WORK AND OVERTIME PREMIUM PAY		
21	Purpose of premium pay provisions	8
22	Premium pay—types and amounts	8
23	Premium pay qualifications	8
24	Paid lunch periods	9
25	Distribution of overtime	9
SECTION V VACATIONS WITH PAY		
26	Eligibility for vacations	9
27	Definitions of terms	10

FIGURE 4–1 (*continued*)

carefully researched and thought-out proposal, offer it to the union, and at the same time announce it publicly to the employees. The bargaining offensive in this instance reverts to the employer, and the bargaining which does occur usually concerns possible or minor modifications in the company offer. The effect of this tactic is to force the union to justify to its constituents any attack on the employer's position, for management has communicated its position directly to the employees. This approach has been utilized with great success by a few large companies. It is known as "Boulwarism," after L. R. Boulware, a former vice president of General Electric Company, who publicized it widely.

Satisfying the Constituents

No matter how smart the union may be or how fair the employer (an employer's being fair does not mean inept bargaining on his part), there will always be some employees in the plant who will be dissatisfied with the results. Usually, they are groups to whom the union promised something that was not obtained. They are the union's problem as well as the employer's. Moreover, difficulties in the home may cause some employees to discover "grievances" which are merely figments of their imagination, for their private lives may have upset them emotionally.

These problems require sincere, sympathetic, and honest treatment by both management and union officials. Grievances must be settled, not won. It does no good to prove that a grievance did not really exist. Pent-up grievances, however imaginary, are the sparks that flame into "quickie" strikes. A real attempt must be made to find the sources of the difficulties and to correct them, even if they are totally unrelated to the grievances presented; otherwise, dissatisfaction continues.

Even under the best conditions, a new relationship between management and labor may be hindered by an occasional "wildcat" stoppage led by irresponsible elements who cannot be controlled by union officials. As elected officers who desire to retain their positions, union leaders cannot be too tough on contract breakers. If, however, wildcat strikes or slowdowns continue despite company patience and good faith, this may be because understanding has degenerated into appeasement. Then a firm management hand, discipline of those who violate the contract, and a "no more nonsense" discussion with the union are usually the best methods of ending the trouble.

THE ECONOMIC SETTING OF COLLECTIVE BARGAINING

The labor relations policies of the textile and pulp and paper industries in the South are completely opposite in most instances despite the fact that both are located in the same region and often in the same or neighboring communities. The textile industry fights unionization tooth and nail, whereas the pulp and paper industry has stressed accommodation, peaceful union recognition, and high wages.

The answers to this seeming paradox lies in the different economics of the two industries. The textile industry has a high labor content, with its ability to operate profitably heavily dependent upon the availability of a large supply of semiskilled labor. Unionization presents a threat to the profitable operation of the industry and to the industry's ability to meet foreign competition, with its much lower labor costs.

In contrast, the economics of the pulp and paper industry is featured by huge investments in buildings, equipment, and timber reserves; a relatively low turnover of capital; and a low percentage of labor costs relative to total costs. With fixed costs so high, there is tremendous pressure on the pulp and paper industry to operate its facilities 24 hours per day, seven days per week. To accomplish this with a minimum of interruptions, the industry has extended voluntary recognition to unions and has paid high wages. The unions in turn have given the companies a relatively free hand in plant operations and have generally cooperated in peaceful settlements. In addition, the unions have aided in recruiting personnel to the often inaccessible locations where mills must be located.

The nature of collective bargaining is always heavily dependent upon its economic setting. The employment relationship is an economic relationship. The character and extent of competition, the relation of wage costs to total costs, the demand for the product, the capacity of the industry to pass on higher costs to the consumer (that is, the elasticity of demand for the product), and the size of the market all directly affect the nature and results of collective bargaining. Misjudging any of these factors can directly and adversely affect the demand for the product and thus for labor. Hence not only the results of bargaining but also the organization of bargaining arrangements (or the lack thereof, as in the case of the textile industry) reflect the economics of the industry. Whether, for example, employers bargain for themselves or through an association, as will be discussed in Chapter 7, depends largely upon these economic variables. The ability of a company to set up subsidiary plants where unions are weaker instead of concentrating them in one area where a strike can close down the entire company can depend on the capacity of the company to afford more than one operation and the investment required to make a plant profitable. A company whose plants manufacture unrelated products has much more bargaining power than does one with interdependent assembly operations and parts plants. A company which supplies parts, such as glass or rubber tires, to another industry which, like the automobile industry, cannot operate without those parts, is usually reluctant to take a strike which could shut down its big customer. In such industries wages are usually very high.

Other examples could be given to show the dominance of the economic setting in collective bargaining. Within the economic constraints, other factors are significant. The social setting of collective bargaining illustrates this fact.

THE SOCIAL SETTING OF COLLECTIVE BARGAINING

The attitudes and issues which develop in the process of collective bargaining are profoundly affected by the social environment in which workers and employers live and work. Although collective bargaining technically concerns only the conditions and terms of work in a particular plant or company, the demands made by workers and the reactions of employers to such demands may reflect broad sociological patterns affecting the entire community, or even the country as a whole. The struggle between management and unions is to some extent a struggle for status—for recognition, respect, and security. This contest is not confined to the factory. It can be seen in the attempts of labor and management to gain the favorable attention of public opinion. It is likewise to be seen in attempts of labor and management groups to influence the election of public officials. Union officials who live in a small-town atmosphere of hostility to unions are not likely to sit down with management with anything other than an attitude of suspicion and distrust.

Ethnic and cultural patterns in the community leave a characteristic imprint on collective bargaining relations. Steelworkers have frequently been Italian-born, or Polish-born; garment workers, Jewish or Italian in background; automobile workers, often Southerners, white or black. These diverse cultural and ethnic backgrounds undoubtedly influence union policies and the course of collective bargaining in particular industries and localities.

Likewise, some of the frictions which develop in a plant may be attributable to deep-rooted tensions in the community growing out of racial conflicts. Antagonism between black workers and white foremen may merely mirror the broader struggle for status of underprivileged black citizens who are discriminated against in the community and of white citizens who have been taught early in life to "keep the Negro in his place."

As of 1974, 23.5% of the work force was under 25 years of age. Youths today are quite different from their counterparts of 40 or 50 years ago. They are American-born, usually of at least two generations, and better educated than ever before. They have grown up in an era of full employment, rising standards of living, and prosperity. They have seen unions stall great industries and union leaders command the respect of management and public officials. But they are questioning many policies of unions and companies. Excessive emphasis on pensions and security, for example, seems unnecessary to them in the light of their experiences and value scales. They want high wages, and they want them now. When unions have not delivered to their satisfaction, they have not hesitated to reject settlements and to stay on strike. Sometimes, such rejection is more a revolt against union leadership than unhappiness with the proposed agreement. But an active, restive, well-educated, and uninhibited rank and file adds a new dimension to collective bargaining.

As these young people grow older, they will undoubtedly become more hesitant to strike, more stable in their relationships. Nevertheless, they will have been affected by their environment, which is different from that of their elders, and this will affect union-management relations. They will, for example, be more used to interracial work forces and less concerned about minority workers in management positions. They will also have different attitudes toward women at work, for already in 1975 women comprised nearly 40% of the labor force, and at that time women accounted for 61% of the growth in the labor force that had occurred during the previous 20 years. This increased participation of women workers has emphasized such matters as equal pay for equal work regardless of sex, synchronized vacations for husband and wife workers, and maternity leave and part-time work opportunities to allow mothers to work and still care for families.

THE COLLECTIVE AGREEMENT

A collective bargaining agreement today is customarily a lengthy document, often drawn in final form by an attorney, which sets forth the basic rules and standards which will govern the relationship of the employer and the employees for the duration of the contract. The contract terms are binding not only on union members but on all employees who are included within the bargaining unit, whether or not they are members of the union. Union contracts customarily include clauses governing wages and hours, vacations, grievance procedures, union security, rights and responsibilities of the management and the union, promotion, layoff and discharge, and various working conditions peculiar to the plant or industry, as indicated by the contract table of contents reproduced in Figure 4–1.

Bargaining during the Life of the Agreement—Grievance Disputes

The typical union-management agreement contains provisions—grievance machinery—for the settlement of disputes arising out of contract interpretation and application. The grievance machinery usually includes a series of steps, with a higher level of union and management authority participating at each step. To induce settlement without a work stoppage, more and more contracts provide for a terminal step of arbitration, to which are referred disputes that the parties cannot settle in any of the earlier stages. This type of arbitration is found in more than 90% of the contracts negotiated in recent years.

The grievance procedure is in fact more than a process which provides for the peaceful settlement of disputes arising out of contract interpretations. It is also a mechanism through which misunderstandings can be straightened out and problems solved. It permits representatives of management and labor to meet regularly and to obtain greater understanding of each other's problems. Finally, it is a vehicle for continued collective bargaining.

Collective bargaining does not end when the agreement is signed. It simply takes a different form. Union officials are just as alert to the possibility of obtaining additional benefits for their membership after a contract is signed as before. If, for example, a union can induce a particular management to make an exception on vacation policy for one worker, that exception can be made the basis of a demand for liberalization of vacations in the next contract negotiations, either with the same company or with other companies with which the union deals. Various groups in the shop may try to gain by direct action or pressure what they failed to achieve in bargaining over the new contract. If a rival for the union leaderership can make gains in this manner, he might insure his election to the top union job next time.

Management may also do more than rest upon the contractual status quo. Plant managers and supervisors, anxious to maintain their control and profit positions, sometimes attempt to water down the agreement in practice. The contract is, in a real sense, only a temporary resting place.

In most instances, bargaining during the life of the contract is different from bargaining over a new contract. This is true because the bargaining after the contract has been signed is basically over the interpretation and administration of the agreement, whereas before the agreement has been signed, it is the language of the agreement which is in dispute. Thus, some observers liken the negotiation of the agreement to the legislative function of writing laws, and the interpretation and administration bargaining which goes on after the agreement has been signed to the judicial function of interpreting laws which the legislature has enacted. Like judges, the parties can substantially alter meaning and intent by interpretation.

Nevertheless, the attitudes of unions and managements toward interpretation and toward bargaining over new contracts are in many ways quite different. For example, whereas, as already noted, most agreements provide for the arbitration of grievance disputes—that is, disputes over contract interpretation—only about 2% provide for the arbitration of disputes over new or reopened agreements. In other words, unions and managements are willing to allow a third party to settle a dispute over an interpretation of an agreement, but when it comes to the actual negotiation of the agreement, they want no outsider to do it for them.

Now this is sensible, because no one is as qualified to write a contract as the parties who have to live with it. On the other hand, if the company is going to get out production, and if the workers are to receive steady pay, then the parties have to agree on a practical method which insures that production will not be interrupted by disputes over contract interpretation and administration. Then, if either party is too dissatisfied with the results of the outside arbitrator's interpretation of the disputed clause in the agreement, that party can attempt to have the contract altered at the next negotiation.

The Steel Industry and National Airlines Arbitration Experiments

Recently there have been some interesting signs of change toward contract arbitration. For many years, the potential of a strike in the steel industry caused customers to increase inventories and led to high production and overtime during the precontract period, then layoffs after agreement was reached and customer inventories were depleted. In addition, American customers of the steel industry placed large orders abroad to insure a supply, thus reducing sales and jobs in the United States.

To solve this problem, the basic steel producers and the Steelworkers have agreed to arbitrate unresolved issues in the next few negotiations. This experimental agreement provides a basic increase to the workers, plus a cost-of-living provision. Thus, if wages are referred to arbitration, the issue will be what, if any, *additional* increase will be awarded.[2]

Similarly, National Airlines and certain air transport unions, including the Machinists, have agreed to arbitrate future unresolved contract issues, again with a guaranteed wage increase provision. National has been beset with so many strikes that its very existence—and the jobs of its employees —have been literally at risk.[3]

Despite such developments, the arbitration of contract disputes has not increased materially. The potential high cost to management of granting a wage increase and possibly arbitrating for more, which seems to be the union price for such a deal, and the reluctance of unions and management to permit outsiders to establish basic conditions and costs, remain impediments to arbitration unless there are overriding reasons to use it.

Typical Grievance Procedure and Cases

Figure 4–2 shows typical grievance machinery from the time a grievance is raised until it is settled by arbitration. Before an arbitration can occur, the arbitrator, or in some cases, the board of arbitrators, must be selected. Some agreements provide either for a permanent arbitrator

---

[2] See Ben Fischer, "The Significance of the Steel No-Strike Agreement," Conference on Labor, New York University, *Proceeding No. 26*, pp. 93–104 (New York: Matthew Bender, 1974.)

[3] "National Airlines Finally Finds Labor Peace," *Business Week*, March 8, 1976, pp. 70–71. Braniff Airlines has also signed an arbitration pact, in this case with the Air Line Pilots Association.

FIGURE 4–2

General Pattern of Grievance Machinery in Large Plants

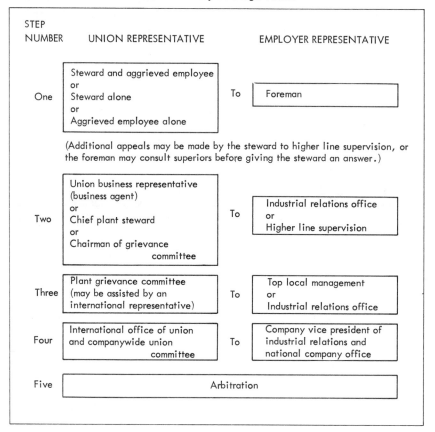

selected by the parties, or for a permanent number of arbitrators who rotate by case. More often, the arbitrator is selected for each case or for each group of cases. Most contracts provide that if the parties cannot agree on a selection, either the Federal Mediation and Conciliation Service or a private, nonprofit organization, the American Arbitration Association, will be asked to submit a panel from which the arbitrator can be chosen, or even to name the arbitrator.

In a certain year, two important holidays—July 4 and May 30 (Memorial Day)—come on Saturdays. What happens if the contract calls for provisions for special pay or for leave with pay on these days, and Saturday is not a workday? The answer is that it all depends upon what the contract says. For if a dispute over contract interpretation goes to an arbitrator, his job is to decide the dispute in the light of what the contract actually says and means.

This dispute arose at the Hanson & Whitney Company of Connecticut, which deals with the Electrical, Radio, and Machine Workers. Here the decision went with the company's contention that it was not obligated to pay for these holidays not worked because the contract stated (1) that the regular workweek was Monday to Friday, inclusive, and (2) that the company would pay for time lost in observance of holidays which were observed during the regular workweek. Obviously, in the light of this language, the union's claim for pay for a Saturday holiday not worked could not stand up.

The same issue arose before the same arbitration board in the case of the New Britain (Connecticut) Gas Company and District 50, since merged with the Steelworkers, but here the language of the contract was quite different. This contract provided that holidays were to be paid whether falling within the workweek or not; and furthermore, that for the purpose of computing overtime pay holiday hours were to accumulate and be counted in determining hours worked. Since the holiday came on Saturday after the employees had worked 40 hours during the week, the arbitrator decided that the language of the contract required not only pay for the Saturday holiday but pay at the overtime rate of time and one half.

Seniority is another area in which disputes are frequently hotly contested. This is especially the case when the issue involves the promotion of a junior man over a senior one under a contract clause which says that both seniority and ability will be factors in promotion.[4] For example, in a case involving Hercules, Incorporated, and the Chemical Workers' Union, the action of the company in promoting an employee with less than top seniority was sustained because the contract read that seniority would prevail *"only if* factors of ability, aptitude and training are relatively equal."* The words *only if* made it clear that seniority was a secondary, not a primary, criterion for promotion. On the other hand, the action of the Southern Bell Telephone Company in promoting a junior employee was overturned by the arbitrator in a dispute with the Communication Workers because the pertinent contract clause read that "seniority shall govern if other necessary qualifications of the individuals are substantially equal"; but the company wrongly interpreted the clause to permit it to promote the best qualified who was not "substantially" superior to the most senior employee in line for promotion.

Among the most difficult cases are those involving discipline. Often the issues are not sufficiently clear, and the evidence is blurred. For example, an employee may have deserved to be discharged for his conduct; but if the employer does not follow the procedure outlined in the contract, the arbitrator may have to reinstate the employee because contract procedure must be followed if an action is to be sustained in

---

[4] Seniority is discussed in Chapter 6. The terms *senior* and *junior* are used to denote length of service with a company, not age or experience.

arbitration. In other cases, union officials will carry discharge cases to arbitration because the rank and file demands that officials fight for the membership, right or wrong. Even if the arbitrator sustains the discharges, the union official can take credit for putting up a good fight.

These cases illustrate not only how grievance disputes are settled but also why contract interpretation is so important to both labor and management during the life of the agreement. By settling disputes over interpretation and administration, and by working out disagreements, labor and management use the grievance machinery to turn a dry contract into a way of working together.

Grievances are important to the union leadership in other ways. They afford an opportunity to gain the workers' loyalty and support by effectively arguing workers' causes with management in the many disputes which are processed through the grievance machinery. Furthermore, operation of the grievance machinery provides opportunities for thousands of workers to serve as union stewards and committeemen, and thus to gain familiarity with the process of collective bargaining. Several hundred thousand union members now serve in these minor positions. By participating in the grievance machinery, these workers are training themselves for future union leadership and at the same time doing something which alleviates the monotony of tending a machine.

Management's representatives in the shop, the foremen, usually find that dealing with a union makes their job much more difficult. Once the union is in, the foremen's commands are subject to union challenge. But the foreman who learns to deal effectively with the union is becoming equipped for a bigger job—for this foreman has learned to deal with people in a situation where not ony command but also leadership achieves results.

Arbitration Loads, Delays, and Problems

In recent years, the arbitration machinery set up by companies and unions has been showing signs of strain. In general this is not true where contracts cover only one plant and one local union. There most disputes continue to be settled by the foreman and the union shop steward, and only a few disputes will go to arbitration. Where multiplant contracts exist, the situation is likely to become more formalized and slower of resolution. Decisions involving one plant affect others, and often local officials, both union and company, are reluctant to settle without checking with their superiors. Frivolous cases often add to the list because local union officials avoid processing them or conceding their lack of merit for fear of alienating constituents.

To attempt to deal with such problems and with their increasing grievance load, the United Steelworkers and the major steel concerns, following the recommendation of a joint committee which studied the matter, established an expedited procedure in 1972. It provides for the elimination of some grievance steps in cases which by agreement involve "an issue of limited contractual significance and complexity" and for the submission of such cases to an arbitrator from a rotating panel of 20 in informal hearings, with no briefs or transcripts. The arbitrator must issue a brief decision within 48 hours after the hearing is completed.

The steel industry experiment to unclog the arbitration process has been adopted in several other industries. The results have generally been favorable, although some managements feel that the resultant easy and cheap access to arbitration has exacerbated, not lessened, the overcrowding of the process.[5]

Arbitrators now possess great power. In three famous cases in 1960, the U.S. Supreme Court ruled that unless a specific exclusion is written into the arbitration clause of a labor agreement, all issues arising between the parties to a contract are arbitrable.[6] Thus, such matters as plant moves, contracting out, and other facets of managerial decisions about which the union may have failed to gain a voice in the contract negotiations, may still be subject to arbitration.

LONG-TERM CONTRACTS

In 1948, a new bargaining style was established when General Motors Corporation and the United Automobile Workers negotiated a two-year contract, and then followed in 1950 with a five-year agreement. In 1951, 70% of the union contracts examined by the Bureau of Labor Statistics were of one year's duration. Five years later, the Bureau reported that only 35% of the contracts in its file were for a period of one year or less, whereas 65% covered periods of two years or more. By 1964, the Bureau's records indicated that contracts for periods of two years or more were the overwhelming favorite of unions and companies, and this practice continued to 1972. The imposition of wage-price controls in 1971 led to a temporary interest on the part of unions in one-year contracts, but the end of controls again marked a return to the long-term trend. The reasons are clear. Both unions and managements prefer to avoid possible interruptions in their relationships every year. Annual negotiations can cause such regular uncertainties in production schedules and deliveries that profits and jobs are endangered, and this is obviously worth avoiding.

The extent to which these longer term contracts—now overwhelmingly for a two- or three-year period—adopt "formula" bargaining seems to

---

[5] Based upon interviews conducted in 1976 in the steel, aluminum, and electrical machinery industries.

[6] *United Steelworkers of America* v. *American Manufacturing Co.*, 361 U.S. 564 (1960); *United Steelworkers* v. *Warrior and Gulf Navigation Co.*, 363 U.S. 574 (1960); and *United Steelworkers* v. *Enterprise Wheel and Car Corp.*, 363 U.S. 593 (1960).

vary with the rate of inflation. The original UAW–General Motors long-term contract provided for quarterly cost-of-living adjustments based upon movements of the consumer price index plus annual increases regardless of price changes. As prices rose in the late 1960s and early 1970s, unions again sought and won automatic cost-of-living adjustments as a condition for signing long-term agreements. These had been abandoned in most industries in the late 1950s or early 1960s, but are now more widespread than ever before, as will be discussed in Chapter 11.

HUMAN RELATIONS COMMITTEES, PRODUCTIVITY BARGAINING, AND CODETERMINATION

Following the 1959 steel strike, the United Steelworkers and the Kaiser Steel Corporation set up a committee composed of three well-known arbitrators plus representatives of each side to try to work out some of the problems which had led to the strike. Later the larger companies in the basic steel industry and the Steelworkers established a joint Human Relations Committee to meet regularly on mutual problems. Human relations committees have obtained much publicity and have had seemingly good results in disposing of troublesome issues without resort to strike. Most of them have worked quietly on particular problems which required considerable analysis and discussion before a settlement could be reached and which therefore could have caused problems in negotiations if not handled carefully. However, the Kaiser program seems to have been overballyhooed. A strike resulted when the initial high payoffs dwindled.

Beginning in the early 1970s, a new union-management emphasis arose—joint committees to improve productivity. Again the steel industry and the United Steelworkers were prominent. Their problem was very real: how to improve productivity so that American steel producers, with their much higher wage costs, could compete with foreign producers and their much lower priced labor. Similarly, locals of the United Rubber Workers in Akron, Ohio, have been working with management to examine production practices and thus stem the flow of work from Akron to newer plants elsewhere. There is little new about such programs of joint labor-management activity; historically, programs of this kind have flourished when jobs are at stake. Even if the programs are successful, the results are likely to be limited because of the basic economic problems which affect the parties involved.

A collective bargaining system, as the next few chapters will emphasize, grows out of the experience of the parties, which, in turn, is based upon the structure and problems of the industry involved, the general economic situation, the personalities at work, and a host of other things. What is applicable in one place may not be in others. There is no panacea. Each situation must be met, examined, and handled, and no two groups do that exactly alike.

As to the use of neutrals, as in the Kaiser plan, there are undoubtedly situations in which an objective study, a different point of view, or a new look can be most helpful and appropriate if a particular problem or problem area is to be handled to successful conclusion. There is, however, no substitute for experience or responsibility. Management and union officials cannot, in the final analysis, share their responsibility and accountability. If a business is not profitable, it is the management's responsibility; if union members are dissatisfied with their contract or its administration, they hold the union leadership accountable. Third parties or neutrals may help to bring agreement, but those responsible must achieve the agreement and live with it.

In the 1976 negotiations with the automobile companies, the United Automobile Workers expressed interest in "codetermination," a policy —initiated in West Germany and subsequently adopted in various forms by a number of European countries—of having workers and/or unions directly participate in company policymaking by being represented on the company board of directors. This UAW interest is atypical of American unions, most of whose leaders believe that participating in management would prejudice their capacity to criticize management actions and thus to represent their constituents. Moreover, through the American system of collective bargaining and the grievance procedure of collective agreements, American unions, both local and national, do participate in key decisions affecting their members' working life and pay, often to a greater extent than do unions abroad, where "workers' councils" are likely to handle local problems and local unions do not exist. Nevertheless, the spread of codetermination throughout Europe is certain to increase interest in more formal systems of participation in management. This, in turn, raises the issues of bargaining scope and managerial prerogatives.

THE SCOPE OF BARGAINING AND MANAGERIAL PREROGATIVES

Union policy with respect to wages has always been phrased in terms of "more—always more." Management fears that unions intend to apply this same policy to the scope of collective bargaining. Court rulings expanding the jurisdiction of arbitrators and rulings by the National Labor Relations Board requiring bargaining over such actions as the contracting-out of work, initiated on purely economic grounds, have, as will be discussed in subsequent chapters, added to management's fears and sharpened the debate over "management's right to manage" and the unions' right to encroach thereon.

Managerial prerogatives may mean different things to different people. For the most part, however, the term is used by the group in society who may be termed the "professional managerial class." These are the managers of large corporations, as distinguished from the stockholders, who are the owners. These people, who include in their ranks the whole array of business executives and administrators from president down to foreman, are a group set apart from both labor and the owners. In a very real sense, the conflict over managerial prerogatives and functions is part of this group's struggle for status and recognition—a struggle which is as important to this group as is the struggle by union leaders for recognition and public respect. Some take the view that the primary function of the union is to limit the power of the managerial class to determine the distribution of the total product of industry and the share individuals and groups have in it.

But the conflict over managerial prerogatives is also a part of the conflict between management's desire and need to innovate and employees' attempts to achieve "security" by institutionalizing the status quo. The history of labor relations is replete with examples of employees, acting through unions, who "win security" by restricting management's freedom to innovate, only to find that their "victory" created a high-cost situation which destroyed the very jobs they sought to protect. For if innovation is blocked in one plant or industry, other companies will innovate, with resulting cost differentials and consequent effects on sales, profits, and employment.

Nevertheless, from one industry to another there is no clear-cut pattern of practice as to what is solely a management function. In Chapters 5 and 6, we shall find that unions have been able to influence—or, on occasion, to control—a wide variety of actual managerial problems which relate to both the wage and the nonwage aspects of collective agreement. Thus, unions assist in advertising and distribution; influence price policies, directly or indirectly; control or limit entrance to trades; act as employment agencies or otherwise control hiring; affect the rate of technological advancement and, therefore, management organization of the factors of production; and in other ways participate in what management traditionally has considered its proper functions. Obviously, it would be very difficult to formulate a definition of managerial functions which would have any real meaning.

Actually, collective bargaining affects all phases of business activity. Paradoxically, the companies which recognize this fact are the ones which have been best able to retain "management's freedom to manage." Before making decisions on plant location, contracting-out, work scheduling, or even new product development and manufacturing, such companies as General Motors and Armstrong Cork consider the employee relations aspects and work to eliminate complications and problems which might otherwise arise. They thus avoid challenges in sensitive areas and are prepared to meet opposition, if it arises, on a factual, nonemotional basis.

Looking at the problem another way, it is important to recognize that unions are, in a real sense, a management-regulating device. The extent to which this management regulating or restraining becomes participation is a matter of degree. This is true despite the fact that most unions disclaim any desire to participate in management as vehemently as management denies the right of labor to participate in management. Yet in the light of the vast participation of unions through collective bargaining machinery in activities which directly or indirectly affect all phases of company management, there is already labor participation in management.

The extent to which labor should participate in management decisions, or whether such participation is socially desirable, remains a matter of debate. Certainly, this is one of the great problems of our time. In fact, the issue of union impingement on managerial prerogatives is merely another aspect of a greater issue—namely, the role of unions in our society. One may therefore agree with the view (often expressed in anger or sorrow by business executives) that there are in fact no limits to union interests in management. Union penetration of former managerial prerogatives is likely to be greatest in the areas most closely associated with industrial relations. Personnel management is thus today much less a sole management function than is business finance. Since, however, industrial relations affect all aspects of a business, union interest in corporate financial methods should not be surprising. Nor is such interest new. The railroad unions, for example, have criticized the financial methods of the railroads for fifty years, charging that they carry an oversized bonded indebtedness which tends to siphon off earnings and thus to permit the railroads to plead inability to pay wage increases. Many other examples could be cited involving production, sales, engineering, and other management functions in which unions have taken an effective interest.

But although unions have taken an *interest* in management functions beyond the personnel field, that interest has not altered management decisions, at least in the mass-production industries. Thus, the decisive considerations in the automobile and steel industries, both before and after the spread of unionism, have been economic and have centered on the advantages which accrue to the largest producers by virtue of their ability to spread their costs. The unions have effected changes and altered ways of thinking, but the basic decisions outside the personnel field are still made by management and controlled by the economics of the given industries. When management has lost this control, or when the economics of the situation has been disregarded, the inevitable result has been economic loss—sales, profits, and employment have declined, or the companies have gone out of business.

SETTING UNION POLICY FOR COLLECTIVE BARGAINING

Who sets union policy in collective bargaining—and how? There is, of course, wide variation among unions, but several clear trends have developed over the years. One is the shift of control from local unions to national unions. This is in line with the trend toward centralization of national union power, which we noted in Chapter 3.

The Shift to National Control

The trend toward national union control of collective bargaining is not new; it was noticeable at the turn of the century. In recent years, however, it has gained momentum, for several reasons.

In the first place, national unions have been forced to take over authority from locals in order to insure that uniform wage and working conditions and policies pertaining thereto will be followed where the national union believes such uniformity is essential. This is especially important when union members travel, as in the case of musicians, actors, or building workers. Although the unions of such workers negotiate on a local basis, the negotiations are often either guided or controlled by the national union to insure uniformity within limits and to prevent jockeying to secure superior settlements.

Even where the tradition of local control is strong, national unions sometimes regulate the limits of local union bargaining. In the Typographical Union local agreements must be submitted to the national headquarters for approval. The United Automobile Workers has created national departments which do the primary bargaining with such multi-plant concerns as General Motors, Ford, and Chrysler.

When collective bargaining goes from the local to the national stage, the power of the local union wanes. Centralization of authority within the United Mine Workers has obviously been furthered by the development of national collective bargaining. On the other hand, regional systems of collective bargaining, such as exist in the parts of the pulp and paper industry, have the effect of creating semiautonomous departments within national unions. Especially if a region is large, it becomes self-sufficient and needs little national assistance in bargaining. Its officers and members are then not likely to submit meekly to close national union supervision. Moreover, even when bargaining is nationwide, purely local conditions are left for local bargaining. The coal miners are a case in point.

Too tight national union control of local bargaining has often brought strong local reactions. Agreements made by national union leaders have on a number of occasions been repudiated by local union members who felt either that their interests were insufficiently considered or that they were not sufficiently consulted beforehand.

Within a single organization, there may be conflict between "high-wage" and "low-wage" locals over the extent of national control. The former, fearful that they will lose business to the latter, are likely to desire strong national control in the interests of uniformity. Because of the marginal character of many employers with whom the low-wage locals deal, the low-wage locals are likely to oppose such policies.

Federation Control

As noted in Chapter 3, certain departments of the AFL–CIO play a role in the collective bargaining process. For many years, the Railway Employees Department coordinated bargaining for the craft unions of the railroad shops; the Building Trades Department and the Metal Trades Department have local or regional affiliates which perform the same task in local or regional bases. By such departmental confederations, craft unions have been able to deal on an industrial basis with employers. But historically the coordinating department official has had little authority or power except to carry out the desires of the national or local unions.

An attempt at more far-reaching coordination, or coalition, has been undertaken by the Industrial Union Department, which has attempted to bring into one bargaining group industrial and craft unions which deal with one company or one industry. Under this coalition program, the representative of the Industrial Union Department assumes a key role in the bargaining, becomes the key strategist, and often the key spokesman as well. The aim of the program is to bring maximum union pressure on the company and to promote union mergers and amalgamations by demonstrating the effectiveness of coalition efforts.[7] If successful, this program would result in taking the bargaining process and its control one step farther from the local union and would, of course, also dilute national union control of bargaining.

Along these same lines, coalitions of unions in Europe, spurred by the integration of the European Community, have been pushing for multinational bargaining on a coalition basis. There have been some meetings between such international union coalitions and major multinational companies, but thus far no bargaining as such on a multinational basis.[8]

---

[7] For an analysis of this program, see William N. Chernish, *Coalition Bargaining*, Major Study No. 45 (Philadelphia: Industrial Research Unit, The Wharton School, University of Pennsylvania, 1969).

[8] For an account of these developments, see the following articles by Herbert R. Northrup and Richard L. Rowan: "Multinational Collective Bargaining Activity: The Factual Record in Chemical, Glass, and Rubber Tires," *Columbia Journal of World Business*, vol. 9 (Spring and Summer 1974), pp. 112–24 and 49–63; "Multinational Bargaining in Food and Allied Industries: Approaches and Prospects," *Wharton Quarterly*, vol. 7 (Spring 1974), pp. 32–40; "Multinational Bargaining in Metals and Electrical Industries: Approaches and Prospects," *Journal of Industrial Relations* (Australia), vol. 17 (March 1975), pp. 1–29; "Multinational Bargaining in the Telecommunications Industry," *British Journal of Industrial Relations*, vol. 13 (July 1975), pp. 257–62; and "Multinational Bargaining Approaches in the Western European Flat Glass Industry," *Industrial and Labor Relations Review*, vol. 30 (October 1976), pp. 32–46.

The Formulation of Demands

Although negotiations may be controlled to a considerable extent by the national officers, it is typically the local members who formulate demands. Actually, most demands other than those for higher wages or specific working conditions are usually articulated by union officials, or in the case of many unions, developed by the leadership. Sometimes union officials even push demands that are not popular with the rank and file. In times of unemployment, it is not uncommon, for example, for union officials to be demanding shorter hours and work division while the working rank and file wants more overtime. In general, however, the leadership must keep its ear to the ground and attempt to articulate what is of interest to the rank and file. Otherwise both the political support of the officials and the opportunities for contract settlement are endangered.

Customarily, demands are formulated at local meetings, in some cases on the basis of leadership proposals, in others after presentation by a special committee, and in still others after direct suggestions from the floor. When more than one local is involved, union rules often call for joint committees of the locals to unify demands. Regional bargaining requires machinery like that once utilized in the Pacific Coast paper industry—in that instance, the locals submitted their amendments to a general meeting held just prior to bargaining conferences. The demands of unions engaged in national bargaining are usually formulated at national conventions (miners, steelworkers) or at special national conferences (railway employees).

One effect of rank-and-file formulation of demands is likely to be that the demands are excessive, both in number and in amount. Everyone has a favorite recipe. This, in turn, leads on occasion either to disgruntlement with the results or to strikes because extraordinary demands either are not met or are insisted upon in the face of employer resistance.

Negotiating Personnel and Their Powers

The negotiating committee in most unions is appointed with an eye to representation of the various groups within the organization. The various crafts, geographic areas, races, and nationalities are likely to be represented on any negotiating committee. It is quite common for union constitutions to require that negotiating committees provide for adequate geographic or trade representation. Craft groups in industrial unions are especially likely to insist on representation. Only a few unions, such as the Laborers' Union, grant almost blanket power to union officials to act automatically as the negotiating committee.

In actual practice, negotiations are frequently carried on by a subcommittee of the negotiating committee. This is often a practical necessity, since negotiating committees are frequently too large and negotiations become unwieldy when all members participate. Some union constitutions provide for the election of a subcommittee. Others do so in practice. In still others, the union president becomes the subcommittee, particularly where he has considerable standing and prestige with both employers and the membership.

The power of negotiating committees or subcommittees varies considerably. At the local level the committee is rarely given full authority to settle without rank-and-file approval of the terms. However, it is quite usual for the rank and file to give a negotiating committee power of settlement after negotiations have proceeded for some time or have reached an impasse where a prompt decision is essential.

In general, it is probable that most local leaders would not want complete power of settlement, The reason is that if they make an agreement without specific rank-and-file approval, they will be held strictly accountable for the results, and the net effect of the accounting may well be defeat for reelection.

On the other hand, most national leaders would prefer the power to settle. They feel that they are capable of securing the best settlement possible, and that the rank and file, which is often without knowledge of the peculiar problems involved in negotiations, will demand more than can possibly be obtained and thus force the union into costly strikes which it has no hope of winning.

The case for granting union officials the power of settlement is formidable. Nevertheless, the requirement that all terms be referred to the rank and file is a power check on union leadership which is probably best retained. Moreover, even in cases where the union leadership possesses the right to settle, the rank and file may effectively curtail that right simply by refusing to work under the new contract. Although rank-and-file rejection of contracts has been alleged to be a serious problem, careful research has demonstrated that it is not pervasive, but that when it occurs, it is the result of a fundamental failure on the part of union officials and management to communicate properly with the rank and file.[9]

There is a great deal of educational value in worker participation in collective bargaining. Except for times when there are political contests within unions, negotiations for new contracts bring the greatest turnouts to meetings and arouse the greatest general worker interest. Service on negotiating committees, participation in discussion of the terms of settlement, and the interest which these activities arouse build union leadership for the future and assure an element of democracy in unions.

[9] Donald R. Burke and Lester Rubin, "Is Contract Rejection a Major Collective Bargaining Problem?" *Industrial and Labor Relations Review*, vol. 26 (January 1973), pp. 820–33.

National collective bargaining, however, does not appear to afford the opportunity for full discussion for settlement on the local level unless it is possible to have the contract discussed and voted upon at local meetings all over the country. With hundreds of locals involved, as in the case of the United Steelworkers, this is impractical. Moreover, the referendum is no substitute, since it does not permit argument and discussion, which are the essence of the educational process. A truly representative national bargaining committee with an effective voice in negotiations appears to be the most practical body to approve or reject contracts where national or regional collective bargaining exists. The difficulty of obtaining effective rank-and-file participation in national collective bargaining is one reason why local strikes have become so common in such industries as automobile manufacturing after the national bargaining has been concluded. Local issues and local participation require consideration that cannot be given at the national level, and a strike may be the only method of effective participation for the local rank and file. Under such circumstances, the settlement of the national contract may be the beginning rather than the end of a company's labor problems. Obviously, if the scope of bargaining is further expanded through coalition bargaining or multinational bargaining, rank-and-file participation will be even more eroded and the resultant problems will increase.

SETTING MANAGEMENT POLICY FOR COLLECTIVE BARGAINING

"When employees want to deal with management through a union, the most fundamental question is how far management should be guided by definite policies."[10] The absence of policies means that all decisions are made on a spur-of-the-moment or opportunist basis. The usual result in such cases is that management sacrifices the long-run need of the business to maintain its competitive position for assurance of uninterrupted production at the moment. For example, in the 1940s and early 1950s, the Studebaker Corporation of South Bend, Indiana,[11] and the

---

[10] Sumner H. Slichter, J. J. Healy, and E. R. Livernash, *The Impact of Collective Bargaining on Management* (Washington, D.C.: Brookings Institution, 1960), p. 10.

[11] When the UAW's late Walter P. Reuther reported in 1945 to General Motors' chief negotiator that Studebaker had granted a substantial wage increase, the General Motors spokesman retorted: "I wouldn't want our plants run like Studebaker's are run" (Robert M. MacDonald, *Collective Bargaining in the Automobile Industry* [New Haven: Yale University Press, 1961], pp. 364–65). Professor MacDonald's study, in contrast to earlier, less incisive ones, found Studebaker featured by costly and poorly administered labor practices, brought on chiefly by top management's inept handling of labor relations and by the inadequate training of supervisors. Unquestionably, Studebaker's inept labor relations policies were a key factor in putting it out of business and destroying the jobs of its employees.

Alexander Smith Carpet Company of Yonkers, New York, were cited as outstanding, liberal companies which handled union relations well. By 1966, both were out of business. Opportunistically attempting to buy good labor relations, these and many other companies allowed their costs to grow until the companies could no longer compete. Not only were the stockholders and the business managers losers—employees lost their jobs, and the local unions representing those employees lost their members.

A management guided by well-thought-out policies does not mean a rigid management. New situations and problems constantly arise, and experimentation is necessary. But such experimentation is far different from action by opportunism, or from complete concern with the immediate and disregard of the future. As the authors of an outstanding work noted:

> A few firms are in a position to dictate the nature of their relationship with the union; many small firms must take what conditions the union offers and get along as best they can; most firms, however, are more or less an equal match for the union, and the quality of their relationship with the union depends on the skill shown in negotiating and administering the agreement. The best goal for most firms is a stable relationship with the union on terms that permit the firm to be competitive and to adapt itself to changing conditions.[12]

This "stable and competitive" relationship can be achieved only if the top management of a company understands the importance of such a relationship and is willing to invest the time, talent, and funds necessary to obtain it. Only top management can make some of the required decisions. For example, will the company take a strike in order to avoid being saddled with a work rule which one day might weaken its competitive position? "Unless top management takes a firm position in advance against accepting uneconomic practices, subordinate officials will tolerate them rather than assume the responsibility of failing to meet production standards."[13]

MANAGEMENT ORGANIZATION

To implement its policies, management must set up an organization capable of handling union relations and other aspects of the personnel function. Because union relations involve time-consuming processes, and talents not necessarily possessed by production or sales executives, a special management representative or department is usually assigned to handle personnel. If union relations are conducted on a part-time or off-hand basis, the net effect is likely to be expensive concessions made to

---

[12] Slichter, Healy, and Livernash, *Impact of Collective Bargaining*, p. 11.
[13] Ibid.

the union "so we can get back to our main business of cutting metal or shuffling paper." Small companies which cannot afford full-time personnel departments often hire skilled lawyers or consultants to handle union relations.

The companies noted for the most successful administration of their labor relations assign this responsibility to executives of stature and resourcefulness, compensate them and afford them status accordingly (for example, name a vice president to the top personnel post), and see that they are a part of the top company councils. Such persons can recommend policies or changes in policies, argue with other top executives about the merits of various issues, and see that the labor relations point of view is considered in basic production and sales policies. Labor problems can then be met and handled before controversies arise.

Keeping Line Supervisors Informed

Equally as important as setting policy and putting effective leadership in charge of union and personnel relations is the need for top management to make clear to its subordinate officials, supervisors, and foremen what it expects of them in handling the union relationship. Unless this is done clearly and effectively, policies at the shop level will bear little relation to the pronouncements from company headquarters, for the foremen will work to "get along" at whatever cost this requires. Such "getting along" can mean quiet but costly concessions which, in practice, whittle away managerial control of the shop, reduce productivity and efficiency, and injure the competitive position of the company.

The best-managed companies, therefore, spend considerable time, effort, and money on foremen selection and training, in an effort to insure effective management, including employee relations management, at the shop level. In such companies, foremen are instructed on techniques of handling people, grievance settlement, and union contract interpretation.

It is most important, also, that top management back up its supervisors and practice what it preaches. If the executives of a company advise the foremen to take a strong stand against a union demand or action and then yield to the union under the threat of a strike, the word will go through the shop grapevine that management does not mean what it says. The union will take the action to mean that it can induce a change in company policy by a show of force, and foremen will see such executive inconsistency as advice to them to concede readily and quietly to union demands.

The Management Bargaining Committee

From the point of view of the employer, bargaining with the union may be on an individual plant basis or on a companywide basis, or the employer may be one of a number who bargain together in an employers' association. If bargaining is between a local union and a single plant of a large corporation, negotiations may be conducted by the local personnel director and/or the plant manager, subject to instructions from company headquarters. On the other hand, if all of a number of company plants are involved, the industrial relations director of the company is likely to conduct negotiations. In regional or industrywide bargaining, employers are usually represented by committees or officers designated by the employers' association. On all levels of collective bargaining negotiations, employer representatives may include the company attorney or consultant, whose function may be to participate actively in negotiations, to give behind-the-scenes advice or in some cases merely to reduce to contract form the bargain reached by the parties.

As with unions, there is considerable diversity in the amount of authority given the management representatives at the bargaining table. In some situations, they may be able to make final decisions on all aspects of the contract; in other situations, they may be able to agree only to minor changes and concessions, and they must obtain the approval of the president before committing the company to anything substantial. Large outlays, such as those involved in the establishment of a pension system, sometimes require approval of the board of directors as well as the president.

Within the management organization, as within the union, there is pulling and hauling for the power of decision making. In some companies, the financial officer exercises powerful influence whenever a money matter is involved; in other companies the dominant voice is that of the top production man; in still others the top sales executive exercises the most influence. The extent to which the advice of the chief personnel official is accepted in such situations is a measure of the standing and influence both of that official and of the personnel function.

Whenever a company must determine whether to take a strike or to accede to a union demand, a decision must be made on the basis of the company's current position and of the prospects and choices involved. Obviously the final determination in such matters must be made by the top executive of the company. In such instances the current sales and the financial and production situations must be evaluated. The decision cannot be made on the basis of industrial relations alone, but must be based upon the total needs of the company. A company which can stockpile inventory is obviously in a stronger position to resist union pressure than is a company which sells a nonstorable service. Automobiles or steel can be warehoused or built ahead; daily newspapers, air transport companies, or restaurants cannot stockpile. The demand for some products can be postponed; the demand for others cannot. Management decisions must reflect the realities of the company's industrial situation.

Because a strike involves losses now, whereas concessions *may* have a serious effect on a company's future competitive position, there is a great temptation for business executives to decide questions involving labor relations on a short-run basis. Yet the failure of management to evaluate correctly the long-run implications of costly concessions made to avoid labor strife has been fatal to many companies. Undue concessions made at the point of a strike threat, or an actual strike, are too often an invitation to further strife. By yielding to such coercion, management is in effect telling union officials and members that a strike threat or a strike pays off. If this feeling becomes general, it can easily result in a long, bitter strike at some future date—if not a series of shorter walkouts—but in any case, it can be quite costly to the business.

Moreover, if a company yields to an uneconomic demand or series of demands, it may be digging its grave by incurring costs which do not permit it to compete in the product market. This can mean not only loss of profits but also loss of jobs and hence union members. A short-run decision which ignores long-run considerations can be disastrous to both employer and union.

Of course, business decisions, like union decisions, are not always based upon economic calculation. Instances of business executives forcing a strike to win leadership over rivals in their own firm are not unknown. Likewise, industrial relations decisions based upon emotions rather than economic facts occur every day in managerial ranks. Business executives, like union leaders, are people, and anything but infallible.

QUESTIONS FOR DISCUSSION

1. If you were the personnel manager of a plant and a union began an organizing campaign, what actions would you take? If you were a business agent of a union, how would you attempt to recruit workers?

2. Why do you think long-term contracts have become so important? What are the economic implications of this development?

3. What are managerial prerogatives? Is it a good idea to define them by law? If you were a manager, how would you protect your prerogatives?

SUGGESTIONS FOR FURTHER READING

Atherton, Wallace N. *Theory of Union Bargaining Goals.* Princeton, N.J.: Princeton University Press, 1973.

Cross, John G. *The Economics of Bargaining.* New York: Basic Books, Inc., 1969.

   Two attempts to present union policy and bargaining in terms of mathematical economics.

Chernish, William N. *Coalition Bargaining.* Major Study No. 45. Philadelphia: Industrial Research Unit, The Wharton School, University of Pennsylvania, 1969.

An analysis, with numerous case studies, of the union drive for expanded bargaining units and its implications.

Recent Initiatives in Labor-Management Cooperation. Washington, D.C.: National Center for Productivity and Quality of Working Life, 1976.

An account of numerous instances in which unions and companies worked together.

Slichter, Sumner H.; Healy, J. J.; and Livernash, E. R. *The Impact of Collective Bargaining on Management,* chaps. 1–2, 21–30. Washington, D.C.: Brookings Institution, 1960.

These chapters of this outstanding work deal with management issues in collective bargaining, grievance handling and arbitration, and managerial handling of industrial relations.

Walton, Richard E., and McKersie, Robert B. *A Behaviorial Theory of Labor Negotiations.* New York: McGraw-Hill Book Co., 1965.

An attempt to describe labor-management negotiations in terms of a social interaction system.

5

The Content of Collective
Bargaining: Wages

COLLECTIVE BARGAINING is basically a method of determining wages and working conditions for employees. In this chapter, we shall examine the wage content of collective bargaining; in the next chapter, the working conditions which form the "industrial jurisprudence" of bargaining will be our subject. Then, in Chapter 7, we shall discuss some key questions resulting from the bargaining process.

WAGE—A COMPLEX TERM

A better insight into the nature of the collective bargaining process is provided by considering just what is encompassed by the term *wage*. There is a natural inclination to use this term as if it were a rather simple component and as if the only variable which had to be determined in setting the wage were its amount. Actually, however, the wage is a highly flexible form of compensation and may vary considerably both as to form and as to content. For example, it may be based on payment by the piece, payment by the hour, or participation in a complex profit-sharing plan. It may or may not include group insurance, pensions, and similar fringe benefits. Thus, a labor-management negotiation may result in a 50-cent-per-hour "package," composed of 40 cents in wages, 5 cents in pension improvements, 3 cents in insurance and miscellaneous benefit improvements, and 2 cents in holiday and vacation allowances.

Only the first item—the change in the wage rate itself—relates directly to what have traditionally been termed wages, whereas the other items of the wage package fall in the category of supplementary or fringe benefits. Moreover, to the company wages are a cost, whereas to the worker they are income. Those who think in terms of social needs regard wages as a right to income, not as payment for work. Demands for guaranteed annual wages reflect the merging of wages paid by the hour and salaries paid by the week, month, or year, with guaranteed income for workers who are at present paid on an hourly basis as well as for salaried workers. The importance of wages is further emphasized by the fact that wages and salaries comprise about 65% of national income, making them a potent factor in national income determination and in their impact on the business cycle and the state of the economy. Some of the major forms of wage payment and management and labor attitudes toward them, will be considered in this chapter. As a background, it will be useful to consider the various types of published wage data, so that the reader may be familiar with the content as well as the limitations of such statistics.

ANALYSIS OF WAGE DATA

The union leader, bargaining with an employer, may be primarily interested in setting a high rate for a particular job in the collective bargaining agreement. The employees, on the other hand, may be more interested in their actual take-home pay. And the employer is likely to be concerned with the overall cost of labor, including all fringe benefits. Because of these varied interests in employee compensation, a number of statistical series are published which analyze wage changes from different points of view. Seven major types of data can be distinguished.

1. *Wage rates* represent the actual price for particular jobs. Because of the great diversity of such rates, not only from industry to industry but also from company to company within the same industry, there are no overall compilations of such rates published regularly by any agency of the government or by private research organizations. However, the Bureau of Labor Statistics of the U.S. Department of Labor publishes studies of wage rates for industries and occupations in states and metropolitan areas.[1] Such studies report the average rates in plants, often by occupation, occupational groups, and area.

2. *Straight-time average hourly earnings* are the average wages earned, exclusive of overtime pay. They include incentive pay, but generally exclude payment for work on weekends, holidays, and late shifts. The Bureau of Labor Statistics also publishes studies of straight-time earnings for particular jobs in various industries.

3. *Gross hourly earnings* include all wage payments to employees, including overtime, premium pay for holidays and weekend pay, and so on, and therefore normally exceed straight-time earnings. Some statistical

---

[1] The U.S. Bureau of Labor Statistics studies are reported or summarized in the *Monthly Labor Review,* published by the U.S. Department of Labor, and often issued in more complete form as separate bulletins. The Bureau's other monthly journal, *Employment and Earnings,* contains the tabulated earnings data.

series report earnings *per hours worked,* and some report earnings *per hours paid for.* If a man is paid for a holiday on which he does not work, should the hours in the holiday be added to hours worked during the rest of the week to obtain the hours figure to divide into total earnings so as to arrive at average hourly earnings? The Bureau of Labor Statistics says yes; the Bureau of the Census says no. As a result, hours of work as used by the Bureau of the Census in its series have averaged about 5% less than hours paid for as reported by the Bureau of Labor Statistics. The most complete gross hourly earnings data are published in the form of a monthly series by the Bureau of Labor Statistics covering 21 broad manufacturing industry groups, about 300 manufacturing industries, and 30 nonmanufacturing industries, including trade, construction, and mining.[2]

4. *Weekly earnings* reflect the average number of hours worked per week in relation to gross earnings per hour. Weekly earnings data are published monthly by the Bureau of Labor Statistics and are also compiled by various state departments of labor and by trade associations.

5. *Weekly take-home-pay* refers to the amount left in the weekly paycheck after deductions for federal income taxes (and in some areas state and/or local income taxes), social security taxes, union dues, health and welfare programs, group insurance, and other benefits. The Bureau of Labor Statistics publishes a monthly calculation of "spendable average weekly earnings," which are defined as gross average weekly earnings less an amount estimated for federal income and social security taxes.[3] By excluding other deductions from paychecks, this average overestimates take-home pay.

6. *Annual earnings* of employees are not published in any regular series. Studies of various industries are made from time to time by the U.S. Bureau of Labor Statistics. In addition, the U.S. Department of Commerce publishes data for 84 industries and industry groups for "full-time equivalent" employees.[4] These are not actual earnings figures but rather computed figures derived by dividing wages and salaries in an industry by the number of full-time workers. For industries having a substantial number of part-time employees, the U.S. Department of Commerce reduces these employees to an equivalent number of full-time employees.

7. *Fringe benefits* run the whole gamut of pay from "coffee-break time" to employer payments for unemployment insurance. There are no reliable statistical series showing the cost of fringe benefits for industry as a whole, or even for all manufacturing industries. Since 1947, the Chamber of Commerce of the United States has made a biennial sample study of the extent and nature of fringe benefits.

---

[2] These data are found each month in *Employment and Earnings.*

[3] Ibid.

[4] Published as a supplement to the U.S. Department of Commerce monthly publication *Survey of Current Business.*

BASIC WAGES

Since many different types of payments are included in labor's total compensation, it is convenient to distinguish two major categories which together make up total compensation: basic wages and supplementary (or fringe) benefits. Basic wages may be defined as the payment for hours actually worked, based on time or output. This includes payment at a higher rate for overtime and premium pay for working night shift, Saturday, or Sunday, and so forth. Supplementary benefits cover all other types of compensation, including vacation pay, Christmas bonuses, pension benefits, dismissal pay, and so on.

Basic Wages: Time Payment

The great majority of American workers are paid by the hour, day, week, or month—that is, by time. For manual workers, rates are typically set by the hour or the day; for white-collar and supervisory workers in private industry, by the week, half month, or month, or, less frequently, by the year. Management employees are often paid at an annual rate. Workers paid on an hourly or daily basis (as well as those who are on an incentive basis where the incentive is computed on the basis of hourly or daily output) are usually referred to as "wage earners." Workers paid by the week or a longer time interval are usually referred to as salaried workers.

Time pay customarily varies to provide extra compensation to employees who have to work at undesirable hours. Nearly all collective bargaining contracts now provide for premium pay at the rate of time and one half for Saturday, or for the sixth day of the week, and double time for Sunday, or the seventh day, and also for extra compensation for evening and night shifts.

Since paying for results is deeply ingrained in managerial philosophy, many employers criticize time payment systems because output and earnings are not directly related. Unions, however, frequently prefer time pay because it compensates workers on a uniform basis and prevents the speedier workers from making it hard for the slower members of the union. Nevertheless, union and managerial attitudes toward the form of wage payment are more the reflection of economic, technological, and historical conditions than of a basic ideological preference for one type of payment rather than another. For example, the United Automobile Workers is widely credited with eliminating incentives in the automobile industry. Yet, incentive plans at the former Studebaker and Kaiser-Willys plants were abandoned at managerial insistence after they became unworkably high-cost—a move reluctantly acquiesced to by local unions after much strife.

Payment on the basis of timework prevails in more than 70% of manufacturing industry, and throughout the building and service trades, the public utilities, and the transportation industry, although the last also incorporates such factors as mileage and trips in its pay scale. Time pay is the most practicable method of payment for most jobs in the business world.

Basic Wages: Incentive Payment

Piecework and other forms of incentive payment relate compensation and output, so that earnings fluctuate more or less in accordance with actual output, thus providing a direct financial stimulus to workers to increase their efforts and output. About 30% of workers in manufacturing receive their basic wages through some form of incentive payment. Such payment is common in apparels, textiles, footwear, and some of the metalworking industries. There is frequent variation, however, even among companies in the same industry. Bonuses and commissions are also frequently paid in retail and wholesale trade as a stimulus to the efforts of individual salesmen.

In general, incentive systems work best in industries where labor cost is a large percentage of total cost, where competition is keen, and where the output of the individual worker is easily discernible. Clothing and textiles are good examples of industries which meet these requirements. In general, incentive compensation is not practical where emphasis is placed on quality rather than quantity, where individual output or performance cannot be measured with precision, and where mechanical contrivances control the speed of employees' work. Automobile assembly, chemical manufacture, and machine tool design are examples of industries in which these conditions apply. Automation and improvement in methods or machine design cause the earnings of employees paid on an incentive basis to increase rapidly and get out of line with the earnings of others in the plant. This is a frequent cause of labor strife. Those receiving the high wages resist change, others resent the out-of-line wages, and management must often take a strike in order to get the incentive rates (and labor costs) back into line. Otherwise a company risks loss of business because of noncompetitive prices resulting from the runaway incentive payments.

Incentive plans vary from simple payment by the piece, or unit of work, to complicated formulas which provide a bonus for production in excess of an established norm. The most common of the latter are standard hour plans. In such a plan, a piecework rate of 40 cents per piece multiplied by a 10-piece-per-hour standard equals $4. Workers would be expected to produce this under normal conditions at a normal work pace. For higher production, a bonus or an incentive would be paid. Incentive plans may be based on an individual's output, which is most common, but also on the output of a related group, or even on the output of an entire plant. Group incentives are applicable only to closely related operations where individual performances are linked. Plantwide incentives have the advantage of keeping all employees interested in high production, but since it is difficult, if not impossible, to relate the work of many employees, for example, maintenance personnel, to output, it is possible for some employees to loaf and still reap the bonus.

Union Attitudes toward Incentive Wage Methods

Union policy toward incentives has always varied considerably from industry to industry, and is far less important in determining the extent of incentives than are the basic economic and technological forces in the industry; or, in the case of steel, than is the historical fact that the industry grew up with this form of payment, in contrast, for example, to the aerospace industry, which started and adhered to a time method of payment. There is no evidence that the United Steelworkers has made any attempts to alter the basic method of payment in the steel industry.

Nonunion competition has historically been an important circumstance conducive to union acceptance of incentives. Nonunion and foreign competition in the men's clothing industry is one of the most important reasons why the union therein not only does not oppose incentives in piecework but has actually promoted them. In addition, the Amalgamated Clothing and Textile Workers, which has been as favorably disposed toward piecework as any union, has promoted its installation because only through piecework could the workers in the clothing industry increase earnings without increasing labor costs. In general, unions accept the method of payment in an industry. They may favor incentives where manual skill and labor costs are extremely important, where nonunion competition exists, where the unit of production can be defined with precision, where standards of work are fairly stable, and where piecework incentives have worked reasonably satisfactorily over a long period of time. The great majority of unions do not take a strong stand either for or against incentives as such, but instead they attempt to exert influence over how incentives work in practice—which, if successful, can have profound effects on the results of incentives.

Union Control of Incentive Systems

The United Mine Workers requires payment for "dead work" and compensation for other unfavorable conditions; the unions in the textile industry fight management on the work load or stretch-out issue without opposing incentives per se; and the United Steelworkers is vitally concerned with methods of computing tonnage rates without attacking the basic system itself. A strong union, by placing numerous restrictions on the incentive system, may succeed in "demoralizing" it—creating substantial inequities in earnings and effort; raising substantially average hourly yields or bonuses; and effectively divorcing productivity from earnings by instituting various guarantees which insure high "incentive" bonuses, whether or not production quotas are met. Usually, union pressure to accomplish this is accompanied by relaxed managerial control and managerial impatience to "get production out of the door no matter what the costs"—which can be substantial.[5]

A union drive to control an incentive system usually takes a number of years. As a rule, the battle for control is waged on two fronts—through negotiation for changes in the contract and through the day-to-day shop operations revolving around rate settings on new jobs and the grievance procedure. By gradually winning guarantees for machine downtime, by negotiating out-of-line rates and then bringing other rates up to those already out of line, by harassing supervision and time-study departments with grievances, and by slowdowns or walkouts at critical delivery periods, the standards can be effectively reduced, and the incentive system can be turned into a featherbedding device for higher pay with less work.

Although sound collective bargaining relationships exist in numerous plants where incentive systems are utilized, there is considerable evidence that incentive plans do complicate industrial relations and can contribute to industrial strife. So many factors, frequently intangible and unmeasurable, affect a worker's earnings that unless mutual goodwill exists, continued bickering is often the result. For example, if a machine breaks down or materials stop flowing, should the worker receive base pay or the average hourly earnings of a previous period?

Another problem arises from the fact that in the average plant an incentive system can be applied to only a part of the employees; maintenance personnel and employees whose speed of work is entirely machine controlled remain on timework. This creates demands for bonuses or wage increases to nonincentive workers in order to equalize earnings. Management sometimes further complicate matters by reducing maintenance on the ground that workers on incentives will "find a way" to produce. Contrary to the belief that incentive pay permits less management, experience demonstrates that installation and effective administration of an incentive system require increased management ability and frequently substantial additions to management payroll in order to provide the staff people—the accountants, time-study experts, and personnel men—who are needed to make the plan work.

Measured Daywork

The realization that incentive systems have disadvantages as well as advantages for management has encouraged the search for a method of

---

[5] Sumner H. Slichter, J. J. Healy, and E. R. Livernash, *The Impact of Collective Bargaining on Management* (Washington, D.C.: Brookings Institution, 1960), pp. 490–529.

wage payment which combines the simplicity of time payment with the control of worker efficiency which is a feature of effective incentive systems. This interest has been furthered by technological advances which reduce worker control over speed or effort. In most plants, however, many employees can raise their efficiency considerably with remarkably little effort. Measured daywork plans offer pay by the hour in association with some type of control of worker efficiency by means of production standards. To make such a system work, management must establish meaningful standards, be able to justify their fairness and objectivity, and adhere to the standards under pressure. If the standards are to be meaningful, they must be met, and those who refuse to meet them must be disciplined. Otherwise, no one will make an effort to meet them. This, in turn, requires managerial objectivity and fairness in setting standards, for if the employees as a whole do not think the standards are fair, then a concerted effort to break them can often succeed.

If, however, management is convinced that the standards are fair, and remains so after carefully evaluating grievances concerning the standards, it must be willing to back up this opinion. To many companies, this means defending their position before arbitrators. Other companies feel even stronger about the need to maintain control over production standards, which can indeed mean control over productivity and hence profits and competitive position. The General Motors Corporation, for example, regards such control as so significant that it prefers to permit unions to strike over production standards in order to exempt such disputes from arbitration. General Motors management believes that this results in better production standards from the company point of view, not only because it leaves production standard determination in the hands of management but, equally important, because the importance of standards setting is emphasized by this procedure. If the standards are set too loose, the cost and competitive position of the plant or operation are jeopardized; if they are set unfairly, a costly strike can occur. Plant management is thus under exacting pressure to set proper standards at all times.

Production Standards and Effective Employee Relations

Loose work standards and inefficient methods not only contribute to the unprofitability of enterprises but also do not usually result in sound employee relations or the absence of strikes. As the authors of the most authoritative book on collective bargaining's impact on management point out:

> Logically it might be expected that a fairly high task level, creating a strong competitive position for a plant, would lead to serious union-management conflict. While the possibility of conflict cannot be ruled out, observation tends to support the view, when reasonably qualified,

that the reverse is true. It is the demoralized incentive plans and the poor daywork plans that are associated with union-management conflict. Efficient plans tend to have satisfactory to good union-management relations.[6]

The reasons for this apparent paradox will become clear, if they are not already, as the reader's study progresses through the many facets of industrial relations and labor economics. Among these reasons are the following:

1. Loose standards, whether incentive or daywork, lead inevitably to high costs and poor competitive position, and result in layoffs and unemployment. The effect is to generate insecurity, poor morale, unrest, and strife.
2. Loose standards are usually preceded by managerial yielding to short strikes, threats of strikes, or slowdowns in order to keep production going. But by yielding to such pressure, management incites more of it. Eventually, the employees go too far, and a long and bitter strike does occur.
3. Loose standards create inequities. People doing similar work are paid different rates or earnings. This creates unhappiness, unrest, and constant demands for changes.
4. Well-run plants, in contrast to poorly run ones, feature uniform treatment of people similarly situated. Threats of force to change what management considers proper are firmly resisted. By experience, employees learn that such action will not yield results; hence, they do not resort to it. Where this is combined with cost-consciousness and sound and humane management, the result is steadier work and well-understood conditions. Feeling secure and knowing where they stand, employees and their union representatives are more likely to work things out with management on a peaceful, logical basis because they have learned that it pays to do it that way.

PROFIT-SHARING PLANS

Incentive systems, whether they be piece-rate or group plans, are generally related to physical production. Profit-sharing plans attempt to go a step further and distribute to workers a share in the profits of a business after all ordinary costs, such as wages, materials, and overhead, have been met. Profits have no necessary or close relation to physical production or employee effort—and this is one of the inherent weaknesses in profit-sharing plans. Employees may exert extra effort, yet profits may decline because competitive conditions compel a reduction in prices; on the other hand, despite a decline in physical production, profits may

---

[6] Ibid., p. 551.

rise because the employer has made a favorable purchase of raw materials, or for many other reasons.

Despite the lack of a close relationship between employee effort and profits, many employers believe that profit sharing is the best means for obtaining maximum cooperation between labor and management and for eliminating friction in labor relations. Profit-sharing plans have existed for over 150 years. Today there are two principal kinds of plans. In cash plans, a division of profits is made on an annual or more frequent basis, and a cash distribution is paid to participating employees. Under existing tax law, such payments are taxed as income in the year they are received. The exact number of such plans is not known, but the Profit Sharing Research Foundation estimated their number in 1974 at about 100,000.[7] The other common form of profit-sharing plan is known as a qualified deferred profit-sharing plan. Under existing tax law, payments made by an employer to a trust for the benefit of employees qualify as deductible business expenses if not in excess of 15% of employee compensation; the employee pays no tax upon the employer payments or the income earned from their investment, and the employee's share is taxed at capital gains rates when the final distribution is made, which may be at his or her retirement from the company. Approximately 190,000 such plans are in effect at present.[8]

Profit-sharing plans are most likely to be found where profits are reasonably large and continuous, the labor force stable, and unions not strong. Obviously if the first two conditions do not prevail, there are few profits to share and few employees to share the profits on a regular basis. In profit-sharing plans, smallness of the firm seems to be an advantage to the employee. A study of such plans for the year 1973 revealed that in companies with less than 100 employees, the percentage of profits distributed averaged 38.4% and cash distributions represented 7.4% of basic pay. By contrast, in companies with over 5,000 employees, the contributions were only 12.4% of profits and cash distributions were only 4.6% of basic pay.[9]

Unions have traditionally opposed profit sharing. Profit sharing (in companies where profits are large) makes employees more difficult to organize, and in an industrial union profit sharing by companies of varying profitability produces wide variations in compensation and therefore may result in dissension among the union membership. Perhaps the major union objection stems from the fact that profits are affected by managerial actions over which collective bargaining normally has no effect. As a consequence, the union may feel that under a profit-sharing

---

[7] Data from Profit Sharing Research Foundation, Evanston, Illinois.

[8] Figure supplied by the Profit-Sharing Council of America, Chicago, Illinois.

[9] *Profit Sharing Experience: 73* (Chicago: Profit Sharing Council of America, 1974), p. 25.

arrangement it must either demand a voice for its members in areas where it has never demanded a voice before, or be willing to have the employees' compensation regulated unilaterally by management decision. Since neither alternative is palatable to most unions, they have generally opposed profit sharing.

On the management side, there is considerable doubt about whether a profit-sharing plan will induce extra effort or loyalty when the individual employee realizes that performance on the job has little or no effect on what he or she receives from the plan. Furthermore, employers also oppose profit sharing with unionized employees because they do not desire to bargain over what share of profits will go to employees, which would be required under the Taft-Hartley Act.

Gain Sharing, Buy-Out Formulas, and Scanlon Plans

Some companies have instituted various kinds of benefit plans in return for employee or union commitments to end restrictive practices. For example, in 1961 American Motors made a contract with the UAW providing for the sharing of profits, with the understanding that the union would yield on certain practices which restricted productive efficiency. However, the company's sales and profit declines, plus union unwillingness to make concessions, ultimately led to the demise of the plan. In the West Coast shipping industry, longshoremen gave up numerous featherbedding practices in return for higher wages and employer contributions to funds providing welfare, disability, and retirement benefits. This seems to have had the desired results, although in 1971–72 other problems, notably jurisdictional disputes with the Teamsters' Union and an intraunion power struggle, broke the period of labor peace which the buy-out formula had induced more than a decade earlier.

The Kaiser Steel plan, noted in the previous chapter, was originally a combination buy-out formula for restrictive practices, a substitute for a demoralized incentive plan, and a public relations device for the company. Wide publicity was given to its monthly bonus distributions. Like many profit-sharing plans, it disintegrated when sales and profits fell and bonuses declined. A bitter strike occurred in 1972 over its terms. Perhaps this was inevitable because the plan was based on an impossible premise: that there was to be no relation between company profitability and work bonuses based on "efficiency." Such a premise obviously ignores the reality of what happens to efficiency when plant utilization declines as a result of lagging sales.

Scanlon plans, developed by the late Joseph Scanlon, onetime Steelworkers' union official, are designed to give employees an incentive to improve production methods and to suggest cost savings. They are often substituted for demoralized incentive plans. A plantwide incentive—or bonus—potential replaces the existing incentive with the aim of producing teamwork efforts to achieve higher efficiency and productivity. "The incentive toward teamwork is provided most commonly by giving the employees a large share (usually three-fourths) of the savings in labor costs. The savings are measured by ascertaining the extent to which the ratio of payroll to sales value of production is reduced below the previous normal ratio."[10]

Scanlon plans require a great deal of mutual trust and cooperation among employees, unions, and management if they are to work. They have been most successful among small firms which have been in trouble competitively, and in which employer-employee relations have been on a high plane of mutual confidence. On the other hand, such plans are not without problems, since bonuses are paid to all, regardless of their contribution to the savings. Moreover, under such plans the parties tend to become overimpressed with initial successes and to believe that necessary overhead, such as industrial and methods engineers, maintenance outlays, and adequate supervision, can be dispensed with because "the worker knows best how to cut costs." Under such conditions a Scanlon plan can become as demoralized as an incentive plan and can result in the payment of bonuses which would not have been paid if proper consideration had been given to the expenses required to maintain future profitability. This seems to have occurred in the case of the widely publicized Scanlon plan at the LaPointe Machine Tool Company, and may well be much more typical of the long-run results of such plans than are the claims of Scanlon enthusiasts.[11]

FORMALIZATION OF WAGE STRUCTURE

In most of American industry, wages are tailored to the job rather than to the man. Management could, of course, attempt to pay each worker an amount equal to management's estimate of the worth of the individual, taking into account his or her age, health, skill, length of service, and similar factors. This practice is followed to some extent with

---

[10] Slichter, Healy, and Livernash, *The Impact of Collective Bargaining*, p. 865. This explanation is given: "Suppose the normal ratio is found to be 35 per cent, which means that if a plant were selling $1 million of goods a year, payroll would normally be $350,000. If the workers by improving their efficiency were able to produce $1 million of goods for a payroll cost of $310,000, three-fourths of the saving or $30,000 would be paid to them as a bonus."

[11] For an analysis of the LaPointe situation, see Herbert R. Northrup and Harvey A. Young, "The Causes of Industrial Peace—Revisited," *Industrial and Labor Relations Review*, vol. 22 (October 1968), pp. 31–47. For a further and very careful critique of the Scanlon approach, see R. B. Gray, "The Scanlon Plan—A Case Study," *British Journal of Industrial Relations*, vol. 9 (November 1971), pp. 291–313. For the favorable side, see F. G. Lesieur (ed.), *The Scanlon Plan* (Cambridge, Mass.: MIT Press, 1958); and "Scanlon Plans in Operation," in *Recent Initiatives in Labor-Management Cooperation* (Washington, D.C.: National Center for Productivity and Quality of Working Life, 1976), pp. 43–50.

respect to supervisory and executive employees and in the hiring of such employees as musicians and radio performers, whose individual talents vary greatly. In a large industrial establishment, however, such piecemeal establishment of a wage structure would be expensive, time-consuming, and impracticable. As a consequence, most industrial establishments have adopted formalized wage structures.

Formal wage structures are generally of two kinds. A "single-rate establishment" pays the same rate to all experienced workers in a job classification. This means that a lower rate may be set for trainees, but once a worker has acquired what is considered the minimum experience necessary to qualify for the job, he or she is paid the same rate as all other experienced workers performing the same work, regardless of variations in length of service and other factors. A "rate range establishment," on the other hand, sets up a range of rates for a particular job and provides that specific rates for individual workers within the range are to be determined by merit and/or length of service.

Job evaluation involves the establishment of a rational internal wage structure. Although such an evaluation may be accomplished in many ways, it is usually done as follows: jobs are described in terms of a formula giving due account to skill, responsibility, working conditions, effort, and so on; then they are grouped into a hierarchy of grades, and wage or salary rates or ranges are established for the grades.

Job evaluation developed as a management device aimed at simplifying the wage structure and its administration and at preventing the "whip-sawing" of rates—that is, using one out-of-line job to gain a wage increase and then using that wage increase to press for others. Except in a few industries, such as steel, job evaluation has not enjoyed formal union support. However, it usually gains union acceptance. This occurs because, although the introduction of a job evaluation plan upsets internal wage relationships and thus is often not politically supportable by union leaders, once the plan is introduced, it stresses payment on a job basis rather than on a personal basis, and hence reduces friction and dissension among the union ranks. For employers, job evaluation simplifies wage administration and helps to prevent individual supervisors from letting individual wage rates get out of line.

Within job evaluation plans, most unions prefer single rates to rate ranges. In the automobile industry, union pressure has virtually eliminated rate ranges. Many employers prefer ranges, with the right to reward merit within the range. Other employers have found that ranges of this type can be maintained only by strict control because otherwise pressure on the foremen to recommend increases within the range soon puts most employees at the top of the range. Some ranges are, in effect, just nominal, for the contract may provide that employees receive a wage increase every few months until they reach the top of the grade. The most effective rate range plans place strict limits on the manner and/or number in the grade who can achieve the top rate and permit automatic increases only to the midpoint of the range—if at all. Since the midpoint of the rate range is, theoretically, the same as a single job rate would be, if an average of the workers' rates in any grade exceeds the midpoint, this means that the plant is paying more for a range rate than it would for a single-rate structure.

SUPPLEMENTARY OR FRINGE BENEFITS

Wage supplements, commonly called fringe benefits, are of two types: those imposed by government, such as social security, and those provided by employers, often pursuant to union agreements, as direct benefits for employees. Government benefits are discussed in Chapter 17. Here we are primarily concerned with fringe benefits as wage supplements. Employers have granted to their employees, health and accident insurance, life insurance, holidays and vacations with pay, pensions, paid sick leave, annual wage guarantees, and many other fringe benefits. Supplemental compensation is now a significant portion of total labor costs, and therefore an important factor in labor negotiations. It is also a source of public concern both because of the billions of dollars involved and because of the impact of such costs and benefits on the level of employment and income in the economy.

The Nature and Extent of Supplementary Benefits

There is no reliable published statistical series showing the cost of all supplementary benefits for industry as a whole, or even for manufacturing industries. This is understandable when we consider that supplementary benefits include such things as pay for "coffee-break" time, suggestion awards, free meals, and a whole gamut of similar benefits. Few employers have the time to calculate the cost of all these miscellaneous benefits. Despite the increasing emphasis placed upon fringe benefits in union negotiations, many employers do not know what their fringe costs are.

Total employee benefit payments of all kinds, including payments made by both governmental and private employers, are estimated to have aggregated $190 billion in 1973 and have undoubtedly increased since that date. (See Table 5–1.) For the purpose of this calculation, benefits are defined broadly and include such fringe payments as pay for vacations, rest periods, holidays, and the like, which are included in most government wage reports as a portion of employee wages. Nevertheless, from the point of view of the employer they represent compensation for time not worked. Total 1975 benefits were estimated at 35.4% of payrolls. This figure is made up of 8.0% for legally required payments; 11.6% for pensions, insurance, and other agreed-upon payments;

TABLE 5–1

Estimated Total Employee Benefits Payments, 1973

Industry	Wages and Salaries (billion dollars)	Benefit Payments	
		Percent	Billion Dollars
Manufacturing	$196.2	30	$ 58.5
Trade (wholesale and retail)	113.2	25	28.5
Services	92.8	20	18.5
Contract construction	42.3	24	10.0
Finance, insurance, and real estate	35.3	37	13.0
Transportation	30.9	31	9.7
Utilities and communication	21.0	35	7.4
Mining	7.4	33	2.4
Agriculture	5.6	18	1.0
Private industry	545.1	27	149.0
Government (federal, state, local)	146.5	28	41.0
Total, all industries	$691.6	27.5	$190.0

Source: *Employee Benefits, 1973* (Washington, D.C.: Chamber of Commerce of the United States, 1974), p. 29.

and 3.6% for rest periods. Vacations, holidays, sick leave, and other time not worked is estimated at 10.1%, and bonuses, profit sharing, and other miscellaneous payments at 2.1%.[12] Twelve years earlier, in 1963, total benefits amounted to only $69 billion, or 22% of payroll.[13]

The escalating magnitude of benefit payments is perhaps best dramatized by the data in Table 5–2, which shows employee benefit costs in 155 companies which have participated in the Chamber of Commerce surveys continuously since 1953. The average benefits for these com-

TABLE 5–2

Comparison of Employee Benefits for 155 Companies, 1955, 1965, 1975

Item	1955	1965	1975
1. As percent of payroll, total 22.7		28.0	40.3
a. Legally required payments (employer's share only) 2.8		4.2	7.1
b. Pension and other agreed-upon payments (employer's share only) 8.2		9.9	14.7
c. Paid rest periods, lunch periods, etc. 2.2		2.6	4.1
d. Payments for time not worked 7.6		9.4	11.9
e. Profit-sharing payments, bonuses, etc. 1.9		1.9	2.5
2. As cents per payroll hour 46.7		86.6	230.9
3. As dollars per year per employee 970		1793	4731

Source: Adapted from *Employee Benefits, 1975*. Washington, D.C.: Chamber of Commerce of the United States, 1976, table 19, p. 27.

---

[12] *Employee Benefits, 1975* (Washington, D.C.: Chamber of Commerce of the United States, 1976), p. 8.

[13] *Employee Benefits, 1973*, p. 29.

panies are somewhat higher than those shown in other surveys because these are larger companies which established their benefit programs earlier than did other companies. As can be seen from Table 5–2, benefits in these companies now amount to over 40% of payroll and cost an estimated $4,731 per employee annually.

The phenomenal growth of benefits since the end of World War II has been attributable to a number of factors. First, during both World War II and during the subsequent wage stabilization efforts, governmental boards attempted to freeze wages but generally adopted a more lenient stance with respect to fringe benefits. Second, NLRB decisions have strengthened union bargaining power with respect to demands for benefits by holding that fringe benefits are mandatory subjects of collective bargaining. Finally, the expansion of employer-sponsored programs has been stimulated by favorable tax treatment accorded under federal income tax legislation which makes employer contributions deductible as an expense and at the same time exempts employee trusts from income tax on the receipt of such payments. These factors, together with a growing acceptance by employers of responsibility for worker security, account for the tremendous growth of benefit plans.

Today fringe benefits are so pervasive in American industry that paid holidays and vacations are almost universally provided, and over 90% of employers make payments for welfare programs of various kinds. Table 5–3 indicates the frequency of various kinds of employee benefit programs in private industry.

Each year, the liberality and variety of coverage of employee benefit programs increase. Whereas health plans once covered only basic hospital care, some now include dental and psychiatric care and free eyeglasses. In 1965, fewer than 2 million workers had dental care coverage; by the end of 1975 the number covered had increased to 25 million. The American Dental Association predicts that by 1980 dental insurance will cover 60 million persons, with most of those covered securing their benefits through employer welfare programs.[14] Another benefit program which has become increasingly popular involves prepaid legal insurance. In August 1973, Congress amended Section 302 of the Taft-Hartley Act so as to permit unions to bargain for legal insurance as an employer-shared benefit. Under the terms of the amendment, insurance policies can now be purchased which entitle the holders to specified kinds of legal services either from an "open panel" of attorneys who will perform the services for the stated fee or from a closed panel of specified attorneys. The current trend seems to be toward the development of closed panel plans sponsored by unions or joint trusts.[15] Since this kind of benefit is

---

[14] *Business Week,* August 4, 1975, p. 28.

[15] Susan T. Mackenzie, *Group Legal Services,* Key Issues Series No. 18, New York State School of Industrial and Labor Relations (Ithaca, N.Y.: Cornell University, 1975), p. 56.

TABLE 5-3

Percent of Workers in Establishments with Formal Provisions for Selected Supplementary Wage Benefits in 229 Standard Metropolitan Statistical Areas: 1972 and 1973

| | Percent with Benefit | | | |
| | Plant Workers | | Office Workers | |
Type of Benefit	1972*	1973†	1972*	1973†
Paid holidays: ‡				
No paid holidays	4	4	Z	Z
6 or more days	89	89	97	97
7 or more days	77	77	86	87
8 or more days	65	65	75	77
9 or more days	43	46	52	55
10 or more days	21	23	31	33
11 or more days	10	12	18	19
12 or more days	6	7	8	8
Paid vacations: §				
2 weeks or more:				
After 1 year of service	28	30	79	80
After 5 years of service	96	95	99	99
3 weeks or more:				
After 5 years of service	19	20	26	27
After 10 years of service	72	74	85	86
After 15 years of service	84	85	93	93
4 weeks or more:				
After 15 years of service	24	27	26	27
After 20 years of service	58	61	69	70
After 25 years of service	65	67	77	77
Health, insurance, and pension plans:				
Life insurance	93	93	97	97
Hospitalization	95	95	97	97
Surgical	95	95	97	97
Medical	88	90	93	93
Major medical	69	72	91	92
Dental insurance	11	12	9	10
Sickness/accident insurance	63	63	47	47
Sick leave (full pay and no waiting period)	22	23	65	65
Sick leave (partial pay and/or waiting period)	13	14	9	9
Retirement pension	78	78	85	84

* Data for half the areas surveyed relate to late 1971 and early 1972; for the remainder, to late 1970 and early 1971.

† About one fifth of the data were collected between July 1970 and June 1971; one half between July 1971 and June 1972; and the remainder between July 1972 and June 1973.

‡ Holidays provided annually. Represents half-day and full-day holidays combined.

§ Such payments as percentages of annual earnings or a flat sum were converted to an equivalent time basis.

Data relate to standard metropolitan statistical areas, as established by the U.S. Office of Management and Budget through January 1968. Data obtained from sample of establishments which employ 50 workers or more, except in 12 of the largest areas where the minimum size was 100 employees for manufacturing, public utilities, and retail trade. Excludes government institutions, and construction and extractive industries. Excludes administrative, executive, and professional employees.

Z = Less than 0.5 percent.

Source: U.S. Bureau of the Census, *Statistical Abstract of the United States*, 96th ed. (Washington, D.C.: Government Printing Office, 1975), p. 368.

relatively new, accurate figures are not available on the extent of legal insurance coverage, but it is believed that millions of workers who otherwise could not have afforded such service have already been provided access to lawyers.

KEY FRINGE ISSUES

In terms of costs, the extent of the problems involved, and pervasiveness, two fringe benefit items, pensions and insurance against illness, are surely the most significant. A third, supplemental unemployment benefits (SUB), deserves special mention because it represents a movement toward guaranteed income for employees in certain industries. A fourth benefit type, the Employee Stock Ownership Plan, is still not very common, but will be discussed below because Congress has elected to provide important advantages to this kind of program.

Pensions

The great growth of pension plans has come in recent years as a result of collective bargaining pressures and benefits conferred under federal tax law. Since 1940, retirement benefits have grown much faster than wages. The percentage of all private nonfarm workers employed in establishments with employer contributions to such plans rose from 53% in 1966 to 65% in 1972.[16] The effectiveness of unions in obtaining the adoption of such plans is demonstrated by the fact that only 9% of employees in unionized groups were in establishments without retirement plans compared to 48% of employees in nonunion groups.[17] As might be expected, most big companies have retirement plans. Of employees in establishments with 500 employees or more, 93% are covered by such plans, compared to only 38% in establishments with less than 100 employees.[18]

At year-end 1973, the latest year for which data are available, close to 35 million persons, including both active workers and retirees, were members of private nongovernmental pension and retirement plans.[19] Overall, about one half of all workers in commerce and industry in the United States and close to three fourths of all government civilian personnel are enrolled in retirement plans other than OASDI (Social Security).[20] In 1974, private noninsured pension funds received $21.1

---

[16] Donald R. Bell, "Prevalence of Private Retirement Plans," *Monthly Labor Review*, vol. 98 (October 1975), p. 17.

[17] Ibid., p. 20.

[18] Ibid., p. 19.

[19] *Life Insurance Fact Book* (New York: Institute of Life Insurance, 1975), p. 35.

[20] Ibid.

billion in contributions and other income and paid out $11.0 billion in benefits.[21] Figure 5–1 shows the growth of pension fund assets and trends in contributions and benefits.

The retirement benefits provided by private pension plans vary a great deal from employer to employer. The pension benefit provided in collectively bargained plans is usually a fixed dollar amount, regardless

FIGURE 5–1

Private Pension Funds: Trends in Assets, Contributions, and Benefits

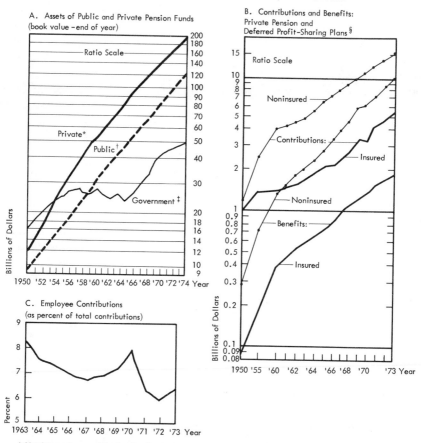

* Noninsured pension funds (includes deferred profit-sharing funds and pension funds of corporations, unions, multiemployer groups, and nonprofit organizations and insured pension funds.

† Civil service and state and local retirement funds.

‡ Railroad Retirement, Federal Old-Age and Survivors Insurance, and Federal Disability Insurance.

§ Note: Excludes federal, state, and local government employees and pension plans for the self-employed but includes railroad plans supplementing the Federal Railroad Retirement program.

Source: Adapted from *Private Pension Funds,* Road Maps of Industry, No. 1775 (New York: The Conference Board, December 1975).

---

[21] *Daily Labor Report,* December 15, 1975, p. B–1.

of the employee's earnings. A formula frequently used to determine the employee's benefit provides a dollar amount (such as $5 or $10) of monthly pension for each year of service the employee has completed at retirement. On the other hand, in plans covering salaried and non-union personnel, the benefit formula is usually related to the employee's earnings and length of service. Many pension plans also make provision for death, termination of employment, or total disability.

Until the enactment of the Employee Retirement Income Security Act of 1974 (ERISA), there was no uniform federally mandated requirement for the vesting of employee retirement benefits. Vesting establishes a right in employees, based upon a predetermined schedule, to receive a retirement benefit at a given age even though they are not working for the company at the time they reach that age. Prior to ERISA, some pension plans required a minimum number of years of service and reaching age 55, 60, or 65 while still in the employ of the company for an employee to receive any benefits. This meant that an employee who left a company after 15 years of service at, say, age 49, would receive nothing under the plan, even upon reaching the age of 65. Most plans did, however, provide some vesting, although not as much as is now required by law. A study made by the U.S. Bureau of Labor Statistics prior to the passage of ERISA found that 90% of all employees covered by private plans were entitled to vested rights or early retirement benefits by age 55 if they had worked 15 years under a plan.[22] Because the inclusion of vesting provisions in a plan greatly increases the cost of the plan to the employer, many companies—particularly smaller establishments—were reluctant to include such features in their retirement programs.

Thus, statistics on the broad coverage of retirement programs in American industry were in some respects illusory because they did not take account of the plight of the worker who voluntarily or involuntarily was separated from his or her covered employer before completing the eligibility requirements under a retirement plan. Another reason why some employees did not receive pensions upon retirement was that inadequate provision had been made for their payment. If insufficient funds are set aside to pay pensions and as a consequence the money is not there when an employee applies for retirement, the employee can depend only upon company solvency. Unfortunately, companies do go out of business without meeting their obligations.

Although some companies have failed to fund pension liabilities adequately, actually the record of private industry has been better in this respect than that of government. Bloated benefits and inadequate funding have rendered New York City pension plans practically insolvent. The Temporary Commission on City Finances recommended major

---

[22] *Business Week,* March 17, 1973, p. 48.

cutbacks in the city's fringe benefits after its investigation revealed that fringe benefits were costing the city $2 for every $3 spent on base pay![23] As will be seen from the discussion in Chapter 17, serious questions have been raised about the solvency of the social security system. Nevertheless, congressional hearings which focused on the inadequacies of a number of private pension plans and on the hardships caused thereby to employees raised a demand for some kind of insurance to protect employees when their employers were unable to meet their pension obligations.

The Employee Retirement Income Security Act

In September 1974, President Ford signed into law what may well be the most important piece of social legislation since passage of the Social Security Act. The new pension reform law—commonly known as ERISA—established a comprehensive framework of safeguards guaranteeing the private pension rights of an estimated 35 million American workers. The new law, which will be administered by both the Treasury Department (Internal Revenue Service) and the Department of Labor, covers all employee benefit plans of private for-profit employers, including multiemployer plans. Although the law's major purpose was to tighten restrictions on private pension plans and to establish federal standards for their administration, certain provisions of the law also apply to profit-sharing, savings, stock bonus, and employee welfare plans. The act is lengthy and highly complex, and it has raised fears among businessmen that its application will greatly increase pension costs and place a heavy reporting burden on small companies. Indeed, in the 18 months following passage of the new law, approximately 5,500 small companies terminated their pension plans.[24] A common complaint among small employers was that the new law required all full-time employees aged 25 or older to be included in a pension plan after one year's service, whereas previously many employers had had five-year waiting periods, thus reducing their overall costs. Although many of the terminations were undoubtedly attributable to the impact of the new law, another contributing cause was the deep recession of 1974–75.

This voluminous act deals with many aspects of retirement programs, but its main impact will be felt in four areas:

1. *Vesting.* The rate at which an employee earns vested rights to his or her pension benefits is no longer a matter for employer (or employer and union) determination. New federal standards apply. The employer has the option of providing vesting under any one of the following three methods:

---

[23] *New York Times,* June 3, 1976, p. 1.

[24] *New York Times,* March 8, 1976, p. 1.

a. Full (100%) vesting after ten years of service, with no vesting prior to the completion of ten years of service.

b. Graded vesting (5 to 15 years) which involves 25% vesting after 5 years of service, plus 5% for each additional year of service up to 10 years (50% vesting after 10 years), plus an additional 10% for each year thereafter (yielding 100% vesting after 15 years of service).

c. The "Rule of 45" (based on age and service): 50% vesting for an employee with at least five years of service when his age and years of service add up to 45, plus 10% for each year thereafter.

These rules are retroactive. That is, in applying the new standards, the employer must now take into account all of the employee's continuous service prior to the enactment of the new law. The act established formulas for funding over a specific period of time the costs of pension benefits earned in the past for which funds had not yet been set aside. Such funding represents an addition to annual operating costs, and for some companies it will cause a significant reduction in operating profits.

2. *Termination Insurance.* The act establishes a Pension Benefit Guaranty Corporation within the U.S. Department of Labor to administer an insurance fund to which all companies with qualified pension plans must contribute. Initially the premiums charged for the insurance are nominal. Employers with their own plans must contribute $1 per worker per year, and multiemployer plans must contribute $.50 per worker per year. The insurance company will pay any deficiency which may develop between the amount necessary to pay all vested benefits and the amount available from a terminating plan's assets. However, only vested rights up to a maximum of $750 per month are insured, and pension increases granted in the five years prior to a plan's termination are insured only to the extent of 20% per year. The insuring corporation has a right to recover from any employer the cost to the corporation of paying benefits to participants or beneficiaries on the employer's behalf. However, the amount recovered cannot exceed 30% of the employer's net worth. The insurance provisions are not applicable to stock bonus, money purchase, and profit-sharing plans, or to plans which do not provide for employer contributions. ERISA's insurance provisions have already benefited some employees of bankrupt corporations. In 1975, 650 retirees of the bankrupt REA Express Company began receiving pension checks from the Pension Benefit Guaranty Corporation, and employees of the bankrupt W. T. Grant Company will presumably also be protected.[25]

3. *Reporting Requirements.* In order to enable federal monitoring of various kinds of plans, the act now requires the filing of detailed information with both the Department of Labor and the Internal Revenue Service as well as detailed disclosure to employee participants in such plans.

---

[25] *New York Times,* February 29, 1976, sec. F, p. 14.

These reporting and disclosure requirements apply to a wide range of benefit plans, including pension, thrift, legal aid, health, education, and insurance plans. Many companies have numerous plans, including some which may no longer be operative except to pay out benefits. The administrative costs involved in such a reporting process can be enormous. Standard Oil of California, for example, has 102 plans covering its U.S. employees and annuitants. It has estimated that reporting costs, including data processing, could run as high as $2.5 million to gear up for the system, and that recurrent administrative costs could jump $750,000 a year.[26]

4. *Fiduciary Standards.* The act establishes federal standards of conduct for fiduciaries involved in administering benefit plans. Fiduciaries are required to "act prudently," to diversify plan assets to minimize the risk of large losses, and are forbidden to participate in conflict-of-interest transactions, including the investment of more than 10% of a pension fund's assets in the employer's securities or property. Management's major concern with these provisions is that the concept of fiduciary has been so broadened that it may be interpreted to include not only trustees and other persons directly involved in the investment and management of funds, but also plan administrators, company executives, and even members of company boards of directors. The act makes fiduciaries personally responsible for breaches of their responsibility and permits plan participants to sue in federal courts to recover losses to individuals or to the plan. In 1974, for the first time in many years, the market value of pension fund assets fell below their book value as a result of the precipitous drop in the stock market.[27] Pension fund managers are fearful that another such decline could expose them to personal liability for losses sustained by pension plans. As a consequence, pension fund managers may become more conservative in their investment policies, with a tendency to shift from equities to fixed-income securities.

Appraisal of ERISA. It will be many years before the full costs and benefits of this monumental legislation can be fully appraised. The insurance and vesting requirements seem to have much merit, although they do impose additional costs upon business and ultimately upon the consumer. ERISA does not provide full "portability" to pension rights, and therefore the frequent job changer can still end up with years of service for various companies but no retirement benefits aside from social security. However, vesting does protect the rights of the employee with longer service.

The reporting and fiduciary provisions seem more likely to provide employment for lawyers and accountants than to accomplish the objective of the legislation, which was "reform" of private pension plans. Most private

---

[26] *Business Week*, March 24, 1975, p. 149.

[27] *Private Pension Funds*, Road Maps of Industry, No. 1775 (New York: The Conference Board, 1975).

plans did not require reform, but one giant plan most certainly does. That plan is the Teamsters' $1.5 billion pension fund, a sizable portion of which has been allocated to bizarre and risky investments, some of which may have been made for the benefit of insiders. Yet, despite numerous congressional investigations, despite passage of the Landrum-Griffin Labor Reform Act of 1959 (which grew out of abuses uncovered in investigations of the Teamsters), little has been done to audit effectively and control the management of billions of pension dollars which are subject to Teamster control. ERISA may likewise founder on the same shoals unless it is given the staff and the funds it needs in order to enforce the reform provisions which Congress has legislated.

Health and Welfare Plans

Privately organized protection against the cost of sickness has grown at a tremendous rate in recent years. Hospitalization insurance has become so popular that by 1971, 181.5 million people, nearly 90% of the civilian resident population, had such protection. Other types of medical care insurance have also become increasingly important, though not so prevalent as hospitalization benefits. Today, surgical expense insurance covers about 95% of those having hospitalization insurance and nearly 90% of those with hospital insurance also have regular medical expense protection. Insurance companies provide about two thirds of this protection, Blue Cross–Blue Shield, the bulk of the rest, with independent plans covering the balance of about 5%.[28]

As the cost of health care has escalated year after year, third-party payments by private insurance, philanthropy, and public (federal, state, and local) funds have been relied upon to assume an ever-larger portion of medical expenses. For example, in 1929, when health spending amounted to only $26 per capita, 88% of the health bill was paid directly by the health resource user. By fiscal 1975, when health care costs had risen to $476 per person, only about one third of such expenditures were paid directly by the health resource user. In 1975 about one quarter of the total health bill was paid for by private insurance plans.[29]

Unions have pushed hard for health insurance coverage under collective bargaining since World War II, and today few contracts exclude such coverage, which tends to be ever more elaborate. New features include psychiatric care, prepaid eye treatment and glasses, prepaid dental care, and annual physical examinations. As in the case of pensions, the costs of such programs have grown enormously, and under union pressure, the bulk of the plans call for the employer to bear all costs for

---

[28] Data from the Health Insurance Institute.

[29] *Health Care Expenditures,* Road Maps of Industry, No. 1780 (New York: The Conference Board, 1976).

employees and their dependents, whereas once the cost of dependents' coverage, especially, was deducted from the workers' paychecks.

For employers, a basic problem with health insurance is that its costs are beyond their control. They bargain generally to provide certain benefits, and then are faced with spiraling hospital and other costs which they must pay. Health care costs have been rising faster than the general cost of living. In 1974 and 1975, the cost of medical services rose 25.3%.[30] In fiscal 1950, the United States was spending $78.35 per person on health care. By fiscal 1972, the medical bill had risen to $394.16 per capita, and it is projected to be as high as $757 per capita by fiscal 1980.[31] Such skyrocketing costs can have serious ramifications for company profit margins. In the automobile industry a 50% increase in five years in the cost of employer contributions to company-paid health care plans led the automobile companies to ask for worker contributions in 1976 bargaining. In 1976, car buyers paid $160 of the car price to finance health insurance for automobile workers. The Big Three automobile companies paid $1,600 a family for health insurance for their workers, compared with a national average of $550 for family health costs. Without major increases in benefits, health insurance costs in the automobile industry between 1975 and 1976 rose over 25% as compared with wage increases of 9%.[32] Although company demands for employee contributions to health care costs were rebuffed in 1976 automobile industry negotiations, it seems evident that the past trend of ever-increasing health care costs cannot go on indefinitely.

The union response to higher medical costs has been support for a new system of national federal health insurance which would transfer the costs to the general taxpayer. Unions also see an additional benefit in national health insurance during strikes, for presumably coverage would not be interrupted. Under private plans funded by employers, the employer can refuse to continue coverage after a strike lasts 30 days because the contractual obligation to do so ceases. This leaves the union with the burden of paying such costs until the strike ends. Apparently the desire to avoid the enormous costs of another month's premium put much pressure on officials of the United Automobile Workers to end the General Motors strike of 1970 when they did.

From the employer's point of view, rising health care costs have led to increased interest in self-insurance, claims monitoring, and prepaid group care. Under prepaid group care, stipulated services are provided by a group of doctors at agreed-upon costs. The best-known plan of

---

[30] *Business Week*, May 17, 1976, p. 144.

[31] *Health Expenditures*, Road Maps of Industry, No. 1722 (New York: The Conference Board, 1973); and *Hospital Statistics, 1975* (Chicago: American Hospital Association, 1975), table 1, p. 4.

[32] Nancy Hicks, "Soaring Cost of Health Insurance Is Debated in Auto Contract Talks," *New York Times,* August 22, 1976, p. 24.

this kind is the Kaiser Foundation Health Plan on the West Coast, which was originally set up to provide care to employees of the wartime Kaiser shipbuilding business. In recent years the federal government has sought to spur the development of the Health Maintenance Organization (HMO). It has provided federal funding for HMOs meeting specified requirements, and it requires that any employer with 25 or more employees who offers a health benefits plan must include the option of membership in federally funded health maintenance organizations in the area. Although the HMO idea has merit, most HMOs have been unsuccessful. The theory is that the HMOs would offer preventive medicine and maintain the patients' health, thereby reducing medical plan expenses. Actually, however, the cost of most HMO plans is higher than what would be charged under other private plans—although admittedly the services are not entirely comparable—and HMOs have found it difficult to secure broad enough membership to remain viable.

Despite their high and rising costs, health insurance programs are not designed to cover accidents or illness occurring, or resulting, directly from employment. This is the function of workers' compensation, the oldest form of social insurance, which is discussed in Chapter 17. In addition, temporary and permanent disabilities are also dealt with under state and federal legislation, and as noted, are also provided for in many pension plans.

Supplemental Unemployment Benefits

Supplemental unemployment benefits (SUB) are company-paid benefits available to about 2.3 million U.S. workers[33] who are members of powerful industrial unions in a few industries. SUB plans are not as widespread as pension and health insurance programs, being confined, for the most part, to industries which deal with the automobile, rubber, and steelworker unions, plus a few others. Essentially most of these plans provide for the establishment of funds, maintained through employer contributions, which pay out benefits over and above what state unemployment compensation programs provide. Under UAW contracts, for example, the combination of SUB payments and state unemployment benefits is designed to pay laid-off workers 95% of their regular take-home wage, less $7.50 a week, the estimated cost of lunches and of transportation to and from work. Depending upon years of service, UAW members can collect SUB for up to one year. However, the duration of benefits is actually determined by a complex formula which depends upon time worked, seniority, and the amount of money per employee in the fund.

One reason that SUB plans have not achieved greater popularity is

---

[33] *Wall Street Journal*, January 2, 1976, p. 16.

that they are significant only to those more recently employed. The senior employees are usually fairly secure and do not want money bargained to go to funds from which they stand to reap little benefit. To accommodate these feelings, some contracts permit senior employees to take layoffs instead of working, as will be noted in the following chapter.

Of even greater significance is the fact that SUB plans cannot really provide guaranteed income in periods of heavy layoffs. In aerospace, for example, where the end of a contract can mean mass layoffs, SUB plans have run out of funds before layoffs hit the senior employees. The result has been that the less senior employees have received SUB benefits while longtime employees have received nothing. In the automobile industry, the sharp downturn in sales in 1974 and 1975 caused the SUB plans at General Motors and Chrysler to run out of funds by April 1975. Commenting on the failure of the SUB program, Irving Bluestone, a UAW vice president, pointed out that the program was developed by the automobile companies and the union to cope with normal employment fluctuations, primarily layoffs associated with model changeovers, and not with "the disaster . . . felt [in 1975] in the auto industry."[34] For many industries, a more equitable system of dealing with widespread layoffs is a program of lump-sum dismissal wages, based upon seniority, or a similar mechanism which recognizes, rather than discriminates against, length of service. Another possibility, which has been suggested by UAW officials, would involve the establishment of two funds, one for older workers and the other for workers with less seniority. The latter might offer less than the 95% pay protection which characterized the usual SUB plans combined with state unemployment compensation benefits.

Employee Stock Plans

Employee stock ownership plans, which encourage ownership by employees of stock in the company which employs them, have been around for many years. Most of the older plans, such as those in effect at IBM, Sears Roebuck, and Texas Instruments, provide for employee purchases of stock of the employing company, often at a discount or with matching funds provided by the employer. The newer plans, which have been sparked by the writing of Louis O. Kelso,[35] a San Francisco lawyer and lay economist, involve an outright contribution by an employer to an employee trust. In such a plan, the company can deduct as a business expense (and thus reduce its income tax) an amount equal to the market value of stock which it contributed to a trust for the benefit of the

---

[34] *Business Week*, February 3, 1975, p. 20.

[35] See, for example, Louis O. Kelso and Patricia Hetter, *How to Turn Eighty Million Workers into Capitalists on Borrowed Money* (New York: Random House, 1967).

employees. The stock is allocated to individual employee accounts according to various formulas, based on salary, length of service, and similar criteria. An employee who retires or leaves the company can either keep the stock which was in his or her account or, if permitted to do so by the plan, can "put" it to the company, which means that the company must buy the stock back at its market value.

In the last few years a special kind of employee stock ownership plan, known as an ESOP, has become popular. ESOPs have become attractive to employers because of the special tax benefits conferred on such plans by ERISA and by the Tax Reduction Act of 1975. Technically, an ESOP is a form of stock bonus plan entitled to certain benefits under the Internal Revenue Code. The plans must meet qualifications spelled out in Section 401 of the code. Proponents of the ESOP claim that it provides an inexpensive method for a company to raise new capital while at the same time providing employees with an interest in the company's equity. The financing aspect of the ESOP, which is probably most meaningful to small- and medium-sized corporations with limited access to capital markets, works as follows: The employee benefit plan borrows money (the loan being guaranteed by the employer company) to purchase stock newly issued by the employer. The employer makes annual contributions of stock to the plan and in addition contributes sufficient cash to cover interest and amortization payments on the loan. Such payments by the company are deductible for purposes of federal income tax, and therefore the company is able to pay off the loan out of pretax earnings. Furthermore, under an ESOP, as with other employee benefit and pension plans, the employee beneficiaries of the plan are not required to pay income tax on the employer contributions until the stock is distributed to the employees, which is usually on retirement.

For the average employee, an ESOP is no substitute for a properly funded pension plan, since the value of the employer's stock, which is the sole asset of the trust, can fluctuate widely. The failure of such corporate giants as the Penn Central Railroad and the W. T. Grant Company raises questions as to the wisdom of tying an employee's security to investment in a single stock. Furthermore, from the employer's point of view, such a plan dilutes equity holdings and therefore may produce dissatisfaction among the company's stockholders.

Whither Fringe Benefit Costs?

Twenty years ago fringe benefits were looked upon by employers as "a little extra benefit to sweeten the pot." Today, the escalating costs of retirement benefits is a major management concern. On the one hand, the decline in the birthrate and the growing number of older persons in our society means that there will be fewer people working to provide the benefits for retirees. Twenty years ago an estimated seven workers were paying social security taxes for every beneficiary. The ratio today is down to three to one, and it is possible that early in the next century it could drop to two to one.[36]

At the same time, the cost of benefits has risen sharply. A survey of fringe benefit costs in 152 companies conducted by the Chamber of Commerce of the United States found that from 1965 to 1975 the cost of providing such benefits rose from 28% to 40.3% of payrolls.[37] In the automobile industry, as noted, benefit costs have risen three times as fast as average hourly earnings and now comprise one third of total labor costs.[38] Not only privately bargained benefits, but also government programs paid for by employers, in whole or in part, have escalated in cost over the years. It is estimated, for example, that social security contributions rose 283% between 1964 and 1974.[39]

Some experts question whether the economy will be able to support and pay for all of the retirement benefits that are now being promised. Figure 5–2 indicates that while the number of beneficiaries collecting benefits has increased by only 69% since 1965, annual contributions are now running at a rate 244% greater than in 1966. It will be noted in Figure 5–2 that annual contributions made by the federal government to support pension plans for civil service and military personnel amount at present to about $18 billion. Some experts predict that such payments could reach $45 billion by 1985.[40] Federal pensions have a built-in inflationary bias by reason of legislation which requires that the level of benefits be raised automatically when the consumer price index jumps 3% or more and holds at that level for at least three months. Thus far, this type of "indexing"[41] has not been adopted in most private plans. A Conference Board study of pension plans in 1,800 companies found that only 4% made cost-of-living adjustments in retirement benefits.[42]

A number of trends have contributed to the steady escalation in benefit costs. First, there has been a trend toward uniformity of benefits between blue-collar unionized workers and white-collar nonunion personnel. Many companies once provided better benefits to nonunion office personnel than to union workers, but over the years such differentials have been eroded. Second, there has been an increasing acceptance of the principle that employee benefits are simply a form of earned compensation. This has had two significant consequences. Since benefits are com-

---

[36] Edmund Faltermayer, "A Steeper Climb up Pension Mountain," *Fortune*, vol. 91 (January 1975), p. 208. See Chapter 17 for a further analysis of this situation.

[37] *Employee Benefits, 1975*, p. 27.

[38] 91 LRR 66, January 26, 1976

[39] *The Two-Way Squeeze, 1975*, Road Maps of Industry, No. 1759 (New York: The Conference Board, 1975).

[40] *U.S. News & World Report*, October 13, 1975, p. 85.

[41] For a discussion of the concept of indexing, see discussion in Chapter 13.

[42] Cited in *U.S. News & World Report*, October 13, 1975, p. 86.

FIGURE 5–2

Explosive Growth in Pension Plans (government and private)

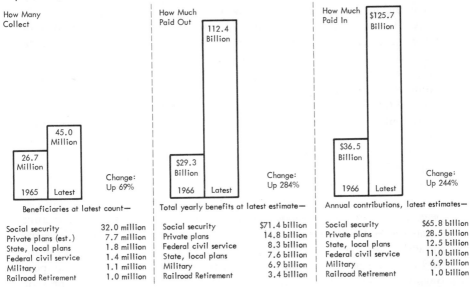

Beneficiaries at latest count—		Total yearly benefits at latest estimate—		Annual contributions, latest estimates—	
Social security	32.0 million	Social security	$71.4 billion	Social security	$65.8 billion
Private plans (est.)	7.7 million	Private plans	14.8 billion	Private plans	28.5 billion
State, local plans	1.8 million	Federal civil service	8.3 billion	State, local plans	12.5 billion
Federal civil service	1.4 million	State, local plans	7.6 billion	Federal civil service	11.0 billion
Military	1.1 million	Military	6.9 billion	Military	6.9 billion
Railroad Retirement	1.0 million	Railroad Retirement	3.4 billion	Railroad Retirement	1.0 billion

Note: Some people collect more than one kind of benefit.

Source: Basic data provided by U.S. Departments of Labor, Defense, and Health, Education, and Welfare; Civil Service Commission; Institute of Life Insurance. Reproduced from *U.S. News & World Report*, March 15, 1976, p. 77, by permission.

pensation, it follows that they should be paid for in full by the employer. Therefore, the proportion of benefit costs paid for by employees has declined steadily over the years. Furthermore, if a benefit—for example, pension rights—is compensation, it ought to be portable. That is, an employee who leaves a company ought to be able to take this right with him because he has already "earned" it. This has led to the principle, now legalized by ERISA, which requires the vesting of pension rights. Third, there has been governmental intervention in the regulation of benefit programs. The extent to which such intervention increases costs to employers is most evident in the application of the new pension legislation.

The recent governmental regulation of pension programs has imposed new financial burdens on companies with retirement plans. The past service funding required by ERISA has increased the liabilities of most companies. It is estimated that unfunded obligations represent one fourth to one third of the net worth of scores of large corporations, with even higher proportions in some cases. For example, the applicable percentage is 46% at Western Union, 53% at Bethlehem Steel, and 86% at Uniroyal.[43] Furthermore, annual amortization charges can sharply reduce

---

[43] Faltermayer, "A Steeper Climb," p. 78.

profits for some companies. A recent study by *Business Week* magazine found that annual amortization charges, based upon a write-off over 40 years—the longest period permitted by ERISA—would amount to 114% of recent pretax earnings at TWA. At Chrysler, LTV, Western Union, and American Motors the annual amortization charge ranged between 22% and 27% of recent five-year average earnings.[44]

The companies which will experience the most pressure from pension liabilities are those in mature and highly unionized industries, such as steel, autos, and metals, and those in industries, which have strong unions but major earnings problems, such as airlines. A rising stock market could ease this burden by increasing the value of pension fund portfolios. However, a decline in the market could diminish the value of such portfolios and put companies in a serious squeeze by requiring additional cash contributions to maintain the fund in an actuarially sound condition. In 1973–74, for example, the stock market debacle cut the value of pension fund equity portfolios by over 30%.[45]

To the sobering problems already existing in the benefit field must be added the possibility of continuing inflation and union demands to index benefits so as to keep pace with rising prices. One writer has put the problem succinctly:

> Pension costs (excluding social security) are now running from 5% to 10% of annual payroll for many companies—a level equivalent to a quarter or more of their annual profits. It is only a matter of time before pension costs rise to 20% to 30% of payroll. This increase will have to be translated into price increases which in turn will fuel more wage increases leading to even higher benefit costs. Where will this spiral end?[46]

WAGE COSTS, FRINGE BENEFITS, AND TAKE-HOME PAY

It is apparent that, bit by bit, American industry is obligating itself to underwrite the economic needs and the economic risks of the worker. Industry today provides a cradle-to-grave security program for employees similar to government programs in England and other countries. As more and more costs go into fringe benefits, payment by the hour for time actually worked will become less important. Does this mean that our traditional modes of payment will eventually be outdated? Many questions which cannot be answered today are a matter of concern to business and labor leaders alike.

At the same time that the employer's cost of employing a worker has been increasing because of fringe benefits, employee take-home pay has been subjected to major deductions in the form of withholding for federal

---

[44] *Business Week,* June 16, 1975, p. 80.

[45] *Business Week,* August 3, 1974, p. 44.

[46] Donald G. Carlson, "Responding to the Pension Reform Law," *Harvard Business Review,* vol. 52 (November–December 1974), p. 144.

income taxes, state income taxes, union dues, charitable contributions, and so on. The result has been a growing gap between spendable earnings and labor costs. For example, assume that a company employs a worker at $230 weekly pay. The company could have, in addition to this direct wage cost, indirect costs associated with the employment of this worker as shown in Table 5-4. On the other side of the coin, the employee's paycheck might well reflect deductions such as those in Table 5-5.

TABLE 5-4
Employer Fringe Benefit Costs

Item	Estimated Weekly Cost to Employer
Federal Old-Age, Survivors, and Disability Insurance tax	$17.50
Unemployment insurance taxes	3.25
Workers' compensation premium	4.50
Private pension contribution	12.00
Group insurance contribution	20.00
Supplemental unemployment benefit plan contribution	4.00
Pay for holidays, vacations, rest periods, and other time not worked	30.00
Employee facilities, services, and other miscellaneous benefits	4.00
Total	$95.25

TABLE 5-5
Employee Deductions from Pay

Item	Estimated Weekly Cost to Employee
Statutory deductions (federal and state income tax withheld; withholding for federal Old-Age, Survivors, and Disability Insurance)	$70.40
Union dues	3.00
Group insurance premiums for dependents' coverage and contributions to company thrift plan and charitable drives	10.00
Total	$83.40

In this company, therefore, the employer looks upon labor costs as $325.25 per week for this particular employee, while the employee only receives $146.60 in his pay envelope. The employee is, of course, aware of these various indirect benefits and of the manner in which his pay has been diverted. The problem facing industry, however, arises from the fact that to a considerable extent, these amounts are likely to be discounted in the employee's thinking. Although "package" settlements, which provide that much of a bargain wage adjustment shall be taken in the form of fringes, are especially popular with employees who are security-conscious, even such employees also tend to think in terms of "take-home" pay—that is, the amount actually received in the pay envelope. Continued emphasis on fringes, therefore, can tend to increase the cost to the employer without increasing the immediate satisfaction of the employee. The same result is produced by the continued growth in statutory deductions from the employee's paycheck. As the wedge between the employee's pay and the employer's cost grows, employees become less willing to work and firms become less willing to hire.

FRINGE BENEFITS AND EMPLOYMENT

A characteristic of many fringe benefits is that they are attached to the individual employee rather than to the overall wage bill of the employer. Thus, the worker receives vacations, holidays, pensions, group insurance, and so on, whether he works 35 hours, 40 hours, or 50 hours per week. Of course, his earnings may change the amount he receives as benefits; but within broad limits, such fringes are often like the government social security program (old age): after a basic amount of payroll cost, there is no additional charge.

This means that fringe benefits can make it cheaper to work employees overtime than to hire new employees. For example, assume that fringe benefits cost an employer 2.38 cents per hour and that government-imposed benefit programs (social security, and unemployment and worker's compensation) add another 15 cents. Add to these the costs of recruiting, indoctrinating, and employing new personnel, which can be substantial, and frequently employers find that it is cheaper to employ existing employees at overtime rates (time and one half) than it would be to hire new employees. This fact accounts for proposals to increase the overtime rate to double time as a means of discouraging overtime.

Fringe benefits, by adding to the employer's marginal costs, may adversely affect both the amount of employment and its character—that is, whether existing employees are worked more hours or new employees are added to the payroll. The cost of security for some may be less employment—and less security—for others. Whether, however, adding to the cost of overtime, and hence to the employer's overall cost, would lessen or increase the propensity to employ is, of course, very doubtful. We shall return to this issue in our discussion of the hours of work question in Chapter 16.

SUMMARY

We have seen that the wage issue is not a simple question of how many cents per hour a worker should be paid. Wages—in the sense used in this text—can encompass a wide range of benefits, from maternity care for a worker's wife to extra pay for working after 6 P.M. Wages are naturally important to a worker because they mean purchasing power for him and his family. But wages also have another dimension in our society which should not be overlooked. The worker, in common with other members of the community, views his wage as a symbol of his standing in the community. It is an aspect of his status in our economic society. That is why such benefits as a third week of paid vacation are so important. If John Jones is at home cutting the lawn while Bill Smith is working at the plant because his company did not give the third week of vacation, you can bet that Mrs. Jones and Mrs. Smith are discussing the injustice of it all and that Bill Smith—and eventually his employer—will hear about it!

In the next chapter, we shall consider other problems arising out of the employer-employee relationship which do not directly involve wages but are important issues in the collective bargaining process.

QUESTIONS FOR DISCUSSION

1. Discuss the various forms of incentive payment. Is it true that unions oppose piecework and favor time payment? Support your answer.
2. Discuss the pros and cons of profit sharing versus gain sharing.
3. Discuss the relationship of fringe benefits as a cost to the employer and a return to the employee. Do you think that fringe benefit costs will continue to rise; and if so, what are some implications of this trend?
4. To what extent, if any, do you think that the federal government should regulate private pension programs? Discuss the possible impact of ERISA on retirement programs.
5. What is an ESOP? Do you think that broad acceptance of such plans by American industry would reduce frictions between management and labor?

SUGGESTIONS FOR FURTHER READING

Burck, Charles G. "There's More to ESOP Than Meets the Eye," *Fortune,* vol. 93 (March 1976), pp. 128–32 et seq.

An authoritative article which discusses the pros and cons of employee stock ownership plans.

Chamber of Commerce of the United States. *Employee Benefits, 1975.* Washington, D.C.: The Chamber, 1976.

A biennial survey of the extent and cost of fringe benefits in participating companies.

Faltermayer, Edmund. "A Steeper Climb up Pension Mountain," *Fortune,* vol. 91 (January 1975), pp. 78–81 et seq.

An article which examines the impact of ERISA on pension costs with specific references to the experience of a number of well-known public corporations.

McGill, Dan M. *Fundamentals of Private Pensions*. 3d ed. Homewood, Ill.: Richard D. Irwin, Inc., 1976.

An exhaustive study of all aspects of private pensions, including the impact of ERISA, by a noted pension expert.

Perham, John C. "The Mess in Public Pensions," *Dun's Review,* vol. 107 (March 1976), pp. 48–50.

An article which presents in graphic detail the unfunded liabilities and potential breakdown facing the pension programs in many cities and states and in the federal government.

Slichter, Sumner H.; Healy, J. J.; and Livernash, E. R. *The Impact of Collective Bargaining on Management,* chaps. 17–20. Washington, D.C.: Brookings Institution, 1960.

These chapters of this outstanding work contain comprehensive and realistic analyses of wage incentives, measured daywork, evaluated wage structures, and other wage structure considerations based upon extensive fieldwork and careful evaluations of the problems encountered. The discussions are still current, although written nearly two decades ago.

6

The Content of
Collective Bargaining:
Industrial Jurisprudence

THE PROCESS of collective bargaining, as we have seen from the previous chapter, is a method of determining the price of labor, that is, of fixing wages. An additional important function of collective bargaining is to formulate the rules and regulations governing the employment relationship.

Where there is no union, management's labor policies may be liberal or restrictive; but in either case, they are *management's* policies. Management is free to discharge, to promote, to hire, or to lay off in any legal manner in which it desires. But when a union represents the employees, these functions and many others which were once the prerogatives of management become subject to a variety of rules. Some of the rules are written into an agreement between union and management; others are simply accepted by both parties and remain unwritten; and still others are embodied in federal, state, or municipal laws, often as a result of pressure by unions or employers. These rules embody the system of "industrial jurisprudence" by which the relations between union and management are regulated.[1]

No Uniformity of Rules

A system of industrial jurisprudence is basically the result of American workers' demands that industrial relations be conducted according to rules which they have a voice in formulating. Only if such rules are in

---

[1] As the term was used by the late Professor Sumner H. Slichter in his pathbreaking book, *Union Policies and Industrial Management* (Washington, D.C.: Brookings Institution, 1941), p. 1. A second edition, completed by Professor Slichter just prior to his death in 1959 and coauthored by Professors J. J. Healy and E. R. Livernash, was published in 1960 under the title, *The Impact of Collective Bargaining on Management* (Washington, D.C.: Brookings Institution).

effect do unions and employees feel that persons equally situated will be guaranteed equal treatment in promotions, layoffs, discipline actions, and meeting technological change; and only if such rules exist can the union in most situations influence substantially the handling of people and maintain its own status as a significant organization capable of exerting effective pressure on managerial decision making.

The type of rules developed in a particular industry or shop reflects the problems encountered there. The industrial pattern—including the extent of product competition, the character of the labor market, the degree of union and nonunion competition, the rate of technological change, and a host of other socioeconomic factors—determines particular union policies. What one union finds suitable in a particular situation, another in a different locale will reject as unworkable. Union policies are a function of their environment. Hence we find a wide variety of policies pursued by various unions.

Union Security

A primary aim of most unions is "union security," and this usually involves some form of compulsory union membership and automatic dues checkoff. Whether a union will demand a "closed shop" (under which employees must join the union as a prerequisite to employment) or a "union shop" (under which the employer may hire anyone he chooses, but after a probationary period of 30–90 days all employees must join the union as a condition of employment) will vary with the type of employment and labor market. In general, the closed shop is found among skilled and strategically located trades and in industries in which employment is casual and intermittent. The closed shop differs from the union shop primarily in that it is not only a means of "union security" but also a method of controlling entrance to the job or trade. Other forms of union security, including methods of "checking off" dues and thus assuring unions of a flow of funds, are described in Table 6–1. Approximately 85% of the more than 20 million persons covered by collective bargaining agreements in private industry work under some form of union security provisions.

In early America, the closed or union shop became a necessary weapon for union survival. Only with such protection could the union count on effective protection from employer discrimination against union members. In many cases the closed- and union-shop provisions were necessary to induce workers to join the union both because of their reluctance to join and their fear of employer retaliation if they did join.

Theoretically, the passage of the National Labor Relations (Wagner) Act in 1935 eliminated much of the need for union security by outlawing employer discrimination against workers because of union membership and by requiring employers to bargain with duly certified unions. Nevertheless, union security demands lost none of their intensity. This was true

TABLE 6–1

Types of Union Security and Checkoff

Union Security Terms	Checkoff Terms
Closed Shop—Employer agrees that all workers must belong to the union to keep their jobs. He further agrees that when hiring new workers he will hire only members of the union.	*Voluntary Irrevocable*—Employer agrees to deduct union dues and other money from the worker's wages only if the worker signs a form authorizing him to do so. This generally requires that the worker's authorization shall not be irrevocable for more than one year or beyond the termination date of the contract, whichever is sooner.
Union Shop—Employer agrees that all workers must belong to the union to keep their jobs. He can hire whom he wants; but the workers he hires must join the union within a specified time (usually 30 days) or lose their jobs.	*Year-to-Year Renewal*—Employer agrees to deduct dues and other money from the worker's wages if the worker signs a checkoff authorization. If the worker does not revoke his authorization at the end of a year or at the contract termination date, it goes into effect for another year.
Modified Union Shop—Employer agrees that all present and future members of the union must remain in the union for the duration of the contract in order to keep their jobs. (Present workers who are not in the union and who do not join the union in the future can keep their jobs without union membership.) The employer further agrees that all new employees must join the union within a specified time (usually 30 days) or lose their jobs.	*Voluntary Revocable*—Employer agrees to deduct union dues and other money from the worker's wages if the worker signs a form authorizing him to do so. The worker can revoke this authorization any time he see fit.
Agency Shop—The employer and the union agree that a worker shall not be forced to join or stay in the union to keep his job. The worker has the choice of joining or not joining. But if he elects not to join he must pay to the union a sum equal to union dues. This sum represents a fee charged him by the union for acting as his agent in collective bargaining and in policing the union contract.	*Automatic*—Employer agrees to deduct dues and other money from the worker's wages automatically and to turn the money over to the union.
Maintenance of Membership—Employer agrees that all present and future members of the union must remain in the union for the duration of the contract in order to keep their jobs. (Workers who are not in the union and who do not join the union in the future can keep their jobs without union membership.)	*Involuntary Irrevocable*—The employer agrees that to secure and keep his job a worker must sign a form authorizing the employer to deduct union dues and other money from his wages.
Revocable Maintenance of Membership—Employer agrees that all present and future members of the union must remain in the union to keep their jobs. But he specifies that workers can leave the union during specified periods (usually 10 days at the end of each year) without losing their jobs.	
Preferential Hiring—Employer agrees that in hiring new workers he shall give preference to union members.	

Source: J. J. Bambrick, *Union Security and Checkoff Provisions,* Studies in Personnel Policy, No. 127 (New York: National Industrial Conference Board, 1952). Mr. Bambrick's definitions have stood the test of time and remain current.

partly because union leaders and members believed, often with considerable justification, that employers were opposed to unions and could circumvent the law; partly because, emotionally, they could not imagine successful unionism without the closed or union shop; and partly because of the rise of rival unionism on a scale theretofore unknown. The existence of a union security provision deters raiding by rival unions and thus gives unions "security" from another angle. The merger of the AFL and the CIO in 1955 further outmoded this union argument in favor of security needs.

Like union arguments in favor of union security, which attempt to couch the issue in terms of the survival of collective bargaining, employer arguments against compulsory unionism are usually set forth in highly emotional language—that is, in terms of individual liberty, the "right to work," or "freedom from domination by union bosses." In actual fact, there are very real power issues involved; power of a union in relation to its members and power of a union in bargaining with management. These are vital concerns of both labor and management.

Power over Members

That the union security issue is concerned with union coercive power over its members seems undeniable. Power over the members involves, of course, the right of a union to fine, discipline, or effectuate the discharge of a member for the violation of union rules or conduct, or for the completely indefensible reasons of opposing, antagonizing, or otherwise offending the union leaders. Students of labor relations have always recognized that a union must have some authority over its members, particularly when a majority has taken a legitimate position in favor of a legitimate objective. Otherwise, anarchy in industrial relations could result. For example, few disagree with the right of a majority to accept a settlement offered by an employer, or to reject the settlement and to choose a strike. But should a union have the power to fine or to discipline a member who crosses a picket line and returns to work during a strike, and thus makes the achievement of the strike goal more difficult for the majority? Should union officials have the authority to spend union dues for political purposes, including the dues of members who oppose the union-endorsed candidate or policies? Should compulsory membership be waived on religious or other conscientious grounds? The courts have ruled in favor of the union position in the fines and religious issues, and in favor of the individual in the political issue, but such problems are far from settled.[2]

---

[2] *National Labor Relations Board* v. *Allis-Chalmers Mfg. Co.*, 388 U.S. 175 (1967), in regard to fines for crossing picket lines. For the requirement that dues may not be used for political purposes if the employee objects, see *International Ass'n of Machinists* v. *Street*, 367 U.S. 740 (1961). On the religious issue, the question of whether compulsory unionism is violative of provisions of the Civil Rights Act of 1964, as amended, is as yet not clear from various court decisions.

The Taft-Hartley Act of 1947 outlawed the closed shop, placed restrictions on other forms of union security, and expressly permitted the states to legislate in this field, regardless of federal law. Once a union security provision was legally negotiated, the union was not restricted in its admission or disciplinary action, but the union could require the discharge of an employee pursuant to a legal union security provision only on the ground that the employee had failed to tender the regularly required initiation fee or dues.

Discharges and Checkoff

Expelling a worker from a union for nonfiscal reasons, or for declining to pay a special fine or assessment, cannot thus expel him from his job unless an employer conspires with a union to violate the Taft-Hartley Act. Undoubtedly, this happens when the parties mutually agree to rid themselves of a "troublemaker." Nevertheless, the existence of this provision has restrained arbitrary union discipline of members, and especially arbitrary union-inspired discharge of members.[3]

The Taft-Hartley Act in this respect did not attempt to protect a person's right to belong to a union. It protected the person's right to remain on the job under a union-shop provision as long as he tendered his regular union dues. The sections of the Landrum-Griffin Act dealing with individual union rights, which are discussed in Chapter 20, added protection to the individual against arbitrary expulsion from the union.

Closely allied to this union security restriction in the Taft-Hartley Act was the act's ban on the compulsory checkoff. The checkoff of membership dues was made lawful only where individual employees execute a written assignment of wages for not longer than one year, or for the duration of the applicable union contract, whichever is shorter. In general practice, such assignments are in effect until revoked. But it is now unlawful for an employer and a union to agree to turn over a portion of an employee's wages to a union without that employee's express written permission—certainly a highly defensible public policy.

Ban on Closed Shop

The Taft-Hartley Act outlawed the closed shop (see Table 6–1 for definitions) and other forms of preemployment preferential treatment of union members. The writers of the act were impressed with the fact that unreasonable denial of work had occurred as a result of union control of hiring, and this they were determined to eliminate.

---

[3] There is still considerable use of union security provision to deny job opportunities, but much less than before Taft-Hartley became law. See, for example, Mack A. Moore, "The Conflict between Union Discipline and Union Security," *Labor Law Journal*, vol. 18 (February 1967), pp. 116–23.

There is general agreement, however, that this provision tended largely to drive the closed shop underground instead of out of existence. We shall examine in following sections of this chapter why control of hiring through the closed shop is so vital to unions in the building, maritime, and other trades where employment is intermittent. In Chapter 3, we also noted how the closed shop is used to bar persons deemed unacceptable to union members—for example, to discriminate against minorities. There is no question that unions in the building trades, for example, have used the power inherent in closed-shop agreements to deny blacks job opportunities.

Despite the obviously discriminatory activities of the building-trades unions, Congress in 1959, while enacting the Landrum-Griffin Act to promote union democracy, actually loosened Taft-Hartley restrictions applying to the construction industry. It legalized "prehire" agreements (that is, arrangements to employ union personnel before a job starts). Such agreements may now make union membership compulsory 7 days after employment (rather than 30 days, as is the Taft-Hartley requirement in other industries), provided that the state law permits union security provisions. Construction union contracts also can require an employer to notify the union of job opportunities and to give the union an opportunity to refer qualified applicants for employment, and can specify minimum training or experience qualifications for employment. The net effect of these provisions was to restore a considerable amount of legality to the actual practices of the construction industry. Then, five years later, in 1964, Congress enacted the Civil Rights Act, Title VII of which forbids discrimination by unions or employers on grounds of race, color, creed, or sex. The net effect has been a flood of lawsuits aimed at unions and contractors in the building industry, and massive federal programs aimed at forcing unions and companies in this industry to open up jobs for blacks and to cease using the closed shop as a device for racial discrimination.

"Right-to-Work" Laws and the Union-Management Power Relationship

In the long run, the most significant provision of Taft-Hartley relating to union security is probably Section 14(b), which provides that "Nothing in this Act shall be construed as authorizing the execution or application of agreements requiring membership in a labor organization as a condition of employment in any State or Territory in which such execution or application is prohibited by State or Territorial Law." This provision ran counter to the usual principle that state laws are superseded by federal legislation on the same subject matter.

Thus, the clear purpose of Section 14(b) was to give states the right to legislate in this field; and 20 have, outlawing union security provisions altogether.[4]

Because of the emotional content of the arguments pro and con on the union security issue, and hence right-to-work laws, some observers have expressed the belief that the issue itself is largely symbolic and political rather than economic and significant in the union-management relationship. In fact, however, the absence of compulsory membership usually results in a loss of union membership varying from 10% to 40%. This deprives the union of considerable numerical strength and financial support—enough to affect a power balance, to pay considerable strike benefits, or to employ a squad of union organizers. Such effects seem considerably more than symbolic.

THE CONTROL OF ENTRANCE TO THE TRADE

Attempts to control entrance to the trade are limited largely to craft unions. Except for a few industrial unions, such as the United Mine Workers, which have been able to utilize license laws in some areas, industrial unions do not find it feasible to control entrance. Their members learn their tasks by experience. The unions permit the employer to recruit the work force, and union control is exerted in other ways.

Craft unions, however, have found that control of entrance is an effective method of increasing their bargaining power. Their efforts to achieve such control take two principal forms: regulation of apprenticeship and support of licensing legislation.

The Regulation of Apprenticeship

Apprenticeship is a way by which young persons who meet certain standards of age, education, and aptitude can learn a trade by working at it under close supervision. Apprentices usually combine such practical learning with appropriately related part-time schooling. Nearly all unions whose membership includes journeymen, for whom apprenticeship is customary, attempt to regulate the terms and conditions under which apprentices are employed. From a pre–World War II figure of 17,300, the number of apprentices grew to a high of 230,283 in 1950, then declined steadily before turning upward in the mid-1960s. As a result of a continued boom, especially in construction, and great pressure and activity to increase the representation of minorities in trades requiring apprenticeship, the number of apprentices rose to an all-time high of nearly 400,000 in 1974. Since then, particularly because of the recession

---

[4] Alabama, Arizona, Arkansas, Florida, Georgia, Iowa, Kansas, Louisiana, Mississippi, Nebraska, Nevada, North Carolina, North Dakota, South Carolina, South Dakota, Tennessee, Texas, Utah, Virginia, and Wyoming. Indiana, which had such a law, repealed it.

in construction, the number has declined somewhat. Table 6–2 gives the relevant figures for 1964 and 1974.

Apprenticeship is only one of the many ways in which a vocational aptitude may be gained. In most occupations, training is acquired on the job, in trade or vocational schools, in the Armed Forces, or in federal or state training courses, or principally, by "picking up the trade"—that is, working with journeymen on a variety of jobs until proficiency is achieved. Only about one fourth of all unions actually participate in apprenticeship regulation. Moreover, most employees who do work in apprenticeable trades have learned their trade without having served

TABLE 6–2
Growth of Apprenticeship in the United States

Number of Apprentices	During 1964	During 1974	Change over the Decade	
			Number	Per-cent
Apprenticeship trades and crafts	250*	415	165	66.0
Registered apprenticeship programs†	13,000	22,000	9,000	69.2
Registered apprentices	223,000	394,000	171,000	76.7
Apprentices completing	26,000	46,000	20,000	76.9
Minorities	4,500*	62,000	57,500	1,277.8
(blacks)	(3,300)*	(32,000)	28,700	869.7
Women	400*	3,700	3,300	825.0
Veterans	78,000*	130,735	52,735	67.6
In building/construction trades	145,000	247,000	102,000	70.3
In metalworking trades	35,000	41,000	6,000	17.1
In graphic arts trades	14,000	13,000	−1,000	−7.1
In personal services trades	2,800	17,000	14,200	507.1
In miscellaneous trades	25,200	76,000	50,800	201.6
Total U.S. civilian labor force	73,091,000	91,011,000	17,920,000	24.5

* Estimated.
† Federally serviced programs only. Does not include state-serviced programs.
  Source: U.S. Department of Labor, Bureau of Apprenticeship and Training; and U.S. Department of Labor, Bureau of Labor Statistics.

an apprenticeship. Thus, studies have estimated that as many as 80% of all carpenters and 30% of all electricians became journeymen without serving apprenticeships.[5] These studies also show that it is more difficult to become a journeyman in the electrical, mechanical, and plumbing trades without formal training than in the carpentry, painting, and trowel trades (bricklaying, cement finishing, and so on).

Nonunion builders have recently begun to establish apprentice pro-

---

[5] See, for example, Howard G. Foster, "Nonapprentice Sources of Training in Construction," *Monthly Labor Review*, vol. 43 (February 1970), pp. 21–26.

grams, and since 1970 they have received the cooperation of the U.S. Department of Labor in so doing. These builders have also initiated a number of innovative training programs which effectively train journeymen much more rapidly than do typical apprentice progams. The basic training method of open shop construction remains, however, on-the-job training, and the number of formal training programs is much higher in construction firms dealing with unions.[6]

Unions control apprenticeship by a variety of regulatory devices. One is to establish qualifications which are both artificially high and subjective. Requirements that applicants be high school graduates, age 17–25, proficient in mathematics, and able to pass exacting tests, have a legitimacy for the advanced mechanical trades but not for the less exacting ones. Indeed, those who can qualify under such rules usually prefer a college education instead of apprentice training. Even if a prospective candidate meets these requirements, he may be subject to interviews which rate him on purely subjective grounds. Opportunities for racial discrimination or for exclusion merely to maintain union craft monopolies are thus present.

Another common method of regulating apprenticeship is to control the proportion of apprentices to journeymen. This protects journeymen against any tendency on the part of employers to displace journeymen with apprentices. Agreements in the building or printing trades normally contain provisions for the employment of one apprentice to every four to eight journeymen. In addition, many unions negotiate agreements which place an absolute limit on the number of apprentices who may be hired.

The number of apprentices can also be controlled by setting apprentice wages at artificially high levels. Thus, a theoretically liberal apprentice-journeyman ratio may be nullified by setting the wages of apprentices so close to those of journeymen that it pays to employ only the latter.

Few unions require the serving of an apprenticeship as a condition of membership. Perhaps more would do so if they completely controlled entrance to their trade. The fact of the matter is, however, that so many Americans either pick up a trade without formal training or have secured their training by other means that unions could not sustain a requirement that apprentice training be an absolute prerequisite to membership.

The reasonableness of union apprentice regulation varies from industry to industry. There has been considerable evidence in certain trades, including building and printing, that union apprentice regulations have been utilized to prevent newcomers from winning a place in the industry; and in other cases, such limitations have actually created artificial short-

---

[6] Herbert R. Northrup and Howard G. Foster, *Open Shop Construction*, Major Study No. 54 (Philadelphia: Industrial Research Unit, The Wharton School, University of Pennsylvania, 1975), chap. 10.

ages of labor. Moreover, in many of these trades, apprentice regulations have been utilized to confine apprentice training to friends or relatives of journeymen.

The exclusion of blacks from apprenticeship programs has been a serious matter because there are few other ways in which blacks can learn the trades requiring the training such programs provide. Not having friends and relatives in such trades, except in the southern trowel trades (bricklaying, plastering, and cement finishing), where there has been a tradition of black craftsmen since slavery days, blacks have been compelled to depend upon formal training if they desire to enter these trades. Informal training based on working with members of the family or friends, or otherwise picking up the trades, a common method of instruction, depends on contacts largely unavailable to blacks. Yet the formal plans in such fields as building construction have in practice been reserved for whites only, with very few exceptions until recently.

Because of this exclusion, combined with a shortage of craftsmen in many cities, the U.S. Department of Labor has instituted plans (termed "Philadelphia Plans" because the first one was instituted there) in key cities throughout the country which require that certain percentages of the work in key crafts be performed by black craftsmen. In addition, where government funds are involved, these plans provide for "learner" and "advanced learner" categories so that journeyman proficiency can be achieved in ways other than through formal apprenticeship.

In addition, the U.S. Department of Labor has funded numerous "Apprentice Outreach Programs" in conjunction with the National Urban League and other organizations. Although these programs have had only limited success, they have contributed substantially to the increased amount of minority participation in apprentice programs, as shown in Table 6–2.[7]

Unions perform some definite service in regard to apprentice training. The existence of a strong union prevents an employer from keeping an apprentice on a task that he has already mastered instead of giving him a well-rounded training. The temptation for employers to confine apprentices to a small section of the mechanic's job is very great, for in such cases they are receiving work of mechanic's quality for apprenticeship wages.

On the other hand, union apprenticeship terms are often obsolete. It is highly doubtful whether three to five years are needed to learn many of the building crafts which require apprenticeships of that duration. The

---

[7] See Richard L. Rowan and Lester Rubin, *Opening the Skilled Construction Trades to Blacks: A Study of the Washington and Indianapolis Plans for Minority Employment*, Labor Relations and Public Policy Series, Report No. 7 (Philadelphia: Industrial Research Unit, The Wharton School, University of Pennsylvania, 1972); and Stephen A. Schneider, "The Apprentice Outreach Program," in Charles R. Perry et al., *The Impact of Government Manpower Programs, in General, and on Minorities and Women*, Manpower and Human Resources Studies, No. 4 (Philadelphia: Industrial Research Unit, The Wharton School, University of Pennsylvania, 1975), chap. 10.

duration could be shortened, but unions fear to do this because their rules and restrictions are based on the number who can be expected to become journeymen after long apprenticeships. Any reduction in the length of apprenticeship would probably be accompanied by a reduction in the percentage of apprentices permitted in union agreements.

Apprentice training as a whole is not likely to be a very efficient method of providing qualified labor when it is needed. Typically, during periods of depression, no apprentices are trained, so that in the periods of prosperity that follow, there is a great shortage of skilled labor. Then in the prosperity period the number of apprentices being trained increases tremendously. By the time some of these apprentices become qualified journeymen, business conditions and opportunities for employment have worsened. Unfortunately, the Bureau of Apprenticeship and Training in the U.S. Department of Labor works very closely with the building-trades unions and is thoroughly committed to the present apprenticeship system.

Licensing Legislation

The great interest of recent years in breaking down barriers to the employment of the disadvantaged and in integrating blacks into all segments of the labor force and society has focused attention on the manpower implications of licensing legislation. Such legislation by states or municipalities has been utilized by many groups in society to limit entrance to occupations, professions, and even trades. Union groups which sponsor such laws include plumbers, electricians, barbers, taxi drivers, and many others. Generally, these groups work closely with employer counterparts, and the laws governing licensing gives unions and employer associations prominent places in their administration. Ostensibly, such laws are enacted in the interest of the safety of the consumer. Actually their real purpose from a union point of view is to limit entry into the trade and to increase union bargaining power by making it more difficult for employers to employ strikebreakers.

Several careful studies of licensing legislation have been made.[8] They indicate that licensing laws are frequently abused and that their value to the consumer varies considerably. For example, such laws may be used as a vehicle for race discrimination, or to restrict artificially the number of qualified mechanics.

---

[8] Among the most important are Benjamin Shimberg et al., *Occupational Licensing: Practices and Policies* (Washington, D.C.: Public Affairs Press, 1973). Note also "Restrictive Licensing of Dental Paraprofessionals," *Yale Law Journal*, vol. 82 (March 1974), pp. 806–26; Elton Rayack, *Professional Power and American Medicine* (Cleveland: World Publishing Co., 1967); F. M. Fletcher, *Market Restraints in the Retail Drug Industry*, Industrial Research Unit Major Study No. 43 (Philadelphia: University of Pennsylvania Press, 1967); and U.S. Department of Health, Education, and Welfare, *State Licensing of Health Occupations*, Public Health Service Publication No. 1758 (Washington, D.C.: Government Printing Office, 1967).

The problem of licensing legislation extends beyond unions. The medical, legal, dental, and other professions which advocate licensing legislation have encountered the same problems. Studies of the practices of physicians and pharmacists indicate that there is considerable use of licensing laws to limit competition and to monopolize services and markets. Licensing laws which are sold to the public as a means of protecting the consumer are easily perverted into tools for enhancing restrictive practices or furthering monopoly control.

CONTROL OF HIRING

In an unorganized labor market the employer controls both hiring and layoffs. When a union enters the picture, it must secure some voice in at least one of these vital matters. Otherwise, the union can be of little service to members who fear discrimination because of union membership or who want hirings and/or layoffs conducted by rules rather than by employer fiat.

Methods of Controlling Hiring

The most common method of controlling hiring is by means of the closed shop, requiring employers to hire only members of the union or, if no union members are available, persons willing to join the union. Some agreements go farther by requiring the employer to hire only through the union office or through a hiring hall which may be controlled by the union, by the union and the employer in cooperation, or by a third body, for example, a government bureau.

Control over layoffs often involves indirect control over hiring, especially if, as on the railroads, employment is declining on a secular basis. In the railroad industry the seniority agreements provide for preference for furloughed workers in rehiring in the order of the furloughed persons' seniority, that is, length of service with the company. If there is a large pool of furloughed workers, the employer's freedom to hire is restricted almost as severely under this type of seniority agreement as under the closed shop.

As in the case of control over entrance to the trade, control over hiring is practiced mainly by the craft unions. The main exceptions involve, first, such control over hiring as results from control over layoffs (for example, seniority provisions); and, second, control over hiring by industrial unions in industries where employment is casual and intermittent or seasonal, as in the maritime or needle trades. Most other unions do not operate in labor markets which permit them to exert control over hiring. Hence, except indirectly through seniority provisions, most industrial unions concentrate on control of layoffs and do not attempt to restrict employer control of hiring.

Hiring Halls

It is quite common in many industries where the average employer is small and the unions are organized on a craft basis for the employer to hire through the union office. Sometimes, this custom arose more as a convenience to employers who wanted a central hiring office than as a means of union control. Generally, however, it resulted from union demands, provoked by special market conditions. In trades or industries where employment is intermittent or casual—for example, building or maritime—hiring through the union is the only method by which the union can secure an equal division of work for its membership and can put an end to systems whereby a small portion of the membership secures the bulk of the available work.

Although unions may demand that employers hire through them in order to avoid abuses, the net effect may be the substitution of new abuses for old. For example, in the building trades the business agent has frequently substituted his favoritism for that of the contracting foreman. The opportunities to use job dispensations as a means of building up one's personal political machine within the union are immense, and the temptation is frequently succumbed to. In order to protect themselves against such methods, the rank and file of many unions may require officials to rotate jobs on a first-come, first-served basis. This, however, can place a heavy burden both on employers and on the most efficient workers. It severely restricts the right of employers to choose workers whom they deem competent. And since, especially in the building trades, where the unions do not control layoffs, the least efficient are the first fired and thus the first in line for new jobs, the efficient workers are at a disadvantage once they are laid off.[9]

Formal hiring halls are most common in the maritime industry. Because employment in this industry is casual, usually a larger labor force is attached to the industry than there are jobs at a given time. This has encouraged a host of antisocial hiring and racketeering practices at the expense of the workers, such as selling jobs, forcing employees to borrow money at exorbitant rates or to patronize retail establishments in which employers have an interest, and so on. Repeated exposures of these practices led the states of New York and New Jersey, in 1953, to establish a bistate waterfront commission to run hiring halls in the Port of New York. On the West Coast, such halls were established in 1934. They are formally under joint union-management control, but since the dispatcher is a union man, the union is the dominant factor in their control. Most seamen's unions also operate hiring halls.

---

[9] For discussions of the pros and cons of union-controlled hiring halls, see Philip Ross, "Origin of the Hiring Hall in Construction," *Industrial Relations*, vol. 11 (October 1972), pp. 366–79; and Northrup and Foster, *Open Shop Construction*, pp. 209–20.

Closed Unions and Hiring Halls

The union which is "closed"—that is, which will not admit new applicants to membership—is generally painted as antisocial. Like all generalizations in labor relations, this is not always so. In the maritime industry, some restriction of entry is actually desirable. One of the causes of favoritism and racketeering in hiring on the waterfront is the fact that, especially in depressed times, unemployed workers drift there, often attracted by the high hourly rates. If the "drifters" are granted free entry into the organization, the hiring hall becomes a vehicle for sharing poverty rather than work. The unions must therefore either refuse admission to newcomers or enforce some sort of seniority regulations which modify rotation schemes and give preference to the workers who have been attached to the industry longest. The former policy is more often pursued because the admission to membership of workers for whom there are no jobs provides a hard core of opposition to incumbent union officers. Moreover, the "unemployed brothers" are likely to congregate in the union hall and to be able to attend all meetings. They thus are in an excellent position to exert an influence on union policy that is out of proportion to their numbers.

THE CONTROL OF LAYOFFS

The interest of a union in layoff policy stems from two sources: the worker's desire to know where he stands—to know what chance he has of retaining his job in case of a reduction in the labor force—and the union's desire to maintain some control in the employment process, which it can do only by a voice either in hiring or in layoffs. Since, for reasons already noted, few unions can control hiring, most unions seek a strong voice in the procedure which governs layoffs. The most common method of handling layoffs is by seniority.

Seniority

Seniority agreements generally provide that employees in a plant or a subdivision thereof shall receive preference in layoffs and rehiring in the order in which they were hired. In some cases, as on the railroads, seniority agreements are quite rigid, the only requirement being ability to perform the job. In other cases, seniority provisions are much weaker, giving the employer the opportunity to select a more competent person over one with greater seniority. A few agreements provide for retention by the employer of a small percentage of personnel in slack times, regardless of seniority, so that the plant will be staffed by a key basic work force. Many agreements place the union shop steward or committeeman at the head of the seniority roster.

Seniority is most common in the railroad, automobile, iron, steel, rubber, electrical products, and other mass-production industries. In the mass-production industries the extent of the seniority district or unit varies considerably. Sometimes the seniority district is the plant, sometimes a plant division, or a department, or an occupation, or some combination thereof. In general, management prefers the smallest possible seniority districts, with no provisions for workers to hold seniority in more than one district. Under such regulations, layoffs and rehiring do not involve much dislocation in the plant and hence do not interfere materially with the efficient organization of personnel.

Union and employee preference as to the size of seniority districts varies considerably. In general, in times of unemployment, skilled workers prefer wide seniority districts and unskilled workers narrow ones. This is because skilled workers can replace unskilled ones, but not vice versa. Hence the wider the seniority district in times of layoffs, the greater the chance for the skilled worker to find a spot by exercising seniority, and the greater the chance that the unskilled worker will be pushed out of a job. In times of prosperity the opposite is likely to be true because expanding employment gives unskilled workers the opportunity to advance in the occupational hierarchy, and this they like to do without sacrificing their seniority in their former jobs. On the other hand, skilled workers see in expanding employment more competition for jobs when times become depressed. Hence they favor narrow seniority districts during prosperous periods.

Seniority and Race

A combination of narrow seniority districts and discriminatory employment practices has been used for many years in the southern pulp and paper and tobacco industries, as well as in the iron and steel industry in many parts of the country, to confine blacks to less desirable jobs in these industries. The seniority practices in these industries were not discriminatory per se. Rather, they were developed out of the needs of the industries. For example, in pulp and paper, a person worked his way up the paper machine hierarchy of jobs to the top job of machine tender. No one else in the plant could bid on any paper machine jobs except the lowest one, no matter how much plantwide seniority he had, unless he was in the paper machine line of progression. The nature of the top job requires long service on the machine. Blacks, however, were employed only for certain jobs, and seniority lines were perverted to deny them the right to bid on even bottom jobs in seniority lines. This led to the development of the "rightful place" doctrine, under which members of the "affected class"—that is, blacks employed before hiring became non-discriminatory—were permitted to advance on the basis of plantwide seniority, instead of occupational seniority, after they were placed in a progression line.[10]

Civil rights and seniority policies have clashed in other areas as well. In the steel industry, blacks were generally hired to do blast furnace work, and although they were permitted to work up to the top jobs in blast furnace departments, they were generally excluded from the rolling mills. The courts have put an end to this practice.[11] Moreover, the Steelworkers and the leading steel producers have signed a consent agreement with the government providing for payments to those discriminated against and for an end to all impediments to the progress of black workers.

The recession of the early 1970s caused a clash between union seniority provisions and company affirmative action plans providing for increased employment and upgrading of minorities. For the most part, the courts ruled that companies were required to follow seniority provisions and lay off the most junior employees although this meant disproportionate hardship to the more recently hired blacks.[12] The issue, however, has not yet been finally settled, and it could lead to a sharp clash between unions and civil rights groups.

In the automobile industry, seniority districts are very broad, since more than half of the jobs are semiskilled. It is easy for persons to move from job to job and for relatively unskilled personnel to master many of the operations. This is a significant reason why the automobile industry is perhaps the largest employer of blacks, who, as we have noted, are relatively less educated and less well represented in jobs requiring a high skill.

Other Effects of Seniority

The widespread use of seniority provisions in industrial relations has other salutary and unfortunate effects. The most important argument in favor of seniority is that it affords the worker knowledge of his position vis-à-vis his fellow workers. Although seniority is frequently confused with security, it should not be, since, if the plant in which the worker holds seniority ceases to operate, seniority is of little value. Moreover, for

---

[10] The key court cases setting forth this principle are *Quarles* v. *Philip Morris, Inc.*, 279 F. Supp. 505 (E.D.Va., 1968); and *U.S.* v. *Local 189, United Papermakers, et al.*, 282 F. Supp 39 (E.D.La., 1968); affirmed, 416 F.2d 980 (5th Cir., 1969); cert. denied, 397 U.S. 919 (1970). The impact of these cases is discussed in Herbert R. Northrup and Richard L. Rowan, *Negro Employment in Southern Industry*, Studies of Negro Employment, vol. IV, parts 1 and 3 (Philadelphia: Industrial Research Unit, The Wharton School, University of Pennsylvania, 1970).

[11] See, for example, *United States* v. *Bethlehem Steel Corp.*, 312 F. Supp. 977 (W.D.N.Y., 1970); 446 F.2d 652 (2d Cir., 1971).

[12] See, for example, *Jersey Central Power & Light Co.* v. *IBEW*, 508 F.2d 687 (3d Cir., 1975).

every worker whom seniority retains on the payroll, another must be discharged. Seniority, however, is an impersonal criterion and rules out the favoritism workers fear so much. And it does have a sort of rough justice, since it gives preference to those who have worked the longest and who presumably have the greatest equity in their jobs.

On the other hand, seniority can put a premium on mediocrity. The person who is least willing and able to take advantage of opportunities in other plants, or who has the least ability and therefore does not receive such opportunities, is the one who stands the greatest chance of reaching the top of a seniority roster. For those who like to get ahead by standing still, seniority is a godsend. For those who yearn for the opportunity to advance quickly on merit, seniority is a bane.

In some instances, seniority may improve managerial efficiency. The fact that employers may no longer discharge workers at will forces them to improve their selection and training facilities. Moreover, union controls prevent the degrading practice of buying favors from foremen and other such favoritism on the job. From the community point of view, seniority gives the not-quite-so-efficient worker an opportunity to improve instead of being cast out or passed over in promotions. It also protects the older worker from being laid off in times of slack employment.

Seniority causes many internal union problems. For example, there is frequently dispute over what constitutes length of service. Occasionally, service is interrupted for one reason or another, and a wide divergence of opinion is likely to arise both between employer and union and among employees as to whether breaks in seniority for one or another reason should be overlooked. Internal union disputes over seniority provisions and their interpretation have resulted in lengthy and costly litigation.

Seniority provisions have an effect on strikes. Generally, senior employees are less willing to strike because they have more to lose. Once on strike, senior employees are likely to be apprehensive at the slightest hint that their jobs are being filled. Junior employees are usually more willing to strike but may be tempted to return to work in order to leap from the bottom to the top of the seniority roster. Once employees return to work, strikes may drag on over the issue of whether the strikebreakers can maintain their place on the seniority roster.

Juniority

Pay to employees who are not working has now reached a stage in some industries where it literally almost pays not to work. In the rubber tire, farm equipment, and automobile industries, for example, the differential which a worker receives for working (that is, wages less paycheck deductions) as compared with what a laid-off employee gets from state unemployment compensation plus supplemental unemployment pay can amount to as little as $10 to $25 per week. In view of this fact, some agreements in these industries permit a senior employee to take a layoff instead of working where the layoff is involuntary and the senior employee's job is directly affected. Thus, the junior employee stays on the job, the senior employee takes leisure with pay. This is the first recognition in union contracts that layoffs may be preferable to working and that the penalty for juniority may be a requirement to stay on the job. At one rubber company, nearly every senior employee involved has taken the layoff instead of accepting a lower rated job. They can accumulate seniority for two years on layoff, which permits some to reach retirement age. Management considers such juniority an advantage because it eliminates multiple bumping and the high costs of retraining and lost production associated with wide shifts in personnel throughout the plant.

Division of Work

Division of work was once much more widely utilized as a layoff control than it is today. The reason is the combination effect of higher layoff benefits and higher paycheck withholding. Division of work can reduce take-home pay very close to the level of benefits paid under state unemployment compensation systems. When supplemental unemployment benefits are added to state benefits, as in the automobile and steel industries, take-home pay under a division-of-work system can even be less than the benefits for not working. Since division of work is also usually less efficient than laying off unnecessary men, it now has little popularity except in special situations, such as in the seasonal garment industry.

There is, however, one situation in the automobile industry where a form of division of work is used and combined with a special form of unemployment pay. Instead of laying off assembly-line workers, companies now often put their labor force on two- or three-day weeks. Employees then receive "short-week pay" to make up some of the lost pay. Manufacturers prefer this because they do not have to slow up the line and reassign each and every job that is left. If, however, business does not improve in time, then layoffs are made and jobs restructured accordingly.

In Europe, division of work, or "short time," is widely used in times of low employment. In such cases, the government pays the difference between the worker's regular wage and what he or she receives for the shorter hours. In Japan, large companies maintain payrolls in depressed time if at all possible, assigning workers to makeup work of various types. Workers in Japan, however, are retired at age 55 with lump-sum payments that provide far less than does the pension of the typical American worker. Thus, lifetime employment there ends at an early retirement age.

Lifetime Security

In 1977, the United Steelworkers developed a proposal for a "lifetime guarantee" of work: essentially, this involves an extension of supplemental unemployment benefits to provide payments for laid-off workers until an early retirement date. Since most senior employees do not suffer unemployment, such a program's cost is highly dependent upon the number of years of seniority that are required for eligibility. Moreover, if requirements for seeking employment are not included, workers involved in a plant closure could be paid many years for not working— an expensive proposition indeed. If this proposal spreads, then labor will become a fixed cost, and this could have a pronounced effect upon the ability of American industry to compete in the world market.

Dismissal Wages

Dismissal compensation is fundamentally a device to mitigate losses resulting from permanent dismissal rather than temporary layoffs. It is utilized in instances in which employees are severed from the payroll as a result of plant abandonment or movement to another area, or as a result of a permanent decrease in the working force. In cases of permanent severance of employees who are near, but have not achieved, the retirement age, a dismissal wage may be used to make up earnings until the employee reaches the age at which he or she is eligible for a pension. Dismissal pay usually provides a schedule of payments based upon length of service. It is very common in the newspaper industry, which has seen many concerns go out of business in recent years. It is also widely used in defense-oriented industries, where heavy layoffs resulting from changes in governmental procurement policies are common. In many other industries, companies and unions have negotiated a dismissal pay schedule after the decision has been made to go out of business or to close a plant.

PROTECTING AGAINST LAYOFFS

Seniority, division of work, and dismissal wages are all means to mitigate the effects of layoffs. But unions also strive to protect their members against layoffs. Among the methods utilized to do this are provisions for retraining, limiting of contracting-out, and "make-work" or "featherbedding" restrictions.

Retraining

Widespread displacement of blue-collar employees in the mass-production industries during the late 1950s generated considerable interest in retraining by industry, unions, and government. The federal government began a program in 1961. Vocational education by government is not new, but the Manpower Development and Training Act of 1962 marked a broader entry into the training and retraining field which was especially aimed at the unemployed and which more recently has been designed to help "disadvantaged" persons, particularly blacks and members of other minority groups, obtain jobs in industry. Other programs have been designed to assist those already employed to qualify, through basic education and/or training for upgrading. These programs are examined in detail in Chapter 15.

From the union point of view, interest in training already displaced workers or those never employed is secondary to attempting to gain retraining for those still on the job but threatened by displacement. In the last decade, the authors have observed an increasing union interest in provisions designed to give training (often at employer expense) to employees to qualify them for new opportunities. In addition, many of the larger companies give employees opportunities to take appropriate training on their own time and at their own expense. If the pace of technological change continues, one may expect a rising interest in such retraining, and perhaps it may become a major focus of union demands in some industries.

Another union proposal—the training of blue-collar personnel for white-collar jobs—meets with more employer resistance. Many blue-collar workers do advance to white-collar jobs. But industry is likely to go slowly to advance union-oriented factory workers to its as yet largely unorganized office work force.

Contracting-Out and Part-Time Work

Few issues in recent years have generated more heat between companies and unions, and among the unions themselves, than has the contracting-out of work. Most manufacturing enterprises do not make everything they assemble. They "contract out" or buy parts from various suppliers. In turn, such companies may make parts for other companies if they have capacity in some departments. The reasons for this are manifold, but basically they fall into two categories: (1) The ability to make parts or items better and cheaper varies among companies; therefore, it is often not good business for a concern to make all of its parts. (2) Some parts or components are not required in sufficient volume to make it profitable for a company to tool up, purchase equipment, or employ or train labor in order to make them itself. And of course, much contracting-out takes place because firms often find parts companies that have lower labor costs and can do the job for less.

From time to time, also, the ability to make parts varies. Capacity might be reached, thus forcing a company to contract out work in order to meet delivery dates. When orders decline, work previously contracted out may be done within the company. Loading and manning factors also may force contracting-out. For example, one department may be overloaded while another is short of work. Yet the short-of-work department may not have the skills or equipment to aid the overloaded one.

In recent years, there has been an increase in another type of contracting-out—that of such services as typing and secretarial work, janitorial tasks, plant guarding, even engineering work, and in some chemical and petroleum concerns, all maintenance work. Companies have found that it is cheaper to pay an agency to supply temporary office help in order to meet peak loads than it is to have employees on the payroll who cannot be kept busy. High wages and fringe benefits have raised the costs of employing guards and janitors to a point where it is economic to contract out such work.

Companies supplying contract labor have had no difficulty in finding workers who desire this type of employment. Temporary employees are the fastest growing segment of the labor force, with almost 10 million persons so occupied. The married woman who wants to work only a few days a week, or a few hours a day while her children are in school, the teacher or fireman who "moonlights" during off-hours for more income, the student putting himself through college, all swell the part-time labor force. Unions in industrial plants are opposed both to contracting-out and to using part-time labor. Being responsive to fears of the people in the plant that contracting-out costs them jobs, and finding that part-timers have little interest in becoming union members or dues payers, unions have naturally put pressure on management to restrict these practices. Some of these restrictions are very tight and deny essential managerial flexibility required to maintain delivery schedules or profitable operations. Other clauses simply require management to notify unions why contracting-out is necessary. Many managements do this anyway, in order to allay fears and otherwise avoid controversy or support for restrictive union demands. The National Labor Relations Board now requires that management bargain at least on the impact of such contracting-out on employees; such decisions can also be subject to arbitration under the contract unless the agreement contains a specific disclaimer to the contrary.

The building-trades unions, in contrast to those in industrial plants, not only are unopposed to contracting-out or to the use of temporary help, but enthusiastically support such measures as a means of furthering the employment of their members. The building-trades unions have worked with a number of contractors to promote the idea of having all maintenance work done by contract labor, and this policy has been adopted by a large number of petroleum and chemical firms. The companies using contract maintenance have been well satisfied with it and believe that it provides a sound solution to their needs for a varying number of maintenance employees at different times. The industrial unions, of course, regard contract maintenance as an invasion of their jurisdiction and as a method of denying work to their members. Because of such opposition, contract maintenance is most likely to be found in new or unorganized plants in the future.

"MAKE-WORK" OR "FEATHERBEDDING"

The insecurity of the worker in modern industry has led employees to "make work" by adopting a variety of policies. These make-work or "featherbedding" arrangements often exist among unorganized as well as organized employees, but the entrance of a union can have the effect of formalizing and strengthening them.

Restrictions on Output

Restrictions on output, direct or indirect, are the most common make-work practice. Formal restrictions are not very common in industry, although reference to them sometimes occurs in union literature or even in collective bargaining contracts. Usually, however, the restrictions are disguised as health protective devices or, more likely, simply based on a tacit understanding among employees. Restrictions, both formal and informal, are more often found under incentive than daywork systems because workers often fear that a "world-beater" among them will earn so much that he or she will force the more average employees either to quit or to work at an exhausting pace.

Restrictions on output and other forms of make-work policies are also the result of fear on the part of employees that they will work themselves out of a job. Most employees believe that there is a given amount of work and that by stretching it out, each employee will receive more. This notion is, of course, fallacious. If employees restrict production, the result is higher costs and higher prices; consumers buy less of the product; and in the end, employment opportunities are diminished. In industries such as building construction, however, the individual worker may stretch out his or her immediate employment by slowing down on the job, even though the long-run effect of the slowdown may well be less work because of resultant high costs.

Limits set on output are usually enforced by social pressure rather than by union rule. True, workers have sometimes been fined for getting out too much work. More often, whether the plant is unionized or not, the speed for work deemed appropriate by the majority is enforced by their refusing to engage in social relationships with other workers who "speed up." The latter, finding themselves outcasts from the groups to which they belong, are likely to conform to the "social output" very quickly.

Limits on output frequently become obsolete as machinery improves and worker efficiency rises. As time passes, such restrictions are often self-defeating. The result may be either loss of membership in the union or inability to organize nonunion shops because the lack of restrictions in the latter establishments can permit the earnings of nonunion employees to rise above the earnings of union employees. Since the national union leadership is likely to be more interested in organizing nonunion shops than is the local union leadership, severe restrictions on output favored by locals are often vigorously opposed by national unions.

Restrictions on output may be effected by indirect methods. Thus, instead of setting a quota, workers may achieve the same results by retarding the speed of performance—for example, by limiting the number of machines an employee may tend or, as in the case of the Painters' Union, limiting the width of the brush or the size of the roller.

Restrictions on output may also be achieved by excessive safety or quality controls. When bus drivers want to slow down, they observe all safety regulations. The result is to put buses an average of 30 minutes behind schedule on moderately long runs.

The 1971 federal Occupational Safety and Health Act provides numerous opportunities for utilizing safety as a means of restricting output or pressuring management. Complaints can be made to the U.S. Department of Labor, and whether they are real or contrived, the complaints must be investigated and sometimes production may be slowed or halted —as will be discussed in Chapter 17. The construction unions have adopted numerous rules in the name of safety which are in fact featherbedding devices. Instances exist in which an operating engineer is paid $300–$400 per week for starting and stopping two or three gasoline engines smaller than those on most home lawn mowers; or in which union electricians must be on hand where temporary lights are used. They are paid $8 to $12 an hour, around the clock, to watch the lights burn.[13]

Unnecessary Work and Unnecessary Employees

Some of the most obvious featherbedding results from union requirements that unnecessary work be done, that work be done by time-consuming methods, or that unnecessary employees be hired. The building, amusement, and railroad industries are characterized by a good deal of such union policies. For example, it is standard practice for the Plumbers' Union to require that pipes be threaded on the job, even though it is far more economical to do the threading in the shop. The International Typographical Union requires that when plates or papier-mâché matrices are exchanged, as they frequently are, the matter be reset, read, and corrected within a stipulated period, and that proof be submitted to the union chairman in the office. The Meat Cutters often require that prewrapped meat be rewrapped on the job. In 1968, the Brotherhood of Railroad Trainmen demanded that railroads eliminate the use of radio

---

[13] For numerous examples, see "Low Productivity: The Real Sin of High Wages," *Engineering News-Record*, February 24, 1972, pp. 20–23.

telephones by crew members and go back to hand signals and lanterns of the age of the coal-burning locomotives. According to the union, this would mean more jobs and would increase safety!

The hiring of unnecessary employees is typified by the manner in which the Brotherhood of Locomotive Firemen and Enginemen was able for years to maintain a "fireman" on diesel engines, even though his firing function did not exist; or by the excessive complements carried by American ships—about one third more than are carried by foreign ships. By refusing to permit workers to do jobs outside of their narrowly defined craft jurisdictions, unions in the building, amusement, and railway industries likewise prevent the most effective utilization of manpower and thus require the hiring of unnecessary employees.

Seniority, Job Ownership, and Featherbedding

Featherbedding was once considered primarily a problem involving craft unions and craft-organized industries. But it appears also in manufacturing enterprises organized by industrial unions. The avenue by which featherbedding most often enters such an industrial situation is through an expansion of the concept of seniority.

The argument goes like this: If a person has seniority in a particular occupation, then he alone can perform the work, even though other persons are qualified to do it. By seniority, he acquires exclusive ownership in his job. Then only a person in that craft can be assigned to the job if the person who "owns" the job is not available.

Similarly, according to this reasoning, if an employee "owns" a job, the employer is no longer permitted to contract it out; and if, in the exercise of what he thinks is his management function, he does so, the employee is entitled to be paid for not working. In a similar view, the National Labor Relations Board has ruled that no contracting-out can be undertaken without consultation with the union—presumably to protect the employees' rights to their seniority.

Few managements could have believed that signing a seniority agreement would mean turning over job ownership as well. Although in the past, industrial unions generally have not sought such an interpretation of seniority, they are doing so increasingly. The pressure is strongest in times of layoffs, when the principle of job ownership can save a worker's job. Of course, the added cost involved may eventually result in additional unemployment, including that of the worker whose job was supposedly saved. But this possibility usually does not seem imminent to those advocating restrictions.

A related idea is that of job confinement—if a job is owned by a particular craft, its limits must be confined or circumscribed. Recently, a strike over this issue occurred at a large machine shop, when some small groups of chippers and flame gaugers were instructed to squirt oil on castings. Through their local unions the groups charged that squirting oil from a can was outside the jurisdiction of their jobs, and demanded that somebody else do the work.

In no industry are job ownership and make-work practices more prevalent than in newspaper publishing. Yet such practices have certainly not brought worker security. Rather, by adding to costs and by decreasing productivity, they contributed to the demise within three years of four newspapers in New York City and of many others elsewhere. To eliminate such practices, to which it had acquiesced earlier, the *Washington Post,* editorially one of the most liberal and prounion newspapers in the nation, literally broke the Pressmen's local with which it dealt in a long strike in 1975–76.

Make-Work Legislation

At the prodding of special interest groups a number of laws have been passed which are ostensibly in the interest of the consumer but which actually go considerably beyond that. In this category are laws which require a "full" railroad crew and which often result in the employment of unneeded personnel. Licensing laws frequently require that a skilled person do an unskilled job—for example, an electrician may be required to replace a light bulb. Unions build on such laws by having skilled craftsmen unload materials, lay pipe, build forms, or break through walls—all jobs that laborers could well perform. In addition, building codes often discriminate against prefabricated materials which are adequate, or even superior to work done on the job, but which can be produced more cheaply in factories.

The most recent addition to such legislation are state and local laws requiring supermarkets to place the price of an item on each unit being sold. Ostensibly, such laws are enacted to protect the consumer and are advocated by consumer groups. Actually, their purpose is to prevent the introduction of electronic scanners which automatically price items at checkout counters. These scanners are made less economic by such laws which prevent the elimination of the clerks used to do the pricing. The fight for these laws has been led by the Retail Clerks and Meat Cutters unions, which have financed the so-called consumer groups. In fact, the result is to add to prices by requiring the supermarkets to keep labor that would otherwise not be needed.[14]

---

[14] As of mid-1976, such restrictive laws were enacted in California, Massachusetts, Connecticut, and Rhode Island, and in 14 cities, including Chicago. These are, of course, all areas where unions are strong. See the *Retail Clerks Advocate,* December 1975, and the *Butcher Workman,* March 1976, for strong statements of the union position. The above issue of the *Advocate* includes an article by Carol Foreman, executive director of the Consumer Federation of America, in support of such legislation; she is now Assistant Secretary of Agriculture. In private life, she is married to an official of the Retail Clerks' union. See Frances Serra, "A Lobbyist for Consumers," *New York Times,* October 31, 1976, sec. F, p. 7.

Comments on "Make-Work"

Make-work rules are a wasteful method of dealing with the problems of unemployment and insecurity, since they add to the cost of production and, as a result, curtail total employment. In many cases, make-work provisions so raise costs that wages are lower than they might otherwise be. An excessive use of make-work rules may seriously limit a union's effectiveness, for it may cause internal dissension between those favoring limits and those favoring higher earnings. Also, as already noted, limits on work may permit nonunion earnings to exceed union earnings and thus prevent a union from organizing nonunion workers who are not interested in decreased earnings.

Make-work rules do not eliminate the intermittent employment which is found in the building and amusement industries, where such rules are common; nor have make-work rules halted the secular decline in railway employment. Actually, by attracting more labor to an industry than is needed, make-work rules aggravate these evils.

Make-work policies present a difficult problem in terms of public policy. One method of attempted regulation is illustrated by the Taft-Hartley Act and a few similar state laws. Section $8(b)(6)$ of the Taft-Hartley Act makes it an unfair labor practice for a union "to cause or attempt to cause an employer to pay or deliver or agree to pay or deliver any money or other thing of value in the nature of an exaction, for services which are not performed or not to be performed." This clause was sometimes referred to as the "antifeatherbedding" provision; but actually, its scope has been construed by the courts and the National Labor Relations Board to be much more limited than the practice of make-work rules which is ordinarily encompassed within the term *featherbedding*. The NLRB has held, however, that Section $8(b)(6)$ prevents a union from forcing an employer to hire unnecessary personnel by picketing.[15]

Although make-work rules are wasteful and costly to the public, it is doubtful whether most such rules can be dealt with effectively by legislation. What agency, for example, is to pass judgment on how fast an employee should work, or how many employees should be required to operate a given machine, or at exactly what point a job requires a skilled worker and at what point little skill is necessary?

To be sure, extreme cases are easy to detect. Legislation, however, would have to leave extraordinary discretion to a government bureau. To do its job, that bureau would be compelled to pass judgment on a

---

[15] *Lathers Local 46* (*Expanded Metal Engineering Co.*), 207 N.L.R.B. 111 (1973); *Teamsters Local 456* (*J. R. Stevenson Corp.*), Case 2–CB–5412, January 21, 1974. If, however, the unnecessary employee is performing a job, as these employees were not, Section $8(b)(6)$ does not apply.

variety of labor relations matters and would thus end up regulating industrial relations to a degree which labor, business, and the public would find undesirable.

There is another aspect to make-work rules and public policy which cannot be ignored. Restriction of output on the part of labor organizations is only one type of such restriction in the economy. Many businesses restrict output in order to keep prices high. Numerous professional societies have urged the enactment of legislation which would permit only licensed personnel to pursue a profession, but the definition of the profession often goes beyond the need for professional competence. In New Jersey the State Bar Association attempted unsuccessfully to have the negotiation of labor-management contracts declared the practice of law. If the attempt had succeeded, nonmembers of the state bar would have been unable to compete with lawyers for the right to aid labor and management unless no compensation were accepted. Farmers continually restrict production, plow under crops, and let fruit rot on the trees in order to bolster prices. Indeed, farmers are often encouraged to do this by law! Should only labor restrictions be regulated?

Before advocating legislation, it is well to realize that many featherbedding practices are the result of managerial mistakes or inadequacies. For example, the fireman issue on the diesel engine arose because railway management believed in 1936 that diesels were only a special-purpose engine that would never replace steam. "Bogus" work in printing derived from the desire of management to charge advertisers a full rate and was once actually encouraged by newspaper publishers. Wasteful ship crew and longshore complements grew out of cost-plus practices during World War II and employer profits on such overstaffing. Numerous other featherbedding rules have resulted from managerial failure to make decisions on a long-run instead of an immediate-profit basis.

TECHNOLOGICAL CHANGE AND AUTOMATION

The introduction of new machinery or methods may be beneficial to union members by easing the physical strains or improving the safety of the job, or by bringing in more work and hence increasing employment. In some cases, unions have agitated for technological improvements. Lighter, faster trucks have created more jobs for truck drivers, and larger, faster airplanes have made jobs for pilots. There are many other such examples.

On the other hand, many technological developments affect workers adversely, at least immediately. They make the job more hazardous or more difficult, or they may reduce employment in particular plants. For example, paint spraying can cause lead poisoning; the substitution of the one-man streetcar for two-man operation certainly made the job of the operator more difficult; the introduction of the continuous strip mill resulted in the abandonment of many hand-rolled steel mills; and the diesel engine eliminated the need for firemen.

Obstruction

The adverse effects of technological change have led a number of unions at various times to oppose shifts in production methods. Opposition to technological change may take several forms. The most common is refusal to work with new machines. Workers can also reduce output, demand prohibitive pay, or even ask for legislation in their fight against change.

Few industrial unions adopt obstruction policies, although occasionally some of their locals may do so. The reason is that the average technological development does not affect all members of an industrial union, and it cannot go "all out" for the interests of a minority of its members. On the other hand, all members of a craft union are likely to be directly affected by an alteration in the methods of production.

In some cases, obstruction has been successful. Thus, the plumbers have prevented the use of pipe-threading machines, and the bricklayers of automatic bricklaying equipment. But this "success" has been limited in the case of the plumbers by the use of tubing instead of piping, and by making connections by soldering and other means which avoid threading; and in the case of the bricklayers, by the use of other means of facing, such as glass, poured concrete, and aluminum.

Opposition to technological change can rarely be successful for long, for if the new methods are superior, some enterprising manager will find a way to use the new technique or to surmount the old one by a substitute process or technology. Then the union will have to decide whether to give up its opposition or to see its members unemployed. At this point, national union leaders, anxious to preserve the union, may find themselves at odds with members or local leaders whose prime objective is to work out their lives—or as long as possible—on the old techniques and methods which they know.

Worker opposition to technological change dates back at least to the industrial revolution, when the textile workers of Lancashire smashed newly installed machines.

> The appearance of something new, whether in the form of a new labor-saving device, a new incentive system, a new kind of supervision, or a new process, seems to sound an alert among men at work; they mount guard, as it were, suspicious in advance that the change bodes them no good. The problem that emerges becomes particularly baffling when time and time again it appears immaterial whether an innovation affects

the workers adversely or not. Indeed, even when it promises them substantial benefit, they still may pull and haul and balk.[16]

Union policies of obstruction are basically reflections of workers' fears that changes will affect them adversely. The unions act to solidify the obstruction or to fight it, but not to create it. Moreover, in many instances, union obstruction has served a good purpose. Opposition of the streetcar motormen to the one-man car led to the invention of the safety-door brake; the fight against the paint spray has helped to develop effective "waterfall" and blower systems to control fumes; and numerous other examples exist of safety measures taken to offset union claims of "health hazards" which, in fact, stem largely from rank-and-file opposition to change.

Perhaps even more important than forcing improvements in machines, union obstruction policies have compelled industry to consider the human costs in introducing new methods. Abandoning a plant or eliminating a skill causes tremendous hardship to those affected. By slowing the process or forcing management to make concessions, union obstruction to technological change has reduced the number of employees rendered temporarily useless by progress. On the other hand, there are many cases, particularly in the building, printing, and other trades, where union obstruction policies have increased consumer costs without apparent benefit to the community.

Competition

If a union finds that a policy of obstruction is failing (usually because nonunion shops are utilizing the new technique and causing unemployment in the union shops), it may attempt to compete with the new method. This takes the form of wage or working rule concessions to employers who retain the techniques or, in rare instances, of the formation of cooperatives by displaced employees who seek to maintain old methods of operation.

Essentially, the policy of competition is a short-run device adopted for the purpose of slowing the advancement of new techniques and preserving the working lives of employees who would otherwise be displaced. If a new technique is sufficiently superior, wage and working rule concessions are not likely to halt its introduction. Nor can cooperative plants producing by less efficient methods hope to compete permanently with more modern plants.

A policy of competition, nevertheless, is not without social benefit. By providing temporary employment for workers who might otherwise

---

[16] B. M. Selekman, *Labor Relations and Human Relations* (New York: McGraw-Hill Book Co., 1947), p. 111.

be unemployed, it mitigates the hardships of change. Moreover, as in the case of obstruction policies, competition forces improvement in new machines, which are often crude when first introduced, and therefore a policy of competition can result in the reduction of costs and prices.

Control

In most cases, opposition to technological advancement and union attempts to compete with new techniques are temporary measures. Sooner or later, the union members must decide whether or not they want the union to survive. If they do, they must work out an agreement with management which permits the use of the new invention. In short, the union must adopt a policy which gives it some control over the working conditions which develop under the new technique.

The policy of control may take many forms. In the supermarket industry, for example, the Amalgamated Meat Cutters and Butcher Workmen has generally obstructed the concept of central meat cutting instead of having butchers in each store. Some locals, however, have provided in their contracts that if central meat cutting is introduced, butchers in the stores will receive the first opportunity for the jobs and their union will be recognized as the bargaining agent in the central plants.[17] In the steel industry, the United Steelworkers has insisted that some of the benefits of machinery go directly to the workers. This has been used as a talking point in wage negotiations and also to implement union arguments that workers laid off as a result of new techniques should be given the first opportunity for new job openings. In other cases, unions have negotiated dismissal compensation for laid-off workers. This tends to lessen rank-and-file opposition to a policy of control. A final method of control is for the union to negotiate high wage rates for work on new machines. Such wage rates slow down the introduction of the new technique by making it relatively more expensive. As a result, the effect on the working force may be temporarily lessened—unless the net effect is to make the whole operation so high-cost that everyone concerned loses his job.

The willingness of a union to adopt a policy of control depends on a variety of factors. Industrial unions are more likely to favor control policies than are craft unions because a new technique often helps one part of the industrial union membership even though it hurts another part. Moreover, craft unions may be unwilling or unable to organize employees operating the new machines, or their members may be unwilling or unable to learn new techniques or to work on new machines.

---

[17] Herbert R. Northrup and Gordon R. Storholm, *Restrictive Labor Practices in the Supermarket Industry,* Industrial Research Unit Study No. 44 (Philadelphia: University of Pennsylvania Press, 1967).

Even if workers are willing and able to be retrained, a new technique may be started in a new plant or industry, and the opportunity to work the new technique may simply be unavailable to those utilizing the old methods of equipment.

Unions are much more willing to accept new techniques and methods if jobs are visibly at stake. The competition of nonunion or foreign plants, or of substitute methods or products, and the consequent loss of sales and jobs, make clear to employees that costs must be lowered if jobs are to be saved. As such competition strikes closer to home, opposition to technological changes tends to decline.

The vast number of technological improvements which have been introduced and their initial ill effect on workers raise the question of why more unions have not adopted policies of obstruction rather than control. The main reason appears to be that most inventions are introduced in times of prosperity and full employment, and indeed contribute to the prosperity. In such times, reemployment of displaced men is more easily effected, and opposition to new techniques is consequently lessened.

Automation Funds and Displacement

Technological developments since World War II have moved along three basic lines. These developments, termed "automation," can be divided into three fundamental groups.[18]

1. The integration by means of mechanical engineering techniques of conventionally separate manufacturing operations into lines of continuous production untouched by human hands.
2. The use of "feedback" control devices or servomechanisms which permit individual operations to be performed, tested, and/or inspected, and controlled without human control by means of electrical engineering or electronic techniques.
3. The development of computing machines which can record and store information and perform complex mathematical operations on such information largely by means of electrical engineering developments.

The effect of automation on labor utilization has been and is potentially spectacular. Labor displacement in some industries has been severe and in other industries promises to have effects that are even more drastic. In the longshore industry, for example, where ships have been loaded and unloaded by substantially the same methods for many years, an innovation known as "containerization" has been developed. This is the principle whereby products to be transported in ships are loaded in large, fully

---

[18] These definitions were first set forth by G. B. Baldwin and G. P. Shultz in "Automation: A New Dimension to Old Problems," in Industrial Relations Research Association, *Annual Proceedings* (Detroit, 1954), pp. 114–28.

enclosed containers at the factory or warehouse and the containers are moved directly by cranes from the dock into the vessel (and unloaded by the same method), thus eliminating all manual loading and unloading of ships at the dockside. Adoption of this method affords major reductions in costs and major improvements in the efficiency of stevedoring operations.

Meat-packing is another industry in which automation has already had profound effects on employment. Manual handling of carcasses has been replaced by conveyors; dressing knives are driven by electric motors; hand curing of bacon and ham has given way to "pickling" by needle injections; automatic machines slice, weigh, and package bacon, and stuff and pack sausage. As a result, employment in the meat-packing industry has declined by about 50,000 in an era in which the consumption of meat has steadily risen.

Such problems have led to special collective bargaining action. The West Coast longshore agreement in effect provided that the employers "buy out" the restrictive practices and opposition to technological change by establishing a fund for improved pension and welfare benefits, provisions for early retirement, and other additions to the welfare package of the longshoremen. After this contract was first negotiated in the early 1950s, employment on West Coast docks actually increased because of general prosperity and its impact on shipping, and because of the requirements of the Vietnam war. A strike in 1971–72 involved other issues and did not end the new rules. It did, however, reveal fear of declining employment incident to the withdrawal from Vietnam.

Armour and Company and the union of meat-packing employees also set up a fund. Its purpose was to study the effects of automation and to attempt to transfer and retrain employees, or to otherwise improve the opportunities of the displaced. As a result of such efforts, some success occurred in the retraining and relocating of displaced packing-house employees.

Automation funds of lesser magnitude, or arrangements of a similar nature, have been developed by the American Federation of Musicians, the International Ladies' Garment Workers' Union, and the East Coast longshoremen's union. In addition, the Kaiser and Scanlon plans, discussed in the preceding chapter, have similar aspects insofar as they are attempts to deal logically and consistently with the problem of technological displacement. Likewise, the efforts of unions in the steel and brewing industries to negotiate long vacations or "sabbaticals" are motivated principally by the desire to mitigate the impact of technology on employment by sharing the work.

But basically, neither automation funds nor the other arrangements discussed emphasize benefits for displaced workers. Rather, the benefits are designed either entirely or primarily for the purpose of sharing the savings of automation with those employees who are retained on the payroll. Thus, such funds are like an extension of the basic policies of unions which concentrate on high wages for those left on the payroll. Since both managements and unions are interested in present and future employees, not former ones, this should not be surprising—but it should also emphasize that automation funds are designed primarily for those who remain to share in the fruits of technology, and not to care for the displaced. In effect, automation funds are a method of union control of technological change; contributions to such funds add to industry's costs of innovating and can therefore slow it down without completely obstructing the innovation.

THE EFFECTS OF UNION ORGANIZATION ON EFFICIENCY

In many firms, prior to the advent of union organization, management depended upon the payment of low wages to keep costs down to a competitive level. Union organization, by removing wage rates from the competitive sphere, can produce a desirable change in emphasis from wage levels to production costs and thereby diminish the divergence in technical standards between the least efficient and the most efficient firms in an industry. If the effect of union wage pressure is to make inefficient managers better innovators, the general level of efficiency in industry will benefit. And of course, to the extent that the least efficient firms are eliminated, an automatic increase occurs in the statistical average efficiency of the surviving firms.

Union organization may increase "social efficiency" by slowing down managerial action designed to displace persons or by forcing managers to consider such things as retraining existing employees instead of replacing them. The net effect can be to prolong the working life of people and thus to add to the overall ability of the population to support itself.

By raising wages in union plants, union organization increases the cost advantage of nonunion competitors and compels union firms to increase efficiency in order to remain in competition. Moreover, the presence of a strong union with alert shop stewards compels management to justify many production methods and rates, and therefore encourages a more careful examination of costs and production policy. Although union wage pressure probably produces a small net gain in labor efficiency, the difficulties encountered by union plants in holding their markets indicate that the gain is insufficient to offset the increased price of labor.

Union influence upon technical efficiency has a time dimension. Probably the greatest increase in efficiency is forthcoming when an industry is newly organized. Then the wastes may be more obvious and abundant; but after a while, when the backlog of waste is largely exhausted, a point of diminishing returns must be reached. Furthermore, as unionism itself matures and its power in industry grows, it is more likely to bring its own wastes to industry. As a general rule, the more strongly entrenched the position of a union in an industry, the less it is concerned with the efficiency of the individual firms under its jurisdiction. Consequently, even though the possibilities of raising the level of industrial efficiency are considerable, there is room for skepticism regarding the contribution which unionism will make in this respect in the future. Managements in the railroad, printing, apparel, and construction industries have been subjected to union wage pressure over a long period, but it is certain that they are not conspicuously more able, thorough, and alert to technological developments than are managements in other industries.

UNFAVORABLE EFFECTS OF UNION RULES

On the whole, union organization probably tends to diminish industrial efficiency rather than to increase it. The rise of unionism has led to a multiplication of union rules and restrictions which limit the freedom of the employer to revise costly operations and to introduce improved techniques of production. There is no immediate prospect of eliminating the many needless make-work rules which are found at present in organized plants in various industries. Although union wage pressure affords some stimulus to invention and technological progress, it is doubtful whether general union wage adjustments occurring more or less simultaneously over a broad area of industry provide much stimulus to the rate of mechanization. Moreover, whatever stimulus is forthcoming from this source tends to be offset by the restrictive influence of union policies which retard the rate of introduction of laborsaving methods and machinery.

Despite the fact that the leaders of organized labor condemn opposition to laborsaving machinery, such opposition is still practiced by individual unions. It is easy for leaders to generalize in sweeping terms about the futility of attempting to stem the advance of progress; but if the individual worker sees in his union a possible barrier to the introduction of a new improvement which threatens his job, he is likely to use the union for that purpose. Union organization has not altered the feelings or attitudes of the average worker toward laborsaving machinery, but it has given him the strength to resist or retard technological change, whereas previously he could only voice weak protest.

Management, by and large, is compelled by the profit motive to be interested in reducing costs and improving the quality of the product. These twin objectives of employers ordinarily place management on the side of efficiency in the collective bargaining process. Unions—at least where nonunion competition is not a major problem—are interested primarily in improving earnings and working conditions, and in introducing order, tenure, and stability into the employment relationship. Although these objectives have important value from the viewpoint of the community and of society, we should recognize that in many cases they will conflict with productive efficiency.

QUESTIONS FOR DISCUSSION

1. Do you feel that a union is ever justified in opposing technological change? Can you support your answer from experience?
2. Why is contracting-out so emotional an issue? How is it concerned with union policy and management rights? Why is it so much more in controversy today than formerly?
3. Why is apprenticeship so important to blacks? What would you do to attempt to increase the number and proportion of black craftsmen?
4.. Seniority has many ramifications. Discuss its relation to job security and union security, and how it can affect these two objectives of most unions. Discuss also the impact of seniority on blacks.

SUGGESTIONS FOR FURTHER READING

Herding, R. *Job Control and Union Structure*. Rotterdam: Rotterdam University Press, 1972.
> A study of union job control and conflict, comparing the United States and West Germany.

Levinson, Harold M., et al. *Collective Bargaining and Technological Change in American Transportation*. Evanston, Ill.: Transportation Center at Northwestern University, 1971.
> A detailed study of the interaction of collective bargaining and technology in the trucking, railroad, maritime, and air transport industries.

Northrup, Herbert R., and Foster, Howard G. *Open Shop Construction*. Major Study No. 54. Philadelphia: Industrial Research Unit, The Wharton School, University of Pennsylvania, 1975, chapter 9.
> A comparison of union and nonunion recruitment and deployment of manpower in the construction industry.

Rowan, Richard L. (ed.) *Readings in Labor Economics and Labor Relations*. 3d ed. Homewood, Ill.: Richard D. Irwin, Inc., 1976, pp. 280–307.
> Four articles dealing with issues in industrial jurisprudence.

Shimberg, Benjamin, et al. *Occupational Licensing: Practices and Policies*. Washington, D.C.: Public Affairs Press, 1973.
> An analysis of how licensing laws affect job entry.

Slichter, Sumner H.; Healy, J. J.; and Livernash, E. R. *The Impact of Collective Bargaining on Management*, chaps. 2–12. Washington, D.C.: Brookings Institution, 1960.
> The basic work on industrial jurisprudence.

Multiunit Bargaining, Strikes, and the Labor Monopoly Issue

IN THIS CHAPTER, we continue our discussion of collective bargaining practices, taking up three of the most controversial issues—multiunit bargaining (often called industrywide bargaining), strikes, and the question of whether unions are monopolies.

MULTIUNIT BARGAINING

Multiunit bargaining is simply a term used to denote a collective bargaining arrangement which covers more than one plant. Multiunit bargaining takes many forms. One such form occurs when a single management controls two or more plants which are organized by a single national union. Negotiations between the United Automobile Workers and the General Motors Corporation or between the United Steelworkers and the United States Steel Corporation are two of the best-known examples of this type of bargaining. Both negotiations are between one management and one union, but they each establish basic wages and employment conditions for many separate plants throughout the country. Moreover, the settlements reached in these bargaining conferences provide the key wage bargains for much of the economy.

A second type of multiunit collective bargaining involves bargaining between one or more national unions and a representative of two or more managements in a single industry. For discussion purposes, such bargaining is usually subdivided on a geographic basis into local, regional, and national types. Local multiunit bargaining is by far the most common. It occurs in service industries of many kinds, building construction, amusements, retail stores, clothing, and many other industries in which the competitive market is predominantly local. Frequently, it is difficult to distinguish the practical difference between the second type of bargaining on a national basis, where the employers are represented by an association or another bargaining representative, and a situation in which a national union bargains at one and the same time with a number of multi-unit employers. This is the situation in the steel industry. Each of the steel companies theoretically bargains independently with the United Steelworkers; but as a practical matter, they all look to the United States Steel Corporation to set the pattern.

Among the industries in which regional multiunit bargaining is common are pulp and paper, lumber, nonferrous metal mining, and maritime and longshore work.

National multicompany bargaining is frequently termed "industrywide" bargaining, but the latter term is inaccurate in most cases. Even the widely known bargaining in the railroad industry, which is national in scope and very inclusive, is not completely industrywide.

National collective bargaining is divisible into two groups. In the first type a sizable segment of an industry throughout the country bargains with a national union or unions. The gradual extension prior to World War I of bituminous coal bargaining from local area to district and then regionwide agreements, climaxed by the "central competitive field" agreements covering mainly Pennsylvania, Ohio, Indiana, and Illinois; the disintegration of this system in the 1920s because the unionized mines could not compete with the nonunion southern mines; and finally, the rise of national bargaining after 1934, afford the most vivid and well-known example of this development. In the late 1940s, this bargaining split into northern and southern groups, but it has merged again.

Railroad history provides another example. Single railway system bargaining developed, under the impetus of union "concerted movements," into regional conferences; then during World War I, when the federal government took over the railroads, national bargaining was adopted. It relapsed into regional bargaining in the early 1920s, but national bargaining was again revived by the railroads in 1931 for the purpose of securing nationwide decreases. Since then, national bargaining has continued.

The railroad and bituminous coal situations have one significant difference which derives from the structure of their respective unions. Bituminous coal deals with one industrial union. Its negotiations settle matters for all employees at one time. The railroads deal with several craft unions. On most occasions the railroad unions have split into two, three, or four groups. National conferences are held with each group by the carriers. A settlement with one group must be made with the demands of the others in mind, thus greatly complicating bargaining.

Quite different from either the bituminous coal or the railroad situations, where most workers in an industry are involved in the national bargaining, is the second type of industrywide bargaining. This is the situation where only one craft of workers bargains, as in the wire-weaving, tile-laying, sprinkler installation, elevator installation and repair, and wallpaper crafts. Despite the fact that only a small segment of a particular employer's work force is involved, the bargaining is national in scope. A small, well-organized craft, desirous of maintaining its standards throughout the country, and an important industry segment providing nationally used products and/or services, participate in these multiunit bargaining arrangements.

Still another type of multiunit collective bargaining cuts across industry lines. In such cases, bargaining occurs between an employers' association, or a division thereof, representing numerous industries and the union or unions holding bargaining rights for the workers in these industries. Bargaining of this type has developed most fully in the San Francisco metropolitan area and has spread to several other western cities and to Hawaii. In San Francisco the aggressiveness and scarcity of labor led employers to organize and bargain on an areawide basis as early as the "Gold Rush" days, but modern master agreements date from the union drives of 1934. Then the use of "whipsaw" tactics by unions—striking employers one at a time in order to raise wages—led to the formation of the San Francisco Employers Council in 1938. Today the Council coordinates all negotiations for its members.

Coordinated, or coalition, bargaining, as noted in previous chapters, has been developed by the AFL–CIO Industrial Union Department as a means of increasing union leverage on companies which deal with a number of unions at various plants throughout the United States and Canada. The IUD has attempted to coordinate efforts of unions to obtain common termination dates of contracts with a particular company, or with several companies in an industry, and then threaten to shut down all the plants if the management refused to deal on a coalition basis. The IUD drive has been resisted for the most part by industry since it is obviously designed to enhance union power at the expense of the employer, but it has achieved some success in electrical manufacturing, metal mining, and a few other instances.[1]

There have also been some attempts to extend bargaining beyond national borders, particularly in the European Common Market. Although such efforts have received widespread publicity, actual bargaining has not occurred because of the reluctance of management to add multinational labor commitments and risks to those already existing at the national and local levels, the like reluctance of national unions to cede authority and power to multinational union bodies, and the different laws and bargaining systems in neighboring countries.[2]

---

[1] William N. Chernish, *Coalition Bargaining*, Major Study No. 45 (Philadelphia: Industrial Research Unit, The Wharton School, University of Pennsylvania, 1969); and Wallace Hendricks, "Conglomerate Mergers and Collective Bargaining," *Industrial Relations*, vol. 15 (February 1976), pp. 75–87.

[2] See the articles by Herbert R. Northrup and Richard L. Rowan cited in Chapter 4, footnote 8.

The Extent of Multiunit Collective Bargaining

Table 7–1 summarizes the findings of a survey on the extent of multiunit collective bargaining. Because of the variations within industries, it has been necessary to include some industries under more than one heading.

In the left-hand column, titled "Single Company," are listed industries in which exist significant numbers of companies having several plants which deal on a companywide basis with unions. These industries are mostly the so-called heavy or basic industries, which are characterized by large investments, mass production, and a small number of large multiplant companies.

It is clear that multiunit bargaining in the United States embraces an enormous portion of American industry. Multiunit bargaining also varies according to issues. Pensions, for example, are bargained nationally in electrical construction, but most other issues are bargained locally. A wide range of such varied practices exists in industry.

Reasons for the Development of Multiunit Collective Bargaining

The reasons for the development of the various types of multiunit collective bargaining vary from industry to industry. Sometimes the union is responsible for initiating such bargaining. In other cases the employers take the initiative.

Equalizing wage costs has been an important reason why unions have supported multiunit collective bargaining. In the railroads, for example, the brotherhoods found that the individual railroads were using the competition of other lines as a reason for objecting to wage increases. This led the brotherhoods to support first regional and then national bargaining. In the needle trades, wages are the most important cost factor. Both the unions and the employers discovered at an early time that unionism could not exist unless it equalized wage costs. This resulted in marketwide bargaining in the various branches of the industry; since most markets are local in scope, bargaining is local in scope. The exceptions are the men's clothing industry, which has expanded into a national bargaining situation, and the work clothes industries, where the union label has induced various manufacturers throughout the country to enter negotiations with the United Garment Workers.

The equalization of competition has played an important role in the development of multiunit collective bargaining in lumber, pulp and paper, pottery, and the various branches of the glass industry. In some of these industries, the initiative was taken by the employers. In metal-jobbing shops of various types, and book and job printing, the pattern is similar to that in the garment trades. Wages are a significant, if not the most significant, cost item; the plant labor force is small; and the degree

TABLE 7–1

Extent of Multiunit Collective Bargaining*

Single Company	Multicompany			Multiindustry
	National	Regional	Local Area	
Automobile	Anthracite	Fishing	Building construc-	San Francisco
Electrical supplies	coal	Canning and	tion	Tacoma
and equip-	Bituminous	preserving	Building materials	Reno
ment	coal	foods	Longshoremen	Sacramento
Farm equipment	Iron and steel	Lumber	Trucking (local de-	Los Angeles
Flat glass	(basic)	Pulp and paper	livery)	Phoenix
Rubber	Railroads	Clay sewer pipe	Warehousing	Denver
Meat-packing	Pottery	Cement	Amusements and	Hawaii
Rayon textiles	Pressed and	Maritime (all	theaters	Albuquerque
Shipbuilding	blown	classes)	Hotels and restau-	
Nonferrous metal	glass	Seamen	rants	
manufactu-	Glass con-	Longshore-	Laundries	
ing	tainers	men	Cleaning and dyeing	
Nonferrous metal	Trucking	Motion-picture	service	
mining	(over the	production	Building service	
Pulp and paper	road)	Hosiery	Retail stores	
Tobacco	Wire-weaving	Cotton textiles	Department stores	
(cigarettes)	Wallpaper	Woolen textiles	Charitable orga-	
	Tile-laying	Dyeing and	nizations	
	Sprinkler fitter	finishing	Metal job shops	
	installa-	textiles	Machine	
	tion	Cotton gar-	Tool and die	
	Elevator instal-	ments	Pattern	
	lation and	Leather	Foundry	
	repair	(tanned,	Steel products	
	Men's and	curried,	(nonbasic)	
	boys'	and fin-	Jewelry and	
	clothes	ished)	silverware	
	Work clothes	Shoes	Newspaper printing	
	Stoves	Trucking	Book and job print-	
			ing	
			Women's clothes	
			Millinery	
			Fur	
			Leather products	
			and gloves	
			Shoes	
			Confectionery	
			products	
			Meat-packing	
			Dairy products	
			Baked goods	
			Malt liquors	
			Beverages	
			(nonalcoholic)	
			Tobacco (cigars)	
			Furniture	
			Knit goods	
			Silk and rayon	
			textiles	
			Paper products	
			(boxes, etc.)	
			Garage main-	
			tenance men	

* Coordinated or coalition bargaining has been attempted in many industries, notably electrical man-ufacturing, nonferrous mining and manufacturing, chemicals, and drugs, but it is widespread only in the first two.

of competition is high. All these factors tend toward the development of multiunit collective bargaining once the workers become unionized.

In industries in which an employee typically works for more than one employer, multiunit collective bargaining is virtually essential for both employer and union. These industries include the maritime trades, the building trades, and the needle trades. In such industries, failure to equalize wages and working conditions would have the effect of permitting some employers to pay higher wages to workers than those paid by other employers. From the union point of view, this is an intolerable situation, and it is equally so from the employers' viewpoint. For example, in the building industry the low-wage employer would be able to outbid high-wage competitors—and solely because the union allowed him a favorable rate. This would injure the union's relations with other employers. Hence the only solution for the unionized employer and the union is multiunit bargaining over the extent of the market. Narrow-market bargaining, which encourages workers to obtain employment in neighboring towns and wait out strikes, and the increasing importance of nonunion construction, which has been growing rapidly at the expense of union construction in recent years, have encouraged demands for wider bargaining units in the industry.[3]

Another reason why both unions and employers prefer multiunit bargaining is that it eases contract enforcement. From the union point of view, this is very important in such industries as building and trucking, or in any other industries where the size of the firm is small and the employees bear a very close personal relationship to their employers. There is a tendency in such industries, particularly when work is slack, for the employer to ask, and often to receive, wage concessions from his workers and to keep the concessions secret from the union. This enables the employer to get more work at the expense of his competitors. It also, however, takes business from the more contract-conscious competitors and threatens the entire union wage structure. Under a multiunit arrangement, it is more difficult to effect such local deals, especially since most arrangements contain explicit provisions enumerating severe penalties for any deals or kickbacks.

Multiunit bargaining simplifies negotiations in industries where there are scores of small employers. It also enables small companies represented by an association to employ skilled attorneys and industrial relations specialists whom they could not afford on an individual plant bargaining basis.

Unions like multiunit bargaining because it makes it more difficult for a rival union to gain a foothold in the industry. A history of bargain-

---

[3] See Herbert R. Northrup and Howard G. Foster, *Open Shop Construction*, Major Study No. 54 (Philadelphia: Industrial Research Unit, The Wharton School, University of Pennsylvania, 1975).

ing with an employers' association will tend to induce the National Labor Relations Board to designate the multiplant group as the appropriate unit for bargaining purposes and thus block the efforts of a rival union to pick off individual plants. Employers also like the protection against rival unions afforded by multiunit bargaining, since the resultant stability of labor relations in the industry may produce moderation on the part of union leaders who feel sufficiently secure against rivals to display economic statesmanship. Of course, if a rival union can win a majority of votes for the entire multiplant unit, it can take over bargaining rights for all of the plants even though it might lack a majority in some of them. This is what a newly formed union, the Association of Western Pulp and Paper Workers, was able to accomplish in the western pulp and paper industry in 1964 after the employees had been represented by AFL–CIO unions for 30 years.

Multiunit bargaining alters the power structure within a union. By concentrating power for negotiations at the national level, the national leaders reduce the importance—and the independence—of the local and regional leadership. National and regional negotiations greatly enhanced the centralization of authority in the United Mine Workers, and in the Steelworkers, among other unions.

One of the most important reasons why employers have initiated or defended multiunit bargaining is the protection it gives them against losses from strikes. In industries such as transportation, building construction, amusements, services, and retail trade, a strike can result in a loss of business which is never regained because the company deals in perishable goods or services. If the union can pick off employers in such industries one at a time, the employers are, more often than not, helpless to prevent the union from achieving even the most outrageous demands. But when the employers form a common front, the power of the union is blunted because a strike means a strike of the entire industry. This, in turn, results in a serious loss of employment to all union members; and, perhaps even more important, no employer benefits from a struck employer's loss of business. Recent efforts by the supermarket industry to control such whipsaw strikes and to enlarge bargaining units are a case in point.[4]

On the other hand, many employers whose employee relations are well controlled oppose multiunit bargaining because it might permit the union to spread throughout the industry gains won from weaker companies. The automobile companies oppose joint bargaining because the larger the group involved, the greater the likelihood of government intervention, which often takes the form of pressure on the companies to give more to avoid a work stoppage.

---

[4] See "Trying to Control the Whipsaw," *Business Week*, April 5, 1976, pp. 77, 79.

Multiunit Bargaining as a Problem

The basic public interest in multiunit bargaining arises out of the effects of work stoppages and wage increases. A strike which shuts down either a whole industry or a major portion thereof causes serious public inconvenience. A wage increase which is achieved by a large number of workers under conditions which insure widespread publicity, such as when the Steelworkers' Union bargains with United States Steel, can result in public dissatisfaction with the large multiunit strike and with the wage bargain. Such settlements, particularly when they are effected by use of the strike weapon on a large scale, may be highly inflationary, give rise to charges of union monopoly, as discussed later in this chapter, and encourage government intervention in negotiations and strikes. Although government intervention is designed to protect the public interest, it has, in fact, often encouraged higher and more inflationary wage settlements because government officials are usually interested primarily in avoiding strikes and pressure employers to offer additional benefits in order to keep the peace.

Multiunit bargaining, by its very nature, tends to remove bargaining from local pressures. Although this may have some advantages in creating an atmosphere conducive to reasonable settlement, it also frequently results in ignoring key local issues, or in referring them back to the plant level for further negotiations. As a result, there has grown up in such industries as automobiles and rubber products a situation which poses a double threat to industrial peace. Negotiations are held on the national level at which basic economic issues (wages, holidays, vacations, and benefits) are settled, together with other items of national significance. Other issues are handled locally after the national negotiations. Management is then faced with bargaining over a host of problems, such as work standards, seniority, and other work rules, which the literature of collective bargaining calls "noneconomic," but which may be very costly indeed. Such items have a direct effect on productivity, the number of labor hours needed, and equipment utilization, all of which help to determine the profitability of the enterprise. Yet, because wages and benefits have already been determined, local managers often have no funds for counteroffers, nor can they do much but oppose further increases in costs. Long local strikes, disgruntled local employees, and a high turnover of local union officials who cannot "produce" for the rank and file are frequent results of multiplant bargaining even though agreement at the national level may have been achieved.

Multiunit bargaining can involve the entire bargaining group in controversies which are of interest only to one plant. Days may be spent in discussing a local issue that will end up being referred back for local determination. If such issues get out of hand, or if one party is spoiling for a fight, all companies may be involved in a strike. When strife occurs the stakes are higher and the damage greater in multiunit bargaining.

STRIKES

To many Americans, the strike epitomizes the union. Headlines are made in industrial disputes. They are the sensational aspects of union policies and managerial counterpolicies. Yet, strikes are surprisingly few in comparison to either man-days worked or the number of collective agreements negotiated. (See Table 7–2.) For example, the average annual

TABLE 7–2
Strikes and Lockouts in the United States, Selected Years, 1917–1975 (private, nonfarm only)

Year	Number of Stoppages	Number of Workers Involved (thousands)	Man-Days Idle (million days)	Percentage of Working Time Lost
1917	4,450	1,227	n.a.	n.a.
1919	3,630	4,160	n.a.	n.a.
1921	2,385	1,099	n.a.	n.a.
1929	921	289	5.4	0.07
1933	1,695	1,168	16.9	0.36
1941	4,288	2,363	23.0	0.32
1944	4,956	2,116	8.7	0.09
1946	4,985	4,600	116.0	1.43
1947	3,693	2,170	34.6	0.41
1952	5,117	3,540	59.1	0.57
1959	3,900	1,850	68.0	0.61
1961	3,367	1,450	16.3	0.12
1967	4,595	2,870	42.1	0.30
1969	5,700	2,480	42.9	0.24
1971	5,138	3,280	47.6	0.26
1973	5,353	2,251	27.9	0.14
1975	5,200	1,800	35.0	0.18

Source: U.S. Department of Labor, Bureau of Labor Statistics.

number of man-days lost in the United States because of strikes during 1935–36—a period of great labor unrest—was 16.9 million, or 0.27% of the total annual estimated working time. In 1946, the worst strike year in our history, man-days lost totaled 116 million, or 1.43% of the annual estimated working time. In 1959, despite the impact of a steel strike that shut down that industry for several months, man-days lost totaled 68 million, or only 0.61% of the annual estimated working time. Almost every hour while strikes occur, a collective bargaining agreement is being peacefully negotiated by a union and a company.

During the latter part of the 1960s, the incidence of strikes began to increase, as unions, strengthened by a tight labor market and pressured by inflation, increased their militancy and sought larger increases, which of course, exacerbated the inflation and contributed to the wage-price freeze of August 1971. The uncertainties of the resultant stabilization period, and the impact of the recession thereafter, kept strikes at a low ebb during the middle 1970s.

Although the strike data in Table 7–2 show minute strike losses, they do not tell the whole story. Those laid off because of strikes, for example, are not included. Thus, in 1971 a strike of 10,000 signalmen shut down the nation's railroads. If this strike had been permitted to continue (Congress enacted a special law ending it), it would have shut down numerous plants dependent on railroads for the movement of goods. Employees laid off from these plants would not have been counted as "workers involved" in a strike—yet they surely were.

The data in Table 7–2 are deficient in another way. They exclude the volatile public sector, in which strikes are illegal, but have been occurring with increasing frequency. Between 1960 and 1974, the number of work stoppages by government employees increased from 36 to 384, the total workers involved from 28,600 to 160,700, and the man-days idle from 58,401 to 1,404,000.[5] The issues, policies, and concepts involved are sufficiently unique that we shall discuss them separately in Chapter 22. It is important here to note, however, that such stoppages not only add to strike idleness but raise serious questions about the appropriateness of strikes.

Strikes have significance far beyond the number of man-days lost because they impact throughout the economy and disadvantage both government and the public. The very right of unions and companies to disrupt the economy is now under serious question. We shall return to this question in Chapters 21 and 22, where these public policy matters are taken up. Here we consider why strikes arise from labor-management disputes.

Classification of Work Stoppages

Strikes may be classified into three general categories: (1) economic strikes, concerning wages, hours, and working conditions; (2) strikes to achieve recognition or to eliminate unfair labor practices by employers; and (3) strikes involving conflicts between unions.

The first category—the "bread-and-butter" type of strike—has consistently been the major type of strike in this country, except during the period from 1934 to 1941, when the great upsurge of union organizing effort pushed to the forefront the second category of strikes. Wages are

---

[5] Data from U.S. Department of Labor, Bureau of Labor Statistics.

the most usual but by no means the only reason for economic strikes. For example, the longest major strike since 1965—that affecting the non-ferrous metal industry—was over an unsuccessful demand of the unions for industrywide and companywide bargaining.

Strikes of the second category are intended to eliminate an unfair labor practice by an employer, such as refusal to bargain or discrimination against union activity. Organization strikes, which also fall into this category, have become relatively unimportant in recent years as a result of the high percentage of organization already achieved in industry, the consequent retardation in the rate of growth of unions, and the existence of peaceful methods of determining a collective bargaining representative under state and federal law. An exception is in the area of public employment.

The third class of strikes is a result of union rivalries over jobs and membership. It includes the jurisdictional strike, which involves a contest between unions over which group of workers will perform a specified piece of work. It also includes the rival union organization strike, in which rival unions seek to compel the employer to recognize one union rather than the other as the exclusive bargaining agent for certain or all of his employees. Despite the fact that both voluntary machinery provided by the AFL–CIO and public methods provided by the National Labor Relations Board and state agencies are available to settle such disputes, they continue to exist. Disputes over construction and maintenance work in industrial plants between industrial and building-trades unions, involving the already discussed contracting-out issue, show no signs of abating.

The Taft-Hartley law makes it an unfair labor practice for a union to engage in a strike or refuse to work on goods, or perform services where an object is "forcing or requiring any employer to assign particular work to employees in a particular labor organization or in a particular trade, craft, or class rather than to employees in another labor organization or in another trade, craft, or class, unless such employer is failing to conform to an order or certification of the Board determining the bargaining representative for employees performing such work." The same law also forbids strikes aimed at compelling an employer to bargain with one union where another union has been certified by the National Labor Relations Board as the proper representative of the employees. Yet such disputes will probably continue to inconvenience the public. The question of whether the Carpenters or the Sheet Metal Workers should install metal frame windows is a small reason to tie up millions of dollars of construction, but to the workers involved, it is a question of who will receive the paycheck. Although jurisdictional and rival union strikes account for less than 6% of all strikes, they have tended to increase in the construction industry, where nearly 40% of all strikes are of this type. This fact, combined with the general strike proneness of the industry, is a basic reason for the increasing tendency to operate nonunion.[6]

Noneconomic Factors in Strikes

There have been a number of attempts to state a theory of industrial disputes in terms of purely economic calculation. The assumption is that such calculation is utilized by the parties to determine whether or not a strike would be advisable. If the parties correctly determine each other's propensity to resist and to concede at given wage rates and strike-length periods, then, according to such analysis, they will come to an agreement without a strike at the precise point beyond which neither would concede further without a strike.[7]

The main fault with this analysis is that it does not go far enough. The decision to strike for higher wages or to accept a peaceful settlement at a lower rate does, in fact, depend to a considerable extent on each party's estimate of the relative resistance or concessions which it can expect from the other. But in addition, such a decision is also influenced by many noneconomic considerations which in some circumstances may make a strike for an additional cent an hour necessary, even though it is unsound on a purely economic basis.

The union is not a purely economic unit; it is a body politic. Its first consideration is always the strength of the organization and/or its leadership. The General Motors strike of 1970 was designed to win a large wage increase for the membership and renown for the United Automobile Workers' new president. The nonferrous metal strike of 1967–68 had as its main objective the strengthening of the bargaining position and

---

[6] The inflationary wages, restrictive work rules, and low productivity of unionized construction are, of course, the key reasons for the movement to the open shop, but strikes add to the problem. Although construction employs only 4% of the nation's civilian work force, and is less than 50% unionized, it regularly accounts for nearly 20% of the total strikes, and about 40% of such strikes are jurisdictional in nature. See U.S. Department of Labor, Bureau of Labor Statistics, *Work Stoppages in Contract Construction, 1962–73*, Bulletin No. 1847 (Washington, D.C.: Government Printing Office, 1975), pp. 1, 32; and Northrup and Foster, *Open Shop Construction*, pp. 220–27.

[7] The late Dr. Allan M. Cartter's book, *Theory of Wages and Employment* (Homewood, Ill.: Richard D. Irwin, Inc., 1959), is a good example. He defines each party's bargaining attitude as follows:

$$\text{"X's bargaining attitude} = \frac{\text{Cost of disagreeing with Y}}{\text{Cost of agreeing on Y's terms}}.$$

... When one's bargaining attitude is equal to unity it is just as costly to disagree as to agree on the other's terms, and we can anticipate that when either party finds itself in this position the bargain may be completed on the other bargainer's offered terms" (page 117).

In fact, even if we ignore noneconomic factors, experienced negotiators will come to an agreement when the cost of agreement somewhat exceeds the cost of disagreement. The cost of agreement is a known factor. The cost of disagreement is relatively unknown because no one can determine the length of a prospective strike.

reputation of the Steelworkers, which had recently merged the Mine, Mill, and Smelter Workers into its ranks. In each case, it took the members many months, even years, to recover their economic losses from the strikes. Yet union leaders talk about "gains" resulting from such strikes—gains which exist only if the union or its leaders are considered separately from the rank and file.

Even where a dispute revolves solely around the size of the wage increase, unions will frequently go out on strike for a few cents more per hour, despite the fact that it is apparent that the wage loss incurred during the strike will far exceed the benefit which may be won in the final settlement. The union—particularly one in the formative stage—may derive more benefit from a wage increase of $2 a day after a strike than it would from a wage increase of $3 without a strike. The union leaders may need the rallying power of a strike to solidify the sentiment of the membership and to consolidate their own control.

Work stoppages may also result from noneconomic preferences of employers. The willingness of employers to take a strike over a principle cannot be measured on an economic calculation chart. What, for example, is it worth to a company to refuse to grant the union shop even if that involves a strike?

Whatever the cause of strikes, the computation of their costs in terms of lost wages or production is not simple. In some industries which produce a perishable or nonreproducible product or service—such as the amusement trades, passenger transportation, and newspaper publishing—business lost can rarely be regained, and therefore the cost of the strike will bear a close relationship to the revenues and wages lost during the walkout. In other industries, time lost by strikes may be made up during the year. Most coal strikes, historically, have not caused miners to lose more working time during an average year than they would otherwise lose from overcapacity in the industry. The average number of days worked per miner per year remained approximately the same in heavy strike years as in years of labor peace. Although this is an extreme case, the situation is somewhat comparable in all industries which produce a storable or postponable product, that is, a product which, if not produced and sold today, can nonetheless be produced and sold tomorrow. This illustrates the point that the "real" cost of strikes is higher in periods of full employment than in periods of less than full employment. For in the latter periods a strike may only determine when idleness, which would occur anyway, will take place.

Strike Tactics

Unions attempt to time a strike so that it will put the greatest pressure on the employer to settle. For this reason, union negotiators attempt to have the term of a collective bargaining agreement end in the employer's busiest season. Employers, of course, prefer to have contract negotiations and any strike action fall in their slack season.

Generally, a strike is preceded by a formal strike vote adopted by the union membership at a meeting at which the last offer of the employer is presented. Occasionally, the membership does not go along with the union leadership and votes to return to work; but usually, most union members support their leadership on a strike vote because they view the vote as a tactical move which psychologically strengthens the hand of their representatives in dealing with the employer.

Strikes sometimes develop without any preliminary formal action. Such unpremediated walkouts, usually called "wildcat" or "quickie" strikes, are generally of short duration and are a way in which workers let off steam which builds up as a result of tensions and grievances in modern industry. In some situations, however, frequent "spontaneous" walkouts of a few hours' duration may be part of a plan by the union leadership to gain concessions from management during the term of the contract without technically violating a no-strike pledge contained in the contract. Although in theory picket lines are informational, they also carry with them a threat of force. In most strikes, workers tend to support the walkout and do not attempt to work. Moreover, employers often do not attempt to operate during a strike unless they do so with salaried employees and supervisors. Where workers attempt to work, however, they are often met with force or threats for which police protection is more likely to be inadequate than protective.[8] The U.S. Supreme Court has strengthened the hands of unions in dealing with members who oppose strikes by ruling that a union could fine employees who crossed picket lines and then institute legal proceedings to collect those fines.[9]

Automation and Strikes

Automation has had a profound effect on union strike tactics in a number of industries. Several strikes in petroleum and chemicals have resulted in severe union defeats, since supervisory employees can keep the plant running at near capacity because of the ease of operating automatic equipment. Long-distance dialing has made telephone strikes ineffective for the same reason. Electric light and power strikes now occur with no interruption of service. To the extent that automation

---

[8] On this point see Frank H. Stewart and Robert J. Townsend, "Strike Violence: The Need for Injunctions," *University of Pennsylvania Law Review*, vol. 114 (February 1966), pp. 459–86; and Northrup and Foster, *Open Shop Construction*, pp. 192–204.

[9] For an analysis of the relevant court and NLRB decisions, see Thomas J. Keeline, *NLRB and Judicial Control of Union Discipline*, Labor Relations and Public Policy Series, Report No. 13 (Philadelphia: Industrial Research Unit, The Wharton School, University of Pennsylvania, 1976).

operates equipment with minimum manual requirements, unions are finding that the strike is becoming an outmoded weapon.

Strike Benefits and Strike Subsidies

Union leaders recognize that the ability of a union to withstand a long strike depends in major part on its members' economic staying power. Since the average union member's savings are quickly exhausted by a strike, most unions pay strike benefits. Some unions, such as the United Automobile Workers, pay benefits to all workers on a strike authorized by the international union executive board. Other unions, such as the United Steelworkers, pay benefits only to those in need. Strike benefits rarely exceed $50 per week and are often less, but even so, they quickly use up large strike funds.

During a strike, unions frequently receive gifts or borrow from other unions to help defray the costs of strike benefits, publicity, legal fees and other expenses which accompany a strike. In large strikes, such fund raising is sometimes coordinated by the AFL–CIO, whose direct resources to assist striking unionists are meager.

The meager amount of most strike benefits once required that the average unionist depend heavily on his own resources. This has changed, since striking workers now have access to food stamps, welfare of various kinds, and on the railroads, in New York and Rhode Island, to unemployment compensation as well. It is estimated that $25 million in tax-supported funds was paid to General Electric strikers in 1969–70, and about $30 million to General Motors strikers later in 1970. In New York in 1971–72, striking telephone workers received $75 per week in unemployment compensation for five months after rejecting a contract that was accepted by sister local unions in every other state. Such subsidization of strikes has become increasingly common and promises to have an increasingly unfortunate impact on collective bargaining in which the strike plays a key role.[10]

In a famous article which drew upon his experience as chairman of the World War II National War Labor Board, the late Professor George W. Taylor described the function of the strike in the collective bargaining system "as the motive power which induces a modification of extreme positions and then a meeting of minds. The acceptability of certain terms of employment is determined in relation to the losses of a work stoppage that can be avoided by agreement. In collective bargaining, economic power provides the final arbitrament."[11]

---

[10] See Armand J. Thieblot, Jr., and Ronald M. Cowin, *Welfare and Strikes: The Use of Public Funds to Support Strikers*, Labor Relations and Public Policy Series, Report No. 6 (Philadelphia: Industrial Research Unit, The Wharton School, University of Pennsylvania, 1972).

[11] George W. Taylor, "Is Compulsory Arbitration Inevitable?" *Proceedings of the First Annual Meeting* (Industrial Relations Research Association, 1948), p. 64.

If, however, one party to the collective bargaining arrangement—labor —is subsidized with public money, then the strike cannot fully perform its function of inducing agreement because it hurts only one party. In such situations, the pressure for settlement from the rank and file is reduced and strikes are likely to last longer.

Employer Strike Funds

Employers, too, have been searching for and finding ways to strengthen one another in a common stand against strong unions. One technique is through mutual assistance pacts, such as the one which exists among major airlines. Under the terms of this pact, airlines which have been shut down by a strike route prospective passengers to other lines. Participating companies share their increased revenue during the strike with the carriers that are shut down. In the newspaper industry, companies have banded together to train white-collar employees in press and other shop operations and to cooperate in printing a newspaper published by a struck company. Where employers bargain on a multicompany basis, courts have sanctioned the right of all employers in a group to lock out if the union strikes one of them.

The right of labor to strike and the right of management to resist strikes by lockout and other measures are rights which are entitled to protection so long as they do not create a war of attrition inimical to the public interest. The continued existence of the right to strike as we know it may well depend upon the moderation with which this weapon is used in the next few years. Unfortunately, the decision to strike and to tie up an entire industry now frequently devolves upon one or two persons, because of the growing scope of multiplant bargaining. The pressures on such leaders of management and labor are often such that considerations other than the general public interest are dominant. This brings us to the important question of whether unions are monopolies. Later we shall again take up the question of whether strikes can be tolerated in our economy (see Chapter 21).

UNIONS AND MONOPOLY POWER

The growing strength of organized labor and the power of unions to shut down large segments of our economy through strikes have led many writers and statesmen to ponder whether restrictive measures are necessary in order to prevent unions from destroying or seriously impairing the free enterprise system in this country. Persons dealing with this problem frequently justify their recommendation for action by labeling unions as monopolies. In some cases, their concern is with the supposed harmful *results* of union bargaining power; in other cases, with the *power* of unions to harm the general public, whether or not it is in fact exercised. Some critics of unions assail the strike as the aspect of unionism most inimical to the public welfare; others attack industry-wide bargaining or the power of exclusive representation granted unions which are certified as bargaining agents under the National Labor Relations Act. One thing emerges clearly from the epithet hurling and name-calling—there is a need for a reexamination of the whole question of whether or not unions are monopolies and, if they are, whether or not unions wield monopoly power which is detrimental to the public welfare.

Aspects of Union Monopoly Power

There are certain ways in which it might be said that unions act like a monopoly:

1. In economic theory, one test of a monopolist, as contrasted with a pure competitor, is the ability to fix prices. Unions and monopolists are alike, since both fix prices and both hope to sell as much of their respective "product" at the fixed price as they can. It is true that the union does not attempt to fix the price of labor with the same objectives in mind as those which motivate a monopolist in setting the price of his product. Presumably, a monopolist fixes a price which will maximize his profit, and in determining this price, he takes account of the fact that the quantity of his product demanded will be less at a higher price than at a lower price. Unions, however, are not profit-making organizations. They are not motivated in all cases by purely economic objectives. Unions do not consistently seek to obtain the highest wage possible or the highest possible income for their membership or the wage consistent with the largest number of jobs for the membership. Often, unions will strike for relatively little above what employers have been willing to concede, even though it is apparent that the strike is bound to cost the membership money when the gains achieved are balanced by the losses sustained during the strike. Moreover, recent studies suggest that in fixing wage rates, except in situations of sharp nonunion competition, unions do not take account of the fact that the higher the wage rate, the smaller may be the employment of union members. In other words, unions do not behave like the calculating monopolist of economic theory.

However, strong unions do, within limits, have the power to fix the price of labor. It is in this "monopoly power" that some writers find a great threat to the continuance of the free enterprise system. This is the thesis of a recent book by W. H. Hutt, who sees strikes and strike threats as disrupting the competitive system and reducing real income and equity.[12] To Hutt, it is the use of this coercive power which in effect makes the union a monopoly, and is a major cause of inflation.[13]

---

[12] W. H. Hutt, *The Strike Threat System* (New Rochelle, N.Y.: Arlington House, 1973).

[13] A further discussion of unions and inflation is found in Chapter 13.

2. A union is like a monopoly because, once certified by the National Labor Relations Board (and unless decertified), a union has, by law, an area of operation in representing workers in a bargaining unit in which competition from other unions is prohibited. Under the Taft-Hartley Act, employees bargain through unions of their own choosing which the employer must recognize as the exclusive bargaining agent. A majority of persons voting in the election determine the bargaining agent for all of the workers in the bargaining unit. As long as a union remains the certified bargaining agent, it has the exclusive right to represent workers in their relations with the employer. When this power is combined with a union shop, which requires new workers to join the union as a prerequisite to holding their jobs, the union has, in effect, obtained a monopoly over job opportunities with the particular employer. Nonunion workers or members of other unions cannot work for the employer. We noted in Chapter 6 how compulsory unionism increased the power of union leaders both over the rank and file and in their relations to the employer.

3. A monopoly which controls the source of supply of a product essential to the public can cause the public serious inconvenience and harm by shutting off the supply of that product. Unions frequently are accused of exercising this type of monopoly power, particularly when a strike shuts down an entire industry. In recent years, there seems to have been a growing feeling in some circles that the basis for this type of union power lies in the practice of multiunit collective bargaining. To many people, major strikes involving multiunit arrangements in steel, automobiles, and other industries seem like battles between Goliaths from which the public is certain to emerge as the major loser.[14]

4. In the public mind, monopoly is frequently associated with great aggrandizement of financial and economic power. The power of large unions to affect economic activity through the use of strikes is well known. Unions have also become great financial institutions. National union assets, including those under union control in welfare funds, now exceed several billion dollars, as we noted in Chapter 3. When a union with assets as large as those of the Teamsters or the United Steelworkers bargains with an individual company which is not one of the major corporations, the scales may be so tipped in favor of the union that the company can do little else but acquiesce to any demands made by the union, however illogical or uneconomic.

5. Under the antitrust laws of the United States, the test of monopoly is the power to restrain interstate commerce. The actions of unions frequently have this effect. As a matter of fact, any large-scale strike is likely to halt the free flow of products in interstate commerce. Furthermore, unions have frequently taken action deliberately aimed at restricting the flow of goods in interstate commerce. Thus, for example, the

---

[14] We shall return to this subject in Chapter 21.

U.S. Supreme Court ruled that it was unlawful for Local No. 3 of the International Brotherhood of Electrical Workers to agree with New York City electrical contractors to purchase equipment only from local manufacturers with whom it had closed-shop agreements and to agree with such manufacturers to sell only to contractors who dealt with Local No. 3. *But the Court, in effect, held that if Local No. 3 accomplished this without conspiring with employers, then it was permissible!*[15]

The extended immunity granted to labor from the antitrust laws was carried to its logical conclusion in other decisions. The American Federation of Musicians was permitted to maintain a nationwide boycott of recordings by refusing to have its members make such recordings;[16] a hod carriers' union was permitted to prevent usage within its jurisdiction of a low-cost cement-mixing machine except under conditions which made the use of such machines financially impossible;[17] building-trades unions were permitted to boycott materials because they were produced by companies where rival unions were bargaining agents or because they were prefabricated instead of being put together on the job;[18] and unions were allowed to picket or boycott a company solely on the ground that it dealt with a rival union and despite the fact that if the employer recognized the picketing or boycotting union, he would violate the National Labor Relations Act.[19] Finally, the Supreme Court refused to declare illegal union action which destroyed a business solely because the union officials disliked the owner.[20]

Recent Trends Bringing Unions under Antitrust Laws

Both the Taft-Hartley Act and the Landrum-Griffin Act restricted aspects of untrammeled union monopoly power.[21] Recent lawsuits undertaken pursuant to these laws against such unions as the Teamsters and the Mine Workers for breach of contract, closing down nonunion operations by force, or other now illegal acts have cost union treasuries hundreds of thousands of dollars. In addition, the U.S. Supreme Court has ruled in a case involving the United Mine Workers that a union forfeits its exemption from the antitrust laws when it is clearly shown that the union has agreed with one set of employers to impose a wage scale on other bargaining units. One group of employers may not conspire to eliminate competitors from an industry, and the union is liable, along

---

[15] *Allen-Bradley Co.* v. *Local 3, International Brotherhood of Electrical Workers,* 325 U.S. 797 (1945).

[16] *United States* v. *American Federation of Musicians,* 318 U.S. 741 (1943).

[17] *United States* v. *International Hod Carriers' Union,* 313 U.S. 539 (1941).

[18] *United States* v. *Building & Construction Trades Council,* 313 U.S. 539 (1941).

[19] *National Labor Relations Board* v. *Publishing Co.,* 97 F.2d 465 (1938).

[20] *Hunt* v. *Crumbach,* 325 U.S. 821 (1945).

[21] See Chapters 19 and 20 for a discussion of these laws.

with the employers, if it becomes a party to the conspiracy.[22] On the other hand, the same Court ruled that it was not illegal to force union stores to refrain from selling meat after 6 P.M. even though the stores remained open.[23] Then in June 1975 the Supreme Court ruled that a local Plumbers' union could be subject to the antitrust laws and treble damages as a result of forcing, by effective picketing, a general contractor, whose employees it neither represented nor sought to represent, to utilize only those plumbing contractors who were parties to agreements with that local union.[24] In effect, the Court likened such subcontractor agreements to a conspiracy to limit competition. We shall examine this issue in more detail in Chapter 18.

Proposals for Change

In summary, then, the charges against unions are that they fix the price of labor through the use of coercion and force, that they have a monopoly of job opportunities, that they can shut down whole industries, that they have become financial giants by reason of their tax-exempt status and their use of the checkoff of dues, and that they hold the power of life or death over thousands of individual businesses. Labor's answer is that despite the alleged power of unions, the average worker with a family still does not have sufficient take-home pay to maintain an adequate standard of living, that the union shop is simply another application of the democratic principle of majority rule, that industrywide bargaining is necessary to stabilize wage rates between competing employers, that the assets of unions are minute compared to the assets of the giant corporations with which they must bargain, and that while some employers may get hurt by union actions, unions use their power to serve millions of workers, not a privileged few.[25]

Unions, however, can hardly expect that their monopoly power can continue to be exercised without restriction in an economy which is generally committed to the principle of fostering competition. Certainly, it is realistic to assume that new regulations of trade unions will come. The direction which such regulation should take, however, is a subject on which there is no unanimity among labor critics. The great danger is that general legislation will be passed which will cause great harm rather than bring improvement.

We noted in Chapter 6 that attempts to legislate against make-work practices are likely to be both ineffective and dangerous to the free

---

[22] *United Mine Workers* v. *Pennington*, 381 U.S. 657 (1965).

[23] *Local 189, Meat Cutters* v. *Jewel Tea Co.*, 381 U.S. 657 (1969).

[24] *Connell Construction Company* v. *Plumbers and Steamfitters Local No. 100*, 421 U.S. 616 (1975).

[25] "The Labor Monopoly Myth," *Labor's Economic Review* (AFL–CIO publication), February 1956.

enterprise system because of the difficulties of distinguishing featherbed-ding from legitimate practices. Likewise, blanket condemnation of multi-unit bargaining—also a favorite of those desiring remedial legislation—could well put small businesses at the mercy of unionism, instead of having the opposite effect. For if small business cannot present a united front against union demands, it often cannot obtain an equitable bargain.

Breaking up unions into local bodies is also a much talked-about remedy. This is a variation of the proposals that the multiunit bargaining which has tied up entire industries be banned. Labor contracts would be required by law to be negotiated only between individual employers and local unions. Obviously, this proposal, if adopted, would also prohibit bargaining through employer associations, which many management spokesmen feel has done much to stabilize labor-management relations. It can be argued that thus breaking up unions might actually cause them to be even more monopolistic in determining the selling price of labor. For example, if there were four or five separate unions in the auto-mobile industry, each dealing with a different employer, each company would still find that it was dealing with a monopoly which could cut off its labor supply. On the other hand, the individual unions would vie with one another to get the highest wage possible from their particular employer. The union in General Motors would be able to push its de-mands without regard to the ability of Ford, Chrysler, or American Motors to meet those demands. Although industrywide strikes might be lessened, the restraint now present in union negotiations, which leads to more or less uniform settlements with the most prosperous as well as the least prosperous companies in the industry, would be removed. The result would probably be a strengthening of the tendency of unions to raise wages and to generate increases in money incomes.

Outlawing compulsory unionism is another proposed solution to union monopoly power. This would probably weaken unions because of its effect on union income, but it would not remove union power over product markets, necessarily reduce the potential for industrywide strikes, or otherwise solve many of the abuses discussed in this chapter.

The problem of union monopoly power thus has many complicated facets. It requires most careful analysis, as well as a general review of existing labor relations law, rather than wholesale attack by oversimpli-fied remedies. In Part Six of this book, we shall discuss our basic labor laws and how they have evolved.

QUESTIONS FOR DISCUSSION

1. Read the decision of the U.S. Supreme Court in the *Connell* case and discuss whether the decision applies only to the construction industry or whether it has wider application.

2. Are unions monopolies? Explain your answer, and compare unions with such aggregations of capital as American Telephone and Telegraph, United States Steel, and General Motors.

3. Do you feel that the future will see more and greater strikes, or fewer? Why? Would you expect such strikes, however many or few, to be accompanied by more or less violence than in the past?

SUGGESTIONS FOR FURTHER READING

deMenil, George. *Bargaining: Monopoly Power versus Union Power.* Cambridge, Mass.: MIT Press, 1971.

A mathematical representation of bargaining where firm monopoly power in the labor market is met by union monopoly power over labor supply.

Hutt, W. H. *The Strike Threat System: The Economic Consequences of Collective Bargaining.* New Rochelle, N.Y.: Arlington House, 1973.

A critique of collective bargaining as a system of enforced monopoly which lowers the standard of living of all.

Rowan, Richard L. (ed.) *Collective Bargaining: Survival in the 70's?* Labor Relations and Public Policy Series, Report No. 5. Philadelphia: Industrial Research Unit, The Wharton School, University of Pennsylvania, 1972.

Includes articles endorsing the application of antitrust laws to unions, evaluating the future of collective bargaining with and without public policy change, and stating the pros and cons of permitting strikers to be supported by public funds.

Stern, Robert N. "Intermetropolitan Patterns of Strike Frequency," *Industrial and Labor Relations Review,* vol. 29 (January 1976), pp. 218–35.

An examination of the factors which cause strikes to have a greater incidence in some areas than in others.

part four

Economics of the Labor Market

8

The Labor Market

IN THE MARKET for labor, as in the market for wheat, buyers and sellers meet and bargain over the price at which a sale is to be made. In the wheat market, one price is ultimately arrived at, determined by supply and demand, which "clears the market." Sellers who want a higher price must accept the market price, or they cannot sell their product; buyers who want to pay less than the market price cannot find sellers. Does the market for labor function like the market for wheat? If not, why not? What is the explanation for the great diversity which exists in rates of wages and salaries? These are the questions which we shall seek to answer in the following discussion.

Definition of the Labor Market

The concept of a "labor market" has been given many definitions by various writers, depending upon their points of view and the problems with which they were attempting to deal. On the one hand, the labor market can be viewed as a process by which supplies of a particular type of labor and demands for that type of labor are balanced or seek to obtain a balance. On the other hand, the labor market can be considered in the sense of a manufacturing or trading center, or some other geographic area. During World War II, the War Labor Board defined a labor market area as one in which the wage structure and levels in an industry were fairly uniform. The War Manpower Commission defined a labor market as the widest area in which employees with fixed addresses would accept employment. Somewhat similar is the definition of a "labor area" given by U.S. Department of Labor, Employment and Training Administration:

A "labor area" consists of a central city or cities and the surrounding territory within commuting distance. It is an economically integrated geographical unit within which workers may readily change jobs without changing their place of residence.[1]

The foregoing definitions have the common characteristic of viewing a labor market as a definite geographic area. Some economists, however, feel that the element of locality as a characteristic of the labor market is of limited significance insofar as the determination of wages is concerned. It is argued that unions often make wage decisions without reference to supply and demand influences in a particular geographic area. Thus, the wage demands of the Rubber Workers' Union in a small town in the Midwest will not be determined by supply and demand factors within the local area or even in the same industry, but may be related to a pattern of wage increases granted by the steel and automobile industries in other parts of the country.

Even though it may be necessary to go beyond a particular geographic area to find the forces or criteria which determine wage levels within that area, the concept of the labor market as a geographic area is still a useful one. In this discussion, the term *labor market* will be used in the sense of the geographic area within which a particular group of employers and wage earners buy and sell services. For some forms of labor, the geographic area may be a town, whereas for other forms of labor, such as a talented violinist, the geographic limits of the labor market may be the entire Western world.

DIFFERENCES BETWEEN LABOR MARKETS AND COMMODITY MARKETS

Labor markets differ from commodity markets. In commodity markets, the product is usually standardized. No. 2 Winter Wheat is No. 2 Winter Wheat anywhere in the world. Not so with the labor effort offered by the individual employee. Individuals vary in interest, motivation, skill, potential, and many other aspects. Furthermore, in the eyes of the seller, each buyer is distinguished from every other buyer. Some workers like to work for a large company, some for a small one. Because the sale of labor involves a continuing rather than a merely temporary relationship with the "buyer," such intangibles are frequently more important in the employee's mind than is the employer's offering price.

Diversity of Rates

Diversity of rates for the same type of labor is the norm, not the exception, in the labor market. As we shall see, differences may exist

---

[1] U.S. Department of Labor, Employment and Training Administration, *Area Trends in Employment and Unemployment, August–September 1975* (Washington, D.C.: Government Printing Office, 1975), p. 13.

between firms, between industries, and between localities. The continued existence of such differentials is attributable in part to imperfections in the flow of information and in part to the variety of influences deriving from both the product market and the labor market which ultimately determine wage levels. Furthermore, because of differences in the skill, experience, and seniority of employees performing the same job, diversity in wage rates for the same job may exist even within a single plant.

Wage Fixing in the Labor Market

Wage fixing, analogous to a quoted price in the product market, is characteristic of the labor market. Whereas it is normally the seller who sets the asking price in the commodity market, in the labor market (in the absence of unions) the buyer of labor normally sets the price. The price that is set tends to be "fixed" for some length of time. Employers do not want wage rates to fluctuate with every change in supply and demand conditions. Stability in wage rates is essential for satisfactory business operations. Constant change in the wage schedule of the average company would cost more than it is worth. Moreover, stability is also desirable from the point of view of employees. Frequent changes in wage rates would cause friction and suspicion and would make employees feel insecure. Therefore, in changing wage rates, employers customarily grant general wage adjustments to all employees instead of adjusting the rates to individual demand and supply conditions, or at least grant individual wage increases according to some plan or custom.

The majority of multiplant companies do relate their wage scales either to those paid by other firms in the area or to rates for the same industry in the area; some, however, pay the same wage scales regardless of the size of the city or the region of the country in which their plants are located, and others have uniform scales for each region or zone. Still others pay community wage rates, but grant the same adjustments, regardless of area. Some companies raise wages with increases in the cost of living and increases in length of service, while other companies do not. Such differences in company wage policies, in employer evaluation of particular jobs, and in stress on various wage factors all contribute to the existence of a diversity of wage rates for any grade of labor in a particular locality.

The labor market, therefore, is not characterized by a norm of pure competition. There is no wage which will clear the market, toward which a labor market under actual conditions, even in the absence of collective bargaining, is tending. The labor market is characterized by stability and a lack of fluidity and by a diversity of rates for similar jobs. A rise in the price of labor offered by a particular employer does not cause employees in other firms who are receiving less than that amount to leave their jobs and flock to the high-wage employer. Sufficiently large differentials will, of course, induce a movement of labor; but within a substantial range, changes in a particular employer's rates may have little effect in causing workers to leave other firms to seek work in the high-wage firm. In order to understand why this is so and why diverse wage rates for the same jobs can continue to coexist in the same area, some understanding of labor mobility is required.

THE NATURE OF LABOR MOBILITY

Labor is not a fluid factor of production. It does not flow readily in response to small changes in its remuneration. One reason is that work—having and keeping a job—is a central status symbol in our profit-oriented society, and changing jobs involves a risk of having no work at all. A second reason is that generally the employee must transport himself to the place of work, and this may require an expenditure of time and money. The inadequate state of our public transportation systems in many of our large cities undoubtedly inhibits the mobility of many low-income job seekers.

Problems of the Job Search

How do job seekers obtain information about potential job openings? Information sources can be divided into two types of networks: informal and formal. Informal networks include referrals from employees, friends, relatives, and other casual sources, and walk-ins or hiring at the gate. Formal networks include state employment agencies, private fee-charging agencies, union hiring halls, newspaper advertisements, and school or college placement bureaus. Most studies have found that employees rely most often upon informal networks. A nationwide survey conducted by the U.S. Bureau of Labor Statistics in January 1973 found that two out of every three workers applied directly to employers without suggestions or referrals by anyone. Not only was this the most frequent method used, but it also proved to be the most effective. Of all persons who applied directly to employers for work, about half found their jobs that way—about double the proportion for the methods with the next highest success ratios.[2]

Of course, job search methods will vary, depending upon the condition of the labor market. In January 1973, when this study was made, the unemployment rate was 5.0% and falling, whereas employment was rising.[3] In a tight labor market, workers are more apt to rely on an informal

---

[2] U.S. Department of Labor, Bureau of Labor Statistics, *Jobseeking Methods Used by American Workers,* Bulletin 1886 (Washington, D.C.: Government Printing Office, 1975), p. 2.

[3] U.S. Department of Labor, *Employment and Earnings,* vol. 20 (August 1973), table A–36, p. 47.

grapevine as a source of job information. On the other hand, in a labor market with high unemployment and fewer job opportunities, workers are more apt to rely on state and private employment services and other formal avenues.

In a perfect labor market, job opportunities would be generally known and available workers would gravitate toward the better-paying jobs for which their skills qualified them. In the actual labor market, this process is only dimly visible because information about various job vacancies and the advantages and disadvantages of particular jobs are not generally known. To a large extent, job attachments result from chance, rather than careful economic appraisal.

Changing Jobs

Even after a worker has found a job, his new status as an employee does not broaden his horizon of knowledge about other job opportunities markedly. Generally, wages, hours, and working conditions in other plants are either vague or unknown to him. Even if employees know that a higher wage can be obtained at a different plant or in a different occupation, they may be reluctant to make a change. One reason is that there is a transfer cost in making such a change. There may be a period of layoff between jobs, or additional training may be required, or perhaps the worker will have to physically move himself and his family to a new city or to a new residence in a different part of a city. All of these costs impose barriers to movement. Since a job change may mean loss of seniority and accrued rights under pension plans, employees are generally reluctant to leave a job as long as they consider their conditions of employment to be generally "fair" even though they may not be the best.

Determinants of Occupational Mobility

Nevertheless, there is still considerable occupational movement in the American economy. Among the 69 million persons working in both January 1972 and January 1973, over 5 million had changed occupations during the year.[4] Although occupational mobility is obviously affected by wars and by economic events, such as the business cycle, over a period of years the percentage of the work force changing occupations has remained relatively constant.[5]

Statistical data suggest definite interrelationships among worker mobility (both voluntary and involuntary) and age, sex, color, education,

---

[4] James J. Byrne, "Occupational Mobility of Workers," *Monthly Labor Review,* vol. 98 (February 1975), p. 54.

[5] The mobility rate of 8.7% was virtually the same in 1972 and 1965. Ibid., p. 58.

type of job, and character of employment. As age increases, mobility decreases. Mobility is slightly higher for men than for women—9% as opposed to 8.2%[6]—but this appears to be primarily attributable to the relatively low mobility rate for black women. The mobility rate of white women is not significantly lower than that of white men. Likewise, few pronounced or consistent racial differences are apparent, except for the relatively low rate for black women.

With respect to education among both men and women, occupational mobility rates are highest for persons with one–three years of college and lowest for persons with eight years of schooling or less. Mobility is lowest in occupations requiring large investments in training time, such as the professions, and in occupations requiring heavy investment in land and/or machinery, such as farming. There appears to be more movement from blue-collar to white-collar occupations than vice versa. The reason is probably the faster growth of white-collar jobs during recent years.[7]

The Relationship between Job Change and Occupational Change

The relationship between occupational change and job change is shown in Table 8–1. As can be seen from the table, workers who

TABLE 8–1

The Relationship between Job Change and Occupation Change

	Men	Women
All persons, 18 years and over, not in school	100.0	100.0
Changed both occupation and employer	8.1	7.6
Changed occupation but not employer	.9	.6
Changed employer but not occupation	6.2	6.8
Changed neither occupation nor employer	84.8	85.0

Source: Adapted from James J. Byrne, "Occupational Mobility of Workers," *Monthly Labor Review*, vol. 98 (February 1975), p. 57.

change occupations are likely to have changed jobs. Furthermore, about 80% of both men and women who had changed occupations had also changed the industry in which they were working.[8] On the whole, persons are less likely to change occupations than to change jobs. Changing occupations often entails a difficult readjustment because a worker's accumulated experience and training may not be as useful in a new field. Job changes occur most frequently in occupations requiring little or no skill, such as those of operatives, service workers, and laborers. Unemployment rates are also relatively high in such occupations.

[6] Ibid., p. 55.

[7] Ibid.

[8] Ibid., p. 57.

One other important factor must be considered in any analysis of job changes—namely, that many of them are not wholly economically motivated. Reasons of health, residence, family, friendship, and many other factors can all contribute in motivating an employee to make a job change. Such noneconomic factors further lessen the correlation between wage changes and employment in the labor market.

Geographic Mobility

Some job changes may require a change of residence. Nearly 20% of the American population has changed residence each year since World War II.[9] Although most moves are made over rather short distances, nevertheless the geographic shifts of the population over time play an important role in determining the condition of labor markets in various parts of the nation.

Age is clearly the most important single determinant of who moves and who does not, with persons in their late teens and early twenties being more mobile than are persons of other ages. Nearly 50% of all persons change residence in their early twenties,[10] a time of life when many persons are still shopping around in the labor market or are just entering the labor force after college. Although age is the best general indicator of who is likely to move, within age groups educational level is probably the best indicator of who is likely to migrate. Among men 25 to 29 years old with less than a high school education, just over 5% can be expected to move from one state to another within a year's time. For men with a graduate school education, this percentage rises to 15%.[11] In other words, the young professor or the aerospace engineer is more likely to move across the country in search of a job than is the automobile mechanic. For many college-educated persons, the job market is national in scope. Furthermore, such persons are likely to have greater knowledge of economic opportunities in other geographic areas than do less educated workers.

Four important trends have characterized the geographic movement of the population since the end of World War II:

1. *Interregional shifts.* During the 1960s, the South experienced significant net in-migration for the first time in this century. Evidence suggests that an important contributing factor to his change was the increasing relative availability of skilled jobs in the South. It is significant that among occupational categories, net in-migration was highest among operatives and craft workers and lowest among nonfarm laborers. Except for the District of Columbia and Maryland, all southern states

---

[9] U.S. Department of Labor, *Manpower Report of the President, 1974* (Washington, D.C.: Government Printing Office, 1974), p. 97.

[10] Ibid., p. 84.

[11] Ibid.

TABLE 8-2
Why Industry Moves to the Sunbelt

| | Manufacturing Costs Are Lower . . . | | | | . . . and So Are Executive Living Costs | |
	Production Workers' Weekly Earnings	All-Industry Weekly Earnings*	Gas Utility Costs (per million BTUs)	State and Local Tax Rates (percent of personal income)	Budget†	Difference from U.S. Average
U.S. average	$192	$164	$0.50	15.6%	$22,475	
Southeast	162	145	0.56	15.3	20,475	−$2,000
Southwest	175	143	0.33	14.3	20,050	−2,425
New England	166	154	1.23	15.8	24,070	+1,595
Mideast	200	171	0.79	17.3	23,175	+700
Great Lakes	223	173	0.65	14.6	22,320	−155
Plains	192	153	0.44	14.5	21,915	−560
Rocky Mountain	195	157	0.36	16.1	21,485	−990
Far West	230	186	0.50	17.4	22,340	−135

* Average earnings adjusted for concentration of high-wage industries in certain states.
† Budget compiled by Bureau of Labor Statistics for a family of four maintaining a "higher level" living standard in 38 representative metropolitan areas.
Source: Data, U.S. Department of Labor, Bureau of Labor Statistics; North Carolina Office of State Planning; American Gas Association, The Tax Foundation, *Business Week* estimates. Reprinted from the May 17, 1976, issue of *Business Week* by special permission. © 1976 by McGraw-Hill, Inc.

registered overall increases in the number of manufacturing employees between 1960 and 1971 despite the relative decline in manufacturing in the national economy.[12] Industry has been attracted to the South by lower wages, taxes, and energy costs (see Table 8–2), and perhaps also by the existence throughout the South (except in Kentucky, New Mexico, and Oklahoma) of state right-to-work laws which may well have deterred union organizing efforts.

2. *Movement from nonmetropolitan areas to metropolitan areas.* From the 1940s through the 1960s, metropolitan areas consistently gained population from nonmetropolitan areas. Since 1970, metropolitan growth has slowed considerably, particularly in the large urban areas.[13] It seems possible that in the years ahead some metropolitan areas—particularly in the Northeast—may actually lose population to nonmetropolitan areas. It is significant that during the decade of the 1960s metropolitan areas in both the Midwest and the Northeast would have actually experienced a net out-migration, had there not been a net inflow of blacks and other minority races.[14]

3. *Movement from cities to suburbs.* The movement of whites from cities to suburbs continues unabated. Between 1960 and 1970, the white population decreased in nine of the ten central cities of the largest metropolitan areas and increased significantly in the suburbs. Not only have people moved to the suburbs, but the locus of jobs has also moved. By 1970, 72% of the employed suburban residents in the 15 largest SMSAs worked in the suburbs. From 1948 to 1967, employment in 39 suburban areas grew from 3.7 million to 8.1 million, while employment in neighboring central cities expanded from 8.9 million to 9.7 million. In other words, the suburban rings absorbed 85% of the new job opportunities in these metropolitan areas.[15]

4. *Black migration from the South to northern cities.* During the 1950s, there was a net out-migration of 1.5 million southern blacks, or about 14% of the 1950 black population of the South. During the 60s, another 1.4 million blacks left, representing about 12% of the 1960 black population of the South. As a result of these massive shifts, the blacks have changed from a predominantly rural population to an overwhelming urban one—in 1970, 81.3% of blacks were classified as urban dwellers.[16] During the 70s, the concentration of blacks in central cities, which are experiencing a decline in job opportunities, has accentuated the dichotomy between primary and secondary labor markets, which are discussed below.

---

[12] Ibid., pp. 70–72.

[13] Ibid., p. 77.

[14] Ibid., p. 78.

[15] Ibid., pp. 80–81.

[16] Ibid., p. 90.

The Trend in Quit Rates

In the labor market, both employer and employee are frequently more interested in job stability than in mobility. The employee prefers stability in job tenure so that he is not exposed to income loss while changing jobs and so that he can build up rights in valuable job fringes based upon seniority. The employer prefers stability because it means that costs of hiring and training new employees are minimized and that he can plan production and operation schedules with the knowledge that adequate personnel is available. Yet, from the point of view of the needs of a dynamic economy with a constantly changing mix of job opportunities, a higher rate of mobility may be required in order to achieve a better utilization of the labor force and to minimize shortages of labor and bottlenecks in production as the economy achieves high employment levels.

Is labor mobility increasing or decreasing in our economy? One way of measuring this trend is to examine so-called quit rates. Voluntary quits are defined as persons who leave the employ of a company upon their own volition for any reason except to retire, enter military service, or transfer to another establishment of the same company. Series of such data per 100 employees are available for manufacturing industries over a long period of years. Unfortunately, they are collected only for manufacturing industries, although labor turnover is undoubtedly higher in some nonmanufacturing industries. As the figures in Table 8–3 reveal, quits are relatively small and tend to vary inversely with layoffs and the rate of unemployment.

There has been considerable controversy in the economic literature as to whether there has been a long-run tendency for the quit rate in manufacturing to decline. Some writers have suggested that seniority rights, pensions, and other benefits of job retention have in effect created a "new industrial feudalism" because workers can no longer afford to quit their jobs. Other investigators have found no evidence of a decline in the quit rate. Of course, the trend in voluntary mobility cannot be determined merely from the quit rates listed in Table 8–3. What is really relevant is the amount of movement as measured by quit rates in relationship to the opportunity or incentives for movement as measured by unemployment rates, interindustry differentials, and similar factors. Burton and Parker conclude, after adjusting for incentives and opportunities for voluntary mobility, that there has been no trend toward declining voluntary mobility in manufacturing industries in the postwar era.[17]

---

[17] John F. Burton, Jr., and John E. Parker, *The New Industrial Feudalism: Secular Trends in Voluntary Labor Mobility*, Occasional Papers No. 33 (A. G. Bush Library of Management, Organization, and Industrial Relations, University of Chicago, 1971), p. 21. See also Paul A. Armknecht and John F. Early, "Quits in Manufacturing: A Study of Their Causes," *Monthly Labor Review*, vol. 95 (November 1972), pp. 31–37.

TABLE 8–3

Quit Rates and Layoff Rates in Manufacturing and Unemployment as Percent of Labor Force (annual averages, selected years, 1955–1975)

| | Per 100 Employees | | Unemploy- |
Year	Quit Rate	Layoff Rate	ment Percent
1955	1.9	1.5	4.4
1960	1.3	2.4	5.5
1965	1.9	1.4	4.5
1966	2.6	1.2	3.8
1967	2.3	1.4	3.8
1968	2.5	1.2	3.6
1969	2.7	1.2	3.5
1970	2.1	1.8	4.9
1971	1.8	1.6	5.9
1972	2.2	1.1	5.6
1973	2.7	.9	4.9
1974	2.3	1.5	5.6
1975	1.4	2.1	8.5

Source: Unemployment rates from U.S. Department of Labor, *Employment and Training Report of the President, 1976* (Washington, D.C.: Government Printing Office, 1976), table A–1, p. 211; quit rates and layoff rates from *Employment and Earnings*, vol. 11 (June 1965), table D–1, p. 55, and vol. 22 (May 1976), table D–1, p. 109.

It is interesting to note that job turnover rates are considerably higher in the United States than in other industrialized countries. For example, turnover rates in manufacturing, measured as the number of separations (quits and layoffs) per 100 employees, were from 70% to 100% higher in the United States during the 1960s than in West Germany, Great Britain, or Italy. In Japan, turnover rates are extremely low because of the custom of "lifetime employment" in which many workers are felt to be committed to employment by a single firm throughout their careers.[18] Compulsory retirement at 55, however, shortens the Japanese worker's career.

LABOR MARKET STRUCTURE

In analyzing various labor markets in this country, we may distinguish them by their geographic location—for example, the West Coast labor market differs materially from that in other parts of the country— or we may distinguish labor markets according to their "structure." A labor market structure has been defined as

a set of "established practices" which are applied consistently in carrying out the various employment functions of recruitment, selection, as-

[18] *Economic Report of the President, 1975* (Washington, D.C.: Government Printing Office, 1975), p. 101.

signment to jobs, wage payment, transfer, separation, and the like. Established practices are created by law, contract, custom, and managerial policy. Their function is to establish the rights and privileges of employees and to introduce certainty and regularity into the handling of personnel—in short, to create a "rule of law" in employment matters. Their main effect is to limit managerial discretion.[19]

In terms of the foregoing definition, labor markets range all the way from the highly structured to the unstructured, depending upon the presence or absence of rules or practices governing the employment relationship.

Structured Labor Markets

It has been estimated that so-called structured labor markets cover about 80% of all employed workers, not including the self-employed, farm laborers, domestic workers, and others performing odd jobs of various types.[20] Structured labor markets fall into three general categories: (1) the market for public employees, which is structured from entry to exit by legislation and administrative rules; (2) the nonunion labor market in the large firm, in which the structuring aspect emanates from the employer's personnel policies, formulated and administered by a personnel department; (3) the labor market, in which "established practices" derive from collective bargaining agreements and union work rules.

The market for public employees is impersonal, technical, and highly classified. Emphasis is placed both on security of tenure and on pay. Entrance requirements are frequently based upon competitive examination. A high proportion of regular, permanent public employees are eligible for civil service status, which carries with it advantages of tenure and opportunities for promotion. However, despite the fact that government, in theory, has unrestricted authority to vary the terms and conditions of employment, as a practical matter the hands of the government administrator in charge of a particular agency are securely tied with the red tape of governmental regulation, so that the public labor market has many of the characteristics of a highly unionized labor market in the private business sector of the economy. The increasing importance of collective bargaining among public employees has further accentuated the formalized structuring of wage and employment practices in this field.[21]

---

[19] Orme W. Phelps, "A Structural Model of the U.S. Labor Market," *Industrial and Labor Relations Review,* vol. 10 (April 1957), p. 403. The writers have drawn heavily on this excellent article for the analysis contained in this section.

[20] U.S. Department of Labor, *Manpower Report, 1974,* p. 114.

[21] See Chapter 22 for a discussion of collective bargaining by government employees.

The nonunion structured labor market dominated by employer personnel policies is to be found in three major areas: the large unorganized industrial firm, which, although somewhat exceptional, still exists; the large unorganized firm in the white-collar industries—banks, department stores, insurance companies, and so on; and nonunion employees outside the bargaining unit in large companies which are organized. Large unorganized industrial firms retain unilateral control over employment policies but, in practice, are likely to follow the rates and policies of their organized competitors so as not to make themselves a target for union organization. In addition, restraints on wages and conditions are imposed by state and federal laws. Large white-collar companies are still the stronghold for structured employment policies dictated by management. This group has become more important in the present decade in terms of share of the total labor market because of the shift of employment toward trade, finance, and related fields, in which this type of structure predominates. White-collar workers who are outside the bargaining unit in organized companies do not have the full protection of the union, but nevertheless benefit in many ways from gains secured by the union for organized employees. Obviously, management cannot afford to have major inequities develop between the two groups of employees, which would either have a bad effect on morale or constitute an invitation to union organization.

Most unionized employment is manual, hourly rated, blue-collar work. The employee may either work on a permanent basis for a large industrial concern or be employed in one of the casual trades, such as construction, where his or her association with any one employer may be brief. The structure of such a labor market is, in theory, bilateral, resulting from the bargain made by the employer and the union. Where the employer is small and the union strong, as in the building trades or the trucking industry, the union may often dictate the rates of pay, the hours of work, job assignments, promotions, and other aspects of the employment relationship. In larger firms the personnel department may still make policy decisions, but these are generally subject to review and consultation with the union through collective bargaining.

Unstructured Labor Markets

The unstructured labor market is, in general, the market of individual bargains, in which there are few if any rules or regulations affecting employment practices, except governmental enactments setting minimum wages, prohibiting discrimination, and so on. This market includes farm labor, domestic help, professional office employees, and employees of small business firms. It has been estimated that the unstructured labor market covers about 20% of the civilian employed labor force (excluding the self-employed, farm laborers, domestic workers, and others performing odd jobs of various types). Employment in unstructured labor markets is apt to be on a personal basis, with little emphasis on formal policies and procedures. Union organization is largely absent, fringe benefits are few, and in many cases the employer is not even subject to the minimal structuring provided by various federal statutes, since such statutes—the Taft-Hartley Act, the Fair Labor Standards Act, and similar laws—provide exemptions for small local businesses.

Internal and External Labor Markets

An employee may progress up the job ladder in a given company (internal market), or he may seek better opportunities with other employers (external market). In some situations in which a large employer dominates an isolated town, there may be no realistic external market for most employees. But even in large industrial areas with many companies competing in the labor market, opportunities for advancement within the internal market of the company are very important to the individual employee. Industries and firms vary widely in the opportunities they provide to new workers to advance up the job ladder. At one extreme, some employers have well-defined career progression steps for qualified employees. On the other hand, one recent examination of advancement opportunities in 11 major manufacturing and nonmanufacturing industries estimated that about one third of the workers involved were in dead-end jobs and that some eight out of nine of these were at the bottom rung of the ladder in either unskilled or semiskilled jobs, while most of the remainder had managed to move a step higher and were working supervisors.[22] Generally advancement—defined in terms of increases in annual earnings—is considerably more rapid in high-wage industries than in low-wage industries, such as textiles and apparels.[23]

Primary and Secondary Labor Markets

In recent years, increasing concern with respect to the high unemployment and low earnings of disadvantaged groups in our urban centers has given rise to a theory of dual labor markets.[24] Under this theory, the urban labor market is divided into two separate sectors, a "primary" market and a "secondary" market, which operate side by side. There is, of course, some movement of workers between the two, but for the most part, disadvantaged workers are denied the opportunity of moving from the secondary to the primary market.

[22] W. J. Grinker, D. D. Cooke, and A. W. Kirsch, *Climbing the Job Ladder: A Study of Employee Advancement in Eleven Industries* (New York: E. F. Shelley and Co., 1970), chap. 1.

[23] U.S. Department of Labor, *Manpower Report, 1974*, p. 116.

[24] See Peter B. Doeringer and Michael J. Piore, *Internal Labor Markets and Manpower Analysis* (Lexington, Mass.: D. C. Heath & Co., 1971).

The primary labor market is characterized by jobs which offer good pay, good working conditions, and steady employment. The secondary market is characterized by jobs which offer irregular employment, low wages, poor working conditions, and low status. Typical are jobs in restaurants and car washes, day labor in construction, private household work, and so on. To some extent, the instability of secondary jobs is matched by the instability of the work force. Since the rewards of secondary employment are low, the penalty for quitting or otherwise losing one's job is also low. Therefore, the secondary market is characterized by frequent job changes and high rates of absenteeism and tardiness. Doeringer and Piore argue that for a variety of socioeconomic reasons, racial minorities tend to be confined to jobs in the secondary labor market, whereas white males have the opportunity to move from secondary to primary jobs, especially as they advance in age from teenage to prime-age workers.[25]

One writer[26] has amplified this theory by pointing out that disadvantaged workers in urban labor markets may actually move in and out of at least four different markets—the secondary labor market, the training sector, the welfare sector, and the irregular economy. (See Figure 8–1.) The last involves various legitimate or illegitimate ways of "hustling," which may involve as many as two fifths of all adults in ghetto neighborhoods. Mobility among the four markets, takes place freely, but only infrequently do these workers move into the primary core labor market.[27]

As a consequence, there can be shortages in the primary job market and continuing irregularity of employment and low earnings in the secondary labor market. Poverty, discrimination, lack of skills—all erect a barrier between the two markets. Recognition of such a barrier implies that reliance cannot be placed simply upon a revival of general business to reduce unemployment among the disadvantaged. Special remedies will be required to deal effectively with this complex problem.[28]

DIVERSITY IN WAGE RATES

We have already observed that even in a local labor market, divergent wage rates may prevail for similar jobs. It is not surprising, then, that diversity is also found when cities are compared with towns or the South with the North, or one industry with another industry. Indeed, diversity of rates is characteristic of the labor market however that term is defined.

---

[25] Ibid.

[26] Bennett Harrison, "Employment, Unemployment, and Structure of the Urban Labor Market," Wharton Quarterly, vol. 6 (Spring 1972), pp. 4–7, 26–31.

[27] Ibid., p. 28.

[28] Manpower policies to deal with the problems of the disadvantaged are considered in Chapter 15.

FIGURE 8–1

The Structure of Urban Labor Markets

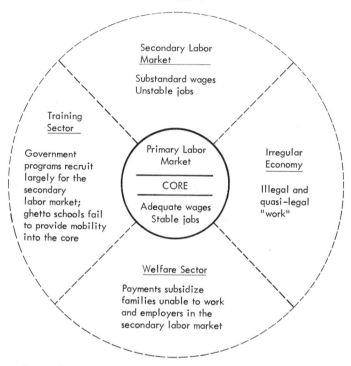

Source: Bennett Harrison, "Employment, Unemployment, and Structure of the Urban Labor Market," *Wharton Quarterly*, vol. 6 (Spring 1972), p. 7. Reproduced by permission.

In the following discussion we shall consider such diversity from four principal points of view: geographic, interindustry, interfirm, and personal.

Geographic Diversity: The North–South Differential

Regional location is an important factor in determining pay levels. It is frequently stated that "wages are lower in the South." This statement is open to several interpretations. The North–South differential may mean that wages in particular industries are lower in the South than in other parts of the country. This is true in some industries, but not in others. Among 26 manufacturing industries studied by the U.S. Bureau of Labor Statistics, the southern wage level ranged from 38.6% below the rest of the country in meat-packing to more than 9% above in synthetic fibers.[29] A study of the compensation of bank employees, conducted in 1973,

---

[29] H. M. Douty, "Wage Differentials: Forces and Counterforces," *Monthly Labor Review*, vol. 91 (March 1968), p. 74.

found that the Northeast region had the highest level of employee compensation ($5.81 an hour), followed in descending order by the North Central ($5.10), the West ($4.96), and the South ($4.72).[30]

The North–South wage differential may suggest that in given occupations, earnings are lower in the South than in the North. Although this may be true as a general statement, the extent of the differential varies markedly, depending upon the occupation. Table 8–2 indicates that the weekly earnings of production workers are lowest in the Southeast sector of the country. On the other hand, a recent study of clerical, computer, and plant workers found that after eliminating the effect of unionization and plant size, pay levels for skilled maintenance workers were actually higher in the South than in the Northeast.[31] As can be seen from Table 8–4, regional differentials are most pronounced for unskilled plant work-

TABLE 8–4

Pay Levels for Occupational Groups in Four Regions, as Percentage of National Average

Occupations	U.S.	Northeast	South	North Central	West
Unskilled plant	100	102	80	109	109
Clerical	100	102	96	100	105
Skilled maintenance	100	95	94	105	106
Technical support	100	101	97	101	101
Professional and administrative	100	101	99	99	102

Source: Harry F. Zeman, "Regional Pay Differentials in White-Collar Occupations," *Monthly Labor Review*, vol. 94 (January 1971), p. 53.

ers, while the differences in the professional and administrative category are insignificant. The high geographic mobility of persons in the latter category, as already mentioned, means that such employees function in a labor market which is national in scope, and therefore their rates are less subject to regional and local influences.

The North–South differential could also be taken to mean that earnings in certain southern states are much lower than those in northern states. This variation is very apparent. In January 1976, the five states whose production workers on manufacturing payrolls had the lowest average weekly earnings were all in the South and Southwest: New Mexico, $148.54; Arkansas, $151.96; North Carolina, $146.46; Mississippi, $149.97; and South Carolina, $153.82. Contrary to what might be expected, however, earnings in Alabama exceeded those in Maine, New

[30] U.S. Department of Labor, *Employee Compensation and Payroll Hours: Banks, 1973*, Bureau of Labor Statistics Report 451 (1976), p. 2.

[31] Stephen E. Baldwin and Robert S. Daski, "Occupational Pay Differences among Metropolitan Areas," *Monthly Labor Review*, vol. 99 (May 1976), p. 29.

Hampshire, and Rhode Island.[32] Likewise, if we examine fringe benefits, we find a regional differential. In 1975, employee benefits as a percent of payroll for all industries averaged 32.7 in the Southeast compared to 36.9 in the Northeast; for all manufacturing, the corresponding figures were 32.2 and 37.5.[33] Of course, such differentials may be attributable not so much to geographic location as to the nature of the industries involved. Furthermore, it is important to note that there is frequently tremendous variation in the rates of compensation within the boundaries of a particular state.

The North–South differential may mean that the average wage of all workers in one region is lower than the average wage of all workers in the other. This is obviously a crude measurement because it compares wages without regard to the intraregional industrial mix and the variations in skills, city size, and other factors which can affect wage levels. One study concluded that average hourly earnings in the non-South are about 25% higher than in the South. About one third of this differential is attributable to regional differences in the labor force as measured by color, age, sex, and education; about one third is related to regional differences in city size; and about one third of the differential remains, after adjusting for labor force composition and city size.[34]

Many explanations have been advanced as to why this residual differential exists. Some claim that southern labor is less efficient, but after adjusting for educational differences, there is little evidence to support this claim. Union leaders argue that the weakness of union organization in the South accounts for the differential, but North–South wage differentials are much too complex and diverse for such a simple explanation. The differentials vary widely in amounts from industry to industry, whether or not the industries are unionized. Another possible reason is an oversupply of labor in the South relative to capital—or to put it another way, a relative shortage of capital—which could affect the productivity of labor.

Although there is considerable evidence that money wages on the average are higher in the North than in the South, it is also known that the cost of living is higher in the North. The question then becomes: Is there a difference in real wages between the two sections? There is no clear-cut answer to this question; the results will depend upon the cities or areas which are compared.[35]

---

[32] U.S. Department of Labor, *Employment and Earnings*, vol. 22 (April 1976), table C–13, pp. 110–13.

[33] Chamber of Commerce of the United States, *Employee Benefits, 1975* (Washington, D.C.: The Chamber, 1976), p. 14.

[34] Victor R. Fuchs, "Hourly Earnings Differentials by Region and Size of City," *Monthly Labor Review*, vol. 90 (January 1967), p. 25.

[35] See Mark L. Ladenson, "The End of the North–South Wage Differential: Comment," *American Economic Review*, vol. 63 (September 1973), pp. 754–56; and P. R. P. Coelho and M. A. Ghali, "The End of the North–South Wage Differential: Reply," ibid., pp. 757–62.

Union Policy and Regional Differentials

In general, union policy has opposed regional wage differentials. The United Mine Workers, for example, has succeeded in equalizing basic wage rates between the northern and southern Appalachian coal regions; the Steelworkers, with the cooperation of United States Steel and Republic Steel, began to eliminate area differentials in the late 1940s, and the job was pretty much completed in the 1950s. The UAW has ended all area differentials at Chrysler and Ford and has fought to eliminate them at General Motors. The Rubber Workers has been unsuccessful in its attempts to eliminate the regional wage spread. In the early 1960s, however, James R. Hoffa was successful in achieving a uniform national rate for over-the-road truck drivers, thereby eliminating several differentials, including one in the South.

On the other hand, many unions have not opposed southern wage differentials where they regard them as justified by certain circumstances. Because of a poor grade of coal and higher transportation costs, the United Mine Workers continues to sanction wage differentials between the Alabama and the Appalachian bituminous areas. The Textile Workers' Union of America has sanctioned differentials between Virginia and the New York metropolitan area.

The difficulty of organizing workers in the South, combined with the low wages of this area, have served as a brake on North–South wage differentials in certain industries. Unable to organize the South, the hosiery and textile workers have seen lower southern rates keep down their wage gains in the North; other unionized mills in the North have either migrated South, where they operate nonunion, or gone out of business. The failure of the United Mine Workers to organize southern coal mines in the 1920s almost destroyed the union. The northern mines were forced to break with the United Mine Workers in order to compete with the low-wage South. The rising number of southern Appalachian mines which now operate nonunion at lower wage and fringe benefit rates is again a severe problem for the UMW.

In these cases, the problem of the regional differential to the union is the problem of union and nonunion competition. The problem of the North–South differential is less acute when the unionized high-wage employers are located in and sell to a market such as the Far West, which, because of distance and geographic factors, is primarily local and is not sensitive to southern competition.

Geographic Diversity: City Size

While average hourly earnings are generally highest in the West and lowest in the South, within each region of this country it has been found that city size has a major impact upon wages no matter what kind of labor is being hired: men or women, white or nonwhite, skilled or unskilled, well schooled or uneducated.

Generally, the bigger the city, the higher the wage. The reasons for this relationship are not fully understood. One study has suggested that there may be some relation between city size and labor productivity.[36] Another contributing factor may be the higher living costs and commuting expenses characteristic of large cities. Whatever the explanation, the fact remains that these differentials do exist, and their existence further attests to the lack of fluidity of labor and capital among geographic areas.

Interindustry Differentials

Marked differences in rates and earnings for similar jobs prevail among various industries, even in the same geographic area. The existence of industrial differentials does not necessarily mean that workers performing comparable jobs are paid at different rates in different industries, though this is sometimes the case. One industry may pay lower rates on the average than another because it requires less skill; because it employs a larger percentage of women, blacks, or part-time workers; because its plants are located in small towns or rural areas rather than in metropolitan areas; or because it lacks union organization.

Table 8–5 suggests that there may have been some broadening of

TABLE 8–5

Average Hourly Earnings of Production or Nonsupervisory Workers on Private Payrolls by Industry Division, Selected Years, 1947–1975 (in dollars)

	1947	1950	1960	1970	1975
Contract construction	1.45	2.02	3.20	5.69	7.24
Mining	1.47	1.93	2.64	4.06	5.89
Durable goods manufacturing	1.28	1.65	2.49	3.79	5.13
Nondurable goods manufacturing	1.15	1.44	2.11	3.26	4.34
Wholesale trade	1.22	1.52	2.31	3.67	4.89
Retail trade	.84	1.06	1.56	2.57	3.33
Finance, insurance, real estate	1.14	1.45	2.09	3.27	4.13

Source: U.S. Department of Labor et al., *Employment and Training Report of the President, 1976* (Washington, D.C.: Government Printing Office, 1976), table C–3, p. 296.

industrial differentials in hourly earnings between 1947 and 1975, at least between the highest paid (contract construction) and the lowest (retail trade). Earnings per hour in construction were 2.2 times as high as those in retail trade in 1975, compared to only 1.8 times in 1947. A similar trend with respect to these industry groups is found when weekly earnings are compared. Weekly earnings in contract construction stood

---

[36] Baldwin and Daski, "Occupational Pay Differences," p. 29.

at $264.98 in 1975, compared to $58.87 in 1947, while weekly earnings in retail trade rose from $33.77 to only $107.89 during the same period.[37]

Differences among industries in earnings can be attributable to such factors as unionization, region, productivity, degree of concentration within an industry, capitalization relative to labor inputs, and average establishment size. The determination of the degree of influence exerted by each of these factors in isolation is rendered difficult because several of these factors are usually interrelated. Thus, for example, it has generally been found that concentrated industries in which a large part of total industry volume is produced by a few firms generally pay higher wages than do less concentrated industries. The theoretical explanation of this circumstance would be that such concentrated industries enjoy higher profits because they exercise a degree of monopoly power in the marketplace and that they could therefore be expected to pay higher wages. It has been found, however, that concentrated industries are also characterized by strong unions, large establishments, and high capital input ratios. Each of these conditions might also be expected to be associated with higher than average wage levels.

Interfirm Differentials

Even within the same industry and geographic locality, different firms will pay different rates for similar jobs. The reason is that employers offer more than a wage to compensate their employees. There may be more "prestige" in working for one employer than another. Or the plant may be newer, or more accessible. Management representatives, such as foremen, may be more skilled in dealing with employees. It takes a mixture of many qualities to build up the reputation of a company as a good place to work. The wage, therefore, is only one part of the total package of benefits which employers hold out to their employees.

Some companies have a deliberate policy of paying more than the market, or more than their competitors, for labor, believing that in the long run this will attract a better type of worker and increase productivity. Most studies have found that establishment size is positively related to the level of wages.[38] Similarly, larger firms tend to pay higher fringe benefits than do smaller firms, particularly among manufacturing industries.[39] However, it is difficult to isolate the effect of size alone on wage rates and earnings. As one book has pointed out, the real relation may be with rate of profit, union power, or occupational skill mix, all of which may vary substantially between large and small firms.[40]

---

[37] U.S. Department of Labor, *Employment and Training Report,* table C–3, p. 296.

[38] See Baldwin and Daski, "Occupational Pay Differences," p. 29.

[39] Chamber of Commerce, *Employee Benefits, 1975,* p. 15.

[40] Albert Rees and George P. Shultz, *Workers and Wages in an Urban Labor Market* (Chicago, Ill.: University of Chicago Press, 1970), p. 7.

Personal Differentials: Sex

While jobs may be alike, no two workers are the same. They bring to their respective jobs different skills, education, motivation, physical strength, and other attributes. We can understand why workers with different educational backgrounds will be compensated at different rates. We may sympathize with the less educated workers and attempt to provide additional training for them, but there is no national policy which frowns on wage differentials based upon such factors. As a matter of national policy, however, we do not approve of wage differentials based solely upon sex or race. Nevertheless, such differentials continue to persist in the labor market.

In 1959, hourly earnings data indicated that females, on the average, earned only 60% as much as the average male worker.[41] More recent figures on median incomes of full-time women workers (see Table 8–6)

TABLE 8–6

Median Incomes of Full-Time Women Workers, by Occupation, 1972

Major Occupation Group	Median Income	Percent of Men's Income
Professional and technical workers	$8,796	68
Nonfarm managers and administrators	7,306	53
Clerical workers	6,039	63
Sales workers	4,575	40
Operatives, including transportation	5,021	58
Service workers (except private household) ...	4,606	59
Private household	2,365	*
Nonfarm laborers	4,755	63

* Percent not shown where median income of men is based on fewer than 75,000 individuals.
Source: Revised tables for the "Fact Sheet on the Earnings Gap" (Washington, D.C.: U.S. Department of Labor, Women's Bureau, March 1974). Reproduced from U.S. Department of Labor, *Manpower Report of the President, 1975* (Washington, D.C.: Government Printing Office, 1975), p. 63.

show little change in this differential, despite both the enactment of antidiscrimination laws during the interim and the movement of some women into higher paid and more responsible positions in industry. The male-female differential varies considerably by industry. It is smallest in government employment and largest in service industries, such as retail trade, where large numbers of women are customarily employed.[42]

---

[41] Victor Fuchs, "Differences in Hourly Earnings between Men and Women," *Monthly Labor Review,* vol. 94 (May 1971), pp. 9–15.

[42] Thomas F. Bradshaw and John F. Stinson, "Trends in Weekly Earnings: An Analysis," *Monthly Labor Review,* vol. 98 (August 1975), p. 26.

The same kind of differential emerges when a comparison is made of the earnings of men and women on an annual basis in particular occupations. Census data indicate that in 1970 men earned more than women in every occupation except public kindergarten teacher. Furthermore median earnings in the top-ranking occupation for women were about one half of those in the top-ranking occupation for men.[43]

A number of reasons have been advanced to explain the differential in earnings between men and women. In the first place, part-time work and discontinuous work experience is much more common for women than for men. In recent years, about one quarter of all employed women held part-time jobs.[44] Part-time work for women is most often found in service and trade categories which are at the bottom of the earnings ladder. Although about seven out of ten women workers have full-time jobs at some time during the year, only about four out of ten maintain full-time jobs throughout the year.[45] Responsibilities with respect to home and child care are obviously contributing factors. Furthermore, the typical work-life cycle of married women with children involves a period of continuous work until the birth of the first child, a period of nonparticipation or partial participation in the labor force until the youngest child reaches school age, and then a more continuous period of work when the mother is in her late thirties or early forties. The result of this discontinuity in work is that, on the average, married women have accumulated only about one half the total years of post-school labor force experience gained by men in the same age group,[46] and this factor translates into lesser earnings, seniority, and promotion.

Some researchers have argued that they could explain nearly all of the sex differential in earnings by controlling for such factors as part-time employment and differences in job responsibilities, education, and length of service. Most studies, however, find that large differentials still remain. The sex stereotyping of jobs is undoubtedly a major factor. Women, like men, are employed as salespeople. The woman, however, is likely to sell dresses in a department store, while the man sells computers for industrial use. An obvious earnings differential results.

In the second place, women at work continue to be concentrated in the lower paying industries and in the lower paying occupational groups, including clerical and service workers. Over the last 30 years, despite affirmative action programs and legislation designed to give women equal access to jobs, the overall job stratification of women has remained remarkably constant. In 1970, as in 1940, the service industry ranked

---

[43] Dixie Sommers, "Occupational Rankings for Men and Women by Earnings," *Monthly Labor Review*, vol. 97 (August 1974), p. 47.

[44] *Monthly Labor Review*, vol. 97 (May 1974), p. 3.

[45] U.S. Department of Labor, *Manpower Report, 1975*, p. 62.

[46] U.S. Department of Labor, *Manpower Report, 1974*, p. 119.

first in employment of women. In 1940, women working in nonagricultural industries were concentrated in three broad occupational groups. Roughly half held service jobs or worked as blue-collar operatives (30 and 21 percent, respectively), and a third were in the white-collar sales group. Thirty years later, working women were still highly concentrated in the same three broad occupational groups, but a much larger proportion were in the clerical-sales field, the professional-technical proportion had edged up, and the service and operative proportions had declined.[47] In 1974, more than one half of all working women were in relatively low-paying clerical and service occupations, while less than 14% of men were in such occupations.[48]

Differentials in earnings related to sex result not so much from the payment of different rates for the same job as from the restriction of job opportunities. When comparisons are made of rates for men and women in the same job in the same establishment, it is found that sex-wage differentials narrow substantially and in some instances disappear.[49]

A recent study charged that although occupational distribution accounts for part of the gap in earnings between men and women, "direct discrimination causes differential behavior between men and women that further increases the gap in earnings."[50] Whether this is true will be further analyzed in Chapter 23, when not only antidiscrimination legislation, but also the Equal Pay Act, will be examined.

Personal Differentials: Race

The earnings of black workers are substantially lower than those of their white counterparts. Here, too, there is considerable variation among industries and occupations. Generally, where blacks and whites do the same work in the same plant, the racial differential, once prevalent, has been eliminated. Blacks, however, tend to be concentrated in the lower paying jobs and in the lower paying industries. Table 8–7 indicates the substantial differential which exists in median weekly earnings of full-time wage and salary workers in various industries.

Has the position of the black worker in the labor market improved over time? Great care must be exercised in analyzing statistics which purport to provide an answer to this question. For example, if we look at the *median* weekly earnings of full-time workers, we find that the earnings gap definitely narrowed over the period 1967–74. Median earn-

[47] E. Waldman and B. J. McEaddy, "Where Women Work—An Analysis by Industry and Occupation," *Monthly Labor Review*, vol. 97 (May 1974), p. 3.

[48] Bradshaw and Stinson, "Trends in Weekly Earnings," p. 26.

[49] John E. Buckley, "Pay Differences between Men and Women in the Same Job," *Monthly Labor Review*, vol. 94 (November 1971), p. 39.

[50] Marianne A. Ferber and Helen M. Lowry, "The Sex Differential in Earnings: A Reappraisal," *Industrial and Labor Relations Review*, vol. 29 (April 1976), p. 386.

TABLE 8-7

Median Weekly Earnings of Full-Time Wage and Salary Workers, by Color, Sex, and Industry, May 1974

| | | Median Weekly Earnings* | | | |
| | All Per-sons | White | | Black | |
Industry		Men	Women	Men	Women
Total	$169	$209	$125	$160	$117
Agriculture	112	119	95	82	—
Mining	226	233	—	—	—
Construction	214	225	140	162	—
Manufacturing	170	205	119	160	109
Durable goods	181	207	128	170	120
Nondurable goods	153	202	112	145	100
Transportation and public utilities	208	230	153	179	135
Wholesale and retail trade	146	186	102	136	100
Wholesale trade	183	221	126	143	—
Retail trade	133	170	97	133	96
Finance, insurance, and real estate	154	229	126	174	122
Private households	54	—	43	—	61
Miscellaneous services	160	206	141	158	122
Business and repair	159	187	117	138	—
Personal services	107	142	96	—	84
Entertainment, recreation	151	176	129	—	—
Professional services	165	222	148	174	132
Public administration	211	232	164	193	153

* Median not shown where number of workers is under 75,000.
Source: Thomas F. Bradshaw and John F. Stinson, "Trends in Weekly Earnings: An Analysis," *Monthly Labor Review*, vol. 98 (August 1975), p. 28.

ings of black full-time workers, equal to only 70% of earnings for white workers in 1967, rose steadily to 81% in 1974.[51] On the other hand, if we use the mean, rather than the median, we find that the gap in earnings actually widened over this same period—from 19% to 21%![52] The difference in result arises from the fact that an arithmetic mean gives greater weight to the heavier concentration of whites in the upper end of the earnings distribution.

Another index of earnings progress is provided by median income of families. Again, the results are not clear. The ratio of the median family income of blacks and other races to that of whites was 54% in 1950 and remained relatively constant until about 1965. It rose to 64% in 1970, but fell to 62% in 1974.[53] The decline since 1970 appears to be attributable to a decline in labor market participation by black married women.

[51] Bradshaw and Stinson, "Trends in Weekly Earnings," p. 26.

[52] Ibid., p. 27.

[53] U.S. Bureau of the Census, *The Social and Economic Status of the Black Population in the United States, 1974*, Current Population Reports, Special Studies, Series P–23, No. 54, July 1975, p. 25.

Between 1970 and 1974, the proportion of black families with wives in the paid labor force declined from 36% to 33%, whereas the proportion for their white counterparts increased from 34% to 37%.[54] Historically, the proportion of black families with multiple wage earners has been greater than that of white families. However, the proportion of black families with two or more earners decreased from 55% in 1970 to 48% in 1974, falling below the 54% observed for white families in 1974.[55]

One area in which blacks have clearly made progress is in occupational status, as can be seen from Table 8–8. Fewer than one out of five blacks

TABLE 8–8
Employment by Occupation Group and Race, 1964 and 1974 (percent distribution)

Occupation Group	1964		1974	
	Whites	Blacks and Other Races	Whites	Blacks and Other Races
Total: Number (thousands)	61,922	7,383	76,620	9,316
Percent	100.0	100.0	100.0	100.0
White-collar workers	47.6	18.8	50.6	32.0
Professional and technical	13.0	6.8	14.8	10.4
Managers and administrators, except farm	11.7	2.6	11.2	4.1
Sales workers	6.6	1.7	6.8	2.3
Clerical workers	16.3	7.7	17.8	15.2
Blue-collar workers	36.1	40.6	33.9	40.2
Craft and kindred	13.7	7.1	13.8	9.4
Operatives	18.4	20.5	15.5	21.9
Nonfarm laborers	4.1	13.0	4.6	8.9
Service workers	10.5	32.3	12.0	25.1
Farm workers	5.8	8.4	3.6	2.7

The data for 1974 are not strictly comparable with those for 1964 as a result of changes in the classification of occupations to accord with the 1970 census. Detail may not add to totals because of rounding.
Source: U.S. Department of Labor, *Manpower Report of the President, 1975* (Washington, D.C.: Government Printing Office, 1975), p. 34.

worked in white-collar occupations in 1964; ten years later about one in three blacks had white-collar jobs. Likewise, gains have been made in the professional and managerial ranks. There has also been a significant reduction in the proportion of blacks in service occupations, particularly private household.

A comparison of earnings for black women and white women on an occupational basis reveals that the racial earnings gap is quite small in most occupations. Indeed, in a few occupational categories, especially in the white-collar sector, black women were reported as earning more than white women. Since they tend, however, to be more concentrated

[54] Ibid., p. 30.
[55] Ibid., p. 31.

in low-skill occupations, their overall earnings average is still lower than that for white women. Black men, on the other hand, trail white men in weekly earnings in nearly every occupation. The percentage gaps vary, however, from less than 10% among professional, technical, and sales workers to over 30% among farm workers.[56]

DIFFERENCES IN OCCUPATIONAL REMUNERATION

In 1974, Harold S. Geneen, chief executive officer of the International Telephone and Telegraph Corporation, received a salary and bonus of $791,000.[57] In the same year, the average white-collar worker in American industry earned only $185 per week, or less than $10,000 per year. (See Table 8–9.) What is the reason for this great disparity of earnings? Does the variation in earnings in a capitalist society reflect differences in ability, or are other factors responsible?

TABLE 8–9
Median Weekly Earnings of Full-Time Wage and Salary Workers by Color, Sex, and Occupation, May 1974

	Median Weekly Earnings*				
	All Per-	White		Black	
Occupation	sons	Men	Women	Men	Women
Total	$169	$209	$125	$160	$117
White-collar workers	185	246	142	214	145
Professional and technical	228	264	188	247	192
Managers and administrators, except farm	250	276	160	229	—
Sales workers	172	224	95	—	—
Retail sales	109	157	90	—	—
Other sales	244	259	156	—	—
Clerical workers	140	195	129	169	133
Blue-collar workers	170	194	109	155	103
Craft and kindred workers	211	216	129	178	—
Operatives, except transport	141	173	108	153	102
Transport equipment operatives	180	190	—	151	—
Nonfarm laborers	149	17	107	140	—
Service workers	114	157	92	138	93
Private household workers	50	—	38	—	61
Other service workers	117	157	95	138	98
Protective service workers	194	200	—	—	—
Waiters, cooks and kindred workers	91	122	82	131	88
All other service workers	115	137	104	134	114
Farm workers	107	114	—	76	—

* Medians not shown where number of workers is under 75,000.
Source: Thomas F. Bradshaw and John F. Stinson, "Trends in Weekly Earnings: An Analysis," *Monthly Labor Review*, vol. 98 (August 1975), p. 27.

[56] Bradshaw and Stinson, "Trends in Weekly Earnings," p. 27.

[57] *Forbes*, vol. 115 (May 15, 1975), p. 234.

In the same year, median weekly earnings of blue-collar workers were $170, while those for service workers were only $114. How can these differentials continue to maintain themselves in the marketplace? Why is there not continual movement from low-paying to high-paying jobs, so that such differentials would be erased over time? The answers to these questions are complex. Economic theorists attempt to explain the differentials which exist in the marketplace in terms of equalizing differences, nonequalizing differences, and by elaborating a theory of noncompeting groups in the labor market.

Equalizing Differences

Not all occupations are equally attractive to workers. Therefore, even if every worker had freedom of choice as to the type of work he would perform, we would expect that certain jobs which were less attractive would have to offer higher pay in order to attract workers, while positions in which working conditions were particularly satisfactory would be able to obtain workers at lower wages. In other words, a part of the differences in wage rates which we observe in the labor market represents a factor which equalizes the attractiveness of various occupations. For example, the low salaries of college professors are partially offset by the short hours of work, the long vacations, and the opportunity for research and study. Women who work as domestics in homes frequently receive more than do women who perform clerical tasks in business because, according to our social mores, working as a servant is looked upon as somewhat degrading, and therefore additional compensation must be offered in these jobs to equalize their attractiveness with other positions that these women might obtain.[58]

Another important equalizing difference is the expense of training. It is not surprising that the best-paid jobs are held by doctors, lawyers, dentists, airline pilots, and others whose occupations require lengthy education and training. The lowest paid workers are generally in unskilled occupations—cooks, charwomen, farm laborers, busboys, and child care workers.[59] The higher earnings generally received by white-collar workers compared to blue-collar workers (see Table 8–9) can be explained in part by differences in educational attainment. The proportions of each group completing 13–15 years of education are about one fifth for professional, managerial, and clerical workers; about one fourth for sales workers; and only 7% for the blue-collar group.[60]

---

[58] From 1970 to 1976, the cost of household maid service has risen considerably faster than the cost of living, reflecting a shortage of household service workers. See *U.S. News & World Report*, May 10, 1976, p. 86.

[59] Sommers, "Occupational Rankings," p. 34.

[60] Robert L. Stein and J. N. Hedges, "Blue-Collar/White-Collar Pay Trends, Earnings, and Family Income," *Monthly Labor Review*, vol. 94 (June 1971), p. 13.

Thus, differences in training costs can explain part of the differential we observe among earnings in various occupations. Most wage differences in the labor market, however, do not seem to be of an equalizing character. Indeed, they are usually the reverse. Instead of the most unattractive work being the best remunerated, it is usually the poorest paid. It is the ditchdigger and the garbage collector—not the movie actor —who receive the least remuneration for their labor.

Nonequalizing Differences

Broad differences in wages prevail which bear no relation to the relative attractiveness of the work involved. The first great source of such differences is the lack of uniformity in physical and mental capabilities among the working population. Even if every worker had freedom of choice to enter any occupation, it is obvious that few would have the talents—physical or mental—to be great scientists, writers, or boxers. The extent to which such abilities are a result of training and environmental factors is still a subject of debate among psychologists, but it is evident that all workers are not equally gifted by inheritance. Those talents which are prized most highly by the community and which are least common among workers tend to be remunerated with the highest earnings.

Another important cause of differences is the fact that all occupations are not equally easy to enter. Even in our free enterprise society, in which class lines are not firmly drawn, social strata emerge which render it difficult for the poor son of a laborer to rise to be the head of a great corporation. Examples of such spectacular success are often cited, but they represent the exception, not the norm.

Differences in ability and in training account for only a part of the wide variations in the compensation of members of the labor force. Sometimes the amount of money a person receives for his work will depend more on who his father is or on what business his relatives control than on his own ability or training. In the corporate world there is frequently no close relation between the compensation of the chief company executive and the productivity of that executive as measured by the earnings record of the company he heads. As an editor of *Forbes* has remarked, "In a way, the whole system makes no sense."[61] He points out that in some cases the chief executives of companies with major financial problems received higher salaries than those paid to the presidents of highly successful enterprises. One reason why the system often "makes no sense" is that under the corporate form of management the chief executive in effect names board members who then pass on the salary of the person to whom they owe their position. Unless a company is in dire straits, the wishes of stockholders in large public

---

[61] *Forbes*, p. 234.

corporations are unlikely to have any significant influence on executive compensation. The possible range of salary for the average chief executive is obviously much greater than that of the production line employee and much more within the sphere of his own personal influence.

Noncompeting Groups

The labor market is characterized by a vast number of noncompeting groups, as will be more fully explained at a later point in this discussion. In terms of occupational differentiation, however, five broad strata can be distinguished in the ranks of employees. At the lowest level, in terms of pay and social position, is the common laborer, working either on the farm or in industry and performing work which requires a minimum of skill and a maximum of brawn. His wages are low because there are very many persons in the labor market who can do such simple work and can do no other. Many workers find an entry into such occupations who would be excluded from other types of positions. Thus, the black, the immigrant, and various other minority or foreign-born groups make up a large proportion of this lowest stratum.

At somewhat higher wages come the semiskilled. These are workers who have ordinarily had some education and have acquired some knowledge of a technical art but who, for one reason or another, have not served the years of apprenticeship necessary to become skilled artisans.

Above them come the skilled workers—carpenters, boilermakers, bakers, and so on. Most of these workers have union cards and the benefit of a considerable period of apprenticeship. That they consider themselves in some respects superior to less skilled fellow workers is demonstrated by the clannishness of the skilled craftsmen in the American Federation of Labor, which, for many years, refused to accept unskilled workers into membership.

The next group on the ladder of social status—the clerical workers—are frequently below the skilled and sometimes below the semiskilled in terms of remuneration in certain job classifications. In 1974, for example, craftsmen, the highest paid classification within the blue-collar group, earned almost twice as much as retail sales workers, who are the lowest paid of the white-collar group. (See Table 8–9.) Nevertheless, in outlook and social allegiance, clerical workers have, in the past, tended to be allied with the professional and capitalist class. This is a major reason why unions found it difficult to make inroads into this group. In recent years, there has been some change in this position, with teachers and other government employees, but the bulk of the white-collar and professional employees have not as yet joined unions.

The top group in the labor market, in terms of pay and social prestige, are the professional workers—the doctors, lawyers, architects, and others who have generally trained for their occupations in college and through advanced study—and the managerial group and self-employed business-men.

Although there is movement among these groups, nevertheless to some extent the strata become self-perpetuating. The greatest barrier to movement up the social ladder is the cost and time required for education and training. As a consequence, the son of a doctor is more likely to become a member of a profession, whereas the son of a common laborer is more likely to become a laborer or, at best, a skilled worker.

If we define as "the skill differential" the percentage difference between the hourly earnings of workers designated as skilled and those designated as unskilled, then most writers would agree that there has been a secular tendency for the skill differential to diminish.[62] Although the emphasis of industrial unions, such as the United Automobile Workers, on cents-per-hour increases, which raise the rates of lower paid workers relative to those of higher paid workers, undoubtedly contributed to the narrowing of the differential between skilled and unskilled, other more basic forces were also at work to bring about this change. Even in the building trades, which are organized and bargain on a craft basis, there has been a marked narrowing of differentials between skilled and unskilled workers.

One basic reason for the relative improvement in the wages of unskilled workers has been that unskilled labor is now being combined with more capital than in the past, with the result that its productivity has been substantially increased.

Another reason for the relative rise in the wages of lower paid workers may be the changing conditions of supply for the two groups in the labor market. On the one hand, there has been a substantial reduction in immigration in the past few decades. In earlier years, when large numbers of immigrants were coming into this country, many of the foreign born could be attracted at low rates to jobs involving manual unskilled work. There is also the possibility that with the rising educational attainment of the labor force, there has been a secular increase in the relative supply of skilled workers or of people who would be inclined to gravitate to such jobs rather than to the unskilled level.

At the same time that the gap between unskilled and skilled workers has been narrowed, the differential between unskilled and white-collar workers has also been reduced and in some cases eliminated. The average hourly earnings of some professional groups are now below those of skilled workers, or even below those of essentially unskilled groups, such as over-the-road truck drivers. On the other hand, as a result of pressure from the craftsmen within their ranks, industrial unions, which once concentrated on raising the rates of the unskilled, are now emphasizing

---

[62] See Melvin W. Reder, "The Occupational Wage Structure," in Campbell R. McConnell (ed.), *Perspectives on Wage Determination* (New York: McGraw-Hill Book Co., 1970), p. 200.

percentage wage adjustments to increase the skill differentials. In some recent settlements, this pressure has resulted in separate and larger adjustments for skilled workers who otherwise threatened not to abide by the union agreement.

Although various studies document the fact that occupational wage differentials have narrowed when measured in terms of hourly or weekly earnings, over the past 30 years such differentials measured in terms of annual earnings have changed very little.[63] Studies by the Bureau of the Census and the Bureau of Labor Statistics, however, indicate that during the 1960s there was a slightly faster rise in pay for white-collar jobs requiring extended educational preparation than in wages for blue-collar and white-collar jobs requiring little or no training. One exception to this trend must be noted: the earnings of laborers rose relative to those of other groups, probably because the compensation of persons at this low level in the pay scale received more impetus from increases in coverage and level of the minimum wage provided under federal law.[64]

UNIONS AND WAGE DIFFERENTIALS

What effect does the advent of a union in a company or industry have on wage differentials? In the individual firm, union organization may cause management to set up job evaluation plans and to eliminate unjustified differentials between similar jobs. In an industry, if a union bargains with a number of the major producers, strong pressure will be exerted for uniformity in rates among the various concerns with which the union has contracts.

The interesting question that remains is: Have unions tended to introduce a new type of differential in the labor market—a differential between union and nonunion companies? Published data generally indicate that wages are higher in union than in nonunion plants within the same industry.[65] This does not necessarily imply that the presence of unions is causally related to the higher level of wages. Unions are more likely to be found in larger plants (in terms of number of employees) and are likely to be more concentrated in metropolitan areas than are nonunion plants. With few exceptions studies have indicated that average earnings are higher in large than in small establishments and higher in metropolitan areas than in smaller communities.

As can be seen from Table 8–10, the size of the wage differential varies considerably by industry, and in a few industries is actually negative.

---

[63] Arthur Sackley and Thomas W. Gavett, "Blue-Collar/White-Collar Pay Trends: Analysis of Occupational Wage Differences," *Monthly Labor Review*, vol. 94 (June 1971), p. 10.

[64] Ibid.

[65] See, for example, Sandra L. Mason, "Comparing Union and Nonunion Wages in Manufacturing," *Monthly Labor Review*, vol. 94 (May 1971), pp. 20–26.

TABLE 8–10

Average Straight-Time Hourly Earnings* of Men in Selected Occupations in Union Establishments as a Percent of the Average for Corresponding Occupations in Nonunion Plants, Selected Manufacturing Industries (average hourly earnings in nonunion plants = 100)

Industry and Pay Periods	Skilled Occu- pations†	Unskilled Occu- pations†
Textile mill products:		
Textile dyeing and finishing—Winter 1965–66 103		116
Apparel and other textile products:		
Men's and boys' shirts, except work, and nightwear—		
October 1968 109		104
Work clothing—February 1968 98		100
Furniture and fixtures:		
Wood household furniture, except upholstered—		
October 1968 105		105
Chemicals and allied products:		
Industrial chemicals—November 1965 100		115
Paints and varnishes—November 1965 100		116
Rubber and plastics products:		
Miscellaneous plastics products—August 1969 96		104
Primary metals industries:		
Gray iron foundries, except pipe and fittings—		
November 1967 106		117
Steel foundries—November 1967 104		115
Nonferrous foundries—June–July 1965 108		118
Machinery, except electrical:		
Construction and related machinery—mid-1966 112		117
General industry machinery—mid-1966 99		101
Metalworking machinery—mid-1966 103		111
Office and computing machine—mid-1966 100		103
Special industry machines—mid-1966 105		118

* Excludes premium pay for overtime and for work on weekends, holidays, and late shifts.
† Pay relatives for skilled and unskilled occupations shown above are averages of regional pay relatives where at least three regions were involved. Regions were held constant within industries in computing relatives for skilled and unskilled jobs.
Source: Sandra L. Mason, "Comparing Union and Nonunion Wages in Manufacturing," *Monthly Labor Review*, vol. 94 (May 1971), p. 22.

It is also worth noting that in this particular compilation, union-nonunion wage differentials were higher for unskilled than for skilled occupations.

The results of a more recent study[66] are set forth in Table 8–11. In this study, data collected in the May 1973 Current Population Survey were used to identify union and nonunion workers and their characteristics and to derive workers' "usual" hourly earnings. With age, education, region, and occupation held constant, the effect of unionization was estimated to be about 12% for all workers. The effect, however, varied substantially from one race-sex group to another. For white men

---

[66] Paul M. Ryscavage, "Measuring Union-Nonunion Earnings Differences," *Monthly Labor Review*, vol. 97 (December 1974), pp. 3–9.

TABLE 8-11

Union-Nonunion Usual Hourly Earnings Differentials by Occupation and Race-Sex Group, Other Factors Constant

Occupation	All Workers	White Men	Black Men	White Women	Black Women
Professional:					
Union	$5.82	$5.63	$4.74	$4.88	$3.75
Nonunion	5.12	5.20	3.92	3.57	3.82
Differential	1.137	1.083	1.209	1.367	0.982
Managerial:					
Union	5.77	5.80	6.48	4.60	3.38
Nonunion	5.25	5.42	4.46	3.37	3.10
Differential	1.099	1.070	1.453	1.365	1.090
Clerical:					
Union	5.04	4.68	4.60	3.77	3.60
Nonunion	4.49	4.35	3.63	3.09	3.93
Differential	1.123	1.076	1.267	1.220	1.188
Sales:					
Union	4.42	4.62	—	0.293	2.82
Nonunion	4.26	4.58	3.55	2.59	2.30
Differential	1.038	1.009	—	1.131	1.226
Craft and kindred worker:					
Union	5.88	5.89	5.06	3.78	5.00
Nonunion	4.55	4.66	4.22	3.02	2.99
Differential	1.292	1.264	1.199	1.252	1.672
Operative:					
Union	4.77	4.81	4.45	3.36	3.17
Nonunion	3.87	3.99	3.54	2.65	2.61
Differential	1.233	1.206	1.257	1.268	1.215
Transportation equipment operative:					
Union	5.24	5.22	4.79	3.63	—
Nonunion	3.65	3.78	3.29	2.55	—
Differential	1.436	1.381	1.456	1.424	—
Laborer:					
Union	4.22	5.00	4.45	3.01	3.21
Nonunion	3.62	3.74	3.47	2.78	2.64
Differential	1.359	1.337	1.282	1.083	1.216
Service:					
Union	3.98	3.86	3.94	2.81	2.94
Nonunion	3.39	3.32	3.04	2.33	2.49
Differential	1.174	1.163	1.296	1.206	1.181

Source: Paul M. Ryscavage, "Measuring Union-Nonunion Earnings Differences," *Monthly Labor Review*, vol. 97 (December 1974), p. 7.

of similar characteristics it was estimated to be about 8%, while among black men the effect of union membership was a 27% advantage in usual hourly earnings. Among black women and white women, the effect was 19% and 22%, respectively.[67] For white men, the largest occupational differentials were in the blue-collar occupations, the next largest in the

---

[67] Ibid., p. 5.

service occupations, and the smallest in white-collar jobs. Among the highest differentials were 34% for nonfarm laborers and 38% for transportation operatives. On the other hand, the differentials for black men were as large in white-collar and service occupations as they were in the blue-collar area.[68]

Comparison of data obtained from various studies conducted by the Bureau of Labor Statistics during the past decade suggests that the union-nonunion wage differential is narrowing.[69] The data, however, refer only to average straight-time earnings and do not reflect changes in fringe benefits. It is well established that the proportion of total employee compensation directed to payments for nonwage benefits is higher in union than in nonunion plants, and this emphasis upon fringe benefits may have been further accentuated during recent years.

It should be apparent from this brief discussion that it is difficult to isolate the precise effect which unionism has on wage differentials because of the concurrent influence of such factors as size of firm and concentration of the industry. Other important factors are the degree of unionization in the industry and in the local area and the structure of collective bargaining.

We shall consider the effect of union organization upon wage rates in more detail in Chapter 13. At this point, however, it can be stated that even those economists who do not believe that unions can alter basic wage relationships so as to be a source of comparative advantage to their members will concede that unions can alter wage relationships to the benefit of their members in three special circumstances: (1) where unions are new and aggressive and may be offsetting prior monopsony power of employers; (2) where there have been periods of substantial unemployment, and in the absence of union contractual arrangements wage rates would tend to fall; and (3) where craft unions control the supply of labor and thereby can push up the wage.

SUPPLY AND DEMAND IN THE LABOR MARKET

We have seen that the labor market differs materially from the market for wheat, which we considered at the beginning of this chapter. Diverse rates, rather than a single rate, typically prevail for a given type of labor in the labor market. There is no one market price—even for a particular grade of labor. Buyers and sellers are able to make bargains at a variety of rates.

How, then, do supply and demand fit into this picture? It will be recalled that we have defined the labor market in terms of geographic area. Because labor is highly immobile, unemployed workers in a labor

[68] Ibid., p. 6.
[69] Mason, "Comparing Wages," p. 22.

market tend to remain in the area rather than to seek jobs in a different market. The existence of this excess labor supply has a downward effect on wages—felt more strongly by nonunion workers than by union workers, but felt by both nonetheless. The workings of supply and demand are clearly seen in the changing fortunes of the college graduate. The ratio of the incomes of college graduates to those of high school graduates—quite stable since World War II—dropped in the early 1970s. In 1969, full-time male workers with four years of college earned 53% more than did male workers with four years of high school. By 1973, the advantage of the college graduate had been reduced to 40%.[70] The increasing proportion of the labor force having a college degree, coupled with a decline in demand on the part of universities and school systems, explains part of this decline. The other major factor has probably been the advantage gained by the high school graduate through union bargaining power.

Supply and demand—two traditional conceptual tools of economists—have not, therefore, been rendered useless by our changed conception of the labor market. Supply and demand do not interact to produce a single rate in the market, but they do influence the level of the whole structure of diverse rates that characterizes the actual labor market. In the next two chapters, we shall consider in detail what demand and supply mean in terms of labor and the labor market.

QUESTIONS FOR DISCUSSION

1. What factors are responsible for the existence of diverse rates for similar jobs in the same labor market? What effect would you expect union organization to have upon such diversity of rates? Why?
2. Discuss the theory of noncompeting groups. Of what value is this theory in explaining actual differences in remuneration in the labor market?
3. If you were an employer, would you pay national rates or community rates if you had plants in both the North and the South?
4. Discuss the trend in the average earnings of women and men in recent years. What factors explain the continuing differential?

SUGGESTIONS FOR FURTHER READING

Edwards, Richard C.; Reich, Michael; and Gordon, David M. (eds.) *Labor Market Segmentation.* Lexington, Mass.: D. C. Heath & Co. 1975.

    A series of essays exploring segmentation of the labor market in terms of large company internal markets and primary and secondary labor markets, and segmentation on the basis of sex.

Foran, Terry G. "Unionism and Wage Differentials," *Southern Economic Journal,* vol. 40 (October 1973), pp. 269–78.

---

[70] *U.S. News & World Report,* October 13, 1975, p. 38.

A concise summary of conflicting views in the literature on the impact of unions on wage differentials.

Mount, R. I., and Bennett, R. E. "Economic and Social Factors in Income Inequality: Race and Sex Discrimination and Status as Elements in Wage Differentials," *American Journal of Economics and Sociology*, vol. 34 (April 1975), pp. 161–74.

Ullman, Joseph C., and Huber, George P. "Are Job Banks Improving the Labor Market Information System?" *Industrial and Labor Relations Review*, vol. 27 (January 1974), pp. 171–85.

An analysis of the effectiveness of job banks in reducing frictional unemployment, aiding the disadvantaged in achieving placement, and facilitating the matching of jobs to applicants.

U.S. Department of Labor, *Manpower Report of the President, 1975.* Washington, D.C.: Government Printing Office, 1975, pp. 55–75.

This report contains a special section on "The Changing Economic Role of Women," which brings together much of the relevant data and statistics with respect to the earnings and occupational status of women.

U.S. Department of Labor, *Occupational Outlook Handbook.* Washington, D.C.: Government Printing Office.

This weighty volume, which is published annually, provides detailed occupational information for thousands of occupations, including required training, typical duties, earnings, and the trends in job opportunities.

U.S. Government, Equal Employment Opportunity Commission. *Job Patterns for Minorities and Women in Private Industry.* Washington, D.C.: Government Printing Office, annually since 1966.

These yearly reports show the number and proportions of minorities and women by industry and location for companies employing 100 or more workers.

9

The Supply of Labor

We HAVE SEEN that the labor market is the area in which the supply and demand for particular types of labor seek to obtain a balance. But what do we mean by the phrase *supply of labor?* What factors are responsible for changes in supply? Over what time period and from what perspective should variations in supply be considered?

Definition of Supply of Labor

For conceptual purposes—as, for example, in drawing the diagram in Figure 9-1 below showing the relationship between the "supply of labor" and wages—it is sometimes convenient to think of labor as being composed of homogeneous units. We might, for example, assume that the difference in wage rates paid for hours of labor offered by different individuals in the labor market is a rough measure of the value of the labor supplied. We could then convert such actual hours into "equivalent hours" by reducing higher paid hours to the equivalent of the lowest paid hour of work offered in the marketplace.[1]

Obviously such an assumption of homogeneity must be used with care; for it is clear that in actuality heterogeneity of labor is the dominating characteristic of the labor market. Not only is there a multitude of types of labor, running the gamut of skills, professions, and trades, but also no two workers are precisely alike, even though they may both work in the same trade side by side at similar machines in the same plant. Yet despite such heterogeneity there is a degree of substitutability of one kind of labor for another, particularly when training, education, and experience can be utilized over time.

---

[1] Milton Friedman, *Price Theory: A Provisional Text* (Chicago: Aldine Publishing Co., 1966), p. 202.

It is the heterogeneity of labor, moreover, which produces many of the problems of labor supply which are matters of national concern today. For example, if all labor were homogeneous, there could not be a shortage of labor (except due to lack of mobility) as long as one man remained unemployed. Yet in the actual labor market we observe continuing unemployment of large numbers of workers, both workers with specialized skills and workers with no skills at all, while at the same time shortages exist for skilled workers in many occupations.

Labor supply can be considered from the short-run as well as the long-run point of view. The short run can be thought of as a period of time in which decisions are made about whether to sell labor services, at what price, and in what amount, such period being shorter than the time dimension in which decisions are made with respect to education, occupational choice, migration, and family size.[2] The important variables within labor supply in the short run, therefore, become: (1) labor effort, which may be of significance in piece-rate industries; (2) hours of work offered per day, per week, and per year; and (3) number of persons in the labor force, which depends upon labor participation rates and the age structure of the population at a given moment of time.

CLASSIFICATIONS OF LABOR SUPPLY

The supply of labor can be considered from four points of view:

The Supply of Labor Available to an Individual Firm. This may be large or small, complex or relatively homogeneous, depending upon the size of the firm, the ramifications of its operations, and the diversity of its products and plant locations. The labor supply of the United States Steel Corporation, for example, would represent a cross section of the working population. By contrast, the supply of labor to the corner drugstore would probably include only pharmacists and youths.

The Supply of Labor Available to an Industry. An industry may be defined, for our purposes, as a group of firms producing approximately the same product. The supply of labor to an industry will ordinarily represent a broader class of skills than the supply of labor to an individual firm because of the variations in the methods of production used by firms making the same product in different parts of the country. The supply of labor to an industry may, however, be quite limited if the industry draws upon a relatively scarce type of skilled labor. For example, there are comparatively few qualified violin makers in this country. Consequently, the supply of labor available to this *entire industry* in the United States is less than the supply of labor available to an individual firm in other industries (for example, the United States Steel Corporation).

---

[2] Belton M. Fleisher, *Labor Economics: Theory and Evidence* (Englewood Cliffs, N.J.: Prentice-Hall, Inc., 1970), p. 37.

The Supply of Labor Available to a Particular Locality. This will represent workers of all types employed in a variety of industries within the particular locality. Unless employment in the locality is highly specialized, the supply of labor will normally include a greater variety of skills and classes of workers than either the supply of labor to an industry or the supply to the average firm. The availability of new workers will depend upon the mobility of workers from other areas and upon the extent to which persons in the area, not normally members of the labor force, can be induced to enter employment.

The Supply of Labor Available in the Economy as a Whole. This is *the* labor force, including workers of all types in all industries in all sections of the country. Since immigration is relatively unimportant, the availability of additional workers in the short run will depend upon the extent to which persons not ordinarily part of the labor force can be attracted into employment.

VARIATIONS IN LABOR SUPPLY

Labor supply is subject to a diversity of influences. Moreover, some influences will affect one element in labor supply (such as hours of work) without affecting another element (such as number of workers available). It is therefore useful to distinguish, on the one hand, the various *causes* of variations in labor supply and, on the other hand, the *components* of labor supply which are subject to variation. We may then select the particular relation between cause of variation and components of labor supply which we wish to study.

The components of labor supply are number of workers, hours of work (that is, length of workday and workweek), and efficiency. Causes of variation in labor supply include variations in the wage rate, family income, willingness to work, physical strength of the worker, conditions of work, and similar factors. A rise in family income, for example, may influence all three components of labor supply. A rise in family income may make it possible for Johnny to go to college, thus reducing the number of men available for work; it may enable the family breadwinner to buy a cottage at the beach and therefore interest him in securing a reduction in the workweek so that he can spend his weekends there; and it may enable him to eat better, and to see the doctor and dentist more regularly, so that his physical efficiency will be improved.

In the following discussion, we shall be primarily concerned with all three components of labor supply but with only one of the causes of variation: the wage rate. Holding the other causes constant (with the exception of family income), and changing only the wage rate, we shall attempt to ascertain how the amount of labor supplied will vary. This is the conventional way of studying changes in labor supply in the labor market.

The Role of Nonwage Factors

It seems probable that the most important single cause of *variation* in the short-run supply of labor is change in the rate of compensation for jobs. The level of wages is, of course, not the only factor employees consider in seeking employment. We know that proximity of the place of employment, congenial atmosphere, employment with friends or relatives, regularity of work, security, and prospects for advancement are all important elements affecting the attractiveness of a job to the individual worker. However, it is the level of wages which normally fluctuates frequently, and it is therefore easier to correlate changes in labor supply with this cause of variation than with others. Any relationship, of course, is going to be rough and approximate; for as we have seen in Chapter 8 in our discussion of the labor market, employees do not normally have accurate information either about existing wage levels in various firms or about changes in such wage levels. Nevertheless, over a period of time, higher wage rates will attract more employees.

The Short-Run Supply of Labor

Variations in labor supply may be considered from either the short-run or the long-run point of view. The short-run supply of labor may be defined as the schedule of the varying amounts of labor that would be supplied at varying wage rates. Geometrically represented, the schedule is a curve on a diagram on which the wage rate is measured along the ordinate (Y axis), and the number of workers, or units of labor, is measured along the abscissa (X axis).

As has already been mentioned, the supply curve may be drawn from the point of view of an individual firm, an industry, a locality, or the economy as a whole. For the purpose of explaining geometric representation of supply conditions, we may assume that Figure 9–1 represents supply curves of labor to a firm. The same type of representation, however, can be used to show supply conditions from the point of view of an industry, a locality, or the economy. Figure 9–1 shows two hypothetical supply curves of labor. The line SS' has been drawn parallel to the X axis and intersects the Y axis at a wage of $100 per week. Since SS' is parallel to OX, it indicates that at a wage of $100 per week the employer anticipates that he can get 20 workers or 40 workers or 70 workers. In other words, as much labor as the employer requires can, within limits, be obtained at the same wage rate. Economists describe this situation by saying that the supply curve of labor is perfectly "elastic." Increasing amounts of labor can be obtained without raising wage rates. As we shall see in the following discussion, this is frequently the case when unemployment exists in the labor market.

Suppose, now, that a war crisis arises suddenly and large numbers of

FIGURE 9–1
Short-Run Supply Curve of Labor to a Firm

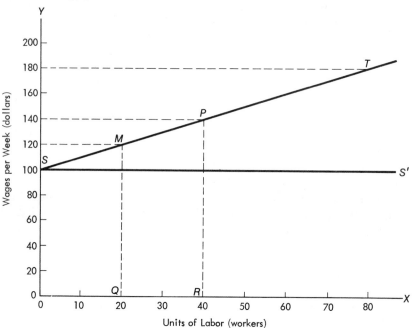

Units of Labor (workers)

workers are drafted into the army. Our employer's supply curve for labor may now be changed abruptly to one which looks like the line *ST* in Figure 9–1. Because of the shortage of labor in the market, the employer now finds that to get more labor, he must offer a progressively higher wage rate to attract workers away from other firms and to draw persons out of retirement into his factory. Thus, while 20 workers (*OQ*) can be hired for a wage of about $120 per week, if the employer wants to double his labor force to 40 workers, he may find that he will have to raise wages to $140 per week (*RP*). Such a supply curve, which correlates higher wage rates with increased labor supply, is known as a supply curve of less than perfect elasticity.[3] This usually means that the supply of labor is limited relative to buyers' demands and that additional workers or additional hours or units of labor can only be obtained by raising rates of pay.

The more "elastic" a supply curve is, the greater will be the increase in labor associated with a given increase in wage rates. Looked at an-

---

[3] The concept of elasticity will be utilized from time to time in the following chapters in connection with both supply curves and demand curves. The elasticity coefficient is equal to the percentage change in quantity divided by the percentage change in price (or wage). Algebraically, this relation can be expressed as $(\Delta Y/\Delta X)$ X/Y, where Y equals quantity and X equals price.

other way, the steeper the slope of the supply curve, the less elastic it will be. In Figure 9–1, curve SS' is more elastic than curve ST, and curve ST has a steeper slope than curve SS'. If the supply curve is vertical, meaning that no matter how much wage rates rise or fall, there will be no change in the amount of labor available, the supply curve is said to be "perfectly inelastic" or of "zero elasticity." On the other hand, if the supply curve is horizontal, as in the case of curve SS' in Figure 9–1, any amount of labor (within limits) can be obtained at a constant wage rate. Such a curve is called "perfectly elastic."

Classification of Variations

Much confusion arises in discussions of labor supply because of a failure to distinguish properly between a shift in the entire supply curve and a movement along the curve. The former should be referred to as a "change in labor supply," since "supply" means the whole schedule. The latter should be designated as a "change in the amount of labor supplied," that is, a movement from one *point* on the supply curve to another. This distinction will be clarified if variations in the availability of workers, labor time, and labor efficiency are considered from the viewpoint of whether they do or do not involve an actual shift in the supply curve:

1. A change occurs in the number of workers available in the market.

a. Such a change may be attributable to factors other than a variation in wage rates. For example, the large withdrawals of troops from Vietnam added thousands of GIs to the ranks of the civilian labor force. Where the change in numbers of workers is attributable to nonwage causes, the whole supply schedule of labor shifts its position, either to the right or to the left, depending on whether there has been an increase or a decrease in the number of workers available at given rates.

b. Additional workers may be induced to enter the labor market by the attraction of high wages. To the extent that this is true, there has been a movement along a given supply curve.

2. A change occurs in hours of work.

a. During World War II, hours of work of nonagricultural employees increased from 41 hours per week in 1940 to a peak of more than 46 hours per week in 1943. In part, the willingness to work these longer hours was motivated by a desire to bring the war to a speedy and successful conclusion. That is, the motive of patriotism would have actuated workers to accept some lengthening of the workweek with no increase in hourly wage rates. To the extent that this was true, there was a shift to the right in the labor supply curve.

b. Workers increase hours of work because of availability of work beyond 40 hours at a premium rate of time and a half. This represents a movement along a given supply curve.

3. A change occurs in efficiency.

a. Lighting is improved in a factory, and as a result, output increases. There has been a movement of the entire supply curve.

b. On the other hand, if additional efficiency is forthcoming simply as a result of a piece-rate system which rewards additional effort with additional compensation, there has merely been a movement along a given supply curve.

The same distinction in terminology, of course, applies to shifts of the demand curve for labor and to movements along that curve.

THE SUPPLY CURVE OF LABOR TO THE FIRM

As has been mentioned, the supply of labor may be considered in relation to a particular firm, an industry, a locality, or the economy as a whole. The last three types of supply curves are "objective." That is, they represent the "actual" changes in the supply of labor which would accompany given changes in the rate of wages, if such variations in supply could be isolated from the general flux in the labor market and measured. The supply curve of labor to the individual firm, however, is of a quite different nature. The supply curve of labor to the individual firm, as this concept is normally used by labor economists, is a subjective concept, not an objective fact. It represents the individual employer's *expectation* of what the relationship of wage rates and labor supply *will be.*

Of course, we could draw up an objective supply curve of labor for the individual firm. The slope of such a curve would reflect, among other things, differences in worker preference for specified combinations of money income and working conditions, attachment of workers to a familiar workplace or residence, and the size of the firm in question. For most economic problems, however, it is more useful to draw up a hypothetical curve analogous to the demand curves which represent employer expectations. These expectations will be derived in part from past experience; and therefore, many of the elements which would determine the shape of the objective supply curve will enter into the employer's estimation of the shape of the supply curve of labor as he imagines it to be.

Labor Supply to a Large Firm

Because the supply curve of labor to the individual firm reflects the estimates of the individual employer, its slope will depend upon the size of the particular firm involved. A very large firm may have to recognize that any attempt by it to obtain more labor is likely to affect the prevailing wage rate in the locality. In order to obtain 1,000 more workers in a local labor market where there may be only 10,000 qualified workers available in all, a large firm will have to raise wage rates sufficiently to induce workers to leave other jobs. Workers will be reluctant to leave jobs in other firms without such an inducement, since by leaving their current employment, they are likely to lose seniority rights and preferential status with regard to future promotion, health benefits, pensions, and so forth. But when the large firm offers higher wages to attract additional workers, this is likely to produce an increase in wage rates in the community generally, since other employers will also find it necessary to raise wages in order to induce employees to remain. The large firm is thus placed in such a position that any increase in rates it may offer to attract additional workers will likewise have to be offered to all employees already on its own payroll; for if other employers raise rates in retaliation, the large firm would not be able to hold its own employees at lower rates. Moreover, if the workers in the large firms are organized, the union will undoubtedly require uniformity of pay among employees of the same skill. Even if the plant were unorganized, management would probably consider it impracticable from the point of view of employee morale to raise rates for new employees without making a corresponding adjustment in the rates of old employees.

The result in such circumstances is that the addition to the total labor cost of the firm incidental to the employment of an additional worker will exceed the direct labor cost or wage paid to that man. In technical language, this means that the marginal cost of labor (that is, the addition to the total cost of labor attributable to the addition of one more unit of labor) will exceed the supply price of labor (that is, the wage offered to the additional worker). Assume that the going rate for labor in the firm is $3 an hour and that 100 men are employed at that wage. In order to attract additional workers, the wage paid to new workers has to be raised to $3.20. The supply price of additional labor, as indicated by the labor supply curve, will therefore be $3.20. But if, as a result of this rise in the wage, all workers already on the payroll have to be given an increase from $3 to $3.20 an hour, the additional cost of $23.20 ($0.20 × 100 + $3.20) attributable to hiring an additional worker will be substantially in excess of his wage ($3.20).

Labor Supply to a Small Firm

The small firm will tend to view its supply curve of labor as being perfectly "elastic" over the relevant range—that is, the employer considers that he can obtain all the additional workers he may need without raising wages. His demand is so small relative to the total supply of workers available that his need for additional workers will not affect wage rates generally. This condition of perfect elasticity may also typify the supply curve for labor in a large firm in times of substantial unemployment. However, the supply curve of the small firm is likely to be perfectly elastic even if there is full employment. For even under conditions of full employment, there are some workers leaving other employment for one reason or another, and the small firm may figure that it can satisfy its needs from this pool of workers without the necessity of paying higher wages to draw men away from other firms. Consequently, if the small firm has been paying $3 an hour to its employees, it estimates that it can get additional workers for $3, and therefore that the marginal cost of the additional labor and its supply price or wage will be the same. The fact that the supply curve for labor to the small firm will tend to be perfectly elastic, while the supply curve to the large firm is more likely to be less than perfectly elastic, influences their respective employment policies. This problem will receive attention in Chapter 10, which deals with the demand for labor.

Why the Labor Supply Curve Slopes Upward

Perhaps the most common cause of an upward slope in the labor supply curve is the need to pay higher wages in order to attract workers away from other firms. As we have seen, insofar as this is the reason for the lack of perfect elasticity in the supply curve, it is more likely to be characteristic of a large than a small firm. But there are other conditions which can produce an upward slope in the labor supply curve, and these are to be found in large and small firms alike. For example, an employer may have to pay penalty rates for overtime if he wishes to get more hours out of his existing labor force. Additional units of labor time have to be remunerated at a higher price, which means that the supply curve for labor to the firm is rising. Another condition which will produce an upward-sloping labor supply curve is a scarcity of qualified workers. If additional workers can be obtained at the prevailing wage, but these workers are less efficient, the firm is, in effect, paying an increased price per "efficiency unit." A further possible reason for an upward-sloping labor supply curve is increased "fringe" expenses made necessary by the employment of additional workers. For example, if the only additional workers available lack necessary skills, the employer may be compelled to expend funds for special training. The result will be that the marginal cost of employing these additional workers will exceed the wages paid to them.

The Effects of Union Organization on the Supply Curve

Union contracts customarily fix the wage rates for particular types of labor for a given period of time, usually a year. Once the rate is fixed in the contract, the employer is obligated to pay it, regardless of the amount of labor he employs. Thus, theoretically, a union contract creates a perfectly elastic supply curve for labor.

In practice, however, the results are sometimes different. In a tight labor market the employer may find that even with a union contract, the only way to get more labor is to hire substandard workers and pay them the union rate or to work more overtime. In both cases, his supply curve of labor would be upward sloping: in the former case, because he has to pay more for less efficient labor; in the latter case, because the additional hours worked would have to be compensated at premium rates.

THE SUPPLY CURVE OF LABOR TO AN INDUSTRY

The elasticity of the supply of labor to an industry will depend primarily upon the mobility of workers who can be drawn into that industry from other sources. Because most skills in modern industry can be acquired fairly quickly, an industry can ordinarily draw workers away from other industries if it offers sufficient inducement in the form of higher wages. The supply curve of labor for an industry will ordinarily be more elastic than the supply curve of labor in a given locality, because there will be less resistance to the movement of workers from industry to industry within a given locality than there will be to movement away from or into the locality. The supply curve of labor for an industry will ordinarily be more elastic than the supply curve of labor for the whole economy, because it will be easier to induce employees to leave other industries to work in this particular industry than it will be to induce additional men, women, and children who are not normally members of the labor force to enter the labor market.

The supply curve of labor for an industry will be of zero elasticity —that is, more workers would not be attracted to the industry no matter how high a wage were offered—only in the rare case when the industry uses a type of highly skilled labor which is not employed by other industries and when the skill is one which cannot be easily acquired in a short period. It should be observed that even if the elasticity of labor supply to a particular industry were zero, an individual employer in such an industry might still imagine that the supply curve of labor to his firm is perfectly elastic. He might calculate that even though the industry as a whole cannot obtain more workers, his own needs are so small relative to the amount of labor available to the industry that he will be able to attract a few additional workers without being compelled to offer a higher wage.

THE SUPPLY CURVE OF LABOR TO A LOCALITY

The slope of the supply curve of labor to a locality will depend in large measure upon the nature and location of the locality in question. If a shortage of labor were to develop in Phoenix, Arizona, additional workers would be attracted from all over the country because of the advantages (other than the job opportunity) which Phoenix has to offer. On the other hand, if a labor shortage were to develop in a little mill town in a backwoods region, even a very high wage rate would not induce many workers to leave their present homes and occupations in order to migrate there.

Although many workers, particularly older ones, are reluctant to sever local ties, nevertheless, as was pointed out in Chapter 8, there is a considerable amount of geographic mobility in this country. During prosperous periods, the rate of mobility out of labor-surplus areas is higher than during periods of depression. But from our observation, it is also true that lower income groups are often the least willing to relocate.

Many of the characteristics of the supply curve of labor to a locality are also true of the supply curve to the economy as a whole; therefore, these aspects can be conveniently considered together in the discussion below.

THE SUPPLY CURVE OF LABOR FOR THE ECONOMY

Discussions of the supply curve of labor for the economy as a whole are generally phrased in terms of reactions to changes in real wage rates. The assumption is made that flows in and out of the labor force, as well as changes in hours and effort forthcoming from individual workers, are made in relation to changes in real wages,[4] rather than in monetary terms. However, there is considerable argument on this point, and some economists speak of a "money illusion" and maintain that workers do in practice react to changes in money rates. In the following discussion, we shall assume that the rise in money rates represents a rise in real wages as well.

For many years, labor economists generally held the view that, except during periods of substantial unemployment, the short-run supply of labor for the economy as a whole was likely to be somewhat inelastic above the prevailing wage. It was assumed that a rise in the wage rate offered would not substantially increase the number of workers available. As soon as all average workers were employed, the amount of labor supplied could be increased only by bringing in submarginal workers or people who were not ordinarily part of the labor force—such as women, youths, and older men. The additions which could be expected from these sources in peacetime, within normal wage ranges, were thought to be relatively small. During World War II, patriotism and the lure of very high wage levels did attract many of these groups into the labor market, but this experience was viewed as an exceptional circumstance.

---

[4] Some economists, such as John M. Keynes, argue that workers, individually and in groups, are more concerned with *relative* than *absolute* real wages. Thus, they may withdraw their labor if their wages fall relative to wages elsewhere, even though they would not withdraw if real wages fell uniformly elsewhere. For a discussion of this point, see James Tobin, "Inflation and Unemployment," *American Economic Review,* vol. 62 (March 1972), p. 3.

In recent years, however, studies of labor market performance have suggested that there is a trend toward growing responsiveness on the part of labor supply. A prime source for the greater degree of elasticity which seems to have evidenced itself in recent years is the growing size and importance of a discretionary labor force. The increased number of part-time workers, the greater participation of women in the labor force, and the growing tendency of older workers to combine early retirement with some reduced rate of participation in the labor force have created a large body of intermittent- or multiple-job holders who flow in and out of the labor force with considerably more rapidity than do members of the primary labor force.[5]

In Figure 9–2, the prevailing wage rate is indicated along the Y axis,

FIGURE 9–2
Short-Run Supply Curve of Labor for the Economy

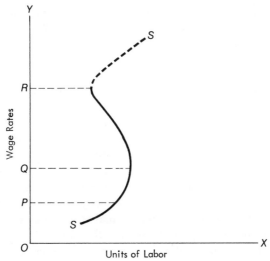

while units of labor supplied are measured along the X axis. The curve lettered SS' represents an approximation to the short-run supply curve of labor for the economy in normal times. If we assume that wage rate OP is a bare subsistence wage, then below that rate, workers will not be strong enough to work as many hours or in as great a number as at wage OP, and the supply curve will therefore reflect this diminution in the number of units of labor supplied by sloping sharply to the left. At and slightly above wage OP, we may assume that earnings are very low relative to the standard of living; and as a consequence, workers with fami-

---

[5] Jacob Mincer, "Labor-Force Participation and Unemployment: A Review of Recent Evidence," in J. F. Burton, Jr., et al., *Readings in Labor Market Analysis* (New York: Holt, Rinehart & Winston, Inc., 1971), pp. 79–105.

lies will be compelled to send their children to work at an early age. Also, many women will have to work at this low wage in order to help their husbands support their families. As the wage rate is raised to a more satisfactory level, men are better able to maintain their families on their own wages. Thus, at a wage of OQ, the earnings of the family bread-winner will be sufficient for children to remain in school for more extended education and for women to remain in the home. Likewise, individual workers will opt for shorter hours and longer vacations so that they can use the higher income for more leisure activities. Consequently, the amount of labor offered on the market will tend to diminish, and the supply curve will slope to the left. As indicated by the discontinuous part of the curve above wage OR, it is possible that at very high wages —as was the case during the war years—women and youths will again be induced to enter the labor market. Likewise, older men who were ready for retirement may postpone the event, and even men over 65 may enter the labor market. Therefore, it is possible that at such high rates the supply curve may again slope to the right.

Economists seek to explain the reactions of labor supply to changes in real wage rates by assuming that at various wage rates individual workers and family units reach a balance between the desire for leisure and the desire for income. If wage rates rise, two offsetting influences come into play. On the one hand, the so-called substitution effect will tend to induce workers to substitute work for leisure, since higher wages now make work more attractive. On the other hand, the so-called income effect may induce a worker to reduce his hours of work because with higher income now he can afford to buy a boat, have a summer cottage, and so on, and he therefore needs additional time to enjoy these acquisitions.[6] The "backward-sloping" portion of the supply curve is explained by the assumption that as real wage rates rise, for numbers of workers the income effect dominates the substitution effect and results both in fewer hours of work being offered by the family bread-winner and in the withdrawal from the market of family members other than the breadwinner.

Statistical Investigations into the Supply Curve for Labor

Various attempts have been made to determine what would happen to labor supply if earnings were lower or higher than the prevailing rate. These studies have generally been based on one of two approaches: (1) labor force size is measured at different moments of time as earnings vary, or (2) simultaneous measurements are made of the labor force and earnings in different labor markets to determine what, if any, is the normal interrelationship. One of the earliest investigations in this field was made by Paul H. Douglas, who used the latter approach and, after

---

[6] The interrelationships between income and leisure are explored in the mathematical appendix at the end of this chapter. See also Chapter 16.

examining earnings and labor force size in 38 large cities, found evidence of an inverse relationship.[7] Clarence D. Long, who published a comprehensive study of this problem, confirms that variations in the proportion of a city's population in the labor force, that is, its participation rate, appear to be inversely associated with variations in its average income per equivalent adult male worker.[8]

A somewhat allied question is the problem of what happens to the labor force in times of depression. If there is an inverse relationship between earnings and labor supply, then, as earnings diminish in times of depression, additional workers should be expected to enter the labor force in an attempt to supplement family income. This "additional workers" theory, as it is called, is held by many economists, but it has been rejected by others. Recent empirical research suggests that labor supply is inversely related to the level of unemployment. This implies that as wages drop and unemployment rises, although some secondary workers enter the labor market in order to supplement family income, more depart or delay their entrance until a more favorable labor market situation develops.[9] Thus, the converse of the "additional workers" theory is the "discouraged workers" theory, which in effect postulates that labor force participation will fall as unemployment rises because lack of jobs in the labor market will cause persons to delay entry into, or to withdraw from, the labor force. The number of discouraged workers can be very large in a severe recession. In the fourth quarter of 1975, about one million persons reported that they wanted jobs but were not actively seeking them because of discouragement over job prospects.[10]

Hours of Work

The slope of the short-run labor supply curve will depend in part upon the relationship between the wage rates and the number of hours employees are willing to work. Here again we are faced with the conflicting influences of the substitution effect and the income effect. A longer workday or a longer workweek not only spells greater fatigue for the worker but also means that he will have less time to devote to his family,

---

[7] Paul H. Douglas, *The Theory of Wages* (New York: Macmillan Co., 1934), chap. 11. See also Paul H. Douglas and Erika Schoenberg, "Studies in the Supply Curve of Labor," *Journal of Political Economy*, vol. 45 (February 1937), pp. 45–79.

[8] Clarence D. Long, *The Labor Force under Changing Income and Employment*, National Bureau of Economic Research, General Series No. 65 (Princeton, N.J.: Princeton University Press, 1958), p. 5. For a more current survey and discussion of earlier studies, see Fleisher, *Labor Economics*, chap. 3, "Evidence Bearing on the Theory of Labor Supply," pp. 56–91.

[9] The U.S. Department of Labor has concluded that it is extremely difficult to substantiate "the additional worker effect" from the available evidence. "There is more concrete evidence of 'the discouraged worker effect' and it appears to be the larger factor." See John E. Bregger, "Unemployment Statistics and What They Mean," *Monthly Labor Review*, vol. 94 (November 1971), p. 26.

[10] *Monthly Labor Review*, vol. 99 (February 1976), p. 7.

recreation, education, and other pursuits. It is understandable, therefore, why premium pay is offered for longer hours of work. On the other hand, we also know that as take-home pay rises, some workers become more interested in a reduction of hours worked so that they can have more time for leisure. It is apparent that this is an area of complex motivation. The subject of hours of work will be discussed in greater detail in Chapter 16.

CHANGES IN EFFICIENCY

The supply of labor can also be varied by changes in the efficiency of workers. Just as an increase in wage rates may increase the amount of labor supplied by inducing additional workers to enter the market, so an increase in wage rates may increase the efficiency of a given work force. When wages are at a very low level, an increase in wages will tend to improve efficiency by contributing to the physical well-being of the workers. Workers who are well fed and afforded proper housing facilities are capable of putting forth more effort than are employees whose incomes are so low that they cannot properly provide for these basic needs. But once wage rates reach a level at which the worker can maintain a satisfactory standard of living, it is doubtful whether further wage increases have much effect on efficiency solely by reason of their reaction on physical well-being.

However, apart from possible improvements in physical condition, a rise in wages may induce employees to work harder. A positive relation between wage increases and increased effort is more likely to be found in piece-rate industries than in industries where payment is by the hour. If the piece rate is raised, the worker can increase his take-home pay by producing more units of product, whereas in an industry where payment is by the hour, the worker is likely to feel that his increased effort would simply increase the employer's profit without any direct, immediate benefit to himself. Thus, it is principally in industries which use incentive pay plans that variations in efficiency are likely to have any close relationship to changes in wage rates. Approximately 30% of the plant workers in manufacturing industries are paid on an incentive basis.

On the whole, under modern industrial conditions in a high-wage economy, wage changes probably have comparatively little effect upon worker efficiency. Because of the high degree of mechanization in American industry, the speed of the production line rather than individual worker effort is the controlling determinant of labor efficiency.

THE LONG-RUN SUPPLY OF LABOR

Classical economists viewed the long-run supply of labor as highly flexible. They believed that labor supply adjusted itself to "the natural price of labor"—that is, the level of real wages which was necessary "to enable laborers one with another to subsist and to perpetuate their race without increase or diminution."[11] This level was conceived of as an equilibrium rate. If real wages rose above this subsistence level, births would increase, deaths would decrease, population would consequently expand, and, with an unchanged demand for labor, wage rates would necessarily fall. On the other hand, a fall in wage rates below the subsistence level would produce an increase in deaths and a decrease in births. Marriages would be postponed, and married persons would delay having children. Consequently, the supply of labor would decline below the equilibrium level, and with the result that wage rates would be bid up to the "natural" wage.

The theory was phrased in terms of a subsistence wage because of the belief, then current, that population tended to increase faster than did the means of subsistence. Population was thought to double every 25 years—thus increasing at a geometric rate—while food production increased only in an arithmetic ratio. However, population was prevented from getting too far out of line with subsistence by certain "positive checks," such as vice, pestilence, war, and famine, and by "preventive checks," such as postponement of marriage.

Although geometric increases in population growth and subsistence wages have characterized the history of many underdeveloped countries, particularly in Asia and Latin America, the experience of the older countries in Europe and more recently of the United States suggests that the highly industrialized Western nations are entering an era of much slower population growth as a result of changes which have occurred in the science of contraception, attitudes toward family size and abortion, and the costs of education and other incidents of child rearing.

POPULATION CHANGE AND THE LABOR FORCE

In 1975, the three basic measures of annual fertility all reached their lowest level in American history. The crude birthrate (births per thousand population) was 14.7, a full 42% lower than it was in 1957. The general fertility rate (births per thousand women between the ages 15 and 49) fell to 66.8, compared to 122.7 in 1957. The total fertility rate (annual births expressed in terms of the implied completed fertility per thousand women) was only about 1.8, less than one half of the rate in 1957.[12] It will be recalled that only a few years ago advocates of ZPG (Zero Population Growth) were calling for a fertility rate of 2.11, which is the minimum required to sustain a stable population. Currently, the

---

[11] David Ricardo, *Principles of Political Economy and Taxation* (Gonner, ed.; London: George Bell & Sons, 1913), p. 70.

[12] U.S. Bureau of the Census, Current Population Reports, "Population Estimates and Projections," Series P–25, No. 632 (July 1976), p. 2.

fertility rate has fallen below that figure! However, this does not mean that population will actually decrease in the near future. The actual number of births depends upon the fertility rate and the number of women of childbearing age in the population. Because of the large number of such women present, there was a natural increase in population in 1975 of over one million, reflecting the excess of births over deaths.[13]

In 1975, the actual number of births fell to 3.1 million, the second lowest number in recent history and a level even lower than that reached during the Great Depression.[14] The decline of over one million births per year from the high reached in 1957 has developed despite the fact that the number of women of childbearing age in the population has steadily increased. It is apparent that fundamental changes in attitudes toward size of family and childbearing are now making their impact felt upon statistics.

The decline in the birthrate affects not only the total increase in population which we are experiencing but also the age composition of the population and the labor force. Persons under 25 now make up about 23% of the labor force, but this proportion will decline to only 18% by 1990.[15] The dramatic increase will be in the young adult group—age 25–34, a group who are entering their prime working years. The U.S. Bureau of the Census projects about 167 million persons of working age (16 and over) in 1980, with slightly over 100 million Americans in the labor force (including the military).[16]

The long-run growth in the supply of labor depends not only on the growth rate of the population—and, in particular, on the increase in men and women of working age in the population—but also on labor participation rates. From 1966 to 1976, the working-age population in the United States increased 19%, while the labor force increased an astounding 26%. If over this period the labor force had increased at only the same rate as population, it would have totaled only 90 million in 1976 (instead of about 95 million), and if employment had remained at the 1976 figure of 88 million, there would have been only 2 million persons classified as unemployed in that year instead of the 7.5 million listed in the unemployed rolls.[17] When the increase in the number of job seekers and jobholders over the past decade is examined, the surprising fact emerges that the male labor force increased by only 16.8% from 1966 to 1976, while the female labor force jumped 42.3%! From 1975 to

---

[13] Ibid.

[14] Ibid., p. 9.

[15] The Conference Board, *The U.S. Economy in 1990* (New York: The Conference Board, 1972), p. 8.

[16] U.S. Department of Labor, *The U.S. Economy in 1980,* Bulletin 1673 (Washington, D.C., 1970), p. 4.

[17] *Wall Street Journal,* September 20, 1976, p. 1.

1976, the labor force increased by 3 million; of that amount, almost 2 million were women.[18]

The fundamental change in women's attitude toward gainful employment in recent years has in effect introduced a high degree of potential elasticity into labor supply. There are an estimated 40 million working-age females in the United States who are not yet among the job seekers, but labor shortages or even reduced family take-home pay requiring the nonworking female to augment family income could easily bring millions more women into the labor market.

Immigration

In considering the various factors which enter into the long-run supply of labor, mention must be made of net immigration. Because of our restrictive immigration policy, the effect of immigration upon the labor supply has been minimal and this is likely to be the case during the 1970s. It is estimated that during the decade of the 70s the labor force will be augmented by about 1 million immigrants.[19] This number represents less than 3% of the increase anticipated in the labor force during the decade.

SUMMARY

We have seen how supply is related to wage rates and have considered the meaning and content of labor supply from the point of view of the firm, the industry, and the economy. In the next chapter, we shall consider the other side of the picture—the demand for labor. After we have explored thoroughly both the demand and the supply for labor and their relationship to wage levels and employment, we shall be prepared in Chapter 11 to tackle the problem of wage determination as it occurs in the labor market.

APPENDIX: THE SUPPLY CURVE OF LABOR

The supply curve can be derived from a consideration of the individual's work-leisure decision. For purposes of this analysis, we assume that an individual's satisfaction depends both on income derived from working and on leisure. His utility function is

$$U = f(y, \Lambda) \tag{1}$$

where y and Λ denote income and leisure, respectively. The decision facing the individual is to allocate hours to work, thus earning income y, or

---

[18] Ibid.

[19] "The U.S. Economy in 1980: A Preview of BLS Projections," *Monthly Labor Review*, vol. 93 (April 1970), p. 27.

to leisure, Λ, the constraints on his ability to maximize satisfaction being the wage rate w and the total number of hours in the day, T. In (1), it is assumed that the individual buys the various commodities in fixed proportions at constant prices, and income is therefore treated as generalized purchasing power.

The rate of substitution of income for leisure is given by

$$-\frac{dy}{d\Lambda} = \frac{\delta f/\delta\Lambda}{\delta f/\delta y} \tag{2}$$

By definition,

$$\Lambda + H = T \tag{3}$$

where H is the number of hours of work performed. The budget constraint is

$$y = wH \tag{4}$$

Substituting (3) and (4) into (1), we have

$$U = f(wH, T - H) \tag{5}$$

The first-order condition for maximization of utility is

$$\frac{dU}{dH} = -\frac{\delta f}{\delta\Lambda} + \frac{\delta f}{\delta y} \cdot w = 0 \tag{6}$$

which yields on substitution into (2)

$$-\frac{dy}{d\Lambda} = \frac{\delta f/\delta\Lambda}{\delta f/\delta y} = w \tag{7}$$

This states that the rate of substitution of income for leisure equals the wage rate. The second-order condition states that

$$\frac{d^2U}{dH^2} = \frac{\delta^2 f}{\delta\Lambda^2} - 2\frac{\delta^2 f}{\delta\Lambda\delta y} + \frac{\delta^2 f}{\delta y^2} w^2 < 0. \tag{8}$$

Equation (7) is a relation based on T and w and is the individual's offer curve for work and states how much he will work at various wage rates.

The same analysis can be presented diagrammatically in terms of indifference curves, as in Figure 9–3. Each curve indicates all combinations of income y and leisure Λ yielding the same satisfaction or utility. Points northeast of any point represent higher levels of utility, and on two curves cross each other. The objective of the consumer is to reach the highest

FIGURE 9–3
The Work-Leisure Decision

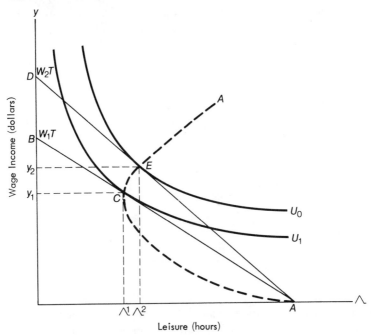

Leisure (hours)

indifference curve possible. The constraint on this is the straight line determined by the wage rate and the number of hours available, T. With a wage rate w_1, the individual can choose between having all T hours of leisure (Point A) and earning income equal to w_1T by working all T hours (Point B). Also, he can trade income for leisure by moving along the line joining the two points A and B. Points on or below the budget line are feasible. The slope of the line is derived by substituting (3) into (4) and differentiating with respect to Λ to obtain $dy/d\Lambda = -w$.

In order to maximize utility, the individual tries to reach the point at which the straight line is just tangential to an indifference curve, as in Point C, which is identical to condition (7). If the wage rate increases to w_2, the budget line changes to AD while the optimum point becomes E. Thus increasing the slope of the budget line changes the amount of leisure consumed. The locus of all the points of tangency yields the labor supply curve AA.

The relationship between the rate and the amount of work offered by the individual, given in Figure 9–4, is usually backward bending. This is based on the hypothesis that as wage rates increase beyond a point, an increase in wage income induces the individual to increase leisure rather than working hours, as the income effect overcomes the substitu-

FIGURE 9–4
Individual Supply Curve of Labor

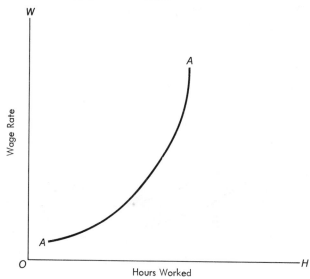

tion effect.[20] Given a homogeneous labor force with a single wage rate, the individual labor supply curves can be aggregated to obtain the labor supply curve for the entire economy.

QUESTIONS FOR DISCUSSION

1. Discuss how recent changes in population growth will affect labor supply in years to come.
2. Under what circumstances will the supply curve of labor to a firm be elastic? Inelastic? Draw a supply curve which is perfectly elastic. Draw a supply curve which is less than perfectly elastic.
3. Discuss the difference between a change in the supply of labor and a change in the amount of labor supplied. What circumstances are likely to cause a change of the former type? Of the latter type?

---

[20] The relationship between the total effect of a wage change on the number of hours worked is given by the Slutsky equation

$$\frac{\delta H}{\delta w} = \left(\frac{\delta H}{\delta w}\right)_{U=\text{const.}} - H\left(\frac{\delta H}{\delta y}\right)_{w=\text{const.}}$$

The first term on the right-hand side is the substitution effect, or the rate at which the individual substitutes work for leisure when the wage rate changes and he moves along the *same* indifference curve. The second term is the income effect, the change in number of hours worked relative to changes in income with the wage rate held constant. The sum of the two is the total effect on number of hours worked for a given change in the wage rate.

SUGGESTIONS FOR FURTHER READING

Barth, Michael C. "Market Effects of a Wage Subsidy," *Industrial and Labor Relations Review,* vol. 27 (July 1974), pp. 572–85.

An attempt to develop a model which predicts the impact on wages and employment of a wage subsidy granted to workers who had been earning less than $3.00 per hour.

Hicks, J. R. *The Theory of Wages.* 2d ed. London: Macmillan & Co., Ltd., 1963, chap. 5, pp. 89–111.

An analysis of factors governing the individual supply of labor expounded from the classical point of view.

Rosen, Shirley, and Welch, Finis. "Labor Supply and Income Redistribution," *Review of Economics and Statistics,* vol. 53 (August 1971), pp. 278–82.

Estimates of labor supply functions bearing on the question of whether or not the provision of unemployment compensation, public assistance grants, and other income supplements creates a withdrawal of recipients from the labor force.

Sawers, Larry. "Urban Poverty and Labor Force Participation: Note," *American Economic Review,* vol. 62 (June 1972), pp. 414–21.

A statistical analysis of labor force participation response on the part of black women and white women in poor and nonpoor areas.

Schweitzer, Stuart O., and Smith, Ralph E. "The Persistence of the Discouraged Worker Effect," *Industrial and Labor Relations Review,* vol. 27 (January 1974), pp. 249–60.

An article which discusses evidence that the discouraged worker effect is intensified by continuing unfavorable experience in the labor market.

U.S. Department of Commerce, Bureau of the Census, *Current Population Reports,* Series P–25. Washington, D.C.: Government Printing Office.

These reports, issued on a continuing basis, are a basic source for data on population growth, with detailed breakdowns with respect to age, sex, color, and so on.

10

The Demand for Labor

DURING THE COURSE of a year, at least 6 million enterprises—3 million farms and as many nonagricultural establishments—use some hired labor. How do these employers decide how much labor to employ and what price to pay for it? What determines whether the employer will hire more men or use machines to perform a particular job? These are problems relating to the demand for labor which we shall consider in the following discussion.

In examining the demand for labor, we shall consider in some detail a theory known as the marginal productivity theory, which attempts to explain the determination of the demand for labor. This theory is widely held by economic theoreticians; but in recent years, it has been attacked as unrealistic by a number of labor economists. Despite such criticism, the marginal productivity theory is still a doctrine to be reckoned with in any study of the functioning of the labor market. It has demonstrated remarkable flexibility, and as will be pointed out in the following discussion, its advocates claim that it is quite compatible with some of the newer theories of wage determination which emphasize the bargaining aspect in wage-employment relationships. In this chapter, we shall consider some of the merits and shortcomings of this theory and compare it with other theories which seek to explain the demand for labor.

THE WAGES FUND THEORY

One of the earliest theories which sought to explain the demand for labor was the so-called wages fund theory, which became popular in England and France in the latter part of the 18th century and the first part of the 19th century. Economists sought to explain the determination of the aggregate amount of funds which employers were prepared to expend in hiring labor. The amount of such funds available for paying wages and salaries was conceived of as substantially fixed at any given period of time. In some discussions, this fund was referred to as "capital."

The wages fund theory declared that the rate of wages is determined by the ratio between this "capital" and the working population.[1] The theory was never clearly formulated, and there was much confusion as to the precise meaning of its terminology. Some formulations of the theory amounted to no more than a truism. To explain the rate of wages by saying that it is a result of the proportion between the number of employees and the amount expended upon their wages by employers is simply to state an arithmetic proposition, not an economic theory. On the other hand, to maintain that there is a definite and fixed fund which is available for payment of wages is clearly erroneous. Wages fund theorists believed that the fund could not be expanded at the expense of profits—that diminution in profits would also reduce the wages fund. But this conclusion rested on the implicit assumption that employers earned only "normal profits," that is, profits at the minimum level necessary to induce an employer to stay in business. As long as there are surplus profits, so that a reduction in profit will not force employers out of business, the wages fund can be expanded by diverting profits to wage and salary payments.

But there is a sense in which the wages fund theory has some validity. In our modern economy, most products are produced by "roundabout" methods of production. That is, the various commodities which constitute the real wage of labor represent the result of a long "period of production." At any given moment, only a certain amount of finished products are emerging from the long production line represented by our entire productive process, just as on the production line at a Ford plant, most of the cars are in an incomplete stage, with only a few ready to be driven off and purchased by consumers.

If the flow of finished products cannot be substantially increased in the short run, an increase in money wages paid to employees may simply produce a rise in prices without augmenting workers' real wages. Thus, in the short run the rate of *real* wages is, to some extent, limited by the size of the "subsistence fund" representing the efforts of past labor which must support current labor until new products emerge from the productive process. However, such a wages fund is flexible over time. Contrary to the view of the proponents of the old wages fund doctrine, an increase in the working population need not reduce the wage rate. On the contrary, when time has permitted the larger number of workers to be better organized so as to achieve a more efficient division of labor, there may be

---

[1] J. S. Mill, *Principles of Political Economy*, Ashley, ed. (London: Longmans, Green & Co., Ltd., 1909), pp. 343–44.

an increase in current output of finished goods which will raise the level of real wages.

The wages fund theory was originally propounded as a means of explaining the determination of the level of real wages. In time, however, it was converted into a doctrine which could be used to prove that attempts by workers to raise their real wages were futile. This perversion of the doctrine ultimately led to its recantation by one of its famous proponents. He conceded that the wages fund was not fixed, that the whole of the capitalists' means was potentially capital (in the sense of advances to labor), and that the amount which actually became capital depended on capitalists' personal expenditures.[2]

THE MARGINAL PRODUCTIVITY THEORY

Following the demise of the wages fund doctrine, the marginal productivity theory became the theory generally applied by economists to explain the functioning of the market for labor. At first, marginal productivity attempted to encompass a theory of wages—that is, it sought to explain the determination of wage levels. This stage of the doctrine is closely associated with the work of John Bates Clark, who, in his influential treatise entitled *Distribution of Wealth*,[3] enunciated a theory which rested on three basic assumptions:

1. Rational employers, in an attempt to maximize profits, will be guided by the marginal productivity of a factor in determining the relationship between a factor's return and its utilization. This premise might be called the "marginal productivity principle" and explains employer demand for the factors of production.
2. Perfect competition exists, so that market forces tend to equalize rates of return for all factors over time.
3. Long-run general equilibrium exists in all markets—which implies a stationary state in which technological progress and changes in demand and supply are absent.[4]

Under the above-stated restrictive conditions, the aggregate labor supply is fixed; and assuming a homogeneous class of labor, it is true that the general level of wages for such labor will be determined by its marginal product.

However, in subsequent writings, other economists attacked the assumptions numbered 2 and 3 above as artificial and remote from the

---

[2] The recantation was made by John Stuart Mill. See Erich Roll, *A History of Economic Thought*, rev. ed. (New York: Prentice-Hall, Inc., 1942), p. 402.

[3] John Bates Clark, *Distribution of Wealth* (London: Macmillan & Co., Ltd., 1899).

[4] See Allan M. Cartter, *Theory of Wages and Employment* (Homewood, Ill.: Richard D. Irwin, Inc., 1959), chaps. 1–3, and especially pp. 18–19.

labor market of reality. In the writings of Alfred Marshall[5] and others, wage determination was explained by the interaction of supply and demand in the marketplace, with marginal productivity being used as a tool to explain the demand for labor. This is the sense in which we shall use the term *marginal productivity* theory in this text. It is *not* a theory of wages; it *is* a theory of demand for factors of production.

According to this theory, employers have a "demand for labor" just as they have a demand for coal, or electricity, or raw materials, or any other of the "means of production" which are required to manufacture a finished product. In considering labor as a means of production, these economists do not, of course, overlook the fact that labor is highly personalized and, therefore, for many problems in the field of labor economics, cannot be treated as the equivalent of so many hours of "energy" on the same level as a lifeless thing like a machine. However, they contend that from the point of view of an employer seeking to operate his plant in the most efficient manner possible, the outlay for labor is a cost of production in the same sense as the outlay for electricity or raw materials. In the employer's calculations, labor becomes merely one of the many factors which can be combined in various proportions to yield varying amounts of physical output.

What determines an employer's demand for labor, according to this theory? Marginal productivity theorists point out that an employer's demand for labor is obviously not determined simply by the physical requirements for production in a given plant. Most plants in our country could physically turn out a larger quantity of goods than they do and could physically utilize larger work forces. The reason they do not do so must be because at some point it becomes unprofitable to produce a larger amount—either because costs rise or prices fall, or both. Therefore, an employer's determination as to actual output must be made with an eye on revenue and costs. Likewise, an employer's utilization of labor must be determined by weighing the cost of employing additional labor against the contribution the added labor is expected to make to the revenue of the firm.

Of course, any such determination made by employers must of necessity be very rough and approximate. The average employer cannot estimate accurately the marginal contribution to revenue which will be made by employment of additional labor. Revenues depend not only upon output but also upon prices; and prices are, of course, subject to constant change and fluctuations in our economy. Nevertheless, these economists argue, as a general rule of economic conduct, it would seem logical to assume that if employers wish to maximize their profits, they will hire additional labor only if its cost is less than the anticipated marginal contribution of the labor to the revenue of the firm.

This principle of weighing marginal revenues contributed by a factor against the added cost incurred through its use is the heart of marginal productivity theory. The marginal productivity theory is generally stated in the form of two propositions: (1) Employers will not ordinarily pay labor (or any other factor of production) more than that factor adds to the revenue of the firm. (2) The forces of competition tend to make employers pay labor (or any other factor) a wage (or price) approximately equal to the full value of its marginal contribution to the revenue of the firm, except in certain special circumstances which we shall consider later in this discussion.

It is important to note that the theory states only a tendency. In a dynamic society such as ours, where prices are always changing, the contribution which employment of additional quantities of labor will make to the revenue of a firm is also subject to continual change. Employers, however, do not change wages or hire or fire workers every time they make a price change. Consequently, the most that can be expected is that whenever employers make adjustments in output, plant size, labor force, or capital equipment, they will do so with the objective in mind of attempting to secure as close an equivalence as possible between the "marginal cost" of a factor of production—that is, the additional cost incurred by employing an additional unit of a factor of production—and the marginal revenue product of the factor—that is, the addition to revenue of the firm attributable to employment of the additional unit of the factor.

The Role of Profit Maximization

The two propositions of the marginal productivity theory stated above are simply logical deductions from a premise basic to the theory, namely that businessmen normally seek to maximize profits. As we shall see later in this chapter, a businessman who finds that with a given amount of labor, he is obtaining a marginal revenue product in excess of the marginal cost of labor, can actually increase his profit by employing more labor until the marginal cost and marginal revenue product of labor are equated. Therefore, if businessmen are interested in maximizing profits, and if they attempt to make estimates of cost and revenue of the marginal type we have considered, there would be some tendency for the wage of labor to approximate the marginal revenue product of labor in the particular firms in which it is employed.

Not all businessmen, however, are motivated by the desire to maximize profits. Recent studies have indicated that the desire for prestige, for power, and for security may be dominant motives in the minds of many employers. Such motives may frequently dictate a policy which is inconsistent with maximizing profit. Some employers may be interested only in "satisficing" profits, rather than in maximizing them. This means that they set a target level of profits based upon a "fair return on investment," which may be less than the maximum profit that can be earned.[6]

Employer motivation is complex. Marginal productivity theorists concede that motives and objectives other than profit maximization influence employer behavior, but they contend nevertheless that the behavior of most employers can best be explained in terms of long-run profit maximization. Critics of the theory, however, take issue with this assumption and argue that noneconomic motivation is so common that a realistic theory cannot be based on profit maximization. Here is the first of the major cleavages between this theory and other theories of labor demand.

Long-Run Adjustments

The marginal productivity theory is a theory of long-run tendencies. Employer behavior which appears uneconomic from the short-run point of view may actually be designed to maximize profits in the long run. Moreover, in the short run, employers cannot freely change the combination of the factors of production. Suppose an employer has been using ten men and a machine to make a product. If the price of labor doubles, he may find that he would be better off using half as much labor and a larger, more complicated machine. But it may be impracticable for him to junk his existing machine immediately, or possibly the larger machine cannot be accommodated in his existing plant. Consequently, several years may elapse before he is able to make the adjustment which the marginal productivity theory states he should make if he wishes to maximize profit.

DEMAND FOR LABOR IN THE INDIVIDUAL FIRM

The marginal productivity theory may be considered from the point of view of the individual firm or of the economy as a whole; or stated another way, marginal productivity principles determine the nature of the demand curve for labor, and the demand curve for labor may be examined from the point of view of the individual employer or of the economy as a whole. In the following discussion, we shall be concerned only with the application of marginal productivity principles by the individual employer. Later in this chapter, we shall consider the problem of applying marginal productivity principles to the economy as a whole.

In the context of individual firm analysis, the marginal contribution of a factor is determined by its effect on the *revenue* of the particular firm. If we say, as a paraphrase of the theory, that employers try to pay

---

[6] See Philip Kotler, *Marketing Management,* 3d ed. (Englewood Cliffs, N.J.: Prentice-Hall, Inc., 1976), p. 252.

labor what it is worth, the term *worth* must be understood in a strictly economic sense, without any moral or social connotations. The advertising executive who thinks up new slogans for dog food has a high worth to his agency because his efforts add a lot to the revenue of the firm. The value of his "product" from the social point of view may be nil. The marginal productivity theory was originally enunciated in terms of a theoretical economy in which perfect competition prevailed. In such a system, factors of production would tend to be allocated in a manner such that the optimum aggregate national product would be obtained, and the value of the marginal product of particular employees would be some index of its social worth. This theoretical problem need not concern us at this point, however. We know that our economy is not perfectly competitive, and that there are no tendencies in that direction to warrant using perfect competition as a norm in our discussion.

The Significance of Monopolistic Competition

In the following analysis, we shall assume—what is a fact—that we have an economy characterized by "monopolistic competition." In such an economy, there are a number of firms in each industry, each firm selling a product which is slightly differentiated from the competing products. Each producer is in competition with other producers; but to some extent, each is a monopolist in his own little market. Hence the term *monopolistic competition.* If the individual producer raises his price, he does not lose all his customers because some customers still prefer his product and will pay the higher price. In other words, although there are competitive products, they are not perfect substitutes in the minds of consumers; and to the extent that such substitution is imperfect, the individual producer is somewhat in the position of a monopolist who can raise his price without losing customers because he has a monopoly of the product. Similarly, when the individual producer lowers his price, he increases his business but does not take away all his competitors' business because some of their customers will remain loyal and buy their products despite this producer's price reduction.

We may assume, therefore, that the average employer with whom we shall be concerned will, in estimating his labor requirements, have in mind the fact that additional units of his product can be sold only at a lower price, which is required in order to take away some of the business from his monopolistic competitors and make it possible to market the larger volume. If additional output can be sold at a lower price, this will also mean that the marginal contribution to revenue made by additional employees will tend to decline. Therefore, the more workers the employer hires, the less he can afford to pay to each additional worker. In geometric terms, this means that the employer will have a downward-sloping demand curve for labor.

Geometry versus Reality

Of course, employers do not normally think in terms of geometric curves. As a matter of fact, they usually would not even have sufficient data to plot a demand curve for labor if they wanted to! The concept of a demand curve for labor is simply an aid which helps economists to understand how employers make decisions involving the employment of labor. The employer must have some rough idea of the various wages he would be willing to pay for varying amounts of labor, based upon his estimates of the additional revenue which such labor could produce for him. The demand curve for labor is simply a geometric representation of this idea.

The demand curve for labor of a hypothetical employer is shown by line *DD* in Figure 10–1. The demand curve for labor shows the various

FIGURE 10–1

The Demand Curve for Labor

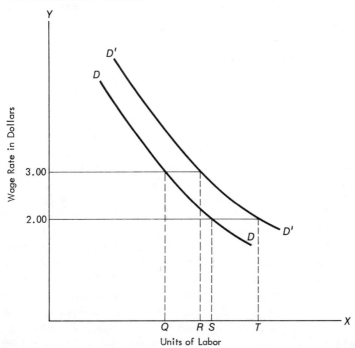

amounts of labor the employer would be willing to employ at various wage levels. As in the preceding chapter, we shall assume, for illustrative purposes, that labor is homogeneous so that we can talk about "units of labor" or "additional labor" without need for concern about personal differences. The lower the wage level, the more labor the individual employer feels he can profitably employ. Thus, at the wage of $3, this employer estimates that he could employ only OQ units of labor, whereas if the wage rate falls to $2, he would employ OS units of labor. Such increases are referred to as changes in the quantity of labor demanded because they involve changes along a given demand curve. Sometimes, however, the entire demand curve for labor will shift. This may happen, for example, when there is an upturn in business, such as occurs during the business cycle. A shift in the demand curve for labor means that at every wage rate the employer is now willing to hire more labor than he was willing to hire previously. For example, in Figure 10–1, if the demand curve shifts to position $D'D'$, then at the wage of $3 the employer will demand OR units of labor instead of the smaller amount OQ indicated by the previous position of the demand curve. This situation involves an *increase in the demand for labor,* whereas increased employment due to a reduction in wage rates is distinguished by economists as an *increase in the quantity of labor demanded.* A similar distinction in terminology was met in the last chapter in connection with changes in supply.

THE LAWS OF PRODUCTION

We have seen that in monopolistic competition the demand curve for labor is downward sloping because of conditions in the market for the employer's product. There is also another and more fundamental reason why the demand curve for labor has this shape. This is found in the so-called laws of production—the law of diminishing returns and the law of scale. These two laws would have the effect of producing a downward-sloping demand curve for labor *even if the employer estimated that he could sell additional units* of his product with no reduction in price. These laws affect the amount of additional *physical* product which can be produced by adding amounts of one factor of production to other factors. They are laws of physical, not monetary, returns.

These laws derive from the firm's "production function," which can be defined as the technical relationship which exists among the various factors or inputs required to produce particular outputs. Two aspects of this relationship can be distinguished: In the first place, we can consider the effect on physical output of increasing all inputs in equal proportions. This measurement gives rise to returns to scale, which theoretically can be decreasing, constant, or increasing. In the second place, we can vary inputs of only one factor while holding other factors constant in amount. In this case, we speak of returns to the variable factor. Here, too, the output results could in theory yield decreasing, constant, or increasing returns. However, as will be explained below, firms always operate in the stretch of the production function where diminishing returns to the factor have set in.

The Law of Diminishing Returns

The law of diminishing returns is concerned with the effect on total output of adding successive amounts of one factor of production to another factor or group of factors which is held constant in amount. Thus, we may wish to know the effect on total product of adding workers to assist in the cultivation of one acre of corn. Or we may wish to know the behavior of total output of shoes as the amount of capital per worker is increased. The universal rule in such cases is that, with a given state of technology, the application of successive units of *any* variable factor to another fixed factor will, after a certain point is reached, yield diminishing returns. Or to put the proposition a little differently, adding units of labor to another factor—say, capital—will, beyond a certain point (that is, the point of diminishing returns), produce diminishing marginal increments in total physical product.

Significance for Marginal Productivity Theory. The law of diminishing returns is of fundamental importance to marginal productivity determination. Its relation to marginal productivity theory can best be illustrated if, for the moment, we direct our attention exclusively to physical product. Suppose that additional units of product can be sold at the same price, so that the employer is concerned primarily with the changes in total physical product attributable to employment of additional labor. Suppose, further, that labor itself is paid in physical product rather than in money. Under these conditions the marginal productivity theory would say that there is a tendency for the wage of labor to equal the marginal physical product it produces.

There could be no such tendency, however, if industry operated in a range of increasing rather than diminishing physical returns. This can be seen from the following example, which illustrates production under increasing returns. If increasing returns prevail, the addition of more labor to a fixed amount of another factor will produce more than proportionate increases in total product, with the result that the marginal physical product of labor will continually rise. The marginal physical product of labor is the increase in total product attributable to the addition of a unit of labor. Suppose that all workers are of equal ability (so that they have to be paid the same wage) and that employment of additional labor increases total product as follows:

Workers	Total Product	Marginal Product
1	4	—
2	10	6
3	17	7
4	25	8

The addition of a fourth worker increases output by 8 units. But the employer could not afford to pay a wage rate equivalent to 8 units of product, since all workers have to be paid the same wage, and payment of an hourly wage of 8 units of output would involve a wage bill of 32 units, which is in excess of total product.

In practice, employers operate within the range of diminishing returns. Therefore, the marginal product of labor will be decreasing, not increasing, as in the above hypothetical example. In the following illustration, the addition of the fourth worker increases total product from 14 units to 17 units:

Workers	Total Product	Marginal Product
1	4	—
2	10	6
3	14	4
4	17	3

The marginal physical product (that is, the increase in total product attributable to the addition of the last unit of the variable factor) of the fourth worker is three units, and the employer can therefore profitably pay up to three units as his wage. Because of diminishing returns, the wage bill will not exhaust total product—the wage bill would be only 12, whereas the total product would be 17. Moreover, there would be a limit to the output of the firm—there would be no incentive to expand output beyond the point at which the marginal product of labor equaled its wage. The demand curve for labor under these circumstances would be downward sloping—even though prices were not affected by increasing output—simply because the marginal contribution to total physical product made by additional workers was declining, and therefore the wage which the employer could afford to pay for such additional labor would also decrease as employment rose.

The Law of Scale

The law of diminishing returns, as we have seen, is concerned with the effect upon total physical output of adding increasing amounts of variable factors to an unchanging amount of a fixed factor. The law of scale, on the other hand, concerns the effect upon total product of increasing *all* factors together. For example, if we double the amount of capital and the quantity of labor and the amount of land, will output likewise double? Will the proportionate increase in total product be greater or less than the proportionate increase in the quantity of factors?

Significance for Marginal Productivity Theory. Why is this problem relevant to marginal productivity determination? The size of the marginal physical product contributed by a particular worker will depend upon the size of the establishment in which he is employed. Take the example of Jones the shoemaker. If Jones is employed in an establishment having only ten employees, the chances are that most of his work will be done by hand. Moreover, he will probably have to make the entire shoe himself, since the number of employees will be too small to permit efficient division of labor. However, as the size of the establishment grows, there will come a point—say, when 100 men are employed—at which it will pay the employer to utilize expensive machinery designed to perform individual operations, such as lasting and cutting. Moreover, the workers can be arranged in a production line, each worker performing only a specialized operation at which he soon becomes highly proficient.

As a result of the introduction of machinery and division of labor, efficiency of operation will increase. Consequently, the physical productivity of a worker in the large factory will be greater than the physical productivity of a worker in the small plant. Here, we have a situation in which an increase in the amount of labor and capital produces a more than proportionate increase in total output. This consequence is fundamentally attributable to the fact that machinery can only be introduced in "chunks." A conveyor belt and production line cannot be advantageously used with only ten employees, and the small firm cannot use half a machine. As the size of a firm grows, various "indivisible" chunks of other factors become profitable to use; and such utilization, impracticable in a smaller plant, may result in a substantial improvement in efficiency.

However, if such improvement were a continuing possibility as a function of increasing scale, there would be no limit to the size of firms. Our economy would be composed of giant monopolies, each supreme in its own field. Obviously, this eventuality has not occurred. The reason is that as a firm grows in size, the problems of organization, supervision, and coordination grow in complexity. Management becomes farther and farther removed from actual operations as the hierarchy of minor officialdom grows. As a consequence, beyond a certain size—which varies by industry—inefficiency develops, and the rate of increase in total product becomes less than proportionate to the increase in the quantity of all factors used.

Another reason for the eventual decline in rate of growth of total output as size of firm grows is that beyond a certain point, it is not possible to increase entrepreneurship in the same proportion as other factors. Executives who can efficiently manage billion-dollar enterprises are few and far between. Consequently, as existing management finds that it must itself coordinate larger quantities of labor and capital, inefficiency develops. This is simply a reflection of the operation of the law of diminishing returns—increasing amounts of labor and capital added to the unchanging factor of entrepreneurship result in diminishing returns in terms of total output.

Thus, the law of scale and the law of diminishing returns set important limitations on the proportion and amount of factors which will be used in individual firms. Were it not for the law of diminishing returns, there would be no limit to the output of a firm; were it not for the law of scale, there would be no limit to the amount of all factors which could profitably be combined under one management. These laws, therefore, play an important role in determining the physical environment in which labor will work and thereby influence the size of physical product which will be attributable to the efforts of particular workers.

MARGINAL PRODUCTIVITY CALCULATIONS

Few employers have ever heard of marginal productivity; yet employees are called upon to apply the principles of this doctrine almost every day in the conduct of their business affairs. The question which is continually presented is: Will the purchase of additional units of a particular productive resource increase the revenue of the firm by an amount in excess of the addition in cost incidental to its employment? If the addition promises to augment profits so calculated, the resource will be acquired; if not, the opportunity to purchase or to employ will be forgone. Obviously, the calculation must ordinarily be approximate.

Determination of the anticipated marginal contribution to the firm attributable to the hiring of an additional worker would be facilitated if three conditions were satisfied: (1) if his employment did not require use of additional material or capital, so that his contribution would be net, without deduction for incidental expenses; (2) if the increment in output attributable to his employment could be measured in distinct, separable, completed physical units; and (3) if the price at which the increased output could be sold could be forecast accurately. In practice, these conditions are never realized, so that at best the employer's calculation of the marginal worth of an employee must remain in the realm of approximation.

In a Robinson Crusoe economy, where Crusoe had merely to evaluate the worth of the services of one man, Friday, the marginal product of labor could be determined with fair precision. In a typical modern factory, however, where thousands of employees, aided by complex machinery, pool their efforts to produce a joint product, the contribution of the individual employee becomes indistinct. Nevertheless, employers must make some estimate of the worth of additional employees. They do not go on hiring workers without limit.

The Nature of Marginal Productivity Calculations

Table 10-1 is intended to clarify and elaborate the nature of the shorthand calculations which the marginal productivity theory assumes employers make in determining the volume of employment in a firm.

TABLE 10–1
Marginal Productivity Calculations

(1)	(2)	(3)	(4)	(5)	(6)	(7)
				Value of		
			Price	Marginal		Marginal
Units		Marginal	per	Physical	Total	Revenue
of	Total	Physical	Unit	Product	Revenue	Product
Labor	Product	Product	(dollars)	(dollars)	(dollars)	(dollars)
1	20	20	5.00	100	100	100
2	50	30	4.00	120	200	100
3	70	20	3.50	70	245	45
4	85	15	3.00	45	255	10
5	95	10	2.00	20	190	−65
6	100	5	1.00	5	100	−90

Few employers would have available such a detailed schedule as is assumed here, but the detailed figures will serve to illustrate more clearly the basic principles involved in marginal productivity determination.

Assume that our factory produces brooms and that the relationships among employment, physical product, and revenue are estimated by the employer to be as shown in Table 10–1. Consider first columns 1, 2, and 3 of Table 10–1. As additional units of labor are added to unchanging amounts of the other factors, the total physical product increases, at first more than in proportion to the increase in labor and subsequently less than in proportion to the increase in labor. Eventually, as more and more labor is hired, total product might actually decrease. This might be attributable to the fact that with, say, ten workers and a limited amount of machinery, the workers would get in one another's way, with the result that total output would be curtailed. The variation in total product and marginal physical product shown in the table reflects the operation of the law of diminishing returns. If labor were paid in brooms and the rate of wages established in the market were 16 brooms, this employer could afford to hire only three workers. With three workers on his force, the employer gets production of 70 brooms, the third employee having increased production by 20 brooms. But the addition of a fourth worker would increase output only to 85 brooms. Fifteen brooms is therefore the marginal physical product attributable to the fourth worker, that is, it is the increment in total physical production attributable to the employment of an additional unit of the variable factor. If wages are paid in brooms, the employer cannot afford to pay this worker 16 brooms when he adds only 15 brooms to the output of the firm.

Value of the Marginal Physical Product of Labor

Since, in a modern capitalist economy, labor is paid in money wages and not in physical product, employers must estimate the money value of the physical contribution made by additional units of labor. The value of the marginal physical product of labor is obtained by multiplying marginal physical product (column 3) by price per unit of product (column 4). This figure would be a fair index of the value to an employer of the additional output produced by additional units of labor if the additional output could be sold without any reduction in price as compared with a smaller output. In other words, if an employer assumed that he could market additional units of product at a constant price, he could afford to pay labor a wage just a trifle less than the price per unit of such additional output and still make a profit. This is the situation which exists under what economists call "perfect competition." In perfect competition, each firm is small and produces only a minor portion of the output in a particular industry. Furthermore, in perfect competition, unlike monopolistic competition, the product of each firm in the industry is indistinguishable from the product of any other firm. As a consequence, the individual employer assumes that if he produces a little more, the addition to the total output of the entire industry will be so slight that it will not affect market price. This situation may exist in the case of farmers producing wheat. Each farmer feels that his output is so small relative to the total output of the industry that he can produce and sell almost any amount of wheat at the same price. In geometric terms, this would mean that if price of product were plotted along the Y axis and quantities expected to be sold along the X axis, the farmer would assume that his demand curve for wheat is horizontal. In perfect competition the individual employer would hire workers until the wage was approximately equal to the value of marginal physical product added by the last worker hired.

The Marginal Revenue Product of Labor

However, under monopolistic competition the value of the marginal physical product of labor is not a fair index of the value to an employer of the additional units produced by added labor because the additional output can be sold only at a lower price, and this lowers not only the price for the additional units but also the price for all other units of the firm's production. Therefore, we must determine what net amount is added to the revenue of the firm by the employment of the additional labor. This figure is supplied by the marginal revenue product (column 7). The marginal revenue product of labor is calculated either by finding the difference between total revenue obtained with a given amount of labor and that obtained with a smaller amount of labor or by subtracting from the value of the marginal physical product the loss in revenue, if any, sustained with respect to units of products produced without use of the additional units of the factor, when the loss is caused by a fall in price because of the augmented output.

If the wage rate for broommakers were established in the market at $30, this firm could afford to employ only three workers. The marginal revenue product (column 7) for the fourth worker is only $10. It would not be profitable for this firm to employ the fourth worker, since his employment would cost the firm more than he adds to revenue. The employment of the third worker results in production of 20 extra units, which can be sold only by taking a reduction in price from $4 to $3.50. The value of the marginal physical product is $70 (column 4 multiplied by column 3). But the reduced price is applicable as well to the 50 units which could have been produced without the extra worker, and therefore the loss of revenue on these units of $25 (50 multiplied by $0.50 equals $25) must be subtracted from $70, leaving $45 as the marginal revenue attributable to the use of the third worker. Thus, it is apparent that in monopolistic competition a worker cannot be paid the value of his marginal physical product, since this would exceed the amount of his marginal revenue contribution to the firm. It is therefore with reference to the marginal revenue product of labor that the employer will make his employment decisions.

CONDITIONS OF PROFIT MAXIMIZATION
IN THE INDIVIDUAL FIRM

The principles of marginal productivity determination elucidated in the foregoing computations are illustrated in geometric form in Figure 10–2. The line marked MRP represents the marginal revenue product obtained from employment of varying amounts of labor. This curve therefore indicates the value to the employer of varying amounts of labor and is identical with his demand curve for labor. For OB units of labor the estimated marginal revenue product is BQ; as more labor is employed, marginal revenue product falls, so that for OD units of labor the marginal revenue product is equal to DL. Suppose, now, that a wage of OA dollars for this type of labor is established in the market. Suppose, further, that the employer can obtain any number of workers he needs at this same wage level. The wage is therefore constant, regardless of the number of units of labor employed. This circumstance is shown by the horizontal line AC. The line is called the supply curve of labor because it indicates the amount of labor that will be supplied at a given wage. It also indicates the average cost to the employer of hiring additional units of labor. Since, in the present case, it has been assumed that each additional unit of labor can be obtained with no increase in price, the average cost and the marginal cost of each unit of labor are identical. The line AC therefore represents both the average cost and the marginal cost of hiring additional labor. At a later point in this discussion, we shall find that under different circumstances the average cost and the marginal cost of labor may diverge.

FIGURE 10–2
Profit Maximization in the Individual Firm

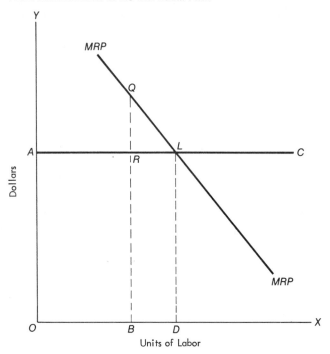

The Determination of Optimum Employment

With a demand curve and a supply curve for labor as shown in Figure 10–2, what amount of labor will yield maximum profits for the employer? Suppose he employs only *OB* units. For this amount the marginal revenue product *BQ* is well above the cost *RB*, and it might therefore be thought that this amount would yield a maximum profit to the employer. But note that if the employer uses a little more labor, although marginal revenue product falls with each additional unit of labor utilized, he can nevertheless increase profits as long as the marginal revenue product of labor remains above its cost. This will be so until we come to the point of intersection of the marginal revenue curve and the wage. For any amount of labor less than *OD*, the employer can increase his profit by using more labor; and for any amount of labor greater than *OD*, the employer will be losing money, since he will be paying labor more in wages than it produces for him in revenue.

The point in equality of marginal revenue product and wage is therefore the point of maximum profit for the employer. Under the assumed circumstances of a horizontal supply curve for labor, the employer who is interested in obtaining the largest profit will seek to utilize that amount of labor for which the marginal revenue product of the last worker employed is approximately equal to his wage. If the employer follows this rule, ordinarily a reduction of wage rates will induce him to increase employment of labor, while an increase in wage rates will induce him to curtail employment of labor. This reaction is to be expected, however, only with a given marginal revenue product curve. If there should be an increase in wage rates concurrently with an increase in demand for labor (that is, a shift to the right of the entire demand curve for labor), then it is quite possible that the wage increase will not produce any reduction in employment and, indeed, may even be associated with an increase in employment. This is frequently the case, as we shall see in our discussion in later chapters of wage changes during the business cycle. Increases in wage rates usually occur in periods when business is booming and the demand for labor is increasing. In such circumstances there is no immediate inducement for employers to curtail employment in response to the increased cost of labor. The marginal productivity theory, therefore, is quite consistent with the observed pattern of wage-employment relationships which develops over the period of the business cycle.

We have seen that maximum profits are obtained by the employer if he attempts to hire an amount of labor such that the marginal revenue product of the last worker hired will approximate his wage. This principle is applicable to all of the factors of production which the employer utilizes. The marginal productivity theory assumes that wherever possible the employer will attempt to obtain maximum output at minimum cost. If he can do this by using more of one factor of production rather than another, he will do so. The decisive consideration in each case is the contribution to revenues in comparison with costs. For maximum profits the employer should utilize the various factors of production so that the ratio of the marginal revenue product of each factor to its cost will equal the ratio of the marginal revenue product to the cost of other factors. Of course, if the employer is able to use an amount of each factor such that its marginal revenue product is equal to its cost, then the former condition of equality of ratios of respective marginal revenue products and costs will automatically be satisfied.[7]

EXPLOITATION OF LABOR

The marginal productivity theory assumes that there is a long-run tendency toward equality between the wage of labor and its marginal revenue product in the individual firm. Normally, the employer obtains his maximum profit by seeking to achieve this position. As we have seen,

---

[7] For a mathematical proof of the propositions stated in this section, see the appendix at the end of this chapter.

if the wage is below the marginal revenue product, it will pay him to increase output and employment to a point where this discrepancy is eliminated and the equality between wage and marginal revenue product is established. However, the marginal productivity theory recognizes that there may be certain situations in which a discrepancy can develop between marginal revenue product and wage which it will be profitable for the employer to maintain, so that there will be no tendency to the normal equilibrium position of equality of wage and marginal revenue product. These exceptions to the general rule are referred to by economists as cases of exploitation of labor.

The term *exploitation* is used by economists simply to denote a condition in which labor is paid a wage less than its marginal revenue product. It is a technical definition without social connotations. It has no necessary connection with the level of wage rates. The distressingly low rates paid to labor in some marginal industries may present an acute labor problem, but the low rate is not in itself any evidence of "exploitation," as the economist uses that term. Indeed, we shall see that exploitation of labor, as we have defined it, is as likely to be encountered where wages are high as where they are low.

A Rising Supply Curve for Labor

Perhaps the most common source of exploitation is the lack of perfect elasticity in the supply curve for labor. In the preceding discussion, it was assumed that the supply curve for labor is horizontal (that is, perfectly elastic); but frequently this will not be the case. For example, a firm may require such a substantial proportion of a particular type of labor in an area that it will have to offer higher wage rates when it wants additional labor, in order to attract workers away from other companies. This is particularly likely in cases of skilled labor which is in short supply. The type of exploitation considered here may therefore be more common where wage rates are high rather than low, since it is a result of scarcity in the labor market. In cases of such short supply a firm, in estimating its labor requirements, will take into account the fact that its demand for labor affects the market price of labor. The firm which is a large enough buyer of a particular class of labor so that its demand will affect the price of labor is termed a *monopsonist* by analogy to a monopolist, who is a large enough seller of a commodity so that his supply will affect the price of a commodity. The monopsonist will assume that he is faced by a rising supply curve for labor, that is, that increasing amounts of labor can be obtained only at successively higher wage rates. This will affect his decision as to the amount of labor he will employ.

In our previous examples, we noted that if an employer can obtain additional workers at the same wage, the average cost of each additional worker and the marginal cost of each additional worker will be the same and will in each case be equal to the wage which is paid the worker. If, however, the employer has to pay higher wages to attract additional workers, the identity between average cost and marginal cost disappears. Suppose that the prevailing wage paid by a firm has been $3 an hour, but that in order to obtain additional workers, the employer finds that he must increase the wage rate to $3.25 per hour. If he pays this rate to new workers, he will also be compelled to pay it to all other workers of the same skill already in the firm, in order to avoid dissatisfaction among his employees. As a consequence, the addition to total wage cost (that is, marginal cost) attributable to hiring an additional worker may under such circumstances be considerably in excess of the wage, or average cost, of the new worker.

In Figure 10–3, units of labor hired by the firm are indicated along

FIGURE 10–3
Exploitation: Upward-Sloping Labor Supply Curve

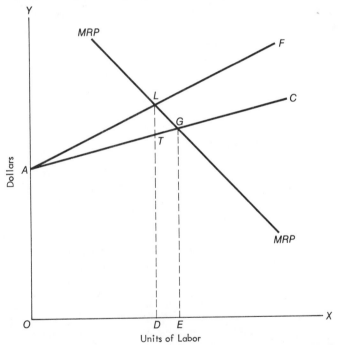

Units of Labor

the X axis, while the cost of labor and its productivity in terms of dollars are indicated along the Y axis. The supply curve of labor (AC) is assumed to be rising to the firm. Each point on this line indicates the wage which will have to be paid to attract the amount of labor indicated along the X axis. The wage paid and the average cost of labor to the individual firm are therefore identical. However, when the average cost of labor is rising, the marginal cost will be greater, as has already been explained, since the marginal cost takes account not only of the higher wage paid to a particular employee but also of the addition to payroll resulting from paying the same higher rate to all employees already employed by the firm. Marginal cost is indicated in Figure 10–3 by the line AF. Obviously, the employer has to take account of these expensive consequences of paying higher rates for new workers; and for this reason, he employs that amount of labor for which the marginal cost of labor and its marginal revenue product are equal. This equality is achieved if OD units of labor are employed. It will be recalled that in our previous example, where the supply curve of labor was constant, the employer also equated marginal cost of labor and marginal revenue product to maximize profits, since the marginal cost of labor and the wage of labor were the same. However, in Figure 10–3, because the supply curve for labor is rising, for OD units of labor the marginal revenue product of labor (DL) will be above the wage paid to labor (DT). If the employer were to expand employment to OE units, which is the point where the wage and the marginal revenue product are equal, he would, under the circumstances set forth here, reduce his profit. Here, then, is a case in which the wage will be less than the marginal revenue product; therefore, exploitation will exist. Under the circumstances shown in Figure 10–3, the employer could not pay labor a wage equal to its marginal revenue product and still maximize profits.

Consequences of Exploitation

We have seen that if the wage of labor is approximately equated with its marginal revenue product, an increase in wage rates will lead the employer to reduce employment until at the smaller output the marginal revenue product of labor is raised to equal the now increased wage. In the case of exploitation attributable to a rising supply curve for labor, however, the effect of a wage increase upon employment will depend on whether there is a rise in the entire supply curve of labor or a change in its slope. If the entire marginal cost and average cost curves for labor shift upward but remain rising supply curves (as would be the case if there were a general increase in wage rates in the area), employment will be reduced in the individual firm, since there will have been a rise in the marginal cost of labor without a concomitant change in the marginal revenue productivity of labor. However, it is also possible that an increase in wage rates may be accompanied by a change in the shape of the supply curve for labor. For example, suppose a union enters the labor market and sets a uniform rate for labor, regardless of the number of workers required (within limits), which is equal to the former marginal cost of labor. In Figure 10–3, this would mean that the supply curve for labor would now be designated by a horizontal line drawn through point L on the marginal revenue product curve. If this were to occur, the employer would still find it profitable to employ the same number of employees (OD), since this amount would be indicated as most profitable by the intersection of the horizontal supply curve for labor and the demand curve for labor. The wage DL thus would be above the former wage DT, but because there would be no change in the marginal cost of labor, employment would be unaffected. All that would occur would be a reduction in the profits of the firm. Here is a case in which workers would benefit from organization.

UNIONS AND MARGINAL PRODUCTIVITY THEORY

A rising supply curve for labor is most typical of skilled wage groups, but these are the very ones which are most likely to be highly unionized. When a trade union sets a minimum wage rate for work of a particular kind, regardless of the number of workers the employer hires to do it, the effect is to make the supply curve for labor to the employer horizontal, or "perfectly elastic," as the economists say. This has the effect of eliminating exploitation attributable to a rising supply curve for labor. But union organization, by reason of its multifarious rules and regulations and restrictions on employer freedom of action, may also make it more difficult for employers to utilize the optimum amount of labor and thus may produce a discrepancy between marginal revenue product and wage.

The correspondence between a worker's wage and his individual contribution to the revenues of the firm depends in some degree upon the ability of the employer to determine the amount of such contribution. This presupposes that the employer can hire and fire at will, rearrange job classifications, change workers from one position to another, substitute machinery for labor, and in general freely alter the combinations of labor and capital within the firm. Unions, however, have restricted many of these former prerogatives of management. Consequently, in firms where unions are strongly entrenched, workers are not freely substitutable, and the task of marginal productivity determination is undoubtedly made more difficult.

The Effects of Union Rules

Union rules which limit the employer's ability to substitute machinery for labor and restrict the freedom of the employer to measure the contribution of labor to the output of the firm may produce a range of indeterminateness in wage-employment relations. For example, many unions are now interested in requiring employers to pay dismissal wages to employees who are displaced as a result of technological change. Suppose that as a result of a wage increase an employer finds that it is profitable to introduce a new machine which will displace ten workers. If the union now compels the employer to pay these displaced workers dismissal wages for some period of time after they are laid off, the employer may decide that it is no longer profitable to introduce the machine. The union insistence on a dismissal wage has obviously not increased the marginal revenue product of the labor involved; yet, it has had the practical effect of enabling the union to raise the wage rates of these workers without producing immediate technological unemployment.

In effect, union rules have produced a range of indeterminateness within which some changes in wage rates may be effected without altering employment. The range of indeterminateness, however, is much narrower than the short-run repercussions of employment would indicate. Any wage adjustment, whether or not it immediately alters employment, does affect profits and the inducement to invest. If these are adversely influenced by union wage demands, wage increases even within the "range of indeterminateness" may cause unemployment in the long run.

THE DEMAND FOR LABOR IN THE ECONOMY

As we have observed earlier in this chapter, the marginal productivity theory in its original form purported to explain the determination of wages in the economy as a whole. It laid down a long list of assumptions and emerged with the conclusion that in equilibrium the wage of labor in the economy as a whole would be equal to the marginal productivity of labor in its least profitable use. This conclusion—and the highly artificial assumptions upon which it was based—did much to bring the theory into disrepute. Moreover, proponents of the theory erroneously reasoned from the existence of unemployment in the labor market to the conclusion that wages were too high and that if wages were only reduced, unemployment could be eliminated.

We have seen that present-day labor economists do not look upon marginal productivity as a theory of wages, but rather as a theory of demand. But even here, limitations must be recognized. As a result of the work of John Maynard Keynes[8] in the field of general equilibrium analysis, it is generally accepted that the marginal productivity theory cannot serve as a general theory of employment and that the theory does not adequately explain the demand for labor in the economy as a whole. The demand curve for labor in the economy as a whole is not simply the sum of the demand curves of all individual firms. The reason is that each individual demand curve for labor is drawn up under the assumption that wages and prices in other firms remain constant. Thus, when the individual employer considers what effect a reduction in wage rates

---

[8] John Maynard Keynes, *The General Theory of Employment, Interest, and Money* (New York: Harcourt, Brace & Co., Inc., 1936).

will have on his labor requirements, he assumes that sales of his product will be unaffected by the reduction in wages. However, when we consider the economy as a whole, a reduction in the wages paid to all labor will affect the demand curve for all labor because wage earners are the principal purchasers of the product of industry. Whereas, for the individual firm, the demand curve for labor may be assumed to be independent of the supply curve for labor, this assumption cannot be made when we are considering the economy as a whole. Therefore, it is possible that a reduction in wage rates might not increase employment at all when the reduction is nationwide, even though increased employment would normally follow a wage reduction in the individual firm.

The demand for labor in the economy as a whole can only be understood by application of the aggregative analysis developed by Keynes, in which attention is given to changes in savings, investment, and national income. However, the fact that marginal productivity analysis has proved inadequate to deal with the demand for labor in the economy as a whole does not necessarily mean that it cannot be used to advantage to explain the demand for labor in the individual firm. Exponents of this theory still contend that it gives a logical explanation of employer behavior in the individual firm.

Furthermore, even from the point of view of the economy as a whole, the marginal productivity theory helps us to understand why the level of wages is high in a country like the United States and low in a country like India. The average level of wages in a particular economy will be determined by the scarcity of labor relative to other factors of production. In the United States, labor has always been in short supply relative to land and capital. As a consequence, the marginal product of labor has remained high. We have seen from previous examples in this chapter that as additional quantities of a factor of production are utilized, its marginal product declines. If labor were more plentiful in the United States, as it is in India, more labor would be used relative to capital, and the marginal product of labor would be less. Employers have been ready to pay, and workers have been able to demand, a high level of wages in this country because the high ratio of land and labor to capital has made the incremental contribution of labor worth a high wage.

CRITIQUE OF THE MARGINAL PRODUCTIVITY THEORY

A number of criticisms have been leveled against the marginal productivity theory. Some of these have merit; others are based in part upon a lack of understanding of what the theory holds. The following are some of the major lines of attack against the marginal productivity theory.

1. Some economists object to the whole notion of marginality and marginal calculations on the ground that "businessmen don't think that

way." It is all very well, they say, to draw up marginal revenue and marginal cost curves and sloping demand curves and rising supply curves, but the fact is that most employers have little or no idea of any points on these curves other than the point at which they are at the time. Although businessmen know their existing prices, they do not know accurately how much their prices will have to be cut to sell additional units, or how much product can be sold at lower prices. Furthermore, factors of production are not easily divisible, so that, as a practical matter, businessmen cannot add one or two or three units of capital to determine how its marginal revenue productivity compares with that of labor. Capital is customarily embodied in "chunks," such as machines and factories, and the employer cannot very well speculate on adding half a machine to his existing equipment. While this can be done to some extent in the long run, when capital can be reinvested in various forms, the fact remains that in the short run the indivisibility of factor units adds to the difficulties of determining marginal contributions.

This means that large areas of indeterminateness are inherent in the practical application of marginal productivity principles, assuming that employers try to apply them at all. Some economists doubt whether employers are even interested in marginal calculations. They point out that when labor costs rise, many businessmen talk about increasing output to reduce *average* costs per unit, whereas according to marginal productivity principles, they should be thinking in terms of decreasing output because of increased *marginal* costs. If businessmen are, in fact, more interested in the behavior of average rather than marginal costs, a substantial revision would be necessitated in marginal productivity doctrine.

Despite these criticisms, advocates of the marginal productivity theory maintain that marginalism still exemplifies the typical economic calculations of the average businessman. They point out that marginal-type calculations are really very simple and are practiced by employers in every aspect of business. For example, if an employer is asked why he does not take on another bookkeeper or purchase a particular machine, his answer will usually be that the added return or revenue or service would not justify the additional expense. Here is an example of the weighing of marginal contributions and marginal costs, which the employer does in a rough sort of way, despite the admitted difficulties in making such calculations. This same sort of rough approximation is all that marginal productivity theorists claim is necessary to make their theory workable in practice.

2. Some economists claim that the market for labor does not function like the ordinary product market and that therefore the marginal productivity theory, which runs in conventional terms of supply and demand for labor, does not give a realistic picture of the labor market. We have already had occasion to consider some peculiarities of the labor

market. Thus, there is typically no one price for a particular type of labor representing an equilibrium of supply and demand. On the contrary, many prices exist side by side, and there is little tendency for such differentials to disappear over time.

Labor economists have made important contributions in pointing out these characteristics of the labor market, but the characteristics do not invalidate supply and demand analysis. Both the volume of unemployment and the number of new job opportunities in a given labor market will have an effect on the whole structure of wage rates in a community, indicating that supply and demand considerations cannot be ignored. The fact that a union may set a wage in a particular market based upon a wage level established by some other union in a distant city does not vitiate the usefulness of marginal productivity theory. Such a wage will probably differ from the wage which would be established in a free labor market; but whatever the wage which is established, it is still possible that the volume of employment at that wage will tend to be determined by the demand curve for labor, which reflects the marginal productivity of labor.

3. A major criticism directed against the marginal productivity theory stems from a fundamental disagreement as to the basic psychology and motivation of employers. Marginal productivity theorists, as we have seen, base their theory on the assumption that employers are motivated by a desire to *maximize* profits. But, as we have already observed, there is some evidence that management in certain companies may desire only a "fair return on investment," or may be motivated by considerations of community respect and other noneconomic objectives. It has even been suggested that the separation of management from ownership which typifies our large corporate business organizations may place management decisions in the hands of executives who are more interested in such objectives as sales, power, prestige, and so forth than in maximum profits.[9] On the other hand, it can be argued that the increased professionalization of management and increased use by management of computers to obtain promptly the complex data necessary for accurate decision making will, if anything, tie business behavior closer to the theoretical goal of profit maximization.

Marginal productivity theorists, of course, recognize that all employers are not profit-minded to the same degree and that any decision in the labor market—as in any line of human endeavor—is the result of a complex of motivations, which may include considerations of prestige, family, security, power, and the like. However, they believe that most businessmen are normally concerned about how they are going to stay in business and that this involves keeping costs down and profits up. They

---

[9] Fritz Machlup, "Theories of the Firm: Marginalist, Behavioral, Managerial," *American Economic Review,* vol. 57 (March 1967), p. 5.

contend, moreover, that managements in large corporations, whose balance sheets and profit and loss statements are made available to stockholders, are particularly interested in making a good showing relative to other large firms in the industry and in other industries. Management's reason for existing is to make profits for stockholder-owners, the usual measure of its success in earnings and dividends. Therefore, marginal productivity theorists state that as a general principle, it is fair to assume that maximization of profits is a dominant employer objective.

THE BARGAINING THEORY OF WAGES

Current interest in the peculiarities of the labor market and the dominant position of unions in shaping wage rates in many industries have led to a revival of interest in the bargaining theory of wages. The roots of this theory are found in the writings of early economists, such as Adam Smith. The most complete recent expositions of a bargaining theory of wages are found in volumes by J. Pen[10] and John Cross.[11]

Basically, the bargaining theory holds that no single principle determines wage rates. In any labor market there may be a diversity of rates for the same type of labor. This diversity develops because of differences in the bargains made by various employers and their employees, or the unions representing the employees. Employers are conceived of as having upper limits above which they will not go in making a wage bargain. This upper limit will differ for various employers. Among the factors determining this upper limit are the productivity of the labor, the profitability of the business, the possibility of utilizing machinery as a substitute for labor, and the possibility that excessive labor costs might require the plant to shut down. The lower limit to the bargain is set by minimum wage rates established by state or federal governments, the possibility of labor moving to other firms or areas, community standards of what is a just wage, and similar considerations.

If the foregoing propositions are all that is involved in the bargaining theory of wages, that theory is quite consistent with the marginal productivity theory. For the latter merely holds that whatever the wage which is set—whether by government, collective bargaining, or market forces—the employer will attempt to adapt to it by employing an amount of labor such that its marginal revenue productivity will be equal to the wage. Some exponents of the bargaining theory overlook this and assume that because the exact level of the wage is indeterminate and may fall anywhere between the upper and the lower level referred to above, therefore the adaptation in terms of employment must also be indetermi-

---

[10] J. Pen, *The Wage Rate under Collective Bargaining* (Cambridge, Mass.: Harvard University Press, 1959).

[11] John Cross, *The Economics of Bargaining* (New York: Basic Books, Inc., 1969).

nate. Marginal productivity theorists deny this and have attempted to integrate the bargaining aspect of wage determination into the general structure of the marginal productivity theory.

For some economists, however, the bargaining theory is much more than just a theory of determination of wage levels. These economists extend bargaining principles to the relationship between wages and employment in the individual firm. They believe that this relationship is much more tenuous and indeterminate than the marginal productivity theory would lead one to believe. Thus, bargaining theorists maintain that a union, by superior bargaining power, may squeeze out monopoly profits for the benefit of organized employees without affecting the volume of employment in the firm. Likewise, they argue that organized labor may achieve wage increases at the expense of the remuneration going to other factors of production which are immobile or lack the benefit of organization to protect their interests.

These conclusions are also not necessarily inconsistent with marginal productivity theory. That theory has always recognized that in the short run, bargaining pressures may squeeze out monopoly profits or increase the remuneration of one group at the expense of another, without affecting employment. Marginal productivity theorists contend, however, that in the long run there is a tendency for adjustments to be made which do affect the volume of employment. Although it may be true that we live in a world consisting of a continuous series of "short runs" and that we never clearly see the long-run effects of particular actions, nevertheless it would seem that any theory of the demand for labor must take account of the fact that short-run reactions to bargaining pressures are not the last word and that changes in location, size, and number of plants, investment in laborsaving machinery, and similar actions are part of the adjustment of employers to changed cost conditions, which take time to work themselves out.

SUMMARY

Theories of the demand for labor tend to evolve as our knowledge of the labor market improves and as the organization of industry and the labor market changes. The marginal productivity theory has held the center of the stage for many years as the accepted theory of labor demand, but recent criticisms indicate that it, too, is subject to revision and possible substitution by other theories. Whether its successor will be the bargaining theory or some other theory remains to be seen. At this point, no other theory has been elaborated in sufficient detail to constitute an adequate substitute.

In this and the preceding chapter, we have examined some of the factors which determine the supply and the demand of labor. We are now prepared to consider wage determination as it actually occurs in the labor market. This is the subject of the following chapter.

APPENDIX

The following analysis derives the marginal productivity theory from a general investigation of the theory of cost and production. Most of the following analysis applies irrespective of the elasticity of demand for the product of the firm under consideration (that is, whether or not the industry is purely competitive). Although the analysis presented is restricted to two factors—capital and labor—it can easily be generalized to include any number of factors.

The maximum output of the product Q, which can be produced by the set of factors (K, L) is given by technical considerations and is represented by the production function.

$$Q = Q(K, L) \tag{1}$$

It is assumed that for each set of inputs there is a maximum output so that the function is single valued and has continuous partial derivatives of desired order. Further, neither marginal physical products can be negative, since otherwise production can be improved for the same input of one factor leaving the other idle, that is,

$$\frac{\delta Q}{\delta K}, \frac{\delta Q}{\delta L} \geq 0 \tag{2}$$

where the two partial derivatives are the marginal physical products of capital and labor respectively. By the assumption of perfect factor markets, unlimited amounts of each input can be purchased at the price r per unit of capital and w for each unit of labor.

The total cost of the firm can be written as

$$C = F + rK + wL \tag{3}$$

where F represents the fixed costs which do not vary with the inputs and output (for example, taxes). (In a particular case F may be zero.) In order to derive the total cost function for different levels of output, it is assumed that for given prices of the factors, and a given production function, the total cost is to be minimized. This will be a function as follows:

$$C = F + V(Q, r, w) . \tag{4}$$

If r and w are regarded as constant, the resulting relationship is the total cost curve.

Given the assumption of total cost minimization, there is an optimum combination of inputs so that the demand for each factor can be written as

$$K = \phi_K(Q, w, r)$$
$$L = \phi_L(Q, w, r)$$
(5)

Substituting into (3), we have,

$$C = F + w\phi_K(Q, w, r) + r\phi_L(Q, w, r) = F + V(Q, w, r) \quad (6)$$

The problem is to minimize

$$C = F + rK + wL \quad (7)$$

subject to

$$Q(K, L) = \bar{Q} = \text{constant.} \quad (8)$$

Mathematically, this is a constrained minimum problem which can be solved by the method of the Lagrangian multiplier. The Lagrangian function is written as

$$G = F + wL + rK - \lambda[Q(K, L) - \bar{Q}] \quad (9)$$

where $(-\lambda)$ is the Lagrangian multiplier whose economic interpretation will be furnished later. For a minimum,

$$\frac{\delta G}{\delta L} = 0 = w - \lambda \frac{\delta Q}{\delta L}$$
$$\frac{\delta G}{\delta K} = 0 = r - \lambda \frac{\delta Q}{\delta K}$$
(10)

which may be written as

$$\frac{1}{\lambda} = \frac{\delta Q/\delta L}{w} = \frac{\delta Q/\delta K}{r} \quad (11)$$

This is the economic law that *for total costs to be a minimum for a given output, the marginal productivity of the last unit of expenditure must be equal for all factors.* It must be noted that this condition is independent of the revenue curve of the firm and holds at every point on the cost curve.

For the optimum defined in (10) to be a proper constrained minimum, secondary necessary and sufficient conditions have to be satisfied.

Mathematically, the secondary conditions are that the bordered Hessian determinant and its principal minors alternate in sign, that is,

$$H = \begin{vmatrix} \dfrac{\delta^2 Q}{\delta K^2} & \dfrac{\delta^2 Q}{\delta K \delta L} & \dfrac{\delta Q}{\delta K} \\[2ex] \dfrac{\delta^2 Q}{\delta L \delta K} & \dfrac{\delta^2 Q}{\delta L^2} & \dfrac{\delta Q}{\delta L} \\[2ex] \dfrac{\delta Q}{\delta K} & \dfrac{\delta Q}{\delta L} & 0 \end{vmatrix} \quad (12)$$

Specifically

$$\frac{\delta^2 Q}{\delta K^2}\left(\frac{\delta Q}{\delta L}\right)^2 - 2\frac{\delta^2 Q}{\delta K \delta L}\frac{\delta Q}{\delta K}\frac{\delta Q}{\delta L} + \frac{\delta^2 Q}{\delta L^2}\left(\frac{\delta Q}{\delta K}\right)^2 < 0 \qquad (13)$$

This condition is usually satisfied if the law of diminishing return holds, that is,

$$\frac{\delta^2 Q}{\delta K^2} \quad \text{and} \quad \frac{\delta^2 Q}{\delta L^2} < 0$$

The economic significance of λ can be clarified by differentiating G in (9) with respect to Q, that is,

$$\frac{\delta G}{\delta Q} = \lambda \qquad (14)$$

This suggests that λ may be a marginal cost. This can be demonstrated easily. Differentiating (7), we can write

$$dC = wdL + rdK \qquad (15)$$

and the total differential of Q in (1) can be written as

$$dQ = \frac{\delta Q}{\delta L}dL + \frac{\delta Q}{\delta K}dK \qquad (16)$$

Dividing (15) by (16), we obtain

$$\frac{\delta C}{\delta Q} = \frac{wdL + rdK}{\dfrac{\delta Q}{\delta L}dL + \dfrac{\delta Q}{\delta K}dK} \qquad (17)$$

Substituting from (10) into (17)

$$\frac{\delta C}{\delta Q} = \frac{\lambda\left[\dfrac{\delta Q}{\delta L}dL + \dfrac{\delta Q}{\delta K}dK\right]}{\dfrac{\delta Q}{\delta L}dL + \dfrac{\delta Q}{\delta K}dK} \qquad (18)$$

or

$$\frac{\delta C}{\delta Q} = \lambda$$

Substituting (18), (10) may be rewritten as

$$w = \frac{\delta C}{\delta Q} \cdot \frac{\delta Q}{\delta L}$$
$$r = \frac{\delta C}{\delta Q} \cdot \frac{\delta Q}{\delta K} \qquad (19)$$

which may be stated as the theorem that *in order for total cost to be minimized for any given output, the price of each factor must be equal to the marginal physical product times marginal cost, irrespective of the revenue function.* Of course, profit maximization requires equality of marginal revenue and marginal cost. Therefore, the theorem can also be stated that in the equilibrium position at which total cost will be minimized, the price of each factor must be equal to its marginal physical product times its marginal contribution to the revenue of the firm.

QUESTIONS FOR DISCUSSION

1. Explain what is meant by marginal productivity. What is the difference between the value of the marginal physical product of labor and the marginal revenue product of labor? Under what circumstances will they be the same?
2. Compare the marginal productivity theory with the bargaining theory of wages. What points of similarity are there in the two theories? What are the merits and shortcomings of each?
3. What conditions may produce a rising supply curve for labor? Will employers apply marginal productivity principles when faced by a rising supply curve of labor? Discuss.

SUGGESTIONS FOR FURTHER READING

Adams, Roy J. "Wage Determination: Reconciling Theory and Practice," *American Journal of Economics and Sociology,* vol. 34 (April 1975), pp. 353–64.

An attempt to reconcile marginal productivity theory with practice by taking into account sociological and psychological variables which affect wage determination.

Fleisher, Belton M. *Labor Economics: Theory and Evidence.* "The Theory of the Demand for Labor: The Competitive Firm," chap. 6, pp. 119–40. Englewood Cliffs, N.J.: Prentice-Hall, Inc., 1970.

A concise mathematical explanation of the derivation of the short-run and long-run demand for labor.

Hicks, J. R. *The Theory of Wages,* 2d ed. London: Macmillan & Co., Ltd., 1963, chap. 1, pp. 1–22. (See also review of chap. 1 by G. F. Shore, ibid., pp. 249–67, and commentary on same by J. R. Hicks, pp. 321–27.)

A classic discussion of the demand for labor from the marginalist point of view with current commentaries on the theory.

McConnell, Campbell R. *Perspectives on Wage Determination,* pp. 7–23. New York, McGraw-Hill Book Co., 1970.

Excerpts from the writings of Ricardo, Mill, Marx, Walker, and Davidson setting forth the wage theories associated with those writers.

Machlup, Fritz. "Theories of the Firm: Marginalist, Behavioral, Managerial," *American Economic Review,* vol. 57 (March 1967), pp. 1–33.

An excellent review and critique of various attacks which have been directed against marginal analysis, together with a bibliography of articles on this subject.

11

Wage Determination under Trade Unionism

IN THE THREE preceding chapters, we have considered the supply of labor, the demand for labor, and the labor market in which these forces operate. Wage determination in the individual firm reflects the various economic forces and circumstances we have examined. Thus, *ceteris paribus,* the wage level in a particular firm will ordinarily be lower if the demand for labor is decreasing than if it is increasing. Wages will be higher when labor is in short supply than where there is a large body of unemployed labor available. Wage rates will tend to be lower in the South than in the North.

When union business agents and management representatives sit down to the conference table to negotiate a new contract, the foregoing circumstances set some limit to the range within which wage rates will finally be set. In this chapter, we shall examine the conditions which cause a particular schedule of rates to be agreed upon by union and management representatives in the individual firm. How are wage rates adjusted in the collective bargaining process? What is the relationship between wage rates in different firms in the same industry? What are the criteria and pertinent economic circumstances which union and management consider in determining wage rates? In discussing wage determination, we shall concentrate our attention on changes in money wage rates, but this should not lead the reader to underestimate the importance of fringe benefits. As we observed in Chapter 5, the practice in union negotiations in recent years has been for so-called package settlements which include improvements in various forms of supplementary compensation as well as in basic pay.

THE INTERNAL WAGE STRUCTURE

In the typical large industrial establishment today, literally hundreds of individual wage rates or wage classifications have to be adjusted as part of a wage negotiation. In our theoretical discussion in earlier chapters, we have talked about "the wage rate in the individual firm." This is obviously a simplification. It would be more correct to talk about a wage structure. The wage structure is the whole complex of rates within the individual firm for all of the various jobs for which persons are employed. This wage structure does not necessarily move as a unit. There may be, of course, wage negotiations where a flat ten cents an hour or a uniform percentage increase is given to all employees; but frequently, exceptions are made for particular groups of employees. There are always individual jobs which get out of line because of the passage of time and the impact of technological change. These require special treatment. Furthermore, there is the pressing problem of keeping a proper relationship between the skilled and the unskilled rates. As a result of these various factors, the wage structure—viewed in terms of the entire schedule of rates from the lowest paid to the highest paid employee—may be compressed or stretched out from one negotiation to the next.

While a great many rates must be altered in the course of a wage negotiation, labor and management do not normally make an issue of every individual rate. This would obviously take too much time. Instead, emphasis is placed upon the key rates in various job clusters. A job cluster may be defined as a stable group of job classifications or work assignments within a firm which are so linked together by technology, the administrative organization of the production process, or social custom that they have common wage-making characteristics.[1] Thus, in a factory, one job cluster may consist of various classes of lathe operators; another job cluster, of sweepers, janitors, and so on; another, of pattern-makers and the like. Each cluster can be viewed as consisting of a key rate and associated rates. In a particular cluster, key rates may be the highest rate, the lowest rate, or sometimes the rate at which the greatest number of workers are employed. These are the rates on which union and management representatives focus in their bargaining negotiations, and once these rates are determined, the associated rates fall into line.

THE EXTERNAL WAGE STRUCTURE

Key rates in the individual firm are not determined in a vacuum. On the contrary, they are hammered out in a collective bargaining relationship where management attempts to safeguard its competitive position in

---

[1] John T. Dunlop, "The Task of Contemporary Wage Theory," in George W. Taylor and Frank C. Pierson (eds.), *New Concepts in Wage Determination* (New York: McGraw-Hill Book Co., 1957), p. 129.

the particular industry of which it is a part. Unless there are extenuating circumstances, management usually tries to keep its rates on a par with the rates of its competitors, on the theory that if its rates are lower, it will lose employees, and if its rates are higher, it will lose business because of the higher costs.

One writer uses the concept of a "wage contour" to elucidate the relationship between the key rates of various individual firms or establishments. "A wage contour is a stable group of wage-determining units which are so linked together by (1) similarity of product markets, (2) resort to similar sources for a labor source, and (3) common labor-market organization (custom) that they have common wage-making characteristics."[2] For example, the basic steel contour for production jobs consists of basic steel producers throughout the nation. By contrast, newspapers in New York City constitute a separate wage contour not directly affected by rates in other cities. The wage contour normally contains one or, in some instances, several key settlements. The contour is composed of rates for a key firm, or key firms, and a group of associated firms. The key settlement may be set by the largest firm, the price leader, or the firm which customarily plays the role of wage relations leader. As we shall see later in this chapter, leader-follower relationships in wage determination are extremely important in our basic industries. Some firms within a wage contour will follow the key settlement closely; others will follow it in varying degree. But this external relationship will have an important bearing on the decision which is made with respect to changes in the key rates in the various job clusters of each establishment's internal wage structure.

The concept of the wage contour helps to explain differences which prevail in rates for similar jobs in different industries. For example, a comparison of hourly rates paid to union drivers in Syracuse, New York, in 1973 showed that in local trucking, drivers received $6.03, whereas in local transit, the rate was only $4.15. On the other hand, in Washington, D.C., the relationship was reversed, with drivers getting $4.62 in local trucking versus $5.39 in local transit.[3] The reason for the variation is that each rate was a reflection of conditions in its own wage contour. Each was a reflection of the product market. Of course, in a perfect labor market, these differences could not prevail because teamsters would tend to move to the higher paying industry, and the lower paying industries would have to raise their rates in order to hold their employees. In actuality, such differences persist over long periods of time because of the orientation of the wage rate determination process in terms of the product market and because of the differences in competitive conditions,

---

[2] Ibid., p. 131.

[3] U.S. Department of Labor, *Handbook of Labor Statistics, 1975* (Washington, D.C.: Government Printing Office, 1975), table 97, p. 247.

profits, and demand conditions in the various industries using this type of labor.

In an important sense, the individual firm can be thought of as an internal labor market within which the pricing and allocation of labor are governed by a set of administrative rules and procedures. The internal market is connected to the external labor market by movement at certain job classifications which constitute "ports of entry and exit" to and from the internal labor market. In some industries, such as the garment industry, there are many such ports of entry, and a considerable flow of workers in and out of the firm occurs at various occupational levels. On the other hand, in a steel plant, skills tend to be more highly specialized and may have to be acquired on the job, so that there are fewer ports of entry.[4] The wage structure which develops within the firm, therefore, reflects the influence of the external labor market but also to an important degree depends upon the specific skills peculiar to the enterprise and upon differentials which develop from long-standing custom.

GENERAL WAGE INCREASES

Much of the friction which develops in collective bargaining involves the issue of "wage increases." What precisely do we mean by this phrase? General wage increases normally have little or no relation to merit. They are usually given to all workers, whether or not the employer is satisfied with their individual performance. The justification for such increases may be an increase in the cost of living or the high profits made by the employer. The performance of the company as a whole is always a consideration, but the performance of the individual worker is not usually at issue in such negotiations. The increases are often but not always uniform for all employees. Many industrial unions prefer to have uniform adjustments for all employees in terms of so many cents per hour because this tends to give the lower paid workers—who represent the bulk of the union membership—a larger percentage increase than is given higher paid workers.

In the 1930s and 1940s, when the advent of industrial unionism first made its impact felt on the wage structure, there was a strong trend toward larger percentage wage adjustments for the lower paid employees. As a result, there was a definite narrowing of occupational differentials. By the early 1950s a slowing of this process was observable; and in recent years, there has been evidence of the maintenance of reasonably stable differentials. This has been partly attributable to an increasing tendency to grant special increases for skilled workers.

What circumstances do unions and management take account of in

---

[4] For an elaboration of this theory, see Peter B. Doeringer and Michael J. Piore, *Internal Labor Markets and Manpower Analysis* (Lexington, Mass.: D. C. Heath & Co., 1971), pp. 2 ff.

determining the amount of a wage increase in an individual firm? In the following discussion, we shall consider some of the principal criteria which seem to play an important part in determining the size of general wage adjustments.

CRITERIA IN GENERAL WAGE ADJUSTMENTS

Intraindustry Comparative Standards

Perhaps the most common standard which is applied by both labor and management to determine whether a wage adjustment should be made in a particular firm is to compare its wage structure with those of other companies in the industry. Because of the importance of the standard of what the other fellow is doing, both union and management representatives usually come to the bargaining table armed with statistics, or at least a working knowledge, of what other firms in the industry are paying. In some industries, employers' associations make such data available; in others, the employer may have to rely on telephone calls to the personnel directors of competing companies. Unions in many cases are able to obtain such data through their international office or through other locals.

Reliance on rates that other companies are paying would, at first glance, seem to put collective bargaining on a factual basis. "If a competitor can afford to pay these rates, why can't you?" is the question which union agents ask employers. The trouble is that statistics—particularly when they are averages—may have little meaning because of shortcomings in their tabulation. Furthermore, the job content of seemingly similar jobs varies considerably from firm to firm. The mere fact that a job classification calls for a stitcher, or a cutter, or a clerk, or a painter, does not mean that the work or the skill required is identical or that the technical conditions will be similar for all employees having similar job descriptions. In the same industry or area the same job title may be used for dozens of dissimilar operations.

Actually, the criterion of intraindustry standards leaves ample room for bargaining. For example, the union may want to compare hourly rates in various plants, while the employer may want to compare weekly earnings. This is frequently the case where a company permits its employees to work some overtime each week at time and a half the regular rate, which gives its employees more take-home pay than that of workers in other plants. Nevertheless, the union will argue that hourly rates should be raised to bring them in line with rates in other plants in the industry.

Wage Leadership. In industries employing the most wage earners—steel, automotive bodies and parts, aircraft, rubber, baked goods, textiles, paper and paperboard, and others—the tendency is for the individual employer to keep his wage rates in line with the rates paid by certain key firms in the industry, a policy which frequently results in an industrywide adjustment of wages whenever circumstances compel revision in such key companies.

The typical structure of an industry in the American economy is that four to eight companies will produce from one half to four fifths of the total output of the industry. Once wage scales have been set in the major companies, the pattern of wage adjustment for most employees in the industry has also been determined.

Wage leadership does not depend upon the existence of national, regional, or other forms of industrywide bargaining. Key wage bargains are important whether wages are determined by collective bargaining or by unilateral company decision in the case of unorganized employees, and can apply to executive personnel as well as the rank and file. For example, in 1974, the soaring cost of living led Manufacturers Hanover Trust Company, one of the largest New York banks, to give a 7% across-the-board hike to all executives. Within weeks, seven other banks gave similar increases.[5]

Although wage leadership has existed in the absence of union organization, union wage pressure has tended to spread and to make explicit uniformity in wage rates as a cardinal basis of management wage policy. There is now double pressure for meeting the other fellow's wage rates: from competitors and from labor itself. Union contracts requiring payment of wages on a par with rates prevailing for work of a similar kind in other firms in the industry hasten the spread of wage increases through an industry. At the same time, however, such pressure may produce a feeling among company executives that upward adjustments should not be made unless other firms in the industry are making them or the union demands them; therefore fewer, though larger, wage adjustments are made.

In some industries, there are not only wage leaders but also "high-wage firms." These companies try to pay more than the going rate for labor. Sometimes, such firms justify this policy on the ground that high wages attract better than average employees. In other cases, the reason for the policy may be to keep a union out. In any case, unions use such differentials to their advantage. In bargaining with other companies in the industry, they will argue that competitors of the high-wage firm should pay wages equal to those paid by the high-wage company. Then, after obtaining such an increase from the other firms, they will go back to the high-wage firm (once it has been organized) and contend that it should maintain its historical differential. Companies which have adopted a policy of higher than average wages as a means of keeping out a union may thus find that they are stuck with the policy when the union organizes their employees.

Unions typically use such a leveling approach in their bargaining

---

[5] *Business Week,* September 7, 1974, p. 42.

strategy. The rates for a particular class of employees may be relatively high in one firm, perhaps because of the length of service of these employees, or perhaps because of unusual conditions under which they have to work. The union will cite the example of these high rates to other firms in the industry, which are likely to be unaware of the special circumstances responsible for them, and will argue that they should meet these rates. In the same way, a "bad settlement" made by one employer in an industry who could not risk a strike for financial reasons can be used by a union as a lever to raise the rates of every other firm in the industry.

Union Attitudes toward Wage Uniformity.   Most unions want uniformity in wage rates for similar jobs throughout an area of competitive production. Unions are dynamic organizations; but paradoxically, one of their major objectives is stability. Frequently, achievement of this aim is dependent upon the elimination of competition among firms in the sphere of wage rates. The more competitive the industry, the smaller the units in the industry, and the less responsible the employers, the greater is the likelihood that union wage policy will seek competitive parity in labor cost as a measure to relieve pressure on the wage structure. In an industry in which there is considerable variation in the size and efficiency of the individual firms, a union must decide whether the welfare of its members can best be served by equalization of hourly rates, piece rates, or labor costs per unit in the various plants under union jurisdiction. In some circumstances, the policy of equalization of wage rates or hourly earnings will provide the maximum incentive to industrial efficiency. The policy may be adopted in the form of uniform wage scales, as in the building and printing industries, where jobs are skilled and occupational rungs clearly defined; or it may take the form of uniformity in plant average hourly earnings, as in the carpet and rug industry, where rapid technology and lack of standardization of operations and product make this the most expedient policy. Such a plan attempts to stabilize earnings while leaving costs to management. Since backward companies must pay as high rates as the most efficient firms, a policy of uniformity in hourly or daily wage rates provides the maximum incentive to adoption of improved machinery by the less efficient companies in an industry.

If, on the other hand, the union decides to equalize piece rates or unit labor cost, the incentive afforded to employers to improve efficiency is reduced unless the union agrees to adjust rates downward as improvements in technique permit greater output. For if piece rates are fixed, the introduction of improved machinery serves merely to increase output per worker, so that labor's earnings, not employers' profits, are augmented by technical advance.

The extent to which a strong union can introduce uniformity of wage rates in an industry is well illustrated by recent developments in the over-the-road trucking industry, where the Teamsters' Union substantially achieved national contracts. While local differentials still remain to some extent, the union has used the device of the long-term contract and common termination dates to achieve its goal of eliminating the great dispersion of rates which formerly existed in this industry. The trend toward wage standardization in the trucking industry has already gone far and is likely to continue.

On the whole, it seems likely that equalization of wage rates will come to be the dominant form of union wage policy. Of course, there must necessarily be variations to suit the peculiarities of individual industries, but the policy of uniformity will probably come to prevail in those industries in which it is practicable because it is best adapted to the political necessities of unionism. It is simple, and its aim of equality in a particularly obvious and just form commends it as a slogan for the rank and file. Its reasonableness is convincing. As one union leader puts it: "If Joe Smith goes into a store to buy a hat, he has to pay the same price for it whether he happens to be an employee of General Motors or American Motors. Then why shouldn't he be paid the same rate for his work?"

Union preference for uniformity in wage rates has already made its impact felt on various aspects of the wage structure of American industry. Within individual firms, unionism has generally eliminated personal differentials in rates or brought them into a formalized, controlled wage scale. Likewise, union organization has tended to reduce or eliminate interfirm differentials in the same product and labor market.

Interindustry Comparative Standards

Wage determination in a particular firm may be affected not only by the settlements of key firms in the same industry, but also by the settlements of major companies in other industries. Some economists are of the opinion that we have reached the stage where a limited number of key wage bargains effectively influence the whole wage structure of the American economy. The concept of key wage bargains was a cornerstone of the Nixon administration's wage and price control plan, which sought to regulate the advance of wages in general by focusing on wage adjustments in the largest firms in the economy. A study of wage changes made during the post–World War II period in 11 basic industries—steel, automotive, electrical, rubber, aluminum, aircraft, farm machinery, copper, petroleum refining, meat-packing, and shipbuilding—found a high degree of uniformity in the size of wage adjustments in those industries.[6]

Two other researchers have found a "contour group" consisting of the following industries: rubber, stone, clay, and glass, primary metals, fabricated metals, nonelectrical machinery, electrical machinery, transportation

---

[6] John E. Maher, "The Wage Pattern in the United States, 1946–1957," *Industrial and Labor Relations Review,* vol. 16 (October 1961), p. 16.

equipment, and instruments.[7] Wages in these industries were found to have moved identically since 1948. In the words of the investigators,

> All of these industries are high-wage industries, have strong industrial unions, typically consist of large corporations that possess considerable market power, and are geographically centered in the Midwestern industrial heartland of the continent.[8]

How are these key wage bargains transmitted from one industry to another? According to one economist who has studied this phenomenon in detail, four important circumstances help produce this uniformity in wage movement:[9]

1. *The Input-Output Nexus.* Many of these industries have close ties with one another because of a buyer-seller relationship. For example, the automotive industry is the largest consumer of rubber and electrical products; aircraft is the largest consumer of aluminum. Buyers and sellers have an understandable interest in each other's wage policies, since a rise in the labor costs and the prices of the supplier industry will ultimately affect the costs and prices of the buyer industry.

2. *Similar Technology.* Most of these industries have high capital-output and capital-labor ratios. Likewise, they are mass-production industries. Most produce capital goods or consumer durable goods. Therefore, they tend to react in similar fashion to current economic changes.

3. *Distribution of Participants.* Most of these industries are clustered in particular geographic areas. Furthermore, the employees in these industries are represented for the most part by a relatively few large national unions.

4. *Institutional Channels of Communication.* Most of the unions involved were originally CIO, and most are now in the AFL–CIO. The leaders of the unions are important, nationally known figures in the labor movement, and there is considerable rivalry among them.

Key wage bargains affect the thinking of unions and management in a variety of industries. Both tend to look to these key agreements as a barometer of the labor market, indicating what workers expect in the way of wage adjustments. In a very real sense, a handful of key negotiators representing management and labor can set trends which will affect the compensation of millions of workers in other industries. Faced with the need to resolve differences, management and union leaders find in key wage bargains a convenient figure upon which they can rationalize a contract. Moreover, union leaders find that they must meet the increase

---

[7] Otto Eckstein and Thomas A. Wilson, "The Determination of Money Wages in American Industry," *Quarterly Journal of Economics*, vol. 76 (August 1962), pp. 384–85.

[8] Ibid. These trends are equally evident today.

[9] Maher, "Wage Pattern," pp. 5–6.

obtained by a union leader in another industry to maintain their personal popularity. The size of the wage increase obtained by various labor leaders is as assiduously studied by their constituents as are the batting averages of baseball players, and if a labor leader wants to stay at the top of the league, he has to keep pace with his rivals in other unions. Union leaders are alert to capitalize on new types of benefits which may have been incorporated into contracts in other industries. Although an estimated 150,000 collective bargaining agreements are in effect in the United States, about 20 unions are responsible for three-quarters of them, and there is a constant exchange of information among these unions.

The variations in wage adjustments among firms and industries reflect differences in profitability, as well as in the ability of management to pass along wage increases in the form of higher prices. The variations may also reflect union rivalries. Leaders of competing unions—whether they are competing for prestige within the labor movement or actually competing for membership—have to avoid falling into a "me, too" policy of simply following another union's lead. Each leader tries to differentiate the benefits gained for his membership by varying the timing of adjustments, the nature and cost of fringe benefits, or the composition of the total negotiated package of benefits.

The Cost of Living

A criterion of major importance in wage negotiations—particularly during periods of rising prices such as we have experienced in recent years—is change in the cost of living. During periods of rising prices, wages typically lag behind prices. This lag is attributed in part to the fact that wages are much "stickier" than prices. In fact, most wages of organized employees are fixed by contract for a given period, frequently a minimum of one year. During the contract period, price increases may rob wage adjustments of much of their value. The extent to which inflation appears to neutralize wage increases is indicated in Table 11–1. Despite large money wage gains achieved by labor in recent years, average spendable weekly earnings were no greater in March 1976 than in 1972, using 1967 dollars as a base.

Data of the type reported in Table 11–1 are often put on the bargaining table, and supposedly they place negotiations on a more concrete basis than would exist if such figures were unavailable. But what do such statistics really mean? Do they mean that the worker sitting across the table from the employer is no better off than he was in 1972 because the cost of living has been eroding his earnings? Not necessarily so.

In the first place, the earnings series reported in Table 11–1 includes part-time as well as full-time workers. Since the proportion of part-time workers has been rising as a proportion of the total labor force, the series tends to understate the increase in the earnings of full-time workers.

TABLE 11-1. Gross and Spendable Weekly Earnings, in Current and 1967 Dollars, 1960–1976 (averages for production or nonsupervisory workers on private nonagricultural payrolls)

Year and month	Private nonagricultural workers						Manufacturing workers					
	Gross average weekly earnings		Spendable average weekly earnings				Gross average weekly earnings		Spendable average weekly earnings			
			Worker with no dependents		Worker with 3 dependents				Worker with no dependents		Worker with 3 dependents	
	Current dollars	1967 dollars	Current dollars	1967 dollars	Current dollars	1967 dollars	Current dollars	1967 dollars	Current dollars	1967 dollars	Current dollars	1967 dollars
1960	$80.67	$90.95	$65.59	$73.95	$72.96	$82.25	$89.72	$101.15	$72.57	$81.82	$80.11	$90.32
1961	82.60	92.19	67.08	74.87	74.48	83.13	92.34	103.06	74.60	83.26	82.18	91.72
1962	85.91	94.82	69.56	76.78	76.99	84.98	96.56	106.58	77.86	85.94	85.53	94.40
1963	88.46	96.47	71.05	77.48	78.56	85.67	99.63	108.65	79.82	87.04	87.04	94.95
1964	91.33	98.31	75.04	80.78	82.57	88.88	102.97	110.84	84.40	90.85	92.18	99.22
1965	95.06	100.59	78.99	83.59	86.30	91.32	107.53	113.79	89.08	94.26	96.78	102.41
1966	98.82	101.67	81.29	83.63	88.66	91.21	112.34	115.58	91.57	94.21	99.45	102.31
1967	101.84	101.84	83.38	83.38	90.86	90.86	114.90	114.90	93.28	93.28	101.26	101.26
1968	107.73	103.39	86.71	83.21	95.28	91.44	122.51	117.57	97.70	93.76	106.75	102.45
1969	114.61	104.38	90.96	82.84	99.99	91.07	129.51	117.95	101.90	92.81	111.44	101.49
1970	119.46	102.72	95.94	82.49	104.61	89.95	133.73	114.99	106.62	91.68	115.90	99.66
1971	127.28	104.93	103.78	85.56	112.41	92.67	142.44	117.43	114.97	94.78	124.24	102.42
1972	136.16	108.67	111.65	89.11	121.09	96.64	154.69	123.46	125.32	100.02	135.56	108.19
1973	145.43	109.26	117.54	88.31	127.41	95.73	166.06	124.76	132.29	99.39	143.20	107.59
1974	154.45	104.57	124.14	84.05	134.37	90.97	176.40	119.43	139.90	94.72	151.25	102.40
1975	163.89	101.67	132.74	82.34	145.93	90.53	189.51	117.56	150.71	93.49	165.33	102.56
1975: March	158.06	100.16	126.68	80.28	137.15	86.91	182.66	115.75	144.51	91.58	156.13	98.94
April	159.22	100.39	127.49	80.38	138.05	87.04	184.00	116.02	145.50	91.74	157.18	99.10
May	160.38	100.68	131.25	82.39	145.37	91.26	185.25	116.29	148.38	93.15	164.12	103.03
June	163.71	101.94	133.60	83.19	147.97	92.14	188.81	117.57	150.81	93.90	166.75	103.83
July	164.89	101.60	134.43	82.83	148.89	91.74	188.55	116.17	150.63	92.81	166.56	102.62
August	166.90	102.52	135.84	83.44	150.47	92.43	191.35	117.54	152.55	93.70	168.62	103.57
September	168.43	102.95	136.88	83.67	151.65	92.70	196.58	120.16	156.36	95.57	172.48	105.43
October	168.69	102.48	137.06	83.27	151.85	92.25	195.51	118.78	155.56	94.51	171.69	104.31
November	169.42	102.31	137.56	83.07	152.41	92.04	197.69	119.38	157.18	94.92	173.30	104.65
December	170.82	102.72	138.52	83.30	153.48	92.29	204.00	122.67	161.85	97.32	177.95	107.01
1976: January	169.92	101.93	139.31	83.57	151.61	90.95	200.30	120.16	161.23	96.72	174.55	104.71
February	171.11	102.40	140.17	83.88	152.53	91.28	201.60	120.65	162.16	97.04	175.52	105.04
March	170.17	101.59	139.49	83.28	151.81	90.63	202.80	121.07	163.01	97.32	176.42	105.33

The earnings, expressed in 1967 dollars, have been adjusted for changes in purchasing power as measured by the Consumer Price Index of the Bureau of Labor Statistics. These series are described in "The Spendable Earnings Series: A Technical Note on its Calculation," *Employment and Earnings and Monthly Report on the Labor Force*, February 1969, pp. 6–13. See also Eric Dmytrow and Janet Grimes, "Changes in the Spendable Earnings Series for 1976: Effects of the Tax Adjustment Act of 1975 and the Social Security Tax Base Change," *Employment and Earnings*, March 1976, pp. 6–13.
Source: *Monthly Labor Review*, vol. 99 (May 1976), table 20, p. 86.

Furthermore, fringe benefits, which have also been rising over time, are not included in the series but represent an important part of the total compensation of full-time workers.

In the second place, it is customary to deflate money earnings by an index to obtain "real" earnings. But the particular index which is customarily used,[10] namely the Consumer Price Index for Urban Wage Earners and Clerical Workers, which is published by the U.S. Department of Labor, is not really a cost-of-living index. The CPI, as it is called, measures the cost of a fixed "market basket" of goods and services, whether or not a particular employee bought or used those goods and services in a given period of time. Thus, the CPI could rise (and real earnings would thereby be reduced) if the cost of health services rises. But a particular employee might not have used health services during the period in question, or if the employee (or his or her family) did use health services, the cost might well have been fully covered by an employer-funded health plan.

Despite its inadequacies, in labor negotiations the CPI has become the standard vehicle for measurement of changes in the cost of living. Furthermore, whether or not an employee's earnings have actually been eroded by increases in the cost of living, rising prices tend to create the impression that the employee is not really improving his position. Thus, "cost of living" becomes a crude slogan voiced by labor when it seeks to improve the perceived real earnings position of union members.

The cost of living may enter into wage negotiations in several ways. In most cases, it is simply another one of the key criteria which unions and management consider in arriving at a wage adjustment. In other situations, the cost of living may affect wage determinations in a much more specific manner. This will be the case where unions and management have already incorporated automatic cost-of-living adjustments or escalator clauses into their collective bargaining agreements. These clauses typically specify a precise relationship between changes in the cost of living and changes in the wage rates to be paid employees covered by the agreements. There is considerable variation in various contracts with respect to the ratio between cost-of-living changes and wage changes. Some contracts are adjustable only upward, but most make wages adjustable both upward and downward in response to changes in a specific cost-of-living index.

Automatic Cost-of-Living Escalator Clauses

Cost-of-living adjustments—commonly called COLAs—may be said to have commenced with the General Motors contract of 1948. Prior to that

---

[10] In 1977, the Department of Labor will publish a new index, to be known as the Consumer Price Index for All Urban Households. However, the current Urban Wage Earners Index will undoubtedly continue as the basis for the calculation of cost-of-living adjustments in most collective bargaining agreements.

time, cost-of-living provisions had been incorporated into various contracts, but in the aggregate covered few workers. The General Motors
settlement, however, started a new trend. By 1950, approximately 2
million workers were covered by COLAs.[11] With a period of relative
price stability during the 60s, COLAs fell into general disuse, but they
regained popularity in the early 70s. At the beginning of 1975, COLA
provisions covered an estimated 7.7 million workers in private industry
and government, representing about 10% of employment in nonagricultural establishments, including government.[12] Escalator coverage is concentrated industrially. At the beginning of 1975, about 75% of the workers
in manufacturing under major agreements[13] with escalator provisions
were found in three major industry groups[14]—94% of the workers under
major agreements in primary metals were covered by COLAs; in electrical
equipment, 86%; and in transportation equipment, 93%.[15]

Although all cost-of-living adjustment provisions attempt to relate
compensatory wage adjustments to changes in the "cost-of-living," these
provisions differ in form as to the measurement, timing, and magnitude
of authorized adjustments. Most COLAs are based on changes in the
monthly levels of the CPI, although contracts in the automobile industry
use a three-month average of a combined U.S.–Canadian consumer price
index. The formula for calculating cost-of-living adjustments affecting the
largest number of workers is one cent for each 0.3-point change in the
CPI,[16] but other contracts use a 0.4-point change, and some contracts use
a percentage change in the CPI. Contracts also vary in the timing of
adjustments. A U.S. Department of Labor survey of major collective
bargaining agreements revealed that out of a total of 678 contracts ex-
piring in 1976 and later years, 357 required quarterly reviews; 111, semi-
annual reviews; 162, annual reviews; and 48, various combinations of the
former.[17]

The factor which generally has the greatest overall effect on the size
of cost-of-living adjustments is the presence or absence of "caps" or
ceilings in the formula. Approximately 2.1 million workers are currently
under contracts with such ceilings.[18] In 1976, fears of renewed inflation
led a number of unions to demand the removal of caps from COLA

---

[11] *Monthly Labor Review,* vol. 82 (December 1959), p. 1324.

[12] Executive Office of the President, Council on Wage and Price Stability, *Cost-of-Living Escalator Clauses and Inflation,* Staff Report (Washington, D.C., August 1975), p. 2.

[13] These agreements include multiplant or multifirm agreements covering 1,000 workers or more, even though individual units may be smaller.

[14] Executive Office of the President, *Cost-of-Living Clauses,* p. 3.

[15] Edward Wasilewski, "Scheduled Wage Increases and Escalator Provisions in 1975," *Monthly Labor Review,* vol. 98 (January 1975), table 1, p. 44.

[16] Peter Kuhmerker, "Scheduled Wage Increases and Escalator Provisions in 1976," *Monthly Labor Review,* vol. 99 (January 1976), p. 43.

[17] Ibid., table 2, p. 45.

[18] Ibid., p. 44.

provisions. On the other hand, management is concerned that unrestricted COLA provisions could in an inflationary period produce uneconomic increases in wages and labor costs and at the same time add fuel to the inflationary spiral.

As might be expected, COLAs are most common in long-term union contracts. Of the 5.8 million workers covered by major agreements with escalator clauses, 5.5 million are under three-year agreements.[19] Unions have demanded the inclusion of such clauses in order to protect their earnings from erosion by inflation during the term of these contracts. In actual practice, however, COLAs have not afforded such protection. Over the whole period from 1968 to 1974, the ratio of average COLA escalator increases to increases in the CPI was slightly less than one half.[20]

Nevertheless, COLAs have contributed a significant share to the earnings of covered workers. In 1975, employees under major contracts with escalators received an average 4.8% wage increase from these escalators.[21]

Ability to Pay

One of the most important considerations affecting wage determination is the basic economic situation in the firm and industry which, for convenience, we can denominate as "ability to pay." When profits and sales are increasing, when the employer needs to hold and attract labor in order to fill a backlog of orders, when prospects for the year ahead are bright, it is not surprising that the employer will favorably consider demands for an upward wage adjustment. On the other hand, if profits have fallen, sales are off, idle capacity exists, unemployment prevails, and there is no immediate prospect of a change for the better in the economic situation of the firm, the employer is understandably loath to increase his costs by agreeing to wage increases. One recent study found that in eight key manufacturing industries money wages over the period 1950–70 were largely determined by rates of profit experienced two to five years prior to each annual wage adjustment. Unemployment rates, by contrast, were found to exert a relatively minor influence on wages in these key industries.[22]

Ability to pay, therefore, is undoubtedly a major consideration in wage negotiations for most firms in good times and bad. The determination of ability to pay is, however, a highly controversial subject. Management, while often pleading inability to pay, is reluctant to make this an issue of fact and permit union representatives to "have a look at the books."

---

[19] Ibid.

[20] Executive Office of the President, *Cost-of-Living Clauses*, p. 29.

[21] Chase Manhattan Bank, *Business in Brief*, No. 126 (February 1976), p. 6.

[22] William A. Howard and N. Arnold Tolles, "Wage Determination in Key Manufacturing Industries, 1950–70," *Industrial and Labor Relations Review*, vol. 27 (July 1974), p. 557.

Management fears in this regard are based on the belief that such a move would be a prelude to union interference in business operations and union encroachment on the whole sphere of managerial prerogatives. In a dispute between the Truitt Manufacturing Company and a steelworkers' union, the U.S. Supreme Court has ruled that refusal by an employer to substantiate a claim of inability to pay increased wages *may* support a finding of failure to bargain in good faith.[23]

There is considerable difference of opinion between unions and management, and among economists as well, as to the extent to which differences in ability to pay should be reflected in differences in wage rates. On the one hand, union representatives frequently argue that workers have to pay the same price for their necessities of life whether they work for a more profitable firm or a less profitable one and, therefore, should be paid the same wage in all companies for similar work. Yet, unions have withdrawn from this position where it appeared that such a policy would force marginal firms out of business and thus produce unemployment among union members.

Management representatives frequently use the ability-to-pay argument to obtain special concessions for their particular firms, particularly where, for one reason or another, their cost of operation is higher than that of competitors. Obviously, the setting of different wage rates in an industry corresponding to the different level of profits in various firms would penalize initiative and good management, and would, in effect, offer a subsidy to the inefficient operators. On the other hand, a strict policy of wage uniformity based on the rates payable by the most efficient producer would force marginal firms out of business. Unions have had to choose between these two extremes and to adapt their wage policies to the peculiar conditions existing in each industry. In most instances, they have made some concessions in the way of differentials for smaller, less profitable firms; but, as has been stated, their preference is for wage uniformity.

Other Criteria in Wage Determination

A number of other criteria are frequently applied by both management and labor in the process of wage determination. For example, when unions seek a reduction in the workweek, the important criterion frequently becomes maintenance of take-home pay despite the reduction in hours worked. In some cases, the new hourly wage rate is simply the arithmetic result obtained by dividing the take-home pay prior to the reduction in hours by the reduced number of hours worked. Improvement in productivity is another circumstance which is receiving greater emphasis from labor in negotiations. We shall have occasion to examine

---

[23] *National Labor Relations Board* v. *Truitt Manufacturing Co.,* 351 U.S. 149 (1956).

the subject of productivity and wages in greater detail in Chapter 13. It is worthy of note, however, that while unions talk a great deal about productivity gains where it suits their purposes, there is no correlation between interindustry differences in productivity gains and wage increases.

The criteria explored in the foregoing discussion play an important role in narrowing the range of possibilities in wage determination. In many cases, however, the wage which is finally agreed upon is a reflection of sheer bargaining power, and talk of intraindustry standards or cost-of-living changes is mere rationalization pressed into service to support demands or concessions which need justification. Even arbitrators write these criteria into their opinions to support decisions already arrived at for other reasons.

It is also important to remember that wage changes are typically arrived at in a series of "rounds." These frequently provide for subsequent wage changes to be made during the term of the contract one, two, or even three years in the future. The relevant criteria and considerations are those that existed at the time the round was negotiated, not when the agreed-upon wage adjustment takes effect.

The Influence of the Product Market on Wage Adjustments

The demand for labor is a derived demand. This proposition simply means that the employer hires labor, not just to utilize its services, but because labor will produce a product for which there is a demand in the marketplace. As we shall see in Chapter 12, where this concept will be discussed more fully, the characteristics of the product market can affect the elasticity of the employer's demand curve for labor, and therefore can influence his decision as to the amount of labor he will utilize and the wages he will be prepared to pay.

In recent years, numerous statistical investigations have been undertaken to determine whether monopoly power in the product market tends to be correlated with larger wage adjustments in the labor market. The criterion of monopoly power frequently used in such studies—which is acknowledged to be subject to many shortcomings—is the so-called concentration ratio—the proportion of the volume of shipments accounted for by the four largest firms in an industry. Even if this imperfect measure of monopoly power is accepted, various statistical investigations have arrived at different conclusions as to the impact of concentration in the product market on the level of wages. On the one hand, Bruce T. Allen concludes that there is considerable evidence that workers in "monopolistic" industries have enjoyed larger wage adjustments than have those in competitive industries.[24] Daniel S. Hamermesh, on the other hand, finds

---

[24] Bruce T. Allen, "Market Concentration and Wage Increases, U.S. Manufacturing, 1947–1964," *Industrial and Labor Relations Review*, vol. 21 (April 1968), pp. 353–65.

that market power does not have any long-term effect on the rate of change of money wages, although it affects the timing of wage hikes over an entire business cycle.[25] And in a recent article, Wallace Hendricks concludes that "on the product market side, the independent effect of concentration on wage levels appears to be small."[26] He postulates that the effect of concentration on wages is highly dependent on the degree of unionization in the industry. Thus, a high level of concentration can have a negative effect on wages when the degree of unionization is low.[27]

While it may be true that the less competitive an industry, the easier it is for the companies in the industry to pass along wage increases, this does not necessarily mean that monopolistic industries are easier targets for unions seeking large wage adjustments. The extent of competition in the product market affects the employer's ability to resist. Large companies in monopolistic industries are much readier to take a strike and to hold out for long periods against union demands than are companies in more competitive industries. One would expect the highest wage adjustments to occur in relatively competitive industries with many small companies and a strong union, such as the trucking industry. Albert Rees has pointed out that in manufacturing it just so happens that almost all strong unions deal with concentrated industries, and so you get evidence of a correlation between "monopoly power" and the size of wage adjustments, but in the economy as a whole, such correlation will not be apparent because there are many competitive industries—such as trucking, construction, and entertainment—which have very strong unions to deal with.[28]

UNION ATTITUDES IN WAGE DETERMINATION

Because strong unions dominate many of our major industries, union attitudes toward wage determination have a significant influence upon the structure of wages in our economy. Union attitudes, as transmitted to management at the bargaining table, are a mixture of basic union needs filtered through and molded by the personalities of the union bargaining representatives. It is up to them to assess properly which of the many possible objectives of union wage policy are in the best interests of the union. They have to weigh the needs of the various groups who make up the membership—the older workers and the younger workers, the full-time workers and the part-time workers—and try to arrive at a "package" to present to management which will satisfy the divergent needs of these

[25] Daniel S. Hamermesh, "Market Power and Wage Inflation," *Southern Economic Journal,* vol. 39 (July 1972), pp. 204–12.

[26] Wallace Hendricks, "Labor Market Structure and Union Wage Levels," University of Illinois Institute of Labor and Industrial Relations, Report No. 248 (Champaign, Ill.: The Institute, 1975), p. 416.

[27] Ibid.

[28] Albert Rees, "Union Wage Gains and Enterprise Monopoly, *Essays on Industrial Relations Research* (Ann Arbor and Detroit: University of Michigan–Wayne State University, Institute of Industrial Relations, 1961), p. 133.

various groups. In any negotiations on behalf of a union, a primary responsibility of a union representative is to set policies which will hold the union together and perpetuate it in the face of stresses within and attacks from without.

What does the membership want? Or to put it more realistically, what might the union representative believe that the membership wants? There are various possible objectives of union wage policy.[29]

1. The largest wage bill, regardless of whether or not all union members are employed.
2. The largest wage bill, including funds from the public support of unemployed union members.
3. The largest private payroll to employed members, deducting from their wage income an amount to pay out-of-work benefits to unemployed members.
4. The largest possible amount of employment for union members.
5. The highest average wage income for each unit of labor affiliated with the union.

Although union leaders can hardly be expected to formulate objectives in this precise fashion, they unquestionably take account of the alternative of more money versus more unemployment, particularly in industries which are characterized by strong nonunion competition or the competition of substitutable products of other industries. The final wage adjustment which union leaders fall back on as the minimum acceptable will be profoundly influenced by political influences within the union, by government pressures, by personal rivalries with other union leaders, and by similar noneconomic forces.

Union Attitudes toward Wage Cuts

Union leaders are elected to secure economic benefits for their constituents. In depressed times, however, they may be faced with employer demands for wage decreases. Generally, unions oppose such demands or yield to them only with the utmost reluctance when employer bargaining power is obviously overwhelming. There are many reasons for this attitude, both economic and political.

A basic reason for union opposition to wage reductions is that there is no assurance that a given change in wages will be associated with the corresponding change in labor cost or with any predictable change in costs or prices. Unit labor cost and wage rates or earnings do not necessarily move together; and in various industries, they have frequently moved in opposite directions.

[29] John T. Dunlop, "Economic Model of a Trade Union," in Campbell R. McConnell (ed.), *Perspectives on Wage Determination* (New York: McGraw-Hill Book Co., 1970), pp. 98–107.

Practically speaking, a union leader can ill afford the political reper-cussions of negotiating a wage cut for the avowed purpose of decreasing unemployment or preventing further unemployment, when neither he nor the employer can be at all certain that lower wages will have the hoped-for results. There is the further fact that most union leaders and the rank-and-file employees do not believe an employer when he pleads inability to pay. All too often, they have heard this complaint raised year after year during contract negotiations; yet, somehow, wage increases were granted, and the employer paid them. When a real crisis arises, the employer may have to take a strike to convince the union that this time he means business!

Unions resist employer demands for wage reductions in depressions because wage policy, by and large, is made by the employed rather than the unemployed union members. Even if there is reason for the leader-ship to believe that the demand for the plant's labor is elastic, the employed members might prefer to pursue a wage policy of maximizing wage rates rather than employment. This is clearly the policy of the United Mine Workers and, generally, of most railway and building-trades unions.

Despite their firm opposition to wage cuts, unions have agreed to them—or to more work at the same pay—on many occasions. There have been special reasons for such action in almost every case. Usually, the crucial factor has been the presence of strong nonunion competition. Currently, this is the situation in the construction industry. Lower hourly rates and less restrictive rules on the part of nonunion employees, and high unemployment among union members, have led to the shaving of rates and the waiver of union rules by many of the craft unions in the construction industry. In 1971, workers in General Motors appliance plants agreed to give up future pay raises for two years because the application of high automobile industry wage scales to these plants had led to a differential of as much as $1 to $2 an hour, compared to the appliance manufacturing plants of companies not affiliated with the automobile industry.

Frequently the near-bankrupt condition of the employer has been the reason for a union's acceptance of wage cuts. This was the motivation of the employees of some airlines which have been suffering huge losses because of mounting fuel costs. Likewise, New York City's financial insolvency has led to negotiations with various unions of public employees to obtain more work for less pay. Another reason for downward adjust-ment of wage levels may be an incentive plan which has led to un-economic wage levels. One study of 12 union concession cases found that the wage incentive system was at issue in 5 cases.[30]

_____
[30] Peter Henle, "Reverse Collective Bargaining? A Look at Some Union Conces-sion Situations," *Industrial and Labor Relations Review*, vol. 26 (April 1973), pp. 956–68.

Unemployment and Union Wage Policies

Unions also accept wage cuts because of pressure from unemployment. This pressure makes itself felt in two ways. The unemployed members of the union may believe that a wage reduction will increase their chances for employment. As their numbers grow, the pressure on the employed members to accede increases. In addition, the existence of high unemployment to some extent reduces the union's bargaining power in negotiation. In some industries, the fear that the unemployed will break a strike, and that the employed will not hold out if a strike is called, has impelled unions to agree to reductions.

As has been pointed out, union leaders are extremely reluctant to accept a wage cut in the hope that it will increase employment. The wage cut means an immediate hardship to union members and to some extent constitutes a blot on the record of the union leadership. The beneficial effects, if any, of the wage reduction may never become evident. Therefore, when a wage *cut* has to be weighed against the possibilities of increased unemployment at existing rates, most union leaders would argue in favor of wage maintenance.

Is there the same emphasis on wages and the same lack of recognition of unemployment reactions when wage *increases* are under consideration? Under what circumstances is a limit set on wage increases by union recognition of the possibility that higher wages would endanger the competitive position of the firm and thereby create unemployment among union members?

There has been some controversy on this subject among economists in recent years. Some economists argue that the effect of a wage increase upon employment is unpredictable before the fact, and that after the increase has been granted, it is impossible to determine the effect of the increase on employment due to the constant fluctuation of business conditions. Therefore, they argue that union leaders cannot normally take employment reactions into consideration in wage negotiations.

Other economists contend that in a number of industries conditions exist which require that union leaders take account of possible employment reactions in making decisions as to wage policy. This is true where an industry is only partially unionized, and imposition of excessive rates on organized firms will cause them to lose business to the nonunion sector of the industry. Similar concern with the employment effects of increased wage costs will also be found in industries characterized by strong competition in the product market and in industries where it is relatively easy for employers to move their plants to other areas.

Such conditions are by no means exceptional. About one out of every five workers in manufacturing is employed in industries where there is clearly no single-firm control of the product market and where competition among firms is keen—textiles, apparels, leather goods, furniture, and lumber. The textile and apparel industries have also been characterized by a movement of new capital into nonunion areas by reason of the high costs imposed by union wage pressure in organized areas. Industries in which union organization is only partial are still important in terms of numbers of workers employed. Nevertheless, although the threat of unemployment obviously affects union wage policy in critical situations, the record shows that it is in periods of high unemployment that the disparity between union and nonunion wage adjustments is greatest. In 1974, for example, with unemployment averaging 5.6% of the civilian labor force, union workers in manufacturing received an average wage hike of 10% while nonunion factory workers gained only 5½%.[31]

Full-Employment Legislation and Union Wage Policy

In Chapter 14, we shall consider proposed federal legislation which would make it a goal of national policy to reduce unemployment to the 3% level, if necessary by casting government as the "employer of last resort." The huge cost of financing such a program would obviously be inflationary, but there is another inflationary effect which is not generally discussed, namely, that removal of concern for the jobs of union members would likewise remove the restraints which possible unemployment resulting from uneconomic wage increases now impose on union leadership. Although, as has been pointed out above, union concern about employment varies, depending upon the particular circumstances of the firm and the industry, nevertheless it remains a factor in union negotiations. With government committed to take up the slack in employment, there is a danger that unions would raise their wage demands and thus trigger a costly wage-price spiral.

Effects of Unions on Wage Adjustments

In Chapter 13, in our discussion of inflation, we shall consider in detail the question of whether or not unions accelerate the rate of wage increases in the American economy. For the purposes of the present discussion, however, it is pertinent to observe that union organization affects the form, size, and frequency of compensation changes in unionized firms.

Unions have profoundly affected the *form* of compensation adjustments in American industry. Supplementary unemployment benefits, cost-of-living adjustments, guaranteed annual wages, pay for employee birthdays, and all kinds of welfare plans—these are some of the diverse ways in which employees have expressed their preferences for wage adjustments through collective bargaining. From 1966 to 1972, organized employees

---

[31] Chase Manhattan Bank, *Business in Brief,* No. 126 (February 1976), p. 6.

showed a higher rate of gain in fringe benefits than did nonunion employees in both manufacturing and nonmanufacturing industries.[32]

Unions also affect the *frequency* of wage adjustments. The timing of wage adjustments is much more formalized for union employees than for nonunion employees. The former almost always receive a wage adjustment annually; the latter may or may not receive such adjustments annually. But in an inflationary economy, nonunion plants which are not tied to long-term contracts, will frequently respond more quickly to changed labor market conditions than will organized establishments.

The *size* of wage adjustments is also affected by the existence of collective bargaining agreements. Nonunion wage adjustments will vary more in amount from year to year because of the fact that nonunion plants are more sensitive to changes in economic conditions. This is likely to be true in both slack and tight labor markets. On the average, however, in any one year a worker in a union factory is likely to receive a smaller percentage but a larger cents-per-hour increase than the nonunion worker, and since the union employee receives increases more frequently, there is some evidence that over a period of years he gains proportionately more than does a nonunion worker. Thus, one study found that over the period from 1966 to 1972, general wage adjustments for nonoffice workers in the private nonfarm economy rose 61% in unionized establishments, compared to 52% in nonunion companies.[33]

POWER ASPECTS OF WAGE DETERMINATION

Wage determination in unionized firms involves a balancing of power. Is it realistic to discuss power in economic terms—particularly with respect to union organizations—or are concepts from the political arena more relevant? On this basic issue, there is considerable disagreement among labor economists. The institutionalists contend that the trade union is ill suited to purely economic analysis and that the union is an essentially political rather than economic institution. Thus, the union may "need" a strike to promote solidarity and loyalty, while from the point of view of any rational economic analysis, there is no economic justification for such action.

Other economists differ sharply with this point of view. John T. Dunlop, for example, concedes that emphasis upon political considerations may have some relevance in understanding the actions of newer unions in which there have been internal factional struggles. He maintains, however, that such situations constitute a minor portion of the spectrum of collective bargaining, and that, by and large, unions must make decisions

---

[32] Paul L. Scheible, "Changes in Employee Compensation, 1966 to 1972," *Monthly Labor Review*, vol. 98 (March 1975), p. 14.

[33] Ibid.

which reflect economic realities in the long run.[34] Furthermore, the lack of objectives held in common by union leaders and union members cannot long endure without membership discontent leading to a change in leadership. On balance, therefore, it seems more meaningful to recognize certain political and irrational elements in union decision making— just as these also exist in business decisions—but nevertheless to view union bargaining demands in an economic context.

Wage determination in unionized firms reflects the union's power to inflict damage by a strike, and the company's ability to withstand a strike and impose a loss of earnings on employees. Even when a strike is not threatened, the power of a union to strike makes itself felt at the bargaining table.

Union bargaining power depends upon three basic elements: the right to strike, the ability to strike successfully, and the amount of loss which can be inflicted on the employer by a strike. The legal right to strike is, of course, a basic prerequisite to union power. If the union contract in question is a two-year contract with a wage reopening after one year and the contract contains a no-strike clause, the union may not be able to strike lawfully to enforce its wage demands during the term of the contract. A strike in violation of a contract may leave the union open to a suit by the employer for damages for breach of contract, or an injunction may be obtained to halt the unlawful work stoppage. Furthermore, when a union strike is unlawful, other unions frequently will not honor the picket line, and therefore the effectiveness of the strike is weakened. Obviously, when such circumstances exist, the union's bargaining power is limited.

If the union has the right to strike, the next consideration is its ability to strike successfully. This will depend upon such circumstances as the cohesiveness of the union, the degree of internal dissension, the possibility of raiding by rival unions, the amount of funds in the union treasury, the ability of the union to pay strike benefits, the extent to which strikers can obtain employment or compensation elsewhere, and, of course, the degree of support by the membership for the union's demands. Even such circumstances as the time of year will affect the union's ability to strike successfully. Employees do not mind losing a few weeks' work on strike in the summertime, but they are loath to do so just before Christmas!

The third important factor which determines the bargaining power of the union is its ability to impose a substantial hardship on the employer by calling a strike. This will depend upon the nature of the employer's business, the position of the firm in the industry, its financial resources, and similar circumstances. If a company is engaged in retail work, for

---

[34] Dunlop, "The Task of Contemporary Wage Theory," pp. 117–39.

example, it is extremely vulnerable to a strike because any business lost through a shutdown cannot be regained at a later date. On the other hand, if an automobile company goes on strike, its permanent loss of business might be negligible. For a time, customers can be supplied out of inventory. Thereafter, many customers will wait for a particular make of car until production is resumed. Sometimes a strike may afford such companies a convenient excuse to curtail production and thus give dealers time to work down excessive inventories.

The power of the union to hurt the employer will depend upon the financial position and the profitability of the company. In some industries, companies work on narrow profit margins and have little working capital. They rely on continuing sales to enable them to meet their bills, and any interruption of production has to be avoided at all costs. In other cases, companies are financially strong and can stand a long strike. Frequently, large companies have a number of plants or branch operations, and if a strike shuts down only part of their operations, they can withstand a long strike by offsetting losses in one area with profits in another.

Just as a union's ability to strike successfully depends in part upon the time of year, so, too, does its ability to impose losses on the employer. The threat of a strike is obviously most effective when the employer is going into his peak season. If contract negotiations break down during a slack season, the employer may not care about a strike, since he may have been thinking in terms of curtailing production and laying off employees anyhow. Both unions and management are keenly aware of the strategic importance of having contract negotiations occur at an advantageous time, and there is always a good deal of sparring over the issue of when a contract should expire or come up for renegotiation.

The loss which can be imposed upon a firm by a strike depends to some extent upon the class of labor involved and its importance in the entire scheme of production. It has long been recognized that the smaller the cost of a factor of production is relative to total costs, and the more essential it is to production, the higher its price can be pushed up without affecting the amount of the factor employers will utilize. In every plant or establishment, there are certain workers with relatively scarce skills who can paralyze production by a walkout. If their wages constitute only a small fraction of the total costs of operation, it is understandable why an employer will frequently be willing to grant such workers large wage increases as the price of uninterrupted production. It was recognition of this principle which led the American Federation of Labor to organize skilled workers along craft lines.

Today, however, even a strike of unskilled workers can be as effective as a walkout of skilled craftsmen. This is the result of two developments: the refusal of other workers to cross a picket line and the decline in the use of strikebreakers. Today, a walkout of janitors and sweepers in a huge industrial establishment can, if the strike is lawful, cause a complete shutdown and a forced layoff of thousands of workers. The right to strike has thus given great power even to unskilled groups who are ready to use this power militantly.

All of the foregoing considerations must be weighed by the union representatives in presenting union demands at the bargaining table. They must estimate, too, just how long a strike might last, what possibility there is of government intervention, and what the chances are that employee dissatisfaction resulting from a long strike might endanger their own positions. Management must likewise consider the strength and weaknesses of its own bargaining position. The wage which is ultimately arrived at will reflect a balancing of these power considerations, the profitability of the firm, general supply and demand conditions, and the personalities of the management and union representatives.

The Changing Balance of Power between Management and Unions

As we view the broad sweep of industrial relations in the American economy, it appears that there have been changing tides in the balance of power between unions and management. Prior to the passage of the Wagner Act in 1935, management clearly had the upper hand and unions found it difficult to organize in many industries. From the Wagner Act until 1947, when the Taft-Hartley Act was passed, union power grew rapidly; unions were able to use boycotts, picketing, secondary pressures on neutral employers, and other coercive actions in addition to the strike. With the passage of the Taft-Hartley Act in 1947 and of the Landrum-Griffin Act[35] in 1959, the pendulum again swung in the direction of management, since these two laws circumscribed many union bargaining weapons and weakened the ability of unions to organize effectively.

The changing fortunes of union and management from 1933 to 1959 were primarily influenced by the intervention of government in the labor market. In recent years, however, there has been some evidence that economic influences and trends have altered the bargaining positions of the protagonists. These developments fall into three major categories:

1. *New Bargaining Techniques.* A major effort to alter the balance of power was mounted by the Industrial Union Department of the AFL–CIO during the decade of the 60s through the use of coalition bargaining. The campaign extended to a number of important industries: petroleum refining, nonferrous metals, metal products, chemicals, electrical equipment, and food processing. In each instance, the initial target situation was one in which a multiplant concern had been conducting separate negotiations with several different locals, frequently affiliated with more

---

[35] The content of the Taft-Hartley and Landrum-Griffin Acts will be considered in Chapters 19 and 20.

than one international union.[36] Although the record of coalition bargaining has thus far been spotty and unions have been unable to compel the enlargement of a bargaining unit's scope when the employer has been opposed to the move, nevertheless maintenance of the status quo has involved a cost to employers. The concept of coalition bargaining may ultimately erode some advantages which now accrue to a company with a number of geographically scattered plants which are under contract with separate unions. In addition, as noted in earlier chapters, unions are attempting to bargain on a multinational basis as a means of coping with the multinational corporation.

Another bargaining technique with important implications for the balance of power is the recently judicially recognized right of the United Transportation Union to strike selectively against any of some 170 railroad carriers which are joined together for multiemployer bargaining.[37] The railroads are extremely vulnerable to whipsawing techniques; presumably the unions are shifting to this form of bargaining pressure because they believe that it will be more effective than industrywide bargaining with a group of employers.

2. *Inflation and Relative Bargaining Power.*   Although rapidly rising prices have deprived wage increases of much of their value in providing workers with additional purchasing power, the fact remains that an inflationary period with a tight labor market for skilled adult males tends to tip the balance of bargaining power in favor of unions. Despite the fact that in 1975 almost 8 million persons, representing 8.5% of the labor force, were unemployed, the unemployment rate for males age 35–64 averaged from 4.3% to 4.9%.[38] This meant that from the union point of view, the threat of layoffs for a significant—and highly influential—segment of the union membership was relatively low. At the same time, rank-and-file militancy was fueled by the steady erosion of real earnings produced by the escalating cost of living. From the employer's point of view, the same inflation provided a mechanism to recoup higher wage costs in the form of higher prices, and therefore management resistance to strike threats was probably weakened. The economic atmosphere produced by inflation with expectations of a continuing rise in prices tends to assist unions in achieving larger settlements in wages and fringe benefits.

3. *Available Sources of Compensatory Income.*   The only justification for a strike as a technique in collective bargaining is that the costs im-

---

[36] George H. Hildebrand, "Bargaining Structure and Relative Power," in Richard L. Rowan (ed.), *Collective Bargaining: Survival in the 70's?* Labor Relations and Public Policy Series, Report No. 5 (Philadelphia: Industrial Research Unit, The Wharton School, University of Pennsylvania, 1972), p. 10.

[37] Ibid., p. 15.

[38] U.S. Department of Labor et al., *Employment and Training Report of the President, 1976* (Washington, D.C.: Government Printing Office, 1976), table A–1, p. 211, and table A–19, p. 241.

posed by a strike on both management and employees will eventually bring about a more reasonable attitude and lead to a compromise settlement. Recent trends, however, have weakened the effectiveness of strike action in achieving this objective. From the union standpoint, strikers have been able to find supplementary sources of income elsewhere, so that the costs to strikers of a prolonged shutdown have been reduced and the duration of strikes has therefore probably been lengthened. In recent years, strikers have found such support from unemployment compensation payments (legal for strikers on the railroads and in two states), welfare payments, food stamps,[39] and, of course, strike funds. In addition, the increasing importance of part-time employment in our economy has provided an opportunity for strikers to obtain some earnings during plant shutdowns by taking such part-time jobs as driving cabs and working as clerks in retail establishments.

At the same time that this trend has become evident, management has been increasing its ability to draw on earnings outside the area of labor conflict. This reserve of management earning power is provided by ownership of businesses in a diversity of industries, some of which may be nonunion and/or overseas. Some multinational corporations derive as much as 50% of their total net profits from abroad. Obviously, a union in the United States would encounter greater difficulty in bringing effective economic pressure to bear upon such a multinational corporation than upon one whose total profit is dependent upon the production which unions can curtail through use of the strike. Little wonder that unions are staunch supporters of a strong antitrust policy against conglomerates!

From the union point of view, the multinational corporation poses the immediate problem of production switching in the event of a strike in a particular plant and the long-run problem of runaway plants on an international basis. Unions are just beginning to attempt to develop strategies capable of dealing with such problems. The logical counterattack would involve internationally coordinated action by unions associated with subsidiaries of the same company in a number of countries. The practical difficulties facing unions which attempt to implement such a strategy are obviously enormous. In several instances, affiliated unions in various countries have tried to coordinate their bargaining efforts against international corporations, with multinational bargaining the aim, but there is no record of real success by unions in such an endeavor.[40]

Whether on balance these trends have tipped the scales in favor of unionism or management depends to some extent upon the criteria which

---

[39] See Armand J. Thieblot, Jr., and Ronald M. Cowin, *Welfare and Strikes: The Use of Public Funds to Support Strikes,* Labor Relations and Public Policy Series, Report No. 6 (Philadelphia: Industrial Research Unit, The Wharton School, University of Pennsylvania, 1972).

[40] See the articles by Herbert R. Northrup and Richard L. Rowan, cited in Chapter 4, footnote 8.

are used to judge success. Is a long strike evidence of the ability of management to resist or of the ability of unions to maintain concerted pressure of long duration? In any case, these trends need to be considered in any current evaluation of the respective bargaining power of unions and management. To the extent that both unions and management have strengthened their staying power, the public may be the loser, and this may shape public attitudes toward proposals to restrict the right to strike.

EFFECTS OF WAGE OR PRICE FIXING BY GOVERNMENT

In Chapter 12, we shall consider in some detail efforts to control wage adjustments through governmental pressure or legislation. Here it is important to note that the existence of such governmental action may change the focus of union interest in collective bargaining. For example, experience has demonstrated that during periods when legislation is in effect placing ceilings on allowable wage increases, unions are likely to demand a return to shorter term contracts rather than a continuation of the trend to three-year contracts which has been much in evidence in recent years. In situations where fringe benefits are exempt from wage regulation, unions show an understandable interest in improving pension, life insurance, and health and welfare plans. Union leaders who can no longer direct their energies toward obtaining the highest possible wage may now focus on obtaining various changes in working rules. These changes in union policy indicate how governmental regulations designed to restrict one phase of the collective bargaining relationship can have unforeseen—and sometimes costly—repercussions upon other aspects of the contractual relationship between labor and management.

SUMMARY

Wage determination in the American economy is a complex process. It reflects the influence of many forces. Thus, if we were trying to explain why a production worker in a steel-fabricating company has a higher hourly wage rate than a production worker in a textile mill, the following are some of the major considerations which would require investigation.

1. The monopoly power of the employer in the product market—Is it easy for the company to pass along to consumers the cost of higher wages?
2. The wage policy of the company—Does it have a policy of paying wages equal to or higher than, those of its competitors or of other firms in its local labor market area?
3. The state of union organization in the plant and industry—Is the employee a union member? What is the bargaining strength of the union,

is its leadership aggressive, does it have to concern itself with non-union competition? What is the extent of collective bargaining among firms with which the employer competes in the product market?

4. The trend of sales and employment in the respective industries—Are there unfilled job vacancies in the plant, is employment increasing, and is the demand for labor strong?

5. The supply of labor in the local labor market—Is there a large pool of qualified but unemployed labor available, or is labor in short supply?

6. The regularity of employment, both over the year and from year to year—Does the high wage rate in the steel company compensate in part for cyclical unemployment incident to the job?

7. The total package of compensation—What other benefits are received by the worker? To what extent can he expect overtime work? How do the two jobs compare when we look at weekly earnings or annual income?

8. Size of firm—Is this a small or large firm, a public corporation or a small family business?

9. Size of labor market—Is the plant located in a large metropolitan area or in a small town?

10. The overall labor force characteristics of the industry or firm—To what extent is the labor force in each firm composed of a high percentage of white, skilled, male workers?

11. Geographic location—Is the plant located in the South or in some other section of the country?

12. The personal characteristics of the employees in question—What is their respective age, race, education, health, and so on?

13. Profitability of the employer—How do the profits of the employer compare with those of other firms in the particular industry? Was this a good year or a bad year? What is the trend in profits both in the firm and in the industry?

14. The job content—To what extent is a high degree of skill or training required to perform the particular job?

All of these considerations enter in varying degrees into the determination of wages. Although we have placed considerable emphasis in this chapter on the role of unions in wage determination, it is important to recognize that the various factors enumerated above will shape and influence the impact which unions can exert upon the level and structure of wages.

QUESTIONS FOR DISCUSSION

1. Discuss the connection between the internal and external wage structure of a firm. What is the significance for collective bargaining of the concept of "wage clusters"?

2. Discuss the significance of key wage bargains in wage determination in the United States.

3. Discuss the interrelationship of monopoly power in the product market and union power in the labor market in terms of the effect of this interrelationship upon the wage level.

4. Discuss the advantages and disadvantages of automatic cost-of-living adjustment provisions in collective bargaining agreements from the viewpoint of the employer and the union.

SUGGESTIONS FOR FURTHER READING

AFL–CIO. *American Federationist*, vol. 83 (March 1976), pp. 1–6.

An article stating the union position on cost-of-living escalator clauses in union contracts.

Executive Office of the President, Council on Wage and Price Stability. *Cost-of-Living Escalator Clauses and Inflation*. Washington, D.C.: Government Printing Office, August 1975.

A review of escalator clauses in American industry and of their possible impact on the price level.

Fogel, Walter, and Lewin, David. "Wage Determination in the Public Sector," in Richard L. Rowan (ed.), *Readings in Labor Economics and Labor Relations*. 3d ed. Homewood, Ill.: Richard D. Irwin, Inc., 1976, pp. 337–52.

An analysis of the special considerations which typify wage determination in the public sector.

Henle, Peter. "Reverse Collective Bargaining? A Look at Some Union Concession Situations," *Industrial and Labor Relations Review*, vol. 26 (April 1973), pp. 956–68.

An analysis of 12 concession situations in which contracts were reopened before expiration and unions agreed to substantial concessions.

U.S. Department of Labor. *The Consumer Price Index: How Will the 1977 Revision Affect It?* Bureau of Labor Statistics Report No. 449. Washington, D.C.: Government Printing Office, 1975.

A concise report explaining the present composition of the CPI and an explanation of how proposed revisions will modify it.

12

Wage Changes and Employment

UNION OFFICIALS, in order to maintain their positions and retain the allegiance and interest of their membership, must constantly seek to obtain new benefits for their members. In view of the strength of organized labor in this country, it seems likely that over the long run the general trend of money wage rates in future years will be upward. What impact will such continuing wage pressure have upon employment?

The effect of wage changes upon employment constitutes one of the most controversial subjects in the field of labor economics. Most union leaders deny that there is any predictable relation between wage increases and employment in the *individual* firm in our dynamic economy. Orthodox economists generally take a contrary view. But when we come to the field of *general* wage adjustments occurring uniformly throughout the economy, we find that many economists argue that such wage adjustments need have no effect upon employment. What is the reason for this divergence in opinion? Under what circumstances will wage increases curtail employment? In this chapter, we shall inquire into the consequences of increases in wage rates upon employment, first from the point of view of the individual firm and second from the point of view of the economy at large. Finally, we shall examine some of the problems created by continuing union wage pressure.

WAGE CHANGES IN THE INDIVIDUAL FIRM

The Short-Run Effects of Wage Increases

Assume that an increase occurs in the rate of wages which an employer is required to pay his labor force. This might be the result of a new union contract or of a minimum wage law or simply of increasing scarcity of labor in the labor market. Assume further that the demand for the product sold by the company remains unchanged, that no new inventions are reducing costs of production in the firm, and that output in the company at the time the wage increase occurred was neither expanding nor contracting but was relatively stable. These various assumptions are generally taken care of by phrasing our inquiry in terms of the effect of a wage increase in the individual firm, "other things being equal."

Orthodox economists assume that the behavior of the employer under such circumstances will conform to the principles of marginal productivity determination, which we examined in Chapter 10. According to the marginal productivity theory, the employer endeavors to hire labor up to the point at which the marginal cost of labor is approximately equal to labor's marginal contribution to the revenue of the firm.

As we have seen in Chapter 10, if the supply of labor is perfectly elastic, the wage and the marginal cost of labor are the same, and the employer will hire labor up to the point of approximate equality between marginal revenue product and wage. It will simplify our analysis if we ignore the complications produced by a rising supply curve for labor and, in the following discussion of employment policy in the individual firm, assume that the employer is faced by a perfectly elastic supply curve for labor so that marginal productivity determination will be made in terms of the wage of labor (which, under these conditions, will be equal to the marginal cost of labor).

Under these circumstances, an employer who wishes to maximize profits will hire labor only up to the point where the last additional worker adds just enough revenue to compensate for the wage he receives. The lower the wage, the larger will be the size of the work force employed, since at low wage rates the employer can afford to keep on the payroll workers whose marginal contribution to the revenues of the firm is comparatively small. When wage costs rise, however, he will be compelled to lay off these men in order to achieve a new equilibrium in which the marginal revenue productivity of the least valuable man employed will be great enough to equal the new higher wage level.

Wage Increases and Layoffs

The pressure on the employer to lay off workers when the wage rate rises comes about in two principal ways. In the first place, when wage costs rise, the employer generally finds it necessary to raise his price for his product in order to cover the increased labor costs. Sometimes, he may find it inexpedient to raise prices but may achieve the same objective by lowering the quality of his product. In either case, whether the price be raised or the quality lowered, he will ordinarily sell a smaller output, even though it is possible that his total sales receipts may increase or remain constant. With a smaller physical production, he will find that he needs fewer employees, and so he will be able to lay off workers whose services are no longer required.

In the second place, when wage rates rise, the employer's profits will immediately be reduced. Therefore, a strong incentive is provided for him to review his entire production setup in an effort to cut costs and save money. Even without a reduction in output, the employer may find it possible, by rescheduling production and rearranging work schedules, to eliminate some workers. Furthermore, if labor becomes more expensive, the employer may find that it is now economically profitable to utilize new laborsaving machinery which will also have the effect of displacing labor. Such substitution of machinery for labor usually takes some time to effect. The employer may have limited space in his plant, or perhaps he may have to defer substitution until his existing machinery is more fully depreciated. Substitution of machinery for labor, therefore, is ordinarily felt most as a long-run consequence of wage increases. It will be considered below in connection with our analysis of the long-run effects of wage pressure.

When labor becomes more expensive, employers are pressed to look over their labor force and decide whether certain jobs need to be performed at all, irrespective of whether they can be performed more cheaply by machines or automated devices. Thus, if labor is cheap, business establishments may employ a porter to clean floors and do odd jobs; but when this kind of labor becomes expensive, they may decide to eliminate this work and call in a contract cleaner on a periodic basis. This basic principle has important social implications. As we shall document in Chapter 16, with every rise in the minimum wage, we have provided an incentive to employers to eliminate certain of the menial jobs at the lowest rung of the wage scale. The minimum wage may be justified as part of a national effort to raise wage standards; yet it is probably responsible for the creation of a substantial amount of hard-core unemployment. For in every society, there are persons whose education, training, and mental abilities are low, and these people can only find employment in jobs whose remuneration is low, corresponding to their low productivity.

Factors Affecting the Elasticity of the Demand for Labor

What determines the elasticity of the demand curve for labor in the short run? Or to put the question in another way: With a given increase in wage rates, what circumstances determine whether the layoffs will be small (inelastic demand) or large (elastic demand)? Many years ago a famous economist, Alfred Marshall, formulated an answer to this question as part of his exposition of the laws of derived demand.[1] It was Marshall's

---

[1] Alfred Marshall, *Principles of Economics,* 8th ed. (New York: Macmillan Co., 1920), pp. 383–86.

theory that the demand for labor is a derived demand. Labor is not wanted for itself but for what it can produce. Therefore, if we want an explanation of the elasticity of demand for labor, we must look to the demand for the final product and the supply of other factors of production, from which the demand for labor is derived.

According to Marshall:

1. *The demand for labor will be the more inelastic the more essential the labor in question is in the production of the final product.* Obviously, the more skilled the worker is, the more likely that the employer will be highly dependent upon his services. Thus, the demand for skilled patternmakers is more likely to be less elastic than the demand for common laborers; and the patternmakers, if they were to go out on strike, would be better able to extract a higher wage from management without layoffs than would the common laborers. In place of the latter class of employees an employer may find that he can operate temporarily by using supervisory help, or he can bring in nonunion employees. In today's labor market, essentiality can result either from a high degree of skill or from a tight control over entrance into a trade exercised by a labor union.

2. *The demand for labor will be the more inelastic the more inelastic the demand for the final product.* The demand curve for the product will have a steep slope, or be "inelastic," when increases in the price of the product produce only a very small decrease in consumer purchases of the product. A classic example of a product with an inelastic demand curve is salt. Even large increases in price would not materially affect sales of this product. If, however, the demand curve for the product is almost horizontal, or "elastic," even a small increase in price will cause sales to fall sharply, with the result that a large curtailment will be required in the labor force of the firm.

The range of possible reactions of employment to a wage increase may be crystallized by considering the difference in the effect of wage increases under two extreme conditions of elasticity of demand for product—first, in a firm with a perfectly inelastic demand curve and, second, in a firm with a perfectly elastic demand curve. In the former case, the increase in costs resulting from a wage adjustment could be passed on completely to consumers in the form of a price rise without affecting sales volume at all. Therefore, no unemployment would be caused by the price rise, although there could still be some unemployment resulting from substitution of factors within the firm. In the latter case, at the other extreme, the firm with the elastic demand curve would be unable to pass any of the price increase on to consumers. The employer would find that to maximize profits, he would be better off selling a smaller volume at the same price and would therefore sharply curtail output and employment.

Firms in monopolistic positions are able to raise the price of their products without affecting sales materially, since consumers cannot shift easily to substitutes. On the basis of the foregoing theoretical analysis, therefore, we should expect that in firms which have an entrenched and protected position in the product market built up through advertising, patents, and sheer size and financial power, wage increases would produce relatively larger price increases and relatively less displacement of labor than in highly competitive companies.

When there are union wage adjustments on an industrywide basis in a well-organized industry, then the demand curve for the product which is relevant is really the demand curve for the product of the entire industry. If, on the other hand, the union has organized only a part of the industry, then the demand curve which is significant is the demand curve for the product of the firms where wage adjustments are being made. The elasticity of demand for the product of these firms is likely to be greater than that for the product of the industry if there is a possibility that rates will not advance to the same extent in nonunion firms and that consumers will therefore substitute a nonunion product for the product of the organized companies.

3. *The demand for labor will be the more inelastic the smaller the ratio of the labor cost in question to the total cost of product.* In some firms, labor costs constitute a relatively small proportion of total costs— frequently less than 10% of total costs. In such firms, if wage rates rise by, say, 5%, total costs would rise by only one half of 1%. If the full increase in total cost were reflected in a price increase, the rise in price would be so small that sales volume, and therefore employment, might not be affected to any significant degree.

But now, suppose that only a portion of the labor force is demanding an increase in wage rates. It is obvious that a small group of workers strategically placed in a company may be able to gain very large increases for themselves, yet from the point of view of management the effect on overall costs may be minor. Of course, management must consider the effect of such wage changes upon the rates of other workers; but nevertheless, it still remains true that there are advantages to be gained in bargaining from being strong but small. From this point of view, small craft unions may well do a better job of wage bargaining for their membership than large industrial unions.

4. *The demand for labor will be the more inelastic the more inelastic the supply of other factors of production.* If the supply of other factors of production that are needed to work with the labor in question is inelastic, a small increase in demand will cause a large increase in the price of such factors. Conversely, a small reduction in demand will cause a sharp fall in the price of such factors. Two influences are at work in this relationship which can be illustrated by the following examples:

a. *The "substitution effect."* Suppose that a union of porters working for a company which cleans floors in various industrial and retail buildings demands a substantial wage increase. Management knows that if it purchases waxing and polishing machines it can speed up floor maintenance work and eliminate a number of porters. However, if a limited number of such machines are available, so that any increase in demand will result in a sharp increase in the price asked for the machines, the bargaining power of the porters in demanding and obtaining wage increases will be improved. In other words, the inelasticity of the supply of this other factor of production will tend to make the demand for the porters' labor more inelastic. Management will then be prepared to pay more for this type of labor rather than substantially curtail the amount of labor employed through increased mechanization.

b. The "output effect." The increase in costs resulting from the adjustment in the wages given to the porters will necessitate an increase in price for services rendered by the floor-cleaning company. Therefore, it is likely that some of its customers will discontinue utilizing its services or will reduce their usage. Assume that the floor-cleaning company has been leasing polishing machines from another firm prior to the wage adjustment. Since the floor-cleaning company's business volume will be reduced as a result of the wage and price adjustments referred to above, it will have less need for polishing machines and may return some to the leasing firm. If the latter has no other place to use the machines and in effect is "stuck" with a fixed supply of them, it might be willing to accept a lower rental just to keep them busy. In other words, a relatively small reduction in demand for this factor of production might cause a substantial drop in its supply price. This is another way of saying that its supply curve is inelastic. If this were so, part of the wage increase gained by the porters could be achieved at the expense of the price paid for the other factor. In other words, an inelastic supply curve for a complementary factor of production would enable the porters to achieve a larger wage adjustment.

Circumstances in Which Wage Increases Do Not Reduce Employment

Suppose that a union were to secure a substantial increase in wages from employers in a particular industry and the employers were then questioned as to the effect the wage adjustment would have on their employment policies. What would be the typical response? The chances are that most of the employers would say that the wage increase would not cause them to cut their labor force; that, on the contrary, they intended to increase employment. They would explain that they had to give the wage increase in order to retain their present labor force and to attract additional workers.

Employers normally grant wage increases when times are good and prices are rising. They make wage changes in a dynamic business environment in which demand and supply conditions are in a continual state of flux. Against such a changing background, it is quite possible that wage increases will not be associated with any immediate diminution in employment. Let us consider briefly the various circumstances under which a wage increase need not have any adverse effect on employment.

1. *When output in the individual firm is increasing.* As we have observed, one avenue by which wage increases affect employment is through the reduction in output which is caused by the increase in product price made to cover the higher wage costs. If, however, output is increasing in the firm at the time the wage increase is made, the effect of employment in the firm may not be altered by the wage increase. Output may be increasing in a firm because of rising demand for its product attributable to a general business revival. During such a period, output, wages, profits, and prices all tend to rise together; and wage increases tend to be associated with increases, not decreases, in employment. Output may also be increasing in a particular firm, even in periods of relative business stability, because the firm is growing, or the demand for the product of the industry is growing, or for similar reasons. Not only does expanding output normally carry with it additional job opportunities, but also, in many industries—such as the steel industry—expanding output is associated with declining labor costs per unit of product. Therefore, if wage *rates* increase at a time when output is expanding in such industries, there may not even be any increase in unit labor costs, since the increase in wage rates may simply be offset by the decline in unit labor costs attributable to the expansion of output.

2. *When productivity is increasing.* As new and more productive machinery is introduced and changes are made in the organization of work, the productivity of labor tends to increase. This means that the employer will find that with a given number of workers, he can now produce a larger output than formerly. Such advance in productivity—which is a continuous process in our dynamic economy—has the effect of reducing labor costs per unit of product. Therefore, if money wage rates are raised at about the same rate that increasing productivity lowers unit labor costs, the two trends may offset each other; and on balance, there may be no net increase in unit labor costs. If the rate of increase in wage rates is no greater than the rate at which technological progress reduces unit labor costs, there will be no increase in unit labor cost, no increase in price, and no reduction in output and employment. However, although wage increases under such circumstances do not produce unemployment, it may eliminate the possibility for any expansion of employment in the firm by preventing technological progress from being reflected in a reduction in price to consumers.

3. *When prices are inflexible.* There are certain situations in which a wage increase, even though it increases labor costs per unit, will not produce a change in the price charged by the individual firm. In such

circumstances, the employer may calculate that even though his profits are being squeezed by failure to adjust prices, he would lose more if he tried to alter his price.

This condition may exist when there are only a few sellers in an industry. In such a situation, known as "oligopoly," the demand curve of the individual firm, as seen by the employer, will often have a "kink" at the prevailing price. This is simply a geometric expression of the fact that each seller in the industry calculates that if he lowers his price, he will merely start a price war and therefore not increase his sales appreciably; whereas if he raises his price, his competitors may not follow suit, with the result that his sales will fall off sharply. Above the prevailing price the demand curve for the product of the individual firm approaches the horizontal, and below the prevailing price the demand curve approaches the vertical—thus producing the so-called kink at the prevailing price. Under such circumstances a rise in wage rates may not produce any change in prices or output. Consequently, employment will not be immediately affected. It must be borne in mind, however, that even when output remains constant, management may still find means of economizing on the use of labor which has become more expensive by reason of the wage increase. For example, in some industries, employers have sought to economize on the use of labor by resorting to the "stretch-out," that is, a worker who formerly tended only one machine is required to operate two machines at the same rate of pay. Through this and similar devices a smaller labor force can be used more intensively, and some workers can be displaced, although output remains unchanged.

4. *When exploitation of labor exists.* As we observed in Chapter 10, a wage increase need not produce unemployment where a condition of exploitation of labor has existed previously. In other words, if an employer has been paying labor less than its marginal revenue product, and the effect of a wage adjustment is to increase the wage rate to the point of equivalence between marginal revenue product and wage, there will be no incentive for the employer to alter his price, output, and employment.

The foregoing analysis indicates that in the dynamic environment of the business world, the connection between wage changes and changes in employment is a very tenuous one. Wage increases do not necessarily produce increases in labor costs per unit of product—they may simply prevent reductions in labor costs attributable to technological change or increasing output from being reflected in price reductions to consumers. Even if the increase in wage rates increases labor costs per unit of product, it still may not affect prices where it is impracticable for the firm to raise prices because of competitive conditions; moreover, even if prices are raised, there need be no reduction in output or employment, if output has been increasing anyway, or if the price increase is negligible because wages constitute such a small proportion of total costs.

The Long-Run Effects of Wage Increases

As we have observed earlier in this chapter, the extent to which wage increases will produce unemployment in the individual firm in the long run can be summarized in the form of four laws. If wages are raised, the resulting unemployment will be smaller in amount:

1. The less elastic the demand for the product.
2. The smaller the substitutability of labor in the process of production.
3. The smaller the proportion which labor costs form of total costs.
4. The less elastic the supply schedules of the complementary factors.[2]

These "laws" are applicable in both the short run and the long run, but it is only in the long run that factors 2 and 4 can exercise their full effect. In essence, these two tendencies reduce to the degree of fluidity of capital. Machinery is ordinarily the complement of labor, as well as its most important substitute. In the long run, capital may not only be substituted for labor (factor 2), but it may also be removed to other industries, or the supply may be altered (factor 4).

At any moment of time, employers, if they have acted rationally, will have pushed their use of labor and capital to the point where they have reached a margin of indifference, that is, it is immaterial to them whether they utilize a unit of capital or a unit of labor at the margin. From this it follows that if the price of labor rises, employers will find two actions profitable: (1) to substitute capital for labor by introducing laborsaving machinery; and (2) to shift from less capitalistic to more capitalistic industries, that is, to industries where the ratio of labor to capital is smaller. These reactions both take time. A full adaptation to an increase in the wage of labor may take years to work itself out. As a consequence, the full effect of wage increases upon the volume of employment can be observed only in the long run.

WAGE PRESSURE AND MECHANIZATION

A major means of improving efficiency and saving labor in our industrial economy has been the machine. Machines, however, are costly, and businessmen will normally invest in laborsaving machinery only if the investment gives promise of paying for itself in a reasonable period of time. A laborsaving machine pays for itself in terms of manpower saved, reduction in spoilage, and so forth. The higher the wage rate of the labor which can be displaced by the machine, the larger the savings which the machine will effect, and the more attractive its purchase becomes.

Businessmen are not uniformly alert to the advantages of using laborsaving machinery. Many laborsaving machines may be in use in some

---

[2] A mathematical exposition of these four rules, which govern the derived demand for labor, is found in the appendix to this chapter.

companies but not utilized by others, either because their labor costs are not high enough to warrant the expenditure on machinery or because management is inefficient and has not sufficient initiative to look around and find out how its costs might be lowered. Undoubtedly, a substantial improvement in the level of industrial efficiency could be obtained if efficient employers were induced to bring their production methods in line with the best in the industry.

Wage pressure may exert this influence in certain circumstances. Wage increases are likely to be most effective as a stimulus to the substitution of machinery for labor in firms where wages, prior to the wage increase, were low, and management relied on low wages rather than efficient methods to compete. Employers are most likely to be sensitive to wage increases in firms where labor costs constitute a large proportion of total costs and where competition is keen and profit margins are slim.

Not all machinery is introduced because of an increase in labor costs. As a matter of fact, it is possible that in our dynamic economy, only a small part of the substitution of machinery for labor which occurs is attributable to changes in wage rates. The reason is that invention is continuously bringing onto the market new machines and devices which have a high laborsaving potential and which, in many cases, would be profitable to use even if the prevailing wage rates were considerably lower. For example, when the "semiautomatic" was introduced into the bottle industry, the Glass Bottle Blowers Association attempted to compete with the machine by accepting a 45% reduction in the hand price on fruit jars, but this substantial wage cut proved ineffective, and the machine continued to be introduced. Here is an example of a machine which would have been profitable to use even at a wage level 45% lower than that which prevailed when it was introduced. Obviously, its introduction did not depend upon wage increases. Many other laborsaving machines fall into the same category. The point is that while wage increases accelerate the introduction of some machinery, a large part of the new machinery which is applied in industry depends upon research and invention which is not significantly influenced by changes in wage rates. The same is true of the modern development of automation, which was discussed in Chapter 6. The widespread application of automation in industry has depended upon our scientific know-how in the field of electronics and control mechanisms reaching a certain stage of development. On the other hand, a high wage level has been a factor in making the application of automation practical.

Wage Pressure and Invention

We have seen that wage increases can affect the rate at which known mechanical improvement are applied by industry. Does the level of wages also affect the rate at which new methods are discovered? In other words, can wage pressure induce invention?

This is a subject upon which there is considerable theoretical discussion and controversy in the economic literature,[3] but very little substantiation in the form of empirical research. The theory of induced invention is usually associated with the name of J. R. Hicks,[4] who suggested that a rise in the rate of wages (the price of labor) relative to the rate of interest (the price of capital) would induce the discovery of methods of production which would save labor. This theory further postulates that the frequency of laborsaving inventions depends upon the rate of increase in wages relative to interest rates. Laborsaving inventions save labor, whereas capital-saving inventions save capital. According to this theory, if interest rates were to rise relative to wages, there would be a greater inducement to save capital; and as a result, the frequency of capital-saving inventions would increase.

Other economists, however, contend that because of the unpredictable nature of the process of invention, wage increases do not necessarily call forth any increase in the number of laborsaving discoveries. According to this view, most inventions will be laborsaving simply because of the continuing high cost of labor as an element of production and because most invention in our society is designed to lighten the arduousness of work.

However, William Fellner finds some statistical support for the concept of induced inventions. He states:

> A good general case can be made for the assumption that a tendency of labor income to rise relative to non-labor income—and hence a tendency for the weight of labor cost to rise in aggregate factor cost—places a premium on following through those research and innovative projects that are tilted more toward a proportionate reduction of labor costs than of capital costs.[5]

Does wage pressure influence the direction of industrial research projects? One would expect to find major emphasis in research to reduce costs in view of the continuing upward pressure of unions on wages, particularly in large companies which support most of the research activity in this country. However, a study conducted by one of the authors suggests that most research funds are allocated to research on new prod-

---

[3] See, for example, Syed Ahmad, "On the Theory of Induced Invention," *Economic Journal*, vol. 76 (June 1966), pp. 344–57; and William Fellner, "Profit Maximization, Utility Minimization, and the Rate and Direction of Innovation," Papers and Proceedings of the Seventy-eighth Annual Meeting of the American Economic Association, *American Economic Review Supplement*, vol. 56 (May 1966), pp. 27–28.

[4] J. R. Hicks, *The Theory of Wages*, 2d ed. (London: Macmillan & Co., Ltd., 1963), chap. 6, pp. 112–35. See also, for a critique of this theory, Gordon F. Bloom, "Note on Hicks' Theory of Invention," *American Economic Review*, vol. 36 (March 1946), pp. 83–96.

[5] William Fellner, "Empirical Support for the Theory of Induced Invention," *Quarterly Journal of Economics*, vol. 85 (1971), p. 603.

ucts and improvement of present products, rather than to new-process research.

This emphasis on product improvement is not entirely inconsistent with major interest on the part of management in reducing labor costs. Very often, a need arises in one industry for a machine to cut costs, and this idea filters back to a supplier, who then devises a new product or a new machine to help fill this need. A new computer is a new-product development from the point of view of the industry making it, yet can be a significant cost-saving development in the industry utilizing it.

Of course, not all invention occurs in the industrial laboratory. Every employer, every foreman—indeed, every employee—is a potential inventor. Anyone who designs a new way of arranging the flow of production, devises a new attachment for a machine which increases man-hour output, adds to the stream of invention. Wage pressure—like any other pressure on profits—tends to make employers look around for new avenues to save money and thus may stimulate some invention. However, it is doubtful whether there is any close relationship between the rate of wages and the frequency of invention, as suggested by Hicks.

UNION WAGE MOVEMENTS AND INDUSTRIAL EFFICIENCY

In earlier chapters, we noted that union organization has tended to accelerate the adoption by management of two important wage practices. The first is uniformity in wage rates. This is the result of the spread of multiunit bargaining and of union interest in the stabilization on an industrywide basis of hourly earnings, piece rates, or labor costs. There is now double pressure for uniformity in rates—from competitors and from labor itself. The second practice is simultaneity in wage adjustments. This is a by-product not only of multiunit bargaining but also of the growing importance of leader-follower relationships in wage policies. Company executives tend to feel that wage adjustments should not be made unless other companies are making them at more or less the same time. As a result of these two practices, wage increases tend to occur more or less simultaneously and to be of a fairly uniform amount in a large number of industries. Obviously, the effect of a wage increase upon efficiency may be quite different when the wage increase takes place in only one firm in an industry than when it occurs throughout an industry. What, then, is the likely effect of these union wage practices on industrial efficiency?

Favorable Effects on Efficiency

The policy of uniformity in wage rates in an industry may hasten the spread of improved methods of production from the more progressive firms to those that are less efficient. In most industries, three or four large companies do most of the business and set the pace for technological development. If unions compel the smaller firms to pay the same rates as the larger firms, the smaller companies will have to keep abreast of the latest developments if they are to survive.

Unfavorable Effects on Efficiency

While uniformity in wage rates probably contributes to an improved standard of industrial efficiency, simultaneity in wage increases probably lessens the effectiveness of the stimulus which is normally forthcoming from wage pressure. If wage rates are raised generally in an industry, the individual employer, knowing that his competitors are faced by the same rise in cost as he, is much more likely to attempt to pass on the increased labor costs in the form of higher prices to consumers, in the expectation that competitors will follow a similar course, than if he alone had been compelled to grant a wage increase. Price increases are more likely to follow industrywide changes in wage levels than changes within a single firm, because the average businessman, although he has a fair conception of the demand curve for his individual product, either has no notion of the demand curve for the product of the industry or else assumes that it is inelastic within the relevant range. Thus, simultaneous union wage changes facilitate shifting the burden of higher labor costs to the consumer. To the extent that this is accomplished, the inducement afforded to management to increase its efficiency is lessened; and as a consequence, neither mechanization nor technological changes of other kinds may follow the wage increase. Profits may not be cut at all by the wage adjustment, but merely be kept from rising as fast as they otherwise would have in good times.

WAGE CHANGES IN THE ECONOMY AS A WHOLE

We have seen that application of the marginal productivity theory to the problem of wage increases in the individual firm indicates that except in unusual cases of product demand and labor supply, the wage increase will result in a reduction of employment, *other things being equal.* The latter assumption is made to rule out the complications which might otherwise be produced by concurrent changes in the demand for the product or in the state of the arts. As mentioned, if a wage increase occurs in a firm at the same time that the demand for the product of the firm is growing and output is expanding, there need not be any immediate curtailment of employment. However, if other things remain equal—and if, in particular, we assume that the change in the supply curve for labor does not produce any change in the demand curve for labor—the wage increase will, according to orthodox economic theory, produce some reduction in employment in the individual firm.

When we come to analyze the effect of *general* changes in wage rates upon employment in the economy as a whole, we can no longer realistically assume that "other things will remain equal." The demand curve for labor in the economy as a whole is not independent of the supply curve for labor. Or to put the same proposition in a less technical way, changes in the amount of wages paid to labor as a whole are bound to affect the aggregate demand for labor. General wage adjustments affect the demand for labor because labor is industry's best customer, and if labor has more or less money to spend, the change in such expenditures may alter the total volume of employment in the economy. Furthermore, changes in wage levels throughout the economy will affect the profitability of investment, with the result that employers may increase or curtail their purchases of capital goods. This, too, will affect the total demand for labor in the economy.

Determinants of Aggregate Spending

What determines the volume of spending in the economy as a whole at any given time? Our understanding of this problem owes much to the theoretical analysis of John Maynard Keynes, a British economist, who developed a new approach to this problem in his famous work *The General Theory of Employment, Interest, and Money,* which was published in 1936.[6] Keynes talks of total spending as "effective demand." Effective demand consists of two types of spending—spending by consumers, which is called consumption, and spending by businessmen for capital expenditures, which is called investment.

According to Keynes, as long as investment and consumption remain constant from one period of time to the next, output and employment will also be unchanged, and a stable level of income will be maintained from period to period, with no tendency to expand or contract. In order to maintain such a steady flow of income through the productive process, the amount of expenditure upon new investment must, according to Keynes, be equal to the amount which people are prepared to save out of their incomes.

For example, suppose that national income is $1,000 billion and that $800 billion of it is derived from the production of consumer goods, while $200 billion is derived from the production of capital goods. Assume further that consumers are prepared to spend annually $800 billion of their $1,000 billion income on consumer goods and to save the remainder. The total value of goods produced—both consumer goods and capital goods—is thus $1,000 billion, while consumers are ready to spend only $800 billion. Under such circumstances, in order to maintain national income at $1,000 billion in succeeding periods, businessmen must be prepared to spend $200 billion annually on new investment. If interest

---

[6] John Maynard Keynes, *The General Theory of Employment, Interest, and Money* (New York: Harcourt, Brace & Co., Inc., 1936).

rates fall and make investment more attractive, businessmen would borrow money from the banks to undertake new investments; and as a result, income and employment would expand. The same reaction would occur if consumers were to increase their consumption. But if we assume that consumption and investment remain constant, then income and employment will remain constant from one period to the next.

The Effects of a General Wage Adjustment: Special Case

Assume that unions obtain a general increase in wage rates throughout the economy. Assume further that the wage increase has no effect on interest rates or on businessmen's inclination to invest, and no effect on consumption. What effect would the wage increase have on employment? The answer is contained in the assumptions, for, as we have observed, if consumption or investment does not change, employment must also remain unchanged. Prices would rise, but output and employment would remain unchanged. A similar result would follow if there were a reduction in wage rates under these restrictive assumptions. In the latter case, there would be a fall in prices, with no alteration in output or employment.

A major contribution made by Keynes was his attack on the contention of classical wage theory that persistent unemployment was voluntary unemployment. Orthodox economists maintained that if wages were lowered sufficiently, unemployment would disappear. Therefore, the persistence of unemployment was due to the perverseness of workers in not accepting a lower wage. As indicated above, Keynes showed that a reduction in *money* wages would not necessarily reduce unemployment. On the other hand, he indicated that a larger volume of employment might be produced by a reduction in *real* wages caused by a rise in prices combined with constant money wages. This notion, that a rise in prices, namely inflation, might be the price which has to be paid to reduce unemployment, has a remarkably current ring to it. In fact, this is the message of the adherents of the so-called Phillips[7] curve, who see a trade-off between unemployment and inflation. As one writer has aptly put it, "Phillips curve doctrine is in an important sense the postwar analogue of Keynesian wage and employment theory."[8]

The Effects of a General Wage Increase on Aggregate Spending

The foregoing examples of possible reactions to a general wage increase and a general wage reduction are admittedly special cases in the general Keynesian theoretical framework. Keynesian theorists do not maintain that a wage increase will not reduce employment, nor do they

---

[7] For a discussion of the Phillips curve, see Chapter 13 below.

[8] James Tobin, "Inflation and Unemployment," *American Economic Review*, vol. 62 (March 1972), p. 4.

contend that a wage reduction will not increase employment. They merely attempt to show by the use of the foregoing type of example that a general wage adjustment need not affect employment at all and that if employment is affected, it is because of the reaction of the wage change upon the real determinants of the volume of employment—namely, the volume of investment and the amount of consumption expenditures. If these variables are affected favorably, so that total spending is maintained or increased, a wage reduction will increase employment, for there will now be the same or a larger aggregate demand to purchase goods whose cost and, presumably, price have been reduced by the wage cut. On the other hand, in the case of a wage increase, employment will increase only if total spending increases more than proportionately to the increase in prices produced by the higher level of costs.

Four possible reactions of total spending may be distinguished as resulting from a general increase in wage rates:

1. The wage increase may expand total spending more than it increases prices. This might happen if a wage increase were made in times of business depression. Both businessmen and workers might take the wage increase as a signal that business revival was under way and so increase their expenditures. As industry increased its output from very low levels, labor costs per unit of output would tend to decline, and the economies in labor costs resulting from such increase in output might offset the increase in labor costs produced by the wage increase, so that there would be, on balance, little or no increase in unit labor costs or in prices. Under such circumstances the increase in total spending would buy a larger volume of goods and services and thus support a larger volume of employment.

The late Professor Sumner H. Slichter believed that this same result might occur during the upswing phase of a business cycle when general "pattern" wage settlements were involved. It was his belief that when general wage adjustments are made in various key industries at more or less the same time, employers are prone to raise prices because they know their competitors have been saddled with similar increases in cost and are likely to follow suit. Slichter contended that when all or most of the firms in an industry increased their prices, the total amount spent on the product of the industry would ordinarily increase because the demand for the product of most basic industries is inelastic. Therefore, in the short run, expenditures would be increased by customers for the product of the industry; and at the same time, the firms in the industry would be paying out more funds for labor. The combined effect of increased spending from these two sources—given a flexible credit system—might well increase the total amount of spending in the economy more than enough to sustain or increase production at the new level of prices.[9]

---

[9] Sumner H. Slichter, "Labor Costs and Prices," in American Assembly, *Wages, Prices, Profits, and Productivity* (New York: Columbia University Press, 1959), p. 173.

2. The wage increase may increase total spending no more than it increases prices. Such a situation might develop if a general wage increase were made throughout the economy at a time when output was at high levels and a point of full employment had been attained. Under such circumstances the wage increase would produce a sharp increase in costs and prices, and there would be little or no effect on employment. The increased spending would, in effect, be dissipated in the form of higher prices.

3. The wage increase may increase total spending, but not as much as it increases prices. When a wage increase occurs during a period of inflation, it frequently causes price adjustments which are greater than the amount which would be required to compensate for the rise in labor costs. Businesses which have been looking for a pretext to raise prices now do so and blame the price rise on "higher labor costs." As a result, even if total spending increases, the rise in the general price level may be so great that the total volume of spending will be insufficient to purchase all of the goods and services offered at the higher price level, and output and employment may therefore decline in particular industries.

4. The wage increase may not increase total spending and may actually diminish it. This could happen if businessmen become alarmed by the rise in costs and prices, and decide to postpone making new investments until prices come down to a more reasonable level. Consumers also may take a similar view. If this attitude of "wait and see" becomes prevalent, total spending may decline despite the higher level of wages, and employment will be reduced as a consequence.

The Effects of a Wage Increase on Borrowing, Investment, and Consumption

How does a general wage increase bring about a change in total spending? Of primary importance to the Keynesian theorists is the effect of the wage increase on the rate of interest. When wages rise, businessmen are compelled to increase their working capital to meet larger cash requirements for payment of wages. For a time, the banks will be willing to increase loans without raising the rate of interest; but as the volume of outstanding loans increases, banks will ultimately raise interest rates and tend to become more selective in the borrowers to whom they will lend funds. At this point, the volume of spending will be affected in two ways. In the first place, the rise in interest rates will make certain investments unprofitable. Businessmen in some industries will curtail purchase of capital goods, and this will be reflected in smaller wage disbursements to employees in these industries. In the second place, refusal by the banks to loan to particular prospective borrowers because of the general tightening of the credit situation will mean that these businessmen will have to revise their plans and curtail contemplated expansion; and this, too, will affect the volume of aggregate spending.

The increase in wage rates may also affect the anticipated profit rate on investment. If the rise in wages increases labor costs, it may increase the number of business failures and result in a reduction of output and unemployment in marginal firms. This may have a depressing effect on the business community. On the other hand, if the wage increase is viewed by businessmen as the beginning of a general upswing in wages and prices, the profitability of present investment will be increased, since presumably capital equipment will, in the future, be produced at even higher costs. Thus, businessmen may be induced to expand current expenditures upon investment.

A third possibility is that the wage increase will stimulate consumption. The initial effect of the wage increase may be to increase the size of the wage bill for industry at large. Furthermore, the rise in prices may tend to shift real income from fixed-income groups to wage earners who obtain wage adjustments. Some economists believe that as a result of such a shift, a larger portion of incomes will now be spent and a smaller portion saved than under the former distribution. If so, the wage increase will be felt in a higher level of spending in the market for consumer goods. On the other hand, some investigations indicate that consumption expenditures are not likely to be significantly affected by shifts in income among various groups. On the whole, it must be admitted that very little is known about the effect of shifts in income on the consumption habits of various groups in the community; and therefore it is premature to predict what effect wage increases would have on this variable.

It can be seen from the foregoing analysis that the net effect of a wage increase on the volume of spending and the volume of employment depends in large measure on the psychological effect which the wage increase has on the economy. If the increase is viewed as the beginning of or part of a sustained upward trend in business, the outcome is likely to be favorable to employment. On the other hand, if businessmen and consumers feel that costs have gotten out of line and defer purchases, the consequences of the wage increase for employment will be adverse. Furthermore, the effect of the wage increase on employment will be more favorable the earlier in a business upturn it occurs. As a boom wears on, the wage increase is more likely to be dissipated in the form of price increases and more likely to produce a rise in interest rates, with a consequent reduction in investment and employment.

Appraisal of the Keynesian Approach

Although there is some feeling that the advocates of the Keynesian theory overemphasize the importance of changes in interest rates as a determinant of the volume of employment, there is no doubt that they have made an important contribution to clearer thinking in this field by directing attention to the effect of general wage adjustments on the volume of total spending. Orthodox theorists tended to assume tacitly that aggregate demand would remain constant whether wage rates increased or decreased. Consequently, they were led to the conclusion that wage increases would produce price increases, reduced output, and contraction of employment. Keynes, however, demonstrated that aggregate demand is capable of expansion and that, as a consequence, it is possible that general wage increases will be reflected in a general increase in the price level, with no reduction in output or employment. Orthodox theorists tended to think in terms of an inelastic supply of money; Keynesian theorists reason in terms of an elastic money supply,[10] which is the product of our modern credit system.

The Keynesian theory and the modern marginal productivity theory are not inconsistent. Each gives us valuable analytic tools to approach the wage-employment relationship from a different point of view and under different circumstances. When we are dealing with macroeconomic problems involving the level of employment in the entire economy, we will find the Keynesian approach more useful, even if we differ with Keynes in his estimate of the effectiveness of the interest rate as a means of stimulating or curtailing investment and employment. On the other hand, when we are concerned with problems in particular firms or even in particular areas—as, for example, in analyzing the effect of minimum wage regulations on southern firms—we shall find the marginal productivity approach more helpful.

WAGE INCREASES AS A RECOVERY MEASURE IN DEPRESSION

An increase in wage rates in one firm will not ordinarily provide a basis for more jobs, since the rise in wage rates simply increases costs without measurably altering the demand for the output of this particular employer. But when wage rates are increased throughout the economy, the effect of these increased disbursements on general consumer demand cannot be ignored. If there are no leakages, and if the banking system expands the quantity of money sufficiently to maintain a higher level of prices without a rise in interest rates, then the rise in wage cost need not reduce employment and may even increase it if the rise in wages and prices is taken as an indication of the end of a deflationary downturn.

The problem is that wage inflation can produce expectations of further wage and price increases which may, in turn, induce unwar-

---

[10] Although money as such does not figure directly in the basic equations of the Keynesian system, Keynes believed that the bank rate and the quantity of money influenced prices indirectly by their influence on the values of the terms in the fundamental equations linking savings, investment, and output. See R. Harrod, "Reassessment of Keynes's Views on Money," *Journal of Political Economy*, vol. 78, no. 4, part 1 (July/August 1970), pp. 617–25.

ranted inventory accumulation, ultimate cutbacks in production, and resultant unemployment. This condition can develop even though official unemployment statistics are still at a high level. Professor Michael Wachter[11] has suggested that officially defined unemployment, which includes women, youth, and part-time workers may not be an accurate measure of labor market tightness and that if we observe the relationship between the unemployment rate for prime-age males and the level of wage rates, there is evidence that in succeeding business cycles the latter has become more sensitive to changes in levels of unemployment so measured. What this means, in effect, is that in our highly complex and interrelated economy, even though unused plant and equipment still exist and official unemployment figures are high, shortages of key types of labor in strategic industries can cause bottlenecks which can abort a recovery.

Wage increases will not significantly enlarge consumption expenditures if the employed workers who receive wage adjustments simply save the additional income or use it to pay off indebtedness to banks. Moreover, even if the wage increases increase consumption, they may merely improve the short-term outlook for business without affecting the views of the business community concerning the profitability of long-term investment in heavy plant and equipment. Because wage increases tend to affect short-term rather than long-term expectations, any favorable reaction upon business expenditures is likely to be reflected in increased inventory accumulation, rather than in the purchase of fixed plant and equipment. Consequently, a recovery movement which is generated by increased wages is likely to be extremely susceptible to speculative influences.

On the whole, relatively few economic theorists favor wage increases as a device to achieve recovery from a depression. An exception is the school of underconsumptionists, who see in depression the cumulative effect of oversaving; in their view, wage increases are essential to eliminate the prime cause of the collapse of business, namely, the deficiency in consumer purchasing power. However, even granting their argument that it is desirable—and even necessary—to raise *consumption* during depression, this in itself is not enough to assure recovery. It is the propensity to *spend*, not alone the propensity to *consume*, that is the crucial factor in the cyclical process. Spending must be stimulated by *all* groups in the community—by employers as well as by consumers. If every increase in expenditure by consumers were accompanied by a decrease in expenditure by employers, it is clear that no stimulus to business recovery would be imparted by wage increases.

Furthermore, in an economy which depends in part upon exporting to other countries, a general increase in labor costs at a time when other

---

[11] Michael L. Wachter, "The Changing Cyclical Responsiveness of Wage Inflation," in *Brookings Papers on Economic Activity* (Washington, D.C.: Brookings Institution, 1976), pp. 115–59.

nations are undergoing the painful process of deflation may have a detrimental effect on employment in export industries. In our highly interrelated modern world, depressions tend to be worldwide, and recovery measures in one country must take account of conditions in other countries. If wages and prices are raised in this country at the same time that consumers in foreign countries find their incomes diminished and prices in their own countries reduced, our export industries will be less able to compete in foreign markets. The depressed condition of these industries will therefore be aggravated by the wage increase. In the absence of a concomitant increase in tariffs, our imports will be stimulated because domestic consumers will find that many articles can now be purchased cheaper abroad than at home. This may produce an unfavorable balance of payments which may require increased interest rates and a tightening in the money supply at the very time when credit restrictions should be relaxed.

WAGE REDUCTIONS AS A RECOVERY MEASURE IN DEPRESSION

Can a reduction in the general level of wages act as a stimulant to start an upturn of employment and investment in depression? Theoretically, a reduction in wage rates might reduce the rate of interest by diminishing the needs of business for cash. The reduction in the rate of interest might induce increased investment by businessmen. But if it were believed that all that was needed to achieve an increase in investment was a reduction in interest rates, it would obviously be sound policy to change such rates directly rather than to seek to influence such rates indirectly through a reduction of wage rates.

A reduction in wage rates in key industries may stimulate investment and employment, particularly where wage rates have gotten out of line in export industries so that such industries have difficulty in competing in the world market. In 1931 in Australia, wage levels were reduced 10% by order of the Commonwealth Arbitration Board, and this wage cut is generally credited with having contributed to Australia's recovery from the depression. Australia's economy is, of course, heavily dependent upon the prosperity of its export industries. To some extent, something of the same nature may have occurred in 1921 in the United States, when recovery seems to have been materially aided by wage and price reductions which brought our high wartime price structure into alignment with world levels.

However, by and large, wage reductions are not an effective recovery measure because of their tendency to produce anticipations of a further fall in wages and prices and because of their adverse consequences for effective demand. Since the immediate effect of a wage reduction is likely to be a decline in wage payments and consumer expenditures, there must be an immediate compensatory increase in spending by business on inventories or capital goods to prevent a shrinkage in total purchasing power. In periods of depression, however, businessmen typically are in a cautious mood and are unlikely to rush into new investment merely because of a wage reduction. Any savings achieved by them in production costs as a result of the wage reduction may simply be used to pay off debt or to build up bank balances. Thus, wage reductions are likely to reduce effective demand, yet hold forth little promise of stimulating the rate of investment.

APPRAISAL OF WAGE POLICY AS A RECOVERY MEASURE

This brief discussion serves to indicate that wage policy is not a very effective or convenient recovery measure. In those special situations where wage policy can be utilized, its effectiveness will depend upon the nature of the particular depression and the basic causes of the maladjustments existing in the economic situation. In 1929, for example, wage reductions could not halt the deflation due to bank failures, nor could they raise the depressed level of long-term expectations. On the other hand, in 1920–21, wage reductions did contribute to recovery because the high wages left over from the war inflation were *themselves* a cause of the ensuing depression.

The fact that there is no certainty that employment will be increased if wage rates are reduced or increased in periods of business recession strengthens the case for wage rigidity. Maintenance of wages may be the best way to maintain consumption expenditures. It is important to maintain consumption during depression because experience has demonstrated that new investment is not likely to revive until inventories have been used up, and this process of depletion takes time. In the three years 1933–35, it is estimated that business inventories declined nearly $4 billion[12] (measured in 1929 prices). This represents a considerable disinvestment and indicates the large amount of slack which needs to be taken up before investment is likely to resume. During the intervening period of adjustment, maintenance of wages is desirable to prevent cumulative contraction. The policy of maintaining wages during depression which was adopted by Sweden in the early 1930s enabled that country to make a quick recovery from the depression. Wages fell less than 5% in Sweden in the worst year of the depression.[13] On the other hand, no country made such drastic cuts in wages and other costs from 1930 to 1933 as the United States, yet no country suffered more intensely from the Great Depression. In the United States, total payrolls in manufacturing, mining, and steam railroads fell by over half from 1929 to 1932.[14]

---

[12] Simon Kuznets, *National Income and Capital Formation, 1919–1935* (New York: National Bureau of Economic Research, 1937), p. 40.

[13] A. Montgomery, *How Sweden Overcame the Depression, 1930–1933*, trans. L. B. Eyre (Stockholm: Alb. Bonniers Boktryckeri, 1938), p. 52.

[14] *Monthly Labor Review*, vol. 57 (September 1940), p. 538.

The severe wage deflation of the Great Depression is not likely to be repeated in the future unless the pattern of our industrial relations undergoes a sharp reversal. Unions characteristically think of wages as income rather than as a cost and consequently have little sympathy for proposals that wages be rendered "flexible" to assist recovery from depression. The experience of the recession in 1938, as well as during the post–World War II period, suggests that the wage rigidity produced by by such union attitudes may produce a cyclical pattern characterized by an extremely sharp fall in production and employment as declining demand impinges upon rigid wage costs. On the other hand, if consumer income is maintained by social security, relief, and supplementary unemployment benefit payments, a fairly rapid recovery can be achieved, since the relative stability of costs and prices attributable to maintenance of wage rates prevents the strengthening of deflationary forces.

APPENDIX

The derivation of the four rules referred to in the text, which determine the derived demand for labor, can be demonstrated as follows:

Consider a good that is produced by the use of two factors, capital K and labor L. The factors are compensated according to the value of their marginal revenue products (as explained in Chapter 10). Let Q be the quantity of the goods produced according to its production function

$$Q = Q(K, L) \tag{1}$$

Also, let p be the price of the good per unit, w the wage rate per unit of labor input, and r the interest rate per unit of capital input. We are interested in computing the derived elasticity of demand for labor λ given that η is the elasticity of demand for the good and μ is the elasticity of supply of capital.

Since the prices of the inputs are equal to their marginal revenue products by the assumption of profit maximization, we have

$$w = p \frac{\delta Q}{\delta L} \qquad r = p \frac{\delta Q}{\delta K} \tag{2}$$

By the definition of elasticity of demand and supply, we write

$$\eta = -\frac{dQ}{dp} \frac{Q}{p}; \mu = \frac{dK}{dr} \frac{K}{r}; \lambda = -\frac{dL}{dw} \frac{L}{w} \tag{3}$$

If we equate total revenue and total costs, we have

$$pQ = wL + rK \tag{4}$$

Substituting from (2) into (4), we obtain

$$Q = L \frac{\delta Q}{\delta L} + K \frac{\delta Q}{\delta K} \tag{5}$$

If the industry under consideration has constant returns to scale, that is, the production function is homogeneous of degree unity, (5) is an identity and can be differentiated partially with respect to K to yield

$$\frac{\delta Q}{\delta K} = L \frac{\delta^2 Q}{\delta K \delta L} + K \frac{\delta^2 Q}{\delta K^2} + \frac{\delta Q}{\delta K} \tag{6}$$

or

$$K \frac{\delta^2 Q}{\delta K^2} = -L \frac{\delta^2 Q}{\delta K \delta L} \tag{6a}$$

The total differential of Q is written as

$$dQ = \frac{\delta Q}{\delta L} dL + \frac{\delta Q}{\delta K} dK \tag{7}$$

which on substitution from (2) yields

$$pdQ = wdL + rdK \tag{8}$$

By considering a change in the labor force by dL, we can rewrite the equality of revenue and costs in (4) in terms of derivatives as

$$pdQ + Qdp = wdL + Ldw + rdK + Kdr \tag{9}$$

Substituting (8) into (9), we obtain

$$Qdp = Ldw + Kdr \tag{10}$$

From the elasticity formulas in (3) and (10) above,

$$\frac{pdQ}{\eta} = \frac{wdL}{\lambda} - \frac{rdK}{\mu} \tag{11}$$

From the definition of elasticity of supply of capital in (3), we can write

$$dK = \frac{K\mu}{r} dr = \frac{K\mu}{r} d\left(p \frac{\delta Q}{\delta K}\right) \tag{12}$$

Substituting (6a) into (12), we can write

$$dK = \frac{K\mu}{r} \left\{ \frac{-rdQ}{Q\eta} + p \frac{\delta^2 Q}{\delta K \delta L} \left(dL - \frac{L}{K} dK \right) \right\} \tag{13}$$

Writing $\alpha = \dfrac{wr}{p^2 Q \dfrac{\delta^2 Q}{\delta K \delta L}}$ and $\beta = \dfrac{wL}{pQ}$, (11) after substitution from (13)

can be written as

$$\frac{pdQ}{\eta} = \frac{wdL}{\alpha} - \frac{rdK}{1-\beta}\left(\frac{1}{\mu} + \frac{\beta}{\alpha}\right) \tag{14}$$

Eliminating dQ, dL, and dK from the above, we have

$$\frac{\lambda - \alpha}{\eta - \lambda} = \left(\frac{\beta}{1-\beta}\right)\left(\frac{\mu + \alpha}{\mu + \eta}\right) \tag{15}$$

or

$$\lambda = \frac{\alpha(\eta + \mu) + \beta\mu(\eta - \alpha)}{\eta + \mu - \beta(\eta - \alpha)}$$

In this equation, η, β, μ correspond to statements 1, 3, and 4 of the formulation on p. 363 for the long-run effects of wage increases, while α, being the elasticity of substitution, explains statement 2. $\frac{\delta^2 Q}{\delta K \delta L}$ gives the rate of change of the marginal product due to one input for a change in the other. If $\frac{\delta^2 Q}{\delta K \delta L}$ is infinite, $\alpha = 0$ and no substitution is possible, thus implying fixed coefficients of production of the Leontief type with the isoquants in Figure 12–1. If $\frac{\delta^2 Q}{\delta K \delta L}$ is zero, α is infinite and the factors are perfect substitutes for each other with the production isoquants being as shown in Figure 12–2. While $\frac{\delta^2 Q}{\delta K \delta L}$ is a rough measure of the elasticity of substitution, it is not independent of the units of Q, K, and L.

FIGURE 12–1
Production Isoquants for Leontief-Type Technology

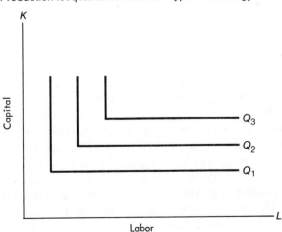

FIGURE 12-2

Production Isoquants Where Perfect Substitutability Exists

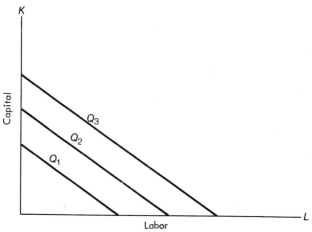

To make it independent of these units, we can multiply it by $\dfrac{p^2Q}{wr}$ and take its reciprocal to obtain a measure increasing with the possibility of substitution.

In order to derive the four rules set out, we differentiate the expression for λ with respect to the four variables η, α, β, and μ.

$$\frac{\delta\lambda}{\delta\eta} = \beta \times \text{a square} \tag{16a}$$

$$\frac{\delta\lambda}{\delta\alpha} = (1 - \beta) \times \text{a square} \tag{16b}$$

$$\frac{\delta\lambda}{\delta\beta} = (\eta - \alpha)(\eta + \mu)(\mu + \alpha) \times \text{a square} \tag{16c}$$

$$\frac{\delta\lambda}{\delta\mu} = \beta(1 - \beta) \times \text{a square.} \tag{16d}$$

A square being always a positive quantity, the signs on the left-hand sides in the above equations are the same as the quantities on the respective right-hand sides.

Since β, the share of labor and total output, is always given by $0 \leq \beta \leq 1$, the expressions in (16a), (16b), and (16d) are always positive. In the case of (16c), we do not have a general rule. So long as μ, the elasticity of supply of capital, is positive and $\eta > \alpha$, that is, the elasticity of demand for the final product is greater than the elasticity of substitution, the third rule is valid. This is almost always true since supply elasticities are positive and the demand for the product is elastic while substitution is difficult.

QUESTIONS FOR DISCUSSION

1. Under what circumstances will a wage increase in a firm have little or no effect on employment in that firm? Under what circumstances will a general increase throughout the economy have little or no effect on employment in the economy?

2. "The effect of a general wage increase on employment in the economy as a whole is simply the sum of the effects of wage increases in all the individual firms in the economy." Discuss the validity of this statement.

3. Discuss the various possible effects of union wage pressure on the level of industrial efficiency. Are the consequences of union wage adjustments likely to differ from the effects of a wage increase in a single firm in an unorganized industry?

SUGGESTIONS FOR FURTHER READING

Gatons, Paul K., and Cebula, Richard J. "Wage-Rate Analysis: Differentials and Indeterminacy," *Industrial and Labor Relations Review,* vol. 25 (January 1972), pp. 207–12.

An attempt to develop a simple model indicating that persistent interregional wage rate differentials are consistent with conventional wage theory and that the existence of a long-run supply range, rather than a curve, introduces an element of indeterminacy into wage rate analysis.

Hicks, J. R. *The Theory of Wages.* 2d ed. London: Macmillan & Co., Ltd., 1963, chap. 6, pp. 112–35.

Statement of the theory which gives major importance to wage pressure as a stimulus to laborsaving invention.

Keynes, John Maynard. *The General Theory of Employment, Interest, and Money.* New York: Harcourt, Brace & Co., Inc., 1936, chap. 19, pp. 257–71.

Statement of the Keynesian theory of the effect of general wage changes.

Sato, R., and Koizumi, T. "Substitutability, Complementarity, and the Theory of Derived Demand," *Review of Economic Studies,* vol. 37 (June 1970), pp. 107–18.

A mathematical analysis and critique of Marshall's four rules of derived demand.

Tobin, James. "Inflation and Unemployment," *American Economic Review,* vol. 62 (March 1972), pp. 1–18.

An outstanding article which compares and analyzes various theories of full employment and employment equilibrium and includes a discussion of Keynesian and Phillips curve analysis.

13

Wages, Productivity, and Inflation

THE AMERICAN ECONOMY faces a productivity crisis. The full impact and nature of this crisis is today becoming apparent to the policymakers of government, to business and union leaders, and to the public at large. The problem arises from the fact that the rate of increase in money wages, which over most of the decade of the 60s had advanced at a rate only slightly in excess of the rate of increase in man-hour output, has now commenced to step ahead of productivity by such large increments as to threaten increases in unit labor costs in excess of 5% per annum.

The rate of annual improvement in productivity is no longer a matter of mere intellectual interest to labor economists. It has become a critical issue, both in labor negotiations and in decisions of public policy. Concrete indicators of the concern which public officials now share as regards this vital issue include former President Richard Nixon's establishment in June 1970 of a National Commission on Productivity to develop recommendations for programs and policies to improve U.S. productivity and former President Gerald Ford's creation of a successor agency, the National Center for Productivity and Quality of Working Life, chaired by the vice president. It is important, therefore, to understand what labor productivity is and how it is measured. In this chapter, we shall consider in detail the nature of productivity, its interrelationships with wages and prices, and the impact of union pressure on inflation. We shall also review various governmental efforts to deal with the problem of inflation.

THE CALCULATION OF PRODUCTIVITY INDEXES

Statistics of increased productivity are generally referred to as showing the increase in productivity of *labor*. This presentation tends to create the impression that in some way, labor is responsible for the increased output and so is entitled to a lion's share of the gains derived from increased productivity. Actually, productivity could just as easily be stated in terms of any other factor used in production, such as dollars of capital invested. Productivity is simply a ratio between output measured in specific units and any input factor, also measured in specific units. For example, most drivers are concerned with the number of miles per gallon they get from their automobiles. This is a simple illustration of output—in this case, mileage—measured in terms of specific input— in this case, gasoline. The same output could be measured in terms of input of tires, or battery, or any of the money, materials, and factors which jointly are responsible for the final output of pleasurable driving. As a matter of custom and convenience, however, statistical series dealing with productivity are usually based upon a comparison over time of output in relation to labor input.[1] It is important to recognize that an index relating labor input and output, such as output per man-hour, reflects the combined influence of many variables, including changes in technology, capital investment, rate of plant utilization, managerial efficiency, and scale of operations as well as changes in the skill, quality, and effort of the labor force.

The most widely used statistics on productivity are those published by the Bureau of Labor Statistics of the U.S. Department of Labor. The Bureau makes available two series, one measuring productivity in terms of output per hour *paid* and the other measuring it in terms of output per hour *worked*. The hours-worked data are derived from a survey of households conducted each month by the Bureau of the Census for the Bureau of Labor Statistics. The hours-paid data are based primarily on a monthly BLS survey of establishment payroll records. Theoretically, the difference between the two measures of labor input is equal to paid vacation time and other paid leave. Since the ratio of hours paid for relative to hours worked is continually rising as a result of the extension of fringe benefits, the productivity index based on hours paid will be lower than the index based on hours worked (that is, the higher the hours input relative to output, the smaller will be the rise in the productivity index). Although most economists agree that hours worked are most useful for productivity calculations, hours paid are more precise for calculations of unit labor cost.

As a result of the difficulties in obtaining and combining outputs of varied plants and industries, practically all statistics of productivity depend upon production data derived either by construction of an index of output or by deflation of a value series. The BLS generally adopts the

---

[1] For a clear and concise explanation of the various concepts and terms used in productivity measurement, it is recommended that the student read U.S. Department of Labor, Bureau of Labor Statistics, *The Meaning and Measurement of Productivity*, Bulletin No. 1714 (Washington, D.C.: Government Printing Office, 1971).

latter technique and measures output in terms of the *constant dollar value of the goods and services produced* in the private sector of the economy. This means that an estimate must be made of the value of the final goods and services produced by the economy, and this figure is then deflated by a price index so as to eliminate the effect of changing prices. The net result, therefore, after such deflation is a figure which, in theory, represents the "real" product of the economy.

Although statistics of labor productivity are frequently carried out to decimal points, they are at best only rough estimates. It is important to recognize that because of the complexity of our economy and the paucity of accurate statistical data concerning its operation, productivity calculations are from beginning to end based upon estimates, inferences, and intelligent guesswork. Nevertheless, over a long period of years, they give a fair indication of the degree of efficiency achieved relative to output in the utilization of labor.

PRODUCTIVITY TRENDS

Since the beginning of this century, there has been a continuous growth in productivity in the American economy. (See Figure 13–1.) As can be seen from Figure 13–2, however, year-to-year improvements in man-hour output have trended downward since about 1965. Output per man-hour in the private economy grew at an annual average rate of 3.2% from

FIGURE 13–1

Productivity in the Private Economy, Farm, and Nonfarm Sectors, 1909–1975

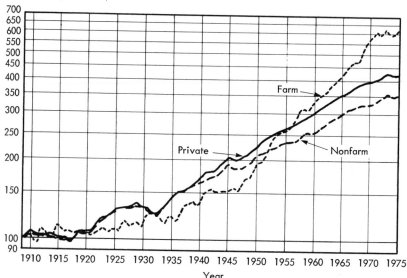

Source: J. R. Norsworthy and L. J. Fulco, "Productivity and Costs in the Private Economy, 1975," *Monthly Labor Review*, vol. 99 (May 1976), p. 9.

FIGURE 13–2

The Decline in Productivity Gains (average annual
percent change)

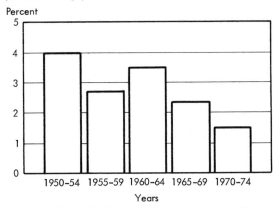

Source: Data, U.S. Department of Labor, Bureau of Labor
Statistics. Chart reproduced from *Nation's Business*, vol. 64
(April 1976), p. 29.

1947 to 1966; then from 1966 to 1975 the annual growth rate dropped
to 1.9%. In 1974, for the first time in the postwar era, output per man-hour
actually declined below the prior year.[2] In 1975, with a better utilization
of plant capacity as a reflection of the business upturn, man-hour output
registered a 1.3% improvement over the prior year.[3] Many economists
forecast a slower rate of productivity improvement in the years ahead.
If this prediction proves true, it would have serious implications in terms
of both our ability to combat inflation at home and our ability to compete
effectively in the international marketplace.

Variations in output per man-hour over the short term must be interpreted with caution because they frequently bear a close relationship
to capacity utilization, particularly in manufacturing. Figure 13–3 shows
the close relationship which exists over time between percentage changes
in output and output per man-hour. Typically, high rates of productivity
gains are registered in early stages of cyclical recovery when previously
unused human and capital resources are tapped. Thus, in the postwar
period, productivity gains were the greatest in the recovery years 1950
(8.1%), 1955 (4.4%), and 1962 (4.7%). Output per man-hour of nonfarm
workers rose 3.4% in 1971, after advancing only 0.6% during 1970, reflecting the revival of production between the two years.[4]

---

[2] U.S. Senate, Report of Committee on Government Operations, *National Productivity and Quality of Working Life Act of 1975*, Senate Report No. 94–335 (Washington, D.C.: Government Printing Office, 1975), p. 2.

[3] J. R. Norsworthy and L. J. Fulco, "Productivity and Costs in the Private Economy,
1975," *Monthly Labor Review*, vol. 99 (May 1976), p. 3.

[4] U.S. Department of Labor, *Manpower Report of the President, 1972* (Washington, D.C.: Government Printing Office, 1972), p. 274.

FIGURE 13-3

Productivity, Private Nonfarm Economy, All Persons, 1967–1976 (percent change over one-quarter span, seasonally adjusted annual rate)

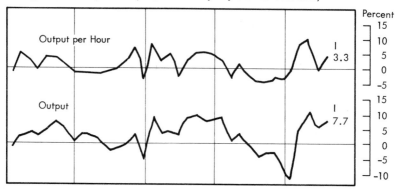

Source: U.S. Department of Labor, Bureau of Labor Statistics, *Chartbook on Prices, Wages, and Productivity*, Washington, D.C., April 1976, chart 16, p. 41.

Diversity in Productivity Performance by Industry

The annual rate of productivity improvement represents an amalgam of many divergent component changes reflecting the different experience of various sectors and industries in the economy. The pace of productivity change has, in the past, consistently been most rapid in agriculture, averaging about 6% per annum, or double the rate of change in nonfarm industries. However, in agriculture, as in other industries, there seems to be a definite slackening in the rate of productivity improvement. Whereas from 1947 to 1968, output per man-hour in the farm sector increased at an average annual rate of 5.9%, from 1969 to 1973 the average annual improvement was only 0.5%.[5] Yields of grain crops have tapered off in recent years, and the increasing utilization of marginally productive land may also have affected labor productivity.

Individual industries in the private nonfarm sector follow quite different patterns in terms of the growth rate in man-hour output. For example, from 1947–73 gas and electric utilities showed an average annual growth of 6.7%; metal cans, 2.3%; air transportation, 7.6%; motor vehicles and equipment, 3.9%; and steel foundries, only 1.4%.[6]

Since the rate of improvement in man-hour output varies among industries, changes in the industry mix can produce an increase or a decrease in the overall rate of productivity even though there has been no change in productivity in any industry. For several decades in the

[5] J. R. Norsworthy and L. J. Fulco, "Productivity and Costs in the Private Economy, 1973," *Monthly Labor Review*, vol. 97 (June 1974), p. 3.

[6] U.S. Department of Labor, Bureau of Labor Statistics, *Handbook of Labor Statistics, 1975*, Bulletin 1865 (Washington, D.C.: Government Printing Office, 1975), pp. 187–200. The Bureau of Labor Statistics publishes output per man-hour statistics for about 35 industries, most of which involve manufacturing or processing.

United States, the shift of workers out of agriculture, where productivity was below average, to manufacturing and other industries, where productivity was higher, has contributed substantially to the overall reported rate of productivity increase. From 1947 to 1966, it is estimated that this shift accounted for about 0.4% of the 3.2% productivity growth per annum in the economy.[7] With the slowdown of the movement from the farms during the period 1966–73, however, this shift accounted for only 0.1% of the productivity trend.[8]

Although in the years ahead this particular shift cannot be counted upon to raise the overall productivity rate, another movement—the shift from goods-producing to service and governmental occupations—may well tend to depress the overall rate of productivity improvement, since productivity has tended to be low in the latter areas. As a matter of fact, economists have calculated that the level of productivity in service industries is about 50% that of manufacturing, and that the rate of year-to-year increase has been 30% to 50% below that in manufacturing.[9]

As pointed out in Chapter 1, an increasing proportion of the American labor force has been employed in government. Some 17% of the civilian labor force already work for federal, state, and local governments, and the percentage is expected to rise during the balance of the decade. This represents a significant portion of the total civilian labor force; yet productivity concepts are difficult to apply to the "output" of such workers. As a consequence, the usual practice of the Bureau of Labor Statistics and the Department of Commerce in constructing overall productivity indexes for the economy is to assume zero productivity growth in government services. Obviously, this assumption has the effect of pulling down the overall rate of productivity growth for the economy as a whole as measured by such indexes.

Measuring the "output" of service industries poses difficult conceptual and statistical problems. Government is, of course, a giant service industry, and the problem of measuring the productivity of governmental agencies presents enormous problems. Nevertheless, because of the need for improved productivity in government and because of the increasing proportion of the labor force which is employed in government—state, local, and federal—the federal government has undertaken a project to measure the productivity of selected departments and agencies whose "output" lends itself to some form of measurement. Table 13–1 indicates the results of such measurement over the period 1967–73. While the productivity of employees in these governmental services increased at an average annual

---

[7] Jerome A. Mark, *Current Developments in Productivity, 1973–74*, U.S. Department of Labor, Report 436 (Washington, D.C.: Government Printing Office, 1975), p. 8.

[8] Ibid., p. 10.

[9] *Business Week*, May 13, 1972, p. 160.

TABLE 13-1

Functional and Summary Indexes of Output per Man-Year for the Measured Portion of the Federal Civilian Government, 1967–1973

[FY 1967=100]

Item	Fiscal year							Rate of change 1967–73[1]
	1967	1968	1969	1970	1971	1972	1973	
Functional groupings:[2]								
Citizens' records	100.0	100.5	103.7	106.7	111.0	116.7	120.0	3.3
Reference services	100.0	102.1	110.7	111.2	111.3	114.2	109.2	1.8
Loans and grants	100.0	105.0	109.4	121.5	135.1	138.1	129.5	5.6
Training and education	100.0	101.6	99.8	97.5	102.8	100.3	101.1	.2
Agriculture and natural resources	100.0	101.2	101.2	102.4	108.0	110.8	111.5	2.0
Regulation	100.0	106.6	114.7	119.6	117.2	116.9	123.0	3.0
Medical services	100.0	102.1	102.4	101.4	100.7	95.3	98.8	–.7
Power	100.0	103.7	123.9	131.9	131.9	138.5	136.5	5.8
Transportation	100.0	110.9	117.7	119.6	113.4	116.7	123.1	2.5
Postal service	100.0	98.3	98.9	99.4	101.6	102.7	108.4	1.3
Specialized manufacturing	100.0	106.5	110.6	120.7	139.8	132.9	128.1	5.2
Standard printing	100.0	98.4	94.4	93.1	87.8	87.2	88.7	–2.4
Procurement and supply	100.0	103.7	114.4	107.7	107.1	106.6	107.6	.7
Overhaul and repair of equipment[3]		100.0	98.7	103.4	110.8	110.6	108.5	[4]2.4
Maintenance of facilities	100.0	102.3	102.6	108.2	110.1	108.2	105.5	1.2
General support services	100.0	106.3	110.1	114.8	128.2	132.4	138.7	5.8
Total of functional groupings	100.0	100.8	102.9	104.0	105.7	106.5	111.1	1.6

[1] Average annual percent change based on linear least squares trend of the logarithms of the index numbers.

[2] The following definitions briefly describe the nature of the organizations classified within each function:

Citizens records—Organizations maintaining records of government obligation to citizens and vice versa, also criminal and hemographic records.

Reference services—Organizations maintaining library or publications services, or developing statistical information for the public.

Loans and grants—Organizations making research grants and various business loans.

Training and education—Organizations overseeing training, education, and social welfare programs.

Agriculture and natural resources—Organizations responsible for overseeing and protecting natural resources.

Regulation—Organizations responsible for enforcing Federal statutes in such areas as interstate commerce, immigration, taxation, and labor.

Medical services—Organizations operating hospitals, clinics, or public health programs.

Power—Organizations responsible for generation, sale, or transmission of electric power.

Transportation—Organizations responsible for operating U.S. canals, and maintaining safe conditions in U.S. airways and waterways.

Postal service—Organization responsible for delivering the mail and providing other services, such as mail insurance and money orders.

Specialized manufacturing—Organizations involved in manufacturing-typed activities, such as printing currency or maps and fish production.

Standard printing—Organizations printing standard text or statistical documents.

Procurement and supply—Organizations responsible for purchasing and distributing supplies.

Overhaul and repair of equipment—Organizations responsible for upkeep of major military equipment.

Maintenance of facilities—Organizations responsible for the operation and upkeep of Federal buildings or installations.

General support services—Organizations performing overall administrative and supportive activities such as personnel, automatic data processing, and budget.

[3] Reference base is fiscal 1968=100.

[4] Rate of change is for fiscal years 1968–73.

Source: U.S. Department of Labor, Bureau of Labor Statistics, *Handbook of Labor Statistics, 1975,* Bulletin 1865 (Washington, D.C.: Government Printing Office, 1975), table 88, p. 201.

rate of 1.6%, employees in the nonfarm economy showed an average annual improvement of about 2.2%.[10]

The Productivity Slowdown

As we have already noted, two circumstances which have probably contributed to the slowdown in the rate of annual improvement in man-hour output since 1966 are the slackening in the shift of employees from agriculture to industry and the increasing share of employment and output represented by service industries. Another factor may be the changing composition of the labor force. Labor force growth accelerated in the late 1960s as the offspring of the "baby boom" era began to enter the labor force for the first time and as women's labor force participation rates rose significantly. New entrants into the labor force typically are less productive because they lack experience, and thus the substantial influx of new entrants may have affected overall productivity rates. The U.S. Department of Labor has estimated that this factor alone may have had an incremental effect in reducing productivity growth to the extent of about 0.3% a year during the latter part of the 1960s.[11]

Other factors which may also have contributed to the productivity slowdown are the leveling off of research and development expenditures, changes in attitude toward work, and a change in the capital-labor ratio. The latter circumstance will be examined in more detail later in this discussion.

Wages, Unit Labor Costs, Productivity, and Prices

During the decade of the 60s, average hourly earnings in the private nonfarm economy rose at an average annual rate of 5.2%, while productivity measured by man-hour output advanced by 2.8% per annum. The result was that unit labor costs rose by about 2.3% annually.[12] Labor cost is the single most important component of price, and in recent years it has constituted about 62½% to 65% of price. As a consequence, there is a fairly close correlation over time between changes in unit labor costs and changes in prices.

Commencing in 1969, the economy has experienced an explosion in unit labor costs. Unit labor costs in the total private economy rose 7.1% in 1969, 6.0% in 1970, 3.1% in 1971, 2.7% in 1972, 5.7% in 1973, 12.3% in 1974, and 7.7% in 1975.[13] These large increases in unit labor costs reflect

---

[10] Mark, *Current Developments*, p. 8.

[11] Jerome Mark, "Productivity and Costs in the Private Economy, 1974," *Monthly Labor Review*, vol. 98 (June 1975), p. 6.

[12] U.S. Department of Labor data.

[13] U.S. Department of Labor et al., *Employment and Training Report of the President, 1976* (Washington, D.C.: Government Printing Office, 1976), table G–2, p. 358.

the influence of two trends. In the first place, the past six years have witnessed a substantial escalation in the magnitude of annual wage adjustments. Table 13–2 shows the size of wage adjustments in recent years

TABLE 13–2
Average Percent Wage-Rate Adjustments in Major Collective Bargaining Settlements, 1970–1975*

Industry Sector and Measure	1970	1971	1972	1973	1974	1975†
All industries:						
First-year adjustment	11.9	11.6	7.3	5.8	9.8	10.2
Average annual change over life of contract	8.9	8.1	6.4	5.1	7.3	7.8
Manufacturing:						
First-year adjustment	8.1	10.9	6.6	5.9	8.7	9.9
Average annual change over life of contract	6.0	7.3	5.6	4.9	6.1	8.1
Nonmanufacturing (except construction):						
First-year adjustment	14.2	12.2	8.2	6.0	10.2	12.0
Average annual change over life of contract	10.2	8.6	7.3	5.4	7.2	7.9
Construction:						
First-year adjustment	17.6	12.6	6.9	5.0	11.0	8.0
Average annual change over life of contract	14.9	10.8	6.0	5.1	9.6	7.4

* Settlements in the private nonfarm economy covering 1,000 workers or more.
† Preliminary.
Data presented in this table exclude increases under escalator provisions, except for those guaranteed in the contract.
Source: U.S. Department of Labor et al. *Employment and Training Report of the President, 1976* (Washington, D.C.: Government Printing Office, 1976), table 3, p. 20.

under major collective bargaining agreements. It should be noted that this refers only to wage adjustments and does not include the cost of various fringe benefits which were also included in these contracts. Although only about one of every five workers in the labor force is a union member and only about one in nine is covered under a major collective bargaining agreement,[14] nevertheless the data included in Table 13–2 are indicative of a stepped-up rate of wage adjustment which has in fact affected all workers, union and nonunion.

At the same time that these large wage and benefit adjustments have been raising unit costs, productivity change—which could produce an offsetting decline in unit costs—has tended to slacken. Thus, most of the increase in wage costs has tended to be reflected in a rise in unit labor costs and ultimately has a major impact on the price level. For example, in 1975, compensation per hour rose 9.1% despite the highest level of unemployment in any post–World War II year. This compares with an

---

[14] Ibid., p. 19.

average annual rate of increase of 5.5% from 1947 to 1975. Since productivity gained only 1.3% in 1975, the result was an increase of 7.7% in unit labor costs.[15] Figure 13–4 shows the interrelationships among hourly compensation, productivity, and unit labor costs.

The balance between wage changes and productivity growth is important, not only because of its impact on the rate of price inflation within the United States, but also because of its influence upon our competitive position in the world market relative to that of other industrial nations. From 1965 to 1970, because of our slow productivity growth, unit labor costs in manufacturing rose more sharply in the United States than in any other countries except Canada and Germany. Japan had the dubious distinction of the most rapidly rising level of money wages of any industrial country, but because it also achieved an astounding annual increment in man-hour output of 14.2%, unit costs rose hardly at all.[16]

From 1970 to 1973, however, a different picture emerges. During this period, productivity gains in Japan and the nine European countries listed in Table 13–3 were greatly exceeded by sharply rising levels of hourly compensation, whereas productivity growth in the United States nearly matched the rise in hourly compensation. Consequently, manufacturing unit labor costs rose much more rapidly in Japan and in Western Europe than in the United States. Recently, there has been some indication that manufacturing costs are again rising more rapidly in the United States than abroad.

The Relation between Productivity and Employment

Increasing productivity is, of course, a manifestation of the dynamic influence of technological change in our economy which over the long run has created more jobs than it has displaced. On the other hand, the year-to-year improvement in productivity has a definite relation to employment which has important implications for governmental policy.

The volume of unemployment in our economy depends upon three major factors:

1. The growth in the labor force.
2. The increase in output per man-hour.
3. The growth of total demand for goods and services.

Changes in the average hours of work are also relevant, though quantitatively less important than the three factors enumerated above. As productivity rises, less labor is required per dollar of total output, or more

---

[15] U.S. Department of Labor, *Employment and Training Report,* p. 18.

[16] U.S. Department of Labor, Bureau of Labor Statistics, *Productivity and the Economy,* Bulletin 1710 (Washington, D.C.: Government Printing Office, 1971), p. 30.

FIGURE 13–4

Hourly Compensation, Unit Labor Cost, and Productivity in the Private Nonfarm Economy and in Manufacturing, 1967–1975

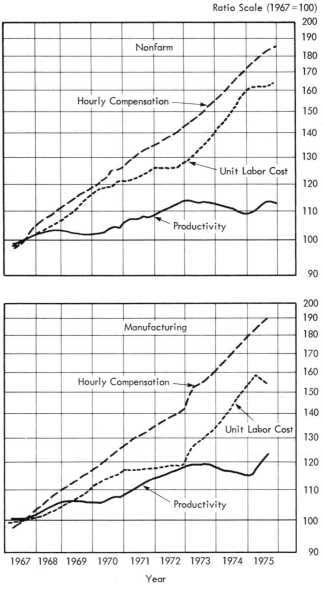

Source: J. R. Norsworthy and L. J. Fulco, "Productivity and Costs in the Private Economy, 1975," *Monthly Labor Review,* vol. 99 (May 1976), p. 5.

TABLE 13–3

Average Annual Percent Change in Manufacturing Productivity and Costs, 12 Countries, 1970–1973

Country	Output per Hour	Output	Aggre-gate Hours	Hourly Compen-sation*	Unit Labor Costs in Na-tional Cur-rency	Unit Labor Costs in U.S. Dollars
United States	5.9	8.0	2.0	6.3	0.4	0.4
Canada	4.9	7.0	2.0	7.8	2.8	4.3
Japan	9.6	8.9	−0.6	18.2	7.9	19.0
Belgium	7.5	4.9	−2.4	16.0	7.9	17.3
Denmark	8.2	6.0	−2.1	14.2	5.5	13.4
France	6.0	6.2	0.2	12.4	6.0	14.3
West Germany	6.1	3.9	−2.1	12.9	6.4	18.1
Italy	7.5	4.6	−2.7	18.4	10.1	13.3
Netherlands	9.0	5.2	−3.5	14.9	5.3	15.0
Sweden	6.3	3.2	−2.9	12.0	5.3	11.8
Switzerland	5.5	3.3	−2.1	11.4	5.6	16.8
United Kingdom	5.1	3.3	−1.8	13.5	7.9	8.9
Eleven foreign countries	6.9	5.5	−1.3	14.0	6.6	15.1
Nine European countries	6.3	4.4	−1.8	13.5	6.8	15.2

* Data for Sweden and the United Kingdom include adjustments for payroll and employment taxes that are not compensation to employees, but are labor costs to employers.

Percent changes computed from the least squares trend of the logarithms of the index numbers.

Source: Patricia Capdevielle and Arthur Neef, "Productivity and Unit Labor Costs in the United States and Abroad," *Monthly Labor Review*, vol. 98 (July 1975), p. 30.

goods and services can be produced with the same number of man-hours. Consequently, if output does not grow, employment will decline; if output increases more rapidly than productivity (less any decline in average hours worked), employment will rise. But we must also take account of the fact that the labor force is growing each year. So unless gross national product (the total expenditure for goods and services in the economy, corrected for price changes) rises more rapidly than the sum of productivity increases and labor force growth (modified by the change in hours of work), the increase in employment will be inadequate to absorb the growth in the labor force, and the rate of unemployment will increase. Only when total production expands faster than the rate of labor force growth *plus* the rate of productivity increase and *minus* the rate at which average annual hours fall will the rate of unemployment be reduced.

FACTORS AFFECTING GROWTH IN OUTPUT PER MAN-HOUR

In the long run, improvement in man-hour output comes primarily from three sources: (1) an increase in the amount of capital per worker; (2) the impact of research and development; and (3) improvement in the quality of the work force. How have these factors influenced productivity in the past, and what is the outlook for the future?

Capital per Worker

Contrary to popular conception, productivity does not depend primarily on human effort. The main reason for increased productivity in the United States is the increased efficiency of machine technology. Not only is the machinery which a worker uses today far more efficient than the machinery in use 50 or 100 years ago, but also the amount of capital used per worker has increased enormously over the years. Figure 13–5

FIGURE 13–5
Capital Invested per Production Worker in Manufacturing Industries

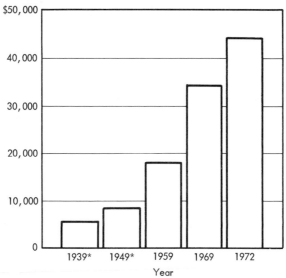

* Estimated.
Source: *Capital Invested in Manufacturing*, Road Maps of Industry, No. 1766 (New York: The Conference Board, 1975).

shows the tremendous increase which occurred from 1939 to 1972 in the amount of capital invested per production worker in manufacturing industries.

Capital invested per production worker in manufacturing industries increased at an average annual rate of 6.7% between 1958 and 1972 and at a higher rate of 8.9% between 1966 and 1972.[17] It appears that the

---

[17] *Capital Invested in Manufacturing*, Road Maps of Industry, No. 1766 (New York: The Conference Board, 1975).

capital-labor ratio grew more rapidly in the United States from 1966 to 1972 than from 1947 to 1966, both in the total private economy and in the nonfarm and manufacturing sectors. In other words, production in the United States not only became more capital intensive between 1966 and 1972, but it did so at a faster rate than was the case between 1947 and 1966. Consequently, changes in the level of capital per worker do not seem to explain the productivity slowdown since 1966.[18]

The rate of man-hour improvement which the American economy will achieve in the decade ahead will depend to a substantial extent upon the maintenance of a high level of new investment in productive plant and equipment. Three major problems face American industry in this regard. In the first place, major demands are being made upon our limited sources of capital for improvements in the quality of life, such as equipment to provide cleaner air and water. Although no one will deny the importance of such efforts, it must be remembered that capital used for such purposes is *not* reflected in a greater output of goods and services. In the second place, numerous studies have documented the fact that the United States could well face a capital shortage in the coming decade. In the third place, research and development expenditures, which provide the opportunities for profitable investment, have tended to taper off in recent years and have declined as a percentage of gross national product.[19] These trends pose major problems to the American economy, particularly when it is considered that a number of our major competitors in the world economy, such as Japan, have higher relative rates of capital spending.

The Quality of Labor

We have seen that there has been a marked reduction in the utilization of unskilled common labor in our modern economy and, on the other hand, a sharp increase in semiskilled, skilled, and professional and technical jobs. Employment of professional and technical workers, who have comprised the fastest growing occupational group during the past decade, will increase about twice as fast as total employment during the decade of the 70s, according to estimates of the U.S. Department of Labor. A further measure of progress in quality of labor is the rising level of educational attainment. Each upcoming generation remains in school longer. For example, in 1950 about 18% of men 30 to 34 years of age had some college experience; by 1970, the ratio had increased to 33%; and by 1990, it is expected to exceed 38%. At present about 23% of women age 30–34 have been to college; by 1990, the proportion will exceed 37%.[20] Figure 13–6 shows the rising educational level of American workers, projected to

---

[18] Mark, "Productivity and Costs," p. 6.

[19] *Research and Development,* Road Maps of Industry, No. 1689 (New York: The Conference Board, 1972).

[20] *The U.S. Economy in 1990* (New York: The Conference Board, 1972), p. 30.

FIGURE 13–6

The Rising Educational Level of Workers: Civilian Labor Force, 18–64 Years of Age

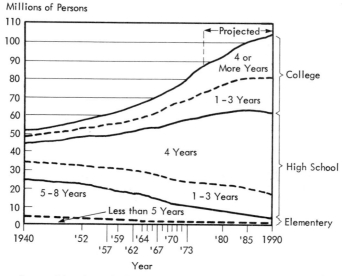

Source: *Educational Attainment of the Work Force,* Road Maps of Industry, No. 1758 (New York: The Conference Board, 1975).

1990. An increase in educational attainment is evidence of an increase in human capital investment. Just as investment in plant and machinery benefits output per man-hour, so, too, does investment in education and the acquisition of specialized skills. The rising level of educational attainment is, therefore, a factor which should contribute to an improvement in man-hour output in the years ahead.

ALTERNATIVE MEANS OF DISTRIBUTING PRODUCTIVITY BENEFITS

Should the gains of increasing productivity be distributed through falling prices or rising money wages? On the whole, reduction in commodity prices would seem by all odds to be the *fairest* method of distributing the benefits of increasing productivity. In large measure, the increasing productivity of labor reflects the combined efforts of the whole community—of savers who contribute the capital equipment, of scientists who pioneer new methods, of entrepreneurs who combine the factors into new and more efficient working teams, and of workers who contribute the skill and brawn to make the technological advances a physical reality. Therefore, if these groups are all to be treated equitably, the increase in productivity representing their joint efforts should be reflected in falling prices, since only in this way can all groups share alike.

Does labor as a group have any special claim to the gains of technological advance that its needs should be given precedence over those of the rest of the community? Labor, as a group, may bear the major share of the inconveniences and dislocations produced by technological change, so that a preferential right to the benefits might be claimed as compensation. However, the particular workers who would get preferential treatment would be those who remain employed at the higher wages, while the ones who actually suffer the "inconveniences and dislocations" would find the buying power of their relief checks reduced by the preferential treatment accorded the more fortunate employed workers. Moreover, labor is not the only group affected by the incidence of technological change. Innovation in one firm may produce bankruptcy in competitors, compelling entrepreneurs to move to other areas to seek new businesses. Similarly, stockholders and bondholders may suffer losses as a result of improved processes in competing firms. Are savers and entrepreneurs also entitled to compensation for the dislocations caused by technological change?

Although it is difficult to prove that labor has any special right to the gains of productivity, some defense of distribution in the form of higher money wages is possible on the ground that unless this method is adopted, the full potentialities of technological progress will not be realized. Some economists believe that the greatest stimulus is afforded to new investment, and adjustment to technological progress is facilitated, when the price level remains relatively stable. Such stability of prices could be achieved by raising money wages as productivity increases. Union leaders recommend this policy, arguing that increased wage payments are necessary to stimulate effective demand and to provide a market for the increased abundance of industrial production.

Other economists, however, maintain that a slowly falling price level is best designed to increase employment and production. They stress the distinction between *productivity* and *production*. Productivity may increase in an industry, yet production may decrease. This occurred in the coal industry, for example, where labor costs were driven up so high as to act as a deterrent to increased production and employment, until recent demands of utilities altered the pattern. Some economists fear that this situation may be duplicated in our economy, with the result that production will not increase fast enough to absorb the workers displaced by technological advance.

Actually, when the problem of distributing the gains of increased productivity is viewed as part of the larger problem of maintaining full employment, there may not be a "best way" of distributing the gains of technological progress. A policy that worked well during the decade of the 20s may not produce the same result during the 70s, account being taken of the rigidities in our labor market resulting from union organization and a possible increase in the importance of administered pricing.

In this complex area of economic analysis, it must be recognized that the effect of reduction in prices or of rising wages upon production and employment will depend upon the stage of the business cycle, businessmen's anticipations, and other circumstances which vary from time to time.

It should also be mentioned that from the practical point of view, little enthusiasm is generated for the policy of falling prices among the general public. Employees, of course, prefer more money in their pay envelope. To trade this for an expectation that prices may fall in the future is to trade a real and present benefit for something which is conjectural and of indeterminate magnitude. Employers also prefer to do business in an economy which has a slight inflationary bias. Such an economic environment is much more propitious for expansion and for taking risks; falling prices have too often been associated with periods of recession and therefore dampen business expectations.

HOW THE GAINS OF INCREASING PRODUCTIVITY HAVE BEEN DISTRIBUTED

Over the last hundred years the typical adjustment of the American economy to technological advance reflected in rising man-hour output has been in the form of rising money wages rather than through a falling price level. No other price series has risen as rapidly as hourly earnings of labor.

The Long-Term Trend in Real Wages

Real wages have risen more or less continuously in this country for over 100 years; during most of this time, union organization was either nonexistent or of negligible importance. As Table 13–4 indicates, in the 61 years from 1914 to 1975 average hourly earnings of production workers in manufacturing rose from 22 cents to $4.72 while real average hourly earnings quadrupled. Since 1967, the rate of advance in real hourly earnings has slowed as the rate of increase in the price level has escalated. Indeed, as can be seen from Table 13–4, real average hourly earnings were actually lower in 1975 than in 1972. It should be cautioned, however, that the figures for hourly earnings are averages and are influenced by the change in the mix of workers which occurred during the years in question. The decline noted in real hourly earnings in the table does not necessarily imply that a typical worker in manufacturing experienced such a diminution. Furthermore, if a price index other than the Consumer Price Index were used to correct money earnings for intervening changes in the price level, a different result might be obtained.

It will be observed that the improvement in real weekly earnings recorded in Table 13–4 is somewhat less on a percentage basis than the

TABLE 13–4
"Real" and Gross Average Hourly and Weekly Earnings of Production Workers in Manufacturing Industries, Selected Years, 1914–1975

Year	In Current Dollars			In 1967 Dollars	
	Hourly Earnings	Weekly Earnings	CPI* 1967 = 100	Hourly Earnings	Weekly Earnings
1914	0.22	10.92	30.1	0.73	36.27
1919	0.47	21.84	51.8	0.91	42.16
1929	0.56	24.76	51.3	1.09	48.27
1933	0.44	16.65	38.8	1.13	42.91
1939	0.63	23.64	41.6	1.51	56.83
1947	1.22	49.17	66.9	1.82	73.50
1948	1.33	53.12	72.1	1.84	73.68
1949	1.34	53.88	71.4	1.87	75.46
1950	1.44	58.32	72.1	1.99	80.89
1951	1.56	63.34	77.8	2.00	81.41
1952	1.65	67.16	79.5	2.07	84.48
1953	1.74	70.47	80.1	2.17	87.98
1954	1.78	70.49	80.5	2.21	87.57
1955	1.86	75.70	80.2	2.31	94.39
1956	1.95	78.78	81.4	2.39	96.78
1957	2.05	81.59	84.3	2.43	96.79
1958	2.11	82.71	86.6	2.43	95.51
1959	2.19	88.26	87.3	2.50	101.10
1960	2.26	89.72	88.7	2.54	101.15
1961	2.32	92.34	89.6	2.58	103.06
1962	2.39	96.56	90.6	2.63	106.58
1963	2.46	99.63	91.7	2.68	108.65
1964	2.53	102.97	92.9	2.72	110.84
1965	2.61	107.53	94.5	2.76	113.79
1966	2.72	112.34	97.2	2.79	115.58
1967	2.83	114.90	100.0	2.83	114.90
1968	3.01	122.51	104.2	2.88	117.57
1969	3.19	129.51	109.8	2.90	117.95
1970	3.36	133.73	116.3	2.88	114.99
1971	3.57	142.00	121.3	2.94	117.06
1972	3.81	155.00	125.3	3.04	123.70
1973	4.07	166.00	133.1	3.06	124.71
1974	4.40	176.00	147.7	2.98	119.16
1975†	4.72	183.00	159.3	2.96	114.88

* Consumer Price Index of U.S. Bureau of Labor Statistics.
† Preliminary.
Source: Data for 1914–66 adapted from The Conference Board, *Economic Almanac, 1967–68* (New York: Macmillan Co., 1967), p. 53; subsequent data from U.S. Bureau of the Census, *Statistical Abstract of the United States, 1975* (Washington, D.C.: Government Printing Office, 1975), table 594, p. 366.

improvement for real hourly earnings. This undoubtedly reflects the influence of a shorter workweek and the fact that workers have chosen to take some of the gains of increasing productivity in the form of leisure time.

Since 1900, real hourly compensation of production workers in manufacturing (average hourly earnings plus fringe benefits deflated by the change in consumer prices) has risen at approximately the same average rate as the average hourly productivity of manufacturing labor. However, the gains of labor extend beyond the increase in purchasing power of hourly earnings; for concomitant with the rise in earnings, there has been a substantial reduction in working time. Furthermore, the average number of days worked in a year has declined substantially through longer vacations and more frequent holidays.

The U.S. Bureau of Labor Statistics now publishes four series indicating trends in real earnings of labor, commencing with the year 1964. The content of these series differs, and their relative movements can vary from year to year. These series are as follows:[21]

1. *Real adjusted average hourly earnings.* This is a monthly series based on average hourly earnings for production and nonsupervisory workers in the private nonfarm economy. The series is adjusted for changes in overtime (in manufacturing only) and shifts in employment among narrowly defined industries. When deflated by the Consumer Price Index, it provides the best measure of changes in real *wage rates.* This is the proper series to use if a comparison is to be made between real wages and productivity, since the data are conceptually and technically consistent with published productivity data.

2. *Real average weekly earnings.* This is a measure of weekly earnings of all production and nonsupervisory workers in the nonfarm private economy deflated by a price index. It is affected by employment and overtime shifts as well as by the average number of hours worked per week. The number of hours could change because of a shift in the overall industrial mix of employment, a change in the number of overtime hours worked, or an increase in the number of part-time workers. This series does not, therefore, measure real earnings of the average worker but only *average earnings for all workers.*

3. *Real compensation to all persons in the total private economy.* This is a measure of real labor payments per hour, but includes supervisory or nonproduction workers, self-employed persons, farm employees, and private household workers. In addition, fringe benefits are included. Unlike series 1, this series is affected by shifts in employment among industries and changes in the amount of overtime worked.

4. *Real spendable earnings.* This is a measure of take-home pay which assumes that the worker has either no dependents or three dependents and is based upon real gross weekly earnings data adjusted for federal income tax and social security tax deductions. The result is affected by the changing mix of workers in the labor force as well as by changes in actual earnings. Therefore, the series does not purport to measure the

---

[21] For a discussion of these series, see Thomas W. Gavett, "Measures of Change in Real Wages and Earnings," *Monthly Labor Review,* vol. 95 (February 1972), pp. 48–53.

spendable earnings of the average worker, but only the *average real spendable earnings of all workers.*

The variance among these series is indicated by the fact that from 1964 to 1970, real compensation per man-hour rose 16.4%; real adjusted average hourly earnings rose 9.3%; real gross weekly earnings rose 4.6%; and real spendable earnings rose 1.2%. If the span 1965–70 is used, real spendable earnings declined by 1.5%![22] This analysis indicates how it is possible to secure a series to substantiate almost any position in economics, particularly when a change in the base period can materially alter the end result!

Labor's Relative Share of National Income

Has the rise in the price of labor given labor as a group a larger share of the increased national income? Some economists answer in the negative. They claim that the percentage of national income going to labor has remained relatively constant over a long period of years, except in deep depression. This statistical record has led some economists to conclude that for the material prosperity of labor as a whole, it makes no great difference whether money wages rise swiftly or slowly, or whether labor is organized or unorganized; for—according to these economists—without regard to these factors, labor's distributive share tends to remain fairly constant over time.[23]

Presumably, the mechanism that would produce this result would follow one or the other of the following avenues: (1) Money wages are pushed up and are followed by price increases, with the result that labor does not succeed in improving its position relative to that of other factors of production. (2) Money wages are pushed up; other prices are not raised correspondingly; and employers suffer a reduction in profits, curtail the use of labor, and substitute capital, with the same result as in (1).

Upon analysis, however, it will be found that the statement that labor's distributive share has remained fairly constant is both ambiguous and inaccurate. In the first place, what is meant by "labor's distributive share"? We can compare the share of compensation of employees as a percentage of national income, as a percentage of privately produced income, or as a percentage of income originating in corporate business, to cite only a few possibilities. As can be seen from Table 13–5, the results shown by the various series are not the same. In the second place, analysis

---

[22] Ibid., pp. 49–50.

[23] For example, in an article appropriately called "A Law That Cannot Be Repealed," Professor Sidney Weintraub presents statistics purporting to prove that since 1900, American business enterprises have spent roughly 50 cents of each dollar of sales revenue on wages and the remainder on interest, rent, profits, and taxes. See *Challenge*, April 1962, p. 18.

TABLE 13–5

Share of Compensation of Employees in Various Income Totals, 1929–1970

Year	As Percent of National Income	As Percent of Income Originating in Corporate Business	As Percent of Income Originating In Private Industry
1929	58.2	74.2	55.6
1930	61.9	78.5	59.0
1931	66.6	87.9	63.2
1932	73.0	101.1	69.3
1933	73.6	101.6	69.5
1934	70.0	88.1	65.6
1935	65.4	83.3	60.8
1936	66.1	79.7	61.3
1937	65.1	79.7	61.0
1938	66.6	82.3	61.8
1939	66.1	80.5	61.6
1940	63.9	75.8	59.5
1941	61.9	72.4	57.6
1942	61.9	71.5	56.8
1943	64.3	72.0	57.6
1944	66.4	73.6	58.8
1945	68.0	76.8	59.8
1946	65.1	79.5	60.1
1947	65.0	77.0	61.3
1948	63.1	74.3	59.5
1949	64.7	75.4	60.7
1950	63.7	73.1	59.8
1951	64.6	73.3	60.3
1952	66.7	76.2	62.3
1953	68.3	77.9	64.2
1954	68.8	79.2	64.6
1955	67.8	76.5	63.6
1956	69.1	78.5	65.1
1957	69.6	79.4	65.6
1958	70.0	80.7	65.6
1959	69.5	78.4	65.3
1960	70.8	80.2	66.6
1961	70.9	80.6	66.5
1962	71.2	80.5	66.7
1963	70.8	80.0	65.4
1964	70.6	79.2	65.2
1965	69.8	75.1	64.6
1966	70.2	77.9	65.2
1967	71.5	79.6	65.8
1968	72.4	79.9	66.7
1969	74.0	82.3	68.6
1970	75.6	84.5	70.1

Source: Gertrude Deutsch, *Relative National Accounts,* Technical Paper No. 4 (New York: National Conference Board, 1964), pp. 19–22; *Economic Report of the President, 1972* (Washington, D.C.: Government Printing Office, 1972), table B–12, p. 209; *Survey of Current Business,* tables on national income, 1964–72.

of the two most comprehensive series—relating employee compensation to national income and to privately produced income—indicates that there has been a definite shift in distribution of income to labor over the period studied.

If we examine the movement of the series which compares employee compensation with national income, it appears that labor's share has increased significantly during the post–World War II period. From about 65% in 1947 (see Table 13–5), labor's share rose to 74.5% in 1973.[24] An important factor in the rising share of labor has been the growth in the supply of capital, which has increased more rapidly than the increase in man-hours worked. Furthermore, rising prices may have adversely affected the income of renters, and thus contributed to an increase in the relative share of labor.

It should be observed that even if labor received only a constant share in national income based on reported statistics, it would still be gaining materially relative to other groups, for in the past 50 years labor has achieved greater gains in leisure time than has any other group. It has been estimated that during the decade of the 1960s about 8% of productivity gains in private industry were taken in the form of paid leisure, with the remaining 92% in higher pay.[25] Furthermore, enormous improvements have been made by labor in various nonwage benefits, so that the real improvement in labor's relative status is substantially greater than is shown by income figures.

Although labor as a whole may have increased its share in national income, this does not mean that all groups within labor have fared equally well. If strong unions, such as the Steelworkers and the Automobile Workers, win large wage increases which set off an inflationary spiral, whereas bank clerks, for example, obtain only small wage increases, the effect may be to redistribute real income from the latter to the former.

WAGE POLICY AND PRODUCTIVITY CHANGES

What is the "best" relationship between wages and productivity, taking account of the institutional rigidities in our economic system and the objective of avoiding inflation? In 1962, the Council of Economic Advisers adopted so-called wage-price guideposts as a standard for the public to use in judging the extent to which private price and wage decisions were consistent with the public interest in a noninflationary economy. From 1962 to 1967—when the Council ceased recommending a specific percentage figure and simply called for "restraint" in wage changes—the Council suggested a norm for wage adjustments approximating the trend rate for productivity in the economy as a whole, or

[24] *Economic Report of the President, 1974* (Washington, D.C.: Government Printing Office, 1974), p. 266.

[25] *Fortune,* vol. 91 (April 1975), p. 97.

about 3.2% per annum. The Council recognized that productivity changes vary substantially from year to year and therefore recommended that the trend rate over a number of years be used as the guide for labor and business to follow in their wage negotiations.

In the words of the President's Council of Economic Advisers:

> The general guide for noninflationary wage behavior is that the rate of increase in wage rates (including fringe benefits) in each industry be equal to the trend rate of overall productivity increase. . . . The general guide for noninflationary price behavior calls for price reduction if the industry's rate of productivity increase exceeds the overall rate, for this would mean declining unit labor costs; it calls for an appropriate increase in price if the opposite relationship prevails; and it calls for stable prices if the two rates of productivity increase are equal.[26]

Any guide to wage policy, however, must recognize that wages are not only a cost and therefore a determinant of prices, but also a price reflecting the influence of supply and demand in the labor market. The Council of Economic Advisers recognized this ambivalent role of wages and spelled out two circumstances in which variations should be permitted in the general guide in order to permit adjustments in the labor market:

1. Wage rate increases should exceed the general guide rate in an industry which would otherwise be unable to attract sufficient labor or where wage rates have been exceptionally low.
2. Wage rate increases should be less than the general rate in an industry which could not provide jobs for its entire labor force even in times of generally full employment, or where wage rates have been exceptionally high.[27]

The rate of productivity change does not bear any necessary relationship to the rate of expansion or contraction in an industry. Therefore, a further modification of the general guide was suggested by the Council to take account of movements of capital into or out of an industry:

1. Prices should rise more rapidly or fall more slowly than indicated by the general wage guide in an industry where the level of profits has been insufficient to attract capital required to finance a needed expansion in capacity, or in which costs other than labor costs have risen.
2. Prices should rise more slowly or fall more rapidly than indicated by the general guide in an industry in which the relation of productive

---

[26] *Economic Report of the President, 1962* (Washington, D.C.: Government Printing Office, 1962), p. 189. The "trend rate" is the annual average percentage change in output per man-hour during the latest five years. A mathematical exposition of the theory upon which the guideposts rest is set forth in the appendix to this chapter.

[27] Ibid.

capacity to full-employment demand shows the desirability of an out-flow of capital, or in which costs other than labor costs have fallen, or where excessive market power created a higher rate of profit than can be earned elsewhere on an investment of comparable risk.[28]

It should be observed that the statement that wage rates should rise at the same pace as man-hour output does not mean that the entire increase in man-hour output should go to labor. If this result were to follow, nothing would be left over to pay a return on the increased amount of capital used to produce the increased output. An example will make this clear. Suppose that employee compensation for the economy as a whole averages $4 per hour and that the value of output per hour averages $6. Suppose that over a period of years, average output per hour rises to $8. If wages are to rise at the same rate as man-hour output, they should rise by one third—from $4 to $5.33 per hour. If wages rose by $2 an hour, equal to the full value of the increase in output per hour, the dollar amount of profits and interest per hour's work would be unchanged. This would mean that the return per unit of capital would actually fall, since the amount of capital used per hour has tended to increase over time and is perhaps the major factor responsible for increasing productivity. It is obvious, therefore, that if labor were to attempt to appropriate for itself the entire increase in man-hour output, there would be little point in investing additional capital in business. Capital formation would be discouraged, and the ultimate result would be a decline in investment and a diminution in job opportunities.

Today the notion that wages should advance only in accordance with increases in productivity is more an intellectual exercise for economists than a practical reality at the bargaining table. With only four exceptions, unit labor costs have increased in every year since 1946.[29] In other words, wages have advanced faster than has output per man-hour despite great strides in technology and mechanization. Labor leaders tend to look at productivity improvement as establishing a floor for wage demands rather than a ceiling.

GOVERNMENTAL WAGE STABILIZATION

If governmental persuasion and governmental wage guidelines do not suffice to temper the size of wage adjustments, can governmental regulation control the movement of wages and prices? The United States

---

[28] Ibid.

[29] Jules Backman, "Emerging Trends," in J. Backman (ed.), *Labor, Technology, and Productivity in the Seventies* (New York: New York University Press, 1974), p. 17.

and a number of foreign nations have attempted this route to stabilization. The problems encountered are discussed in the following section.

World War II Wage Stabilization

In 1939, the United States possessed a relatively large volume of unused resources, both labor and plant. Under these circumstances, the country was able to commence war production without serious inflation at the outset. Nevertheless, new purchasing power created by increased employment in war industry caused purchasing power to expand at a more rapid rate than output of civilian goods. This, plus shortages of key skills, products, and equipment, tended to push prices up before unused resources of men and machines were fully employed.

At the time of the Japanese attack on Pearl Harbor on December 7, 1941, the National Defense Mediation Board, an agency to deal with strikes which interfered with defense production, had already been established. This agency, however, was threatening to fall apart. President Franklin D. Roosevelt therefore convened a special Labor–Management Conference, which resulted in the establishment of the National War Labor Board (WLB).

Until October 1942, the WLB had no authority over voluntary wage adjustments. During the first nine months of its existence, however, when its sole concern was with cases involving disputes between labor and management, the WLB developed its basic stabilization program, which was later applied both to voluntary requests for wage adjustments (submitted either by management alone in nonunion plants or jointly by union and management in union plants) and to cases in which the WLB decided disputes between unions and management.

The core of this program was the so-called Little Steel Formula. Basically, this formula provided that establishments which had not had an increase of 15% in average straight-time hourly earnings since January 1941 (equivalent to the rise in living costs between January 1941 and May 1942), should be permitted to increase wages to this amount. It is noteworthy that wages were thus stabilized at this level without regard to increases in the cost of living which followed after May 1942.

Wages are, however, almost never, in the strict sense of the word, stabilized. Rather, wages are restrained. Thus, although the WLB stabilized basic wage rates in accordance with the Little Steel Formula, wages continued to rise throughout the World War II period. This happened because workers received wage increases on account of promotions, by changing jobs, by receiving merit or length-of-service increases, or by alteration of piece rates. Then, too, workers increased their earnings (without altering wage rates) by working overtime and by working evening or night shifts, for which a bonus or "shift differential" was paid. Finally, although wage rates were stabilized, the WLB permitted the institution and liberalization of fringe benefits, such as vacations, holidays, and health and welfare plans; and the WLB granted wage adjustments to eliminate inequities and substandards, and to aid in war production.

Dispute Cases versus Stabilization

To stabilize wages and settle labor disputes at the same time is both conflicting and complementary. It is conflicting in that frequently a dispute can most easily be settled by ignoring stabilization. "Quickie" strikes during World War II were frequently strikes against stabilization rather than against the employer, who was often willing to pay higher wages but was not permitted to do so. If, however, stabilization is ignored in order to settle a dispute, obviously the way would be clear to circumvent stabilization simply by invoking a dispute.

The Effects of World War II Stabilization

The rise in the cost of living between January 1941 and July 1945 was approximately 33.3%. During the same period, basic wage rates increased about 24%; straight-time hourly earnings, adjusted for employment shifts, 40.5%; gross hourly earnings, 51.2%; and gross weekly earnings, 70.5%.[30]

In terms of spendable earnings, the increases were much smaller. Inflation control involves the use of taxes and credit controls as well as of wage and price controls. Between January 1941 and July 1945, the average worker supporting a wife and two children had increases in spendable earnings (real earnings less federal taxes) of 24%; the average single worker's spendable earnings increased only 11.6%.

On the basis of these data, a good case can be made that wages during World War II were stabilized about as well as could be expected. Partially, perhaps, because wages and prices were controlled well and decontrolled too fast, a dramatic wage-price spiral featured the immediate postwar years, pushing consumer prices up at a rapid rate. When it appeared that wages and prices were approaching stability, the Korean War began, and a new wage-price spiral commenced.

WAGE STABILIZATION DURING THE KOREAN WAR

When the Korean War started in June 1950, the United States had been experiencing a decade of war and postwar prosperity of unprecedented magnitude, and full employment of manpower and equipment.

---

[30] National War Labor Board, *Termination Report,* vol. 1 (Washington, D.C.: Government Printing Office, n.d.), p. 55.

The inflationary impact of the Korean War was immediate—but immediate more because of psychological than because of basic economic factors. For despite full employment, war expenditures in bulk did not occur until *after* the greatest price increases. Inflation resulted, not from a shortage of supply relative to demand, but because people *expected* shortages to occur and because they *expected* prices and wages to be stabilized.

Although wage and price control legislation was enacted soon after the Communists invaded South Korea, President Harry S Truman's administration did not invoke it until a serious wage-price spiral had already occurred. Once price and wage controls were invoked, the runaway course of inflation was halted. In view of the psychological character of the inflation and the lack of any genuine supply shortage relative to demand, it is logical to assume that the slowness to invoke controls was a costly mistake. Once controls were invoked, however, they worked quite differently from those of World War II.

The Wage Stabilization Board

Wage stabilization during the Korean War was administered by the Wage Stabilization Board. Whereas the War Labor Board of World War II was created as an agency with power to act only in dispute cases and later was granted authority over voluntary wage adjustments, the Wage Stabilization Board was created to control voluntary wage adjustments and later was given limited control over dispute cases. Although a dispute case—the Steelworkers–Big Steel controversy—just about put the finishing touches on the work of the Wage Stabilization Board, most of the controversies before the WSB were cases in which employers and unions joined forces in an endeavor to obtain special consideration.

In general, the approach of the War Labor Board of World War II was to set policy on the basis of its decision in individual cases, particularly dispute cases. The approach of the Wage Stabilization Board was quite different. After wages and prices were temporarily frozen on January 25, 1951, the WSB began promulgating regulations governing the conditions under which merit, length of service, promotion, inequity, and other increases could be granted without specific WSB approval. Unions and managements which wanted permission for larger increases than were allowed by the general regulations then had to request specific permission from the WSB. As requests were granted, the general regulations were changed, so that although *initial* policy was set by general regulations, specific cases modified the regulations and resulted in new ones.

In a real sense, the wage stabilization picture during the Korean War resembled a game of leapfrog. A general regulation setting a permissive wage increase ceiling was laid down. A special case came up, and the increase permitted jumping the ceiling. Soon after the price-wage freeze on January 25, 1951, these "leaps" proceeded rapidly; then, for a while, they slowed down. In the end, they took one big leap—the steel case—and then wage stabilization virtually collapsed. Wage controls were anything but a conspicuous success during the Korean War.

ANALYSIS OF THE WAGE CONTROLS OF WORLD WAR II AND OF THE KOREAN WAR

Why did wage controls work quite differently during World War II than during the Korean War? There are several reasons, grounded in the different character of the two periods and of unions and employers during those periods.

We have already noted some of the different economic and psychological conditions of the two periods. The differences in the psychological conditions were as important as, if not more important than, the differences in the economic conditions. World War II was an all-out effort psychologically. Contributing to inflation was unpatriotic. Nearly everyone was involved emotionally in the war effort. The Korean War, by contrast, was a partial effort, psychologically and emotionally as well as economically and militarily, especially as soon as the hopes for easy victory faded. Under those conditions, concern with the general problem of inflation was decidedly secondary in most people's minds.

Different as were the economic and psychological conditions during World War II and the Korean War, they were no more different than were the attitudes of management and labor. During World War II, management still fought unions on the prime issues of wages, fringes, and union security. Indeed, management of the early 1940s can truly be said not to have accepted unions as a permanent institution. Consequently, management fought unions hard on the crucial issues of wages. *It appears quite clear in retrospect that wage stabilization succeeded so well during World War II because employers feared that wage increases would be ruinous to them and therefore supported stabilization.*

By the time the Korean War broke out, managements, especially of large companies, had found that they could live with unions, even with large wage increases, fringes, and the granting of union security. Consequently, these employers were more interested in labor peace than in wage stabilization. The president of General Motors argued before the Wage Stabilization Board against freezing the cost-of-living and annual improvement increases in his agreement with the United Automobile Workers at least as vehemently as did the president of the UAW.

The unions of the Korean War had changed since the beginning of World War II as much as employers. At the start of World War II, unions were new in most industries, insecure and unaccepted. They gladly accepted union security in place of wage increases, and then fringes to keep wage rates stable.

By the time the Korean War began, unions had gained acceptance, security, fringes, and large wage increases after surviving the postwar labor strife rather handily. Being responsive to their membership, the unions saw no answer but wage increases to offset the effects of rising prices on union members. With management anxious to cooperate, the unions obtained what they wanted.

"Stabilization" by Big Bargains

During World War II the government, acting through the War Labor Board, a tripartite agency, composed of an equal number of labor, management, and public representatives, established its stabilization norm—the Little Steel Formula—and stuck to it, with some yielding on the fringes. The nature of the then current war, the economic and psychological situations, and the prevailing character of labor and management relations made that possible.

During the Korean War the government adopted no such independent position. Essentially, what the Wage Stabilization Board did was to take the top national bargains and turn them into governmental policy. When a bargain exceeded such policy it was sometimes turned down; but often, it was approved as a special case. The nature of the then current war, the economic and psychological situations, and the prevailing character of labor and management relations again made that possible.

The effect of stabilizing at "big bargain" levels, as the Korean War WSB did, is undoubtedly to push wages of some companies higher than would occur otherwise. For once the top limits are set, unions, in response to the membership, push for the limit. It would probably be accurate to state that the Korean War stabilization program was not only started too late but was also maintained too late. For after the institution of controls stopped the psychological inflation, in the absence of serious supply-demand disequilibriums, the controls tended to push wages up to the big bargains rather than to keep them stabilized.

THE NIXON ADMINISTRATION WAGE AND PRICE CONTROLS

The comparative experience of wage controls during World War II and the Korean War sheds much light on the difficulties faced by an economy which attempts to control wages. Lacking similarity with the economic conditions of World War II, and lacking also the patriotic and psychological factors involved therein, one could predict great problems in any attempt to control—or more accurately, to restrain—wages. Yet, by the end of the summer of 1971, it was apparent that some strong action needed to be taken by government to check the escalation of expectations with respect to wages and prices. Each round of wages was becoming larger than the preceding one, and despite large money wage adjustments, weekly spendable earnings of employees were no higher than in 1965. Against this background, George Meany, president of the AFL–CIO, publicly stated that organized labor would accept wage and price controls provided that the controls covered profits, rents, interests, and all prices.

The second quarter of 1971 brought with it a rapid deterioration in the U.S. balance-of-payments position. The trade balance, which had improved briefly in the first quarter fell sharply in the spring. There was a strong outflow of funds from the United States, and speculation was rife that there would be devaluation. The nation was faced by a deteriorating position in world markets, a 6% unemployment rate, and a mounting level of wages and prices.

On August 15, 1971, President Nixon—who had heretofore been an outspoken critic of governmental wage and price regulation—announced a dramatic change in policy. The United States suspended the convertibility of the dollar into gold or other reserve assets for the first time since 1934. It imposed a temporary surcharge on dutiable imports. Prices, wages, and rents were frozen for 90 days. The international measures and the wage-price controls were both designed to create conditions in which a more expansive budget policy would be safer and more effective in dealing with the persistent problem of unemployment. The imposition of such controls represented a unique chapter in American economic policy, since the action was taken when the nation was not formally at war and the economy was operating at significantly less than full capacity in both the product and labor markets.

At the end of the 90-day period, the president unveiled the outlines of the continuing wage and price control procedure, which became known as "Phase II." The administration sought to control wages and prices in the economy primarily through stringent controls on large companies.[31] A major reason for this emphasis was the desire to avoid the establishment of a huge governmental bureaucracy. Responsibility for price controls was delegated to a 7-member Commission composed wholly of public members, while wage controls were to be administered by a 15-member tripartite Pay Board consisting of representatives of labor, business, and the public.

The announced goal of the administration was to reduce inflation to about a 2½% per annum price rise by the end of 1972. With this rate of permissible price increases and with an assumed rate of productivity advance of 3%, the Pay Board initially set its standard for permissible wage adjustments at 5.5%. Recognizing that it would be presented with

---

[31] At the end of six months of operation under Phase II, the Cost of Living Council lifted controls from 5 million small businesses, leaving only 1.5 million large companies subject to wage and price constraints (*Business Week,* May 6, 1972, p. 23).

some hardship cases, the Board further decreed that it would, in special cases, permit wage adjustments in excess of 5.5% but no greater than 7% if such adjustments were necessary to bring the cumulative increase during the last three years to 7% per year, or to preserve certain limited traditional relationships with wages in other trades or industries, or to attract labor in shortage situations.

The problem raised by fringe benefits caused a further modification of the Pay Board's goals. Congress gave the Board a mandate to exclude contributions to fringe benefit plans that were not "unreasonably inconsistent" with the 5.5% standard. The Board interpreted this to permit fringe benefits contributions of up to 0.7% of total compensation. Therefore, as a practical matter, this allowance had to be added to the 5.5% wage standard.

The Board soon found that the only hope for its continued existence was to play the law of averages. Some contracts would have to be approved even though they violated the standards, but it was hoped that there would be a sufficient number of contracts below the standard so that the overall goals of stabilization could be achieved. Thus, the Board approved a 16% single-year wage-fringe increase under the bituminous coal contract. In January 1972, the Board vetoed 12% increases requested under aerospace contracts but approved 8.3% first-year increases and further agreed that the unpaid balance could be added to second-year adjustments provided for under the contract. A major stumbling block was presented by the West Coast Longshoremen's contract, which provided for a 20.9% increase in wages. After much controversy, the Board disallowed the amount requested but agreed to approve 14.9%, even though this was far in excess of the standards set by the Board.

Organized Labor and Phase II Stabilization

From the day the Pay Board was established, it was involved in acrimonious conflict with organized labor. At first, the labor members refused to serve at all, until President Nixon, in a memorandum to George Meany, AFL–CIO president, agreed that the Pay Board would be autonomous and that the Cost of Living Council, appointed by the president to supervise the stabilization effort, would not "approve, revise, veto, or revoke standards or criteria developed by the Pay Board." Once the Board was in operation, the labor members frequently found themselves outvoted by the public and business members of the Board. Finally, on March 22, 1972, all of the labor members except Frank Fitzsimmons, president of the Teamsters' Union, resigned from the Board. In leaving the Board, Meany charged that it was not really tripartite but represented a coalition of business and political interests. He further criticized the entire stabilization program as a one-sided affair in which profits were permitted to increase, interest rates were not regulated, and workers found their wages controlled while the prices they paid for the necessities continued to rise. President Nixon then reconstituted the Pay Board with a corresponding reduction of business members and stated that it consist of five public members, one labor representative, and one business member. The newly constituted Board continued to operate through the balance of 1972. Then, on January 11, 1973, the president unexpectedly announced the termination of both the Pay Board and the Price Commission and the initiation of a so-called Phase III in which existing wage and price regulations were made advisory and the administrative functions of the two agencies were given to an expanded Cost of Living Council, except with respect to construction, food processing and retailing, and health services.

Phase III was intended to be a transitional stage in the process of removing mandatory wage and price controls. The shift failed because a new surge in inflation began, sparked by mounting fuel and energy costs that brought with them increasing pressure to reinstate tougher controls. Finally, in June 1973, a new price freeze was promulgated for 60 days. This freeze covered only prices, with wages to be adjusted under existing standards and procedures. At the expiration of the price freeze, Phase IV was begun. Under Phase IV, the freeze was lifted on a sectoral basis as sectors were placed under regulations similar to those that prevailed during Phase II, though somewhat more stringent. Phase IV commenced with the announced intention of achieving decontrol on a sector-by-sector basis. The end of controls came on April 30, 1974.

Appraisal of the Phase II Wage Stabilization

The effectiveness of the price and wage controls imposed under authority of the Economic Stabilization Act in August 1971 and continuing for more than 32 months will be long debated and probably never resolved. The reason for an inconclusive judgment is that there is no way of accurately simulating the course of events which would have occurred in the absence of controls. One thing is certain: if wages and prices should again begin to escalate at a potentially dangerous rate, there will be those who will point to the Nixon stabilization as evidence of the success of controls, and an equally vociferous group who will cite the same experiment as evidence of their failure.

It is clear that the Pay Board did not achieve its announced objective of holding wage increases to 5.5%. First-year increases approved by the Board in 1972 in new collective bargaining agreements covering more than 1,000 employees averaged about 7%. Furthermore, it seems clear that powerful unions could be reasonably certain of doing better than 7% while companies with nonunion employees were likely to be frozen at the 5.5% limit. The power of labor unions in Congress was not lost on Board members. When the unions could not obtain retroactivity through the Pay Board, they succeeded in persuading Congress to write it into law.

The Phase II control system and the systems that followed relied on wage controls to attain price stability. Price controls were based on markups and pass-throughs. If costs rose, prices could also rise. The success of the whole program, therefore, hinged on wage controls.[32] The wage controls, however, were not entirely effective. The Pay Board undoubtedly reduced some increases below what they would otherwise have been, but on the other hand the effect of the general wage increase standard was undoubtedly to raise some increases above what they would otherwise have been.[33] The rate of consumer price inflation during the first year of controls was held to about 3% over the rate of the previous year, but it rose to 11.5% in the eight months before controls ended and then to 12.2% in the eight months after they ended.[34] One must agree with the judgment of the Council of Economic Advisers concerning the stabilization program that "whatever contribution it may have made was probably concentrated in its first 16 months, when the economy was operating well below its potential." As the boom intensified, the controls only served to cause misallocation of resources and shortages. "Thus, the net benefit of the controls system, however evaluated, had become extremely small by the beginning of 1974, and legal termination of controls only ratified the inevitable process of dismantling them in response to public and market pressures."[35]

Lessons Learned from Wage Controls

Certain lessons can be gained from our experience with wage controls. Comprehensive wage controls, which rely on general guidelines, involve the least administrative cost, but because of their generality they tend to be inappropriate to many cases, and require special exemptions to deal with special situations. On the other hand, wage controls which proceed on a case-by-case basis may be less arbitrary, but are likely to give rise to creeping wage inflation achieved with a high cost of administration. Whatever the form of wage controls, employees know that they will eventually end, and that the end of controls is inevitably followed by a catch-up period which seems to bring back all the ills

---

[32] Daniel J. B. Mitchell, "The Impact and Administration of Wage Controls," in John Kraft and Blaine Roberts (eds.), *Wage and Price Controls: The U.S. Experiment* (New York: Praeger Publishers, Inc., 1975), p. 38.

[33] Daniel Quinn Mills, *Government, Labor, and Inflation* (Chicago: University of Chicago Press), 1975, pp. 70–71.

[34] Marvin H. Kosters, *Controls and Inflation* (Washington, D.C.: American Enterprise Institute for Public Policy Research, 1975), p. 1.

[35] *Economic Report of the President, 1975* (Washington, D.C.: Government Printing Office, 1975), pp. 228–29.

the controls sought to eliminate. A specialized board, operating with the cooperation of both unions and management, such as the Construction Industry Stabilization Committee, may, however, be effective for short periods in reducing negotiated increases below those that would occur otherwise. Even in this case, however, the increasing impact of nonunion construction may have been a greater restraint than controls.

THE LABOR DILEMMA

The American economy faces a dilemma. As a nation we have as objectives two goals which may be incompatible: full employment and price stability. In 1975, there were 7.8 million persons unemployed in the United States.[36] Furthermore, millions more were underemployed or were denied the benefits of full employment. Massive governmental efforts to reduce such unemployment, to cut down the idleness of our teenagers, and to lessen the poverty and despair in our slums have called for the expenditures of vast sums of money which will add fuel to the fires of inflation. On the other hand, primary emphasis upon controlling inflation would require continuing wage and price controls and restrictive fiscal and monetary policy which would hamper efforts to stimulate business recovery and increase employment opportunities.

The Concept of the Phillips Curve

In recent years it has become common to talk about a "trade-off" between a given rate of price increase and the rate of unemployment. The idea is that if unemployment is lowered below a certain critical rate, then a predictable rate of price inflation will result. On this theory, some level of unemployment may be "necessary" to buy price stability.

The theoretical basis for this relationship derives from work done by Professor A. W. Phillips, who sought to represent by a curve the relation between changes in money wages and employment in the British economy.[37] Other writers expanded upon this work and derived a modified application purporting to show a trade-off relationship between unemployment and changes in the price level.[38] An example of this relationship is shown in Figure 13–7. According to this figure, in order to reduce unemployment to a 3% rate, the economy would have to assume a 5% annual rate of increase in prices.

In the 1970s, however, it soon became apparent that the Phillips

---

[36] U.S. Department of Labor, *Employment and Training Report*, table A–1, p. 211.

[37] A. W. Phillips, "The Relation between Unemployment and the Rate of Change of Money Wages in the United Kingdom, 1861–1957," *Economica*, vol. 25 (November 1958), pp. 283–99.

[38] See Jerome C. Darnell, "Another Look at the Trade-Off between Inflation and Unemployment," *Conference Board Record*, vol. 7 (January 1970), pp. 18–19.

FIGURE 13–7

Modified Phillips Curve

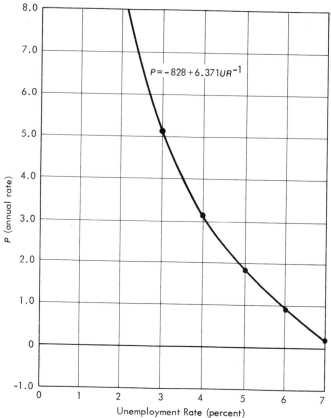

Source: Jerome C. Darnell, "Another Look at the Trade-Off between Inflation and Unemployment," *Conference Board Record*, vol. 7 (January 1970), p. 21.

curve did not fit the data. In fact, high unemployment seemed to be associated with high rates of inflation, rather than vice versa. Some economists sought to rehabilitate the concept by claiming that structural changes in the labor force—particularly the influx of youth and women —had caused the Phillips curve to "shift to the right," meaning that for any percentage reduction in unemployment a higher rate of price inflation had to be accepted. But even this tenuous explanation fails to account for years of "stagflation" in which the economy experienced double-digit inflation along with high levels of unemployment.

This is not to deny that there may be some relationship between changes in the price level and changes in the level of unemployment. However, inflation can be the result of many causes, and there is certainly no fixed relationship between the rate of inflation and changes in the number of jobs or in the level of money wages. Furthermore, as a guide to public policy, the Phillips curve fails to take account of the fact that some programs designed to reduce unemployment can be highly inflationary, whereas others may be less so.

UNIONS AND WAGE INFLATION

Much of the discussion on the wage-price-inflation issue tends to cast unions as the villains of the piece. The reasoning is that if it were not for the bargaining strength and the "exorbitant" wage demands of the unions, wage rates would not be pushed up as fast, and therefore the dilemma with its unpalatable consequences would never have to be faced. There are really two logical steps in this reasoning which require examination. First, is it true that unions make wage rates higher than they would otherwise be? Second, to what extent is price inflation primarily the result of cost-push or of demand-pull factors?

Do Unions Accelerate the Rise in Wage Levels? Negative View

Those who contend that unions have not caused wage rates generally to rise any faster than they would have in the absence of union organization emphasize that changes in wage rates, like changes in prices, are simply the reflection of more fundamental developments in the underlying forces which determine supply and demand in the marketplace. They claim that the sharp increases in money wage rates which occurred in the post–World War II period and are recurring now are the result of the increase in the supply and velocity of money which made itself felt through an expanding demand for goods of all kinds. The growth of consumer credit, large expenditures on plant and equipment, high farm incomes, rising governmental expenditures, and similar circumstances contributed to the inflation, which in turn produced a shortage of labor and high wage rates.

Wage Gains among Unorganized Workers

We have spoken earlier of unions as mere avenues through which inflationary forces transmit their impact to wages and prices. In support of this position, it may be observed that money wage rates seem to have risen as fast, if not faster, in previous periods of inflation, when union organization was a negligible factor in the labor market. For example, in the period from 1917 to 1921, organized labor represented less than 12% of the labor force, as contrasted with 25% in the post–World War II period. Yet increases in money wage rates generally in these two postwar periods of inflation were strikingly similar.

Another illuminating comparison is provided by the steel industry. Workers in this industry actually made larger percentage gains in money and real hourly earnings during the period 1914–20, when union organization was negligible, than during the period 1939–48, when the CIO United Steelworkers spearheaded a drive for wage increases in the industry.[39]

That union organization is not necessary to give workers large increases in money wages if the necessary factors are present—high demand for labor and/or shortage of labor supply—is illustrated by comparing gains in wages and salaries in largely organized and largely unorganized sectors of the economy. For example, average hourly earnings of employees (production or nonsupervisory) in manufacturing, a highly organized sector of the economy, increased from $2.61 in 1965 to $4.96 in December 1975, or 90%. During the same period, average hourly earnings in services increased from $2.05 to $4.22, or 105%; in wholesale and retail trade, from $2.03 to $3.84, or 89%; and in finance, insurance, and real estate, from $2.39 to $4.22, or 77%.[40] Employees in the latter three largely unorganized sectors of the economy have done as well or better than their counterparts in heavily organized manufacturing industries.

Anyone who has sought to hire a maid or someone to perform housework can attest to the fact that without the aid of union organization, domestic servants have probably achieved greater gains in hourly earnings during the past decade than have the members of the United Automobile Workers! Indeed, it can be argued that rather than accelerating increases in the wage level, union organization has inhibited such increases, relative to those of nonunion employees, primarily because of the lag produced by the term of existing wage contracts. Union wage adjustments, as a consequence, tend to follow rather than to lead nonunion wage adjustments during an inflationary period in the economy.

Do Unions Accelerate the Rise in Wage Levels? Affirmative View

A number of economists have concluded that unions do push up money wages to a level higher than that which would exist in a nonunion economy. Most of the empirical studies which have been conducted with respect to this problem concern the immediate post–World War II era, but the conclusions would seem to hold for our more recent experience. H. Gregg Lewis, for example, concludes that the average union/nonunion relative wage was approximately 10–15% higher than it would have been in the absence of union organization.[41] Albert Rees concludes that "strong American unions seem to be able to raise the relative earnings of

[39] Albert Rees, "Postwar Wage Determination in the Basic Steel Industry," *American Economic Review,* vol. 41 (June 1951), p. 400.

[40] U.S. Department of Labor, Bureau of Labor Statistics, *Employment and Earnings, U.S., 1909–72,* Bulletin 1312–9 (Washington, D.C.: Government Printing Office, 1972), table 7, p. xi; and *Employment and Earnings,* vol. 22 (March 1976), table C–8, p. 106.

[41] H. Gregg Lewis, *Unionism and Relative Wages in the United States* (Chicago: University of Chicago Press, 1963), p. 5.

their members by 15% to 25%.[42] Arthur Ross, examining the period 1933–45, concluded that the groups of employees who experienced the greatest increases in unionism also showed the greatest relative increases in wages.[43] On the other hand, Richard Lester, using different terminal dates for a similar study, namely 1935 and 1948, found no correspondence between increases in wages and changes in the extent of unionism.[44] In a more recent study, Terry G. Foran concludes that although continuing unionism is not a sufficient condition for creating differential wage changes, new unionism and its post–World War II counterpart, quasi–new unionism, is sufficient.[45] On this theory, a governmental wage freeze which inhibits normal union activity gives rise after the end of the stabilization effort to a new wave of union wage pressure which Foran finds can push up wages in the union sector faster than the increases which occur in the nonunion sector.

Since the principal business of trade unions is to get more money for union members, it would be strange if unions did not have some effect on the wage level. Evidence of the ability of unions to force high wage levels on employers is found in the history of many companies in the coal, hosiery, cotton textile, garment, and shoe industries, which were forced out of business because unions compelled them to pay wages above the nonunion scale. However, in certain circumstances, long-term union contracts can retard the rate of increase of union wages, while nonunion employees, unfettered by such contracts, may be able to capitalize more quickly on the opportunities afforded by a tight labor market.

Have wages simply been chasing prices up, or have wages been pushing prices up? A number of economists contend that given conditions in the market favorable to the exercise of union bargaining power, union organization results in a greater inflation in wages and prices than would occur in a nonunion economy. The following are some of the reasons advanced in support of this contention:

1. First and foremost is the dominant position of labor unions in our key industries. Between 80% and 100% of employees are under union contracts in the aluminum, steel, coal- and metal-mining, automobile and automobile parts, agricultural equipment, rubber products, shipbuilding, building construction, longshoring, railroad, and trucking industries. With such complete control of the labor force in these industries, unions are in a position to exact higher rates than would be the case in a free

---

[42] Albert Rees, *The Economics of Trade Unions* (Chicago: University of Chicago Press, 1962), p. 77.

[43] Arthur M. Ross, "The Influence of Unionism upon Earnings," *Quarterly Journal of Economics*, vol. 62 (February 1948), pp. 263–86.

[44] Richard Lester, "The Influence of Unionism upon Earnings," ibid., pp. 783–87.

[45] Terry G. Foran, "Unionism and Wage Differentials," *Southern Economic Journal*, vol. 40 (October 1973), p. 277.

labor market. Furthermore, since bargaining tends to be on a multiunit basis, all or most of the employers of the industry have their labor costs raised more or less simultaneously. As a result, there is a natural inclination to raise prices, since each producer knows that his competitor "is in the same boat" and will welcome a chance to pass on increased costs to consumers.

It is significant, too, that the industries in which unions are strongest are key industries from which wage and price changes fan out rapidly in the entire economy. As one writer has put it: "Strong textile unionism and weak auto unionism would produce a different wage atmosphere."[46] Economists who believe that unions create an inflationary bias in wage changes stress the fact that a comparison of the size of wage changes in union and nonunion companies will not reveal a significant differential, because it is well known that nonunion companies, in order to avoid union organization, keep their wages abreast of, and frequently exceed, wage adjustments being made in organized firms in their particular industry.

2. In the second place, in a highly unionized economy, key wage bargains spread rapidly from one industry to another, even though supply and demand conditions within the "follower" industries may not justify the same increase as that granted in the "leader" industry. Union workers are strong believers in uniformity of wages—that is, uniformity with the highest wage rate paid. This is particularly true where members of one international union may be employed in a number of industries. If a profitable firm in one industry employing members of a particular union gives a large wage adjustment, the cry immediately goes up from the membership to obtain the same increase for all members of the union. Whereas, in a nonunion economy, wage adjustments are likely to spread gradually by affecting local supply and demand conditions, and to vary in size depending upon the profitability of the particular firm and local conditions, in a unionized economy, key wage adjustments leap rapidly from one industry to another. Thus, it is possible that wage increases may spread more rapidly and may be more likely to produce price increases in a unionized economy than in a free labor market.

3. Events indicate that unions will press for further advances in wage rates even when profits are declining and unemployment is growing in an industry or in the economy. Wages rose in each of the years 1949, 1954, 1958, 1970, and 1974 despite falling demand for labor and relatively high unemployment. Historical data indicate that there was a much closer relationship between wage changes and varying levels of unemployment prior to 1930, when unions were still weak, than in the last 20 years, when unions have become major factors in the labor market. Although there is room for disagreement as to the influence of unions on the level of money wage rates in periods of rapid expansion, there

---

[46] Lloyd G. Reynolds, "Structural Determinants of Cost Inflation and Remedial Measures," *Monthly Labor Review*, vol. 82 (August 1959), p. 873.

seems to be little doubt that unions hold up wages in periods of severe contraction and, in fact, tend to push up wages even in periods of business recession.

4. The existence of union contractual arrangements with employers was until recently a factor which on the whole retarded the wage-price spiral by producing a minimum time lag during which wage rates could not be negotiated. The stabilizing effect of such contracts has,

TABLE 13–6

Indexes of Money and Real Adjusted* Average Hourly Earnings, Private Nonfarm Economy, and Average Effective† General Wage Increases, Major Collective Bargaining Agreements, and Year-to-Year Changes, 1965–1974

| | Indexes (1965 = 100) | | | | Year-to-Year Percent Changes in Real Earnings and Wage Rates | |
| | Adjusted Average Hourly Earnings, Private Nonfarm Economy | | Average Effective General Wage Changes, Major Union Agreements | | Adjusted Average Hourly Earnings | Average Effective General Wage Changes |
Year	Money	Real	Money	Real		
1965	100.0	100.0	100.0	100.0	—	—
1966	104.1	100.9	103.6	100.4	0.9	0.4
1967	109.2	103.2	108.2	102.3	2.3	1.9
1968	116.0	105.2	114.2	103.5	1.9	1.2
1969	123.7	106.4	120.0	103.3	1.1	−0.2
1970	131.9	107.1	128.8	104.6	0.1	1.3
1971	141.3	110.0	139.1	108.3	2.7	3.5
1972	150.4	113.4	147.4	111.2	3.1	2.7
1973	160.0	114.2	157.7	112.6	0.7	1.2
1974‡	172.9	110.6	172.2	110.2	−3.2	−2.1
Average annual percent increase, 1965–74..	6.2	1.1	6.2	1.1	—	—

* Average hourly earnings of production and nonsupervisory workers in private nonfarm establishments adjusted for overtime (manufacturing only) and interindustry employment shifts.
† Increases resulting from negotiations during the year, deferred increases, and escalator adjustments in agreements affecting 1,000 workers or more, excluding government.
‡ Preliminary.
Source: U.S. Department of Labor, Bureau of Labor Statistics. Reproduced from Executive Office of the President, Council on Wage and Price Stability, *Staff Report* (Washington, D.C.: Government Printing Office, 1975), p. 48.

however, been gradually eroded by the spread of automatic escalator clauses, as discussed in Chapter 11. Table 13–6 contains two sets of indexes of money and real wages for the years 1965–74. The first set relates to the adjusted average hourly earnings of production or nonsupervisory workers in the private nonfarm economy. About two thirds of the workers in this category are estimated to be nonunion, so that this series can serve as a rough index of wage changes for unorganized employees. The second set of indexes relates to average effective general wage changes under major collective bargaining agreements. The changes include those negotiated during the year, increases agreed to in prior years, and escalator adjustments. As is obvious from Table 13–6, there is a remarkable similarity in movement of the two series over the whole period, with each registering an increase of 72% in hourly earnings. It is significant, however, that in the 1970s workers under collective agreements have fared better in protecting and improving their real earnings than have workers in the other group. It seems possible that the increasing use of escalator clauses in union contracts may be responsible for this trend.

The Effects of Cost-of-Living Provisions in Union Contracts

As we mentioned in Chapter 11, the sharp upturn in prices in recent years has renewed organized labor's interest in automatic cost-of-living adjustment provisions. Do escalator clauses in union contracts *cause* inflation? The answer would seem to be no. Considered alone, cost-of-living adjustment clauses do not initiate inflation, but they can *intensify* an inflationary trend attributable to other factors. By reducing or eliminating the normal time lag in making wage adjustments, they would lower a barrier to spiraling incomes and labor costs. Whereas wage rates are most commonly negotiated annually in the absence of long-term agreements, wages are frequently adjusted quarterly pursuant to cost-of-living clauses in long-term contracts. Furthermore, the very existence of escalator clauses in labor contracts in key industries may increase the inflationary expectations of employers and labor in other sectors of the economy, and thus result in larger wage settlements than might otherwise be arrived at.

The inflationary potential of escalator clauses has been recognized by many foreign countries since the end of World War II, and many governments—among them France, Australia, Austria, Belgium, Norway, Denmark, Sweden, and Finland—have taken steps either to prohibit this type of automatic adjustment or to restrict it in order to lessen its tendency to feed inflationary forces. In this country, limitations on escalator clauses have been introduced into collective bargaining agreements primarily at the insistence of management. Business must have known costs in order to project prices and production for the future. An open-end escalator clause introduces an element of uncertainty into management planning which businessmen have been trying to avoid by placing ceilings or other limitations on cost-of-living adjustments in labor contracts.

THE DEBATE OVER "INDEXING"

Despite the problems which can be generated by widespread use of escalator clauses in collective bargaining agreements, some economists have advocated that the concept of "indexing"—that is, linking contract prices to changes in the cost of living—be extended to all forms of long-term contractual arrangements, including wages, rents, and interest on bonds and savings deposits. At the same time, the federal income tax system would be adjusted so that corporate and individual income gains that merely reflect the impact of inflation would not be taxed away.

The major argument in favor of indexing is fairness. Indexing is already being applied to many segments of the population (see Figure 13–8). Those who do not have the benefit of such clauses—and this is particularly true of the poor—in effect have income transferred from them to more

FIGURE 13–8
Recipients of Indexed Income

MILLIONS WHO ALREADY GET "INDEXED" INCOME—

Major groups with wages or benefits that automatically rise with increases in the cost of living—

Social Security beneficiaries	31,300,000
Food-stamp recipients	19,200,000
Union members in private industry with "escalation" contracts	7,000,000
Aged, blind, disabled on federal aid	4,100,000
Retired federal workers or their survivors	1,400,000
Retired military personnel or their survivors	1,047,000
Railroad-retirement beneficiaries	1,000,000
Postal workers	600,000
Disabled coal miners, widows and dependents	507,000

AND THAT'S NOT ALL: Thousands of schoolteachers, firemen, sanitation workers and other State and local-government employes have "cost of living" contracts. In addition, Congress and practically all federal employes except the President now enjoy semiautomatic pay raises based on changes in private pay.

Source: Government agencies

Reproduced from *U.S. News & World Report*, August 18, 1975, p. 44, by permission.

favored groups in times of inflation. The economist Milton Friedman, a strong advocate of indexing, argues that without indexing unions try both to catch up with past inflation and to anticipate future price rises in their wage contracts. He contends further that indexing would foster a quicker and less painful response to anti-inflationary policies, because wage hikes would slacken in tandem with prices.[47]

Even if indexing has some merits when the economy is slowing, there is great danger that it would contribute to inflation when the economy is overheated. Moreover, if an energy shortage or a drought is reflected

---

[47] *Business Week*, May 25, 1974, p. 148.

in sharp increases in prices, there is a real question whether it is sound to adopt a system which seeks to maintain real incomes when the necessities of the situation may require a tightening of belts. Furthermore, as Arthur F. Burns, chairman of the Federal Reserve System, has pointed out, "By making it easier for many people to live with inflation, escalator arrangements would gravely weaken the discipline that is needed to conduct business and government affairs prudently and efficiently.[48]

Nevertheless, indexing is spreading in this country—and in the world. Currently, the House Labor Standards Subcommittee is considering the advisability of indexing the minimum wage. If enacted, such a measure would build inflationary pressures into the entire scale of wage rates in the economy (see Chapter 16). On the pension front, recent settlements in the aluminum, can, and steel industries have accepted the concept of cost-of-living escalators for pensions. Indexing already covers retired federal employees, and broad extension of this principle could lead to mushrooming pension costs. Indexing experiments are also under way in Finland, Israel, Chile, Brazil, and Belgium. The last country has had a relatively long experience with indexing and is currently reporting double-digit inflation.[49]

APPRAISAL OF THE DILEMMA

Continuing inflation—particularly at an accelerated rate—is intolerable, since it would erode the standard of living of fixed-income groups, endanger the stability of the dollar in international commerce, and might eventually lead to coercive controls in our society. Inflation in the United States is a policy packed with political dynamite; for if the middle-class citizens of America rightly or wrongly come to conclude that wage pressure by organized labor is responsible for the erosion of their savings, then they might be led to sponsor and support restrictive measures which would spell the end of a free labor market as we know it.

On the other hand, a high rate of unemployment is also an intolerable condition for our society. But this depends upon who is unemployed: Is it the breadwinner of the family? Or is it the part-timer, the youth, the married woman with a working husband who is anxious to reenter the labor force? If the present 7% unemployment rate were concentrated among family breadwinners, there might be a different focus of public policy today. However, the nature of our unemployment has changed substantially in recent years. In the next chapter, we shall consider the significance of this change which explains why continuing emphasis will probably be placed upon control of inflation in this country.

---

[48] *U.S. News & World Report,* August 18, 1975, p. 44.

[49] Ibid., p. 45.

APPENDIX: INFLATION, UNEMPLOYMENT, AND THE PHILLIPS CURVE

The Wage, Price, and Productivity Relationship

The equilibrium in the labor market is determined by the interaction of the demand and the supply of labor, which are represented by the following equations:

$$\text{Demand: } w = f(L) \text{ or } W = P \cdot f(L) \tag{1}$$

$$\text{Supply: } \quad w = g(L) \text{ or } W = P \cdot g(L) \tag{2}$$

where w is the real wage rate, W is the money wage rate, P is the price level, and $f(L)$ and $g(L)$ are the functional forms of the demand and supply equations for labor. (Recall that the demand for labor is obtained by setting the marginal productivity of labor equal to the wage rate while the supply of labor is determined by the aggregate trade-off between work and leisure.) Equating demand to supply gives the labor market equilibrium

$$f(L) = g(L) \text{ or } P \cdot f(L) = P \cdot g(L) \tag{3}$$

The basic wage-price-productivity relationship can be derived from a version of the labor market equilibrium condition in (1). For any given L, the price level is given by

$$P = \frac{W}{f(L)} \tag{4}$$

FIGURE 13–9
Equilibrium in the Labor Market

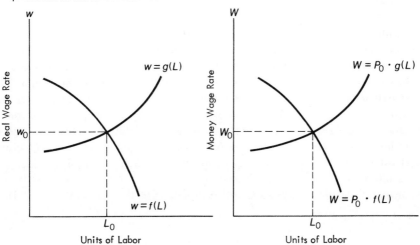

Real Wage Rate

$w = g(L)$

w_0

$w = f(L)$

L_0

Units of Labor

Money Wage Rate

$W = P_0 \cdot g(L)$

W_0

$W = P_0 \cdot f(L)$

L_0

Units of Labor

If the money wage rate, W, and the marginal productivity of labor grow at the same rate, there will be no change in the equilibrium price level, P. For example, if the initial price level, P_1, is given by

$$P_1 = \frac{W}{[f(L)]_1}$$

and both W and $f(L)$ grow at $a\%$ annually, the wage and marginal productivity after one year are $W_2 = W_1[1 + a/100]$ and $[f(L)]_2 = [f(L)]_1 [1 + a/100]$, respectively. In logarithmic terms, (4) can be written as

$$\log_e P = \log_e W - \log_e[f(L)] \tag{5}$$

Differentiating with respect to time, we obtain

$$\dot{P} = \dot{W} - [\dot{f(L)}] \tag{6}$$

where dots denote percentage rates of growth of the respective variables for small changes. Thus

$$\dot{P} = \frac{dP/dt}{P}$$

Equation (6) indicates that if W and $f(L)$ grow at the same rate so that $\dot{W} = [\dot{f(L)}]$, $\dot{P}$ will be 0, that is, the equilibrium price level will remain unchanged. Alternatively, since the real wage w is just W/P, the growth rate in real wage is given by

$$\dot{w} = \dot{W} - \dot{P} \tag{7}$$

If money wages grow as fast as productivity and P remains unchanged so that $\dot{P} = 0$, (7) combined with (6) yields

$$w = \dot{W} - \dot{P} = [\dot{f(L)}] \tag{8}$$

The noninflationary rule for wages states that *the real wage rate can grow as fast as productivity with no change in the equilibrium price level.*

The analysis can be extended to consider the unit labor cost and the labor share of output. The labor cost per unit of real output c can be written as

$$c = \frac{WL}{Q} = \frac{W}{Q/L} \tag{9}$$

where L is the total labor force employed. Taking logarithms we obtain,

$$\log_e c = \log_e W - \log_e(Q/L) \tag{10}$$

or differentiating,

$$\dot{c} = \dot{W} - (\dot{Q/L})$$

This implies that unit labor cost remains constant if the money wage rate and labor productivity increase at the same rate.

The labor share of total output can be written as

$$S_L = \frac{WL}{PQ} = \frac{w}{Q/L} \tag{11}$$

As demonstrated earlier, if the real wage w and the productivity Q/L change by the same percentage, the equilibrium price level remains unchanged. Taking logarithms and differentiating,

$$\overset{\bullet}{S_L} = \overset{\bullet}{w} - (\overset{\bullet}{Q/L}) \tag{12}$$

Hence, if w and Q/L change by the same rate, the labor share of output remains constant—$\overset{\bullet}{S_L} = 0$.

The wage-price-productivity analysis above formed the basis for the Council of Economic Advisers' wage-price guideposts referred to in this chapter. According to the general guidepost, in industries where productivity increased more than average, prices should fall, and in other industries where the productivity change was relatively slow, prices should rise, maintaining overall price stability. This implies that all wages grow at about the same rate. With bars indicating economy-wide averages, the wage guidepost says

$$\overset{\bullet}{W_i} = \overline{(\overset{\bullet}{Q/L})} \tag{13}$$

By this criterion, wages in every industry i should grow as fast as the average labor productivity. Unit labor costs in industry i will grow at the rate

$$\overset{\bullet}{c_i} = \overset{\bullet}{W_i} - (\overset{\bullet}{Q/L})_i = \overline{(\overset{\bullet}{Q/L})} - (\overset{\bullet}{Q/L})_i \tag{14}$$

Hence, if industry i has productivity growing faster than average, its labor costs fall and according to the guidepost its prices should fall to preserve constant relative shares of labor and capital. Conversely, for industries with slower than average productivity growth, the guidepost recommends a price rise. Thus, on the average, a constant price level would be maintained.

QUESTIONS FOR DISCUSSION

1. How have the gains of increased productivity been distributed in the postwar years? From the point of view of achieving maximum employment in our economy, what is the "best" method of distributing such gains?

2. What is meant by "labor productivity"? How does this concept differ from "labor efficiency"? What factors have produced the increase in output per man-hour in American industry?

3. Are union organization, full employment, and price stability compatible in

a free labor market? Discuss the economic and political implications of this question.

4. Union leaders maintain that cost-of-living escalator clauses in union contracts are beneficial to the economy because they help to maintain the real purchasing power of the worker's dollar. Discuss the validity of this statement with particular relation to the problem of inflation.

5. Discuss the pros and cons of indexing as a national policy.

SUGGESTIONS FOR FURTHER READING

Backman, Jules (ed.). *Labor, Technology, and Productivity in the Seventies.* New York: New York University Press, 1974.

A series of authoritative articles dealing with various aspects of the interrelationships among wages, prices, and productivity.

Greenberg, Leon. *A Practical Guide to Productivity Measurement.* Washington, D.C.: Bureau of National Affairs, Inc., 1975.

A concise text by the former executive director of the National Commission on Productivity which explains how productivity concepts can be applied and measured in individual firms.

Industrial Relations Research Association. *Collective Bargaining and Productivity.* Madison, Wis.: The Association, 1975.

A series of articles discussing productivity issues within the collective bargaining context. Several of the articles deal with productivity bargaining.

Kosters, Marvin H. *Controls and Inflation: The Economic Stabilization Program in Retrospect.* Domestic Affairs Studies. Washington, D.C.: American Enterprise Institute for Public Policy Research, 1975.

Mills, Daniel Quinn. *Government, Labor, and Inflation: Wage Stabilization in the United States.* Chicago: University of Chicago Press, 1975.

Two studies of wage stabilization which are carefully done but differ in emphasis and conclusions.

Ulman, Lloyd, and Flanagan, Robert J. *Wage Restraint: A Study of Income Policies in Western Europe.* Berkeley: University of California Press, 1971.

An excellent study of attempts to restrain increases in wages and prices in the United Kingdom, the Netherlands, Sweden, Denmark, France, West Germany, and Italy.

14

Unemployment and Poverty in a High-Employment Economy

In the previous and earlier chapters of this text, we referred to the paradoxical problem facing this nation, namely, that while total employment records all-time highs, we face continuing high levels of unemployment and persistent poverty affecting millions of our citizens. The 1974–75 recession, with its sharp increase in unemployment, focused national attention on these issues and raised questions about the validity of long-standing concepts and methods of measuring unemployment. In this chapter, we shall examine these two problems—unemployment and poverty—and shall consider their nature, measurement, and probable causes.

THE EXTENT OF UNEMPLOYMENT

Unemployment of some amount is a normal concomitant of a free labor market. Irregularity of employment is, in a sense, one of the costs which a system of free enterprise exacts in return for the privileges it bestows. Thus, the American worker has greater liberty than a worker anywhere else in the world to shift his place of employment in order to benefit his economic welfare. This is no idle gift—indeed, as we have seen from our discussion of the labor market, it is a privilege frequently exercised by the American worker. But the freedom of the worker to quit and to move is balanced by the freedom of the employer to fire, with the result that the individual employee is subjected to the vicissitudes of his current employer's business fortunes.

Thus, employment and unemployment typically fluctuate over time. A major determinant of the volume of unemployment is the level of business activity. At the depth of the Great Depression in 1933, one in every four persons was unemployed. On the other hand, in 1953 only about 1.8 million persons were unemployed out of a total civilian labor force of 63 million, or about 2.9% of the labor force.[1] Although the period following World War II was one of rapid economic growth and rising levels of real income, the unemployment rate averaged 4.7% from 1947 through 1973. Only during World War II (1944), when 17% of the total labor force were in the Armed Forces, did the rate ever come close to 1%.[2]

In 1975, the number of unemployed averaged about 7.8 million, representing an unemployment rate of about 8.5%. This was the highest rate of unemployment experienced by the economy in the post–World War II era. Despite the unemployment caused by a severe recession, total employment reached 84,783,000, down slightly from 1974, but still the second highest level of employment in the nation's history.[3] The number of persons who experience some unemployment during a given year is roughly three to four times the average number of unemployed throughout the year. An estimated 18.3 million persons were unemployed at some time during 1974.[4]

The labor force and the rolls of the employed and unemployed are in a state of constant flux. The potential expansion and contraction of the labor force are illustrated by the data which show that more than 10 million out of a total of about 59 million persons not in the labor force during the fourth quarter of 1975 worked at some time during the preceding 12 months.[5]

The recession of 1974–75 heightened interest in governmental policies to achieve full employment, but public discussion revealed that there is no agreement as to what full employment is, how unemployment should be defined, and whether progress should be measured by monitoring employment or unemployment. The problem of defining unemployment has been complicated by the changing nature of the labor force. For example, not only have more women entered the labor force, but also the percentage of women in the labor force has risen from 27% in 1947 to 39% in 1975.[6] Other factors which have complicated the definition of unemployment are the increasing volume of part-time employment and the substantial fluctuations in the number of persons who enter and leave the labor force, frequently in response to changing conditions

---

[1] U.S. Department of Labor, *Employment and Training Report of the President, 1976* (Washington, D.C.: Government Printing Office, 1976), table A–1, p. 211.

[2] *Economic Report of the President, 1975* (Washington, D.C.: Government Printing Office, 1975), pp. 86–87.

[3] U.S. Department of Labor, *Employment and Training Report*, p. 211.

[4] U.S. Department of Labor, Bureau of Labor Statistics, *Work Experience of the Population in 1974*, Special Labor Force Report, June 1975, p. 1.

[5] Julius Shiskin, "Employment and Unemployment: The Doughnut or the Hole?" *Monthly Labor Review*, vol. 99 (February 1976), p. 7.

[6] U.S. Department of Labor, *Employment and Training Report*, pp. 211–12.

in the labor market. There is general agreement that unemployment is a serious national problem. But should the inability of a college student to obtain work in the summer be given the same weight in unemployment statistics as the loss of a job by the family breadwinner?

Since unemployment statistics are used for many purposes, it seems likely that no single unemployment measure can serve all needs. In order to meet the varying needs of data users, the U.S. Bureau of Labor Statistics regularly publishes a variety of unemployment rates and indicators in its Employment Situation press releases and in *Employment and Earnings,* a monthly publication.

THE MEASUREMENT OF UNEMPLOYMENT

Unemployment statistics are watched with great interest from month to month by government, business, and the public. Obviously, such current information cannot be provided by a comprehensive survey of every household in the United States. Therefore, a sampling technique must be used. Each month some 1,000 pollsters from the U.S. Bureau of the Census descend upon 47,000 households across the nation to gather data about employment, unemployment, and participation in the labor force.[7] One fourth of the 47,000 households in the sample are replaced each month so that no single household is visited in more than four consecutive surveys. The sample covers every state and the District of Columbia and is designed to reflect urban, rural, and industrial areas in proportion to their presence in the nation as a whole.

The interviewers all work from a standard questionnaire which has been carefully worded to avoid bias. The respondents are never specifically asked whether they are unemployed. Furthermore, they are given no opportunity to decide their own labor force status. The actual classification of individuals as employed, unemployed, or not in the labor force is made in the computer from official criteria which have been programmed into the machine. Final data from the survey (commonly known as the CPS) are then turned over to the Labor Department's Bureau of Labor Statistics. Although this sampling technique can undoubtedly be improved, it is not the Bureau's data-gathering methods which have been subjected to major criticism, but rather the definition of unemployment itself.

The Bureau of Labor Statistics has announced that it does not intend to propose any modifications of the unemployment definitions which are the basis for the CPS survey.[8] It does concede, however, that there

---

[7] The Bureau of Labor Statistics has announced that it expanded its data base to 50,000 households in 1976 and will expand further to 70,000 at some future date.

[8] Julius Shiskin, "Unemployment: Measurement Problems and Recent Trends," U.S. Department of Labor, Bureau of Labor Statistics, Report 445 (Washington, D.C.: Government Printing Office, 1975), p. 6.

are a number of problem areas, and with respect to these it proposes to tighten definitions and to provide additional data through special studies. These areas are the following:

The Job Search. Here the issue is whether information elicited on job-seeking activity can be sharpened so as to identify casual job seekers who may not be serious in their efforts to find a job. A special survey to learn more about the intensity and frequency of efforts made by the unemployed to find work was conducted by the Bureau of Labor Statistics in fiscal 1976–77.

Secondary Workers. The issue here involves the propriety of including among the unemployed, on the same basis as heads of households needing full-time work, such persons as full-time students and others seeking part-time work. There has been a steady uptrend over the years in the proportion of husband-wife families with more than one worker. The proportion rose from 43% in 1959 to 57% in 1974.[9] Over the same period, the proportion of unemployed husbands with another worker in the family rose from 49% to 57%.[10] The employment of additional family members provides an important cushion against the economic impact of the family head's unemployment. On the other hand, the unemployment rates for secondary workers—particularly youth—are typically high and can distort overall unemployment statistics.

Discouraged Workers. The Bureau of Labor Statistics defines discouraged workers as persons who want a job but have not sought work in the past four weeks because they believed that none was available. The issue is whether these discouraged workers should be counted as unemployed. Under present procedures they are excluded, although the Bureau does publish separate data for this group, who are classified as not being in the labor force. The discouraged workers group consists largely of youth, women, and elderly persons; not many men of prime working age are included. Blacks—and particularly black youth—tend to be overrepresented relative to their proportion of the population. In the fourth quarter of 1975, about 1 million persons reported that they wanted jobs but did not seek them because of discouragement over job prospects. Two thirds of this group were women. A larger group of 4.3 million persons reported that they wanted jobs but did not look for them for a variety of reasons, such as school attendance, family responsibilities, or illness.[11]

The number of persons in this category may depend in part upon the duration of unemployment compensation payments. In September 1975, 5.6 million out of 7.5 million unemployed were receiving unemployment compensation, while approximately 200,000 had used up their benefits. The Labor Department estimated that as of January 1, 1977, a

---

[9] Ibid., p. 4.

[10] Ibid., p. 5.

[11] Shiskin, "Employment and Unemployment," p. 7.

total of 2.1 million persons will have used up their benefits.[12] Many of these persons may then drop out of the labor market because of discouragement about job prospects.

The "Subemployed." A fourth major issue is whether a new "subemployment" concept is needed which could combine low earners with the unemployed. Two categories of persons are involved:

1. Workers on part-time for economic reasons (such as slack work or inability to find full-time work). The extra hours these men and women would work if they could find full-time employment represent a surplus of unutilized labor which is not reflected in the aggregate unemployment statistics, because such persons are classified as "employed." In 1975, over 3.5 million persons who worked part-time wanted full-time jobs but were on shortened work schedules, primarily because of slack work loads.[13]

2. Workers who take low-wage employment simply because they cannot find work in their usual field. A typical case is that of a Ph.D. in sociology who is driving a taxi. Should he be classified as employed or unemployed? Obviously, classifying persons on the basis of their views of the kind of job they are really qualified for would open up a hornet's nest of qualitative judgments; yet many persons do take jobs that are really a form of "disguised unemployment."

In addition to these categories, which are viewed as problems by the Bureau of Labor Statistics, another large group is also largely neglected in current statistical surveys. These are persons with physical handicaps, who are presently treated as unemployable rather than unemployed, and are therefore excluded from the labor force. The U.S. Department of Labor has estimated that there are about 5 to 7 million handicapped workers who could be placed in industrial occupations. In considering statistics of unemployment, it is important to bear in mind that concepts of employability alter with the changing needs of the economy and that tomorrow we may consider persons to be unemployed who today are deemed unemployable.

The foregoing analysis indicates that in addition to the official statistics of the unemployed, our economy comprises another large body of people who might be called "the invisible unemployed." The existence of the invisible unemployed complicates the problem of devising a policy to reduce unemployment. As government moves through appropriate monetary, fiscal, and manpower policies to reduce unemployment, it finds that it is to some extent on a treadmill. For the more successful it is in expanding the number of jobs and reducing the supply of unemployed labor, the more likely are the members of the invisible unemployed to seek jobs in the labor market. In other words, the labor force participa-

---

[12] *Fortune*, November 1975, p. 22.

[13] U.S. Department of Labor, *Employment and Training Report*, p. 28.

tion rate tends to increase when jobs are plentiful and wages are high.

In theory, this tendency is offset to some extent by the so-called additional worker effect, which holds that secondary workers are induced to enter the labor market as principal breadwinners lose their jobs or take a pay cut, and conversely, that they leave the labor market when the principal breadwinner's earnings are restored. The U.S. Bureau of Labor Statistics concludes, however, that "it is extremely difficult to substantiate the 'additional worker effect' from available labor force data. There is more accurate concrete evidence of the 'discouraged worker effect' and it appears to be the larger factor."[14]

The wide range of results produced by different measures of the severity of unemployment is graphically shown in Figure 14-1. As can be seen from Figure 14-1, data for the third quarter of 1975 produce measures ranging from a low value of 3.1 for series U-1 to a high of 10 for series U-7. The rationale for these various measures is as follows:

U-1 measures the number of persons employed 15 weeks or longer as a percentage of the civilian labor force on the theory that unemployment beyond this period becomes a serious financial problem.

U-2 is the number of persons unemployed because they lost their last jobs, taken as a percentage of the labor force. Unemployment which accompanies entry or reentry into the labor force or voluntary job leaving are treated as less serious and thus omitted.

U-3, which measures only the number of household heads unemployed as a percentage of all household heads in the civilian labor force, assumes that unemployment of family breadwinners has the most serious repercussions on the economy.

U-4 measures the number of unemployed seeking full-time jobs as a percentage of all those in the full-time labor force. It thus treats as less important the problems faced by part-time workers or discouraged workers.

U-5 is the official, regularly published total unemployment rate for all workers age 16 or over. This series represents the total number of persons not working but available for and seeking work as a percentage of the civilian labor force. It makes no value judgments about the relative importance of a person's need for work. It only requires that job-seeking take place.

U-6 includes, as a percentage of the labor force, the number of unemployed persons seeking full-time work plus one half of the number of unemployed persons seeking part-time work and one half of the number of persons employed involuntarily on part-time schedules who usually have or desire full-time work. This is obviously an effort

---

[14] See John E. Bregger, "Unemployment Statistics and What They Mean," *Monthly Labor Review,* vol. 94 (November 1971), p. 26.

FIGURE 14–1

Unemployment Indicators, 1953–1975

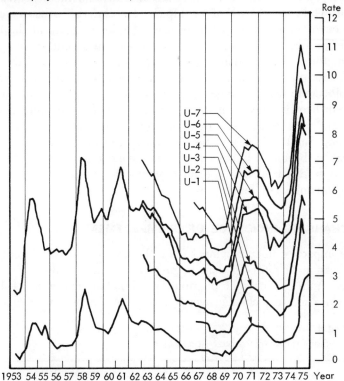

Selected quarterly unemployment rates:
U–1 15 weeks or longer.
U–2 Job losers.
U–3 Household heads.
U–4 Full-time job seekers.
U–5 Unemployed total.
U–6 Full-time + ½ part-time job seekers.
U–7 Full-time + ½ part-time + discouraged workers.
    Source: Data, U.S. Department of Labor, Bureau of Labor Statistics, December 5, 1975. Chart, Julius Shiskin, "Employment and Unemployment: The Doughnut or the Hole?" *Monthly Labor Review,* vol. 99 (February 1976), chart 1, p. 6.

to give some weight to the unemployment problems of part-time workers.

U–7 is the same as U–6, except that the number of discouraged workers is added to both the unemployed and the labor force components. Many critics of existing unemployment statistics believe that this is the only true measure and that discouraged workers, who do not actively seek work because they believe that none is available, should be given the same weight as those who are active job seekers.[15]

---

[15] For a discussion of the foregoing measures of unemployment, see Shiskin, "Employment and Unemployment," pp. 3–10.

It is apparent from the foregoing discussion that a single overall unemployment ratio can be a deceptive statistic and must be read with caution. The overall rate of unemployment can rise because of a decrease in the number of jobs or because the denominator of the fraction —the labor force—is increasing faster than employment. Thus, changes in labor force participation rates and changes in the size of the Armed Forces, by affecting the size of the civilian labor force, can alter the unemployment rate. Changes in the age-sex composition of the labor force can likewise have a material effect on the level of unemployment. The overall rate can remain constant from period to period, yet hide an increasing trend of joblessness among one sector of the labor force which happens to be offset by increasing employment by another. Finally, it must be emphasized that the unemployment rate reflects more people looking for jobs, not fewer jobs.

THE CHANGING INCIDENCE OF UNEMPLOYMENT

The impact of unemployment upon the economy was different during the recession of 1974–75 than in previous business downturns. As can be seen from the percent distribution tabulation in Table 14–1, there has been a gradual change over the years in the burden of unemploy-

TABLE 14–1
Unemployment Highs in Postwar Recessions

Age and Sex	Unemployment Rates (seasonally adjusted, quarterly averages)					
	1949 IV	1954 III	1958 II	1961 II	1971 III	1975 II
All workers	7.0	6.0	7.4	7.0	6.0	8.7
Both sexes, 16 to 19 years ...	15.0	13.7	16.3	16.3	17.0	20.2
Men, 20 to 24 years	11.1	11.0	13.7	11.9	10.3	14.7
Men, 25 years and over	5.9	4.9	6.2	5.5	3.5	5.7
Women, 20 to 24 years	8.6	7.8	9.9	11.0	9.1	12.8
Women, 25 years and over ..	5.3	4.8	6.2	6.1	5.0	7.4

	Percent Distribution					
	1949 IV	1954 III	1958 II	1961 II	1971 III	1975 II
Total unemployment	100.0	100.0	100.0	100.0	100.0	100.0
Both sexes, 16 to 19 years ...	15.1	14.1	13.9	16.1	25.5	22.0
Men, 20 to 24 years	12.1	8.9	10.3	10.1	12.8	13.4
Men, 25 years and over	50.5	49.6	48.7	44.2	29.2	30.3
Women, 20 to 24 years	5.4	5.0	5.0	6.0	9.3	9.6
Women, 25 years and over ..	16.9	22.3	22.1	23.7	23.3	24.6

These are the actual highs of the seasonally adjusted unemployment rates and do not necessarily reflect the National Bureau of Economic Research troughs. Detail may not add to totals because of rounding.
Source: U.S. Department of Labor et al., *Employment and Training Report of the President, 1976* (Washington, D.C.: Government Printing Office, 1976), table 5, p. 27.

ment among men, women, and teenagers of both sexes. Whereas men 25 years and over constituted a smaller proportion of the unemployed in the last two recessions than in earlier years, women and teenagers have borne the brunt of recent unemployment. Figure 14–2 vividly por-

FIGURE 14–2
Unemployment and Unemployment Rates, 1973–1976

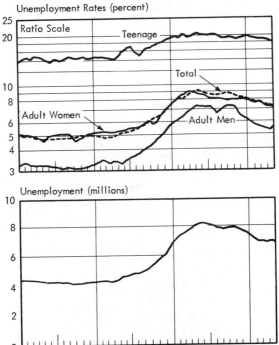

Source: Data, U.S. Department of Labor, Bureau of Labor Statistics. Chart, Chase Manhattan Bank, *Business in Brief,* June 1976, p. 2.

trays the drastic difference in unemployment rates between the most stable segment of the labor force—adult men—and the most volatile—teenagers.

Just as the incidence of unemployment was uneven for various demographic groups, it also varied widely among industries and occupations. (See Figure 14–3.) In general, unemployment rates reached abnormally high levels for workers whose jobs were in goods-producing industries. Among industries, construction experienced the most serious relative impact, with more than one in five construction workers out of work at one point during 1975.[16] Blue-collar joblessness more than doubled as a result of the recession, rising from a low point of 5.2% during 1973

---

[16] U.S. Department of Labor, *Employment and Training Report,* p. 27.

FIGURE 14–3

How Unemployment Compared by Group in 1975

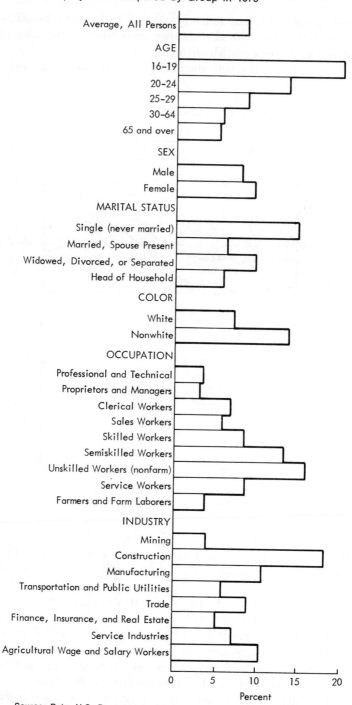

Percent

Source: Data, U.S. Department of Labor, Bureau of Labor Statistics. Chart, reprinted by permission from *Nation's Business*, vol. 64 (May 1976), p. 26. Copyright 1976 by *Nation's Business*, Chamber of Commerce of the United States.

to a peak of 12.6% in the second quarter of 1975.[17] White-collar unemployment was considerably lower, but nevertheless rose from less than 3% in 1973 to a postwar high of 5% in 1975.[18]

The severity of unemployment in 1975 can be better appreciated when it is compared with that of previous postwar recessions. The total rate of unemployment during the second quarter of 1975 reached 8.7%. During the next most serious recession, that of 1957–58, unemployment in the trough did not exceed 7.4%. As compared to the 1971 downturn, there was a sharp increase in unemployment of long duration. In 1971, out of a total unemployment of about 5 million, 1.2 million, or 24%, were unemployed 15 weeks or longer. In 1975, out of a total unemployment of 7.8 million, 2.5 million, or 32%[19] were unemployed for more than 15 weeks.

One important fact which emerges from a study of the changing incidence of unemployment over time is that changes in the composition of the labor force can produce a gradually increasing rate of unemployment *even though business activity is maintained at a high level.* Steady increases in the participation rates of women and fast growth in the population age 16–24 have made the labor force noticeably younger and more female as time has passed. Since these groups tend to experience higher rates of unemployment than do males over 24, their increasing proportion in the labor force creates a kind of "creeping unemployment" which can make the national goal of reducing unemployment much more difficult to achieve. On the other hand, to the extent that government and service employment continues to grow in relative importance, greater stability is introduced into the overall employment rate. Furthermore, the end of the baby boom and the gradual shrinkage which will follow in the teenage population will tend to reduce the rate of teenage unemployment.

WHO ARE THE UNEMPLOYED?

Unemployment statistics are made by individuals. Who are the unemployed? Who is the typical unemployed person? What are the conditions or circumstances which typify the bulk of our employment? Figure 14–3 shows graphically the groups which experience the highest rate of unemployment. The following discussion details this experience.

Unskilled Workers

The unemployed person is likely to be unskilled. As can be seen from Figure 14–3, the unemployment rate for unskilled workers (nonfarm

---

[17] Ibid.

[18] Ibid., p. 28.

[19] Ibid., table A–29, p. 253.

laborers) is greater than that for any other group. This is true year after year without variation. The second highest rate is that for operatives and kindred semiskilled workers. By contrast, the rate for professional, technical, and managerial personnel until 1970 averaged less than 2%. Since then, the rate for this group increased to over 3% in 1975, although it was still well below the rates for most other groups. The higher rate of unemployment among this group reflects sharp cutbacks in defense, aerospace production, and government-financed research.

Youth

Unemployment has always been substantially higher among young persons than among adults. Teenagers, for example, include a large proportion of new entrants into the labor market, and they customarily have a period of unemployment associated with "shopping around" for satisfactory positions. Frequently they begin their working careers by taking part-time jobs which may be temporary or seasonal. Since young people have fewer family commitments than older workers, they change their jobs more often in search of the "right" job. Furthermore, they tend to be more vulnerable to layoffs because of inexperience and lack of seniority.

In recent years, however, the sharp increase in the incidence of unemployment among this group has created a problem of grave concern to our nation. In the second quarter of 1975, about 3.7 million youth—divided equally between teenagers and those in their early twenties—were jobless. Youth in these age groups comprised only one fourth of the civilian labor force but accounted for almost one half of all unemployed workers.[20] In recent years, the teenage unemployment rate has averaged nearly 5 times that of workers over 25 while the rate for 20–24-year-olds has been 2½ times that of the older group.[21]

The unemployment problem is particularly acute among black teenagers. In 1975, the unemployment rate among black youth age 16–19 was 38%, compared to 18% for white youth.[22] With over one out of every three black youth unemployed, the potential for violence and juvenile delinquency in our central cities is greatly magnified. Unless productive employment can be found for the youth of our nation, we shall reap a bitter harvest of social unrest and delinquency. Alleviation of the problem may require revision of our minimum wage laws to provide exemptions for youth as well as increased emphasis upon vocational education in our schools.

---

[20] Janice N. Hedges, "Youth Unemployment in the 1974–75 Recession," *Monthly Labor Review*, vol. 99 (January 1976), p. 50.

[21] Ibid., p. 49.

[22] Ibid., table 3, p. 52.

The Uneducated

The relationship between education and unemployment must be approached with caution because apparent correlations may in fact be attributable to causes other than lack of education. For example, data for March 1974 indicate that the rate of unemployment for workers 16 years and over with less than five years of elementary school education was 5.3%, while the rate for those with one to three years of high school was 9.6%.[23] Does this mean that the more education a worker has, the more likely he is to be unemployed? The answer is no. The comparison actually involves two quite different groups of workers. Persons in the former category tend to be more mature older workers who completed their formal education ten or more years ago and have since acquired the skills and experience necessary to maintain stable jobs. The latter group includes the high school dropouts who have neither the education, the skills, and possibly not even the motivation, to find permanent jobs in the labor market.

In general, however, broad statistical comparisons of unemployed and employed tend to show higher unemployment rates for the group with lesser educational attainment. One reason is that workers with minimum educational achievements tend to be employed as blue-collar workers, laborers, and in various occupations which are more exposed to the vicissitudes of the business cycle. Over the past decade, however, the relative advantage of education as insurance against unemployment has tended to diminish. For example, in 1959 the median education of the employed was 12 years and of the unemployed 9.9 years. Since then, the average education of the unemployed has risen, so that by 1974 the difference between the median education of the employed (12.5) and the unemployed (12.1) no longer had statistical significance.[24] The increase in the unemployment rate for well-educated persons in recent years reflects, on the one hand, the high jobless rate among engineers, technical personnel, and other white-collar workers associated with aerospace and defense industries and, on the other hand, the high rate of unemployment among young high school graduates.

The college graduate in our society can still look forward to a career marked by less unemployment than that of the high school graduate, primarily because of the difference in the occupations to which the two groups will gravitate. Nevertheless, recent trends lend support to the thesis that the education mix and the job mix may be out of balance. In the academic year ending in June 1976, about 1.3 million persons received bachelor's, master's, or doctoral degrees, nearly double the level

---

[23] U.S. Department of Labor, Bureau of Labor Statistics, "Educational Attainment of Workers, March 1974," Special Labor Force Report 175 (Washington, D.C., 1975), table K, p. A–20.

[24] Ibid., p. 65.

of 1966. During the same period, however, the number of professional, technical, and managerial jobs in the United States grew by barely more than a third.[25] It is not surprising, therefore, that the history major with a Ph.D. may have as much difficulty in finding a job as the high school dropout!

Older Workers

Unemployment among older workers poses a special problem. The difficulty is not so much in the rate of unemployment as in its duration once it occurs. In 1975, men age 55–64 had a lower unemployment rate than did any other age group.[26] This low rate reflects two factors: the unemployment rate for older workers is likely to be low because most of these older employees are protected by seniority. On the other hand, published rates may understate the actual experience of unemployment by older workers because once employees in the upper age groups lose their jobs they are more inclined than others to withdraw from the labor force, and therefore they are not counted among the unemployed.

When senior workers are laid off, they frequently find that their skills have become obsolete. Moreover, they are unwilling to move to new areas because of community and family ties. The average duration of their unemployment, therefore, tends to be high. In 1975, 25% of the unemployed in the 55–64 age category and 32% of those 65 and over had been jobless for at least 27 weeks, in contrast with 13% for employees 20–24 years old.[27] Because of both inclination and inability to obtain full-time work, many older employees take part-time employment. For example, for the age group 65 and over, the proportion of males who had part-time employment rose from 40% in 1966 to 45% in 1974; for the comparable female group, the figure rose from 53% to 61%.[28]

Black Workers

In 1975, the unemployment rate for white employees was 7.8%; for blacks and other minorities, it was 13.9%.[29] Blacks, both male and female, show a higher unemployment rate than do whites in every age group. (See Table 14–2.) During the entire post–World War II period, the simple ratio of black and white unemployment rates has shown consistent stability at about two to one. This stability is rather remarkable when it is considered that during this period there has been a reduction in

---

[25] *Time,* March 29, 1976, p. 46.

[26] U.S. Department of Labor, *Employment and Training Report,* table A–19, p. 241.

[27] Shirley H. Rhine, "The Senior Worker—Employed and Unemployed," *Conference Board Record,* vol. 13 (May 1976), p. 9.

[28] Ibid., p. 9.

[29] U.S. Department of Labor, *Employment and Training Report,* table A–18, p. 239.

TABLE 14–2
Unemployment Rates by Sex, Age, and Race

	Blacks and Other Races		Whites	
	August 1975	August 1976	August 1975	August 1976
Males 16 years and over 12.9		11.7	6.5	5.7
Males 20–64 years 11.0		9.4	5.6	4.9
Females 16 years and over 14.7		14.8	8.9	8.6
Females 20–64 years 12.7		12.5	7.8	7.6

Source: *Employment and Earnings,* vol. 23 (September 1976), table A–10, p. 28.

job discrimination because of federal and state legislation and a narrowing of earnings differentials between the races. One explanation which has been suggested is that two movements within the black unemployment figures have balanced each other. On the one hand, the relative unemployment rate of black youths with little experience has increased, whereas on the other hand, the unemployment rate of experienced black workers has declined.[30]

In attempting to determine the full incidence of unemployment among the black population, it is important to recognize that conventional definitions and measurement techniques may underestimate the true amount of unemployment. Blacks are undoubtedly heavily represented in the category of subemployed and discouraged workers. In 1974, blacks, who constitute about 12% of the population of working age, accounted for 20% of the unemployed and 24% of all discouraged workers.[31]

A number of reasons have been advanced for the high unemployment rate among nonwhite workers. A major cause is their heavy concentration in occupations where there is typically a great deal of unemployment, such as unskilled farm and nonfarm labor, semiskilled production jobs, and service work. In 1975, 8.7% of blacks were employed as nonfarm laborers, compared to 4.4% for whites; 25.8% were in service work, compared to 12.3% for whites; 20% in operative jobs, compared to 14.6%. On the other hand, only 34.2% of blacks were employed in white-collar jobs compared to 51.7% for white employees.[32]

Lack of education is another major cause for the high incidence of unemployment among nonwhites. In recent years, increased school enrollment by black teenagers and higher retention rates have resulted in rising educational attainment levels. By 1974, the proportion of blacks

[30] Robert J. Flanagan, "On the Stability of the Racial Unemployment Differential," *American Economic Review,* Papers and Proceedings of the 88th Annual Meeting (May 1976), p. 307.

[31] Shiskin, "Unemployment," p. 5.

[32] U.S. Department of Labor, *Employment and Training Report,* table A–16, p. 237.

20 to 24 years old who had completed high school reached 72%, a figure which represented a faster rise than the rise in the proportion for the comparable group of whites. In 1974, however, a sizable education gap still existed, since 85% of whites in the 20–24 age group had completed high school.[33]

As has already been pointed out, a particularly serious unemployment problem afflicts black teenagers. Many of these youth are dropouts from school or have failed to receive a sound training in the three R's in schools in slum areas. Lacking both a good education and occupational skills, a large proportion of these young people will suffer high unemployment rates throughout their lives.

There is no simple answer to the problem of black unemployment. It must be attacked on a broad front. Success in reducing the rate of unemployment depends upon the degree of cooperation forthcoming from business and organized labor, both of which have been guilty of discriminatory practices. It is apparent that even if all blacks who want to work were given jobs, their rate of unemployment would be disproportionately high as long as they were concentrated in industries and occupations which have the least stability over the business cycle. Better education and improved training, therefore, are essential to any real solution of this problem.

OCCUPATIONAL CHARACTERISTICS OF THE UNEMPLOYED

In some occupations, unemployment is part of the normal routine of the ebb and flow of work. Take, for example, the construction industry, which has an unemployment rate more than twice that of all workers (see Table 14–3). Construction is subject to sharp seasonal swings; projects are short term, and the worker has only a passing attachment to any particular employer. The high hourly rates paid in this industry are intended to compensate workers—in part, at least—for the loss of income they regularly suffer in the intervals between jobs.

In manufacturing, fluctuations in employment are closely tied to the level of activity in the particular industry and to the stage of the general business cycle. The automobile industry is an example of an industry which is subject to major swings in demand by consumers and in which employment fluctuates from month to month and from year to year.

In Chapter 1, we commented on the shift in employment that is occurring between goods-producing and service-producing industries. As service-oriented employment grows in our economy, it will tend to introduce a greater degree of employment stability over the cycle than

---

[33] U.S. Department of Commerce, Bureau of the Census, *The Social and Economic Status of the Black Population in the United States, 1974,* Current Population Reports, P–23, No. 54 (Washington, D.C., 1975), pp. 1–2.

TABLE 14–3

Unemployment Rates of Persons 16 Years and Over by Major Industry Group: Annual Averages, 1948–1975

Year	Total unem-ployed	Experienced wage and salary workers												
		Total	Agricul-ture	Nonagricultural private wage and salary workers										
				Total	Mining	Con-struc-tion	Manufacturing			Trans-porta-tion and public utilities	Whole-sale and retail trade	Finance, insur-ance, real estate	Service indus-tries	Govern-ment
							Total	Durable goods	Non-durable goods					
	Unemployment rate													
1948	3.8	4.3	5.5	4.5	3.0	8.7	4.2	4.0	4.4	3.5	4.7	1.8	4.8	2.2
1949	5.9	6.8	7.1	7.3	8.9	13.9	8.0	8.1	7.8	5.9	6.2	2.1	6.7	3.1
1950	5.3	6.0	9.0	3.9	6.7	12.2	6.2	5.7	6.7	4.6	6.0	2.2	6.4	3.0
1951	3.3	3.7	4.3	3.9	4.0	7.2	3.8	3.0	4.7	2.3	3.9	1.5	4.2	1.8
1952	3.0	3.3	4.8	3.6	3.8	6.7	3.5	2.6	4.1	2.3	3.5	1.7	3.6	1.6
1953	2.9	3.2	5.6	3.4	4.4	7.2	3.1	2.9	3.8	2.2	3.4	1.7	3.4	1.5
1954	5.5	6.2	8.9	6.7	14.4	12.9	7.1	7.3	6.9	5.6	5.7	2.3	5.5	2.2
1955	4.4	4.8	7.2	5.1	6.8	10.9	4.7	4.4	5.2	4.0	4.5	2.3	5.2	2.0
1956	4.1	4.4	7.3	4.7	5.8	10.0	4.7	4.4	5.3	3.3	4.5	1.7	4.6	1.7
1957	4.3	4.6	6.9	4.9	5.9	10.9	5.1	4.9	5.7	3.3	4.6	1.8	4.2	1.9
1958	6.8	7.3	10.3	7.9	10.9	15.3	9.3	10.6	7.7	6.1	6.8	2.8	5.3	2.5
1959	5.5	5.7	9.0	6.1	9.7	13.4	6.1	6.2	6.0	4.4	5.9	2.5	5.1	2.2
1960	5.5	5.7	8.3	6.2	9.5	13.5	6.2	6.4	6.1	4.6	5.9	2.4	6.2	2.4
1961	6.7	6.8	9.6	7.5	11.1	15.7	7.8	8.5	6.8	5.3	7.3	3.3	5.5	2.5
1962	5.5	5.6	7.5	6.1	7.7	13.5	5.8	5.7	6.0	4.1	6.3	3.0	5.7	2.1
1963	5.7	5.6	9.2	6.1	7.3	13.3	5.7	5.5	6.0	4.2	6.2	2.7	5.3	2.2
1964	5.2	5.0	7.5	5.4	6.7	11.2	5.0	4.7	5.4	3.5	5.7	2.6	4.6	2.1
1965	4.5	3.5	6.6	4.6	3.5	10.1	4.0	3.5	4.7	2.9	5.0	2.3	3.9	1.9
1966	3.8	3.6	6.9	3.9	3.4	7.1	3.2	2.7	3.8	2.0	4.4	2.1	3.9	1.8
1967	3.8	3.4	6.3	3.9	3.1	6.6	3.6	3.4	4.1	2.3	4.2	2.2	3.6	1.8
1968	3.6	3.3	6.0	3.0	2.9	6.9	3.3	3.0	3.7	1.9	4.0	2.1	3.5	1.9
1969	3.5	3.3	6.0	3.5	3.1	6.0	3.3	3.0	3.7	2.2	4.1	2.2	3.9	2.2
1970	4.9	4.8	7.5	5.2	4.1	9.7	5.6	5.7	5.4	3.8	5.3	2.8	4.7	2.2
1971	5.9	5.7	7.9	6.2	4.1	10.4	6.8	7.0	6.5	3.5	6.4	3.3	5.6	2.9
1972	5.6	5.3	7.6	5.7	2.9	10.3	5.6	5.4	5.7	3.0	6.4	3.4	5.3	2.9
1973	4.9	4.5	6.9	4.8	2.9	8.8	4.3	3.9	4.9	3.2	6.4	2.7	4.8	2.7
1974	5.6	5.3	7.3	5.7	3.2	10.6	5.7	5.4	6.2	3.0	6.4	3.1	5.1	3.0
1975	8.5	8.2	10.3	9.2	4.0	18.1	10.9	11.3	10.4	5.6	8.7	4.9	7.1	4.0

Source: U.S. Department of Labor et al., *Employment and Training Report of the President, 1976* (Washington, D.C.: Government Printing Office, 1976), table A–22, p. 245.

exists when a greater proportion of persons are employed as production workers in goods-producing industries. Industries such as construction and durable and nondurable goods manufacturing had unemployment rates in 1975 higher than the average for the entire private economy.

Furthermore, as can be seen from Table 14–4, white-collar workers have unemployment rates less than those of blue-collar workers. The shift in employment from blue- to white-collar workers should also tend to stabilize employment.

THE LOCATION OF UNEMPLOYMENT

One of the characteristics of our unemployment problem is pockets of unemployment that persist in various depressed areas of the country. For example, Appalachia is a region which continues to have persistent unemployment reflecting the effects of the migration of coal mining from the area and the lack of any other industry to take up the slack in manpower. While Appalachia is more than half rural, many urban areas are also trouble spots. In September 1975, the U.S. Department of Labor listed 135 major labor areas as areas of substantial unemployment—the highest figure since classification began in May 1955. In addition, 93 other labor areas (not major areas) fell into the substantial unemployment category.[34]

There is considerable variation in unemployment on a regional basis, reflecting the varied fortunes of local industry and the limited mobility of labor. Thus, in 1975 Michigan reported that 12.5% of its civilian labor force was unemployed, while the rate in neighboring Illinois was only 7.1%. Louisiana reported unemployment of 7.4%, while Texas registered only 5.6%. In Buffalo, the rate was 11.9%, compared to 7.8% in Cleveland.[35]

Unemployment in the Cities

In the last few years, Americans have suddenly become aware that their large central cities are literally decaying. Poverty, crime, inadequate housing, and unemployment—all of these ills seem to have crowded into the central cities. The problems of the central cities have been further complicated by the gravitation of large numbers of blacks to these areas, while white workers and their families moved to the suburbs. In 1960, 53% of blacks and only 32% of whites lived in central cities. By 1974, the

---

[34] U.S. Department of Labor, Employment and Training Administration, *Area Trends in Employment and Unemployment, August–September 1975* (Washington, D.C.: Government Printing Office, 1975), p. 1.

[35] U.S. Department of Labor, Bureau of Labor Statistics, News Release 76–811, May 12, 1976. On April 16, 1976, the Bureau of Labor Statistics began monthly publication of unemployment estimates for the 50 states and 200 large Standard Metropolitan Statistical Areas.

TABLE 14-4

Unemployment Rates of Persons 16 Years and Over by Occupation Group: Annual Averages, 1958–1975

Unemployment rate

Year	Total unemployed	Experienced workers															Persons with no previous work experience
		White-collar workers					Blue-collar workers					Service workers			Farmers and farm laborers	
		Total	Professional and technical	Managers and administrators	Sales workers	Clerical workers	Total	Craft and kindred workers	Operatives			Nonfarm laborers	Total	Private household workers	Other service workers		
									Total	Except transport	Transport equipment						
1958	6.8	3.1	2.0	1.7	4.1	4.4	10.2	6.8	11.0	(*)	(*)	15.0	6.9	5.6	7.4	3.2	-----
1959	5.5	2.6	1.7	1.3	3.8	3.7	7.6	5.3	7.6	(*)	(*)	12.6	6.1	5.2	6.4	2.6	-----
1960	5.5	2.7	1.7	1.4	3.8	3.8	7.8	5.3	8.0	(*)	(*)	12.6	5.8	5.3	6.0	2.7	-----
1961	6.7	3.3	2.0	1.8	4.3	4.6	9.2	6.3	9.6	(*)	(*)	14.7	7.2	6.4	7.4	2.8	-----
1962	5.5	2.8	1.7	1.5	4.3	4.0	7.4	5.1	7.5	(*)	(*)	12.5	6.2	5.8	6.5	2.3	-----
1963	5.7	2.9	1.8	1.5	4.3	4.0	7.3	4.8	7.5	(*)	(*)	12.4	6.1	5.8	6.3	3.0	-----
1964	5.2	2.6	1.7	1.4	3.5	3.7	6.3	4.1	6.6	(*)	(*)	10.8	6.0	5.4	6.1	3.1	-----
1965	4.5	2.3	1.5	1.1	3.4	3.3	5.3	3.6	5.5	(*)	(*)	8.6	5.3	4.7	5.5	2.6	-----
1966	3.8	2.0	1.3	1.0	2.8	2.9	4.2	2.8	4.4	(*)	(*)	7.4	4.6	4.1	4.8	2.2	-----
1967	3.8	2.2	1.3	.9	3.2	3.1	4.4	2.5	5.0	(*)	(*)	7.6	4.5	3.9	4.6	2.3	-----
1968	3.6	2.0	1.2	1.0	2.9	3.0	4.1	2.4	4.5	(*)	(*)	7.2	4.4	3.6	4.6	2.1	-----
1969	3.5	2.1	1.3	.9	2.9	3.0	3.9	2.2	4.4	(*)	(*)	6.7	4.2	4.2	4.3	1.9	-----
1970	4.9	2.8	2.0	1.3	4.3	4.0	6.2	3.8	7.1	(*)	(*)	9.5	5.3	4.5	5.5	2.6	-----
1971	5.9	3.5	2.9	1.6	4.3	4.7	7.4	4.7	8.3	(*)	(*)	10.3	6.3	4.0	6.6	2.6	-----
1972	5.6	3.4	2.4	1.8	3.7	4.7	6.5	4.3	6.9	7.6	4.7	10.3	6.3	4.0	6.6	2.6	-----
1973	4.9	2.9	2.2	1.4	3.7	4.2	5.3	3.7	5.7	6.1	4.1	8.4	5.7	4.4	5.9	2.5	-----
1974	5.6	3.3	2.3	1.8	4.2	4.6	6.7	4.4	7.5	8.2	5.1	10.1	6.3	4.4	6.5	2.5	-----
1975	8.5	4.7	3.2	3.0	5.8	6.6	11.7	8.3	13.2	14.7	8.5	15.6	8.6	5.4	8.9	3.5	-----

* Data not available.

Source: U.S. Department of Labor et al., *Employment and Training Report of the President, 1976* (Washington, D.C.: Government Printing Office, 1976), table A-21, p. 244.

percentage of the black population which lived in central cities had risen to 58%, while the percentage for white had fallen to 26%.[36]

The great majority of the nation's unemployed are concentrated in metropolitan areas, with especially high rates of unemployment among blacks, youth, and in particular, black youth. Most major labor forces—teenagers, adult men, household heads, whites, and blacks—residing in metropolitan areas suffer higher rates of unemployment than do their counterparts elsewhere (see Figure 14–4). The only major group with a

FIGURE 14–4
Unemployment Tends to Be More Severe in Metropolitan Than in Nonmetropolitan Areas

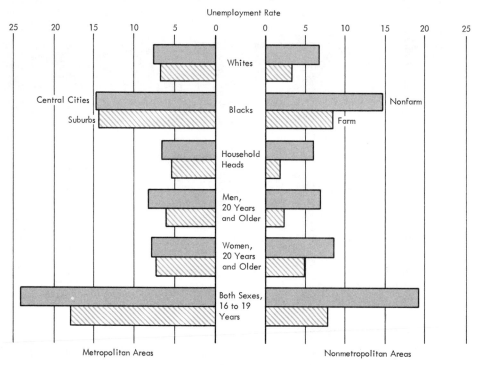

1975 annual average.
Source: U.S. Department of Labor et al., *Employment and Training Report of the President, 1976* (Washington, D.C.: Government Printing Office, 1976), p. 32.

lower incidence of unemployment in metropolitan than in nonmetropolitan areas are adult women. This probably reflects the greater opportunities that exist for women in urban settings.[37]

In 1975, within metropolitan areas, joblessness was more prevalent

---

[36] Bureau of the Census, *Social and Economic Status of the Black Population*, p. 9; also U.S. Department of Labor, Bureau of Labor Statistics, *Social and Economic Conditions of Negroes in the United States*, Report 332 (Washington, D.C., 1967), p. 13.

[37] U.S. Department of Labor, *Employment and Training Report*, p. 311.

among central city residents than among suburban residents (9.6% versus 8.0%, respectively). This was not true for blacks, however. Unemployment in recent times seems to have been striking blacks in the suburbs at about the same rate as in the city.[38]

Why is unemployment higher in our central cities than in our suburban areas? The answer is not to be found in a numerical lack of jobs. The fact is that the central city usually has a larger total number of jobs than does the rest of the metropolitan area in which it is located. Furthermore, the percentage of jobs located in the central city is generally greater than the percentage of the area's population living there. Many suburban residents commute to jobs in the central city, but there is less reverse commutation to the expanding employment centers in the suburbs.

The primary problem of the job market in the central city is the lack of correspondence between the job requirements and the skills available among central city residents. The businesses which have been growing in the central cities—finance, insurance, real estate, business service, and so on—require a preponderance of professional, administrative, and clerical white-collar employees. At the same time, there has been little growth in central city blue-collar employment, and in some cities an actual decline has occurred in this category. Unfortunately, a high proportion of central city residents lack the necessary education and training to qualify for the available white-collar jobs, while the blue-collar jobs which they can handle are declining or are available only on a sporadic basis at low wages.

We have seen from an earlier discussion in this chapter that a change in the composition of the work force can itself produce an increase in the rate of unemployment. This same development can be seen at work in the central city. The labor force of the central city contains a high proportion of nonwhite workers who traditionally have a higher incidence of unemployment. Likewise, the central city has a high proportion of newcomers—from other regions and often from other countries—who usually experience more difficulty in obtaining jobs. In poverty neighborhoods, a high proportion of households have women heads, who frequently can accept only part-time or casual employment. For these and other reasons which have been discussed in Chapter 8, central city residents may be cut off from the primary labor market and are subjected to the vicissitudes and high unemployment rates of the secondary labor market.

Unemployment Amid Labor Shortages

One of the paradoxes of the labor market today is that despite the highest level of unemployment in the postwar era, employers are unable

---

[38] Ibid., p. 31.

to find suitable applicants for thousands of jobs. In November 1975, the U.S. Labor Department's Employment Service listed 244,000 job openings across the nation. Since only a fraction of all job openings are reported to the Employment Service, government officials estimate that there were as many as a million job openings during the month.[39]

There are four reasons why jobs go begging even at the depths of a recession. In the first place, the loss of income for laid-off employees is softened by unemployment compensation. Many of the unemployed do not make a real effort to look around until they have exhausted these benefits. In the second place, many of the openings may exist in another area or state and require that the employee and his or her family move. The relative immobility of labor makes the matching of jobs to applicants more difficult. Third, many of the jobs are low-paying or are viewed as relatively undesirable. For example, at this writing short-order cooks and live-in help are extremely difficult to find. Finally, there is a shortage of highly skilled employees, such as machinists, welders, technical health care specialists, and—oddly enough—experienced secretaries.

This analysis indicates that the labor market is actually considerably tighter than overall statistics would seem to indicate. Unemployment is concentrated among groups who to a large extent are new entrants and therefore lack skills and training which match the needs of the market-place. This growing disparity has developed despite the fact that new entrants are better educated than ever before in our history. Unfortunately, education is not the equivalent of job training. As a matter of fact, the Department of Labor has warned that "the job mix and education mix are . . . out of balance" and that new kinds of jobs will be needed in order to provide employment for the growing numbers of high school graduates.[40] One economist attributes the paradox of un-filled jobs and high unemployment to what he calls a "twist" in the labor market which seems to have developed since World War II and which has reduced the demand for low-skilled and poorly educated workers more rapidly than the supply of such workers has decreased, while the demand for high-skilled, well-educated workers has risen more rapidly than the supply of such workers has increased. The result has been "an increasing concentration of economic hardship—in the form of unemployment, underemployment and declining labor force participation—in the lower levels of the labor market . . ."[41] It is apparent that manpower training and manpower policy will be of increasing importance in the years ahead if we are to achieve any substantial success in reducing

---

[39] *Business Week*, January 19, 1976, p. 16.

[40] U.S. Department of Labor, Bureau of Labor Statistics, *Educational Attainment of Workers, March 1969 and 1970* (Washington, D.C., 1970), p. 15.

[41] Charles C. Killingsworth, "The Outlook for the Economy," *Proceedings of the N.Y.U. Twenty-eighth Annual Conference on Labor* (New York: Matthew Bender, 1976), pp. 9–10.

overall unemployment rates. Current efforts of the federal government in this area will be discussed in Chapter 15.

International Comparison of Unemployment Rates

Although there are obvious difficulties in comparing unemployment rates in the United States with those of other industrialized nations because of differences in definition, measurement, and currency valuation, nevertheless policymakers in this country have tended to look at the lower rates abroad with envy. It is a fact that over the ten-year period 1962–72 the United States experienced a higher average rate of unemployment than did any other major industrialized nation except Canada. (See Table 14–5.) In 1975, the U.S. rate was likewise the highest, but other countries also experienced sharply rising unemployment.

TABLE 14–5

Unemployment Rates, Adjusted to U.S. Concepts, in Selected Industrial Countries, 1962–1975 (percent;* seasonally adjusted)

Country	1962–1972 Average	1973	1974	1975 I	1975 II	1975 III	1975 IV
United States	4.7	4.9	5.6	8.1	8.7	8.6	8.5
Canada	5.1	5.6	5.4	7.0	7.3	7.2	7.1
Japan	1.3	1.3	1.4	1.7	1.8	1.9	†2.2
France	2.1	2.9	3.1	3.9	4.2	4.4	‡4.6
West Germany	0.6	1.0	2.1	3.2	4.0	4.6	‡4.6
Italy	3.6	3.8	3.1	3.0	4.0	3.6	—
Great Britain	3.1	2.9	2.9	3.5	4.3	5.6	5.7

* Unemployment as percent of the civilian labor force.
† October.
‡ October–November average.
The quarterly adjusted data for the European countries make use of annual adjustment factors and should be viewed as approximate indicators under U.S. concepts. These data should be viewed as approximate only because of the difficulty in adjusting very disparate concepts.
Source: *Economic Report of the President, 1976* (Washington, D.C.: Government Printing Office, 1976), p. 131.

There are a number of possible reasons for this difference in performance. In the United States a rising percentage of women have entered the labor force in recent years, and many have not been able to find jobs or have obtained only temporary employment. In the countries listed in Table 14–5, by contrast, all except for Great Britain and Canada have actually experienced a decline in the participation of women in the labor force over the past 15 years.[42] Some nations have also done a better job than the United States in retraining unemployed workers and in providing public works projects promptly to take up slack in employment.

---

[42] *Wall Street Journal,* March 22, 1976, p. 1.

Although unemployment measured against the labor force has been high in the United States, this country has done a better job than most foreign economies in terms of job generation relative to population. Over the last 15 years, the percentage of working-age persons actually holding jobs has remained relatively constant in the United States, while it has declined in all of the European nations and Japan.[43]

POVERTY AND UNEMPLOYMENT

How many poor are there in the American economy? What are the causes of poverty? Are we making progress in eliminating it? The answers to these questions would not in any case be easy, but they are further complicated by the difficulty in adequately defining the concept of poverty. As one writer has aptly put it:

> Depending upon how poverty is defined, one can conclude that it is not a serious problem in the United States, that it is an insoluble problem, that we now are making great strides toward eliminating it, that we are not making any progress at all—or almost anything in between these extreme alternatives.[44]

Most statistics used by governmental agencies are based upon a so-called poverty index which was developed by the Social Security Administration in 1964. For families of three or more persons, the poverty level was set at three times the cost of an economy food plan designed by the U.S. Department of Agriculture to provide minimum nutritional needs for "emergency or temporary use when funds are low." Annual revisions of the poverty income cutoff for family groups of various sizes and for various geographic areas were formerly based upon price changes of the items in the economy food budget. Since 1969, the poverty cutoffs have been revised to reflect upward movements in the overall Consumer Price Index.[45]

In 1974, the poverty threshold, based upon this definition, was $5,038, for an urban family of four. Some 24.3 million persons, or about 12% of the population, fell below the threshold.[46] From 1959 to 1969, the Ameri-

---

[43] Ibid.

[44] Victor R. Fuchs, "Redefining Poverty and Redistributing Income," *Public Interest,* No. 8 (Summer 1967), p. 88. One difficulty with conventional definitions of poverty is that they are based upon income and do not take account of assets which an individual may own. Thus, a retired farmer who owns his farm mortgage-free and owns stocks and bonds may be a member of the "poverty" group, yet be living quite comfortably.

[45] U.S. Department of Commerce, Bureau of the Census, *Revision in Poverty Statistics, 1959 to 1968,* Current Population Reports, Special Studies, Series P–23, No. 28 (August 12, 1969), p. 1.

[46] U.S. Department of Commerce, Bureau of the Census, *Money Income and Poverty Status of Families and Persons in the United States, 1974,* Current Population Reports, P–60, No. 99 (Washington, D.C., July 1975), p. 1.

can economy seemed to be making substantial progress in reducing the percentage classified as being below the poverty level. In 1959, 39.5 million persons, or 22.4% of the population, were below the poverty level, while in 1969 there were only 24.3 million, representing 12.2% of the population (see Figure 14–5). In 1970, however, the absolute number

FIGURE 14–5
Persons below the Poverty Level, 1959–1974

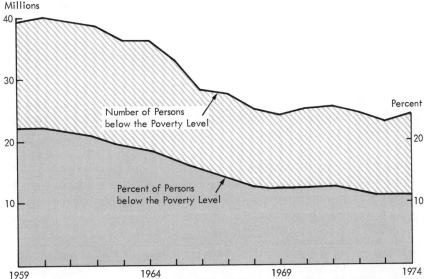

Source: U.S. Department of Commerce, Bureau of the Census, *Consumer Income, Characteristics of the Population below the Poverty Level, 1974,* Current Population Reports, P–60, No. 102 (Washington, D.C., January 1976), figure 1, cover.

of persons in poverty increased for the first time since 1959, and the recent recession has added many persons to the poverty rolls. In terms of numbers and percentage of the population, little progress has been made since 1969. Of course, if we used a fixed-income standard in terms of dollars without annual revision to take account of changes in the Consumer Price Index, poverty would tend to "disappear" as a consequence of the upward escalation in wages and prices.

Unfortunately, there is considerable evidence that poverty has become self-perpetuating. Studies indicate that about 70% of the families which are in poverty in a given year are also in poverty the following year. Of the remaining 30%, about 11% were dissolved by death and other causes, leaving only 19% who escaped from poverty. Of this 19%, however, 8% were still within $1,000 of the poverty line, 4% were within $2,000 of the poverty line, and only 7% were more than $2,000 away from the poverty line.[47] Because of their higher incidence of illness and insecure job tenure, families who escape from poverty in any one year also have a significant probability of falling back into poverty in succeeding years.

Another way of looking at poverty is to examine the relative distribution of income in the United States over time. The "poor" can thus be thought of as those at the bottom of the income distribution structure. Some economists would focus attention on how far those at the bottom are from the median income group. Using the definition of the poor as "any family whose income is less than half of the median family income," Victor Fuchs has found that the proportion of families with less than half of the median income has remained constant at about 20% throughout the postwar period.[48] Thurow and Lucas likewise conclude that the pattern of American income distribution has been approximately constant when changes are measured in relative terms during the postwar period. They point out, however, that as average incomes have risen, the real income gap between the rich and the poor when measured in constant dollars has actually widened.[49]

It appears that despite our efforts as a nation to effect some income transfer from the wealthy to the poor, there has been relatively little change in the proportions of national income received by various income groups. The accompanying table shows the percentages of income that went to various categories of families during the period 1947–74.

Group	1947	1950	1960	1970	1974
Lowest fifth	5.1	4.5	4.8	5.4	5.4
Second fifth	11.8	11.9	12.2	12.2	12.0
Middle fifth	16.7	17.4	17.8	17.6	17.6
Fourth fifth	23.2	23.6	24.0	23.8	24.1
Highest fifth	43.3	42.7	41.3	40.9	41.0

Source: U.S. Bureau of the Census, *Statistical Abstract of the United States, 1975*, 96th ed. (Washington, D.C.: Government Printing Office, 1975), table 636, p. 392.

THE PROFILE OF POVERTY

New Census Bureau data afford a clear picture of the nature and characteristics of poverty in the United States.

---

[47] Lester Thurow and Robert Lucas, "The American Distribution of Income: A Structural Problem," a study prepared for the use of the Joint Economic Committee of the Congress of the United States (Washington, D.C.: Government Printing Office, 1972), p. 13.

[48] Fuchs, "Redefining Poverty," p. 89. When the Fuchs figures are brought up-to-date through 1974, the same conclusion holds. See Richard Perlman, *The Economics of Poverty* (New York: McGraw-Hill Book Co., 1976), p. 15.

[49] Thurow and Lucas, "American Distribution," p. 1.

The Location of Poverty

Poverty is increasingly becoming a phenomenon of our large metropolitan areas. For example, the 1970 Census revealed that outside the South, 94% of the black poor and 56% of the white poor lived in metropolitan areas.[50] Furthermore, in 1974, of all the black poor living in metropolitan areas, 82% resided in central cities.[51] In 1974, of 24.3 million persons in poverty in the United States, two out of five lived in the central cities of metropolitan areas.[52] Moreover, it appears that the concentration of poor persons in central cities is growing over time. In 1959, about 56% of all poor persons lived in nonmetropolitan areas; by 1974, that percentage had fallen to 40%. The reverse trend is evident for the central cities of metropolitan areas. In 1959, only 27% of all poor persons lived in such central cities, but by 1974 the proportion had risen to over 36%.[53]

Of course, not all persons in poverty live in central cities or even in metropolitan areas. In the South, for example, poverty is much more a rural phenomenon than in the North. In 1970, about 65% of the South's black poor and 63% of its white poor lived in nonmetropolitan areas.[54] In 1970, the South had 46% of the nation's poor persons, almost the same percentage as in 1959,[55] indicating that despite the region's rapid growth in employment and production in recent years, poverty remains a persistent problem.

The Families and Racial Composition of the Poor

The majority of the poor in 1974 were black, of Spanish origin, elderly, or in families headed by women.[56] Each year from 1970 to 1974, families headed by women constituted an increasing proportion of all poor families. The percentage rose from 37% of all poor families in 1970 to 46% in 1974.[57] In 1974, about 44% of all poor families headed by women were black, up from 40% in 1969.[58] Employment opportunities for persons of minority races, the elderly, and women who head households are fre-

---

[50] Ray Marshall, "Some Rural Economic Development Problems in the South," *Monthly Labor Review*, vol. 95 (February 1972), p. 28.

[51] U.S. Department of Commerce, Bureau of the Census, *Consumer Income, Characteristics of the Population below the Poverty Level, 1974*, Current Population Reports, P–60, No. 102 (Washington, D.C., January 1976), p. 19.

[52] Ibid.

[53] Ibid., p. 21.

[54] Marshall, "Rural Economic Development," p. 28.

[55] Ibid., p. 28.

[56] Bureau of the Census, *Consumer Income, 1974*, P–60, No. 102, p. 2.

[57] Ibid., p. 6.

[58] Ibid., p. 7.

quently limited, and this is a major factor contributing to the poverty of these groups. Poverty in the United States is also an affliction of the young. In 1974, about one third of all poor persons were under the age of 14.[59]

In terms of racial composition, there are substantially more white poor than black poor, but the black poor tend to be much more concentrated in our metropolitan areas. In 1974, out of a total of 24.3 million poor, 16.3 million were white, and the remainder black and minority races.[60] Thus, while blacks and other minority races represented only 11.4% of the total population in 1974, they constituted about one third of all persons below the poverty level. Blacks have less schooling on the average than do whites, but their poverty seems to be largely independent of their lower educational attainment since their poverty rates are higher at every educational level.[61]

Poverty and Unemployment

In recent years there has been no relationship between the level of unemployment in the economy and the number of persons below the poverty level. Indeed, in 1959 and in 1974 the percentage of the labor force unemployed was virtually the same (5.5% in 1959; 5.6% in 1974), yet, as can be seen from Figure 14–5, there was a substantial reduction in both the number and the percentage of the poor. A possible reason for the decline in the number of poor persons is that the more liberal current unemployment compensation payments have helped keep unemployed persons off the welfare rolls.

Contrary to popular impression, a large proportion of the persons classified as poor are actually employed. In 1974, the head of the household in 2.7 million out of a total of 5.1 million poor families worked at some time during the year.[62] However, jobs for the poor generally offer erratic employment. Only 980,000 family heads had year-round full-time work in 1974; of the female family heads who worked, about 45% worked less than one-half year.[63] A study made in 1970 found that about 50% of the heads of poor families who worked during the year were employed as farmers and farm laborers, nonfarm laborers, and in service, including private households.[64] These occupations characteristically provide irregular employment at low wages.

---

[59] Ibid., p. 1.

[60] Ibid., p. 3.

[61] Perlman, "Economics of Poverty," p. 39.

[62] Bureau of the Census, *Consumer Income, 1974*, P–60, No. 102.

[63] Ibid., pp. 5–6.

[64] U.S. Department of Commerce, Bureau of the Census, *Consumer Income,* Current Population Reports, P–60, No. 77 (Washington, D.C., May 1971), p. 5.

Programs to Eliminate Poverty

Efforts to reduce and ultimately to eliminate poverty have followed three general courses of action.

The first involves the stimulation of economic growth in the hope that as production and employment rise, the poor and the disadvantaged will benefit along with all other members of our society. This policy has in fact had considerable effect if we measure progress by the number of poor households or poor persons falling within the conventional definition of poverty as prescribed by the Social Security Administration. However, the relative stability of the poverty rolls in the past five years suggests that we may have reached a core group of poverty persons whose economic status is not necessarily improved as a result of general prosperity. For example, households headed by women with young children, disabled persons, and elderly persons, who together constitute a substantial proportion of the poor, are not too likely to be helped by improvement in the labor market.

The second course involves training programs to enable members of poverty groups to obtain gainful employment. Obviously, such programs cannot be very helpful to mothers who must stay at home, the aged, the disabled, and children. Nevertheless, although only a small percentage of the total poor population is represented by employable males, the provision of adequate jobs for such men could have a multiplier effect by removing their families from welfare rolls. In New York City, the number of employable males has been estimated at 20–25% of all welfare recipients.[65] Training programs can be a meaningful avenue to reduce poverty, particularly with respect to those poor persons, both male and female, with actual or potential attachment to the labor force. This group consists largely of the poorly educated, the less skilled, and persons who are exposed to discrimination because of their race. It is noteworthy that in 1970 about 31% of poverty families were headed by persons with less than eight years of elementary school education.[66]

The third course involves various forms of income transfer payments in which funds are in effect taken by taxation from the more well-to-do and given to the poor as outright grants. One of the most important of such programs is AFDC (Aid to Families with Dependent Children). As indicated in Table 14–6, the number of families in the AFDC program has increased substantially over time, with the sharpest rise occurring between 1965 and 1971, when the number of AFDC families almost tripled. Since such payments, as well as food stamps, are not subject to

---

[65] Leonard A. Lecht, *Poor Persons in the Labor Force: A Universe of Need*, report prepared for the U.S. Department of Labor, Manpower Administration (October 1970), p. I–5.

[66] Bureau of the Census, *Consumer Income*, P–60, No. 77, p. 5.

TABLE 14–6

AFDC Families, Recipients, and Cash Payments, Selected Years, 1950–1975

		AFDC Families*		AFDC Cash Payments		
			Percent of All Female-Headed	Annual Total	Monthly Average per Recipient†	
Year	AFDC Recipients (thousands)	Number (thousands)	Families with Children	(millions of current dollars)	Current Dollars	December 1974 Dollars‡
1950	2,233	651	51.3	547	21	44
1955	2,192	602	32.2	612	24	46
1960	3,073	803	38.3	994	28	49
1965	4,396	936	40.2	1,644	33	54
1970	9,659	2,394	81.8	4,857	50	65
1971	10,653	2,783	82.7	6,230	52	66
1972	11,065	3,005	83.5	7,020	54	66
1973	10,815	3,068	80.8	7,292	57	64
1974	11,006	3,219	78.9	7,991	66	66
1975	11,300	3,395	77.1	—	71	68

* Excludes families with unemployed fathers. The number of AFDC families is for December of each year except 1975, which is for September. The percents are based on the number of female-headed families in March of each year except for 1955, which refers to April.
† Data are for December of each year except 1975, which are for September.
‡ Deflated by the consumer price index.
AFDC refers to the Aid to Families with Dependent Children program.
Source: *Economic Report of the President, 1976* (Washington, D.C.: Government Printing Office, 1976), table 29, p. 97.

federal income tax, even a seemingly low level of payments is the equivalent of a much higher level of taxable income. The Council of Economic Advisers has estimated that in 1975 a hypothetical AFDC family of four (consisting of a woman and three children) was eligible for AFDC payments and food stamps which together were the equivalent of a taxable income of $5,815.[67]

An antipoverty concept which is achieving growing acceptance is the so-called negative income tax. Advocates of this idea would use the federal income tax system as a means for redistributing income. Filing an income tax return, for the poor, would take the place of the current means test. Persons with incomes higher than the minimum support level would pay a tax, while persons with incomes below that level would receive a benefit payment through the tax system.

A controversial aspect of such support programs has been the question of their effect on the incentive to work. It is difficult to devise an income transfer program with adequate basic income guarantees and at the same time to assure that persons with earnings from work will

[67] *Economic Report of the President, 1976* (Washington, D.C.: Government Printing Office, 1976), p. 96.

receive a higher total income than that of those who do not work. Income support programs therefore usually include some formula to provide an incentive for earning additional income. Some critics contend, however, that in many states and cities where relatively liberal welfare benefits are paid, we may have pushed the "welfare rate" above the "market rate" for persons with limited skills. For these persons, therefore, it does not pay to work.[68]

How can we win the battle against poverty? Substantial progress has already been made in reducing the number of poor, both white and non-white. But more work and effort are needed, not only from the government, but also from business, labor, and various social and philanthropic agencies. Fortunately, we are not dealing with a problem of mass poverty, such as that which typifies many underdeveloped countries, nor are we faced by poverty resulting from large-scale unemployment. Poverty in this country is a problem of certain specific people whose personal, social, demographic, and environmental characteristics must be changed in order to enable them to escape from poverty.

It is obvious that mere financial assistance to needy families is not enough. We must improve the "employability" of these underprivileged groups so that they can raise their incomes through productive work. This calls for the expansion of employment opportunities in depressed areas and the strengthening of federal, state, and local training programs. These same programs are also necessary to reduce hard-core unemployment and upgrade the skills of our substandard employed. A number of federal programs have made an encouraging start in these directions. Manpower programs will be discussed in detail in Chapter 15. Finally, in view of the high proportion of female-headed households on the welfare rolls, we may have to recognize that reestablishment of the husband-wife form of family status may be an essential condition precedent to the elimination of residual poverty, especially in our central cities.

TYPES OF UNEMPLOYMENT

Unemployment can be classified into various types, either from the point of view of the individuals concerned or from the point of view of economists who look at the phenomenon of unemployment as it affects the economy as a whole.

Unemployment from the Worker's Point of View

Table 14–7 classifies the total amount of unemployment which existed in 1975 on the basis of the reasons given by unemployed persons to the

---

[68] See, for example, Blanche Bernstein et al., *Obstacles to Employment of Employable Welfare Recipients* (New York: New York School for Social Research, 1974).

TABLE 14–7
Reasons for Unemployment, 1975

Year and Reason for Unemployment	Total Unemployed (thousands)	Percent Distribution of Unemployed					
		Total	Both Sexes, 16 to 19 Years	Male, 20 Years and Over	Female, 20 Years and Over	Whites	Blacks and Other Races
Total: Number 7,830	7,830	1,752	3,428	2,649	6,371	1,459
Percent ...... —	100.0	100.0	100.0	100.0	100.0	100.0
Lost last job 4,341	55.4	25.5	74.9	50.0	56.0	52.8
Left last job 812	10.4	8.7	8.5	13.9	10.9	7.9
Reentered labor force 1,865	23.8	29.9	14.5	31.9	23.5	25.4
Never worked before 812	10.4	35.8	2.1	4.2	9.6	13.8

Source: U.S. Department of Labor, *Employment and Training Report of the President, 1976* (Washington, D.C.: Government Printing Office, 1976), table A–25, p. 247.

survey interviewer. The "job losers" referred to in the table include persons on layoff, whether temporary or indefinite, as well as those who lose their jobs permanently. Persons who voluntarily leave their jobs and immediately start to look for other work are termed "job leavers." The relative proportions of these two groups and new job seekers will vary over the year. For example, as might be expected, the number of unemployed who are new entrants to the labor market rises sharply in June of each year when the school year ends. As can be seen from the table, in 1975 over half of the unemployed had actually lost jobs.

Economic Classifications of Unemployment

Economists customarily classify unemployment into various categories, such as cyclical, technological, and seasonal, which we shall consider in the following discussion. Obviously, any such categorization is arbitrary. For example, technological unemployment—the displacement of labor attributable to mechanization and automation—is frequently distinguished from cyclical unemployment—the unemployment associated with the rise and fall of business activity over the cycle. In actuality, it is almost impossible to separate these two kinds of unemployment, for the typical unemployment problem is the complex result of a number of diverse factors. Nevertheless, such classification is useful in pointing out a direction for public policy and in enabling economists, trade-union officials, and other persons concerned with the problem of unemployment to attack this complex phenomenon in an orderly manner.

CYCLICAL UNEMPLOYMENT

The outstanding source of unemployment in our modern economy is the recurrent fluctuation in business which has been called the business cycle. Although the business cycle has characterized American industrial development almost since its inception, mass unemployment of a cyclical nature is a comparatively recent problem. Prior to 1929, the number of unemployed in industry did not exceed 5 million per annum. Yet, it is estimated that approximately 13 million workers were unemployed in 1933. The figure of 13 million understates the tragedy of unemployment, for another 25 million persons were directly or indirectly dependent upon these unemployed.

The causes of the business cycle constitute a separate field of study which is outside the scope of our immediate inquiry in this book. It is pertinent to this discussion, however, to observe certain definite characteristics in the fluctuations of employment which customarily develop in boom and depression. Thus, for example, it is well established that the durable goods-producing industries experience more extreme variations in output and employment over the cycle than do the industries producing nondurable goods. In the recent recession, employment declined by a total of 2.4 million jobs from September 1974 to April 1975—the largest consecutive monthly drop since 1945. Over 50 percent of the employment decline occurred in the durable goods-producing industries.[69] Housing and automobile production were particularly hard hit, and a decline in production in these industries has a multiplied effect upon the many companies in diverse industries which supply materials, parts, and services for these two critical industries.

During the 1974–75 recession, industries traditionally staffed by men were hit especially hard. Of the nonagricultural payroll jobs for men which were cut back during the recession, three out of every four were in the goods-producing sector of the economy.[70] As a consequence, the resulting net decline in payroll jobs for men was larger than for women, both absolutely and proportionately.

Women tend to be concentrated in the service-producing sector of the economy, which historically has been less affected by cyclical downturns. This was also true of the 1974–75 downturn, which saw relatively stable employment in the service sector.[71] In fact, state and local governments actually exhibited significant growth in employment throughout the recession! It would seem that the gradual shift in employment from the goods-producing to the service-producing and governmental sectors

---

[69] Robert W. Bednarzik, "The Plunge of Employment during the Recent Recession," *Monthly Labor Review,* vol. 98 (December 1975), p. 3.

[70] Ibid., p. 7.

[71] Ibid., p. 3.

would tend to have a stabilizing effect upon employment over the cycle. Although the economy has seemed less susceptible in recent years to the extreme depression-boom pattern of the 1920s and 1930s cycles, nevertheless, a cyclical pattern in employment and unemployment still persists.

SECULAR TRENDS IN EMPLOYMENT

Secular trends are long-term trends which may take perhaps 50 years to run their course. They are distinguishable from cyclical movements, which on the average do not exceed ten years in duration. Secular trends in employment within an industry are due to the influence of technological change, population growth, and competition from other industries.

Secular trends are at work not only in particular industries but also in the economy as a whole, and perhaps also in the world at large. Thus, wars, changes in the gold supply, new patterns of consumer demand, and population shifts will all affect secular employment trends.

One of the most disturbing secular problems facing the United States is that some industries which contributed substantially to employment growth in the post–World War II years now show slackening or declining growth. These industries include automobile production, education, health care, and construction. Automobiles of the future will be smaller, will require less material from other industries, and thus will create fewer job opportunities in supplier companies. Furthermore, because of increased costs, automobile owners are keeping their cars longer, which reduces the demand for new cars and employment opportunities in this basic industry. Similarly, the once booming education industry has been deflated by the declining birthrate; mounting health care costs have reduced hospital construction; and construction in general has been inhibited by high costs and saturation of demand in many areas. What new industry will take up the slack created by the decline affecting these major areas of employment?

TECHNOLOGICAL UNEMPLOYMENT

Technological unemployment is that displacement of labor by machinery and improved methods of production which is attributable to advances of the arts and sciences or to improvements in the technique of management. This definition does not make technological unemployment synonymous with all kinds of displacement of labor by machinery. For example, suppose that a minimum wage is imposed on an industry, doubling the wage rates it has to pay. Employers would now find it profitable to introduce machines already known and in use in other industries but which it had hitherto not been profitable to utilize in this particular industry operating at a low wage rate. Some labor will be displaced by the introduction of the machines, but it would be misleading to attribute this to technological change. The unemployment in this case is attributable to the rise in the price of labor and would have occurred even in a stationary state where technological progress was absent. Thus, for the purpose of precise analytic reasoning, it is important to distinguish "substitution" unemployment from "technological" unemployment. In actual practice, however, it is usually impossible to separate the two, so that any figures for technological unemployment are likely to comprise a substantial amount of substitution unemployment as well.

The Possibility of Permanent Technological Unemployment

Can laborsaving machinery produce permanent technological unemployment? The answer to this question will depend upon whether we are considering a particular firm or industry, on the one hand, or the economy as a whole, on the other. In a particular firm or industry, the effect of a laborsaving machine on employment will depend upon the rate of introduction of the machine, the laborsaving capacity of the machine, the extent to which the skills of the old workers are still useful under the new method of production, and the elasticity of demand for the product.

Whether laborsaving machinery can produce permanent technological unemployment in the economy as a whole has long been the subject of controversy in the literature. According to economic theory, the effect of a laborsaving invention is to raise the marginal product of capital relative to labor and thus reduce labor's relative share of the national income. Some writers have seized on this possibility to argue that a decline in the relative share of labor will mean a shift of income from those classes which save little to those which save more, so that consumer purchasing power will be diminished, a deflationary influence will be exerted on the consumer goods industries, and the equilibrium level of employment will therefore be reduced.[72] This conclusion, however, rests on an erroneous major premise and is not borne out by historical evidence. While most inventions are laborsaving, there has been no long-run trend toward a reduction of labor's share of the national income. The effect of a laborsaving invention in reducing the relative share of labor is only temporary. Since the invention also increases the marginal productivity of capital, and therefore the expectation of profits, investment will increase and thereby raise the marginal productivity of labor and the level of employment.

Technological Progress and Employment Opportunities

The kind of technological progress we have experienced in the past has expanded employment opportunities for two reasons. In the first

---

[72] Joan Robinson, *Essays in the Theory of Employment* (New York: Macmillan Co., 1937), p. 135.

place, the production of laborsaving machinery has itself constituted a major form of new investment and has contributed directly to a rise in employment in the durable goods industries. In the second place, the invention of a laborsaving device, such as the gasoline engine, which ushered in the automobile age, has created a tremendous tide of secondary investment. Thus, the gasoline engine gave rise to road construction, gas stations, tire plants, motels, and so on. Therefore, even though technological change as we have known it has produced serious problems of dislocation of communities, obsolescence of skills, and large-scale unemployment, at the same time, it has also opened up extensive new job opportunities.

What about automation? Is this just a new version of laborsaving invention—or is it something different which may therefore have quite different repercussions upon employment? Automation means continuous automatic production, linking together more than one already mechanized operation, with the product automatically transferred between two or among several operations. Automation has reduced the number of workers required in many offices and plants, but it has created many new jobs in industries which manufacture and assemble the intricate machines and complicated controls which make automation possible.

On the other hand, it is possible that automation does not create as much secondary investment as did some of the earlier developments in technology, because it involves not so much a substitution of machinery for labor as a linking and integration of already mechanized operations and the application of electronic controls. Furthermore, the immediate impact of automation can be serious in an economy striving to reduce already high levels of unemployment; for automation can render whole plants obsolete and can substantially alter the skill requirements of the job market.

Despite the fact that automation presents acute and peculiar problems with respect to the level of employment, it seems likely that in the long run—as one branch of the stream of technological progress—automation will provide a net benefit to the economy in terms both of employment and of standard of living. It is well to remember that 30 years ago, nuclear fission was an abstract theory; today, several hundred thousand workers are employed in the production and application of nuclear products. Who is to say what new products, what new avenues of production and distribution, automation will open up?

SEASONAL UNEMPLOYMENT

Seasonal unemployment is due to variations in business during the year caused by climatic or other seasonal changes in supply and by changing seasonal demands reflecting custom, habit, and style factors. Seasonal fluctuations in the demand for and supply of labor cause large flows of persons into unemployment. For example, the unemployment rate of construction workers tends to be 133% larger in February than in August.[73] The unemployment of young people has a strong seasonal component, related mainly to the search for jobs during school vacations.

Agriculture, of course, reflects the direct influence of the weather, and therefore it, as well as the processing industries related to agricultural output, is peculiarly susceptible to seasonal variations in production and employment. Seasonal variations can also be found in a wide range of industries, such as automobile production, women's hats, and Christmas cards.

The seasonality of the pattern of demand for labor in agriculture has given rise to a migratory labor force, moving from one area to another, following the cycle of crops. These people, who are generally in the very low income brackets and are unable to form fixed associations or community ties, present a serious political and sociological problem with which no relief agency has as yet been able to cope effectively.

Within any large state or area—if industry is diversified—opposite seasonal variations tend to counteract one another, so that the net seasonal fluctuations in total employment may be relatively small in consequence. For the country as a whole, such a balancing will always occur; but because of the distances involved and the insufficient mobility of labor, a substantial amount of seasonal unemployment may remain. Statistical techniques have been developed to eliminate the influence of seasonality from data of employment, production, and sales, so as to permit analysis of such statistics free from the distortion of seasonal variations, which tend to obscure long-term trends.

FRICTIONAL UNEMPLOYMENT

Frictional unemployment is attributable to time lost in changing jobs rather than to a lack of job opportunities. Frictional unemployment, defined broadly enough, could encompass almost all types of unemployment, since the cyclical unemployed, the seasonal worker, and the victim of declining demand in a particular industry must all take time to find new jobs. Frictional unemployment, however, is generally associated with joblessness of relatively short duration. Some idea of the magnitude of frictional unemployment can be gained from examination of the duration-of-unemployment data published by the U.S. Bureau of Labor Statistics. These reveal that in 1974, when total unemployment amounted to 5 million, 4 million persons were unemployed for periods of less than 15 weeks. Over 2.5 million persons were unemployed for periods of less than five weeks.[74] It seems likely that with a labor force of about 93

---

[73] *Economic Report of the President, 1975,* p. 91.

[74] U.S. Department of Labor, Bureau of Labor Statistics, *Handbook of Labor Statistics, 1975* (Washington, D.C.: Government Printing Office, 1975), table 67, p. 162.

million persons, a changing pool of about 3–4 million employees who are in the process of changing jobs can be expected.

To some extent the volume of frictional unemployment reflects the ability of workers to withstand some unemployment while they are looking around for a job. The high wages earned by employees while they are at work and the unemployment compensation benefits those involuntarily unemployed receive while they are out of work enable them to take more time while looking for a new job and to find an opening which will improve their ultimate income, instead of being compelled to take the first job opening available.

Frictional unemployment is a reflection of freedom of movement in the labor market coupled with some degree of immobility. To some extent, it also reflects movement in and out of the labor market. Since the end of World War II, there has been a major increase in the proportion of teenagers and married women age 20 or over in the labor force (from 20% in 1950 to 31% in 1974). Both groups have relatively high rates of labor force entry and reentry because of school or home responsibilities. As a result, labor force entrants and reentrants have probably accounted for an increasing proportion of the labor force and of the unemployed since World War II, and hence for a higher level of frictional unemployment.[75]

DEMAND VERSUS STRUCTURAL UNEMPLOYMENT

The definition and classification of types of unemployment constitute more than a useful exercise in orderly thinking. The classification of unemployment as one type or another can have important ramifications in terms of policy decisions, for a remedy which is applicable to one kind of unemployment may not be appropriate if the unemployment is attributable to other causes.

Because of the difficulty in classifying the unemployment which exists from time to time, discussions by economists and public officials have proceeded primarily on the basis of the comparative effectiveness of reducing total unemployment by (1) measures to raise aggregate demand, via tax policy, expenditure increase, or monetary expansion; or (2) measures to improve the employability of the unemployed via retraining, education, placement, and other labor market policies. Those emphasizing the former represent the "inadequate demand" school; those stressing the latter represent the "structural" point of view. It should be emphasized that adherents of these two points of view recognize that this is not an all-black or all-white situation and that there must be a judicious mixture of the two policies.

Advocates of the "inadequate demand" approach contend that hard-

---

[75] *Economic Report of the President, 1975*, p. 89.

core unemployment represents only an insignificant part of total unemployment and that a large part of it—attributable to such factors as obsolescence, automation, and changes in demand—would disappear if proper tax, spending, and credit policies produced an appropriate expansion of demand. Economists holding this position do not discount the worth of training programs, but emphasize that mere training does not produce jobs. For jobs to be created, there must be an effective demand for goods and services. On the other hand, structuralists hold that for certain participants in the labor market unemployment tends to persist even in tight labor markets. They stress the need for special training and relocation programs and fear that if the nation tries to solve the structural unemployment problem by expansion of effective demand, the result will be inflation rather than the solution of the problem of persistent and continuing unemployment among specific groups.

Although the debate continues between the two approaches, recent events have tended to buttress the position argued by the structuralists. As was pointed out in Chapter 13, the apparent shift of the Phillips curve, or its inapplicability to current economic conditions, has placed new constraints on monetary policy designed to eliminate unemployment through changes in aggregate demand. Furthermore, data on the changing nature of the labor force focus attention upon particular groups who are likely to have continuing high rates of unemployment. In the past 15 years, as a result of the baby boom, the number of teenagers in the labor force increased from 4.8 to 8.8 million.[76] Obviously, the absorption of these new entrants into the labor market poses special problems because of their lack of skills. Likewise, many of the new entrants are women and blacks, with similar problems of inadequate skills and training. In the case of women, many of them are seeking to earn a second income in families that already have a breadwinner. In 1975, nearly half of all husband-wife families had two workers or more.[77] These women tend to change jobs frequently and to move in and out of the unemployment category. Teenagers may alternate between a few weeks' work in a car wash and a few weeks on the unemployment rolls. Even with the high unemployment of 1975, in November of that year a third of the 8 million persons counted as jobless had been out of work for less than five weeks.[78] It seems obvious that changes in the composition of the labor force have created groups of employees with characteristics which lend themselves to higher rates of unemployment than apply to the more stable older members of the work force. In November 1975, for example, the unemployment rate for married men was only 4.6%.[79]

---

[76] *Business Week*, March 22, 1976, p. 116.

[77] Howard Hayghe, "Families and the Rise of Working Wives—An Overview," *Monthly Labor Review*, vol. 99 (May 1976), p. 12.

[78] *Time*, January 12, 1976, p. 56.

[79] Ibid.

THE CHALLENGE OF A HIGH-EMPLOYMENT ECONOMY

In 1946, Congress enacted the Employment Act of 1946. This statute provides:

> It is the continuing policy and responsibility of the federal govern-ment to use all practicable means consistent with its needs and obligations and other essential considerations of national policy, with the assistance and cooperation of industry, agriculture, labor, and state and local govern-ments, to coordinate and utilize all its plans, functions, and resources, for the purpose of creating and maintaining, in a manner calculated to foster and promote free competitive enterprise and the general welfare, condi-tions under which there will be afforded useful employment opportunities, including self-employment, for those able, willing and seeking to work and to promote maximum employment, production, and purchasing power.

This act charges the president with the responsibility for formulating a program to achieve its objectives. To assist the president in carrying out this responsibility, a Council of Economic Advisers was created in the Executive Office of the President. The Council prepares for the president annually, for submission by him to Congress, an Economic Report, which includes relevant data on current levels of employment, purchasing power, and production, and recommendations for such legislative actions as may best effectuate the purposes of the act.

The Employment Act of 1946 is not a *full*-employment act. Its aim has been interpreted to be *high-level* employment, and the content of that concept has tended to change over time, reflecting what appears to be a growing difficulty in reducing the volume of unemployment. For many years the accepted goal was a 4% norm. Recently, however, the Ford administration forecast unemployment rates for the balance of the decade as follows: 7.9% in 1976; 7.2% in 1977; 6.5% in 1978; 5.8% in 1979; 5.1% in 1980.[80]

The fact is that except in periods of wartime activity, the percentage of unemployment relative to the civilian labor force has not fallen below 4%. If we exclude from consideration the years 1951–53, which marked large-scale participation by the United States in the Korean War, and the years 1966–69, during which we were heavily involved in the Vietnam conflict, and confine ourselves to times of normal peacetime activity, unemployment rates have generally exceeded 4%.

The difficulty in reducing unemployment can be illustrated by the following calculation. In order to reduce the 8.3% unemployment rate which prevailed in early 1976 to approximately 5% by 1985, the creation of 37 million new jobs would be required—8 million to take care of the current unemployed; 15 million to accommodate the normal population

---

[80] *BNA Daily Labor Report,* December 8, 1975, p. A–2.

increase; and 12 million more to compensate for the jobs which will be lost through the substitution of machinery for labor. Yet in the ten years 1964–74, only 16.5 million jobs were created, and most of these were in low-paying industries.[81]

Despite these difficulties, a number of bills have been introduced in Congress which would target 3% unemployment as a goal of national policy. The Economic Policy Committee of the AFL–CIO has also endorsed the target of 3% unemployment.[82]

The Humphrey-Hawkins bill, which carried the formidable title "The Full Employment and Balanced Growth Act of 1976," accepts the concept that the federal government should be the employer of last resort and that if private industry cannot provide employment, then government should. Obviously, the implementation of such legislation would be very costly. But the proponents of such legislation argue that unemployment is also costly. In 1975, an estimated $75 billion was lost in tax revenues because of high unemployment. Furthermore, about $23 billion was paid out in unemployment compensation benefits for which no productive work was performed. And in addition, a $12 billion tax reduction bill was enacted primarily to stimulate the economy and reduce unemployment. Thus, our present manner of reacting to unemployment involves high costs. And one must not ignore the effects of unemployment on individuals in terms of social pathology; for unemployment is often reflected in higher rates of suicide, divorce, mental breakdown, and crime.

The major problem which proponents of the Humphrey-Hawkins approach tend to minimize, however, is the impact of such legislation on inflation. A nonpartisan study made in May 1975 by the Library of Congress concluded that an attempt to get the overall unemployment rate down to 3% within 18 months would push inflation back up to a 12–13% annual rate initially, and even more later.[83] Long before the 3% rate could be reached, severe shortages of skilled technical and professional workers would develop, leading to lowered productivity and inflationary wage boosts. The development of an inflationary psychology in the economy would ultimately lead to a new recession and perhaps to even higher unemployment than was experienced in 1975. The seemingly simple solution provided by the Humphrey-Hawkins bill is actually fraught with difficulty.

Should public policy be targeted at high employment or low unemployment? The two concepts are not simply opposite sides of the same coin. In fact, the two measures are calculated in quite different ways. As we have seen, unemployment data to a great extent measure a state

[81] *New York Times,* January 1, 1976, p. 17.

[82] BNA *Daily Labor Report,* December 8, 1975, p. A–2.

[83] *Time,* January 12, 1976, p. 57.

of mind, and are compared with the labor force, which is itself an obscure concept. Employment, on the other hand, is more concrete and is usually measured as a percentage of population. The latter concept is much more clear-cut and much easier to measure than are its counterparts in unemployment statistics. Moreover, there is no simple relationship between the movement of the two ratios over time. For example, in 1974 the unemployment ratio averaged 5.6%, which was relatively high by historical standards. At the same time, the percentage of the working-age population which had jobs averaged 57%, exceeding any previous year since World War II.[84] According to the employment ratio, the economy was more fully employed than ever before. According to the unemployment ratio, it was a long way from full employment and government compensatory action seemed to be needed. Which is the appropriate index to trigger public policy action? The way in which government officials answer this question in the years ahead may well determine the shape of our national economic and fiscal policies.

QUESTIONS FOR DISCUSSION

1. Would the achievement of full employment eliminate poverty in the United States? Discuss the characteristics of poverty in the United States and possible measures to deal with it effectively.

2. Should American public policy be geared to maximization of the number of jobs or to reduction of unemployment? Are the two goals consistent?

3. "Hard-core unemployment is not made of rock, but of ice, and melts when total demand expands." Discuss the validity of this quotation.

4. Discuss the merits and deficiencies of the definition of unemployment used by the Bureau of the Census. In your opinion, what groups are excluded by this definition who should be counted among the unemployed?

5. Discuss the meaning of the following concepts: poverty; invisible unemployment; frictional unemployment.

6. Discuss the characteristics of the typical unemployed person. Of what significance is the shift in employment from goods-producing to service industries?

SUGGESTIONS FOR FURTHER READING

Gilroy, Curtis L. "Black and White Unemployment: The Dynamics of the Differential," *Monthly Labor Review*, vol. 97 (February 1974), pp. 38–47.
    An analysis of the ratio of black to white unemployment during the various phases of the business cycle.

———. "Investment in Human Capital and Black-White Unemployment," *Monthly Labor Review*, vol. 98 (July 1975), pp. 13–21.
    A study of unemployment which purports to show that differences in

---

[84] *New York Times*, May 9, 1975, p. 12.

the quantity and quality of education account for most of the unemployment differential between blacks and whites in 1960 and 1970.

Klein, Deborah P. "Gathering Data on Residents of Poverty Areas," *Monthly Labor Review*, vol. 98 (February 1975), pp. 38–44.

This article analyzes the location of poverty areas and the characteristics of their residents.

Shiskin, Julius. "Employment and Unemployment: The Doughnut or the Hole?" *Monthly Labor Review*, vol. 99 (February 1976), pp. 3–10.

This outstanding article by the Commissioner of Labor Statistics discusses the advantages and disadvantages of various possible measurements of unemployment.

U.S. Department of Labor. *Hidden Unemployment*. Reprint 2867. Washington, D.C., 1973, pp. 8–37.

A reprint of various articles on the concept of hidden unemployment which appeared in the *Monthly Labor Review*, March 1973.

15

Manpower Planning by Business and Government

"MANPOWER PLANNING" as a concept is both new and old. It is new in both its micro and macro aspects in the emphasis placed upon it as an urgent function of business and government; it is old in that business and government have long engaged in manpower planning, both formally and informally. In recent years, however, rapid technological advancement, the changing nature of the business environment, increased competitive pressures from abroad, and the continued scarcity of some skilled personnel in the face of persistent unemployment have led companies to attempt to do a more effective job of forecasting their manpower requirements and the potential sources and means of fulfilling these needs.

Historically, government interest in manpower planning has been concerned with providing for educational needs—until recently very largely local and state functions—and with encouraging particular types of manpower development—vocational and agricultural education, military officer training, and particularly obvious technical needs, for example, meteorologists for airports. In addition, the Armed Forces have effectively trained personnel requiring many types of skills, such as airplane pilots, mechanics of all descriptions, and cooks. Also, through the Bureau of Apprentice Training, U.S. Department of Labor, formal apprenticeship training has been encouraged, and through the Office of Education, U.S. Department of Health, Education, and Welfare, educational activities have been furthered generally.

In the 1960s, government entered the manpower planning field massively. The persistence of structural unemployment, the civil rights movement, and the desire to eliminate poverty spurred great interest in the need to fit persons to jobs. The employment services of the states and the federal government were obviously inadequate to perform this function. A myriad of agencies came into being, and billions of dollars were spent on manpower development, planning, and upgrading and associated programs. Yet structural unemployment was far from overcome. Growing dissatisfaction with the extensive fragmentation and complexity of the so-called categorical programs of the 1960s—that is, programs designated and funded by Congress—resulted in the passage of the Comprehensive Employment and Training Act (CETA) in 1973. Although the purpose of the new legislation was to provide training and employment opportunities through a decategorized and decentralized system, CETA still operates to a large extent through categorical programs and with substantial federal government involvement.

MANPOWER PLANNING AT THE FIRM

A management publication defines manpower planning as "a process intended to assure an organization that it will have the proper number of properly qualified and motivated employees in its work force at some specified future time to carry on the work that will have to be done."[1]

Since firms engage in manpower planning for a variety of objectives, and since their manpower needs vary, their manpower planning activities vary considerably. In general, however, manpower planning at the firm, or micro level, may be said to have four aspects: (1) forecasting, (2) inventorying, (3) determining problem areas, and (4) planning for future needs.

Forecasting. To do planning of any type, it is necessary to estimate future requirements. This, in turn, involves judgments concerning matters both internal and external to the firm's control. The general state of business, industrial developments, and other factors affecting a firm's product demand must be estimated and projected in terms of the quantity and quality of labor required for the firm's production and sales. Obviously, the farther into the future the firm projects, the less precise the results are likely to be. To aid in these projections, companies develop mathematical models of future production based on different assumptions, often using general economic models, such as the Wharton Econometric Model, and project manpower on the basis of various assumptions as to future business conditions.

Inventorying. The second step involves essentially an examination of the company's existing human resources in order to determine whether they are employed optimally and to assess the extent to which they can meet the firm's future needs. The most comprehensive manner in which this is accomplished is by use of sophisticated data processing systems. Characteristics, capabilities, experience, educational attainment, and such

---

[1] Walter S. Wikstrom, *Manpower Planning: Evolving Systems,* Report No. 521 (New York: The Conference Board, 1971), p. 1.

pertinent aspects for the future as age, supervisory ratings, and so on, can all be put on tape and retrieved by modern computers in any part or form desired. Such inventorying received a strong impetus in the early 1960s, when companies were reexamining their black and other minority race employees, hoping to discover educational backgrounds and/or skills which had heretofore been ignored.

Determining Problem Areas.   The third basic step involves a comparison of projected future manpower needs with the resources estimated to be available from current manpower. To the extent that this comparison is accurate, it can demonstrate where shortages of numbers or skills are likely to exist in the future. It will, of course, be obvious to the reader that the longer the projection, the more risky in terms of accuracy becomes the comparative projection.

Planning for Future Needs.   With the scarcities estimated, planning programs are required to overcome problems. Such programs can include the training of existing or newly recruited manpower, intensive recruitment of persons with particular skills or educational backgrounds, the transfer of key personnel from one sector of the firm to another where the need is greater, and new programs of compensation and motivation in order to increase employee interest in upgrading or personnel development.

The New Emphasis

All the activities summarized above have, as already noted, been practiced by personnel departments for years, as they strove to overcome labor shortages or attempted to insure an adequate manpower supply. What differentiates the situation today from that of previous eras is (1) the pressure to employ minorities and women; (2) the changing demographic composition of the labor force, and in many labor markets, the changing racial mix as well; and (3) the impact on the labor force of rapid technological developments.

Government Civil Rights Impact.   To comply with government directives about minority labor force utilization, employers must have considerable knowledge about such workers—their availability, their relative size in the labor force and the population, the degree of training they will have to be given to make them eligible for work or promotion—and must plot this knowledge against the firm's projected labor force requirements.[2] In order to provide this information to governmental authorities

---

[2] We shall discuss government equal employment opportunity programs in Chapter 23. It should be noted here that government contractors, which include almost every concern of large size, must go beyond open doors to take "affirmative action" in employing minorities, women, and older and handicapped workers. This is often construed as a virtual requirement to train unqualified persons in order to qualify them.

and to defend their practices, many firms have been compelled to develop more detailed manpower and training programs than they would otherwise have done. The increased emphasis on female employee utilization will also expand the need for effective planning of labor resources.

For the first time, many companies now incorporate manpower planning in all future planning, whereas in the past the assumption was made (not always correctly) that manpower would be available for future needs. Nevertheless, such manpower planning, despite pressure from government involving the utilization of minorities, females and older and handicapped workers, remains relatively undeveloped. A survey by the Conference Board in 1971 stated:

> In the course of this study line managers and personnel specialists in 84 companies were interviewed concerning their manpower planning priorities. Only 24 companies reported anything that they considered to be a manpower planning system. Most of these firms were larger organizations selected for the study because it was known that they had recognized and responded to a need for more effective manpower planning. And, in most of those cases, their manpower planning systems were only about five years old [as of 1971].[3]

One reason why even the threat of sanctions concerning the utilization of minorities and women has not spurred greater efforts to plan manpower is that the imponderables loom so large. The needs for manpower in the future depend upon so much that is extraneous to the firm: the general state of politics within the country and throughout the world; the general state of business; the character and quality of the labor force in the firm's plant areas; technology bearing upon the firm's products; changes in the character of demand by the overall population; and many others. Such plans as are made must, by the nature of the problem, be flexible—but flexible or not, such planning seems essential if manpower is not to be a major constraint of effective firm success, not only for reasons of civil rights policy, but also because of the changing labor force and technological developments.

The Changing Labor Force. Western Electric Company, the manufacturing arm of American Telephone and Telegraph Company, has major plants in the Newark and Chicago areas. These plants were once surrounded by enclaves of European immigrants and their families. Many such immigrants brought with them skills acquired in their European training, and they encouraged their sons and daughters to seek employment at Western Electric's plants. The company could count on a labor supply that was imbued with mechanical interest and background.

Now the areas around these plants are peopled by black migrants from the rural South and second-generation urban blacks. Schools have

---

[3] Wikstrom, *Manpower Planning*, p. 5. Our debt to this excellent study is heavy.

deteriorated, family mechanical background is largely absent, family structure and motivation are weaker. Obviously, the type, degree, intensity, and scope of training required to create a labor force out of the current supply are far different and undoubtedly much more expensive and lengthy than was the case 20 years ago. To be successful, manpower planning must integrate such training with the nature of the jobs that will be required in the future. Perhaps jobs can be altered to fit more closely the background of the labor force.[4] Certainly, however, a company in similar circumstances can meet neither its own manpower needs nor government-imposed civil rights requirements unless it plans in terms of the changed labor force now available to it.

The demographic factors in the labor force also require careful planning. General Motors opened a new facility at Lordstown, Ohio, to produce its Vega subcompact. It found that the labor force was composed almost exclusively of young people—under 30 years of age and for the most part under 25. In view of the labor force characteristics resulting from the birthrates of past decades (as described in Chapter 1), this should not have been surprising. General Motors found the young employees less inclined to accept management direction, demanding of lax work habits (ten minutes' break each hour!), and quick to strike. The character of the labor force, lacking an older-worker mix, upset production goals until declining production needs, experience with unemployment, and aging changed the employees' outlook. A better age mix in the labor force might have averted these difficulties.[5]

Technology and Planning. The rapidly changing technology of recent years has been both an incentive for and a hindrance to manpower planning at the firm level. The incentive comes from the need for the knowledge and skills required in new technology which may involve exotic metals; advanced electronic, mechanical, hydraulic, or pneumatic skills; or various combinations of all of these. How to plan for the acquisition of these skills, and to what extent, involves much careful thought. At the same time, constant changes in technology and its varied usage with different product combinations can discourage any long-range forecasts.

Such problems are typical of the aerospace industry, which is frequently requested to build products, or to incorporate systems into products, which have never before even been designed. Such, in effect, was the job of the companies which prepared the hardware and systems

----

[4] On Western Electric's racial policies, see Theodore V. Purcell and Daniel P. Mulvey, *The Negro in the Electrical Manufacturing Industry,* Racial Policies of American Industry, Report No. 27 (Philadelphia: Industrial Research Unit, The Wharton School, University of Pennsylvania, 1971), especially pp. 105–6.

[5] *New York Times,* April 2, 1972; *Business Week,* March 4, 1972, pp. 69–70, and April 1, 1972, pp. 22–23; and personal investigation by one of the authors in 1976.

for the Apollo moon landing program. They were required to develop the capacity to handle metals and plastics especially designed for the project. This meant extensive, worldwide recruiting of specialists, plus intensive training. Indeed, because of its constant work at the frontier of knowledge and because of the tremendous fluctuations of employment which result from the awarding and completion of government contracts, the aerospace industry is without peer in training. Manpower planning in this industry must include reliance on training departments which can impart knowledge of all kinds quickly and effectively.

Unfortunately, training in this industry frequently brings skills to a high level and then discards them. Thus, when building the C–5A, the world's largest airplane, which also has one of the most advanced radar, control, and navigational systems of any airplane, Lockheed Aircraft Corporation discovered that it could find no electromechanical mechanics sufficiently capable of maintaining the equipment utilized in the manufacturing process. Sixty especially well qualified mechanics were given two years of on-the-job training plus 1,000 hours of classroom instruction. Two years after this expensive but necessary program was completed, the work on the 81 planes ordered by the Air Force was completed, and the mechanics had to be laid off. If a new order for complicated aircraft work is received, the company may have to go through the whole process again.

FIRM MANPOWER PLANNING AND UNEMPLOYMENT

To what extent can manpower planning at the firm level alleviate unemployment? The answer would seem to depend upon the character of the unemployment. Seasonal unemployment has been an early and reasonably successful target of manpower planning by companies. Part of the reason has been union pressure. Requirements to lay off by seniority, with attendant high costs of "bumping" (as described in Chapter 6), have induced many companies to plan their production in a manner that will smooth out seasonal peaks and valleys. Where that cannot be accomplished, other companies have employed special seasonal workers. For example, one construction concern utilizes college students to handle its peak summer needs and maintains a permanent year-round force. Some companies employ part-time workers to meet their peak Christmas or Easter load. The need for such workers and their usefulness in manpower planning are attested to by the number of successful concerns in the business of supplying part-time labor. In the automobile industry, "short-week" pay, under supplemental unemployment benefit plans, has induced companies to plan shutdowns of assembly lines for a few days per week instead of layoffs. This is a form of division of work, as noted in Chapter 6, that avoids reassignment of worker schedules and duties.

Insofar as unemployment is attributable to long-term business declines, company manpower planning, by proper forecasting, can contribute to the handling of the problem by allowing the labor force to decline by attrition, but it cannot solve the problem. The cure is new business, and manpower planning can basically aid by training employees to handle new duties. If, however, the sales are not forthcoming, manpower planning cannot solve the problem, except to give advance warning and some retraining to the individuals affected.

Much the same is true of cyclical unemployment. The real problem is to avoid the downturns by a product mix or some other such program. Manpower planning is a dependent variable geared to business needs; it is not an end in itself.

Business manpower planning has done its best service against unemployment in structural unemployment matters. Spurred by government pressure and the civil rights revolution, industry alone, or in combination with government, has devised programs which have brought into the labor market thousands of employees whose prior education and skill had heretofore marked them as unfit for all but the most menial work. This has involved a shift in the prior training role of industry. Historically, private industry has built upon the employee's past education by training, motivating, and developing him on the job and throughout his working life.[6] Partly as a result of the increasing complexity of industrial jobs and partly because of the failure of the American educational system to provide large numbers in our society with appropriate tools for work—particularly, effective communications, arithmetic, and work habit skills—industry has also increasingly assumed the pretraining educational role. This has been done to provide firms with an effective labor force and to meet their affirmative action requirements in minority employment. Training of the disadvantaged is a new, but growing, aspect of manpower planning.

A major problem in industry training of the disadvantaged to meet manpower requirements is that it is necessarily cyclical. Thus, Chrysler Corporation was compelled to curtail a major program when car sales declined in 1970; it had no jobs available for trainees, and so it could not in good conscience train them. Similarly, the extraordinary training capacity of the aerospace industry, which was beginning to show excellent results in training the hard core, ceased to be utilized when the industry's employment fell by 50% after 1969.

An effective attack on structural unemployment obviously involves both private and public manpower planning and attendant training. We therefore turn to a review of the manpower planning activities of the federal government.

---

[6] See Charles A. Myers, *The Role of the Private Sector in Manpower Development,* Policy Studies in Employment and Welfare, No. 10 (Baltimore: Johns Hopkins Press, 1971).

FEDERAL MANPOWER PROGRAMS

The antecedents of manpower programs can be found in the New Deal of the 1930s, but the current phase began with the Area Redevelopment Act of 1961 and the Manpower Development and Training Act (MDTA) of 1962. Manpower training as a distinct program at the federal level came into being in the 1960s and received its initial recognition in the Area Redevelopment Act of 1961, which provided job-oriented training programs for unemployed and underemployed persons. In 1962, Congress enacted MDTA, which has been broadened through subsequent amendments to provide institutional and on-the-job training for the unemployed, disadvantaged youth, and older workers; experimental and demonstration programs; and various supportive services. In 1964, the second major enabling legislation in manpower programs, the Equal Opportunity Act (EOA), was passed by Congress, creating a range of programs for poverty communities, including the Job Corps, the Neighborhood Youth Corps, and other programs for welfare recipients.

The 1967 amendments to the Social Security Act authorized the creation of the Work Incentive Program (WIN) to provide "employability development" services for selected recipients in the Aid to Families with Dependent Children (AFDC) category. In response to the increasing rate of unemployment, in July 1971 Congress passed the Emergency Employment Act, providing funding for public service employment for unemployed persons during periods of high unemployment.

The Comprehensive Employment and Training Act (CETA), signed into law on December 28, 1973, is designed to provide "job training and employment opportunities for economically disadvantaged, unemployed, and underemployed persons" to enable them to secure self-sustaining, unsubsidized employment. The new manpower law replaced the earlier mandated categorical programs with a system whereby local prime sponsors would assume control and determine the nature of local manpower programs. The only categorical programs that were maintained were WIN and Job Corps. Thus, CETA has decentralized the decision-making process for selecting programs and their clientele.

MANPOWER PROGRAMS PRIOR TO CETA: THE CATEGORICAL PROGRAMS

A major purpose of a national manpower program is to improve labor market operations by enhancing the competitive position of individuals facing barriers to employment, such as the lack of job skills, deficiencies in basic education, absence of supportive services, and social-psychological handicaps. In the evaluation of the impact of the categorical programs, these programs have been classified into the following four major groups, based on their manpower service mix and their expected short-term economic impact:[7]

1. Skill training programs.
   a. MDTA institutional training.
   b. MDTA on-the-job training.
2. Job development programs.
   a. Job Opportunities in the Business Sector (JOBS).
   b. Public Service Careers (PSC).
   c. Apprenticeship Outreach Program (AOP).
   d. Public Employment Program (PEP).
3. Employability development programs.
   a. Opportunities Industrialization Centers (OIC).
   b. Concentrated Employment Program (CEP).
   c. Work Incentive Program (WIN).
   d. Job Corps.
4. Work experience programs.
   a. Neighborhood Youth Corps (NYC).
   b. Operation Mainstream.

Many of these categorical programs have been maintained despite the shift in administration to local and state officials. Although CETA replaced the earlier mandated categorical programs to encourage greater flexibility, local prime sponsors are continuing such programs largely unchanged.[8] The following are brief descriptions of some of the major programs:

MDTA Institutional Training—classroom occupational training and related supportive services for unemployed persons 16 years of age and older who cannot reasonably be expected to obtain full-time employment with their present skills, and for underemployed persons who are working but who, with training, could obtain higher level employment. Training relevant to the local labor market, as determined by the state employment service, is usually provided at skills centers or at public or private vocational schools.

MDTA On-the-Job Training—occupational training for unemployed and underemployed persons who cannot reasonably be expected to obtain appropriate full-time employment without MDTA assistance. Such training is generally conducted through private industry—local employers, national groups, such as unions or nonprofit organizations—in the

---

[7] For a detailed analysis of the manpower programs of the 1960s, see Charles R. Perry et al., *The Impact of Government Manpower Programs in General, and on Minorities and Women,* Manpower and Human Resources Studies No. 4 (Philadelphia: Industrial Research Unit, The Wharton School, University of Pennsylvania, 1975).

[8] William Mirengoff and Lester Rindler, *The Comprehensive Employment and Training Act: Impact on People, Places, Programs* (Washington, D.C.: National Academy of Sciences, 1976), p. 13.

regular work environment. The private firms are reimbursed by the federal government, either directly or through the states, for the costs of instruction, and the trainees are on the payrolls of the employers.

The JOBS Program—training and employment for disadvantaged persons. The Department of Labor administers this program in cooperation with the National Alliance of Businessmen. The program consists of a contract component and a noncontract, or voluntary, component. Under the former, private employers, either individually or in groups, enter into contracts with the Department of Labor, for the employment and training of disadvantaged persons. The contracts provide for reimbursement by government of the extraordinary costs in hiring, training, and retraining disadvantaged persons. Under the noncontract component, private employers pledge to hire specific numbers of disadvantaged persons without cost to the government.

The Opportunities Industrialization Centers Program (OIC)—motivational and basic work orientation, basic education, skills training, and job placement assistance to unemployed and underemployed persons who have not been attracted to public agency–sponsored manpower programs. OIC is unique in that it was started by a group of private citizens without federal funding. The program emphasizes minority group leadership.

Concentrated Employment Program (CEP)—a system of packaging and delivering manpower services to disadvantaged residents of a locally defined CEP area. The Manpower Administration works through a single contract with a single sponsor (usually a Community Action Agency) to provide counseling, basic education, training, job development and placement, and other resources.

The Work Incentive Program (WIN)—recipients of welfare under the Aid to Families with Dependent Children (AFDC) program given training and supportive services with the objective of moving them from welfare dependence to economic self-sufficiency. At the federal level, this program is administered jointly by the Departments of Labor and Health, Education, and Welfare. At the state level, the state employment services, under contract with the Department of Labor, sponsor the program. This is one of the two categorical programs that have been maintained since the passage of CETA.

The Job Corps—special services for disadvantaged young men and women age 14–21 to train them to become productive citizens and to assist them in finding jobs, entering college, or enrolling in the Armed Services. The program utilizes residential urban and rural conservation centers and nonresidential skill-training centers which permit the youths to remain near or in their home communities. Job Corps centers are run by state and federal agencies, private industry, and public or nonprofit agencies. This youth program is still in operation despite CETA.

The Neighborhood Youth Corps (NYC)—opportunities to students from low-income families to earn sufficient funds to remain in school while receiving useful work experience and some supportive services. NYC also provides work experience training and supportive services for youths from low-income families who have dropped out of school.

Operation Mainstream—work training and employment activities, with necessary supportive services, for chronically unemployed needy adults who have poor employment prospects and who are unable—because of age, lack of employment opportunity, or other reasons—to secure appropriate employment or training assistance under other programs. Participants must be 22 years of age or older, and 40% of those enrolled must be 55 or older.

As shown in Table 15–1, over 11 million individuals enrolled in the

TABLE 15–1

Enrollment and Expenditures, Federal Manpower Program, Fiscal Years 1963–1974

Program	Total Enrollment (in thousands)	Total Expenditures (in thousands)
MDTA	2,519.1	$ 3,567,775
Neighborhood Youth Corps	5,762.2	3,721,401
Operation Mainstream	180.1	490,436
Public Service Careers	160.1	339,946
Concentrated Employment Program	650.4	1,096,812
Work Incentive Program	997.7	886,427
JOBS	394.1	848,034
Job Corps	230.4	874,505
Public Employment Program	672.9	2,482,142*
Total	11,572.3	$14,366,600

* Includes $44,010,000 allotted under Title II and $237,110,000 allotted under Title III–A of the Comprehensive Employment and Training Act of 1973.

Source: *Manpower Report of the President, 1975* (Washington, D.C.: Government Printing Office, 1975), table F–1, p. 317.

categorical manpower programs between the 1963 and the 1974 fiscal years. Over $14 billion was spent on these programs during that time span.

Evaluation of the Categorical Programs

In their assessment of the manpower programs of the 1960s, Perry et al. investigated both the economic and the noneconomic impact of these programs.[9] The economic effects were measured by changes in employment, hourly wages, and gross earnings, while the noneconomic benefits which accrued to the individual during the training process

---

[9] Perry, *Government Manpower Programs.*

were distinguished from the benefits experienced after participation in the program.

Perry et al. found that "the evaluative literature clearly and uniformly suggests that, as a group, participants in manpower programs have enjoyed higher average annual earnings in the immediate post-training period than they did just prior to their training experience."[10] They also found that the magnitude of the increase in earnings varied both within and among programs; greater earnings gains were acquired by participants in skill-training programs as opposed to participants in work experience programs.

Although there is no consistent pattern in the changes in hourly earnings of enrollees in the various programs, the available data on wage rates earned by manpower program participants before and after enrollment generally indicate wage gains that compare favorably with basic wage trends in the national economy. Perry et al. also determined that with the possible exception of participants in work experience programs for youth and the elderly, program enrollees achieved substantial improvements in employment—increases in both aggregate employment rates and greater employment stability. "Overall, these changes were more important than wage rate gains in explaining both the gross and net pre-/post-training earnings increases recorded by program participants. . . ."[11]

As to the differential impact of manpower programs on women and minorities, it was found that:

> The available data on the earnings, wages and employment of manpower program participants by sex and/or race suggest that, overall, such programs have had a limited but positive effect in breaking down labor market barriers confronting women and minorities. Data on pre- and post-program levels of participant earnings, wages, and employment do not contain significant and persistent differentials between men and women and between whites and minorities. Moreover, data on pre-/post-program changes in these variables generally indicate that participation in a manpower program was associated with a narrowing of these differentials in percent and, in some cases, absolute terms.[12]

Evaluators of manpower programs have often alluded to the potential changes in the psychological, emotional, and environmental well-being of program participants. Although such "noneconomic" benefits may not be the main objectives of the programs, these gains may have a long-lasting impact on the participants. The noneconomic benefits of manpower programs include such items as the supportive services received

---

[10] Ibid., p. 76.

[11] Ibid., p. 77.

[12] Ibid., pp. 77–78.

by participants while enrolled in the programs and changes in the participants' work ethic, job satisfaction, and schooling. Measurements of noneconomic gains remain imprecise, but such gains may be among the most significant contribution of manpower programs.[13]

In terms of performing their basic task—that is, moving the disadvantaged into the mainstream of employment—the government manpower programs have been considerably less than an unqualified success. The greater the skill training that a program has provided, the smaller has been the involvement of minorities and the disadvantaged. Thus, such programs as the NYC and the CEP have catered mainly to the deeply disadvantaged, but have offered little in constructive job training. Moreover, much of the JOBS program has obtained minorities and the disadvantaged basically unskilled work which has been the first to be eliminated when the business cycle turns down.

A major difficulty in evaluating government manpower programs is the paucity of data. Although the government has spent many millions for evaluation studies, a review of studies disclosed that few of them provided actual data and that even fewer set up control groups or utilized other methodology that could lead to definitive conclusions. It has been clear, however, that the turnover in many of these government manpower programs has been inordinately high, that more often than not clients were not trained for specific jobs and did not obtain jobs related to their training, and that the output of the programs has been small for the billions expended.[14]

CETA

CETA was enacted to incorporate three basic concepts (see Figure 15–1). First, the major responsibility for the planning and operations of programs under CETA is decentralized and shifted from federal control to state and local officials designated as prime sponsors. The underlying assumption of this change is that local officials are closer to the people and can sponsor employment and training services suited to the needs of their particular areas. Second, CETA attempts to consolidate and coordinate funding through local prime sponsors, replacing the previous network of direct contracts from the Department of Labor by many diverse local sponsoring organizations, without any overall management for local areas as a whole. Third, the funding under CETA is decategorized—that is, it theoretically permits the local government units to develop their own programs and to spend the money allotted accordingly, instead of requiring these units to use funds for a categorized

---

[13] Ibid., pp. 80–98.

[14] Ibid.; and Eli Ginzberg, *The Manpower Connection* (Cambridge, Mass.: Harvard University Press, 1975).

FIGURE 15–1

Summary of the Comprehensive Employment and Training Act

The Comprehensive Employment and Training Act of 1973 (PL 93–203, as amended) has seven titles:

Title I establishes a program of financial assistance to state and local governments (prime sponsors) for comprehensive manpower services. Prime sponsors are cities and counties of 100,000 or more, and consortia, defined as any combination of government units in which one member has a population of 100,000 or more. A state may be a prime sponsor for areas not covered by local governments.

The prime sponsor must submit a comprehensive plan acceptable to the Secretary of Labor. The plan must set forth the kinds of programs and services to be offered and give assurances that manpower services will be provided to unemployed, underemployed, and disadvantaged persons most in need of help.

The sponsor must also set up a planning council representing local interests to serve in an advisory capacity.

The mix and design of services is to be determined by the sponsor, who may continue to fund programs of demonstrated effectiveness or set up new ones.

Eighty percent of the funds authorized under this title are apportioned in accordance with a formula based on previous levels of funding, unemployment, and low income. The 20 percent not under the formula are to be distributed as follows: 5 percent for special grants for vocational education, 4 percent for state manpower services, and 5 percent to encourage consortia. The remaining amount is available at the Secretary's discretion.

State governments must establish a state manpower services council to review the plans of prime sponsors and make recommendations for coordination and for the cooperation of state agencies.

Title II provides funds to hire unemployed and underemployed persons in public service jobs in areas of substantial unemployment. Title III provides for direct federal supervision of manpower programs for Indians, migrant and seasonal farm workers, and special groups, such as youth, offenders, older workers, persons of limited English-speaking ability, and other disadvantaged. This title also gives the Secretary the responsibility for research, evaluation, experimental and demonstration projects, labor market information, and job-bank programs. Title IV continues the Job Corps. Title V establishes a National Manpower Commission. Title VI, added in December 1974 under the Emergency Jobs and Unemployment Assistance Act, authorizes a one-year appropriation of $2.5 billion for a public service employment program for all areas, not just for areas of substantial unemployment. Title VII contains provisions applicable to all programs, such as prohibitions against discrimination and political activity.

Source: William Mirengoff and Lester Rindler, *The Comprehensive Employment and Training Act: Impact on People, Places, Programs* (Washington, D.C.: National Academy of Sciences, 1976), p. 3.

program, which is defined as one described and written into law by Congress.

Prime Sponsors

Prime sponsors are responsible for operating CETA employment and training programs to serve the needs of their communities, and are generally one of the following: states, cities, or communities with populations of at least 100,000, or combinations of units of government, called consortia, in which one member jurisdiction has a population of 100,000 or more. Defining a consortium as a prime sponsor encourages broad coverage of labor market areas that may extend beyond the boundaries of local government jurisdictions; CETA regulations provide that a special incentive bonus may be offered to those local government units that wish to combine as a program sponsor.[15] CETA in effect turns over the programs to local political leaders.

Eligibility

Any person who is economically disadvantaged, unemployed, or underemployed is eligible to participate in a program offered under Title I. An economically disadvantaged person is defined as a member of a family which receives cash welfare payments or whose annual income in relation to family size does not exceed the poverty level determined in accordance with the criteria established by the Office of Management and Budget. Any person living in an area of substantial unemployment who has been unemployed for at least 30 days, or is underemployed, is eligible to participate in Title II programs.

Soon after the enactment of CETA, the economy declined significantly. Title VI, authorized by the Emergency Jobs and Unemployment Assistance Act, was designed to respond quickly to cyclical unemployment— thus, Title VI was intended to make the greatest impact on creating public service jobs for an emergency period. Eligibility for Title VI program participation is open to any person in a high unemployment area who resides in the prime sponsor's jurisdiction and has been unemployed for at least 30 days—15 days under certain conditions.

Characteristics of Participants

CETA regulations require that, to the extent feasible, Title I programs should be aimed at "those most in need" within the broad categories of eligible persons. For programs under Titles II and VI, special consideration must be given to persons who have been out of work the longest period of time.

Table 15–2 compares the socioeconomic characteristics of CETA participants with those of enrollees in the former categorical programs and the national unemployment population. Title I program participants have the same characteristics as those in pre-CETA categorical programs. Title I program enrollees have been predominantly young and members of minority groups, and overwhelmingly in the economically disadvantaged

---

[15] U.S. Department of Labor et al., *Employment and Training Report of the President, 1976* (Washington, D.C.: Government Printing Office, 1976), p. 89.

TABLE 15–2

Characteristics of Participants in CETA and Other Programs and of the Unemployed Population* (percent)

Characteristic	Categorical Programs	CETA Title I	CETA Title II	CETA Title VI	U.S. Un-employed Population
Total	100.0	100.0	100.0	100.0	100.0
Sex:					
Men	57.7	54.4	65.8	70.2	54.9
Women	42.3	45.6	34.2	29.8	45.1
Age:					
Under 22 years	63.1	61.7	23.7	21.4	34.8
22 to 44 years	30.5	32.1	62.9	64.8	46.0
45 years and over	6.2	6.1	13.4	13.8	19.1
Education:					
8 years and under	15.1	13.3	9.4	8.4⎰	15.1
9 to 11 years	51.1	47.6	18.3	18.2⎱	28.9
12 years and over	33.6	39.1	72.3	73.3	56.0
Economically disadvantaged	86.7	77.3	48.3	43.6	†
Race:					
White‡	54.9	54.6	65.1	71.1	81.1
Black	37.0	38.5	21.8	22.9	
American Indian	3.5	1.3§	1.0	1.1	18.9
Other	4.6	5.6	12.1	4.9	
Spanish-speaking	15.4	12.5	16.1	12.9	6.5
Limited English-speaking ability .	†	4.1§	8.0	4.6	†
Veterans:					
Special Vietnam era .... ⎱15.3⎰		5.2	11.3	12.5	7.5
Other		4.4	12.6	14.6	9.4

* Data on categorical programs are for fiscal 1974, the final year of their operation. For CETA programs and the U.S. unemployed population, data are for fiscal 1975.
† Not available.
‡ Includes Spanish-speaking Americans.
§ Special programs for Indians and those with limited English-speaking ability are also part of Title III of CETA.
Detail may not add to totals because of rounding.
Source: *Employment and Training Report of the President, 1976* (Washington, D.C.: Government Printing Office, 1976), p. 100.

category. Although public service employment under Title II was initially intended to be a developmental tool to assist the unemployed and under-employed to secure unsubsidized jobs, depressed economic conditions in 1975 led to the temporary use of Title II funds as a countercyclical tool to assist the rising numbers of unemployed. Title VI of CETA, in contrast, was originally aimed at providing emergency countercyclical public service employment. The characteristics of Titles II and VI program clients were thus more like those of the unemployed labor force than were the characteristics of Title I participants. Mirengoff and Rindler found:

> There is a trend toward serving a broader economic group of clients and a weakening of forces that have concentrated manpower programs

on the disadvantaged. Factors associated with this trend are the spread of programs to the suburbs, the conscious policy of prime sponsors to extend the client base, the change in eligibility requirements, and the reshuffling of program content.

The decline in the economy is having an impact on the selection of clients. The shift toward enrollment of adult heads of households and the recently unemployed reflects this trend.[16]

Although all sponsor plans recognize the disadvantaged as a priority group, the study conducted by Mirengoff and Rindler found that a broader socioeconomic group is being admitted into CETA programs as a result of pressures at the local level as well as the changing climate.

Funding

In addition to the actual amount of funding allotted for CETA programs, three facts are worthy of note. (1) Since the level of unemployment significantly affects the distribution of CETA funds, prime sponsors have become very conscious of the method by which unemployment is measured. In attempting to gain more funds, local prime sponsors may stress the technical deficiencies in the estimates of the number unemployed and of low income. (2) "Despite its billing as a comprehensive manpower program, CETA accounts for only 56 percent of all federal manpower program funds."[17] (3) Although CETA is intended to be a decategorized program, more than half of the funds appropriated are specifically earmarked. However, nearly 90 percent of the funds are now administered by local and state prime sponsors."[18]

Table 15–3 summarizes the number of individuals enrolled in CETA programs under each title, and the monetary appropriations for manpower programs in the 1975 fiscal year. Participants in Title I programs comprise 47% of first-time enrollment in CETA programs, while utilizing 40% of total CETA funds.

Appraisal of CETA

Among the assumptions underlying the decentralization concept is the view that local communities are better equipped than a distant federal department to identify their own employment and training needs, to design and operate programs meant to meet those needs, and to alter plans in response to changes in the labor market. One way of measuring local flexibility is to compare the mix of services originally planned by

---

[16] Mirengoff and Rindler, *Comprehensive Employment*, pp. 138–39.

[17] Ibid., p. 21.

[18] Ibid., p. 45.

TABLE 15-3

First-Time Enrollments and Obligations for Work and Training Programs
Administered by the Department of Labor, Fiscal Year 1975 (thousands)

Program	First-Time Enrollments	Obligations
Total	2,761.9	$4,109,000
Comprehensive Employment and Training Act	2,394.5	3,967,100
Title I	1,126.0	1,585,100
Title II	227.1	668,800
Title III*	69.6	229,400
Title IV (Job Corps)	45.8	210,400
Title VI	157.0	872,300
Summer youth program†	716.2	390,600
Section 3(a) Transition (Emergency Employment Act programs)‡	52.8	10,500
Older Americans Act, Title IX	7.0	12,000
Work Incentive Program§	360.4	129,900

* Includes Indian (Sec. 302), Migrant (Sec. 303), and Operation Mainstream (Sec. 304) programs.
† Authorized under Title III, Section 304, of CETA. Reflects activity in fiscal year 1975.
‡ Funds made available to provide for the orderly transition of programs funded under legislation predating CETA.
§ Authorized by the 1967 amendments to Title IV of the Social Security Act.
Source: *Employment and Training Report of the President, 1976* (Washington, D.C.: Government Printing Office, 1976), table F-1, p. 339.

prime sponsors with the changes made in the program mix as the year progressed. A comparison of planned and actual program activity reveals that as unemployment worsened, there was a shift away from classroom training and an increased stress on work experience activities.[19] Table 15-4 indicates CETA program activities by title for the 1975 fiscal year.

An effective evaluation of CETA must not only measure the number and costs of placements, but must also place adequate stress on the quality of placements and the stability of participants' past program employment. The Department of Labor is collecting longitudinal data tracking the earnings, employment, and job stability of a national sample of CETA participants for three years after their termination from the program, and the experiences of a control group of nonparticipants during the same period. This information is still not available for analysis.[20] Thus, analysis is limited to short-run changes in the placement of terminees from manpower programs.

Of the 658,000 individuals who enrolled in and left programs under Titles I, II, and VI of CETA in 1975, 202,300, or 31%, were reported as leaving the program for unsubsidized employment. Of this group, 10%

[19] U.S. Department of Labor, *Employment and Training Report,* p. 98.
[20] Ibid., p. 101.

TABLE 15–4

CETA Activity under Titles I, II, and VI, Fiscal Year 1975

Activity	Total	Title I	Title II	Title VI
Total individuals served	1,510,100	1,126,000	227,100	157,000
Cumulative enrollment by selected program activity:*†				
Classroom training	297,900	292,000	5,100	800
On-the-job training	76,500	73,800	2,400	300
Public service employment	361,200	29,800	211,500	119,900
Work experience	609,700	562,200	10,700	36,800
Other activities‡	88,000	86,900	1,100	—
Current enrollment, as of June 30, 1975* .	852,000	572,700	156,200	123,100
Current enrollment by selected program activity, June 30, 1975:*				
Classroom training	127,200	124,200	2,700	300
On-the-job training	41,100	39,400	1,400	300
Public service employment	262,200	20,700	147,000	94,500
Work experience	329,800	297,200	4,600	28,000
Other activities‡	36,700	36,200	500	—
Total terminations	658,000	553,300	70,900	33,800
Direct placements	64,200	62,900	1,000	300
Indirect placements	98,400	84,500	9,700	4,200
Self-placements	39,700	28,600	5,900	5,300
Other positive terminations	198,300	170,800	21,900	5,600
Nonpositive terminations	257,400	206,600	32,400	18,400

* Exclusive of enrollees not yet assigned to a specific program activity.

† Some enrollees counted in more than one program activity.

‡ Includes activities and services, such as job restructuring, removal of artificial barriers to employment, and development and implementation of affirmative action plans.

Source: *Employment and Training Report of the President, 1976* (Washington, D.C.: Government Printing Office, 1976), table F–2, p. 339.

or 64,000 enrollees, received no employment or training services under CETA, but instead were immediately placed in jobs as a direct result of applying for CETA programs, and another 40,000 individuals found jobs through their own efforts. In addition to those entering employment, another 30% (over 198,000) noted other positive terminations (that is, entered school or the Armed Forces). Thus, placements and other positive terminations totaled 61% of all persons who left the program.

If one looks beyond the official data, however, some serious questions may be raised about the potential CETA programs. As noted above, the programs are literally in the hands of the local politicians, who have thus acquired a significant source of funding at a time when local government, and particularly big-city government, is in serious financial difficulty. There is nothing wrong with such control, except that such local control exacerbates the temptation to utilize funds where needed rather than for the most appropriate training purposes. Thus, the beleaguered government of New York City sought to use CETA funds to "retrain" employees whom it was forced to lay off because of financial difficulties. Manpower training under CETA could easily become a patronage haven or a means of getting work performed through federal funding that might otherwise be performed by regular municipal employees.

A serious shortcoming of CETA program administration is that business is not well represented in program design. There are, to be sure, business and labor advisory groups, but these seem to be more window dressing than substance. As a result, there is insufficient consideration of what is needed in training to insure success in placement. Discussions with employers by the authors show that very few employers even know about CETA programs, and that those who do, have a very low opinion of the training given by CETA groups. The widespread impression in the business community seems to be that CETA program graduates are likely to be very marginal employees. The result is that such trainees are likely to be employed only as a last resort, when the labor market is very tight, or when employers are pressed by a government agency to achieve affirmative action goals.

CONTINUING FEDERAL PROGRAMS FOR SPECIAL GROUPS

In addition to performing general oversight functions specified under CETA, the Department of Labor operates programs and activities for the more disadvantaged members of society. Section 301 of Title III requires the Secretary of Labor to provide special or additional services for youth, offenders, older workers, persons of limited English-speaking ability, and others who are determined by the Secretary to be particularly disadvantaged in the labor market.

Although CETA has tried to place greater emphasis on programs covering all segments of the labor force rather than the disadvantaged alone, federal manpower policy still includes the operation of specific programs aimed at distinct disadvantaged groups. Under this policy, Indians and Alaskan natives comprise a major target group for CETA programming. Special programs for youth include the continued operation of Job Corps centers and special summer programs for low-income youth. Thus, the shift toward enrolling adult heads of households and recently unemployed in programs under Titles II and VI is a direct response to the rising unemployment rate, but special programs for the disadvantaged have been maintained under Title III. Altogether, CETA prime sponsors—that is, state and local governments—are expected to spend about $2 billion in federal funds allocated to them in 1977. This is in addition to the summer jobs for youth, WIN, Job Corps, and other categorical programs. As Figure 15–2 shows, the outlays for such programs have been increasing, regardless of performance, and apparently will continue to do so. Moreover, if a law is passed guaranteeing employment to all, the funding of all governmental manpower programs will increase in the hope that training will successfully bring the program

FIGURE 15–2

Outlays for Training, Employment, and Social Services

Billions of Dollars

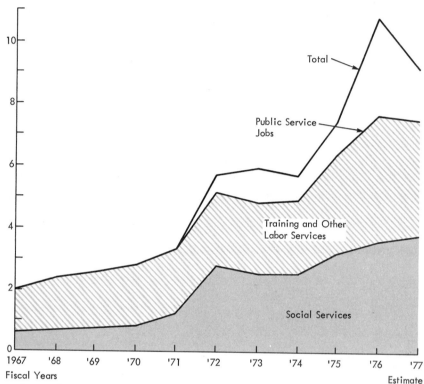

Source: Executive Office of the President, Office of Management and Budget, *The United States Budget in Brief, Fiscal Year 1977* (Washington, D.C.: Government Printing Office, 1976), p. 35.

participants into self-supporting employment—a hope that seems a bit optimistic despite some past successes. The problem, of course, is that the alternative—simply handing out money to unemployed workers in accordance with our current practice—may have worse consequences. Perhaps legislative debate will give rise to some compromise solution which will require unemployed persons, as a condition of receiving unemployment compensation, to perform various kinds of constructive work in parks, streets, and various public institutions.

QUESTIONS FOR DISCUSSION

1. Why do some firms engage in manpower planning and others not at all? Compare how you would spend funds on manpower planning if you were managing an aerospace firm or a steel company.

2. Identify the goals of federal manpower programs with respect to different segments of society. On what basis would you evaluate a specific program to determine its effectiveness?

3. How does the stage of the business cycle affect the need for and the nature of manpower training programs? Can manpower training be an effective anticyclical device?

4. How can manpower planning affect the trade-off relationship between inflation and unemployment?

5. Discuss the pros and cons of having the federal government become the "employer of last resort."

SUGGESTIONS FOR FURTHER READING

Ginzberg, Eli. *The Manpower Connection*. Cambridge, Mass.: Harvard University Press, 1975.

An evaluation of the role of manpower programs by one of the leading authorities in the field.

Mirengoff, William (ed.). *Transition to Decentralized Manpower Programs: Eight Area Manpower Programs*. Washington, D.C.: National Academy of Sciences, 1976.

Mirengoff, William, and Rindler, Lester. *The Comprehensive Employment and Training Act: Impact on People, Places, Programs*. Washington, D.C.: National Academy of Sciences, 1976.

The first two studies of the structure of government manpower programs under CETA.

Perry, Charles R., et al. *The Impact of Government Manpower Programs in General and on Minorities and Women*. Manpower and Human Resources Studies No. 4. Philadelphia: Industrial Research Unit, The Wharton School, University of Pennsylvania, 1975.

The most thorough study of the impact and effectiveness of government manpower programs prior to the enactment of CETA.

U.S. Department of Labor and U.S. Department of Health, Education, and Welfare. *Employment and Training Report of the President*. Annual. Washington, D.C.: Government Printing Office.

Contains comprehensive data and information relating to government manpower programs.

Wikstrom, Walter S. *Manpower Planning: Evolving Systems*. Report No. 521. New York: The Conference Board, 1971.

An excellent analysis of industrial manpower planning.

part five

Minimum Wages, Maximum Hours, and Government Security Programs

16

Minimum Wages and
Maximum Hours

THE ESTABLISHMENT of minimum wages and maximum hours for the work force has long been a function of government. The rationale is both humanitarian and economic. This chapter examines the movements for ever higher minimum wages and for limiting hours of work, and discusses the economic consequences of such legislation.

THE FEDERAL FAIR LABOR STANDARDS ACT

The basic minimum wage law, the Fair Labor Standards Act (FLSA), often termed the wage and hour law, was first enacted in 1938 and has since been amended several times. The original minimum wage was set at 25 cents per hour. As of January 1, 1976, the legal minimum wage was set at $2.30 per hour, with lower minima for special work groups. The history of the act is summarized in Figure 16–1. Since its passage, the act has also regulated hours of work by requiring that all work over a standard workweek, set since 1940 at 40 hours, be paid for at the rate of time and one half the regular wage.

The Fair Labor Standards Act never covered all employees. As a result of amendments of the last decade, the U.S. Department of Labor estimates that approximately 49.8 million workers are covered by the act. About 5 million more are covered by similar state legislation. Those outside the federal law's purview include principally employees of small farms and small or intrastate businesses; state and municipal employees who were covered by the 1966 and 1974 amendments, found unconstitutional by the U.S. Supreme Court;[1] and managerial, supervisory, pro-

---

[1] *The National League of Cities et al. v. W. J. Usery, Jr., Secretary of Labor,* 96 S. Ct. 2465 (1976).

FIGURE 16–1

Federal Minimum Wage History

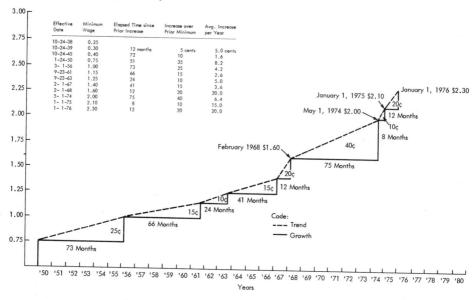

fessional, and outside sales personnel, whose compensation generally would in any case be unaffected by minimum wage legislation. Table 16–1 summarizes the coverage of the Fair Labor Standards Act.

Superminimum and Prevailing Wages

In addition to the FLSA, there are special *superminimum* wage laws, or prevailing wage laws which govern the wages of particular groups. Thus, under a complex formula, airline pilots are paid wages in excess of $25,000 per year (some earn more than $90,000), and their hours may not exceed 85 per month.

A second superminimum wage law, known as the Davis-Bacon Act, was first passed in 1931. As later amended, it requires contractors engaged in construction work valued at $2,000 or more, and paid for by federal funds, to compensate employees on the basis of "prevailing wages." In 1965, by the O'Hara-McNamara Services Act, the Davis-Bacon type of regulation was extended to government-contract on-site services other than construction—for example, machinery installation.[2]

The Secretary of Labor determines prevailing minimum rates for the

---

[2] For an analysis of this law and its administration, see Armand J. Thieblot, Jr., *The Davis-Bacon Act*, Labor Relations and Public Policy Series, Report No. 10 (Philadelphia: Industrial Research Unit, The Wharton School, University of Pennsylvania, 1975). Forty-two states have similar laws. See Armand J. Thieblot, Jr., "The 'Little Davis-Bacon Acts': Prevailing Wage Laws of the States," report prepared for the Merit Shop Foundation, Inc., 1975.

TABLE 16-1

Estimated Number of Employed Wage and Salary Workers in the Civilian Labor Force Classified by Their Status under the Minimum Wage Provisions of the Fair Labor Standards Act, by Industry Division, July 1976 (in thousands)

Industry Division	Number of Employed Wage and Salary Workers in the Civilian Labor Force				Number of Nonsupervisory Employees Subject to the Minimum Wage Provisions of the FLSA*					Number of Nonsupervisory Employees Not Subject to the Minimum Wage Provisions of the FLSA§
	Total	Activities Generally Exempt under Section 13(a)(1) of FLSA*		Nonsupervisory Employees, Excluding Outside Sales Workers	Total	Subject Prior to the 1966 Amendments†	Subject as a Result of the 1966 Amendments†	Subject as a Result of the 1974 Amendments†		
		Executive, Administrative and Professional Personnel	Outside Sales Workers							
Total civilian labor force	81,482	15,165	1,979	64,338	49,673	35,677	10,238	3,758		16,643
Private sector	66,387	9,349	1,979	55,059	47,369	35,677	9,623	2,069		9,669
Agriculture‡	1,446	71	—	1,375	597	—	572	25		778
Mining	758	84	—	674	670	670	—	—		4
Contract construction	3,659	366	3	3,290	3,273	2,674	599	—		20
Manufacturing	18,694	2,177	378	16,139	16,083	15,986	60	37		434
Transportation and public utilities	4,503	512	6	3,985	3,921	3,818	103	—		70
Wholesale trade	4,194	596	710	2,888	2,878	2,770	108	—		720
Retail trade	12,890	1,276	116	11,498	8,227	4,188	3,438	601		3,387
Finance, insurance, and real estate	4,243	613	737	2,893	2,766	2,661	105	—		864
Service industries (except private households)	14,221	3,654	29	10,538	7,680	2,910	4,638	132		2,887
Private households	1,779	—	—	1,779	1,274	—	—	1,274		505
Federal government	2,746	442	—	2,304	2,304	—	615	1,689		—

* Section 13(a)(1) exempts from the minimum wage and overtime provisions of the Fair Labor Standards Act ". . . any employee employed in a bona fide executive, administrative, or professional capacity (including any employee employed in the capacity of academic administrative personnel, or teacher in elementary or secondary schools), or in the capacity of outside salesman. . . ." Included are all employees in the specified activities, whether employed in covered or non-covered establishments.

† Relates to currently employed workers who would have been subject under criteria in effect prior to the 1974 amendments.

‡ Based upon average annual employment.

§ Includes state and municipal employees covered by the 1974 amendments but excluded by the decision of the U.S. Supreme Court in *The National League of Cities v. Usery, Secretary of Labor*, 96 S. Ct. 2465 (1976).

Source: U.S. Department of Labor, Employment Standards Administration.

various crafts under the Davis-Bacon Act procedure. As interpreted by Secretaries since 1931, "prevailing" is usually synonymous with "union." Building-trades unions have found the Davis-Bacon Act a valuable tool to prevent undercutting of their wages and to assist in extending the union rate to a wider area. Not infrequently, the union rate has been determined to be prevailing in a locality not even unionized but in addition paying considerably less than the union rate which actually prevails in a large city some miles away.

A third superminimum wage law is the Public Contracts, or Walsh-Healey Act, which was enacted in 1936, two years prior to the passage of the Fair Labor Standards Act, as a means of filling part of the gap left by the demise of the NRA. The Walsh-Healey Act provided, among other things, that for all government in-plant contracts in excess of $10,000, wages should not be less than the "prevailing minimum" as established by the Secretary of Labor. The wage-setting mechanisms of this law were rendered inoperative in 1964 by a court decision,[3] thus ending a very controversial government activity.[4]

State Minimum Wage Laws

State minimum wage laws were originally enacted to cover employment of women and children only, but since World War II, states have increasingly enacted laws of general application. Only the latter type are now operative, since the Civil Rights Act of 1964, by outlawing sex as well as race discrimination, prohibits such distinctions. In 1976, 40 states, Puerto Rico, the District of Columbia, and Guam had minimum wage laws. Kansas and Louisiana had wage boards, but no minima in effect.

Table 16–2 lists the states which have minimum wage laws and gives the rates currently in effect. Some of these laws set a statutory minimum; others permit the rates to be adjusted by administrative procedures which allow the establishment of different rates for different industries, and within limits, the raising of rates without new legislative sanction. Still other laws establish rates by reference to the federal Fair Labor Standards Act.

---

[3] The Secretary used data collected by the U.S. Bureau of Labor Statistics to determine prevailing wages. Since these were gathered for other BLS purposes on promise to cooperating employers that no individual company would be identified, their source could not be given to those who wanted to check them, thus denying due process in a proceeding. See *Wirtz* v. *Baldor Electric Co.*, 337 Fed. 518 (D.C. Cir. 1964).

[4] Two studies shed much light on the Walsh-Healey Act and its procedure: Herbert C. Morton, *Public Contracts and Private Wages: Experience under the Walsh-Healey Act* (Washington, D.C.: Brookings Institution, 1965); and Carroll L. Christensen and Richard A. Myren, *Wage Policy under the Walsh-Healey Public Contracts Act: A Critical Review* (Bloomington: University of Indiana Press, 1966).

TABLE 16–2
Basic Minimum Wage and Overtime Premium Pay Provisions Applicable to
Nonagricultural Employment under State Laws, January 1, 1977

Jurisdiction (state)	Basic Minimum Rate (per hour)	Premium Pay after Designated Hours	
		Daily	Weekly
Alaska	$2.80[a]	8	40
Arkansas (applicable to employers of 5 or more)	2.00	8	7th day
California	2.50	8	—
Colorado	1.00–1.25		40–42
Connecticut	2.31[a]		40
Delaware	1.60		
District of Columbia	2.48–2.70[d]		40
Georgia (applicable to employers of six or more, or employers with annual sales of $40,000 or more)	1.25		
Guam	2.05		40
Hawaii	2.40		40
Idaho	1.60[e]	8	48
Illinois (applicable to employers of five or more full-time employees)	2.10[d]		
Indiana (applicable to employers of four or more in any workweek)	1.25[e]		
Kentucky	1.60		44–48 7th day
Maine (*except* hospital and nursing home employees; and *except* employers of less than four)	2.30[a]		40
Maryland	2.30		40
Massachusetts	2.00		40
Michigan (applicable to employers of four or more at any one time within any calendar year; if employer has four or more at any one time, he is covered by the law for remainder of such calendar year)	2.30[e]		40[c]
Minnesota	1.80[d]		
Montana	2.00		40
Nebraska (applicable to employers of four or more at any one time)	1.60		
Nevada	2.30[d]	8	48
New Hampshire	2.30[a d]		
New Jersey	2.50[d]		40
New Mexico	2.30[c]		48
New York	2.30[a d]		40
North Carolina (applicable to employers of four or more at any one time)	2.00[e]		50[b]
North Dakota	2.10–2.30		48
Ohio	1.60		40
Oklahoma (applicable to employers of ten or more full-time employees at any one location)	1.80		
Oregon	2.30[d]		40
Pennsylvania	2.30		40
Puerto Rico	0.65–1.60	8 d.t. statutory rest day d.t.	48 d.t.

TABLE 16–2 (continued)

Jurisdiction (state)	Basic Minimum Rate (per hour)	Premium Pay after Designated Hours	
		Daily	Weekly
Rhode Island	2.30		48
South Dakota	2.00 e		
Texas	1.40		
Utah	1.20–1.35		
Vermont (applicable to employers of two or more)	2.30 a		40
Virginia (applicable to employers of more than four)	2.00		
Washington	2.30 d		
West Virginia (applicable to employers of six or more in any calendar week at one location).	2.00		44
Wisconsin	2.30 c d		
Wyoming	1.60 e		

General note: Many of these laws establish lower minima for agricultural and domestic workers.

ᵃ Increases in minimum rates linked to the federal rate: Alaska's rate increases by 50 cents above the federal minimum; Connecticut's provides an increase of ½ of 1% above the federal minimum; Maine matches federal increases up to $3.00; New York and Vermont equal the federal rate; New Hampshire uses the federal rate by reference; and Wisconsin's rate may not fall below 90% of the federal minimum.

ᵇ North Carolina overtime provisions apply to employees not assured premium under FLSA.

ᶜ Effective later than January 1, 1977, for all or some covered workers.

ᵈ Lower youth minimum rates.

ᵉ Youth under 16 (Idaho and North Carolina) or under 18 (balance noted) exempted.

dt = double time.

Source: U.S. Department of Labor, Employment Standards Administration.

Minimum Wages and Employment—The Theory

Minimum wage legislation means higher wage costs to the individual employer affected by such legislation. Economic theory tells us that if an employer finds that labor has become more expensive, he will try to economize in its use or to get more work out of his labor force. There may be some workers who can be dropped from the payroll simply by rescheduling work or changing the assignment of duties. In some cases, it may be possible to eliminate jobs which no longer "pay" at the higher wage rate. The most effective way of reducing labor costs is, of course, through substituting machinery for labor. The lower the wage paid prior to the establishment of the minimum wage, and the greater the increase in costs imposed by such legislation, the greater the incentive to the employer to introduce laborsaving machinery.

In many cases, the process of mechanization will involve the purchase of machinery which was already known and in use in the industry but which was not adopted at the low-wage level. Sometimes, however, the wage increase will cause employers to introduce machinery which it would have been profitable to introduce even at a lower wage level but which management failed to adopt because of inefficiency and reliance on the payment of substandard wages as a means of competition. In other words, the imposition of a minimum wage may provide the "shock" which compels inefficient management to look around in the industry and bring its production methods in line with more efficient firms in order to survive. This will involve the adoption not only of laborsaving machinery but also of methods and layouts which will reduce overhead, material costs, insurance expense, and other outlays. It should be remembered that the introduction of laborsaving machinery is sometimes a long-term process. Some employers may not be able to utilize the newest machinery in an antiquated plant and may have to delay the purchase of machinery until they can move to a new location; other employers may try to get a few more years out of old equipment before making the large capital expenditure required for modern machinery. As a result, the displacement of labor through the introduction of laborsaving machinery may not occur until several years after the imposition of the minimum wage; and if business meanwhile increases, there may be no unemployment observable at all.

Another avenue by which a minimum wage may react upon employment is through the effect of the wage increase on price. Large companies frequently have big advertising budgets and are able to obtain a higher price for their products by building up the idea of quality in consumers' minds. Small companies, on the other hand, must often compete primarily on the basis of price. If a minimum wage raises the labor costs of smaller concerns, it puts them at a substantial competitive disadvantage. If they raise prices to compensate for the increase in costs, some part of their business will tend to shift to their larger competitors, and they may eventually be forced out of business. If this result occurs, the total volume of employment in the industry may be lowered after the shift of business is effected, even though some labor displaced in small companies is employed by larger ones. The reason is that the larger concerns are likely to be more mechanized, and a dollar's sales in such companies will require employment of a smaller amount of labor than in the smaller, low-wage plants.

It should be noted that if a minimum wage law produces unemployment, the incidence of unemployment may be expected to fall most heavily upon those with the least skills—that is, upon those employees whose wages have been below the legal minimum and who have the most difficulty in finding jobs. It will be recalled that in our analysis of unemployment in Chapter 14, it was pointed out that a disproportionate share of the persistent unemployment in recent years has fallen upon the unskilled group. Our succeeding analysis will attempt to determine whether this unemployment has been partially a result of minimum wage legislation.

Minimum wage legislation affects not only employer efficiency but employee efficiency as well. Workers who in 1938 received less than the minimum of 25 cents per hour obviously had difficulties in making ends meet. Similarly, in 1976, workers who earned less than the $2.30-per-hour minimum had difficulty in providing adequate food, clothing, shelter, and medical care for themselves and their families. The establishment of a minimum wage which eliminates substandard wages is likely to have some beneficial effect on the health, efficiency, and morale of workers which may be reflected in improved man-hour production. Also, the higher cost of labor makes employers more labor-conscious and is likely to cause management to devote more time and effort to training workers and selecting new employees more carefully. The net result may be better productivity, which will tend, in part, to offset the higher wage costs, so that the rise in unit labor costs will be less than the rise in wage rates. To the extent that this is true, the effect of the wage increase on employment will be lessened.

In general, economic theorists conclude that imposition of a minimum wage will tend to produce some unemployment in the individual firm affected by such legislation. The amount of the unemployment will vary from firm to firm, depending upon the magnitude of the wage increase, the importance of labor costs relative to total costs, the ability of the employer to reduce costs other than labor costs, the extent to which the business of the firm falls off if it increases prices, the effect of the wage increase on man-hour output, and the extent to which the company introduces laborsaving machinery. As has already been mentioned, however, the tendency toward reduction of employment may not be observable because of counteracting changes in the business scene.

Empirical Studies—The 25-Cent Minimum of 1938

Fortunately, we can do more than theorize about the imposition of a minimum wage. We have empirical studies which shed light on what actually occurred when minimum wage laws were imposed, starting with the imposition of the 25-cent-per-hour minimum in 1938.

Two weeks after the 25-cent-per-hour minimum went into effect (this was the initial requirement of the Fair Labor Standards Act of 1938), the administrator of the act reported to the president that, in all, between 30,000 and 50,000 persons, or less than 0.05% of the workers affected by the law, lost their employment for reasons probably traceable to the act. Of these workers, about 90% were concentrated in a few industries in the South, such as pecan shelling, tobacco stemming, lumbering, and bagging. Other industries which were seriously affected by the minimum wage included cottonseed crushing, seamless hosiery, and cotton garments.[5]

---

[5] See, for example, U.S. Department of Labor, Bureau of Labor Statistics, *Hours and Earnings of Employees of Independent Tobacco Stemmeries*, Serial No. 1388 (Washington, D.C.: Government Printing Office, 1941); and J. F. Moloney, "Some Effects of the Fair Labor Standards Act upon Southern Industry," *Southern Economic Journal*, vol. 9 (July 1942), pp. 5–23. Also A. F. Hinrichs, "Effects of the 25 Cent Minimum Wage on Employment in the Seamless Hosiery Industry," *Journal of the American Statistical Association*, vol. 35 (March 1940), pp. 13–23; and H. M. Douty, "Minimum Wage Regulation in the Seamless Hosiery Industry," *Southern Economic Journal*, vol. 15 (October 1948), pp. 176–89.

Firms reacted to the higher minimum by substituting machinery for labor, narrowing wage differentials, weeding out inefficient workers, and improving personnel policies to increase labor efficiency. A principal effect was technological unemployment, especially in tobacco stemming, pecan shelling and cottonseed crushing. Some unemployment was offset by improved business conditions, and later, the defense boom.

The 75-Cent Minimum of 1949

The situation when the 75-cent minimum was established was similar to that of 1938. The same industries were affected in largely the same manner, and the economic upswing resulting from the Korean War obscured and probably offset the employment impact of the higher minimum.

The $1 Minimum of 1956

The $1 minimum wage had a more severe and direct effect on employment than did previous legislation. Employment in industries which had substantial employment at rates under $1 declined even in 1956–57, when the economy was strong. Sixteen of the so-called high-impact industries suffered a 10–25% drop in employment, with unskilled workers especially hard hit.[6] Because lower rated employees received increases required by law, but lesser or no increases were granted to higher rated jobs, wage schedules were compressed.[7]

The 1961 Amendments

In 1961, Congress raised the minimum for previously covered workers to $1.15 as of September 1, 1961, and $1.25 as of September 1, 1963. In addition, the act was extended to 3.6 million additional workers, mostly in retail trade. For those newly covered, overtime payments were waived for three years, and mimima were set at $1 as of September 1, 1961; $1.15, four years later; and $1.25 as of September 1, 1966. As a result, approximately 15% of those covered in 1961 received wage increases, but this included nearly 67% of those in the 15 southern industries which had been affected by every change in the Fair Labor Standards Act since

---

[6] U.S. Department of Labor, Wage and Public Contracts Division, *Studies of the Effects of the $1.00 Minimum Wage* (Washington, D.C.: Government Printing Office, 1959). See also Harry M. Douty, "Some Effects of the $1.00 Minimum Wage in the United States," *Economica*, vol. 27 (May 1960), pp. 137–47. For a critique of the Department of Labor studies, see George Macesich and Charles T. Stewart, Jr., "Recent Department of Labor Studies of Minimum Wage Effects," *Southern Economic Journal*, vol. 26 (April 1960), pp. 281–90.

[7] Ibid.; and David E. Kaun, "Economics of the Minimum Wage: The Effects of the Fair Labor Standards Act, 1945–1960" (unpublished doctoral dissertation, Stanford University, 1963).

1938. In 1963, the increase in the minimum to $1.25 affected directly an estimated additional 2.6 million workers, again primarily in the South. In October 1960, for example, average hourly earnings in the southern lumber industry were $1.18 per hour; by June 1962, these earnings had risen to $1.27 under the impact of the minimum, with 63% of the employees receiving wage increases. Employment in this industry continued on a downward trend, dropping 32,000 between October 1960 and June 1962.[8]

The 1961 and 1963 increases brought under the minimum wage act low-wage retail employees who had not been covered since the 1949 amendments. Employment in retailing continued its expansion; but in nonmetropolitan areas of the South, employment in covered retail trade declined from 160,000 in June 1961 to 143,000 in June 1962, while employment in retail trade in these areas in establishments *not* covered by the FLSA rose from 549,000 to 574,000.[9]

The 1965 Amendments

The 1965 amendments, which raised the minimum wage to $1.60 per hour in two steps for those already within the purview of the law and in several steps for those newly brought within its coverage, were enacted in a period of great prosperity and rising employment. Government sponsors of higher minimum wage laws hailed the results as contributing to the fight against poverty without substantially affecting employment. A more careful examination of the available data indicates that the consequences of the 1965 amendments included employment declines in some newly affected industries, such as laundries and agriculture;[10] employment in other newly affected industries, including motels and hotels, restaurants, and hospitals, continued to expand. Drugstores reacted by abolishing lunch counters and soda fountains and reducing employment by 12%, mainly affecting marginal employees, including many blacks.[11]

The impact of the changes in minimum wage legislation in the 1960s, like the impact in previous prosperous times, was often more likely to be felt after some time lag, rather than immediately. Mechanization takes

---

[8] U.S. Department of Labor, *Report Submitted to the Congress in Accordance with the Requirements of Section 4(d) of the Fair Labor Standards Act* (Washington, D.C.: Government Printing Office, January 1963), pp. vii, 35, and 40.

[9] U.S. Department of Labor, *Effects of Minimum Wage Rates Established under the Fair Labor Standards Act in Retail Trade in the United States and Puerto Rico: A Study of Changes in Wage Structure of a Matched Sample of Retail Establishments, 1961–1962* (Washington, D.C.: Government Printing Office, November 1963), p. 5.

[10] Agricultural employment was also affected by the cutting off of imported Mexican labor. Reducing supply is, of course, another way of raising wages.

[11] F. M. Fletcher, "The Negro in the Drugstore Industry," in Gordon F. Bloom et al., *Negro Employment in Retail Trade*, Studies of Negro Employment, vol. 6, part three (Philadelphia: Industrial Research Unit, The Wharton School, University of Pennsylvania, 1972), pp. 17–18.

time. Equipment installed as a result of higher minima may not be in place until a year or more after the effective date of the change in the law. Moreover, the impact is often delayed when the law becomes effective because the times are prosperous and business is expanding. When the business cycle turns downward, then marginal employees are let go, or not hired. Moreover, the impact is likely to be especially hard on the young, the black, the disadvantaged, and the untrained—often one and the same. Empirical studies of the effects of the federal law and of the state laws[12] amply support the theoretical economic expectation that adverse employment results follow from higher minimum wages and that such results are likely to be heavily felt during an economic downturn if the minimum wage is raised during a period of full employment.

The 1974 Amendments

In 1974, the act was amended again to provide for a three-step increase to $2.30 for workers covered prior to 1966 and a slower progression for workers covered for the first time in 1966 or 1974. Thus, the former group reached the new minimum on January 1, 1976; the latter group will achieve it in two steps, one and two years later.

The impact of the 1974 amendments is difficult to determine at this writing. It is likely, however, that they have added to the severe problems encountered by youth and the disadvantaged to obtain jobs in this period. The increases in the minimum wage occurred during the sharpest economic recession since World War I, a recession which was accompanied by escalating costs and inflation. Therefore, the studies of this period will probably find that, if business continues to improve, the higher minimum rates hindered the job search of the disadvantaged, as discussed in the following section, but that general business conditions were more significant during the depths of the recession in determining the employment of marginal workers.

Minimum Wages, Poverty, and Youth

The U.S. Department of Labor reported in 1968 that the $1.60 minimum wage meant that "for the first time in the history of the Fair Labor Standards Act, the statutory minimum wage will yield an above-poverty

---

[12] A good summary of studies and their findings in this period in regard to minimum wages and employment, including studies of state legislation, is found in John M. Peterson and Charles T. Stewart, Jr., *Employment Effects of Minimum Wage Rates* (Washington, D.C.: American Enterprise Institute for Public Policy Research, 1969). See also Patrick M. Lenihan, "The Economic Effects of Minimum Wage Orders [in Wisconsin]" (unpublished Ph.D. dissertation, University of Wisconsin, 1967); James E. Estes, *The Minimum Wage and Its Impact on South Carolina*, Bureau of Business and Economic Research, Report No. 18 (Columbia: College of Business Administration, University of South Carolina, 1968); and M. Z. Wolfson, "A Reexamination of the Wage and Employment Effects of the Minimum Wage on the Southern Pine Industry" (unpublished Ph.D. dissertation, University of Illinois, 1971).

wage."[13] This is perhaps a correct statement for those who receive the wage, but it ignores the possible impact on employment, not only of the marginal employees already on industry's rolls, but of a perhaps more important group, the submarginal population which even in prosperity finds great difficulty in obtaining work. Moreover, this statement ignores the potential impact of the minimum wage on youth employment.

A subsequent study of the U.S. Bureau of Labor Statistics found that both higher minimum wages and the extension of minimum wage coverage to retail trade, services, and agriculture had probably contributed to an unemployment rate of 16–17-year-olds five times that of those 25 years of age and older, and also to an unemployment rate of 18–19-year-olds higher than the average. One reason for this is that a higher proportion of youngsters work in the newly covered industries than in the labor force as a whole. Often they are marginal employees, easily replaced by other, more productive workers at higher minimum wage rates or by machines. In some cases, such as the already noted phasing out of drugstore soda fountains, "youth work" has simply been eliminated. The study concluded that a youth differential in the minimum wage would greatly aid employment of young persons.[14] A youth differential in some form is found in some state minimum wage laws and was advocated by many persons prior to the 1974 amendments.

There is also considerable evidence that increases in minimum wages have not only had adverse effects on the volume of employment of youths and of other marginal employees, for example, blacks and other minorities with poor educational backgrounds, but have also increased the vulnerability of such groups to cyclical unemployment. Such groups, for example, are disproportionately put on reduced workweeks when recessions occur;[15] moreover, teenagers, especially minority teenagers, are now obtaining less employment even when employment is growing at a good pace. They are also more likely to suffer unemployment in periods of short-term employment changes.[16] The persistently high rate

---

[13] U.S. Department of Labor, Wage and Hour and Public Contracts Divisions, *Minimum Wages and Maximum Hours Standards under the Fair Labor Standards Act* (Washington, D.C.: Government Printing Office, 1968), p. 2.

[14] Thomas W. Gavett, "Youth Unemployment and Minimum Wages," *Monthly Labor Review*, vol. 93 (March 1970), pp. 3–15. See also T. G. Moore, "The Effect of Minimum Wages on Teenage Unemployment Rates," *Journal of Political Economy*, vol. 79 (July–August 1971), pp. 897–902.

[15] Robert M. Bednarzik, "Involuntary Part-Time Work," *Monthly Labor Review*, vol. 98 (September 1975), pp. 12–18.

[16] Marvin Kosters and Finis Welch, "The Effects of Minimum Wages on the Distribution of Changes in Aggregate Employment," *American Economic Review*, vol. 62 (June 1972), p. 320. A mathematical model designed by these authors as the basis for their analysis is set forth in the appendix to this chapter. See also Finis Welch, "Minimum Wage Legislation in the United States," *Economic Inquiry* (formerly *Western Economic Journal*), vol. 12 (September 1974), pp. 285–318; and Philip G. Cotterill and Walter J. Wadycki, "Teenagers and the Minimum Wage in Retail Trade," *Journal of Human Resources,* vol. 11 (Winter 1976), pp. 69–85.

of unemployment among teenagers, noted in Chapter 14, is, of course, indicative of the sensitivity of teenagers to unemployment. In that chapter, as well as in several others, we have noted that the unemployment rate of blacks has consistently been twice that of whites, and that the unemployment rate of black teenagers has been four to five times that of white adult males.

A youth differential has been opposed, particularly by the AFL–CIO, which is on record "that the minimum wage represents a floor under wages and that no one—young, old, black or white, male or female—should be asked to work for less than the wage floor."[17] The AFL–CIO is also a strong supporter of an ever higher minimum and of an extension of the act's coverage to all workers not now within its purview. The federation's reasoning relies heavily upon the minimum wage as a cure for poverty, while at the same time denying any causal relationship between rising minimum wages and unemployment in general, or youth unemployment in particular.

In future years, as we have noted throughout this text, the greatest employment opportunities will occur in the professional and technical occupations. Among the manual occupations, the need for skilled mechanics will also increase. But the number of unskilled jobs will remain relatively stationary, despite a tremendous increase in unskilled additions to the labor market. It seems even more apparent, therefore, that the higher the wage minimum, the greater will be the effort to substitute machinery for unskilled work or to recast methods somehow so as to make the unskilled increasingly unnecessary, particularly in manufacturing enterprises. To push for even higher minimums in spite of these labor market facts, as Congress and various state legislatures continue to do, is likely to make unemployed victims of those who are supposed to become higher paid beneficiaries of a minimum wage law.

There is another concern about raising the minimum wage which is of great significance. Although the imposition of a higher minimum does tend to narrow wage differentials because it is likely to result in increases in the lowest wage with smaller increases, or even no increases, for the higher paid, nevertheless it does tend to exert an upward pressure on wages above the minimum, both in industries directly affected and in all other industries competing for labor. This adds still another inflationary push to the economy, in which inflationary tendencies are already so strong. To the extent that an upward revision in the minimum wage results in price increases, it will again hurt most the low-wage groups for whom the minimum is urged as a benefit.

---

[17] *Fair Labor Standards Amendments of 1971*, hearings before the Subcommittee on Labor of the Committee on Labor and Public Welfare, U.S. Senate, 92d Cong., 1st sess., on S. 1861 and S. 2259, 1971 (Washington, D.C.: Government Printing Office, 1971), part 1, p. 70. A complete statement of the AFL–CIO's position is found in pp. 75–116 of these hearings. It was the AFL–CIO's unremitting pressure which prevented a youth differential in the 1974 amendments.

It is very likely, therefore, that our concern with poverty is in conflict with the policy of a steadily rising minimum wage. Perhaps minimum wages should continue to rise, and perhaps the resulting unemployment should be tolerated. In such case, it should be understood that one of the costs of minimum wage legislation is increased public welfare, training, rehabilitation, and subsidy payments to those who are priced out of the labor market.

Indexing Proposals

A number of proposals have been made to tie increases in the minimum wage to increases in the cost of living. The argument for such "indexing" is that the poor suffer disproportionately from inflation, and that therefore, they, like many more affluent union members, should be protected in this manner. Unfortunately, if such a proposal were adopted, it could aggravate the adverse employment effects discussed above. One reason why the unemployment effects of increased minimum wages are not more severe is that inflation somewhat obviates their impact over time by raising the costs of other factors. If minimum wages were tied to the cost of living, this would not occur. Moreover, as with social security, discussed in the following chapter, Congress would probably be pressured to increase the minimum rates *in addition* to the cost-of-living adjustments, further aggravating adverse employment effects.

THE SHORTER WORKWEEK

From colonial days to 1950, the average workweek gradually declined from a norm of "sunup to sundown," or about 70 hours per week, to a norm of 40 hours. This is required by the Fair Labor Standards Act unless the employer pays time and one half the regular rate. The normal workday has become 8 hours, with time and one half required by most union contracts and by the Public Contracts (Walsh-Healey) Act, but not by the FLSA, for work beyond 8 hours (unless it brings the weekly total to over 40 hours). State laws which limited the hours of women, or denied them access to nightwork or hazardous jobs, were rendered inoperative because they were in conflict with the nondiscriminatory provisions in regard to sex of Title VII of the Civil Rights Act of 1964.

THE ARGUMENTS FOR SHORTER HOURS

Legislation and union bargaining power have been the principal forces in the history of hours reduction. More recently, other factors, such as long commuting time in metropolitan areas and special hours for specially situated employees, have led to hours reduction and/or hours restructuring. Shorter hours have been advocated for a number of reasons, but those relating to the impact on employment are the most significant today.

Health and Leisure

Shorter hours have frequently been advocated as a health measure. This is the primary basis for the regulation of hours for women and the regulation of hours in dangerous trades. The regulation of hours in transportation is also partly based on this argument, although here the health and safety of both the consumer and the worker are protected. Since these arguments are more applicable to a longer workweek than 40 hours, they are infrequently used today, except with respect to dangerous or very strenuous occupations.

Purchasing Power Theory

Organized labor has traditionally put forth the argument that increased leisure with earnings maintained would permit workers the time to spend more as consumers and thus would bolster the economy. Other proponents of a shorter workweek support this argument and also maintain that more leisure would be helpful in encouraging citizens to participate in political and civil affairs.

During recent years, it has been customary for union leaders to overemphasize the purchasing power theory of the business cycle. Obviously, if workers were employed 12 hours a day, they would not have much time to do anything else besides eat and sleep, and they would not make very good customers for that part of industry which does not produce absolute necessities. Since only a very small portion of industry produces absolute necessities, it is also obvious that demand must exist for the miscellaneous luxuries, semiluxuries, and other things which make up America's high living standard. Shortening the working day, so long as it does not impair earnings, may make workers better customers for the essentials and nonessentials of modern capitalist production.

Certainly, the five-day week and shorter working hours have greatly expanded spending for leisure. Moreover, the employee who works shorter hours receives a greater exposure to advertising over radio, television, and other media, and this may make him more desirous of spending to "keep up" or to enjoy the latest conveniences or luxuries.

But how much more the average worker's family will spend on consumer goods if his or her hours are reduced below 40 is not easy to determine. This leisure argument assumes that the increased costs resulting from decreasing the hours will not adversely affect employment and therefore will not adversely affect consumer expenditures; and it also assumes that the shorter hour movement will not be simply a device to increase overtime pay. Where actual hours are not reduced but merely made more expensive by penalty overtime payments, the increased leisure argument is irrelevant; for here, the worker's take-home pay, not the worker's leisure, is increased.

Efficiency and Productivity

Historically, the reduction in hours of work has been accompanied by increases in productivity. As a result, the increased costs occasioned by shorter hours have not led to higher prices—at least over long periods of time. The fact that shorter hours and increased productivity have marched hand in hand has given birth to the argument that reduced hours increase efficiency and/or productivity and hence absorb the increased costs of shorter hours, even if the shorter hours are accompanied by wage adjustments sufficient to maintain weekly earnings.

Productivity and worker efficiency are not necessarily synonymous terms. Productivity is not a measurement of the worker alone but of the worker and his or her equipment. It is a statistic commonly measured by dividing output by man-hours worked. As already noted, rising labor productivity is largely a manifestation of the joint contribution of increasing capital, improved managerial technique, and scientific advance.

On the other hand, labor efficiency, as defined here, refers to changes in output resulting solely from changes in labor effort or input, other factors being held constant. Hence an increase in labor efficiency will result in an increase in productivity, but an increase in productivity does not necessarily mean that labor efficiency has increased.

Shorter Hours and Efficiency. Unfortunately, few studies have been made of the effect of hours on labor efficiency, and those which are available deal mainly with increases in hours above 40 rather than with reductions below 40. In addition, most of the more important studies which attempt to relate efficiency and hours of work were made during World War II, when conditions were quite abnormal. Moreover, such factors as changing attitudes toward work and the affluent work force make one hesitant to draw conclusions applicable to the current situation from the results of World War II experiences.

Nevertheless, the studies did show that a seven-day workweek caused output to fall as worker fatigue accumulated from continued overtime, with spoilage, accidents, and absenteeism rising as time went on. On the other hand, an increase to a six-day week from a five-day week resulted in rising output despite increased absenteeism. The study of the U.S. Bureau of Labor Statistics concluded that "the addition of the sixth day had no disadvantageous effect on output, provided daily hours were held to eight."[18] Other studies support the conclusion that the 48-hour week

---

[18] U.S. Department of Labor, Bureau of Labor Statistics, *Hours of Work and Output,* Bulletin 917 (Washington, D.C.: Government Printing Office, 1947).

was best for war production and that adding the sixth day had no ill effect unless the daily hours were excessive. It should be noted again, however, that different results might occur if the six-day week were inaugurated in peacetime.

After the war, many of the plants covered by the BLS survey resumed a normal five-day week. Although the increase in hours by the addition of a sixth day had resulted in an almost proportionate increase in weekly output in most cases, the decrease in hours was accompanied by a less than proportionate decrease in production. As in the increase of the workweek, so, too, in the decrease—absenteeism among men was little affected by the shift. Women's absences increased after both changes, in the latter instance probably because they lost interest in the work and were preparing for a resumption of household duties. The most logical explanation advanced for the observed improvement in efficiency as hours of work were reduced was that workers who were paid on an incentive basis wished to make up lost take-home pay brought about by the elimination of time and a half for the sixth day.

The 36-Hour-Week Experience in Akron

Large segments of the rubber tire industry, especially in Akron, have worked on a six-hour day, six-day week schedule since the 1930s. The results have been relatively unsatisfactory to both employees and companies, both in terms of earnings and productivity, so that only a few plants are still operating these hours. Moreover, tire manufacturing is now no longer concentrated in Akron, but rather in newer plants, particularly in the South, where the eight-hour day has always been utilized.

One of the authors has been interviewing a company official over the last 30 years on the effects of the six-hour day. This official's company has always been disappointed with results of the six-hour day insofar as improved efficiency is concerned; but the official has also noted that wage rates are higher and plants are older in Akron than in other areas, and that therefore comparisons between the six-hour day in Akron and the eight-hour day in other rubber tire plants are difficult to make. The last plant of this company which was on the six-day schedule converted to eight hours in 1967. A few years later, the last tire plants outside Akron changed from the 36-hour week to the standard 40-hour week, and in 1972, Firestone also converted. It is likely that the 36-hour week will shortly disappear from the industry.

A striking consequence of short work schedules, such as have existed in Akron, is their propensity to encourage moonlighting. According to one study: "In Akron the best guesses hold that 16 to 20 percent of the rubber workers hold a second job, not a *part*-time job but a *full*-time job. About another 40 percent hold down a second, merely part-time employment."[19] A second study found that "the incidence of dual wage or job holding is significantly higher for . . . 36-hour Akron rubber workers than for . . . 40-hour rubber workers located outside of Akron," and that "total multijobholding is significantly related to the length of the primary job workweek."[20] Actually, the desire of members of the United Rubber Workers to hold on to the 36-hour week has been a direct function of moonlighting. The leaders of the United Rubber Workers made a determined attempt at the 1956 convention to eliminate the six-hour day and go back to the 40-hour week. They were defeated precisely because the Akron workers did not want to give up the extra income they gained from holding two jobs and working many hours over 40 per week. In the last several years, however, the plants have hired thousands of young employees who desire more opportunity for earnings on their primary job and who have not as yet developed outside income interests. The votes of these new employees are tipping the balance in favor of the 8-hour day, 40-hour week. In 1972, when the Firestone local of the United Rubber Workers voted 2,356 to 977 to give up the 36-hour week, one supporter of the change commented, "A lot of the guys in the shop who were talking down . . . [the 40-hour week] were the ones who had two jobs. They'll just have to give one up now."[21]

As of now, only the Goodyear Tire and Rubber, General Tire, and Mohawk Rubber companies remain on the six-day week. Goodyear finds some advantages as well as disadvantages. It can expand shifts from six to eight without paying overtime during heavy vacation schedules; and it can cut down to 30 hours when orders decline. On the other hand, the six-hour shifts mean additional fringe costs, since these costs, as noted in Chapter 5, are largely a function of number of employees, not hours worked. In addition, six-hour day shifts may well be less efficient because of the larger number of start-up and readying-to-quit periods in which production is usually low.

The high fringe costs to employers and the potential higher earnings of employees on 8-hour shifts have led to the gradual abandonment of the rubber industry's 6-hour day, 36-hour week. The experience under it is not conclusive as to the shorter workweek; it does, however, point up some of the basic economic problems involved.

The Construction Industry

The powerful unions in the construction industry have pushed their standard workweek below 40 hours and their workday to 7 hours or less.

---

[19] Sebastian de Grazia, *Of Time, Work, and Leisure* (New York: Twentieth Century Fund, 1962), p. 71.

[20] John C. Deiter, *Multijobholding and the Short Workweek Issue* (Ann Arbor, Mich.: University Microfilms, Inc., 1965), p. 81.

[21] *Business Week*, March 18, 1972, p. 67.

In fact, however, this is largely a method of increasing compensation by making additional employment available at penalty overtime—time and one half or double time. The extreme case was that of the New York City electricians, who won a 25-hour week—but a guarantee of at least 5 hours overtime. In a real sense, this is not hours reduction but rather one aspect of union wage policy. It has not been emulated significantly in other industries where unions have less than the enormous power which they have exhibited in construction. Undoubtedly, such policies have contributed to the expansion of nonunion construction, which now accounts for a majority of employees in the industry.[22]

Moonlighting

People working at more than one job—"moonlighting"—is not a new phenomenon. In 1975, about 3.9 million workers, 4.7% of all employed persons, held two jobs or more.[23] This rate has been fairly constant for several years. Since in order to avoid taxes or union or employer censure, many moonlighters do not report their second activity, the actual number of moonlighters is probably considerably greater. A majority of moonlighters are found among professional, self-employed, government-employed, education, and farming groups, but more recently the number of moonlighting blue-collar workers has been increasing.

In times of unemployment, moonlighting is often attacked as a contributor to that unemployment. The studies which have been made of moonlighting, however, do not bear this out. The largest segment of moonlighters are those with a special skill which is in demand or those who have a strong desire to enhance their incomes. Their moonlighting activity supplements their basic income from the primary job but is usually insufficient as a primary means of support. Moonlighting does not vary with employment or unemployment trends.[24]

Moonlighting is a further indication of the preference of many persons for additional income rather than additional leisure. The grievances in nearly any company inevitably include complaints from some workers that they did not receive a fair share of overtime work—"the golden hours" at time and one half or double time. The following comment of a then union research director, which was delivered two decades ago, is still relevant:

> Aside from the workers' desire for their paid holidays and paid vacations there is no evidence in recent experience that workers want shorter

---

[22] Herbert R. Northrup and Howard G. Foster, *Open Shop Construction*, Major Study No. 54 (Philadelphia: Industrial Research Unit, The Wharton School, University of Pennsylvania, 1975).

[23] Kopp Michelotti, "Multiple Jobholders in May 1975," *Monthly Labor Review*, vol. 98 (November 1975), pp. 56–62.

[24] Ibid., pp. 59–60.

daily or *weekly* hours. The evidence is all on the other side. Hundreds of local and national officials have testified that the most numerous and persistent grievances are disputes over the sharing of overtime work. The issue usually is not that someone has been made to work, but that he has been deprived of a chance to make overtime pay.[25]

HOURS REDUCTION AND EMPLOYMENT

There are two points of view from which reduction in hours of work per day or per week can be examined as a remedy for unemployment. The first is a reduction in hours without a change in the basic wage rate, so that the workers previously employed now receive fewer hours of work and correspondingly reduced earnings. The second is the effect of a shortening of hours with compensatory increases in basic rates, so that earnings for the shorter working time remain undiminished. No one now seriously advocates the first approach. Nevertheless, a short analysis of the possible effects on unemployment of a reduction in hours without compensatory change in base rates will point up the economic relationships between hours reduction and employment, and will also help to clarify those relationships where compensatory wage adjustments are involved.

Shorter Hours with Unchanged Basic Wage Rates

It is not unusual for persons to assume logic and correctness in the statement attributed to Samuel Gompers that "if anyone is out of work, the hours of work are too long." The idea is that if hours are only reduced sufficiently, unemployment can be automatically eliminated.

A realistic look at the supply factors shows that the effect of shortening hours, even without the compensatory adjustments in wage rates which unions demand, cannot be assessed by a mere arithmetic calculation. For example, it might be thought that as long as basic rates are unchanged, unit labor costs should likewise remain constant. But employers will have to add new workers who will require training and who may be less skilled than those already employed, so that the immediate effect of the plan is probably to produce some decline in the efficiency of labor. Moreover, in some industries, work sharing produces technical difficulties. The balance of operations may not be workable with two 6-hour shifts instead of one 8-hour shift—or, for that matter, there just might not be enough demand for two shifts of 32 or 35 hours where one of 40 hours now suffices.

Even if unit labor costs do not change, capital costs per unit of output will be increased in those plants which operate fewer hours per week

[25] George Brooks, "The History of Organized Labor's Drive for Shorter Hours of Work," *AFL–CIO Conference on Shorter Hours of Work*, published in Special Report No. 1, *Daily Labor Report*, No. 177 (September 11, 1956), p. 13.

after the shorter hour program is inaugurated. The rise in fixed costs per unit will force marginal firms out of business and thus add to the amount of unemployment. Moreover, the reduction in profits in all plants will make entrepreneurs somewhat more reluctant to invest; and therefore, in the long run the level of employment may be further reduced.

On the demand side, the shortening of the hours of work of employed labor may provide job opportunities for persons formerly on relief or receiving unemployment benefits. Where there are no compensatory wage adjustments, the earnings of those formerly employed full time will be reduced, and therefore an increase in consumer demand can only follow if the newly employed workers greatly expand purchases over what they had consumed, while receiving unemployment benefits or on relief, to an extent greater than the drop in expenditures by those formerly employed 40 hours and now working and earning less.

Reduction in Hours with Compensatory Wage Increases

On the whole, a program of shorter hours is unacceptable to labor unless it is accompanied by compensatory wage adjustments, so that labor income is maintained. In advocating such a policy to reduce unemployment, organized labor has shown its customary bias in emphasizing the role of demand conditions and ignoring the more immediate repercussions of the increased hourly price of labor on costs and business profits.

Employers, by and large, can be expected to react to a program of reduced hours with compensatory hourly wage increases as they would react to any increase in marginal cost. Prices will tend to rise; a smaller output will be demanded; and ultimately, a new equilibrium will be established at a lower level of output. In order to think this through, let us assume that the demand for labor under these circumstances in a particular firm has an elasticity of unity. If the union raises hourly rates 5% and reduces hours of work by 5%, it will have duplicated the readjustment that the employer himself would have made to the changed cost conditions. But since a new equilibrium has been established at the higher unit price of labor, there is no incentive to hire any additional labor. It is therefore clear that if the demand curve for labor in a particular firm has an elasticity of unity or greater, the reemployment objective of the shorter hour movement must fail of accomplishment.

On the whole, it seems likely that in depression periods, when management is extremely sensitive to cost increases of any kind, the demand for labor is elastic, at least in an upward direction. That is, a given percentage increase in wage rates will produce a more than proportionate reduction in employment. Although there is room for disagreement as to the precise value of the elasticity of demand for labor, it seems likely that the reduction in hours must be substantially greater than the percentage increase in hourly wage rates if the immediate effect of the institution of the shorter workweek is not to increase the volume of employment. The effect of the shorter hours of work with compensatory wage adjustments will depend upon the relationships among three factors: (1) the percentage decrease in the hours of work, (2) the percentage increase in hourly rate, and (3) the elasticity of demand for labor. Thus, if the elasticity of demand for labor were equal to minus two (that is, the volume of employment diminishes 2% with each increase of 1% in wage rates), and if the increase in hourly rates were 5%, then the percentage reduction in hours would have to be more than 10% if more workers were to be hired.

The Effects of Increasing the Number of Shifts

Suppose that a plant in a continuous-process industry has been accustomed to run continuously for five days a week, using three eight-hour shifts. If this plant were to change to four shifts of six hours each, it would appear that employment would be increased. However, if each worker now employed a shorter number of hours wishes to keep his or her pay undiminished, it is evident that there will be a rise in labor cost per unit, despite the fact that the number of shifts has increased. The increased labor costs will be reflected in higher prices and a reduced total output, so that ultimately no permanent increase in employment may result from this changeover.

But there are circumstances in which the addition of another shift may tend to increase employment. The substitution of two six-hour shifts for a previous eight-hour day, or perhaps for a longer day including some employment at overtime, will tend to reduce capital costs per unit by allowing management to work capital longer while labor works shorter hours. The decrease in total unit costs attributable to this influence will tend to offset the increase in unit labor costs occasioned by shortening the hours of work with compensatory wage increases, so that, on balance, profits may be unimpaired.

Although the more intensive use of capital is a favorable factor, it should be recognized that if the increase in the number of shifts does increase employment, it will have this effect only after a series of highly complicated long-run influences are set in motion. The spreading of overhead will not affect marginal costs, while the reduction of hours with increases in basic hourly rates will raise marginal costs. Hence, as far as immediate price and output reactions are concerned, the change in the number of shifts does not alter the picture. Some plants will be forced out of business, while other plants, in which the proportion of labor costs is relatively low and that of overhead costs is relatively high, will find their profits increased by the changeover to additional shifts. Ultimately, the number of plants in the industry undergoing the change will diminish, with a larger volume of business concentrated in a smaller number of firms, each using capital more intensively than was true before the shorter hour program was inaugurated.

The ability to inaugurate an additional shift will vary considerably from industry to industry; and in those firms attempting it, the benefits obtained will vary, depending upon the importance of overhead costs. In some plants where equipment is antiquated, working additional shifts may mean increasingly frequent breakdowns without adequate time for repairs. In industries which do not operate continuously, the amount of reemployment which can be provided by a shortening of hours of work will depend in part upon the availability of unused machinery and equipment. To the extent that less efficient equipment is brought into use, the upward pressure on costs is intensified.

Interindustry Shifts

A program of shorter hours with undiminished take-home pay would produce important changes in the demand for particular industries. The increased availability of leisure would probably be reflected in an increased demand for sporting goods and other recreational goods by which leisure can be made more enjoyable. Likewise, the effect of the increased wage disbursements—assuming that there is some initial reemployment—would operate to stimulate the consumer goods industries. At the same time, however, the nondurable consumer goods industries would experience the greatest increases of cost relative to the rest of the economy, since it appears that the nondurable consumer goods industries have higher ratios of wages to value added than do the capital goods industries. Thus, insofar as the effect on costs is concerned, the former industries would be hardest hit by the combination of shorter hours and increased wage rates; while the capital goods industries, having a higher ratio of capital costs, would be the ones to benefit most from the addition of extra shifts.

This combination of altered cost and demand positions would ultimately produce some readjustment in the distribution of the total labor force among the various industries in the economy. The net effect upon employment can only be conjectural. If wage disbursements increase initially as a result of the shorter hours of work with compensatory wage rate increases, it appears that a larger proportion of the national income would be spent on nondurable consumer goods than before the hours program was instituted. Two factors will contribute to this result. On the one hand, the total income of wage earners will increase if there is some reemployment; and the income of working people, particularly during periods of large-scale unemployment, is likely to be spent on the products of the nondurable consumer goods industries. But as we have seen, these are the very industries which will feel most of the impact of the shorter hour program. Therefore, prices will rise in these industries relative to the general price level; but because of the relatively inelastic demand typical of these industries, the total receipts of the nondurable consumer goods industries will probably increase. This augmented volume of expenditure concentrated in these industries will probably support a larger volume of employment than prevailed under the previous distribution of expenditures, since the nondurable consumer goods industries are likely to be more labor-employing than other industries. At the same time, since the proportion of labor costs to total costs is less in the capital goods industries than in the nondurable consumer goods industries, and since the adjustments resulting from the changeover to more shifts with shorter hours per employee may lead to a more efficient allocation of output concentrated in fewer plants, prices of machines should rise less than in proportion to consumer goods prices. This would stimulate the demand for laborsaving machinery and thus increase the volume of investment and employment.

Shortages of Skilled Labor

Any general uniform reduction in hours per week is likely to increase the number of bottlenecks which develop in production and is therefore likely to raise a barrier to full employment. A shortage of skilled workers in a key industry can have repercussions which produce unemployment throughout the economy. If the shorter hour program is applied to skilled workers, management is faced by three alternatives, all of which are likely to react unfavorably upon employment generally. Management can, of course, employ the same skilled workers as before, but now pay them additional overtime because of the shortening of the basic workweek. This would have the same effect as a wage increase and would therefore raise costs and prices. On the other hand, management can attempt to hire other workers and train them to fill these jobs; but such workers will, on the average, be less experienced and make more mistakes, so that labor cost per unit will tend to rise through their employment. Lastly, if management is unwilling or unable to find additional skilled help, bottlenecks and shortages will develop which will cause stoppages, depriving even the unskilled of their jobs.

The shortage of skilled labor is often a regional or local problem. It can be especially severe in small towns having available only a limited pool of labor. Thus a program of shorter hours must be undertaken with caution. On the other hand, it is conceivable that in some industries, a reasonable shortening of hours, even if it does produce some rise in costs, could be accomplished without too difficult a readjustment. An appreciation of the various possible repercussions of a shorter hour program indicates the danger of any general uniform shortening of hours accomplished by legislative decree.

THE NATURE OF UNEMPLOYMENT

Any attempt to utilize shortening of hours as a means of curbing unemployment must consider the nature of the unemployment. That of the early 1970s impacted disproportionately on youth, the unskilled, and blacks, who are often one and the same person. Certainly, merely reducing hours of work cannot accomplish the miracle of finding jobs for those who do not have the background, education, training, means, or motivation to accept even unskilled jobs in industry. Nor will reducing hours transfer people from the high-unemployment inner cores of the cities to the new manufacturing plants in the suburbs and rural areas.

A reduction in hours will not solve the unemployment problems of the disadvantaged, unless it is accompanied by an extraordinarily successful training program which would have to be both more successful and more expensive than the record of such programs described in Chapter 15, and which would also have to be combined with a remarkable improvement in labor mobility. Moreover, the costs of such retraining programs, combined with the cost burden imposed by the shorter workweek, as set forth below, is more likely to discourage than to encourage employment. Dividing up work—and almost by necessity, raising its costs —is not likely therefore to raise employment.

COSTS OF THE SHORTER HOUR PROGRAM

Figure 16–2 shows the hourly increases required to maintain weekly pay as a 40-hour schedule drops to 32. An increase of about 14% is needed to offset a five-hour decline, and an increase of more than 25% is needed to accomplish an eight-hour decline.

Even this is not the whole story. Suppose that the workweek is reduced to 35 hours but that business requires 40 hours of work to meet

FIGURE 16–2
Rising Cost of a Shorter Workweek

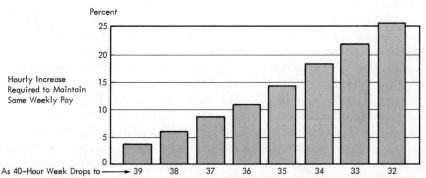

Percent

Hourly Increase Required to Maintain Same Weekly Pay

As 40–Hour Week Drops to ———➤ 39   38   37   36   35   34   33   32

its commitments. Then, five hours must be worked at time and one half. As calculated in Table 16–3, this would mean an increase not of 14% but of 21.3%! Obviously, such wage increases cannot be borne by a significant segment of American industry—and equally obviously, such wage increases would therefore be likely to create unemployment, not employment.

TABLE 16–3
Cost of Reduction in Workweek

Cost of reduction in workweek:
1. No loss of pay for employee.
2. No loss of production for employer.
Assume rate of pay = $5 per hour; for 40-hour week, weekly pay = $200.
1. If work week is lowered to 35 hours.
No loss of pay for employee; hourly rate now raised to $5.71 to equal $200 weekly take-home pay.
Increase in hourly rate 14.2%.
2. If employer requires 40-hour week:
Five hours must be worked overtime; time and one half of $5.71 = $8.57, 35 hours @ $5.71 plus 5 hours @ $8.57 = $242.50.
Increase in weekly rate 21.3%.

AUTOMATION AND HOURS

Because automation increases productivity, it is often argued, particularly in times of high unemployment, that hours should be reduced to offset the higher output per man-hour. Actually, automation has tended to increase employment, not to reduce it, as such an argument implies. Changes resulting from automation have accentuated unemployment problems in some areas and among some labor groups, but at the same time, jobs and industries have been created elsewhere, with the impacts varying considerably. Technological progress does not proceed smoothly throughout industry, but rather develops at widely different paces and in quite different ways from industry to industry.

On the other hand, a general hours reduction would fall on both highly and lightly automated industries, on industries for which technological unemployment is a problem, and on industries which are growing as a result of changing technology. A general hours reduction would give a bonus to the fully employed—or threaten their employment. It would seek, against heavy economic odds, to help those not fully employed.

To succeed in creating employment, a reduction in hours from 40 to 35, with pay maintained, would require a minimum productivity increase of 15%—a most unlikely development. But even if such an increase in productivity occurred, it would probably be insufficient because the substantial investment in expensive equipment required by automation greatly increases fixed costs. To the extent that a shorter workweek keeps this equipment idle, fixed costs per unit during operating periods increase and tend to offset decreases in costs resulting from increases in productivity.

A shorter workweek, with take-home pay maintained, would so increase costs that automation could well be discouraged except in the larger, wealthier firms. This could accelerate a trend toward economic concentration and possibly increase rather than diminish technological unemployment.

The most desirable manner of attaining full employment is by high-volume production, so that labor is fully employed 40 hours a week and the community benefits from technological progress in the form of a rising level of real income. From the point of view of maximizing national welfare, increasing leisure for labor by reducing hours of work below 40 a week can hardly be preferred to raising real income for the whole community. Moreover, it must be reiterated that there is no guarantee that a reduction in the workweek will increase employment. The crux of the problem is whether full employment could in fact be attained at the 35-hour level or whether the rise in costs attributable to the program of shorter hours with less work would not so depress business confidence that investment would be discouraged and perhaps even greater unemployment would prevail with the shorter workweek.

OVERTIME PAY AND EMPLOYMENT

Because it is sometimes cheaper to pay the existing labor force time and one half to work overtime rather than to employ additional workers, proposals have been made to increase the overtime rate to double time or more. The rationale is that this would encourage spreading of the work.

Fringe Benefit Costs, Overtime Costs, and Turnover Costs

We noted in Chapter 5 that fringe benefit costs have risen rapidly and substantially. Moreover, fringe benefits, such as hospitalization, and many governmental benefits, such as social security, are employee-related, not hours-related. In addition, state unemployment benefit systems, as will be explained in Chapter 17, penalize companies with excessive turnover and hence favor long hours, not more employees.[26] We also noted in Chapter 5 that the Ford Motor Company was able to maintain its supplemental unemployment benefits during the recent recession, unlike General Motors and Chrysler, because Ford found it more economical to use

---

[26] On this subject, in general, see Joseph W. Garbarino, "Fringe Benefits and Overtime as Barriers to Expanding Employment," *Industrial and Labor Relations Review,* vol. 17 (April 1964), pp. 426–42; and particularly the comment thereon by Robert M. MacDonald and the reply by Professor Garbarino, ibid., vol. 19 (July 1966), pp. 562–72. See also Ronald G. Ehrenberg, *Fringe Benefits and Overtime Behavior,* Lexington, Mass.: D. C. Heath & Co., 1973); and Agis Solpukas. "Auto Layoffs Keep On despite Overtime," *New York Times,* May 10, 1976.

overtime rather than employ additional personnel during previous prosperous years.

On the other hand, overtime costs have risen too, because the base
by which time and one half is figured has risen sharply. In other words,
if a wage is increased from $4 to $5 per hour, overtime increases from $6
to $7.50. Overtime costs can, therefore, rise as fast as fringe costs.

Such an analysis is, however, unrealistic because (1) it assumes that
the employer is certain that he knows how long he will need a new
employee (or overtime), and (2) it ignores training and layoff costs. The
average employer often hesitates to add to the labor force until he feels
reasonable assurance that he has need of an employee for a longer period.
In the meantime, he will usually use overtime work to fill his needs.

Finding, interviewing, processing, and training new personnel can cost
several hundred dollars per employee. The Occupational Safety and
Health Act discussed in Chapter 17, adds to this expense because employers must be certain that an employee with an illness or a disability
has that disability noted before he or she is hired. Otherwise, the company might be held liable at a later date.

After all this money is expended, the employee may quit or prove
unsatisfactory. Then, if a layoff occurs, new expenses mount. In a large
New England plant studied by one of the authors, each time one person
was laid off, three to five "bumps" occurred as a result of the working
of the plant seniority system. The plant management estimated that each
layoff cost $750–$1,000 because of the upset, retraining, and lost time
involved! Naturally, in such a situation, management will prefer to utilize
overtime rather than hire new employees if it is uncertain as to the length
of time for which additional work hours are needed.

The amount of overtime in industry varies substantially with the business cycle. Thus in the recession month of May 1975, 2 million fewer
employees were working 41 hours or longer than during the same month
in the boom year of 1974.[27] Whether there is a trend toward more overtime is not at all clear. If, however, overtime costs are increased, any
beneficial employment effect would probably be more than offset by
the increased labor costs that could preclude either overtime work or
additional employment.

TIME-OFF ARRANGEMENTS

The persistent call for a shorter workweek on the part of union officials
led to an agreement in 1973 between the United Automobile Workers
and the International Harvester, John Deere, and Caterpillar Tractor
companies to give workers who meet certain attendance requirements
time off. The idea was that this would discourage absenteeism and also

---

[27] Janice N. Hedges, "Long Workweeks and Premium Pay," *Monthly Labor
Review*, vol. 99 (April 1976), p. 8.

spread some work. The companies found that the experience was unsatisfactory because employees with poor attendance records continued to be absent, and so the result was just more time off for the more diligent employees with no compensating attendance improvements.[28]

In the 1976 bargaining with the automobile companies, the United Automobile Workers won a demand for seven days off that will obviously push the economy toward the four-day week. The avowed purpose was to divide up work. The union has a more than academic interest in this concept, not only because several thousand automobile workers have remained unemployed since the peak sales of the pre–oil crisis period, but also because more work division is envisioned to mean more union members and therefore more union dues. The serious question is whether the results will in fact follow the union script. Economic theory and past history would indicate otherwise.

In the 1973 negotiation, the UAW won limits on overtime with the same objective. The severe recession which followed and the continued desire of working members to enjoy more overtime and income, not less, made this demand quite academic. Then, after a month's strike against the Ford Motor Company in September–October 1976, the UAW gained seven additional days off per year with no loss of income for its members. This was in addition to regular vacations and holidays. The UAW also won additional time off at International Harvester, Caterpillar, and Deere after a short strike at the last.

Thus the four-day week is closer, and it is spreading throughout major manufacturing industries. But this will probably add to the inflationary bias in the economy and make competition with the rest of the world more difficult. Time off with pay, by its very nature, not only reduces productivity; it also increases labor costs, particularly because of high fringe benefits and payroll taxes which are attached to the individual regardless of hours worked. As already noted, union interest in such spread-the-work schemes is enhanced by the prospect that increased employment will mean more dues-paying members. On the other hand, the resultant higher costs to the companies must be reflected in prices, especially when, as in this case, the impact on productivity is negative. The net result could well be decreased demand and a net reduction in both the number of employees and the number of dues-paying union members.

REARRANGED AND FLEXIBLE WORKWEEKS

Much publicity was given a few years ago to the idea of rearranged workweeks—four 10-hour days being the usual arrangement. Yet by mid-1974 only 2% of the full-time employees in the labor force were working

---

[28] Interview with officials of the three companies by one of the authors, March 1976.

on this basis,[29] and there has been no increase since then. Flexible work schedules are now quite common in Europe and are gaining ground in the United States. Under such arrangements, employees can report for work or leave work on a flexible basis, but are usually required to be at work during a core period. Most such arrangements apply to salaried workers only.

Despite the allure of three-day weekends, the rearranged workweek failed to win a substantial following, in part because of legal and union restraints, in part because of institutional restraints. The Public Contracts (Walsh-Healey) Act requires the payment of time and one half for all work in excess of eight hours in one day. Most union contracts have similar provisions, which make the ten-hour day prohibitively expensive.

Although employees saw the rearranged workweek as guaranteeing the three-day weekend, this was not necessarily the case. Managements looked for greater utilization of capital by having an expanded work force employed ten hours, five days per week, but each employee working only four days. Thus, an employee works Monday–Thursday one week, Tuesday–Friday another, Wednesday–Friday and the following Monday during the third week, and so on. The three-day weekend does not occur for an individual regularly, because the plant or office is working, with the fifth day a "swing" one. This is how insurance companies are operating a four-day week.

Much of the literature in favor of the rearranged workweek stressed greater leisure as a by-product. In fact, many used it to achieve greater income. A government study for May 1974 found that those on a four-day week were twice as likely as all full-time workers to hold a second job.[30] As Figure 16–3 demonstrates, this same study also found that four-day workers constituted only about 10% of those usually working ten-hour days. The great bulk were five-day workers on overtime.

Despite the failure of the restructured workweek to win a substantial following, we may be a lot closer to achieving a four-day week than we realize. In 1971, a new federal law required the celebration of five holidays on Mondays, thus assuring five additional three-day weekends. Perhaps more significant is the increase in absenteeism in plants on Mondays and Fridays. Workers may be opting for leisure and three-day weekends more than the data reveal.

CONCLUDING REMARKS

Whenever unemployment becomes a serious problem, the question of shorter hours will come to the fore. Nevertheless, a reduction of the

---

[29] U.S. Department of Labor, Bureau of Labor Statistics, *The Revised Workweek: Results of a Pilot Study of 16 Firms*, Bulletin 1846 (Washington, D.C.: Government Printing Office, 1975), p. 1.

[30] Janice N. Hedges, "How Many Days Make a Workweek?" *Monthly Labor Review*, vol. 98 (April 1975), p. 32.

FIGURE 16–3
Proportion of Wage and Salary Workers Who Usually
Work Ten-Hour Days, by Number of Days Worked, 1974

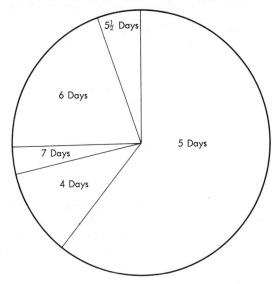

Less than 0.5 worked 4½ days.
Source: U.S. Bureau of Labor Statistics.

workweek seems at best a poor remedy for the problem of unemployment, and certainly no solution for the disadvantaged in our society who are without jobs. If our society decides to take improvement in productivity in the form of reduced hours of work rather than in disposable income, economic growth can be impaired. Hence, a further reduction in hours could well curtail rather than expand employment. It remains to be seen whether daily hours will increase in the future to accommodate new demands for leisure without reducing the workweek.

APPENDIX[31]

The model [designed by Drs. Kosters and Welch to demonstrate that minimum wages make teenagers and blacks more vulnerable to cyclical unemployment and less likely to gain in the upward cycle movement of employment] is estimated one equation at a time without imposing the constraints of internal consistency, $\Sigma_i \beta_{it} = \Sigma \gamma_{it} = 1$ and $\Sigma_i \eta_{pi} \gamma_{it} = \Sigma \eta_{ri} \beta_{it} = 0$. The estimation technique is nonlinear. We simply iterate over values of η_p and η_r to minimize the residual sum of squares. The typical equation (omitting subscript, i) is

---

[31] Reproduced by permission from Marvin Kosters and Finis Welch, "The Effects of Minimum Wages on the Distribution of Changes in Aggregate Employment," *American Economic Review*, vol. 62 (June 1972), pp. 330–33.

$$E_t = \gamma_0 Z_{1t} + \beta_0 Z_{2t} + U_t$$

where Z_1 and Z_2 are constructs that are respectively proportional to E_{pt} and E_{rt}, where the factors of proportionality are of the form

$$log \ (Z_{1t}/E_{pt}) = \eta_p \ log \ M_t + t \ log \ (1 + r)$$
$$log \ (Z_{2t}/E_{rt}) = \eta_r \ log \ M_t + t \ log \ (1 + r)$$

There are 60 observations and 4 parameters, γ_0, β_0, η_{pi}, η_{ri} are estimated. For particular values of η_p and η_r, Z_1, and Z_2 are computed and the OLS regression of E_{it} on Z_1 and Z_2 is then calculated. Iterating over η_p and η_r, that solution is selected to minimize the residual sum of squares.

The standard errors of $\hat{\gamma}_0$ and $\hat{\beta}_0$ are computed as though the regression of E_i on Z_1 and Z_2 were of the standard form except that degrees of freedom are 56 instead of 58. The standard errors of η_{pi} and η_{ri} are computed heuristically to measure the sensitivity of the residual sum of squares to the constraints $\eta_{pi} = 0$ and $\eta_{ri} = 0$. Specifically, to compute the standard error of $\hat{\eta}_p$ we first estimate the equation as described above and then impose the constraint, $\eta_{pi} = 0$ and iterate on η_{ri} to minimize the residual sum of squares. Let Q_0 represent the unconstrained residual sum of squares, and let Q_1 represent the constrained sum of squares. Then compute

$$``F_{1,56} = \frac{Q_1 - Q_0}{Q_0/56},$$
$$``t_{56}" = (``F_{1,56}")^{1/2},$$

and

$$\sigma(\hat{\eta}_p) = \frac{\hat{\eta}_p}{``t_{56}"}$$

The standard error of $\hat{\eta}_r$ is computed the same way.

The employment data are quarterly averages computed from seasonally adjusted monthly data reported in *Employment and Earnings*. The minimum wage and coverage data were provided by the U.S. Department of Labor. . . . The minimum wage data are reported in Kosters and Welch.[32]

The quarterly growth rates in employment for each of the groups are computed as observed growth rates between the years 1956–III to 1957–II and one decade later, 1966–III to 1967–II. This period was chosen because overall unemployment rates were similar in both years. The relative growth rate, r_i, is the quarterly growth rate of employment in this group relative to that of aggregate employment over the decade. They are:

---

[32] M. Kosters and F. Welch, *The Effects of Minimum Wages on the Distribution of Changes in Aggregate Employment*, RM–6273–OEO, RAND Corp., Santa Monica, Calif., September 1970.

	White Males	Nonwhite Males	White Females	Nonwhite Females
Adults	−.0023	−.0003	.0023	.0027
Teenagers	.0077	.0029	.0071	.0063

Quarterly growth rate in aggregate employment = .0035.

QUESTIONS FOR DISCUSSION

1. Is there a competitive tendency toward reduction of hours of work? Evaluate the importance of governmental legislation and union organization in shortening hours of work.

2. Discuss the relationship of hours reduction and efficiency. What are the advantages and disadvantages of a six-hour shift? Of the four-day, ten-hour week?

3. Do you favor a minimum wage differential for teenagers? Explain your answer.

4. Evaluate minimum wages as a poverty cure.

SUGGESTIONS FOR FURTHER READING

Ehrenberg, Ronald G. *Fringe Benefits and Overtime Behavior.* Lexington Books. Lexington, Mass.: D. C. Heath & Co., 1971.

An econometric and theoretical analysis of the relationship between fringe benefit costs and the use of overtime to supply additional labor.

Evans, Archibald A. *Flexibility in Working Life.* Paris: Organization for Economic Cooperation and Development, 1973.

Fleuter, Douglas L. *The Workweek Revolution: A Guide to the Changing Workweek.* Reading, Mass.: Addison-Wesley Publishing Co., 1975.

U.S. Department of Labor, Bureau of Labor Statistics. *The Revised Workweek: Results of a Pilot Study of 16 Firms.* Washington, D.C.: Government Printing Office, 1975.

Three studies of flexible and rearranged workweeks.

Hedges, Janice N. "How Many Days Make a Workweek?" *Monthly Labor Review,* vol. 98 (April 1975), pp. 29–36.

————. "Long Workweeks and Overtime Pay," *Monthly Labor Review,* vol. 99 (April 1976), pp. 7–12.

Michelotti, Kopp. "Multiple Jobholders in May 1975," *Monthly Labor Review,* vol. 98 (November 1975), pp. 56–62.

Three articles discussing different aspects of the workweek.

Kosters, Marvin, and Welch, Finis. "The Effects of Minimum Wages on the Distribution of Changes in Aggregate Employment," *American Economic Review,* vol. 62 (June 1972), pp. 323–32.

Peterson, John M., and Stewart, Charles T. *Employment Effects of Minimum Wage Rates.* Washington, D.C.: American Enterprise Institute for Public Policy Research, 1969.

Welch, Finis. "Minimum Wage Legislation in the United States," *Economic*

Inquiry (formerly *Western Economic Journal*), vol. 12 (September 1974), pp. 285–318.

Three excellent studies of the impact of the minimum wage on employment.

Owen, John D. "Workweeks and Leisure: An Analysis of Trends, 1948–75," *Monthly Labor Review*, vol. 99 (August 1976), pp. 3–8.

An excellent historical analysis of the trend in workweeks since World War II.

17

Government Programs for Security against Old Age, Unemployment, and Accident or Illness

In Chapter 5, we discussed those "fringe benefits" which were designed to protect employees against the expenses or loss of income occasioned by old age, unemployment, or ill health. Self-help and private means have been the traditional methods employed by Americans to guard against such eventualities. Even today, after 30 years of accelerated growth of public welfare and social insurance, private means cover a significant proportion of the population.

The depression which began in 1929 forcefully called attention to the need for an overall, national, or social approach to the problems caused by loss of income to the family. To be sure, prior to 1929 some attack had already been begun on the problem of supplying an income to the family when the breadwinner could no longer produce a paycheck, but the pre-1929 approach was confined largely to compensating the worker for loss sustained in accidents suffered at the place of work—workers' compensation. It was not until 1935, with the passage of the Social Security Act, that an overall program was begun to deal with loss of income because of old age, death of the breadwinner, or unemployment. In almost every election year, beginning with 1950, significant amendments have been enacted. Despite the many changes, the two-pronged "insurance-assistance" approach to the alleviation of economic security which was originally adopted remains in effect.

Table 17–1 summarizes the American social security system and illustrates the complicated nature and administration of the various laws. A detailed analysis of all facets of this vast program would involve another book the size of this one. Here, we shall concentrate on the principal "insurance" features and key economic and industrial relations issues. In

TABLE 17–1
A Summary of the American Social Security System

> *Administered directly by the federal government:*
> "Social Security" (old-age, survivors, disability, and health insurance—OASDHI).
> Railroad programs, including retirement, unemployment, and disability insurance.
> Veterans programs providing pensions, compensation, annuities, and burial awards.
> *Administered under state laws:*
> Unemployment insurance, including programs for federal employees and ex-servicemen.
> Workers' compensation and state temporary disability insurance.
> *Public Aid:* Included here are welfare programs which provide money payments and services to needy families financed from general revenues. Means tests are generally required. The following programs are included:
> *Administered under state laws, usually in conformance to some federal standards:*
> Food Stamps (administered under Department of Agriculture)
> Surplus food distributions (administered under Department of Agriculture)
> Aid to Families with Dependent Children
> Aid to the Blind
> Old-Age Assistance
> Emergency Aid
> Aid to the Permanently and Totally Disabled
> Work Relief
> Work Incentive program (administered under Department of Labor)
> *Administered by the states and localities without federal funds:*
> Public assistance and general assistance (sometimes called "relief").

this connection, it is important to note two things: a combination of congressional generosity in greatly expanding benefits and of demographic changes in reducing the birthrate threatens the fiscal integrity of the basic old-age benefit system; and the burgeoning welfare load (see Table 17–2) constantly exerts pressure on the "insurance" aspects to take over part of the welfare aspects and to thus blur the historic distinction between the two.

THE OLD-AGE, SURVIVORS, DISABILITY, AND HEALTH INSURANCE PROGRAM (OASDHI)

OASDHI is an all federally administered program, covering over 90% of all employed persons and providing the following types of benefits:

Retirement benefits:
Primary monthly benefit to retired worker (reduced benefit, ages 62–64; full benefit, age 65).
Monthly benefit to his wife if 62 or older (reduced if claimed before age 65).

TABLE 17–2
Spending on Social Programs Has Soared

		Millions of Dollars (fiscal years)			
	1960	*1970*	*1973*	*1975* *(esti-* *mated)*	*1976* *(pro-* *posed)*
Cash income maintenance					
Social security	$11,018	$29,685	$48,288	$63,511	$70,063
Unemployment compensation ..	2,375	3,369	5,362	14,697	18,162
Federal civilian retirement	1,821	4,192	6,954	7,125	8,646
Veterans' compensation and pensions	3,312	5,229	6,401	7,671	7,707
Public assistance to the aged, blind, and disabled	1,449	1,979	2,041	4,713	5,458
Aid to families with dependent children	612	2,163	3,922	4,196	4,084
Benefits for disabled miners ...	—	10	952	964	973
Total	$20,587	$46,627	$73,920	$102,877	$115,093
Helping people buy essentials					
Medicare	—	7,149	9,479	13,904	14,991
Medicaid	—	2,727	4,600	6,767	7,156
Food stamps	—	577	2,208	3,672	3,860
Housing	279	1,279	1,420	2,153	2,646
Higher education student aid...	498	1,625	3,880	2,104	2,325
Total	777	13,357	21,587	28,600	30,978
Total	$21,364	$59,984	$95,507	$131,477	$146,071

Source: Data, Brookings Institution. Reprinted from the February 17, 1975 issue of *Business Week* by special permission. © 1975 by McGraw-Hill, Inc.

Monthly benefit to his dependent children under 18 or disabled.
Monthly benefit to wife, whatever age, if caring for child.
Monthly benefit to dependent husband, if 62 or over (reduced if claimed before age 65).

Survivors' benefits:
Monthly benefit to widow, 60 or older.
Monthly benefit to widow or divorced wife, whatever age, if caring for dependent children.
Monthly benefit to child under 18 or disabled.
Monthly benefit to dependent widower, 62 or older.
Monthly benefit to dependent widow, 62 or over.
Burial benefit in lump sum to widow or widower, or to person who paid burial expenses.

Disability benefits:
Monthly benefit to worker if totally disabled for work.
Monthly benefits for same dependents as under retirement benefits.
Monthly benefit to disabled widows and widowers between ages 50 and 62.

Medical benefits:

Hospital, nursing, and outpatient service.

Voluntary supplementary coverage.

OASDHI is thus designed to provide a pension for those retired or disabled, survivorship benefits for those who lose their breadwinner or primary social security recipient, and medical benefits for the aged. These benefits are not limited by life insurance, private pensions, or other private arrangements, except that those who earn stipulated amounts as employees or self-employed persons cannot collect full social security until they reach their seventies.

All benefits are based upon the monthly payment to the worker who retires at age 65 or over; this is called the primary insurance amount. That amount, in turn, is determined by the worker's average monthly wage. While there is more than one method of computing the average monthly wage, it will usually be figured as follows: The total of creditable earnings in covered employment and self-employment after 1950, or age 21, if later, and until age 65 is divided by the number of months elapsing in this period, except that the five years of lowest earnings are omitted, as well as any years for which a disability freeze was in effect. Retired workers who start collecting benefits at 62, 63, or 64 receive less than the primary insurance amount. The full amount, however, is payable to eligible disabled workers, regardless of age.

The monthly benefits for dependents of a retired or disabled worker, the survivors of a deceased worker, or the disabled widow or widower of a deceased worker are equal to specified fractions of the primary insurance amount. Table 17–3 shows the benefit schedules enacted in 1976. Congress has increased benefits at least every two years, on election years,

TABLE 17–3

Examples of Monthly Retirement Benefits for Various Pay Brackets—OASDHI

Average Yearly Earnings	For Workers Retired at 65	For Workers and Spouse Retired at 65
$ 923 or less	$107.90	$161.90
1,200	138.90	208.40
2,000	180.70	271.10
3,000	223.20	341.20
4,000	262.60	448.80
5,000	304.50	561.90
5,600	328.50	609.10
6,000	344.10	631.30
6,600	368.10	666.30
7,000	385.60	687.20
7,600	412.70	722.20
8,000	427.80	748.70

Benefits and taxes are subject to automatic cost-of-living increases.
Source: Social Security Administration.

and has provided automatic cost-of-living increases as well, which increased benefits by 8% in 1975 and 6.4% in 1976.

Financing

The OASDHI program is paid for by equal contributions from both employer and employee in covered employment. Self-employed persons covered by the program pay three quarters as much as the total of employer and employee contributions on the same amount of earnings. The tax rate keeps growing (see Table 17–4). Initially, the employee

TABLE 17–4
Social Security Taxes—Past, Present, and Projected

Year	Maximum Employee Tax (matched by employer)	Maximum Self-Employed Tax
1937	$ 30.00	—
1953	54.00	$ 81,00
1959	120.00	180.00
1965	174.00	259.20
1971	405.60	585.00
1974	772.20	1,042.80
1980	1,179.75	1,579.50
2000	3,386.25	4,462.50
2011	6,705.00	7,650.00

Source: U.S. Department of Health, Education, and Welfare data.

tax was 1% on the first $3,000 of earnings. In 1977, the combined employer-employee tax was 11.7% on the first $16,500 of employee earnings. This included a 1.8% tax for Medicare.

The OASDHI taxes are collected by the payroll deduction method for the employed, and with income taxes for the self-employed, under the administration of the Internal Revenue Service. The bulk of the taxes collected are deposited in the OASI Trust Fund of the U.S. Treasury. The balance goes into separate Disability Insurance, Health Insurance, and Supplementary Medical Insurance Trust funds. All expenses and benefits of the program come from these tax receipts. The reserve portions of the trust funds, approximately 2%, are invested in interest-bearing U.S. government securities. In 1975, the reserve fund contained $45.9 billion. In 1976, however, the combined payroll taxes into the trust fund totaled about $72.8 billion, while payments to beneficiaries came to $78.2 billion. That $5.6 billion deficit was supplied by the reserve fund. Obviously, only a few years of such deficits, and the reserve fund will be depleted. Figure 17–1 illustrates the financial crisis social security will face if this trend should continue. Table 17–5 presents figures demonstrating how quickly this deficit may accrue.

FIGURE 17–1

Under Present Law, Benefits Will Far Outstrip Taxable Wages

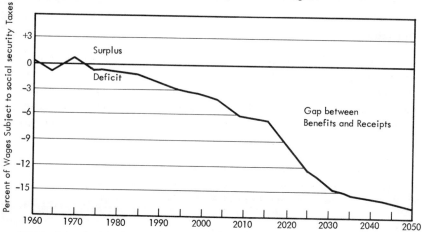

Source: Data, Social Security Administration. Reprinted from the July 19, 1976 issue of *Business Week* by special permission. © 1976 by McGraw-Hill, Inc.

TABLE 17–5

Social Security Finances Increasing Deficit

Year	Income*	Outgo*	Deficit*
1975 .... 66.5		69.6	3.1
1976 .... 72.8		78.2	5.6
1977 .... 82.3		87.4	5.1
1978 .... 91.7		97.5	5.8
1979 ....100.9		107.1	6.2
1980 ....109.8		116.8	7.0
1981 ....117.6		126.6	9.0
1982 ....125.3		136.8	11.5
1983 ....133.4		148.0	14.6
1984 ....141.8		160.3	18.5

* In billions of dollars.

Source: U.S. House of Representatives, Ways and Means Committee, Subcommittee on Social Security.

Administration

The OASDHI is a wholly federal government–administered program, with the exceptions that initial determinations of disability are made by state agencies and that medical expense benefits are administered through fiscal intermediaries, such as Blue Cross and private insurance carriers. Two departments of the federal government share these administrative functions—the Treasury and the Department of Health, Education, and Welfare. The Internal Revenue Service of the Treasury collects the taxes, and the Secretary of the Treasury is the managing trustee of the trust funds. The Treasury also issues benefit checks, and appropriations are made from the funds to cover administrative expenses.

All other administrative functions are handled by the Social Security Administration, which is now a division of the Department of Health, Education, and Welfare. Centralized records are kept in Baltimore, Maryland, and field offices are located throughout the United States. In addition, research and actuarial divisions are attached to the Social Security Administration in Washington, as is an appeals council which hears cases involving claimants who are dissatisfied with interpretations of eligibility or amount of benefits due.

CURRENT OASDHI ISSUES

Most students of social security favor, in principle, the widest possible coverage of an insurance program and the narrowest possible coverage of an assistance program. This preference is based upon both social and economic grounds. The social reasons are grounded in the democratic belief that older persons have a right to spend their final years in dignity, with an income based upon earned right rather than an income secured on the basis of demonstrated need. Under an insurance system, the worker and his or her employer, or the self-employed person, contribute during the worker's life a given amount of money to support those already retired who had previously worked. These contributions entitle the worker to receive similar retirement benefits. By complying with the published rules of the insurance system, the retirement income is earned. Need is not a factor.

In contrast, assistance is based upon need, which means that need has to be defined. Even with the best of intentions, different administrators will define need differently. In other instances, favoritism or political pressure may determine who receives assistance and who does not. The aged are a significant group worth pleasing to the ambitious politician, sometimes without proper consideration for the general welfare. Under such circumstances, need can be redefined in terms of political regularity, with consequent degradation of the older person in real need.

The economic grounds for preferring an insurance program to an assistance program are closely related to the social ones. Insurance is paid for by the beneficiaries or their employers under a system of taxation that is clearly earmarked for a specific purpose. Assistance comes out of general taxation, which permits liberality without tying costs to benefits, or costs to responsibilities. In the long run, assistance is likely to be found to be less efficient and more expensive, with those employed burdened with the care of an increasing older population that has not provided for its own retirement by insurance.

The framers of the Social Security Act envisioned Old-Age Assistance as a temporary measure to protect those not previously covered by OASDHI. Yet, as Table 17–2 shows, almost $5.5 billion was expended on assistance to the aged, blind, and disabled in 1976, and the aged accounted for a large portion of that. Because of the burgeoning costs of aid to dependent children (see also Table 17–2), there has developed considerable support to commingle all insurance and aid programs and to provide both by general taxes. We believe that this would be unfortunate, but now funding for *both* the insurance and aid programs are in trouble: the aid programs because of their costs to cities and states; and the insurance programs because, as already noted, of congressional generosity and demographic changes.

The present method of financing old-age and survivor benefits is actually a practical compromise between two extremes: pay as you go and level premium. The latter would require a uniform contribution rate at all times, much higher to meet current outlays in earlier years and lower than necessary for the same purposes in later years. Because of the enormous reserve fund, with its potential deflationary impact, which level-premium financing would require, it has not been adopted. Rather, the plan intended to set taxes on an increasing basis which will divide costs over the years and build up a large but not enormous (for the job to be done) reserve. The fund can, however, absorb short-term fluctuations only. As seen in Figure 17–1 and Table 17–5, the reserve fund established under this system will soon be depleted and payroll taxes and taxable income will continue to increase. The root causes lie in the 1972 amendments.

The Impact of the 1972 Amendments

The 1972 amendments increased benefits by 20% without increasing payroll taxes and then set up an "indexing," or cost-of-living, arrangement, for the future benefit increases. Both actions were financially irresponsible. The increase was based upon demographic predictions that were clearly erroneous and obsolete at the time that they were used and have become more so since then, as demonstrated by Figure 17–2; and upon an indexing system that inflated benefits over and above any inflationary compensation. As summarized by Professor Kaplan:

> Unfortunately there were two severe problems with the 1972 amendments that have contributed greatly to the current problems with the system. First, the future cost projections were made using an obsolete set of demographic assumptions that bore little relation to the recent experience of sharply declining birth rates. The demographic projections had been developed in the early 1960s and were not modified until 1974. Figure [17–2] shows, along with the actual birth rate, the low and high birth rates (per 1,000) assumed by the Social Security Administration's Actuary Office from 1964 until the trustees report in 1974. One can see

FIGURE 17–2

Actual Birth Rates and Social Security Projections,
1964–1975

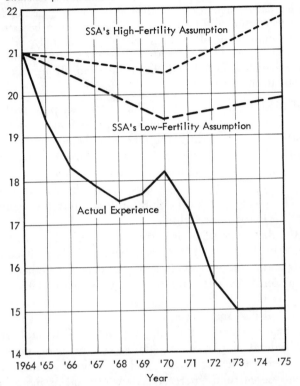

Source: Francisco Bayo, *United States Population Projections for OASDHI Cost Estimates*, U.S. Department of Health, Education, and Welfare, Social Security Administration, Office of the Actuary, Actuarial Study No. 62 (December 1966), p. 7, and U.S. Department of Health, Education, and Welfare, Public Health Service, *Monthly Vital Statistics Report*, various issues. Chart from Robert S. Kaplan, *The Financial Crisis in the Social Security System* (Washington, D.C.: American Enterprise Institute for Public Policy Research, 1976), p. 6. Reproduced by permission.

that the actual birth rate declined steadily from the assumed levels until, by 1972, the assumed birth rate (an average of the high and low projections) was 30 percent higher than the actual rate. After 1972, the birth rate dropped even further.

Since the future costs of the system depend crucially upon the number of workers available to be taxed to support the future retired workers, a severe decline in current births will eventually cause sharply higher tax rates on these future workers. If Congress had used realistic birth rate assumptions in 1972, it would likely have seen that the system was already in deficit, even before the 20 percent across-the-board increase.

Naturally, this generous benefit increase, coupled with ever-decreasing birth rates, has contributed to the large deficits now forecasted for the system in the twenty-first century.

The second problem with the 1972 amendments arose when Congress legislated an indexing method that overcompensates for inflation. This defect causes the future cost of the system to be extremely sensitive to future *levels* of inflation which are, naturally, very difficult to forecast. A properly indexed system's cost should depend on productivity and demographic factors but should be relatively insensitive to purely monetary phenomena.[1]

With inflation, a worker's wage is likely to keep pace with increasing prices. Basing an individual's benefits on his average indexed monthly earnings rather than indexing the benefits themselves, would deflate them to coincide with the worker's average buying power throughout his or her working life, and would in fact provide protection against inflation in a manner superior to that accomplished for most income recipients. This change, or "decoupling" as it is referred to, could possibly halve the deficit in the reserve fund.

Even if the decoupling flaw is corrected, the problems associated with the declining birthrate are being magnified by other difficulties. Local governments and nonprofit associations may choose whether to enter into or remain under OASDHI, and some have recently left, thus further eroding the tax base. Federal civil service workers receive not only federal pensions but also social security if they work at least seven years in the private sector. This "double dipping" into the federal treasury has given some federal employees, including congressmen, pensions larger than their preretirement salaries, and is obviously an unwarranted drain on the reserve fund. Increased longevity means more benefits for longer periods, and pressure for benefits at an earlier age than 65 add to the costs at the lower end.

All this has raised questions about the method of paying for social security and old age. Pay-as-you-go is based upon a dangerous assumption, since it assumes that future generations and Congresses will be willing to levy special taxes at a much higher rate than present rates. The cost of retirement is both a present one and a future one. By levying all the cost of those retired at the time of retirement, pay-as-you-go adherents would have us, in effect, live off our depreciation. What we would be doing would be analogous to the factory owner who takes no heed of machine depreciation until the machine wears out. Then he must charge the cost of a new machine against the profits of a single year, instead of spreading the cost over many years. Proper provision

---

[1] Robert S. Kaplan, *Financial Crisis in the Social Security System,* Domestic Affairs Studies (Washington, D.C.: American Enterprise Institute for Public Policy Research, 1976), p. 5.

for the aged requires that the costs of retirement be divided between the future and the present.

"Earmarked" Taxes versus General Revenues

A question that is repeatedly raised is whether OASDHI benefits should be financed from general revenues rather than by means of an "earmarked" tax, as is the situation at present. Those who favor the use of general revenues point out that the present OASDHI tax is regressive in nature in that lower income and middle-income families pay a higher proportion of their incomes than do families with higher incomes. They also point out that the use of general revenues would permit a greater degree of fiscal flexibility in that taxes or benefits could be raised or lowered independently. On a more immediate and short-term basis, this could permit the financing of recent substantial increases in benefits.

On the other hand, proponents of our present system of an earmarked tax argue that the use of general revenues would remove the restraints inherent in a program where taxes and benefits are directly tied together. Removal of these restraints could permit an escalation of benefits and taxes. Moreover, proponents argue that it would be difficult to draw a logical line as to how much of the program should be financed from general revenues, that pressures would mount for the increased use of general revenues, and that ultimately, the entire program would be financed on this basis. Finally, general revenue financing could well result in a merger of assistance and insurance and abrogate an individual's "earned right" to specific benefits.

There is a need to integrate private and public pension systems. In Chapter 5, we noted how the private pension system has expanded and benefits have inflated. A combination of social security and private pensions has created a sizable group of beneficiaries receiving retirement income near or above their final working earnings. It is doubtful whether the bulk of the labor force should foot this bill, or whether it is in the public interest that this occur. Any reorganization of the social security system should, it would seem, contain provisions for reasonable limits on combined private and public benefits. As we shall see in Chapter 22, this is an especially critical problem in the public sector.

MEDICARE

Medicare is a hospital and medical insurance program for the aged which is composed of two parts, as set forth in Figure 17–3. Part A, the "basic coverage," is financed by payroll taxes added to the basic social security taxes. Part B, the "supplementary coverage," is paid for by contributions from beneficiaries and federal funds from general reve-

FIGURE 17–3
Medicare—What It Meant as of July 1, 1976

Part A Basic Coverage	Part B Supplementary Coverage
(Financed by increased social security taxes.)	(Voluntary insurance financed by individual monthly premiums of $5.80 and federal funds from general revenues; individual pays first $60 of his or her total annual costs and 20% of the cost of all services totaling more than $60.)
Hospital care Full coverage after the first $104 for up to 60 days in each period of illness;* coverage up to 30 additional days, for which the patient pays $26 a day. "Lifetime reserve" of 60 days toward which patient pays $52 a day. Psychiatric care is included for up to 60 days in each period of illness, with a lifetime limit of 190 days.	*Physician's care* Physicians' and surgeons' (including certain dental surgeons') fees. (100% reimbursement for radiological or pathological services by physicians to patients in hospitals.) *Home nursing care* Up to 100 home health visits each year in addition to those allowed under the basic plan, without any requirement for prior hospitalization.
Nursing home care Posthospital care for 20 days in each period of illness at no cost to patient, plus 80 additional days, for which patient pays $13 per day.	*Other health services and supplies* Coverage includes cost of outpatient charges, X rays and other diagnostic tests, radiological treatments, casts, splints, artificial limbs, and ambulance service.
Home nursing care Up to 100 visits by nurses or technicians in each period of illness at no cost to patient.	*Out-of-hospital benefits* Yearly limit for treatment of mental, psychoneurotic, and personality disorders is $250.

* A period of illness, as defined by the bill, normally starts with the first day of hospitalization and ends whenever the patient has spent 60 consecutive days without hospital or nursing home care.
Source: U.S. Department of Health, Education, and Welfare.

nues, as noted in Figure 17–3. Eligibility is basically the same as for the social security system. The payroll taxes for the Medicare program are included in the tabulations depicted in Table 17–4.

One of the most controversial aspects of the Medicare program is its costs. Partially because estimates were based on existing utilization prior to the program's enactment, despite the generally known propensity for the availability of prepaid medical care to enhance its usage, costs have greatly exceeded any forecasts with $14 billion paid out in 1975 (see Table 17–2) and the trend moving upward rapidly. Overutilization and malingering have undoubtedly contributed to this problem, but the most significant item has been the rising cost of medical services and hospital labor costs. The cost of medical care has been advancing faster than other elements of living expense, and with the advent of Medicare, that cost rose quite sharply with the demand for services. (See Figure 17–4.)

FIGURE 17–4
The Rising Costs of Medical Care

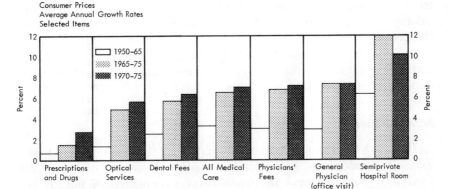

Medical Care By Type of Service

Total Expenditures for Personal Health Care

Fiscal 1950
$10.4 Billion = 100%

Fiscal 1975
$103.2 Billion = 100%

All Other Services
Hospital Care
Prescriptions and Drugs
Dental Services
Physician Services

Consumer Prices
Average Annual Growth Rates
Selected Items

1950–65
1965–75
1970–75

Prescriptions and Drugs   Optical Services   Dental Fees   All Medical Care   Physicians' Fees   General Physician (office visit)   Semiprivate Hospital Room

Personal health care spending has grown from $10.4 billion in fiscal 1950 to $103.2 billion in fiscal 1975, an almost tenfold increase. About 15% of the growth in health care spending can be attributed to the increase in population. Increased use of health resources, technological improvements, and other factors account for about 37 percent. But the largest portion of the growth in expenditures is due to inflation—to the higher prices of health services.

The consumer price index for health care has been rising faster than have prices for all consumer items. Medical care prices advanced at an average rate of 3.5% a year between 1950 and 1965, compared to 1.8% for all consumer prices. The rate of increase for health care prices almost doubled to 6.5% annually between 1965 and 1975; for all consumer items, the annual average price rise was 5.5%. Although health care prices have continued to rise, there has not been very much acceleration in the rate of increase over the last five years. Indeed, the rate of increase for some prices—such as that for a semiprivate hospital room, the fastest rising component—actually slowed somewhat in the last five years.

Health care costs are not uniform throughout the country. For example, a typical four-person family living in Los Angeles would have spent a total of $901 on medical care in 1974, compared to about $650 for a similar family in Buffalo, St. Louis, Cincinnati, or Pittsburgh. Moreover, costs vary significantly, sometimes by 10% or more, in metropolitan areas as geographically close as Milwaukee and Chicago, or Cleveland and Cincinnati.

Source: The Conference Board, *Road Maps of Industry,* March 1976.

Still another issue of the federal government's program for providing health care is the cost of Medicaid—provided for under Title 19 of the Social Security Act. Under this program, the federal government provides financial assistance to the states that provide medical assistance for individuals who are on welfare or who are "medically needy." As of 1975, Medicaid was in effect in all states except Arizona. The cost of Medicaid was originally expected to involve a federal outlay of under $1 billion per year, but by 1975 it had reached $6 billion. Part of the problem is attributable to the fact that the states were allowed to establish their own standards as to who would be considered "medically needy." Liberal state standards greatly expanded the number of potential beneficiaries, until the federal government restricted beneficiaries to persons whose income is no more than 133% of the maximum welfare payment in the state.

UNEMPLOYMENT COMPENSATION

Unemployment compensation (or "insurance": both terms are used) is part of the broad spectrum of social insurance programs, and provides cash benefits to regularly employed members of the labor force who become involuntarily unemployed and who are able and willing to accept suitable jobs. Although unemployment compensation was established by the Social Security Act of 1935, the federal government does not exert great influence over either the administration or the funding of the program. Funding is not raised from general revenues but rather from a tax imposed on employers.

Administration

Unemployment compensation is primarily a state-administered program. The federal act provided an incentive to the states to establish their own unemployment insurance plans by imposing a federal tax, 90% of which could be offset by employer taxes paid under state laws meeting certain general standards. The tax, of 3.0% on the first $3,000 of an employee's annual wages was originally imposed on all employers having eight or more employees in covered employment in 20 weeks of the year. All of these conditions have by now changed, but the principles remain the same.

All of the states have approved unemployment insurance programs. There is, however, wide variation among the states with respect to specific provisions. Employers who are subject to these programs pay their state tax and receive credit against their federal tax. The remaining federal tax (about 0.4% of the covered payroll) is used by the federal government for federal and state administration (including the operation of public employment offices) and to bolster the reserves of the state programs. The state taxes are deposited in the unemployment trust fund in the federal treasury, and from these monies the states make weekly payments to unemployed persons covered by the state laws. Separate accounts are maintained for each state.

Operations

The Social Security Act did not establish or make mandatory unemployment compensation laws. It was enabling legislation allowing the states to do so, imposing a tax structure which greatly encouraged them to do so, and establishing minimum conditions for their programs if they participated. Each state determines specific qualifications for benefits (for example, allowable reasons for job separation), specific interpretation of terms (for example, "able to work," "available for work"), and other conditions, such as allowable earnings when unemployed.

The federal act does stipulate situations where a state cannot deny aid to an otherwise eligible applicant, particularly if he refuses to accept new work because:

1. The job opening is available because of a strike or lockout.
2. The wages or conditions are substantially less favorable than those prevailing for similar work in the locality.
3. The job requires an individual to join a company-dominated union, or to resign from or refrain from joining a bona fide labor organization.

When a worker is unemployed, he reports to the local employment office, where he may file a claim for benefits if the office cannot place him in a suitable job. These are paid to the worker on a weekly basis in an amount and for a period determined by state law. Generally, the amount is about 50% of past earnings, subject to a maximum, which varied among the states from $80 to $150 per week as of January 1977.

The state agency which administers this program is generally either a part of a state department of labor or an independent department or board. These agencies operate through approximately 2,000 local employment offices, which not only handle the unemployment claims but provide job-finding and other services. Federal functions are mostly handled by the U.S. Department of Labor, although the Treasury Department maintains and invests the trust fund. Separate funds and programs now exist for railroad employees, ex-servicemen, and federal civilian employees.

Subject to these and other federal requirements, the states have considerable discretion in deciding who shall be covered, the amount and duration of benefits, the taxes to be paid, and the procedures to be used for handling claims. For example, a state may include in its own program a provision whereby an employer with a low-unemployment history may pay a lower tax, or it may adopt a standard tax rate which is different (higher) than the federal rate of 2.7%.

Coverage

Unemployment insurance is provided for only covered employment. This historically included primarily industrial and commercial workers in private industry, and excluded from coverage agricultural workers, domestics, certain casual labor, employees in some governmental and nonprofit organizations, the self-employed, and employees in small firms. Over the years, however, the states added coverage on employers with only a single worker, domestics and agricultural workers, and other excluded groups.

In 1970 and 1976, Congress amended the Employment Security Act to require that the states conform to federal rules as to coverage. This has brought coverage to sizable numbers of farm workers, domestics, and small business and government employees. In total, about 90% of all those employed are now within the purview of state or federal unemployment insurance legislation.

Eligibility

Eligibility conditions, like all other aspects of the individual state provisions, vary greatly, but there are usually these four:

1. The period of unemployment must be longer than some waiting period (usually one week).
2. The claimant must have qualified for benefits by having worked some minimum time or earned a minimum amount in covered jobs. (Usually 15 weeks or $500, sometimes in more than one fiscal quarter.)
3. The individual must have a continuing attachment to the labor force indicated by registration for work at an employment office (and sometimes be "actively seeking work" or show "willingness to accept suitable work").
4. Most states refuse benefits to those who terminate their employment under specified conditions.

The general purpose of these qualifications is to restrict benefits to those who become unemployed through no fault of their own. It is generally held that an employee who voluntarily leaves his job or is terminated through his own fault should take the consequences. The disqualifying reasons include: discharge for misconduct or cause, dishonesty or criminal acts, voluntarily leaving without good cause, refusal of suitable work, participation or involvement in a labor dispute, customary layoffs of short and known duration, quitting to attend school or become self-employed, and fraudulent misrepresentation. All of these disqualifications are subject to greatly different conditions under state laws. The eligibility conditions relating to the disqualification of strikers are discussed below.

Financing

Not all states actually charge employers at the legal maximum rate, and most states reduce the rates charged employers who have good employment histories. This is known as "experience rating," and is designed to encourage employment-stabilizing practices. The tax is imposed entirely on the employer in all states except the following, where the additional rates indicated are charged the employees:

Alaska	0.3%–0.9%	Puerto Rico	0.5%
California	1.0%	Rhode Island	1.0%
New Jersey	1.0%		

Employee contributions are usually earmarked for disability insurance, which is discussed later in this chapter.

The 1970 and 1976 amendments raised the taxable base for federal purposes to $6,000. It is expected that most states will do likewise.

The federal share of the unemployment compensation tax (0.07%) is first used for annual appropriations to the states to cover the costs of administration of the unemployment compensation laws. The entire costs of administration are covered by these grants because all funds collected from taxes on employers or employees must be used for payment of benefits. Federal grants are also made to the states for the costs of administering the state employment offices, through which unemployment compensation benefits are handled. Since the costs of administration prior to the 1950s proved to be less than anticipated, the federal government developed a substantial surplus from its tax share. The Administrative Financing Act of 1954 utilized these surpluses to protect the solvency of the insurance funds. It provides for the automatic appropriation to the Federal Unemployment Trust Fund of the annual excess of federal unemployment tax collections over employment security administrative expenses. These excess collections are used first to establish and maintain a $550 million fund in the federal unemployment account available for non-interest-bearing loans to state agencies with depleted reserves. The excess collections beyond $550 million are used to establish a $250 million reserve for administrative expenses. Finally, any excess tax collections are returned to the states.

During recessions, states suffering severe unemployment have been compelled to "borrow" from the federal treasury to make payments to the unemployed. A lengthy, severe depression would surely require some reexamination of the entire financing issue.

Benefit Duration

Benefits become available in all states except five after a one-week waiting period. Connecticut requires a two-week wait, and Delaware, Kentucky, Maryland, and Nevada do not require any wait. Benefits in most states last for 26 weeks, although some last longer, and Congress has several times provided for extended benefits during recessions, providing for a maximum of 13 weeks on top of the regular period up to a total of 39 weeks. Such extended benefits become payable to all states when the national insured unemployment rate[2] exceeds 4.5% for three consecutive months, and they continue until the rate drops below 4.5% for a like period. High unemployment in the 1970s gave rise to emergency bills which extended coverage to as much as 65 weeks and gave benefits to those otherwise uncovered up to 39 weeks.

Unemployment Compensation and Strikers

Of particular significance for the study of labor relations and labor economics is the impact of unemployment compensation on strikes. As in other aspects of the program, there is considerable variation among the states. The railroad program is the most liberal in this regard, paying compensation to strikers, and those otherwise involved in strikes, from the moment the strike starts, regardless of the circumstances. Some $69.6 million was thus expended between 1953 and 1975 by the railroads to finance strikes against themselves.[3]

Among the states, New York and Rhode Island pay benefits after waiting periods of seven and eight weeks, respectively; 14 states pay benefits if the employer locks out his employees; and other states pay benefits even to employees who may be indirectly involved in the strike. For example, if a worker's plant is shut down for lack of parts because of a strike called by his union in an adjoining, related plant, the worker is eligible for these latter benefits.

In Chapter 7, we discussed the questionable public policy of supporting strikes from the public treasury. Unemployment compensation for strikers seems, if anything, less justified, for it provides not only for public financial support of strikers, but in addition, requires the employer to finance the strike through his taxes, which in turn are increased as a result of the payment of benefits to the strikers!

Other Unemployment Compensation Issues

Closely related to the use (or misuse) of unemployment compensation is that of eligibility in general. Since the purpose of unemployment insurance is to protect persons who are genuinely attached to the labor force from hardships incurred when they are temporarily unemployed and seeking other work, eligibility conditions must be set. As these conditions

---

[2] "Insured unemployment rate" is the rate of unemployment among workers covered by unemployment compensation.

[3] Data from U.S. Railroad Retirement Board.

have steadily become less stringent, and benefits have become both more liberal and more widely supplemented, abuses have become more widespread. Not working at public expense in effect becomes more nearly equated with working.

The problem arises because we are witnessing two parallel revolutions which affect unemployment insurance. There is steady pressure and a noticeable trend toward payment of higher benefits for longer periods of more uniform duration. At the same time, as noted in Chapter 1, an extraordinary growth in part-time secondary workers in the labor force has occurred. For persons with only marginal attachment to the labor force, the temptation presented by larger benefits paid for as long as 65 weeks can lead to an increase in malingering and other undesirable practices, which, in the past, have never been problems of any magnitude in the system. The federal-state system will have to balance protection against fraud and malingering against requirements of fairness.

Since eligibility is related to employment within a particular state, workers would lose rights by moving from one state to another if it were not for the existence of an Interstate Benefit Plan whereby workers who qualify for benefits in one state may draw their benefits in another. The original home state pays the benefits, and the state in which the worker then dwells acts as the agent for the transaction. All 50 states cooperate in this plan. The Interstate Benefit Plan, however, does not help a worker who would qualify for benefits only if his or her credits in both states were totaled. As a result, a "basic plan for combining wages" has been subscribed to by the states. This plan provides for the totaling of credits where that is necessary to make determinations for eligibility. Still another problem arises when a worker is eligible for benefits but would be eligible for the maximum benefits only by combining wages in the states. The Extended Interstate Benefit Plan for Combining Wages, adopted by the states, is specifically designed to handle this problem.

Again, however, as the services provided by unemployment compensation laws are expanded, so, too, is the opportunity to benefit without seriously looking for work. A laid-off New York housewife finds it pleasant to collect benefits while enjoying the Florida sun when her working husband is on a 4 weeks' vacation from his job. Attachment to the labor force is now often defined loosely enough to permit such perversions of the intent of the law.

Vacation and retirement also give rise to troublesome questions. Several states permit benefits to be paid if the worker is on vacation without pay, through no fault of his own. On the other hand, a state may refuse payment on the ground that the employment relationship still continues during vacation or that the worker on vacation is not available for work.

Another abuse affects those who retire but claim they are looking for work. In many states, workers and executives collect 26–39 weeks of unemployment insurance after retirement—and never return to the labor market. The 1976 amendments restricted unemployment payments to retired persons and recipients of social security, but provided that such restrictions would not be effective before 1979!

The root cause of abuse is that income from unemployment compensation—or from supplemental unemployment benefits—is not subject to federal or state income taxes. If such compensation and benefits were taxed like wages, the net return to the worker would not so closely approximate income from working, and much of the abuse might well disappear.

Perhaps the most serious problem relating to the unemployment compensation system is that the system itself may encourage both the extent and the duration of unemployment among employees permanently attached to the labor market. Several studies have confirmed that increases in benefits are associated with increased duration of unemployment,[4] and there is widespread concern that this problem will increase as benefits rise and the practice of living off them becomes more common. Unless such tendencies are halted, for example by taxing benefit income, the whole unemployment compensation system will have to be reexamined.

WORKERS' COMPENSATION[5]

Workers' compensation was the first type of social insurance to be developed extensively in the United States. It is designed to assure prompt payment of benefits to employees injured on the job or afflicted by occupational diseases; or in the case of a fatality in industry, to pay benefits to dependents. Such compensation does not cover accident or injury outside working hours, but only such accidents as occur on or pertain to the job.

The first state workers' compensation law was passed in New York in 1909. By 1948, this type of legislation had been enacted by all of the states and Puerto Rico. Special federal compensation laws cover civilian government employees, longshoremen and harbor workers, private employees in the District of Columbia, and since 1969, coal miners.

Workers' compensation legislation, however, does not completely cover the American work force. Some states fail to provide coverage for certain types of accidents or diseases; and agricultural, domestic, and certain other workers are usually excluded from coverage of these laws. In New Jersey, South Carolina, and Texas, workers' compensation acts

---

[4] The information on this subject and studies relating thereto were reviewed in a conference held at the University of Pittsburgh under the auspices of the U.S. Department of Labor, April 8–9, 1976. Professor Arnold Katz kindly made the papers prepared for the conference available to the authors.

[5] Formerly known as "workmen's compensation."

are elective rather than compulsory. In these states, employers may refuse to operate under the compensation act if they prefer to risk suit for damages by injured workers. In a few states, the laws are compulsory as to some employments and elective as to others. When employers elect not to come under a compensation act, employees are remitted to their old remedies at common law, and must prove that the employer was negligent. In such circumstances, however, the employer loses his common-law defenses—contributory negligence, the fellow-servant doctrine, and assumption of the risk.

Besides agricultural and domestic workers, compensation laws usually exclude casual employment. In addition, railway employees come under the Federal Employers' Liability Act (FELA) rather than under workers' compensation. And maritime employees come under the Jones Act, which gives them the same rights that railroad workers have under the FELA. These two employee groups claim that they are able to collect more compensation by negligence suits than by compensation laws because of the fact that juries are generally sympathetic to them and unsympathetic to railroad and shipping concerns. As of January 1976, in one fourth of the jurisdictions, private employers who have less than a specified number of employees, varying from 2 to 15, are excluded from compulsory coverage of compensation legislation.[6]

Compensation laws are limited not only as to persons and employers included but also as to injuries covered. For example, some states exclude coverage if the employee is under the influence of alcohol or drugs, or if the accident is caused by willful misconduct or gross negligence. In addition, a large number of states restrict coverage, to some extent, for occupational disease.

The Nature of Benefits

Workers' compensation laws provide two basic types of benefits: (1) cash payments for loss of income or death and (2) medical services, including rehabilitation, or cash payments for these services.

Most of the acts provide cash benefits based upon a percentage of the worker's wage up to a specified maximum. A few states vary the payments with the worker's marital status and number of dependents. The periods during which the compensation is paid vary tremendously, and the maximum weekly payments range from $50 in Oklahoma to $358 in Alaska.[7]

---

[6] The basic data for this section of the chapter are taken from Chamber of Commerce of the United States, *Analysis of Workmen's Compensation Laws* (1975 ed.); and A. S. Hribal and G. M. Minor, "Workers' Compensation—1975 Enactments," *Monthly Labor Review*, vol. 99 (January 1976), pp. 30–36.

[7] John R. Emshwiller, "Compensation Rift: Labor and Employers Clash over Changes in Disability Payments," *Wall Street Journal*, August 2, 1976, pp. 1, 29.

Death benefits also vary considerably. In some states, in the District of Columbia, and under the federal compensation acts, payments are made to the widow until she is employed and/or remarried, and to children until they reach a specified age. In other states, death benefits are limited to payments for periods ranging from 300 to 1,000 weeks, but these states can continue to pay to children until they reach a specified age. Death benefits are usually based upon a percentage of the average weekly wage of the deceased worker, but Oklahoma pays a lump sum, and Kansas pays a flat pension. Widower dependency is now also increasingly assumed.

Thirty-three states, the District of Columbia, and the federal acts make permanent total disability payments for life or for the entire period of the disability. The remaining jurisdictions limit the time from 330 weeks to 550 weeks or limit the total amount of payments. Payments also vary in some states according to the number of dependents, and Kansas disallows payments to social security recipients.

Twenty states, the District of Columbia, and the federal acts make temporary total disability payments for the entire period of disability. In the other states, the payments are limited from 208 to 1,000 weeks and are in various amounts. Some temporary total disability recipients are also paid additional benefits for dependent children.

Most compensation laws provide payments for permanent partial disability. Two categories of such injuries are generally recognized— scheduled and nonscheduled. The former category includes specific injuries such as the loss of use of an arm or leg; the latter includes more general injuries, such as an injury to the head or back. Most states provide specific payments for scheduled injuries, and the maximum payable for such injuries varies considerably. For example, for the loss of an arm at the shoulder, a specified amount is payable. Payments for nonscheduled injuries are generally related to the loss of earning power; and in many cases, they exceed payments for scheduled injuries.

All the compensation acts require that medical aid be furnished to the injured employee. Approximately half of the states confine medical benefits for occupational diseases and accidents as to duration or cost, or both. In addition, all acts require the employer to furnish artificial limbs and other necessary appliances.

Before any cash payments are made, nearly all states require a waiting period of one week after the injury. Medical benefits begin immediately, however, and compensation may be retroactive to the date of injury if the disability continues beyond the waiting period.

Administration

To make certain that benefit payments will be paid when due, the states require that the covered employer obtain insurance or give proof of his qualifications to carry his own risk, which is known as self-insurance. In most of the states, the employer is permitted to insure with private insurance companies. State insurance systems exist in 18 states and Puerto Rico. In six of these states and in Puerto Rico, the system is called "exclusive," because employers are required to insure in the monopolistic state fund. Competitive state funds exist in 12 states, where employers may choose whether they will insure their risks in the state fund or with private insurance companies, or qualify as "self-insurers" with the privilege of carrying their own risks.

In most states, a specific agency has been established to administer the act. In five states, however, there is no administrative agency empowered to supervise the compensation law, and injured workers can look only to the courts to enforce their claims. In states where the law is administered by a commission or a board, the state agency usually has exclusive jurisdiction over the determination of facts, with appeals to the courts limited to questions of law. In a few states, however, the courts can consider the issues anew.

Second-Injury Funds and Special Provisions

A second injury to an employee who has already sustained an injury —such as the loss of a limb—may cause an employee to be totally disabled. If an employer were held responsible for the resulting total disability, this would encourage hiring discrimination against the handicapped. Therefore, nearly all states have second-injury funds which limit the employer's liability to the disability caused by the second injury alone. The difference between the disability for the loss as a whole, and what the loss would have been in the absence of a prior injury, is made up from the fund.

Financing

Unlike the situation for other social insurances, the funds for worker's compensation are not provided for by specific taxes levied upon employer or employee, or both. There is no central fund from which compensation is payable to eligible injured workers. Rather, the employee's compensation claim is against his employer, who must insure the risk. In nearly all jurisdictions, workers make no direct contributions to costs.

Workers' Compensation Problems

The complicated benefit system, the costly and inefficient overlapping among compensation and other insurance programs, inadequate coverage because of the large numbers of excluded categories, the failure to make provision for all occupational diseases, and the number of laws which are elective—all have been criticized for many years. These problems remain, but more recently questions of high awards and abuse to avoid working have been added to them.

Administration is perhaps the weakest phase of workers' compensation. There is tremendous variation from state to state in the caliber of administration. Some states make an excellent effort to see that claims are promptly paid, that workers know their rights, and that final reports are received from insurance companies on benefits paid, how benefits were computed, and the nature of the injury for which benefits were paid. Unfortunately, such good administration is apparently relatively uncommon. Many states collect little pertinent information. The majority of employed workers apparently do not know their rights, and state administrators make no real effort to correct this lack of information. Only a few states attempt to find out how promptly workers are paid, how much is paid for medical expenses, how adequate benefits are to take the place of lost wages, and for what purpose benefits are paid. Moreover, inordinately expensive administration is the rule rather than the exception. It has been estimated that a large percentage of the cost of workers' compensation goes for administration.

Since both insurance companies and employers have an interest in keeping costs at a minimum, and since most workers are not too well informed of their rights, the pressure to keep benefits down, to avoid expansion of coverage, and to pay the very least allowable in compensation is dominant in most state legislatures and most state administrative agencies. Moreover, since the individual is usually left to obtain his own benefits, he frequently becomes involved in litigation and lawyers' fees if he is to protect his rights, or else faces loss of benefits because of ignorance of his rights. In other instances, benefits have been delayed by attempts of insurance companies to transfer doubtful jurisdictional cases to the state jurisdiction which pays the least benefit. On the other hand, sometimes compensation costs can get out of line because of excessive liberality of state administrations, or because of intense pressure from unions in behalf of their members. This last situation is becoming quite common in heavily unionized areas where union-associated lawyers often work with union officials to gain maximum benefits, regardless of the merits of the case.[8] Moreover, in a survey of employers in the chemical and aerospace industries in 1976, one of the authors found that employees regularly increased compensation claims when employment was on a downturn or when a strike was threatened.

The creation of the National Commission on State Workmen's Compensation and its voluminous reports in 1972 and thereafter acted as a tremendous spur to state legislatures to improve their compensation laws or face the threat of a federal takeover of the field. Such legislation is

---

[8] Ibid.

now pending and is a key goal of the AFL–CIO. Although many state laws are still deficient, most states now pay generous benefits. The problem of high costs may be more serious now than that of inadequate benefits. In addition, the passage of the federal Occupational Safety and Health Act in 1970 has made workers much more conscious of their rights and probably more prone to press compensation claims. If federal law preempts the workers' compensation field, one may expect more liberality and higher costs, which could, like all costs, react unfavorably in terms of unemployment for the worker while seeking to protect him or her against injury.

THE OCCUPATIONAL SAFETY AND HEALTH ACT OF 1970 (OSHA)

The prime objective of workers' compensation legislation is, of course, the payment of benefits to those injured on the job. If, however, its social purpose is to be achieved, it should encourage safe working practices which will prevent injuries; and it must provide the means to rehabilitate workers who have been injured so that they can, insofar as possible, become self-supporting once more.

There can be no doubt that workers' compensation has encouraged safe working practices. The insurance rate which is charged to the employer is determined by the accident frequency and severity record of his business. Substantial savings in insurance costs accrue to the employer whose plant safety record is of high quality. The larger insurance companies in the compensation field provide safety counseling as part of their services. In addition, most states provide for safety inspections. Many employers have found that they can regain all of their costs spent on safety by reduced costs in compensation through fewer work injuries.

Unfortunately, relatively few businesses have had adequate safety programs. Estimates of the Bureau of Labor Statistics indicate that only one third of all workers were subject to planned, organized safety efforts prior to 1970. Consequently, American industry averaged 2 million disabling injuries and 14,000 deaths, with an estimated direct economic loss of 250 million man-days of work—representing full-time employment of about 1 million persons for one year—despite the fact that the severity and the frequency of injuries per man-hour worked have, for the most part, declined over the years.

Although accident prevention is obviously socially more desirable than compensation after injury, most workers' compensation administrators either have had no authority to enforce safety regulations or no funds to spend on safety, or no interest in the subject. In some states industrial health and safety programs and law enforcement are assigned to one department, compensation administration to another.

Workers' compensation legislation has been less a stimulation to rehabilitation than to accident prevention. Only about one third of the state laws contain specific provisions for tiding permanently impaired workers over a period of vocational rehabilitation. A few other states make liberal provisions for the same purpose, although not unlimited ones. Usually, however, the awards for rehabilitation are meager, and insufficient to accomplish the task.

This need to improve business safety practices led Congress to enact the Occupational Safety and Health Act of 1970 (OSHA) "to assure so far as possible every working man and woman in the Nation safe and healthful working conditions and to preserve our human resources." It covers virtually all industry and employment in the country not covered by special laws, such as the Coal Mine Health and Safety Act. OSHA charges employers with maintaining safe and healthful places of work and with complying with safety and health standards under the act; employees likewise have the duty to comply with such standards and rules. The Secretary of Labor is responsible for promulgating and enforcing health and safety standards; if any employer is cited for a violation, he may contest it before a new three-man quasi-judicial body, the Occupational Safety and Health Review Commission. Orders of the Commission are reviewable in the U.S. Courts of Appeals.

OSHA has virtually created a new right for workers—the right of a safe and healthful place of employment. The failure of employers to comply can mean fines or business shutdowns. Moreover, inspections must be made upon employee complaints, and plants are subject to unannounced inspections at any time by a new force of federal inspectors. Representatives of employees—usually union representatives—have the right to accompany inspectors on their rounds.

A controversial aspect of this new law is its potential for becoming a tool of industrial warfare.[9] As noted in Chapter 6, it is an old tactic of unions to use safety as a defense of featherbedding or as a means of harassing an employer. On the other hand, many union complaints about health and safety are genuine. An examination of union and company publications since mid-1970[10] clearly demonstrates that unions believe that OSHA provides a mechanism to increase their interest in health and safety and to enhance their right to an effective voice in working conditions affecting health and safety, whereas employers fear that this interest will be used as a wedge to increase union penetration into managerial functions and to force additional wage and benefit concessions.

One certain effect of OSHA is a greater interest in health and safety standards. Safety practices, plant housekeeping, and top-management interest in accident prevention have all been enhanced. On the other

---

[9] Legislation designed to effectuate noise abatement and to protect hearing, as well as various state and federal environmental laws, have similar impacts on labor relations.

[10] By one of the authors.

hand, although OSHA has caused great interest in industrial health problems, and in particular, concern about cancer-causing chemicals, it has apparently been bogged down in the administration of minor safety matters, such as the distance of safety railings from walls, and has been very slow to develop standards for protection against possible harmful products.

Part of the problem involves, of course, the speed with which the government should move to protect workers and consumers. Complete safety can be achieved only if all productive activity ceases, and even then, careless individuals will surely injure themselves. Moreover, there are serious questions as to the costs and benefits involved in industrial health. On the one hand, the government may ban production of a chemical and save or lengthen several lives—perhaps several thousand; on the other hand, this act may throw more people out of work. Meanwhile, the same government subsidizes the raising of tobacco whose products are perhaps much more cancer-inducing than are the banned chemicals. The policy problem is further complicated because the effects of exposure to alleged cancer-causing chemicals are difficult to prove and because the facts are not at all clear. For example, those exposed to such chemicals may not show signs of cancer until many years later, and even then may also have been heavy smokers or have dwelt in cities in which noxious smog is heavy. Meanwhile, the administrators are pressured by stories in the press which may not be accurate, by companies and unions, and by politicians, all anxious for action. The costs of inaction can be heavy in human misery; the costs of action can involve outlays of billions of dollars and a decline in employment and in the competitiveness of American industry, as funds are spent for safety and health and not to increase productivity. OSHA may well be the most significant and far-reaching labor legislation ever enacted.

DISABILITY LEGISLATION

Disability legislation is of two types; permanent and total, and temporary. Permanent and total disability legislation is, as discussed above, part of the old-age, survivors, disability, and health insurance (OASDHI) legislation. Essentially, it involves the payment of old-age benefits earlier than they would otherwise be due, without reduction of benefits, when the covered employee has become disabled and is no longer able to work. The OASDHI program also provides the same disability benefits for dependents as they would receive under retirement benefits and for benefits to disabled widows and widowers between ages 50 and 62.

Temporary disability insurance is payable for a fixed period, for example, 26 weeks. Whereas workers' compensation pays compensation for occupational injuries and illnesses, temporary disability insurance is designed to provide compensation for injuries and illnesses contracted away from, and not related to, the job. Finally, although every state has a workers' compensation law, temporary disability insurance laws have been enacted by only four states—California, New Jersey, New York, and Rhode Island. The Railroad Unemployment Insurance Act also provides temporary disability benefits for nonoccupational as well as occupational disability. Thus, nearly all temporary disability insurance is covered by private welfare programs, including union-management ones.

Although the first state disability law was enacted by Rhode Island in 1942, there has been no new legislation since 1950. Disagreement over the character of such laws—that is, whether they should be incorporated into unemployment or workers' compensations; whether they should be state- or federal-financed, or both; and the relative roles of private and public carriers—seems to have prevented their expansion in the 1950s. By then, private employer and union-management plans took over and interest in legislation lagged. Rather, the focus of debate has turned to health insurance.

THE HEALTH INSURANCE ISSUE

The plethora of social insurance and welfare programs still find, after a quarter of a century of agitation, no all-inclusive health insurance program. Older persons are covered by Medicare and Medicaid, with the burgeoning welfare load made more costly by the latter. An ever-increasing number of persons are covered by private health insurance, but proposals before Congress in 1977 indicate quite clearly the increased likelihood that millions of Americans not now covered by federal programs may be brought within their purview in the near future. A key difference among the various proposals is that one group would integrate into the proposed federal plan, and use the many private plans and organizations already in the health field. Thus Blue Cross–Blue Shield, various prepaid group medical plans, and private carriers would have a role, with the federal government a reinsurer and supplier where private insurance was unavailable; the other approach would monopolize the field, or nearly so, and create an entirely new federal plan. It would, of course, be far more expensive to the taxpayer.

The basic issue before the American people regarding health expenditures can be stated in terms of opportunity cost: What does one wish to give up to improve health care? Burgeoning medical costs are illustrated in Figure 17–4. Although proponents of new federal health insurance programs claim that the costs involved with their proposals are substantially substitutes for existing costs, this is not too likely, because the very availability of prepaid medical programs creates an enlarged demand for services. Consequently, any new program creates a supply shortage and increased costs. A very real question is whether the facilities and medical personnel should not be built up before dramatic new programs are incorporated into the system. Most of all, basic decisions should be made as to the extent of our national resources that we should divert to health care instead of economic growth, housing, old-age benefits, or other equally praiseworthy and sound economic ventures and programs.

In the final analysis, of course, political pressures will probably determine the nature of future health insurance programs, as has been the case in the past. The impact of inflation and huge federal budget deficits, and the obvious distaste of the average taxpayer for new costly programs, has slowed the development of what may be the most expensive benefit of all—national health insurance.

CONCLUDING REMARKS

The American social security system is a rare blend of public and private systems. Today, as a result of congressional overgenerosity and changing demographic patterns, much of it is in deep fiscal difficulty. Other new programs, such as the Occupational Safety and Health Act, which could be even more expensive in terms of real costs, have been launched but have not reached maturity. On the horizon may be the most expensive program of all—national health insurance.

The current American system of security is both generous and meager in part. Whether, if carefully planned and considered, it could be more satisfactory, remains to be determined. Unless, however, some hard decisions are made, costs looked at squarely and honestly, and priorities determined, it could prove more burdensome than supportive.

QUESTIONS FOR DISCUSSION

1. Do you believe that OASDHI should continue to be financed by payroll taxes or from general funding? Explain your answer.
2. Regardless of your answer to the previous question, how would you plan to deal with the current and future deficits in OASDHI?
3. If you were administering the Occupational Safety and Health Act, how would you set standards for the safety of workers involved in the production of chemicals which could possibly be cancer-causing?
4. What is the role of unemployment compensation? Should the program be federalized? Should strikers ever receive benefits? Explain your answers.
5. What are the shortcomings and strong features of workers' compensation? What will be the likely impact of the Occupational Safety and Health Act of 1970 on workers' compensation laws in the long term?
6. Are you in favor of national health insurance? If so, what "insurance package" do you advocate? How would you defend your position when it is alleged that such insurance would be too costly?

SUGGESTIONS FOR FURTHER READING

Campbell, Colin D. *Over-indexed Benefits: The Decoupling Proposals for Social Security.*

Kaplan, Robert S. *Financial Crisis in the Social Security System.*
Washington, D.C.: American Enterprise Institute for Public Policy Research, 1976.
Two timely, well-written pamphlets dealing with the deficit-ridden social security system, the causes of the deficits and proposed remedies.

Davis, Karen. *National Health Insurance: Benefits, Costs, and Consequences.* Washington, D.C.: Brookings Institution, 1975.
An analysis of the inadequacies and inequities of the current system of health care and of the possible effects of a national health insurance program and the costs thereof.

National Commission on State Workmen's Compensation Laws. *Compendium on Workmen's Compensation; Report to the President and the Congress;* and various technical papers. Washington, D.C.: Government Printing Office, 1972.
These studies are without doubt the most complete available for all aspects of workers' compensation. They provide the basic source of knowledge on the subject and have had, and continue to have, significant impact on the future of the state system of laws.

Smith, Robert S. *The Occupational Safety and Health Act: Its Goals and Achievements.* Washington D.C.: American Enterprise Institute for Public Policy Research, 1976.
A critical analysis of OSHA, with a proposal for utilizing a cost-benefit approach to safety and industrial health problems and enforcement.

U.S. Department of Health, Education, and Welfare. *Social Security Programs in the United States.* Social Security Administration, various years.
A detailed explanation of social security and unemployment compensation programs, issued whenever the laws are modified.

part six

Government Control of
Labor Relations

18

Governmental Control of the Weapons of Conflict

AMERICANS pride themselves on having maintained free collective bargaining and a free labor market in a world which is becoming increasingly regimented and collectivized. But the degree of freedom in our collective bargaining is relative. It is relatively unrestricted when compared with labor relations in the Soviet Union and other countries in the Communist bloc. On the other hand, an appraisal of the development of labor relations in this country reveals a patchwork of judicial decisions, laws, and regulations which have continually eroded and narrowed the field of individual action. In this chapter, we shall examine in detail some of the major weapons of conflict in the struggle for power between unions and management and shall consider how governmental and judicial controls have attempted to curtail their use.

LABOR AND THE COURTS IN EARLY AMERICA

The basic economic and social environment in the United States has, on the whole, been hostile to the development of union organization. In a land of opportunity, rich in natural resources and capable of providing a high standard of living to its wage earners, trade unions have been unable to draw their membership from a proletariat with strong class allegiance, as in most European nations. On the contrary, class lines have been fluid; and even among wage earners, there has been continuing respect and support for the institution of private property. Union leaders have come to recognize this difference in outlook among our workers and have had to adopt a new kind of unionism—antisocialist and business-oriented—in order to attract and retain membership.

This same strength of private property rights which is a product of the free enterprise of the American environment is reflected in the attitude of both employers and courts toward union organization. In their struggle for recognition of the right to organize, unions have had to combat not only antagonistic employers, vehemently committed to defending their right to run their own businesses without interference from their employees, but also an unfriendly judiciary and an inimical common law. Members of the judiciary tended to be selected from the propertied classes of the community and therefore reflected a conservative attitude in their opinions in labor disputes. But even had their personal predilections been liberal, the fact remains that the controlling precedents of common law were generally restrictive of organized labor's actions.

Our common law, which is based upon the customs of the land as reflected in the accumulated decisions of the judiciary, has its roots in English history. In the 18th century, English courts outlawed labor combinations which exerted pressure to increase wages or to secure the closed shop as a means toward that end. British courts and statesmen considered such combinations among workers to be inimical to the public interest because they interfered with the free working of market forces. In the famous *Philadelphia Cordwainers* case of 1806, and in numerous other cases during the next 30 years, American state courts adopted this same viewpoint and held that concerted action by combinations of workers to better their wages and working conditions represented an illegal conspiracy against the public and against employers.

Then in 1842, in the case of *Commonwealth* v. *Hunt*,[1] the Supreme Judicial Court of Massachusetts decided that a strike in support of a closed shop was not, per se, illegal; and that unless it could also be shown that the worker's objectives were bad, the conspiracy doctrine did not apply. Although the conspiracy doctrine continued to be utilized occasionally for some years to break up strikes, the decision in *Commonwealth* v. *Hunt* dealt it a blow from which it never recovered.

Judicial Tests of Legality

After the decision in *Commonwealth* v. *Hunt*, many courts tended to judge the legality of union activity on the basis of "motive" and "intent." This proved to be a highly subjective standard, which frequently reflected the prejudices of the individual judge rather than the facts of the case. Equally unsatisfactory was the so-called means test, which attempted to draw the line between permissible and unlawful union activity on the basis of whether or not the union action involved peaceful persuasion or unlawful intimidation. A further theory utilized by courts in labor cases in these early years was the doctrine of restraint

---

[1] 4 Metcalf 111 (1842).

of trade. This doctrine assumed much greater importance in judicial decisions with the subsequent enactment of the Sherman Antitrust Act, which will be discussed later. The doctrine of restraint of trade, however, also existed in common law. In general, the common-law doctrine was based on the premise that everyone should have equal access to the market and that when two or more persons combined to block access to the market and thereby inflicted injury upon the public, a conspiracy in restraint of trade existed. All restraints, whether inspired by labor or by industry, were not considered illegal per se. The legality of such restraints was held to depend upon their "reasonableness," which was determined by the courts by weighing the extent of coercion exercised, if any, and the effect of the restraint on the volume of business and access to the market.

The Injunction

By the latter part of the 19th century, the courts had generally recognized the right of employees to organize in unions without civil or criminal liability. However, the use of concerted economic weapons—the strike, the boycott, and picketing—was generally held to be unlawful on the basis of one of the theories referred to above. The most effective weapon management was able to utilize to restrain such action by unions was the injunction.

The major objective of organized labor in the latter part of the 19th century and the early 20th century was to free itself from the shackles of the injunction. The injunction is a legal technique developed in equity courts to provide relief against continuing injury where recovery in the form of monetary damages does not suffice. Upon a showing that "irreparable damage" might occur to the party requesting the relief unless certain acts of the defendant are stopped, the judge may issue an order forbidding the defendant to do such acts. If the defendant disobeys the court order, he may be fined or imprisoned for contempt of court.

The effectiveness of the injunction was based upon the speed with which it could be secured and the manner in which it could be applied. An employer could go into court and secure what is known as an ex parte injunction by alleging that grave and irreparable damage would occur to his business or property if the injunction were not granted. Such an ex parte injunction could be obtained by the employer or his attorney appearing before a single judge, without notice to the union and giving the judge only his side of the story. If the judge granted the request for an injunction—as he usually did—he would issue an order of the court forbidding the union officers and members to do a long list of prohibited acts. Such an order would completely tie up union organizational activities, and at the same time leave the employer free to dischage union members and otherwise act to destroy union organization in his plant before the union could be heard in court. By the time the case was brought to a hearing to determine whether the injunction should be dissolved or made permanent, the employer could often whip the union. If union officials violated any part of the injunction, they could be held in contempt of court and fined or jailed by the court, without trial by jury. This was true whether or not the injunction was made permanent.

The application of injunctions to labor disputes developed rapidly after the *Debs* case of 1895.[2] In that case, Eugene Debs, the leader of the strike,[3] was enjoined by an order obtained by the U.S. government from continuing a boycott of Pullman cars which, the government alleged, interfered with interstate commerce and the transportation of the mails. Although injunctions had been used in labor disputes prior to this time, the case focused nationwide attention on the injunction technique as a weapon against union organizational activities.

A further development which contributed to the popularity of the injunction as a management tool in labor disputes was the so-called yellow-dog contract. This is a contract which an employer requires a worker to sign, stating that as a condition of employment, he agrees not to join a union. The phrase *yellow dog* was applied by unionists at an early date to workers who signed such contracts, and the contracts have been known by that appellation ever since.

In practice, employers made no real attempt to enforce such contracts against the individual workers who signed them. The importance of the contracts was that if they were legal, then attempts by union organizers to compel workers who had signed such contracts to join a union were deliberate efforts to cause a breach of the contracts, and such action could be enjoined by the courts. Unionists maintained that because workers had no choice but to sign such agreements, the agreements were without force or effect. The majority of state courts rejected this view, holding that inequality of bargaining power did not preclude enforcement of contracts. The New York courts, however, accepted labor's point of view.

Because of the generally antagonistic attitude of the courts, labor unions attempted at an early date to secure the passage of legislation which would outlaw yellow-dog contracts and thus curb the use of this effective antiunion organization weapon. Between 1890 and 1914, no less than 14 states enacted legislation making it a misdemeanor or otherwise unlawful for employers (1) to exact yellow-dog contracts from their employees and (2) to interfere with the right of the employees to join or otherwise belong to a legitimate union. In addition, in 1898, Congress

---

[2] *In re Debs,* 158 U.S. 654, 15 S. Ct. 900 (1895).

[3] The strike involved an abortive attempt to establish industrial unionism on the railroads.

passed the Erdman Act, which contained similar provisions for the benefit of operating employees of the railroads.

The courts, however, rejected this legislation, which contained the principles of the Wagner Act 40 years before that law was conceived. The Supreme Court found that both the state laws and the pertinent section of the Erdman Act were unconstitutional because the 5th and 14th amendments to the Constitution guarantee freedom of contract as a property right.[4] According to the courts, an employer had a constitutional right to request his employees to sign yellow-dog contracts and to enforce such contracts, and also to discharge his employees because of union activities. In short, the courts held that furthering union activities or even preventing interference therewith was not a sufficient promotion of the general welfare to permit interference with the sanctity of contracts, even if they were yellow-dog contracts. Furthermore, in 1917, in the *Hitchman Coal and Coke* case,[5] the U.S. Supreme Court completely supported the enforceability of yellow-dog contracts. It ruled that a court of equity could issue an injunction restraining attempts to organize employees who were bound by contracts not to join a labor union. Needless to say, these decisions caused unionists to take an extremely jaundiced view of the judiciary and to redouble their efforts to curb judicial interference in labor-management relations.

THE APPLICATION OF THE ANTITRUST LAWS TO ORGANIZED LABOR

Section I of the Sherman Act of 1890 states: "Every contract, combination in the form of trust, or otherwise, or conspiracy in restraint of trade or commerce among the several States, or with foreign nations, is hereby declared to be illegal." For some years after this act was passed, there was speculation as to whether or not this broad statutory language applied to labor. Finally, in 1908, in the case of *Loewe* v. *Lawlor*,[6] commonly known as the *Danbury Hatters* case, the U.S. Supreme Court ruled that a nationwide boycott organized by the union to persuade wholesalers and retailers to refrain from buying the company's products was an illegal restraint on commerce. The Court interpreted the statutory phrase "restraint of trade or commerce" to apply to interference by a union with the interstate shipment of goods. The Court ordered the union to pay treble damages amounting to over half a million dollars, and individual members of the union were held responsible for their share of the damages.

---

[4] *Coppage* v. *Kansas*, 236 U.S. 1, 35 S. Ct. 240 (1915), which nullified the state laws; and *Adair* v. *United States*, 208 U.S. 161, 28 S. Ct. 277 (1908), which nullified Section 10 of the Erdman Act.

[5] *Hitchman Coal and Coke Co.* v. *Mitchell*, 245 U.S. 229, 38 S. Ct. 65 (1917).

[6] 208 U.S. 274, 28 S. Ct. 301 (1908).

Labor leaders were justifiably concerned about this decision and immediately commenced pressure for exemption of labor from the antitrust laws. This drive culminated in the passage of the Clayton Act of 1914. Section 6 of that act declared:

> ... nothing contained in the antitrust laws shall be construed to forbid the existence and operation of labor ... organizations, instituted for the purposes of mutual help, and not having capital stock or conducted for profits, or to forbid or restrain individual members of such organizations from lawfully carrying out the legitimate objects thereof; nor shall such organizations, or the members thereof, be held or construed to be illegal combinations or conspiracies in restraint of trade under the antitrust laws.

Section 20 of the Clayton Act barred the issuance of federal injunctions prohibiting such activities as strikes, boycotts, or picketing "in any case between an employer and employees, or between employers and employees, or between employees, or between persons employed and persons seeking employment, involving or growing out of, a dispute concerning terms or conditions of employment." This same section concludes with a broad statement that none of the acts specified in this paragraph shall be considered violations "of any law of the United States."

Despite this broad language, the U.S. Supreme Court in 1921 in the case of *Duplex Printing Company* v. *Deering*[7] held that the Clayton Act did not give labor unions a complete exemption from the antitrust laws. The case involved a secondary boycott of products of Duplex carried out for the most part by persons who did not stand in a direct employment relationship with Duplex. Construing the language of Section 20 of the Clayton Act narrowly, the Court held that the defendants were not entitled to exemption from the Sherman Act. As a result of this decision, which appeared to nullify congressional intent, employers stepped up their use of the injunction as a weapon to curb labor's organizing efforts.

OTHER LEGAL IMPEDIMENTS TO ORGANIZATION

Another major impediment to organization provided by the common law was the freedom of an employer to refuse employment to workers because of union activity. Employers thus could maintain what might be called an "antiunion closed shop." In furtherance of antiunion activities, employers were, in the absence of legislation, free to engage in blacklisting of union members and to utilize labor spies to ferret out union sympathizers. The common law did provide that a worker might not be hounded or libeled in order to prevent him from seeking security or maintaining employment, but this protection proved of little value because the employer also had the right to advise other employers that

---

[7] 254 U.S. 443, 41 S. Ct. 172 (1921).

he had discharged a man because of his union or "radical" sympathies or activities.

More than one half of the states now have laws which outlaw the blacklist, and six states require employers, upon demand, to give discharged employees a truthful statement of the reasons for discharge. These state laws against blacklisting, however, have not been easily enforced, although in at least one case, such a law was used by workers to secure an injunction against the use of the blacklist.[8] It was almost impossible to prevent one employer from telling another over the telephone that Jones, Smith, and Brown were "radical unionists," so that when these three applied for employment to the second employer, they were refused a job on the ground that no vacancies were available. It was not until the passage of the National Labor Relations Act in 1935 that effective protection against blacklisting was finally achieved.

STRIKES, BOYCOTTS, AND PICKETING AND THE COURTS BEFORE 1932

As has been pointed out in the discussion thus far, the courts (in years prior to 1932) tended to interpret both the common law and the statutory law in a manner unfavorable to the development of organized labor. The practical effect of such an antagonistic attitude on the part of the judiciary can best be appreciated by examining its impact on the major weapons a union can utilize to achieve its objectives—the strike, the boycott, and picketing. From the point of view of federal law, it is convenient to consider judicial interpretation prior to 1932 and after 1932, since in that year Congress enacted the Norris–La Guardia Act, which drastically altered the power of federal courts to intervene in labor disputes.

Strikes

Workers on strike do not ordinarily regard themselves as having terminated their employment relationship. They have left their work temporarily, and in concert, in order to secure more favorable terms of employment. But they regard themselves as having a vested or property right in their jobs. The courts, however, have not recognized this right until very recently—and then only in a modified form. On the whole, courts have been more ready to accept ideas concerning employer property rights than employee property rights—at least until recently.

As we pointed out at the beginning of this chapter, after the courts abandoned the theory of conspiracy, they continued to regulate union conduct by looking into the motives or intent of union conduct. In the

[8] E. E. Witte, *The Government in Labor Disputes* (New York: McGraw-Hill Book Co., 1932), pp. 212–20.

case of strikes, this involved an analysis of the purpose or objective of the walkout.

Courts have frequently enjoined the continuance of a strike where the purpose of the strike was to force the employer to cooperate in committing an illegal act. They have also taken similar action in cases where, after weighing the damage done by a strike against the objective sought, they have concluded that the strike was "unjustified." This is, of course, a highly subjective criterion, but it has been widely applied in a variety of circumstances. For example, prior to 1932, judges frequently found sympathetic strikes unlawful. These are strikes by one group of workers in support of another, such as a strike of plumbers out of sympathy for striking gravediggers. Judges have found no possible justification for inflicting loss on the employers of plumbers merely because of a dispute between gravediggers and their employers. Likewise, despite the pathbreaking case of *Commonwealth* v. *Hunt*, many state courts, if not the majority, have condemned strikes to obtain a closed shop. The reason is that the closed shop is regarded as monopolistic and as attaching a condition to the right of a worker to obtain employment.

On the other hand, in the case of strikes against technological change and jurisdictional strikes, courts have usually adopted a "hands-off" attitude. Although most courts have indicated that they regard strikes aimed at preventing technological advance as harmful to society, they have recognized the problems that such progress often creates for workers and have usually not interfered, in the absence of legislative enactment, with the attempts of unions to retard technological change. Likewise, in the case of jurisdictional strikes—which are contests between unions over which group of workers shall perform a specified piece of work—most courts have declined to enjoin strikes per se. They have regarded jurisdictional strikes as a matter for regulation by the legislative branch of the government.

Lockouts

A lockout is an act by an employer or employers locking out employees from their jobs in an effort to compel them to accede to the terms of employment desired by management. In contrast to the strike, where numbers and relationships may under the conspiracy doctrine make a difference, a lockout under common law may be practiced without legal restriction, whether by a single employer or by employers in combination. What one employer may do, all may do. There is, however, one exception to this common-law principle, and that is that a lockout in violation of a collective agreement may be enjoined. On the other hand, an employer who is a member of an association and obligated thereby to cooperate with his fellow employers may be sued if he fails to cooperate in the lockout activities. Limitations on the right to lock out imposed by statute and judicial decision are discussed later in this chapter.

Boycotts

Economic pressure by unions can be exerted in other ways than by strikes. One of the most familiar of labor's weapons has always been the boycott. In a certain sense, all strikes are boycotts. For when workers are on strike, they are "boycotting" their employer and urging all others to do likewise. Such a strike would thus qualify as a "primary" boycott —primary because the strikers are exerting pressure directly on the employer on whom they are making their demands.

Generally, however, strikes are not considered as coming within the meaning of boycotts. In public discussions, the term *boycott* is used almost exclusively to mean an organized refusal to deal with someone in order to induce him to change some practice he follows. Such a boycott may be in the form of a "we do not patronize" list or of other types of pressure designed to prevent sales of particular products, or it may be a refusal to handle certain goods.

Illustrations of such pressures are readily found in everyday union activity. For example, the United Automobile Workers resorted to a nationwide boycott of Kohler products in a long-drawn-out battle against this manufacturer of plumbing wares. In another case, the same union asked its members not to use fishing tackle manufactured by a firm which allegedly had locked out members of the United Steelworkers. Union building-trades workers have usually refused to handle materials manufactured under nonunion conditions.

Boycotts of these types are not as simple as strikes because they can involve pressure on third parties. For example, if the United Automobile Workers picketed a store which was selling fishing tackle purchased from the aforementioned firm, it would be engaging in a "secondary boycott"—that is, it would be applying pressure on a third party in order to aid the Steelworkers' fight against the manufacturer directly involved in the dispute.

Before 1932, a majority of American courts held the secondary boycott to be unlawful per se—"as if it were a separate category of tort liability."[9] Other courts, however, recognized that labor had an interest in maintaining standards and therefore had a right to engage in boycotts for this purpose. For example, some courts have upheld labor's rights to boycott nonunion products on the ground that the distribution of goods produced under nonunion conditions would depress standards won by the union.

---

[9] Charles O. Gregory, *Labor and the Law,* 2d rev. ed. (New York: W. W. Norton & Co., Inc., 1961), p. 122.

Picketing before the Norris–La Guardia Act

One of the most controversial questions of public policy in the field of labor relations today concerns the extent to which picketing by labor unions should be regulated. A companion question upon which conflicting views are found in the field of labor law involves the extent to which such limitations on the right to picket are constitutionally permissible.

Picketing is a familiar form of pressure utilized by unions which has become an indispensable adjunct of the strike. Picketing usually involves the patrolling of a struck establishment by one or more persons bearing signs or placards stating that the workers are on strike or that the employer is unfair to organized labor, or words of similar effect. The average worker will not pass a picket line. This is based partly on his fear of social ostracism; partly on the feeling that unless he supports the group on strike, they may not support him someday when his union is out on the street; partly on the fear of physical violence; and sometimes on the fear of sanctions contained in the constitution of his own union. Whatever the motivations, it is clear that the picket line is a most effective weapon. In our highly unionized economy a picket line, staffed even by a small group in a large company, can completely paralyze a plant or an establishment because other union workers who are employed in the plant, or deliver its supplies, will not cross the picket line.

Picketing may be thought of in two ways. It is a form of expression, letting the public and labor supporters know that a controversy exists and giving labor's side of that controversy. It is also a form of pressure intended to dissuade persons from patronizing or entering a place of business.

At first, the courts took the view that picketing per se was illegal. Later, they grudgingly conceded that picketing was legal as long as it was conducted peacefully and did not bar entrance to and exit from the plant, and as long as it did not obstruct traffic on a public thoroughfare. But while the courts conceded the legality of picketing, they also severely regulated it, often limiting the number of pickets permitted and generally outlawing "stranger picketing"—that is, picketing by persons not employees of the plant. The attitude of the courts on stranger picketing was conditioned by their belief that workers had no interest in a labor controversy unless they were employees of the plant itself, a theory which ignores the relation of labor conditions in one plant with those in another.

Those who believed in labor's right to picket freely did not generally support picketing which prevented entrance into and exit from a plant, or picketing which obstructed ordinary commerce on a public thoroughfare. They took the view, however, that picketing was a form of expression and hence, if peacefully conducted, was protected by the First Amendment, as are other forms of communication. That viewpoint, however, was almost unanimously rejected by the courts prior to 1932. Indeed, the tendency right up to the passage of the Norris–La Guardia Act was to limit rather than to expand the right of labor to picket in support of its interests.

THE NORRIS–LA GUARDIA ACT

In 1932, when the membership of the American Federation of Labor was the lowest in 20 years, the AFL achieved its greatest legislative triumph to date. After almost 50 years of sustained effort, the AFL succeeded in making the federal judiciary "neutral" in labor disputes. The law which accomplished this result was the Norris–La Guardia Anti-Injunction Act, passed by a Democratic-controlled House of Representatives and a Republican Senate, and signed by a Republican president, Herbert Hoover.

We have seen how labor had been frustrated in its aim of securing the passage of legislation which would effectively make lawful the use of union tactics deemed necessary by labor for its survival and successful growth. The Norris–La Guardia Act represented a new approach to this problem. It did not legalize union action; it simply deprived the federal courts of jurisdiction in most situations involving labor disputes. It reflected an essentially laissez-faire philosophy. The law should intervene only to prevent damage to tangible property and to preserve public order; otherwise, the disputants should be left to their own resources to work out their problems. Both labor and business would now be free to promote their own interests in the field of labor policy through self-help, without interference from the courts. The act thus represented a reaction to judicial policymaking, which had produced the anomalous result of making the same action enjoinable in one state and not in another. Henceforth, all federal courts were barred from passing judgment as to the lawfulness or unlawfulness of the objectives of labor's actions. This same principle was soon extended to many state courts, for the federal act was immediately copied by a dozen or more state legislatures.

The Norris–La Guardia Act commences with a statement of public policy which affirms the right of workers to engage in collective bargaining through unions of their own choosing. Yellow-dog contracts are declared to be against this public policy, and the federal courts are instructed not to enforce such contracts. Then, Section 4 of the act states:

> No court of the United States shall have jurisdiction to issue any restraining order or temporary or permanent injunction in any case involving or growing out of any labor dispute. . . .

The act defines "labor dispute" in the broadest possible way so as to preclude judicial constructions, such as whittled away the effect of the Clayton Act:

> The term "labor dispute" includes any controversy concerning terms or conditions of employment, or concerning the association or representation of persons in negotiating, fixing, maintaining, changing or seeking to arrange terms or conditions of employment, regardless of whether or not the disputants stand in the proximate relation of employer and employee.

It will be observed that Congress specifically took account of the fact that organized labor had a valid interest in conditions of employment even where it did not represent a single employee and that although such a situation did not involve a dispute technically between "an employer" and its "employees," nevertheless the protection afforded by the Norris–La Guardia Act was applicable.

The Norris–La Guardia Act has been aptly called "the last monument to the spirit of complete free enterprise for unions."[10] It left unions pretty much free to use their tactical weapons without judicial interference.[11] As we shall see, a "liberalized" Supreme Court interpreted the statute broadly so as to confer almost complete immunity on labor leaders in labor disputes. The act, in effect, outlawed injunctions in labor disputes except where violence was involved. As long as violence was not used, unions could resort to threats, coercion, boycotts, picketing, strikes, and so on, without fear of federal court action. Moreover, even where violence was involved, the granting of injunctions was severely restricted by statutory prohibitions. Some labor critics say that the act went too far in freeing unions from court intervention and that the problems we face today in terms of abuse of union tactics would not have resulted had the Norris–La Guardia Act attempted to make a distinction between lawful and unlawful union objectives, as did the Clayton Act. This is a debatable issue which we shall understand better after discussing the Norris–La Guardia Act and its aftermath.

The Norris–La Guardia Act and the Courts

With a single piece of legislation, Congress thus repealed a century of judicial interpretation and created laissez-faire, or economic free enterprise, for organized labor as well as for business. Henceforth, the courts were not to interfere with strikes, boycotts, and picketing which were conducted peacefully and were otherwise within the law. Moreover, by defining "labor dispute" in a broad fashion, Congress insured labor's right to engage in sympathy strikes, secondary boycotts, stranger picketing, and other activities where nonemployees of a concern come to the aid of the concern's employees in labor disputes directly or by applying pressure upon third parties.

---

[10] Gregory, *Labor and the Law*, p. 197.

[11] However, the Norris–La Guardia Act does not apply to employees of local and state governments or of the federal government. For a discussion of strikes by such employees, see Chapter 22.

The Reversal of Sherman Act Decisions

The combined effect of the Norris–La Guardia Act and the liberalized view of labor disputes which the Supreme Court adopted after 1937 resulted in a revision of precedents on the application of the Sherman Act to organized labor. Commencing in 1940, the Supreme Court handed down a group of landmark decisions which seemed to delineate the legal status of unions under the antitrust laws. Three leading cases—*Apex Hosiery Co.* v. *Leader,*[12] *United States* v. *Hutcheson,*[13] and *Allen-Bradley Co.* v. *Local 3, International Brotherhood of Electrical Workers*[14] broadly defined the permissible limits of concerted union activity, and suggested that unions are subject to the antitrust laws under existing legislation only:

1. Where the union intends to achieve some commercial restraint primarily and not as a by-product of its essential intent to advance its own cause.
2. Where union activity is not in the course of a labor dispute as broadly defined by the Norris–La Guardia Act.
3. Where a union combines with some nonlabor group to achieve some direct commercial restraint.

The extended immunity granted to labor from the antitrust laws and the injunction was followed to its logical conclusion in other decisions, to which we have already referred in Chapter 7. Their combined effect was to permit unions to perform many acts which the law classifies as illegal when done by other groups or organizations within the community. It is not surprising, therefore, that this line of decisions, together with the tremendous growth in economic power of organized labor in the past few decades, produced a demand in some circles for new legislation which would "subject labor to the antitrust laws."

Then on June 7, 1965, the U.S. Supreme Court handed down two landmark decisions which seemed to indicate that unions might not be as immune from antitrust liability as was generally thought. Both of these cases were brought by employers against unions alleging violations of Sections 1 and 2 of the Sherman Antitrust Act. In the *Pennington* case,[15] the employer alleged that the United Mine Workers had conspired with large coal operators to force smaller operators, including the plaintiff, out of business by raising wage rates and fringe benefits in the big companies and then forcing these rates on the smaller companies with the knowledge that the latter would have to close down. Although the

[12] 310 U.S. 469, 60 S. Ct. 982 (1940).

[13] 312 U.S. 219, 61 S. Ct. 463 (1941).

[14] 325 U.S. 797, 65 S. Ct. 1533 (1945).

[15] *United Mine Workers* v. *Pennington,* 381 U.S. 657 (1965). In subsequent decisions since this case, federal courts relying on the *Pennington* precedent have found the United Mine Workers in violation of the Sherman Act and have assessed treble damages.

case was remanded for a new trial because of an error in the instruction given to the jury by the trial judge, the Supreme Court held that if the United Mine Workers had in fact conspired with the major coal operators to drive the smaller operators out of business by requiring them to sign wage agreements which they could not afford, it would be guilty of a violation of the Sherman Act.

The *Pennington* case is of paramount importance for two reasons. In the first place, it reversed the generally accepted assumption which prevailed until that time that any union action relating to wage agreements with employers was exempt from the antitrust laws. The *Pennington* decision indicates that a union agreement with one employer or group of employers with respect to wages, hours, or working conditions that the union will seek to negotiate with *other* employers is not exempt from prosecution. In the second place, the trial court left it to the jury to determine as a *question of fact* whether there was a purpose among the alleged conspirators to impose a national contract upon the small producers with the intent of restraining trade and driving them out of business or whether the purpose was to improve working conditions, compensation, and other legitimate union objectives. This sounds very much like the old judicial tests of legality of union action which sought to determine "motive" and "intent."

In the *Jewel Tea* case,[16] decided on the same day, the company claimed that the Meat Cutters Union had violated the Sherman Act by negotiating agreements with Chicago food stores which provided that meat could not be sold before 9 A.M. or after 6 P.M., even if there were no butchers in the store. Jewel maintained that the union's insistence on the marketing-hours provision was part of a conspiracy between the union and the Associated Food Retailers of Greater Chicago, which represented the independent food stores and meat dealers. Although the company lost its case before the High Court, the actual decision represented a loss for organized labor; for the Court's opinion made it clear that if the trial judge had not found, as a question of fact, that there was an intimate connection between hours of work and hours of sale, the agreement negotiated by the union might well have been a violation of the Sherman Act. Here again, as in the *Pennington* case, the Supreme Court has indicated that findings of fact arrived at in a courtroom by a jury or by a trial judge sitting without a jury can impose liability on unions under the antitrust laws, even though the subject matter involves an issue which unions can reasonably believe is a proper subject for collective bargaining.

Further erosion of the immunity of unions from the antitrust laws was signaled by the decision of the Supreme Court in the *Connell* case.[17]

---

[16] *Local 189, Amalgamated Meat Cutters* v. *Jewel Tea Co.*, 381 U.S. 674 (1965).

[17] *Connell Construction Co.* v. *Plumbers Local 100*, 95 S. Ct. 1830 (1975).

In that case, the Court held that a construction union violated the anti-trust laws by forcing a general contractor, whose employees they were not trying to organize, to sign an agreement that he would let subcontracts only to mechanical subcontractors with whom the union had labor contracts. The union argued that its action was protected under Section 8(e) of the Taft-Hartley Act, which permits a union and an employer in the construction industry to make an agreement relating to the contracting or subcontracting of work to be done at the site. The Supreme Court held that the exemption applied only to an employer whom the union was attempting to organize and that the agreement in question indiscriminately excluded nonunion subcontractors from a portion of the market, even if their competitive advantages were not derived from substandard wages and working conditions, but rather from more efficient operating methods. The Court apparently feared that sanctioning the type of agreement in question would grant to construction unions an "almost unlimited organizational weapon."

Although critics of the power of organized labor have drawn some comfort from these recent cases, the cry "Bring organized labor under the antitrust laws" is still voiced in management circles. It is doubtful, however, whether any such broad extension represents a satisfactory solution for the field of labor problems. Our existing antitrust laws have not been particularly successful in preventing monopoly in industry, and court decisions have been notably unsuccessful in clarifying in businessmen's minds what is lawful and unlawful in this complicated field of law.

What is needed is specific legislation aimed at eliminating particular abuses upon which there is general agreement that governmental action is required. For example, consideration should be given to a comprehensive review of the Norris–La Guardia Act to adapt it to the current labor scene. It should be remembered that when that act was passed, there was no Wagner Act or Taft-Hartley Act; and furthermore, organized labor had not achieved its present position of strength in industry at large. Many labor experts agree that the original purpose of the Norris–La Guardia Act has long since been fulfilled and that the statute is in many respects obsolete.

PICKETING AFTER THE NORRIS–LA GUARDIA ACT

As we have seen, the passage of the Norris–La Guardia Act in 1932 substantially limited the power of the federal courts to issue injunctions in labor disputes. State courts, however, continued to enjoin picketing under a variety of circumstances and for a variety of reasons, except where the power of state courts had been circumscribed by the enactment of state "little Norris–La Guardia acts," modeled after the federal statute.

Picketing and Free Speech

Commencing in 1937, a series of cases were brought before the U.S. Supreme Court involving the question of whether picketing could be restricted by state legislatures and courts or whether it was protected from such regulation as a form of free speech guaranteed by the First Amendment of the federal Constitution. These cases are of major interest to students of labor problems not only because they concern a major union weapon—picketing—but also because they indicate how the changing views of the Supreme Court may influence the pattern of state legislative and judicial control of labor relations and thus profoundly affect the evolution of collective bargaining in our society. As will appear more fully in the following discussion, it seems in retrospect that the Supreme Court first became intrigued with the idea of treating picketing as a form of free speech entitled to constitutional protection and then retreated from this position when it recognized the coercive elements present in picketing and the legitimate right of the states to limit picketing in certain instances to protect the public interest.

In 1937, in a case which affirmed the right of a state to enact a "little Norris–La Guardia Act," Justice Louis D. Brandeis remarked: "Members of a union might without special statutory authorization by a State make known the facts of a labor dispute, for freedom of speech is guaranteed by the Federal Constitution."[18] This statement was misconstrued by many lawyers and judges to mean that picketing was a form of free speech guaranteed by the Constitution. Actually, Justice Brandeis merely said that union members might make known the facts of a dispute, without stating what means they might use for this purpose. He did not say that union members had a constitutional right to make facts known by means of a picket line. Nevertheless, three years later, in the case of *Thornhill* v. *Alabama*,[19] the Supreme Court completely accepted the doctrine that picketing was a form of free speech. An Alabama law, which termed picketing a form of loitering and made it a misdemeanor, was held unconstitutional on the ground that picketing is a form of speech protected by the First Amendment and that a penal statute which makes picketing a misdemeanor without regard to the manner in which it is conducted is unconstitutional on its face. In the companion case of *Carlson* v. *California*,[20] the Supreme Court elaborated the doctrine of picketing as a form of speech in the following words: "Publicizing the facts of a labor dispute in a peaceful way through appropriate means, whether by pamphlet, by word of mouth or by banner, must now be regarded as within that liberty of communication which is secured to every person by the Fourteenth Amendment against abridgement by a

---

[18] *Senn* v. *Tile Layers' Protective Union*, 301 U.S. 468, 57 S. Ct. 857 (1937).

[19] 310 U.S. 88, 60 S. Ct. 736 (1940).

[20] 310 U.S. 106, 113; 60 S. Ct. 746, 749 (1940).

State." And in 1941, in *American Federation of Labor* v. *Swing*,[21] the U.S. Supreme Court held unconstitutional a decision of the Illinois Supreme Court enjoining peaceful stranger picketing of a beauty parlor when none of the employees of the beauty parlor were members of the union conducting the picketing.

However, the notion that picketing is merely a form of free speech did not prove very satisfactory, in view of the coercive elements usually present in picketing. As a result, the U.S. Supreme Court slowly began to modify its views. In 1941, the Supreme Court refused to set aside an Illinois injunction which forbade all picketing by a milk drivers' union where there had been a background of previous violence.[22] In three important cases handed down in 1950, the Supreme Court held that the state courts could constitutionally restrict picketing which had as its objective action which violated a state statute or was deemed contrary to public policy.[23]

Subsequently, in *Vogt* v. *Teamsters*,[24] the Supreme Court upheld the action of a Wisconsin court in enjoining simple stranger picketing, a decision which fully acknowledged the retreat from the *Thornhill* doctrine and amounted, as the dissenters observed, to "formal surrender." Speaking for a majority of the Supreme Court, Justice Felix Frankfurter stated that picketing is fully subject to the right of the states to balance the social interests between employers and unions, provided only that states' policies are rational. Although Justice Frankfurter noted that states could not, under the *Thornhill* doctrine, proscribe all picketing per se, he made it clear that state courts and legislatures are free to decide whether to permit or suppress any particular picket line for any reason other than a blanket policy against picketing.[25]

In May 1968, in the *Logan Valley Plaza* case,[26] the Supreme Court, again expressly equating picketing with the right of free speech under

---

[21] 312 U.S. 321, 61 S. Ct. 568 (1941).

[22] *Milk Wagon Drivers* v. *Meadowmoor Dairies, Inc.*, 312 U.S. 287, 61 S. Ct. 552 (1941).

[23] *Building Service International Union* v. *Gazzam*, 339 U.S. 532, 70 S. Ct. 784 (1950); *Hughes* v. *Superior Court of State of California*, 339 U.S. 460, 70 S. Ct. 718 (1950); *International Brotherhood of Teamsters* v. *Hanke*, 339 U.S. 470, 70 S. Ct. 773 (1950).

[24] 354 U.S. 284, 77 S. Ct. 31 (1956).

[25] However, states cannot enact laws restricting peaceful picketing in a manner which deprives workers of rights guaranteed under the Taft-Hartley Act. Thus, for example, the U.S. Supreme Court has held unlawful a Virginia statute which imposed a fine on any person participating in picketing who was not a "bona fide" employee of the business or industry being picketed. Such a law against stranger picketing would be inconsistent with the Taft-Hartley Act, which makes no distinction as to whether a person picketing is an employee or not. See *Waxman* v. *Commonwealth of Virginia*, 371 U.S. 4 (1962).

[26] *Amalgamated Food Employees Local 590* v. *Logan Valley Plaza*, 88 S. Ct. 1601 (1968).

the First Amendment, voided an injunction by a state court against picketing carried on by a union against a tenant of a shopping center in the parking lot of the center. Although conceding that the First Amendment was intended only to protect freedom of speech against encroachment by federal, state, or local government and did not extend to restrictive action by individuals, the Court reasoned that because the shopping center was "open to the public," it was in effect a "public area."

Had this decision stood, it would have greatly extended the effective area of union picketing. However, a retreat from this position began in *Lloyd Corp.* v. *Tanner*,[27] in which the Supreme Court held that the First Amendment did not give individuals the right to distribute anti–Vietnam War leaflets in a shopping mall. Finally, in *Hudgens* v. *NLRB*,[28] the Court held that the First Amendment did not give a union the right to enter upon private property and picket a store in a shopping mall where the union had a dispute with the management of the retail outlet. In reaching this decision, the Court confirmed the fact that *Logan Valley Plaza* had been overruled.[29] The Court sent the dispute back to the NLRB with instructions to resolve the conflict between rights under Section 7 of the NLRA and private property rights within the context of the NLRA and without reference to the First Amendment.

Federal Government Regulation of Picketing

A number of the cases referred to above arose as the result of efforts of state courts and legislatures to prohibit or restrict picketing. The federal government has also passed legislation restricting labor's right to picket. These restrictions are embodied in the Taft-Hartley Act and the Landrum-Griffin Act, which we shall consider in detail in Chapters 19 and 20. In 1951, in a decision[30] consistent with its changed viewpoint toward picketing, the U.S. Supreme Court held that the provisions of the Taft-Hartley Act banning certain types of picketing in connection with secondary boycotts, did not violate constitutional guarantees of free speech.

The Present Status of Picketing

In light of the changing views of the U.S. Supreme Court on the subject, neither labor nor management today can be wholly certain as

---

[27] 407 U.S. 551 (1972).

[28] 44 Law Week 4281 (March 3, 1976).

[29] In the words of the Court, "the rationale of *Logan Valley* did not survive the Court's opinion in the *Lloyd* case"! Ibid., at 4285.

[30] *International Brotherhood of Electrical Workers* v. *National Labor Relations Board*, 341 U.S. 694 (1951).

to the legality of a given picket line. Some broad criteria seem, however, to have evolved. In general, the legality of picketing depends upon behavior (Is there violence?), effect (Did the pickets egress?), and objective (Was the picketing designed to support an illegal strike or an illegal secondary boycott?). It is in the last area that the most difficult questions arise. In a way we have come full circle, and in a manner reminiscent of decisions following *Commonwealth* v. *Hunt,* courts are again determining the legality of union action by attempting to determine union motives and intent.

BOYCOTTS AFTER THE NORRIS–LA GUARDIA ACT

We have seen that the Norris–La Guardia Act deprived the federal courts of jurisdiction in most cases involving labor disputes. However, its effect upon such union tactics as boycotts was even broader, for the U.S. Supreme Court interpreted the Norris–La Guardia Act as not only depriving the federal courts of jurisdiction to enjoin labor tactics enumerated in Section 4 of that act but also as making such acts lawful for all purposes under federal law. This momentous decision was enunciated by the Court in the *Hutcheson* case,[31] which involved a secondary boycott organized by a carpenters' union against the Anheuser-Busch Brewing Company. The Court held that because of the intervention of the Norris–La Guardia Act, which had "infused new spirit" into the Clayton Act, such union conduct did not violate the Sherman Act, even though in 1908 it had reached a contrary conclusion on similar facts in the *Danbury Hatters* case.

As a result of a more liberal judicial attitude reflecting the spirit of the Norris–La Guardia and Wagner acts, by the late 1930s and early 1940s union boycotts were no longer repressed by federal courts. The outcome was a major expansion in the use of the secondary boycott by organized labor. Strategically placed unions, particularly in the field of distribution, were able to expand their sphere of organization by bringing pressure on persons whose only relation to the dispute was that they did business with the particular employer involved. The Teamsters exerted additional pressure on nonunion employers by obtaining "hot cargo" agreements, in which employers agreed not to deal with nonunion employers.

The abuses which arose from the widespread use of such tactics by organized labor, together with the rash of strikes in 1947, led to a demand for restrictive labor legislation. The Taft-Hartley Act, passed in that year, had as one of its prime objectives the outlawing of all secondary boycotts. As we shall observe in our discussion of this act in Chapter 19, the provisions directed against secondary boycotts were poorly drawn

---

[31] *United States* v. *Hutcheson,* 312 U.S. 219, 61 S. Ct. 463 (1941).

and left many loopholes. Additional statutory restrictions aimed at closing these loopholes were incorporated in the Landrum-Griffin Act, which will be analyzed in Chapter 20.

LIMITATIONS ON THE RIGHT TO STRIKE

Writers are often prone to equate the right to strike with democracy and a free labor market. It has been said that preservation of the right to strike is what distinguishes our economy from those of Communist nations and that if this right is compromised, then other individual rights will also suffer. Actually, however, the right to strike has been limited in a number of important respects by the Taft-Hartley and Landrum-Griffin acts, and yet economic democracy still flourishes in our country. The change from the era of uninhibited union action under the Norris–La Guardia Act is rather remarkable and is deserving of closer scrutiny.

Strike action can be divided into two general categories—primary and secondary. A primary strike is a strike which occurs in connection with a labor dispute and directly involves the employer of the striking workers. A secondary strike is a strike which is aimed at an employer other than the employer of the striking workers. Suppose the carpenters on a construction job strike for higher wages. This is a primary strike directed against their employer, who, let us say, is the general contractor on the job. Now, a nonunion flooring subcontractor brings in nonunion workers to put down asphalt tile flooring in the building. The carpenters go on strike in protest against the use of nonunion workers on the job. This is a secondary strike.

While it is difficult to generalize in such a complicated field, it can be said that the law generally permits primary strike activity and prohibits secondary strike activity. A similar rule applies to picketing. There are, however, important exceptions. All secondary strike activity is not unlawful; and on the other hand, many kinds of primary strike activity are either prohibited or subject to limitations under our statutes. Let us examine some of the major types of primary strike activity which are restricted by federal law.

Strikes against Public Policy as Set Forth in Federal Statutes

In this category would fall strikes which directly violate or compel an employer to violate restrictive provisions contained in such labor laws as the Taft-Hartley law. Thus, for example, it is unlawful for a union to strike to compel an employer to recognize one union when another union has already been certified as the collective bargaining agency by the NLRB. The NLRB has held that it is unlawful for a union to strike to compel an employer to sign a "hot cargo" contract in the construction industry, even though the statute expressly permits such contracts if voluntarily made. A strike for a closed shop is unlawful under the Taft-Hartley Act, and it is also unlawful in many states under common law.

Strikes Arising out of Jurisdictional Disputes

The Taft-Hartley Act makes it an unfair labor practice for a union to engage in a strike to force or require any employer to assign particular work to employees in a particular labor organization or in a particular trade, craft, or class rather than to employees in another labor organization or in another trade, craft, or class, unless such employer is failing to conform to an order or certification of the NLRB determining the bargaining representative for employees performing such work. The law further provides that whenever it is charged that there has been a violation of this section, "the Board is empowered and directed to hear and determine the dispute out of which such unfair labor practice shall have arisen." The U.S. Supreme Court has held that this provision means that the Board must inquire into the merits of the dispute and then make a binding award of the work.[32] The Board has discretionary authority to seek an injunction against jurisdictional strikes in violation of the statute. As a result of these statutory provisions, the NLRB is now required to determine jurisdictional disputes by what amounts to compulsory arbitration.

Strikes during the Term of a Valid Collective Bargaining Agreement

The Taft-Hartley Act specifically prohibits strikes called before the end of a 60-day-notice period prior to the expiration of collective bargaining agreements. This provision was included in the law in order to give conciliation agencies sufficient time to meet with the parties and attempt to resolve disputes before a walkout occurred. Quite apart from this provision, a strike to compel a change in the terms of a contract prior to the expiration date of the contract has been held to be unlawful under the Taft-Hartley Act. This is true whether or not the contract contains a no-strike agreement. A strike in violation of a collective bargaining agreement is not protected concerted activity under the Taft-Hartley Act and may constitute an unfair labor practice.[33] A strike during the term of a contract over grievances or in protest over unfair employer labor practices is not, however, unlawful (unless in violation of a no-strike clause).

Suppose that a collective bargaining agreement contains both a no-

---

[32] *National Labor Relations Board* v. *Radio Engineers Union,* 364 U.S. 578 (1961).

[33] *United Mine Workers of America* (Boone County Coal Corp.), 117 NLRB 1095 (1957); enforcement denied, 257 F. (2d) 211 (D.C. Cir. 1958). Cf. *Boeing Airplane Co.* v. *National Labor Relations Board,* 174 F. (2d) 988 (D.C. Cir. 1949).

strike agreement on the part of the union and a commitment by union and management to submit certain types of disputes to binding arbitration. Suppose further that such a dispute arises, goes to arbitration, and the union loses. The union then strikes. What are the employer's rights? Section 301 of the Taft-Hartley Act provides that suits for violation of contracts between an employer and a union may be brought in any district court of the United States. The remedy of the employer in such a situation would be to sue for damages for breach of contract, but a victory in such a suit might represent a hollow triumph if the union were permitted to continue its strike. However, the blanket prohibitions of the Norris–La Guardia Act against the use of injunctions in labor disputes seemed to bar the injunction as a remedy available in federal courts to employers caught in such an impasse. This was the conclusion which the U.S. Supreme Court reached in 1962 in the leading case of *Sinclair Refining Co. v. Atkinson.*[34]

In a strong dissent, Justice Brennan warned that

> ... this decision deals a crippling blow to the cause of grievance arbitration itself. ... since unions cannot be enjoined by a federal court from striking in open defiance of their undertakings to arbitrate, employers will pause long before committing themselves to obligations enforceable against them but not against their unions.[35]

The one-sided doctrine embodied in the *Sinclair* decision did not stand for long. Eight years later, Justice Brennan delivered the majority opinion in the *Boys Markets* case,[36] expressly overruling the *Sinclair* decision. In the *Boys Markets* case, the union contract contained a no-strike clause and a provision that all controversies concerning the interpretation or application of the contract should be resolved by arbitration. A dispute over nonunion supervisors handling products in a store precipitated a strike by the union. After the company unsuccessfully sought arbitration of the dispute, it applied to court for an injunction against the strike. After various court proceedings, the Supreme Court held that an injunction could be issued by a federal court despite the prohibitions contained in the Norris–La Guardia Act.

Management officials hailed this decision as "clearing the air," but unfortunately the air did not remain clear for long! In July 1976, in the *Buffalo Forge*[37] case, a similar set of facts was before the Supreme Court, except that here the union engaged in a sympathy strike with a sister union, rather than because of any grievance with the employer company. The union contract contained a no-strike clause as well as a pro-

---

[34] 370 U.S. 195 (1962).

[35] 370 U.S. 195, 227 (1962).

[36] *Boys Markets, Inc. v. Retail Clerks, Local 770,* 398 U.S. 235 (1970).

[37] *Buffalo Forge Co. v. United Steelworkers of America,* 44 Law Week 5346 (July 1976).

vision for the arbitration of disputes arising over the interpretation of provisions of the contract, including the no-strike clause. Despite the similarities to the *Boys Markets* case, the Supreme Court held that a federal court could not issue an injunction because it was not clear that the sympathy strike was an arbitrable issue under the contract.

This decision, which seems to narrow significantly the application of *Boys Markets*, has great significance for labor relations, particularly in the coal industry, where wildcat strikes have been rampant and union locals have honored picket lines set up by roving pickets, despite the fact that contracts contained arbitration and no-strike clauses. At this writing, a number of district courts, citing *Buffalo Forge*, have refused to issue restraining orders against United Mine Worker locals, and the resulting litigation is likely to lead to still another Supreme Court ruling in this confused area of labor law.

The Partial Strike

Suppose that as a negotiating tactic with an employer a union does not strike but simply engages in harassing activities, such as slowdowns, quickie strikes, or refusals to work overtime? The validity of this last tactic was at issue in a recent case[38] in which a union, while in negotiations with an employer for renewal of an expired collective bargaining agreement, refused to permit its members to work overtime. The NLRB denied relief under the Taft-Hartley Act, so the employer appealed to the Wisconsin Employment Relations Commission, which held that such action was an unfair labor practice under the state labor relations act and therefore enjoined the union from taking it. When the issue reached the U.S. Supreme Court, the Court ruled that since the partial strike was neither protected nor prohibited under the Taft-Hartley Act, it was the intent of Congress to leave such action wholly unregulated, and therefore neither the Wisconsin Commission nor the state court had authority to interfere with the union action. This surprising decision, which overruled an earlier Supreme Court holding,[39] implies that even where Congress has not acted to regulate union activity, states may be barred from imposing restraints on union conduct.

Strikes against the Government and National Emergency Strikes

Most governmental bodies—federal, state, and municipal—forbid strikes by employees on the ground that such strikes are against the sovereign and therefore against the public interest. Section 305 of the

---

[38] *Lodge 76 International Association of Machinists* v. *Wisconsin Employment Relations Commission*, 44 Law Week 5026, June 25, 1976.

[39] *Auto Workers* v. *Wisconsin Employment Relations Board*, 336 U.S. 245 (1948).

Taft-Hartley Act makes it unlawful for any individual employed by the United States or any agency thereof, including wholly owned government corporations, to participate in any strike. The problem of government employees and the right to strike will be more fully explored in Chapter 22.

The Taft-Hartley Act contains provisions enabling the government to obtain a temporary injunction in cases involving strikes which imperil or threaten to imperil the national health or safety. After such an injunction is obtained, the strike action becomes unlawful. These provisions will be discussed in Chapter 21.

Summary

The foregoing brief outline describes the status of strikes in interstate commerce where federal labor laws are applicable. Where state law is applicable to a local dispute, the results will depend upon the provisions of that state statute, or upon common law in the absence of an applicable statute. Basically, courts, in the absence of statutes to guide them, still apply the old rule of ends and means. If the ends are illegal, the court is likely to enjoin the strike, no matter how peaceful the means used may be. This result reflects the historical judicial attitude that a strike is fundamentally an intentional tortious interference with an advantageous business relationship and therefore should only be permitted if it is carried on for a proper purpose. Strikes to improve working conditions are generally held to be for a valid purpose, but a strike for a closed shop may still be held lawful in one state and illegal in another.

LIMITATIONS ON THE RIGHT TO LOCK OUT

Labor legislation in this country has gradually deprived employers of most of the effective tactical weapons which they used in the past to combat efforts of unions to organize their employees. We have seen how the Norris–La Guardia Act outlawed the yellow-dog contract and barred injunctions against unions in federal court—thus eliminating two devices which had been widely used to discourage union organizing efforts. Likewise, the unfair labor practice provisions of the Wagner and Taft-Hartley laws restricted other tactics frequently utilized by antiunion employers, such as discriminatory hiring and firing practices, spying on employees, and antiunion speeches. While this restrictive legislation was primarily intended to prevent employers from obstructing the efforts of employees to organize and bargain through representatives of their own choosing, it also has the effect of weakening the tactical position of employers who reach an impasse in bargaining with unions over economic issues. For example, the Norris–La Guardia Act and the state statutes patterned after it have made it extremely difficult to halt mass picketing, vandalism, and other violence which sometimes results from efforts of management to bring employees through a picket line into a struck plant. As a consequence, most employers are reluctant to run a plant with strikebreakers, even though they have a legal right to do so. The Norris–La Guardia Act, therefore, tends to make the picket line a more effective weapon for imposing economic losses upon the employer and consequently gives the union a strategic advantage in collective bargaining.

There is another effective employer tactical weapon which is relatively little used and about which little has been written. That is the right to lock out. In some respects, the employer's right to lock out his employees may be thought of as paralleling the employees' right to withhold their services through strike action. Just as the right to strike has been subjected to restrictions where it contravenes certain purposes, so the employer's right to shut down operations has been held to be a limited managerial prerogative. Although, with minor exceptions,[40] there are no statutory prohibitions against use of the lockout, nevertheless, as a result of decisions of the NLRB and the courts, the lockout has been so circumscribed by restrictions that an employer involved in a labor dispute would be ill advised to shut down his plant without first obtaining competent legal advice.

In the first place, it is clear that an employer cannot use the lockout as a device to avoid union organization. The Taft-Hartley Act prohibits discharges of employees where the purpose is to discourage membership in a labor organization. Since an employer cannot discharge individual employees in order to deter unionization, it is not surprising that both the NLRB and the courts have held that he cannot shut down an entire plant and lay off all employees in order to accomplish the same result. Of course, employers will generally point to some economic reason for the shutdown, while union spokesmen will claim that the action was taken to break the union. Cases which come before the NLRB on this issue usually involve complex factual situations susceptible to either interpretation, which tends to complicate the problem presented to the Board for determination.

In the second place, the rule has been established that an employer cannot seek to avoid his commitment under an existing union contract or to wrest bargaining concessions from a union by shutting down his plant and moving to another area. In such cases, the NLRB has usually required the employer to offer employment to the former employees at the new location, to pay their moving expenses to such new location, and in

---

[40] The Taft-Hartley Act prohibits lockouts (and strikes) for a period of 60 days after notice is given of a proposed modification or expiration of a collective bargaining agreement (Section 8[d][4]). In addition, lockouts (and strikes) which imperil the national health and safety are subject to injunction for a limited period of time during the fact-finding procedure prescribed by Section 206 of the Taft-Hartley Act.

addition, to make the employees whole for the loss they may have suffered by reason of the unlawful discharge.

In the third place, the NLRB for many years looked upon the lockout as a lawful employer weapon only where unusual economic circumstances justified it as a *defensive* measure against a threatened strike. The Board condemned lockouts by individual employers undertaken in the course of collective bargaining negotiations to bring pressure on the union for a satisfactory settlement. Although the union could strike to enforce its demands, the NLRB had generally taken the position that a lockout in such circumstances would interfere with the protected concerted activities of the employees. For example, in the *American Brake Shoe*[41] case, the Board said that if an anticipatory lockout were to be permitted as lawful, the employer would be immunized from effective strike action and the employees' right to strike would be rendered virtually meaningless.

However, in 1965, in the *American Shipbuilding*[42] case, the U.S. Supreme Court held that a company did not violate the Taft-Hartley Act when, after an impasse had been reached in contract negotiations, it shut down its plant and laid off employees for the purpose of bringing pressure to bear on the union, which was threatening to strike during the company's busiest season. In subsequent decisions, the NLRB has stated that it views this decision as obliterating any distinction between offensive and defensive lockouts. Nevertheless, it seems that some significant differences still remain. If a lockout is defensive, that is, invoked either by a multiemployer group in response to a whipsawing strike against one member of the group or by an individual employer in anticipation of a threatened strike, employers may continue to operate by using replacements for locked-out employees. However, if the lockout is offensive, that is, invoked in support of a bargaining position without regard to a strike or threatened strike, then the employer is probably in violation of the Taft-Hartley Act if he continues to operate by using replacements for locked-out employees.

Because of the uncertainty which still surrounds the law of lockout, it is used infrequently by employers, and then only rarely do employers seek to operate with replacements. Therefore, much of the fear which the NLRB apparently shares with respect to an unrestricted lockout policy seems to be unwarranted; for a lockout still deprives the employer of the opportunity to carry on business. It precipitates what the employer normally hopes to avoid and therefore is not likely to be widely used, regardless of a more liberal trend in the decisions. It is most likely to be resorted to in multiemployer bargaining situations and in cases

---

[41] 116 NLRB 832.

[42] 380 U.S. 300 (1965).

where an individual employer wishes to forestall a union which is prone to resort to quickie strikes and violence.

ARBITRATION OR GOVERNMENT PROCESS

There are two principal avenues through which disputes between labor and management can be resolved. The first involves resort to arbitration procedures, which to an increasing extent are being included in collective bargaining agreements as the final step in the orderly resolution of disputes arising under the contract. The second avenue involves an appeal to the National Labor Relations Board and ultimately to the courts.

There are a number of compelling reasons for favoring the first alternative as a matter of public policy. As will be pointed out in the next chapter, the NLRB is faced with a mounting load of cases, which makes prompt resolution of disputes difficult to achieve. Arbitrators develop a special expertise with relation to particular industries and firms and can frequently make a more satisfactory decision with respect to complex issues than the NLRB. Finally, there is the danger that continual resort to government to resolve problems in the field of labor relations will erode the process of collective bargaining. Voluntary arbitration appears to be a much more salutary, prompt, and effective way of settling many disputes which do not threaten the existence of the union itself.

In recent years, in a succession of cases, both the courts and the NLRB have spoken out in favor of deferral to the private arbitration system where there appears to be an overlap between that system and the applicable labor law. Thus, in *United Steelworkers* v. *Warrior & Gulf Navigation Co.*,[43] the Supreme Court held that when a party sought to compel arbitration in a suit under Section 301 of the Labor-Management Relations Act, the courts should resolve questions of interpretation of the arbitration clause by applying a strong presumption in favor of arbitrability. As we observed in the earlier discussion in this chapter, the Supreme Court's decision in the *Boys Markets* case will also strengthen the process of arbitration. The National Labor Relations Board has set forth four criteria to guide it in determining when to defer to private arbitration. The Board will defer to arbitration when:

1. The contract provides grievance and arbitration machinery.
2. There is no showing that the alleged unilateral action has been taken to undermine the union.
3. There is a claim of privilege under the contract by the respondent.

---

[43] 363 U.S. 574 (1960).

4. It appears that an arbitrator's interpretation of the contract would resolve the controversy as well as the Board's interpretation would.[44]

The Board's action in this regard seems to be on firm ground. A number of commentators contend that deferral should be further broadened so that a broad range of discipline cases could be handled through the arbitration procedure. Most labor economists would agree with this opinion of a former Board chairman:

> I think that when parties have voluntarily agreed upon a mechanism for the adjustment of their disputes, then to the widest extent possible we ought to permit that machinery to operate and not complicate the situation by permitting either party to side-step those processes and instead look to government in the form of this Board to decide the merits of their disputes.[45]

QUESTIONS FOR DISCUSSION

1. What is meant by the term *injunction*? Discuss the manner in which the injunction has been used to impede labor's organizational efforts. To what extent can employers still use the injunction in labor disputes?
2. Should all picketing be treated as a form of free speech? Discuss the changing attitude of the U.S. Supreme Court on this issue.
3. What are the points of similarity between the strike and the lockout? In what ways do the two actions differ? Should employers have the same freedom to lock out as unions have to strike?
4. Should unions be subject to the antitrust laws? Discuss the validity of the tests established by the *Pennington* and *Jewel Tea* cases as criteria for determining whether or not the Sherman Act prohibitions are applicable to concerted action by employees.

SUGGESTIONS FOR FURTHER READING

Abodeely, John E. "Injunctive Powers under the National Labor Relations Act," in Richard L. Rowan (ed.), *Collective Bargaining: Survival in the 70's?* Philadelphia: Industrial Research Unit, The Wharton School, University of Pennsylvania, 1972, pp. 106–26.

A discussion of the merits and demerits of broadened use of the injunction in labor relations, with particular reference to the power of the NLRB to seek injunctive relief under Sections 10(*j*) and 10(*l*) of the Taft-Hartley Act.

Cohen, Laurence J. "Labor and the Antitrust Laws: A New Look at a Recurring Issue," in *Labor Law Developments, 1976*, 22d Annual Institute,

---

[44] *Joseph Schlitz Brewing Co.*, 175 NLRB 23. These criteria were affirmed in *Collyer Insulated Wire*, 192 NLRB 150, in which the NLRB stated that these guidelines would set the Board's policy in similar cases in the future.

[45] Remarks at the Conference of Western States Employer Association Executives, 167 D.L.R. D–1 (1971).

Southwestern Legal Foundation, Dallas, Texas. New York: Matthew
Bender, 1976, pp. 157–90.

An up-to-date analysis of the changing views of the U.S. Supreme
Court toward application of the antitrust laws to unions, including a
critique of the *Connell* case by an attorney who represents unions.

Handsaker, Morrison L., and Handsaker, Marjorie L. "Remedies and Penalties
for Wildcat Strikes: How Arbitrators and Federal Courts Have Ruled,"
Industrial Relations Law Digest, vol. 16 (July 1973), pp. 49–68.

A condensation of an article explaining how courts, including the U.S.
Supreme Court, and arbitrators have dealt with wildcat strikes in violation
of collective bargaining agreements.

Rosen, Samuel D. "Area Standards Picketing," *Labor Law Journal,* vol. 23
(February 1972), pp. 67–79.

A discussion which, although primarily concerned with the problems
posed by area standards picketing, provides an excellent classification of
the various types of picketing.

Scott, Manuelo A. "The Invisible Hand and the Clenched Fist: Is There a
Safe Way to Picket under the First Amendment?" *Industrial Relations
Law Digest,* vol. 18 (Summer 1975), pp. 71–83.

An analysis of the decisions of the Supreme Court which attempt to
deal with the problem of whether picketing involves speech or conduct.

19

The Taft-Hartley Act

SINCE ITS ENACTMENT in 1947, the Labor-Management Relations Act of 1947—more popularly known as the Taft-Hartley Act—has been the subject of controversy. Although at its inception it was most criticized by labor leaders, who characterized it as a "slave labor law," it is now widely condemned by businessmen, who argue that the NLRB has interpreted the act in a manner inconsistent with the intent of Congress. In this chapter, we shall consider in detail various provisions of this act and its effect upon employers, unions, individual employees, and the general public. Since the Taft-Hartley Act is, in form, an amendment of the earlier National Labor Relations Act, or Wagner Act, as it is commonly known, we shall commence our discussion with a brief consideration of the Wagner Act.

*

THE WAGNER ACT

Legislative Background and Statutory Policy

The Wagner Act was enacted largely because of the failure of American employers to modernize their concepts of industrial relations by giving employees an opportunity to participate in the determination of wages, hours, and working conditions. The failure of industry to alter its long-standing policies and to recognize unions of its employees voluntarily was all the more remarkable in view of the ample warnings that if industry did not act, government would be compelled to do so. Commencing in 1885, a long list of government commissions, agencies, and (in later years) statutes contained governmental endorsement of the principle of collective bargaining. In 1898, Congress passed the Erdman

Act, which contained provisions making discrimination against union activity on the railroads a misdemeanor. Although this provision was declared unconstitutional, later railway legislation, including the Railway Labor Act of 1926, endorsed unionism and collective bargaining. Between 1890 and 1914, no less than 14 states enacted legislation similar to the Erdman Act, only to have the courts declare such laws unconstitutional. Both the Norris–La Guardia Act of 1932 and the National Industrial Recovery Act of 1933 contained statements of policy endorsing the right of employees to bargain through representatives of their own choosing, but neither act contained effective penalties in case of employer disinclination to conform to these statutory purposes.

In 1935, Congress passed the Wagner Act, which, in retrospect, appears to be the most significant labor law ever enacted in the United States. Congress virtually ordered employers to stop interfering with the efforts of unions to organize their employees. It put the power of the federal government behind the union organizer, assuring him that employees could choose whether or not to join a union without fear of employer interference. Moreover, in contrast to earlier legislation, the Wagner Act provided an effective mechanism to secure compliance by employers. The Wagner Act, therefore, required a completely new orientation of employer industrial relations policies.

The heart of the substantive provisions of the Wagner Act is contained in Section 7, which states the statutory policy in these words: "Employees shall have the right to self-organization, to form, join, or assist labor organizations, to bargain collectively through representatives of their own choosing, and to engage in concerted activities, for the purpose of collective bargaining or other mutual aid or protection."

The administration of the Wagner Act was given to a three-man National Labor Relations Board. The NLRB developed a large staff to enable it to carry on its work, including attorneys, investigators, hearing officers, review officers, and the many clerical personnel required to perform the detailed work in a nationwide administrative agency. The NLRB had jurisdiction only over employers engaged in interstate commerce. The Supreme Court has given the phrase *interstate commerce* an elastic definition, so that the jurisdiction of the Board has been held to apply not only to companies actively engaged in shipping products across state lines, but also to intrastate businesses which use a substantial quantity of raw materials shipped across state lines or sell products a substantial portion of which are destined for shipment across state lines.

Unfair Labor Practices

The Wagner Act was passed at a time when the labor market was vastly different from that which exists in industry today. Organized labor numbered only 4 million union members, primarily concentrated in the construction trades, transportation, mining, and the needle trades. The great basic industries of the country were either unorganized or were characterized by bargaining with company unions dominated by management. In 1935, for example, such industries as basic steel, agricultural implements, petroleum refining, rubber products, electrical machinery, and meat-packing had from 50% to 80% of their employees covered by company unions.[1] Employers were openly hostile to unions and used every weapon at their command to prevent union organization. Lockouts, intimidation, blacklists, yellow-dog contracts, spying, and discrimination were commonplace.

In drafting the Wagner Act, Congress recognized that business hostility to unions was a fact to be reckoned with and that pious pronouncements of policy in favor of union organization, unbuttressed by sanctions against violators of congressional policy, would achieve nothing. The act therefore enumerated so-called employer unfair practices and made such conduct unlawful. Furthermore, it empowered the NLRB to issue cease and desist orders against such illegal conduct, and to enforce such orders in the courts. During the 12 years of the Wagner Act administration until its amendment in 1947, employees and their representatives filed more than 45,000 charges of unfair labor practices against employers with the NLRB. It is therefore apparent that protection of employees against management unfair labor practices constituted a major function of the Board.

The unfair labor practices prohibited by the Wagner Act (in each case directed against employers) are the following:

1. *To interfere with, restrain, or coerce employees in the exercise of rights guaranteed in Section 7.* This is an all-inclusive provision which actually covers all of the more specific unfair labor practices enumerated below. However, it was aimed at such employer practices as spying on unions, questioning employees about their union affiliation, using blacklists or yellow-dog contracts, or favoring one union over another.

A major problem which arose under this section involved the question of freedom of speech. Since unions were weak during the early years of the Wagner Act, the NLRB considered the effect of antiunion speeches by employers as an important part of a totality of conduct which might interfere with the rights of employees under the act. Employers complained that the NLRB went too far in its zeal to protect employees and actually deprived employers of rights of free speech guaranteed by the Constitution.

2. *To dominate or interfere with the formation or administration of any labor organization or contribute financial or other support to it.* This

---

[1] H. A. Millis and E. C. Brown, *From the Wagner Act to Taft-Hartley* (Chicago: University of Chicago Press, 1950), p. 110.

section was designed to prevent the formation or use of company unions which were supported by and subservient to the employer. As has been mentioned, company unions were commonly used by employers in the early 1930s as a device to deter legitimate independent unionism; but as a result of the effective enforcement of this provision, employer-controlled company unions gradually disappeared from the labor scene.

3. *By discrimination in regard to hire or tenure of employment or any term or condition of employment to encourage or discourage membership in any labor organization.* This section was designed to make it unlawful for employers to use blacklists, yellow-dog contracts, or other devices to discourage membership in unions. Employers were forbidden to inquire of job applicants whether they were union members or favored unions, and employers could not fire employees because of union membership or lawful concerted activities protected under the act.

A proviso was included in this section permitting an employer who had entered into an agreement with a union duly representing his employees to require membership in the union as a condition of employment. This was the so-called closed-shop proviso, which was amended by the Taft-Hartley Act.

4. *To discharge or otherwise discriminate against an employee because he has filed charges or given testimony under the act.* This section was deemed necessary by Congress in order to assure protection to employees who invoked the provisions of the act against employers.

5. *To refuse to bargain collectively with the representatives of employees duly chosen pursuant to other provisions of the act.* This section of the law was inserted to require employers to meet and negotiate with representatives of their employees. It is clear from the legislative history of the act that Congress did not intend to compel employers to agree to anything; it did want to assure that they would at least sit down and bargain. The language of this section aroused violent criticism from management spokesmen, who objected to the fact that the obligation to bargain was imposed only on them and not on unions. Furthermore, they criticized the manner in which the NLRB established criteria as to what was "good-faith" bargaining, claiming that such rules, in effect, required employers to come to an agreement contrary to the original statutory purpose.

The prohibition of specific unfair labor practices in the Wagner Act ushered in a new era in labor relations. Whereas in earlier years labor leaders found the power of the courts interfering with their organizing activities, with the advent of the Wagner Act the courts, in effect, became an ally of labor, standing ready to enforce valid orders of the NLRB in cases where the Board found an employer guilty of unfair labor practices and the employer ignored the Board's cease and desist order. Despite the act's shortcomings, and despite the delays attendant upon its enforcement, the act's procedures for handling unfair labor practices represented such an improvement from organized labor's point of view over pre–Wagner Act conditions that organizing activity was greatly enhanced.

In a typical unfair labor practice case under the Wagner Act, the NLRB received a complaint from the union in behalf of an individual worker alleging some violation of the act. A field examiner of the Board investigated the case, and if the Board found that there was sufficient evidence to warrant a hearing, it set down the case for hearing and, if necessary, issued such subpoenas as were needed for the appearances of records and persons. In more than three quarters of the cases, however, settlement was achieved by informal methods before the hearing actually took place.

Hearings under the Wagner Act were conducted under the best accepted methods of administrative process. The NLRB was always careful to give all interested parties due notice and the right of hearing. However, the Board did act as both judge and prosecutor, which seemed unfair to some critics. Criticism of this feature of the law's administration ultimately led to establishment of the position of independent General Counsel under the Taft-Hartley Act, whose job is to initiate complaints and bring them before the Board.

Representation Cases

Equally as important as unfair labor practice cases in the work of the NLRB, and every bit as controversial as a result of the split in the American labor movement which existed until 1955, have been representation cases. Section 9(a) of the Wagner Act provided that "representatives . . . selected for the purposes of collective bargaining by the majority of the employees in a unit appropriate for such purposes, shall be the exclusive representatives of all the employees in such unit for the purposes of collective bargaining. . . ." This provision, with important additions which we shall consider at a later point in the discussion, was carried over into the Taft-Hartley Act.

Congress adopted the majority rule principle basically because experience had shown that it was the only practical method. The representative of the majority is thus the representative of all the employees in the bargaining unit, whether or not they are union members, just as a congressman represents all persons in his district, regardless of whether they are members of his party or whether they voted for him or his opponent in the last election. If minority representation were permitted in collective bargaining, the employer would be constantly faced with demands from one group or another desirous of attracting support. Obviously, under such a setup, neither collective bargaining nor a business would stand much chance of survival. The NLRB has further determined that majority means a majority of the employees voting, not a majority of those eligible. This compels all interested groups to vie in getting out the vote. As a result, votes cast in NLRB elections averaged 80–90% of those eligible, as compared with the average of 50–65% of those eligible who vote in national elections.

In order to determine whether or not a particular union was the representative of workers in a plant, the NLRB held elections by secret ballot among the employees. The names of the union or unions seeking certification were placed on the ballot along with "no union." If a union won a majority of the votes cast, it was certified as the collective bargaining agent with which the employer had to bargain as the exclusive representative of the employees involved. If "no union" received a majority, no certification was made.

Bargaining Unit Problems

One of the most difficult kinds of problems faced by the NLRB involved deciding which employees were eligible to vote in an election to determine the bargaining agent and which groups of employees should have the right to separate choice of bargaining agents. Congress delegated these problems, known as questions of the "appropriate bargaining unit," to the NLRB, giving it almost unlimited authority[2] in Section 9(b) of the Wagner Act, which stated that "the Board shall decide in each case whether, in order to insure to employees the full benefit of their right to self-organization and to collective bargaining, and otherwise to effectuate the policies of this Act, the unit appropriate for the purposes of collective bargaining shall be the employer unit, craft unit, plant unit, or subdivision thereof." This wide authority was given to the NLRB in the belief, based on experience of the National Recovery Administration labor boards, that the various problems which arose were not foreseeable and could best be determined by the NLRB.

Although the Board decided each case on the merits, it grouped the facts determining its bargaining unit decisions around two basic criteria —the history of collective bargaining, if any, and the mutuality of interests of the employees. A typical bargaining unit was composed of production and maintenance employees in a single plant. Foremen and supervisors were excluded from the production workers' unit because of their peculiar relation to management. Likewise, office, clerical, and white-collar workers were separated from production and maintenance employees, as were professional employees. In addition, guards and watchmen were placed in separate units because of their unique position, and temporary employees were often deemed outside the bargaining unit

---

[2] This authority has been restricted to some extent in the Taft-Hartley Act with respect to craft units, guards, and professional employees. See subsequent discussion in this chapter.

because they had no permanent status in the plant. All these decisions were based on the fact that production and maintenance employees have a basic common denominator which is lacking among other plant groups, especially since many of the latter have a special and different relation to the employer.

The Effects of AFL–CIO Rivalry

The determination of the bargaining unit was complicated by the rivalry between the AFL and the CIO. The struggle between these two groups was bitterly fought in cases involving the question of whether employees should be represented on a craft or on an industrial basis. During the early years of the Wagner Act, the CIO concentrated its organizing drives in the great basic industries of the country—steel, automobile, electrical, chemical, oil, and so on—and sought to organize companies on an industrial basis. This drive brought it into conflict with the AFL, which frequently represented strategically placed craft groups in such industries. In resolving the issue of the appropriate bargaining unit, where both an industrial union and a craft union claimed the right to represent a particular group of workers, the NLRB would consider the claims of both parties; and if it found, upon the basis of all the circumstances, that the craft could logically lay claim to consideration as a separate bargaining unit, and if there was reasonable doubt as to whether the majority of this craft preferred representation by the craft union or the industrial union, the Board permitted the workers in the craft to determine the issue for themselves. The Board accomplished this by providing that the workers in the craft would have a choice in an election of voting for the craft union, the industrial union, or no union, whereas the other production workers could vote only for the industrial union or no union.

When Congress passed the Wagner Act, it did not, of course, foresee the split in the labor movement. Therefore, it anticipated that in those situations where employees wanted to be represented by a union, a petition for an election would be filed with the Board by the union (normally an AFL affiliate), and a prompt, peaceful determination of the question of representation would be made through the administrative procedures of the Board.

This procedure broke down when AFL and CIO unions engaged in a bitter struggle with each other over the right to represent employees in given bargaining units. Instead, the plant became a battleground, with both employer and employees as casualties. If one union felt confident enough to move for an early election, the other union would use all sorts of pressures to defer it. If it appeared that one union was successfully signing up members in a plant, the other union might institute a boycott of the products of the company, picket the premises, threaten workers, or use similar pressures to weaken the hold of the rival union. The employer could do nothing to protect his business or employees against such tactics, for the Norris–La Guardia Act had deprived employers of their most effective weapon—the injunction. Since the Wagner Act imposed no prohibition on the activities of unions similar to the unfair labor practices proscribed for employers, employees had no way to protect themselves against such union pressures.

Even after one union was certified as the exclusive bargaining agent, there was nothing in the Wagner Act which prohibited a rival union from continuing its organizing and harassing activities, including picketing and boycotting. Employers were bound by the results of an NLRB election; but a rival union which lost an election was not bound by such results as a practical matter, since it could still attempt to achieve through economic pressure what it could not accomplish through peaceful procedures under the act.

The Wagner Act, Union Growth, and Strikes

That the Wagner Act achieved its basic purpose in compelling a change in employer policy toward unions cannot be doubted. In 1935, when the act became law, union membership stood at 3.9 million. In 1947, when the Wagner Act was amended, union membership exceeded 15 million. Although this union growth must be attributed to many factors, it was without a doubt substantially hastened by the Wagner Act. If the Wagner Act is judged in terms of fulfillment of its stated policy of "encouraging the practice and procedure of collective bargaining," it was eminently successful.

On the other hand, the Wagner Act cannot be said to have minimized the causes of industrial disputes except in one important respect. The representation procedure of the act provided a peaceful and democratic means of determining whether a union had the right to represent a group of employees. The substitution of NLRB procedure for the use of force in determining this question was one of the great contributions of the act.

Insofar as strikes generally are concerned, however, the Wagner Act had little contribution to make. Congress gave the NLRB no authority to interfere in disputes over the terms and conditions of employment. Once the union was certified as the bargaining agent and the employer's conduct was purged of unfair labor practices, the Wagner Act left matters to the parties themselves. But since the protection of the act spurred union activity, the period 1935–41 saw a great surge of union growth. A combination of immature unions and managements inexperienced in industrial relations resulted in numerous strikes which more mature and experienced parties might have avoided. Critics of the Wagner Act blamed either the act or its administration by the NLRB as the cause of the strife. Proponents of the act blamed management opposition to both the act and unions as the cause. Perhaps a more accurate analysis would place the blame mainly on the growing pains of unions and the learning pains of management.

THE TAFT-HARTLEY ACT

The Wagner Act was under severe public criticism from its enactment in 1935 until its amendment 12 years later. Repeated attempts to modify the Wagner Act were bottled up in congressional committees, but finally, in 1946, the stage was set for new labor legislation by an unprecedented wave of strikes. In that year, time lost through strikes reached an all-time high of 116 million man-days—a figure three times higher than in the previous year or in 1937, the two worst years up to that time for which such statistics are available. Then followed the congressional elections of November 1946, which reflected strong public dissatisfaction with current labor policies and which were interpreted by Congress as a mandate for corrective labor legislation. On June 23, 1947, the Labor-Management Relations Act—more popularly known as the Taft-Hartley Act—was passed by Congress over President Truman's veto.

Thus ended an important stage in the development of national labor policy in this country. The attitude of government toward collective bargaining by employees had passed through a succession of stages from active hostility in the early 1800s, when labor organizations were prosecuted as conspiracies, to active encouragement of union organization under the Wagner Act. Enactment of the Taft-Hartley law represented a new stage in government treatment of both management and labor. The metamorphosis which had occurred in public thinking on the subject of collective bargaining is well exemplified by a comparison of the original phraseology of Section 7 of the Wagner Act with its revised wording in the Taft-Hartley Act: "Employees shall have the right to self-organization ... for the purpose of collective bargaining or other mutual aid or protection, *and shall also have the right to refrain from any or all of such activities....*" Whereas, formerly, the weight of government influence had been placed behind union organization activities, the Taft-Hartley Act appeared to place the government in the position of a neutral, recognizing the right of employees to organize or not to organize. In theory, the government was to be not a partisan but a policeman, protecting both management and labor from unfair labor practices. However, as we shall observe in the later discussion, critics have alleged that the actual administration of the act has deviated from this apparent statutory policy.

The Taft-Hartley Act also qualified the principle that organized labor should be free to use its economic weapons without restriction. Secondary boycotts, strikes, and picketing for certain purposes were all subjected to regulation by the act. In this and other respects which will be discussed in the text, the Taft-Hartley Act established the principle that law, protecting the interest of management, labor, and the public, plays a necessary role in labor relations.

The Scope and Administration of the Act

The Labor-Management Relations Act of 1947 was, in form, an amendment of the Wagner Act. Title I incorporated the text of the Wagner Act—with, however, a number of major modifications and additions. Title II, which dealt with the conciliation of labor disputes and national emergency strikes, is discussed in Chapter 21. Title III authorized suits by and against unions, and Title IV created a joint committee to study and report on basic problems affecting friendly labor relations and productivity. Administration of the act remained under the National Labor Relations Board, but a number of important changes were made in the composition and power of the NLRB. Section 3 of the act enlarged the Board from three to five members. To remedy the oft-repeated charge made against the Board under the Wagner Act that it was both judge and prosecutor, the prosecuting function was removed from the Board and vested in a General Counsel who in this respect was made completely independent of the Board. In the handling of cases the General Counsel has final authority, subject neither to appeal to the Board nor to appeal to the courts, both as to the institution of formal unfair labor practice proceedings and as to the dismissal of charges. However, the General Counsel is subject to the Board's direction in matters of basic policy, such as the determination of what categories of employers and employees are covered by the act.

In 1961, in order to keep abreast of its mounting load of representation cases, the Board delegated its powers in election cases to its regional directors. Since that date, the holding of elections and the initial resolution of election issues have been handled by staff personnel in the Board's 43 regional and field offices under the supervision of the regional directors and with limited review by the Board itself. In unfair labor practice cases, the General Counsel investigates charges and if he deems them meritorious, issues a complaint. Hearings are held before an Administrative Law Judge, with the General Counsel presenting evidence of the alleged violation. If exceptions are filed to the judge's decision, the Board reviews the proceedings and either adopts or modifies his determinations.

Although collective bargaining is today firmly established in American industry, the total case load handled by the Board continues to mount year after year. In the fiscal year ending June 30, 1976, 49,335 cases were filed with the Board, including 34,509 unfair labor practice charges.[3]

---

[3] *Forty-First Annual Report of the National Labor Relations Board for the Fiscal Year ended June 30, 1976* (Washington, D.C.: Government Printing Office, 1976), pp. 1, 11.

The proportion of the Board's total case load allocated to unfair labor practice cases continues to mount year after year. Unfair labor practice charges which in 1965 constituted about 56% of the Board's incoming cases had risen to about 70% by 1976. The 34,509 unfair labor practice charges filed in 1976 were more than double the 15,933 filed ten years before. Of the unfair labor practice charges filed, 23,496 alleged violations by employers while 10,898 alleged unlawful conduct on the part of unions.[4] It is important to recognize that most unfair labor practice charges are filed by the parties as a bargaining tactic and are found by the Board to be without merit. The highest level of cases found to have merit was 36.6%, in 1966; in 1976, the percentage was 31.2%.[5]

The NLRB closed a total of 46,136 cases in 1976, of which 32,406 involved unfair labor practice charges.[6] The NLRB has concentrated its efforts on the voluntary disposition of unfair labor practice cases through its regional offices. In fiscal 1976, 27,588 such cases were closed in this manner, and only 3.2% of the unfair labor practice cases closed went to the five-man Board for decision as contested cases.[7]

The Extent of the Act's Coverage

Although the coverage of the Taft-Hartley Act is extremely broad, nevertheless certain employers, employees, and types of business are excluded from its application either by statutory definition or administrative determination.

Local Business. Under both the original Wagner Act and the Taft-Hartley Act, the NLRB was granted jurisdiction extending to any business "affecting commerce." Because of its limited budget, however, the Board has never exercised fully the powers granted to it by Congress. In 1950, 1954, and 1958, the Board laid down general standards intended to exclude "local businesses" from its jurisdiction. These standards, based upon sales volume and similar criteria, were intended to keep the Board from being inundated with a flood of cases involving small companies with relatively few employees.

The action of the Board in thus limiting its jurisdiction nullified in practice certain aspects of the protection which the act attempted to afford to small employers. For example, the Taft-Hartley Act makes it an unfair labor practice to coerce an employer or a self-employed person to join a union. Obviously, this provision is most meaningful in the case of small employers or self-employed persons working without hired help; yet the Board would not ordinarily take jurisdiction of such cases because

---

[4] Ibid., p. 11.

[5] Ibid., p. 13.

[6] Ibid., p. 9.

[7] Ibid.

the business involved would not normally meet the Board's jurisdictional requirements. To make matters worse, the U.S. Supreme Court held in a series of decisions that state labor relations boards had no power to act in cases involving interstate commerce where the National Labor Relations Board had refused to assert jurisdiction. The net result of NLRB policy and the Supreme Court's interpretation of the law was the creation of a no-man's-land in the field of labor relations where the small employer was without a forum to hear his case. This serious defect in the administration of the Taft-Hartley Act was not remedied until the passage of the Landrum-Griffin Act in 1959.

Supervisors. The Taft-Hartley Act made important changes in the definition of the word *employee,* as this term was used in the Wagner Act, with the result that supervisors were excluded from the protective coverage of the act. Under the Wagner Act the NLRB vacillated as to whether or not that act protected the right of supervisors to form unions and engage in collective bargaining, but it consistently held that the act protected supervisors as employees from discriminatory practices by employers. Under the Taft-Hartley Act, however, supervisors were deprived of both of these protections and were therefore compelled to rely solely on economic weapons to achieve their objectives. Supervisors could still join unions, but employers were free to use any means to intimidate and forestall such organization. In practice, the Taft-Hartley Act dealt unions of supervisors a hard blow. After its enactment, contracts of the Foreman's Association of America with the Ford Motor Company and other important firms were not renewed. However, the act has had little effect in printing and other industries in which it was customary to include foremen in unions of employees. In the years since the Taft-Hartley Act was passed, management has done much to upgrade foremen, so that some writers contend that the once controversial issue of excluding foremen from the protection of the act is now largely moot.[8]

Agricultural Workers. The term *employee* is defined in the act to exclude "any individual employed as an agricultural laborer." Therefore, no governmental protection is afforded to agricultural employees who may wish to form unions. In the late 1960s, Cesar Chavez made headlines with his United Farmworkers Organizing Committee (UFWOC) by using picketing, boycotts, and similar tactics to organize workers in the California grape and lettuce fields. Chavez's organizing activities focused attention on the glaring deficiencies in existing law as far as agricultural workers were concerned and gave rise to a demand for a new labor law to cover such workers. For example, UFWOC attempted to organize employees in the lettuce industry even though their employers had valid

---

[8] For a discussion of the effects of the act on foremen, see J. E. Moore, "The National Labor Relations Board and Supervisors," *Labor Law Journal,* vol. 21 (April 1970), pp. 190–205.

contracts with the Teamsters' Union. Growers found that they were caught in the cross fire between the two organizations with no means to determine the true wishes of the employees. Since UFWOC was not technically a labor organization as defined under the Taft-Hartley Act, it was not barred from utilizing the secondary boycott, secondary picketing, and other coercive tactics denied to conventional unions.

In 1975, California enacted landmark labor legislation covering agricultural workers and providing for a state-supervised system of elections by employees to determine bargaining representatives. The law did not, however, outlaw secondary boycotts. At present, bills are pending in Congress which would establish a separate labor law for agricultural employees or bring them under the coverage of the Taft-Hartley Act. One of the controversial issues delaying the passage of such legislation is the question of whether agricultural workers should be covered by the same secondary boycott provisions that apply to other workers subject to the Taft-Hartley Act. The UFWOC, which is now affiliated with the AFL–CIO, has argued that since it is in a formative stage of organization and opposed by employers hostile to unionization, it needs the secondary boycott to pressure those employers. On the other hand, secondary boycotts, by their very nature, pressure third parties and consumers, not the direct employer. Thus, the UFWOC boycotts have been aimed either at forcing supermarkets not to carry farm products produced on non-UFWOC-unionized farms or at inducing supermarkets to pressure farm operators to unionize their employees. The result is that the supermarkets, although having no dispute with their own employees, become embroiled in a far-off dispute and that consumers may be denied the opportunity to purchase what they desire.

Health Care Workers. The Taft-Hartley Act contained an exemption for employees of nonprofit hospitals. The growth of unions in this field in recent years led to the passage in 1974 of Public Law 93–360, which eliminated this exemption. The activity in this industry is attested by the fact that in fiscal 1976, 2,974 cases involving the health care industry were filed with the Board.[9]

In assuming jurisdiction over the health care industry, Congress preempted the field, and thus nullified in interstate commerce laws which several states had adopted to deal with hospital labor problems. As we shall note in Chapter 21, several of these laws provided for fact-finding and/or compulsory arbitration to settle hospital labor disputes. Whereas Congress might have permitted such legislation to continue to operate, thus enabling experimentation with different forms, it chose not to do so. An immediate effect was a long, costly hospital strike in New York City in 1976, which could have been avoided if the state law providing for arbitration had not been superseded.

---

[9] *Forty-First Annual Report of the NLRB*, p. 217.

Government Employees. The term *employer* in the law excludes "the United States or any wholly owned government corporation, or any Federal Reserve Bank, or any State or political subdivision thereof." Employees working for such employers are not covered by the act. Collective bargaining by government employees is a relatively new development; its present rapid development could not have been foreseen in 1947.

HOW THE EMPLOYER WAS AFFECTED

In form, the Taft-Hartley Act retained the five unfair labor practices specified in the Wagner Act; and therefore, to a casual reader, it might appear that the employer is still subject to the same restrictions as under the Wagner Act. Actually, however, newly added provisions in the law were intended to afford the employer important new freedoms.

Free Speech

The Taft-Hartley Act accepted in principle employers' complaints on the "free speech" issue. Under the original Wagner Act the employer was prohibited from interfering with employee organization activities. This was so construed that practically any opinion expressed by an employer against union organization was held to be an unfair labor practice. In the years immediately prior to the passage of the Taft-Hartley Act, however, the Board modified its views so as to permit some employer opinions to be stated in the interest of preserving the right of free speech. During the time of the Wagner Act, NLRB policy toward employer free speech went through three distinct phases:

> The first was characterized by the requirement that the employer maintain strict neutrality by remaining silent; the second, by the concession that the employer could express his antiunion views, so long as they were not accompanied by threats or promises, and so long as employees were not required to listen; and the third, by the refinement that the employer could make noncoercive antiunion speeches to compulsory audiences of his employees, provided that similar opportunities were afforded union representatives to express their views.[10]

The Taft-Hartley Act attempted to clarify employer rights of free speech by specifically providing in Section 8(c), that the expression of any views, arguments, or opinions could not be considered evidence of an unfair labor practice unless there was an actual threat of reprisal or force, or promise of benefit.

---

[10] Joseph Shister, Benjamin Aaron, and C. W. Summers (eds.), *Public Policy and Collective Bargaining*, Industrial Relations Research Association Publication No. 27 (New York: Harper & Row, 1962), p. 35.

The Board, however, has restricted the application of Section 8(c) by holding that it applies only to unfair labor practice cases and not to elections. With respect to the latter, the Board has adopted the concept that it has the responsibility to maintain "laboratory conditions" during an election, and if in its judgment such conditions have not been maintained, it will set aside the results of the election, whether or not the conduct complained of constituted an unfair labor practice. The result has been that neither employers nor unions can exercise as much freedom in campaigning for employee votes as they could during the Wagner Act period before Congress enacted legislation designed to guarantee their rights of free speech![11]

Appeals courts have tended to defer to the Board's judgment regarding the impact of campaign tactics on employee voting behavior because of the Board's supposed expertise in these matters. The fact is, however, that the Board has never attempted to determine empirically whether a particular course of conduct—by employers or unions—has a coercive effect and has preferred to rely on its own "reasonable judgment." As a consequence, some writers contend that the supposed expertise of the Board in this area is a fiction.[12]

Designation of the Union as Bargaining Agent through Authorization Cards

One of the most controversial issues of the Board's administration of the act involves its use of union authorization cards as a means of determining the collective bargaining representative. Under the Wagner Act the Board was authorized to hold secret ballot elections "or utilize any other suitable method" to determine the representative of the employees. The Taft-Hartley amendments deleted the quoted phrase, which led most management spokesmen to believe that the secret ballot election was the only permissible method of determining the bargaining representative. However, the Board maintains that in cases where the employer's unfair conduct has made the secret ballot a nullity, it is useless to hold a runoff election, since presumably the same unfair conduct will have vitiated the results of such an election. Therefore, the Board relies on authorization cards solicited by the union from employees in which employees are to indicate their consent to the union's acting as their bargaining representative.

Are authorization cards a valid indication of employee preference?

---

[11] R. E. Williams, P. A. Janus, and K. C. Huhn, *NLRB Regulation of Election Conduct,* Labor Relations and Public Policy Series, Report No. 8 (Philadelphia: Industrial Research Unit, The Wharton School, University of Pennsylvania, 1974), p. 10.

[12] Julius G. Getman and Stephen B. Goldberg, "The Myth of Labor Board Expertise," *University of Chicago Law Review,* vol. 39 (Summer 1972), p. 682.

The Fourth Circuit has declared that they are "inherently unreliable" and that "an employer could not help but doubt the results of a card check."[13] There seems to be little doubt that signature cards are inferior to an election and that employees frequently change their minds after signing an authorization card, the significance of which may not have been fully understood by them. The Board itself has expressed its reservations concerning authorization cards but, on the other hand, has felt that this device was necessary where a secret ballot could no longer reflect employee free choice because of unfair conduct on the part of the employer.

The Supreme Court in the *Gissel Packing* case[14] affirmed the Board's right to use authorization cards. The Court stated that use of a bargaining order based upon signature cards was appropriate:

1. In exceptional cases marked by outrageous and pervasive unfair labor practices of such a nature that their coercive effects cannot be eliminated by the application of traditional remedies.
2. In cases such as *Gissel Packing*, marked by less pervasive practices which nevertheless still have the tendency to undermine majority strength and impede the election process. The Board's use of cards in such instances is appropriate if there is a showing that at one point the union had a majority representation in the bargaining unit.

Suppose that a union offers to prove it has signed authorization cards from a majority of employees in the bargaining unit and asks for recognition as bargaining representative. What are the employer's options? In such a case, the employer may (1) extend voluntary recognition to the union so that the union becomes the uncertified bargaining agent for the employees; or (2) petition the Board for an election; or (3) do nothing. As long as the employer does not engage in unfair labor practices designed to undermine the position of the union, he can shift to the union the burden of petitioning for an election, and a bargaining order will not be issued by the Board.[15] This represents a change of position by the Board from earlier NLRB decisions which attempted to determine whether or not there was "good faith doubt" on the part of the employer as to the majority status of the union.

Although bargaining orders based on authorization cards represent only a minority of the representation cases handled by the Board,[16]

---

[13] *Logan Packing,* 66 LRRM 2596.

[14] *NLRB* v. *Gissel Packing Co.,* 395 U.S. 575 (1969).

[15] *Linden Lumber Co.* v. *NLRB,* 419 U.S. 301 (1974).

[16] During the period 1962–75, the Gissel-type remedy based on authorization cards accounted for only 2.2% of the total number of bargaining relationships established by the Board. See Douglas S. McDowell and Kenneth C. Huhn, *NLRB Remedies for Unfair Labor Practices,* Labor Relations and Public Policy Series, Report No. 12 (Philadelphia: Industrial Research Unit, The Wharton School, University of Pennsylvania, 1976), p. 202.

nevertheless they continue to be a source of criticism by employers. A frequently voiced complaint is that the bargaining order can give a union a second chance at winning representation even when it has been defeated in an election. In one recent case the union had secured only a bare majority of signatures to authorization cards—48 out of 94 employees—and then went on to lose an election by a vote of 50 to 42. Nevertheless, the U.S. Court of Appeals for the District of Columbia affirmed a Board order to the employer to bargain with the union because the company had made threats that the plant might have to close if the union won bargaining rights.[17]

Such a result can be justified only if the Board applies comparable standards to union organizers' efforts to obtain employee signatures to authorization cards and to employers' communications with employees prior to and during elections. The record suggests, however, that the NLRB has not done this, but instead has applied stricter standards to employer tactics during elections than to union tactics. Since 1969, not only have unions filed objections about employer tactics during elections almost twice as frequently as employers have filed objections against union tactics, but also the union success rate before the Board has been approximately three times that of employers.[18] Union polling of employees about how they will vote is held to be unobjectionable, but the same conduct by an employer will upset an election.[19] Likewise, employer visits to employee homes to urge them to reject the union are deemed inherently coercive, without regard to what is said, whereas union visits are unobjectionable as long as what is said is noncoercive.[20] Some movement toward a more equal standard is evidenced by a 1973 decision of the U.S. Supreme Court which overruled a long line of Board decisions and held that a union's offer to waive initiation fees for all employees who sign authorization cards interferes with the employee's right to refrain from union activity.[21]

The Board has been more concerned about employer threats and promises because in its view these are more likely to be carried out. It is also important, however, to recognize the pressure which can be applied to an employee by a union organizer who suggests that if the employee does not sign the card, and if the union wins, the employee will face a wrathful regime.

---

[17] *Amalgamated Clothing Workers of America* v. *NLRB; NLRB* v. *Jimmy Richard Co.*, C.A.D.C., Nos. 74–1608 and 74–1668 (December 8, 1975).

[18] John H. Smither, "Does the Goalpost Move When Employers Kick about Union Misconduct during Elections?" *Labor Law Journal*, vol. 25 (September 1974), p. 578. See also Williams et al., *NLRB Regulation*, for a detailed analysis of this situation.

[19] See *Springfield Discount*, 195 NLRB 57, 71 L C par. 23,897 (CA–7 1972).

[20] *Canton, Carp's Inc.* 127 NLRB 513 (1960).

[21] *Savair Manufacturing*, 95 S. Ct. 495 (1973).

Reinstatement

Section 10(c) of the act prohibited the Board from ordering reinstatement or back pay in any case where the discharge was made "for cause." The NLRB has continued to order reinstatement where circumstances warrant this remedy for workers illegally discharged. Unfortunately, there are still more violations of the act involving a discriminatory discharge by an employer than any other type of unfair labor practice. In the fiscal year ending June 30, 1976, the Board awarded back pay to 7,238 workers, amounting to $11.6 million;[22] 2,796 accepted reinstatement, about 67% of those offered this remedy.[23]

Union spokesmen complain that the remedial powers available to the Board to deal with unlawful discharge cases are wholly inadequate. It is unlikely that a hostile employer is dissuaded from firing a union organizer by the knowledge that two or three years in the future he may have to reinstate the worker with back pay plus 6%. Moreover, company opposition can make reinstatement an empty remedy. One study found that 55% of the employees reinstated had left their jobs within four months.[24] The NLRB has, however, concluded that it lacks statutory power to award compensatory or punitive damages.

Procedural Privileges

Employers were also granted important procedural rights. Whereas previously, employers could petition for an election only when confronted with demands for bargaining rights by two or more competing unions, they could now seek an election whenever a union made a demand for recognition. The grant of this privilege to the employer restrained premature claims of representation by unions attempting to organize a plant; for if the union failed to secure a majority vote in an election called by the employer, the act prohibited the holding of another election for 12 months. The right to request an election has frequently been utilized by employers. During the fiscal year ending June 30, 1976, employers petitioned for elections in 300 cases.[25]

Another important right provided in the Taft-Hartley Act is the privilege of suing unions in federal court for breach of contract. Section 301(a) of the act provides:

> Suits for violation of contracts between an employer and a labor organization representing employees in an industry affecting commerce as

---

[22] *Forty-First Annual Report of the NLRB*, p. 15.

[23] Ibid.

[24] E. C. Stephens and W. Chaney, "A Study of the Reinstatement Remedy under the National Labor Relations Act," *Labor Law Journal*, vol. 25 (January 1974), p. 36.

[25] *Forty-First Annual Report of the NLRB*, p. 230.

defined in this Act, or between any such labor organizations, may be brought in any district court of the United States having jurisdiction of the parties without respect to the amount in controversy or without regard to the citizenship of the parties.[26]

Furthermore, Section 303 of the act provides that whoever is injured in his business or property by reason of certain enumerated unfair labor practices of a labor organization may sue in federal district court "and shall recover the damages by him sustained and the cost of the suit." Contrary to the grim prognostications of union leaders, there has been no rush by employers to sue unions[27] in federal court.

One direct result of the inclusion of Section 301(a) in the Taft-Hartley Act has been an increase in the frequency of clauses in labor contracts protecting the union against financial liability in the event of unauthorized strikes. Contrary to expectations, however, there appears to have been no reduction in the frequency of no-strike clauses in labor agreements negotiated since enactment of the Taft-Hartley amendments.

Although the intent of Congress in including Section 301 may have been to provide a remedy for breaches of collective bargaining agreements, the courts have taken a broad view of the statutory language and have applied this section to union no-raiding agreements and to such intraunion matters as a breach of charter. Moreover, the Supreme Court has indicated that while retirement benefits due to retirees are not a mandatory subject for bargaining under the Taft-Hartley Act, retirees have a federal remedy under Section 301 for breach of contract if their benefits are changed unilaterally.[28]

Good-Faith Bargaining

It will be recalled that the Wagner Act provided that it was an unfair labor practice for an employer to refuse to bargain collectively with representatives of his employees. The statute did not set forth the requirements of bargaining in good faith, but the NLRB gradually developed a series of rules which, in the eyes of employers, erroneously interpreted the statute and required the employer to make counterproposals and thereby accede to union demands. The Taft-Hartley amendments added a new provision, Section 8(d), which defined the obligation to bargain and stated further that the obligation "does not compel either

---

[26] While Section 301(a) is considered above in connection with employer procedural rights, it should be noted that equal rights are accorded to unions to bring suits against employers.

[27] The Landrum-Griffin Act amendments to the Taft-Hartley Act broadened this provision so that today an employer can sue a union for damages sustained as the result of any activity or conduct defined as an unfair labor practice in Section 8(b)(4) of the Taft-Hartley Act, as amended.

[28] *Allied Chemical Workers* v. *Pittsburgh Plate Glass Co.,* 404 U.S. 157.

party to agree to a proposal or require the making of a concession." Despite this statutory instruction, the NLRB has nevertheless tended to view a refusal to make a counterproposal as evidence of bad faith.

A classic test of the meaning of the statutory language was posed by the 1960 case involving negotiations between the International Union of Electrical Workers and the General Electric Company. The company, in accordance with a long-standing policy which has become known as "Boulwarism,"[29] offered a complete package of benefits to the union and then, except for minor modifications, sought to stand by this offer. The IUE, after a short strike, finally signed a contract with GE, but then filed a charge with the NLRB alleging that the company had not bargained in good faith. Four and one-half years after the 1960 three-year agreement was signed and 18 months after GE, the IUE, and 100 other unions had peacefully arrived at successor three-year contracts, the NLRB ruled that GE was guilty of bargaining in bad faith![30]

In finding a violation of Section $8(a)(5)$ of the Taft-Hartley Act, the NLRB rested its conclusion upon an alleged "totality of conduct" by the company which in its opinion tended to "freeze" its bargaining stance, even though the company had admittedly made certain concessions from its first offer and even though the Board found that the company was at all times willing and anxious to sign a new contract. This case raised serious questions in the minds of employers, management consultants, and lawyers as to whether it is any longer possible for employers to engage in so-called tough bargaining with unions.

The Board has attempted to use the good-faith bargaining provisions of the act to compel a company to sign a contract containing a provision which it strongly objected to. In the *H. K. Porter* case,[31] the Board found that a company had failed to bargain in good faith when it refused to sign a contract containing a union dues checkoff. A subsequent hearing on this case before the circuit court raised the issue of whether the company could be forced to grant the checkoff clause, and the court held that the Board had the authority to order the company to do so. The NLRB then ordered the company to grant the checkoff. Such action is very close to compulsory arbitration. However, upon appeal, the U.S. Supreme Court held that the Board was without power to enter such an order.[32] The Court stated that although the Board did have the power to require

---

[29] See Herbert R. Northrup, *Boulwarism* (Ann Arbor, Mich.: Bureau of Industrial Relations, University of Michigan, 1964).

[30] *General Electric Co.*, 150 NLRB 192 (1964). The decision of the Board was subsequently upheld by the U.S. Circuit Court of Appeals, and the U.S. Supreme Court denied review (*NLRB* v. *General Electric Co.*, CA 2d [1969], 72 LRRM 2530, cert. denied U.S. Supreme Ct. [1970] 73 LRRM 2600).

[31] *NLRB* v. *H. K. Porter Company, Inc.*, 153 NLRB 1370 (1965), enf. 363 F.2d 272 (D.C. Cir., 1966).

[32] *H. K. Porter Company, Inc.* v. *NLRB*, 397 U.S. 99 (1970) reversing 414 F.2d 1123 (C.A.D.C.), enfg. 172 NLRB No. 72.

employers and unions to negotiate, it was without power to compel a company or a union to agree to any substantive contractual provision of a collective bargaining agreement.

Although the *H. K. Porter* case stands as a brake on the authority of the Board to write collective bargaining agreements for the parties, the line between dictating the substance of contracts and merely requiring the parties to negotiate is a fine one. Relying on the good-faith bargaining requirements of the act, the Board not only tells employers and unions when they must make concessions but has also set up a complicated set of rules governing what they can and cannot bargain about. First, the parties have a mandatory obligation to bargain about rates of pay, wages, hours, and other conditions of employment. This language has been broadly construed by the Board and the courts to include such matters as Christmas bonuses, employee stock purchase plans, and employee discounts on purchases of the employer's product.

Perhaps most significant is the fact that the U.S. Supreme Court supported the contention of the Board that a company had a mandatory obligation under the Taft-Hartley Act to bargain with union representatives concerning an economically motivated decision to subcontract work which had theretofore been performed by the employees in the bargaining unit. In the now-famous *Fibreboard Paper Products* case,[33] the Court affirmed the order of the Board requiring the company to resume the subcontracted operation and to reinstate the displaced employees with back pay. This decision was greeted with dismay by employers on the grounds that the requirement to bargain about what they considered to be vital management decisions with respect to operation of the business would result in endless delays and deprive business of flexibility in an era when change and prompt reaction to change were the keynotes of business. On the other hand, the Board contended that where subcontracting impinges upon work which the bargaining unit is qualified to do, the union should have an opportunity to discuss with the employer the proposed decision to give this work to others.

A distinction can be made between requiring an employer to bargain about the decision to subcontract and requiring him to bargain about the impact of such a decision. There is no question that legitimate union interests are involved in the latter case. In the former, however, except in rare instances of runaway shops, the issues are usually financial and managerial, and it is doubtful whether the union can contribute anything substantive in terms of alternatives to justify the delay and restriction of flexibility which the mandatory obligation imposes upon employers. Nevertheless, as the law now stands, employers have an obligation to bargain about the decision to subcontract, and in addition the Board

---

[33] *Fibreboard Paper Products Corp. v. NLRB,* 57 LRRM 2609, 379 U.S. 203 (1964).

has expanded its *Fibreboard* doctrine to require bargaining about a decision to automate and, in certain circumstances, about decisions to close down partial operations of a company. In a *General Motors Corp.*[34] case, however, a majority of the Board held that a decision to sell an enterprise is not a mandatory subject of bargaining under Section 8(a)(5).

A second class of bargaining subjects falls in a prohibited category. These are items, such as the closed shop, which Congress has declared contrary to public policy. Finally, there are matters which may be classified as "nonmandatory subjects," such as an employer demand that the union contract contain a clause calling for a prestrike secret vote of the employees as to the employer's last offer. The Supreme Court has held that the parties can talk about such subjects, but that if either party insists upon inclusion of such matters in a contract, it violates the good-faith bargaining requirement of the law![35]

The good-faith bargaining requirement of the Taft-Hartley Act has been the subject of so much litigation, has resulted in so many controversial decisions, and has caused so much delay in collective bargaining negotiations that employers, unions, and the Board alike agree that a change is desirable. As to what that change should be, however, there is no agreement. Many economists believe that the distinctions between mandatory and nonmandatory bargaining are satisfactory for the courtroom but not for the smoke-filled conference room, and that collective bargaining would benefit if the Section 8(a)(5) provision were scrapped. Employers would like to eliminate the power of the Board in this area, which they believe infringes on the right to manage their business. Employer opposition also stems from the fact that the Board has used this section of the law to require bargaining with a union even where it may have lost an election, as we observed in our earlier discussion.

On the other hand, unions and the Board are concerned by the fact that the simple order to bargain is not effective in compelling a truly recalcitrant employer to deal with the union, except after what may be years of litigation. Numerous study commissions have taken note of the inadequacy of the Board's power under Section 8(a)(5) and have observed that the resultant delays have frequently been injurious to the rights of employees. Some labor experts believe that new remedies need to be fashioned, such as making the benefits of a contract retroactive to the date of the first refusal of the employer to bargain in good faith. Likewise, in cases where employers have been found in violation of Section 8(a)(5) and have not agreed to the terms of a contract, unions have requested that the Board provide a remedy which would make their members whole for the wages and benefits which might have accrued if

---

[34] *General Motors Corp.* 191 NLRB 951, enf. 470 F.2d 422, 81 LRRM 2439 (D.C. Cir. 1972).

[35] *National Labor Relations Board* v. *Wooster Division of Borg-Warner Corp.,* 356 U.S. 342, 78 S. Ct. 718 (1958).

the employers had bargained in good faith. Both of these remedies would amount to compulsory arbitration, since the Board would be put in the position of writing a contract which the parties had never mutually agreed to. Thus far, the Board has declined to take such drastic action and has relied primarily on cease and desist orders.

HOW UNIONS WERE AFFECTED

Unfair Labor Practices

The Wagner Act sought to overcome the disparity of bargaining power between employers and employees which existed at the time of its enactment. Therefore, its restrictive provisions were all directed at employers, while unions were left free to engage in strikes, picketing, and various forms of coercion short of violence, in order to achieve organization of the workers. For this reason the Wagner Act was criticized as being a one-sided law. The Taft-Hartley Act was designed to remedy this one-sidedness. It proceeded on the assumption that substantial equality of bargaining power had been achieved and that therefore both union and management should be subject to similar prohibitions regarding unfair practices.[36] The bulk of unfair labor practice cases handled by the Board continue to be brought against employers, but a substantial number now involve complaints against unions. In the fiscal year ended June 30, 1976, a total of 10,898 unfair labor practice charges were filed against unions.[37]

The unfair labor practices to which unions are subject are six in number, enumerated in Section 8(b) of the act:

1. *Restraint or Coercion.* It was made an unfair labor practice for a union to restrain or coerce employees in the exercise of the rights guaranteed them in Section 7. That section guarantees employees the right to bargain collectively through representatives of their own choosing and also the right to refrain from such activity (except where a union shop has been authorized by law). Most of the unfair labor practice charges filed against unions involve alleged violations of Section 7. In fiscal 1976, 7,266 charges were filed alleging illegal restraint and coercion of employees by unions.[38] Among the union activities which have been found violative are mass picketing, the blocking of ingress to and egress from struck plants, and threatened physical violence toward employees. On the other hand, the Supreme Court, by a divided vote, sustained the Board's holding that a union did not violate Section 7 when it imposed and subsequently instituted court proceedings to enforce fines against

---

[36] Despite this change in emphasis, more than 80% of the Board's time under the Taft-Hartley Act has been spent in handling cases submitted by unions, not employers.

[37] *Forty-First Annual Report of the NLRB*, p. 11.

[38] Ibid.

members who crossed a lawful picket line in support of the union's authorized strike.[39]

2. *Illegal Demands for Union Security.* It was made an unfair labor practice for a union to cause an employer to discriminate against an employee for nonmembership in the union unless there was a union security contract with the employer which was recognized under the act. The closed shop was prohibited, even though both employer and employees were satisfied with its operation. This prohibition, if enforced, could have had far-reaching effects upon labor relations in view of the fact that prior to enactment of the Taft-Hartley law, in the neighborhood of 4.8 million employees worked under closed-shop arrangements.[40] However, on the whole, closed-shop industries have either ignored or circumvented the prohibition. This part of the law imposes no penalties and therefore is not brought into operation unless an individual employee charges an unfair labor practice.

A union-shop provision in a collective agreement was recognized under the act if the provision allowed at least 30 days after hiring before new employees were required to become members of the union. However, such a security provision could not be legally negotiated until the NLRB held a special election to determine the wishes of the majority of the employees in the bargaining unit with respect to the union shop. In October 1951, after a period of four years during which the NLRB held 46,146 union-shop elections, of which 97% authorized the union shop, the act was revised by the so-called Taft-Humphrey amendment so as to permit voluntary union-shop contracts without elections. However, even if a union and an employer agreed to a union-shop clause, its inclusion in a collective bargaining agreement was prohibited under the act if the particular state in which the business was located imposed more drastic conditions on union security clauses or forbade them entirely. Despite dire predictions by labor leaders, evidence is not clear that this provision of the act seriously weakened the labor movement, although it did accelerate the enactment of "right-to-work" laws by a number of states. As of September 1976, compulsory unionism was prohibited in 20 states.

As was pointed out in Chapter 6, the Taft-Hartley Act makes it illegal for a union or an employer to enforce a union security clause against anyone for any reason other than nonpayment of dues or initiation fees. The inclusion of this clause in the act is evidence of the concern of Congress that the union shop, by giving the union a monopoly of job opportunities in the particular establishment, might be used as a club to intimidate workers who disagreed with the policies of union officials.

3. *Refusal to Bargain.* It was made an unfair practice for a union to

---

[39] *NLRB* v. *Allis Chalmers Manufacturing Co.*, 338 U.S. 175.

[40] *Monthly Labor Review*, vol. 64 (May 1947), p. 766.

refuse to bargain collectively with an employer. This provision was apparently directed at those unions which had become so powerful that their "bargaining" activities consisted of presenting demands with a "take it or leave it" attitude. It is doubtful, however, whether this provision has brought about any change of attitude by unions in negotiations, since the act makes it clear that the obligation to bargain in good faith does not compel a union (or an employer) to "agree to a proposal or require the making of a concession." Furthermore, union bargaining by ultimatum seems to have been sanctioned by the NLRB under certain circumstances, yet denied to employers. (See *General Electric* case, above.)

For example, in one case,[41] the Board held that the union involved did not refuse to bargain in good faith by giving the employer an ultimatum backed by a strike threat to sign certain contract proposals immediately, without any further opportunity to consult with its bargaining agent. The ultimatum was the culmination of protracted bargaining which had extended over a period of five months and had resulted in an impasse.

4. *Illegal Strikes and Boycotts.* Section 8(b)(4) of the act made it an unfair labor practice for a union to engage in or to encourage any strike[42] or refusal by employees to use, manufacture, transport, work, or handle goods if an object of such action were one of the following:

a. To require an employer or self-employed person to join a union or an employer organization. The purpose of this clause was to prevent unions from forcing independent businessmen, such as plumbers and bakery deliverymen, to join a union. Congress believed that the economic independence of these groups should be protected, even though their hours of work and their earnings might affect the standards of employees who worked for hire in the same occupation.

b. To force the employer or any other person to cease dealing in the products of another employer or to cease doing business with any other person. This clause was directed at the so-called secondary boycott. If employees in plant A strike to compel employer A to grant higher wages or to grant a union shop, this involves direct action against the employer primarily involved in the dispute; but if the employees, having a grievance against employer A, picket or induce a strike in company B, which uses the products of plant A, then a secondary boycott or secondary action is involved. Congress not only made the secondary boycott an unfair labor practice, but it also directed the NLRB to seek federal court injunctions against its continuance under certain circumstances, and furthermore, it authorized damage suits to be brought in federal courts by employers against unions which engaged in secondary

---

[41] *Lumber and Sawmill Workers' Union,* 47 LRRM 1287.

[42] The act defined "strike" to include a concerted stoppage or slowdown.

boycotts. Congress thus condemned secondary boycotts because they unduly widened the area of industrial disputes by interrupting the operations of employers only remotely connected with the chief cause of the controversy.

Congress may also have been concerned about the secondary boycott because it had become a potent weapon in the hands of strong labor unions to force union membership on unwilling employees. Since the national labor policy now stated that employees should have the right to join or to refrain from joining a union (unless there was a compulsory union-shop provision in effect), it is not surprising that Congress found it necessary to restrict boycotts in order to make employee rights of self-determination effective.

Union leaders objected vehemently to these provisions of the act. They pointed out that the act even outlawed such traditional union action as a concerted refusal to handle "scab" products made in a nonunion shop or in a shop in which a strike was in progress. Even where one nonunion employer threatened the working standards of an otherwise fully organized industry, a refusal on the part of employees in the organized plants to handle or process goods intended for or coming from the nonunion plant would violate the act.

While it is clear from the foregoing discussion that the Taft-Hartley Act effectively curtailed many forms of union secondary boycott activity, nevertheless it also left major loopholes. For example, the act did not expressly forbid boycott action applied through inducement of employees individually, or through supervisors, or through employees of railroads, municipalities, and governmental agencies. Another loophole resulted from NLRB rulings on "hot cargo" agreements. After some vacillation the Board held that "hot cargo" agreements could validly be included in collective bargaining agreements and presumably could be enforced by appropriate court action. The fact that they were sanctioned as a subject of collective bargaining and were included in contracts enforceable in law strengthened the hands of unions in making secondary boycott action effective.

One of the most difficult problems arising in connection with the ban on secondary boycotts was the determination of where primary action ended and secondary action began. For example, if a picket line around plant A in which a labor dispute existed prevented drivers from employer B from entering and picking up merchandise, was the picket line unlawful because of its effect on employees of employer B? The NLRB has answered no, since the strike against A is privileged activity, and the repercussions on B are only incidental. But suppose that the primary dispute is with a trucking company. Can the employees of that company picket the trucks they are loading and unloading on the premises of employer A? This raises the question of the so-called ambulatory situs—the trucks are in a sense an extension of the employer's business site. The Board has ruled that such picketing is permissible where it is confined to one employer and conducted at the only place where the union could picket effectively.[43]

In the subsequent *Moore Drydock* case,[44] the Board developed a set of standards in which picketing of the secondary employer's premises is permissible if:

1. The picketing is strictly limited to times when the *situs* of dispute is located on the secondary employer's premises.
2. At the time of the picketing the primary employer is engaged in his normal business at the situs.
3. The picketing is limited to places reasonably close to the location of the *situs*.
4. The picketing discloses clearly that the dispute is with the primary employer.[45]

These standards sought to balance the conflicting interests of the union and the neutral employer. However, in subsequent decisions the Board has seemed to move away from the *Moore* standards and has permitted secondary picketing under circumstances seemingly in conflict with the *Moore* doctrine.[46]

Another situation in which the line between primary and secondary action is blurred is the so-called common situs problem, which has been a major source of friction in the construction industry, where it is customary for a general contractor and various subcontractors to work on the same premises. Suppose that employees of the general contractor or union subcontractors picket the premises in protest over another subcontractor's use of nonunion labor. Under the Board and court interpretations of Section 8(b)(4)(A), such action has been held to be a secondary boycott. It is not surprising that the building-trades unions are the most frequent users of the secondary boycott technique. For the fiscal year 1976, NLRB records show that 1,694 secondary boycott charges were filed with the Board.[47] Unions in the building and construction field were involved in a large number of such complaints. The building-trades unions contend that no secondary boycott action is involved because there is really only one employer—the general contractor—and because all of his subcontractors are so related to him by the nature of the work

---

[43] *Schultz Refrigerated Service, Inc.,* 87 NLRB 502 (1949).

[44] *Sailor's Union* (Moore Drydock Co.), 92 NLRB 547 (1950).

[45] 92 NLRB at 549.

[46] For a discussion of this subject, see Ralph M. Dereshinsky, *The NLRB and Secondary Boycotts,* Labor Relations and Public Policy Series, Report No. 4 (Philadelphia: Industrial Research Unit, The Wharton School, University of Pennsylvania, 1972), particularly pp. 5–49.

[47] *Forty-First Annual Report of the NLRB,* p. 208.

that the concept of a "neutral employer" in this situation is unrealistic. In *NLRB* v. *Denver Building Trades Council*,[48] the Supreme Court held in effect that the general contractor on a jobsite was a neutral in the labor disputes of the nonunion subcontractor to whom he had subcontracted part of the total job. The building-trades unions sought to overturn this decision through congressional action, and finally, after 25 years of effort, succeeded in getting Congress to enact a so-called common situs bill which exempted most large construction projects from the restraints imposed by this section of the Taft-Hartley law, and could have otherwise greatly expanded the picketing rights of the powerful construction unions. President Ford, however, vetoed the bill.

c. To force or require an employer (including the employer of the strikers) to recognize or bargain with one union if another union is the certified bargaining agent, or to force another employer (not the employer of the strikers) to recognize an uncertified union. This clause was intended to protect employers from strikes by an uncertified union, aimed at compelling the employer to deal with it rather than with another union already certified. Under the Wagner Act, many companies found themselves in a disastrous dilemma as a result of rivalry between CIO and AFL unions. If the employer yielded to the pressure of the uncertified union, he violated the Wagner Act and was subject to sanctions for so doing. If he did not yield, his business could be destroyed. He could get no injunction or court relief against the picketing because of the anti-injunction provisions of the Norris–La Guardia Act. The dilemma to the employees was as real. Because they had exercised their right of free choice, they stood to lose their jobs through the efforts of the union which they had rejected.

The attempts on the part of unions to nullify the right of workers to join unions of their own choosing were indefensible and completely at variance with the basic principles of the Wagner Act. Such activities were also, of course, part of the basic conflict between the principle of exclusive jurisdiction upon which American unionism had been built and the principle of self-determined organization which the Wagner Act made law.

The Taft-Hartley Act made such strikes illegal and made it mandatory for the NLRB to seek injunctive relief in the courts, if, after a preliminary investigation, there was reason to believe that the union was engaging in a strike prohibited by this section.

d. To force or require an employer to assign particular work to employees in one union or craft rather than to employees in another union or craft. This clause was intended to outlaw the so-called jurisdictional strike. Such strikes, growing out of controversies as to which craft had the right to perform a particular job, were particularly common in

---

[48] 341 U.S. 675 (1950).

the construction industry and evoked widespread public criticism. As a direct result of the enactment of the Taft-Hartley law, the building-trades unions set up machinery to adjust jurisdictional disputes among the various crafts.

A union which engaged in any of the activities banned in the above four situations committed an unfair labor practice and rendered itself liable in damages to anyone whose business or property was injured as a result of the strike. Moreover, when a charge was filed alleging that a union was engaging in activities under *a*, *b*, or *c* above, it was made mandatory that the Board seek an injunction against the union, if the Board had reasonable cause to believe that the charge was true. In the case of jurisdictional disputes, however, the Board had to hear and decide such cases itself unless, within ten days after a charge was filed, the parties agreed to voluntary adjustment. The mandatory injunction provision mentioned above did not apply to jurisdictional disputes, but the NLRB could seek an injunction in situations where such relief was appropriate.

In the fiscal year ended June 30, 1976, injunctions were granted in 11 cases involving jurisdictional disputes, most of them in the building and construction industry.[49] It is obvious from this record that the machinery set up by the building trades to handle their disputes is not fully effective.

Although the Board has often been attacked for injecting itself into the substance of collective bargaining, it religiously refrained from making determinations of work assignments in jurisdictional dispute cases coming before it. In 1961, however, in the *Columbia Broadcasting* case,[50] which involved a dispute between a union of television technicians and a union of stage employees over which union would control the work of providing electric lighting for television shows, the Supreme Court held that the NLRB could not "duck" this responsibility imposed upon it by Congress and that it must make an affirmative award of disputed work in such cases. The assumption by the Board of the role of arbiter in such disputes will add pressure on unions to settle such controversies through their own dispute machinery.

5. *Excessive Initiation Fees.* It was made an unfair labor practice for a union which had a union-shop agreement to charge membership fees in an amount which the Board found excessive or discriminatory under all the circumstances. In a number of cases, the Board has ordered a union to reduce its admission fees, but the total effect of this provision has been minor.

6. *Featherbedding.* It was made an unfair labor practice for a union

---

[49] *Forty-First Annual Report of the NLRB*, p. 173.

[50] *National Labor Relations Board* v. *Radio and Television Broadcast Engineers' Union*, 364 U.S. 573, 81 S. Ct. 330 (1961).

to "cause or attempt to cause an employer to pay or deliver or agree to pay or deliver any money or other thing of value, in the nature of an exaction, for services which are not performed or not to be performed." This clause is sometimes referred to as the "antifeatherbedding" provision, and as noted in Chapter 6, it has resulted in some successful NLRB restrictions against payment where no work is performed. If, however, some work is performed in return for the compensation—even though it is mere standing around during a recorded broadcast—then the statutory requirement of "services which are not performed" is not satisfied, and the provision is not applicable. Thus, the Supreme Court ruled that the practice of the International Typographical Union in requiring pay for setting so-called bogus type which is not used and the practice of the American Federation of Musicians of requiring pay for "standby orchestras" when outside bands play in local theaters were both lawful under this provision.

Loyalty Affidavit

One of the provisions of the act which initially provoked much controversy, but today attracts little attention, was directed at Communist officers who exercised positions of power in a few American unions. Section 9(b) of the act disqualified a labor organization both as a bargaining agent and as a complainant under the act unless there was on file with the Board an affidavit executed by each officer of the local and the parent international union affirming that such officer was not a member of the Communist party. This provision strengthened the hand of non-Communist elements in unions and helped to pave the way for the decline of Communist influence in the American labor movement.

Miscellaneous Regulations Applicable to Unions

The act required unions to file various reports showing officer salaries, initiation fees, constitutions, and bylaws. These provisions were subsequently repealed by the Landrum-Griffin Act, which imposed more rigorous requirements. The act also made it unlawful for any labor organization to make a contribution or expenditure in connection with any election to any federal political office. The prohibition as to contributions corresponded to a similar prohibition applicable to corporations under the Corrupt Practices Act. The act also sought to impose some restrictions on the administration of union health and welfare funds. Section 302 of the act permitted welfare funds maintained by employer contributions only when the payments were held in trust and the fund was administered jointly by employer and employee representatives, with neutral persons available to settle possible disputes. Subsequent investigations of corruption and mismanagement in the administration of funds of this type led to enactment of the Teller Act in 1958, the Landrum-Griffin Act in 1959, and sections of the Employee Retirement Income Security Act in 1974.

HOW THE INDIVIDUAL WORKER WAS AFFECTED

A major objective claimed by the framers of the Taft-Hartley Act was to protect individual employees from the arbitrary power wielded by some labor leaders. Consequently, a number of important new privileges were granted to employees, with corresponding limitations on unions, on the theory that the actions of the latter have not always been truly representative of the will of the workers in the collective bargaining unit.

Elections

The Taft-Hartley Act made a number of important changes in election procedure. Under the original Wagner Act procedure, if two or more unions were on the ballot in an election to choose a bargaining representative, the employees voting in a "runoff" election did not have an opportunity to cast a negative vote (that is, "no union") in the runoff, unless the no-union choice had received a plurality of votes cast in the first election. In other words, the employees were limited in the runoff election to a choice between two unions, even though one of these unions might have run in third place. Later the NLRB changed this procedure by requiring the two highest choices to be placed on the runoff ballot, so that the no-union choice could appear on the runoff ballot even if it had not received a plurality of votes in the first election. The Taft-Hartley Act made this procedure a matter of law.

The act also gave employees the right to seek elections to decertify a bargaining representative which no longer represented the majority of workers. In decertification elections held under the act, the bargaining representative has been decertified in about two out of every three elections, indicating that in many cases unions in the course of time cease to represent the will of the workers.

Representation elections still require a major portion of the Board's time. In fiscal 1976, the Board conducted 8,632 secret ballot representation elections.[51] Table 19–1 indicates how the number of elections held annually has risen steadily over the years, while the percentage won by unions has tended to decline.

The Taft-Hartley Act also made an important change in the rule governing the right of employees on strike to vote in representation

---

[51] *Forty-First Annual Report of the NLRB*, p. 236.

TABLE 19-1
Results of NLRB Representation Elections,
Selected Years, 1936–1976

Fiscal Year	Total Elections	Percent Won by Unions
1936	31	81
1940	1,192	77
1945	4,919	83
1950	5,619	74
1955	4,215	68
1960	6,380	59
1965	7,576	61
1967	7,882	60
1970	8,074	55
1974	8,368	51
1975	8,061	50
1976	8,638	48

Source: National Labor Relations Board data.

elections. Under the Wagner Act the Board had ruled that in a strike caused by employer unfair labor practices, only strikers were eligible to vote, since they were entitled to reinstatement; whereas in a strike over economic issues, both replacements and strikers were eligible to vote. The Taft-Hartley Act, however, contained a specific provision that "employees on strike who are not entitled to reinstatement shall not be eligible to vote." In an economic strike the employer has the legal right to fill the jobs of strikers with permanent replacements. Therefore, in an economic strike, strikers who are replaced could lose the right to vote in a representation election. This provision was attacked by union spokesmen, who claimed that it would enable antiunion employers to provoke a strike, recruit nonunion replacements, and then call for an election. The strikebreakers could elect "representatives," which would bar an independent, effective union from calling an election for a year, or they might vote for decertification of the existing union. This provision was amended by the Landrum-Griffin Act, as explained in Chapter 20.

Ban on the Compulsory Checkoff

The act prohibited the compulsory checkoff, the method by which union dues are deducted by the employer from the worker's wages and paid directly to the union treasury. The checkoff of membership dues was made lawful only where individual employees executed a written assignment of wages for not longer than one year or for the duration of the applicable union contract, whichever was shorter.

Bargaining Unit Problems

Under the Taft-Hartley Act, as under the Wagner Act, the NLRB continued to be vested with authority to determine the appropriate bargaining unit. This authority, however, was limited in the case of professional employees, craft workers, and guards.

Craft-Industrial Problems.   As we have noted in our discussion of the Wagner Act, one of the most difficult problems faced by the NLRB was the contest between AFL and CIO unions as to whether the appropriate bargaining unit should be a craft or an industrial unit. Congress, of course, had been concerned primarily with the question of whether employees wanted *any* union to represent them, rather than with the question of *which* union. This highly explosive issue was dumped into the lap of the NLRB with little statutory guidance to assist it in its determination. Section 9(*b*) of the Wagner Act simply directed the Board to "decide in each case whether, in order to insure to employees the full benefit of their right to self-organization, and otherwise to effectuate the policies of the Act, the unit appropriate for the purposes of collective bargaining shall be the employer unit, craft unit, plant unit, or subdivision thereof."

In making such determinations, the NLRB found that it had to weigh and balance two often conflicting objectives of labor policy: self-determination and stability in industrial relations. Self-determination, which favored craft severance, could, if carried to an extreme, result in the fragmentation of collective bargaining into a myriad of small, ineffective units. Moreover, it raised the problems of multiplicity of negotiations, more jurisdictional disputes, and the possible weakening of industrial unions. On the other hand, the policy of stability, which was frequently synonymous with favored treatment for industrial unions, could mean that individual crafts would be submerged in a large union without regard to their peculiar problems. Moreover, preference for larger industrial unions could lead to dissatisfaction among substantial groups of employees within the union.

The Board wrestled with this problem throughout the Wagner Act period. In the early years, it tended to favor large industrial unions as most conducive to effective collective bargaining. Then, in 1937, this trend was reversed, and the *Globe* doctrine[52] evolved, which in most instances allowed craftworkers in initial representation elections to determine whether they wanted to be in a plantwide union or to have separate craft unions. The Board was for a time more reluctant to allow craft severance where craftworkers had already been included in a large

---

[52] The *Globe* doctrine, which involves the principle of self-determination by a particular group of employees as to their bargaining unit, is so called because it was first enunciated in the case of the *Globe Machine and Stamping Co.*, 3 NLRB 294 (1937).

industrial union; but in 1942 the Board's policy shifted, and severance was permitted where a "true" craft was involved.

However, the Board's policies on bargaining units did not satisfy either the CIO or the AFL. The Taft-Hartley Act sought to settle this issue by writing into law the restriction that the Board might not decide that a craft unit was inappropriate on the ground that an industrial unit had already been established by a prior Board determination, unless a majority of employees in the proposed craft unit voted against the craft unit.

Under its present practice, the Board now considers all relevant factors to determine a severance issue, such as whether the employees sought are skilled journeymen craftsmen or constitute a functionally distinct department; the bargaining history of the plant and the industry; the extent to which the employees have established or maintained their separate identity; the integration of the production process; and the qualifications of the union seeking severance.[53]

The Extent of the Bargaining Unit. The power of the Board to determine the appropriate bargaining unit can have a material effect upon the ability of unions to organize the unit in question. Generally, the smaller the unit, the easier it is for the union to obtain a majority of the employees, but fragmentation of bargaining units would create a difficult problem for employers, who might find that they have to bargain with many different unions in a multiunit organization. In both the retail industry and the insurance industry, the Board originally opted for wider geographic units, but under present practice in the retail chain store field the Board will find the individual store to be the appropriate unit where there is substantial autonomy in each store and no material interchange of employees. Similarly in the insurance field, the Board has moved in the direction of holding the district office, rather than a statewide unit, to be appropriate for bargaining purposes.[54] With respect to the private health care industry, the Board in May 1975 issued decisions in eight cases which established guidelines for appropriate units for collective bargaining. The Board has concluded that the basic appropriate units in health care institutions should include all registered nurses as a separate unit, with all other professionals in a different unit.[55]

Since the determination of the appropriate bargaining unit is a typical kind of administrative decision involving the application of expertise, the Board can exercise wide discretion in its weighing of the relevant issues and can obviously consider the impact of the unit determination on collective bargaining, as long as the extent to which

---

[53] These criteria were enunciated in *Mallinckrodt Chemical Works,* 64 LRRM 1011.

[54] *Metropolitan Life Insurance Co.,* 56 NLRB 1635.

[55] *Mercy Hospitals of Sacramento,* 217 NLRB 131, p. 58.

employees have organized is not controlling. The power of the Board in this area is particularly impressive because it is normally not subject to court review. Although Section 10 of the act provides for court review in the case of any person "aggrieved by a final order of the Board," the Supreme Court has decided that certifications of a bargaining agent are not "final orders" in this sense and therefore cannot be appealed to the courts.[56] Normally, the only way an employer can obtain judicial review of an NLRB order in an election case is to refuse to bargain with the union certified by the Board. When the union brings an unfair labor practice charge, the NLRB's order to bargain can be appealed, and at such time the certification of the bargaining agent and the record of the election are subject to review by the court. However, this process is not open to a union that wishes to challenge an election ruling.

Discrimination against Minority Groups

The extent to which the NLRB should involve itself in attempting to curb discrimination on the basis of race or sex has become the subject of increasing litigation and controversy under the act. The Taft-Hartley Act does not expressly refer to racial or sexual discrimination, and indeed, it is doubtful whether Congress had this problem in mind in 1947. Section $8(a)(3)$ does provide that an employer is not justified in discriminating against an employee for nonmembership in a labor organization if he has reasonable grounds for believing that such membership was not available to the employee on the same terms and conditions generally applicable to other members. At first glance, this appears to mean that a union-shop contract cannot be applied to black employees unless blacks are fully and equally admitted with whites to union membership. Section $8(b)(1)$, however, provides that a union shall have the right to prescribe its own rules with respect to the acquisition or retention of membership. Moreover, the Senate-House Conference Report expressly declared that the act did not disturb arrangements in which blacks were relegated to an auxiliary local.[57]

For many years the Taft-Hartley Act had little or no effect upon discrimination against blacks practiced by unions or employers. As public opinion focused more and more on this problem, however, the NLRB gradually evolved a set of doctrines to deal with this problem, either in terms of an unfair labor practice or as a consideration in election procedures.

---

[56] If, however, a Board certification violates an express provision of the statute, for example, by improperly grouping together professional and nonprofessional employees in the same bargaining unit, the courts will set aside the action of the Board (*Leedom* v. *Kyne*, 358 U.S. 184, 79 S. Ct. 180 [1958]).

[57] Any other interpretation would have alienated southern Democrats who were among the act's most ardent supporters.

1. *Unfair Labor Practices.*   Under the Miranda doctrine,[58] the Board has held that a labor organization, when acting as an exclusive bargaining agent, has an obligation to refrain from taking any "unfair" action against employees in matters affecting their employment. A white local which fails to process a black employee's grievance[59] violates this doctrine, as does a union which establishes separate all-white and all-black locals and divides the work unfairly. In a recent case the Board has extended the doctrine to discrimination on the basis of sex. In *Pacific Maritime Association*[60] the Board found that the Longshoremen and Warehousemen's Union breached its duty of fair representation by denying women the use of its dispatch facilities on the basis of their sex. Employers who practiced racial discrimination have also been found guilty of unfair labor practices under the act. The relationship between the grant of an exclusive bargaining power to a union and its duty to represent all employees fairly is perhaps more understandable than the relationship between the employer's duty not to discriminate to deter unionization and his obligation to treat all races equally. Nevertheless, a federal court has found the latter obligation consistent with the purposes of the act because racial discrimination would create industrial unrest and induce apathy on the part of minority employees which would deter them from asserting their full rights under the act.[61] If this interpretation is sustained by the Supreme Court, the Board could become the focal point for a flood of cases alleging that employers are parties to racial discrimination, despite the fact that Congress has provided another remedy for such cases under Title VII of the Civil Rights Act of 1964. (See Chapter 23.)

Suppose that black employees in a union believe they are being subjected to discriminatory racial employment practices and that the union will not act to eliminate such conditions. Can such employees picket the employer in their off-duty hours in an effort to deal directly with the employer concerning their grievances? The answer is no. The Supreme Court has held that the Taft-Hartley Act does not protect concerted activity by minority employees seeking to bargain directly with their employer over such grievances because such activity abridges the authority of the exclusive union bargaining agent. The Court has held that minority employees would have to seek a remedy under Title VII of the Civil Rights Act.[62]

2. *Election and Certification.*   The Board has held that it cannot

---

[58] *Miranda Fuel Co.*, 51 LRRM 1584 (1962).

[59] *Metal Workers Union* (Hughes Tool), 56 LRRM 1289 (1964).

[60] *Pacific Maritime Association*, 85 LRRM 1389 (1974).

[61] *United Packinghouse, Food, and Allied Workers* v. *NLRB*, 70 LRRM 2489 (D.C. Cir., February 7, 1969).

[62] *Emporium Capwell Co.* v. *Western Addition Community Organization*, 420 U.S. 50 (1975).

constitutionally certify a union shown to be engaging in unlawful racial discrimination, but it will not investigate allegations of such discrimination until after an election has been held and the union involved has received a majority of the votes.[63] Once the union has been certified as the bargaining agent, proof that it discriminates on the basis of race is a sufficient defense by an employer against a bargaining order and can lead to its loss of certification. Oddly enough, the Board has ruled that sex discrimination is not sufficient to justify withholding a bargaining order from a union and must be raised in an unfair labor practice proceeding based on an allegation that the union had breached its duty of fair representation.[64]

Other Procedural Safeguards

Among other important rights given to individual employees to strengthen their positions relative to the union was the power to sue the union for damages resulting from an illegal strike. Also, the employee was given the right to present grievances directly to his or her employer and to have such grievances adjusted without the intervention of the union representative. The adjustment could not be inconsistent with the terms of the collective bargaining agreement, and the union was given the right to have its representative present at the adjustment.

HOW THE PUBLIC WAS AFFECTED

One of the major reasons for enactment of the Taft-Hartley Act was the general recognition of the public and lawmakers that some means had to be devised to protect the community from stoppages of the flow of essential commodities and services, such as characterized the wave of strikes in 1946. The Wagner Act itself had contained no prohibition against strikes of any kind; instead, it provided a peaceful alternative to the costly strikes which had been fought over the denial of basic rights of union recognition. In 1937, 60% of the workers on strike were involved in organizational disputes; in 1945, only 22%.[65] Thus, the Wagner Act was successful in reducing this particular form of work stoppage. At the same time, however, strikes over economic issues—wages, hours, and working conditions—increased in importance. Moreover, industrywide bargaining led to walkouts involving an entire industry instead of merely one plant. Thus, the same number of strikes in 1946 as in 1937 produced four times as many man-days lost in the later year. The Taft-Hartley Act attempted by a number of procedures and pro-

---

[63] *Bekins Moving and Storage Company of Florida, Inc.*, 211 NLRB 7, 86 LRRM 1323 (1974).

[64] *Bell and Howell Co.*, 213 NLRB 79, 87 LRRM 1172 (1974).

[65] National Labor Relations Board, *Eleventh Annual Report* (Washington, D.C.: Government Printing Office, 1946), p. 2, n. 1.

hibitions to narrow and restrict the use of the strike weapon by organized labor.

Prohibited Strikes

Certain types of strikes deemed unduly oppressive to employers and the public were outlawed. These have been considered earlier in the chapter. They included secondary strikes and boycotts, jurisdictional disputes, and strikes to upset the certification of a rival union. Under the act, any person injured in his business or property as a result of such unlawful strikes may bring suit for damages against the offending union.

Strikes against the federal government were likewise forbidden, and any individual employed by the United States who went on strike was subject to immediate discharge and loss of civil service status. We shall discuss this section in Chapter 22.

Strikes called in violation of no-strike clauses in collective bargaining agreements were not prohibited, but the act provided a procedure whereby the union could be sued by the employer in federal court for damages due to breach of contract. It was hoped that by facilitating the bringing of suits against unions, the act would make for stricter observance of such clauses and thus lessen the number of work stoppages.

National Emergency Strikes

Finally, the Taft-Hartley Act established procedures to govern so-called national emergency strikes. These procedures, which are discussed in Chapter 21, do not forbid such strikes, but merely provide for their postponement.

APPRAISAL OF THE TAFT-HARLEY ACT

Whether the Taft-Hartley Act is a "good" or a "bad" law depends in large measure upon the standard by which it is judged. If it is deemed desirable to afford greater freedom and privileges of self-determination to the individual worker, then it would seem that the act constituted a rather hesitant advance in labor legislation. On the other hand, if one believes that progressive social policy requires strengthening labor organizations on the theory that all but a few unions are still at a disadvantage in bargaining with employers, then the various restrictions imposed upon the activities of unions appear less desirable.

Standards, therefore, affect one's view of the act, and such standards frequently reflect the social bias of the individual. However, one standard is at hand which lends itself to a fairly objective appraisal. That standard is the extent to which the act facilitated the process of effective collective bargaining.

Ways in Which the Act Encouraged Effective
Collective Bargaining

Effective collective bargaining may be defined as bargaining which in general represents the will of the majority of workers. The decertification procedure provided by the Taft-Hartley Act enabled employees to rid themselves of a union which because of corrupt leadership or other causes no longer represented the majority of workers. Likewise, the Communist affidavit requirements may have served to lessen industrial disputes which reflected, not the bona fide grievances of workers, but rather the intrigues of Communist officials. The prohibition against the closed shop and restrictions on the union shop were intended to eliminate such practices as the selling of jobs through the issuance of work permits, which benefited the union bosses rather than the union membership, but these provisions were largely ineffective.

Effective collective bargaining also assumes a balance of power between labor and management. Under the Wagner Act, however, the balance of power in some industries had been so turned in labor's favor that individual employers had no choice but to accept the union's demands. The Taft-Hartley Act sought to remedy this situation by imposing an obligation to bargain upon both the union and the employer. On the premise that effective collective bargaining requires responsible parties to the agreement, the act made unions subject to court actions for breach of contract. This premise, however, ignored the fact that sound industrial relations are not built by running to the courts. Furthermore, as we have already observed in the prior discussion, the plethora of Board and Court decisions on what constitutes good-faith bargaining has probably been detrimental to the establishment of sound voluntary bargaining relations.

Effective collective bargaining assumes that the democratic privilege of self-determination of wages, hours, and working conditions will be reasonably exercised so as not to inconvenience the public by widespread work stoppages. Such union devices as the secondary boycott, jurisdictional strikes, and industrywide strikes in essential industries unnecessarily burden the public. Therefore, the Taft-Hartley Act narrowed the use of the strike weapon within limits deemed consistent with the public interest.

Ways in Which the Act Impeded Effective
Collective Bargaining

The act enabled employers to delay the peaceful determination of a bargaining representative through the NLRB machinery and therefore encouraged unions to strike to obtain recognition. An employer could delay an election for the certification of a bargaining representative by charging the union with unfair labor practices, and since most organizing campaigns usually involve some "high-pressure" salesmanship by union advocates, a prima facie case of coercion frequently could be made. On the other hand, recent NLRB rulings restrict the employer's right of free speech.

The act was intended to restore the balance of power in collective bargaining relations. But Congress had in mind the circumstances which existed in highly organized industries, without fully recognizing that in some areas, organization was still in an incipient state and that in such areas the act gave an antiunion employer power to prevent the emergence of effective collective bargaining. Particularly potent in this respect were the provisions which guaranteed the employer "free speech" and enabled him to sue a union in federal court (and thus weaken it financially) and to charge it with unfair labor practices in organizing. Under other provisions of the act an employer could provoke a walkout over economic issues and then be free to replace the strikers with nonunion men. The act stated that strikers could not vote in an election, but strikebreakers were given this privilege. Antiunion employers could thus use a strike over wages to change the bargaining representative in their plants. Again, recent administration of the act has realtered this power balance, and in particular, has left small employers with little recourse to resist large unions.

The Taft-Hartley Act represented a step in the direction of government dictation of the content of collective bargaining agreements. The act told employers and unions what they could and what they could not include in contracts with respect to welfare plans, union security clauses, and checkoff dues. While this approach is probably unavoidable if the act's purpose of protecting employees is to be made effective, in the long run this trend may prove detrimental to the continuation of voluntary collective bargaining. As we shall see in the next chapter, the Landrum-Griffin Act takes an even bigger step in this direction and subjects the internal affairs of union organizations to governmental regulation.

Effect of the Act on the Growth of Union Organization

There is no question that the rate of union growth has slowed in recent years and that from 1947 to the present, contrary to experience in prior years, unions have grown at a slower rate than has the labor force. It is doubtful whether the blame for labor's organizing woes can be put on the Taft-Hartley Act, although labor leaders find this legislation a convenient excuse for lack of progress. As we observed in Chapter 2, it seems likely that more fundamental developments may be responsible for the decline of union membership, among them the shift in employment from manufacturing to service industries; the tremendous growth in white-collar employment; the geographic shift of industry to the Midwest and the South, where public opinion has been more hostile to union organization than in other sections; the lack of aggressive union leadership; and the increasing difficulty of union organization now that most large companies are organized and that unions must seek new members in the smaller companies.

Criticism of Administration of the Act by the NLRB

Many critics of our present labor policy have aimed their attack, not against the Taft-Hartley Act, but rather against the manner in which the NLRB has administered it. It should be recognized that the NLRB is more than an administrative body carrying out the mandate of Congress. It is also a policymaking body, and almost necessarily so; for the Taft-Hartley Act merely sets forth rules in general terms, and it is the function of the Board to amplify this language so that it is applicable to the multitude of diverse cases which are presented to it for decision.

In recent years the Board has been subject to sharp attack by management spokesmen for alleged bias in favor of labor. The record shows that various Board decisions have restricted management prerogatives and favored unions in a number of critical areas:

1. Blunting restrictions on union tactical weapons, such as the picket line.
2. Restricting employer counterweapons, such as employer free speech.
3. Defining the bargaining unit to facilitate organizing efforts of unions.
4. Relying on card checks as opposed to secret ballot elections in cases where employers have been accused of unfair labor practices.
5. Restricting management prerogatives in such areas as subcontracting.

Although it is true that the Board seems to have tipped the balance in favor of organized labor in these areas, it is also true that, in general, the Board's views on these controversial issues have been upheld by the U.S. Supreme Court.

There is no question that the composition of the Board, as changed by presidential appointments from time to time, has made a difference in its attitude toward labor and management. In some ways, this makes the evolution of labor policy more responsive to changing public attitudes, as evidenced by changing national administrations. On the other hand, Board members are called upon to carry out quasi-judicial functions, and therefore many critics contend that they should be appointed for life so that they are not subject to political influences.

The lack of regard for *stare decisis* by the Board has made it difficult for management and labor leaders alike to make policy decisions with any assurance that these will comply with what the Board considers lawful practice. Many lawyers argue that if the Board wishes to change a long-standing policy, it should do so by utilizing the process of the Administrative Procedures Act, which requires due notice and an opportunity to argue the merits of the new policy. The Board, on the contrary, simply uses a particular case as a vehicle to change its policy, which can be obviously unfair to the participants in that case.

Suggestions for Reform

Proposals for changing both the act and the Board have been forthcoming in increasing numbers in recent years from labor, management, members of the bar, labor economists, and members of the NLRB itself. Many of the suggested reform measures make a distinction between the two basic functions of the Board. The first is the determination—by secret ballot elections—and occasionally by card checks—whether employees in an appropriate bargaining unit wish to have unions represent them in collective bargaining negotiations with employers. This is a typical administrative function in which the Board has developed considerable expertise. The Board conducts about 9,000 elections every year, and most are run without incident. Since its inception, the NLRB has conducted more than 200,000 elections in which approximately 27 million voters have cast their ballots for or against representation. Today about four out of every five elections are conducted on an amicable basis by agreement between the employer and the union.

Although the Board's decisions on appropriate bargaining units have frequently been attacked and its use of card checks rather than secret ballot elections in limited cases has aroused the ire of employers, the fact remains that it has handled the overall election procedure with reasonable efficiency. The median time from the filing of a representation petition to the date of the election has averaged about 49 days—certainly a creditable performance for an administrative agency. By contrast, in unfair labor practice cases, the median time from the filing of a charge to the date of the Board decision has averaged 332 days.[66] It is doubtful whether a labor court would improve on the Board's performance in representation matters, but the Board could certainly reduce the number of time-consuming postelection protests by formulating some clear-cut rules and by permitting the parties wider latitude to express their views in preelection activities.[67]

A second function of the Board is to prevent and to remedy unfair labor practices, whether committed by unions or by employers. It is in this area that the Board is particularly vulnerable. The accusation has continually been made that the Board, with a membership which changes with shifts in political power on the national scene, cannot be judicial; yet

---

[66] Betty S. Murphy, "The First Eight Months: An Overview," in *Labor Law Developments, 1976,* 22d Annual Institute, Southwestern Legal Foundation, Dallas, Texas, 1976 (New York: Matthew Bender, 1976), p. 120.

[67] See Williams et al., *NLRB Regulation.*

in the unfair labor practice area, it must make what are in effect judicial decisions. Suggestions for reform run the gamut from forming a labor court to giving the federal courts jurisdiction over unfair labor practice cases.[68]

Justice must be timely, or it is not justice. This aphorism is as true in labor relations as it is in the courts of law. Reinstatement which comes three years later to an employee who has been wrongfully discharged may be an empty victory. Yet in Section $8(a)(3)$ unfair labor practice discharge cases, the median number of days between the filing of the charge and the issuance of a circuit court enforcement order has been about 855![69]

Union spokesmen argue that the best way to expedite the handling of unfair labor practice cases is to reduce the case load and that this will happen only when the Board is given the power to assess penalties which are stringent enough to deter unfair labor practices on the part of employers. The AFL–CIO, for example, recommends that the Board should have the power to disqualify from federal government contracts or orders employers who deliberately and repeatedly violate the act. At this writing, a bill (H.R. 8409) has been introduced in Congress under which employers whose NLRA violations fall within the bill's coverage would be barred from federal contract awards for three years. Such legislation suffers from overkill; unfortunately, enforcement of the bill's sanctions woud penalize innocent employees, as well as the employer, by limiting employment opportunities. Moreover, there is considerable doubt that stricter penalties would speed up NLRB processes or alter the conduct of the parties.[70]

Another frequent suggestion is that the Board be given power to grant injunctive relief. At present, if a party violates a Board order, the Board must seek to enforce the order in a federal court of appeals. It is at this stage that the longest delays occur, since on the average an additional 396 days are required before a court of appeals renders its decision in such cases.[71]

In January 1976, a blue-ribbon task force of 27 members, nominated from the ranks of labor, management, the academic community, and agency officials, was sworn in to conduct a two-year study of NLRB procedures. It is to be hoped that the task force will not conclude that

---

[68] Fritz Lyne, "The National Labor Relations Board and Suggested Alternatives," *Labor Law Journal*, vol. 23 (July 1971), p. 411.

[69] Charles J. Morris, "The Need for New and Coherent Regulatory Mechanisms," in Richard L. Rowan (ed.), *Collective Bargaining: Survival in the 70's?* (Philadelphia: Industrial Research Unit, The Wharton School, University of Pennsylvania, 1972), p. 44.

[70] See McDowell and Huhn, *NLRB Remedies*, Chapter 16, for a thorough discussion of these points.

[71] *Harvard Law Review*, vol. 84 (1971), pp. 1670, 1673.

current problems in the administration of the act can be solved by the invention of new—and more severe—penalties. The result of such action may well be to produce even more protracted litigation than now exists. The real need is not for new remedies but for more certainty in the application of the law. Much of the delay in the disposition of unfair labor practice and representation cases is attributable to uncertainty as to the limits of legal conduct by the parties. The greatest contribution that could be made to the effective and speedy application of the act would be the clear enunciation by the Board of the rules and criteria applicable in areas of labor law which are at present clothed in confusing verbiage and doubt.

QUESTIONS FOR DISCUSSION

1. What is meant by the term *unfair labor practice?* How are charges of unfair labor practices handled by the NLRB? How does the Taft-Hartley Act differ from the Wagner Act in its approach toward unfair labor practices?

2. What is meant by "mandatory" and "nonmandatory" subjects of collective bargaining? Give examples of each. Does this distinction make sense in practical collective bargaining? Do you think that the "good-faith" bargaining provisions of the Taft-Hartley Act should be repealed?

3. In what way have recent decisions by the NLRB tended to facilitate union organization? Is this action consistent with the statutory purposes set forth in the Taft-Hartley Act?

4. Discuss the actual and potential effects of the Taft-Hartley Act upon collective bargaining.

5. In what respects, if any, do you think the Taft-Hartley Act should be changed? How would you implement your decision?

SUGGESTIONS FOR FURTHER READING

Getman, Julius G.; Goldberg, Stephen B.; and Herman, Jeanne B. *Union Representation Elections: Law and Reality.* New York: Russell Sage Foundation, 1976.

> A critical analysis questioning and testing some of the basic assumptions underlying the NLRB decisions concerning permissible conduct during union organizing campaigns.

McDowell, Douglas S., and Huhn, Kenneth C. *NLRB Remedies for Unfair Labor Practices.* Labor Relations and Public Policy Series, Report No. 12. Philadelphia: Industrial Research Unit, The Wharton School, University of Pennsylvania, 1976.

> An analysis of the problems involved in the NLRB's application of remedies for unfair labor practices.

Morris, Charles J. (ed.) *The Developing Labor Law.* Washington, D.C.: Bureau of National Affairs, Inc., 1971, with annual supplements.

The most comprehensive review of NLRB and related statute case law, kept up-to-date by annual supplementary volumes.

Murphy, Betty S. "The NLRB in Its Fortieth Year," *Labor Law Journal*, vol. 26 (September 1975), pp. 551–58.

A review of the Board's accomplishments and of the principal problems facing it, by its present chairman.

National Labor Relations Board. *Annual Reports*. Washington, D.C.: Government Printing Office.

The annual reports of the Board, covering operations of the fiscal year ended June 30, are excellent sources for statistics, as well as providing a summary of action taken by the NLRB on key issues.

Swift, Robert A. *The NLRB and Management Decision Making*. Labor Relations and Public Policy Series, Report No. 9. Philadelphia: Industrial Research Unit, The Wharton School, University of Pennsylvania, 1974.

An analysis of the manner in which the NLRB has impacted management decision making in four areas: subcontracting, automation, relocation, and plant closure.

Williams, Robert E., et al. *NLRB Regulation of Election Conduct*, Labor Relations and Public Policy Series, Report No. 8. Philadelphia: Industrial Research Unit, The Wharton School, University of Pennsylvania, 1974.

A detailed analysis of the NLRB policies and standards for setting aside representation elections based on postelection objections.

20

The Landrum-Griffin Act

IN THE PRECEDING CHAPTERS, we have seen how the role of law and government has evolved in the field of union-management relations. The Norris–La Guardia Act was essentially laissez-faire in attitude. The purpose of the statute was to prevent law—in the form of the court injunction—from interfering with union-management relations. Then came the Wagner Act, in which the force of law was used to assist organized labor. Government power was committed to protect the right to organize and to restrict employer interference with that right. Union tactics were left virtually unregulated. As a result of its favored position, organized labor grew so strong that abuses developed, and the need was recognized for restrictions on the power of unions. The Taft-Hartley Act was passed, with government now placed in the role of policing certain actions of both labor and management. However, abuses in the internal administration of unions continued to come to light. Since much of the power wielded by unions over individual workers stems from union monopoly over job opportunities provided under both the Wagner and the Taft-Hartley acts, government has felt a responsibility to safeguard the rights of individual union members. As a result, the conduct of internal union affairs has come to be viewed as a federal problem.

The regulation of internal union procedures is a major purpose of the Labor-Management Reporting and Disclosure Act of 1959, more popularly known as the Landrum-Griffin Act. Passage of this law marked the culmination of the well-publicized hearings of the Senate Select Committee on Improper Activities in the Labor or Management Field (McClellan Committee), which revealed that many union officials were guilty of coercion, violence, and the denial of basic rights to union members; that small employers were being victimized through the use of secondary boycotts, extortion, picketing, and similar techniques; and that employers were guilty of interfering with employee rights through the use of "sweetheart" contracts and the bribery of union officials by hired consultants.

THE SCOPE AND COVERAGE OF THE ACT

The Landrum-Griffin Act comprises seven different sections, called "titles," each of which deals with a different phase of the act's coverage. Title I contains a bill of rights for members of labor organizations. Title II requires unions and employers to file various reports with the Secretary of Labor. Title III requires unions to file reports relating to so-called trusteeships over other labor organizations. Title IV contains detailed provisions with respect to the term of office of union officials, election procedures, and procedures for the removal of union officers. Title V contains provisions relating to the fiduciary responsibility of union officials, requires the bonding of such officials, prohibits loans by unions to employees of such organizations resulting in a total indebtedness in excess of $2,000, and prohibits certain classes of persons with records of crime or Communist affiliation from holding union office. Title VI contains a number of miscellaneous provisions, among them a prohibition against extortionate picketing and a grant of power to the Secretary of Labor to investigate violations of the act. Title VII contains a number of amendments to the Taft-Hartley Act relating to federal-state jurisdiction, the voting rights of economic strikers, and secondary boycotts and recognition picketing.

The act grants to the Secretary of Labor broad powers to investigate possible violations of the law and to institute appropriate civil or criminal action. This authorization does not, however, apply to the bill-of-rights section or to the amendments of the Taft-Hartley Act. In the case of violations of the former section, union members must bring their own civil actions in the U.S. district courts. As to the latter category, enforcement is the responsibility of the National Labor Relations Board. A special office—now called the Labor-Management Services Administration—was established in the U.S. Department of Labor to handle the day-to-day administration of the act. In 1974, this office reported that 53,486 annual reports of labor organizations were on file pursuant to the requirements of the act.[1]

Like its predecessor, the Taft-Hartley Act, the Landrum-Griffin Act relates to employers and labor organizations in industries "affecting commerce." However, the scope of the Landrum-Griffin Act is broadened

---

[1] U.S. Department of Labor, Labor-Management Services Administration, *Compliance, Enforcement, and Reporting in 1974 under the Labor-Management Reporting and Disclosure Act* (Washington, D.C.: Government Printing Office, 1975), p. 25.

by the fact that many of its provisions are applicable to employees and employers covered by the Railway Labor Act, who were expressly excluded from the Taft-Hartley provisions. The definition of "employer" includes anyone considered an employer under any federal law. The definition is thus the most comprehensive to be found in federal law.

HOW THE EMPLOYER WAS AFFECTED

The Landrum-Griffin Act imposes new obligations as well as new benefits upon employers.

Restrictions on Employers

Although the McClellan Committee devoted most of its attention to abuses of labor organizations, it uncovered a number of examples of malpractice by employers in their dealings with employees and unions. Thus, some companies paid union officials in order to obtain so-called sweetheart contracts, which permitted the continuation of substandard working conditions; or companies conspired with officials of a "friendly" union to permit organizing of the company's workers to the exclusion of other, more belligerent unions. The committee also found evidence that some companies were interfering with the rights of employees to organize by using so-called labor consultants. The committee noted that the Taft-Hartley Act could not deal effectively with such activity because the NLRB had no power to act against independent contractors serving as labor consultants.

Title II of the Landrum-Griffin Act requires employers to file annual reports with the Secretary of Labor disclosing payments and loans to unions, union officers, shop stewards, and employees of unions. The reporting requirement applies to payments and loans, whether direct or indirect, whether in cash or other things of value, but excludes deductions of union dues pursuant to a checkoff and certain other classes of "valid" employer payments. Other subsections require reports by employers of payments to employees, employee committees, or labor consultants which might affect the free choice of employees to exercise their right to organize and bargain collectively. In addition, Title V of the law expands Section 302 of the Taft-Hartley Act by broadening the types of payments which are criminal offenses.

Benefits of the Landrum-Griffin Act to Employers

Although the reporting requirements of the Landrum-Griffin Act are onerous to employers already burdened by the reporting requirements of many other federal agencies, nevertheless the benefits to employers conferred by the new law far outweigh the disadvantages.

Despite some weakening of the provisions of the act by NLRB and court decisions, the sections of the act further restricting secondary boycotts and organizational picketing by unions are of substantial importance to employers. So also are the sections aimed at eliminating the so-called no-man's-land in NLRB jurisdiction.

Restrictions on Union Secondary Boycotts

We observed in the preceding chapter that although the Taft-Hartley Act purported to outlaw secondary boycotts, many loopholes developed in practice. Thus, if a Teamster business agent attempted to persuade X's employees not to handle the goods manufactured by Y, this was unlawful; yet the Taft-Hartley Act did not prohibit the business agent from warning X directly that he had better not handle Y's product! Likewise, the Taft-Hartley Act permitted boycott action applied through inducement of employees individually, instead of in concert, and inducement of employees of railroads, municipalities, and governmental agencies. The Landrum-Griffin Act closed all of these loopholes.

Under the Taft-Hartley Act, it was common practice for unions to induce employers to sign collective bargaining agreements which contained a so-called hot cargo clause. In accepting this provision, the employer agreed that his employees would not handle the goods of anyone with whom the union was having a labor dispute. The Landrum-Griffin Act makes it an unfair labor practice for any labor organization and any employer to enter into such agreements. Two exceptions are provided in the statute; agreements in the construction industry relating to the contracting or subcontracting of work done at the construction site and agreements relating to jobbers, subcontractors, and the like in the apparel and clothing industry.

The legislative history of the act suggests that Congress, in providing an exemption for the construction industry, intended to permit agreements in which, for example, a union agreed with a general contractor that the latter would not employ nonunion subcontractors on the job. It is doubtful whether there was any intent to legalize efforts by unions to bar the use of prefabricated materials at a construction site. Nevertheless, in a much-criticized decision,[2] in which four justices dissented, the U.S. Supreme Court has held that an agreement with a general contractor forbidding union members from handling premachined doors on the construction site was not unlawful and was permitted under the construction industry exemption. Both the NLRB and the Supreme Court held that the clause in question had work preservation as its

---

[2] *Brotherhood of Carpenters and Joiners* (National Woodwork Manufacturers Association) 149 NLRB 646 (1964) rev'd in part 354 F2d 594 (7 Cir. 1965), rev'd in part 386 U.S. 612 (1967).

object and that therefore the enforcement of the contract was primary, rather than secondary, in its effect. This case established the "work-preservation" doctrine as the main criterion for determining the legality or illegality of activity under Section 8(e).

Two other rules are also relevant in determining the legality of product boycotts in the construction industry. The first involves the concept of "medium of transmission." Suppose that an employer has signed a hot cargo agreement with a union providing that employees do not have to handle products made or distributed by nonunion workers. If the union calls on the employer to comply with the contract, such action is deemed lawful, but if the union appeals to employees not to handle the product, that action is unlawful![3] A second doctrine involves the concept of "right of control." Suppose that a union attempts to pressure an employer to stop using preassembled products on the jobsite. If the employer has the right to specify other materials, the dispute is viewed as primary, since the employer has the "right of control." This is frequently the case where the dispute is with the general contractor. If, however, a subcontractor is involved who by reason of his contract with the general contractor must use certain specified materials, then the union dispute is really with the third party—the general contractor. Therefore, the union action is deemed secondary, and is unlawful.[4]

It is obvious from the foregoing discussion that the efforts by Congress to close secondary boycott loopholes have again failed. Product boycotts still remain a potent factor in the construction industry and have contributed to the high cost of union construction projects which has resulted in a slowdown of activity in a vital industry and high unemployment among union members.

The effect of statutory restrictions against secondary boycotts has also been weakened by interpretations of the Board and the courts of the so-called publicity proviso. This proviso appears in the amended Section 8(b)(4) of the National Labor Relations Act after an enumeration of prohibitions on various forms of strikes and boycotts. The proviso states:

> Provided further, that for the purposes of this paragraph (4) only, nothing contained in such paragraph shall be construed to prohibit publicity, other than picketing, for the purpose of truthfully advising the public, including consumers and members of a labor organization, that a product or products are produced by an employer with whom the labor organization has a primary dispute and are distributed by another employer, as long as such publicity does not have the effect of inducing any in-

---

[3] See *NLRB* v. *Carpenters and Joiners Local 1976*, 113 NLRB 123 (1955), 241 F2d 147 (1957), 357 U.S. 93 (1959).

[4] For an excellent discussion of these cases, see M. J. Fox, Jr., R. H. C. Even, and J. G. Hamilton, "Product Boycotts in the Construction Industry and the NLRB 'Right-of-Control' Doctrine," *Labor Law Journal*, vol. 27 (April 1976), pp. 230–44.

dividual employed by any person other than the primary employer in the course of his employment to refuse to pick up, deliver, or transport any goods, or not to perform any services, at the establishment of the employer engaged in such distribution.

Since the above-mentioned proviso specifically excludes "picketing" from protected union activity, it was generally assumed that picketing in connection with secondary boycott action was unlawful even when directed to the public. However, in a decision handed down by a divided Court, the Supreme Court has indicated that this is not so. In the case before the Court, a Teamsters' union, which had a primary dispute with an organization of fruit packers, set up picket lines in front of retail stores which sold fruit purchased from the packers. The picket signs advised consumers not to buy the fruit because it was nonunion. Pickets were instructed not to patrol delivery entrances or exits, and other precautions were taken not to interfere with the flow of merchandise in and out of the stores. No employees stopped work, and deliveries were not affected. Nevertheless, the NLRB found that the union action was unlawful secondary boycott action intended to force the stores to cease doing business with the packers. However, when the case reached the Supreme Court, the Court reversed the Board and held that so-called consumer picketing at neutral stores for the purpose of persuading customers to cease buying *products* of a struck primary employer does not violate the law, even though it may cause economic loss to the stores of the neutral third party.[5] The Court concluded that Congress had not intended to ban all consumer picketing and that it was necessary to distinguish between a union appeal to the public not to trade with the secondary employer (presumably unlawful) and what the Court found existed in the present case—a union appeal to the public not to buy the merchandise of the primary employer.

Although the *Tree Fruits* decision was greeted with dismay by management spokesmen, who argued that it emasculated the proviso of Section 8(b)(4), the loophole so opened has been a narrow one and has been restricted by subsequent decisions. Nevertheless, if an identifiable consumer product is involved and the issues elicit strong support from the labor movement generally, a product boycott can bring even a large corporation to its knees where normal organizing attempts have failed. In 1974, the Amalgamated Clothing Workers of America organized the Farah Manufacturing Company, one of the nation's largest men's and boys' slacks manufacturers, as a result of a boycott, even though it had been previously unable to shut down a single company plant with pickets during a 20-month organizing struggle. As a result of the boycott conducted at retail stores, Farah sales dropped nearly 25% in 1973, resulting in an $8 million loss.[6]

---

[5] *National Labor Relations Board* v. *Fruit Packers Local 760*, 377 U.S. 58 (1964).

[6] *Business Week*, April 6, 1974, p. 63.

The success of the boycott in the Farah case has caused concern among other southern nonunion plants that unions now have an effective way of forcing union recognition outside the law. They argue that although the boycott with attendant picketing is supposedly informational and aimed at consumers, in actual fact it carries an implied threat of trouble and harassment to retailers who continue to carry the boycotted product, and therefore comes close to an illegal secondary boycott involving neutrals in a labor dispute.

In June 1976, the Amalgamated Clothing and Textile Workers Union, newly created from the merger of the Amalgamated Clothing Workers and the Textile Workers Union, launched a major national boycott against the J. P. Stevens Company, the second largest textile manufacturer in the United States. This corporation has fought union organization over a long period of years and has been found 15 times to have committed various unfair labor practices.[7] Although the AFL-CIO has pledged its support in the boycott effort, the boycott will be more difficult to implement against Stevens than it was against Farah. The latter sells consumer products and is therefore vulnerable to a consumer boycott. Stevens, however, sells the bulk of its products as intermediate goods to other manufacturers. Under present law, the union cannot lawfully urge the public not to buy finished goods of another manufacturer simply because they contain certain Stevens materials.

Restrictions on Picketing

Although the Landrum-Griffin amendments were intended to tighten the restrictions on secondary boycotts, it appears that the new language contains its own "loopholes." The same can be said of the Landrum-Griffin restrictions on picketing. The act makes extortionate picketing —picketing intended to "shake down" an employer for the personal profit of a union agent rather than for the benefit of employees—a federal offense. Furthermore, in perhaps the most controversial section of the law, major restrictions are imposed upon recognition and organizational picketing. The act makes it an unfair labor practice for a labor organization to picket or threaten to picket an employer where an object thereof is forcing or requiring an employer to recognize or bargain with a labor organization as the representative of his employees, or forcing or requiring the employees of an employer to accept or select such labor organization as their collective bargaining representative, unless such labor organization is currently certified as the representative of such employees, under any of the following circumstances:

> (A) Where an employer has lawfully recognized another union and the question of representation may not be legally raised at this time.

---

[7] *Business Week,* June 14, 1976, p. 28.

(B)   Where a Taft-Hartley Act election has been held within the past 12 months.

(C)   Where the picketing has been conducted without a petition for a representation election being filed within a reasonable period of time, not to exceed 30 days from commencement of the picketing.

The application of these provisions is made subject to a so-called consumer picketing proviso, which has been the source of much controversy. It states, in substance, that nothing in subparagraph (C), quoted above,

> ... shall be construed to prohibit any picketing or other publicity for the purpose of truthfully advising the public (including consumers) that an employer does not employ members of, or have a contract with, a labor organization, unless an effect of such picketing is to induce any individual employed by any other person in the course of his employment, not to pick up, deliver or transport any goods or not to perform any services.

The scope and meaning of these provisions are by no means clear, and a definitive interpretation of the foregoing language must await determination by the Supreme Court. Meanwhile, the National Labor Relations Board, in a series of influential decisions, has laid down these guidelines, based upon its construction of the statutory language:

1. *Informational Picketing.* If the sole object of the picketing is to inform the public, and recognition of the union is not an objective of the picketing, the picketing is lawful and is not barred by any of the subsections enumerated above. Furthermore, even if such picketing interferes with deliveries or pickups, it is lawful nonetheless.[8]

2. *Dual-Purpose Picketing.* A picket line frequently has as its purpose both informing the public and securing recognition by an employer. Such picketing is presumably unlawful where the circumstances set out in subsections (A) and (B) above prevail. If (A) or (B) is not applicable, such picketing is entitled to the protection of the proviso to subsection (C) unless it interferes with deliveries and so forth.[9] The NLRB has further held that mere isolated interferences with deliveries are not enough to make the picketing illegal. Despite the fact that the consumer picketing proviso expressly refers to "*an* effect" and "*any* individual" (italics added), the NLRB has read the language as if Congress were concerned only with a "substantial" effect and has held that there is a violation of the law only if picketing has "disrupted, interfered with or curtailed the employer's business."[10]

3. *Recognition Picketing.* Picketing intended to compel the employer to recognize the union as the bargaining representative for his employees is subject to the prohibitions of subsection (C), and the picketing will be enjoined if it continues more than 30 days without

---

[8] *Crown Cafeteria,* 49 LRRM 1648, reversing 47 LRRM 1321 (1962).

[9] Ibid.

[10] *Barker Bros. Corp. and Gold's, Inc.,* 51 LRRM 1053 (1962).

the filing of a petition for an election. The Board has held, however, that so-called union standards picketing is not recognition picketing. Therefore, even if an employer has signed a contract with another certified labor organization, it is not unlawful, according to the NLRB, for another union to picket where the signs carried by the pickets merely state that the employer pays wages lower than the standards set by the picketing union, and there is no attempt by the union to obtain recognition from the employer.[11]

It is apparent from the foregoing brief outline that the NLRB has greatly narrowed the scope of the restrictive provisions contained in the Landrum-Griffin Act as they apply to picketing. Many of the key decisions have been handed down by a divided Board. The application of the statute is obviously not clear to the members of the Board, and it is even more uncertain to the average union member. Gone are the simple days when the Norris–La Guardia Act granted automatic immunity to such action. By contrast, a union leader who today determines to place a picket line around a plant needs a lawyer at his side to guide him. The legality of the picketing may depend upon the wording of the placards which the pickets carry and how people react to them. It may depend upon the relationship between the employer and the union, between the employer and a rival union, or between the employer and other employers with whom the union has a dispute. Most of all, the lawfulness of the picket line may hinge upon what the NLRB interprets the objective and purpose of the picket line to be.[12] To the average laboring man, such examination of motives and objectives seems like a return to the old doctrine of lawful and unlawful objectives, motives, and other mystical criteria which courts found so convenient in the past to justify injunctions against union activity.

Elimination of the Jurisdictional No-Man's-Land

Another important employer benefit conferred by the Landrum-Griffin Act is the elimination of the so-called no-man's-land created by the refusal of the National Labor Relations Board to assert jurisdiction over

---

[11] *Claude Everett Construction Co.,* 49 LRRM 1757 (1962).

[12] The *Crown Cafeteria* case is a good illustration of how subjective judgments —which reflect the particular bias of the Board member or judge—now determine the lawfulness or unlawfulness of a picket line. In that case a union picketed a new cafeteria which had refused to hire through a union hiring hall or to sign a contract. The picket signs were addressed to "members of organized labor and their friends," stated that the cafeteria was "nonunion," and asked them not to patronize it. No stoppage of deliveries or services took place. In its first hearing of this case, a majority of the NLRB concluded that despite what was said on the signs, the picketing was really conducted for recognition purposes and was therefore not protected by the consumer picketing proviso (47 LRRM 1321). Subsequently, two new members were appointed to the Board, and upon reconsideration of the case the Kennedy Board held that the picketing was lawful because it was conducted merely to advise the public and caused no stoppages (49 LRRM 1648).

certain labor disputes which did not meet its jurisdictional standards. Under the Taft-Hartley Act the NLRB found that it had neither the time nor the money required to handle the great number of labor disputes involving small employers; it therefore imposed certain jurisdictional limitations on itself, stating in effect that it would not become involved in a dispute if the employer's sales volume was less than a certain prescribed figure. But when the small employer then went to the state court for relief, the U.S. Supreme Court ruled that the state court had no right to hear the case if the NLRB *could* have taken jurisdiction, even if it *did* not! As a consequence, small employers were denied a forum to give them relief from coercive union tactics, even though their larger competitors were protected by the NLRB.

The Landrum-Griffin Act seeks to solve this problem by amending the Taft-Hartley Act so as to permit the states to assert jurisdiction over labor disputes in interstate commerce over which the NLRB declines to take jurisdiction. The law authorizes the NLRB to decline to assert jurisdiction over any labor disputes which it determines would have only a slight impact upon interstate commerce, but it cannot reduce its jurisdiction below the standards prevailing on August 1, 1959. The Board is free, of course, to expand its jurisdiction at any time. The states have always had jurisdiction over labor disputes in intrastate commerce and over cases involving violence, mass picketing, or other coercive conduct. This jurisdiction has now been broadened to include cases in interstate commerce which formerly fell in the "no-man's-land" area.

Although the Landrum-Griffin Act appears to have eliminated the question of conflicting jurisdiction over cases of labor disputes, it does not necessarily follow that either management or labor will find that turning these problems back to the states is wholly satisfactory. At this writing, only 25 states and Puerto Rico have comprehensive codes regulating labor relations. In the remaining states, parties excluded from the protection of the Taft-Hartley Act by reason of the Board's jurisdictional standards do not have recourse to comprehensive labor laws governing labor-management relations. In such cases, these excluded parties will have to rely upon common-law doctrines or their own economic power. The small businessman and the weak union are thus still penalized by lack of size. This problem can be met only by the enactment of labor relations laws in all of the states or by a major expansion of the personnel of the NLRB so as to enable that agency to enlarge its jurisdiction. Neither of these possibilities appears to be very likely at this time.

HOW UNIONS WERE AFFECTED

The Landrum-Griffin Act is based upon the premise that unions and officials of unions have in many instances disregarded the rights of individual employees and that individual union members have been powerless to protect themselves against such tactics. The act therefore contains numerous restrictions on unions and union officials while conferring new rights and privileges upon individual union members.

Restrictions on Internal Union Affairs

The Landrum-Griffin Act repeals those provisions of the Taft-Hartley Act which required the filing of information as to the union's constitution, bylaws, and financial reports and also the filing of non-Communist affidavits. It substitutes new provisions requiring more detailed reports concerning the internal operation and financial condition of the union. Most important is the change in approach relative to enforcement. Whereas the Taft-Hartley Act punished failure to file required reports with a denial of the right to use the procedures of the National Labor Relations Board, the Landrum-Griffin Act imposes direct and severe criminal penalties.

Every labor organization is required to adopt a constitution and bylaws and to file a copy with the Secretary of Labor. Furthermore, to the extent that the constitution and bylaws do not cover these points, the union must file a detailed statement as to qualifications for, or restrictions on, membership; procedures with respect to such matters as the levying of assessments; audit of the financial transactions of the organization; the discipline or removal of officers and agents for breaches of trust; the imposition of fines and suspensions, and expulsions of members; and numerous other details as to the internal administration of the union. Have these and other provisions in the act had much of an impact upon union constitutions? Based on a study of 43 labor union constitutions, both before and after the 1959 effective date of the act, Professors Philip Ross and Philip Taft conclude that there has been little substantive amendment of union constitutions in response to the provisions of the act. However, they also conclude that the provisions of the act and its attendant threat of Department of Labor intervention may, at least, foster habits of constitutional care and an extension of due process guarantees to organized minorities within a union.[13]

Unions must also file annual financial reports which, in addition to the usual balance sheet, must disclose loans aggregating more than $250 made to any officer, employee, or member; direct and indirect loans to any business enterprise; payments, including reimbursed expenses, to officers and employees who during the fiscal year received more than $10,000 in union compensation; and "other disbursements including the purposes thereof."

The objective of Congress in requiring financial reports by unions to

---

[13] Philip Ross and Philip Taft, "The Effect of the LMRDA upon Union Constitutions," *New York University Law Review*, vol. 43 (April 1968), pp. 305–33.

be filed with the government was to improve the financial practices of such organizations and to make significant financial transactions of the union open to the scrutiny of the union membership. Unfortunately, there is considerable evidence that reports are simply being filed and not used, and that little change has occurred in the internal financial practices of unions.

Restrictions on Union Officials

Under the provisions of many state laws, officers and directors of business corporations are held accountable to strict standards of fiduciary responsibility. The Landrum-Griffin Act applies this principle to union officials, stating that officers, agents, stewards, and other representatives of labor unions must conduct themselves in accordance with the rules of law generally applicable to the dealings of a trustee with other people's money. The act establishes a new federal crime—embezzlement or other unlawful conversion of a union's assets by an officer or employee of the union—punishable by a fine of up to $10,000, imprisonment of up to five years, or both. Drawing on the principle of minority stockholder suits in corporation law, the act provides that if an officer or other union representative is accused of violating his fiduciary responsibilities and the union fails to take action against such officer or representative within a reasonable time after being requested to do so by a union member, the latter may, with the court's permission, bring his own suit in state or federal court for an accounting, and attorney's fees may be awarded out of any recovery. In addition, the act establishes detailed bonding requirements for officers, agents, shop stewards, or other representatives of employees of a union who handle funds or other property of the union.

A major objective of the 1959 legislation was to stamp out racketeering, crime, and corruption in labor unions. To this end the act contains provisions designed to bring to light possible conflicts of interest and similar shadowy transactions through which unscrupulous union officials and employers sacrifice the welfare of employees to personal advantage. Thus, the Landrum-Griffin Act requires officers and employees of labor unions (other than employees performing exclusively clerical or custodial duties) who have engaged in certain transactions enumerated in the act to file annual reports with the Secretary of Labor, covering not only themselves but their wives and minor children, and disclosing payments, stock, or other interests acquired in or from companies which the union represents or seeks to represent. The filing of false reports is made punishable by a fine of up to $10,000, a year in jail, or both. These reports, as well as the reports which employers and labor consultants must file, as discussed previously, are required to be available for public inspection.

Experience has demonstrated that the filing of reports is not a cure for corruption. The act lacks the machinery to attack deeply embedded corruption, because it relies primarily on the emergence of union reformers, or at least on complaints by rank-and-filers. Unfortunately, most union members—like the average citizen—are little inclined to risk involvement by actively fighting corruption when it does not tangibly affect them. Moreover, the big money—and therefore major opportunities for the manipulation of funds—resides in the pension trusts, and the Landrum-Griffin Act is not designed to deal adequately with this problem. As we have observed in Chapter 5, the new pension law passed in 1975, the Employee Retirement Income Security Act, technically provides government with the legal tools to deal with such problems, but budgetary restrictions on manpower have hampered effective enforcement of that law.

Under the Landrum-Griffin Act, persons convicted of serious crimes are barred for a period of five years after conviction from holding any union position other than a clerical or custodial job. This provision was included in the act because the Senate's McClellan Committee had found that a number of unions were under the control of gangsters and hoodlums. Unfortunately, however, the mere fact that the government or individual union members can sue to oust an officer with a criminal record does not permit the NLRB to deny certification to a union with such officers when it uses the processes of the Board in a representation procedure. Furthermore, the Landrum-Griffin Act lists certain crimes as a bar to holding office, but presumably a union leader convicted of a crime not on the prohibited list would not be barred from continuing to hold office. The act imposes a similar prohibition against members of the Communist party and against ex-Communists for a period of five years after they have quit the party. Violation of these provisions—with respect both to criminals and to Communists—is punishable by a fine of not more than $10,000 or by imprisonment for not more than one year, or both.

Trusteeships

The constitutions of many international unions authorize the international officers to suspend the normal processes of government of local unions and other subordinate bodies to supervise their internal activity and to assume control of their property and funds. These so-called trusteeships have been widely used by responsible officials to prevent corruption, mismanagement of funds, and the infiltration of Communists, and to preserve order and integrity within the union. The hearings before the McClellan Committee, however, revealed that trusteeships have been used in some cases as a means of consolidating the power of corrupt union officials, of plundering and dissipating the resources of local unions, and of preventing the growth of competing political elements within the organization. For example, the McClellan Committee found that of the Teamsters' 892 locals, 113 were under "trusteeship"!

Title III of the act requires national or international unions to file reports with the Secretary of Labor concerning all trusteeships. According to the reports on file, there were 435 active trusteeships as of June 30, 1974.[14] The act expressly limits trusteeships so that they can be established only in accordance with the constitution and bylaws of the national or international union and can be imposed only for the purpose of "correcting corruption or financial malpractice, assuring the performance of collective bargaining agreements or other duties of a bargaining representative, restoring democratic procedures, or otherwise carrying out the legitimate objects of such labor organizations." In order to limit the duration of trusteeships without imposing a fixed term which would interfere with the legitimate activities of the union, the act merely provides that after a period of 18 months a trusteeship shall be "presumed invalid," and the court is directed to decree its discontinuance unless it is shown by clear and convincing proof that continuation is necessary for an allowable purpose. However, as was pointed out in Chapter 3, despite this provision, the United Mine Workers maintained trusteeships imposed in the 1920s until 1972. The U.S. Department of Labor filed a suit in 1964 to bar these trusteeships, but the cases were allowed to languish for eight years. Finally, in 1972, after the UMW had been exposed for numerous transgressions, two district courts issued orders disestablishing the trusteeships and ordering free elections in the affected districts.[15]

Restrictions on Union Organizing and Bargaining Tactics

As has already been pointed out, the Landrum-Griffin Act imposes prohibitions and limitations on the use of picketing and boycott tactics by unions. Union spokesmen believe that if the amendments to the Taft-Hartley Act had been brought in as a separate enactment in a different session of Congress, less restrictive provisions would have resulted. However, since the picketing and boycott sections were considered as part of an overall labor reform program aimed primarily at a few corrupt unions, the entire package was adopted into law.

Special Privileges for Unions in the Construction Industry

The casual and occasional nature of the employment relationship between employer and employees in the construction industry caused

---

[14] U.S. Department of Labor, *Compliance, Enforcement, and Reporting*, p. 24.

[15] *Monborne et al.* v. *United Mine Workers et al.*, Civil Action No. 71–690, U.S. Dis. Ct., W. Dis. Pa. (May 14, 1972); and *Hodgson* v. *United Mine Workers et al.*, Civil Action No. 3071–64, U.S. Dis. Ct., D.C. (May 24, 1971). For a discussion of the administration of the trusteeship provision, see Janice R. Bellace, "Union Trusteeships: Difficulties in Applying, Sections 302 and 304(*c*) of the Landrum-Griffin Act, *American University Law Review*, vol. 25 (Winter 1970), pp. 337–69.

many problems to develop in that industry because of the restrictive provisions of the Taft-Hartley Act. The Landrum-Griffin Act—in one of its few provisions intended to loosen restrictions on unions—recognizes these problems and amends the Taft-Hartley Act so as to make lawful so-called prehire agreements in the construction industry. Such agreements may now make union membership compulsory 7 days after employment (rather than 30 days, as is the case in other industries) in states where union shops are permitted. Union contracts can also require an employer to notify the union of job openings and to give the union an opportunity to refer qualified applicants for such employment, and can specify minimum training or experience qualifications for employment.

HOW THE INDIVIDUAL WORKER WAS AFFECTED

A major objective of the Landrum-Griffin Act was to rid unions of gangster control and of corrupt practices generally. The legislators believed that if they could provide union members with information about what was happening to union funds and about other vital aspects of union activities, and if they could protect individual rights through a bill of rights and procedures insuring secret elections, union members would rid themselves of untrustworthy or corrupt officers.

The Bill of Rights

Title I of the law purports to legislate into the internal laws and procedures of unions certain of the essential guarantees contained in the Bill of Rights of the Constitution of the United States. The act provides that every member of a union shall have equal rights to nominate candidates, to vote in elections or referenda of the union, to attend membership meetings, and to participate in the deliberations and voting upon the business of such meetings, subject to reasonable rules and regulations in the union's constitution and bylaws. Furthermore, every member is guaranteed the right to meet and assemble freely with other members; to express views, arguments, or opinions; and to express at meetings of the labor organization his views upon candidates in a union election or upon any other business before the meeting, subject to the organization's established and reasonable rules pertaining to the conduct of meetings.

The act seeks to limit the extent to which union dues and assessments can be raised without the approval of the membership. The act also states that except for nonpayment of dues, no member of any union may be fined, suspended, expelled, or otherwise disciplined by such organization or by any officer thereof unless such member has been served with written specific charges, given a reasonable time to prepare his defense, and afforded a full and fair hearing. Furthermore, unions are prohibited from limiting the right of any union member to sue in court, except that such member may be required to exhaust reasonable hearing procedures (not to exceed a four month's lapse of time) within the union before instituting legal or administrative proceedings against the union or its officers.

Many persons who favored the adoption of other sections of the Landrum-Griffin Act opposed the inclusion of the bill of rights in this enactment. They questioned whether unions should—or could—operate as model democratic institutions. Unions, they argued, are fighting organizations; in many disputes with employers the very existence of the union may be in danger. In such cases, organizations typically require strong direction from the top.

Claims have been made that the Landrum-Griffin Act, by encouraging dissent within the local union, has promoted some unrest and factionalism within unions which has tended to spill over into contract negotiation and grievance settlement, causing contracts to be rejected by the rank and file at a greater rate than heretofore. Furthermore, some employers have expressed concern that union representatives who may now have to contend more strongly to maintain their jobs as union officials will be more inclined to make extreme demands and less likely to strike a bargain which might subject them to criticism by their rivals. A recent study, however, found no support for this contention and concluded that the existence of the act is cited as an excuse by unions and employers who have lost touch with the rank and file.[16]

The act significantly omits any criminal penalties for violation of the bill-of-rights section, except where there is use of force or threat of violence. As a consequence, the enforcement of rights, from the point of view of the individual member, is difficult. Civil remedies, such as an injunction, cannot offer very effective relief to a member who has been denied the right to speak at a meeting that has already been held.

Fair Elections

Under both the Taft-Hartley Act and the Railway Labor Act, the union which is the bargaining agent has the power, in conjunction with the employer, to fix an employee's wages, hours, and working conditions. The individual employee has no right to negotiate directly with the employer if he is dissatisfied with the contract made by his union representatives. The federal government, which conferred these exclusive rights upon unions, has an obligation to insure that the union officials who wield this power are responsive to the desires of the membership

---

[16] Donald R. Burke and Lester Rubin, "Is Contract Rejection a Major Collective Bargaining Problem?" *Industrial and Labor Relations Review,* vol. 26 (January 1973), pp. 820–33.

they represent. The best assurance of this is free and periodic elections —a fact recognized by the AFL–CIO Ethical Practices Committee, which wrote into its code a requirement for frequent elections.

With these principles in mind, the legislators incorporated into the Landrum-Griffin Act detailed provisions relating to union elections. Every national or international union, except a federation of national or international unions, is required to elect its officers not less than once every five years[17] either by secret ballot among the members in good standing or at a convention of delegates chosen by secret ballot. Local unions are required to elect officers not less often than once every three years by secret ballot among the members in good standing. Officers of intermediate bodies between the internationals and the locals must be elected not less often than once every four years by secret ballot among the members in good standing or by labor organization officers representative of such members who have been elected by secret ballot.

The act provides that in any election required to be held by secret ballot, a reasonable opportunity shall be given for the nomination of candidates; and that every member in good standing shall be eligible to be a candidate, subject to reasonable qualifications uniformly imposed (except for Communists and persons convicted of certain crimes, who are barred from holding office). Union members are guaranteed the right to vote for, or otherwise to support, the candidate of their own choice without being subject to penalty, discipline, improper interference, or reprisal. All candidates have to be treated equally, and every bona fide candidate is given the right, once within 30 days prior to the union election in which he is a candidate, to inspect the list of names and addresses of "all members of the labor organization who are subject to a collective bargaining agreement requiring membership therein as a condition of employment."[18] Unions are forbidden to spend dues money in support of any candidate, and employers are likewise forbidden to spend money in support of candidates for union office. Detailed requirements are spelled out in the act as to the manner of sending election

---

[17] Although the intent of this provision was to insure that control of the presidency be periodically returned to the membership for a vote, there is evidence that the specification of the five-year maximum interval has probably lengthened rather than shortened the convention interval! See Marvin Snowbarger and Sam Pintz, *A Quantitative Appraisal of Presidential Turnover Rates before and after the Landrum-Griffin Act* (San Jose State College: Institute for Business and Economic Research, 1970).

[18] In 20 states which have so-called right-to-work laws, compulsory unionism is unlawful. In these states, it would appear that the lists referred to above would not have to be maintained by the union or made available to candidates. While the language of this particular section raises questions about both its applicability and its usefulness, another section of the act requires unions to "refrain from discrimination in favor of or against any candidate with respect to the use of lists of members." Therefore, if *any* list of members is available, even in the right-to-work states, it presumably must be made available on equal terms to all candidates.

notices, counting votes, and other safeguards to insure a fair election. The act also establishes a procedure insuring that union officers guilty of serious misconduct may be removed by secret ballot elections.

The Secretary of Labor has ruled that unions may prescribe reasonable rules and regulations with respect to voting eligibility. They may "in appropriate circumstances defer eligibility to vote by requiring a reasonable period of prior membership, such as six months or a year, or by requiring apprentice members to complete their apprenticeship training, as a condition of voting."

More LMRDA civil actions—54 in number—were brought by or against the Secretary of Labor during the 1974 fiscal year than in any previous year since the law was enacted. As can be seen from Table 20–1, most of the litigation under the act involves election procedures. It is noteworthy that approximately 90% of all election complaints investigated by the Secretary of Labor relate to the election of *local* officers. Very few complaints—with a few notable exceptions—involve the election of intermediate or national officers. In one significant case, however, an investigation found that James B. Carey, longtime president of the International Union of Electrical, Radio, and Machine Workers, whose "re-election" had been announced, was in fact defeated by 23,316 votes. Carey promptly "resigned."

More notorious was the disputed and much-publicized 1969 election of international officers of the United Mine Workers, after which Joseph A. Yablonski, the defeated opposition candidate for president, and two members of his family were murdered. Yablonski, hitherto a member of the entrenched "machine," had challenged W. A. "Tony" Boyle, the incumbent president, and after a vitriolic campaign—in which frequent charges were made that the election was being "fixed"—succeeded in winning 37% of the votes. Three weeks later came the murders. After the election, the Secretary of Labor undertook an intensive investigation and brought suit to set aside the election. In May 1972, a federal judge ruled that a new election must be held. In the second election, held under strict Department of Labor monitorship, Boyle lost to an insurgent, Arnold Miller, by 15,000 votes. Boyle was later convicted and jailed for conspiracy in the murder of Yablonski.

The Labor Department has been sharply criticized for its failure to institute an investigation of alleged irregularities which were brought to its attention by a formal request on July 9, 1969, five months before the election. However, George P. Shultz, who was then serving as Secretary of Labor, responded by stating:

> Although the Secretary of Labor does have the power under Section 601(a) of the Labor-Management Reporting and Disclosure Act of 1959 (LMRDA) to investigate election irregularities at any time, it is the Department of Labor's long-established policy not to undertake investi-

TABLE 20-1
LMRDA Suits Filed by or against the Secretary of Labor, by Fiscal Year and Type*

Type of Suit	Fiscal Year														1960–1974
	1961	1962	1963	1964	1965	1966	1967	1968	1969	1970	1971	1972	1973	1974	
Election	14	9	15	25	12	35	15	23	29	34	35	23	16	32	317†
Subpoena	3	4	8	3	8	5	2	1	0	3	3	6	0	3	49
Defensive	6	3	9	4	1	5	5	2	1	3	3	1	5	6	54
Reporting	2	1	4	6	0	4	4	6	3	5	5	14	11	13	78
Trusteeship	0	0	1	0	1	1	0	1	0	0	0	0	0	0	4
Agreements	0	0	0	0	1	0	0	0	0	0	0	0	0	0	1
Miscellaneous	0	0	0	0	0	0	0	1	0	0	0	0	0	0	1‡
Totals	25	17	37	38	23	50	26	34	33	45	46	44	32	54	504

* No suits were filed prior to fiscal year 1961.
† A fiscal 1974 civil suit which charged Longshoremen's Local 795 of Gulfport, Mississippi, with violating Title IV election requirements also charged the International Longshoremen's Association with violating Title III trusteeship provisions. For statistical purposes, this action is classified as an election suit.
‡ Sec. 504 suit, *U.S.* v. *Jalas.*
Source: U.S. Department of Labor, Labor-Management Services Administration, *Compliance, Enforcement, and Reporting in 1974 under the Labor-Management Reporting and Disclosure Act* (Washington, D.C.: Government Printing Office, 1975), p. 3.

gation of this kind without having a valid complaint under section 402(*a*) after an election has been completed.[19]

Perhaps a more active role by the Department of Labor would have established a climate in which the opposition forces would have had a fair chance in the election. As it was, in the words of the attorney for the Yablonski forces, "The Yablonski election was not lost on election day; it was lost, I believe, on the day that Secretary Shultz decided not to investigate the pre-election conduct of the UMWA. Boyle and his cohorts were free from that moment on to take action unhindered and unwatched."[20]

As a result of litigation and various court decisions relating to election procedures, guidelines are gradually emerging as to the kind of eligibility requirements which unions can impose as a condition of voting in an election. In general, the courts have held that such requirements violate the act if their effect in a particular case is to reduce those eligible to vote to a very small percentage of the membership. For example, in one case involving the Glass Bottle Blowers, the Supreme Court held unreasonable a union rule that only members who had attended 75% of monthly meetings over the last two years could be candidates for office or vote in union elections. It found that such a rule disqualified 490 out of the local union's 500 members! Similarly, the courts have ruled that qualifications in the National Maritime Union and in a local of the Hotel and Restaurant Workers' Union which bar a majority of the membership from seeking office violate the Landrum-Griffin Act.[21] Undoubtedly, the act has paved the way for at least challenging well-entrenched union officials and for ousting them when they obviously attempt to steal elections.

The perpetuation of what are, in effect, union dictatorships depends upon stifling democratic elections at the local level. The late Senator Robert A. Taft once said that "the employee has a good deal more of an opportunity to select his employer than he has to select his labor-union leader." Certain unions—particularly the Teamsters—have been able to keep the ruling clique in power by various devices which have disqualified opposition candidates or put them at a substantial disadvantage in obtaining votes. The Landrum-Griffin Act strikes at these unfair methods and attempts to insure free and honest elections in unions. The safeguards contained in the law permit rank-and-file union members to express their wishes more freely than was possible in the past, and

---

[19] Joseph L. Rauh, Jr., "LMRDA—Enforce It or Repeal It," *Georgia Law Review*, vol. 5 (Summer 1971), pp. 645–46.

[20] Ibid., p. 647.

[21] See *Wirtz* v. *Local 153, Glass Bottle Blowers Association*, 389 U.S. 463 (1967); *Wirtz* v. *National Maritime Union*, U.S. Dis. Ct., So. Dis., N.Y. (April 24, 1968), 68 LRRM 2349; and *Wirtz* v. *Hotel, Motel, and Club Employees Union*, 88 S. Ct. 1743 (1968).

in some cases such union members have done so. In most unions, however, there is general apathy among the membership with respect to union elections. On the other hand, among union leaders there is a strong desire for power and a repugnance to resuming the status of ordinary worker-members. It seems clear that without active interest on the part of union members, legislation will not suffice to make unions democratic. It is not surprising that there has been no significant change in the turnover rate of presidents of national and international unions since the passage of the act. Moreover, such turnover as does occur seems to be confined to a leadership group, giving credence to what has been called "the iron law of oligarchy."[22]

As we have noted at the beginning of this section, Congress apparently believed that if it could provide union members with information about the operation of their unions and protect individual rights through the requirement of democratic procedures, union members themselves would rid their unions of corruption. Congress thus assumed that a democratic union would be less inclined to corruption. Experience suggests, however, that this relationship does not always hold. On the one hand, some dictatorial unions have handled tremendous trust funds without a hint of corruption. On the other hand, some unions with substantial local autonomy have been infected with corruption. Corruption in a union may be more closely related to economic factors in the industry—such as severe competition and a highly mobile labor force—than to election procedures contained in the union constitution.

Voting by Strikers

Through an amendment of the Taft-Hartley Act, the Landrum-Griffin law eliminates the so-called union-busting provision contained in the Taft-Hartley Act. Section 9(c)(3) of that act provided that employees on strike who were not entitled to reinstatement were ineligible to vote. This provision had the effect of preventing any "economic striker" (an employee striking for higher wages, better conditions, or any reason other than his employer's unfair labor practices) who had been replaced by a new employee hired during the strike from voting in an NLRB election conducted during the strike. For example, in a case in the rubber industry the United Rubber Workers was certified as the bargaining representative in an NLRB election. Following months of fruitless negotiations for a contract, the union struck, and the company replaced the strikers with new employees. Thereafter, the employer filed for a new election and succeeded in throwing out the union, because the strikers were not permitted to vote. Under the amendment added by the Landrum-

---

[22] Leon Applebaum and Harry R. Blaine, "The 'Iron Law' Revisited: Oligarchy in Trade Union Locals," *Labor Law Journal*, vol. 26 (September 1975), p. 599.

Griffin Act, such economic strikers retain their right to vote in any NLRB election conducted within 12 months of the start of the strike, subject to regulations established by the NLRB. In applying this statutory provision, the NLRB has ruled that it will presume that economic strikers have retained their interest in struck jobs, that replacements were employed on a permanent basis, and that both therefore are eligible to vote. This means that the mere fact that a striking worker has taken a job elsewhere does not mean that he cannot vote in an election held in the company at which he and other union members are on strike. The NLRB places the burden of proof on the party challenging his vote to show that he is disqualified from voting.

HOW THE PUBLIC WAS AFFECTED

Because the Landrum-Griffin Act deals primarily with the internal administration of unions, its impact upon the general public has been somewhat limited. It was hoped, however, that the procedures it requires, by eliminating corrupt influences in unions, together with the provisions designed to tighten restrictions on picketing and boycotts, would reduce the area of industrial strife. There is little evidence one way or the other that this has occurred.

Beyond this is the strengthening of democratic processes in the nation as a whole which comes from the practice of unionism under conditions where each union member is free to speak his mind and to help determine the overall policies of union government. Democracy is not something which can be carried out on rare occasions—like a treasured antique—and then put back in mothballs. It must be lived daily to survive. We cannot expect democracy in government to survive when employees in their daily lives see democratic forces subverted through intimidation and corruption.

APPRAISAL OF THE ACT

The Landrum-Griffin Act is a law with a very limited purpose. Its primary object is the reform of labor unions. It does not purport to be a law covering the broad aspects of collective bargaining, as did the Taft-Hartley Act. Nor is it intended to effect a broad revision of that act. Its provisions amending the Taft-Hartley Act were added as an accident of its legislative history and for the most part bear some relation to the abuses which were the main object of the legislators' concern.

Interestingly enough, it is the amendments of the Taft-Hartley Act —particularly those which deal with restrictions on picketing and secondary boycotts—that have given rise to the most litigation and controversy. The main body of the Landrum-Griffin law has been incorporated into our industrial life with a minimum of court action. This does not mean that the act has reformed unionism or that many abuses do not exist. The fact is, however, that the U.S. Department of Labor has been called upon to handle fewer complaints of violation of the act than many labor experts had anticipated.

Analysis of the legislative history of the Landrum-Griffin Act indicates that three basic principles motivated the legislators in drafting it:

1. There should be a minimum of interference by government in the internal affairs of any private organization; only essential standards of conduct should be established by legislation.
2. Given the maintenance of minimum democratic safeguards and the availability of detailed essential information about the union, individual members are fully competent to regulate union affairs.
3. Remedies for abuses should be direct. Where the law prescribes standards, sanctions for violations should also be direct.

There can be little argument with the first principle, although there will be considerable dispute as to whether the Landrum-Griffin Act goes far enough in implementing minimum standards. When the act was passed, union spokesmen contended that the provisions relative to disclosure would enable labor spies to obtain confidential information about the union's financial condition and to hamstring internal operation of the union. They further contended that the bill-of-rights provision would convert the union into a debating society and weaken it as a fighting organization. Neither of these contentions has been supported by subsequent experience under the act.

However, eight members of the House Labor Committee filed a minority report bitterly attacking the proposed labor reform bill for its omission of a guarantee of civil rights. In their words, "if there is to be a bill of rights in this legislation it must most assuredly include a guarantee of equal rights—the right of every workingman to join a union and not to be segregated within that union because of race, creed, color, or national origin." It was a fact of political life in 1959 that the Labor Reform bill probably could not have been passed if it had incorporated a civil rights provision. Today, however, the civil rights movement is much stronger, and federal and state laws passed in the intervening years have incorporated the view expressed by the minority report. The Civil Rights Act of 1964 has gone a long way toward broadening the bill of rights of the Landrum-Griffin Act by providing explicit guarantees of such rights to members of labor organizations. Furthermore, as noted in the previous chapter, the NLRB and the courts have interpreted various provisions of the Taft-Hartley Act to preclude racial discrimination in labor relations.[23]

With respect to the second principle, some skeptics wonder whether

---

[23] For a discussion of civil rights and labor relations, see Chapter 23.

the rank-and-file union member is really concerned about graft and corruption in his union any more than the average citizen really concerns himself about graft and corruption in government. Surveys have indicated, for example, that many Teamster members, despite the disclosure of corruption among their officers, still approve their leadership because the leadership has "produced" for them in terms of high wages and excellent working conditions. Perhaps the conditions affecting the relationship between the average worker and his union are such that we should not expect democratic action to flourish in the union environment. Nevertheless, the maintenance of minimum democratic safeguards seems necessary to protect the rights of individuals and to insure that union action reflects the desire of the membership.

On the subject of the third principle, the Landrum-Griffin Act takes a different approach from that of the Taft-Hartley Act. The latter penalized a union's violation of various provisions of the law by denying the union access to the procedures of the NLRB. This had the effect of punishing all the union members for the violations of their officials. The Landrum-Griffin Act, by contrast, imposes direct sanctions in the form of fines, imprisonment, and/or civil remedies through court action to insure compliance with the act. This is certainly a more mature and realistic approach. Moreover, these sanctions have been used. Since the passage of the Landrum-Griffin Act, more than 1,000 persons have been indicted for criminal violations of the act and almost 800 convictions have resulted.

The type of legislation embodied in the Landrum-Griffin Act was probably inevitable. Abuses in other aspects of business life—such as the securities market, banking, and drugs—have likewise brought forth detailed federal regulation. Unions thus far have been remarkably free from such internal regulation, despite the fact that they enjoy unique benefits and privileges under the income tax laws and the antitrust laws. No association or organization can long expect to enjoy such privileges without assuming major obligations.

Unions in our society are no longer mere private clubs or fraternal organizations whose internal affairs and admission and fiscal policies are matters of concern to their membership only. On the contrary, they bear a strong resemblance to public utilities or government entities, which are subject to legal control of their internal affairs. When a union is certified as a collective bargaining agent, it has conferred upon it a government-sanctioned monopoly and the unusual powers that flow from this privilege. It is incumbent upon government, which granted this power to unions, to insure that it is not abused.

Unions have an obligation to maintain democratic processes. They control the conditions under which their members spend most of their productive lives. More and more, they have a captive audience. A truck driver may move from one city to another, but he cannot long escape the far-flung power of the Teamsters' Union. The Landrum-Griffin Act takes a long step in the direction of attempting to insure democratic conditions in unions. Its success in achieving this objective will depend upon the support afforded this legislation by union leaders who profess to be interested in "clean" union government and, most important, upon the rank-and-file union membership who must want democratic government enough to use the tools which Congress has given them.

QUESTIONS FOR DISCUSSION

1. It has been said that a union is an organization that must always be ready for battle. Can such an organization function effectively on a democratic basis? Do you consider the operation of most large corporations to be democratic? Why should unions be held to this standard? Discuss.

2. Discuss the so-called bill of rights of the Landrum-Griffin Act. In what way could these provisions handicap union action? Should the bill of rights have been broadened to include other rights, such as the right of free admission to a union? Discuss.

3. Assuming that there were abuses in the internal administration of unions, do you think that the power of the federal government should be invoked to curb such abuses? What other measures might have been taken to accomplish the same objective?

SUGGESTIONS FOR FURTHER READING

Bellace, Janice R. "Union Trusteeships: Difficulties in Applying Sections 302 and 304(c) of the Landrum-Griffin Act," *The American University Law Review,* vol. 25 (Winter 1976), pp. 337–69.

    An analysis of the criteria which courts have applied in determining legitimate utilization of trusteeships by unions.

Brinker, Paul A., and Taylor, Benjamin J. "The Secondary Boycott Maze," *Labor Law Journal,* vol. 25 (July 1974), pp. 418–27.

    An article which reviews the history and exercise of secondary boycotts and concludes that they may serve a valid function in labor relations in certain circumstances.

Dereshinsky, Ralph M. *The NLRB and Secondary Boycotts,* Labor Relations and Public Policy Series, Report No. 4. Philadelphia: Industrial Research Unit, The Wharton School, University of Pennsylvania, 1972.

    This concise monograph summarizes the law with respect to common-situs picketing, consumer boycotts, and hot cargo agreements and concludes that secondary boycotts should be entirely outlawed.

Duerr, Patrick T. "Developing a Standard for Secondary Consumer Picketing," *Labor Law Journal,* vol. 26 (September 1975), pp. 585–93.

    An attempt to derive some workable standards in consumer picketing, based on the *Tree Fruits* case and subsequent NLRB decisions.

Klock, Joseph J., and Palzer, Doris. "Democracy in the UMW?" *Labor Law Journal,* vol. 25 (October 1974), pp. 625–31.

Shortcomings of the Landrum-Griffin Act as evidenced by its application to the government of the United Mine Workers.

U.S. Department of Labor, Labor-Management Services Administration. *Compliance, Enforcement, and Reporting under the Labor-Management Reporting and Disclosure Act.* Annual Reports. Washington, D.C.: Government Printing Office.

Annual reports which contain detailed statistical breakdowns of activities of the LMWP.

21

The Government in Labor Disputes—Mediation, Emergency Disputes, and State Legislation

THE PREVIOUS chapters have been concerned with key federal legislation. These laws, however, are only part of the total role of the federal government in labor disputes. In this chapter, we shall discuss how the federal government attempts to settle labor disputes or to prevent them from erupting. In addition, we shall discuss how 50 states and some municipalities play a significant role in labor disputes in the private sector by means of "little Taft-Hartley acts," "little Landrum-Griffin laws," and other legislation.

MEDIATION OR CONCILIATION—THE FEDERAL SERVICE

The principal mediation agency in the United States is the Federal Mediation and Conciliation Service. (See Figure 21–1 for definitions.) It dates from the Act of 1913 which created the U.S. Department of Labor. This law contained a paragraph authorizing the Secretary of Labor to mediate labor disputes and to appoint "commissioners of conciliation" for that purpose. This phase of the U.S. Department of Labor's work quickly expanded until a special division was set up in the Department known as the United States Conciliation Service, with headquarters in Washington, D.C., and regional offices in the principal industrial centers of the nation. In 1947, the Conciliation Service, as a division of the Department of Labor, was abolished by the Taft-Hartley Act, and an independent agency, the Federal Mediation and Conciliation Service, whose functions remained basically the same, was substituted for it. This was done largely at the behest of employer groups who felt that if the Conciliation Service were to remain a division of

FIGURE 21–1

Definitions

Mediation and *Conciliation* are used interchangeably to mean an attempt by a third party, typically a government official, to bring disputants together by persuasion and compromise. The mediator or conciliator is not vested with power to force a settlement.

Strike Notice laws require the union and company to notify each other and certain public officials a specified number of days prior to striking or locking out.

Strike Vote laws require an affirmative vote of either the union members or the employees in the bargaining unit before a strike may be called.

Fact Finding involves investigation of a dispute by a panel, which issues a report setting forth the causes of the dispute. Usually, but not always, recommendations for settling the dispute are included in the report. Laws requiring fact finding usually provide that the parties maintain the status quo and refrain from strikes or lockouts until a stipulated period after the fact finders' report has been made. Once the procedure has been complied with, however, the parties are free to strike and to lock out.

Compulsory Arbitration requires the submission of an unsettled labor dispute to a third party or board for determination. Strikes or lockouts are completely forbidden, and the arbitrator's decision is binding on the parties for a stated length of time.

Seizure involves temporary state control of a business which is or threatens to be shut down by a work stoppage. Strikes or lockouts are forbidden during the period of seizure, which lasts until the threat of work stoppage has abated.

the Department of Labor, the conciliators themselves would inevitably reflect the prolabor bias of the Department.

In establishing a separate Mediation and Conciliation Service, the Taft-Hartley Act gave the Service the statutory base it previously lacked. In addition, Section 201 of the Taft-Hartley Act set forth the policy of the federal government as the peaceful settlement of labor disputes by collective bargaining. Section 203 directed the Service to minimize work stoppages by mediation and the encouragement of voluntary arbitration; Section 204 admonished labor and industry to cooperate fully with the efforts of the Service to settle strikes; and Section 205 established a labor-management advisory panel for the Service. Finally, Section 8(*d*) of the Taft-Hartley Act required labor and mangement to notify each other of intent to modify a collective agreement at least 60 days prior to the termination date of the agreement, and to notify the Service and any appropriate state agency 30 days later if no agreement had been reached.

The Mediation and Conciliation Service may be called into a dispute by either labor or management, or it may proffer its services. It has, however, no authority to force itself upon a recalcitrant employer or union. Of course, as a federal agency, it carries with it the prestige of the government, so that refusal to participate in a conference called by the Service is unusual.

Mediators often perform a valuable contribution in preventing strikes by bringing the parties together when bargaining has failed. A clever mediator can obtain concessions from the parties by adroit maneuvering, or otherwise find a basis for agreement when it is lacking, as, for example, when the bargaining adversaries are no longer able to communicate directly with each other, or are afraid to do so.

To accomplish their tasks despite a lack of authority, mediators must time their participation in a dispute correctly. If they enter the dispute too early or too often, the parties may prefer to save concessions for mediation instead of getting down to the business of seeking agreement. If mediators come in too late, the parties' positions may have become too hardened to permit concessions. Mediation is an art, and a valuable one. It cannot be squandered loosely if it is to be effective. The fact that the Mediation Service has been able to attract some excellent men during the last two decades has helped it to increase its ability to accomplish its important task.

State Mediation Agencies

Although almost all states have provisions in their laws for the adjustment of labor disputes, in only a few is this made a full-time job. Nor is this surprising, considering that in many states, there would not be enough work to keep even a single conciliator occupied, let alone a board or a commission. Other states prefer to leave adjustment work to the Federal Mediation and Conciliation Service, with such assistance as the state industrial commissioner or the state department of labor can render. The states which, in contrast to the general rule, are most active in the adjustment of labor disputes are California, Connecticut, Massachusetts, Michigan, Minnesota, New Jersey, New York, Pennsylvania, and Wisconsin. In all of these states a special agency devotes full time to the job.

The job of the state mediator is no different from that of his federal counterpart. He must be capable of bringing about an agreement by conciliation and persuasion, without authority or power to force compliance with his wishes. The fact that most states have not paid staff mediators anything in excess of a very modest income has made it difficult to find persons who are willing to perform this valuable service. Nevertheless, over the last several years both authors have encountered some able state mediators who have been most helpful in critical disputes.

Municipal Adjustment Agencies

A number of municipalities have at one time or another established machinery for the adjustment of labor disputes. Most of these agencies have depended upon the volunteer services of public-spirited citizens and have ceased to exist after these citizens retired. Their success has been varied. Experienced mediators have not been available to municipalities, and inexperienced ones have frequently done more harm than good. Strikes which occur on the outskirts of a city or in its suburbs may vitally affect a city, yet be outside the jurisdiction of its adjustment agency. And if state and federal agencies are already in operation, the intrusion of a municipal board may only complicate matters.

Louisville, Kentucky; Toledo, Ohio; and New York City have had the most active municipal mediation agencies. New York City maintains a special labor secretary to the mayor who attempts mediation; and if unsuccessful, he can refer the dispute for further mediation to a panel composed of one labor, one industry, and one public member.

The Jurisdictional Hodgepodge in Mediation

A recurring problem in mediation is the competition of mediators to obtain recognition in settling disputes. It is by no means uncommon to find federal and state mediators, and occasionally, municipal mediators as well, competing for the job of settling a dispute. The Taft-Hartley Act specifically permits such dual mediation. In recent years, a "code of ethics" has required that mediators cooperate at least on a pro forma basis, but the urge "to get in on the glory" is strong. Moreover, the existence of mediators from different jurisdictions gives labor and management the opportunity to "shop around" in order to try and have the mediation work done by the one judged most sympathetic to the viewpoint of one of the parties.

Mediation is certainly unlikely to be more effective because of the participation by more mediators in a single dispute. The authors have experienced both cooperation and lack of cooperation among state and federal mediators in various disputes. For the most part, mediators have cooperated with one another as reasonable people working toward a common goal should. There continues to be, however, evidence of lack of cooperation from time to time.

ADJUSTMENT IN RAILWAY AND AIR TRANSPORT

Mediation in the railway and air transport industries is conducted by an agency especially set up for this purpose—the National Mediation Board. Moreover, under the procedure set forth in the Railway Labor Act which governs these two industries, mediation is combined with a strike notice and fact-finding procedure. This separate treatment has its historical roots in a series of laws dating back to 1888. Since then, railway labor problems have generally been governed by procedures different from those in other industries. An exception to this rule is the

Labor-Management Reporting and Disclosure Act (Landrum-Griffin), which, unlike the basic provisions of the Taft-Hartley Act, applies to both railway and air transport.

The Railway Labor Act makes it the duty of labor and management to exert every reasonable effort to "make and maintain agreements concerning rates of pay and working conditions" and to attempt to adjust all differences by peaceful methods. A three-man, nonpartisan National Mediation Board then attempts mediation if the parties cannot agree among themselves. The Board is further instructed to urge voluntary arbitration if mediation proves unsuccessful. If arbitration is refused and the dispute is such as "substantially to interrupt interstate commerce," the Board is instructed to notify the president, who can create a special emergency board to investigate and publish findings. During the pendency of these various proceedings and until 30 days after the report of the emergency board, neither party may alter "the conditions out of which the dispute arose," except by mutual agreement. The parties, however, are under no legal obligation to accept the recommendations of the emergency board, and strikes or lockouts are permissible after the waiting period has expired.

A unique aspect of the Railway Labor Act is its requirement for the compulsory arbitration of grievances and of other disputes arising out of the interpretation of agreements. The agency charged with this task (for the railroads only) is the National Railroad Adjustment Board. This Board is a bipartisan agency composed of 36 members, half of whom are paid and compensated by the carriers and half by the unions "national in scope." (Thus, smaller organizations of workers have no representation on the Adjustment Board.) The work of the Adjustment Board is divided into four divisions, each of which has jurisdiction over certain crafts. If a division deadlocks, referees are appointed by the National Mediation Board or by the division if it can agree on a selection.

The Railway Labor Act also provides elaborate safeguards for the free choice of employee representatives by setting forth a list of unfair labor practices similar to those contained in the National Labor Relations Act prior to the Taft-Hartley amendments. Enforcement is, however, different from that under the National Labor Relations Act, in that violations are punishable by criminal penalties and prosecution is under the jurisdiction of the U.S. Department of Justice. Because of the difficulties of proving willful intent to commit an unfair labor practice before a jury, there have been no convictions and only one trial for unfair labor practices. There have, however, been a number of court actions to force employers or unions to cease alleged unfair labor practices and to bargain in good faith.

Until 1951, the Railway Labor Act prohibited all types of union security and checkoff agreements. This prohibition was placed in the act in 1934 to prevent company unions from obtaining union security and automatic dues support from reluctant workers, and it had the support of the so-called standard unions. By 1951, the company unions had been ousted by defeats in representation elections, and the standard unions were able to persuade Congress to legalize union security and checkoff provisions. Unlike the Taft-Hartley Act, the Railway Labor Act provides no machinery for decertifying unions or for voting out union security provisions.

The Railway Labor Act also provides formal machinery for the selection of employee representatives. The National Mediation Board is required to make determinations in this regard, and usually does so by representation elections. The bargaining unit under the Railway Labor Act is limited to a "craft or class," but the National Mediation Board has wide discretion in determining the definition of craft or class and in determining voting eligibility in representation elections.

Prior to World War II, the Railway Labor Act was hailed as a "model law," and frequent suggestions were made to enact similar legislation for industry generally. Since 1940, however, a number of strikes or near strikes, which were averted only by presidential action or by special legislation outside the procedures of the Railway Labor Act, have caused many former advocates of the "model law" concept to take a second and deeper look at the Railway Labor Act.

The effect of the elaborate procedure of the Railway Labor Act is to make collective bargaining completely perfunctory prior to the emergency board stage. Neither party tends to concede anything from its original position for fear of prejudicing its case before the emergency board. The procedure of the Railway Labor Act, which is supposed to supplement collective bargaining, has been used instead as a substitute for collective bargaining. Because they know that an important dispute is likely to end up before an emergency board, railway labor and management have just gone through the motions of bargaining until the emergency board hearings took place.

Such a development is probably inevitable. It is the easy way out for the parties to let someone else make the decision for them. In that way, they avoid the responsibility and, under the emergency board procedure, still remain free to act if the board's recommendation is unsatisfactory. In 1963, President John F. Kennedy and Congress refused to permit a strike over the fireman issue, and Congress enacted a special compulsory arbitration law to settle it. Other aspects of the same dispute were settled under the aegis of President Lyndon B. Johnson by mediation in 1964. Since then, Congress has passed special legislation several times to terminate strikes by railway employees. In these cases, the procedure of the Railway Labor Act failed to produce a settlement—as has occurred in most major disputes under the act's jurisdiction since 1940.

Experience under the state laws, which also have a fact-finding procedure, is similar to that under the Railway Labor Act.[1] Moreover, nowhere has the appointment of fact-finding or emergency boards been confined to emergencies by any realistic or even generous use of the term *emergency*. In the case of the Railway Labor Act, for example, a dispute on a small railroad can apparently as easily cause the appointment of an emergency board as a dispute affecting most of the railroads in the nation. Once the appointment of an emergency or fact-finding board becomes commonplace, the public loses interest; and it is then exceedingly difficult, if not impossible, to rally public opinion behind the settlement in the manner which proponents of the fact-finding procedure claim could be effective.

THE TAFT-HARTLEY ACT AND NATIONAL EMERGENCIES

The emergency disputes law which is applicable to industries not covered by the Railway Labor Act is found in provisions of the Taft-Hartley Act. Title I of this law requires that a 60-day notice be given by either union or management to the other party if a change in the collective agreement is contemplated and that such notices also be sent to appropriate federal and state mediation services. This procedure has become perfunctory, since unions generally automatically give notice in order to be free to strike if negotiations do not result in agreement. These notices have, of course, alerted the mediation agencies that a strike could occur, but it is possible that they may also have induced mediation where it was unnecessary.

Title II of the Taft-Hartley Act also requires that the president appoint a Board of Inquiry to investigate and report, without recommendations, on the issues of a dispute which "threatens" the national health or safety. The president can then direct the Attorney General to petition a federal district court for an injunction to prevent or terminate the strike or lockout. If the injunction is granted, the conditions of work and pay are frozen for the time being, and the parties are obliged to make every effort to settle their differences with the assistance of the Conciliation Service. If these efforts fail, at the end of 60 days the Board of Inquiry is required to make a public report on the status of the dispute, again without recommendations. The National Labor Relations Board is then required within 15 days to poll employees as to whether they will accept the last offer of the employer and to certify the result to the Attorney General within 5 days. The injunction must then be dissolved. By this time, 80 days will have elapsed since the first application

[1] For an analysis of these state laws, see Herbert R. Northrup, *Compulsory Arbitration and Government Intervention in Labor Disputes* (Washington, D.C.: Labor Policy Association, 1966), pp. 263–94.

for an injunction. If the majority of workers refuse the employer's last offer, then the president can submit the complete report to Congress, with or without recommendations for action.

As of January 1, 1977, boards of inquiry had been appointed under this section on 34 different occasions. In 16 cases a strike vote on the employer's last offer was taken; and in 8 cases, strikes occurred after the machinery of the act had been completely utilized.

The Taft-Hartley Act thus provides no ultimate sanctions against a national emergency strike after the fact-finding period has elapsed, other than the implied threat of possible congressional action and the force of public opinion. Experience under the Taft-Hartley Act has emphasized what experience under the Railway Labor Act had already demonstrated —fact-finding reports have relatively little effect in mobilizing public sentiment so as to compel the settlement of labor disputes unless there is really a grave national emergency affecting the entire country, or most of it.

The Last-Offer Vote

The last-offer vote has often been utilized to gain the unions more. They have simply told their memberships to vote no and they will obtain more, and this has happened in all cases in which a last-offer vote occurred, more often without a strike than with one. It has also happened in eight of the nine cases in which a vote was held under a similar procedure of the now defunct Pennsylvania Utility Arbitration Act (see Table 21–1). (The only exception occurred the day before the Korean War wage stabilization program was scheduled to become effective, in 1951. The workers voted to accept a settlement for fear of having their wages frozen at pre-last-offer levels.) This was to be expected. An offer, once made, is rarely withdrawn, so why not vote no and probably get more?

TABLE 21–1
Last-Offer Votes: Experience under Taft-Hartley and Pennsylvania Laws to July 1, 1976

	Number of Votes	Last Offer Accepted	Last Offer Rejected
Law			
Taft-Hartley Act	16	0*	15
Pennsylvania Utility Arbitration Act.......	9	1†	8

* In one case the employees rejected a subsequent and higher offer after the "last" offer had been rejected. In another case the union asked employees to boycott the vote; no one voted from this group.
† Vote conducted on January 24, 1951, just prior to 1951 Korean War wage freeze. Employees feared that to reject it would mean freezing existing wages.
Source: National Labor Relations Board and Pennsylvania State Labor Relations Board.

Actually, there have been four cases in which the last-offer vote served the purpose of inducing agreement. The late Professor George W. Taylor noted that the steel industry settled in 1960 partially because management believed that the "last" offer would be rejected.[2] In the 1962 Lockheed case the union settled without the union shop because it feared that the employees would not support its insistence on this demand in the last-offer vote. Similarly, in the 1966 strikes of the United Automobile Workers at General Electric's jet engine plant in Evendale, Ohio, and of the Steelworkers at Union Carbide's defense work facility at Kokomo, Indiana, last-minute withdrawals of demands and settlements were probably triggered by the belief of these unions that the employees might accept the companies' last offers.[3]

PROPOSALS FOR EMERGENCY STRIKE LAWS

The Taft-Hartley emergency procedure has been least successful in the industry which has caused the most invocations of the procedure —stevedoring. Twelve of the 35 times that the machinery has been used have involved longshoremen or associated groups. In 8 of these 12 cases, the strike resumed after the 80-day cooling-off period ended. In 1972, the West Coast longshoremen called off their strike only after Congress passed special legislation which would have ordered the men back to work and set up a special compulsory arbitration board unless the parties settled by a given date—which they did.

Experience under the Railway Labor Act and the failures of the Taft-Hartley Act in longshore disputes have induced many persons over the years to advocate compulsory arbitration legislation for all transportation industry disputes. The problem is how to protect the public and industry from the crippling impact of such strikes and others which affect the public interest and at the same time avoid destroying the capacity of union and management to settle most disputes through collective bargaining. Thus far, such compulsory procedures have lacked success when tried in various states or in other democratic countries because of the role of the strike, paradoxically, in inducing settlement and because of the impact on bargaining of withdrawing the right to strike.[4]

---

[2] George W. Taylor, "The Adequacy of Taft-Hartley in Public Emergency Disputes," *The Annuals*, vol. 333 (January 1961), p. 79.

[3] Another form of strike vote legislation requires an affirmative vote of employees before they strike. The War Labor Disputes (Smith-Connally) Act of World War II and several state laws incorporated this idea, but unions made it a vote of confidence, and thus assured an overwhelming strike vote as a vote of confidence of employees for their negotiators. See Northrup, *Compulsory Arbitration,* pp. 295–99, for a description of these laws.

[4] For a history and analysis of various forms of compulsory settlement legislation, in the United States and abroad, see Northrup, *Compulsory Arbitration.*

In Chapter 7, we noted that if a strike hurts only one of the parties, as when the other is subsidized by welfare, the strike does not serve its purpose of motivating agreement—it no longer acts, as Professor George W. Taylor put it, "as the motive power which induces a modification of extreme positions and then a meeting of minds. The acceptability of certain terms of employment is determined in relation to the losses of a work stoppage that can be avoided by an agreement. In collective bargaining, economic power provides the final arbitrament."[5]

Dr. Taylor then described what occurs when third-party determination or intervention is substituted for the collective bargaining system:

> When the rights to strike and to lockout are withdrawn, as during a war or under compulsory arbitration, a most important inducement to agree is removed. The penalties for failing to agree—stoppage of production and employment—are waived. Even more devastating consequences result. Each party is reluctant to make any "concessions" around the bargaining table. That might "prejudice" its case before whatever Board is set up to deal with labor disputes. In addition, the number of issues is kept large and formidable. Demands that customarily "wash out" in negotiations are carefully preserved for submission to the Board. Why not? There is everything to gain and nothing to lose by trying to get one's unusual demands approved without cost.[6]

There are, however, situations when the strike does not serve its purpose. This can occur if a strike exerts greater pressure upon the public or the government than it does on the parties. "The parties can hold out longer than the public or the government. In consequence, a strike which creates a public emergency exerts primary pressure upon the government to intervene and also to specify the terms upon which production is to be resumed."[7] Such situations are typified by railroad strikes or shutdowns of other key transportation services, for example, New York City subways, or utility or government services upon which a significant sector of the public depends for the orderly working of their daily livelihood.

The American system basically depends upon restraint of the parties to avoid confrontations in areas where strikes are considered intolerable —that is where they impact more on the public than on the parties themselves. The question today is whether that dependence is misplaced.

In an endeavor to protect the public and at the same time to encourage, rather than to discourage, settlement by the parties themselves, the various states and many foreign democratic countries and their political subdivisions have enacted various ingeniously drawn laws incorporating

---

[5] George W. Taylor, "Is Compulsory Arbitration Inevitable?" *Proceedings of the First Annual Meeting, Industrial Relations Research Association, 1948,* p. 64.

[6] Ibid. See also Northrup, *Compulsory Arbitration,* pp. 182–84.

[7] Taylor, "Is Compulsory Arbitration Inevitable?" p. 65.

fact finding, seizure, compulsory arbitration, and various combinations of these procedures.[8] (See Figure 21–1 for definitions.) None of these procedures has succeeded both in preventing strikes *and* in encouraging the parties to settle their disputes without regular intervention. Fact finding, such as occurs under the Railway Labor Act, is the least successful because it inhibits the collective bargaining process without providing alternative means of settlement. Hence, when the procedure has been completed, a legal strike can still occur. Seizure holds the strike in abeyance, but does not resolve anything. Moreover, an employer finds it very difficult to understand when government seizes a facility temporarily and negotiates a costly agreement which the employer must then agree to in order to repossess his property.

Compulsory arbitration is, of course, designed as a substitute for strikes. It has been used for most of this century as such in Australia and New Zealand. There collective bargaining as we know it occurs but little. Instead, disputes are submitted to arbitration courts for determination. Yet strikes in those countries are not only common, but actually occur much more frequently there than in the United States. They are usually short and are designed to pressure employers to grant more than was won at the arbitration court. Although such strikes are illegal, penalties are assessed relatively rarely. Politicians do not like to fine powerful unions or masses of employees.[9]

There is thus no easy answer. If the right to strike is curtailed, and other procedures are substituted for strikes, the collective bargaining method of settlement will probably inevitably be inhibited, and thus the procedure adopted to prevent strikes will be regularly utilized. Its effectiveness in preventing strikes will probably then decline. Nevertheless, in an age of technological and industrial interdependence, this could be the lesser of two evils. Moreover, if wage and price stabilization were to be reinstituted, collective bargaining would be restrained, and strikes to breach government wage order or ceilings would be illegal. Under such circumstances, we would be moving closer to a new era in which government determination of the conditions of employment could be more significant than our present system of collective bargaining.

---

[8] See Northrup, *Compulsory Arbitration,* esp. pp. 215–441, for an analysis of this experience.

[9] For excellent analyses of the situation in Australia and New Zealand, see Kingsley Laffer, "Does Compulsory Arbitration Prevent Strikes? The Australian Experience," in Richard L. Rowan (ed.), *Collective Bargaining: Survival in the 70's?* Labor Relations and Public Policy Series, Report No. 5 (Philadelphia: Industrial Research Unit, The Wharton School, University of Pennsylvania, 1972), pp. 154–78; Noel S. Woods, "The Industrial Relations Situation in New Zealand," *Journal of Industrial Relations,* vol. 12 (November 1970), pp. 360–65; and A. J. Geare, "Strike Sanctions and Penalties under New Zealand's Industrial Relations Law," *Journal of Industrial Relations,* vol. 18 (March 1976), pp. 45–57.

STATE LABOR RELATIONS ACTS

In 1937, the year in which the Supreme Court sanctioned the Wagner Act, Massachusetts, New York, Pennsylvania, Utah, and Wisconsin adopted legislation patterned on the Wagner Act.

In 1939, however, the Pennsylvania and Wisconsin laws were amended to incorporate restrictions on employers and unions, as well as on employees, and later the Utah law was likewise amended, thus foreshadowing the Taft-Hartley Act. Laws modeled on the Taft-Hartley Act are now in effect in 13 states[10] and the Territory of Guam; those resembling the Wagner Act are found in 4 states[11] and Puerto Rico. A number of states have also enacted limited purpose legislation, some of the Landrum-Griffin type. In 1975, California enacted a comprehensive labor relations law applicable only to agriculture, the first of its type. The Hawaiian law has always covered agriculture as well as industry.

Jurisdiction

Coverage of the state labor relations acts is limited by (1) the extent of federal preemption and (2) restrictions imposed in the state laws. Between the passage of the Taft-Hartley Act in 1947 and the enactment of the Landrum-Griffin Act of 1959, the jurisdiction of state laws was severely limited to intrastate commerce business not within the purview of the Taft-Hartley law. Amendments contained in the Landrum-Griffin Act specifically gave the states jurisdiction over cases which might fall within the Taft-Hartley Act's jurisdiction, but which the National Labor Relations Board declined to accept under its jurisdictional standards of August 1, 1959. Thereafter, the jurisdictions of many state laws, as will be discussed in the following chapter, were expanded to encompass public employees and/or employees of hospitals and other nonprofit institutions. But the National Labor Relations Board assumed jurisdiction over universities and some quasi–health care institutions, and then in 1974 Congress amended the Taft-Hartley Act to place voluntary hospitals and other such health care units under NLRB control, thus further limiting state jurisdiction.

In the private sector, state activity has tended to stagnate despite the passage of a few new laws in the last decade.[12] State agencies handle annually less than 8% of the 50,000 cases which come before the National

---

[10] Colorado, Hawaii, Kansas, Michigan, Minnesota, North Dakota, Oregon, Pennsylvania, South Dakota, Utah, Vermont, West Virginia, and Wisconsin.

[11] Connecticut, Massachusetts, New York, and Rhode Island. (Massachusetts regulates union entrance requirements and union security provisions but remains basically a Wagner type without union unfair labor practices.)

[12] See Harold A. Katz and Bruce S. Feldacker, "The Decline and Fall of State Regulation of Labor Relations," *Labor Law Journal*, vol. 20 (June 1968), pp. 327–45.

Labor Relations Board, and one half of these are New York State labor relations cases. Moreover, the typical state case involves a small shop with few employees.

Unfair Labor Practices

Both the "little Wagner acts" and the "little Taft-Hartley acts" follow the unfair labor practice provisions of the federal act insofar as employer unfair labor practice provisions are concerned. Some also include in their proscriptions specific prohibitions against the blacklist, employer espionage, and other matters which were included within the Taft-Hartley Act's general restrictions on the restraint of employees for union activity. The unfair labor practices in the "little Taft-Hartley laws" which are directed against employees and unions may be divided into four categories:

1. Prohibitions of violence and similar activities which were almost universally unlawful before the passage of the labor relations acts—for example, sit-down strikes, sabotage, and mass picketing.
2. Restrictions on peaceful tactics, such as picketing and organizing campaigns, especially where coercion is alleged.
3. Limitations, on union objectives which make illegal all efforts to achieve a forbidden objective, such as a make-work rule.
4. Regulation of the internal affairs of unions, such as financial matters, election procedure, and eligibility for union office.

Many of these laws thus contain provisions which are similar to those in both the Taft-Hartley Act and the Landrum-Griffin Act, including the provision in the latter law designed to safeguard the finances and the rights of workers in their relationship with unions. Most provisions controlling union and employee conduct are, however, designed to limit strikes, picketing, or boycotts, or to preclude union interference with the peaceful designation of a bargaining agent.

Representation Disputes

The representation procedure is, in general, similar in most states to that provided under the Taft-Hartley Act. Decertification procedure is not, however, always provided for, although Pennsylvania and Wisconsin, for example, do have something similar.

Administration

Administration of the state labor relations acts is vested in several different types of administrative establishments. In some, typified by the state labor relations boards of New York and Pennsylvania, a single-purpose agency modeled on the National Labor Relations Board was created to handle only unfair labor practice and representation matters arising under the labor relations acts of the states. A second type of administration agency, such as that in Colorado, Wisconsin, or North Dakota, is multipurpose. It administers the labor relations act in addition to several other functions—such as the mediation of labor disputes, or even functions like workers' compensation, safety, minimum wages, and other protective legislation. As in the case of the National Labor Relations Board, state labor relations agencies cannot enforce their own orders, but must apply to the courts for enforcement.

Specific Laws Regulating Weapons of Conflict

Besides these comprehensive state laws which have been discussed, many states have enacted legislation outlawing or controlling the weapons of conflict in labor-management relations. Thus, 11 states bar the picketing of homes;[13] 2, of courts;[14] 18 prohibit mass picketing, or blocking plant entrances;[15] and 6 forbid picketing by a union representing only a minority of employees, or by a group that is ineligible to raise a representative election question before the appropriate state agency.[16] Many of these laws are designed to protect individuals or small businesses from coercive union activity.

The constitutionality of many of these provisions remains in doubt, especially in cases in which the Taft-Hartley Act has jurisdiction. As was noted in previous chapters, governmental regulation of the weapons of conflict involves the difficult question of coercion and free speech, as well as a conflict of state and federal jurisdiction. Hence it is not surprising that the law is unsettled in these areas of social policy.

On the other side, 16 relatively new laws prohibit or discourage the recruiting of replacements for strikers.[17] Such laws have also been enacted by several cities. The purpose of these laws is, of course, to strengthen union bargaining power by making it more difficult to replace strikers. Organized labor has secured the passage of laws in 13 states[18] making it illegal to require the submission to lie-detector tests

---

[13] Alabama, Arkansas, Colorado, Connecticut, Florida, Hawaii, Illinois, Kansas, Michigan, North Dakota, and South Dakota.

[14] Louisiana and Massachusetts.

[15] Arkansas, Colorado, Florida, Georgia, Hawaii, Kansas, Maine, Michigan, Mississippi, Nebraska, New Mexico, North Dakota, South Carolina, South Dakota, Texas, Utah, Virginia, and Wisconsin.

[16] California, Massachusetts, Michigan, New Mexico, Oregon, and Texas.

[17] California, Delaware, Hawaii, Illinois, Iowa, Louisiana, Maine, Maryland, Massachusetts, Michigan, Minnesota, New Jersey, Oklahoma, Pennsylvania, Rhode Island, and Washington.

[18] Alaska, California, Connecticut, Delaware, Hawaii, Idaho, Maryland, Massachusetts, Minnesota, New Jersey, Oregon, Rhode Island, and Washington.

as a condition of employment, and in three other states,[19] requiring the licensing of lie-detector machine operators. There is considerable controversy in industry concerning the reliability of such tests and machines. Finally, in this specific law area, we should note again the existence of 20 state "right-to-work" laws,[20] which were examined in Chapter 6 and which outlaw compulsory unionism.

"Little Norris–La Guardia Acts"

Laws similar to the Norris–La Guardia Act have been enacted by 25 states[21] and Puerto Rico. As on the national scene, these laws have caused the number of injunctions issued in labor disputes to decline sharply. There is, however, tremendous variation in these anti-injunction laws, partly because many have been amended over the years to permit curbs on boycotts, picketing, and other weapons of conflict, and also because some state courts have tended to interpret the laws very narrowly, while others have interpreted them very broadly.

"Little Landrum-Griffin Laws"—Reporting, Disclosure, and Democracy

State labor relations acts in a number of jurisdictions provide for safeguards of union finances and members' rights. Reporting and disclosure laws involving union finances are also in effect in other states;[22] but in nearly all cases, enforcement mechanisms are lacking.

In addition, five states—California, Massachusetts, New York, Washington, and Wisconsin—have enacted legislation requiring disclosure about the activities of health and welfare funds set up by labor-management agreements. These laws require full disclosure of the income, disbursements, and operations of the covered funds, but they all lack effective enforcement mechanisms. Connecticut, which once had such a law, repealed it in 1967. As noted in Chapter 3, even the federal law, enacted in 1962, appears inadequate to police effectively the burgeoning welfare funds amassed by unions, and more stringent national legislation

---

[19] Arkansas, Florida, and Nevada.

[20] Alabama, Arizona, Arkansas, Florida, Georgia, Iowa, Kansas, Louisiana, Mississippi, Nebraska, Nevada, North Carolina, North Dakota, South Carolina, South Dakota, Tennessee, Texas, Utah, Virginia and Wyoming.

[21] Arizona, Colorado, Connecticut, Hawaii, Idaho, Illinois, Indiana, Kansas, Louisiana, Maine, Maryland, Massachusetts, Minnesota, Montana, New Jersey, New Mexico, New York, North Dakota, Oregon, Pennsylvania, Rhode Island, Utah, Washington, Wisconsin, and Wyoming.

[22] Alabama, Connecticut, Florida, Hawaii, Kansas, Massachusetts, Minnesota, New York, Oregon, South Dakota, Texas, Utah, and Wisconsin. The reporting requirements of the laws of Hawaii, Kansas, Massachusetts, Utah, and Wisconsin are not separate laws but are included in the "little Taft-Hartley laws" of these states.

is likely to be passed. The states do not appear to have either the will or the means to police union government, so that this has become and will continue to be a federal task except in special cases.

An unusual law is that enacted in 1952 by both New Jersey and New York to regulate waterfront conditions in the Port of New York. It established a bistate Authority to control crime on the waterfront by barring those convicted of felonies from serving as waterfront union officials and by regulating waterfront hiring practices. Although considerable success has been achieved by this Authority, particularly in bringing stability and fairness in the hiring of longshoremen, the Authority's own reports emphasize that crime on the waterfront, in the Port of New York as in many other ports, still flourishes. Pilfering, loansharking, and "kickbacks" remain problems difficult to eliminate in a labor market where more workers want jobs than there are jobs available and where the opportunities for preying on the job seeker, the customer, and the public are great. The persistence of similar organized thievery at New York airports has resulted in a move to place these areas under the control of the Waterfront Commission, but no legislation has resulted.

The two most comprehensive state laws aimed at furthering union democracy are the Minnesota Labor Union Democracy Act of 1943 and the New York Labor and Management Improper Practices Act of 1959. The Minnesota law regulates the details of union elections, providing that they must be held at least once every four years by secret ballot. The state can disqualify the union as a bargaining agent in case of violation. The law also gives the state the right to appoint a temporary labor referee to take charge of the union and to conduct a fair election. Although widely heralded when enacted, this law has never been invoked or utilized.

The New York law is very similar to the financial reporting sections of the Landrum-Griffin Act. It requires financial reporting by both employers and unions, imposes a fiduciary obligation on union officers and agents, and forbids conflict-of-interest transactions. The law also applies to employers and to labor relations consultants in a manner similar to that of the Landrum-Griffin Act by requiring annual reports on expenditures related to interference, restraint, or other attempts to sway employees away from their right to choose unions as bargaining agents.

The passage of the Landrum-Griffin Act immediately after New York enacted its legislation has tended to overshadow the New York law. Because of the Landrum-Griffin Act's broad coverage, few unions are outside its purview. Congress decided, however, not to bar concurrent state legislation, for it provided in Section 603(a) of the Landrum-Griffin Act that "except as explicitly provided to the contrary, nothing in this statute shall reduce or limit the responsibilities of any labor organization . . . or take away any right or bar any remedy to which members of a labor organization are entitled under any other federal law or law of any state." Whether a concurrent law like New York's Labor and Management Improper Practices Act can be significant, given the far-reaching character of the Landrum-Griffin Act, remains doubtful. Since Congress decided to exercise the full scope of federal jurisdiction in regulating internal union affairs, the states have not found it desirable to legislate further in this field.

Limits on Union Political Expenditures

A final group of laws aimed at controlling union finances are those which limit a union's right to utilize regular union income from membership dues, fees, and so forth, for political purposes. Four states—Pennsylvania, Texas, Indiana, and Wisconsin—limit union political contributions. The restrictions of the first two are rather narrow, of the last two rather broad. Like the proscriptions of the Taft-Hartley Act, however, their aim is to force unions to raise money for political purposes voluntarily and directly, instead of utilizing dues money, which may be collected from employees who oppose the aims for which or the people to whom the contribution is given. In general, these laws have been ineffective.

THE DECLINE OF STATE LABOR LEGISLATION

Despite their variety, state labor laws are today relatively insignificant, and indeed, often dormant. Federal preemption and the desire of unions and companies for uniform regulations have insured this result. Although many state laws have been poorly designed and unwisely administered, the takeover by the federal government is not without its adverse consequences. By permitting the states wider latitude, Congress and the courts could have utilized them as experimental laboratories for various forms of regulation and labor legislation. Instead, as is illustrated by the 1974 amendments to the Taft-Hartley Act providing for federal control of hospital labor disputes, many state laws, some of which have worked well for many years, have been stripped of most of their jurisdiction by acts of Congress.

The diversity of interests in the various states insures a wide variety of approaches to problems. Excessive federal preemption rules out experimentation, new solutions, and experience, all of which might well contribute to improved labor relations nationally. The one area seemingly left to the states is state and local public employment, since the Supreme Court has apparently ruled out federal intrusion for such employees.[23] The following chapter discusses public policy in this important field.

---

[23] *National League of Cities et al.* v. *W. J. Usery, Jr., Secretary of Labor*, 96 S. Ct. 2465 (1976).

QUESTIONS FOR DISCUSSION

1. Is mediation a difficult job to perform? Explain your answer.

2. Do you think that legislation can be devised which would both protect the country against strikes in emergency situations and maintain normal collective bargaining relationships? What type of legislation would be most advantageous to accomplish these two objectives? Explain your answer.

3. Does state labor legislation now on the books provide a comprehensive body of labor law for intrastate business? Do you think it should? Explain your answer.

4. Do you think that Congress should have permitted state laws affecting hospital labor relations to continue to operate without limit? Explain your answer.

SUGGESTIONS FOR FURTHER READING

Katz, Harold A., and Feldacker, Bruce S. "The Decline and Fall of State Regulation of Labor Relations," *Labor Law Journal*, vol. 20 (June 1969), pp. 327–45.

    An excellent summary of the various state laws regulating labor relations and the reasons for their declining significance.

Lewin, Jeff L. " 'Representatives of Their Own Choosing': Practical Consideration in the Selection of Bargaining Representatives for Seasonal Farmworkers," *Industrial Relations Law Journal*, vol. 1 (Spring 1976), pp. 55–117.

    An analysis of some problems arising under the pioneer California farm labor law by a protagonist of the union viewpoint.

Maggiolo, Walter A. *Techniques of Mediation in Labor Disputes*. Dobbs Ferry, N.Y.: Oceana Publications, 1971.

Simkin, William E. *Mediation and the Dynamics of Collective Bargaining*. Washington: Bureau of National Affairs, Inc., 1971.

    The former head of the Federal Mediation and Conciliation Service and a veteran mediator discuss the role of mediation, its nature and problems, and techniques and strategies used by mediators.

Rowan, Richard L. (ed.) *Collective Bargaining: Survival in the 70's?* Labor Relations and Public Policy Series, Report No. 5. Philadelphia: Industrial Research Unit, The Wharton School, University of Pennsylvania, 1972, pp. 129–306.

    A series of articles by several government, business, union, and academic authorities on mediation, emergency strikes, the Australian compulsory arbitration experience, and transportation labor problems.

22

Public Policy and the Public Employer

THE 20TH CENTURY has witnessed a rapid growth in the number of government employees, and more recently, a rising incidence of public sector unionism and strikes. Initially, labor relations scholars tended to regard such activities as growing pains associated with the development of private sector–like collective bargaining in the public sector. That public sector bargaining involves some fundamental differences from its counterpart in the private sector is now becoming increasingly clear. This chapter reviews public sector collective bargaining and analyzes the public policy problems relating thereto.

GOVERNMENT EMPLOYMENT

Over the past two decades, government employment has grown more rapidly than the total labor force. In 1975, as was pointed out in Chapter 1, the federal government employed 2.7 million civilians, 2.2 million were in the Armed Forces, and 12.0 million employees worked for local and state governments. Excluding Armed Forces personnel, the combined federal, state, and local governments employed 14,773,000 workers in 1975—more than 19% of nonagricultural employment. Table 22–1 and Figure 22–1 show the contribution made by the different levels of government to the growth of the public sector. The federal government continues to be the single largest employer, but the total number of workers employed by the states has exceeded federal employment since 1972.

Although the public sector labor force increased rapidly between 1950 and 1970, this rate of growth is not expected to be maintained. Public education employment comprised 40.8% of all civilian govern-

681

TABLE 22–1

Government Employment as a Percentage of Total
Nonagricultural Employment, Selected Years, 1940–1975

Year	Total	Federal	State and Local
1940 . . . . .13.0		3.1	9.9
1945 . . . . .14.7		7.0	7.8
1950 . . . . .13.3		4.3	9.0
1955 . . . . .13.6		4.3	9.3
1960 . . . . .15.4		4.2	11.2
1965 . . . . .16.6		3.9	12.7
1970 . . . . .17.7		3.9	13.9
1975 . . . . .19.2		3.6	15.6

Source: U.S. Department of Labor, Bureau of Labor Statistics.

ment employment in 1970. The education sector, which grew most rapidly between 1950 and 1970, is expected to advance much more slowly in response to the declining birthrate. Unless new major federal activities are developed, federal civilian employment will increase only slightly; and the Armed Forces, in the absence of an international crisis, will stabilize. Faced with monumental problems in meeting the costs of government payrolls, local governments have sought to reduce the size of the public labor force, not only by decreasing the number of new hires, but by laying off as well.

UNIONS AND STRIKES IN GOVERNMENT

Public employee unionism is not new, but its growth in recent years has been phenomenal. In the 16 years between 1956 and 1972, the proportion of government employees among all union members increased from 5% to 12%. Since the mid-1950s, the public sector unions have been the only ones in the labor movement to increase memberships at a rate faster than the increase in the labor force. Between 1960 and 1975, the American Federation of State, County, and Municipal Employees (AFSCME) saw its membership increase from 185,000 to 700,000; the American Federation of Government Employees (AFGE), the largest union of federal employees, from 70,000 to 325,000; and the American Federation of Teachers (AFT), from 56,000 to 440,000.[1] By 1971, various unions in the postal service claimed to represent virtually all eligible workers under their jurisdiction. Symbolic of the changing role of governments employee unions was the election of the presidents of both AFSCME and AFGE to the AFL–CIO Executive Council.

In addition to these "regular unions," other organizations have been acting as bargaining agents for government employees and are growing

---

[1] Data from U.S. Department of Labor, Bureau of Labor Statistics.

FIGURE 22–1

Government Employment, 1946–1974

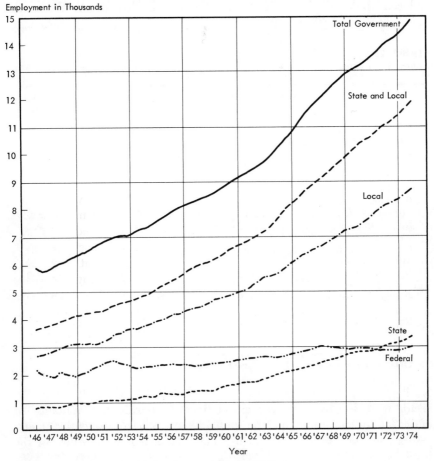

Source: U.S. Department of Labor, Bureau of Labor Statistics.

rapidly. Thus, chapters of the Policemen's Benevolent Association serve police officers in this regard, and the National Education Association, claiming 1.5 million members, once the only professional organization of public school teachers, now represents in collective bargaining (or "professional negotiations," as NEA spokesmen euphemistically term the process) many thousands more teachers than does its union rival, the American Federation of Teachers. Moreover, NEA chapters have conducted strikes, staffed picket lines, and otherwise acted as militantly as have AFT locals.

The employees in the public sector are today represented by a multitude of unions, quasi unions, and associations, which combined, make the public sector more highly organized than its private counterpart. Such diversity of organizations also adds to the negotiation problems and contributes to the difficulties of peaceful settlement. As shown in Table 22–2, over 40% of all work stoppages in 1974 in the government

TABLE 22–2
Work Stoppages in Government, by Union Affiliation and Recognition Status, 1974

	Number of Stoppages in Year	Workers Involved	Days Idle during Year
Total*	384	160,700	1,404,200
All unions and associations:			
Officially recognized	334	137,700	1,289,100
Not recognized	27	21,700	112,300
No information	3	500	1,000
AFL–CIO:			
Officially recognized	143	58,400	630,100
Not recognized	17	12,400	82,300
No information	2	400	700
Other unions:			
Officially recognized	33	13,900	84,500
Not recognized	5	8,300	24,900
No information	0	0	0
Employee associations			
Officially recognized	158	65,300	574,400
Not recognized	5	1,000	500
No information	1	100	300
No union	20	900	1,800

* Because of rounding, sums of individual items may not equal totals.
Source: U.S. Department of Labor, Bureau of Labor Statistics.

sector were led by employee associations. Moreover, the militancy of employee organizations in the public service has frequently "manifested itself in a determination to achieve union goals regardless of the law."[2]

The result has been conflict: between public employee unions and political leaders and between unions and those groups seeking enhanced control over governmental decisions affecting them. Some disputes have been settled, but only under the threat of a disruption of governmental services. Others—more than a few—have been settled only after an illegal strike that creates the atmosphere of a crisis if not the fact itself. And those disputes involving highly charged political issues, such as a police civilian review board or school decentralization plan, or touching society's most sensitive nerves by pitting a union of one race against a citizenry of another, have frequently left an ugly residue of racial and ethnic tension. The effects of such labor disputes on the social and

---

[2] Harry H. Wellington and Ralph K. Winter, Jr., *The Unions and the Cities*, Studies of Unionism in Government (Washington, D.C.: Brookings Institution, 1971), p. 35.

political fabric of New York City—and of the events of Memphis on the nation—surely demonstrate this deadly potential.[3]

THE STRIKE RECORD

The rising militancy of public workers, as indicated by their propensity to strike despite the fact that most strikes of public workers are illegal, is illustrated by the data in Table 22–3. These figures do not include such job actions as work slowdowns or refusals to work overtime—often used by municipal unions to protest budgetary required layoffs of government workers. In 1960, there were 36 stoppages of government employees involving 28,600 employees and 58,400 man-days idle; in 1974, the figures were 384 stoppages, 160,700 employees, and 1,404,000 man-days. The bulk of the stoppages have been in local government. As shown in Table 22–4, teachers have had the highest incidence of strikes, but police officers, fire fighters, sanitation workers, doctors, nurses, and various types of clerical and manual workers have all been involved in stoppages. Federal employees rarely engage in work stoppages, although well-advertised actions of airport traffic controllers and postal workers have disrupted air travel and postal service in recent years. As in industry as a whole, the major dispute behind work stoppages in the public sector involved general wage changes. Over 10% of stoppages in the public sector, however, compared with 5% of total industry stoppages, arose from union organization and security matters.

COMPENSATION

Historically, the public sector paid lower wages than the private one, but it provided more liberal benefits. For example, the cost attributable to various benefits almost doubled the total labor cost of New York City employees. Moreover, the 1960s saw changes in the relative wages offered in the private and public sector, undoubtedly as a result of the rising power of public employee organizations. The Federal Pay Comparability Act of 1970 requires that the president maintain federal employee pay rates comparable with private enterprise pay rates for the same levels of work. Successive salary increases voted by Congress at the urging of the strong lobby of the federal employee unions, plus "catch-up" increases to conform to the Pay Comparability Act, have resulted in substantial annual gains. Benefits to state and municipal government workers have also continued to rise, sometimes to such an extent, as in the case of pensions, that the fiscal integrity of local government bodies is in doubt. Faced with increasing problems in balancing the city's budget, New York City in 1976 was required to negotiate with major

---

[3] Ibid.

TABLE 22-3
Work Stoppages by Level of Government,* 1960, 1970, and 1974

Year	Total			State Government			Local Government		
	Number of Stoppages	Total Workers Involved	Man-Days Idle	Number of Stoppages	Total Workers Involved	Man-Days Idle	Number of Stoppages	Total Workers Involved	Man-Days Idle
1960	36	28,600	58,400	3	970	1,170	33	27,600	57,200
1970	412†	333,500	2,023,200	23	8,800	44,600	386	168,900	1,330,500
1974	384‡	160,700	1,404,200	34	24,700	86,400	348	135,400	1,316,300

* Includes stoppages lasting a full day or shift or longer and involving six or more workers.
† Includes three stoppages of federal employees affecting 155,800 workers and resulting in 648,300 man-days of idleness.
‡ Includes two stoppages of federal employees affecting 500 workers and resulting in 1,400 man-days of idleness.
Source: U.S. Department of Labor, Bureau of Labor Statistics.

TABLE 22-4
Government Employee Work Stoppages by Occupation, 1974

	Stoppages Beginning in Year		Workers Involved		Days Idle during Year	
	Number	Percentage	Number	Percentage	Number	Percentage
All occupations	384	100.0	160,700	100.0	1,404,200	100.0
Teachers	133	34.6	60,100	37.4	538,000	38.3
Nurses	1	0.3	100	0.1	13,000	0.9
Other professions	3	0.8	200	0.1	1,200	0.1
Clerical	4	1.0	400	0.3	1,000	0.1
Sanitation workers	8	2.1	200	0.1	1,600	0.1
Craft workers	6	1.6	300	0.2	1,000	0.1
Blue collar and manual .	107	27.9	26,700	16.6	140,600	10.0
Police officers	12	3.1	1,500	0.9	4,500	0.3
Fire fighters	11	2.9	4,300	2.7	55,200	3.9
Other protective	6	2.9	1,600	1.0	8,700	0.6
Service workers	3	0.8	400	0.3	1,700	0.1
Professional, technical, and clerical	11	2.0	4,300	2.7	55,200	3.9
Clerical and blue collar ...	30	7.8	12,200	7.6	313,000	22.3
Professional, technical, and blue collar.....	41	10.7	40,100	25.0	256,900	18.3
Protective and blue collar ...	8	2.1	11,200	7.0	57,500	40.9

Source: U.S. Department of Labor, Bureau of Labor Statistics.

municipal unions in an attempt to reduce benefits attained in prior contracts, or face bankruptcy. Many other cities are also in a precariously
tight fiscal situation.

PENSIONS—A SPECIAL CASE

As noted in Chapter 5, pensions were once considered a gratuity
awarded upon retirement for loyal service. Now, pensions are considered
deferred wages that the employee has earned but can collect only upon
retirement. The revised concept of pensions raises serious questions
concerning the validity of the "pay-as-you-go" financing of many government pension plans.

The levels and kinds of benefits provided in public retirement systems and the financing of those benefits are subject to decisions made
under pressure in a political atmosphere. In addition to agreeing to the
pension benefits of government employees, elected officials also legislate such benefits for themselves. Elected officials also sometimes find
it more politically acceptable to raise their wages in the form of deferred
income instead of a standard pay increase. One reason for New York
City's financial problems—its liberal pension program—is illustrated by
the calculation that Mayor Abraham Beame can retire on a pension of
about $71,200 annually, or $10,000 more than he would receive in
salary if he continues as mayor![4]

High benefit levels for government workers are not restricted to those
elected to office; if he retires at age 65 after 30 or more years of service,
a married male employee of New York City will draw retirement income, net after taxes, inclusive of social security for himself and his
wife, when she is 65, that will be greater than his aftertax income in
his final year of work.[5]

> The benefit levels of the public plans are, as of January 1, 1972,
> approximately double those prevailing in private industry. Many of the
> public employees do not, however, have the dual coverage of Social
> Security. When that is taken into account, the combined benefits pro-
> vided to the employees of state and local governments are approximately
> one-third higher than are provided by the plans in private industry.[6]

The funding problem for state and local governments is one of the
most important of the unsolved conflicts. Insufficient funding initially
reduces taxpayers' costs and is therefore politically popular, but it
threatens the solvency of the funds. Government pension plans represent

---

[4] *U.S. News & World Report,* May 10, 1976, p. 8.

[5] Robert Tilove, *Public Employee Pension Funds* (New York: Columbia University Press, 1976), pp. 277–78.

[6] Ibid., p. 339.

continuing costs to taxpayers. Some have claimed that underfunding, which usually arises from liberalizing benefits and letting future generations of legislators and taxpayers decide how to meet the fiscal obligations, represents no real problem because of the funds' claim on tax revenues. This argument, however, ignores the increased benefit liberalization that is encouraged by a policy of significant and continued underfunding.[7] Government pension plans are not covered by the Pension Reform Act (ERISA); thus, in view of current fiscal problems, the liberal pension benefits previously negotiated by public sector unions may never be realized.

Federal civil service pensions are extremely liberal by any yardstick. Civil service employees with 30 years of service can retire at age 65 on a full pension; they can then take a job in private industry and become eligible for a second pension under social security legislation, as approximately 40% of the early civil service retirees do. Moreover, civil service pensions have been subject to an extraordinary cost-of-living arrangement whereby a 3% increase in the Consumer Price Index provides them with a 4% pension increase![8] This was eliminated as of 1977.

Even in disability matters, the federal system is questionably beneficial. Whereas private plans usually provide for disability benefits if the employee cannot perform *any* job, the federal system pays such benefits if the employee cannot perform *his current* job. A warehouse worker with a bad back who can do a lighter job can thus retire on disability. No wonder, then, that disability retirements in the federal system are about 50% higher than in private industry.

PUBLIC SECTOR BARGAINING

In the private sector, collective bargaining, theoretically, is a means of achieving labor peace, of increasing worker participation in determining the terms and conditions of employment, of giving employees a force through which to work in political arenas, and of equalizing or increasing employee bargaining power vis-à-vis that of the employer.[9] Although collective bargaining works imperfectly even in the private sector, there remains a strong presumption that collective bargaining may still be preferred to other methods of solving labor-management disputes, for example, compulsory arbitration, primarily because it permits the parties themselves to determine their own industrial fate.

---

[7] Louis M. Kohlmeier, *Conflicts of Interest: State and Local Pension Fund Asset Management* (New York: Twentieth Century Fund, 1976), p. 51.

[8] As an example, former Speaker of the House Carl Albert retired with a pension of $51,000 per year, plus cost-of-living increases (*New York Times,* July 8, 1976, p. 28).

[9] See Wellington and Winter, *Unions and Cities,* pp. 8–9.

SOVEREIGNTY AND STRIKES

The argument for transferring the private sector bargaining system to the public sector is formidable and has wide support. Moreover, it has overcome many decades of traditional opposition based on the theory of sovereignty. For many years the assumption was that since the government represents the sovereign power, it alone could set the terms and conditions for the employment of its employees. Critics quickly pointed out that sovereign authorities can delegate and share authority. As early as 1912, with the passage of the Lloyd–La Follette Act, the federal government conceded to its employees the right to petition, to confer, or to request changes in their conditions of employment; without interference; this was generally interpreted to mean approval of federal employee unionism. Nevertheless, many states and municipalities questioned the right of public employees to unionize, or declined to bargain, or even to confer, with representatives of employees. Often, government leaders who did bargain refused to sign contracts, limiting arguments to verbal understandings or else posting the results of "agreements" on bulletin boards as managerial decisions.[10]

A second traditional argument advanced against permitting collective bargaining for government employees is that strikes would inevitably result (as they have); and that strikes against government are both insurrectionary and intolerable because they interrupt vital services. In the post–World War II period, several states passed laws forbidding strikes of government employees and providing for severe penalties for such strikers. The tone of these laws was similar to that of the Taft-Hartley Act of 1947 which states:

> It shall be unlawful for any individual employed by the United States or any agency thereof including wholly-owned government corporations to participate in any strike. Any individual employed by the United States or by any such agency, who strikes, shall be discharged immediately from his employment, and shall forfeit his civil service status, if any, and shall not be eligible for reemployment for three years by the United States or any such agency.

Opponents of the traditional ban against strikes of public employees have noted quite correctly, that strikes are not insurrections, that many public workers provide less essential services than do private workers, and that the status of employees should not change because private interests sell their companies to public agencies, or vice versa. There is certainly much truth in these assertions. A massive withdrawal of minor government clerks not only poses no inconvenience to the public, but

---

[10] Court decisions of recent years would appear to invalidate state laws or local ordinances which deny public employees the right to join unions. On the other hand, in the absence of specific legislation to the contrary, no public body is required to bargain with a union of its employees. For details see ibid., pp. 69–82.

may actually benefit the public by illustrating the nonessential character of much government work. On the other hand, a strike of privately operated railroads could cause tremendous inconvenience, or even a national emergency. Finally, as many transit systems are sold to public bodies, should their employees lose the right to strike? When private companies purchase public power plants, as they have on several occasions, do the employees then obtain the right to strike? In each case, a strike has the same impact on the public, whether the striking employees are from the public or the private sector.

Arguments on these narrow grounds have set the tone of public policy since the late 1950s. The federal government, by executive order, and a majority of the states, by legislation, have encouraged collective bargaining on the private sector model. Although the federal government and most states do not legalize strikes of government employees, seven states[11] have enacted legislation allowing a limited opportunity for legal strikes by certain types of public employees. Whatever the legislation, the penalties invoked in the event of an illegal strike are not generally enforced, and the laws forbidding strikes are ignored for the most part both by unions and by government agencies.

FEDERAL EMPLOYEE REGULATION

Although a few state laws encouraging public employee bargaining antedated modern federal action, it was Executive Order 10988, issued by President John F. Kennedy on January 17, 1962, that set the tone for current policy. Even though the Lloyd–La Follette Act of 1912, as already noted, gave federal employees the right to join unions, prior to the Kennedy order the federal government did not have a consistent program of union recognition and collective bargaining for its employees. Some agencies, such as the Tennessee Valley Authority, recognized unions and dealt with them as exclusive bargaining agents, even signing contracts with them. Others, which had less discretion in determining conditions of employment, dealt with unions in much the same manner, but did not sign contracts. In such cases, notices embodying the substance of what had been agreed to with the government employees' union were sometimes posted on bulletin boards over the signature of the agency or department manager. Many agencies, however, neither recognized nor dealt with unions.

The Kennedy order provided for three separate forms of recognition—exclusive, formal, and informal—depending on the extent to which employees designated unions to represent them. Bargaining was necessarily restricted in scope because Congress established wages and benefits, and compulsory union membership was not permitted.

---

[11] Alaska, Hawaii, Minnesota, Montana, Oregon, Pennsylvania, and Vermont.

On October 29, 1969, President Nixon modified federal policy by Executive Order 11491. It provides for exclusive representation only, based upon majority rule. The Nixon order sets forth unfair labor practices and standards of union conduct on the Taft-Hartley and Landrum-Griffin models, and designates the Assistant Secretary of Labor for Labor-Management Relations to administer changes pursuant to these sections and also to make bargaining unit determinations. The federal government's policy toward work stoppages by its employees is specified in Section 19(b)(4) of the order, which makes it an unfair labor practice for a public employee labor organization to "call" or engage in a strike, work stoppage, or slowdown; to picket an agency in a labor-management dispute; or to condone any such activity by failing to take affirmative action to stop it. With a few highly publicized exceptions in the past several years, the absolute ban on work stoppages by federal employees has been respected by employee organizations.

The extent of organization in the federal government has mushroomed dramatically since the Kennedy order. More than 1 million, or 53%, of the nonpostal federal employees were covered by union agreements in 1975. The magnitude of union representation of eligible employees is not indicated by the percentage figures, however, since these are based on total federal employment. But of the 2,704 units covered by agreements in 1975, the American Federation of Government Employees (AFGE) represented 1,724 units; the National Federation of Federal Employees (NFFE), 690; the National Treasury Employees Union (NTEU), 101; the National Association of Government Employees (NAGE), 333; the Machinists (IAM), 96; and the AFL–CIO Metal Trades Council (MTC), 51.[12]

Under the Nixon executive order, the scope of bargaining continues to be limited, and compulsory union membership banned.[13] Federal government employee unions have historically lobbied for higher wages and benefits through legislative action. The smaller scope of bargaining, particularly in view of the oft-demonstrated influence of these unions with Congress, is therefore not necessarily a disadvantage. The Postal Reorganization Act of 1970 may, however, presage a change of method toward greater bargaining and less legislation.

Subchapter II of the 1970 postal law, which abolished the Post Office Department and set up an independent government corporation to handle

---

[12] "More Than One Million Non-postal Federal Employees Were Covered by Union Agreements in November 1975," *Daily Labor Report* No. 34 (February 19, 1976), pp. A–1, A–2.

[13] For good summaries of the federal public employee bargaining arrangements, see Lee C. Shaw, "The Development of Federal and State Laws," in Sam Zagoria (ed.), *Public Workers and Public Unions* (Englewood Cliffs, N.J.: Prentice-Hall, Inc., 1972), pp. 24–26; and Harriet E. Berger, "The Old Order Giveth Away to the New: A Comparison of Executive Order 10988 with Executive Order 11491," *Labor Law Journal,* vol. 21 (February 1970), pp. 79–87.

the mails, puts postal employees under the Taft-Hartley Act instead of under Executive Order 11491, insofar as representation and unfair labor practices are concerned. The postal law, however, prohibits strikes, outlaws all union security arrangements except the voluntary checkoff, and provides for fact finding and, if required, compulsory arbitration, to resolve impasses. Of major significance is Subchapter II's provision that wages, hours, and working conditions are to be negotiated by postal unions which have exclusive bargaining rights. Moreover, whereas Executive Orders 10988 and 11491 both contain strong management rights clauses, Subchapter II instead appears to make union proposals restricting technological changes or limiting subcontracting matters of mandatory bargaining.[14]

The Federal Pay Comparability Act of 1970 also increases the scope of bargaining for federal employees. The law transfers to the president the establishment of salaries of classified federal employees but retains a veto for Congress. Unions are given a very substantial role in the steps which precede the president's determination:

> A Federal Employee Pay Council is established, with five members of employee organizations. Their views are to be sought and given "thorough consideration" by the President's agents (the Office of Management and Budget and the Civil Service Commission) on such matters as the coverage of the annual BLS survey (which serves as the basis for comparison with private enterprise levels for the same levels of work), the process of comparing statutory pay rates with these levels, and the actual adjustments proposed to achieve comparability. The report to the President by his agents is to include the views thus presented. An independent Advisory Committee on Federal Pay is also established. For presidential appointment of the three members, persons are to be recommended by the Director of the Federal Mediation and Conciliation Service who are "generally recognized for their impartiality, knowledge, and experience in the field of labor relations and pay policy." The advisory committee is to review the annual report of the President's agents, consider further views presented in writing by employee organizations, the President's agents, and other government officials, and report its findings and recommendations to the President.[15]

The first two years after Executive Order 11491 saw a dramatic turn toward the bargaining table by federal employee organizations. Whereas these unions had previously been content to organize workers and to represent them in grievance procedures, requests for FMCS assistance have increased. Mediators found that the parties were unusually inexperienced in contract negotiations, that many issues involved questions of negotiability under the management's rights clauses in the executive order, and

---

[14] Shaw, "Federal and State Laws," p. 25.

[15] Joseph P. Goldberg, "Public Employee Developments in 1971," *Monthly Labor Review*, vol. 95 (January 1972), pp. 56–57.

that delays were caused by the inability to determine who in the bureaucracy could make specific decisions. Thus, in 1973, W. J. Usery, Jr., then director of FMCS, issued a new policy for mediators to follow in federal bargaining disputes.

> ... Our Service will become an *active advocate* of collective bargaining in the Federal Government in units where unions have been appropriately recognized as certified bargaining agents. ...
>
> Accordingly, we must recognize two important differences in the way mediators must work in Federal Government negotiations: (1) During negotiations, more time must be devoted to patiently educating the parties to their roles and responsibilities, and (2) more time must be devoted to ascertaining, and dealing with, the real decisionmakers, especially within their agencies.[16]

The procedure leaves open to the unions their effective lobbying privileges in case they do not like the president's determination. This two-bites-at-the-apple procedure—bargaining and political maneuvering—is one of the factors that distinguishes the public sector situation from the private. Although the above procedure purports to further bargaining and to decrease lobbying, it would appear to do that only if the unions are satisfied with the results of bargaining.

STATE AND MUNICIPAL REGULATION

As of January 1977, 26 states had enacted general public employee bargaining laws;[17] 15 had passed legislation covering teachers;[18] 9, special laws for firemen and/or policemen;[19] and others, separate laws for particular groups, such as transit[20] or facilities formerly operated privately. Some states, such as Pennsylvania, had both general legislation and special laws for specific classes of public employees.

The general public employee legislation is of two kinds: the most common kind provides for required collective bargaining on the Taft-Hartley Act model; a minority of states, however, require only that the

---

[16] Jerome H. Ross, "Federal Mediation in the Public Sector," *Monthly Labor Review*, vol. 99 (February 1976), p. 42.

[17] Alaska, California, Connecticut, Delaware, Florida, Hawaii, Illinois, Indiana, Iowa, Maine, Massachusetts, Michigan, Minnesota, Missouri, Montana, Nebraska, Nevada, New Jersey, New York, Ohio, Oregon, Pennsylvania, Rhode Island, South Dakota, Texas, Vermont, and Wisconsin.

[18] Alabama, Alaska, Connecticut, Delaware, Florida, Idaho, Indiana, Kansas, Maryland, Nebraska, North Dakota, Oklahoma, Rhode Island, Vermont, and Washington.

[19] Firemen only: Georgia, Idaho, Kentucky, Utah, and Wyoming. Firemen and policemen: Oklahoma, Pennsylvania, Rhode Island, and Texas.

[20] For transit, see Darold T. Barnum, "From Public to Private: Labor Relations in Urban Transit," *Industrial and Labor Relations Review*, vol. 25 (October 1971), pp. 95–115.

public bodies "meet and confer" with representatives of employees. The trend is definitely for the latter to be supplanted by the former. In some states, agencies were created to administer the legislation; in other states, the legislation provided that existing administrative bodies were to assume these duties, which include bargaining unit determination, unfair labor practice enforcement, and in many cases, the application of impasse resolution techniques.

Bargaining Unit Problems

The inexperience of state and local administrators has led to a large number of fragmented bargaining units and a host of concomitant problems familiar to students of labor relations in the construction, railroad, printing, maritime, air transport, and amusement industries, which are organized on a craft union basis. Except in a few cities, such as Philadelphia, recognition has usually been given to unions on an extent-of-organization basis, regardless of administrative efficiency or employee affinity of interest. Then as other employees unionize, new units are recognized. The result has been exacerbated union rivalries, attempts of one union to gain increases in excess of another, and in many cases, almost continual turmoil. New York City is an extreme example of this problem.[21]

Inexperienced public officials have also failed to give heed to private sector experience in other ways. Professional and clerical employees have sometimes been submerged into units dominated by blue-collar workers, causing unrest, dissatisfaction, and recruitment difficulties. Confidential employees (for example, secretaries to administrators), supervisory employees, and even middle-management personnel have been placed in bargaining units, with the result that their value to management has been dissipated. In other situations, governmental units have negotiated increases with unions and not provided increases for supervisory and managerial personnel, causing the latter to unionize in order to seek redress, as they have in Pennsylvania. And as in the 1930s in the private sector, collective bargaining in the public sector has sometimes so enhanced union power and deflated that of supervisors and lower management that the latter have sought unions of their own, quit their jobs, or ceased to attempt to work effectively.

The Scope of Bargaining

Of major importance in the public sector has been the scope of bargaining. This is now primarily a state and local problem, for the executive orders have limited the scope of bargaining in the federal service. Teach-

---

[21] See A. H. Raskin, "Politics Upends the Bargaining Table," in Zagoria, *Public Workers,* pp. 138–42.

ers negotiate about classroom size, curricula, and student discipline; professors demand the right to elect department heads; social workers strike against more stringent welfare regulations and demand that restrictions be placed on case loads; policemen, firemen, nurses, and others negotiate terms affecting the scope of their work and the extent and degree of protection afforded the public. As a result, the public employee unions assume considerable power over and above other interest groups to determine the extent and quality of public service. In the words of Wellington and Winter: "When this occurs, the scope of bargaining in the public sector must be regulated in a manner that will adequately limit the role of unions in the political decision-making process."[22]

Civil Service Conflicts

Collective bargaining in most government sectors is superimposed on existing civil service regulations. These regulations often set forth rules for promotion, pay increases, and job protection. Sometimes this results in restrictions on what may be bargained, conflicts in the locus of authority, or bargaining for improvements over and above what is provided automatically by law. Thus, if the promotion process is set forth in law, it cannot be altered by bargaining unless there is further enabling legislation. On the other hand, employees who have processed grievances through the collective bargaining grievance machinery have, if not satisfied, started the process all over again via civil service procedures. Contrary and conflicting rulings have resulted. In Pennsylvania, where teachers receive automatic wage increases of $300 each year, their unions bargain for how much above these increases they should receive. It remains to be seen, in view of these conflicts, whether collective bargaining and civil service rules and procedures can continue to coexist and, if so, in what form.[23]

Union Security Clauses

Although government employee unions have pushed increasingly for union security clauses, most regulation proscribes any form of the union and closed shop, or even less stringent forms of union organization, but the checkoff of dues under individual authorizations is more often permitted. Compulsory union memberhip is prohibited both by the federal executive order and the Postal Reorganization Act, and most state statutes are similar. Kentucky and Washington, however, authorize the union

---

[22] Wellington and Winter, *Unions and Cities,* p. 142.

[23] For a further analysis of the problems associated with the imposition of collective bargaining on existing civil service regulations, see U.S. Department of Labor, Labor-Management Services Administration, *Collective Bargaining in Public Employment and the Merit System* (Washington, D.C.: Government Printing Office, 1972).

shop, and Alaska may do so. Moreover, a few states, such as Connecticut, provide for the agency shop, and Pennsylvania authorizes maintenance of membership agreements.

Since civil service regulations provide for continuity of employment—and indeed, often tenure—compulsory union membership with the threat of discharge for nonpayment of dues runs directly counter to such regulations. Considerable litigation has therefore resulted from union security provisions or contracts in public employment in various states. The U.S. Supreme Court is expected to give a decisive ruling in a pending case.[24]

In part because of their desire to legalize union security clauses, government employee unions have been pushing federal legislation designed either to place public employees under the Taft-Hartley Act or to establish a similar federal law and agency for public employees. In view of the U.S. Supreme Court's decision in striking down federal minimum wage laws for state and municipal employees, as discussed in Chapter 16, it would appear that the federal government can enact such legislation only for federal employees.

Impasse Resolution

Although most of the states have established public policy through legislation which prohibits work stoppages of government employees, limited work stoppages of such employees have been legalized in some states.[25] In 1967, the Vermont legislators became the first to give public employees, except teachers, the right to strike as long as there was no danger to health, safety, or welfare; not even policemen or firemen were denied this right. A 1973 amendment to the Vermont statute, however, restricts the legality of such strikes to: (1) work stoppages occurring after a fact-finding report, (2) disputes not subject to final and binding arbitration, and (3) strikes that do not endanger the public health, safety, or welfare.

In 1970, two highly publicized laws allowing public employee strikes were passed in Hawaii and Pennsylvania. The Hawaii law covers all public employees, while the Pennsylvania statute excludes policemen, firemen, prison and mental health guards, and court employees. Both states established two principal requirements for a legal work stoppage of public employees: good-faith mediation and fact-finding efforts had to be exhausted, and the stoppage must not endanger public health, safety, or welfare.

An Alaska statute, passed in 1972, allows strikes of public employees but makes their legality contingent upon the essentiality of the employ-

---

[24] The Court is expected to rule by mid-1977 on this issue.

[25] For a discussion of state laws on public work stoppages, see Jerome T. Barrett, "Public Sector Strikes—Legislative and Court Treatment," *Monthly Labor Review*, vol. 97 (September 1974), pp. 19–22.

ees' functions. In 1973, Minnesota and Oregon passed laws dealing with the right of public employees to strike. The Minnesota law, which covers all public employees, does not legalize strikes of public employees, but provides that the failure to utilize arbitration in an interest dispute with "nonessential" public employees may result in a court's refusal to enjoin a strike if it does not create a clear and present danger to public health or safety. The Oregon statute allows strikes of all public employees except policemen, firemen, and guards at correctional and mental institutions, and requires that impasses be referred through binding arbitration. A statute passed in Montana in 1973 covers all public employees other than nurses and teachers. The Montana law makes no mention of strikes; however, a state district court has interpreted the act as granting public employees the right to strike.

Thus, in the last nine years, a number of states have become receptive to the concept of legalized public employee strikes. Nevertheless, the most common type of impasse resolution procedure is mediation followed by fact finding. Since this does not supply a final resolution unless accepted by both parties, and since strikes have occurred increasingly, many jurisdictions are moving toward compulsory arbitration. Policemen and firemen favor this approach, undoubtedly because their pleas generally seem to fall upon sympathetic arbitral ears.

The principal reason why compulsory arbitration has not gained more adherents is that it removes final fiscal authority from the electorate to a third party who is not responsible to that electorate. Thus, in Pennsylvania generous arbitration awards for policemen or firemen have compelled elected officials to alter town budgets and curtail some services in order to provide the policemen and firemen with the compensation ordered by arbitrators pursuant to the state law. Perhaps the solution is to devise comprehensive regulations limiting the scope of arbitral authority, but this is difficult to accomplish.

Experiments have been instituted which modify the collective bargaining process in the public sector. In 1972, the Michigan and Wisconsin legislatures enacted statutes providing for final-offer arbitration.[26] The Wisconsin statute forces the arbitrator to select the entire final-offer package of one or the other of the parties, while in Michigan a final-offer-by-issue system is prescribed. In either case, final-offer arbitration seems to alter the balance of power of the disputing parties—giving more power to the weaker party.

A number of states, including New York, provide penalties for strikers, or for officials of unions and/or unions which engage in strikes. Such penalties include checkoff revocations, fines, and jail terms. They have not deterred strikes. It may be that they are not sufficiently harsh. More often, however, politicians decline to invoke penalties, and this is always

---

[26] See James L. Stern et al., *Final Offer Arbitration* (Lexington, Mass.: D. C. Heath and Co., 1975).

likely to be the case. The reason is clear: politics, not economics, is supreme in public employee collective bargaining—a major reason why strikes in the public service cannot serve the purpose of motivating agreement. Table 22–5 compares the types of settlement ending work

TABLE 22–5
Work Stoppages by Type of Settlement, 1974

	Stoppages Ending in 1974		Workers Involved	Days Idle
	Number	Percentage		
All industry	6,031	100.0	2,795,000	49,881,000
Formal settlement reached	4,905	81.3	2,474,300	47,049,100
No formal settlement reached				
Short protest or sympathy strike	533	8.8	158,900	274,800
Strike broken	236	3.9	32,100	1,087,700
Work resumed under court injunction	210	3.5	96,700	341,400
Employer out of business	45	0.8	3,900	224,800
No information	110	1.8	29,100	903,100
Government	381	100.0	160,400	1,396,000
Formal settlement reached	297	80.0	130,100	1,266,400
No formal settlement reached				
Short protest or sympathy strike	28	7.3	12,200	12,900
Strike broken	24	6.3	5,000	46,500
Work resumed under court injunction	32	8.4	13,200	70,200
Employer out of business	—	—	—	—
No information	—	—	—	—

Source: U.S. Department of Labor, Bureau of Labor Statistics.

stoppages of government workers and of industry as a whole in 1974. In both categories, approximately 80% of the disputes reached a formal settlement. In 8.4% of the government strikes, compared with 3.5% for all industry, work was resumed under a court injunction.

STRIKE POLICY IN PUBLIC EMPLOYMENT

In the private sector, as we have noted in previous chapters, collective bargaining is theoretically constrained by economic realities and the fact that the strike induces settlement by hurting both parties. Of course, this system works haltingly, and it works better in some periods and in some industries than in others. Moreover, government policy, by such actions as intervention in disputes which enhances the power of one of the parties too greatly, or paying welfare to strikers, often inhibits the effectiveness of the system.

Nevertheless, the constraints are real. The construction unions seemed to be able to gain unlimited increases in the late 1960s; yet in 1972, their leaders were attempting to hold local unions in line because of the widespread loss of work to nonunion competitors. Periodically, unions have negotiated wage decreases, fought for tariffs to exclude foreign competitors, or otherwise demonstrated their concern for economic constraints. These same constraints have forced employers to endure long strikes in order to maintain economic viability.

The demand for labor in the private sector is thus elastic in varying degrees. To the extent that unions push up wages, they risk a trade-off for unemployment. Some, such as the United Mine Workers, have done this almost with impunity; yet in nearly all cases, the elasticity of demand for labor reduces union wage push.

In the public sector, however, it has generally been assumed that the demand for services is usually inelastic. Indeed, a service is likely to be performed by government because it is a natural monopoly. Union wage pushes in the public sector are likely to be resisted only slightly because of this inelasticity. And when a strike occurs, the clamor for resumption of service is likely to be overwhelming: the strike hurts the public before it hurts the union. *Politically*, the union cannot be resisted.

It is the political factor which gives the unions such power in the public sector. Opposing the union in a tense situation is likely to win a politician few new friends and many enemies. The public wants the service; that it will be obtained at the expense of deterioration in other services is not usually immediately discernible. To an ambitious politician who desires to remain in office or go on to better things, there is often really no choice.

Political alliances between public employees and incumbent politicians are not new. With the former in strong unions, however, such alliances take on new meaning. Through both economic and political means, public employees are able to exert powerful pressure to enhance their economic well-being.

This is particularly true where the impact of concessions shows up later. Pension benefits can sometimes be given at little present cost, but at phenomenal later costs, at a time, perhaps, when a new incumbent will have to wrestle with the resultant revenue problems.

The rise in earnings gains means that priority for government service allocation has been passing from a variety of interest groups to unions. There comes a time, however, when local governments are forced to slash their payrolls in an attempt to attain fiscal solvency. As one study noted:

> When a firm's costs rise and internal economizing is unsuccessful, it must receive higher prices from consumers or accept lower profits. Since large city governments don't make profits, they must receive higher

"prices" to continue operating at the same level. Governments "raise prices" by increasing taxes—the price of public services to citizens. This solution has fallen on hard times, however. Taxpayers across the land are "revolting" against increased levies. . . .

If no other source of funds can be tapped, the only alternative for a government is to slash expenditures and services. If the price of theater tickets or dinners goes up, people generally go out less often. In sum, the taxpayers of large cities face a Hobson's choice. If wage changes raise the cost of police protection and city taxpayers refuse to fork over higher taxes, "somebody else"—the state house or even the White House —must foot the bill or there will be less protection. The same goes for schools, streets, and social welfare. The laws of economics apply just as clearly to governments as to firms. Public employees cannot be paid more unless greater sacrifices are made.[27]

In the mid-1970s, the financial plight of some local governments was so great that public sentiment changed significantly, to the point where it became politically acceptable to withstand a strike of public employee unions. New York City, during this era of retrenchment, was forced to lay off many public employees, and its unions negotiated to maintain the benefits obtained in prior contracts rather than to obtain huge wage increases. In Massachusetts state employees struck for three days, but when the state held firm and threatened stiff fines, they went back to work with nothing gained except progress in negotiations. In San Francisco, where some city workers struck for 36 days against pay cuts, the stoppage had only a minor impact. It has become increasingly obvious to union leaders and members that local governments do not have unlimited funds and that strikes can be lost as well as won.

Another reason for believing that strikes should not play a part in public employee bargaining is the extent to which race can exacerbate such situations. Teachers' strikes in New York, garbage collectors' strikes in Memphis and Atlanta, and public hospital employees' strikes in Charleston, South Carolina, have been just a few such strikes with strong racial overtones. The extent of blacks in municipal work and of whites in municipal authority indicate a potential for public employee strikes to become racial conflicts. On that ground alone, it would seem better not to consider public employee strikes as proper methods of impasse resolution.

Given the political and economic power of public employees, and the explosive environment, it seems unrealistic to suppose that public employee strikes can contribute to the public good. It must be recognized that such strikes will occur. It must also be recognized that other forms of settlement, for example, compulsory arbitration, are imperfect instru-

---

[27] James L. Freund, "Wage Pressures on City Hall: Philadelphia Experiences Perspective," *Federal Reserve Bank of Philadelphia Business Review*, March 1972, p. 17.

ments, often yielding unsatisfactory results. Certainly, we need new social experimentation and social engineering to provide us with new tools to resolve the problems of public employees. But to transfer to the public sector the collective bargaining mechanism developed in the private sector ignores the fundamental institutional differences between the two. As Wellington and Winter conclude:

> We believe that in the cities, counties and states [as well as in the federal government] there are other claimants with needs at least as pressing as those of the public employees. Such claimants can never have the power the unions will win if we mindlessly import into the public sector all the collective bargaining practices developed in the private sector. Make no mistake about it, government is not "just another industry."[28]

QUESTIONS FOR DISCUSSION

1. What are the features of public employment which distinguish it from private employment? How should these features influence public policy determination?
2. Why have most union activity and strikes in the public sector occurred in the cities? Have municipal unions been successful and, if so, by what criteria?
3. How will the Federal Pay Comparability Act affect salary determination and collective bargaining in the public service?
4. Do you think that compulsory unionism should be permitted or encouraged in government service? Explain your answer.

SUGGESTIONS FOR FURTHER READING

Chickering, A. Lawrence (ed.). *Public Employee Unions: A Study of the Crisis in Public Sector Labor Relations.* San Francisco: Institute for Contemporary Studies, 1976.

A series of essays by scholars, union officials, and mayors giving a current and realistic account of the nature and problems of public employee relations.

Perry, Charles R. *The Labor Relations Climate and Management Rights in Urban School Systems.* Labor Relations and Public Policy Series, Report No. 11. Philadelphia: Industrial Research Unit, The Wharton School, University of Pennsylvania, 1974.

An analysis of how teachers have been able to increase salaries, decrease hours and work loads, and assume management functions in large cities, utilizing a case study of Philadelphia for in-depth examination.

Stern, James L., et al. *Final Offer Arbitration.* Lexington Books. Lexington, Mass.: D. C. Heath and Co., 1975.

---

[28] Wellington and Winter, *Unions and Cities,* p. 202.

A study of the experience of several states with arbitration which limits the discretion of the arbitrator.

Stieber, Jack. *Public Employee Unionism*. Studies of Unionism in Government. Washington: Brookings Institution, 1973.

A broad, factual survey of the public employee union movement.

Tilove, Robert. *Public Employee Pension Funds*. New York: Columbia University Press, 1976.

A detailed analysis of the public employee pension system by an outstanding expert in the field.

Wellington, Harry H., and Winter, Ralph K., Jr. *The Unions and the Cities*. Studies of Unionism in Government. Washington, D.C.: Brookings Institution, 1971.

A careful analysis of the necessary differences between private and public employee union policy.

23

Civil Rights and Equal
Pay Legislation

THE CIVIL RIGHTS ACT of 1964, as amended in 1972, makes it unlawful for a company, union, employment agency, or joint labor-management apprentices committee to discriminate because of religion, race, sex, or national origin. Similar legislation exists in nearly all states outside the South. In addition, federal and state laws proscribe discrimination on the basis of age, protect the handicapped, and Vietnam veterans, and require that equal pay be paid for equal work regardless of sex. Obviously, such legislation profoundly affects the employment process and the collective bargaining relationship.

TITLE VII OF THE CIVIL RIGHTS ACT OF 1964, AS AMENDED

In previous chapters we have pointed out that, despite great gains, black citizens and other minorities are disproportionately concentrated in the lower income positions, are disproportionately represented among the unemployed, and suffer numerous educational and income disadvantages. This remains true despite a decade of great gains for minorities in which they progressed more rapidly than did the population as a whole. One reason for the progress was the sustained high prosperity of the 1960s with its concomitant labor shortages and therefore employment opportunities for virtually all members of the work force. Another reason was the concentration of private and public efforts on civil rights, especially nondiscriminatory employment. The key legislation was Title VII of the Civil Rights Act of 1964, the Equal Employment Opportunity Title. In 1972, this title was amended to expand its coverage and to enhance the powers of its administrative agency.

704

Legislative and Administrative Background

Since World War II, the federal government through presidential executive orders and the states via legislation have attempted to deal with the problems of employment discrimination and unequal opportunity. On June 25, 1941, President Franklin D. Roosevelt issued Executive Order 8802, the first of several of this type. It established the President's Committee on Fair Employment Practice, which operated throughout the war period. Although the Committee held hearings, dramatized the issue of black employment, and undoubtedly contributed to the increase in the utilization of black manpower, its lack of statutory authority prevented it from securing compliance with its orders when discriminating employers or unions balked. Thus, it failed to make an appreciable change in the employment practices of the railroads or of the West Coast shipbuilding industry, where employers' discrimination was buttressed by active union support, if not leadership.

The President's Committee on Fair Employment Practice ended its life in 1945, after being denied funds by Congress. It was followed by a succession of committees whose jurisdiction was limited to establishments doing business under contracts with the federal government. These committees were first set up by President Harry S Truman and then reorganized by each succeeding president. Initially, they relied on persuasion and publicity. Moreover, they lacked jurisdiction over unions, which are not a party to government controls, but which, particularly in the construction industry, are often, as the suppliers of labor under closed-shop contracts, the focal point of discrimination.

Executive Order 10925, issued by President Kennedy on March 6, 1961, and the subsequent Order 11246 of President Johnson, which successive presidents have kept in effect, introduced a new concept, "affirmative action," which requires that employers doing business with the government actively seek out minorities. This concept has had a profound impact on employer hiring and promoting policies; it will be discussed later, after a review of the basic law, Title VII of the Civil Rights Act of 1964, as amended.

New York, the first state to take action in this field, enacted its non-discrimination law in 1945. Since then, nearly all states outside the South have enacted similar laws. Such legislation operates similarly to that on the federal level, which is described later. Like state labor relations activities, and in spite of the fact that federal law relating to civil rights specifically reserves a place for state laws, state equal opportunity legislation appears to have declined in significance during recent years. The same is true for the municipal ordinances which several large cities have enacted to deal with equal opportunity. Where a federal law exists, it apparently takes over despite congressional attempts to safeguard state action.

Coverage and Content

Title VII, as amended, applies to interstate employers of 15 or more persons, to unions which have 15 or more members, and to employment agencies. States and local governments are covered by Title VII, except for employees directly chosen by elected officials as advisers, cabinet members, or personal staff members. The U.S. Civil Service Commission is directed by Title VII to enforce an equal employment policy consistent with Title VII for federal agencies and employees. Title VII's general coverage is further enhanced by reference to Landrum-Griffin's definition of employers who are designated as being in interstate commerce, which, as noted in Chapter 20, is the most comprehensive such definition to be found in major labor legislation. Finally, the 1972 amendments specifically brought state and municipal employees and private and public nonreligious educational institutions within Title VII's purview.

The basic proscriptions of the law are set forth in Figure 23–1. The coverage of the law extends to joint labor-management committees or other organizations controlling apprenticeship—thus closing a loophole found in many state fair employment laws. It permits religion, sex, or national origin to be utilized where valid occupational classification calls for such a distinction (for example, a model, a Kosher butcher, or a teacher in a girls' school or a religious seminary), but the 1972 amendments define "religion" to include all aspects of religious observance, practice, and belief so as to require employers to make reasonable accommodations for employees whose "religion" may include observances, practices, and beliefs which conflict with standard employment schedules. This has involved difficulties in continuous-operations industries where employees decline to work on their Sabbath (not necessarily Sunday) despite the need to staff the operations on that day.

Administration

The act established an Equal Employment Opportunity Commission, a five-man independent agency appointed by the president with the consent of the Senate. Like other federal agencies, this Commission is empowered to establish regional offices and to appoint staff pursuant to civil service regulations, to subpoena records, and to prescribe rules and regulations for carrying out its duties. The 1972 amendments also provided for the appointment of an independent EEOC General Counsel on the NLRB model, who is responsible for litigation, and with the concurrence of the EEOC chairman, for the appointment of regional attorneys.

Charges must be filed with the EEOC by, or on behalf of, an aggrieved individual within 180 days of the occurrence of the alleged unlawful

Discrimination because of Race, Color, Religion, or National Origin

Sec. *703.* (*a*) It shall be an unlawful employment practice for an employer—

(1) to fail or refuse to hire or to discharge any individual, or otherwise to discriminate against any individual with respect to his compensation, terms, conditions, or privileges of employment, because of such individual's race, color, religion, sex, or national origin; or

(2) to limit, segregate, or classify his employees in any way which would deprive or tend to deprive any individual of employment opportunities or otherwise adversely affect his status as an employee, because of such individual's race, color, religion, sex, or national origin.

(*b*) It shall be an unlawful employment practice for an employment agency to fail or refuse to refer for employment, or otherwise to discriminate against, any individual because of his race, color, religion, sex, or national origin, or to classify or refer for employment any individual on the basis of his race, color, religion, sex, or national origin.

(*c*) It shall be an unlawful employment practice for a labor organization—

(1) to exclude or to expel from its membership, or otherwise to discriminate against, any individual because of his race, color, religion, sex, or national origin;

(2) to limit, segregate, or classify its membership, or in any way to classify or fail or refuse to refer for employment any individual, in any way which would deprive or tend to deprive any individual of employment opportunities, or would limit such employment opportunities or otherwise adversely affect his status as an employee or as an applicant for employment, because of such individual's race, color, religion, sex, or national origin; or

(3) to cause or attempt to cause an employer to discriminate against an individual in violation of this section.

(*d*) It shall be an unlawful employment practice for any employer, labor organization, or joint labor-management committee controlling apprenticeship or other training or retraining, including on-the-job training program, to discriminate against any individual because of his race, color, religion, sex, or national origin in admission to, or employment in any program established to provide apprenticeship or other training.

* * * * *

Other Unlawful Employment Practices

Sec. *704.* (*a*) It shall be an unlawful employment practice for an employer to discriminate against any of his employees or applicants for employment, for an employment agency or joint labor-management committee controlling apprenticeship or other training or retraining, including on-the-job training programs, to discriminate against any individual, or for a labor organization to discriminate against any member thereof or applicant for membership, because he has opposed any practice made an unlawful employment practice by this title, or because he has made a charge, testified, assisted, or participated in any manner in an investigation, proceeding, or hearing under this title.

(*b*) It shall be an unlawful employment practice for an employer, labor organization, or employment agency or joint labor-management committee controlling apprenticeship or other training or retraining, including on-the-job training programs, to print or publish or cause to be printed or published any notice or advertisement relating to employment by such an employer or membership in or any classification or referral for employment by such a labor organization, or relating to any classification or referral for employment by such an employment agency, indicating any preference, limitation, specification, or discrimination, based on race, color, religion, sex, or national origin, except that such a notice or advertisement may indicate a preference, limitation, specification, or discrimination based on religion, sex or national origin when religion, sex, or national origin is a bona fide occupational qualification for employment.

practice. Where there is a state law or a municipal ordinance proscribing discrimination or providing for a means of relief, no action may be taken by the EEOC until it has notified the state or local agency and given it 60 days to act, or, if the state or local agency is in its first year of existence, 120 days to act. The law specifically permits state laws to exist concurrently, provided that such laws do not require or permit the doing of any act which would be an unlawful employment practice. Moreover, the Commission is urged to enter into agreements with state agencies for the utilization of the latter's services to carry out the functions of the federal law. Records are required to be kept by employers, unions, and employment agencies so as to provide information on compliance with the act.

Where there is no state or municipal agency, or where the latter has not acted to the satisfaction of the EEOC, the Commission attempts to settle the matter by conciliation. The records and proceedings of conciliation activities are confidential and cannot be made part of later proceedings except by consent of the parties. If the EEOC feels that conciliation has been unsuccessful, it may bring a civil action in a U.S. District Court for redress of the alleged violation. If the respondent is a state or a local government body, however, the conduct of any court action becomes a function of the U.S. Attorney General rather than of the EEOC's General Counsel. The court may order redress, elimination of the violation, "such affirmative action as may be appropriate," damages, back pay, and so on. Even though no court action is brought by the EEOC or the Attorney General, an individual who feels aggrieved may initiate his own case in court. In that case, the EEOC or the Attorney General may participate as intervenors if "the case is of general public importance." Federal government employees can file charges in court if they are dissatisfied with actions taken by the U.S. Civil Service Commission in regard to alleged discrimination.

An additional section (707) permits the EEOC to bring a civil action where it believes that any person or group of persons is engaged in a pattern or practice of resistance to the full enjoyment of any of the rights guaranteed by Title VII, requesting relief, including an injunction, to overcome such resistance. Before proceeding to court, the Commission may hold a public hearing, examine witnesses, and make findings. Individuals subpoenaed or otherwise objecting to an investigation may appeal to the courts within 20 days after being served.

Relation to Other Laws

As we have noted, the Civil Rights law drafters were very careful to consider the effect of the new law on similar state and local enactments. But there is no mention of Taft-Hartley, Landrum-Griffin, or other federal statutes. For example, a union may be charged with an unlawful employment practice by the Equal Employment Opportunity Commission for discriminating against minorities at the same time that it is being certified as the bargaining agent for these same discriminated-against employees by the National Labor Relations Board. The Equal Opportunity title also sheds no light on whether picketing or boycotts by racial groups are "labor disputes" within the meaning of the Norris–La Guardia Act, a decision which judges have to make before deciding whether such demonstrations can be enjoined. In a key case, the U.S. Supreme Court ruled that employees who picket a store and attempt to bargain directly with their employer about alleged discrimination, in disregard of a no-strike provision in the union contract, may be disciplined and/or discharged.[1]

Nor is the EEOC the sole federal authority to combat discrimination. Persons who feel aggrieved may file a case under the arbitration clause of a union contract, under Title VII of the EEOC, with state or municipal agencies, with the Office of Federal Contract Compliance Programs pursuant to Executive Order 11246, or if they can allege an unfair labor practice, they may go to the NLRB, or they may charge that safety violations are involved and go to the Occupational Safety and Health Administration, or if they lose in any one of these jurisdictions, they may try another. In 1972, the House of Representatives proposed making EEOC the sole federal authority to combat discrimination proscribed by Title VII, but this provision was deleted from the the final bill. Hence such litigation can be kept alive almost indefinitely.

The EEOC's Impact

Although it is impossible to separate the impact of the EEOC from that of other factors, for example, the national concern with civil rights matters in the 1960s and the tight labor market of that period, it seems that the EEOC has had a profound impact on hiring practices and employment patterns, both as to race and as to sex. As a result of EEOC's existence and activities, thousands of women and minorities have had improved opportunities and work status, and thousands more have received back pay because of alleged discrimination by companies or unions. EEOC has either directly litigated or supported cases which have developed the "rightful place" doctrine, thus preventing the impact of past discrimination from continuing unabated.[2] Its work has voided the use of questionable tests to maintain discrimination.[3] EEOC has upset seniority systems which discriminate against minorities in such

---

[1] *Emporium Capwell Co.* v. *Western Additional Community Organization,* 420 U.S. 50 (1975).

[2] *Quarles* v. *Philip Morris, Inc.,* 279 F. Supp. 505 (E.D. Va. 1968).

[3] *Griggs* v. *Duke Power Co.,* 401 U.S. 424 (1971).

industries as paper manufacturing, iron and steel, and trucking.[4] In addition, EEOC-inspired or -directed litigation has not only won thousands of dollars in back pay for employees who were allegedly discriminated against by such corporate giants as American Telephone and Telegraph and United Airlines,[5] but has also forced these companies to agree to give minorities and women preference in hiring and promotion in order to achieve agreed-upon goals. And the EEOC has had a leading part in litigation to combat the discriminatory practices of the construction unions.[6] Numerous other key litigations and actions could be cited in support of the impact which EEOC has had during its more than a decade of existence.

Administratively, however, the EEOC has been less successful. Its case backlog has become enormous, exceeding 120,000 unresolved matters; its regional offices have been charged with incompetence and corruption;[7] and its administrative problems have been compounded by turnover of Commission chairmen and members so that direction has been lacking.

Looking at these administrative shortcomings, and more importantly, at the fact that blacks and women are still far short of equality in the workplace, a number of critics have concluded that the EEOC and government enforcement of civil rights in general have failed in their prime objective of improving the economic well-being of minorities and women. This, for example, has been the principal contention of another government agency, the U.S. Civil Rights Commission.[8] Yet the reasoning behind such claims is fundamentally simplistic. These claims assume that if inequality continues to exist, it is because employment discrimination is the prime cause and because the EEOC and other government enforcement agencies in the civil rights field are not doing a proper job.

Effective government support and enforcement of equal employment opportunity appear necessary if we are to achieve equal employment. This has been documented innumerable times. Equally well documented, however, is the fact that such government action is insufficient in itself to achieve equality. It cannot overcome inadequate training and education;

---

[4] *U.S.* v. *Local 189, United Papermakers et al.*, 282 F. Supp. 39 (E.D. La. 1968); affirmed 416 F.2d 980 (CA.5, 1969); cert. denied, 397 U.S. 919 (1970); *U.S.* v. *Bethlehem Steel Corp.*, 446 F.2d 652 (CA.2, 1971); and *Franks* v. *Bowman Transportation Co.*, 96 S. Ct. 1251 (1976).

[5] *EEOC* v. *American Telephone & Telegraph Co.*, 365 F. Supp. 1105 (E.D. Pa. 1973); *EEOC* v. *United Airlines* (U.S. D. Ct. N.D. Ill., April 14, 1976).

[6] Significant cases are *Local 53* v. *Vogler*, 407 F.2d 1047 (CA.5, 1969); *Dobbins* v. *Local 212, IBEW*, 292 F. Supp. 413 (S.D. Ohio 1968); and *EEOC* v. *Locals 638 et al., Sheet Metal Workers International Association* (CA.2, March 8, 1976). For numerous other EEOC and state commission cases, see *FEP Cases*, any of the various volumes.

[7] The General Accounting Office has issued several reports on EEOC administration, all quite critical.

[8] *Federal Civil Rights Enforcement Effort* (Washington, D.C.: Government Printing Office, 1970). Several similar follow-up reports have been issued.

its effectiveness is limited when employment is declining; it cannot immediately offset a history of discrimination; it cannot move people from one location to jobs in another location; and it cannot reorder the job structure of an industry to a marked degree, although it can, and has, recast discriminatory upgrading policies and seniority systems.

The situation in the aerospace industry is a case in point. In 1966, 21 of the largest companies in this industry employed 788,022 persons in 127 establishments, or about two thirds of the industry's total.[9] Of these employees, 179,436 were classified as professionals in 1966, of whom only 0.8%, or 1,435, were black. This looks like a highly discriminatory pattern of employment. Moreover, by a few years later, these same companies had, if conventional ratings are utilized, improved little. Their total professional employment had declined a bit, to 179,041; their black professional complement had increased slightly, to 1,598; but the percentage of black employees was still only 0.9%.

But if one looks at the total situation, a different picture emerges. In 1966, when these 21 companies in the aerospace industry had a professional black ratio of only 0.8%, they employed approximately 40% of all black professionals in manufacturing industries reporting to the EEOC. Moreover, throughout the 1960s and well into the 1970s, only 2% of all engineering students were blacks,[10] and the situation was similar in many other professions, so that even improvements of well over 100% per year will require many years to affect significantly the total black ratio available for work. Lack of training in the past has had similar, although less dramatic, effects in slowing minority catch-up in many trades.

Perhaps the real problem in assessing the extent of success which the EEOC has experienced is the fact that different people, differently placed, view the matter by quite different standards. This "gap in understanding" that Professor Bernard E. Anderson noted between the management in public utilities and the EEOC is equally applicable in all industries:

> The commission, being an enforcement agency, looks to the statistical record for evidence that equal employment, in fact, exists in business firms. Corporate managers, however, often emphasize company progress in changing the focus, direction, and energy devoted to equal employment issues. Such changes within the business firm may not result in significant numerical gains in the number of black workers employed or promoted during a one- or two-year period. The modification of tra-

---

[9] Herbert R. Northrup et al., *Negro Employment in Basic Industry*, Studies of Negro Employment, vol. 1 (Philadelphia: Industrial Research Unit, The Wharton School, University of Pennsylvania, 1970), part three, pp. 165–66, 172–73; part eight, pp. 726–28.

[10] Robert Kiehl, *Opportunities for Blacks in the Profession of Engineering*, a study prepared for the Manpower Administration, U.S. Department of Labor (Newark: Foundation for the Advancement of Graduate Study in Engineering, 1970), pp. 13–14.

ditional employment practices is no less real to corporate managers even though the results may not meet EEOC measurement criteria. To management, changes in the employment process that might result in long term gains for black workers are often considered more important than short term gains in numbers employed. The difference of opinion between EEOC and industry representatives regarding the meaning and relative importance of affirmative action programs and affirmative action results is one of the most difficult issues in the equal employment area today.[11]

The OFCCP and Affirmative Action

Perhaps more significant in terms of achieving equal employment than the work of the EEOC are the rules and regulations adopted pursuant to Executive Order 11246, particularly General Order No. 4 of the Office of Federal Contract Compliance Programs. The OFCCP, which administers the executive order, has set standards above and beyond Title VII which must be adhered to by government contractors. It requires (1) an analysis of all major job classifications and an explanation of why minorities may be underutilized; (2) the establishment of goals, targets, and affirmative action commitments designed to relieve any shortcoming identified; and (3) the development and supply of data to government organizations, including not only racial-occupational figures in great detail but also progression charts, seniority rosters, and an analysis by race of applicants for the various jobs.

Most concerns, and certainly those of any significant size are federal contractors. As a result, they are under constant pressure to increase and to upgrade their minority employment and to engage in other types of affirmative action. The latter would include recruiting visits to secondary schools with high black enrollment and to black colleges in order to obtain recruits for white-collar jobs, advertising for employees in black community newspapers, and the ending of recruitment restricted either to walk-ins or to referrals by the families of previous employees. Affirmative action might instigate special training courses for the transfer and upgrading of black employees into certain all-white departments in the plant. It can involve special programs for the hard core as described above. It might carry out special recruitment to increase the proportion of black foremen. It usually also involves the appointment of a company executive called an "Equal Employment Opportunity Coordinator." By making this either a full-time position or one in which the executive has major responsibility, the government hopes to prevent the normal production, sales, or other executive duties from crowding out attention to equal employment.

---

[11] Bernard E. Anderson, *Negro Employment in Public Utilities,* Studies of Negro Employment, vol. 3 (Philadelphia: Industrial Research Unit, The Wharton School, University of Pennsylvania, 1970), p. 207.

In the construction industry, the OFCCP has set specific goals by craft in many cities pursuant to its "Philadelphia Plan" concept. This marks the first in-depth attack on the invidious union-management discrimination which has been so pervasive in construction and which has denied blacks a reasonable share of much skilled construction work. Unfortunately, there has been little consistency of results from city to city.

THE NEED FOR EDUCATION AND TRAINING

Regardless of the powers vested in EEOC, OFCCP, or various state agencies, equality on the job will not be possible as long as a disproportionate number of blacks and other minorities continue to be uneducated, unskilled, and untrained. Until this inequality has been remedied, black workers will continue to be overrepresented among the unemployed, the underemployed, and the unskilled. Professor Charles C. Killingsworth has noted, despite the heritage of slavery and years of discrimination "and despite the continuing necessity for efforts to eliminate racial discrimination, there appears to be a reasonable basis for doubting that this factor is the principal *present* source of economic disadvantage for the Negro. If it is not, then continuing insistence that it is may well divert attention and effort from other more important sources and remedial measures."[12]

DISCRIMINATION IN REGARD TO SEX, AGE, THE HANDICAPPED, AND VIETNAM VETERANS

The year 1964 was a banner one for the feminists. In June the "equal pay for equal work" law, enacted in 1963, became effective. And then, just a few weeks later, Congress passed the Equal Opportunity law, which forbade discrimination by sex as well as by race, color, creed, or national origin. This law, as noted, became effective in mid-1965. In addition, sex discrimination is outlawed by most state antidiscrimination legislation.

Equal Pay for Equal Work

The Equal Pay law was enacted as an amendment to the Fair Labor Standards Act. Therefore, its coverage is identical with that of the federal minimum wage law (see Table 16–1, p. 499). It is administered and enforced by the Employment Standards Division of the U.S. Department of Labor.

The Equal Pay law, in brief, provides that it is illegal to pay women less than men (or conversely, men less than women) for doing the same

---

[12] Charles C. Killingsworth, *Jobs and Income for Negroes* (Washington, D.C.: National Manpower Policy Task Force and University of Michigan, 1968), pp. 31–32.

work, and that it is unlawful for a union or its agents to cause or attempt to cause an employer to discriminate in wages on the basis of sex. Furthermore, the elimination of existing differentials by a wage reduction is prohibited. The act contains a general exception for differentials based on any factor other than sex. In addition, three specific exemptions—wage differentials based on merit, seniority, and piece rates or incentives—are specifically permitted.

The Equal Pay law has been rigorously enforced so that the once relatively common practice of having separate female jobs and rates of pay, or even specifying such in collective agreements, has been discarded.[13] Moreover, Title VII of the Civil Rights Act has, as noted, opened up thousands of jobs to women where before they were not even considered. These include not only top professional and managerial positions, but also such jobs as coal mining, craftwork in construction, and a host of factory jobs which were once strictly male preserves. Companies doing business with the federal government must now have an affirmative action program for women, as well as for minorities. The tempo of such advancement is likely to increase as more and more women enter graduate business schools and the professions, or decide to do skilled manual work.

Age Discrimination

In 1967, Congress enacted the Age Discrimination in Employment Act, which became effective six months later. This law is administered under the Secretary of Labor by the Employment Standards Division, the same agency which enforces the Fair Labor Standards and Equal Pay acts. The law applies to companies and unions employing, or having a membership of, 25 persons or more, and to employment agencies. The law's general coverage is otherwise similar to that of the Fair Labor Standards Act. Similar laws have been enacted by 39 states, the District of Columbia, Guam, Puerto Rico, and the Virgin Islands. Six of these laws, however, apply only to public sector employment.

Until the early 1970s, these laws were not utilized to any great extent, but since then there have been significant litigations which have created both great interest and much more use of the laws. The federal law resulted in back pay of approximately $20,000,000, as of mid-1976, for employees who were found to have been discriminated against.[14] Employers have learned that they can no longer specify younger workers for jobs or solve layoff problems by pushing out older workers. Retirement under

---

[13] For a detailed analysis of the record of the Equal Pay law from the point of view of its enforcers, see Albert H. Ross and Frank V. McDermott, Jr., "The Equal Pay Act of 1963," *Boston College Industrial and Commercial Law Review*, vol. 16 (November 1974), pp. 1–73.

[14] From the annual reports to Congress of the U.S. Department of Labor, Employment Standards Division, in regard to the Age Discrimination Act of 1967.

a nondiscriminatory pension plan is, however, not a violation of the age discrimination law. Given the projected increase of the population in the 40–65 age bracket, it is likely that the federal and state laws covering older workers will become, if anything, increasingly important. The Age Discrimination in Employment Act is being especially used by white, middle managers and professionals to protect their jobs in economic downturns.

Discrimination against the Handicapped

The 1973 amendments to the Rehabilitation Act, among other changes, prohibited employment discrimination against the handicapped. These provisions are administered through the government's purchasing activities and the Office of Federal Contract Compliance Programs. The OFCCP has established regulations which call upon all government contractors to hire the handicapped affirmatively, although goals and timetables had not been established by early 1977. In addition, contractors are required to *accommodate* their workplaces and jobs so that handicapped workers do not have barriers preventing their working—which if enforced for older buildings, could cost billions of dollars. A key problem yet to be decided is the definition of the term *handicapped,* and the determination of the extent of mental deficiency which will be covered by the law. A preliminary survey of large companies by the Industrial Research Unit of The Wharton School in 1976 found them taking measures to employ the physically handicapped, but quite perplexed as to what should be done in regard to the mentally handicapped, who are also included in the law's coverage.

The Vietnam Era Veterans Readjustment Act

Amendments to this law in 1974 apply to contractors and are administered by OFCCP in the same manner as the law relating to the handicapped. These regulations also require affirmative action.

DISCRIMINATION—CONCLUDING REMARKS

There are thus a myriad of federal and state laws governing discrimination against, and requiring affirmative action for, various groups. Indeed, in any meeting, it is often difficult to find anyone who is not a member of a protected class when it is noted that all minorities, women, persons aged 40–65, persons with any mental or physical handicap, and Vietnam Era veterans are among those protected. Employers are especially at risk since the refusal to hire or to promote must be carefully documented and proved when a member of a protected class is involved, lest the action be the basis of a lawsuit. Moreover, a good performance, for example, in employing blacks, does not protect an employer who has failed to show a good record in regard to another group, for example, older workers. Liability exists separately for each group. The danger, of course, is that we are moving toward a quota society in which membership in a protected class will be more important than merit on the job. Yet paradoxically, the purpose of antidiscrimination legislation is to insure employment and promotion on the basis of merit, without regard to race, sex, age, handicapped condition, or service in the Armed Forces.

QUESTIONS FOR DISCUSSION

1. How has the Equal Opportunity law altered racial patterns in the South? In northern cities? Explain your answer.

2. Assume that you are a construction employer and that you hire through unions. Two of them have never referred a black to you. What is your status under the Equal Opportunity law, and what can you do to avoid being charged with an unlawful employment practice without encouraging union antagonism?

3. Which act is more likely to affect employment opportunities for women, the Equal Pay Act or the Equal Opportunity Act?

4. What is your concept of "affirmative action"? Explain your answer in terms of blacks, women, older workers, the handicapped, and Vietnam Era veterans.

SUGGESTIONS FOR FURTHER READING

Age Discrimination in Employment Act of 1967. U.S. Department of Labor, Employment Standards Division. Annual reports.

　　A report discussing the act, the problems, and the current status of enforcement is issued each year.

Gardner, William F. "The Development of the Substantive Principles of Title VII Law: The Defendant's View," *Alabama Law Review*, vol. 26 (Fall 1973), pp. 1–118.

Summers, Clyde W. "Work Sharing as an Alternative to Layoffs by Seniority: Title VII Remedies in Recession," *University of Pennsylvania Law Review*, vol. 124 (April 1976), pp. 893–941.

　　Two well-written articles from different points of view on key equal employment issues.

Glazer, Nathan. *Affirmative Discrimination: Ethnic Inequality and Public Policy.* New York: Basic Books, Inc., 1975.

　　A critical analysis of the affirmative action concept by one of the nation's leading sociologists.

Hildebrand, George H. "Evaluating the Impact of Affirmative Action: A Look at the Federal Compliance Program (A Symposium)," *Industrial and Labor Relations Review*, vol. 29 (July 1976), pp. 485–584.

　　An attempt, largely by mathematically inclined economists, to evaluate the OFCCP's activities and results.

Northrup, Herbert R.; Rowan, Richard L.; et al. *Studies of Negro Employment*. Philadelphia: Industrial Research Unit, The Wharton School, University of Pennsylvania, 1970–74.

Seven volumes describing black employment patterns in 24 industries, analyzing the reasons for such patterns, and comparing and contrasting the different industrial patterns.

Ross, Albert H., and McDermott, Frank V., Jr. "The Equal Pay Act of 1963: A Decade of Enforcement," *Boston College Industrial and Commercial Law Review,* vol. 16 (November 1974), pp. 1–74.

The most complete account and analysis of the Equal Pay law by lawyers representing its administrators.

part seven

Concluding Observations

24

Some Labor Problems of the Future

THROUGHOUT THIS BOOK, we have stressed the new trends and developments which have modified the context and environment of labor economics during recent years and which promise to affect conditions much more substantially during the balance of this decade. By way of a summary and conclusion, attention is directed to some of these factors once again.

UNEMPLOYMENT—AND INFLATION

From the end of the Korean War in the early 1950s until almost the mid-1960s, the United States was plagued with unemployment which regularly exceeded 5% of the labor force and rose to over 7% in times of recession. Then, under the impetus of government fiscal policy, including a tax decrease, and a business boom, unemployment fell below 4% in 1965 and remained below that figure for several years. But the unemployment and poverty in our large cities and among minority groups continued to remain high, and to complicate the problem, prices moved steadily upward. It was apparent that increased demand wiped out much of the basic unemployment in society. Yet, the remaining unemployment proved hard core and difficult to overcome; and further increases in demand not only did not reach the remaining unemployed but in addition accentuated the inflationary aspects of a high-level economy.

The overstimulation of the economy led to double-digit inflation and serious unemployment. Both were materially improved under the moderate policies of the Ford administration, but there are strong forces which would guarantee everyone a job either by more stimulation of the economy or by making the government the employer of last resort. Neither policy seems to give sufficient recognition to the structural character of much of the unemployment or to the impact which federally guaranteed employment could have on union policy, our system of collective bargaining, and inflation. The acceptable compromise between unemployment and inflation has yet to be developed, and our failure to find it could leave the economy with too much of both to be tolerated or socially accepted.

Both the private and the public sectors of our economy have recognized the problem and have attempted to alleviate the structural defects which aggravate inflation and impede employment. That only the surface has been scratched is obvious; and that much more needs to be learned about how to make the hard-core unemployed become self-reliant members of our society is equally clear. The fact that blacks, our largest minority racial group, make up so disproportionate a number of the disadvantaged unemployed both complicates the problem and makes its solution more urgent. The race issue is the most serious internal social problem of our age. Finding jobs for blacks and making them productive, job-filling members of our society is undoubtedly the key to the solution of this problem.

Most persons agree that a key element in any program to rehabilitate the hard-core unemployed is a major revision of the nation's welfare programs and an improvement of the schools, particularly in the inner cities. Welfare reform has been talked about for at least a decade, but the rolls continue to rise. Meanwhile, the public schools—especially, but not only, in the inner cities—continue to produce graduates who cannot read or write adequately and who each year seem to do less well on reading and mathematics achievement tests. The school situation continues to worsen despite ever-higher teachers' salaries and massive expenditures for remedial education and training programs which are designed to teach those whom the schools failed to teach in the first place. Meanwhile, studies fail to demonstrate, for example, that such programs do indeed improve literacy sufficiently to insure job improvement, or that the billions of dollars spent on government training programs substantially enhance job opportunity or performance, although there have been some successes.

The great lesson of the Civil Rights Act and similar legislation is not that some discrimination continues. It is rather that now, when so many opportunities are open to blacks and other minorities, many are unqualified to accept those opportunities. What is needed is not training in general, but more training for specific jobs and, above all, for upgrading. It may well be that such training can be done only by industry, and that government should spend less directly and attempt through subsidies to increase training in industry.

Such problems also pose major challenges for unions. Seniority programs devised in another era need change and flexibility if they are to survive. Moreover, unions have generally not been oriented toward helping the hard-core unemployed; they have been more concerned with obtaining maximum benefits for their already employed members. Can union leaders continue to maintain this attitude in view of the nature of the unemployment problem? Can employed union members simply shut their eyes to the fact that union wage policies may restrict employment opportunities? What positive programs for stimulating employment can union leaders logically espouse?

Minimum Wages and Shorter Hours

In the area of governmental policy a new look has yet to be taken at the impact of minimum wage laws. All available data point to a major problem of structural unemployment concentrated among the poorly educated, the least skilled, and the minority group members of the labor force. When we raise minimum wage rates, as we seem to do at regular intervals, these workers are the first to lose their jobs. Are those men and women better off when employed at what society concedes to be sub-standard rates of pay? Or should they be either unemployed on temporary grants under our unemployment compensation system or consigned to relief? Or should they be paid a government subsidy and kept at work? In a similar vein, is not the regular advocacy of a substantially shorter workweek without pay reduction ill conceived by reason of its costly burden on employers and its resultant probable impact on employment?

Security and Costs

How much "security" do we crave, and what will it cost? If government-sponsored prepaid medical care is adopted, what will the resultant increased taxes do to the prospects for expansion in our economy and hence to the prospects for a decrease in the rate of unemployment? If, as seems likely, ever-larger fringe benefits induce a preference among employers for overtime rather than new hires, is our security system building more security for the majority and continued insecurity for those unemployed?

Year after year, in prosperity as well as in depression, the welfare costs of our major cities have risen, and the number of people on relief have increased. Why cannot welfare recipients be made self-supporting members of society? Are welfare and minimum wage legislation related? How about welfare policies and the impact thereon of union wage policies?

To alleviate poverty, some would make cash handouts in the form of a "negative income tax." This would perhaps simplify record keeping and the administration of welfare, but it would not provide either the dignity or the self-reliance of an income-producing job. Moreover, more cash handouts would seem to be inflationary in an economy already concerned about inflation. Would further inflation mean an ever-higher negative income tax, and thus would the costs, as in welfare, keep rising?

Collective Bargaining and Unionism

What about collective bargaining in an economy where unemployment, job security, retraining, civil rights, and manpower utilization become the key issues? Can management and unions really deal with these problems as they have dealt with wage issues? If they cannot, what are the alternatives? What has the government to offer as a solution? These very problems are most serious and are certainly not solved in the one industry—railroads—where the government has intervened longest and most consistently.

Can the labor movement contribute to the solution of the basic problems of which unemployment is the central issue? Many observers doubt it. They note that unions have already accomplished their big job: attaining recognition of the dignity of labor. The fact that unions have essentially done the job they set out to do is the very fact that may now bring about their eventual downfall. The late Sumner H. Slichter made this point many times in urging labor to take a broader view of its role in the American economy.

For two decades, unions had a major appeal to workers because union leadership was attuned to the current needs of the labor force. Unions were growing, and their very growth was a dynamic factor of appeal. But after the mid-1950s, unions first lost ground both in terms of total members and proportion of the labor force unionized; then, despite the prosperity which greatly increased union membership in the mid-1960s, union membership gains failed to keep pace with the growth of the labor force. This leaves the union movement in the private sector heavily dependent upon the business cycle for growth, membership, and income.

The failure of unions to grow may be blamed on many things. Some AFL–CIO adherents blame it on managerial opposition to unions, although this does not explain why unions grew despite the same opposition in earlier years. The late Walter Reuther claimed that the "standpat" leadership of George Meany was at the root of the problem, but his attempt to create "a new labor movement" was very unsuccessful.

Actually, unions may well be suffering from the same inability to please that has harassed many once-popular public figures. Old appeals do not always bring the same results in the entertainment field, the advertising field, the political field, or the union field. Unions have been strangely unable to appeal to many of the new recruits to the labor force. Throughout the 1970s, the labor force will continue to see more additions from the quite young, the older worker, the part-time worker, the previously rural worker, the more highly educated worker, the relatively affluent worker, and the "middle-class-minded" worker. The old appeals that brought workers into unity in unionism in the 1930s are not appropriate to the new workers of the 1970s, even where these workers are occupying jobs of onetime union adherents. Yet, unions have been strangely unable to adapt themselves to the appeals that would be meaningful to the prospective member of the 1970s. When the new workers are in the unions, often as a result of compulsory unionism, the degree of rejection of contracts testifies to the communication gap between leaders and the rank and file.

Beyond the union-centered inability to meet the new prospect on his own terms, there is an added dimension which we noted in our description of trends in the labor force. This is the fact that the mix of work has changed as well. Even if there had been no change in the ideas and attitudes of the production worker to whom the union had the greatest appeal in the last generation, a significant shift in ratio toward the predominance of white-collar work has been taking place for at least the last 30 years, and this shift is accelerating daily. This shift is well recognized by union mentors, but not so well seen is what to do about it. At one union convention after another the subject of the organization of white-collar workers is discussed. By now, it is generally conceded that new appeals—and, indeed, new appealers—must be found if the white-collar people are to be organized. Large sums of money have been appropriated for organizing campaigns, and studies have been undertaken to determine the type of appeal which will interest white-collar workers, without evident success.

But if the big unions ever do seriously tackle the organization of white-collar workers in the private sector, they face a risk far greater than the declining membership rolls that now plague them. The risk is that the unions will have to undergo a change in their own philosophies to become consonant with the contemplated changes in appeals. It is as though a producer were seeking some new advertising technique to reach a new sales market. He sometimes finds—as the unions may, too—that it takes more than just a new appeal; often, it really requires a new product before the sale is won. If this might be the case in the unions' quest for members in the white-collar ranks, then we could expect the most revolutionary changes in the trends of union thinking.

What would happen, on the other hand, if the union official who is trying desperately to attract white-collar employees to membership should start talking like a conservative in politics after all the years of enunciating a party line in political matters that was so clearly liberal? Would this cause a loss in present membership, or would it bring out a new interest and approval from present members? Nobody knows. The problem is that in many crucial matters of wages and hours and working conditions, there is a broad disparity between what white-collar workers believe and what unions have for many years proclaimed as the belief of their membership. In order to maintain an appeal to both groups, the union would, in effect, have to espouse two philosophies and finally accept a split personality that might be disastrous in its appeal either to blue-collar workers or to white-collar workers.

On the other hand, it is equally difficult for today's union leadership to appeal to the poverty-stricken or for the union rank and file to concern itself with the problems of the poor. With union members having middle-class income, their concerns are less and less those of the slum population and more and more those of the typical suburbanite. A labor movement that has successfully carried its members so fast and so far up the income ladder finds it more and more difficult to represent, or even to communicate with, the downtrodden.

The race issue portends a severe problem for union leadership. Like most other white people, union leaders failed to sense the black mood and the impending crises which have turned once prounion black leaders into sharp critics of unionism. The AFL–CIO has adopted a liberal program. But it has had difficulty selling this program to many of its constituent unions and to the rank and file. Racial antagonism among unionized workers remains strong in many places, and several key unions, particularly in the building trades, have obstructed, rather than furthered, employment opportunities for blacks. The paucity of blacks among the top echelon and key leadership of American unions is further illustrative of the gap between organized labor and the black community.

Government Employee Unionism

The one area where unions have made remarkable advances is in the public sector. Were it not for these gains, union membership would have fallen back considerably farther in relation to the expansion of the labor force. Public employee unionism has been regarded—by unions, government officials, and many academicians—as merely an extension of collective bargaining in the private sector. The analysis in Chapter 22 points up the questionable nature of this conception. The economic constraints and the political pressures are too different in the public sector for the private analogy to be valid. Yet public employee unions continue to exert pressure in the same manner as unions in the private sector, and these unions lobby hard and successfully for legislation which, seemingly uncritically, insures that private sector tactics and strategy will be employed in public bargaining. Will this impact on the labor movement generally? Suppose, which it is not difficult to believe, that the public, weary of strikes and interruptions in public services, and angered by the inflationary wage increases brought by unionism to public employees, moves to end the freedom to strike in the private as well as the public sectors? Now that the extraordinarily liberal pensions extant in the public sector (retirement after 20 years service at age 50 at half the last year's salary, including overtime) have become common knowledge, will these matters continue to be left to private deals in the public *or* the private sector? In short, will the excesses of public employee bargaining lead to a drastic curtailment of all collective bargaining?

Unionism and the Service Economy

Over the years, unionism and collective bargaining have survived and prospered primarily in manufacturing industry. Tremendous union gains in wages and benefits have been matched by increases in productivity, so that the public did not pay the total costs. Union strikes inconvenienced the public, but not too severely, because manufactured goods could be stockpiled ahead of the strikes or shortages made up after their cessation.

Now the economy is a service one, with unionism spreading particularly into the governmental and quasi-governmental sectors, such as hospitals. Strikes and substantial wage increases engendered by union power have a direct and profound impact on the public. When essential services are impaired, the public is both immediately affected and profoundly disturbed. Sharply rising wage increases have not been offset by productivity increases in the service sectors. Rather, they have been followed by sharp increases in taxes and/or sharp curtailment of services. Strikes followed by higher school taxes, less frequent garbage collection, or $200 per day rent for semiprivate hospital rooms, do not endear the collective bargaining mechanism to the public. It may well be, as these trends continue, that we are observing the demise of the American industrial relations system as we have known it, and that even before the end of this decade, it will be a far different one.

Union Political Power

The great success of the politically oriented public employee unions and the increasing political power and political successes of the labor movement have led to increasing reliance by unions on political solutions. In the legislative halls of both Congress and the states, unions are lobbying hard for legislation which regulates shop conditions, such as the Occupational Safety and Health Act, and for stringent administration of such legislation. Such laws not only accomplish union objectives of improving working conditions, but provide unions with greater leverage in union-management relations. What cannot be won at the bargaining table can thus be won in the legislative halls; or at the very least, the balance of power can be shifted toward the union side.

Bills to guarantee full employment are certain to generate increasing, and perhaps overwhelming, union power in relation to management. The greatest restraint on union wage demands is the fear of their impact on employment. Guarantees of full employment remove that fear and that restraint. But the seemingly inevitable consequence is inflation and the imposition of wage and price controls, perhaps on a permanent basis. This already appears to be in effect in the United Kingdom and other European countries. It means a labor movement that participates in government and, increasingly, in management decision making, and a far different system than we have had in the past. Whether it will be a better system, or really solve the problems of unemployment and inflation, remains to be demonstrated. The evidence from Europe is certainly neither positive nor heartening. Instead of making old concepts work better, or else developing new ones, the United States seems to be about to adopt many concepts that have already been found wanting in other countries.

The Need for New Concepts

The need for new concepts is not confined to the labor movement but exists on all fronts, in view of the changing direction of the use of the labor force. For example, trends point to an ever-larger percentage of the labor force being occupied in producing "public goods" instead of private products. All one has to do is to look about his city, town, or state to see an increasing share of our productive forces going into such channels as road construction, schools, universities, and hospitals. Today, education boasts the biggest payroll in the country; hospitals employ over 2 million persons—more than twice the number employed in the basic steel industry. The trend of employment in these fields is increasing; that of manufacturing is declining.

We have already noted the importance of this shift for collective bargaining and for the labor movement. But what relevance does this have for historical measurements of productivity? Will the concept really be useful for comparable purposes over time when the product of today is ever more one of governmental or quasi-public services? Will this trend accentuate the possibility of inflation because, as otherwise unemployed labor is used in this kind of project, more dollars are put into the income stream as part of payment of wages, but no product emerges that is immediately usable to offset the increased purchasing power? Inefficiency in the private sector leads to fewer sales, smaller profits, and even the disappearance of companies. Managements that fail to produce profits in the private sector lose their jobs. What constraints occur in the public and nonprofit sectors under similar circumstances, and what are the implications for government labor policy and collective bargaining? Will failure just mean rescue by the taxpayers, as in the case of New York City?

GOVERNMENTAL INTERVENTION

The same questions may be asked of our governmental labor policies. Are our laws attuned to the economy of the 1970s or to that of the 1930s? The labor policy of the United States has developed slowly and haltingly. No one court decision or legislative act can be singled out as representing the beginning of governmental labor policy. Much of our present policy, it is true, stems from the Great Depression and the period of the Roosevelt administration, during which great strides were made toward formulating our present labor policies. Nevertheless, each period of history has made some contribution to the present status of labor legislation and governmental action. For example, even the most revolutionary of all labor laws—the National Labor Relations Act—had its roots in state and railway labor legislation of the 1890s.

At various stages of American labor history, different aspects of labor policy have been stressed by legislators and labor leaders. For example, the encouragement of collective bargaining by protecting the right of labor to organize was of prime importance in our labor policy in the period from the birth of the National Recovery Administration to enactment of the National Labor Relations Act. Restraints on union activities were especially emphasized in the post–World War II era, representing, in part, a reaction to certain excesses of unions during the period of unrestricted union organization. The protection of minority group rights was the dominant theme of the 1960s. Women's rights, safety and health, and public employee bargaining are key collective bargaining issues of the 1970s. Labor policy is thus continually evolving. Laws are passed which at the time may represent majority thinking. But majority thinking is not static, and as views alter, labor legislation reflects the changing trend in public opinion.

It is natural to assume, therefore, that labor policy will continue to evolve in the future. While many future developments cannot be predicted, certain trends are already evident. Thus, for example, a developing labor policy will undoubtedly continue to grapple with the amount and coverage of minimum wages and social security, the extent of the workweek, the issue of emergency strikes, the rights of public employees, and the rights of union members of minority groups and women—all issues which have been before the public for several decades. To these are now added working conditions on the job, including health and safety, and perhaps the fundamental right to be working. As in the past, when new laws or new rights are enacted, little consideration is given to their impact on old ones, or to conflicts of purpose and administration among the old and the new.

Actually, the United States has no labor policy but rather a patchwork of policies, comprehensive but not consistent. There is, for example, no uniformity of treatment among the states. State labor relations, workers' compensation, unemployment insurance, and minimum wage laws differ widely. The accident of location determines the extent of employee protection. Although the Landrum-Griffin Act did define some areas of delegation between federal and state laws, great inconsistencies occur in such areas as picketing, boycotts, mediation, and strike control legislation. Moreover, when the states do attempt to act, the federal government often preempts the field without consideration of consequences.

The inconsistency of federal legislation, as noted in previous chapters, is very real. For example, the Norris–La Guardia Act conflicts with the Taft-Hartley Act, and the latter law with the Landrum-Griffin Act. There have been cases in which persons have been sentenced to jail for actions which violated the Landrum-Griffin Act and yet have been recognized as legitimate union officials by the Taft-Hartley Act. This means that management has been required to deal with law violators and racketeers, or itself violate a law.

Welfare legislation adds a further inconsistency. Thus, even though a strike may be contrary to public policy or even illegal, the strikers may be aided by being given food stamps, welfare payments, or in two states and on the railroads, unemployment compensation. Whether collective bargaining can survive if strikers are subsidized by the public purse, or in any case, whether the welfare system should be diverted to care for otherwise well-paid workers who exercise their right to strike, are questions that have not received full consideration by Congress and by the various state legislators.

Although the Civil Rights law was made consistent with state legislation of the same type, its relation to the Taft-Hartley Act was not given serious consideration. Other inconsistencies exist in the coverage of various laws. Railway and airline employers and employees who come under the Railway Labor Act have rights and duties different from those of their fellow employees and employers who come under the National Labor Relations Act. Likewise, the railway industry has a separate social security system, while airline pilots have a special (and extraordinary) minimum wage law.

There is also inconsistency of purpose between the two current goals of labor policy: promoting collective bargaining and regulating certain union activities. It remains doubtful whether the government at both the federal and state levels can continue to maintain both a spur to union growth and a strong deterrent to certain activities which can affect union growth. And, of course, the impact of full employment legislation on collective bargaining and labor legislation seems to have received no consideration at all in the legislative process.

Inconsistency a Part of the Democratic Process

The fact that there are basic conflicts in the national labor policy should not be surprising. Indeed, all things considered, perhaps it is surprising that there are not more inconsistencies in existing legislation. Labor legislation is enacted in response to the pressure of public opinion and influences exerted by various interest groups. In some states, labor's political position is strong; in others, it is weak. State labor laws reflect this fact.

Moreover, neither labor nor industry alone can command sufficient votes to sway Congress. When in disagreement over legislation, both must appeal for support to that huge, vague group known as the "middle class," which holds the balance of power in our society, insofar as such a balance exists. As the electorate shifts first one way and then another, the complexion of Congress and state legislatures changes. Legislation in the highly controversial field of labor relations reflects these changes.

Nevertheless, there is a real need for a general overhauling of our disjointed system of conflicting and overlapping labor laws. Even if agreement could not be reached as to the basis on which such laws should be improved, it might at least be possible to achieve a greater degree of uniformity than now exists among the various laws. Unfortunately, however, the achievement of even such limited agreement is not too likely in view of the basic conflicts of interest, not only between labor and industry, but also within both labor and industry groups. The present system of "push and pull" of pressure groups to secure labor legislation favorable to themselves is likely to remain with us for some time to come.

The Need for Defining the Roles of Unions and Management

In Chapter 4, we considered the problem of defining the scope of managerial prerogatives. We need not repeat the considerations there discussed. Suffice it to say that the problem of preserving entrepreneurial freedom to manage business while affording union members security will be telescoped in importance in coming years by the ever-growing extent of union demands. Although union leaders, by and large, believe in the maintenance of the American system of free enterprise, their continuing search for means to afford security to their membership must inevitably produce a narrowing of the area of business initiative. Layoffs, technological change, and production policies are likely to be moved more and more into the orbit of union consultation and control. Union attempts to prove management's ability to pay higher wages and other benefits will lead to increasing interest by unions in company accounting systems and managerial policies.

No one can say where the ever-widening scope of union demands will end. It is safe to hazard a guess, however, that labor and management in the United States will ultimately work out a *modus vivendi* which will differ from that reached in other countries and which will reflect the peculiar character of American democracy and the American industrial environment. Such a compromise must recognize the basic need of the worker to feel secure in his job and to participate fully in the industrial process. At the same time, it is important that management be left free to plan, to invent, and to improve production methods so that not only labor but also the public at large may benefit from the efficiency of the capitalist system.

The decades ahead will continue to witness a step-up in the tempo of the economic struggle between the United States and the Soviet Union. Soviet spokesmen have clearly stated their objective of surpassing the United States in economic production. Their success in space and their demonstrated capacity to produce sophisticated war matériel are proof that their aims cannot be taken lightly. More immediately, the competition of the European Common Market countries and of Japan insures that the United States risks a high-cost position in world markets, with resultant loss of business and unemployment, unless our costs are brought into line and inflation controlled.

This very real threat raises the question of whether the American economy can any longer afford the make-work rules, the restrictions imposed on new laborsaving devices, the slowdowns and walkouts which have become an accepted part of the labor-management scene in recent years. What is needed is a "new look" for labor, a new rapprochement between labor and management, a new recognition by both labor and management that preservation of our way of life requires not only a willingness to fight but also a willingness to produce.

The need for a consistent policy is also demonstrated by the conflicts of a clean environment versus growth and jobs. To what extent should the economy sacrifice the latter for the former? What is the role, if any, of unions in reaching such an accommodation?

The need for increased efficiency in production is accentuated by the rapid rise of overseas competition. We cannot meet this threat by raising tariffs. The only sound answer is an accelerated rate of increase in output per man-hour in this country through application of the most advanced technology. Can labor leaders rise to this challenge—and if so, can they convince their membership of the necessity for abandoning traditional policies in sharp conflict with the present needs of the nation? Never before in our history has there been such a need for forceful, farseeing labor leadership!

The Need for Defining the Roles of Industry and Government

The problem of demarcating the respective scopes of unions and management has its counterpart in the larger social question of the proper balance between individual initiative and government control. This basic issue is met not only in debates over the merits of government control or the stabilization of wages, but also in the development of labor policy. It seems clear that in coming years, union organizations will attempt to saddle industry with new and heavy obligations growing out of the worker's need for security. Unions have seized upon the idea that industry should provide for depreciation of the human machine in the same way that it provides for depreciation of capital equipment. This idea has been given concrete form in demands for liberalized pensions, health insurance, life insurance, free dental care, and other benefits. The basic question is whether such benefits, assuming that they are justified, should be provided by industry or government—and in either case, how much of our national income should be devoted to security.

The notion that industry, on its own initiative, should amortize its human costs in the same manner as it has customarily amortized its mechanical costs is an attractive one, yet, it must be recognized that there are definite shortcomings to this view. The primary difficulty in having pensions, supplementary unemployment benefits, or other plans financed and administered by individual firms without an overall supervision has been recognized. But the result has been the passage of very complex and potentially costly legislation which has forced many small firms to cease offering pensions to their employees. Here again, is an example of legislation which, like strong unions, forces many gains for workers upon employers, but in turn extracts a cost—less security and unemployment for those who do not participate or who are forced out of work as a result. Strong unions have already demonstrated their ability to require employers to make enormous contributions to employee welfare funds, but their very success has often brought damaging unemployment and less security to many members of the work force. The history of industrial relations in the bituminous coal industry is an extreme case in point.

A further element of unfairness in leaving the settlement of pensions and other aspects of a welfare program to the process of collective bargaining is that the costs of such programs must ultimately be borne by all consumers in the form of lower real income, since—to the extent that companies bear the cost of pension plans—costs and prices of their products will tend to rise. This means that the public generally must pay for the disproportionate benefits which may be obtained by strong unions in particular industries. Moreover, as long as welfare plans remain a matter for collective bargaining, there will be constant rivalry among unions in various industries to increase the benefits obtained for their membership, in order to outdo other unions. The consequences of such rivalry upon industrial costs, profits, and employment could be serious.

The alternative to individual company welfare plans is government benefits under an expanded and liberalized social security program. This approach has the advantage of enabling workers to share equally in benefits, regardless of whether they are organized or unorganized, members of strong unions or of weak unions. Moreover, the principle has already been established under the Social Security Act that workers should contribute to support of the cost of the program—a principle which seems to commend itself for its fairness. Unfortunately, as we found in Chapter 17, social security is in deep trouble as a result of changing demographic developments and the lack of restraint of Congress in raising benefits.

Even without congressional mismanagement, an all-government pension system is not necessarily desirable. It means rising taxes, an ever-increasing bureaucracy, and growing government intervention in all aspects of our lives. It would also insure that unions would increase their political activity since, like government employee unions, they would have to marshal their political forces in order to achieve fringe benefit gains.

Employee demands for protection against insecurity thus present industry with a challenge and a dilemma. Either industry must accept its responsibilities and take the initiative in developing a broad program designed to protect workers from the risks and hazards of industrial life—with unforeseen consequences for costs, profits, and employment —or labor may take the other road, which leads to increasing government regulation and taxation of industry, and to increasing dependence by workers upon the government to solve their problems. The decisions made with respect to this aspect of labor policy thus have profound repercussions upon the pattern of American economic life and influence the nature of the balance which is ultimately struck between government regulation and individual enterprise in our economy.

Labor Policy in a Democracy

A cornerstone of our democratic form of government has been the use of national policy to control great aggrandizements of power. As a nation, we have long recognized that when particular groups become so powerful that their actions can seriously interfere with market processes and endanger the public interest, government regulation may be required. Thus, the Sherman Antitrust Act recognized the evils inherent in combinations of corporations designed to restrain trade or monopolize an industry. Likewise, our graduated income tax and heavy estate tax were intended, in part, to restrict the concentration of economic and political power which would flow from the amassing of great fortunes passed on from generation to generation without tax.

With this history of the role of governmental regulation in our democratic society, it seems almost inevitable that the extent of regulation of unions will expand as they grow in strength and economic power. To date, the function of government has been primarily to police the use of bargaining power by management and labor. The Wagner Act sought to prevent large, strongly entrenched corporations from using their power to throttle unions in their infancy by resort to discriminatory practices. Then, as unions grew in membership and strength, the need for such one-sided intervention in the labor market lessened; and Congress enacted the Taft-Hartley Act in an effort to pare down some of the rights given unions and to equalize bargaining power in the labor market, and the Landrum-Griffin Act to protect members from arbitrary union power. The Civil Rights law, like Landrum-Griffin, is primarily designed to protect individual employees—here members of minority groups.

It might be thought that with the development of strong union organization and the achievement of relative equality in bargaining power between industry and labor, government could now withdraw to the sidelines and let the parties fight it out. Unfortunately, however, the very equality of power between the parties in mass-production industries where strong unions confront large corporations, each with extensive financial resources, increases the possibility of prolonged work stoppages, with their attendant inconvenience to the public. Although, as has been pointed out in the earlier discussion in this text, few such stoppages actually create national emergencies, nevertheless, the stoppages are serious enough to give rise to a hue and cry that something should be done to prevent such interference with the orderly flow of production, or in the case of public employees, with the orderly operation of government.

There are, of course, some persons who believe that the only way to deal with this problem of the battle of the giants is to restore the working of a free market by breaking up unions and large corporations—by "atomizing" competition, as it is called—so that the unions and corporations which are left to deal with each other will be too small to have a serious effect on the market or the public by reason of their occasional disputes. This possibility, whether or not desirable in theory, is plainly impractical. Our industrial system, as now constituted, is too dependent upon our large, integrated corporations to warrant such a change; and as long as corporate units remain large, union organizations will also be large, in order to bargain most effectively for their membership.

The struggle between strong unions and large corporations will continue to lead to a demand by the public for further government regulation of union activities. The pressure for such action is growing as inflation plagues us; for many people have come to believe—either rightly or wrongly—that union demands for wage increases, backed up by the threat of the strike, have been a major cause of the upward trend in prices since World War II. The result may be further restriction of certain rights— such as the right to strike—which unions believe are fundamental to our democracy.

There are few absolute rights in our society. Rights are implicit with obligations. We cherish freedom of speech, but a man cannot yell "fire" without cause in a crowded theater. A democratic society can afford to give rights and privileges to groups only if those rights and privileges will not be abused and the rights of the public will be respected. Congress has prevented railway and longshore strikes since the middle 1960s by a variety of stopgap laws. The more powerful organizations become, the greater is the damage that they can inflict upon society by abuse of their rights, and therefore the more circumspect must society be to see that such organizations respect their obligations to the community. Today the existence of nonunion and foreign competition is a powerful brake on possible abuses of union bargaining power in many industries, just as the existence of strong competition is a brake on the abuses of corporate power. If unions gradually eliminate such nonunion competition, the chances for abuse of power will be accentuated, and a real test will be presented for enlightened labor leadership. Unless union leaders exercise real self-restraint in the exercise of their powers, they may find that government will prescribe the restraints for them.

Labor policy in a democracy must also recognize that government regulation is not a panacea. Every walkout which inconveniences the public should not be met with the demand that "there ought to be a law." Free unionism and free collective bargaining are institutions which are worth preserving. By contrast, the growth of government bureaucracy and the intervention of government in the labor market are tendencies which should not be lightly encouraged. In labor policy, as in other national policies, we must follow the middle road. As a general rule, labor and industry should be given every opportunity to work out their problems without government regulation, except in situations where injury to the public is apparent and substantial, and justification from the point of view of legitimate union conduct is lacking.

The obligations of unions in a free society have yet to be clearly defined. The Landrum-Griffin Act is a step in this direction. The Civil Rights law is another. Future delineation of the obligations of unions and of the rights of union members would help to clarify, in part, the role of government and of industry as well. Especially needed is a clear policy involving public employee unionism and bargaining. Whatever the ultimate role which government, industry, and unions will play in our society, we may be sure that it will follow a pattern reflecting the needs of our highly integrated industrial economy and the traditional concepts of our democratic society.

QUESTIONS FOR DISCUSSION

1. Write a short statement of what you think the national labor policy should encompass. How does actual policy differ from this?
2. What is the major labor problem today, and why do you think it is so significant?

SUGGESTIONS FOR FURTHER READING

Rowan, Richard L. (ed.) *Readings in Labor Economics and Labor Relations.* 3d ed. Homewood, Ill.: Richard D. Irwin, Inc., 1976, pp. 475–532.
Several articles and excerpts from basic labor laws provide a foundation for evaluating national labor policy.

Shaffer, Bertram. "Some Alternatives to Existing Labor Policies," *Labor Law Journal*, vol. 27 (June 1976), pp. 370–78.
An incisive critique of existing labor relations policies.

Indexes

Index of Authors Cited

Index of Subjects

This book has been set in 10 and 9 point Caledonia, leaded 2 points. Part numbers are 24 point (small) Helvetica Medium and part titles are 24 point (small) Helvetica regular. Chapter numbers are 42 point Venus Medium Extended and chapter titles are 18 point Helvetica. The size of the type page is 27 by 46½ picas.